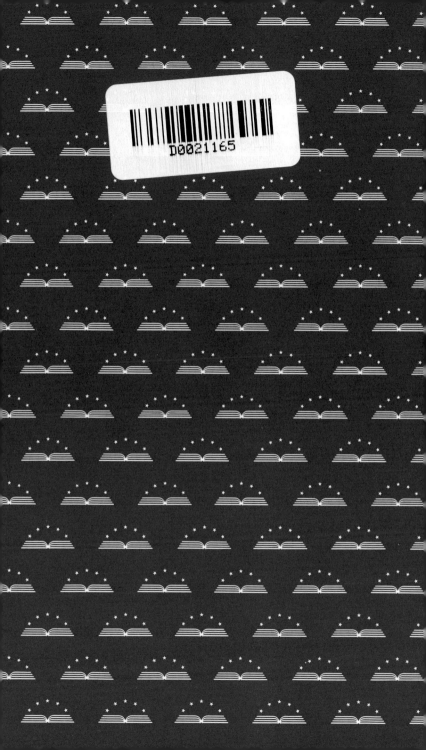

EDITH WHARTON

EDITH WHARTON

NOVELLAS AND OTHER WRITINGS
Madame de Treymes
Ethan Frome
Summer
Old New York
The Mother's Recompense
A Backward Glance

THE LIBRARY OF AMERICA

49869

CYNTHIA GRIFFIN WOLFF
WROTE THE NOTES AND SELECTED
THE TEXTS FOR THIS VOLUME

Grateful acknowledgment is made to the National Endowment for the Humanities, the Ford Foundation, and the Andrew W. Mellon Foundation for their generous support of this series.

Contents

MADAME DE TREYMES

I

JOHN DURHAM, while he waited for Madame de Malrive to draw on her gloves, stood in the hotel doorway looking out across the Rue de Rivoli at the afternoon brightness of the Tuileries gardens.

His European visits were infrequent enough to have kept unimpaired the freshness of his eye, and he was always struck anew by the vast and consummately ordered spectacle of Paris: by its look of having been boldly and deliberately planned as a background for the enjoyment of life, instead of being forced into grudging concessions to the festive instincts, or barricading itself against them in unenlightened ugliness, like his own lamentable New York.

But today, if the scene had never presented itself more alluringly, in that moist spring bloom between showers, when the horse-chestnuts dome themselves in unreal green against a gauzy sky, and the very dust of the pavement seems the fragrance of lilac made visible—today for the first time the sense of a personal stake in it all, of having to reckon individually with its effects and influences, kept Durham from an unrestrained yielding to the spell. Paris might still be—to the unimplicated it doubtless still was—the most beautiful city in the world; but whether it were the most lovable or the most detestable depended for him, in the last analysis, on the buttoning of the white glove over which Fanny de Malrive still lingered.

The mere fact of her having forgotten to draw on her gloves as they were descending in the hotel lift from his mother's drawing-room was, in this connection, charged with significance to Durham. She was the kind of woman who always presents herself to the mind's eye as completely equipped, as made up of exquisitely cared for and finely-related details; and that the heat of her parting with his family should have left her unconscious that she was emerging gloveless into Paris, seemed, on the whole, to speak hopefully for Durham's future opinion of the city.

Even now, he could detect a certain confusion, a desire to draw breath and catch up with life, in the way she dawdled

3

over the last buttons in the dimness of the porte-cochère, while her footman, outside, hung on her retarded signal.

When at length they emerged, it was to learn from that functionary that Madame la Marquise's carriage had been obliged to yield its place at the door, but was at the moment in the act of regaining it. Madame de Malrive cut the explanation short. "I shall walk home. The carriage this evening at eight."

As the footman turned away, she raised her eyes for the first time to Durham's.

"Will you walk with me? Let us cross the Tuileries. I should like to sit a moment on the terrace."

She spoke quite easily and naturally, as if it were the most commonplace thing in the world for them to be straying afoot together over Paris; but even his vague knowledge of the world she lived in—a knowledge mainly acquired through the perusal of yellow-backed fiction—gave a thrilling significance to her naturalness. Durham, indeed, was beginning to find that one of the charms of a sophisticated society is that it lends point and perspective to the slightest contact between the sexes. If, in the old unrestricted New York days, Fanny Frisbee, from a brown stone door-step, had proposed that they should take a walk in the Park, the idea would have presented itself to her companion as agreeable but unimportant; whereas Fanny de Malrive's suggestion that they should stroll across the Tuileries was obviously fraught with unspecified possibilities.

He was so throbbing with the sense of these possibilities that he walked beside her without speaking down the length of the wide alley which follows the line of the Rue de Rivoli, suffering her even, when they reached its farthest end, to direct him in silence up the steps to the terrace of the Feuillants. For, after all, the possibilities were double-faced, and her bold departure from custom might simply mean that what she had to say was so dreadful that it needed all the tenderest mitigation of circumstance.

There was apparently nothing embarrassing to her in his silence: it was a part of her long European discipline that she had learned to manage pauses with ease. In her Frisbee days she might have packed this one with a random fluency; now she was content to let it widen slowly before them like the spacious prospect opening at their feet. The complicated beauty of this prospect, as they moved toward it between the symmetrically clipped limes of the lateral terrace, touched him anew through her nearness, as with the hint of some vast impersonal power, controlling and regulating her life in ways he could not guess, putting between himself and her the whole width of the civilization into which her marriage had absorbed her. And there was such fear in the thought—he read such derision of what he had to offer in the splendour of the great avenues tapering upward to the sunset glories of the Arch—that all he had meant to say when he finally spoke compressed itself at last into an abrupt unmitigated: "Well?"

She answered at once—as though she had only awaited the call of the national interrogation—"I don't know when I have been so happy."

"So happy?" The suddenness of his joy flushed up through his fair skin.

"As I was just now—taking tea with your mother and sisters."

Durham's "Oh!" of surprise betrayed also a note of disillusionment, which she met only by the reconciling murmur: "Shall we sit down?"

He found two of the springy yellow chairs indigenous to the spot, and placed them under the tree near which they had paused, saying reluctantly, as he did so: "Of course it was an immense pleasure to *them* to see you again."

"Oh, not in the same way. I mean—" she paused, sinking into the chair, and betraying, for the first time, a momentary inability to deal becomingly with the situation. "I mean," she resumed, smiling, "that it was not an event for them, as it was for me."

"An event?"—he caught her up again, eagerly; for what, in the language of any civilization, could that word mean but just the one thing he most wished it to?

"To be with dear, good, sweet, simple, real Americans again!" she burst out, heaping up her epithets with reckless prodigality.

Durham's smile once more faded to impersonality, as he rejoined, just a shade on the defensive: "If it's merely our

Americanism you enjoyed—I've no doubt we can give you all you want in that line."

"Yes, it's just that! But if you knew what the word means to me! It means—it means—" she paused as if to assure herself that they were sufficiently isolated from the desultory groups beneath the other trees—"it means that I'm *safe* with them: as safe as in a bank!"

Durham felt a sudden warmth behind his eyes and in his throat. "I think I do know——"

"No, you don't, really; you can't know how dear and strange and familiar it all sounded: the old New York names that kept coming up in your mother's talk, and her charming quaint ideas about Europe—their all regarding it as a great big innocent pleasure ground and shop for Americans; and your mother's missing the home-made bread and preferring the American asparagus—I'm so tired of Americans who despise even their own asparagus! And then your married sister's spending her summers at—where is it?—the Kittawittany House on Lake Pohunk——"

A vision of earnest women in Shetland shawls, with spectacles and thin knobs of hair, eating blueberry-pie at unwholesome hours in a shingled dining-room on a bare New England hilltop, rose pallidly between Durham and the verdant brightness of the Champs Elysées, and he protested with a slight smile: "Oh, but my married sister is the black sheep of the family—the rest of us never sank as low as that."

"Low? I think it's beautiful—fresh and innocent and simple. I remember going to such a place once. They have early dinner—rather late—and go off in buckboards over terrible roads, and bring back goldenrod and autumn leaves, and read nature books aloud on the piazza; and there is always one shy young man in flannels—only one—who has come to see the prettiest girl (though how he can choose among so many!) and who takes her off in a buggy for hours and hours——" She paused and summed up with a long sigh: "It is fifteen years since I was in America."

"And you're still so good an American."

"Oh, a better and better one every day!"

He hesitated. "Then why did you never come back?"

Her face altered instantly, exchanging its retrospective light for the look of slightly shadowed watchfulness which he had known as most habitual to it.

"It was impossible—it has always been so. My husband would not go; and since—since our separation—there have been family reasons."

Durham sighed impatiently. "Why do you talk of reasons? The truth is, you have made your life here. You could never give all this up!" He made a discouraged gesture in the direction of the Place de la Concorde.

"Give it up! I would go tomorrow! But it could never, now, be for more than a visit. I must live in France on account of my boy."

Durham's heart gave a quick beat. At last the talk had neared the point toward which his whole mind was straining, and he began to feel a personal application in her words. But that made him all the more cautious about choosing his own.

"It is an agreement—about the boy?" he ventured.

"I gave my word. They knew that was enough," she said proudly; adding, as if to put him in full possession of her reasons: "It would have been much more difficult for me to obtain complete control of my son if it had not been understood that I was to live in France."

"That seems fair," Durham assented after a moment's reflection: it was his instinct, even in the heat of personal endeavour, to pause a moment on the question of "fairness." The personal claim reasserted itself as he added tentatively: "But when he *is* brought up—when he's grown up: then you would feel freer?"

She received this with a start, as a possibility too remote to have entered into her view of the future. "He is only eight years old!" she objected.

"Ah, of course it would be a long way off?"

"A long way off, thank heaven! French mothers part late with their sons, and in that one respect I mean to be a French mother."

"Of course—naturally—since he has only you," Durham again assented.

He was eager to show how fully he took her point of view, if only to dispose her to the reciprocal fairness of taking his when the time came to present it. And he began to think that the time had now come; that their walk would not have thus resolved itself, without excuse or pretext, into a tranquil session beneath the trees, for any purpose less important than that of giving him his opportunity.

He took it, characteristically, without seeking a transition. "When I spoke to you, the other day, about myself—about what I felt for you—I said nothing of the future, because, for the moment, my mind refused to travel beyond its immediate hope of happiness. But I felt, of course, even then, that the hope involved various difficulties—that we can't, as we might once have done, come together without any thought but for ourselves; and whatever your answer is to be, I want to tell you now that I am ready to accept my share of the difficulties." He paused, and then added explicitly: "If there's the least chance of your listening to me, I'm willing to live over here as long as you can keep your boy with you."

II

WHATEVER Madame de Malrive's answer was to be, there could be no doubt as to her readiness to listen. She received Durham's words without sign of resistance, and took time to ponder them gently before she answered, in a voice touched by emotion: "You are very generous—very unselfish; but when you fix a limit—no matter how remote—to my remaining here, I see how wrong it is to let myself consider for a moment such possibilities as we have been talking of."

"Wrong? Why should it be wrong?"

"Because I shall want to keep my boy always! Not, of course, in the sense of living with him, or even forming an important part of his life; I am not deluded enough to think that possible. But I do believe it possible never to pass wholly out of his life; and while there is a hope of that, how can I leave him?" She paused, and turned on him a new face, a face in which the past of which he was still so ignorant showed itself like a shadow suddenly darkening a clear pane. "How can I make you understand?" she went on urgently. "It is not only because of my love for him—not only, I mean, because of my own happiness in being with him; that I can't, in imagination, surrender even the remotest hour of his future; it is because, the moment he passes out of my influence, he passes under that other—the influence I have been fighting against every hour since he was born!—I don't mean, you know," she added, as Durham, with bent head, continued to offer her the silent fixity of his attention, "I don't mean the special personal influence—except inasmuch as it represents something wider, more general, something that encloses and circulates through the whole world in which he belongs. That is what I meant when I said you could never understand! There is nothing in your experience—in any American experience—to correspond with that far-reaching family organization, which is itself a part of the larger system, and which encloses a young man of my son's position in a network of accepted prejudices and opinions. Everything is prepared in advance—his political and religious convictions, his judgements of people, his sense of honour, his ideas of women, his whole view of life. He is taught to see vileness and corruption in every one not of his own way of thinking, and in every idea that does not directly serve the religious and political purposes of his class. The truth is n't a fixed thing: it's not used to test actions by, it's tested by them, and made to fit in with them. And this forming of the mind begins with the child's first consciousness; it's in his nursery stories, his baby prayers, his very games with his playmates! Already he is only half mine, because the Church has the other half, and will be reaching out for my share as soon as his education begins. But that other half is still mine, and I mean to make it the strongest and most living half of the two, so that, when the inevitable conflict begins, the energy and the truth and the endurance shall be on my side and not on theirs!"

She paused, flushing with the repressed fervour of her utterance, though her voice had not been raised beyond its usual discreet modulations; and Durham felt himself tingling with the transmitted force of her resolve. Whatever shock her words brought to his personal hope, he was grateful to her for speaking them so clearly, for having so sure a grasp of her purpose.

Her decision strengthened his own, and after a pause of deliberation he said quietly: "There might be a good deal to urge on the other side—the ineffectualness of your sacrifice, the probability that when your son marries he will inevitably be absorbed back into the life of his class and his people; but I can't look at it in that way, because if I were in your place I believe I should feel just as you do about it. As long as there was a fighting chance I should want to keep hold of my half, no matter how much the struggle cost me. And one reason why I understand your feeling about your boy is that I have the same feeling about *you*: as long as there's a fighting chance of keeping my half of you—the half he is willing to spare me—I don't see how I can ever give it up." He waited again, and then brought out firmly: "If you'll marry me, I'll agree to live out here as long as you want, and we'll be two instead of one to keep hold of your half of him."

He raised his eyes as he ended, and saw that hers met them through a quick clouding of tears.

"Ah, I am glad to have had this said to me! But I could never accept such an offer."

He caught instantly at the distinction. "That does n't mean that you could never accept *me*?"

"Under such conditions——"

"But if I am satisfied with the conditions? Don't think I am speaking rashly, under the influence of the moment. I have expected something of this sort, and I have thought out my side of the case. As far as material circumstances go, I have worked long enough and successfully enough to take my ease and take it where I choose. I mention that because the life I offer you is offered to your boy as well." He let this sink into her mind before summing up gravely: "The offer I make is made deliberately, and at least I have a right to a direct answer."

She was silent again, and then lifted a cleared gaze to his. "My direct answer then is: if I were still Fanny Frisbee I would marry you."

He bent toward her persuasively. "But you will be—when the divorce is pronounced."

"Ah, the divorce——" She flushed deeply, with an instinctive shrinking back of her whole person which made him straighten himself in his chair.

"Do you so dislike the idea?"

"The idea of divorce? No—not in my case. I should like anything that would do away with the past—obliterate it all—make everything new in my life!"

"Then what——?" he began again, waiting with the patience of a wooer on the uneasy circling of her tormented mind.

"Oh, don't ask me; I don't know; I am frightened."

Durham gave a deep sigh of discouragement. "I thought your coming here with me today—and above all your going with me just now to see my mother—was a sign that you were *not* frightened!"

"Well, I was not when I was with your mother. She made everything seem easy and natural. She took me back into that clear American air where there are no obscurities, no mysteries——"

"What obscurities, what mysteries, are you afraid of?"

She looked about her with a faint shiver. "I am afraid of everything!" she said.

"That's because you are alone; because you've no one to turn to. I'll clear the air for you fast enough if you'll let me."

He looked forth defiantly, as if flinging his challenge at the great city which had come to typify the powers contending with him for her possession.

"You say that so easily! But you don't know; none of you know."

"Know what?"

"The difficulties——"

"I told you I was ready to take my share of the difficul- ties—and my share naturally includes yours. You know Amer- icans are great hands at getting over difficulties." He drew himself up confidently. "Just leave that to me—only tell me exactly what you're afraid of."

She paused again, and then said: "The divorce, to begin with—they will never consent to it."

He noticed that she spoke as though the interests of the whole clan, rather than her husband's individual claim, were to be considered; and the use of the plural pronoun shocked his free individualism like a glimpse of some dark feudal survival.

"But you are absolutely certain of your divorce! I've con- sulted—of course without mentioning names——"

She interrupted him, with a melancholy smile: "Ah, so have I. The divorce would be easy enough to get, if they ever let it come into the courts."

"How on earth can they prevent that?"

"I don't know; my never knowing how they will do things is one of the secrets of their power."

"Their power? What power?" he broke in with irrepressible contempt. "Who are these bogeys whose machinations are going to arrest the course of justice in a—comparatively— civilized country? You've told me yourself that Monsieur de Malrive is the least likely to give you trouble; and the others are his uncle the abbé, his mother and sister. That kind of a syndicate doesn't scare me much. A priest and two women *contra mundum!*"

She shook her head. "Not *contra mundum*, but with it,

their whole world is behind them. It's that mysterious solidarity that you can't understand. One does n't know how far they may reach, or in how many directions. I have never known. They have always cropped up where I least expected them."

Before this persistency of negation Durham's buoyancy began to flag, but his determination grew the more fixed.

"Well, then, supposing them to possess these supernatural powers; do you think it's to people of that kind that I'll ever consent to give you up?"

She raised a half-smiling glance of protest. "Oh, they're not wantonly wicked. They'll leave me alone as long as——"

"As I do?" he interrupted. "Do you want me to leave you alone? Was that what you brought me here to tell me?"

The directness of the challenge seemed to gather up the scattered strands of her hesitation, and lifting her head she turned on him a look in which, but for its underlying shadow, he might have recovered the full free beam of Fanny Frisbee's gaze.

"I don't know why I brought you here," she said gently, "except from the wish to prolong a little the illusion of being once more an American among Americans. Just now, sitting there with your mother and Katy and Nannie, the difficulties seemed to vanish; the problems grew as trivial to me as they are to you. And I wanted them to remain so a little longer; I wanted to put off going back to them. But it was of no use— they were waiting for me here. They are over there now in that house across the river." She indicated the grey sky-line of the Faubourg, shining in the splintered radiance of the sunset beyond the long sweep of the quays. "They are a part of me—I belong to them. I must go back to them!" she sighed.

She rose slowly to her feet, as though her metaphor had expressed an actual fact and she felt herself bodily drawn from his side by the influences of which she spoke.

Durham had risen too. "Then I go back with you!" he exclaimed energetically; and as she paused, wavering a little under the shock of his resolve: "I don't mean into your house— but into your life!" he said.

She suffered him, at any rate, to accompany her to the door of the house, and allowed their debate to prolong itself through the almost monastic quiet of the quarter which led thither. On the way, he succeeded in wresting from her the confession that, if it were possible to ascertain in advance that her husband's family would not oppose her action, she might decide to apply for a divorce. Short of a positive assurance on this point, she made it clear that she would never move in the matter; there must be no scandal, no *retentissement*, nothing which her boy, necessarily brought up in the French tradition of scrupulously preserved appearances, could afterward regard as the faintest blur on his much-quartered escutcheon. But even this partial concession again raised fresh obstacles; for there seemed to be no one to whom she could entrust so delicate an investigation, and to apply directly to the Marquis de Malrive or his relatives appeared, in the light of her past experience, the last way of learning their intentions.

"But," Durham objected, beginning to suspect a morbid fixity of idea in her perpetual attitude of distrust—"but surely you have told me that your husband's sister—what is her name? Madame de Treymes?—was the most powerful member of the group, and that she has always been on your side."

She hesitated. "Yes, Christiane has been on my side. She dislikes her brother. But it would not do to ask her."

"But could no one else ask her? Who are her friends?"

"She has a great many; and some, of course, are mine. But in a case like this they would be all hers; they wouldn't hesitate a moment between us."

"Why should it be necessary to hesitate between you? Suppose Madame de Treymes sees the reasonableness of what you ask; suppose, at any rate, she sees the hopelessness of opposing you? Why should she make a mystery of your opinion?"

"It's not that; it is that, if I went to her friends, I should never get her real opinion from them. At least I should never know if it *was* her real opinion; and therefore I should be no farther advanced. Don't you see?"

Durham struggled between the sentimental impulse to soothe her, and the practical instinct that it was a moment for unmitigated frankness.

"I'm not sure that I do; but if you can't find out what Madame de Treymes thinks, I'll see what I can do myself."

"Oh—*you!*" broke from her in mingled terror and admiration; and pausing on her doorstep to lay her hand in his before she touched the bell, she added with a half-whimsical flash of regret: "Why did n't this happen to Fanny Frisbee?"

III

WHY HAD it not happened to Fanny Frisbee?
    Durham put the question to himself as he walked back along the quays, in a state of inner commotion which left him, for once, insensible to the ordered beauty of his surroundings. Propinquity had not been lacking: he had known Miss Frisbee since his college days. In unsophisticated circles, one family is apt to quote another; and the Durham ladies had always quoted the Frisbees. The Frisbees were bold, experienced, enterprising: they had what the novelists of the day called "dash." The beautiful Fanny was especially dashing; she had the showiest national attributes, tempered only by a native grace of softness, as the beam of her eyes was subdued by the length of their lashes. And yet young Durham, though not unsusceptible to such charms, had remained content to enjoy them from a safe distance of good-fellowship. If he had been asked why, he could not have told; but the Durham of forty understood. It was because there were, with minor modifications, many other Fanny Frisbees; whereas never before, within his ken, had there been a Fanny de Malrive.

He had felt it in a flash, when, the autumn before, he had run across her one evening in the dining-room of the Beau-rivage at Ouchy; when, after a furtive exchange of glances, they had simultaneously arrived at recognition, followed by an eager pressure of hands, and a long evening of reminiscence on the starlit terrace. She was the same, but so mysteriously changed! And it was the mystery, the sense of unprobed depths of initiation, which drew him to her as her freshness had never drawn him. He had not hitherto attempted to define the nature of the change: it remained for his sister Nannie to do that when, on his return to the Rue de Rivoli, where the family were still sitting in conclave upon their recent visitor, Miss Durham summed up their groping comments in the phrase: "I never saw anything so French!"

Durham, understanding what his sister's use of the epithet implied, recognized it instantly as the explanation of his own feelings. Yes, it was the finish, the modelling, which Madame de Malrive's experience had given her that set her apart from the fresh uncomplicated personalities of which she had once been simply the most charming type. The influences that had lowered her voice, regulated her gestures, toned her down to harmony with the warm dim background of a long social past—these influences had lent to her natural fineness of perception a command of expression adapted to complex conditions. She had moved in surroundings through which one could hardly bounce and bang on the genial American plan without knocking the angles off a number of sacred institutions; and her acquired dexterity of movement seemed to Durham a crowning grace. It was a shock, now that he knew at what cost the dexterity had been acquired, to acknowledge this even to himself; he hated to think that she could owe anything to such conditions as she had been placed in. And it gave him a sense of the tremendous strength of the organization into which she had been absorbed, that in spite of her horror, her moral revolt, she had not reacted against its external forms. She might abhor her husband, her marriage, and the world to which it had introduced her, but she had become a product of that world in its outward expression, and no better proof of the fact was needed than her exotic enjoyment of Americanism.

The sense of the distance to which her American past had been removed was never more present to him than when, a day or two later, he went with his mother and sisters to return her visit. The region beyond the river existed, for the Durham ladies, only as the unmapped environment of the Bon Marché; and Nannie Durham's exclamation on the pokiness of the streets and the dulness of the houses showed Durham, with a start, how far he had already travelled from the family point of view.

"Well, if this is all she got by marrying a Marquis!" the young lady summed up as they paused before the small sober hotel in its high-walled court; and Katy, following her mother through the stone-vaulted and stone-floored vestibule, murmured: "It must be simply freezing in winter."

In the softly-faded drawing-room, with its old pastels in old frames, its windows looking on the damp green twilight of a garden sunk deep in blackened walls, the American ladies might have been even more conscious of the insufficiency of their friend's compensations, had not the warmth of her welcome precluded all other reflections. It was not till she had gathered them about her in the corner beside the tea-table, that Durham identified the slender dark lady loitering negligently in the background, and introduced in a comprehensive murmur to the American group, as the redoubtable sister-in-law to whom he had declared himself ready to throw down his challenge.

There was nothing very redoubtable about Madame de Treymes, except perhaps the kindly yet critical observation which she bestowed on her sister-in-law's visitors: the unblinking attention of a civilized spectator observing an encampment of aborigines. He had heard of her as a beauty, and was surprised to find her, as Nannie afterward put it, a mere stick to hang clothes on (but they *did* hang!), with a small brown glancing face, like that of a charming little inquisitive animal. Yet before she had addressed ten words to him—nibbling at the hard English consonants like nuts—he owned the justice of the epithet. She was a beauty, if beauty, instead of being restricted to the cast of the face, is a pervasive attribute informing the hands, the voice, the gestures, the very fall of a flounce and tilt of a feather. In this impalpable *aura* of grace Madame de Treymes' dark meagre presence unmistakably moved, like a thin flame in a wide quiver of light. And as he realized that she looked much handsomer than she was, so, while they talked, he felt that she understood a great deal more than she betrayed. It was not through the groping speech which formed their apparent medium of communication that she imbibed her information: she found it in the air, she extracted it from Durham's look and manner, she caught it in the turn of her sister-in-law's defenceless eyes—for in her presence Madame de Malrive became Fanny Frisbee again!—she put it together, in short, out of just such unconsidered indescribable trifles as differentiated the quiet felicity of her dress from Nannie and Katy's "handsome" haphazard clothes.

Her actual converse with Durham moved, meanwhile, strictly in the conventional ruts: had he been long in Paris, which of the new plays did he like best, was it true that

American *jeunes filles* were sometimes taken to the Boulevard theatres? And she threw an interrogative glance at the young ladies beside the tea-table. To Durham's reply that it depended how much French they knew, she shrugged and smiled, replying that his compatriots all spoke French like Parisians, enquiring, after a moment's thought, if they learned it, *là bas, des nègres*, and laughing heartily when Durham's astonishment revealed her blunder.

When at length she had taken leave—enveloping the Durham ladies in a last puzzled penetrating look—Madame de Malrive turned to Mrs. Durham with a faintly embarrassed smile.

"My sister-in-law was much interested; I believe you are the first Americans she has ever known."

"Good gracious!" ejaculated Nannie, as though such social darkness required immediate missionary action on some one's part.

"Well, she knows *us*," said Durham, catching, in Madame de Malrive's rapid glance, a startled assent to his point.

"After all," reflected the accurate Katy, as though seeking an excuse for Madame de Treymes' unenlightenment, "*we* don't know many French people, either."

To which Nannie promptly if obscurely retorted: "Ah! but we couldn't and *she* could!"

IV

MADAME DE TREYMES' friendly observation of her sister-in-law's visitors resulted in no expression on her part of a desire to renew her study of them. To all appearances, she passed out of their lives when Madame de Malrive's door closed on her; and Durham felt that the arduous task of making her acquaintance was still to be begun.

He felt also, more than ever, the necessity of attempting it; and in his determination to lose no time, and his perplexity how to set most speedily about the business, he bethought himself of applying to his cousin Mrs. Boykin.

Mrs. Elmer Boykin was a small plump woman, to whose vague prettiness the lines of middle age had given no meaning: as though whatever had happened to her had merely added to the sum total of her inexperience. After a Parisian residence of twenty-five years, spent in a state of feverish servitude to the great artists of the Rue de la Paix, her dress and hair still retained a certain rigidity in keeping with the directness of her gaze and the unmodulated candour of her voice. Her very drawing-room had the hard bright atmosphere of her native skies, and one felt that she was still true at heart to the national ideals in electric lighting and plumbing.

She and her husband had left America owing to the impossibility of living there with the finish and decorum which the Boykin standard demanded; but in the isolation of their exile they had created about them a kind of phantom America, where the national prejudices continued to flourish unchecked by the national progressiveness: a little world sparsely peopled by compatriots in the same attitude of chronic opposition toward a society chronically unaware of them. In this uncontaminated air Mr. and Mrs. Boykin had preserved the purity of simpler conditions, and Elmer Boykin, returning rakishly from a Sunday's racing at Chantilly, betrayed, under his "knowing" coat and the racing-glasses slung ostentatiously across his shoulder, the unmistakable cut of the American business man coming "up town" after a long day in the office.

It was a part of the Boykins' uncomfortable but determined

attitude—and perhaps a last expression of their latent patriotism—to live in active disapproval of the world about them, fixing in memory with little stabs of reprobation innumerable instances of what the abominable foreigner was doing; so that they reminded Durham of persons peacefully following the course of a horrible war by pricking red pins in a map. To Mrs. Durham, with her gentle tourist's view of the European continent, as a vast Museum in which the human multitudes simply furnished the element of costume, the Boykins seemed abysmally instructed, and darkly expert in forbidden things; and her son, without sharing her simple faith in their omniscience, credited them with an ample supply of the kind of information of which he was in search.

Mrs. Boykin, from the corner of an intensely modern Gobelin sofa, studied her cousin as he balanced himself insecurely on one of the small gilt chairs which always look surprised at being sat in.

"Fanny de Malrive? Oh, of course: I remember you were all very intimate with the Frisbees when they lived in West Thirty-third Street. But she has dropped all her American friends since her marriage. The excuse was that de Malrive didn't like them; but as she's been separated for five or six years, I can't see—. You say she's been very nice to your mother and the girls? Well, I dare say she is beginning to feel the need of friends she can really trust; for as for her French relations——! That Malrive set is the worst in the Faubourg. Of course you know what *he* is; even the family, for decency's sake, had to back her up, and urge her to get a separation. And Christiane de Treymes——"

Durham seized his opportunity. "Is she so very reprehensible too?"

Mrs. Boykin pursed up her small colourless mouth. "I can't speak from personal experience. I know Madame de Treymes slightly—I have met her at Fanny's—but she never remembers the fact except when she wants me to go to one of her *ventes de charité*. They all remember us then; and some American women are silly enough to ruin themselves at the smart bazaars, and fancy they will get invitations in return. They say Mrs. Addison G. Pack followed Madame d'Alglade around for a whole winter, and spent a hundred thousand francs at her stalls; and at the end of the season Madame d'Alglade asked her to tea, and when she got there she found *that* was for a charity too, and she had to pay a hundred francs to get in."

Mrs. Boykin paused with a smile of compassion. "That is not *my* way," she continued. "Personally I have no desire to thrust myself into French society—I can't see how any American woman can do so without loss of self-respect. But any one can tell you about Madame de Treymes."

"I wish you would, then," Durham suggested.

"Well, I think Elmer had better," said his wife mysteriously, as Mr. Boykin, at this point, advanced across the wide expanse of Aubusson on which his wife and Durham were islanded in a state of propinquity without privacy.

"What's that, Bessy? Hah, Durham, how are you? Didn't see you at Auteuil this afternoon. You don't race? Busy sightseeing, I suppose? What was that my wife was telling you? Oh, about Madame de Treymes."

He stroked his pepper-and-salt moustache with a gesture intended rather to indicate than to conceal the smile of experience beneath it. "Well, Madame de Treymes has not been like a happy country—she's had a history: several of 'em. Some one said she constituted the *feuilleton* of the Faubourg daily news. *La suite au prochain numéro*—you see the point? Not that I speak from personal knowledge. Bessy and I have never cared to force our way"——He paused, reflecting that his wife had probably anticipated him in the expression of this familiar sentiment, and added with a significant nod: "Of course you know the Prince d'Armillac by sight? No? I'm surprised at that. Well, he's one of the choicest ornaments of the Jockey Club: very fascinating to the ladies, I believe, but the deuce and all at baccara. Ruined his mother and a couple of maiden aunts already—and now Madame de Treymes has put the family pearls up the spout, and is wearing imitation for love of him."

"I had that straight from my maid's cousin, who is employed by Madame d'Armillac's jeweller," said Mrs. Boykin with conscious pride.

"Oh, it's straight enough—more than *she* is!" retorted her husband, who was slightly jealous of having his facts reinforced by any information not of his own gleaning.

"Be careful of what you say, Elmer," Mrs. Boykin inter-posed with archness. "I suspect John of being seriously smit-ten by the lady."

Durham let this pass unchallenged, submitting with a good grace to his host's low whistle of amusement, and the sar-donic enquiry: "Ever do anything with the foils? D'Armillac is what they call over here a *fine lame*."

"Oh, I don't mean to resort to bloodshed unless it's abso-lutely necessary; but I mean to make the lady's acquaintance," said Durham, falling into his key.

Mrs. Boykin's lips tightened to the vanishing point. "I am afraid you must apply for an introduction to more fashionable people than *we* are. Elmer and I so thoroughly disapprove of French society that we have always declined to take any part in it. But why should not Fanny de Malrive arrange a meeting for you?"

Durham hesitated. "I don't think she is on very intimate terms with her husband's family——"

"You mean that she's not allowed to introduce *her* friends to them," Mrs. Boykin interjected sarcastically; while her husband added, with an air of portentous initiation: "Ah, my dear fellow, the way they treat the Americans over here—that's another chapter, you know."

"How some people can *stand* it!" Mrs. Boykin chimed in; and as the footman, entering at that moment, tendered her a large coronetted envelope, she held it up as if in illustration of the indignities to which her countrymen were subjected.

"Look at that, my dear John," she exclaimed—"another card to one of their everlasting bazaars! Why, it's at Madame d'Armillac's, the Prince's mother. Madame de Treymes must have sent it, of course. The brazen way in which they com-bine religion and immorality! Fifty francs admission—*rien que cela!*—to see some of the most disreputable people in Eu-rope. And if you're an American, you're expected to leave at least a thousand behind you. Their own people naturally get off cheaper." She tossed over the card to her cousin.

"There's your opportunity to see Madame de Treymes."

"Make it two thousand, and she'll ask you to tea," Mr. Boy-kin scathingly added.

V

I n the monumental drawing-room of the Hôtel de Malrive—it had been a surprise to the American to read the
name of the house emblazoned on black marble over its still
more monumental gateway—Durham found himself surrounded by a buzz of feminine tea-sipping oddly out of keeping with the wigged and cuirassed portraits frowning high on
the walls, the majestic attitude of the furniture, the rigidity of
great gilt consoles drawn up like lords-in-waiting against the
tarnished panels.

It was the old Marquise de Malrive's "day," and Madame
de Treymes, who lived with her mother, had admitted
Durham to the heart of the enemy's country by inviting him,
after his prodigal disbursements at the charity bazaar, to come
in to tea on a Thursday. Whether, in thus fulfilling Mr. Boykin's prediction, she had been aware of Durham's purpose,
and had her own reasons for falling in with it; or whether she
simply wished to reward his lavishness at the fair, and permit
herself another glimpse of an American so picturesquely em-
bodying the type familiar to French fiction—on these points
Durham was still in doubt.

Meanwhile, Madame de Treymes being engaged with a
venerable Duchess in a black shawl—all the older ladies
present had the sloping shoulders of a generation of shawl-
wearers—her American visitor, left in the isolation of his un-
importance, was using it as a shelter for a rapid survey of the
scene.

He had begun his study of Fanny de Malrive's situation
without any real understanding of her fears. He knew the repugnance to divorce existing in the French Catholic world,
but since the French laws sanctioned it, and in a case so flagrant as his injured friend's, would inevitably accord it with
the least possible delay and exposure, he could not take seriously any risk of opposition on the part of the husband's family. Madame de Malrive had not become a Catholic, and since
her religious scruples could not be played on, the only
weapon remaining to the enemy—the threat of fighting the
divorce—was one they could not wield without self-injury.

24

Certainly, if the chief object were to avoid scandal, common sense must counsel Monsieur de Malrive and his friends not to give the courts an opportunity of exploring his past; and since the echo of such explorations, and their ultimate transmission to her son, were what Madame de Malrive most dreaded, the opposing parties seemed to have a common ground for agreement, and Durham could not but regard his friend's fears as the result of over-taxed sensibilities. All this had seemed evident enough to him as he entered the austere portals of the Hôtel de Malrive and passed, between the faded liveries of old family servants, to the presence of the dreaded dowager above. But he had not been ten minutes in that presence before he had arrived at a faint intuition of what poor Fanny meant. It was not in the exquisite mildness of the old Marquise, a little grey-haired bunch of a woman in dowdy mourning, or in the small neat presence of the priestly uncle, the Abbé who had so obviously just stepped down from one of the picture-frames overhead: it was not in the aspect of these chief protagonists, so outwardly unformidable, that Durham read an occult danger to his friend. It was rather in their setting, their surroundings, the little company of elderly and dowdy persons—so uniformly clad in weeping blacks and purples that they might have been assembled for some mortuary anniversary—it was in the remoteness and the solidarity of this little group that Durham had his first glimpse of the social force of which Fanny de Malrive had spoken. All these amiably chatting visitors, who mostly bore the stamp of personal insignificance on their mildly sloping or aristocratically beaked faces, hung together in a visible closeness of tradition, dress, attitude and manner, as different as possible from the loose aggregation of a roomful of his own countrymen. Durham felt, as he observed them, that he had never before known what "society" meant; nor understood that, in an organized and inherited system, it exists full-fledged where two or three of its members are assembled.

Upon this state of bewilderment, this sense of having entered a room in which the lights had suddenly been turned out, even Madame de Treymes' intensely modern presence threw no illumination. He was conscious, as she smilingly rejoined him, not of her points of difference from the others,

but of the myriad invisible threads by which she held to
them; he even recognized the audacious slant of her little
brown profile in the portrait of a powdered ancestress beneath which she had paused a moment in advancing. She was
simply one particular facet of the solid, glittering, impenetrable body which he had thought to turn in his hands and look
through like a crystal; and when she said, in her clear staccato
English, "Perhaps you will like to see the other rooms," he felt
like crying out in his blindness: "If I could only be sure of
seeing *anything* here!" Was she conscious of his blindness, and
was he as remote and unintelligible to her as she was to him?
This possibility, as he followed her through the nobly-
unfolding rooms of the great house, gave him his first hope of
recoverable advantage. For, after all, he had some vague traditional lights on her world and its antecedents; whereas to
her he was a wholly new phenomenon, as unexplained as a
fragment of meteorite dropped at her feet on the smooth
gravel of the garden-path they were pacing.

She had led him down into the garden, in response to his
admiring exclamation, and perhaps also because she was sure
that, in the chill spring afternoon, they would have its em-
bowered privacies to themselves. The garden was small, but
intensely rich and deep—one of those wells of verdure and
fragrance which everywhere sweeten the air of Paris by wafts
blown above old walls on quiet streets; and as Madame de
Treymes paused against the ivy bank masking its farther
boundary, Durham felt more than ever removed from the
normal bearings of life.

His sense of strangeness was increased by the surprise of his
companion's next speech.

"You wish to marry my sister-in-law?" she asked abruptly;
and Durham's start of wonder was followed by an immediate
feeling of relief. He had expected the preliminaries of their
interview to be as complicated as the bargaining in an Eastern
bazaar, and had feared to lose himself at the first turn in a
labyrinth of "foreign" intrigue.

"Yes, I do," he said with equal directness; and they smiled
together at the sharp report of question and answer.

The smile put Durham more completely at his ease, and
after waiting for her to speak, he added with deliberation: "So

far, however, the wishing is entirely on my side." His scrupulous conscience felt itself justified in this reserve by the conditional nature of Madame de Malrive's consent.

"I understand; but you have been given reason to hope——"

"Every man in my position gives himself his own reasons
for hoping," he interposed with a smile.

"I understand that too," Madame de Treymes assented.
"But still—you spent a great deal of money the other day at
our bazaar."

"Yes: I wanted to have a talk with you, and it was the readiest—if not the most distinguished—means of attracting your
attention."

"I understand," she once more reiterated, with a gleam of
amusement.

"It is because I suspect you of understanding everything
that I have been so anxious for this opportunity."

She bowed her acknowledgement, and said: "Shall we sit a
moment?" adding, as he drew their chairs under a tree: "You
permit me, then, to say that I believe I understand also a little
of our good Fanny's mind?"

"On that point I have no authority to speak. I am here only
to listen."

"Listen, then: you have persuaded her that there would be
no harm in divorcing my brother—since I believe your religion does not forbid divorce?"

"Madame de Malrive's religion sanctions divorce in such a
case as——"

"As my brother has furnished? Yes, I have heard that your
race is stricter in judging such *écarts*. But you must not
think," she added, "that I defend my brother. Fanny must
have told you that we have always given her our sympathy."

"She has let me infer it from her way of speaking of you."

Madame de Treymes arched her dramatic eyebrows. "How
cautious you are! I am so straightforward that I shall have no
chance with you."

"You will be quite safe, unless you are so straightforward
that you put me on my guard."

She met this with a low note of amusement.

"At this rate we shall never get any farther; and in two
minutes I must go back to my mother's visitors. Why should

we go on fencing? The situation is really quite simple. Tell me just what you wish to know. I have always been Fanny's friend, and that disposes me to be yours."

Durham, during this appeal, had had time to steady his thoughts; and the result of his deliberation was that he said, with a return to his former directness: "Well, then, what I wish to know is, what position your family would take if Madame de Malrive should sue for a divorce." He added, without giving her time to reply: "I naturally wish to be clear on this point before urging my cause with your sister-in-law."

Madame de Treymes seemed in no haste to answer; but after a pause of reflection she said, not unkindly: "My poor Fanny might have asked me that herself."

"I beg you to believe that I am not acting as her spokesman," Durham hastily interposed. "I merely wish to clear up the situation before speaking to her in my own behalf."

"You are the most delicate of suitors! But I understand your feeling. Fanny also is extremely delicate: it was a great surprise to us at first. Still, in this case—" Madame de Treymes paused—"since she has no religious scruples, and she had no difficulty in obtaining a separation, why should she fear any in demanding a divorce?"

"I don't know that she does: but the mere fact of possible opposition might be enough to alarm the delicacy you have observed in her."

"Ah—yes: on her boy's account."

"Partly, doubtless, on her boy's account."

"So that, if my brother objects to a divorce, all he has to do is to announce his objection? But, my dear sir, you are giving your case into my hands!" She flashed an amused smile on him.

"Since you say you are Madame de Malrive's friend, could there be a better place for it?"

As she turned her eyes on him he seemed to see, under the flitting lightness of her glance, the sudden concentrated expression of the ancestral will. "I am Fanny's friend, certainly. But with us family considerations are paramount. And our religion forbids divorce."

"So that, inevitably, your brother will oppose it?"

She rose from her seat, and stood fretting with her slender boot-tip the minute red pebbles of the path.

"I must really go in: my mother will never forgive me for deserting her."

"But surely you owe me an answer?" Durham protested, rising also.

"In return for your purchases at my stall?"

"No: in return for the trust I have placed in you."

She mused on this, moving slowly a step or two toward the house.

"Certainly I wish to see you again; you interest me," she said smiling. "But it is so difficult to arrange. If I were to ask you to come here again, my mother and uncle would be surprised. And at Fanny's——"

"Oh, not there!" he exclaimed.

"Where then? Is there any other house where we are likely to meet?"

Durham hesitated; but he was goaded by the flight of the precious minutes. "Not unless you'll come and dine with me," he said boldly.

"Dine with you? *Au cabaret?* Ah, that would be diverting—but impossible!"

"Well, dine with my cousin, then—I have a cousin, an American lady, who lives here," said Durham, with suddenly-soaring audacity.

She paused with puzzled brows. "An American lady whom I know?"

"By name, at any rate. You send her cards for all your charity bazaars."

She received the thrust with a laugh. "We do exploit your compatriots."

"Oh, I don't think she has ever gone to the bazaars."

"But she might if I dined with her?"

"Still less, I imagine."

She reflected on this, and then said with acuteness: "I like that, and I accept—but what is the lady's name?"

VI

ON THE WAY home, in the first drop of his exaltation, Durham had said to himself: "But why on earth should Bessy invite her?"

He had, naturally, no very cogent reasons to give Mrs. Boykin in support of his astonishing request, and could only, marvelling at his own growth in duplicity, suffer her to infer that he was really, shamelessly "smitten" with the lady he thus proposed to thrust upon her hospitality. But, to his surprise, Mrs. Boykin hardly gave herself time to pause upon his reasons. They were swallowed up in the fact that Madame de Treymes wished to dine with her, as the lesser luminaries vanish in the blaze of the sun.

"I am not surprised," she declared, with a faint smile intended to check her husband's unruly wonder. "I wonder *you* are, Elmer. Didn't you tell me that Armillac went out of his way to speak to you the other day at the races? And at Madame d'Alglade's sale—yes, I went there after all, just for a minute, because I found Katy and Nannie were so anxious to be taken—well, that day I noticed that Madame de Treymes was quite *empressée* when we went up to her stall. Oh, I didn't buy anything: I merely waited while the girls chose some lampshades. They thought it would be interesting to take home something painted by a real Marquise, and of course I didn't tell them that those women *never* make the things they sell at their stalls. But I repeat I'm not surprised: I suspected that Madame de Treymes had heard of our little dinners. You know they're really horribly bored in that poky old Faubourg. My poor John, I see now why she's been making up to you! But on one point I am quite determined, Elmer; whatever you say, I shall *not* invite the Prince d'Armillac."

Elmer, as far as Durham could observe, did not say much; but, like his wife, he continued in a state of pleasantly agitated activity till the momentous evening of the dinner.

The festivity in question was restricted in numbers, either owing to the difficulty of securing suitable guests, or from a desire not to have it appear that Madame de Treymes' hosts attached any special importance to her presence; but the

smallness of the company was counterbalanced by the multiplicity of the courses.

The national determination not to be "downed" by the despised foreigner, to show a wealth of material resource obscurely felt to compensate for the possible lack of other
distinctions—this resolve had taken, in Mrs. Boykin's case,
the shape—or rather the multiple shapes—of a series of culi-
nary feats, of gastronomic combinations, which would have
commanded her deep respect had she seen them on any other
table, and which she naturally relied on to produce the same
effect on her guest. Whether or not the desired result was
achieved, Madame de Treymes' manner did not specifically declare; but it showed a general complaisance, a charming will-
ingness to be amused, which made Mr. Boykin, for months
afterward, allude to her among his compatriots as "an old
friend of my wife's—takes potluck with us, you know. Of
course there's not a word of truth in any of those ridiculous
stories."

It was only when, to Durham's intense surprise, Mr. Boykin hazarded to his neighbour the regret that they had not
been so lucky as to "secure the Prince"—it was then only that
the lady showed, not indeed anything so simple and unprepared as embarrassment, but a faint play of wonder, an under-
flicker of amusement, as though recognizing that, by some
odd law of social compensation, the crudity of the talk might
account for the complexity of the dishes.

But Mr. Boykin was tremulously alive to hints, and the
conversation at once slid to safer topics, easy generalizations
which left Madame de Treymes ample time to explore the
table, to use her narrowed gaze like a knife slitting open
the unsuspicious personalities about her. Nannie and Katy
Durham, who, after much discussion (to which their hostess
candidly admitted them), had been included in the feast, were
the special objects of Madame de Treymes' observation. During dinner she ignored in their favour the other carefully-
selected guests—the fashionable art-critic, the old Legitimist
general, the beauty from the English Embassy, the whole impressive marshalling of Mrs. Boykin's social resources—and
when the men returned to the drawing-room, Durham found
her still fanning in his sisters the flame of an easily-kindled

enthusiasm. Since she could hardly have been held by the intrinsic interest of their converse, the sight gave him another swift intuition of the working of those hidden forces with which Fanny de Malrive felt herself encompassed. But when Madame de Treymes, at his approach, let him see that it was for him she had been reserving herself, he felt that so graceful an impulse needed no special explanation. She had the art of making it seem quite natural that they should move away together to the remotest of Mrs. Boykin's far-drawn salons, and that there, in a glaring privacy of brocade and ormolu, she should turn to him with a smile which avowed her intentional quest of seclusion.

"Confess that I have done a great deal for you!" she exclaimed, making room for him on a sofa judiciously screened from the observation of the other rooms.

"In coming to dine with my cousin?" he enquired, answering her smile.

"Let us say, in giving you this half hour."

"For that I am duly grateful—and shall be still more so when I know what it contains for me."

"Ah, I am not sure. You will not like what I am going to say."

"Shall I not?" he rejoined, changing colour.

She raised her eyes from the thoughtful contemplation of her painted fan. "You appear to have no idea of the difficulties."

"Should I have asked your help if I had not had an idea of them?"

"But you are still confident that with my help you can surmount them?"

"I can't believe you have come here to take that confidence from me?"

She leaned back, smiling at him through her lashes. "And all this I am to do for your *beaux yeux*?"

"No—for your own: that you may see with them what happiness you are conferring."

"You are extremely clever, and I like you." She paused, and then brought out with lingering emphasis: "But my family will not hear of a divorce."

She threw into her voice such an accent of finality that

Durham, for the moment, felt himself brought up against an insurmountable barrier, but, almost at once, his fear was mitigated by the conviction that she would not have put herself out so much to say so little.

"When you speak of your family, do you include yourself?" he suggested.

She threw a surprised glance at him. "I thought you understood that I am simply their mouthpiece."

At this he rose quietly to his feet with a gesture of acceptance. "I have only to thank you, then, for not keeping me longer in suspense."

His air of wishing to put an immediate end to the conversation seemed to surprise her. "Sit down a moment longer," she commanded him kindly; and as he leaned against the back of his chair, without appearing to hear her request, she added in a low voice: "I am very sorry for you and Fanny—but you are not the only persons to be pitied."

"The only persons?"

"In our unhappy family." She touched her breast with a sudden tragic gesture. "I, for instance, whose help you ask— if you could guess how I need help myself!"

She had dropped her light manner as she might have tossed aside her fan, and he was startled at the intimacy of misery to which her look and movement abruptly admitted him. Perhaps no Anglo-Saxon fully understands the fluency in self-revelation which centuries of the confessional have given to the Latin races, and to Durham, at any rate, Madame de Treymes' sudden avowal gave the shock of a physical abandonment.

"I am so sorry," he stammered—"is there any way in which I can be of use to you?"

She sat before him with her hands clasped, her eyes fixed on his in a terrible intensity of appeal. "If you would—if you would! Oh, there is nothing I would not do for you. I have still a great deal of influence with my mother, and what my mother commands we all do. I could help you—I am sure I could help you; but not if my own situation were known. And if nothing can be done it must be known in a few days."

Durham had reseated himself at her side. "Tell me what I

can do," he said in a low tone, forgetting his own preoccupations in his genuine concern for her distress.

She looked up at him through tears. "How dare I? Your race is so cautious, so self-controlled—you have so little indulgence for the extravagances of the heart. And my folly has been incredible—and unrewarded." She paused, and as Durham waited in a silence which she guessed to be compassionate, she brought out below her breath: "I have lent money—my husband's, my brother's—money that was not mine, and now I have nothing to repay it with."

Durham gazed at her in genuine astonishment. The turn the conversation had taken led quite beyond his uncomplicated experiences with the other sex. She saw his surprise, and extended her hands in deprecation and entreaty. "Alas, what must you think of me? How can I explain my humiliating myself before a stranger? Only by telling you the whole truth—the fact that I am not alone in this disaster, that I could not confess my situation to my family without ruining myself, and involving in my ruin some one who, however undeservedly, has been as dear to me as—as you are to——"

Durham pushed his chair back with a sharp exclamation.

"Ah, even that does not move you!" she said.

The cry restored him to his senses by the long shaft of light it sent down the dark windings of the situation. He seemed suddenly to know Madame de Treymes as if he had been brought up with her in the inscrutable shades of the Hôtel de Malrive.

She, on her side, appeared to have a startled but uncomprehending sense of the fact that his silence was no longer completely sympathetic, that her touch called forth no answering vibration; and she made a desperate clutch at the one chord she could be certain of sounding.

"You have asked a great deal of me—much more than you can guess. Do you mean to give me nothing—not even your sympathy—in return? Is it because you have heard horrors of me? When are they not said of a woman who is married unhappily? Perhaps not in your fortunate country, where she may seek liberation without dishonour. But here—! You who have seen the consequences of our disastrous marriages—you

who may yet be the victim of our cruel and abominable system; have you no pity for one who has suffered in the same
way, and without the possibility of release?" She paused, laying her hand on his arm with a smile of deprecating irony. "It
is not because you are not rich. At such times the crudest way
is the shortest, and I don't pretend to deny that I know I am
asking you a trifle. You Americans, when you want a thing,
always pay ten times what it is worth, and I am giving you
the wonderful chance to get what you most want at a
bargain."

Durham sat silent, her little gloved hand burning his coat-
sleeve as if it had been a hot iron. His brain was tingling with
the shock of her confession. She wanted money, a great deal
of money: that was clear, but it was not the point. She was
ready to sell her influence, and he fancied she could be
counted on to fulfil her side of the bargain. The fact that he
could so trust her seemed only to make her more terrible to
him—more supernaturally dauntless and baleful. For what
was it that she exacted of him? She had said she must have
money to pay her debts; but he knew that was only a pretext
which she scarcely expected him to believe. She wanted the
money for some one else; that was what her allusion to a
fellow-victim meant. She wanted it to pay the Prince's gambling debts—it was at that price that Durham was to buy the
right to marry Fanny de Malrive.

Once the situation had worked itself out in his mind, he
found himself unexpectedly relieved of the necessity of weighing the arguments for and against it. All the traditional forces
of his blood were in revolt, and he could only surrender himself to their pressure, without thought of compromise or
parley.

He stood up in silence, and the abruptness of his movement caused Madame de Treymes' hand to slip from his arm.

"You refuse?" she exclaimed; and he answered with a bow:
"Only because of the return you propose to make me."

She stood staring at him, in a perplexity so genuine and
profound that he could almost have smiled at it through his
disgust.

"Ah, you are all incredible," she murmured at last, stooping
to repossess herself of her fan; and as she moved past him to

rejoin the group in the farther room, she added in an incisive undertone: "You are quite at liberty to repeat our conversation to your friend!"

VII

DURHAM did not take advantage of the permission thus strangely flung at him. Of his talk with her sister-in-law he gave to Madame de Malrive only that part which concerned her.

Presenting himself for this purpose, the day after Mrs. Boykin's dinner, he found his friend alone with her son; and the sight of the child had the effect of dispelling whatever illusive hopes had attended him to the threshold. Even after the governess's descent upon the scene had left Madame de Malrive and her visitor alone, the little boy's presence seemed to hover admonishingly between them, reducing to a bare statement of fact Durham's confession of the total failure of his errand.

Madame de Malrive heard the confession calmly; she had been too prepared for it not to have prepared a countenance to receive it. Her first comment was: "I have never known them to declare themselves so plainly——" and Durham's baffled hopes fastened themselves eagerly on the words. Had she not always warned him that there was nothing so misleading as their plainness? And might it not be that, in spite of his advisedness, he had suffered too easy a rebuff? But second thoughts reminded him that the refusal had not been as unconditional as his necessary reservations made it seem in the repetition; and that, furthermore, it was his own act, and not that of his opponents, which had determined it. The impossibility of revealing this to Madame de Malrive only made the difficulty shut in more darkly around him, and in the completeness of his discouragement he scarcely needed her reminder of his promise to regard the subject as closed when once the other side had defined its position.

He was secretly confirmed in this acceptance of his fate by the knowledge that it was really he who had defined the position. Even now that he was alone with Madame de Malrive, and subtly aware of the struggle under her composure, he felt no temptation to abate his stand by a jot. He had not yet formulated a reason for his resistance: he simply went on feeling, more and more strongly with every precious sign of her participation in his unhappiness, that he could neither owe his escape from it to such a transaction, nor suffer her, innocently, to owe hers.

The only mitigating effect of his determination was in an increase of helpless tenderness toward her; so that, when she exclaimed, in answer to his announcement that he meant to leave Paris the next night: "Oh, give me a day or two longer!" he at once resigned himself to saying: "If I can be of the least use, I'll give you a hundred."

She answered sadly that all he could do would be to let her feel that he was there—just for a day or two, till she had readjusted herself to the idea of going on in the old way; and on this note of renunciation they parted.

But Durham, however pledged to the passive part, could not long sustain it without rebellion. To "hang round" the shut door of his hopes seemed, after two long days, more than even his passion required of him; and on the third he despatched a note of good-bye to his friend. He was going off for a few weeks, he explained—his mother and sisters wished to be taken to the Italian lakes: but he would return to Paris, and say his real farewell to her, before sailing for America in July.

He had not intended his note to act as an ultimatum: he had no wish to surprise Madame de Malrive into unconsidered surrender. When, almost immediately, his own messenger returned with a reply from her, he even felt a pang of disappointment, a momentary fear lest she should have stooped a little from the high place where his passion had preferred to leave her; but her first words turned his fear into rejoicing.

"Let me see you before you go: something extraordinary has happened," she wrote.

What had happened, as he heard from her a few hours later—finding her in a tremor of frightened gladness, with her door boldly closed to all the world but himself—was nothing less extraordinary than a visit from Madame de Treymes, who had come, officially delegated by the family, to announce that Monsieur de Malrive had decided not to oppose his wife's suit for divorce. Durham, at the news, was almost afraid to show himself too amazed; but his small signs of alarm and wonder were swallowed up in the flush of Madame de Malrive's incredulous joy.

"It's the long habit, you know, of not believing them—of looking for the truth always in what they *don't* say. It took me hours and hours to convince myself that there's no trick under it, that there can't be any," she explained.

"Then you *are* convinced now?" escaped from Durham; but the shadow of his question lingered no more than the flit of a wing across her face.

"I am convinced because the facts are there to reassure me. Christiane tells me that Monsieur de Malrive has consulted his lawyers, and that they have advised him to free me. Maître Enguerrand has been instructed to see my lawyer whenever I wish it. They quite understand that I never should have taken the step in face of any opposition on their part—I am so thankful to you for making that perfectly clear to them!—and I suppose this is the return their pride makes to mine. For they *can* be proud collectively——" She broke off, and added, with happy hands outstretched: "And I owe it all to you—Christiane said it was your talk with her that had convinced them."

Durham, at this statement, had to repress a fresh sound of amazement; but with her hands in his, and, a moment after, her whole self drawn to him in the first yielding of her lips, doubt perforce gave way to the lover's happy conviction that such love was after all too strong for the powers of darkness.

It was only when they sat again in the blissful after-calm of their understanding, that he felt the pricking of an unappeased distrust.

"Did Madame de Treymes give you any reason for this change of front?" he risked asking, when he found the distrust was not otherwise to be quelled.

"Oh, yes: just what I've said. It was really her admiration of *you*—of your attitude—your delicacy. She said that at first she hadn't believed in it: they're always looking for a hidden motive. And when she found that yours was staring at her in the actual words you said: that you really respected my scruples, and would never, never try to coerce or entrap me—something in her—poor Christiane!—answered to it, she told me, and she wanted to prove to us that she was capable of understanding us too. If you knew her history you'd find it wonderful and pathetic that she can!"

Durham thought he knew enough of it to infer that Madame de Treymes had not been the object of many conscientious scruples on the part of the opposite sex; but this increased rather his sense of the strangeness than of the pathos of her action. Yet Madame de Malrive, whom he had once inwardly taxed with the morbid raising of obstacles, seemed to see none now; and he could only infer that her sister-in-law's actual words had carried more conviction than reached him in the repetition of them. The mere fact that he had so much to gain by leaving his friend's faith undisturbed was no doubt stirring his own suspicions to unnatural activity; and this sense gradually reasoned him back into acceptance of her view, as the most normal as well as the pleasantest he could take.

VIII

THE UNEASINESS thus temporarily repressed slipped into the final disguise of hoping he should not again meet Madame de Treymes; and in this wish he was seconded by the decision, in which Madame de Malrive concurred, that it would be well for him to leave Paris while the preliminary negotiations were going on. He committed her interests to the best professional care, and his mother, resigning her dream of the lakes, remained to fortify Madame de Malrive by her mild unimaginative view of the transaction, as an uncomfortable but commonplace necessity, like house-cleaning or dentistry. Mrs. Durham would doubtless have preferred that her only son, even with his hair turning grey, should have chosen a Fanny Frisbee rather than a Fanny de Malrive; but it was a part of her acceptance of life on a general basis of innocence and kindliness, that she entered generously into his dream of rescue and renewal, and devoted herself without after-thought to keeping up Fanny's courage with so little to spare for herself.

The process, the lawyers declared, would not be a long one, since Monsieur de Malrive's acquiescence reduced it to a formality; and when, at the end of June, Durham returned from Italy with Katy and Nannie, there seemed no reason why he should not stop in Paris long enough to learn what progress had been made.

But before he could learn this he was to hear, on entering Madame de Malrive's presence, news more immediate if less personal. He found her, in spite of her gladness in his return, so evidently preoccupied and distressed that his first thought was one of fear for their own future. But she read and dispelled this by saying, before he could put his question: "Poor Christiane is here. She is very unhappy. You have seen in the papers——?"

"I have seen no papers since we left Turin. What has happened?"

"The Prince d'Armillac has come to grief. There has been some terrible scandal about money and he has been obliged to leave France to escape arrest."

"And Madame de Treymes has left her husband?"

"Ah, no, poor creature: they don't leave their husbands—they can't. But de Treymes has gone down to their place in Brittany, and as my mother-in-law is with another daughter in Auvergne, Christiane came here for a few days. With me, you see, she need not pretend—she can cry her eyes out."

"And that is what she is doing?"

It was so unlike his conception of the way in which, under the most adverse circumstances, Madame de Treymes would be likely to occupy her time, that Durham was conscious of a note of scepticism in his query.

"Poor thing—if you saw her you would feel nothing but pity. She is suffering so horribly that I reproach myself for being happy under the same roof."

Durham met this with a tender pressure of her hand; then he said, after a pause of reflection: "I should like to see her."

He hardly knew what prompted him to utter the wish, unless it were a sudden stir of compunction at the memory of his own dealings with Madame de Treymes. Had he not sacrificed the poor creature to a purely fantastic conception of conduct? She had said that she knew she was asking a trifle of him; and the fact that, materially, it would have been a trifle, had seemed at the moment only an added reason for steeling himself in his moral resistance to it. But now that he had gained his point—and through her own generosity, as it still appeared—the largeness of her attitude made his own seem cramped and petty. Since conduct, in the last resort, must be judged by its enlarging or diminishing effect on character, might it not be that the zealous weighing of the moral anise and cummin was less important than the unconsidered lavishing of the precious ointment? At any rate, he could enjoy no peace of mind under the burden of Madame de Treymes' magnanimity, and when he had assured himself that his own affairs were progressing favourably, he once more, at the risk of surprising his betrothed, brought up the possibility of seeing her relative.

Madame de Malrive evinced no surprise. "It is natural, knowing what she has done for us, that you should want to show her your sympathy. The difficulty is that it is just the one thing you *can't* show her. You can thank her, of course, for ourselves, but even that at the moment——"

"Would seem brutal? Yes, I recognize that I should have to choose my words," he admitted, guiltily conscious that his capability of dealing with Madame de Treymes extended far beyond her sister-in-law's conjecture.

Madame de Malrive still hesitated. "I can tell her; and when you come back tomorrow——"

It had been decided that, in the interests of discretion—the interests, in other words, of the poor little future Marquis de Malrive—Durham was to remain but two days in Paris, withdrawing then with his family till the conclusion of the divorce proceedings permitted him to return in the acknowledged character of Madame de Malrive's future husband. Even on this occasion, he had not come to her alone; Nannie Durham, in the adjoining room, was chatting conspicuously with the little Marquis, whom she could with difficulty be restrained from teaching to call her "Aunt Nannie." Durham thought her voice had risen unduly once or twice during his visit, and when, on taking leave, he went to summon her from the inner room, he found the higher note of ecstasy had been evoked by the appearance of Madame de Treymes, and that the little boy, himself absorbed in a new toy of Durham's bringing, was being bent over by an actual as well as a potential aunt.

Madame de Treymes raised herself with a slight start at Durham's approach: she had her hat on, and had evidently paused a moment on her way out to speak with Nannie, without expecting to be surprised by her sister-in-law's other visitor. But her surprises never wore the awkward form of embarrassment, and she smiled beautifully on Durham as he took her extended hand.

The smile was made the more appealing by the way in which it lit up the ruin of her small dark face, which looked seared and hollowed as by a flame that might have spread over it from her fevered eyes. Durham, accustomed to the pale inward grief of the inexpressive races, was positively startled by the way in which she seemed to have been openly

stretched on the pyre; he almost felt an indelicacy in the ravages so tragically confessed.

The sight caused an involuntary readjustment of his whole
view of the situation, and made him, as far as his own share in
it went, more than ever inclined to extremities of self-disgust.
With him such sensations required, for his own relief, some
immediate penitential escape, and as Madame de Treymes
turned toward the door he addressed a glance of entreaty to
his betrothed.

Madame de Malrive, whose intelligence could be counted
on at such moments, responded by laying a detaining hand
on her sister-in-law's arm.

"Dear Christiane, may I leave Mr. Durham in your charge
for two minutes? I have promised Nannie that she shall see
the boy put to bed."

Madame de Treymes made no audible response to this request, but when the door had closed on the other ladies she
said, looking quietly at Durham: "I don't think that, in this
house, your time will hang so heavy that you need my help in
supporting it."

Durham met her glance frankly. "It was not for that reason
that Madame de Malrive asked you to remain with me."

"Why, then? Surely not in the interest of preserving appearances, since she is safely upstairs with your sister?"

"No; but simply because I asked her to. I told her I wanted
to speak to you."

"How you arrange things! And what reason can you have
for wanting to speak to me?"

He paused a moment. "Can't you imagine? The desire to
thank you for what you have done."

She stirred restlessly, turning to adjust her hat before the
glass above the mantelpiece.

"Oh, as for what I have done——!"

"Don't speak as if you regretted it," he interposed.

She turned back to him with a flash of laughter lighting up
the haggardness of her face. "Regret working for the happiness of two such excellent persons? Can't you fancy what a
charming change it is for me to do something so innocent
and beneficent?"

He moved across the room and went up to her, drawing

down the hand which still flitted experimentally about her hat.

"Don't talk in that way, however much one of the persons of whom you speak may have deserved it."

"One of the persons? Do you mean me?"

He released her hand, but continued to face her resolutely. "I mean myself, as you know. You have been generous—extraordinarily generous."

"Ah, but I was doing good in a good cause. You have made me see that there is a distinction."

He flushed to the forehead. "I am here to let you say whatever you choose to me."

"Whatever I choose?" She made a slight gesture of deprecation. "Has it never occurred to you that I may conceivably choose to say nothing?"

Durham paused, conscious of the increasing difficulty of the advance. She met him, parried him, at every turn: he had to take his baffled purpose back to another point of attack.

"Quite conceivably," he said: "so much so that I am aware I must make the most of this opportunity, because I am not likely to get another."

"But what remains of your opportunity, if it is n't one to me?"

"It still remains, for me, an occasion to abase myself——" He broke off, conscious of a grossness of allusion that seemed, on a closer approach, the real obstacle to full expression. But the moments were flying, and for his self-esteem's sake he must find some way of making her share the burden of his repentance.

"There is only one thinkable pretext for detaining you: it is that I may still show my sense of what you have done for me."

Madame de Treymes, who had moved toward the door, paused at this and faced him, resting her thin brown hands on a slender sofa-back.

"How do you propose to show that sense?" she enquired.

Durham coloured still more deeply: he saw that she was determined to save her pride by making what he had to say of the utmost difficulty. Well! he would let his expiation take that form, then—it was as if her slender hands held out to him the fool's cap he was condemned to press down on his own ears.

"By offering in return—in any form, and to the utmost—any service you are forgiving enough to ask of me."

She received this with a low sound of laughter that scarcely rose to her lips. "You are princely. But, my dear sir, does it not occur to you that I may, meanwhile, have taken my own way of repaying myself for any service I have been fortunate enough to render you?"

Durham, at the question, or still more, perhaps, at the tone in which it was put, felt, through his compunction, a vague faint chill of apprehension. Was she threatening him or only mocking him? Or was this barbed swiftness of retort only the wounded creature's way of defending the privacy of her own pain? He looked at her again, and read his answer in the last conjecture.

"I don't know how you can have repaid yourself for anything so disinterested—but I am sure, at least, that you have given me no chance of recognizing, ever so slightly, what you have done."

She shook her head, with the flicker of a smile on her melancholy lips. "Don't be too sure! You have given me a chance and I have taken it—taken it to the full. So fully," she continued, keeping her eyes fixed on his, "that if I were to accept any farther service you might choose to offer, I should simply be robbing you—robbing you shamelessly." She paused, and added in an undefinable voice: "I was entitled, wasn't I, to take something in return for the service I had the happiness of doing you?"

Durham could not tell whether the irony of her tone was self-directed or addressed to himself—perhaps it comprehended them both. At any rate, he chose to overlook his own share in it in replying earnestly: "So much so, that I can't see how you can have left me nothing to add to what you say you have taken."

"Ah, but you don't know what that is!" She continued to smile, elusively, ambiguously. "And what's more, you wouldn't believe me if I told you."

"How do you know?" he rejoined.

"You did n't believe me once before; and this is so much more incredible."

He took the taunt full in the face. "I shall go away unhappy unless you tell me—but then perhaps I have deserved to," he confessed.

She shook her head again, advancing toward the door with the evident intention of bringing their conference to a close; but on the threshold she paused to launch her reply.

"I can't send you away unhappy, since it is in the contemplation of your happiness that I have found my reward."

IX

THE NEXT DAY Durham left with his family for England, with the intention of not returning till after the divorce should have been pronounced in September.

To say that he left with a quiet heart would be to overstate the case: the fact that he could not communicate to Madame de Malrive the substance of his talk with her sister-in-law still hung upon him uneasily. But of definite apprehensions the lapse of time gradually freed him, and Madame de Malrive's letters, addressed more frequently to his mother and sisters than to himself, reflected, in their reassuring serenity, the undisturbed course of events.

There was to Durham something peculiarly touching—as of an involuntary confession of almost unbearable loneliness—in the way she had regained, with her re-entry into the clear air of American associations, her own fresh trustfulness of view. Once she had accustomed herself to the surprise of finding her divorce unopposed, she had been, as it now seemed to Durham, in almost too great haste to renounce the habit of weighing motives and calculating chances. It was as though her coming liberation had already freed her from the garb of a mental slavery, as though she could not too soon or too conspicuously cast off the ugly badge of suspicion. The fact that Durham's cleverness had achieved so easy a victory over forces apparently impregnable, merely raised her estimate of that cleverness to the point of letting her feel that she could rest in it without farther demur. He had even noticed in her, during his few hours in Paris, a tendency to reproach herself for her lack of charity, and a desire, almost as fervent as his own, to expiate it by exaggerated recognition of the disinterestedness of her opponents—if opponents they could still be called. This sudden change in her attitude was peculiarly moving to Durham. He knew she would hazard herself lightly enough wherever her heart called her; but that, with the precious freight of her child's future weighing her down, she should commit herself so blindly to his hand stirred in him the depths of tenderness. Indeed, had the actual course of events been less auspiciously regular, Madame de Malrive's

48

confidence would have gone far toward unsettling his own; but with the process of law going on unimpeded, and the other side making no sign of open or covert resistance, the fresh air of good faith gradually swept through the inmost recesses of his distrust.

It was expected that the decision in the suit would be reached by mid-September; and it was arranged that Durham and his family should remain in England till a decent interval after the conclusion of the proceedings. Early in the month, however, it became necessary for Durham to go to France to confer with a business associate who was in Paris for a few days, and on the point of sailing for Cherbourg. The most zealous observance of appearances could hardly forbid Durham's return for such a purpose; but it had been agreed between himself and Madame de Malrive—who had once more been left alone by Madame de Treymes' return to her family—that, so close to the fruition of their wishes, they would propitiate fate by a scrupulous adherence to usage, and communicate only, during his hasty visit, by a daily interchange of notes.

The ingenuity of Madame de Malrive's tenderness found, however, the day after his arrival, a means of tempering their privation. "Christiane," she wrote, "is passing through Paris on her way from Trouville, and has promised to see you for me if you will call on her today. She thinks there is no reason why you should not go to the Hôtel de Malrive, as you will find her there alone, the family having gone to Auvergne. She is really our friend and understands us."

In obedience to this request—though perhaps inwardly regretting that it should have been made—Durham that afternoon presented himself at the proud old house beyond the Seine. More than ever, in the semi-abandonment of the *morte saison*, with reduced service, and shutters closed to the silence of the high-walled court, did it strike the American as the incorruptible custodian of old prejudices and strange social survivals. The thought of what he must represent to the almost human consciousness which such old houses seem to possess, made him feel like a barbarian desecrating the silence of a temple of the earlier faith. Not that there was anything venerable in the attestations of the Hôtel de Malrive, except in so far as, to a sensitive imagination, every concrete embodiment of a past order of things testifies to real convictions once suffered for. Durham, at any rate, always alive in practical issues to the view of the other side, had enough sympathy left over to spend it sometimes, whimsically, on such perceptions of difference. Today, especially, the assurance of success—the sense of entering like a victorious beleaguerer receiving the keys of the stronghold—disposed him to a sentimental perception of what the other side might have to say for itself, in the language of old portraits, old relics, old usages dumbly outraged by his mere presence.

On the appearance of Madame de Treymes, however, such considerations gave way to the immediate act of wondering how she meant to carry off her share of the adventure. Durham had not forgotten the note on which their last conversation had closed: the lapse of time serving only to give more precision and perspective to the impression he had then received.

Madame de Treymes' first words implied a recognition of what was in his thoughts.

"It is extraordinary, my receiving you here; but *que voulez vous*? There was no other place, and I would do more than this for our dear Fanny."

Durham bowed. "It seems to me that you are also doing a great deal for me."

"Perhaps you will see later that I have my reasons," she returned, smiling. "But before speaking for myself I must speak for Fanny."

She signed to him to take a chair near the sofa-corner in which she had installed herself, and he listened in silence while she delivered Madame de Malrive's message, and her own report of the progress of affairs.

"You have put me still more deeply in your debt," he said as she concluded; "I wish you would make the expression of this feeling a large part of the message I send back to Madame de Malrive."

She brushed this aside with one of her light gestures of deprecation. "Oh, I told you I had my reasons. And since you are here—and the mere sight of you assures me that you are as well as Fanny charged me to find you—with all these preliminaries disposed of, I am going to relieve you, in a small measure, of the weight of your obligation."

Durham raised his head quickly. "By letting me do something in return?"

She made an assenting motion. "By asking you to answer a question."

"That seems very little to do."

"Don't be so sure! It is never very little to your race." She leaned back, studying him through half-dropped lids.

"Well, try me," he protested.

She did not immediately respond; and when she spoke, her first words were explanatory rather than interrogative.

"I want to begin by saying that I believe I once did you an injustice, to the extent of misunderstanding your motive for a certain action."

Durham's uneasy flush confessed his recognition of her meaning. "Ah, if we must go back to *that*——"

"You withdraw your assent to my request?"

"By no means; but nothing consolatory you can find to say on that point can really make any difference."

"Will not the difference in my view of you perhaps make a difference in your own?"

She looked at him earnestly, without a trace of irony in her eyes or on her lips. "It is really I who have an *amende* to make, as I now understand the situation. I once turned to you for help in a painful extremity, and I have only now learned to understand your reasons for refusing to help me."

"Oh, my reasons——" groaned Durham.

"I have learned to understand them," she persisted, "by being so much, lately, with Fanny."

"But I never told her!" he broke in.

"Exactly. That was what told *me*. I understood you through her, and through your dealings with her. There she was—the woman you adored and longed to save; and you would not lift a finger to make her yours by means which would have seemed—I see it now—a desecration of your feeling for each other." She paused, as if to find the exact words for meanings she had never before had occasion to formulate. "It came to me first—a light on your attitude—when I found you had never breathed to her a word of our talk together. She had

confidently commissioned you to find a way for her, as the
mediaeval lady sent a prayer to her knight to deliver her from
captivity, and you came back, confessing you had failed, but
never justifying yourself by so much as a hint of the reason
why. And when I had lived a little in Fanny's intimacy—at a
moment when circumstances helped to bring us extraordinarily close—I understood why you had done this; why you had
let her take what view she pleased of your failure, your passive
acceptance of defeat, rather than let her suspect the alternative
offered you. You couldn't, even with my permission, betray
to any one a hint of my miserable secret, and you couldn't,
for your life's happiness, pay the particular price that I asked."
She leaned toward him in the intense, almost childlike, effort
at full expression. "Oh, we are of different races, with a different point of honour; but I understand, I see, that you are
good people—just simply, courageously *good!*"

She paused, and then said slowly: "Have I understood you?
Have I put my hand on your motive?"

Durham sat speechless, subdued by the rush of emotion
which her words set free.

"That, you understand, is my question," she concluded
with a faint smile; and he answered hesitatingly: "What can it
matter, when the upshot is something I infinitely regret?"

"Having refused me? Don't!" She spoke with deep seriousness, bending her eyes full on his: "Ah, I have suffered—
suffered! But I have learned also—my life has been enlarged.
You see how I have understood you both. And that is something I should have been incapable of a few months ago."

Durham returned her look. "I can't think that you can ever
have been incapable of any generous interpretation."

She uttered a slight exclamation, which resolved itself into a
laugh of self-directed irony.

"If you knew into what language I have always translated
life! But that," she broke off, "is not what you are here to
learn."

"I think," he returned gravely, "that I am here to learn the
measure of Christian charity."

She threw him a new, odd look. "Ah, no—but to show it!"
she exclaimed.

"To show it? And to whom?"

She paused for a moment, and then rejoined, instead of answering: "Do you remember that day I talked with you at Fanny's? The day after you came back from Italy?"

He made a motion of assent, and she went on: "You asked me then what return I expected for my service to you, as you called it; and I answered, the contemplation of your happiness. Well, do you know what that meant in my old language—the language I was still speaking then? It meant that I knew there was horrible misery in store for you, and that I was waiting to feast my eyes on it: that's all!"

She had flung out the words with one of her quick bursts of self-abandonment, like a fevered sufferer stripping the bandage from a wound. Durham received them with a face blanching to the pallor of her own.

"What misery do you mean?" he exclaimed.

She leaned forward, laying her hand on his with just such a gesture as she had used to enforce her appeal in Mrs. Boykin's boudoir. The remembrance made him shrink slightly from her touch, and she drew back with a smile.

"Have you never asked yourself," she enquired, "why our family consented so readily to a divorce?"

"Yes, often," he replied, all his unformed fears gathering in a dark throng about him. "But Fanny was so reassured, so convinced that we owed it to your good offices——"

She broke into a laugh. "My good offices! Will you never, you Americans, learn that we do not act individually in such cases? That we are all obedient to a common principle of authority?"

"Then it was not you——"

She made an impatient shrugging motion. "Oh, you are too confiding—it is the other side of your beautiful good faith!"

"The side you have taken advantage of, it appears?"

"I—we—all of us. I especially!" she confessed.

X

THERE WAS another pause, during which Durham tried to steady himself against the shock of the impending revelation. It was an odd circumstance of the case, that though Madame de Treymes' avowal of duplicity was fresh in his ears, he did not for a moment believe that she would deceive him again. Whatever passed between them now would go to the root of the matter.

The first thing that passed was the long look they exchanged: searching on his part, tender, sad, undefinable on hers. As the result of it he said: "Why, then, did you consent to the divorce?"

"To get the boy back," she answered instantly; and while he sat stunned by the unexpectedness of the retort, she went on: "Is it possible you never suspected? It has been our whole thought from the first. Everything was planned with that object."

He drew a sharp breath of alarm. "But the divorce—how could that give him back to you?"

"It was the only thing that could. We trembled lest the idea should occur to you. But we were reasonably safe, for there has only been one other case of the same kind before the courts." She leaned back, the sight of his perplexity checking her quick rush of words. "You didn't know," she began again, "that in that case, on the remarriage of the mother, the courts instantly restored the child to the father, though he had—well, given as much cause for divorce as my unfortunate brother?"

Durham gave an ironic laugh. "Your French justice takes a grammar and dictionary to understand."

She smiled. "*We* understand it—and it isn't necessary that you should."

"So it would appear!" he exclaimed bitterly.

"Don't judge us too harshly—or not, at least, till you have taken the trouble to learn our point of view. You consider the individual—we think only of the family."

"Why don't you take care to preserve it, then?"

"Ah, that's what we do; in spite of every aberration of the

individual. And so, when we saw it was impossible that my brother and his wife should live together, we simply transferred our allegiance to the child—we constituted *him* the family."

"A precious kindness you did him! If the result is to give him back to his father."

"That, I admit, is to be deplored; but his father is only a fraction of the whole. What we really do is to give him back to his race, his religion, his true place in the order of things."

"His mother never tried to deprive him of any of those inestimable advantages!"

Madame de Treymes unclasped her hands with a slight gesture of deprecation.

"Not consciously, perhaps; but silences and reserves can teach so much. His mother has another point of view——"

"Thank heaven!" Durham interjected.

"Thank heaven for *her*—yes—perhaps; but it would not have done for the boy."

Durham squared his shoulders with the sudden resolve of a man breaking through a throng of ugly phantoms.

"You have n't yet convinced me that it won't have to do for him. At the time of Madame de Malrive's separation, the court made no difficulty about giving her the custody of her son; and you must pardon me for reminding you that the father's unfitness was the reason alleged."

Madame de Treymes shrugged her shoulders. "And my poor brother, you would add, has not changed; but the circumstances have, and that proves precisely what I have been trying to show you: that, in such cases, the general course of events is considered, rather than the action of any one person."

"Then why is Madame de Malrive's action to be considered?"

"Because it breaks up the unity of the family."

"*Unity*——!" broke from Durham; and Madame de Treymes gently suffered his smile.

"Of the family tradition, I mean: it introduces new elements. You are a new element."

"Thank heaven!" said Durham again.

She looked at him singularly. "Yes—you may thank heaven. Why is n't it enough to satisfy Fanny?"

"Why is n't what enough?"

"Your being, as I say, a new element; taking her so completely into a better air. Why should n't she be content to begin a new life with you, without wanting to keep the boy too?"

Durham stared at her dumbly. "I don't know what you mean," he said at length.

"I mean that in her place——" she broke off, dropping her eyes. "She may have another son—the son of the man she adores."

Durham rose from his seat and took a quick turn through the room. She sat motionless, following his steps through her lowered lashes, which she raised again slowly as he stood before her.

"Your idea, then, is that I should tell her nothing?" he said.

"Tell her *now*? But, my poor friend, you would be ruined!"

"Exactly." He paused. "Then why have you told *me*?"

Under her dark skin he saw the faint colour stealing. "We see things so differently—but can't you conceive that, after all that has passed, I felt it a kind of loyalty not to leave you in ignorance?"

"And you feel no such loyalty to her?"

"Ah, I leave her to you," she murmured, looking down again.

Durham continued to stand before her, grappling slowly with his perplexity, which loomed larger and darker as it closed in on him.

"You don't leave her to me; you take her from me at a stroke! I suppose," he added painfully, "I ought to thank you for doing it before it's too late."

She stared. "I take her from you? I simply prevent your going to her unprepared. Knowing Fanny as I do, it seemed to me necessary that you should find a way in advance—a way of tiding over the first moment. That, of course, is what we had planned that you should n't have. We meant to let you marry, and then—. Oh, there is no question about the result: we are certain of our case—our measures have been taken *de loin*." She broke off, as if oppressed by his stricken silence.

"You will think me stupid, but my warning you of this is the only return I know how to make for your generosity. I could not bear to have you say afterward that I had deceived you twice."

"Twice?" he looked at her perplexedly, and her colour rose.

"I deceived you once—that night at your cousin's, when I tried to get you to bribe me. Even then we meant to consent to the divorce—it was decided the first day that I saw you." He was silent, and she added, with one of her mocking gestures: "You see from what a *milieu* you are taking her!"

Durham groaned. "She will never give up her son!"

"How can she help it? After you are married there will be no choice."

"No—but there is one now."

"*Now?*" She sprang to her feet, clasping her hands in dismay. "Have n't I made it clear to you? Have n't I shown you your course?" She paused, and then brought out with emphasis: "I love Fanny, and I am ready to trust her happiness to you."

"I shall have nothing to do with her happiness," he repeated doggedly.

She stood close to him, with a look intently fixed on his face. "Are you afraid?" she asked with one of her mocking flashes.

"Afraid?"

"Of not being able to make it up to her——?"

Their eyes met, and he returned her look steadily.

"No; if I had the chance, I believe I could."

"I know you could!" she exclaimed.

"That's the worst of it," he said with a cheerless laugh.

"The worst——?"

"Don't you see that I can't deceive her? Can't trick her into marrying me now?"

Madame de Treymes continued to hold his eyes for a puzzled moment after he had spoken; then she broke out despairingly: "Is happiness never more to you, then, than this abstract standard of truth?"

Durham reflected. "I don't know—it's an instinct. There does n't seem to be any choice."

"Then I am a miserable wretch for not holding my tongue!"

He shook his head sadly. "That would not have helped me; and it would have been a thousand times worse for her."

"Nothing can be as bad for her as losing you! Are n't you moved by seeing her need?"

"Horribly—are not *you*?" he said, lifting his eyes to hers suddenly.

She started under his look. "You mean, why don't I help you? Why don't I use my influence? Ah, if you knew how I have tried!"

"And you are sure that nothing can be done?"

"Nothing, nothing: what arguments can I use? We abhor divorce—we go against our religion in consenting to it—and nothing short of recovering the boy could possibly justify us."

Durham turned slowly away. "Then there is nothing to be done," he said, speaking more to himself than to her.

He felt her light touch on his arm. "Wait! There is one thing more——" She stood close to him, with entreaty written on her small passionate face. "There is one thing more," she repeated. "And that is, to believe that I am deceiving you again."

He stopped short with a bewildered stare. "That you are deceiving me—about the boy?"

"Yes—yes; why should n't I? You're so credulous—the temptation is irresistible."

"Ah, it would be too easy to find out—"

"Don't try, then! Go on as if nothing had happened. I have been lying to you," she declared with vehemence.

"Do you give me your word of honour?" he rejoined.

"A liar's? I have n't any! Take the logic of the facts instead. What reason have you to believe any good of me? And what reason have I to do any to you? Why on earth should I betray my family for your benefit? Ah, don't let yourself be deceived to the end!" She sparkled up at him, her eyes suffused with mockery; but on the lashes he saw a tear.

He shook his head sadly. "I should first have to find a reason for your deceiving me."

"Why, I gave it to you long ago. I wanted to punish you—and now I've punished you enough."

"Yes, you've punished me enough," he conceded.

The tear gathered and fell down her thin cheek. "It's you who are punishing me now. I tell you I'm false to the core. Look back and see what I've done to you!"

He stood silent, with his eyes fixed on the ground. Then he took one of her hands and raised it to his lips.

"You poor, good woman!" he said gravely.

Her hand trembled as she drew it away. "You're going to her—straight from here?"

"Yes—straight from here."

"To tell her everything—to renounce your hope?"

"That is what it amounts to, I suppose."

She watched him cross the room and lay his hand on the door.

"Ah, you poor, good man!" she said with a sob.

ETHAN FROME

I HAD THE STORY, bit by bit, from various people, and, as generally happens in such cases, each time it was a different story.

If you know Starkfield, Massachusetts, you know the post-office. If you know the post-office you must have seen Ethan Frome drive up to it, drop the reins on his hollow-backed bay and drag himself across the brick pavement to the white colonnade: and you must have asked who he was.

It was there that, several years ago, I saw him for the first time; and the sight pulled me up sharp. Even then he was the most striking figure in Starkfield, though he was but the ruin of a man. It was not so much his great height that marked him, for the "natives" were easily singled out by their lank longitude from the stockier foreign breed: it was the careless powerful look he had, in spite of a lameness checking each step like the jerk of a chain. There was something bleak and unapproachable in his face, and he was so stiffened and grizzled that I took him for an old man and was surprised to hear that he was not more than fifty-two. I had this from Harmon Gow, who had driven the stage from Bettsbridge to Starkfield in pre-trolley days and knew the chronicle of all the families on his line.

"He's looked that way ever since he had his smash-up; and that's twenty-four years ago come next February," Harmon threw out between reminiscent pauses.

The "smash-up" it was—I gathered from the same informant—which, besides drawing the red gash across Ethan Frome's forehead, had so shortened and warped his right side that it cost him a visible effort to take the few steps from his buggy to the post-office window. He used to drive in from his farm every day at about noon, and as that was my own hour for fetching my mail I often passed him in the porch or stood beside him while we waited on the motions of the distributing hand behind the grating. I noticed that, although he came so punctually, he seldom received anything but a copy of the *Bettsbridge Eagle*, which he put without a glance into his sagging pocket. At intervals, however, the post-

master would hand him an envelope addressed to Mrs. Zenobia—or Mrs. Zeena—Frome, and usually bearing conspicuously in the upper left-hand corner the address of some manufacturer of patent medicine and the name of his specific.
These documents my neighbour would also pocket without a
glance, as if too much used to them to wonder at their number and variety, and would then turn away with a silent nod
to the post-master.

Every one in Starkfield knew him and gave him a greeting
tempered to his own grave mien; but his taciturnity was respected and it was only on rare occasions that one of the older
men of the place detained him for a word. When this happened he would listen quietly, his blue eyes on the speaker's
face, and answer in so low a tone that his words never
reached me; then he would climb stiffly into his buggy,
gather up the reins in his left hand and drive slowly away in
the direction of his farm.

"It was a pretty bad smash-up?" I questioned Harmon,
looking after Frome's retreating figure, and thinking how
gallantly his lean brown head, with its shock of light hair,
must have sat on his shoulders before they were bent out of
shape.

"Wust kind," my informant assented. "More'n enough to
kill most men. But the Fromes are tough. Ethan'll likely touch
a hundred."

"Good God!" I exclaimed. At the moment Ethan Frome,
after climbing to his seat, had leaned over to assure himself of
the security of a wooden box—also with a druggist's label on
it—which he had placed in the back of the buggy, and I saw
his face as it probably looked when he thought himself alone.
"*That* man touch a hundred? He looks as if he was dead and
in hell now!"

Harmon drew a slab of tobacco from his pocket, cut off a
wedge and pressed it into the leather pouch of his cheek.
"Guess he's been in Starkfield too many winters. Most of the
smart ones get away."

"Why didn't *he*?"

"Somebody had to stay and care for the folks. There warn't
ever anybody but Ethan. Fust his father—then his mother—
then his wife."

"And then the smash-up?"

Harmon chuckled sardonically. "That's so. He *had* to stay then."

"I see. And since then they've had to care for him?"

Harmon thoughtfully passed his tobacco to the other cheek. "Oh, as to that: I guess it's always Ethan done the caring."

Though Harmon Gow developed the tale as far as his mental and moral reach permitted, there were perceptible gaps between his facts, and I had the sense that the deeper meaning of the story was in the gaps. But one phrase stuck in my memory and served as the nucleus about which I grouped my subsequent inferences: "Guess he's been in Starkfield too many winters."

Before my own time there was up I had learned to know what that meant. Yet I had come in the degenerate day of trolley, bicycle and rural delivery, when communication was easy between the scattered mountain villages, and the bigger towns in the valleys, such as Bettsbridge and Shadd's Falls, had libraries, theatres and Y.M.C.A. halls to which the youth of the hills could descend for recreation. But when winter shut down on Starkfield, and the village lay under a sheet of snow perpetually renewed from the pale skies, I began to see what life there—or rather its negation—must have been in Ethan Frome's young manhood.

I had been sent up by my employers on a job connected with the big power-house at Corbury Junction, and a long-drawn carpenters' strike had so delayed the work that I found myself anchored at Starkfield—the nearest habitable spot—for the best part of the winter. I chafed at first, and then, under the hypnotising effect of routine, gradually began to find a grim satisfaction in the life. During the early part of my stay I had been struck by the contrast between the vitality of the climate and the deadness of the community. Day by day, after the December snows were over, a blazing blue sky poured down torrents of light and air on the white landscape, which gave them back in an intenser glitter. One would have supposed that such an atmosphere must quicken the emotions as well as the blood; but it seemed to produce no change except that of retarding still more the sluggish pulse of Starkfield. When I had been there a little longer, and had seen this phase of crystal clearness followed by long stretches of sunless cold; when the storms of February had pitched their white tents about the devoted village, and the wild cavalry of March winds had charged down to their support; I began to understand why Starkfield emerged from its six months' siege like a starved garrison capitulating without quarter. Twenty years earlier the means of resistance must have been far fewer, and the enemy in command of almost all the lines of access between the beleaguered villages; and, considering these things, I felt the sinister force of Harmon's phrase: "Most of the smart ones get away." But if that were the case, how could any combination of obstacles have hindered the flight of a man like Ethan Frome?

During my stay at Starkfield I lodged with a middle-aged widow colloquially known as Mrs. Ned Hale. Mrs. Hale's father had been the village lawyer of the previous generation, and "lawyer Varnum's house," where my landlady still lived with her mother, was the most considerable mansion in the village. It stood at one end of the main street, its classic portico and small-paned windows looking down a flagged path between Norway spruces to the slim white steeple of the Congregational church. It was clear that the Varnum fortunes were at the ebb, but the two women did what they could to preserve a decent dignity; and Mrs. Hale, in particular, had a certain wan refinement not out of keeping with her pale old-fashioned house.

In the "best parlour," with its black horse-hair and mahogany weakly illuminated by a gurgling Carcel lamp, I listened every evening to another and more delicately shaded version of the Starkfield chronicle. It was not that Mrs. Ned Hale felt, or affected, any social superiority to the people about her; it was only that the accident of a finer sensibility and a little more education had put just enough distance between herself and her neighbours to enable her to judge them with detachment. She was not unwilling to exercise this faculty, and I had great hopes of getting from her the missing facts of Ethan Frome's story, or rather such a key to his character as should co-ordinate the facts I knew. Her mind was a store-house of innocuous anecdote, and any question about her acquaintances brought forth a volume of detail; but on the subject of Ethan Frome I found her unexpectedly reticent. There was no hint of disapproval in her reserve; I merely felt in her an insurmountable reluctance to speak of him or his affairs, a low "Yes, I knew them both . . . it was awful . . ." seeming to be the utmost concession that her distress could make to my curiosity.

So marked was the change in her manner, such depths of sad initiation did it imply, that, with some doubts as to my delicacy, I put the case anew to my village oracle, Harmon Gow; but got for my pains only an uncomprehending grunt.

"Ruth Varnum was always as nervous as a rat; and, come to think of it, she was the first one to see 'em after they was picked up. It happened right below lawyer Varnum's, down at the bend of the Corbury road, just round about the time that Ruth got engaged to Ned Hale. The young folks was all friends, and I guess she just can't bear to talk about it. She's had troubles enough of her own."

All the dwellers in Starkfield, as in more notable communities, had had troubles enough of their own to make them comparatively indifferent to those of their neighbours; and though all conceded that Ethan Frome's had been beyond the common measure, no one gave me an explanation of the look in his face which, as I persisted in thinking, neither poverty nor physical suffering could have put there. Nevertheless, I might have contented myself with the story pieced together from these hints had it not been for the provocation of Mrs. Hale's silence, and—a little later—for the accident of personal contact with the man.

On my arrival at Starkfield, Denis Eady, the rich Irish grocer, who was the proprietor of Starkfield's nearest approach to a livery stable, had entered into an agreement to send me over daily to Corbury Flats, where I had to pick up my train for the Junction. But about the middle of the winter Eady's horses fell ill of a local epidemic. The illness spread to the other Starkfield stables and for a day or two I was put to it to find a means of transport. Then Harmon Gow suggested that Ethan Frome's bay was still on his legs and that his owner might be glad to drive me over.

I stared at the suggestion. "Ethan Frome? But I've never

even spoken to him. Why on earth should he put himself out for me?"

Harmon's answer surprised me still more. "I don't know as he would; but I know he wouldn't be sorry to earn a dollar."

I had been told that Frome was poor, and that the saw-mill and the arid acres of his farm yielded scarcely enough to keep his household through the winter; but I had not supposed him to be in such want as Harmon's words implied, and I expressed my wonder.

"Well, matters ain't gone any too well with him," Harmon said. "When a man's been setting round like a hulk for twenty years or more, seeing things that want doing, it eats inter him, and he loses his grit. That Frome farm was always 'bout as bare's a milkpan when the cat's been round; and you know what one of them old water-mills is wuth nowadays. When Ethan could sweat over 'em both from sun-up to dark he kinder choked a living out of 'em; but his folks ate up most everything, even then, and I don't see how he makes out now. Fust his father got a kick, out haying, and went soft in the brain, and gave away money like Bible texts afore he died. Then his mother got queer and dragged along for years as weak as a baby; and his wife Zeena, she's always been the greatest hand at doctoring in the county. Sickness and trouble: that's what Ethan's had his plate full up with, ever since the very first helping."

The next morning, when I looked out, I saw the hollow-backed bay between the Varnum spruces, and Ethan Frome, throwing back his worn bearskin, made room for me in the sleigh at his side. After that, for a week, he drove me over every morning to Corbury Flats, and on my return in the afternoon met me again and carried me back through the icy night to Starkfield. The distance each way was barely three miles, but the old bay's pace was slow, and even with firm snow under the runners we were nearly an hour on the way. Ethan Frome drove in silence, the reins loosely held in his left hand, his brown seamed profile, under the helmet-like peak of the cap, relieved against the banks of snow like the bronze image of a hero. He never turned his face to mine, or answered, except in monosyllables, the questions I put, or such slight pleasantries as I ventured. He seemed a part of the mute melancholy landscape, an incarnation of its frozen woe, with all that was warm and sentient in him fast bound below the surface; but there was nothing unfriendly in his silence. I simply felt that he lived in a depth of moral isolation too remote for casual access, and I had the sense that his loneliness was not merely the result of his personal plight, tragic as I guessed that to be, but had in it, as Harmon Gow had hinted, the profound accumulated cold of many Starkfield winters.

Only once or twice was the distance between us bridged for a moment; and the glimpses thus gained confirmed my desire to know more. Once I happened to speak of an engineering job I had been on the previous year in Florida, and of the contrast between the winter landscape about us and that in which I had found myself the year before; and to my surprise Frome said suddenly: "Yes: I was down there once, and for a good while afterward I could call up the sight of it in winter. But now it's all snowed under."

He said no more, and I had to guess the rest from the inflection of his voice and his sharp relapse into silence.

Another day, on getting into my train at the Flats, I missed a volume of popular science—I think it was on some recent discoveries in bio-chemistry—which I had carried with me to read on the way. I thought no more about it till I got into the sleigh again that evening, and saw the book in Frome's hand.

"I found it after you were gone," he said.

I put the volume into my pocket and we dropped back into our usual silence; but as we began to crawl up the long hill from Corbury Flats to the Starkfield ridge I became aware in the dusk that he had turned his face to mine.

"There are things in that book that I didn't know the first word about," he said.

I wondered less at his words than at the queer note of resentment in his voice. He was evidently surprised and slightly aggrieved at his own ignorance.

"Does that sort of thing interest you?" I asked.

"It used to."

"There are one or two rather new things in the book: there have been some big strides lately in that particular line of research." I waited a moment for an answer that did not come; then I said: "If you'd like to look the book through I'd be glad to leave it with you."

He hesitated, and I had the impression that he felt himself about to yield to a stealing tide of inertia; then, "Thank you—I'll take it," he answered shortly.

I hoped that this incident might set up some more direct communication between us. Frome was so simple and straightforward that I was sure his curiosity about the book was based on a genuine interest in its subject. Such tastes and acquirements in a man of his condition made the contrast more poignant between his outer situation and his inner needs, and I hoped that the chance of giving expression to the latter might at least unseal his lips. But something in his past history, or in his present way of living, had apparently driven him too deeply into himself for any casual impulse to draw him back to his kind. At our next meeting he made no allusion to the book, and our intercourse seemed fated to remain as negative and one-sided as if there had been no break in his reserve.

Frome had been driving me over to the Flats for about a week when one morning I looked out of my window into a thick snow-fall. The height of the white waves massed against the garden-fence and along the wall of the church showed that the storm must have been going on all night, and that the drifts were likely to be heavy in the open. I thought it probable that my train would be delayed; but I had to be at the power-house for an hour or two that afternoon, and I decided, if Frome turned up, to push through to the Flats and wait there till my train came in. I don't know why I put it in the conditional, however, for I never doubted that Frome would appear. He was not the kind of man to be turned from his business by any commotion of the elements; and at the appointed hour his sleigh glided up through the snow like a stage-apparition behind thickening veils of gauze.

I was getting to know him too well to express either wonder or gratitude at his keeping his appointment; but I exclaimed in surprise as I saw him turn his horse in a direction opposite to that of the Corbury road.

"The railroad's blocked by a freight-train that got stuck in a drift below the Flats," he explained, as we jogged off into the stinging whiteness.

"But look here—where are you taking me, then?"

"Straight to the Junction, by the shortest way," he answered, pointing up School House Hill with his whip.

"To the Junction—in this storm? Why, it's a good ten miles!"

"The bay'll do it if you give him time. You said you had some business there this afternoon. I'll see you get there."

He said it so quietly that I could only answer: "You're doing me the biggest kind of a favour."

"That's all right," he rejoined.

Abreast of the schoolhouse the road forked, and we dipped down a lane to the left, between hemlock boughs bent inward to their trunks by the weight of the snow. I had often walked that way on Sundays, and knew that the solitary roof showing through bare branches near the bottom of the hill was that of Frome's saw-mill. It looked exanimate enough, with its idle wheel looming above the black stream dashed with yellow-white spume, and its cluster of sheds sagging under their white load. Frome did not even turn his head as we drove by, and still in silence we began to mount the next slope. About a mile farther, on a road I had never travelled, we came to an orchard of starved apple-trees writhing over a hillside among outcroppings of slate that nuzzled up through the snow like animals pushing out their noses to breathe. Beyond the orchard lay a field or two, their boundaries lost under drifts; and above the fields, huddled against the white immensities of land and sky, one of those lonely New England farm-houses that make the landscape lonelier.

"That's my place," said Frome, with a sideway jerk of his lame elbow; and in the distress and oppression of the scene I did not know what to answer. The snow had ceased, and a flash of watery sunlight exposed the house on the slope above us in all its plaintive ugliness. The black wraith of a deciduous creeper flapped from the porch, and the thin wooden walls, under their worn coat of paint, seemed to shiver in the wind that had risen with the ceasing of the snow.

"The house was bigger in my father's time: I had to take down the 'L,' a while back," Frome continued, checking with

a twitch of the left rein the bay's evident intention of turning
in through the broken-down gate.

I saw then that the unusually forlorn and stunted look of
the house was partly due to the loss of what is known in New
England as the "L": that long deep-roofed adjunct usually
built at right angles to the main house, and connecting it, by
way of store-rooms and tool-house, with the wood-shed and
cow-barn. Whether because of its symbolic sense, the image it
presents of a life linked with the soil, and enclosing in itself
the chief sources of warmth and nourishment, or whether
merely because of the consolatory thought that it enables the
dwellers in that harsh climate to get to their morning's work
without facing the weather, it is certain that the "L" rather
than the house itself seems to be the centre, the actual hearth-
stone, of the New England farm. Perhaps this connection of
ideas, which had often occurred to me in my rambles about
Starkfield, caused me to hear a wistful note in Frome's words,
and to see in the diminished dwelling the image of his own
shrunken body.

"We're kinder side-tracked here now," he added, "but there
was considerable passing before the railroad was carried
through to the Flats." He roused the lagging bay with another twitch; then, as if the mere sight of the house had let
me too deeply into his confidence for any farther pretence of
reserve, he went on slowly: "I've always set down the worst of
mother's trouble to that. When she got the rheumatism so
bad she couldn't move around she used to sit up there and
watch the road by the hour; and one year, when they was six
months mending the Bettsbridge pike after the floods, and
Harmon Gow had to bring his stage round this way, she
picked up so that she used to get down to the gate most days
to see him. But after the trains begun running nobody ever
come by here to speak of, and mother never could get it
through her head what had happened, and it preyed on her
right along till she died."

As we turned into the Corbury road the snow began to fall
again, cutting off our last glimpse of the house; and Frome's
silence fell with it, letting down between us the old veil of
reticence. This time the wind did not cease with the return of
the snow. Instead, it sprang up to a gale which now and then,

from a tattered sky, flung pale sweeps of sunlight over a landscape chaotically tossed. But the bay was as good as Frome's word, and we pushed on to the Junction through the wild white scene.

In the afternoon the storm held off, and the clearness in the west seemed to my inexperienced eye the pledge of a fair evening. I finished my business as quickly as possible, and we set out for Starkfield with a good chance of getting there for supper. But at sunset the clouds gathered again, bringing an earlier night, and the snow began to fall straight and steadily from a sky without wind, in a soft universal diffusion more confusing than the gusts and eddies of the morning. It seemed to be a part of the thickening darkness, to be the winter night itself descending on us layer by layer.

The small ray of Frome's lantern was soon lost in this smothering medium, in which even his sense of direction, and the bay's homing instinct, finally ceased to serve us. Two or three times some ghostly landmark sprang up to warn us that we were astray, and then was sucked back into the mist; and when we finally regained our road the old horse began to show signs of exhaustion. I felt myself to blame for having accepted Frome's offer, and after a short discussion I persuaded him to let me get out of the sleigh and walk along through the snow at the bay's side. In this way we struggled on for another mile or two, and at last reached a point where Frome, peering into what seemed to me formless night, said: "That's my gate down yonder."

The last stretch had been the hardest part of the way. The bitter cold and the heavy going had nearly knocked the wind out of me, and I could feel the horse's side ticking like a clock under my hand.

"Look here, Frome," I began, "there's no earthly use in your going any farther—" but he interrupted me: "Nor you neither. There's been about enough of this for anybody."

I understood that he was offering me a night's shelter at the farm, and without answering I turned into the gate at his side, and followed him to the barn, where I helped him to unharness and bed down the tired horse. When this was done he unhooked the lantern from the sleigh, stepped out again into the night, and called to me over his shoulder: "This way."

Far off above us a square of light trembled through the screen of snow. Staggering along in Frome's wake I floundered toward it, and in the darkness almost fell into one of the deep drifts against the front of the house. Frome scrambled up the slippery steps of the porch, digging a way through the snow with his heavily booted foot. Then he lifted his lantern, found the latch, and led the way into the house. I went after him into a low unlit passage, at the back of which a ladder-like staircase rose into obscurity. On our right a line of light marked the door of the room which had sent its ray across the night; and behind the door I heard a woman's voice droning querulously.

Frome stamped on the worn oil-cloth to shake the snow from his boots, and set down his lantern on a kitchen chair which was the only piece of furniture in the hall. Then he opened the door.

"Come in," he said; and as he spoke the droning voice grew still. . .

It was that night that I found the clue to Ethan Frome, and began to put together this vision of his story. . . . . .
. . . .
. . . .

I

THE VILLAGE lay under two feet of snow, with drifts at the windy corners. In a sky of iron the points of the Dipper hung like icicles and Orion flashed his cold fires. The moon had set, but the night was so transparent that the white house-fronts between the elms looked grey against the snow, clumps of bushes made black stains on it, and the basement windows of the church sent shafts of yellow light far across the endless undulations.

Young Ethan Frome walked at a quick pace along the deserted street, past the bank and Michael Eady's new brick store and Lawyer Varnum's house with the two black Norway spruces at the gate. Opposite the Varnum gate, where the road fell away toward the Corbury valley, the church reared its slim white steeple and narrow peristyle. As the young man walked toward it the upper windows drew a black arcade along the side wall of the building, but from the lower openings, on the side where the ground sloped steeply down to the Corbury road, the light shot its long bars, illuminating many fresh furrows in the track leading to the basement door, and showing, under an adjoining shed, a line of sleighs with heavily blanketed horses.

The night was perfectly still, and the air so dry and pure that it gave little sensation of cold. The effect produced on Frome was rather of a complete absence of atmosphere, as though nothing less tenuous than ether intervened between the white earth under his feet and the metallic dome overhead. "It's like being in an exhausted receiver," he thought. Four or five years earlier he had taken a year's course at a technological college at Worcester, and dabbled in the laboratory with a friendly professor of physics; and the images supplied by that experience still cropped up, at unexpected moments, through the totally different associations of thought in which he had since been living. His father's death, and the misfortunes following it, had put a premature end to Ethan's studies; but though they had not gone far enough to be of much practical use they had fed his fancy and made him aware of huge cloudy meanings behind the daily face of things.

As he strode along through the snow the sense of such meanings glowed in his brain and mingled with the bodily flush produced by his sharp tramp. At the end of the village he paused before the darkened front of the church. He stood there a moment, breathing quickly, and looking up and down the street, in which not another figure moved. The pitch of the Corbury road, below lawyer Varnum's spruces, was the favourite coasting-ground of Starkfield, and on clear evenings the church corner rang till late with the shouts of the coasters; but to-night not a sled darkened the whiteness of the long declivity. The hush of midnight lay on the village, and all its wakening life was gathered behind the church windows, from which strains of dance-music flowed with the broad bands of yellow light.

The young man, skirting the side of the building, went down the slope toward the basement door. To keep out of range of the revealing rays from within he made a circuit through the untrodden snow and gradually approached the farther angle of the basement wall. Thence, still hugging the shadow, he edged his way cautiously forward to the nearest window, holding back his straight spare body and craning his neck till he got a glimpse of the room.

Seen thus, from the pure and frosty darkness in which he stood, it seemed to be seething in a mist of heat. The metal reflectors of the gas-jets sent crude waves of light against the whitewashed walls, and the iron flanks of the stove at the end of the hall looked as though they were heaving with volcanic fires. The floor was thronged with girls and young men. Down the side wall facing the window stood a row of kitchen chairs from which the older women had just risen. By this time the music had stopped, and the musicians—a fiddler, and the young lady who played the harmonium on Sundays—were hastily refreshing themselves at one corner of the supper-table which aligned its devastated pie-dishes and ice-cream saucers on the platform at the end of the hall. The guests were preparing to leave, and the tide had already set toward the passage where coats and wraps were hung, when a young man with a sprightly foot and a shock of black hair shot into the middle of the floor and clapped his hands. The signal took instant effect. The musicians hurried to their instruments, the dancers—some already half-muffled for departure—fell into line down each side of the room, the older spectators slipped back to their chairs, and the lively young man, after diving about here and there in the throng, drew forth a girl who had already wound a cherry-coloured "fascinator" about her head, and, leading her up to the end of the floor, whirled her down its length to the bounding tune of a Virginia reel.

Frome's heart was beating fast. He had been straining for a glimpse of the dark head under the cherry-coloured scarf and it vexed him that another eye should have been quicker than his. The leader of the reel, who looked as if he had Irish blood in his veins, danced well, and his partner caught his fire. As she passed down the line, her light figure swinging from hand to hand in circles of increasing swiftness, the scarf flew off her head and stood out behind her shoulders, and Frome, at each turn, caught sight of her laughing panting lips, the cloud of dark hair about her forehead, and the dark eyes which seemed the only fixed points in a maze of flying lines.

The dancers were going faster and faster, and the musicians, to keep up with them, belaboured their instruments like jockeys lashing their mounts on the home-stretch; yet it seemed to the young man at the window that the reel would never end. Now and then he turned his eyes from the girl's face to that of her partner, which, in the exhilaration of the dance, had taken on a look of almost impudent ownership. Denis Eady was the son of Michael Eady, the ambitious Irish grocer, whose suppleness and effrontery had given Starkfield its first notion of "smart" business methods, and whose new brick store testified to the success of the attempt. His son seemed likely to follow in his steps, and was meanwhile applying the same arts to the conquest of the Starkfield maidenhood. Hitherto Ethan Frome had been content to think him a mean fellow; but now he positively invited a horse-whipping. It was strange that the girl did not seem aware of it: that she

could lift her rapt face to her dancer's, and drop her hands
into his, without appearing to feel the offence of his look and
touch.

Frome was in the habit of walking into Starkfield to fetch
home his wife's cousin, Mattie Silver, on the rare evenings
when some chance of amusement drew her to the village. It
was his wife who had suggested, when the girl came to live
with them, that such opportunities should be put in her way.
Mattie Silver came from Stamford, and when she entered the
Fromes' household to act as her cousin Zeena's aid it was
thought best, as she came without pay, not to let her feel too
sharp a contrast between the life she had left and the isolation
of a Starkfield farm. But for this—as Frome sardonically reflected—it would hardly have occurred to Zeena to take any
thought for the girl's amusement.

When his wife first proposed that they should give Mattie
an occasional evening out he had inwardly demurred at having to do the extra two miles to the village and back after his
hard day on the farm; but not long afterward he had reached
the point of wishing that Starkfield might give all its nights to
revelry.

Mattie Silver had lived under his roof for a year, and from
early morning till they met at supper he had frequent chances
of seeing her; but no moments in her company were compa-
rable to those when, her arm in his, and her light step flying
to keep time with his long stride, they walked back through
the night to the farm. He had taken to the girl from the first
day, when he had driven over to the Flats to meet her, and
she had smiled and waved to him from the train, crying out
"You must be Ethan!" as she jumped down with her bundles,
while he reflected, looking over her slight person: "She don't
look much on house-work, but she ain't a fretter, anyhow."
But it was not only that the coming to his house of a bit of
hopeful young life was like the lighting of a fire on a cold
hearth. The girl was more than the bright serviceable creature
he had thought her. She had an eye to see and an ear to hear:
he could show her things and tell her things, and taste the
bliss of feeling that all he imparted left long reverberations
and echoes he could wake at will.

It was during their night walks back to the farm that he

felt most intensely the sweetness of this communion. He had
always been more sensitive than the people about him to the
appeal of natural beauty. His unfinished studies had given
form to this sensibility and even in his unhappiest moments
field and sky spoke to him with a deep and powerful per-
suasion. But hitherto the emotion had remained in him as a
silent ache, veiling with sadness the beauty that evoked it.
He did not even know whether any one else in the world
felt as he did, or whether he was the sole victim of this
mournful privilege. Then he learned that one other spirit
had trembled with the same touch of wonder: that at his
side, living under his roof and eating his bread, was a creature to whom he could say: "That's Orion down yonder;
the big fellow to the right is Aldebaran, and the bunch of
little ones—like bees swarming—they're the Pleiades . . ."
or whom he could hold entranced before a ledge of granite
thrusting up through the fern while he unrolled the huge
panorama of the ice age, and the long dim stretches of succeeding time. The fact that admiration for his learning mingled with Mattie's wonder at what he taught was not the
least part of his pleasure. And there were other sensations,
less definable but more exquisite, which drew them together
with a shock of silent joy: the cold red of sunset behind
winter hills, the flight of cloud-flocks over slopes of golden
stubble, or the intensely blue shadows of hemlocks on sunlit
snow. When she said to him once: "It looks just as if it was
painted!" it seemed to Ethan that the art of definition could
go no farther, and that words had at last been found to utter
his secret soul. . . .

As he stood in the darkness outside the church these memories came back with the poignancy of vanished things.
Watching Mattie whirl down the floor from hand to hand, he
wondered how he could ever have thought that his dull talk
interested her. To him, who was never gay but in her presence, her gaiety seemed plain proof of indifference. The face
she lifted to her dancers was the same which, when she saw
him, always looked like a window that has caught the sunset.
He even noticed two or three gestures which, in his fatuity,
he had thought she kept for him: a way of throwing her head
back when she was amused, as if to taste her laugh before she

let it out, and a trick of sinking her lids slowly when anything charmed or moved her.

The sight made him unhappy, and his unhappiness roused his latent fears. His wife had never shown any jealousy of Mattie, but of late she had grumbled increasingly over the house-work and found oblique ways of attracting attention to the girl's inefficiency. Zeena had always been what Starkfield called "sickly," and Frome had to admit that, if she were as ailing as she believed, she needed the help of a stronger arm than the one which lay so lightly in his during the night walks to the farm. Mattie had no natural turn for house-keeping, and her training had done nothing to remedy the defect. She was quick to learn, but forgetful and dreamy, and not disposed to take the matter seriously. Ethan had an idea that if she were to marry a man she was fond of the dormant instinct would wake, and her pies and biscuits become the pride of the county; but domesticity in the abstract did not interest her. At first she was so awkward that he could not help laughing at her; but she laughed with him and that made them better friends. He did his best to supplement her unskilled efforts, getting up earlier than usual to light the kitchen fire, carrying in the wood overnight, and neglecting the mill for the farm that he might help her about the house during the day. He even crept down on Saturday nights to scrub the kitchen floor after the women had gone to bed; and Zeena, one day, had surprised him at the churn and had turned away silently, with one of her queer looks.

Of late there had been other signs of his wife's disfavour, as intangible but more disquieting. One cold winter morning, as he dressed in the dark, his candle flickering in the draught of the ill-fitting window, he had heard her speak from the bed behind him.

"The doctor don't want I should be left without anybody to do for me," she said in her flat whine.

He had supposed her to be asleep, and the sound of her voice had startled him, though she was given to abrupt explosions of speech after long intervals of secretive silence.

He turned and looked at her where she lay indistinctly outlined under the dark calico quilt, her high-boned face taking a greyish tinge from the whiteness of the pillow.

"Nobody to do for you?" he repeated.

"If you say you can't afford a hired girl when Mattie goes."

Frome turned away again, and taking up his razor stooped to catch the reflection of his stretched cheek in the blotched looking-glass above the wash-stand.

"Why on earth should Mattie go?"

"Well, when she gets married, I mean," his wife's drawl came from behind him.

"Oh, she'd never leave us as long as you needed her," he returned, scraping hard at his chin.

"I wouldn't ever have it said that I stood in the way of a poor girl like Mattie marrying a smart fellow like Denis Eady," Zeena answered in a tone of plaintive self-effacement.

Ethan, glaring at his face in the glass, threw his head back to draw the razor from ear to chin. His hand was steady, but the attitude was an excuse for not making an immediate reply.

"And the doctor don't want I should be left without anybody," Zeena continued. "He wanted I should speak to you about a girl he's heard about, that might come——"

Ethan laid down the razor and straightened himself with a laugh.

"Denis Eady! If that's all I guess there's no such hurry to look round for a girl."

"Well, I'd like to talk to you about it," said Zeena obstinately.

He was getting into his clothes in fumbling haste. "All right. But I haven't got the time now; I'm late as it is," he returned, holding his old silver turnip-watch to the candle.

Zeena, apparently accepting this as final, lay watching him in silence while he pulled his suspenders over his shoulders and jerked his arms into his coat; but as he went toward the door she said, suddenly and incisively: "I guess you're always late, now you shave every morning."

That thrust had frightened him more than any vague insinuations about Denis Eady. It was a fact that since Mattie Silver's coming he had taken to shaving every day; but his wife always seemed to be asleep when he left her side in the winter darkness, and he had stupidly assumed that she would not notice any change in his appearance. Once or twice in the past he had been faintly disquieted by Zenobia's way of letting things happen without seeming to remark them, and then, weeks afterward, in a casual phrase, revealing that she had all along taken her notes and drawn her inferences. Of late, however, there had been no room in his thoughts for such vague apprehensions. Zeena herself, from an oppressive reality, had faded into an insubstantial shade. All his life was lived in the sight and sound of Mattie Silver, and he could no longer conceive of its being otherwise. But now, as he stood outside the church, and saw Mattie spinning down the floor with Denis Eady, a throng of disregarded hints and menaces wove their cloud about his brain. . .

II

As the dancers poured out of the hall Frome, drawing back behind the projecting storm-door, watched the segregation of the grotesquely muffled groups, in which a moving lantern ray now and then lit up a face flushed with food and dancing. The villagers, being afoot, were the first to climb the slope to the main street, while the country neighbours packed themselves more slowly into the sleighs under the shed.

"Ain't you riding, Mattie?" a woman's voice called back from the throng about the shed, and Ethan's heart gave a jump. From where he stood he could not see the persons coming out of the hall till they had advanced a few steps beyond the wooden sides of the storm-door; but through its cracks he heard a clear voice answer: "Mercy no! Not on such a night."

She was there, then, close to him, only a thin board between. In another moment she would step forth into the night, and his eyes, accustomed to the obscurity, would discern her as clearly as though she stood in daylight. A wave of shyness pulled him back into the dark angle of the wall, and he stood there in silence instead of making his presence known to her. It had been one of the wonders of their intercourse that from the first, she, the quicker, finer, more expressive, instead of crushing him by the contrast, had given him something of her own ease and freedom; but now he felt as heavy and loutish as in his student days, when he had tried to "jolly" the Worcester girls at a picnic.

He hung back, and she came out alone and paused within a few yards of him. She was almost the last to leave the hall, and she stood looking uncertainly about her as if wondering why he did not show himself. Then a man's figure approached, coming so close to her that under their formless wrappings they seemed merged in one dim outline.

"Gentleman friend gone back on you? Say, Matt, that's tough! No, I wouldn't be mean enough to tell the other girls. I ain't as low-down as that." (How Frome hated Denis's

banter!) "But look at here, ain't it lucky I got the old man's
cutter down there waiting for us?"

Frome heard the girl's voice, gaily incredulous: "What on
earth's your father's cutter doin' down there?"

"Why, waiting for me to take a ride. I got the roan colt
too. I kinder knew I'd want to take a ride to-night," Eady, in
his triumph, tried to put a sentimental note into his bragging
voice.

The girl seemed to waver, and Frome saw her twirl the end
of her scarf irresolutely about her fingers. Not for the world
would he have made a sign to her, though it seemed to him
that his life hung on her next gesture.

"Hold on a minute while I unhitch the colt," Denis called
to her, springing toward the shed.

She stood perfectly still, looking after him, in an attitude
of tranquil expectancy torturing to the hidden watcher.
Frome noticed that she no longer turned her head from
side to side, as though peering through the night for another figure. She let Denis Eady lead out the horse, climb
into the cutter and fling back the bearskin to make room
for her at his side; then, with a swift motion of flight, she
turned about and darted up the slope toward the front of the
church.

"Good-bye! Hope you'll have a lovely ride!" she called back
to him over her shoulder.

Denis laughed, and gave the horse a cut that brought him
quickly abreast of her.

"Come along! Get in quick! It's as slippery as thunder
on this turn," he cried, leaning over to reach out a hand.

She laughed back at him: "Good-night! I'm not getting in."

By this time they had passed beyond Frome's earshot and
he could only follow the shadowy pantomime of their silhou-
ettes as they continued to move along the crest of the slope
above him. He saw Eady, after a moment, jump from the
cutter and go toward the girl with the reins over one arm.
The other he tried to slip through hers; but she eluded him
nimbly, and Frome's heart, which had swung out over a black
void, trembled back to safety. A moment later he heard
the jingle of departing sleigh bells and discerned a figure ad-

vancing alone toward the empty expanse of snow before the church.

In the black shade of the Varnum spruces he caught up with her and she turned with a quick "Oh!"

"Think I'd forgotten you, Matt?" he asked with sheepish glee.

She answered seriously: "I thought maybe you couldn't come back for me."

"Couldn't? What on earth could stop me?"

"I knew Zeena wasn't feeling any too good to-day."

"Oh, she's in bed long ago." He paused, a question struggling in him. "Then you meant to walk home all alone?"

"Oh, I ain't afraid!" she laughed.

They stood together in the gloom of the spruces, an empty world glimmering about them wide and grey under the stars. He brought his question out.

"If you thought I hadn't come, why didn't you ride back with Denis Eady?"

"Why, where *were* you? How did you know? I never saw you!"

Her wonder and his laughter ran together like spring rills in a thaw. Ethan had the sense of having done something arch and ingenious. To prolong the effect he groped for a dazzling phrase, and brought out, in a growl of rapture: "Come along."

He slipped an arm through hers, as Eady had done, and fancied it was faintly pressed against her side; but neither of them moved. It was so dark under the spruces that he could barely see the shape of her head beside his shoulder. He longed to stoop his cheek and rub it against her scarf. He would have liked to stand there with her all night in the blackness. She moved forward a step or two and then paused again above the dip of the Corbury road. Its icy slope, scored by innumerable runners, looked like a mirror scratched by travellers at an inn.

"There was a whole lot of them coasting before the moon set," she said.

"Would you like to come in and coast with them some night?" he asked.

"Oh, *would* you, Ethan? It would be lovely!"

"We'll come to-morrow if there's a moon."

She lingered, pressing closer to his side. "Ned Hale and Ruth Varnum came just as *near* running into the big elm at the bottom. We were all sure they were killed." Her shiver ran down his arm. "Wouldn't it have been too awful? They're so happy!"

"Oh, Ned ain't much at steering. I guess I can take you down all right!" he said disdainfully.

He was aware that he was "talking big," like Denis Eady; but his reaction of joy had unsteadied him, and the inflection with which she had said of the engaged couple "They're so happy!" made the words sound as if she had been thinking of herself and him.

"The elm *is* dangerous, though. It ought to be cut down," she insisted.

"Would you be afraid of it, with me?"

"I told you I ain't the kind to be afraid," she tossed back, almost indifferently; and suddenly she began to walk on with a rapid step.

These alterations of mood were the despair and joy of Ethan Frome. The motions of her mind were as incalculable as the flit of a bird in the branches. The fact that he had no right to show his feelings, and thus provoke the expression of hers, made him attach a fantastic importance to every change in her look and tone. Now he thought she understood him, and feared; now he was sure she did not, and despaired. To-night the pressure of accumulated misgivings sent the scale drooping toward despair, and her indifference was the more chilling after the flush of joy into which she had plunged him by dismissing Denis Eady. He mounted School House Hill at her side and walked on in silence till they reached the lane leading to the saw-mill; then the need of some definite assurance grew too strong for him.

"You'd have found me right off if you hadn't gone back to have that last reel with Denis," he brought out awkwardly. He could not pronounce the name without a stiffening of the muscles of his throat.

"Why, Ethan, how could I tell you were there?"

"I suppose what folks say is true," he jerked out at her, instead of answering.

She stopped short, and he felt, in the darkness, that her face was lifted quickly to his. "Why, what do folks say?"

"It's natural enough you should be leaving us," he floundered on, following his thought.

"Is that what they say?" she mocked back at him; then, with a sudden drop of her sweet treble: "You mean that Zeena—ain't suited with me any more?" she faltered.

Their arms had slipped apart and they stood motionless, each seeking to distinguish the other's face.

"I know I ain't anything like as smart as I ought to be," she went on, while he vainly struggled for expression. "There's lots of things a hired girl could do that come awkward to me still—and I haven't got much strength in my arms. But if she'd only tell me I'd try. You know she hardly ever says anything, and sometimes I can see she ain't suited, and yet I don't know why." She turned on him with a sudden flash of indignation. "You'd ought to tell me, Ethan Frome—you'd ought to! Unless *you* want me to go too——"

Unless he wanted her to go too! The cry was balm to his raw wound. The iron heavens seemed to melt and rain down sweetness. Again he struggled for the all-expressive word, and again, his arm in hers, found only a deep "Come along."

They walked on in silence through the blackness of the hemlock-shaded lane, where Ethan's saw-mill gloomed through the night, and out again into the comparative clearness of the fields. On the farther side of the hemlock belt the open country rolled away before them grey and lonely under the stars. Sometimes their way led them under the shade of an overhanging bank or through the thin obscurity of a clump of leafless trees. Here and there a farmhouse stood far back among the fields, mute and cold as a grave-stone. The night was so still that they heard the frozen snow crackle under their feet. The crash of a loaded branch falling far off in the woods reverberated like a musket-shot, and once a fox barked, and Mattie shrank closer to Ethan, and quickened her steps.

At length they sighted the group of larches at Ethan's gate, and as they drew near it the sense that the walk was over brought back his words.

"Then you don't want to leave us, Matt?"

He had to stoop his head to catch her stifled whisper: "Where'd I go, if I did?"

The answer sent a pang through him but the tone suffused him with joy. He forgot what else he had meant to say and pressed her against him so closely that he seemed to feel her warmth in his veins.

"You ain't crying are you, Matt?"

"No, of course I'm not," she quavered.

They turned in at the gate and passed under the shaded knoll where, enclosed in a low fence, the Frome grave-stones slanted at crazy angles through the snow. Ethan looked at them curiously. For years that quiet company had mocked his restlessness, his desire for change and freedom. "We never got away—how should you?" seemed to be written on every headstone; and whenever he went in or out of his gate he thought with a shiver: "I shall just go on living here till I join them." But now all desire for change had vanished, and the sight of the little enclosure gave him a warm sense of continuance and stability.

"I guess we'll never let you go, Matt," he whispered, as though even the dead, lovers once, must conspire with him to keep her; and brushing by the graves, he thought: "We'll always go on living here together, and some day she'll lie there beside me."

He let the vision possess him as they climbed the hill to the house. He was never so happy with her as when he abandoned himself to these dreams. Half-way up the slope Mattie stumbled against some unseen obstruction and clutched his sleeve to steady herself. The wave of warmth that went through him was like the prolongation of his vision. For the first time he stole his arm about her, and she did not resist. They walked on as if they were floating on a summer stream.

Zeena always went to bed as soon as she had had her supper, and the shutterless windows of the house were dark. A dead cucumber-vine dangled from the porch like the crape streamer tied to the door for a death, and the thought flashed through Ethan's brain: "If it was there for Zeena—" Then he had a distinct sight of his wife lying in their bedroom asleep, her mouth slightly open, her false teeth in a tumbler by the bed . . .

They walked around to the back of the house, between the rigid gooseberry bushes. It was Zeena's habit, when they came back late from the village, to leave the key of the kitchen door under the mat. Ethan stood before the door, his head heavy with dreams, his arm still about Mattie. "Matt——" he began, not knowing what he meant to say.

She slipped out of his hold without speaking, and he stooped down and felt for the key.

"It's not there!" he said, straightening himself with a start.

They strained their eyes at each other through the icy darkness. Such a thing had never happened before.

"Maybe she's forgotten it," Mattie said in a tremulous whisper; but both of them knew that it was not like Zeena to forget.

"It might have fallen off into the snow," Mattie continued, after a pause during which they had stood intently listening.

"It must have been pushed off, then," he rejoined in the same tone. Another wild thought tore through him. What if tramps had been there—what if . . .

Again he listened, fancying he heard a distant sound in the house; then he felt in his pocket for a match, and kneeling down, passed its light slowly over the rough edges of snow about the doorstep.

He was still kneeling when his eyes, on a level with the lower panel of the door, caught a faint ray beneath it. Who could be stirring in that silent house? He heard a step on the stairs, and again for an instant the thought of tramps tore through him. Then the door opened and he saw his wife.

Against the dark background of the kitchen she stood up tall and angular, one hand drawing a quilted counterpane to her flat breast, while the other held a lamp. The light, on a level with her chin, drew out of the darkness her puckered throat and the projecting wristbone of the hand that clutched the quilt, and deepened fantastically the hollows and prominences of her high-boned face under its ring of crimping-pins. To Ethan, still in the rosy haze of his hour with Mattie, the sight came with the intense precision of the last dream before waking. He felt as if he had never before known what his wife looked like.

She drew aside without speaking, and Mattie and Ethan passed into the kitchen, which had the deadly chill of a vault after the dry cold of the night.

"Guess you forgot about us, Zeena," Ethan joked, stamping the snow from his boots.

"No. I just felt so mean I couldn't sleep."

Mattie came forward, unwinding her wraps, the colour of the cherry scarf in her fresh lips and cheeks. "I'm so sorry, Zeena! Isn't there anything I can do?"

"No; there's nothing." Zeena turned away from her. "You might 'a' shook off that snow outside," she said to her husband.

She walked out of the kitchen ahead of them and pausing in the hall raised the lamp at arm's-length, as if to light them up the stairs.

Ethan paused also, affecting to fumble for the peg on which he hung his coat and cap. The doors of the two bedrooms faced each other across the narrow upper landing, and to-night it was peculiarly repugnant to him that Mattie should see him follow Zeena.

"I guess I won't come up yet awhile," he said, turning as if to go back to the kitchen.

Zeena stopped short and looked at him. "For the land's sake—what you going to do down here?"

"I've got the mill accounts to go over."

She continued to stare at him, the flame of the unshaded lamp bringing out with microscopic cruelty the fretful lines of her face.

"At this time o' night? You'll ketch your death. The fire's out long ago."

Without answering he moved away toward the kitchen. As he did so his glance crossed Mattie's and he fancied that a fugitive warning gleamed through her lashes. The next moment they sank to her flushed cheeks and she began to mount the stairs ahead of Zeena.

"That's so. It *is* powerful cold down here," Ethan assented; and with lowered head he went up in his wife's wake, and followed her across the threshold of their room.

III

THERE WAS some hauling to be done at the lower end of the wood-lot, and Ethan was out early the next day.

The winter morning was as clear as crystal. The sunrise burned red in a pure sky, the shadows on the rim of the wood-lot were darkly blue, and beyond the white and scintillating fields patches of far-off forest hung like smoke.

It was in the early morning stillness, when his muscles were swinging to their familiar task and his lungs expanding with long draughts of mountain air, that Ethan did his clearest thinking. He and Zeena had not exchanged a word after the door of their room had closed on them. She had measured out some drops from a medicine-bottle on a chair by the bed and, after swallowing them, and wrapping her head in a piece of yellow flannel, had lain down with her face turned away. Ethan undressed hurriedly and blew out the light so that he should not see her when he took his place at her side. As he lay there he could hear Mattie moving about in her room, and her candle, sending its small ray across the landing, drew a scarcely perceptible line of light under his door. He kept his eyes fixed on the light till it vanished. Then the room grew perfectly black, and not a sound was audible but Zeena's asthmatic breathing. Ethan felt confusedly that there were many things he ought to think about, but through his tingling veins and tired brain only one sensation throbbed: the warmth of Mattie's shoulder against his. Why had he not kissed her when he held her there? A few hours earlier he would not have asked himself the question. Even a few minutes earlier, when they had stood alone outside the house, he would not have dared to think of kissing her. But since he had seen her lips in the lamplight he felt that they were his.

Now, in the bright morning air, her face was still before him. It was part of the sun's red and of the pure glitter on the snow. How the girl had changed since she had come to Starkfield! He remembered what a colourless slip of a thing she had looked the day he had met her at the station. And all the first winter, how she had shivered with cold when the northerly gales shook the thin clapboards and the snow beat like hail against the loose-hung windows!

He had been afraid that she would hate the hard life, the cold and loneliness; but not a sign of discontent escaped her. Zeena took the view that Mattie was bound to make the best of Starkfield since she hadn't any other place to go to; but this did not strike Ethan as conclusive. Zeena, at any rate, did not apply the principle in her own case.

He felt all the more sorry for the girl because misfortune had, in a sense, indentured her to them. Mattie Silver was the daughter of a cousin of Zenobia Frome's, who had inflamed his clan with mingled sentiments of envy and admiration by descending from the hills to Connecticut, where he had married a Stamford girl and succeeded to her father's thriving "drug" business. Unhappily Orin Silver, a man of far-reaching aims, had died too soon to prove that the end justifies the means. His accounts revealed merely what the means had been; and these were such that it was fortunate for his wife and daughter that his books were examined only after his impressive funeral. His wife died of the disclosure, and Mattie, at twenty, was left alone to make her way on the fifty dollars obtained from the sale of her piano. For this purpose her equipment, though varied, was inadequate. She could trim a hat, make molasses candy, recite "Curfew shall not ring to-night," and play "The Lost Chord" and a pot-pourri from "Carmen." When she tried to extend the field of her activities in the direction of stenography and book-keeping her health broke down, and six months on her feet behind the counter of a department store did not tend to restore it. Her nearest relations had been induced to place their savings in her father's hands, and though, after his death, they ungrudgingly acquitted themselves of the Christian duty of returning good for evil by giving his daughter all the advice at their disposal, they could hardly be expected to supplement it by material aid. But when Zenobia's doctor recommended her looking about for some one to help her with the house-work the clan instantly saw the chance of exacting a compensation from Mattie. Zenobia, though doubtful of the girl's efficiency, was tempted by the freedom to find fault without much risk of losing her; and so Mattie came to Starkfield.

Zenobia's fault-finding was of the silent kind, but not the less penetrating for that. During the first months Ethan alternately burned with the desire to see Mattie defy her and trembled with fear of the result. Then the situation grew less strained. The pure air, and the long summer hours in the open, gave back life and elasticity to Mattie, and Zeena, with more leisure to devote to her complex ailments, grew less watchful of the girl's omissions; so that Ethan, struggling on under the burden of his barren farm and failing saw-mill, could at least imagine that peace reigned in his house.

There was really, even now, no tangible evidence to the contrary; but since the previous night a vague dread had hung on his sky-line. It was formed of Zeena's obstinate silence, of Mattie's sudden look of warning, of the memory of just such fleeting imperceptible signs as those which told him, on certain stainless mornings, that before night there would be rain.

His dread was so strong that, man-like, he sought to postpone certainty. The hauling was not over till mid-day, and as the lumber was to be delivered to Andrew Hale, the Starkfield builder, it was really easier for Ethan to send Jotham Powell, the hired man, back to the farm on foot, and drive the load down to the village himself. He had scrambled up on the logs, and was sitting astride of them, close over his shaggy greys, when, coming between him and their steaming necks, he had a vision of the warning look that Mattie had given him the night before.

"If there's going to be any trouble I want to be there," was his vague reflection, as he threw to Jotham the unexpected order to unhitch the team and lead them back to the barn.

It was a slow trudge home through the heavy fields, and when the two men entered the kitchen Mattie was lifting the coffee from the stove and Zeena was already at the table. Her husband stopped short at sight of her. Instead of her usual calico wrapper and knitted shawl she wore her best dress of brown merino, and above her thin strands of hair, which still preserved the tight undulations of the crimping-pins, rose a hard perpendicular bonnet, as to which Ethan's clearest notion was that he had had to pay five dollars for it at the Bettsbridge Emporium. On the floor beside her stood his old valise and a bandbox wrapped in newspapers.

"Why, where are you going, Zeena?" he exclaimed.

"I've got my shooting pains so bad that I'm going over to Bettsbridge to spend the night with Aunt Martha Pierce and see that new doctor," she answered in a matter-of-fact tone, as if she had said she was going into the storeroom to take a look at the preserves, or up to the attic to go over the blankets.

In spite of her sedentary habits such abrupt decisions were not without precedent in Zeena's history. Twice or thrice before she had suddenly packed Ethan's valise and started off to Bettsbridge, or even Springfield, to seek the advice of some new doctor, and her husband had grown to dread these expeditions because of their cost. Zeena always came back laden with expensive remedies, and her last visit to Springfield had been commemorated by her paying twenty dollars for an electric battery of which she had never been able to learn the use. But for the moment his sense of relief was so great as to preclude all other feelings. He had now no doubt that Zeena had spoken the truth in saying, the night before, that she had sat up because she felt "too mean" to sleep: her abrupt resolve to seek medical advice showed that, as usual, she was wholly absorbed in her health.

As if expecting a protest, she continued plaintively: "If you're too busy with the hauling I presume you can let Jotham Powell drive me over with the sorrel in time to ketch the train at the Flats."

Her husband hardly heard what she was saying. During the winter months there was no stage between Starkfield and Bettsbridge, and the trains which stopped at Corbury Flats were slow and infrequent. A rapid calculation showed Ethan that Zeena could not be back at the farm before the following evening. . . .

"If I'd supposed you'd 'a' made any objection to Jotham Powell's driving me over—" she began again, as though his silence had implied refusal. On the brink of departure she was always seized with a flux of words. "All I know is," she continued, "I can't go on the way I am much longer. The pains are clear away down to my ankles now, or I'd 'a' walked in to Starkfield on my own feet, sooner 'n put you out, and asked Michael Eady to let me ride over on his wagon to the Flats, when he sends to meet the train that brings his groceries. I'd 'a' had two hours to wait in the station, but I'd sooner 'a' done it, even with this cold, than to have you say——"

"Of course Jotham'll drive you over," Ethan roused himself to answer. He became suddenly conscious that he was looking at Mattie while Zeena talked to him, and with an effort he turned his eyes to his wife. She sat opposite the window, and the pale light reflected from the banks of snow made her face look more than usually drawn and bloodless, sharpened the three parallel creases between ear and cheek, and drew querulous lines from her thin nose to the corners of her mouth. Though she was but seven years her husband's senior, and he was only twenty-eight, she was already an old woman.

Ethan tried to say something befitting the occasion, but there was only one thought in his mind: the fact that, for the first time since Mattie had come to live with them, Zeena was to be away for a night. He wondered if the girl were thinking of it too. . . .

He knew that Zeena must be wondering why he did not offer to drive her to the Flats and let Jotham Powell take the lumber to Starkfield, and at first he could not think of a pretext for not doing so; then he said: "I'd take you over myself, only I've got to collect the cash for the lumber."

As soon as the words were spoken he regretted them, not only because they were untrue—there being no prospect of his receiving cash payment from Hale—but also because he knew from experience the imprudence of letting Zeena think he was in funds on the eve of one of her therapeutic excursions. At the moment, however, his one desire was to avoid the long drive with her behind the ancient sorrel who never went out of a walk.

Zeena made no reply: she did not seem to hear what he had said. She had already pushed her plate aside, and was measuring out a draught from a large bottle at her elbow.

"It ain't done me a speck of good, but I guess I might as well use it up," she remarked; adding, as she pushed the empty bottle toward Mattie: "If you can get the taste out it'll do for pickles."

IV

As soon as his wife had driven off Ethan took his coat and cap from the peg. Mattie was washing up the dishes, humming one of the dance tunes of the night before. He said "So long, Matt," and she answered gaily "So long, Ethan"; and that was all.

It was warm and bright in the kitchen. The sun slanted through the south window on the girl's moving figure, on the cat dozing in a chair, and on the geraniums brought in from the door-way, where Ethan had planted them in the summer to "make a garden" for Mattie. He would have liked to linger on, watching her tidy up and then settle down to her sewing; but he wanted still more to get the hauling done and be back at the farm before night.

All the way down to the village he continued to think of his return to Mattie. The kitchen was a poor place, not "spruce" and shining as his mother had kept it in his boyhood; but it was surprising what a homelike look the mere fact of Zeena's absence gave it. And he pictured what it would be like that evening, when he and Mattie were there after supper. For the first time they would be alone together indoors, and they would sit there, one on each side of the stove, like a married couple, he in his stocking feet and smoking his pipe, she laughing and talking in that funny way she had, which was always as new to him as if he had never heard her before.

The sweetness of the picture, and the relief of knowing that his fears of "trouble" with Zeena were unfounded, sent up his spirits with a rush, and he, who was usually so silent, whistled and sang aloud as he drove through the snowy fields. There was in him a slumbering spark of sociability which the long Starkfield winters had not yet extinguished. By nature grave and inarticulate, he admired recklessness and gaiety in others and was warmed to the marrow by friendly human intercourse. At Worcester, though he had the name of keeping to himself and not being much of a hand at a good time, he had secretly gloried in being clapped on the back and hailed as "Old Ethe" or "Old Stiff"; and the cessation of such familiarities had increased the chill of his return to Starkfield.

There the silence had deepened about him year by year. Left alone, after his father's accident, to carry the burden of farm and mill, he had had no time for convivial loiterings in the village; and when his mother fell ill the loneliness of the house grew more oppressive than that of the fields. His mother had been a talker in her day, but after her "trouble" the sound of her voice was seldom heard, though she had not lost the power of speech. Sometimes, in the long winter evenings, when in desperation her son asked her why she didn't "say something," she would lift a finger and answer: "Because I'm listening"; and on stormy nights, when the loud wind was about the house, she would complain, if he spoke to her: "They're talking so out there that I can't hear you."

It was only when she drew toward her last illness, and his cousin Zenobia Pierce came over from the next valley to help him nurse her, that human speech was heard again in the house. After the mortal silence of his long imprisonment Zeena's volubility was music in his ears. He felt that he might have "gone like his mother" if the sound of a new voice had not come to steady him. Zeena seemed to understand his case at a glance. She laughed at him for not knowing the simplest sick-bed duties and told him to "go right along out" and leave her to see to things. The mere fact of obeying her orders, of feeling free to go about his business again and talk with other men, restored his shaken balance and magnified his sense of what he owed her. Her efficiency shamed and dazzled him. She seemed to possess by instinct all the household wisdom that his long apprenticeship had not instilled in him. When the end came it was she who had to tell him to hitch up and go for the undertaker, and she thought it "funny" that he had not settled beforehand who was to have his mother's clothes and the sewing-machine. After the funeral, when he saw her preparing to go away, he was seized with an unreasoning dread of being left alone on the farm; and before he knew what he was doing he had asked her to stay there with him. He had often thought since that it would not have happened if his mother had died in spring instead of winter . . .

When they married it was agreed that, as soon as he could straighten out the difficulties resulting from Mrs. Frome's long illness, they would sell the farm and saw-mill and try their luck in a large town. Ethan's love of nature did not take the form of a taste for agriculture. He had always wanted to be an engineer, and to live in towns, where there were lectures and big libraries and "fellows doing things." A slight engineering job in Florida, put in his way during his period of study at Worcester, increased his faith in his ability as well as his eagerness to see the world; and he felt sure that, with a "smart" wife like Zeena, it would not be long before he had made himself a place in it.

Zeena's native village was slightly larger and nearer to the railway than Starkfield, and she had let her husband see from the first that life on an isolated farm was not what she had expected when she married. But purchasers were slow in coming, and while he waited for them Ethan learned the impossibility of transplanting her. She chose to look down on Starkfield, but she could not have lived in a place which looked down on her. Even Bettsbridge or Shadd's Falls would not have been sufficiently aware of her, and in the greater cities which attracted Ethan she would have suffered a complete loss of identity. And within a year of their marriage she developed the "sickliness" which had since made her notable even in a community rich in pathological instances. When she came to take care of his mother she had seemed to Ethan like the very genius of health, but he soon saw that her skill as a nurse had been acquired by the absorbed observation of her own symptoms.

Then she too fell silent. Perhaps it was the inevitable effect of life on the farm, or perhaps, as she sometimes said, it was because Ethan "never listened." The charge was not wholly unfounded. When she spoke it was only to complain, and to complain of things not in his power to remedy; and to check a tendency to impatient retort he had first formed the habit of not answering her, and finally of thinking of other things while she talked. Of late, however, since he had had reasons for observing her more closely, her silence had begun to trouble him. He recalled his mother's growing taciturnity, and wondered if Zeena were also turning "queer." Women did, he knew. Zeena, who had at her fingers' ends the pathological chart of the whole region, had cited many cases of the kind while she was nursing his mother; and he himself knew of certain lonely farm-houses in the neighbourhood where stricken creatures pined, and of others where sudden tragedy had come of their presence. At times, looking at Zeena's shut face, he felt the chill of such forebodings. At other times her silence seemed deliberately assumed to conceal far-reaching intentions, mysterious conclusions drawn from suspicions and resentments impossible to guess. That supposition was even more disturbing than the other; and it was the one which had come to him the night before, when he had seen her standing in the kitchen door.

Now her departure for Bettsbridge had once more eased his mind, and all his thoughts were on the prospect of his evening with Mattie. Only one thing weighed on him, and that was his having told Zeena that he was to receive cash for the lumber. He foresaw so clearly the consequences of this imprudence that with considerable reluctance he decided to ask Andrew Hale for a small advance on his load.

When Ethan drove into Hale's yard the builder was just getting out of his sleigh.

"Hello, Ethe!" he said. "This comes handy."

Andrew Hale was a ruddy man with a big grey moustache and a stubbly double-chin unconstrained by a collar; but his scrupulously clean shirt was always fastened by a small diamond stud. This display of opulence was misleading, for though he did a fairly good business it was known that his easy-going habits and the demands of his large family frequently kept him what Starkfield called "behind." He was an old friend of Ethan's family, and his house one of the few to which Zeena occasionally went, drawn there by the fact that Mrs. Hale, in her youth, had done more "doctoring" than any other woman in Starkfield, and was still a recognised authority on symptoms and treatment.

Hale went up to the greys and patted their sweating flanks.

"Well, sir," he said, "you keep them two as if they was pets."

Ethan set about unloading the logs and when he had

finished his job he pushed open the glazed door of the shed which the builder used as his office. Hale sat with his feet up on the stove, his back propped against a battered desk strewn with papers: the place, like the man, was warm, genial and untidy.

"Sit right down and thaw out," he greeted Ethan.

The latter did not know how to begin, but at length he managed to bring out his request for an advance of fifty dollars. The blood rushed to his thin skin under the sting of Hale's astonishment. It was the builder's custom to pay at the end of three months, and there was no precedent between the two men for a cash settlement.

Ethan felt that if he had pleaded an urgent need Hale might have made shift to pay him; but pride, and an instinctive prudence, kept him from resorting to this argument. After his father's death it had taken time to get his head above water, and he did not want Andrew Hale, or any one else in Starkfield, to think he was going under again. Besides, he hated lying; if he wanted the money he wanted it, and it was nobody's business to ask why. He therefore made his demand with the awkwardness of a proud man who will not admit to himself that he is stooping; and he was not much surprised at Hale's refusal.

The builder refused genially, as he did everything else: he treated the matter as something in the nature of a practical joke, and wanted to know if Ethan meditated buying a grand piano or adding a "cupolo" to his house; offering, in the latter case, to give his services free of cost.

Ethan's arts were soon exhausted, and after an embarrassed pause he wished Hale good-day and opened the door of the office. As he passed out the builder suddenly called after him: "See here—you ain't in a tight place, are you?"

"Not a bit," Ethan's pride retorted before his reason had time to intervene.

"Well, that's good! Because I *am*, a shade. Fact is, I was going to ask you to give me a little extra time on that payment. Business is pretty slack, to begin with, and then I'm fixing up a little house for Ned and Ruth when they're married. I'm glad to do it for 'em, but it costs." His look appealed to Ethan for sympathy. "The young people like things nice.

You know how it is yourself: it's not so long ago since you fixed up your own place for Zeena."

Ethan left the greys in Hale's stable and went about some other business in the village. As he walked away the builder's last phrase lingered in his ears, and he reflected grimly that his seven years with Zeena seemed to Starkfield "not so long."

The afternoon was drawing to an end, and here and there a lighted pane spangled the cold grey dusk and made the snow look whiter. The bitter weather had driven every one indoors and Ethan had the long rural street to himself. Suddenly he heard the brisk play of sleigh-bells and a cutter passed him, drawn by a free-going horse. Ethan recognised Michael Eady's roan colt, and young Denis Eady, in a handsome new fur cap, leaned forward and waved a greeting. "Hello, Ethe!" he shouted and spun on.

The cutter was going in the direction of the Frome farm, and Ethan's heart contracted as he listened to the dwindling bells. What more likely than that Denis Eady had heard of Zeena's departure for Bettsbridge, and was profiting by the opportunity to spend an hour with Mattie? Ethan was ashamed of the storm of jealousy in his breast. It seemed unworthy of the girl that his thoughts of her should be so violent.

He walked on to the church corner and entered the shade of the Varnum spruces, where he had stood with her the night before. As he passed into their gloom he saw an indistinct outline just ahead of him. At his approach it melted for an instant into two separate shapes and then conjoined again, and he heard a kiss, and a half-laughing "Oh!" provoked by the discovery of his presence. Again the outline hastily disunited and the Varnum gate slammed on one half while the other hurried on ahead of him. Ethan smiled at the discomfiture he had caused. What did it matter to Ned Hale and Ruth Varnum if they were caught kissing each other? Everybody in Starkfield knew they were engaged. It pleased Ethan to have surprised a pair of lovers on the spot where he and Mattie had stood with such a thirst for each other in their hearts; but he felt a pang at the thought that these two need not hide their happiness.

He fetched the greys from Hale's stable and started on his long climb back to the farm. The cold was less sharp than earlier in the day and a thick fleecy sky threatened snow for the morrow. Here and there a star pricked through, showing behind it a deep well of blue. In an hour or two the moon would push up over the ridge behind the farm, burn a gold-edged rent in the clouds, and then be swallowed by them. A mournful peace hung on the fields, as though they felt the relaxing grasp of the cold and stretched themselves in their long winter sleep.

Ethan's ears were alert for the jingle of sleigh-bells, but not a sound broke the silence of the lonely road. As he drew near the farm he saw, through the thin screen of larches at the gate, a light twinkling in the house above him. "She's up in her room," he said to himself, "fixing herself up for supper"; and he remembered Zeena's sarcastic stare when Mattie, on the evening of her arrival, had come down to supper with smoothed hair and a ribbon at her neck.

He passed by the graves on the knoll and turned his head to glance at one of the older headstones, which had interested him deeply as a boy because it bore his name.

SACRED TO THE MEMORY OF
ETHAN FROME AND ENDURANCE HIS WIFE,
WHO DWELLED TOGETHER IN PEACE
FOR FIFTY YEARS.

He used to think that fifty years sounded like a long time to live together; but now it seemed to him that they might pass in a flash. Then, with a sudden dart of irony, he wondered if, when their turn came, the same epitaph would be written over him and Zeena.

He opened the barn-door and craned his head into the ob-scurity, half-fearing to discover Denis Eady's roan colt in the stall beside the sorrel. But the old horse was there alone, mumbling his crib with toothless jaws, and Ethan whistled cheerfully while he bedded down the greys and shook an extra measure of oats into their mangers. His was not a tuneful throat, but harsh melodies burst from it as he locked the barn and sprang up the hill to the house. He reached the kitchen-porch and turned the door-handle; but the door did not yield to his touch.

Startled at finding it locked he rattled the handle violently; then he reflected that Mattie was alone and that it was natural she should barricade herself at nightfall. He stood in the darkness expecting to hear her step. It did not come, and after vainly straining his ears he called out in a voice that shook with joy: "Hello, Matt!"

Silence answered; but in a minute or two he caught a sound on the stairs and saw a line of light about the door-frame, as he had seen it the night before. So strange was the precision with which the incidents of the previous evening were repeating themselves that he half expected, when he heard the key turn, to see his wife before him on the threshold; but the door opened, and Mattie faced him.

She stood just as Zeena had stood, a lifted lamp in her hand, against the black background of the kitchen. She held the light at the same level, and it drew out with the same distinctness her slim young throat and the brown wrist no bigger than a child's. Then, striking upward, it threw a lustrous fleck on her lips, edged her eyes with velvet shade, and laid a milky whiteness above the black curve of her brows.

She wore her usual dress of darkish stuff, and there was no bow at her neck; but through her hair she had run a streak of crimson ribbon. This tribute to the unusual transformed and glorified her. She seemed to Ethan taller, fuller, more womanly in shape and motion. She stood aside, smiling silently, while he entered, and then moved away from him with something soft and flowing in her gait. She set the lamp on the table, and he saw that it was carefully laid for supper, with fresh dough-nuts, stewed blueberries and his favourite pickles in a dish of gay red glass. A bright fire glowed in the stove and the cat lay stretched before it, watching the table with a drowsy eye.

Ethan was suffocated with the sense of well-being. He went out into the passage to hang up his coat and pull off his wet boots. When he came back Mattie had set the teapot on the table and the cat was rubbing itself persuasively against her ankles.

"Why, Puss! I nearly tripped over you," she cried, the laughter sparkling through her lashes.

Again Ethan felt a sudden twinge of jealousy. Could it be his coming that gave her such a kindled face?

"Well, Matt, any visitors?" he threw off, stooping down carelessly to examine the fastening of the stove.

She nodded and laughed "Yes, one," and he felt a blackness settling on his brows.

"Who was that?" he questioned, raising himself up to slant a glance at her beneath his scowl.

Her eyes danced with malice. "Why, Jotham Powell. He came in after he got back, and asked for a drop of coffee before he went down home."

The blackness lifted and light flooded Ethan's brain. "That all? Well, I hope you made out to let him have it." And after a pause he felt it right to add: "I suppose he got Zeena over to the Flats all right?"

"Oh, yes; in plenty of time."

The name threw a chill between them, and they stood a moment looking sideways at each other before Mattie said with a shy laugh: "I guess it's about time for supper."

They drew their seats up to the table, and the cat, un-bidden, jumped between them into Zeena's empty chair. "Oh, Puss!" said Mattie, and they laughed again.

Ethan, a moment earlier, had felt himself on the brink of eloquence; but the mention of Zeena had paralysed him. Mat-tie seemed to feel the contagion of his embarrassment, and sat with downcast lids, sipping her tea, while he feigned an insatiable appetite for dough-nuts and sweet pickles. At last, after casting about for an effective opening, he took a long gulp of tea, cleared his throat, and said: "Looks as if there'd be more snow."

She feigned great interest. "Is that so? Do you suppose it'll interfere with Zeena's getting back?" She flushed red as the question escaped her, and hastily set down the cup she was lifting.

Ethan reached over for another helping of pickles.

"You never can tell, this time of year, it drifts so bad on the Flats." The name had benumbed him again, and once more he felt as if Zeena were in the room between them.

"Oh, Puss, you're too greedy!" Mattie cried.

The cat, unnoticed, had crept up on muffled paws from Zeena's seat to the table, and was stealthily elongating its body in the direction of the milk-jug, which stood between Ethan and Mattie. The two leaned forward at the same moment and their hands met on the handle of the jug. Mattie's hand was underneath, and Ethan kept his clasped on it a moment longer than was necessary. The cat, profiting by his unusual demonstration, tried to effect an unnoticed retreat, and in doing so backed into the pickle-dish, which fell to the floor with a crash.

Mattie, in an instant, had sprung from her chair and was down on her knees by the fragments.

"Oh, Ethan, Ethan—it's all to pieces! What will Zeena say?"

But this time his courage was up. "Well, she'll have to say it to the cat, any way!" he rejoined with a laugh, kneeling down at Mattie's side to scrape up the swimming pickles.

She lifted stricken eyes to him. "Yes, but, you see, she never meant it should be used, not even when there was company; and I had to get up on the step-ladder to reach it down from the top shelf of the china-closet, where she keeps it with all her best things, and of course she'll want to know why I did it——"

The case was so serious that it called forth all of Ethan's latent resolution.

"She needn't know anything about it if you keep quiet. I'll get another just like it to-morrow. Where did it come from? I'll go to Shadd's Falls for it if I have to!"

"Oh, you'll never get another even there! It was a wedding present—don't you remember? It came all the way from Philadelphia, from Zeena's aunt that married the minister. That's why she wouldn't ever use it. Oh, Ethan, Ethan, what in the world shall I do?"

She began to cry, and he felt as if every one of her tears were pouring over him like burning lead. "Don't, Matt, don't—oh, *don't!*" he implored her.

She struggled to her feet, and he rose and followed her helplessly while she spread out the pieces of glass on the kitchen dresser. It seemed to him as if the shattered fragments of their evening lay there.

"Here, give them to me," he said in a voice of sudden authority.

She drew aside, instinctively obeying his tone. "Oh, Ethan, what are you going to do?"

Without replying he gathered the pieces of glass into his broad palm and walked out of the kitchen to the passage. There he lit a candle-end, opened the china-closet, and, reaching his long arm up to the highest shelf, laid the pieces together with such accuracy of touch that a close inspection convinced him of the impossibility of detecting from below that the dish was broken. If he glued it together the next morning months might elapse before his wife noticed what had happened, and meanwhile he might after all be able to match the dish at Shadd's Falls or Bettsbridge. Having satisfied himself that there was no risk of immediate discovery he went back to the kitchen with a lighter step, and found Mattie disconsolately removing the last scraps of pickle from the floor.

"It's all right, Matt. Come back and finish supper," he commanded her.

Completely reassured, she shone on him through tear-hung lashes, and his soul swelled with pride as he saw how his tone subdued her. She did not even ask what he had done. Except when he was steering a big log down the mountain to his mill he had never known such a thrilling sense of mastery.

V

THEY FINISHED supper, and while Mattie cleared the table Ethan went to look at the cows and then took a last turn about the house. The earth lay dark under a muffled sky and the air was so still that now and then he heard a lump of snow come thumping down from a tree far off on the edge of the wood-lot.

When he returned to the kitchen Mattie had pushed up his chair to the stove and seated herself near the lamp with a bit of sewing. The scene was just as he had dreamed of it that morning. He sat down, drew his pipe from his pocket and stretched his feet to the glow. His hard day's work in the keen air made him feel at once lazy and light of mood, and he had a confused sense of being in another world, where all was warmth and harmony and time could bring no change. The only drawback to his complete well-being was the fact that he could not see Mattie from where he sat; but he was too indolent to move and after a moment he said: "Come over here and sit by the stove."

Zeena's empty rocking-chair stood facing him. Mattie rose obediently, and seated herself in it. As her young brown head detached itself against the patch-work cushion that habitually framed his wife's gaunt countenance, Ethan had a momentary shock. It was almost as if the other face, the face of the superseded woman, had obliterated that of the intruder. After a moment Mattie seemed to be affected by the same sense of constraint. She changed her position, leaning forward to bend her head above her work, so that he saw only the foreshortened tip of her nose and the streak of red in her hair; then she slipped to her feet, saying "I can't see to sew," and went back to her chair by the lamp.

Ethan made a pretext of getting up to replenish the stove, and when he returned to his seat he pushed it sideways that he might have a view of her profile and of the lamplight falling on her hands. The cat, who had been a puzzled observer of these unusual movements, jumped up into Zeena's chair, rolled itself into a ball, and lay watching them with narrowed eyes.

Deep quiet sank on the room. The clock ticked above the

dresser, a piece of charred wood fell now and then in the stove, and the faint sharp scent of the geraniums mingled with the odour of Ethan's smoke, which began to throw a blue haze about the lamp and to hang its greyish cobwebs in the shadowy corners of the room.

All constraint had vanished between the two, and they began to talk easily and simply. They spoke of every-day things, of the prospect of snow, of the next church sociable, of the loves and quarrels of Starkfield. The commonplace nature of what they said produced in Ethan an illusion of long-established intimacy which no outburst of emotion could have given, and he set his imagination adrift on the fiction that they had always spent their evenings thus and would always go on doing so . . .

"This is the night we were to have gone coasting, Matt," he said at length, with the rich sense, as he spoke, that they could go on any other night they chose, since they had all time before them.

She smiled back at him. "I guess you forgot!"

"No, I didn't forget; but it's as dark as Egypt outdoors. We might go to-morrow if there's a moon."

She laughed with pleasure, her head tilted back, the lamp-light sparkling on her lips and teeth. "That would be lovely, Ethan!"

He kept his eyes fixed on her, marvelling at the way her face changed with each turn of their talk, like a wheat-field under a summer breeze. It was intoxicating to find such magic in his clumsy words, and he longed to try new ways of using it.

"Would you be scared to go down the Corbury road with me on a night like this?" he asked.

Her cheeks burned redder. "I ain't any more scared than you are!"

"Well, *I'd* be scared, then; I wouldn't do it. That's an ugly corner down by the big elm. If a fellow didn't keep his eyes open he'd go plumb into it." He luxuriated in the sense of protection and authority which his words conveyed. To prolong and intensify the feeling he added: "I guess we're well enough here."

She let her lids sink slowly, in the way he loved. "Yes, we're well enough here," she sighed.

Her tone was so sweet that he took the pipe from his mouth and drew his chair up to the table. Leaning forward, he touched the farther end of the strip of brown stuff that she was hemming. "Say, Matt," he began with a smile, "what do you think I saw under the Varnum spruces, coming along home just now? I saw a friend of yours getting kissed."

The words had been on his tongue all the evening, but now that he had spoken them they struck him as inexpressibly vulgar and out of place.

Mattie blushed to the roots of her hair and pulled her needle rapidly twice or thrice through her work, insensibly drawing the end of it away from him. "I suppose it was Ruth and Ned," she said in a low voice, as though he had suddenly touched on something grave.

Ethan had imagined that his allusion might open the way to the accepted pleasantries, and these perhaps in turn to a harmless caress, if only a mere touch on her hand. But now he felt as if her blush had set a flaming guard about her. He supposed it was his natural awkwardness that made him feel so. He knew that most young men made nothing at all of giving a pretty girl a kiss, and he remembered that the night before, when he had put his arm about Mattie, she had not resisted. But that had been out-of-doors, under the open irresponsible night. Now, in the warm lamplit room, with all its ancient implications of conformity and order, she seemed infinitely farther away from him and more unapproachable.

To ease his constraint he said: "I suppose they'll be setting a date before long."

"Yes. I shouldn't wonder if they got married some time along in the summer." She pronounced the word *married* as if her voice caressed it. It seemed a rustling covert leading to enchanted glades. A pang shot through Ethan, and he said, twisting away from her in his chair: "It'll be your turn next, I wouldn't wonder."

She laughed a little uncertainly. "Why do you keep on saying that?"

He echoed her laugh. "I guess I do it to get used to the idea."

He drew up to the table again and she sewed on in silence,

with dropped lashes, while he sat in fascinated contemplation of the way in which her hands went up and down above the strip of stuff, just as he had seen a pair of birds make short perpendicular flights over a nest they were building. At length, without turning her head or lifting her lids, she said in a low tone: "It's not because you think Zeena's got anything against me, is it?"

His former dread started up full-armed at the suggestion. "Why, what do you mean?" he stammered.

She raised distressed eyes to his, her work dropping on the table between them. "I don't know. I thought last night she seemed to have."

"I'd like to know what," he growled.

"Nobody can tell with Zeena." It was the first time they had ever spoken so openly of her attitude toward Mattie, and the repetition of the name seemed to carry it to the farther corners of the room and send it back to them in long repercussions of sound. Mattie waited, as if to give the echo time to drop, and then went on: "She hasn't said anything to *you*?"

He shook his head. "No, not a word."

She tossed the hair back from her forehead with a laugh. "I guess I'm just nervous, then. I'm not going to think about it any more."

"Oh, no—don't let's think about it, Matt!"

The sudden heat of his tone made her colour mount again, not with a rush, but gradually, delicately, like the reflection of a thought stealing slowly across her heart. She sat silent, her hands clasped on her work, and it seemed to him that a warm current flowed toward him along the strip of stuff that still lay unrolled between them. Cautiously he slid his hand palm-downward along the table till his finger-tips touched the end of the stuff. A faint vibration of her lashes seemed to show that she was aware of his gesture, and that it had sent a counter-current back to her; and she let her hands lie motionless on the other end of the strip.

As they sat thus he heard a sound behind him and turned his head. The cat had jumped from Zeena's chair to dart at a mouse in the wainscot, and as a result of the sudden movement the empty chair had set up a spectral rocking.

"She'll be rocking in it herself this time to-morrow," Ethan thought. "I've been in a dream, and this is the only evening we'll ever have together." The return to reality was as painful as the return to consciousness after taking an anæsthetic. His body and brain ached with indescribable weariness, and he could think of nothing to say or to do that should arrest the mad flight of the moments.

His alteration of mood seemed to have communicated itself to Mattie. She looked up at him languidly, as though her lids were weighted with sleep and it cost her an effort to raise them. Her glance fell on his hand, which now completely covered the end of her work and grasped it as if it were a part of herself. He saw a scarcely perceptible tremor cross her face, and without knowing what he did he stooped his head and kissed the bit of stuff in his hold. As his lips rested on it he felt it glide slowly from beneath them, and saw that Mattie had risen and was silently rolling up her work. She fastened it with a pin, and then, finding her thimble and scissors, put them with the roll of stuff into the box covered with fancy paper which he had once brought to her from Bettsbridge.

He stood up also, looking vaguely about the room. The clock above the dresser struck eleven.

"Is the fire all right?" she asked in a low voice.

He opened the door of the stove and poked aimlessly at the embers. When he raised himself again he saw that she was dragging toward the stove the old soap-box lined with carpet in which the cat made its bed. Then she recrossed the floor and lifted two of the geranium pots in her arms, moving them away from the cold window. He followed her and brought the other geraniums, the hyacinth bulbs in a cracked custard bowl and the German ivy trained over an old croquet hoop.

When these nightly duties were performed there was nothing left to do but to bring in the tin candlestick from the passage, light the candle and blow out the lamp. Ethan put the candlestick in Mattie's hand and she went out of the kitchen ahead of him, the light that she carried before her making her dark hair look like a drift of mist on the moon.

"Good night, Matt," he said as she put her foot on the first step of the stairs.

She turned and looked at him a moment. "Good night, Ethan," she answered, and went up.

When the door of her room had closed on her he remembered that he had not even touched her hand.

VI

THE NEXT MORNING at breakfast Jotham Powell was between them, and Ethan tried to hide his joy under an air of exaggerated indifference, lounging back in his chair to throw scraps to the cat, growling at the weather, and not so much as offering to help Mattie when she rose to clear away the dishes.

He did not know why he was so irrationally happy, for nothing was changed in his life or hers. He had not even touched the tip of her fingers or looked her full in the eyes. But their evening together had given him a vision of what life at her side might be, and he was glad now that he had done nothing to trouble the sweetness of the picture. He had a fancy that she knew what had restrained him . . .

There was a last load of lumber to be hauled to the village, and Jotham Powell—who did not work regularly for Ethan in winter—had "come round" to help with the job. But a wet snow, melting to sleet, had fallen in the night and turned the roads to glass. There was more wet in the air and it seemed likely to both men that the weather would "milden" toward afternoon and make the going safer. Ethan therefore proposed to his assistant that they should load the sledge at the wood-lot, as they had done on the previous morning, and put off the "teaming" to Starkfield till later in the day. This plan had the advantage of enabling him to send Jotham to the Flats after dinner to meet Zenobia, while he himself took the lumber down to the village.

He told Jotham to go out and harness up the greys, and for a moment he and Mattie had the kitchen to themselves. She had plunged the breakfast dishes into a tin dish-pan and was bending above it with her slim arms bared to the elbow, the steam from the hot water beading her forehead and tightening her rough hair into little brown rings like the tendrils on the traveller's joy.

Ethan stood looking at her, his heart in his throat. He wanted to say: "We shall never be alone again like this." Instead, he reached down his tobacco-pouch from a shelf of the

dresser, put it into his pocket and said: "I guess I can make
out to be home for dinner."

She answered "All right, Ethan," and he heard her singing
over the dishes as he went.

As soon as the sledge was loaded he meant to send Jotham
back to the farm and hurry on foot into the village to buy the
glue for the pickle-dish. With ordinary luck he should have
had time to carry out this plan; but everything went wrong
from the start. On the way over to the wood-lot one of the
greys slipped on a glare of ice and cut his knee; and when
they got him up again Jotham had to go back to the barn for
a strip of rag to bind the cut. Then, when the loading finally
began, a sleety rain was coming down once more, and the
tree trunks were so slippery that it took twice as long as usual
to lift them and get them in place on the sledge. It was what
Jotham called a sour morning for work, and the horses, shivering and stamping under their wet blankets, seemed to like it
as little as the men. It was long past the dinner-hour when the
job was done, and Ethan had to give up going to the village
because he wanted to lead the injured horse home and wash
the cut himself.

He thought that by starting out again with the lumber as
soon as he had finished his dinner he might get back to the
farm with the glue before Jotham and the old sorrel had had
time to fetch Zenobia from the Flats; but he knew the chance
was a slight one. It turned on the state of the roads and on
the possible lateness of the Bettsbridge train. He remembered
afterward, with a grim flash of self-derision, what importance
he had attached to the weighing of these probabilities . . .

As soon as dinner was over he set out again for the wood-
lot, not daring to linger till Jotham Powell left. The hired man
was still drying his wet feet at the stove, and Ethan could only
give Mattie a quick look as he said beneath his breath: "I'll be
back early."

He fancied that she nodded her comprehension; and with
that scant solace he had to trudge off through the rain.

He had driven his load half-way to the village when Jotham
Powell overtook him, urging the reluctant sorrel toward the
Flats. "I'll have to hurry up to do it," Ethan mused, as the
sleigh dropped down ahead of him over the dip of the school-

house hill. He worked like ten at the unloading, and when it was over hastened on to Michael Eady's for the glue. Eady and his assistant were both "down street," and young Denis, who seldom deigned to take their place, was lounging by the stove with a knot of the golden youth of Starkfield. They hailed Ethan with ironic compliment and offers of conviviality; but no one knew where to find the glue. Ethan, consumed with the longing for a last moment alone with Mattie, hung about impatiently while Denis made an ineffectual search in the obscurer corners of the store.

"Looks as if we were all sold out. But if you'll wait around till the old man comes along maybe he can put his hand on it."

"I'm obliged to you, but I'll try if I can get it down at Mrs. Homan's," Ethan answered, burning to be gone.

Denis's commercial instinct compelled him to aver on oath that what Eady's store could not produce would never be found at the widow Homan's; but Ethan, heedless of this boast, had already climbed to the sledge and was driving on to the rival establishment. Here, after considerable search, and sympathetic questions as to what he wanted it for, and whether ordinary flour paste wouldn't do as well if she couldn't find it, the widow Homan finally hunted down her solitary bottle of glue to its hiding-place in a medley of cough-lozenges and corset-laces.

"I hope Zeena ain't broken anything she sets store by," she called after him as he turned the greys toward home.

The fitful bursts of sleet had changed into a steady rain and the horses had heavy work even without a load behind them. Once or twice, hearing sleigh-bells, Ethan turned his head, fancying that Zeena and Jotham might overtake him; but the old sorrel was not in sight, and he set his face against the rain and urged on his ponderous pair.

The barn was empty when the horses turned into it and, after giving them the most perfunctory ministrations they had ever received from him, he strode up to the house and pushed open the kitchen door.

Mattie was there alone, as he had pictured her. She was bending over a pan on the stove; but at the sound of his step she turned with a start and sprang to him.

"See, here, Matt, I've got some stuff to mend the dish with! Let me get at it quick," he cried, waving the bottle in one hand while he put her lightly aside; but she did not seem to hear him.

"Oh, Ethan—Zeena's come," she said in a whisper, clutching his sleeve.

They stood and stared at each other, pale as culprits.

"But the sorrel's not in the barn!" Ethan stammered.

"Jotham Powell brought some goods over from the Flats for his wife, and he drove right on home with them," she explained.

He gazed blankly about the kitchen, which looked cold and squalid in the rainy winter twilight.

"How is she?" he asked, dropping his voice to Mattie's whisper.

She looked away from him uncertainly. "I don't know. She went right up to her room."

"She didn't say anything?"

"No."

Ethan let out his doubts in a low whistle and thrust the bottle back into his pocket. "Don't fret; I'll come down and mend it in the night," he said. He pulled on his wet coat again and went back to the barn to feed the greys.

While he was there Jotham Powell drove up with the sleigh, and when the horses had been attended to Ethan said to him: "You might as well come back up for a bite." He was not sorry to assure himself of Jotham's neutralising presence at the supper table, for Zeena was always "nervous" after a journey. But the hired man, though seldom loth to accept a meal not included in his wages, opened his stiff jaws to answer slowly: "I'm obliged to you, but I guess I'll go along back."

Ethan looked at him in surprise. "Better come up and dry off. Looks as if there'd be something hot for supper."

Jotham's facial muscles were unmoved by this appeal and, his vocabulary being limited, he merely repeated: "I guess I'll go along back."

To Ethan there was something vaguely ominous in this stolid rejection of free food and warmth, and he wondered what had happened on the drive to nerve Jotham to such stoicism. Perhaps Zeena had failed to see the new doctor or had not liked his counsels: Ethan knew that in such cases the first person she met was likely to be held responsible for her grievance.

When he re-entered the kitchen the lamp lit up the same scene of shining comfort as on the previous evening. The table had been as carefully laid, a clear fire glowed in the stove, the cat dozed in its warmth, and Mattie came forward carrying a plate of dough-nuts.

She and Ethan looked at each other in silence; then she said, as she had said the night before: "I guess it's about time for supper."

VII

ETHAN WENT OUT into the passage to hang up his wet garments. He listened for Zeena's step and, not hearing it, called her name up the stairs. She did not answer, and after a moment's hesitation he went up and opened her door. The room was almost dark, but in the obscurity he saw her sitting by the window, bolt upright, and knew by the rigidity of the outline projected against the pane that she had not taken off her travelling dress.

"Well, Zeena," he ventured from the threshold.

She did not move, and he continued: "Supper's about ready. Ain't you coming?"

She replied: "I don't feel as if I could touch a morsel."

It was the consecrated formula, and he expected it to be followed, as usual, by her rising and going down to supper. But she remained seated, and he could think of nothing more felicitous than: "I presume you're tired after the long ride."

Turning her head at this, she answered solemnly: "I'm a great deal sicker than you think."

Her words fell on his ear with a strange shock of wonder. He had often heard her pronounce them before—what if at last they were true?

He advanced a step or two into the dim room. "I hope that's not so, Zeena," he said.

She continued to gaze at him through the twilight with a mien of wan authority, as of one consciously singled out for a great fate. "I've got complications," she said.

Ethan knew the word for one of exceptional import. Almost everybody in the neighbourhood had "troubles," frankly localized and specified; but only the chosen had "complications." To have them was in itself a distinction, though it was also, in most cases, a death-warrant. People struggled on for years with "troubles," but they almost always succumbed to "complications."

Ethan's heart was jerking to and fro between two extremities of feeling, but for the moment compassion prevailed. His

wife looked so hard and lonely, sitting there in the darkness
with such thoughts.

"Is that what the new doctor told you?" he asked, instinctively lowering his voice.

"Yes. He says any regular doctor would want me to have an
operation."

Ethan was aware that, in regard to the important question
of surgical intervention, the female opinion of the neighbourhood was divided, some glorying in the prestige conferred by
operations while others shunned them as indelicate. Ethan,
from motives of economy, had always been glad that Zeena
was of the latter faction.

In the agitation caused by the gravity of her announcement
he sought a consolatory short cut. "What do you know about
this doctor anyway? Nobody ever told you that before."

He saw his blunder before she could take it up: she wanted
sympathy, not consolation.

"I didn't need to have anybody tell me I was losing ground
every day. Everybody but you could see it. And everybody in
Bettsbridge knows about Dr. Buck. He has his office in
Worcester, and comes over once a fortnight to Shadd's Falls
and Bettsbridge for consultations. Eliza Spears was wasting
away with kidney trouble before she went to him, and now
she's up and around, and singing in the choir."

"Well, I'm glad of that. You must do just what he tells
you," Ethan answered sympathetically.

She was still looking at him. "I mean to," she said. He was
struck by a new note in her voice. It was neither whining nor
reproachful, but drily resolute.

"What does he want you should do?" he asked, with a
mounting vision of fresh expenses.

"He wants I should have a hired girl. He says I oughtn't to
have to do a single thing around the house."

"A hired girl?" Ethan stood transfixed.

"Yes. And Aunt Martha found me one right off. Everybody
said I was lucky to get a girl to come away out here, and I
agreed to give her a dollar extry to make sure. She'll be over
to-morrow afternoon."

Wrath and dismay contended in Ethan. He had foreseen an

immediate demand for money, but not a permanent drain on his scant resources. He no longer believed what Zeena had told him of the supposed seriousness of her state: he saw in her expedition to Bettsbridge only a plot hatched between herself and her Pierce relations to foist on him the cost of a servant; and for the moment wrath predominated.

"If you meant to engage a girl you ought to have told me before you started," he said.

"How could I tell you before I started? How did I know what Dr. Buck would say?"

"Oh, Dr. Buck——" Ethan's incredulity escaped in a short laugh. "Did Dr. Buck tell you how I was to pay her wages?"

Her voice rose furiously with his. "No, he didn't. For I'd 'a' been ashamed to tell *him* that you grudged me the money to get back my health, when I lost it nursing your own mother!"

"*You* lost your health nursing mother?"

"Yes; and my folks all told me at the time you couldn't do no less than marry me after——"

"Zeena!"

Through the obscurity which hid their faces their thoughts seemed to dart at each other like serpents shooting venom. Ethan was seized with horror of the scene and shame at his own share in it. It was as senseless and savage as a physical fight between two enemies in the darkness.

He turned to the shelf above the chimney, groped for matches and lit the one candle in the room. At first its weak flame made no impression on the shadows; then Zeena's face stood grimly out against the uncurtained pane, which had turned from grey to black.

It was the first scene of open anger between the couple in their sad seven years together, and Ethan felt as if he had lost an irretrievable advantage in descending to the level of recrimination. But the practical problem was there and had to be dealt with.

"You know I haven't got the money to pay for a girl, Zeena. You'll have to send her back: I can't do it."

"The doctor says it'll be my death if I go on slaving the way I've had to. He doesn't understand how I've stood it as long as I have."

"Slaving!——" He checked himself again, "You sha'n't lift a

hand, if he says so. I'll do everything round the house my-self——"

She broke in: "You're neglecting the farm enough already," and this being true, he found no answer, and left her time to add ironically: "Better send me over to the almshouse and done with it . . . I guess there's been Fromes there afore now."

The taunt burned into him, but he let it pass. "I haven't got the money. That settles it."

There was a moment's pause in the struggle, as though the combatants were testing their weapons. Then Zeena said in a level voice: "I thought you were to get fifty dollars from Andrew Hale for that lumber."

"Andrew Hale never pays under three months." He had hardly spoken when he remembered the excuse he had made for not accompanying his wife to the station the day before; and the blood rose to his frowning brows.

"Why, you told me yesterday you'd fixed it up with him to pay cash down. You said that was why you couldn't drive me over to the Flats."

Ethan had no suppleness in deceiving. He had never before been convicted of a lie, and all the resources of evasion failed him. "I guess that was a misunderstanding," he stammered.

"You ain't got the money?"

"No."

"And you ain't going to get it?"

"No."

"Well, I couldn't know that when I engaged the girl, could I?"

"No." He paused to control his voice. "But you know it now. I'm sorry, but it can't be helped. You're a poor man's wife, Zeena; but I'll do the best I can for you."

For a while she sat motionless, as if reflecting, her arms stretched along the arms of her chair, her eyes fixed on va-cancy. "Oh, I guess we'll make out," she said mildly.

The change in her tone reassured him. "Of course we will! There's a whole lot more I can do for you, and Mattie——"

Zeena, while he spoke, seemed to be following out some elaborate mental calculation. She emerged from it to say: "There'll be Mattie's board less, anyhow——"

Ethan, supposing the discussion to be over, had turned to go down to supper. He stopped short, not grasping what he heard. "Mattie's board less—?" he began.

Zeena laughed. It was an odd unfamiliar sound—he did not remember ever having heard her laugh before. "You didn't suppose I was going to keep two girls, did you? No wonder you were scared at the expense!"

He still had but a confused sense of what she was saying. From the beginning of the discussion he had instinctively avoided the mention of Mattie's name, fearing he hardly knew what: criticism, complaints, or vague allusions to the imminent probability of her marrying. But the thought of a definite rupture had never come to him, and even now could not lodge itself in his mind.

"I don't know what you mean," he said. "Mattie Silver's not a hired girl. She's your relation."

"She's a pauper that's hung onto us all after her father'd done his best to ruin us. I've kep' her here a whole year: it's somebody else's turn now."

As the shrill words shot out Ethan heard a tap on the door, which he had drawn shut when he turned back from the threshold.

"Ethan—Zeena!" Mattie's voice sounded gaily from the landing, "do you know what time it is? Supper's been ready half an hour."

Inside the room there was a moment's silence; then Zeena called out from her seat: "I'm not coming down to supper."

"Oh, I'm sorry! Aren't you well? Sha'n't I bring you up a bite of something?"

Ethan roused himself with an effort and opened the door. "Go along down, Matt. Zeena's just a little tired. I'm coming."

He heard her "All right!" and her quick step on the stairs; then he shut the door and turned back into the room. His wife's attitude was unchanged, her face inexorable, and he was seized with the despairing sense of his helplessness.

"You ain't going to do it, Zeena?"

"Do what?" she emitted between flattened lips.

"Send Mattie away—like this?"

"I never bargained to take her for life!"

He continued with rising vehemence: "You can't put her out of the house like a thief—a poor girl without friends or money. She's done her best for you and she's got no place to go to. You may forget she's your kin but everybody else'll remember it. If you do a thing like that what do you suppose folks'll say of you?"

Zeena waited a moment, as if giving him time to feel the full force of the contrast between his own excitement and her composure. Then she replied in the same smooth voice: "I know well enough what they say of my having kep' her here as long as I have."

Ethan's hand dropped from the door-knob, which he had held clenched since he had drawn the door shut on Mattie. His wife's retort was like a knife-cut across the sinews and he felt suddenly weak and powerless. He had meant to humble himself, to argue that Mattie's keep didn't cost much, after all, that he could make out to buy a stove and fix up a place in the attic for the hired girl—but Zeena's words revealed the peril of such pleadings.

"You mean to tell her she's got to go—at once?" he faltered out, in terror of letting his wife complete her sentence.

As if trying to make him see reason she replied impartially: "The girl will be over from Bettsbridge to-morrow, and I presume she's got to have somewheres to sleep."

Ethan looked at her with loathing. She was no longer the listless creature who had lived at his side in a state of sullen self-absorption, but a mysterious alien presence, an evil energy secreted from the long years of silent brooding. It was the sense of his helplessness that sharpened his antipathy. There had never been anything in her that one could appeal to; but as long as he could ignore and command he had remained indifferent. Now she had mastered him and he abhorred her. Mattie was her relation, not his: there were no means by which he could compel her to keep the girl under her roof. All the long misery of his baffled past, of his youth of failure, hardship and vain effort, rose up in his soul in bitterness and seemed to take shape before him in the woman who at every turn had barred his way. She had taken everything else from him; and now she meant to take the one thing that made up for all the others. For a moment such a flame of hate rose in him that it ran down his arm and clenched his fist against her. He took a wild step forward and then stopped.

"You're—you're not coming down?" he said in a bewildered voice.

"No. I guess I'll lay down on the bed a little while," she answered mildly; and he turned and walked out of the room.

In the kitchen Mattie was sitting by the stove, the cat curled up on her knees. She sprang to her feet as Ethan entered and carried the covered dish of meat-pie to the table.

"I hope Zeena isn't sick?" she asked.

"No."

She shone at him across the table. "Well, sit right down then. You must be starving." She uncovered the pie and pushed it over to him. So they were to have one more evening together, her happy eyes seemed to say!

He helped himself mechanically and began to eat; then disgust took him by the throat and he laid down his fork.

Mattie's tender gaze was on him and she marked the gesture.

"Why, Ethan, what's the matter? Don't it taste right?"

"Yes—it's first-rate. Only I—" He pushed his plate away, rose from his chair, and walked around the table to her side. She started up with frightened eyes.

"Ethan, there's something wrong! I *knew* there was!"

She seemed to melt against him in her terror, and he caught her in his arms, held her fast there, felt her lashes beat his cheek like netted butterflies.

"What is it—what is it?" she stammered; but he had found her lips at last and was drinking unconsciousness of everything but the joy they gave him.

She lingered a moment, caught in the same strong current; then she slipped from him and drew back a step or two, pale and troubled. Her look smote him with compunction, and he cried out, as if he saw her drowning in a dream: "You can't go, Matt! I'll never let you!"

"Go—go?" she stammered. "Must I go?"

The words went on sounding between them as though a torch of warning flew from hand to hand through a black landscape.

Ethan was overcome with shame at his lack of self-control

in flinging the news at her so brutally. His head reeled and he had to support himself against the table. All the while he felt as if he were still kissing her, and yet dying of thirst for her lips.

"Ethan what has happened? Is Zeena mad with me?"

Her cry steadied him, though it deepened his wrath and pity. "No, no," he assured her, "it's not that. But this new doctor has scared her about herself. You know she believes all they say the first time she sees them. And this one's told her she won't get well unless she lays up and don't do a thing about the house—not for months——"

He paused, his eyes wandering from her miserably. She stood silent a moment, drooping before him like a broken branch. She was so small and weak-looking that it wrung his heart; but suddenly she lifted her head and looked straight at him. "And she wants somebody handier in my place? Is that it?"

"That's what she says to-night."

"If she says it to-night she'll say it to-morrow."

Both bowed to the inexorable truth: they knew that Zeena never changed her mind, and that in her case a resolve once taken was equivalent to an act performed.

There was a long silence between them; then Mattie said in a low voice: "Don't be too sorry, Ethan."

"Oh, God—oh, God," he groaned. The glow of passion he had felt for her had melted to an aching tenderness. He saw her quick lids beating back the tears, and longed to take her in his arms and soothe her.

"You're letting your supper get cold," she admonished him with a pale gleam of gaiety.

"Oh, Matt—Matt—where'll you go to?"

Her lids sank and a tremor crossed her face. He saw that for the first time the thought of the future came to her distinctly. "I might get something to do over at Stamford," she faltered, as if knowing that he knew she had no hope.

He dropped back into his seat and hid his face in his hands. Despair seized him at the thought of her setting out alone to renew the weary quest for work. In the only place where she was known she was surrounded by indifference or animosity; and what chance had she, inexperienced and untrained, among the million bread-seekers of the cities? There came back to him miserable tales he had heard at Worcester, and the faces of girls whose lives had begun as hopefully as Mattie's. . . . It was not possible to think of such things without a revolt of his whole being. He sprang up suddenly.

"You can't go, Matt! I won't let you! She's always had her way, but I mean to have mine now——"

Mattie lifted her hand with a quick gesture, and he heard his wife's step behind him.

Zeena came into the room with her dragging down-at-the-heel step, and quietly took her accustomed seat between them.

"I felt a little mite better, and Dr. Buck says I ought to eat all I can to keep my stren'th up, even if I ain't got any appetite," she said in her flat whine, reaching across Mattie for the teapot. Her "good" dress had been replaced by the black calico and brown knitted shawl which formed her daily wear, and with them she had put on her usual face and manner. She poured out her tea, added a great deal of milk to it, helped herself largely to pie and pickles, and made the familiar gesture of adjusting her false teeth before she began to eat. The cat rubbed itself ingratiatingly against her and she said "Good Pussy," stooped to stroke it and gave it a scrap of meat from her plate.

Ethan sat speechless, not pretending to eat, but Mattie nibbled valiantly at her food and asked Zeena one or two questions about her visit to Bettsbridge. Zeena answered in her every-day tone and, warming to the theme, regaled them with several vivid descriptions of intestinal disturbances among her friends and relatives. She looked straight at Mattie as she spoke, a faint smile deepening the vertical lines between her nose and chin.

When supper was over she rose from her seat and pressed her hand to the flat surface over the region of her heart. "That pie of yours always sets a mite heavy, Matt," she said, not ill-naturedly. She seldom abbreviated the girl's name, and when she did so it was always a sign of affability.

"I've a good mind to go and hunt up those stomach powders I got last year over in Springfield," she continued.

"I ain't tried them for quite a while, and maybe they'll help the heartburn."

Mattie lifted her eyes. "Can't I get them for you, Zeena?" she ventured.

"No. They're in a place you don't know about," Zeena answered darkly, with one of her secret looks.

She went out of the kitchen and Mattie, rising, began to clear the dishes from the table. As she passed Ethan's chair their eyes met and clung together desolately. The warm still kitchen looked as peaceful as the night before. The cat had sprung to Zeena's rocking-chair, and the heat of the fire was beginning to draw out the faint sharp scent of the geraniums. Ethan dragged himself wearily to his feet.

"I'll go out and take a look round," he said, going toward the passage to get his lantern.

As he reached the door he met Zeena coming back into the room, her lips twitching with anger, a flush of excitement on her sallow face. The shawl had slipped from her shoulders and was dragging at her down-trodden heels, and in her hands she carried the fragments of the red glass pickle-dish.

"I'd like to know who done this," she said, looking sternly from Ethan to Mattie.

There was no answer, and she continued in a trembling voice: "I went to get those powders I'd put away in father's old spectacle-case, top of the china-closet, where I keep the things I set store by, so's folks sha'n't meddle with them—" Her voice broke, and two small tears hung on her lashless lids and ran slowly down her cheeks. "It takes the step-ladder to get at the top shelf, and I put Aunt Philura Maple's pickle-dish up there o' purpose when we was married, and it's never been down since, 'cept for the spring cleaning, and then I always lifted it with my own hands, so's 't it shouldn't get broke." She laid the fragments reverently on the table. "I want to know who done this," she quavered.

At the challenge Ethan turned back into the room and faced her. "I can tell you, then. The cat done it."

"The *cat*?"

"That's what I said."

She looked at him hard, and then turned her eyes to Mattie, who was carrying the dish-pan to the table.

"I'd like to know how the cat got into my china-closet," she said.

"Chasin' mice, I guess," Ethan rejoined. "There was a mouse round the kitchen all last evening."

Zeena continued to look from one to the other; then she emitted her small strange laugh. "I knew the cat was a smart cat," she said in a high voice, "but I didn't know he was smart enough to pick up the pieces of my pickle-dish and lay 'em edge to edge on the very shelf he knocked 'em off of."

Mattie suddenly drew her arms out of the steaming water. "It wasn't Ethan's fault, Zeena! The cat *did* break the dish; but I got it down from the china-closet, and I'm the one to blame for its getting broken."

Zeena stood beside the ruin of her treasure, stiffening into a stony image of resentment. "*You* got down my pickle-dish—what for?"

A bright flush flew to Mattie's cheeks. "I wanted to make the supper-table pretty," she said.

"You wanted to make the supper-table pretty; and you waited till my back was turned, and took the thing I set most store by of anything I've got, and wouldn't never use it, not even when the minister come to dinner, or Aunt Martha Pierce come over from Bettsbridge—" Zeena paused with a gasp, as if terrified by her own evocation of the sacrilege. "You're a bad girl, Mattie Silver, and I always known it. It's the way your father begun, and I was warned of it when I took you, and I tried to keep my things where you couldn't get at 'em—and now you've took from me the one I cared for most of all—" She broke off in a short spasm of sobs that passed and left her more than ever like a shape of stone.

"If I'd 'a' listened to folks, you'd 'a' gone before now, and this wouldn't 'a' happened," she said; and gathering up the bits of broken glass she went out of the room as if she carried a dead body . . .

VIII

WHEN ETHAN was called back to the farm by his father's illness his mother gave him, for his own use, a small room behind the untenanted "best parlour." Here he had nailed up shelves for his books, built himself a box-sofa out of boards and a mattress, laid out his papers on a kitchen-table, hung on the rough plaster wall an engraving of Abraham Lincoln and a calendar with "Thoughts from the Poets," and tried, with these meagre properties to produce some likeness to the study of a "minister" who had been kind to him and lent him books when he was at Worcester. He still took refuge there in summer, but when Mattie came to live at the farm he had had to give her his stove, and consequently the room was uninhabitable for several months of the year.

To this retreat he descended as soon as the house was quiet, and Zeena's steady breathing from the bed had assured him that there was to be no sequel to the scene in the kitchen. After Zeena's departure he and Mattie had stood speechless, neither seeking to approach the other. Then the girl had returned to her task of clearing up the kitchen for the night and he had taken his lantern and gone on his usual round outside the house. The kitchen was empty when he came back to it; but his tobacco-pouch and pipe had been laid on the table, and under them was a scrap of paper torn from the back of a seedsman's catalogue, on which three words were written: "Don't trouble, Ethan."

Going into his cold dark "study" he placed the lantern on the table and, stooping to its light, read the message again and again. It was the first time that Mattie had ever written to him, and the possession of the paper gave him a strange new sense of her nearness; yet it deepened his anguish by reminding him that henceforth they would have no other way of communicating with each other. For the life of her smile, the warmth of her voice, only cold paper and dead words!

Confused motions of rebellion stormed in him. He was too young, too strong, too full of the sap of living, to submit so easily to the destruction of his hopes. Must he wear out all his years at the side of a bitter querulous woman? Other possibilities had been in him, possibilities sacrificed, one by one, to Zeena's narrow-mindedness and ignorance. And what good had come of it? She was a hundred times bitterer and more discontented than when he had married her: the one pleasure left her was to inflict pain on him. All the healthy instincts of self-defence rose up in him against such waste . . .

He bundled himself into his old coon-skin coat and lay down on the box-sofa to think. Under his cheek he felt a hard object with strange protuberances. It was a cushion which Zeena had made for him when they were engaged— the only piece of needlework he had ever seen her do. He flung it across the floor and propped his head against the wall . . .

He knew a case of a man over the mountain—a young fellow of about his own age—who had escaped from just such a life of misery by going West with the girl he cared for. His wife had divorced him, and he had married the girl and prospered. Ethan had seen the couple the summer before at Shadd's Falls, where they had come to visit relatives. They had a little girl with fair curls, who wore a gold locket and was dressed like a princess. The deserted wife had not done badly either. Her husband had given her the farm and she had managed to sell it, and with that and the alimony she had started a lunch-room at Bettsbridge and bloomed into activity and importance. Ethan was fired by the thought. Why should he not leave with Mattie the next day, instead of letting her go alone? He would hide his valise under the seat of the sleigh, and Zeena would suspect nothing till she went upstairs for her afternoon nap and found a letter on the bed . . .

His impulses were still near the surface, and he sprang up, re-lit the lantern, and sat down at the table. He rummaged in the drawer for a sheet of paper, found one, and began to write.

"Zeena, I've done all I could for you, and I don't see as it's been any use. I don't blame you, nor I don't blame myself. Maybe both of us will do better separate. I'm going to try my luck West, and you can sell the farm and mill, and keep the money——"

His pen paused on the word, which brought home to him

the relentless conditions of his lot. If he gave the farm and mill to Zeena what would be left him to start his own life with? Once in the West he was sure of picking up work—he would not have feared to try his chance alone. But with Mattie depending on him the case was different. And what of Zeena's fate? Farm and mill were mortgaged to the limit of their value, and even if she found a purchaser—in itself an unlikely chance—it was doubtful if she could clear a thousand dollars on the sale. Meanwhile, how could she keep the farm going? It was only by incessant labour and personal supervision that Ethan drew a meagre living from his land, and his wife, even if she were in better health than she imagined, could never carry such a burden alone.

Well, she could go back to her people, then, and see what they would do for her. It was the fate she was forcing on Mattie—why not let her try it herself? By the time she had discovered his whereabouts, and brought suit for divorce, he would probably—wherever he was—be earning enough to pay her a sufficient alimony. And the alternative was to let Mattie go forth alone, with far less hope of ultimate provision . . .

He had scattered the contents of the table-drawer in his search for a sheet of paper, and as he took up his pen his eye fell on an old copy of the *Bettsbridge Eagle*. The advertising sheet was folded uppermost, and he read the seductive words: "Trips to the West: Reduced Rates."

He drew the lantern nearer and eagerly scanned the fares; then the paper fell from his hand and he pushed aside his unfinished letter. A moment ago he had wondered what he and Mattie were to live on when they reached the West; now he saw that he had not even the money to take her there. Borrowing was out of the question: six months before he had given his only security to raise funds for necessary repairs to the mill, and he knew that without security no one at Starkfield would lend him ten dollars. The inexorable facts closed in on him like prison-warders hand-cuffing a convict. There was no way out—none. He was a prisoner for life, and now his one ray of light was to be extinguished.

He crept back heavily to the sofa, stretching himself out with limbs so leaden that he felt as if they would never move again. Tears rose in his throat and slowly burned their way to his lids.

As he lay there, the window-pane that faced him, growing gradually lighter, inlaid upon the darkness a square of moon-suffused sky. A crooked tree-branch crossed it, a branch of the apple-tree under which, on summer evenings, he had some-times found Mattie sitting when he came up from the mill. Slowly the rim of the rainy vapours caught fire and burnt away, and a pure moon swung into the blue. Ethan, rising on his elbow, watched the landscape whiten and shape itself under the sculpture of the moon. This was the night on which he was to have taken Mattie coasting, and there hung the lamp to light them! He looked out at the slopes bathed in lustre, the silver-edged darkness of the woods, the spectral purple of the hills against the sky, and it seemed as though all the beauty of the night had been poured out to mock his wretchedness . . .

He fell asleep, and when he woke the chill of the winter dawn was in the room. He felt cold and stiff and hungry, and ashamed of being hungry. He rubbed his eyes and went to the window. A red sun stood over the grey rim of the fields, behind trees that looked black and brittle. He said to himself: "This is Matt's last day," and tried to think what the place would be without her.

As he stood there he heard a step behind him and she entered.

"Oh, Ethan—were you here all night?"

She looked so small and pinched, in her poor dress, with the red scarf wound about her, and the cold light turning her paleness sallow, that Ethan stood before her without speaking.

"You must be frozen," she went on, fixing lustreless eyes on him.

He drew a step nearer. "How did you know I was here?"

"Because I heard you go down stairs again after I went to bed, and I listened all night, and you didn't come up."

All his tenderness rushed to his lips. He looked at her and said: "I'll come right along and make up the kitchen fire."

They went back to the kitchen, and he fetched the coal and kindlings and cleared out the stove for her, while she brought in the milk and the cold remains of the meat-pie. When warmth began to radiate from the stove, and the first ray of sunlight lay on the kitchen floor, Ethan's dark thoughts melted in the mellower air. The sight of Mattie going about her work as he had seen her on so many mornings made it seem impossible that she should ever cease to be a part of the scene. He said to himself that he had doubtless exaggerated the significance of Zeena's threats, and that she too, with the return of daylight, would come to a saner mood.

He went up to Mattie as she bent above the stove, and laid his hand on her arm. "I don't want you should trouble either," he said, looking down into her eyes with a smile.

She flushed up warmly and whispered back: "No, Ethan, I ain't going to trouble."

"I guess things'll straighten out," he added.

There was no answer but a quick throb of her lids, and he went on: "She ain't said anything this morning?"

"No. I haven't seen her yet."

"Don't you take any notice when you do."

With this injunction he left her and went out to the cow-barn. He saw Jotham Powell walking up the hill through the morning mist, and the familiar sight added to his growing conviction of security.

As the two men were clearing out the stalls Jotham rested on his pitch-fork to say: "Dan'l Byrne's goin' over to the Flats to-day noon, an' he c'd take Mattie's trunk along, and make it easier ridin' when I take her over in the sleigh."

Ethan looked at him blankly, and he continued: "Mis' Frome said the new girl'd be at the Flats at five, and I was to take Mattie then, so's 't she could ketch the six o'clock train for Stamford."

Ethan felt the blood drumming in his temples. He had to wait a moment before he could find voice to say: "Oh, it ain't so sure about Mattie's going——"

"That so?" said Jotham indifferently; and they went on with their work.

When they returned to the kitchen the two women were already at breakfast. Zeena had an air of unusual alertness and activity. She drank two cups of coffee and fed the cat with the scraps left in the pie-dish; then she rose from her seat and, walking over to the window, snipped two or three yellow leaves from the geraniums. "Aunt Martha's ain't got a faded leaf on 'em; but they pine away when they ain't cared for," she said reflectively. Then she turned to Jotham and asked: "What time'd you say Dan'l Byrne'd be along?"

The hired man threw a hesitating glance at Ethan. "Round about noon," he said.

Zeena turned to Mattie. "That trunk of yours is too heavy for the sleigh, and Dan'l Byrne'll be round to take it over to the Flats," she said.

"I'm much obliged to you, Zeena," said Mattie.

"I'd like to go over things with you first," Zeena continued in an unperturbed voice. "I know there's a huckaback towel missing; and I can't make out what you done with that match-safe 't used to stand behind the stuffed owl in the parlour."

She went out, followed by Mattie, and when the men were alone Jotham said to his employer: "I guess I better let Dan'l come round, then."

Ethan finished his usual morning tasks about the house and barn; then he said to Jotham: "I'm going down to Starkfield. Tell them not to wait dinner."

The passion of rebellion had broken out in him again. That which had seemed incredible in the sober light of day had really come to pass, and he was to assist as a helpless spectator at Mattie's banishment. His manhood was humbled by the part he was compelled to play and by the thought of what Mattie must think of him. Confused impulses struggled in him as he strode along to the village. He had made up his mind to do something, but he did not know what it would be.

The early mist had vanished and the fields lay like a silver shield under the sun. It was one of the days when the glitter of winter shines through a pale haze of spring. Every yard of the road was alive with Mattie's presence, and there was hardly a branch against the sky or a tangle of brambles on the bank in which some bright shred of memory was not caught. Once, in the stillness, the call of a bird in a mountain ash was so like her laughter that his heart tightened and then grew large; and all these things made him see that something must be done at once.

Suddenly it occurred to him that Andrew Hale, who was a kind-hearted man, might be induced to reconsider his refusal and advance a small sum on the lumber if he were told that Zeena's ill-health made it necessary to hire a servant. Hale, after all, knew enough of Ethan's situation to make it possible for the latter to renew his appeal without too much loss of pride; and, moreover, how much did pride count in the ebullition of passions in his breast?

The more he considered his plan the more hopeful it seemed. If he could get Mrs. Hale's ear he felt certain of success, and with fifty dollars in his pocket nothing could keep him from Mattie . . .

His first object was to reach Starkfield before Hale had started for his work; he knew the carpenter had a job down the Corbury road and was likely to leave his house early. Ethan's long strides grew more rapid with the accelerated beat of his thoughts, and as he reached the foot of School House Hill he caught sight of Hale's sleigh in the distance. He hurried forward to meet it, but as it drew nearer he saw that it was driven by the carpenter's youngest boy and that the figure at his side, looking like a large upright cocoon in spectacles, was that of Mrs. Andrew Hale. Ethan signed to them to stop, and Mrs. Hale leaned forward, her pink wrinkles twinkling with benevolence.

"Mr. Hale? Why, yes, you'll find him down home now. He ain't going to his work this forenoon. He woke up with a touch o' lumbago, and I just made him put on one of old Dr. Kidder's plasters and set right up into the fire."

Beaming maternally on Ethan, she bent over to add: "I on'y just heard from Mr. Hale 'bout Zeena's going over to Bettsbridge to see that new doctor. I'm real sorry she's feeling so bad again! I hope he thinks he can do something for her? I don't know anybody round here's had more sickness than Zeena. I always tell Mr. Hale I don't know what she'd 'a' done if she hadn't 'a' had you to look after her; and I used to say the same thing 'bout your mother. You've had an awful mean time, Ethan Frome."

She gave him a last nod of sympathy while her son chirped

to the horse; and Ethan, as she drove off, stood in the middle of the road and stared after the retreating sleigh.

It was a long time since any one had spoken to him as kindly as Mrs. Hale. Most people were either indifferent to his troubles, or disposed to think it natural that a young fellow of his age should have carried without repining the burden of three crippled lives. But Mrs. Hale had said "You've had an awful mean time, Ethan Frome," and he felt less alone with his misery. If the Hales were sorry for him they would surely respond to his appeal . . .

He started down the road toward their house, but at the end of a few yards he pulled up sharply, the blood in his face. For the first time, in the light of the words he had just heard, he saw what he was about to do. He was planning to take advantage of the Hales' sympathy to obtain money from them on false pretences. That was a plain statement of the cloudy purpose which had driven him in headlong to Starkfield.

With the sudden perception of the point to which his madness had carried him, the madness fell and he saw his life before him as it was. He was a poor man, the husband of a sickly woman, whom his desertion would leave alone and destitute; and even if he had had the heart to desert her he could have done so only by deceiving two kindly people who had pitied him.

He turned and walked slowly back to the farm.

IX

A<small>T THE KITCHEN DOOR</small> Daniel Byrne sat in his sleigh behind a big-boned grey who pawed the snow and swung his long head restlessly from side to side.

Ethan went into the kitchen and found his wife by the stove. Her head was wrapped in her shawl, and she was reading a book called "Kidney Troubles and Their Cure" on which he had had to pay extra postage only a few days before.

Zeena did not move or look up when he entered, and after a moment he asked: "Where's Mattie?"

Without lifting her eyes from the page she replied: "I presume she's getting down her trunk."

The blood rushed to his face. "Getting down her trunk—alone?"

"Jotham Powell's down in the wood-lot, and Dan'l Byrne says he darsn't leave that horse," she returned.

Her husband, without stopping to hear the end of the phrase, had left the kitchen and sprung up the stairs. The door of Mattie's room was shut, and he wavered a moment on the landing. "Matt," he said in a low voice; but there was no answer, and he put his hand on the door-knob.

He had never been in her room except once, in the early summer, when he had gone there to plaster up a leak in the eaves, but he remembered exactly how everything had looked: the red and white quilt on her narrow bed, the pretty pin-cushion on the chest of drawers, and over it the enlarged photograph of her mother, in an oxydized frame, with a bunch of dyed grasses at the back. Now all these and other tokens of her presence had vanished, and the room looked as bare and comfortless as when Zeena had shown her into it on the day of her arrival. In the middle of the floor stood her trunk, and on the trunk she sat in her Sunday dress, her back turned to the door and her face in her hands. She had not heard Ethan's call because she was sobbing; and she did not hear his step till he stood close behind her and laid his hands on her shoulders.

"Matt—oh, don't—oh, *Matt!*"

She started up, lifting her wet face to his. "Ethan—I thought I wasn't ever going to see you again!"

He took her in his arms, pressing her close, and with a trembling hand smoothed away the hair from her forehead.

"Not see me again? What do you mean?"

She sobbed out: "Jotham said you told him we wasn't to wait dinner for you, and I thought——"

"You thought I meant to cut it?" he finished for her grimly.

She clung to him without answering, and he laid his lips on her hair, which was soft yet springy, like certain mosses on warm slopes, and had the faint woody fragrance of fresh sawdust in the sun.

Through the door they heard Zeena's voice calling out from below: "Dan'l Byrne says you better hurry up if you want him to take that trunk."

They drew apart with stricken faces. Words of resistance rushed to Ethan's lips and died there. Mattie found her handkerchief and dried her eyes; then, bending down, she took hold of a handle of the trunk.

Ethan put her aside. "You let go, Matt," he ordered her.

She answered: "It takes two to coax it round the corner"; and submitting to this argument he grasped the other handle, and together they manœuvred the heavy trunk out to the landing.

"Now let go," he repeated; then he shouldered the trunk and carried it down the stairs and across the passage to the kitchen. Zeena, who had gone back to her seat by the stove, did not lift her head from her book as he passed. Mattie followed him out of the door and helped him to lift the trunk into the back of the sleigh. When it was in place they stood side by side on the door-step, watching Daniel Byrne plunge off behind his fidgety horse.

It seemed to Ethan that his heart was bound with cords which an unseen hand was tightening with every tick of the clock. Twice he opened his lips to speak to Mattie and found no breath. At length, as she turned to re-enter the house, he laid a detaining hand on her.

"I'm going to drive you over, Matt," he whispered.

She murmured back: "I think Zeena wants I should go with Jotham."

"I'm going to drive you over," he repeated; and she went into the kitchen without answering.

At dinner Ethan could not eat. If he lifted his eyes they rested on Zeena's pinched face, and the corners of her straight lips seemed to quiver away into a smile. She ate well, declaring that the mild weather made her feel better, and pressed a second helping of beans on Jotham Powell, whose wants she generally ignored.

Mattie, when the meal was over, went about her usual task of clearing the table and washing up the dishes. Zeena, after feeding the cat, had returned to her rocking-chair by the stove, and Jotham Powell, who always lingered last, reluctantly pushed back his chair and moved toward the door.

On the threshold he turned back to say to Ethan: "What time'll I come round for Mattie?"

Ethan was standing near the window, mechanically filling his pipe while he watched Mattie move to and fro. He answered: "You needn't come round; I'm going to drive her over myself."

He saw the rise of the colour in Mattie's averted cheek, and the quick lifting of Zeena's head.

"I want you should stay here this afternoon, Ethan," his wife said. "Jotham can drive Mattie over."

Mattie flung an imploring glance at him, but he repeated curtly: "I'm going to drive her over myself."

Zeena continued in the same even tone: "I wanted you should stay and fix up that stove in Mattie's room afore the girl gets here. It ain't been drawing right for nigh on a month now."

Ethan's voice rose indignantly. "If it was good enough for Mattie I guess it's good enough for a hired girl."

"That girl that's coming told me she was used to a house where they had a furnace," Zeena persisted with the same monotonous mildness.

"She'd better ha' stayed there then," he flung back at her; and turning to Mattie he added in a hard voice: "You be ready by three, Matt; I've got business at Corbury."

Jotham Powell had started for the barn, and Ethan strode down after him aflame with anger. The pulses in his temples throbbed and a fog was in his eyes. He went about his task without knowing what force directed him, or whose hands and feet were fulfilling its orders. It was not till he led out the sorrel and backed him between the shafts of the sleigh that he once more became conscious of what he was doing. As he passed the bridle over the horse's head, and wound the traces around the shafts, he remembered the day when he had made the same preparations in order to drive over and meet his wife's cousin at the Flats. It was little more than a year ago, on just such a soft afternoon, with a "feel" of spring in the air. The sorrel, turning the same big ringed eye on him, nuzzled the palm of his hand in the same way; and one by one all the days between rose up and stood before him . . .

He flung the bearskin into the sleigh, climbed to the seat, and drove up to the house. When he entered the kitchen it was empty, but Mattie's bag and shawl lay ready by the door. He went to the foot of the stairs and listened. No sound reached him from above, but presently he thought he heard some one moving about in his deserted study, and pushing open the door he saw Mattie, in her hat and jacket, standing with her back to him near the table.

She started at his approach and turning quickly, said: "Is it time?"

"What are you doing here, Matt?" he asked her.

She looked at him timidly. "I was just taking a look round—that's all," she answered, with a wavering smile.

They went back into the kitchen without speaking, and Ethan picked up her bag and shawl.

"Where's Zeena?" he asked.

"She went upstairs right after dinner. She said she had those shooting pains again, and didn't want to be disturbed."

"Didn't she say good-bye to you?"

"No. That was all she said."

Ethan, looking slowly about the kitchen, said to himself with a shudder that in a few hours he would be returning to it alone. Then the sense of unreality overcame him once more, and he could not bring himself to believe that Mattie stood there for the last time before him.

"Come on," he said almost gaily, opening the door and putting her bag into the sleigh. He sprang to his seat and bent over to tuck the rug about her as she slipped into the place at his side. "Now then, go 'long," he said, with a shake of the reins that sent the sorrel placidly jogging down the hill.

"We got lots of time for a good ride, Matt!" he cried, seeking her hand beneath the fur and pressing it in his. His face tingled and he felt dizzy, as if he had stopped in at the Starkfield saloon on a zero day for a drink.

At the gate, instead of making for Starkfield, he turned the sorrel to the right, up the Bettsbridge road. Mattie sat silent, giving no sign of surprise; but after a moment she said: "Are you going round by Shadow Pond?"

He laughed and answered: "I knew you'd know!"

She drew closer under the bearskin, so that, looking sideways around his coat-sleeve, he could just catch the tip of her nose and a blown brown wave of hair. They drove slowly up the road between fields glistening under the pale sun, and then bent to the right down a lane edged with spruce and larch. Ahead of them, a long way off, a range of hills stained by mottlings of black forest flowed away in round white curves against the sky. The lane passed into a pine-wood with boles reddening in the afternoon sun and delicate blue shadows on the snow. As they entered it the breeze fell and a warm stillness seemed to drop from the branches with the dropping needles. Here the snow was so pure that the tiny tracks of wood-animals had left on it intricate lace-like patterns, and the bluish cones caught in its surface stood out like ornaments of bronze.

Ethan drove on in silence till they reached a part of the wood where the pines were more widely spaced; then he drew up and helped Mattie to get out of the sleigh. They passed between the aromatic trunks, the snow breaking crisply under their feet, till they came to a small sheet of water with steep wooded sides. Across its frozen surface, from the farther bank, a single hill rising against the western sun threw the long conical shadow which gave the lake its name. It was a shy secret spot, full of the same dumb melancholy that Ethan felt in his heart.

He looked up and down the little pebbly beach till his eye lit on a fallen tree-trunk half submerged in snow.

"There's where we sat at the picnic," he reminded her.

The entertainment of which he spoke was one of the few

that they had taken part in together: a "church picnic" which, on a long afternoon of the preceding summer, had filled the retired place with merry-making. Mattie had begged him to go with her but he had refused. Then, toward sunset, coming down from the mountain where he had been felling timber, he had been caught by some strayed revellers and drawn into the group by the lake, where Mattie, encircled by facetious youths, and bright as a blackberry under her spreading hat, was brewing coffee over a gipsy fire. He remembered the shyness he had felt at approaching her in his uncouth clothes, and then the lighting up of her face, and the way she had broken through the group to come to him with a cup in her hand. They had sat for a few minutes on the fallen log by the pond, and she had missed her gold locket, and set the young men searching for it; and it was Ethan who had spied it in the moss . . . That was all; but all their intercourse had been made up of just such inarticulate flashes, when they seemed to come suddenly upon happiness as if they had surprised a butterfly in the winter woods . . .

"It was right there I found your locket," he said, pushing his foot into a dense tuft of blueberry bushes.

"I never saw anybody with such sharp eyes!" she answered.

She sat down on the tree-trunk in the sun and he sat down beside her.

"You were as pretty as a picture in that pink hat," he said.

She laughed with pleasure. "Oh, I guess it was the hat!" she rejoined.

They had never before avowed their inclination so openly, and Ethan, for a moment, had the illusion that he was a free man, wooing the girl he meant to marry. He looked at her hair and longed to touch it again, and to tell her that it smelt of the woods; but he had never learned to say such things.

Suddenly she rose to her feet and said: "We mustn't stay here any longer."

He continued to gaze at her vaguely, only half-roused from his dream. "There's plenty of time," he answered.

They stood looking at each other as if the eyes of each were straining to absorb and hold fast the other's image. There were things he had to say to her before they parted, but he could not say them in that place of summer memories, and he turned and followed her in silence to the sleigh. As they drove away the sun sank behind the hill and the pine-boles turned from red to grey.

By a devious track between the fields they wound back to the Starkfield road. Under the open sky the light was still clear, with a reflection of cold red on the eastern hills. The clumps of trees in the snow seemed to draw together in ruffled lumps, like birds with their heads under their wings; and the sky, as it paled, rose higher, leaving the earth more alone.

As they turned into the Starkfield road Ethan said: "Matt, what do you mean to do?"

She did not answer at once, but at length she said: "I'll try to get a place in a store."

"You know you can't do it. The bad air and the standing all day nearly killed you before."

"I'm a lot stronger than I was before I came to Starkfield."

"And now you're going to throw away all the good it's done you!"

There seemed to be no answer to this, and again they drove on for a while without speaking. With every yard of the way some spot where they had stood, and laughed together or been silent, clutched at Ethan and dragged him back.

"Isn't there any of your father's folks could help you?"

"There isn't any of 'em I'd ask."

He lowered his voice to say: "You know there's nothing I wouldn't do for you if I could."

"I know there isn't."

"But I can't——"

She was silent, but he felt a slight tremor in the shoulder against his.

"Oh, Matt," he broke out, "if I could ha' gone with you now, I'd ha' done it——"

She turned to him, pulling a scrap of paper from her breast. "Ethan—I found this," she stammered. Even in the failing light he saw it was the letter to his wife that he had begun the night before and forgotten to destroy. Through his astonishment there ran a fierce thrill of joy. "Matt—" he cried; "if I could ha' done it, would you?"

"Oh, Ethan, Ethan—what's the use?" With a sudden

movement she tore the letter in shreds and sent them flut-
tering off into the snow.

"Tell me, Matt! Tell me!" he adjured her.

She was silent for a moment; then she said, in such a low
tone that he had to stoop his head to hear her: "I used to
think of it sometimes, summer nights, when the moon was so
bright I couldn't sleep."

His heart reeled with the sweetness of it. "As long ago as
that?"

She answered, as if the date had long been fixed for her:
"The first time was at Shadow Pond."

"Was that why you gave me my coffee before the others?"

"I don't know. Did I? I was dreadfully put out when you
wouldn't go to the picnic with me; and then, when I saw you
coming down the road, I thought maybe you'd gone home
that way o' purpose; and that made me glad."

They were silent again. They had reached the point where
the road dipped to the hollow by Ethan's mill and as they
descended the darkness descended with them, dropping down
like a black veil from the heavy hemlock boughs.

"I'm tied hand and foot, Matt. There isn't a thing I can
do," he began again.

"You must write to me sometimes, Ethan."

"Oh, what good'll writing do? I want to put my hand out
and touch you. I want to do for you and care for you. I want
to be there when you're sick and when you're lonesome."

"You mustn't think but what I'll do all right."

"You won't need me, you mean? I suppose you'll marry!"

"Oh, Ethan!" she cried.

"I don't know how it is you make me feel, Matt. I'd a'most
rather have you dead than that!"

"Oh, I wish I was, I wish I was!" she sobbed.

The sound of her weeping shook him out of his dark anger,
and he felt ashamed.

"Don't let's talk that way," he whispered.

"Why shouldn't we, when it's true? I've been wishing it
every minute of the day."

"Matt! You be quiet! Don't you say it."

"There's never anybody been good to me but you."

"Don't say that either, when I can't lift a hand for you!"

"Yes; but it's true just the same."

They had reached the top of School House Hill and Stark-field lay below them in the twilight. A cutter, mounting the road from the village, passed them by in a joyous flutter of bells, and they straightened themselves and looked ahead with rigid faces. Along the main street lights had begun to shine from the house-fronts and stray figures were turning in here and there at the gates. Ethan, with a touch of his whip, roused the sorrel to a languid trot.

As they drew near the end of the village the cries of children reached them, and they saw a knot of boys, with sleds behind them, scattering across the open space before the church.

"I guess this'll be their last coast for a day or two," Ethan said, looking up at the mild sky.

Mattie was silent, and he added: "We were to have gone down last night."

Still she did not speak and, prompted by an obscure desire to help himself and her through their miserable last hour, he went on discursively: "Ain't it funny we haven't been down together but just that once last winter?"

She answered: "It wasn't often I got down to the village."

"That's so," he said.

They had reached the crest of the Corbury road, and between the indistinct white glimmer of the church and the black curtain of the Varnum spruces the slope stretched away below them without a sled on its length. Some erratic impulse prompted Ethan to say: "How'd you like me to take you down now?"

She forced a laugh. "Why, there isn't time!"

"There's all the time we want. Come along!" His one desire now was to postpone the moment of turning the sorrel toward the Flats.

"But the girl," she faltered. "The girl'll be waiting at the station."

"Well, let her wait. You'd have to if she didn't. Come!"

The note of authority in his voice seemed to subdue her, and when he had jumped from the sleigh she let him help her out, saying only, with a vague feint of reluctance: "But there isn't a sled round anywheres."

"Yes, there is! Right over there under the spruces."

He threw the bearskin over the sorrel, who stood passively by the roadside, hanging a meditative head. Then he caught Mattie's hand and drew her after him toward the sled.

She seated herself obediently and he took his place behind her, so close that her hair brushed his face. "All right, Matt?" he called out, as if the width of the road had been between them.

She turned her head to say: "It's dreadfully dark. Are you sure you can see?"

He laughed contemptuously: "I could go down this coast with my eyes tied!" and she laughed with him, as if she liked his audacity. Nevertheless he sat still a moment, straining his eyes down the long hill, for it was the most confusing hour of the evening, the hour when the last clearness from the upper sky is merged with the rising night in a blur that disguises landmarks and falsifies distances.

"Now!" he cried.

The sled started with a bound, and they flew on through the dusk, gathering smoothness and speed as they went, with the hollow night opening out below them and the air singing by like an organ. Mattie sat perfectly still, but as they reached the bend at the foot of the hill, where the big elm thrust out a deadly elbow, he fancied that she shrank a little closer.

"Don't be scared, Matt!" he cried exultantly, as they spun safely past it and flew down the second slope; and when they reached the level ground beyond, and the speed of the sled began to slacken, he heard her give a little laugh of glee.

They sprang off and started to walk back up the hill. Ethan dragged the sled with one hand and passed the other through Mattie's arm.

"Were you scared I'd run you into the elm?" he asked with a boyish laugh.

"I told you I was never scared with you," she answered.

The strange exultation of his mood had brought on one of his rare fits of boastfulness. "It *is* a tricky place, though. The least swerve, and we'd never ha' come up again. But I can measure distances to a hair's-breadth—always could."

She murmured: "I always say you've got the surest eye . . ."

Deep silence had fallen with the starless dusk, and they leaned on each other without speaking; but at every step of their climb Ethan said to himself: "It's the last time we'll ever walk together."

They mounted slowly to the top of the hill. When they were abreast of the church he stooped his head to her to ask: "Are you tired?" and she answered, breathing quickly: "It was splendid!"

With a pressure of his arm he guided her toward the Norway spruces. "I guess this sled must be Ned Hale's. Anyhow I'll leave it where I found it." He drew the sled up to the Varnum gate and rested it against the fence. As he raised himself he suddenly felt Mattie close to him among the shadows.

"Is this where Ned and Ruth kissed each other?" she whispered breathlessly, and flung her arms about him. Her lips, groping for his, swept over his face, and he held her fast in a rapture of surprise.

"Good-bye—good-bye," she stammered, and kissed him again.

"Oh, Matt, I can't let you go!" broke from him in the same old cry.

She freed herself from his hold and he heard her sobbing. "Oh, I can't go either!" she wailed.

"Matt! What'll we do? What'll we do?"

They clung to each other's hands like children, and her body shook with desperate sobs.

Through the stillness they heard the church clock striking five.

"Oh, Ethan, it's time!" she cried.

He drew her back to him. "Time for what? You don't suppose I'm going to leave you now?"

"If I missed my train where'd I go?"

"Where are you going if you catch it?"

She stood silent, her hands lying cold and relaxed in his.

"What's the good of either of us going anywheres without the other one now?" he said.

She remained motionless, as if she had not heard him. Then she snatched her hands from his, threw her arms about his neck, and pressed a sudden drenched cheek against his face. "Ethan! Ethan! I want you to take me down again!"

"Down where?"

"The coast. Right off," she panted. "So 't we'll never come up any more."

"Matt! What on earth do you mean?"

She put her lips close against his ear to say: "Right into the big elm. You said you could. So 't we'd never have to leave each other any more."

"Why, what are you talking of? You're crazy!"

"I'm not crazy; but I will be if I leave you."

"Oh, Matt, Matt—" he groaned.

She tightened her fierce hold about his neck. Her face lay close to his face.

"Ethan, where'll I go if I leave you? I don't know how to get along alone. You said so yourself just now. Nobody but you was ever good to me. And there'll be that strange girl in the house . . . and she'll sleep in my bed, where I used to lay nights and listen to hear you come up the stairs . . ."

The words were like fragments torn from his heart. With them came the hated vision of the house he was going back to—of the stairs he would have to go up every night, of the woman who would wait for him there. And the sweetness of Mattie's avowal, the wild wonder of knowing at last that all that had happened to him had happened to her too, made the other vision more abhorrent, the other life more intolerable to return to . . .

Her pleadings still came to him between short sobs, but he no longer heard what she was saying. Her hat had slipped back and he was stroking her hair. He wanted to get the feeling of it into his hand, so that it would sleep there like a seed in winter. Once he found her mouth again, and they seemed to be by the pond together in the burning August sun. But his cheek touched hers, and it was cold and full of weeping, and he saw the road to the Flats under the night and heard the whistle of the train up the line.

The spruces swathed them in blackness and silence. They might have been in their coffins underground. He said to himself: "Perhaps it'll feel like this . . ." and then again: "After this I sha'n't feel anything . . ."

Suddenly he heard the old sorrel whinny across the road, and thought: "He's wondering why he doesn't get his supper. . ."

"Come," Mattie whispered, tugging at his hand.

Her sombre violence constrained him: she seemed the embodied instrument of fate. He pulled the sled out, blinking like a night-bird as he passed from the shade of the spruces into the transparent dusk of the open. The slope below them was deserted. All Starkfield was at supper, and not a figure crossed the open space before the church. The sky, swollen with the clouds that announce a thaw, hung as low as before a summer storm. He strained his eyes through the dimness, and they seemed less keen, less capable than usual.

He took his seat on the sled and Mattie instantly placed herself in front of him. Her hat had fallen into the snow and his lips were in her hair. He stretched out his legs, drove his heels into the road to keep the sled from slipping forward, and bent her head back between his hands. Then suddenly he sprang up again.

"Get up," he ordered her.

It was the tone she always heeded, but she cowered down in her seat, repeating vehemently: "No, no, no!"

"Get up!"

"Why?"

"I want to sit in front."

"No, no! How can you steer in front?"

"I don't have to. We'll follow the track."

They spoke in smothered whispers, as though the night were listening.

"Get up! Get up!" he urged her; but she kept on repeating: "Why do you want to sit in front?"

"Because I—because I want to feel you holding me," he stammered, and dragged her to her feet.

The answer seemed to satisfy her, or else she yielded to the power of his voice. He bent down, feeling in the obscurity for the glassy slide worn by preceding coasters, and placed the runners carefully between its edges. She waited while he seated himself with crossed legs in the front of the sled; then she crouched quickly down at his back and clasped her arms about him. Her breath in his neck set him shuddering again, and he almost sprang from his seat. But in a flash he remembered the alternative. She was right: this was better than parting. He leaned back and drew her mouth to his. . .

Just as they started he heard the sorrel's whinny again, and the familiar wistful call, and all the confused images it brought with it, went with him down the first reach of the road. Half-way down there was a sudden drop, then a rise, and after that another long delirious descent. As they took wing for this it seemed to him that they were flying indeed, flying far up into the cloudy night, with Starkfield immeasurably below them, falling away like a speck in space . . . Then the big elm shot up ahead, lying in wait for them at the bend of the road, and he said between his teeth: "We can fetch it; I know we can fetch it——"

As they flew toward the tree Mattie pressed her arms tighter, and her blood seemed to be in his veins. Once or twice the sled swerved a little under them. He slanted his body to keep it headed for the elm, repeating to himself again and again: "I know we can fetch it"; and little phrases she had spoken ran through his head and danced before him on the air. The big tree loomed bigger and closer, and as they bore down on it he thought: "It's waiting for us: it seems to know." But suddenly his wife's face, with twisted monstrous lineaments, thrust itself between him and his goal, and he made an instinctive movement to brush it aside. The sled swerved in response, but he righted it again, kept it straight, and drove down on the black projecting mass. There was a last instant when the air shot past him like millions of fiery wires; and then the elm . . .

The sky was still thick, but looking straight up he saw a single star, and tried vaguely to reckon whether it were Sirius, or—or— The effort tired him too much, and he closed his heavy lids and thought that he would sleep. . . The stillness was so profound that he heard a little animal twittering somewhere near by under the snow. It made a small frightened *cheep* like a field mouse, and he wondered languidly if it were hurt. Then he understood that it must be in pain: pain so excruciating that he seemed, mysteriously, to feel it shooting through his own body. He tried in vain to roll over in the direction of the sound, and stretched his left arm out across the snow. And now it was as though he felt rather than heard the twittering; it seemed to be under his palm, which rested on something soft and springy. The thought of the animal's suffering was intolerable to him and he struggled to raise himself, and could not because a rock, or some huge mass, seemed to be lying on him. But he continued to finger about cautiously with his left hand, thinking he might get hold of the little creature and help it; and all at once he knew that the soft thing he had touched was Mattie's hair and that his hand was on her face.

He dragged himself to his knees, the monstrous load on him moving with him as he moved, and his hand went over and over her face, and he felt that the twittering came from her lips . . .

He got his face down close to hers, with his ear to her mouth, and in the darkness he saw her eyes open and heard her say his name.

"Oh, Matt, I thought we'd fetched it," he moaned; and far off, up the hill, he heard the sorrel whinny, and thought: "I ought to be getting him his feed. . ."

.   .   .   .
.   .   .   .
.   .   .   .

THE QUERULOUS DRONE ceased as I entered Frome's kitchen, and of the two women sitting there I could not tell which had been the speaker.

One of them, on my appearing, raised her tall bony figure from her seat, not as if to welcome me—for she threw me no more than a brief glance of surprise—but simply to set about preparing the meal which Frome's absence had delayed. A slatternly calico wrapper hung from her shoulders and the wisps of her thin grey hair were drawn away from a high forehead and fastened at the back by a broken comb. She had pale opaque eyes which revealed nothing and reflected nothing, and her narrow lips were of the same sallow colour as her face.

The other woman was much smaller and slighter. She sat huddled in an arm-chair near the stove, and when I came in she turned her head quickly toward me, without the least corresponding movement of her body. Her hair was as grey as her companion's, her face as bloodless and shrivelled, but amber-tinted, with swarthy shadows sharpening the nose and hollowing the temples. Under her shapeless dress her body kept its limp immobility, and her dark eyes had the bright witch-like stare that disease of the spine sometimes gives.

Even for that part of the country the kitchen was a poor-looking place. With the exception of the dark-eyed woman's chair, which looked like a soiled relic of luxury bought at a country auction, the furniture was of the roughest kind. Three coarse china plates and a broken-nosed milk-jug had been set on a greasy table scored with knife-cuts, and a couple of straw-bottomed chairs and a kitchen dresser of unpainted pine stood meagrely against the plaster walls.

"My, it's cold here! The fire must be 'most out," Frome said, glancing about him apologetically as he followed me in.

The tall woman, who had moved away from us toward the dresser, took no notice; but the other, from her cushioned niche, answered complainingly, in a high thin voice: "It's on'y just been made up this very minute. Zeena fell asleep and slep' ever so long, and I thought I'd be frozen stiff before I could wake her up and get her to 'tend to it."

I knew then that it was she who had been speaking when we entered.

Her companion, who was just coming back to the table with the remains of a cold mince-pie in a battered pie-dish, set down her unappetising burden without appearing to hear the accusation brought against her.

Frome stood hesitatingly before her as she advanced; then he looked at me and said: "This is my wife, Mis' Frome." After another interval he added, turning toward the figure in the arm-chair: "And this is Miss Mattie Silver. . ."

. . . .

Mrs. Ned Hale, tender soul, had pictured me as lost in the Flats and buried under a snow-drift; and her satisfaction on seeing me safely restored to her the next morning made me feel that my peril had caused me to advance several degrees in her favour.

Great was her amazement, and that of old Mrs. Varnum, on learning that Ethan Frome's old horse had carried me to and from Corbury Junction through the worst blizzard of the winter; greater still their surprise when they heard that his master had taken me in for the night.

Beneath their exclamations of wonder I felt a secret curiosity to know what impressions I had received from my night in the Frome household, and divined that the best way of breaking down their reserve was to let them try to penetrate mine. I therefore confined myself to saying, in a matter-of-fact tone, that I had been received with great kindness, and that Frome had made a bed for me in a room on the ground-floor which seemed in happier days to have been fitted up as a kind of writing-room or study.

"Well," Mrs. Hale mused, "in such a storm I suppose he felt he couldn't do less than take you in—but I guess it went hard with Ethan. I don't believe but what you're the only stranger has set foot in that house for over twenty years. He's that proud he don't even like his oldest friends to go there; and I don't know as any do, any more, except myself and the doctor . . ."

"You still go there, Mrs. Hale?" I ventured.

"I used to go a good deal after the accident, when I was first married; but after a while I got to think it made 'em feel worse to see us. And then one thing and another came, and my own troubles . . . But I generally make out to drive over there round about New Year's, and once in the summer. Only I always try to pick a day when Ethan's off somewheres. It's bad enough to see the two women sitting there—but *his* face, when he looks round that bare place, just kills me . . . You see, I can look back and call it up in his mother's day, before their troubles."

Old Mrs. Varnum, by this time, had gone up to bed, and her daughter and I were sitting alone, after supper, in the austere seclusion of the horse-hair parlour. Mrs. Hale glanced at me tentatively, as though trying to see how much footing my conjectures gave her; and I guessed that if she had kept silence till now it was because she had been waiting, through all the years, for some one who should see what she alone had seen.

I waited to let her trust in me gather strength before I said: "Yes, it's pretty bad, seeing all three of them there together."

She drew her mild brows into a frown of pain. "It was just awful from the beginning. I was here in the house when they were carried up—they laid Mattie Silver in the room you're in. She and I were great friends, and she was to have been my brides-maid in the spring . . . When she came to I went up to her and stayed all night. They gave her things to quiet her, and she didn't know much till to'rd morning, and then all of a sudden she woke up just like herself, and looked straight at me out of her big eyes, and said . . . Oh, I don't know why I'm telling you all this," Mrs. Hale broke off, crying.

She took off her spectacles, wiped the moisture from them, and put them on again with an unsteady hand. "It got about the next day," she went on, "that Zeena Frome had sent Mattie off in a hurry because she had a hired girl coming, and the folks here could never rightly tell what she and Ethan were doing that night coasting, when they'd ought to have been on their way to the Flats to ketch the train . . . I never knew myself what Zeena thought—I don't to this day. Nobody knows Zeena's thoughts. Anyhow, when she heard o' the accident she came right in and stayed with Ethan over to the minister's, where they'd carried him. And as soon as the doctors said that Mattie could be moved, Zeena sent for her and took her back to the farm."

"And there she's been ever since?"

Mrs. Hale answered simply: "There was nowhere else for her to go;" and my heart tightened at the thought of the hard compulsions of the poor.

"Yes, there she's been," Mrs. Hale continued, "and Zeena's done for her, and done for Ethan, as good as she could. It was a miracle, considering how sick she was—but she seemed to be raised right up just when the call came to her. Not as she's ever given up doctoring, and she's had sick spells right along; but she's had the strength given her to care for those two for over twenty years, and before the accident came she thought she couldn't even care for herself."

Mrs. Hale paused a moment, and I remained silent, plunged in the vision of what her words evoked. "It's horrible for them all," I murmured.

"Yes: it's pretty bad. And they ain't any of 'em easy people either. Mattie *was*, before the accident; I never knew a sweeter nature. But she's suffered too much—that's what I always say when folks tell me how she's soured. And Zeena, she was always cranky. Not but what she bears with Mattie wonderful—I've seen that myself. But sometimes the two of them get going at each other, and then Ethan's face'd break your heart . . . When I see that, I think it's *him* that suffers most . . . anyhow it ain't Zeena, because she ain't got the time . . . It's a pity, though," Mrs. Hale ended, sighing, "that they're all shut up there'n that one kitchen. In the summertime, on pleasant days, they move Mattie into the parlour, or out in the door-yard, and that makes it easier . . . but winters there's the fires to be thought of; and there ain't a dime to spare up at the Fromes'."

Mrs. Hale drew a deep breath, as though her memory were eased of its long burden, and she had no more to say; but suddenly an impulse of complete avowal seized her.

She took off her spectacles again, leaned toward me across the bead-work table-cover, and went on with lowered voice: "There was one day, about a week after the accident, when they all thought Mattie couldn't live. Well, I say it's a pity she *did*. I said it right out to our minister once, and he was shocked at me. Only he wasn't with me that morning when she first came to . . . And I say, if she'd ha' died, Ethan might ha' lived; and the way they are now, I don't see's there's much difference between the Fromes up at the farm and the Fromes down in the graveyard; 'cept that down there they're all quiet, and the women have got to hold their tongues."

THE   END

SUMMER

I

A GIRL came out of lawyer Royall's house, at the end of the one street of North Dormer, and stood on the doorstep.

It was the beginning of a June afternoon. The springlike transparent sky shed a rain of silver sunshine on the roofs of the village, and on the pastures and larchwoods surrounding it. A little wind moved among the round white clouds on the shoulders of the hills, driving their shadows across the fields and down the grassy road that takes the name of street when it passes through North Dormer. The place lies high and in the open, and lacks the lavish shade of the more protected New England villages. The clump of weeping-willows about the duck pond, and the Norway spruces in front of the Hatchard gate, cast almost the only roadside shadow between lawyer Royall's house and the point where, at the other end of the village, the road rises above the church and skirts the black hemlock wall enclosing the cemetery.

The little June wind, frisking down the street, shook the doleful fringes of the Hatchard spruces, caught the straw hat of a young man just passing under them, and spun it clean across the road into the duck-pond.

As he ran to fish it out the girl on lawyer Royall's doorstep noticed that he was a stranger, that he wore city clothes, and that he was laughing with all his teeth, as the young and careless laugh at such mishaps.

Her heart contracted a little, and the shrinking that sometimes came over her when she saw people with holiday faces made her draw back into the house and pretend to look for the key that she knew she had already put into her pocket. A narrow greenish mirror with a gilt eagle over it hung on the passage wall, and she looked critically at her reflection, wished for the thousandth time that she had blue eyes like Annabel Balch, the girl who sometimes came from Springfield to spend a week with old Miss Hatchard, straightened the sunburnt hat over her small swarthy face, and turned out again into the sunshine.

"How I hate everything!" she murmured.

The young man had passed through the Hatchard gate, and she had the street to herself. North Dormer is at all times an empty place, and at three o'clock on a June afternoon its few able-bodied men are off in the fields or woods, and the women indoors, engaged in languid household drudgery.

The girl walked along, swinging her key on a finger, and looking about her with the heightened attention produced by the presence of a stranger in a familiar place. What, she wondered, did North Dormer look like to people from other parts of the world? She herself had lived there since the age of five, and had long supposed it to be a place of some importance. But about a year before, Mr. Miles, the new Episcopal clergyman at Hepburn, who drove over every other Sunday—when the roads were not ploughed up by hauling—to hold a service in the North Dormer church, had proposed, in a fit of missionary zeal, to take the young people down to Nettleton to hear an illustrated lecture on the Holy Land; and the dozen girls and boys who represented the future of North Dormer had been piled into a farm-waggon, driven over the hills to Hepburn, put into a way-train and carried to Nettleton. In the course of that incredible day Charity Royall had, for the first and only time, experienced railway-travel, looked into shops with plate-glass fronts, tasted cocoanut pie, sat in a theatre, and listened to a gentleman saying unintelligible things before pictures that she would have enjoyed looking at if his explanations had not prevented her from understanding them. This initiation had shown her that North Dormer was a small place, and developed in her a thirst for information that her position as custodian of the village library had previously failed to excite. For a month or two she dipped feverishly and disconnectedly into the dusty volumes of the Hatchard Memorial Library; then the impression of Nettleton began to fade, and she found it easier to take North Dormer as the norm of the universe than to go on reading.

The sight of the stranger once more revived memories of Nettleton, and North Dormer shrank to its real size. As she looked up and down it, from lawyer Royall's faded red house at one end to the white church at the other, she pitilessly took its measure. There it lay, a weather-beaten sunburnt village of the hills, abandoned of men, left apart by railway, trolley, telegraph, and all the forces that link life to life in modern communities. It had no shops, no theatres, no lectures, no "business block"; only a church that was opened every other Sunday if the state of the roads permitted, and a library for which no new books had been bought for twenty years, and where the old ones mouldered undisturbed on the damp shelves. Yet Charity Royall had always been told that she ought to consider it a privilege that her lot had been cast in North Dormer. She knew that, compared to the place she had come from, North Dormer represented all the blessings of the most refined civilization. Everyone in the village had told her so ever since she had been brought there as a child. Even old Miss Hatchard had said to her, on a terrible occasion in her life: "My child, you must never cease to remember that it was Mr. Royall who brought you down from the Mountain."

She had been "brought down from the Mountain"; from the scarred cliff that lifted its sullen wall above the lesser slopes of Eagle Range, making a perpetual background of gloom to the lonely valley. The Mountain was a good fifteen miles away, but it rose so abruptly from the lower hills that it seemed almost to cast its shadow over North Dormer. And it was like a great magnet drawing the clouds and scattering them in storm across the valley. If ever, in the purest summer sky, there trailed a thread of vapour over North Dormer, it drifted to the Mountain as a ship drifts to a whirlpool, and was caught among the rocks, torn up and multiplied, to sweep back over the village in rain and darkness.

Charity was not very clear about the Mountain; but she knew it was a bad place, and a shame to have come from, and that, whatever befell her in North Dormer, she ought, as Miss Hatchard had once reminded her, to remember that she had been brought down from there, and hold her tongue and be thankful. She looked up at the Mountain, thinking of these things, and tried as usual to be thankful. But the sight of the young man turning in at Miss Hatchard's gate had brought back the vision of the glittering streets of Nettleton, and she felt ashamed of her old sun-hat, and sick of North Dormer, and jealously aware of Annabel Balch of Springfield, opening her blue eyes somewhere far off on glories greater than the glories of Nettleton.

"How I hate everything!" she said again.

Half way down the street she stopped at a weak-hinged gate. Passing through it, she walked down a brick path to a queer little brick temple with white wooden columns supporting a pediment on which was inscribed in tarnished gold letters: "The Honorius Hatchard Memorial Library, 1832."

Honorius Hatchard had been old Miss Hatchard's great-uncle; though she would undoubtedly have reversed the phrase, and put forward, as her only claim to distinction, the fact that she was his great-niece. For Honorius Hatchard, in the early years of the nineteenth century, had enjoyed a modest celebrity. As the marble tablet in the interior of the library informed its infrequent visitors, he had possessed marked literary gifts, written a series of papers called "The Recluse of Eagle Range," enjoyed the acquaintance of Washington Irving and Fitz-Greene Halleck, and been cut off in his flower by a fever contracted in Italy. Such had been the sole link between North Dormer and literature, a link piously commemorated by the erection of the monument where Charity Royall, every Tuesday and Thursday afternoon, sat at her desk under a freckled steel engraving of the deceased author, and wondered if he felt any deader in his grave than she did in his library.

Entering her prison-house with a listless step she took off her hat, hung it on a plaster bust of Minerva, opened the shutters, leaned out to see if there were any eggs in the swallow's nest above one of the windows, and finally, seating herself behind the desk, drew out a roll of cotton lace and a steel crochet hook. She was not an expert workwoman, and it had taken her many weeks to make the half-yard of narrow lace which she kept wound about the buckram back of a disintegrated copy of "The Lamplighter." But there was no other way of getting any lace to trim her summer blouse, and since Ally Hawes, the poorest girl in the village, had shown herself in church with enviable transparencies about the shoulders, Charity's hook had travelled faster. She unrolled the lace, dug the hook into a loop, and bent to the task with furrowed brows.

Suddenly the door opened, and before she had raised her eyes she knew that the young man she had seen going in at the Hatchard gate had entered the library.

Without taking any notice of her he began to move slowly about the long vault-like room, his hands behind his back, his short-sighted eyes peering up and down the rows of rusty bindings. At length he reached the desk and stood before her.

"Have you a card-catalogue?" he asked in a pleasant abrupt voice; and the oddness of the question caused her to drop her work.

"A *what*?"

"Why, you know———" He broke off, and she became conscious that he was looking at her for the first time, having apparently, on his entrance, included her in his general short-sighted survey as part of the furniture of the library.

The fact that, in discovering her, he lost the thread of his remark, did not escape her attention, and she looked down and smiled. He smiled also.

"No, I don't suppose you *do* know," he corrected himself. "In fact, it would be almost a pity———"

She thought she detected a slight condescension in his tone, and asked sharply: "Why?"

"Because it's so much pleasanter, in a small library like this, to poke about by one's self—with the help of the librarian."

He added the last phrase so respectfully that she was mollified, and rejoined with a sigh: "I'm afraid I can't help you much."

"Why?" he questioned in his turn; and she replied that there weren't many books anyhow, and that she'd hardly read any of them. "The worms are getting at them," she added gloomily.

"Are they? That's a pity, for I see there are some good ones." He seemed to have lost interest in their conversation, and strolled away again, apparently forgetting her. His indifference nettled her, and she picked up her work, resolved not to offer him the least assistance. Apparently he did not need it, for he spent a long time with his back to her, lifting down, one after another, the tall cobwebby volumes from a distant shelf.

"Oh, I say!" he exclaimed; and looking up she saw that he had drawn out his handkerchief and was carefully wiping the edges of the book in his hand. The action struck her as an unwarranted criticism on her care of the books, and she said irritably: "It's not my fault if they're dirty."

He turned around and looked at her with reviving interest. "Ah—then you're not the librarian?"

"Of course I am; but I can't dust all these books. Besides, nobody ever looks at them, now Miss Hatchard's too lame to come round."

"No, I suppose not." He laid down the book he had been wiping, and stood considering her in silence. She wondered if Miss Hatchard had sent him round to pry into the way the library was looked after, and the suspicion increased her resentment. "I saw you going into her house just now, didn't I?" she asked, with the New England avoidance of the proper name. She was determined to find out why he was poking about among her books.

"Miss Hatchard's house? Yes—she's my cousin and I'm staying there," the young man answered; adding, as if to disarm a visible distrust: "My name is Harney—Lucius Harney. She may have spoken of me."

"No, she hasn't," said Charity, wishing she could have said: "Yes, she has."

"Oh, well——" said Miss Hatchard's cousin with a laugh; and after another pause, during which it occurred to Charity that her answer had not been encouraging, he remarked: "You don't seem strong on architecture."

Her bewilderment was complete: the more she wished to appear to understand him the more unintelligible his remarks became. He reminded her of the gentleman who had "explained" the pictures at Nettleton, and the weight of her ignorance settled down on her again like a pall.

"I mean, I can't see that you have any books on the old houses about here. I suppose, for that matter, this part of the country hasn't been much explored. They all go on doing Plymouth and Salem. So stupid. My cousin's house, now, is remarkable. This place must have had a past—it must have been more of a place once." He stopped short, with the blush of a shy man who overhears himself, and fears he has been voluble. "I'm an architect, you see, and I'm hunting up old houses in these parts."

She stared. "Old houses? Everything's old in North Dormer, isn't it? The folks are, anyhow."

He laughed, and wandered away again.

"Haven't you any kind of a history of the place? I think there was one written about 1840: a book or pamphlet about its first settlement," he presently said from the farther end of the room.

She pressed her crochet hook against her lip and pondered. There was such a work, she knew: "North Dormer and the Early Townships of Eagle County." She had a special grudge against it because it was a limp weakly book that was always either falling off the shelf or slipping back and disappearing if one squeezed it in between sustaining volumes. She remembered, the last time she had picked it up, wondering how anyone could have taken the trouble to write a book about North Dormer and its neighbours: Dormer, Hamblin, Creston and Creston River. She knew them all, mere lost clusters of houses in the folds of the desolate ridges: Dormer, where North Dormer went for its apples; Creston River, where there used to be a paper-mill, and its grey walls stood decaying by the stream; and Hamblin, where the first snow always fell. Such were their titles to fame.

She got up and began to move about vaguely before the shelves. But she had no idea where she had last put the book, and something told her that it was going to play her its usual trick and remain invisible. It was not one of her lucky days.

"I guess it's somewhere," she said, to prove her zeal; but she spoke without conviction, and felt that her words conveyed none.

"Oh, well——" he said again. She knew he was going, and wished more than ever to find the book.

"It will be for next time," he added; and picking up the volume he had laid on the desk he handed it to her. "By the way, a little air and sun would do this good; it's rather valuable."

He gave her a nod and smile, and passed out.

II

THE HOURS of the Hatchard Memorial librarian were from three to five; and Charity Royall's sense of duty usually kept her at her desk until nearly half-past four.

But she had never perceived that any practical advantage thereby accrued either to North Dormer or to herself; and she had no scruple in decreeing, when it suited her, that the library should close an hour earlier. A few minutes after Mr. Harney's departure she formed this decision, put away her lace, fastened the shutters, and turned the key in the door of the temple of knowledge.

The street upon which she emerged was still empty: and after glancing up and down it she began to walk toward her house. But instead of entering she passed on, turned into a field-path and mounted to a pasture on the hillside. She let down the bars of the gate, followed a trail along the crumbling wall of the pasture, and walked on till she reached a knoll where a clump of larches shook out their fresh tassels to the wind. There she lay down on the slope, tossed off her hat and hid her face in the grass.

She was blind and insensible to many things, and dimly knew it; but to all that was light and air, perfume and colour, every drop of blood in her responded. She loved the roughness of the dry mountain grass under her palms, the smell of the thyme into which she crushed her face, the fingering of the wind in her hair and through her cotton blouse, and the creak of the larches as they swayed to it.

She often climbed up the hill and lay there alone for the mere pleasure of feeling the wind and of rubbing her cheeks in the grass. Generally at such times she did not think of anything, but lay immersed in an inarticulate well-being. Today the sense of well-being was intensified by her joy at escaping from the library. She liked well enough to have a friend drop in and talk to her when she was on duty, but she hated to be bothered about books. How could she remember where they were, when they were so seldom asked for? Orma Fry occasionally took out a novel, and her brother Ben was fond of what he called "jography," and of books relating to trade and bookkeeping; but no one else asked for anything except, at intervals, "Uncle Tom's Cabin," or "Opening a Chestnut Burr," or Longfellow. She had these under her hand, and could have found them in the dark; but unexpected demands came so rarely that they exasperated her like an injustice. . . .

She had liked the young man's looks, and his short-sighted eyes, and his odd way of speaking, that was abrupt yet soft, just as his hands were sunburnt and sinewy, yet with smooth nails like a woman's. His hair was sunburnt-looking too, or rather the colour of bracken after frost; his eyes grey, with the appealing look of the shortsighted, his smile shy yet confident, as if he knew lots of things she had never dreamed of, and yet wouldn't for the world have had her feel his superiority. But she did feel it, and liked the feeling; for it was new to her. Poor and ignorant as she was, and knew herself to be—humblest of the humble even in North Dormer, where to come from the Mountain was the worst disgrace—yet in her narrow world she had always ruled. It was partly, of course, owing to the fact that lawyer Royall was "the biggest man in North Dormer"; so much too big for it, in fact, that outsiders, who didn't know, always wondered how it held him. In spite of everything—and in spite even of Miss Hatchard—lawyer Royall ruled in North Dormer; and Charity ruled in lawyer Royall's house. She had never put it to herself in those terms; but she knew her power, knew what it was made of, and hated it. Confusedly, the young man in the library had made her feel for the first time what might be the sweetness of dependence.

She sat up, brushed the bits of grass from her hair, and looked down on the house where she held sway. It stood just below her, cheerless and untended, its faded red front divided from the road by a "yard" with a path bordered by gooseberry bushes, a stone well overgrown with traveller's joy, and a sickly Crimson Rambler tied to a fan-shaped support, which Mr. Royall had once brought up from Hepburn to please her. Behind the house a bit of uneven ground with clothes-lines strung across it stretched up to a dry wall, and beyond the wall a patch of corn and a few rows of potatoes strayed vaguely into the adjoining wilderness of rock and fern.

Charity could not recall her first sight of the house. She had been told that she was ill of a fever when she was brought down from the Mountain; and she could only remember waking one day in a cot at the foot of Mrs. Royall's bed, and opening her eyes on the cold neatness of the room that was afterward to be hers.

Mrs. Royall died seven or eight years later; and by that time Charity had taken the measure of most things about her. She knew that Mrs. Royall was sad and timid and weak; she knew that lawyer Royall was harsh and violent, and still weaker. She knew that she had been christened Charity (in the white church at the other end of the village) to commemorate Mr. Royall's disinterestedness in "bringing her down," and to keep alive in her a becoming sense of her dependence; she knew that Mr. Royall was her guardian, but that he had not legally adopted her, though everybody spoke of her as Charity Royall; and she knew why he had come back to live at North Dormer, instead of practising at Nettleton, where he had begun his legal career.

After Mrs. Royall's death there was some talk of sending her to a boarding-school. Miss Hatchard suggested it, and had a long conference with Mr. Royall, who, in pursuance of her plan, departed one day for Starkfield to visit the institution she recommended. He came back the next night with a black face; worse, Charity observed, than she had ever seen him; and by that time she had had some experience.

When she asked him how soon she was to start he answered shortly, "You ain't going," and shut himself up in the room he called his office; and the next day the lady who kept the school at Starkfield wrote that "under the circumstances" she was afraid she could not make room just then for another pupil.

Charity was disappointed; but she understood. It wasn't the temptations of Starkfield that had been Mr. Royall's undoing; it was the thought of losing her. He was a dreadfully "lonesome" man; she had made that out because she was so "lonesome" herself. He and she, face to face in that sad house, had sounded the depths of isolation; and though she felt no particular affection for him, and not the slightest gratitude, she pitied him because she was conscious that he was superior to the people about him, and that she was the only being between him and solitude. Therefore, when Miss Hatchard sent for her a day or two later, to talk of a school at Nettleton, and to say that this time a friend of hers would "make the necessary arrangements," Charity cut her short with the announcement that she had decided not to leave North Dormer.

Miss Hatchard reasoned with her kindly, but to no purpose; she simply repeated: "I guess Mr. Royall's too lonesome."

Miss Hatchard blinked perplexedly behind her eye-glasses. Her long frail face was full of puzzled wrinkles, and she leant forward, resting her hands on the arms of her mahogany armchair, with the evident desire to say something that ought to be said.

"The feeling does you credit, my dear."

She looked about the pale walls of her sitting-room, seeking counsel of ancestral daguerreotypes and didactic samplers; but they seemed to make utterance more difficult.

"The fact is, it's not only—not only because of the advantages. There are other reasons. You're too young to understand——"

"Oh, no, I ain't," said Charity harshly; and Miss Hatchard blushed to the roots of her blonde cap. But she must have felt a vague relief at having her explanation cut short, for she concluded, again invoking the daguerreotypes: "Of course I shall always do what I can for you; and in case . . . in case . . . you know you can always come to me. . . ."

Lawyer Royall was waiting for Charity in the porch when she returned from this visit. He had shaved, and brushed his black coat, and looked a magnificent monument of a man; at such moments she really admired him.

"Well," he said, "is it settled?"

"Yes, it's settled. I ain't going."

"Not to the Nettleton school?"

"Not anywhere."

He cleared his throat and asked sternly: "Why?"

"I'd rather not," she said, swinging past him on her way to her room. It was the following week that he brought her up the Crimson Rambler and its fan from Hepburn. He had never given her anything before.

The next outstanding incident of her life had happened two years later, when she was seventeen. Lawyer Royall, who hated to go to Nettleton, had been called there in connection with a case. He still exercised his profession, though litigation languished in North Dormer and its outlying hamlets; and for once he had had an opportunity that he could not afford to refuse. He spent three days in Nettleton, won his case, and came back in high good-humour. It was a rare mood with him, and manifested itself on this occasion by his talking impressively at the supper-table of the "rousing welcome" his old friends had given him. He wound up confidentially: "I was a damn fool ever to leave Nettleton. It was Mrs. Royall that made me do it."

Charity immediately perceived that something bitter had happened to him, and that he was trying to talk down the recollection. She went up to bed early, leaving him seated in moody thought, his elbows propped on the worn oilcloth of the supper table. On the way up she had extracted from his overcoat pocket the key of the cupboard where the bottle of whiskey was kept.

She was awakened by a rattling at her door and jumped out of bed. She heard Mr. Royall's voice, low and peremptory, and opened the door, fearing an accident. No other thought had occurred to her; but when she saw him in the doorway, a ray from the autumn moon falling on his discomposed face, she understood.

For a moment they looked at each other in silence; then, as he put his foot across the threshold, she stretched out her arm and stopped him.

"You go right back from here," she said, in a shrill voice that startled her; "you ain't going to have that key tonight."

"Charity, let me in. I don't want the key. I'm a lonesome man," he began, in the deep voice that sometimes moved her.

Her heart gave a startled plunge, but she continued to hold him back contemptuously. "Well, I guess you made a mistake, then. This ain't your wife's room any longer."

She was not frightened, she simply felt a deep disgust; and perhaps he divined it or read it in her face, for after staring at her a moment he drew back and turned slowly away from the door. With her ear to her keyhole she heard him feel his way down the dark stairs, and toward the kitchen; and she listened for the crash of the cupboard panel. But instead she heard him, after an interval, unlock the door of the house, and his heavy steps came to her through the silence as he walked down the path. She crept to the window and saw his bent figure striding up the road in the moonlight. Then a belated sense of fear came to her with the consciousness of victory, and she slipped into bed, cold to the bone.

A day or two later poor Eudora Skeff, who for twenty years had been the custodian of the Hatchard library, died suddenly of pneumonia; and the day after the funeral Charity went to see Miss Hatchard, and asked to be appointed librarian. The request seemed to surprise Miss Hatchard: she evidently questioned the new candidate's qualifications.

"Why, I don't know, my dear. Aren't you rather too young?" she hesitated.

"I want to earn some money," Charity merely answered.

"Doesn't Mr. Royall give you all you require? No one is rich in North Dormer."

"I want to earn money enough to get away."

"To get away?" Miss Hatchard's puzzled wrinkles deepened, and there was a distressful pause. "You want to leave Mr. Royall?"

"Yes: or I want another woman in the house with me," said Charity resolutely.

Miss Hatchard clasped her nervous hands about the arms of her chair. Her eyes invoked the faded countenances on the wall, and after a faint cough of indecision she brought out: "The . . . the housework's too hard for you, I suppose?"

Charity's heart grew cold. She understood that Miss Hatchard had no help to give her and that she would have to fight her way out of her difficulty alone. A deeper sense of isolation overcame her; she felt incalculably old. "She's got to be talked to like a baby," she thought, with a feeling of compassion for Miss Hatchard's long immaturity. "Yes, that's it," she said aloud. "The housework's too hard for me: I've been coughing a good deal this fall."

She noted the immediate effect of this suggestion. Miss Hatchard paled at the memory of poor Eudora's taking-off, and promised to do what she could. But of course there were people she must consult: the clergyman, the selectmen of North Dormer, and a distant Hatchard relative at Springfield. "If you'd only gone to school!" she sighed. She followed Charity to the door, and there, in the security of the threshold, said with a glance of evasive appeal: "I know Mr. Royall is . . . trying at times; but his wife bore with him; and you must always remember, Charity, that it was Mr. Royall who brought you down from the Mountain."

Charity went home and opened the door of Mr. Royall's "office." He was sitting there by the stove reading Daniel Webster's speeches. They had met at meals during the five days that had elapsed since he had come to her door, and she had walked at his side at Eudora's funeral; but they had not spoken a word to each other.

He glanced up in surprise as she entered, and she noticed that he was unshaved, and that he looked unusually old; but as she had always thought of him as an old man the change in his appearance did not move her. She told him she had been to see Miss Hatchard, and with what object. She saw that he was astonished; but he made no comment.

"I told her the housework was too hard for me, and I wanted to earn the money to pay for a hired girl. But I ain't going to pay for her: you've got to. I want to have some money of my own."

Mr. Royall's bushy black eyebrows were drawn together in a frown, and he sat drumming with ink-stained nails on the edge of his desk.

"What do you want to earn money for?" he asked.

"So's to get away when I want to."

"Why do you want to get away?"

Her contempt flashed out. "Do you suppose anybody'd stay at North Dormer if they could help it? You wouldn't, folks say!"

With lowered head he asked: "Where'd you go to?"

"Anywhere where I can earn my living. I'll try here first, and if I can't do it here I'll go somewhere else. I'll go up the Mountain if I have to." She paused on this threat, and saw that it had taken effect. "I want you should get Miss Hatchard and the selectmen to take me at the library: and I want a woman here in the house with me," she repeated.

Mr. Royall had grown exceedingly pale. When she ended he stood up ponderously, leaning against the desk; and for a second or two they looked at each other.

"See here," he said at length, as though utterance were difficult, "there's something I've been wanting to say to you; I'd ought to have said it before. I want you to marry me."

The girl still stared at him without moving. "I want you to marry me," he repeated, clearing his throat. "The minister'll be up here next Sunday and we can fix it up then. Or I'll drive you down to Hepburn to the Justice, and get it done there. I'll do whatever you say." His eyes fell under the merciless stare she continued to fix on him, and he shifted his weight uneasily from one foot to the other. As he stood there before her, unwieldy, shabby, disordered, the purple veins distorting the hands he pressed against the desk, and his long orator's jaw trembling with the effort of his avowal, he seemed like a hideous parody of the fatherly old man she had always known.

"Marry you? Me?" she burst out with a scornful laugh. "Was that what you came to ask me the other night? What's come over you, I wonder? How long is it since you've looked at yourself in the glass?" She straightened herself, insolently conscious of her youth and strength. "I suppose you think it would be cheaper to marry me than to keep a hired girl. Everybody knows you're the closest man in Eagle County; but I guess you're not going to get your mending done for you that way twice."

Mr. Royall did not move while she spoke. His face was ash-coloured and his black eyebrows quivered as though the blaze of her scorn had blinded him. When she ceased he held up his hand.

"That'll do—that'll about do," he said. He turned to the door and took his hat from the hat-peg. On the threshold he paused. "People ain't been fair to me—from the first they ain't been fair to me," he said. Then he went out.

A few days later North Dormer learned with surprise that Charity had been appointed librarian of the Hatchard

Memorial at a salary of eight dollars a month, and that old Verena Marsh, from the Creston Almshouse, was coming to live at lawyer Royall's and do the cooking.

III

IT WAS NOT in the room known at the red house as Mr.
Royall's "office" that he received his infrequent clients.
Professional dignity and masculine independence made it necessary that he should have a real office, under a different roof;
and his standing as the only lawyer of North Dormer required that the roof should be the same as that which sheltered the Town Hall and the post-office.

It was his habit to walk to this office twice a day, morning
and afternoon. It was on the ground floor of the building,
with a separate entrance, and a weathered name-plate on the
door. Before going in he stepped in to the post-office for his
mail—usually an empty ceremony—said a word or two to
the town-clerk, who sat across the passage in idle state, and
then went over to the store on the opposite corner, where
Carrick Fry, the storekeeper, always kept a chair for him, and
where he was sure to find one or two selectmen leaning on
the long counter, in an atmosphere of rope, leather, tar and
coffee-beans. Mr. Royall, though monosyllabic at home, was
not averse, in certain moods, to imparting his views to his
fellow-townsmen; perhaps, also, he was unwilling that his
rare clients should surprise him sitting, clerkless and unoccupied, in his dusty office. At any rate, his hours there were not
much longer or more regular than Charity's at the library; the
rest of the time he spent either at the store or in driving about
the country on business connected with the insurance companies that he represented, or in sitting at home reading
Bancroft's History of the United States and the speeches of
Daniel Webster.

Since the day when Charity had told him that she wished
to succeed to Eudora Skeff's post their relations had undefin-
ably but definitely changed. Lawyer Royall had kept his
word. He had obtained the place for her at the cost of considerable manœuvering, as she guessed from the number of rival
candidates, and from the acerbity with which two of them,
Orma Fry and the eldest Targatt girl, treated her for nearly a
year afterward. And he had engaged Verena Marsh to come
up from Creston and do the cooking. Verena was a poor old

widow, doddering and shiftless: Charity suspected that she came for her keep. Mr. Royall was too close a man to give a dollar a day to a smart girl when he could get a deaf pauper for nothing. But at any rate, Verena was there, in the attic just over Charity, and the fact that she was deaf did not greatly trouble the young girl.

Charity knew that what had happened on that hateful night would not happen again. She understood that, profoundly as she had despised Mr. Royall ever since, he despised himself still more profoundly. If she had asked for a woman in the house it was far less for her own defense than for his humiliation. She needed no one to defend her: his humbled pride was her surest protection. He had never spoken a word of excuse or extenuation; the incident was as if it had never been. Yet its consequences were latent in every word that he and she exchanged, in every glance they instinctively turned from each other. Nothing now would ever shake her rule in the red house.

On the night of her meeting with Miss Hatchard's cousin Charity lay in bed, her bare arms clasped under her rough head, and continued to think of him. She supposed that he meant to spend some time in North Dormer. He had said he was looking up the old houses in the neighbourhood; and though she was not very clear as to his purpose, or as to why anyone should look for old houses, when they lay in wait for one on every roadside, she understood that he needed the help of books, and resolved to hunt up the next day the volume she had failed to find, and any others that seemed related to the subject.

Never had her ignorance of life and literature so weighed on her as in reliving the short scene of her discomfiture. "It's no use trying to be anything in this place," she muttered to her pillow; and she shrivelled at the vision of vague metropolises, shining super-Nettletons, where girls in better clothes than Belle Balch's talked fluently of architecture to young men with hands like Lucius Harney's. Then she remembered his sudden pause when he had come close to the desk and had his first look at her. The sight had made him forget what he was going to say; she recalled the change in his face, and jumping up she ran over the bare boards to her washstand, found the matches, lit a candle, and lifted it to the square of looking-glass on the white-washed wall. Her small face, usually so darkly pale, glowed like a rose in the faint orb of light, and under her rumpled hair her eyes seemed deeper and larger than by day. Perhaps after all it was a mistake to wish they were blue. A clumsy band and button fastened her un-bleached night-gown about the throat. She undid it, freed her thin shoulders, and saw herself a bride in low-necked satin, walking down an aisle with Lucius Harney. He would kiss her as they left the church. . . . She put down the candle and covered her face with her hands as if to imprison the kiss. At that moment she heard Mr. Royall's step as he came up the stairs to bed, and a fierce revulsion of feeling swept over her. Until then she had merely despised him; now deep hatred of him filled her heart. He became to her a horrible old man. . . .

The next day, when Mr. Royall came back to dinner, they faced each other in silence as usual. Verena's presence at the table was an excuse for their not talking, though her deafness would have permitted the freest interchange of confidences. But when the meal was over, and Mr. Royall rose from the table, he looked back at Charity, who had stayed to help the old woman clear away the dishes.

"I want to speak to you a minute," he said; and she followed him across the passage, wondering.

He seated himself in his black horse-hair armchair, and she leaned against the window, indifferently. She was impatient to be gone to the library, to hunt for the book on North Dormer.

"See here," he said, "why ain't you at the library the days you're supposed to be there?"

The question, breaking in on her mood of blissful abstraction, deprived her of speech, and she stared at him for a moment without answering.

"Who says I ain't?"

"There's been some complaints made, it appears. Miss Hatchard sent for me this morning——"

Charity's smouldering resentment broke into a blaze. "I know! Orma Fry, and that toad of a Targatt girl—and Ben

Fry, like as not. He's going round with her. The low-down sneaks—I always knew they'd try to have me out! As if anybody ever came to the library, anyhow!"

"Somebody did yesterday, and you weren't there."

"Yesterday?" she laughed at her happy recollection. "At what time wasn't I there yesterday, I'd like to know?"

"Round about four o'clock."

Charity was silent. She had been so steeped in the dreamy remembrance of young Harney's visit that she had forgotten having deserted her post as soon as he had left the library.

"Who came at four o'clock?"

"Miss Hatchard did."

"Miss Hatchard? Why, she ain't ever been near the place since she's been lame. She couldn't get up the steps if she tried."

"She can be helped up, I guess. She was yesterday, anyhow, by the young fellow that's staying with her. He found you there, I understand, earlier in the afternoon; and he went back and told Miss Hatchard the books were in bad shape and needed attending to. She got excited, and had herself wheeled straight round; and when she got there the place was locked. So she sent for me, and told me about that, and about the other complaints. She claims you've neglected things, and that she's going to get a trained librarian."

Charity had not moved while he spoke. She stood with her head thrown back against the window-frame, her arms hanging against her sides, and her hands so tightly clenched that she felt, without knowing what hurt her, the sharp edge of her nails against her palms.

Of all Mr. Royall had said she had retained only the phrase: "He told Miss Hatchard the books were in bad shape." What did she care for the other charges against her? Malice or truth, she despised them as she despised her detractors. But that the stranger to whom she had felt herself so mysteriously drawn should have betrayed her! That at the very moment when she had fled up the hillside to think of him more deliciously he should have been hastening home to denounce her short-comings! She remembered how, in the darkness of her room, she had covered her face to press his imagined kiss closer; and her heart raged against him for the liberty he had not taken.

"Well, I'll go," she said suddenly. "I'll go right off."

"Go where?" She heard the startled note in Mr. Royall's voice.

"Why, out of their old library: straight out, and never set foot in it again. They needn't think I'm going to wait round and let them say they've discharged me!"

"Charity—Charity Royall, you listen——" he began, getting heavily out of his chair; but she waved him aside, and walked out of the room.

Upstairs she took the library key from the place where she always hid it under her pincushion—who said she wasn't careful?—put on her hat, and swept down again and out into the street. If Mr. Royall heard her go he made no motion to detain her: his sudden rages probably made him understand the uselessness of reasoning with hers.

She reached the brick temple, unlocked the door and entered into the glacial twilight. "I'm glad I'll never have to sit in this old vault again when other folks are out in the sun!" she said aloud as the familiar chill took her. She looked with abhorrence at the long dingy rows of books, the sheep-nosed Minerva on her black pedestal, and the mild-faced young man in a high stock whose effigy pined above her desk. She meant to take out of the drawer her roll of lace and the library register, and go straight to Miss Hatchard to announce her resignation. But suddenly a great desolation overcame her, and she sat down and laid her face against the desk. Her heart was ravaged by life's cruellest discovery: the first creature who had come toward her out of the wilderness had brought her anguish instead of joy. She did not cry; tears came hard to her, and the storms of her heart spent themselves inwardly. But as she sat there in her dumb woe she felt her life to be too desolate, too ugly and intolerable.

"What have I ever done to it, that it should hurt me so?" she groaned, and pressed her fists against her lids, which were beginning to swell with weeping.

"I won't—I won't go there looking like a horror!" she muttered, springing up and pushing back her hair as if it stifled her. She opened the drawer, dragged out the register, and turned toward the door. As she did so it opened, and the young man from Miss Hatchard's came in whistling.

IV

HE STOPPED and lifted his hat with a shy smile. "I beg your pardon," he said. "I thought there was no one here."

Charity stood before him, barring his way. "You can't come in. The library ain't open to the public Wednesdays."

"I know it's not; but my cousin gave me her key."

"Miss Hatchard's got no right to give her key to other folks, any more'n I have. I'm the librarian and I know the by-laws. This is my library."

The young man looked profoundly surprised.

"Why, I know it is; I'm so sorry if you mind my coming."

"I suppose you came to see what more you could say to set her against me? But you needn't trouble: it's my library to-day, but it won't be this time tomorrow. I'm on the way now to take her back the key and the register."

Young Harney's face grew grave, but without betraying the consciousness of guilt she had looked for.

"I don't understand," he said. "There must be some mistake. Why should I say things against you to Miss Hatchard —or to anyone?"

The apparent evasiveness of the reply caused Charity's indignation to overflow. "I don't know why you should. I could understand Orma Fry's doing it, because she's always wanted to get me out of here ever since the first day. I can't see why, when she's got her own home, and her father to work for her; nor Ida Targatt, neither, when she got a legacy from her step-brother on'y last year. But anyway we all live in the same place, and when it's a place like North Dormer it's enough to make people hate each other just to have to walk down the same street every day. But you don't live here, and you don't know anything about any of us, so what did you have to meddle for? Do you suppose the other girls'd have kept the books any better'n I did? Why, Orma Fry don't hardly know a book from a flat-iron! And what if I don't always sit round here doing nothing till it strikes five up at the church? Who cares if the library's open or shut? Do you suppose anybody ever comes here for books? What they'd

180

like to come for is to meet the fellows they're going with—if
I'd let 'em. But I wouldn't let Bill Sollas from over the hill
hang round here waiting for the youngest Targatt girl, because I know him . . . that's all . . . even if I don't know
about books all I ought to. . . ."

She stopped with a choking in her throat. Tremors of rage
were running through her, and she steadied herself against
the edge of the desk lest he should see her weakness.

What he saw seemed to affect him deeply, for he grew red
under his sunburn, and stammered out: "But, Miss Royall, I
assure you . . . I assure you . . ."

His distress inflamed her anger, and she regained her voice
to fling back: "If I was you I'd have the nerve to stick to what
I said!"

The taunt seemed to restore his presence of mind. "I hope I
should if I knew; but I don't. Apparently something disagreeable has happened, for which you think I'm to blame. But I
don't know what it is, because I've been up on Eagle Ridge
ever since the early morning."

"I don't know where you've been this morning, but I know
you were here in this library yesterday; and it was you that
went home and told your cousin the books were in bad
shape, and brought her round to see how I'd neglected
them."

Young Harney looked sincerely concerned. "Was that what
you were told? I don't wonder you're angry. The books *are* in
bad shape, and as some are interesting it's a pity. I told Miss
Hatchard they were suffering from dampness and lack of air;
and I brought her here to show her how easily the place could
be ventilated. I also told her you ought to have some one to
help you do the dusting and airing. If you were given a
wrong version of what I said I'm sorry; but I'm so fond of old
books that I'd rather see them made into a bonfire than left to
moulder away like these."

Charity felt her sobs rising and tried to stifle them in
words. "I don't care what you say you told her. All I know is
she thinks it's all my fault, and I'm going to lose my job, and
I wanted it more'n anyone in the village, because I haven't got
anybody belonging to me, the way other folks have. All I
wanted was to put aside money enough to get away from

here sometime. D'you suppose if it hadn't been for that I'd have kept on sitting day after day in this old vault?"

Of this appeal her hearer took up only the last question. "It *is* an old vault; but need it be? That's the point. And it's my putting the question to my cousin that seems to have been the cause of the trouble." His glance explored the melancholy penumbra of the long narrow room, resting on the blotched walls, the discoloured rows of books, and the stern rosewood desk surmounted by the portrait of the young Honorius. "Of course it's a bad job to do anything with a building jammed against a hill like this ridiculous mausoleum: you couldn't get a good draught through it without blowing a hole in the mountain. But it can be ventilated after a fashion, and the sun can be let in: I'll show you how if you like. . . ." The architect's passion for improvement had already made him lose sight of her grievance, and he lifted his stick instructively toward the cornice. But her silence seemed to tell him that she took no interest in the ventilation of the library, and turning back to her abruptly he held out both hands. "Look here— you don't mean what you said? You don't really think I'd do anything to hurt you?"

A new note in his voice disarmed her: no one had ever spoken to her in that tone.

"Oh, what *did* you do it for then?" she wailed. He had her hands in his, and she was feeling the smooth touch that she had imagined the day before on the hillside.

He pressed her hands lightly and let them go. "Why, to make things pleasanter for you here; and better for the books. I'm sorry if my cousin twisted around what I said. She's excitable, and she lives on trifles: I ought to have remembered that. Don't punish me by letting her think you take her seriously."

It was wonderful to hear him speak of Miss Hatchard as if she were a querulous baby: in spite of his shyness he had the air of power that the experience of cities probably gave. It was the fact of having lived in Nettleton that made lawyer Royall, in spite of his infirmities, the strongest man in North Dormer; and Charity was sure that this young man had lived in bigger places than Nettleton.

She felt that if she kept up her denunciatory tone he would

secretly class her with Miss Hatchard; and the thought made her suddenly simple.

"It don't matter to Miss Hatchard how I take her. Mr. Royall says she's going to get a trained librarian; and I'd sooner resign than have the village say she sent me away."

"Naturally you would. But I'm sure she doesn't mean to send you away. At any rate, won't you give me the chance to find out first and let you know? It will be time enough to resign if I'm mistaken."

Her pride flamed into her cheeks at the suggestion of his intervening. "I don't want anybody should coax her to keep me if I don't suit."

He coloured too. "I give you my word I won't do that. Only wait till tomorrow, will you?" He looked straight into her eyes with his shy grey glance. " You can trust me, you know—you really can."

All the old frozen woes seemed to melt in her, and she murmured awkwardly, looking away from him: "Oh, I'll wait."

V

THERE HAD never been such a June in Eagle County. Usually it was a month of moods, with abrupt alternations of belated frost and midsummer heat; this year, day followed day in a sequence of temperate beauty. Every morning a breeze blew steadily from the hills. Toward noon it built up great canopies of white cloud that threw a cool shadow over fields and woods; then before sunset the clouds dissolved again, and the western light rained its unobstructed brightness on the valley.

On such an afternoon Charity Royall lay on a ridge above a sunlit hollow, her face pressed to the earth and the warm currents of the grass running through her. Directly in her line of vision a blackberry branch laid its frail white flowers and blue-green leaves against the sky. Just beyond, a tuft of sweet-fern uncurled between the beaded shoots of the grass, and a small yellow butterfly vibrated over them like a fleck of sunshine. This was all she saw; but she felt, above her and about her, the strong growth of the beeches clothing the ridge, the rounding of pale green cones on countless spruce-branches, the push of myriads of sweet-fern fronds in the cracks of the stony slope below the wood, and the crowding shoots of meadowsweet and yellow flags in the pasture beyond. All this bubbling of sap and slipping of sheaths and bursting of calyxes was carried to her on mingled currents of fragrance. Every leaf and bud and blade seemed to contribute its exhalation to the pervading sweetness in which the pungency of pine-sap prevailed over the spice of thyme and the subtle perfume of fern, and all were merged in a moist earth-smell that was like the breath of some huge sun-warmed animal.

Charity had lain there a long time, passive and sun-warmed as the slope on which she lay, when there came between her eyes and the dancing butterfly the sight of a man's foot in a large worn boot covered with red mud.

"Oh, don't!" she exclaimed, raising herself on her elbow and stretching out a warning hand.

"Don't what?" a hoarse voice asked above her head.

"Don't stamp on those bramble flowers, you dolt!" she retorted, springing to her knees. The foot paused and then descended clumsily on the frail branch, and raising her eyes she saw above her the bewildered face of a slouching man with a thin sunburnt beard, and white arms showing through his ragged shirt.

"Don't you ever *see* anything, Liff Hyatt?" she assailed him, as he stood before her with the look of a man who has stirred up a wasp's nest.

He grinned. "I seen you! That's what I come down for."

"Down from where?" she questioned, stooping to gather up the petals his foot had scattered.

He jerked his thumb toward the heights. "Been cutting down trees for Dan Targatt."

Charity sank back on her heels and looked at him musingly. She was not in the least afraid of poor Liff Hyatt, though he "came from the Mountain," and some of the girls ran when they saw him. Among the more reasonable he passed for a harmless creature, a sort of link between the mountain and civilized folk, who occasionally came down and did a little wood-cutting for a farmer when hands were short. Besides, she knew the Mountain people would never hurt her: Liff himself had told her so once when she was a little girl, and had met him one day at the edge of lawyer Royall's pasture. "They won't any of 'em touch you up there, f'ever you was to come up. . . . But I don't s'pose you will," he had added philosophically, looking at her new shoes, and at the red ribbon that Mrs. Royall had tied in her hair.

Charity had, in truth, never felt any desire to visit her birthplace. She did not care to have it known that she was of the Mountain, and was shy of being seen in talk with Liff Hyatt. But today she was not sorry to have him appear. A great many things had happened to her since the day when young Lucius Harney had entered the doors of the Hatchard Memorial, but none, perhaps, so unforeseen as the fact of her suddenly finding it a convenience to be on good terms with Liff Hyatt. She continued to look up curiously at his freckled weather-beaten face, with feverish hollows below the cheekbones and the pale yellow eyes of a harmless animal. "I wonder if he's related to me?" she thought, with a shiver of disdain.

"Is there any folks living in the brown house by the swamp, up under Porcupine?" she presently asked in an indifferent tone.

Liff Hyatt, for a while, considered her with surprise; then he scratched his head and shifted his weight from one tattered sole to the other.

"There's always the same folks in the brown house," he said with his vague grin.

"They're from up your way, ain't they?"

"Their name's the same as mine," he rejoined uncertainly.

Charity still held him with resolute eyes. "See here, I want to go there some day and take a gentleman with me that's boarding with us. He's up in these parts drawing pictures."

She did not offer to explain this statement. It was too far beyond Liff Hyatt's limitations for the attempt to be worth making. "He wants to see the brown house, and go all over it," she pursued.

Liff was still running his fingers perplexedly through his shock of straw-colored hair. "Is it a fellow from the city?" he asked.

"Yes. He draws pictures of things. He's down there now drawing the Bonner house." She pointed to a chimney just visible over the dip of the pasture below the wood.

"The Bonner house?" Liff echoed incredulously.

"Yes. You won't understand—and it don't matter. All I say is: he's going to the Hyatts' in a day or two."

Liff looked more and more perplexed. "Bash is ugly sometimes in the afternoons."

"I know. But I guess he won't trouble me." She threw her head back, her eyes full on Hyatt's. "I'm coming too: you tell him."

"They won't none of them trouble you, the Hyatts won't. What d'you want a take a stranger with you, though?"

"I've told you, haven't I? You've got to tell Bash Hyatt."

He looked away at the blue mountains on the horizon; then his gaze dropped to the chimney-top below the pasture.

"He's down there now?"

"Yes."

He shifted his weight again, crossed his arms, and continued to survey the distant landscape. "Well, so long," he said at last, inconclusively; and turning away he shambled up the hillside. From the ledge above her, he paused to call down: "I wouldn't go there a Sunday"; then he clambered on till the trees closed in on him. Presently, from high overhead, Charity heard the ring of his axe.

She lay on the warm ridge, thinking of many things that the woodsman's appearance had stirred up in her. She knew nothing of her early life, and had never felt any curiosity about it: only a sullen reluctance to explore the corner of her memory where certain blurred images lingered. But all that had happened to her within the last few weeks had stirred her to the sleeping depths. She had become absorbingly interesting to herself, and everything that had to do with her past was illuminated by this sudden curiosity.

She hated more than ever the fact of coming from the Mountain; but it was no longer indifferent to her. Everything that in any way affected her was alive and vivid: even the hateful things had grown interesting because they were a part of herself.

"I wonder if Liff Hyatt knows who my mother was?" she mused; and it filled her with a tremor of surprise to think that some woman who was once young and slight, with quick motions of the blood like hers, had carried her in her breast, and watched her sleeping. She had always thought of her mother as so long dead as to be no more than a nameless pinch of earth; but now it occurred to her that the once-young woman might be alive, and wrinkled and elf-locked like the woman she had sometimes seen in the door of the brown house that Lucius Harney wanted to draw.

The thought brought her back to the central point in her mind, and she strayed away from the conjectures roused by Liff Hyatt's presence. Speculations concerning the past could not hold her long when the present was so rich, the future so rosy, and when Lucius Harney, a stone's throw away, was bending over his sketch-book, frowning, calculating, measuring, and then throwing his head back with the sudden smile that had shed its brightness over everything.

She scrambled to her feet, but as she did so she saw him coming up the pasture and dropped down on the grass to wait. When he was drawing and measuring one of "his houses," as she called them, she often strayed away by herself into the woods or up the hillside. It was partly from shyness that she did so: from a sense of inadequacy that came to her most painfully when her companion, absorbed in his job, forgot her ignorance and her inability to follow his least allusion, and plunged into a monologue on art and life. To avoid the awkwardness of listening with a blank face, and also to escape the surprised stare of the inhabitants of the houses before which he would abruptly pull up their horse and open his sketch-book, she slipped away to some spot from which, without being seen, she could watch him at work, or at least look down on the house he was drawing. She had not been displeased, at first, to have it known to North Dormer and the neighborhood that she was driving Miss Hatchard's cousin about the country in the buggy he had hired of lawyer Royall. She had always kept to herself, contemptuously aloof from village love-making, without exactly knowing whether her fierce pride was due to the sense of her tainted origin, or whether she was reserving herself for a more brilliant fate. Sometimes she envied the other girls their sentimental preoccupations, their long hours of inarticulate philandering with one of the few youths who still lingered in the village; but when she pictured herself curling her hair or putting a new ribbon on her hat for Ben Fry or one of the Sollas boys the fever dropped and she relapsed into indifference.

Now she knew the meaning of her disdains and reluctances. She had learned what she was worth when Lucius Harney, looking at her for the first time, had lost the thread of his speech, and leaned reddening on the edge of her desk. But another kind of shyness had been born in her: a terror of exposing to vulgar perils the sacred treasure of her happiness. She was not sorry to have the neighbors suspect her of "going with" a young man from the city; but she did not want it known to all the countryside how many hours of the long June days she spent with him. What she most feared was that the inevitable comments should reach Mr. Royall. Charity was instinctively aware that few things concerning her escaped the eyes of the silent man under whose roof she lived; and in spite of the latitude which North Dormer accorded to courting couples she had always felt that, on the day when she showed too open a preference, Mr. Royall might, as she phrased it, make her "pay for it." How, she did not know; and her fear was the greater because it was undefinable. If she had been accepting the attentions of one of the village youths she would have been less apprehensive: Mr. Royall could not prevent her marrying when she chose to. But everybody knew that "going with a city fellow" was a different and less straightforward affair: almost every village could show a victim of the perilous venture. And her dread of Mr. Royall's intervention gave a sharpened joy to the hours she spent with young Harney, and made her, at the same time, shy of being too generally seen with him.

As he approached she rose to her knees, stretching her arms above her head with the indolent gesture that was her way of expressing a profound well-being.

"I'm going to take you to that house up under Porcupine," she announced.

"What house? Oh, yes; that ramshackle place near the swamp, with the gipsy-looking people hanging about. It's curious that a house with traces of real architecture should have been built in such a place. But the people were a sulky-looking lot—do you suppose they'll let us in?"

"They'll do whatever I tell them," she said with assurance.

He threw himself down beside her. "Will they?" he rejoined with a smile. "Well, I should like to see what's left inside the house. And I should like to have a talk with the people. Who was it who was telling me the other day that they had come down from the Mountain?"

Charity shot a sideward look at him. It was the first time he had spoken of the Mountain except as a feature of the landscape. What else did he know about it, and about her relation to it? Her heart began to beat with the fierce impulse of resistance which she instinctively opposed to every imagined slight.

"The Mountain? I ain't afraid of the Mountain!"

Her tone of defiance seemed to escape him. He lay breast-down on the grass, breaking off sprigs of thyme and pressing them against his lips. Far off, above the folds of the nearer hills, the Mountain thrust itself up menacingly against a yellow sunset.

"I must go up there some day: I want to see it," he continued.

Her heart-beats slackened and she turned again to examine his profile. It was innocent of all unfriendly intention.

"What'd you want to go up the Mountain for?"

"Why, it must be rather a curious place. There's a queer colony up there, you know: sort of outlaws, a little independent kingdom. Of course you've heard them spoken of; but I'm told they have nothing to do with the people in the valleys—rather look down on them, in fact. I suppose they're rough customers; but they must have a good deal of character."

She did not quite know what he meant by having a good deal of character; but his tone was expressive of admiration, and deepened her dawning curiosity. It struck her now as strange that she knew so little about the Mountain. She had never asked, and no one had ever offered to enlighten her. North Dormer took the Mountain for granted, and implied its disparagement by an intonation rather than by explicit criticism.

"It's queer, you know," he continued, "that, just over there, on top of that hill, there should be a handful of people who don't give a damn for anybody."

The words thrilled her. They seemed the clue to her own revolts and defiances, and she longed to have him tell her more.

"I don't know much about them. Have they always been there?"

"Nobody seems to know exactly how long. Down at Creston they told me that the first colonists are supposed to have been men who worked on the railway that was built forty or fifty years ago between Springfield and Nettleton. Some of them took to drink, or got into trouble with the police, and went off—disappeared into the woods. A year or two later there was a report that they were living up on the Mountain.

Then I suppose others joined them—and children were born. Now they say there are over a hundred people up there. They seem to be quite outside the jurisdiction of the valleys. No school, no church—and no sheriff ever goes up to see what they're about. But don't people ever talk of them at North Dormer?"

"I don't know. They say they're bad."

He laughed. "Do they? We'll go and see, shall we?"

She flushed at the suggestion, and turned her face to his. "You never heard, I suppose—I come from there. They brought me down when I was little."

"You?" He raised himself on his elbow, looking at her with sudden interest. "You're from the Mountain? How curious! I suppose that's why you're so different. . . ."

Her happy blood bathed her to the forehead. He was praising her—and praising her because she came from the Mountain!

"Am I . . . different?" she triumphed, with affected wonder.

"Oh, awfully!" He picked up her hand and laid a kiss on the sunburnt knuckles.

"Come," he said, "let's be off." He stood up and shook the grass from his loose grey clothes. "What a good day! Where are you going to take me tomorrow?"

VI

THAT EVENING after supper Charity sat alone in the kitchen and listened to Mr. Royall and young Harney talking in the porch.

She had remained indoors after the table had been cleared and old Verena had hobbled up to bed. The kitchen window was open, and Charity seated herself near it, her idle hands on her knee. The evening was cool and still. Beyond the black hills an amber west passed into pale green, and then to a deep blue in which a great star hung. The soft hoot of a little owl came through the dusk, and between its calls the men's voices rose and fell.

Mr. Royall's was full of a sonorous satisfaction. It was a long time since he had had anyone of Lucius Harney's quality to talk to: Charity divined that the young man symbolized all his ruined and unforgotten past. When Miss Hatchard had been called to Springfield by the illness of a widowed sister, and young Harney, by that time seriously embarked on his task of drawing and measuring all the old houses between Nettleton and the New Hampshire border, had suggested the possibility of boarding at the red house in his cousin's absence, Charity had trembled lest Mr. Royall should refuse. There had been no question of lodging the young man: there was no room for him. But it appeared that he could still live at Miss Hatchard's if Mr. Royall would let him take his meals at the red house; and after a day's deliberation Mr. Royall consented.

Charity suspected him of being glad of the chance to make a little money. He had the reputation of being an avaricious man; but she was beginning to think he was probably poorer than people knew. His practice had become little more than a vague legend, revived only at lengthening intervals by a summons to Hepburn or Nettleton; and he appeared to depend for his living mainly on the scant produce of his farm, and on the commissions received from the few insurance agencies that he represented in the neighbourhood. At any rate, he had been prompt in accepting Harney's offer to hire the buggy at a dollar and a half a day; and his satisfaction with the bargain had manifested itself, unexpectedly enough, at the end of the first week, by his tossing a ten-dollar bill into Charity's lap as she sat one day retrimming her old hat.

"Here—go get yourself a Sunday bonnet that'll make all the other girls mad," he said, looking at her with a sheepish twinkle in his deep-set eyes; and she immediately guessed that the unwonted present—the only gift of money she had ever received from him—represented Harney's first payment.

But the young man's coming had brought Mr. Royall other than pecuniary benefit. It gave him, for the first time in years, a man's companionship. Charity had only a dim understanding of her guardian's needs; but she knew he felt himself above the people among whom he lived, and she saw that Lucius Harney thought him so. She was surprised to find how well he seemed to talk now that he had a listener who understood him; and she was equally struck by young Harney's friendly deference.

Their conversation was mostly about politics, and beyond her range; but tonight it had a peculiar interest for her, for they had begun to speak of the Mountain. She drew back a little, lest they should see she was in hearing.

"The Mountain? The Mountain?" she heard Mr. Royall say. "Why, the Mountain's a blot—that's what it is, sir, a blot. That scum up there ought to have been run in long ago—and would have, if the people down here hadn't been clean scared of them. The Mountain belongs to this township, and it's North Dormer's fault if there's a gang of thieves and outlaws living over there, in sight of us, defying the laws of their country. Why, there ain't a sheriff or a tax-collector or a coroner'd durst go up there. When they hear of trouble on the Mountain the selectmen look the other way, and pass an appropriation to beautify the town pump. The only man that ever goes up is the minister, and he goes because they send down and get him whenever there's any of them dies. They think a lot of Christian burial on the Mountain—but I never heard of their having the minister up to marry them. And they never trouble the Justice of the Peace either. They just herd together like the heathen."

He went on, explaining in somewhat technical language how the little colony of squatters had contrived to keep the law at bay, and Charity, with burning eagerness, awaited young Harney's comment; but the young man seemed more concerned to hear Mr. Royall's views than to express his own.

"I suppose you've never been up there yourself?" he presently asked.

"Yes, I have," said Mr. Royall with a contemptuous laugh. "The wiseacres down here told me I'd be done for before I got back; but nobody lifted a finger to hurt me. And I'd just had one of their gang sent up for seven years too."

"You went up after that?"

"Yes, sir: right after it. The fellow came down to Nettleton and ran amuck, the way they sometimes do. After they've done a wood-cutting job they come down and blow the money in; and this man ended up with manslaughter. I got him convicted, though they were scared of the Mountain even at Nettleton; and then a queer thing happened. The fellow sent for me to go and see him in gaol. I went, and this is what he says: 'The fool that defended me is a chicken-livered son of a —— and all the rest of it,' he says. 'I've got a job to be done for me up on the Mountain, and you're the only man I seen in court that looks as if he'd do it.' He told me he had a child up there—or thought he had—a little girl; and he wanted her brought down and reared like a Christian. I was sorry for the fellow, so I went up and got the child." He paused, and Charity listened with a throbbing heart. "That's the only time I ever went up the Mountain," he concluded.

There was a moment's silence; then Harney spoke. "And the child—had she no mother?"

"Oh, yes: there was a mother. But she was glad enough to have her go. She'd have given her to anybody. They ain't half human up there. I guess the mother's dead by now, with the life she was leading. Anyhow, I've never heard of her from that day to this."

"My God, how ghastly," Harney murmured; and Charity, choking with humiliation, sprang to her feet and ran upstairs. She knew at last: knew that she was the child of a drunken convict and of a mother who wasn't "half human," and was glad to have her go; and she had heard this history of her origin related to the one being in whose eyes she longed to appear superior to the people about her! She had noticed that

Mr. Royall had not named her, had even avoided any allusion that might identify her with the child he had brought down from the Mountain; and she knew it was out of regard for her that he had kept silent. But of what use was his discretion, since only that afternoon, misled by Harney's interest in the outlaw colony, she had boasted to him of coming from the Mountain? Now every word that had been spoken showed her how such an origin must widen the distance between them.

During his ten days' sojourn at North Dormer Lucius Harney had not spoken a word of love to her. He had intervened in her behalf with his cousin, and had convinced Miss Hatchard of her merits as a librarian; but that was a simple act of justice, since it was by his own fault that those merits had been questioned. He had asked her to drive him about the country when he hired lawyer Royall's buggy to go on his sketching expeditions; but that too was natural enough, since he was unfamiliar with the region. Lastly, when his cousin was called to Springfield, he had begged Mr. Royall to receive him as a boarder; but where else in North Dormer could he have boarded? Not with Carrick Fry, whose wife was paralysed, and whose large family crowded his table to overflowing; not with the Targatts, who lived a mile up the road, nor with poor old Mrs. Hawes, who, since her eldest daughter had deserted her, barely had the strength to cook her own meals while Ally picked up her living as a seamstress. Mr. Royall's was the only house where the young man could have been offered a decent hospitality. There had been nothing, therefore, in the outward course of events to raise in Charity's breast the hopes with which it trembled. But beneath the visible incidents resulting from Lucius Harney's arrival there ran an undercurrent as mysterious and potent as the influence that makes the forest break into leaf before the ice is off the pools.

The business on which Harney had come was authentic; Charity had seen the letter from a New York publisher commissioning him to make a study of the eighteenth century houses in the less familiar districts of New England. But incomprehensible as the whole affair was to her, and hard as she found it to understand why he paused enchanted before certain neglected and paintless houses, while others, refurbished and "improved" by the local builder, did not arrest a glance, she could not but suspect that Eagle County was less rich in architecture than he averred, and that the duration of his stay (which he had fixed at a month) was not unconnected with the look in his eyes when he had first paused before her in the library. Everything that had followed seemed to have grown out of that look: his way of speaking to her, his quickness in catching her meaning, his evident eagerness to prolong their excursions and to seize on every chance of being with her.

The signs of his liking were manifest enough; but it was hard to guess how much they meant, because his manner was so different from anything North Dormer had ever shown her. He was at once simpler and more deferential than any one she had known; and sometimes it was just when he was simplest that she most felt the distance between them. Education and opportunity had divided them by a width that no effort of hers could bridge, and even when his youth and his admiration brought him nearest, some chance word, some unconscious allusion, seemed to thrust her back across the gulf.

Never had it yawned so wide as when she fled up to her room carrying with her the echo of Mr. Royall's tale. Her first confused thought was the prayer that she might never see young Harney again. It was too bitter to picture him as the detached impartial listener to such a story. "I wish he'd go away: I wish he'd go tomorrow, and never come back!" she moaned to her pillow; and far into the night she lay there, in the disordered dress she had forgotten to take off, her whole soul a tossing misery on which her hopes and dreams spun about like drowning straws.

Of all this tumult only a vague heart-soreness was left when she opened her eyes the next morning. Her first thought was of the weather, for Harney had asked her to take him to the brown house under Porcupine, and then around by Hamblin; and as the trip was a long one they were to start at nine. The sun rose without a cloud, and earlier than usual she was in the kitchen, making cheese sandwiches, decanting buttermilk into a bottle, wrapping up slices of apple pie, and accusing Verena of having given away a basket she needed, which had always hung on a hook in the passage. When she came out into the porch, in her pink calico, which had run a little in the washing, but was still bright enough to set off her dark tints, she had such a triumphant sense of being a part of the sunlight and the morning that the last trace of her misery vanished. What did it matter where she came from, or whose child she was, when love was dancing in her veins, and down the road she saw young Harney coming toward her?

Mr. Royall was in the porch too. He had said nothing at breakfast, but when she came out in her pink dress, the basket in her hand, he looked at her with surprise. "Where you going to?" he asked.

"Why—Mr. Harney's starting earlier than usual today," she answered.

"Mr. Harney, Mr. Harney? Ain't Mr. Harney learned how to drive a horse yet?"

She made no answer, and he sat tilted back in his chair, drumming on the rail of the porch. It was the first time he had ever spoken of the young man in that tone, and Charity felt a faint chill of apprehension. After a moment he stood up and walked away toward the bit of ground behind the house, where the hired man was hoeing.

The air was cool and clear, with the autumnal sparkle that a north wind brings to the hills in early summer, and the night had been so still that the dew hung on everything, not as a lingering moisture, but in separate beads that glittered like diamonds on the ferns and grasses. It was a long drive to the foot of Porcupine: first across the valley, with blue hills bounding the open slopes; then down into the beech-woods, following the course of the Creston, a brown brook leaping over velvet ledges; then out again onto the farm-lands about Creston Lake, and gradually up the ridges of the Eagle Range. At last they reached the yoke of the hills, and before them opened another valley, green and wild, and beyond it more blue heights eddying away to the sky like the waves of a receding tide.

Harney tied the horse to a tree-stump, and they unpacked their basket under an aged walnut with a riven trunk out of which bumblebees darted. The sun had grown hot, and behind them was the noonday murmur of the forest. Summer

insects danced on the air, and a flock of white butterflies
fanned the mobile tips of the crimson fireweed. In the valley
below not a house was visible; it seemed as if Charity Royall
and young Harney were the only living beings in the great
hollow of earth and sky.

Charity's spirits flagged and disquieting thoughts stole
back on her. Young Harney had grown silent, and as he lay
beside her, his arms under his head, his eyes on the network
of leaves above him, she wondered if he were musing on what
Mr. Royall had told him, and if it had really debased her in
his thoughts. She wished he had not asked her to take him
that day to the brown house; she did not want him to see the
people she came from while the story of her birth was fresh in
his mind. More than once she had been on the point of suggesting that they should follow the ridge and drive straight to
Hamblin, where there was a little deserted house he wanted
to see; but shyness and pride held her back. "He'd better
know what kind of folks I belong to," she said to herself, with
a somewhat forced defiance; for in reality it was shame that
kept her silent.

Suddenly she lifted her hand and pointed to the sky.
"There's a storm coming up."

He followed her glance and smiled. "Is it that scrap of
cloud among the pines that frightens you?"

"It's over the Mountain; and a cloud over the Mountain
always means trouble."

"Oh, I don't believe half the bad things you all say of the
Mountain! But anyhow, we'll get down to the brown house
before the rain comes."

He was not far wrong, for only a few isolated drops had
fallen when they turned into the road under the shaggy flank
of Porcupine, and came upon the brown house. It stood alone
beside a swamp bordered with alder thickets and tall bul-
rushes. Not another dwelling was in sight, and it was hard to
guess what motive could have actuated the early settler who
had made his home in so unfriendly a spot.

Charity had picked up enough of her companion's erudition to understand what had attracted him to the house. She
noticed the fan-shaped tracery of the broken light above the
door, the flutings of the paintless pilasters at the corners, and

the round window set in the gable; and she knew that, for reasons that still escaped her, these were things to be admired and recorded. Still, they had seen other houses far more "typical" (the word was Harney's); and as he threw the reins on the horse's neck he said with a slight shiver of repugnance: "We won't stay long."

Against the restless alders turning their white lining to the storm the house looked singularly desolate. The paint was almost gone from the clapboards, the window-panes were broken and patched with rags, and the garden was a poisonous tangle of nettles, burdocks and tall swamp-weeds over which big blue-bottles hummed.

At the sound of wheels a child with a tow-head and pale eyes like Liff Hyatt's peered over the fence and then slipped away behind an out-house. Harney jumped down and helped Charity out; and as he did so the rain broke on them. It came slantwise, on a furious gale, laying shrubs and young trees flat, tearing off their leaves like an autumn storm, turning the road into a river, and making hissing pools of every hollow. Thunder rolled incessantly through the roar of the rain, and a strange glitter of light ran along the ground under the increasing blackness.

"Lucky we're here after all," Harney laughed. He fastened the horse under a half-roofless shed, and wrapping Charity in his coat ran with her to the house. The boy had not reappeared, and as there was no response to their knocks Harney turned the door-handle and they went in.

There were three people in the kitchen to which the door admitted them. An old woman with a handkerchief over her head was sitting by the window. She held a sickly-looking kitten on her knees, and whenever it jumped down and tried to limp away she stooped and lifted it back without any change of her aged, unnoticing face. Another woman, the unkempt creature that Charity had once noticed in driving by, stood leaning against the window-frame and stared at them; and near the stove an unshaved man in a tattered shirt sat on a barrel asleep.

The place was bare and miserable and the air heavy with the smell of dirt and stale tobacco. Charity's heart sank. Old derided tales of the Mountain people came back to her, and

the woman's stare was so disconcerting, and the face of the
sleeping man so sodden and bestial, that her disgust was
tinged with a vague dread. She was not afraid for herself; she
knew the Hyatts would not be likely to trouble her; but she
was not sure how they would treat a "city fellow."

Lucius Harney would certainly have laughed at her fears.
He glanced about the room, uttered a general "How are
you?" to which no one responded, and then asked the
younger woman if they might take shelter till the storm was
over.

She turned her eyes away from him and looked at Charity.

"You're the girl from Royall's, ain't you?"

The colour rose in Charity's face. "I'm Charity Royall," she
said, as if asserting her right to the name in the very place
where it might have been most open to question.

The woman did not seem to notice. "You kin stay," she
merely said; then she turned away and stooped over a dish in
which she was stirring something.

Harney and Charity sat down on a bench made of a board
resting on two starch boxes. They faced a door hanging on a
broken hinge, and through the crack they saw the eyes of the
tow-headed boy and of a pale little girl with a scar across her
cheek. Charity smiled, and signed to the children to come in;
but as soon as they saw they were discovered they slipped
away on bare feet. It occurred to her that they were afraid of
rousing the sleeping man; and probably the woman shared
their fear, for she moved about as noiselessly and avoided
going near the stove.

The rain continued to beat against the house, and in one or
two places it sent a stream through the patched panes and ran
into pools on the floor. Every now and then the kitten mewed
and struggled down, and the old woman stooped and caught
it, holding it tight in her bony hands; and once or twice the
man on the barrel half woke, changed his position and dozed
again, his head falling forward on his hairy breast. As the
minutes passed, and the rain still streamed against the windows, a loathing of the place and the people came over Charity. The sight of the weak-minded old woman, of the cowed
children, and the ragged man sleeping off his liquor, made the
setting of her own life seem a vision of peace and plenty. She

thought of the kitchen at Mr. Royall's, with its scrubbed floor and dresser full of china, and the peculiar smell of yeast and coffee and soft-soap that she had always hated, but that now seemed the very symbol of household order. She saw Mr. Royall's room, with the high-backed horsehair chair, the faded rag carpet, the row of books on a shelf, the engraving of "The Surrender of Burgoyne" over the stove, and the mat with a brown and white spaniel in a moss-green border. And then her mind travelled to Miss Hatchard's house, where all was freshness, purity and fragrance, and compared to which the red house had always seemed so poor and plain.

"This is where I belong—this is where I belong," she kept repeating to herself; but the words had no meaning for her. Every instinct and habit made her a stranger among these poor swamp-people living like vermin in their lair. With all her soul she wished she had not yielded to Harney's curiosity, and brought him there.

The rain had drenched her, and she began to shiver under the thin folds of her dress. The younger woman must have noticed it, for she went out of the room and came back with a broken teacup which she offered to Charity. It was half full of whiskey, and Charity shook her head; but Harney took the cup and put his lips to it. When he had set it down Charity saw him feel in his pocket and draw out a dollar; he hesitated a moment, and then put it back, and she guessed that he did not wish her to see him offering money to people she had spoken of as being her kin.

The sleeping man stirred, lifted his head and opened his eyes. They rested vacantly for a moment on Charity and Harney, and then closed again, and his head drooped; but a look of anxiety came into the woman's face. She glanced out of the window and then came up to Harney. "I guess you better go along now," she said. The young man understood and got to his feet. "Thank you," he said, holding out his hand. She seemed not to notice the gesture, and turned away as they opened the door.

The rain was still coming down, but they hardly noticed it: the pure air was like balm in their faces. The clouds were rising and breaking, and between their edges the light streamed down from remote blue hollows. Harney untied the horse, and they drove off through the diminishing rain, which was already beaded with sunlight.

For a while Charity was silent, and her companion did not speak. She looked timidly at his profile: it was graver than usual, as though he too were oppressed by what they had seen. Then she broke out abruptly: "Those people back there are the kind of folks I come from. They may be my relations, for all I know." She did not want him to think that she regretted having told him her story.

"Poor creatures," he rejoined. "I wonder why they came down to that fever-hole."

She laughed ironically. "To better themselves! It's worse up on the Mountain. Bash Hyatt married the daughter of the farmer that used to own the brown house. That was him by the stove, I suppose."

Harney seemed to find nothing to say and she went on: "I saw you take out a dollar to give to that poor woman. Why did you put it back?"

He reddened, and leaned forward to flick a swamp-fly from the horse's neck. "I wasn't sure——"

"Was it because you knew they were my folks, and thought I'd be ashamed to see you give them money?"

He turned to her with eyes full of reproach. "Oh, Charity——" It was the first time he had ever called her by her name. Her misery welled over.

"I ain't—I ain't ashamed. They're my people, and I ain't ashamed of them," she sobbed.

"My dear . . . " he murmured, putting his arm about her; and she leaned against him and wept out her pain.

It was too late to go around to Hamblin, and all the stars were out in a clear sky when they reached the North Dormer valley and drove up to the red house.

VII

SINCE HER reinstatement in Miss Hatchard's favour Charity had not dared to curtail by a moment her hours of attendance at the library. She even made a point of arriving before the time, and showed a laudable indignation when the youngest Targatt girl, who had been engaged to help in the cleaning and rearranging of the books, came trailing in late and neglected her task to peer through the window at the Sollas boy. Nevertheless, "library days" seemed more than ever irksome to Charity after her vivid hours of liberty; and she would have found it hard to set a good example to her subordinate if Lucius Harney had not been commissioned, before Miss Hatchard's departure, to examine with the local carpenter the best means of ventilating the "Memorial."

He was careful to prosecute this inquiry on the days when the library was open to the public; and Charity was therefore sure of spending part of the afternoon in his company. The Targatt girl's presence, and the risk of being interrupted by some passer-by suddenly smitten with a thirst for letters, restricted their intercourse to the exchange of commonplaces; but there was a fascination to Charity in the contrast between these public civilities and their secret intimacy.

The day after their drive to the brown house was "library day," and she sat at her desk working at the revised catalogue, while the Targatt girl, one eye on the window, chanted out the titles of a pile of books. Charity's thoughts were far away, in the dismal house by the swamp, and under the twilight sky during the long drive home, when Lucius Harney had consoled her with endearing words. That day, for the first time since he had been boarding with them, he had failed to appear as usual at the midday meal. No message had come to explain his absence, and Mr. Royall, who was more than usually taciturn, had betrayed no surprise, and made no comment. In itself this indifference was not particularly significant, for Mr. Royall, in common with most of his fellow-citizens, had a way of accepting events passively, as if he had long since come to the conclusion that no one who lived in North Dormer could hope to modify them. But to

Charity, in the reaction from her mood of passionate exaltation, there was something disquieting in his silence. It was
almost as if Lucius Harney had never had a part in their lives:
Mr. Royall's imperturbable indifference seemed to relegate
him to the domain of unreality.

As she sat at work, she tried to shake off her disappointment at Harney's non-appearing. Some trifling incident had
probably kept him from joining them at midday; but she was
sure he must be eager to see her again, and that he would not
want to wait till they met at supper, between Mr. Royall and
Verena. She was wondering what his first words would be,
and trying to devise a way of getting rid of the Targatt girl
before he came, when she heard steps outside, and he walked
up the path with Mr. Miles.

The clergyman from Hepburn seldom came to North Dormer except when he drove over to officiate at the old white
church which, by an unusual chance, happened to belong to
the Episcopal communion. He was a brisk affable man, eager
to make the most of the fact that a little nucleus of "church-
people" had survived in the sectarian wilderness, and resolved
to undermine the influence of the ginger-bread-coloured Baptist chapel at the other end of the village; but he was kept
busy by parochial work at Hepburn, where there were paper-
mills and saloons, and it was not often that he could spare
time for North Dormer.

Charity, who went to the white church (like all the best
people in North Dormer), admired Mr. Miles, and had even,
during the memorable trip to Nettleton, imagined herself
married to a man who had such a straight nose and such a
beautiful way of speaking, and who lived in a brown-stone
rectory covered with Virginia creeper. It had been a shock to
discover that the privilege was already enjoyed by a lady with
crimped hair and a large baby; but the arrival of Lucius
Harney had long since banished Mr. Miles from Charity's
dreams, and as he walked up the path at Harney's side she
saw him as he really was: a fat middle-aged man with a baldness showing under his clerical hat, and spectacles on his
Grecian nose. She wondered what had called him to North
Dormer on a weekday, and felt a little hurt that Harney
should have brought him to the library.

It presently appeared that his presence there was due to Miss Hatchard. He had been spending a few days at Springfield, to fill a friend's pulpit, and had been consulted by Miss Hatchard as to young Harney's plan for ventilating the "Memorial." To lay hands on the Hatchard ark was a grave matter, and Miss Hatchard, always full of scruples, and of scruples about her scruples (it was Harney's phrase), wished to have Mr. Miles's opinion before deciding.

"I couldn't," Mr. Miles explained, "quite make out from your cousin what changes you wanted to make, and as the other trustees did not understand either I thought I had better drive over and take a look—though I'm sure," he added, turning his friendly spectacles on the young man, "that no one could be more competent—but of course this spot has its peculiar sanctity!"

"I hope a little fresh air won't desecrate it," Harney laughingly rejoined; and they walked to the other end of the library while he set forth his idea to the Rector.

Mr. Miles had greeted the two girls with his usual friendliness, but Charity saw that he was occupied with other things, and she presently became aware, by the scraps of conversation drifting over to her, that he was still under the charm of his visit to Springfield, which appeared to have been full of agreeable incidents.

"Ah, the Coopersons . . . yes, you know them, of course," she heard. "That's a fine old house! And Ned Cooperson has collected some really remarkable impressionist pictures. . . ." The names he cited were unknown to Charity. "Yes; yes; the Schaefer quartette played at Lyric Hall on Saturday evening; and on Monday I had the privilege of hearing them again at the Towers. Beautifully done . . . Bach and Beethoven . . . a lawn-party first . . . I saw Miss Balch several times, by the way . . . looking extremely handsome. . . ."

Charity dropped her pencil and forgot to listen to the Targatt girl's sing-song. Why had Mr. Miles suddenly brought up Annabel Balch's name?

"Oh, really?" she heard Harney rejoin; and, raising his stick, he pursued: "You see, my plan is to move these shelves away, and open a round window in this wall, on the axis of the one under the pediment."

"I suppose she'll be coming up here later to stay with Miss Hatchard?" Mr. Miles went on, following on his train of thought; then, spinning about and tilting his head back: "Yes, yes, I see—I understand: that will give a draught without materially altering the look of things. I can see no objection."

The discussion went on for some minutes, and gradually the two men moved back toward the desk. Mr. Miles stopped again and looked thoughtfully at Charity. "Aren't you a little pale, my dear? Not overworking? Mr. Harney tells me you and Mamie are giving the library a thorough overhauling." He was always careful to remember his parishioners' Christian names, and at the right moment he bent his benignant spectacles on the Targatt girl.

Then he turned to Charity. "Don't take things hard, my dear; don't take things hard. Come down and see Mrs. Miles and me some day at Hepburn," he said, pressing her hand and waving a farewell to Mamie Targatt. He went out of the library, and Harney followed him.

Charity thought she detected a look of constraint in Harney's eyes. She fancied he did not want to be alone with her; and with a sudden pang she wondered if he repented the tender things he had said to her the night before. His words had been more fraternal than lover-like; but she had lost their exact sense in the caressing warmth of his voice. He had made her feel that the fact of her being a waif from the Mountain was only another reason for holding her close and soothing her with consolatory murmurs; and when the drive was over, and she got out of the buggy, tired, cold, and aching with emotion, she stepped as if the ground were a sunlit wave and she the spray on its crest.

Why, then, had his manner suddenly changed, and why did he leave the library with Mr. Miles? Her restless imagination fastened on the name of Annabel Balch: from the moment it had been mentioned she fancied that Harney's expression had altered. Annabel Balch at a garden-party at Springfield, looking "extremely handsome" . . . perhaps Mr. Miles had seen her there at the very moment when Charity and Harney were sitting in the Hyatts' hovel, between a drunkard and a half-witted old woman! Charity did not know exactly what a garden-party was, but her glimpse of the flower-edged lawns of Nettleton helped her to visualize the scene, and envious recollections of the "old things" which Miss Balch avowedly "wore out" when she came to North Dormer made it only too easy to picture her in her splendour. Charity understood what associations the name must have called up, and felt the uselessness of struggling against the unseen influences in Harney's life.

When she came down from her room for supper he was not there; and while she waited in the porch she recalled the tone in which Mr. Royall had commented the day before on their early start. Mr. Royall sat at her side, his chair tilted back, his broad black boots with side-elastics resting against the lower bar of the railings. His rumpled grey hair stood up above his forehead like the crest of an angry bird, and the leather-brown of his veined cheeks was blotched with red. Charity knew that those red spots were the signs of a coming explosion.

Suddenly he said: "Where's supper? Has Verena Marsh slipped up again on her soda-biscuits?"

Charity threw a startled glance at him. "I presume she's waiting for Mr. Harney."

"Mr. Harney, is she? She'd better dish up, then. He ain't coming." He stood up, walked to the door, and called out, in the pitch necessary to penetrate the old woman's tympanum: "Get along with the supper, Verena."

Charity was trembling with apprehension. Something had happened—she was sure of it now—and Mr. Royall knew what it was. But not for the world would she have gratified him by showing her anxiety. She took her usual place, and he seated himself opposite, and poured out a strong cup of tea before passing her the tea-pot. Verena brought some scrambled eggs, and he piled his plate with them. "Ain't you going to take any?" he asked. Charity roused herself and began to eat.

The tone with which Mr. Royall had said "He's not coming" seemed to her full of an ominous satisfaction. She saw that he had suddenly begun to hate Lucius Harney, and guessed herself to be the cause of this change of feeling. But she had no means of finding out whether some act of hostility on his part had made the young man stay away, or whether he simply wished to avoid seeing her again after their drive back from the brown house. She ate her supper with a studied show of indifference, but she knew that Mr. Royall was watching her and that her agitation did not escape him.

After supper she went up to her room. She heard Mr. Royall cross the passage, and presently the sounds below her window showed that he had returned to the porch. She seated herself on her bed and began to struggle against the desire to go down and ask him what had happened. "I'd rather die than do it," she muttered to herself. With a word he could have relieved her uncertainty: but never would she gratify him by saying it.

She rose and leaned out of the window. The twilight had deepened into night, and she watched the frail curve of the young moon dropping to the edge of the hills. Through the darkness she saw one or two figures moving down the road; but the evening was too cold for loitering, and presently the strollers disappeared. Lamps were beginning to show here and there in the windows. A bar of light brought out the whiteness of a clump of lilies in the Hawes's yard: and farther down the street Carrick Fry's Rochester lamp cast its bold illumination on the rustic flower-tub in the middle of his grass-plot.

For a long time she continued to lean in the window. But a fever of unrest consumed her, and finally she went downstairs, took her hat from its hook, and swung out of the house. Mr. Royall sat in the porch, Verena beside him, her old hands crossed on her patched skirt. As Charity went down the steps Mr. Royall called after her: "Where you going?" She could easily have answered: "To Orma's," or "Down to the Targatts'"; and either answer might have been true, for she had no purpose. But she swept on in silence, determined not to recognize his right to question her.

At the gate she paused and looked up and down the road. The darkness drew her, and she thought of climbing the hill and plunging into the depths of the larch-wood above the pasture. Then she glanced irresolutely along the street, and as she did so a gleam appeared through the spruces at Miss Hatchard's gate. Lucius Harney was there, then—he had not gone down to Hepburn with Mr. Miles, as she had at first imagined. But where had he taken his evening meal, and what had caused him to stay away from Mr. Royall's? The light was positive proof of his presence, for Miss Hatchard's servants were away on a holiday, and her farmer's wife came only in the mornings, to make the young man's bed and prepare his coffee. Beside that lamp he was doubtless sitting at this moment. To know the truth Charity had only to walk half the length of the village, and knock at the lighted window. She hesitated a minute or two longer, and then turned toward Miss Hatchard's.

She walked quickly, straining her eyes to detect anyone who might be coming along the street; and before reaching the Frys' she crossed over to avoid the light from their window. Whenever she was unhappy she felt herself at bay against a pitiless world, and a kind of animal secretiveness possessed her. But the street was empty, and she passed unnoticed through the gate and up the path to the house. Its white front glimmered indistinctly through the trees, showing only one oblong of light on the lower floor. She had supposed that the lamp was in Miss Hatchard's sitting-room; but she now saw that it shone through a window at the farther corner of the house. She did not know the room to which this window belonged, and she paused under the trees, checked by a sense of strangeness. Then she moved on, treading softly on the short grass, and keeping so close to the house that whoever was in the room, even if roused by her approach, would not be able to see her.

The window opened on a narrow verandah with a trellised arch. She leaned close to the trellis, and parting the sprays of clematis that covered it looked into a corner of the room. She saw the foot of a mahogany bed, an engraving on the wall, a wash-stand on which a towel had been tossed, and one end of the green-covered table which held the lamp. Half of the lamp-shade projected into her field of vision, and just under it two smooth sunburnt hands, one holding a pencil and the other a ruler, were moving to and fro over a drawing-board.

Her heart jumped and then stood still. He was there, a few feet away; and while her soul was tossing on seas of woe he had been quietly sitting at his drawing-board. The sight of those two hands, moving with their usual skill and precision, woke her out of her dream. Her eyes were opened to the disproportion between what she had felt and the cause of her agitation; and she was turning away from the window when one hand abruptly pushed aside the drawing-board and the other flung down the pencil.

Charity had often noticed Harney's loving care of his drawings, and the neatness and method with which he carried on and concluded each task. The impatient sweeping aside of the drawing-board seemed to reveal a new mood. The gesture suggested sudden discouragement, or distaste for his work, and she wondered if he too were agitated by secret perplexities. Her impulse of flight was checked; she stepped up on the verandah and looked into the room.

Harney had put his elbows on the table and was resting his chin on his locked hands. He had taken off his coat and waistcoat, and unbuttoned the low collar of his flannel shirt; she saw the vigorous lines of his young throat, and the root of the muscles where they joined the chest. He sat staring straight ahead of him, a look of weariness and self-disgust on his face: it was almost as if he had been gazing at a distorted reflection of his own features. For a moment Charity looked at him with a kind of terror, as if he had been a stranger under familiar lineaments; then she glanced past him and saw on the floor an open portmanteau half full of clothes. She understood that he was preparing to leave, and that he had probably decided to go without seeing her. She saw that the decision, from whatever cause it was taken, had disturbed him deeply; and she immediately concluded that his change of plan was due to some surreptitious interference of Mr. Royall's. All her old resentments and rebellions flamed up, confusedly mingled with the yearning roused by Harney's nearness. Only a few hours earlier she had felt secure in his comprehending pity; now she was flung back on herself, doubly alone after that moment of communion.

Harney was still unaware of her presence. He sat without moving, moodily staring before him at the same spot in the wall-paper. He had not even had the energy to finish his packing, and his clothes and papers lay on the floor about the portmanteau. Presently he unlocked his clasped hands and stood up; and Charity, drawing back hastily, sank down on the step of the verandah. The night was so dark that there was not much chance of his seeing her unless he opened the window, and before that she would have time to slip away and be lost in the shadow of the trees. He stood for a minute or two looking around the room with the same expression of self-disgust, as if he hated himself and everything about him; then he sat down again at the table, drew a few more strokes, and threw his pencil aside. Finally he walked across the floor, kicking the portmanteau out of his way, and lay down on the bed, folding his arms under his head, and staring up morosely at the ceiling. Just so, Charity had seen him at her side, on the grass or the pine-needles, his eyes fixed on the sky, and pleasure flashing over his face like the flickers of sun the branches shed on it. But now the face was so changed that she hardly knew it; and grief at his grief gathered in her throat, rose to her eyes and ran over.

She continued to crouch on the steps, holding her breath and stiffening herself into complete immobility. One motion of her hand, one tap on the pane, and she could picture the sudden change in his face. In every pulse of her rigid body she was aware of the welcome his eyes and lips would give her; but something kept her from moving. It was not the fear of any sanction, human or heavenly; she had never in her life been afraid. It was simply that she had suddenly understood what would happen if she went in. It was the thing that *did* happen between young men and girls, and that North Dormer ignored in public and snickered over on the sly. It was what Miss Hatchard was still ignorant of, but every girl of Charity's class knew about before she left school. It was what had happened to Ally Hawes's sister Julia, and had ended in her going to Nettleton, and in people's never mentioning her name.

It did not, of course, always end so sensationally; nor, perhaps, on the whole, so untragically. Charity had always suspected that the shunned Julia's fate might have its compensations. There were other worse endings that the village knew of, mean, miserable, unconfessed; other lives that went on drearily, without visible change, in the same cramped setting of hypocrisy. But these were not the reasons that held her back. Since the day before, she had known exactly what she would feel if Harney should take her in his arms: the melting of palm into palm and mouth on mouth, and the long flame burning her from head to foot. But mixed with this feeling was another: the wondering pride in his liking for her, the startled softness that his sympathy had put into her heart. Sometimes, when her youth flushed up in her, she had imagined yielding like other girls to furtive caresses in the twilight; but she could not so cheapen herself to Harney. She did not know why he was going; but since he was going she felt she must do nothing to deface the image of her that he carried away. If he wanted her he must seek her: he must not be surprised into taking her as girls like Julia Hawes were taken. . . .

No sound came from the sleeping village, and in the deep darkness of the garden she heard now and then a secret rustle of branches, as though some night-bird brushed them. Once a footfall passed the gate, and she shrank back into her corner; but the steps died away and left a profounder quiet. Her eyes were still on Harney's tormented face: she felt she could not move till he moved. But she was beginning to grow numb from her constrained position, and at times her thoughts were so indistinct that she seemed to be held there only by a vague weight of weariness.

A long time passed in this strange vigil. Harney still lay on the bed, motionless and with fixed eyes, as though following his vision to its bitter end. At last he stirred and changed his attitude slightly, and Charity's heart began to tremble. But he only flung out his arms and sank back into his former position. With a deep sigh he tossed the hair from his forehead; then his whole body relaxed, his head turned sideways on the pillow, and she saw that he had fallen asleep. The sweet expression came back to his lips, and the haggardness faded from his face, leaving it as fresh as a boy's.

She rose and crept away.

VIII

S HE HAD LOST the sense of time, and did not know how late it was till she came out into the street and saw that all the windows were dark between Miss Hatchard's and the Royall house.

As she passed from under the black pall of the Norway spruces she fancied she saw two figures in the shade about the duck-pond. She drew back and watched; but nothing moved, and she had stared so long into the lamp-lit room that the darkness confused her, and she thought she must have been mistaken.

She walked on, wondering whether Mr. Royall was still in the porch. In her exalted mood she did not greatly care whether he was waiting for her or not: she seemed to be floating high over life, on a great cloud of misery beneath which everyday realities had dwindled to mere specks in space. But the porch was empty, Mr. Royall's hat hung on its peg in the passage, and the kitchen lamp had been left to light her to bed. She took it and went up.

The morning hours of the next day dragged by without incident. Charity had imagined that, in some way or other, she would learn whether Harney had already left; but Verena's deafness prevented her being a source of news, and no one came to the house who could bring enlightenment.

Mr. Royall went out early, and did not return till Verena had set the table for the midday meal. When he came in he went straight to the kitchen and shouted to the old woman: "Ready for dinner——" then he turned into the dining-room, where Charity was already seated. Harney's plate was in its usual place, but Mr. Royall offered no explanation of his absence, and Charity asked none. The feverish exaltation of the night before had dropped, and she said to herself that he had gone away, indifferently, almost callously, and that now her life would lapse again into the narrow rut out of which he had lifted it. For a moment she was inclined to sneer at herself for not having used the arts that might have kept him.

She sat at table till the meal was over, lest Mr. Royall should remark on her leaving; but when he stood up she rose also, without waiting to help Verena. She had her foot on the stairs when he called to her to come back.

"I've got a headache. I'm going up to lie down."

"I want you should come in here first; I've got something to say to you."

She was sure from his tone that in a moment she would learn what every nerve in her ached to know; but as she turned back she made a last effort of indifference.

Mr. Royall stood in the middle of the office, his thick eyebrows beetling, his lower jaw trembling a little. At first she thought he had been drinking; then she saw that he was sober, but stirred by a deep and stern emotion totally unlike his usual transient angers. And suddenly she understood that, until then, she had never really noticed him or thought about him. Except on the occasion of his one offense he had been to her merely the person who is always there, the unquestioned central fact of life, as inevitable but as uninteresting as North Dormer itself, or any of the other conditions fate had laid on her. Even then she had regarded him only in relation to herself, and had never speculated as to his own feelings, beyond instinctively concluding that he would not trouble her again in the same way. But now she began to wonder what he was really like.

He had grasped the back of his chair with both hands, and stood looking hard at her. At length he said: "Charity, for once let's you and me talk together like friends."

Instantly she felt that something had happened, and that he held her in his hand.

"Where is Mr. Harney? Why hasn't he come back? Have you sent him away?" she broke out, without knowing what she was saying.

The change in Mr. Royall frightened her. All the blood seemed to leave his veins and against his swarthy pallor the deep lines in his face looked black.

"Didn't he have time to answer some of those questions last night? You was with him long enough!" he said.

Charity stood speechless. The taunt was so unrelated to what had been happening in her soul that she hardly understood it. But the instinct of self-defense awoke in her.

"Who says I was with him last night?"

"The whole place is saying it by now."

"Then it was you that put the lie into their mouths. —Oh, how I've always hated you!" she cried.

She had expected a retort in kind, and it startled her to hear her exclamation sounding on through silence.

"Yes, I know," Mr. Royall said slowly. "But that ain't going to help us much now."

"It helps me not to care a straw what lies you tell about me!"

"If they're lies, they're not my lies: my Bible oath on that, Charity. I didn't know where you were: I wasn't out of this house last night."

She made no answer and he went on: "Is it a lie that you were seen coming out of Miss Hatchard's nigh onto midnight?"

She straightened herself with a laugh, all her reckless insolence recovered. "I didn't look to see what time it was."

"You lost girl . . . you . . . you . . . Oh, my God, why did you tell me?" he broke out, dropping into his chair, his head bowed down like an old man's.

Charity's self-possession had returned with the sense of her danger. "Do you suppose I'd take the trouble to lie to *you*? Who are you, anyhow, to ask me where I go to when I go out at night?"

Mr. Royall lifted his head and looked at her. His face had grown quiet and almost gentle, as she remembered seeing it sometimes when she was a little girl, before Mrs. Royall died.

"Don't let's go on like this, Charity. It can't do any good to either of us. You were seen going into that fellow's house . . . you were seen coming out of it. . . . I've watched this thing coming, and I've tried to stop it. As God sees me, I have. . . ."

"Ah, it *was* you, then? I knew it was you that sent him away!"

He looked at her in surprise. "Didn't he tell you so? I thought he understood." He spoke slowly, with difficult pauses, "I didn't name you to him: I'd have cut my hand off sooner. I just told him I couldn't spare the horse any longer; and that the cooking was getting too heavy for Verena. I guess he's the kind that's heard the same thing before. Anyhow, he took it quietly enough. He said his job here was about done, anyhow; and there didn't another word pass between us. . . . If he told you otherwise he told you an untruth."

Charity listened in a cold trance of anger. It was nothing to her what the village said . . . but all this fingering of her dreams!

"I've told you he didn't tell me anything. I didn't speak with him last night."

"You didn't speak with him?"

"No. . . . It's not that I care what any of you say . . . but you may as well know. Things ain't between us the way you think . . . and the other people in this place. He was kind to me; he was my friend; and all of a sudden he stopped coming, and I knew it was you that done it—*you!*" All her unreconciled memory of the past flamed out at him. "So I went there last night to find out what you'd said to him: that's all."

Mr. Royall drew a heavy breath. "But, then—if he wasn't there, what were you doing there all that time?—Charity, for pity's sake, tell me. I've got to know, to stop their talking."

This pathetic abdication of all authority over her did not move her: she could feel only the outrage of his interference.

"Can't you see that I don't care what anybody says? It's true I went there to see him; and he was in his room, and I stood outside for ever so long and watched him; but I dursn't go in for fear he'd think I'd come after him. . . ." She felt her voice breaking, and gathered it up in a last defiance. "As long as I live I'll never forgive you!" she cried.

Mr. Royall made no answer. He sat and pondered with sunken head, his veined hands clasped about the arms of his chair. Age seemed to have come down on him as winter comes on the hills after a storm. At length he looked up.

"Charity, you say you don't care; but you're the proudest girl I know, and the last to want people to talk against you. You know there's always eyes watching you: you're handsomer and smarter than the rest, and that's enough. But till lately you've never given them a chance. Now they've got it, and they're going to use it. I believe what you say, but they won't. . . . It was Mrs. Tom Fry seen you going in . . . and two or three of them watched for you to come out again. . . . You've been with the fellow all day long every day since he come here . . . and I'm a lawyer, and I know how hard slander dies." He paused, but she stood motionless, without giving him any sign of acquiescence or even of attention. "He's a pleasant fellow to talk to—I liked having him here myself. The young men up here ain't had his chances. But there's one thing as old as the hills and as plain as daylight: if he'd wanted you the right way he'd have said so."

Charity did not speak. It seemed to her that nothing could exceed the bitterness of hearing such words from such lips.

Mr. Royall rose from his seat. "See here, Charity Royall: I had a shameful thought once, and you've made me pay for it. Isn't that score pretty near wiped out? . . . There's a streak in me I ain't always master of; but I've always acted straight to you but that once. And you've known I would—you've trusted me. For all your sneers and your mockery you've always known I loved you the way a man loves a decent woman. I'm a good many years older than you, but I'm head and shoulders above this place and everybody in it, and you know that too. I slipped up once, but that's no reason for not starting again. If you'll come with me I'll do it. If you'll marry me we'll leave here and settle in some big town, where there's men, and business, and things doing. It's not too late for me to find an opening. . . . I can see it by the way folks treat me when I go down to Hepburn or Nettleton. . . ."

Charity made no movement. Nothing in his appeal reached her heart, and she thought only of words to wound and wither. But a growing lassitude restrained her. What did anything matter that he was saying? She saw the old life closing in on her, and hardly heeded his fanciful picture of renewal.

"Charity—Charity—say you'll do it," she heard him urge, all his lost years and wasted passion in his voice.

"Oh, what's the use of all this? When I leave here it won't be with you."

She moved toward the door as she spoke, and he stood up and placed himself between her and the threshold. He seemed suddenly tall and strong, as though the extremity of his humiliation had given him new vigour.

"That's all, is it? It's not much." He leaned against the

door, so towering and powerful that he seemed to fill the narrow room. "Well, then—look here. . . . You're right: I've no claim on you—why should you look at a broken man like me? You want the other fellow . . . and I don't blame you. You picked out the best when you seen it . . . well, that was always my way." He fixed his stern eyes on her, and she had the sense that the struggle within him was at its highest. "Do you want him to marry you?" he asked.

They stood and looked at each other for a long moment, eye to eye, with the terrible equality of courage that sometimes made her feel as if she had his blood in her veins.

"Do you want him to—say? I'll have him here in an hour if you do. I ain't been in the law thirty years for nothing. He's hired Carrick Fry's team to take him to Hepburn, but he ain't going to start for another hour. And I can put things to him so he won't be long deciding. . . . He's soft: I could see that. I don't say you won't be sorry afterward—but, by God, I'll give you the chance to be, if you say so."

She heard him out in silence, too remote from all he was feeling and saying for any sally of scorn to relieve her. As she listened, there flitted through her mind the vision of Liff Hyatt's muddy boot coming down on the white bramble-flowers. The same thing had happened now; something transient and exquisite had flowered in her, and she had stood by and seen it trampled to earth. While the thought passed through her she was aware of Mr. Royall, still leaning against the door, but crestfallen, diminished, as though her silence were the answer he most dreaded.

"I don't want any chance you can give me: I'm glad he's going away," she said.

He kept his place a moment longer, his hand on the door-knob. "Charity!" he pleaded. She made no answer, and he turned the knob and went out. She heard him fumble with the latch of the front door, and saw him walk down the steps. He passed out of the gate, and his figure, stooping and heavy, receded slowly up the street.

For a while she remained where he had left her. She was still trembling with the humiliation of his last words, which rang so loud in her ears that it seemed as though they must echo through the village, proclaiming her a creature to lend herself to such vile suggestions. Her shame weighed on her like a physical oppression: the roof and walls seemed to be closing in on her, and she was seized by the impulse to get away, under the open sky, where there would be room to breathe. She went to the front door, and as she did so Lucius Harney opened it.

He looked graver and less confident than usual, and for a moment or two neither of them spoke. Then he held out his hand. "Are you going out?" he asked. "May I come in?"

Her heart was beating so violently that she was afraid to speak, and stood looking at him with tear-dilated eyes; then she became aware of what her silence must betray, and said quickly: "Yes: come in."

She led the way into the dining-room, and they sat down on opposite sides of the table, the cruet-stand and japanned bread-basket between them. Harney had laid his straw hat on the table, and as he sat there, in his easy-looking summer clothes, a brown tie knotted under his flannel collar, and his smooth brown hair brushed back from his forehead, she pictured him as she had seen him the night before, lying on his bed, with the tossed locks falling into his eyes, and his bare throat rising out of his unbuttoned shirt. He had never seemed so remote as at the moment when that vision flashed through her mind.

"I'm so sorry it's good-bye: I suppose you know I'm leaving," he began, abruptly and awkwardly; she guessed that he was wondering how much she knew of his reasons for going.

"I presume you found your work was over quicker than what you expected," she said.

"Well, yes—that is, no: there are plenty of things I should have liked to do. But my holiday's limited; and now that Mr. Royall needs the horse for himself it's rather difficult to find means of getting about."

"There ain't any too many teams for hire around here," she acquiesced; and there was another silence.

"These days here have been—awfully pleasant: I wanted to thank you for making them so," he continued, his colour rising.

She could not think of any reply, and he went on: "You've been wonderfully kind to me, and I wanted to tell you. . . . I

wish I could think of you as happier, less lonely. . . . Things
are sure to change for you by and by. . . ."

"Things don't change at North Dormer: people just get
used to them."

The answer seemed to break up the order of his pre-
arranged consolations, and he sat looking at her uncertainly.
Then he said, with his sweet smile: "That's not true of you. It
can't be."

The smile was like a knife-thrust through her heart: everything in her began to tremble and break loose. She felt her
tears run over, and stood up.

"Well, good-bye," she said.

She was aware of his taking her hand, and of feeling that
his touch was lifeless.

"Good-bye." He turned away, and stopped on the threshold. "You'll say good-bye for me to Verena?"

She heard the closing of the outer door and the sound of
his quick tread along the path. The latch of the gate clicked
after him.

The next morning when she arose in the cold dawn and
opened her shutters she saw a freckled boy standing on the
other side of the road and looking up at her. He was a boy
from a farm three or four miles down the Creston road, and
she wondered what he was doing there at that hour, and why
he looked so hard at her window. When he saw her he
crossed over and leaned against the gate unconcernedly.
There was no one stirring in the house, and she threw a shawl
over her night-gown and ran down and let herself out. By the
time she reached the gate the boy was sauntering down the
road, whistling carelessly; but she saw that a letter had been
thrust between the slats and the crossbar of the gate. She took
it out and hastened back to her room.

The envelope bore her name, and inside was a leaf torn
from a pocket-diary.

DEAR CHARITY:

I can't go away like this. I am staying for a few days at Creston
River. Will you come down and meet me at Creston pool? I will
wait for you till evening.

IX

CHARITY sat before the mirror trying on a hat which Ally Hawes, with much secrecy, had trimmed for her. It was of white straw, with a drooping brim and a cherry-coloured lining that made her face glow like the inside of the shell on the parlour mantelpiece.

She propped the square of looking-glass against Mr. Royall's black leather Bible, steadying it in front with a white stone on which a view of the Brooklyn Bridge was painted; and she sat before her reflection, bending the brim this way and that, while Ally Hawes's pale face looked over her shoulder like the ghost of wasted opportunities.

"I look awful, don't I?" she said at last with a happy sigh.

Ally smiled and took back the hat. "I'll stitch the roses on right here, so's you can put it away at once."

Charity laughed, and ran her fingers through her rough dark hair. She knew that Harney liked to see its reddish edges ruffled about her forehead and breaking into little rings at the nape. She sat down on her bed and watched Ally stoop over the hat with a careful frown.

"Don't you ever feel like going down to Nettleton for a day?" she asked.

Ally shook her head without looking up. "No, I always remember that awful time I went down with Julia—to that doctor's."

"Oh, Ally——"

"I can't help it. The house is on the corner of Wing Street and Lake Avenue. The trolley from the station goes right by it, and the day the minister took us down to see those pictures I recognized it right off, and couldn't seem to see anything else. There's a big black sign with gold letters all across the front—'Private Consultations.' She came as near as anything to dying. . . ."

"Poor Julia!" Charity sighed from the height of her purity and her security. She had a friend whom she trusted and who respected her. She was going with him to spend the next day—the Fourth of July—at Nettleton. Whose business was it but hers, and what was the harm? The pity of it was that

girls like Julia did not know how to choose, and to keep bad
fellows at a distance. . . . Charity slipped down from the
bed, and stretched out her hands.

"Is it sewed? Let me try it on again." She put the hat
on, and smiled at her image. The thought of Julia had vanished. . . .

The next morning she was up before dawn, and saw the
yellow sunrise broaden behind the hills, and the silvery lustre
preceding a hot day tremble across the sleeping fields.

Her plans had been made with great care. She had announced that she was going down to the Band of Hope
picnic at Hepburn, and as no one else from North Dormer
intended to venture so far it was not likely that her absence
from the festivity would be reported. Besides, if it were she
would not greatly care. She was determined to assert her
independence, and if she stooped to fib about the Hepburn
picnic it was chiefly from the secretive instinct that made her
dread the profanation of her happiness. Whenever she was
with Lucius Harney she would have liked some impenetrable
mountain mist to hide her.

It was arranged that she should walk to a point of the
Creston road where Harney was to pick her up and drive her
across the hills to Hepburn in time for the nine-thirty train to
Nettleton. Harney at first had been rather lukewarm about
the trip. He declared himself ready to take her to Nettleton,
but urged her not to go on the Fourth of July, on account of
the crowds, the probable lateness of the trains, the difficulty
of her getting back before night; but her evident disappointment caused him to give way, and even to affect a faint enthusiasm for the adventure. She understood why he was not
more eager: he must have seen sights beside which even a
Fourth of July at Nettleton would seem tame. But she had
never seen anything; and a great longing possessed her to
walk the streets of a big town on a holiday, clinging to his
arm and jostled by idle crowds in their best clothes. The only
cloud on the prospect was the fact that the shops would be
closed; but she hoped he would take her back another day,
when they were open.

She started out unnoticed in the early sunlight, slipping

through the kitchen while Verena bent above the stove. To avoid attracting notice, she carried her new hat carefully wrapped up, and had thrown a long grey veil of Mrs. Royall's over the new white muslin dress which Ally's clever fingers had made for her. All of the ten dollars Mr. Royall had given her, and a part of her own savings as well, had been spent on renewing her wardrobe; and when Harney jumped out of the buggy to meet her she read her reward in his eyes.

The freckled boy who had brought her the note two weeks earlier was to wait with the buggy at Hepburn till their return. He perched at Charity's feet, his legs dangling between the wheels, and they could not say much because of his presence. But it did not greatly matter, for their past was now rich enough to have given them a private language; and with the long day stretching before them like the blue distance beyond the hills there was a delicate pleasure in postponement.

When Charity, in response to Harney's message, had gone to meet him at the Creston pool her heart had been so full of mortification and anger that his first words might easily have estranged her. But it happened that he had found the right word, which was one of simple friendship. His tone had instantly justified her, and put her guardian in the wrong. He had made no allusion to what had passed between Mr. Royall and himself, but had simply let it appear that he had left because means of conveyance were hard to find at North Dormer, and because Creston River was a more convenient centre. He told her that he had hired by the week the buggy of the freckled boy's father, who served as livery-stable keeper to one or two melancholy summer boarding-houses on Creston Lake, and had discovered, within driving distance, a number of houses worthy of his pencil; and he said that he could not, while he was in the neighbourhood, give up the pleasure of seeing her as often as posible.

When they took leave of each other she promised to continue to be his guide; and during the fortnight which followed they roamed the hills in happy comradeship. In most of the village friendships between youths and maidens lack of conversation was made up for by tentative fondling; but Harney, except when he had tried to comfort her in her trouble on their way back from the Hyatts', had never put his arm about her, or sought to betray her into any sudden caress. It seemed to be enough for him to breathe her nearness like a flower's; and since his pleasure at being with her, and his sense of her youth and her grace, perpetually shone in his eyes and softened the inflections of his voice, his reserve did not suggest coldness, but the deference due to a girl of his own class.

The buggy was drawn by an old trotter who whirled them along so briskly that the pace created a little breeze; but when they reached Hepburn the full heat of the airless morning descended on them. At the railway station the platform was packed with a sweltering throng, and they took refuge in the waiting-room, where there was another throng, already dejected by the heat and the long waiting for retarded trains. Pale mothers were struggling with fretful babies, or trying to keep their older offspring from the fascination of the track; girls and their "fellows" were giggling and shoving, and passing about candy in sticky bags, and older men, collarless and perspiring, were shifting heavy children from one arm to the other, and keeping a haggard eye on the scattered members of their families.

At last the train rumbled in, and engulfed the waiting multitude. Harney swept Charity up on to the first car and they captured a bench for two, and sat in happy isolation while the train swayed and roared along through rich fields and languid tree-clumps. The haze of the morning had become a sort of clear tremor over everything, like the colourless vibration about a flame; and the opulent landscape seemed to droop under it. But to Charity the heat was a stimulant: it enveloped the whole world in the same glow that burned at her heart. Now and then a lurch of the train flung her against Harney, and through her thin muslin she felt the touch of his sleeve. She steadied herself, their eyes met, and the flaming breath of the day seemed to enclose them.

The train roared into the Nettleton station, the descending mob caught them on its tide, and they were swept out into a vague dusty square thronged with seedy "hacks" and long curtained omnibuses drawn by horses with tasselled fly-nets over their withers, who stood swinging their depressed heads drearily from side to side.

A mob of 'bus and hack drivers were shouting "To the Eagle House," "To the Washington House," "This way to the Lake," "Just starting for Greytop;" and through their yells came the popping of fire-crackers, the explosion of torpedoes, the banging of toy-guns, and the crash of a firemen's band trying to play the Merry Widow while they were being packed into a waggonette streaming with bunting.

The ramshackle wooden hotels about the square were all hung with flags and paper lanterns, and as Harney and Charity turned into the main street, with its brick and granite business blocks crowding out the old low-storied shops, and its towering poles strung with innumerable wires that seemed to tremble and buzz in the heat, they saw the double line of flags and lanterns tapering away gaily to the park at the other end of the perspective. The noise and colour of this holiday vision seemed to transform Nettleton into a metropolis. Charity could not believe that Springfield or even Boston had anything grander to show, and she wondered if, at this very moment, Annabel Balch, on the arm of as brilliant a young man, were threading her way through scenes as resplendent.

"Where shall we go first?" Harney asked; but as she turned her happy eyes on him he guessed the answer and said: "We'll take a look round, shall we?"

The street swarmed with their fellow-travellers, with other excursionists arriving from other directions, with Nettleton's own population, and with the mill-hands trooping in from the factories on the Creston. The shops were closed, but one would scarcely have noticed it, so numerous were the glass doors swinging open on saloons, on restaurants, on drugstores gushing from every soda-water tap, on fruit and confectionery shops stacked with strawberry-cake, cocoanut drops, trays of glistening molasses candy, boxes of caramels and chewing-gum, baskets of sodden strawberries, and dangling branches of bananas. Outside of some of the doors were trestles with banked-up oranges and apples, spotted pears and dusty raspberries; and the air reeked with the smell of fruit and stale coffee, beer and sarsaparilla and fried potatoes.

Even the shops that were closed offered, through wide expanses of plate-glass, hints of hidden riches. In some, waves of silk and ribbon broke over shores of imitation moss from

which ravishing hats rose like tropical orchids. In others, the
pink throats of gramophones opened their giant convolutions in a soundless chorus; or bicycles shining in neat ranks
seemed to await the signal of an invisible starter; or tiers of
fancy-goods in leatherette and paste and celluloid dangled
their insidious graces; and, in one vast bay that seemed to
project them into exciting contact with the public, wax ladies
in daring dresses chatted elegantly, or, with gestures intimate
yet blameless, pointed to their pink corsets and transparent
hosiery.

Presently Harney found that his watch had stopped, and
turned in at a small jeweller's shop which chanced to be still
open. While the watch was being examined Charity leaned
over the glass counter where, on a background of dark blue
velvet, pins, rings and brooches glittered like the moon and
stars. She had never seen jewellery so near by, and she longed
to lift the glass lid and plunge her hand among the shining
treasures. But already Harney's watch was repaired, and he
laid his hand on her arm and drew her from her dream.

"Which do you like best?" he asked leaning over the
counter at her side.

"I don't know. . . ." She pointed to a gold lily-of-the-
valley with white flowers.

"Don't you think the blue pin's better?" he suggested, and
immediately she saw that the lily of the valley was mere trum-
pery compared to the small round stone, blue as a mountain
lake, with little sparks of light all round it. She coloured at her
want of discrimination.

"It's so lovely I guess I was afraid to look at it," she said.

He laughed, and they went out of the shop; but a few steps
away he exclaimed: "Oh, by Jove, I forgot something," and
turned back and left her in the crowd. She stood staring
down a row of pink gramophone throats till he rejoined her
and slipped his arm through hers.

"You mustn't be afraid of looking at the blue pin any
longer, because it belongs to you," he said; and she felt a little
box being pressed into her hand. Her heart gave a leap of joy,
but it reached her lips only in a shy stammer. She remembered other girls whom she had heard planning to extract
presents from their fellows, and was seized with a sudden

dread lest Harney should have imagined that she had leaned over the pretty things in the glass case in the hope of having one given to her. . . .

A little farther down the street they turned in at a glass doorway opening on a shining hall with a mahogany staircase, and brass cages in its corners. "We must have something to eat," Harney said; and the next moment Charity found herself in a dressing-room all looking-glass and lustrous surfaces, where a party of showy-looking girls were dabbing on powder and straightening immense plumed hats. When they had gone she took courage to bathe her hot face in one of the marble basins, and to straighten her own hat-brim, which the parasols of the crowd had indented. The dresses in the shops had so impressed her that she scarcely dared look at her reflection; but when she did so, the glow of her face under her cherry-coloured hat, and the curve of her young shoulders through the transparent muslin, restored her courage; and when she had taken the blue brooch from its box and pinned it on her bosom she walked toward the restaurant with her head high, as if she had always strolled through tessellated halls beside young men in flannels.

Her spirit sank a little at the sight of the slim-waisted waitresses in black, with bewitching mob-caps on their haughty heads, who were moving disdainfully between the tables. "Not f'r another hour," one of them dropped to Harney in passing; and he stood doubtfully glancing about him.

"Oh, well, we can't stay sweltering here," he decided; "let's try somewhere else—" and with a sense of relief Charity followed him from that scene of inhospitable splendour.

The "somewhere else" turned out—after more hot tramping, and several failures—to be, of all things, a little open-air place in a back street that called itself a French restaurant, and consisted in two or three rickety tables under a scarlet-runner, between a patch of zinnias and petunias and a big elm bending over from the next yard. Here they lunched on queerly flavoured things, while Harney, leaning back in a crippled rocking-chair, smoked cigarettes between the courses and poured into Charity's glass a pale yellow wine which he said was the very same one drank in just such jolly places in France.

Charity did not think the wine as good as sarsaparilla, but she sipped a mouthful for the pleasure of doing what he did, and of fancying herself alone with him in foreign countries. The illusion was increased by their being served by a deep-bosomed woman with smooth hair and a pleasant laugh, who talked to Harney in unintelligible words, and seemed amazed and overjoyed at his answering her in kind. At the other tables other people sat, mill-hands probably, homely but pleasant looking, who spoke the same shrill jargon, and looked at Harney and Charity with friendly eyes; and between the table-legs a poodle with bald patches and pink eyes nosed about for scraps, and sat up on his hind legs absurdly.

Harney showed no inclination to move, for hot as their corner was, it was at least shaded and quiet; and, from the main thoroughfares came the clanging of trolleys, the incessant popping of torpedoes, the jingle of street-organs, the bawling of megaphone men and the loud murmur of increasing crowds. He leaned back, smoking his cigar, patting the dog, and stirring the coffee that steamed in their chipped cups. "It's the real thing, you know," he explained; and Charity hastily revised her previous conception of the beverage.

They had made no plans for the rest of the day, and when Harney asked her what she wanted to do next she was too bewildered by rich possibilities to find an answer. Finally she confessed that she longed to go to the Lake, where she had not been taken on her former visit, and when he answered, "Oh, there's time for that—it will be pleasanter later," she suggested seeing some pictures like the ones Mr. Miles had taken her to. She thought Harney looked a little disconcerted; but he passed his fine handkerchief over his warm brow, said gaily "Come along, then," and rose with a last pat for the pink-eyed dog.

Mr. Miles's pictures had been shown in an austere Y.M.C.A. hall, with white walls and an organ; but Harney led Charity to a glittering place—everything she saw seemed to glitter—where they passed, between immense pictures of yellow-haired beauties stabbing villains in evening dress, into a velvet-curtained auditorium packed with spectators to the last limit of compression. After that, for a while, everything was merged in her brain in swimming circles of heat and

blinding alternations of light and darkness. All the world has
to show seemed to pass before her in a chaos of palms and
minarets, charging cavalry regiments, roaring lions, comic po-
licemen and scowling murderers; and the crowd around her,
the hundreds of hot sallow candy-munching faces, young,
old, middle-aged, but all kindled with the same contagious
excitement, became part of the spectacle, and danced on the
screen with the rest.

Presently the thought of the cool trolley-run to the Lake
grew irresistible, and they struggled out of the theatre. As
they stood on the pavement, Harney pale with the heat, and
even Charity a little confused by it, a young man drove by in
an electric run-about with a calico band bearing the words:
"Ten dollars to take you round the Lake." Before Charity
knew what was happening, Harney had waved a hand, and
they were climbing in. "Say, for twenny-five I'll run you out
first to see the ball-game and back," the driver proposed with
an insinuating grin; but Charity said quickly: "Oh, I'd rather
go rowing on the Lake." The street was so thronged that
progress was slow; but the glory of sitting in the little carriage
while it wriggled its way between laden omnibuses and trolleys made the moments seem too short. "Next turn is Lake
Avenue," the young man called out over his shoulder; and as
they paused in the wake of a big omnibus groaning with
Knights of Pythias in cocked hats and swords, Charity looked
up and saw on the corner a brick house with a conspicuous
black and gold sign across its front. "Dr. Merkle; Private
Consultations at all hours. Lady Attendants," she read; and
suddenly she remembered Ally Hawes's words: "The house
was at the corner of Wing Street and Lake Avenue . . .
there's a big black sign across the front. . . ." Through all the
heat and the rapture a shiver of cold ran over her.

X

THE LAKE at last—a sheet of shining metal brooded over by drooping trees. Charity and Harney had secured a boat and, getting away from the wharves and the refreshment-booths, they drifted idly along, hugging the shadow of the shore. Where the sun struck the water its shafts flamed back blindingly at the heat-veiled sky; and the least shade was black by contrast. The Lake was so smooth that the reflection of the trees on its edge seemed enamelled on a solid surface; but gradually, as the sun declined, the water grew transparent, and Charity, leaning over, plunged her fascinated gaze into depths so clear that she saw the inverted tree-tops interwoven with the green growths of the bottom.

They rounded a point at the farther end of the Lake, and entering an inlet pushed their bow against a protruding tree-trunk. A green veil of willows overhung them. Beyond the trees, wheat-fields sparkled in the sun; and all along the horizon the clear hills throbbed with light. Charity leaned back in the stern, and Harney unshipped the oars and lay in the bottom of the boat without speaking.

Ever since their meeting at the Creston pool he had been subject to these brooding silences, which were as different as possible from the pauses when they ceased to speak because words were needless. At such times his face wore the expression she had seen on it when she had looked in at him from the darkness, and again there came over her a sense of the mysterious distance between them; but usually his fits of abstraction were followed by bursts of gaiety that chased away the shadow before it chilled her.

She was still thinking of the ten dollars he had handed to the driver of the run-about. It had given them twenty minutes of pleasure, and it seemed unimaginable that anyone should be able to buy amusement at that rate. With ten dollars he might have bought her an engagement ring; she knew that Mrs. Tom Fry's, which came from Springfield, and had a diamond in it, had cost only eight seventy-five. But she did not know why the thought had occurred to her. Harney would never buy her an engagement ring: they were friends and comrades, but no more. He had been perfectly fair to her: he had never said a word to mislead her. She wondered what the girl was like whose hand was waiting for his ring. . . .

Boats were beginning to thicken on the Lake and the clang of incessantly arriving trolleys announced the return of the crowds from the ball-field. The shadows lengthened across the pearl-grey water and two white clouds near the sun were turning golden. On the opposite shore men were hammering hastily at a wooden scaffolding in a field. Charity asked what it was for.

"Why, the fireworks. I suppose there'll be a big show." Harney looked at her and a smile crept into his moody eyes. "Have you never seen any good fireworks?"

"Miss Hatchard always sends up lovely rockets on the Fourth," she answered doubtfully.

"Oh——" his contempt was unbounded. "I mean a big performance like this: illuminated boats, and all the rest."

She flushed at the picture. "Do they send them up from the Lake, too?"

"Rather. Didn't you notice that big raft we passed? It's wonderful to see the rockets completing their orbits down under one's feet." She said nothing, and he put the oars into the rowlocks. "If we stay we'd better go and pick up something to eat."

"But how can we get back afterward?" she ventured, feeling it would break her heart if she missed it.

He consulted a time-table, found a ten o'clock train and reassured her. "The moon rises so late that it will be dark by eight, and we'll have over an hour of it."

Twilight fell, and lights began to show along the shore. The trolleys roaring out from Nettleton became great luminous serpents coiling in and out among the trees. The wooden eating-houses at the Lake's edge danced with lanterns, and the dusk echoed with laughter and shouts and the clumsy splashing of oars.

Harney and Charity had found a table in the corner of a balcony built over the Lake, and were patiently awaiting an unattainable chowder. Close under them the water lapped the piles, agitated by the evolutions of a little white steamboat trellised with coloured globes which was to run passengers up and down the Lake. It was already black with them as it sheered off on its first trip.

Suddenly Charity heard a woman's laugh behind her. The sound was familiar, and she turned to look. A band of showily dressed girls and dapper young men wearing badges of secret societies, with new straw hats tilted far back on their square-clipped hair, had invaded the balcony and were loudly clamouring for a table. The girl in the lead was the one who had laughed. She wore a large hat with a long white feather, and from under its brim her painted eyes looked at Charity with amused recognition.

"Say! if this ain't like Old Home Week," she remarked to the girl at her elbow; and giggles and glances passed between them. Charity knew at once that the girl with the white feather was Julia Hawes. She had lost her freshness, and the paint under her eyes made her face seem thinner; but her lips had the same lovely curve, and the same cold mocking smile, as if there were some secret absurdity in the person she was looking at, and she had instantly detected it.

Charity flushed to the forehead and looked away. She felt herself humiliated by Julia's sneer, and vexed that the mockery of such a creature should affect her. She trembled lest Harney should notice that the noisy troop had recognized her; but they found no table free, and passed on tumultuously.

Presently there was a soft rush through the air and a shower of silver fell from the blue evening sky. In another direction, pale Roman candles shot up singly through the trees, and a fire-haired rocket swept the horizon like a portent. Between these intermittent flashes the velvet curtains of the darkness were descending, and in the intervals of eclipse the voices of the crowds seemed to sink to smothered murmurs.

Charity and Harney, dispossessed by newcomers, were at length obliged to give up their table and struggle through the throng about the boat-landings. For a while there seemed no escape from the tide of late arrivals; but finally Harney secured the last two places on the stand from which the more privileged were to see the fireworks. The seats were at the end of a row, one above the other. Charity had taken off her hat to have an uninterrupted view; and whenever she leaned back to follow the curve of some dishevelled rocket she could feel Harney's knees against her head.

After a while the scattered fireworks ceased. A longer interval of darkness followed, and then the whole night broke into flower. From every point of the horizon, gold and silver arches sprang up and crossed each other, sky-orchards broke into blossom, shed their flaming petals and hung their branches with golden fruit; and all the while the air was filled with a soft supernatural hum, as though great birds were building their nests in those invisible tree-tops.

Now and then there came a lull, and a wave of moonlight swept the Lake. In a flash it revealed hundreds of boats, steel-dark against lustrous ripples; then it withdrew as if with a furling of vast translucent wings. Charity's heart throbbed with delight. It was as if all the latent beauty of things had been unveiled to her. She could not imagine that the world held anything more wonderful; but near her she heard someone say, "You wait till you see the set piece," and instantly her hopes took a fresh flight. At last, just as it was beginning to seem as though the whole arch of the sky were one great lid pressed against her dazzled eye-balls, and striking out of them continuous jets of jewelled light, the velvet darkness settled down again, and a murmur of expectation ran through the crowd.

"Now—now!" the same voice said excitedly; and Charity, grasping the hat on her knee, crushed it tight in the effort to restrain her rapture.

For a moment the night seemed to grow more impenetrably black; then a great picture stood out against it like a constellation. It was surmounted by a golden scroll bearing the inscription, "Washington crossing the Delaware," and across a flood of motionless golden ripples the National Hero passed, erect, solemn and gigantic, standing with folded arms in the stern of a slowly moving golden boat.

A long "Oh-h-h" burst from the spectators: the stand creaked and shook with their blissful trepidations. "Oh-h-h," Charity gasped: she had forgotten where she was, had at last forgotten even Harney's nearness. She seemed to have been caught up into the stars. . . .

The picture vanished and darkness came down. In the

obscurity she felt her head clasped by two hands: her face was drawn backward, and Harney's lips were pressed on hers. With sudden vehemence he wound his arms about her, holding her head against his breast while she gave him back his kisses. An unknown Harney had revealed himself, a Harney who dominated her and yet over whom she felt herself possessed of a new mysterious power.

But the crowd was beginning to move, and he had to release her. "Come," he said in a confused voice. He scrambled over the side of the stand, and holding up his arm caught her as she sprang to the ground. He passed his arm about her waist, steadying her against the descending rush of people; and she clung to him, speechless, exultant, as if all the crowding and confusion about them were a mere vain stirring of the air.

"Come," he repeated, "we must try to make the trolley." He drew her along, and she followed, still in her dream. They walked as if they were one, so isolated in ecstasy that the people jostling them on every side seemed impalpable. But when they reached the terminus the illuminated trolley was already clanging on its way, its platforms black with passengers. The cars waiting behind it were as thickly packed; and the throng about the terminus was so dense that it seemed hopeless to struggle for a place.

"Last trip up the Lake," a megaphone bellowed from the wharf; and the lights of the little steamboat came dancing out of the darkness.

"No use waiting here; shall we run up the Lake?" Harney suggested.

They pushed their way back to the edge of the water just as the gang-plank was lowered from the white side of the boat. The electric light at the end of the wharf flashed full on the descending passengers, and among them Charity caught sight of Julia Hawes, her white feather askew, and the face under it flushed with coarse laughter. As she stepped from the gang-plank she stopped short, her dark-ringed eyes darting malice.

"Hullo, Charity Royall!" she called out; and then, looking back over her shoulder: "Didn't I tell you it was a family party? Here's grandpa's little darling come to take him home!"

A snigger ran through the group; and then, towering above them, and steadying himself by the hand-rail in a desperate effort at erectness, Mr. Royall stepped stiffly ashore. Like the young men of the party, he wore a secret society emblem in the buttonhole of his black frock-coat. His head was covered by a new Panama hat, and his narrow black tie, half undone, dangled down on his rumpled shirt-front. His face, a livid brown, with red blotches of anger and lips sunken in like an old man's, was a lamentable ruin in the searching glare.

He was just behind Julia Hawes, and had one hand on her arm; but as he left the gang-plank he freed himself, and moved a step or two away from his companions. He had seen Charity at once, and his glance passed slowly from her to Harney, whose arm was still about her. He stood staring at them, and trying to master the senile quiver of his lips; then he drew himself up with the tremulous majesty of drunkenness, and stretched out his arm.

"You whore—you damn—bare-headed whore, you!" he enunciated slowly.

There was a scream of tipsy laughter from the party, and Charity involuntarily put her hands to her head. She remembered that her hat had fallen from her lap when she jumped up to leave the stand; and suddenly she had a vision of herself, hatless, dishevelled, with a man's arm about her, confronting that drunken crew, headed by her guardian's pitiable figure. The picture filled her with shame. She had known since childhood about Mr. Royall's "habits": had seen him, as she went up to bed, sitting morosely in his office, a bottle at his elbow; or coming home, heavy and quarrelsome, from his business expeditions to Hepburn or Springfield; but the idea of his associating himself publicly with a band of disreputable girls and bar-room loafers was new and dreadful to her.

"Oh——" she said in a gasp of misery; and releasing herself from Harney's arm she went straight up to Mr. Royall.

"You come home with me—you come right home with me," she said in a low stern voice, as if she had not heard his apostrophe; and one of the girls called out: "Say, how many fellers does she want?"

There was another laugh, followed by a pause of curiosity,

during which Mr. Royall continued to glare at Charity. At length his twitching lips parted. "I said, 'You—damn— whore!' " he repeated with precision, steadying himself on Julia's shoulder.

Laughs and jeers were beginning to spring up from the circle of people beyond their group; and a voice called out from the gangway: "Now, then, step lively there—all *aboard!*" The pressure of approaching and departing passengers forced the actors in the rapid scene apart, and pushed them back into the throng. Charity found herself clinging to Harney's arm and sobbing desperately. Mr. Royall had disappeared, and in the distance she heard the receding sound of Julia's laugh.

The boat, laden to the taffrail, was puffing away on her last trip.

XI

AT TWO O'CLOCK in the morning the freckled boy from
Creston stopped his sleepy horse at the door of the red
house, and Charity got out. Harney had taken leave of her at
Creston River, charging the boy to drive her home. Her mind
was still in a fog of misery, and she did not remember very
clearly what had happened, or what they had said to each
other, during the interminable interval since their departure
from Nettleton; but the secretive instinct of the animal in
pain was so strong in her that she had a sense of relief when
Harney got out and she drove on alone.

The full moon hung over North Dormer, whitening the
mist that filled the hollows between the hills and floated trans-
parently above the fields. Charity stood a moment at the gate,
looking out into the waning night. She watched the boy drive
off, his horse's head wagging heavily to and fro; then she
went around to the kitchen door and felt under the mat for
the key. She found it, unlocked the door and went in. The
kitchen was dark, but she discovered a box of matches, lit a
candle and went upstairs. Mr. Royall's door, opposite hers,
stood open on his unlit room; evidently he had not come
back. She went into her room, bolted her door and began
slowly to untie the ribbon about her waist, and to take off her
dress. Under the bed she saw the paper bag in which she had
hidden her new hat from inquisitive eyes. . . .

She lay for a long time sleepless on her bed, staring up at
the moonlight on the low ceiling; dawn was in the sky when
she fell asleep, and when she woke the sun was on her face.

She dressed and went down to the kitchen. Verena was
there alone: she glanced at Charity tranquilly, with her old
deaf-looking eyes. There was no sign of Mr. Royall about the
house and the hours passed without his reappearing. Charity
had gone up to her room, and sat there listlessly, her hands
on her lap. Puffs of sultry air fanned her dimity window curtains and flies buzzed stiflingly against the bluish panes.

At one o'clock Verena hobbled up to see if she were not

coming down to dinner; but she shook her head, and the old
woman went away, saying: "I'll cover up, then."

The sun turned and left her room, and Charity seated herself in the window, gazing down the village street through
the half-opened shutters. Not a thought was in her mind; it
was just a dark whirlpool of crowding images; and she
watched the people passing along the street, Dan Targatt's
team hauling a load of pine-trunks down to Hepburn, the
sexton's old white horse grazing on the bank across the way,
as if she looked at these familiar sights from the other side of
the grave.

She was roused from her apathy by seeing Ally Hawes
come out of the Frys' gate and walk slowly toward the red
house with her uneven limping step. At the sight Charity recovered her severed contact with reality. She divined that Ally
was coming to hear about her day: no one else was in the
secret of the trip to Nettleton, and it had flattered Ally profoundly to be allowed to know of it.

At the thought of having to see her, of having to meet her
eyes and answer or evade her questions, the whole horror of
the previous night's adventure rushed back upon Charity.
What had been a feverish nightmare became a cold and unescapable fact. Poor Ally, at that moment, represented North
Dormer, with all its mean curiosities, its furtive malice, its
sham unconsciousness of evil. Charity knew that, although all
relations with Julia were supposed to be severed, the tender-
hearted Ally still secretly communicated with her; and no
doubt Julia would exult in the chance of retailing the scandal
of the wharf. The story, exaggerated and distorted, was probably already on its way to North Dormer.

Ally's dragging pace had not carried her far from the Frys'
gate when she was stopped by old Mrs. Sollas, who was a
great talker, and spoke very slowly because she had never
been able to get used to her new teeth from Hepburn. Still,
even this respite would not last long; in another ten minutes
Ally would be at the door, and Charity would hear her greeting Verena in the kitchen, and then calling up from the foot
of the stairs.

Suddenly it became clear that flight, and instant flight, was
the only thing conceivable. The longing to escape, to get

away from familiar faces, from places where she was known, had always been strong in her in moments of distress. She had a childish belief in the miraculous power of strange scenes and new faces to transform her life and wipe out bitter memories. But such impulses were mere fleeting whims compared to the cold resolve which now possessed her. She felt she could not remain an hour longer under the roof of the man who had publicly dishonoured her, and face to face with the people who would presently be gloating over all the details of her humiliation.

Her passing pity for Mr. Royall had been swallowed up in loathing: everything in her recoiled from the disgraceful spectacle of the drunken old man apostrophizing her in the presence of a band of loafers and street-walkers. Suddenly, vividly, she relived again the horrible moment when he had tried to force himself into her room, and what she had before supposed to be a mad aberration now appeared to her as a vulgar incident in a debauched and degraded life.

While these thoughts were hurrying through her she had dragged out her old canvas school-bag, and was thrusting into it a few articles of clothing and the little packet of letters she had received from Harney. From under her pincushion she took the library key, and laid it in full view; then she felt at the back of a drawer for the blue brooch that Harney had given her. She would not have dared to wear it openly at North Dormer, but now she fastened it on her bosom as if it were a talisman to protect her in her flight. These preparations had taken but a few minutes, and when they were finished Ally Hawes was still at the Frys' corner talking to old Mrs. Sollas. . . .

She had said to herself, as she always said in moments of revolt: "I'll go to the Mountain—I'll go back to my own folks." She had never really meant it before; but now, as she considered her case, no other course seemed open. She had never learned any trade that would have given her independence in a strange place, and she knew no one in the big towns of the valley, where she might have hoped to find employment. Miss Hatchard was still away; but even had she been at North Dormer she was the last person to whom

Charity would have turned, since one of the motives urging
her to flight was the wish not to see Lucius Harney. Travelling back from Nettleton, in the crowded brightly-lit train, all
exchange of confidence between them had been impossible;
but during their drive from Hepburn to Creston River she
had gathered from Harney's snatches of consolatory talk—
again hampered by the freckled boy's presence—that he
intended to see her the next day. At the moment she had
found a vague comfort in the assurance; but in the desolate
lucidity of the hours that followed she had come to see the
impossibility of meeting him again. Her dream of comradeship was over; and the scene on the wharf—vile and disgraceful as it had been—had after all shed the light of truth
on her minute of madness. It was as if her guardian's words
had stripped her bare in the face of the grinning crowd and
proclaimed to the world the secret admonitions of her
conscience.

She did not think these things out clearly; she simply followed the blind propulsion of her wretchedness. She did not
want, ever again, to see anyone she had known; above all, she
did not want to see Harney. . . .

She climbed the hill-path behind the house and struck
through the woods by a short-cut leading to the Creston
road. A lead-coloured sky hung heavily over the fields, and in
the forest the motionless air was stifling; but she pushed on,
impatient to reach the road which was the shortest way to the
Mountain.

To do so, she had to follow the Creston road for a mile or
two, and go within half a mile of the village; and she walked
quickly, fearing to meet Harney. But there was no sign of
him, and she had almost reached the branch road when she
saw the flanks of a large white tent projecting through the
trees by the roadside. She supposed that it sheltered a travelling circus which had come there for the Fourth; but as she
drew nearer she saw, over the folded-back flap, a large sign
bearing the inscription, "Gospel Tent." The interior seemed to
be empty; but a young man in a black alpaca coat, his lank
hair parted over a round white face, stepped from under the
flap and advanced toward her with a smile.

"Sister, your Saviour knows everything. Won't you come in

and lay your guilt before Him?" he asked insinuatingly, putting his hand on her arm.

Charity started back and flushed. For a moment she thought the evangelist must have heard a report of the scene at Nettleton; then she saw the absurdity of the supposition.

"I on'y wish't I had any to lay!" she retorted, with one of her fierce flashes of self-derision; and the young man murmured, aghast: "Oh, Sister, don't speak blasphemy. . . ."

But she had jerked her arm out of his hold, and was running up the branch road, trembling with the fear of meeting a familiar face. Presently she was out of sight of the village, and climbing into the heart of the forest. She could not hope to do the fifteen miles to the Mountain that afternoon; but she knew of a place half-way to Hamblin where she could sleep, and where no one would think of looking for her. It was a little deserted house on a slope in one of the lonely rifts of the hills. She had seen it once, years before, when she had gone on a nutting expedition to the grove of walnuts below it. The party had taken refuge in the house from a sudden mountain storm, and she remembered that Ben Sollas, who liked frightening girls, had told them that it was said to be haunted.

She was growing faint and tired, for she had eaten nothing since morning, and was not used to walking so far. Her head felt light and she sat down for a moment by the roadside. As she sat there she heard the click of a bicycle-bell, and started up to plunge back into the forest; but before she could move the bicycle had swept around the curve of the road, and Harney, jumping off, was approaching her with outstretched arms.

"Charity! What on earth are you doing here?"

She stared as if he were a vision, so startled by the unexpectedness of his being there that no words came to her.

"Where were you going? Had you forgotten that I was coming?" he continued, trying to draw her to him; but she shrank from his embrace.

"I was going away—I don't want to see you—I want you should leave me alone," she broke out wildly.

He looked at her and his face grew grave, as though the shadow of a premonition brushed it.

"Going away—from me, Charity?"

"From everybody. I want you should leave me."

He stood glancing doubtfully up and down the lonely forest road that stretched away into sun-flecked distances.

"Where were you going?"

"Home."

"Home—this way?"

She threw her head back defiantly. "To my home—up yonder: to the Mountain."

As she spoke she became aware of a change in his face. He was no longer listening to her, he was only looking at her, with the passionate absorbed expression she had seen in his eyes after they had kissed on the stand at Nettleton. He was the new Harney again, the Harney abruptly revealed in that embrace, who seemed so penetrated with the joy of her presence that he was utterly careless of what she was thinking or feeling.

He caught her hands with a laugh. "How do you suppose I found you?" he said gaily. He drew out the little packet of his letters and flourished them before her bewildered eyes.

"You dropped them, you imprudent young person— dropped them in the middle of the road, not far from here; and the young man who is running the Gospel tent picked them up just as I was riding by." He drew back, holding her at arm's length, and scrutinizing her troubled face with the minute searching gaze of his short-sighted eyes.

"Did you really think you could run away from me? You see you weren't meant to," he said; and before she could answer he had kissed her again, not vehemently, but tenderly, almost fraternally, as if he had guessed her confused pain, and wanted her to know he understood it. He wound his fingers through hers.

"Come—let's walk a little. I want to talk to you. There's so much to say."

He spoke with a boy's gaiety, carelessly and confidently, as if nothing had happened that could shame or embarrass them; and for a moment, in the sudden relief of her release from lonely pain, she felt herself yielding to his mood. But he had turned, and was drawing her back along the road by which she had come. She stiffened herself and stopped short.

"I won't go back," she said.

They looked at each other a moment in silence; then he answered gently: "Very well: let's go the other way, then."

She remained motionless, gazing silently at the ground, and he went on: "Isn't there a house up here somewhere—a little abandoned house—you meant to show me some day?" Still she made no answer, and he continued, in the same tone of tender reassurance: "Let us go there now and sit down and talk quietly." He took one of the hands that hung by her side and pressed his lips to the palm. "Do you suppose I'm going to let you send me away? Do you suppose I don't understand?"

The little old house—its wooden walls sun-bleached to a ghostly gray—stood in an orchard above the road. The garden palings had fallen, but the broken gate dangled between its posts, and the path to the house was marked by rose-bushes run wild and hanging their small pale blossoms above the crowding grasses. Slender pilasters and an intricate fan-light framed the opening where the door had hung; and the door itself lay rotting in the grass, with an old apple-tree fallen across it.

Inside, also, wind and weather had blanched everything to the same wan silvery tint: the house was as dry and pure as the interior of a long-empty shell. But it must have been exceptionally well built, for the little rooms had kept something of their human aspect: the wooden mantels with their neat classic ornaments were in place, and the corners of one ceiling retained a light film of plaster tracery.

Harney had found an old bench at the back door and dragged it into the house. Charity sat on it, leaning her head against the wall in a state of drowsy lassitude. He had guessed that she was hungry and thirsty, and had brought her some tablets of chocolate from his bicycle-bag, and filled his drinking-cup from a spring in the orchard; and now he sat at her feet, smoking a cigarette, and looking up at her without speaking. Outside, the afternoon shadows were lengthening across the grass, and through the empty window-frame that faced her she saw the Mountain thrusting its dark mass against a sultry sunset. It was time to go.

She stood up, and he sprang to his feet also, and passed his arm through hers with an air of authority. "Now, Charity, you're coming back with me."

She looked at him and shook her head. "I ain't ever going back. You don't know."

"What don't I know?" She was silent, and he continued: "What happened on the wharf was horrible—it's natural you should feel as you do. But it doesn't make any real difference: you can't be hurt by such things. You must try to forget. And you must try to understand that men . . . men sometimes . . ."

"I know about men. That's why."

He coloured a little at the retort, as though it had touched him in a way she did not suspect.

"Well, then . . . you must know one has to make allowances. . . . He'd been drinking. . . ."

"I know all that, too. I've seen him so before. But he wouldn't have dared speak to me that way if he hadn't . . ."

"Hadn't what? What do you mean?"

"Hadn't wanted me to be like those other girls. . . ." She lowered her voice and looked away from him. "So's 't he wouldn't have to go out. . . ."

Harney stared at her. For a moment he did not seem to seize her meaning; then his face grew dark. "The damned hound! The villainous low hound!" His wrath blazed up, crimsoning him to the temples. "I never dreamed—good God, it's too vile," he broke off, as if his thoughts recoiled from the discovery.

"I won't never go back there," she repeated doggedly.

"No——" he assented.

There was a long interval of silence, during which she imagined that he was searching her face for more light on what she had revealed to him; and a flush of shame swept over her.

"I know the way you must feel about me," she broke out, ". . . telling you such things. . . ."

But once more, as she spoke, she became aware that he was no longer listening. He came close and caught her to him as if he were snatching her from some imminent peril: his impetuous eyes were in hers, and she could feel the hard beat of his heart as he held her against it.

"Kiss me again—like last night," he said, pushing her hair back as if to draw her whole face up into his kiss.

XII

O NE AFTERNOON toward the end of August a group of girls sat in a room at Miss Hatchard's in a gay confusion of flags, turkey-red, blue and white paper muslin, harvest sheaves and illuminated scrolls.

North Dormer was preparing for its Old Home Week. That form of sentimental decentralization was still in its early stages, and, precedents being few, and the desire to set an example contagious, the matter had become a subject of prolonged and passionate discussion under Miss Hatchard's roof. The incentive to the celebration had come rather from those who had left North Dormer than from those who had been obliged to stay there, and there was some difficulty in rousing the village to the proper state of enthusiasm. But Miss Hatchard's pale prim drawing-room was the centre of constant comings and goings from Hepburn, Nettleton, Springfield and even more distant cities; and whenever a visitor arrived he was led across the hall, and treated to a glimpse of the group of girls deep in their pretty preparations.

"All the old names . . . all the old names. . . ." Miss Hatchard would be heard, tapping across the hall on her crutches. "Targatt . . . Sollas . . . Fry: this is Miss Orma Fry sewing the stars on the drapery for the organ-loft. Don't move, girls . . . and this is Miss Ally Hawes, our cleverest needle-woman . . . and Miss Charity Royall making our garlands of evergreen. . . . I like the idea of its all being home-made, don't you? We haven't had to call in any foreign talent: my young cousin Lucius Harney, the architect—you know he's up here preparing a book on Colonial houses—he's taken the whole thing in hand so cleverly; but you must come and see his sketch for the stage we're going to put up in the Town Hall."

One of the first results of the Old Home Week agitation had, in fact, been the reappearance of Lucius Harney in the village street. He had been vaguely spoken of as being not far off, but for some weeks past no one had seen him at North Dormer, and there was a recent report of his having left

Creston River, where he was said to have been staying, and gone away from the neighbourhood for good. Soon after Miss Hatchard's return, however, he came back to his old quarters in her house, and began to take a leading part in the planning of the festivities. He threw himself into the idea with extraordinary good-humour, and was so prodigal of sketches, and so inexhaustible in devices, that he gave an immediate impetus to the rather languid movement, and infected the whole village with his enthusiasm.

"Lucius has such a feeling for the past that he has roused us all to a sense of our privileges," Miss Hatchard would say, lingering on the last word, which was a favourite one. And before leading her visitor back to the drawing-room she would repeat, for the hundredth time, that she supposed he thought it very bold of little North Dormer to start up and have a Home Week of its own, when so many bigger places hadn't thought of it yet; but that, after all, Associations counted more than the size of the population, didn't they? And of course North Dormer was so full of Associations . . . historic, literary (here a filial sigh for Honorius) and ecclesiastical . . . he knew about the old pewter communion service imported from England in 1769, she supposed? And it was so important, in a wealthy materialistic age, to set the example of reverting to the old ideals, the family and the homestead, and so on. This peroration usually carried her half-way back across the hall, leaving the girls to return to their interrupted activities.

The day on which Charity Royall was weaving hemlock garlands for the procession was the last before the celebration. When Miss Hatchard called upon the North Dormer maidenhood to collaborate in the festal preparations Charity had at first held aloof; but it had been made clear to her that her non-appearance might excite conjecture, and, reluctantly, she had joined the other workers. The girls, at first shy and embarrassed, and puzzled as to the exact nature of the projected commemoration, had soon become interested in the amusing details of their task, and excited by the notice they received. They would not for the world have missed their afternoons at Miss Hatchard's, and, while they cut out and sewed and draped and pasted, their tongues kept up such an accompaniment to the sewing-machine that Charity's silence sheltered itself unperceived under their chatter.

In spirit she was still almost unconscious of the pleasant stir about her. Since her return to the red house, on the evening of the day when Harney had overtaken her on her way to the Mountain, she had lived at North Dormer as if she were suspended in the void. She had come back there because Harney, after appearing to agree to the impossibility of her doing so, had ended by persuading her that any other course would be madness. She had nothing further to fear from Mr. Royall. Of this she had declared herself sure, though she had failed to add, in his exoneration, that he had twice offered to make her his wife. Her hatred of him made it impossible, at the moment, for her to say anything that might partly excuse him in Harney's eyes.

Harney, however, once satisfied of her security, had found plenty of reasons for urging her to return. The first, and the most unanswerable, was that she had nowhere else to go. But the one on which he laid the greatest stress was that flight would be equivalent to avowal. If—as was almost inevitable—rumours of the scandalous scene at Nettleton should reach North Dormer, how else would her disappearance be interpreted? Her guardian had publicly taken away her character, and she immediately vanished from his house. Seekers after motives could hardly fail to draw an unkind conclusion. But if she came back at once, and was seen leading her usual life, the incident was reduced to its true proportions, as the outbreak of a drunken old man furious at being surprised in disreputable company. People would say that Mr. Royall had insulted his ward to justify himself, and the sordid tale would fall into its place in the chronicle of his obscure debaucheries.

Charity saw the force of the argument; but if she acquiesced it was not so much because of that as because it was Harney's wish. Since that evening in the deserted house she could imagine no reason for doing or not doing anything except the fact that Harney wished or did not wish it. All her tossing contradictory impulses were merged in a fatalistic acceptance of his will. It was not that she felt in him any ascendency of character—there were moments already when she knew she was the stronger—but that all the rest of life had become a mere cloudy rim about the central glory of their passion. Whenever she stopped thinking about that for a moment she felt as she sometimes did after lying on the grass and staring up too long at the sky; her eyes were so full of light that everything about her was a blur.

Each time that Miss Hatchard, in the course of her periodical incursions into the work-room, dropped an allusion to her young cousin, the architect, the effect was the same on Charity. The hemlock garland she was wearing fell to her knees and she sat in a kind of trance. It was so manifestly absurd that Miss Hatchard should talk of Harney in that familiar possessive way, as if she had any claim on him, or knew anything about him. She, Charity Royall, was the only being on earth who really knew him, knew him from the soles of his feet to the rumpled crest of his hair, knew the shifting lights in his eyes, and the inflexions of his voice, and the things he liked and disliked, and everything there was to know about him, as minutely and yet unconsciously as a child knows the walls of the room it wakes up in every morning. It was this fact, which nobody about her guessed, or would have understood, that made her life something apart and inviolable, as if nothing had any power to hurt or disturb her as long as her secret was safe.

The room in which the girls sat was the one which had been Harney's bedroom. He had been sent upstairs, to make room for the Home Week workers; but the furniture had not been moved, and as Charity sat there she had perpetually before her the vision she had looked in on from the midnight garden. The table at which Harney had sat was the one about which the girls were gathered; and her own seat was near the bed on which she had seen him lying. Sometimes, when the others were not looking, she bent over as if to pick up something, and laid her cheek for a moment against the pillow.

Toward sunset the girls disbanded. Their work was done, and the next morning at daylight the draperies and garlands were to be nailed up, and the illuminated scrolls put in place in the Town Hall. The first guests were to drive over from Hepburn in time for the midday banquet under a tent in Miss Hatchard's field; and after that the ceremonies were to begin.

Miss Hatchard, pale with fatigue and excitement, thanked her young assistants, and stood in the porch, leaning on her crutches and waving a farewell as she watched them troop away down the street.

Charity had slipped off among the first; but at the gate she heard Ally Hawes calling after her, and reluctantly turned.

"Will you come over now and try on your dress?" Ally asked, looking at her with wistful admiration. "I want to be sure the sleeves don't ruck up the same as they did yesterday."

Charity gazed at her with dazzled eyes. "Oh, it's lovely," she said, and hastened away without listening to Ally's protest. She wanted her dress to be as pretty as the other girls'— wanted it, in fact, to outshine the rest, since she was to take part in the "exercises"—but she had no time just then to fix her mind on such matters. . . .

She sped up the street to the library, of which she had the key about her neck. From the passage at the back she dragged forth a bicycle, and guided it to the edge of the street. She looked about to see if any of the girls were approaching; but they had drifted away together toward the Town Hall, and she sprang into the saddle and turned toward the Creston road. There was an almost continual descent to Creston, and with her feet against the pedals she floated through the still evening air like one of the hawks she had often watched slanting downward on motionless wings. Twenty minutes from the time when she had left Miss Hatchard's door she was turning up the wood-road on which Harney had overtaken her on the day of her flight; and a few minutes afterward she had jumped from her bicycle at the gate of the deserted house.

In the gold-powdered sunset it looked more than ever like some frail shell dried and washed by many seasons; but at the back, whither Charity advanced, drawing her bicycle after her, there were signs of recent habitation. A rough door made of boards hung in the kitchen doorway, and pushing it open she entered a room furnished in primitive camping fashion. In the window was a table, also made of boards, with an earthenware jar holding a big bunch of wild asters. Two canvas chairs stood near by, and in one corner was a mattress with a Mexican blanket over it.

The room was empty, and leaning her bicycle against the house Charity clambered up the slope and sat down on a rock under an old apple-tree. The air was perfectly still, and from where she sat she would be able to hear the tinkle of a bicycle-bell a long way down the road. . . .

She was always glad when she got to the little house before Harney. She liked to have time to take in every detail of its secret sweetness—the shadows of the apple-trees swaying on the grass, the old walnuts rounding their domes below the road, the meadows sloping westward in the afternoon light—before his first kiss blotted it all out. Everything unrelated to the hours spent in that tranquil place was as faint as the remembrance of a dream. The only reality was the wondrous unfolding of her new self, the reaching out to the light of all her contracted tendrils. She had lived all her life among people whose sensibilities seemed to have withered for lack of use; and more wonderful, at first, than Harney's endearments were the words that were a part of them. She had always thought of love as something confused and furtive, and he made it as bright and open as the summer air.

On the morrow of the day when she had shown him the way to the deserted house he had packed up and left Creston River for Boston; but at the first station he had jumped off the train with a hand-bag and scrambled up into the hills. For two golden rainless August weeks he had camped in the house, getting eggs and milk from the solitary farm in the valley, where no one knew him, and doing his cooking over a spirit-lamp. He got up every day with the sun, took a plunge in a brown pool he knew of, and spent long hours lying in the scented hemlock-woods above the house, or wandering along the yoke of the Eagle Ridge, far above the misty blue valleys that swept away east and west between the endless hills. And in the afternoon Charity came to him.

With part of what was left of her savings she had hired a bicycle for a month, and every day after dinner, as soon as her guardian started to his office, she hurried to the library, got out her bicycle, and flew down the Creston road. She knew that Mr. Royall, like everyone else in North Dormer, was perfectly aware of her acquisition: possibly he, as well as the rest of the village, knew what use she made of it. She did not care:

she felt him to be so powerless that if he had questioned her she would probably have told him the truth. But they had never spoken to each other since the night on the wharf at Nettleton. He had returned to North Dormer only on the third day after that encounter, arriving just as Charity and Verena were sitting down to supper. He had drawn up his chair, taken his napkin from the side-board drawer, pulled it out of its ring, and seated himself as unconcernedly as if he had come in from his usual afternoon session at Carrick Fry's; and the long habit of the household made it seem almost natural that Charity should not so much as raise her eyes when he entered. She had simply let him understand that her silence was not accidental by leaving the table while he was still eating, and going up without a word to shut herself into her room. After that he formed the habit of talking loudly and genially to Verena whenever Charity was in the room; but otherwise there was no apparent change in their relations.

She did not think connectedly of these things while she sat waiting for Harney, but they remained in her mind as a sullen background against which her short hours with him flamed out like forest fires. Nothing else mattered, neither the good nor the bad, or what might have seemed so before she knew him. He had caught her up and carried her away into a new world, from which, at stated hours, the ghost of her came back to perform certain customary acts, but all so thinly and insubstantially that she sometimes wondered that the people she went about among could see her. . . .

Behind the swarthy Mountain the sun had gone down in waveless gold. From a pasture up the slope a tinkle of cow-bells sounded; a puff of smoke hung over the farm in the valley, trailed on the pure air and was gone. For a few minutes, in the clear light that is all shadow, fields and woods were outlined with an unreal precision; then the twilight blotted them out, and the little house turned gray and spectral under its wizened apple-branches.

Charity's heart contracted. The first fall of night after a day of radiance often gave her a sense of hidden menace: it was like looking out over the world as it would be when love had gone from it. She wondered if some day she would sit in that same place and watch in vain for her lover. . . .

His bicycle-bell sounded down the lane, and in a minute she was at the gate and his eyes were laughing in hers. They walked back through the long grass, and pushed open the door behind the house. The room at first seemed quite dark and they had to grope their way in hand in hand. Through the window-frame the sky looked light by contrast, and above the black mass of asters in the earthern jar one white star glimmered like a moth.

"There was such a lot to do at the last minute," Harney was explaining, "and I had to drive down to Creston to meet someone who has come to stay with my cousin for the show."

He had his arms about her, and his kisses were in her hair and on her lips. Under his touch things deep down in her struggled to the light and sprang up like flowers in sunshine. She twisted her fingers into his, and they sat down side by side on the improvised couch. She hardly heard his excuses for being late: in his absence a thousand doubts tormented her, but as soon as he appeared she ceased to wonder where he had come from, what had delayed him, who had kept him from her. It seemed as if the places he had been in, and the people he had been with, must cease to exist when he left them, just as her own life was suspended in his absence.

He continued, now, to talk to her volubly and gaily, deploring his lateness, grumbling at the demands on his time, and good-humouredly mimicking Miss Hatchard's benevolent agitation. "She hurried off Miles to ask Mr. Royall to speak at the Town Hall tomorrow: I didn't know till it was done." Charity was silent, and he added: "After all, perhaps it's just as well. No one else could have done it."

Charity made no answer: she did not care what part her guardian played in the morrow's ceremonies. Like all the other figures peopling her meagre world he had grown non-existent to her. She had even put off hating him.

"Tomorrow I shall only see you from far off," Harney continued. "But in the evening there'll be the dance in the Town Hall. Do you want me to promise not to dance with any other girl?"

Any other girl? Were there any others? She had forgotten even that peril, so enclosed did he and she seem in their secret world. Her heart gave a frightened jerk.

"Yes, promise."

He laughed and took her in his arms. "You goose—not even if they're hideous?"

He pushed the hair from her forehead, bending her face back, as his way was, and leaning over so that his head loomed black between her eyes and the paleness of the sky, in which the white star floated . . .

Side by side they sped back along the dark wood-road to the village. A late moon was rising, full orbed and fiery, turning the mountain ranges from fluid gray to a massive blackness, and making the upper sky so light that the stars looked as faint as their own reflections in water. At the edge of the wood, half a mile from North Dormer, Harney jumped from his bicycle, took Charity in his arms for a last kiss, and then waited while she went on alone.

They were later than usual, and instead of taking the bicycle to the library she propped it against the back of the wood-shed and entered the kitchen of the red house. Verena sat there alone; when Charity came in she looked at her with mild impenetrable eyes and then took a plate and a glass of milk from the shelf and set them silently on the table. Charity nodded her thanks, and sitting down fell hungrily upon her piece of pie and emptied the glass. Her face burned with her quick flight through the night, and her eyes were dazzled by the twinkle of the kitchen lamp. She felt like a night-bird suddenly caught and caged.

"He ain't come back since supper," Verena said. "He's down to the Hall."

Charity took no notice. Her soul was still winging through the forest. She washed her plate and tumbler, and then felt her way up the dark stairs. When she opened her door a wonder arrested her. Before going out she had closed her shutters against the afternoon heat, but they had swung partly open, and a bar of moonlight, crossing the room, rested on her bed and showed a dress of China silk laid out on it in virgin whiteness. Charity had spent more than she could afford on the dress, which was to surpass those of all the other girls; she had wanted to let North Dormer see that she was worthy of Harney's admiration. Above the dress, folded on the pillow, was the white veil which the young women who took part in the exercises were to wear under a wreath of asters; and beside the veil a pair of slim white satin shoes that Ally had produced from an old trunk in which she stored mysterious treasures.

Charity stood gazing at all the outspread whiteness. It recalled a vision that had come to her in the night after her first meeting with Harney. She no longer had such visions . . . warmer splendours had displaced them . . . but it was stupid of Ally to have paraded all those white things on her bed, exactly as Hattie Targatt's wedding dress from Springfield had been spread out for the neighbours to see when she married Tom Fry. . . .

Charity took up the satin shoes and looked at them curiously. By day, no doubt, they would appear a little worn, but in the moonlight they seemed carved of ivory. She sat down on the floor to try them on, and they fitted her perfectly, though when she stood up she lurched a little on the high heels. She looked down at her feet, which the graceful mould of the slippers had marvellously arched and narrowed. She had never seen such shoes before, even in the shop-windows at Nettleton . . . never, except . . . yes, once, she had noticed a pair of the same shape on Annabel Balch.

A blush of mortification swept over her. Ally sometimes sewed for Miss Balch when that brilliant being descended on North Dormer, and no doubt she picked up presents of cast-off clothing: the treasures in the mysterious trunk all came from the people she worked for. There could be no doubt that the white slippers were Annabel Balch's. . . .

As she stood there, staring down moodily at her feet, she heard the triple click-click-click of a bicycle-bell under her window. It was Harney's secret signal as he passed on his way home. She stumbled to the window on her high heels, flung open the shutters and leaned out. He waved to her and sped by, his black shadow dancing merrily ahead of him down the empty moonlit road; and she leaned there watching him till he vanished under the Hatchard spruces.

XIII

THE TOWN HALL was crowded and exceedingly hot. As Charity marched into it, third in the white muslin file headed by Orma Fry, she was conscious mainly of the brilliant effect of the wreathed columns framing the green-carpeted stage toward which she was moving and of the unfamiliar faces turning from the front rows to watch the advance of the procession.

But it was all a bewildering blur of eyes and colours till she found herself standing at the back of the stage, her great bunch of asters and goldenrod held well in front of her, and answering the nervous glance of Lambert Sollas, the organist from Mr. Miles's church, who had come up from Nettleton to play the harmonium, and sat behind it, running his conductor's eye over the fluttered girls.

A moment later Mr. Miles, pink and twinkling, emerged from the background, as if buoyed up on his broad white gown, and briskly dominated the bowed heads in the front rows. He prayed energetically and briefly and then retired, and a fierce nod from Lambert Sollas warned the girls that they were to follow at once with "Home, Sweet Home." It was a joy to Charity to sing: it seemed as though, for the first time, her secret rapture might burst from her and flash its defiance at the world. All the glow in her blood, the breath of the summer earth, the rustle of the forest, the fresh call of birds at sunrise, and the brooding midday languors, seemed to pass into her untrained voice, lifted and led by the sustaining chorus.

And then suddenly the song was over, and after an uncertain pause, during which Miss Hatchard's pearl-grey gloves started a furtive signalling down the hall, Mr. Royall, emerging in turn, ascended the steps of the stage and appeared behind the flower-wreathed desk. He passed close to Charity, and she noticed that his gravely set face wore the look of majesty that used to awe and fascinate her childhood. His frock-coat had been carefully brushed and ironed, and the ends of his narrow black tie were so nearly even that the tying must have cost him a protracted struggle. His appearance

struck her all the more because it was the first time she had
looked him full in the face since the night at Nettleton, and
nothing in his grave and impressive demeanour revealed a
trace of the lamentable figure on the wharf.

He stood a moment behind the desk, resting his finger-tips
against it, and bending slightly toward his audience; then he
straightened himself and began.

At first she paid no heed to what he was saying: only
fragments of sentences, sonorous quotations, allusions to
illustrious men, including the obligatory tribute to Honorius
Hatchard, drifted past her inattentive ears. She was trying to
discover Harney among the notable people in the front row;
but he was nowhere near Miss Hatchard, who, crowned by a
pearl-grey hat that matched her gloves, sat just below the
desk, supported by Mrs. Miles and an important-looking unknown lady. Charity was near one end of the stage, and from
where she sat the other end of the first row of seats was cut
off by the screen of foliage masking the harmonium. The
effort to see Harney around the corner of the screen, or
through its interstices, made her unconscious of everything
else; but the effort was unsuccessful, and gradually she found
her attention arrested by her guardian's discourse.

She had never heard him speak in public before, but she
was familiar with the rolling music of his voice when he read
aloud, or held forth to the selectmen about the stove at Carrick Fry's. Today his inflections were richer and graver than
she had ever known them: he spoke slowly, with pauses that
seemed to invite his hearers to silent participation in his
thought; and Charity perceived a light of response in their
faces.

He was nearing the end of his address . . . "Most of you,"
he said, "most of you who have returned here today, to take
contact with this little place for a brief hour, have come only
on a pious pilgrimage, and will go back presently to busy
cities and lives full of larger duties. But that is not the only
way of coming back to North Dormer. Some of us, who went
out from here in our youth . . . went out, like you, to busy
cities and larger duties . . . have come back in another way—
come back for good. I am one of those, as many of you
know. . . ." He paused, and there was a sense of suspense in

the listening hall. "My history is without interest, but it has its lesson: not so much for those of you who have already made your lives in other places, as for the young men who are perhaps planning even now to leave these quiet hills and go down into the struggle. Things they cannot foresee may send some of those young men back some day to the little township and the old homestead: they may come back for good. . . ." He looked about him, and repeated gravely: "For *good*. There's the point I want to make . . . North Dormer is a poor little place, almost lost in a mighty landscape: perhaps, by this time, it might have been a bigger place, and more in scale with the landscape, if those who had to come back had come with that feeling in their minds—that they wanted to come back for *good* . . . and not for bad . . . or just for indifference. . . .

"Gentlemen, let us look at things as they are. Some of us have come back to our native town because we'd failed to get on elsewhere. One way or other, things had gone wrong with us . . . what we'd dreamed of hadn't come true. But the fact that we had failed elsewhere is no reason why we should fail here. Our very experiments in larger places, even if they were unsuccessful, ought to have helped us to make North Dormer a larger place . . . and you young men who are preparing even now to follow the call of ambition, and turn your back on the old homes—well, let me say this to you, that if ever you do come back to them it's worth while to come back to them for their good. . . . And to do that, you must keep on loving them while you're away from them; and even if you come back against your will—and thinking it's all a bitter mistake of Fate or Providence—you must try to make the best of it, and to make the best of your old town; and after a while—well, ladies and gentlemen, I give you my recipe for what it's worth; after a while, I believe you'll be able to say, as I can say today: 'I'm glad I'm here.' Believe me, all of you, the best way to help the places we live in is to be glad we live there."

He stopped, and a murmur of emotion and surprise ran through the audience. It was not in the least what they had expected, but it moved them more than what they had expected would have moved them. "Hear, hear!" a voice cried out in the middle of the hall. An outburst of cheers caught up the cry, and as they subsided Charity heard Mr. Miles saying to someone near him: "That was a *man* talking——" He wiped his spectacles.

Mr. Royall had stepped back from the desk, and taken his seat in the row of chairs in front of the harmonium. A dapper white-haired gentleman—a distant Hatchard—succeeded him behind the goldenrod, and began to say beautiful things about the old oaken bucket, patient white-haired mothers, and where the boys used to go nutting . . . and Charity began again to search for Harney. . . .

Suddenly Mr. Royall pushed back his seat, and one of the maple branches in front of the harmonium collapsed with a crash. It uncovered the end of the first row and in one of the seats Charity saw Harney, and in the next a lady whose face was turned toward him, and almost hidden by the brim of her drooping hat. Charity did not need to see the face. She knew at a glance the slim figure, the fair hair heaped up under the hat-brim, the long pale wrinkled gloves with bracelets slipping over them. At the fall of the branch Miss Balch turned her head toward the stage, and in her pretty thin-lipped smile there lingered the reflection of something her neighbour had been whispering to her. . . .

Someone came forward to replace the fallen branch, and Miss Balch and Harney were once more hidden. But to Charity the vision of their two faces had blotted out everything. In a flash they had shown her the bare reality of her situation. Behind the frail screen of her lover's caresses was the whole inscrutable mystery of his life: his relations with other people—with other women—his opinions, his prejudices, his principles, the net of influences and interests and ambitions in which every man's life is entangled. Of all these she knew nothing, except what he had told her of his architectural aspirations. She had always dimly guessed him to be in touch with important people, involved in complicated relations— but she felt it all to be so far beyond her understanding that the whole subject hung like a luminous mist on the farthest verge of her thoughts. In the foreground, hiding all else, there was the glow of his presence, the light and shadow of his face, the way his short-sighted eyes, at her approach, widened and deepened as if to draw her down into them; and, above all, the flush of youth and tenderness in which his words enclosed her.

Now she saw him detached from her, drawn back into the unknown, and whispering to another girl things that provoked the same smile of mischievous complicity he had so often called to her own lips. The feeling possessing her was not one of jealousy: she was too sure of his love. It was rather a terror of the unknown, of all the mysterious attractions that must even now be dragging him away from her, and of her own powerlessness to contend with them.

She had given him all she had—but what was it compared to the other gifts life held for him? She understood now the case of girls like herself to whom this kind of thing happened. They gave all they had, but their all was not enough: it could not buy more than a few moments. . . .

The heat had grown suffocating—she felt it descend on her in smothering waves, and the faces in the crowded hall began to dance like the pictures flashed on the screen at Nettleton. For an instant Mr. Royall's countenance detached itself from the general blur. He had resumed his place in front of the harmonium, and sat close to her, his eyes on her face; and his look seemed to pierce to the very centre of her confused sensations. . . . A feeling of physical sickness rushed over her— and then deadly apprehension. The light of the fiery hours in the little house swept back on her in a glare of fear. . . .

She forced herself to look away from her guardian, and became aware that the oratory of the Hatchard cousin had ceased, and that Mr. Miles was again flapping his wings. Fragments of his peroration floated through her bewildered brain. . . . "A rich harvest of hallowed memories. . . . A sanctified hour to which, in moments of trial, your thoughts will prayerfully return. . . . And now, O Lord, let us humbly and fervently give thanks for this blessed day of reunion, here in the old home to which we have come back from so far. Preserve it to us, O Lord, in times to come, in all its homely sweetness—in the kindliness and wisdom of its old people, in the courage and industry of its young men, in the piety and purity of this group of innocent girls——" He flapped a white wing in their direction, and at the same moment

Lambert Sollas, with his fierce nod, struck the opening bars of "Auld Lang Syne." . . . Charity stared straight ahead of her and then, dropping her flowers, fell face downward at Mr. Royall's feet.

XIV

NORTH DORMER's celebration naturally included the villages attached to its township, and the festivities were to radiate over the whole group, from Dormer and the two Crestons to Hamblin, the lonely hamlet on the north slope of the Mountain where the first snow always fell. On the third day there were speeches and ceremonies at Creston and Creston River; on the fourth the principal performers were to be driven in buck-boards to Dormer and Hamblin.

It was on the fourth day that Charity returned for the first time to the little house. She had not seen Harney alone since they had parted at the wood's edge the night before the celebrations began. In the interval she had passed through many moods, but for the moment the terror which had seized her in the Town Hall had faded to the edge of consciousness. She had fainted because the hall was stiflingly hot, and because the speakers had gone on and on. . . . Several other people had been affected by the heat, and had had to leave before the exercises were over. There had been thunder in the air all the afternoon, and everyone said afterward that something ought to have been done to ventilate the hall. . . .

At the dance that evening—where she had gone reluctantly, and only because she feared to stay away, she had sprung back into instant reassurance. As soon as she entered she had seen Harney waiting for her, and he had come up with kind gay eyes, and swept her off in a waltz. Her feet were full of music, and though her only training had been with the village youths she had no difficulty in tuning her steps to his. As they circled about the floor all her vain fears dropped from her, and she even forgot that she was probably dancing in Annabel Balch's slippers.

When the waltz was over Harney, with a last hand-clasp, left her to meet Miss Hatchard and Miss Balch, who were just entering. Charity had a moment of anguish as Miss Balch appeared; but it did not last. The triumphant fact of her own greater beauty, and of Harney's sense of it, swept her apprehensions aside. Miss Balch, in an unbecoming dress, looked sallow and pinched, and Charity fancied there was a worried expression in her pale-lashed eyes. She took a seat near Miss Hatchard and it was presently apparent that she did not mean to dance. Charity did not dance often either. Harney explained to her that Miss Hatchard had begged him to give each of the other girls a turn; but he went through the form of asking Charity's permission each time he led one out, and that gave her a sense of secret triumph even completer than when she was whirling about the room with him. . . .

She was thinking of all this as she waited for him in the deserted house. The late afternoon was sultry, and she had tossed aside her hat and stretched herself at full length on the Mexican blanket because it was cooler indoors than under the trees. She lay with her arms folded beneath her head, gazing out at the shaggy shoulder of the Mountain. The sky behind it was full of the splintered glories of the descending sun, and before long she expected to hear Harney's bicycle-bell in the lane. He had bicycled to Hamblin, instead of driving there with his cousin and her friends, so that he might be able to make his escape earlier and stop on the way back at the deserted house, which was on the road to Hamblin. They had smiled together at the joke of hearing the crowded buckboards roll by on the return, while they lay close in their hiding above the road. Such childish triumphs still gave her a sense of reckless security.

Nevertheless she had not wholly forgotten the vision of fear that had opened before her in the Town Hall. The sense of lastingness was gone from her and every moment with Harney would now be ringed with doubt.

The Mountain was turning purple against a fiery sunset from which it seemed to be divided by a knife-edge of quivering light; and above this wall of flame the whole sky was a pure pale green, like some cold mountain lake in shadow. Charity lay gazing up at it, and watching for the first white star. . . .

Her eyes were still fixed on the upper reaches of the sky when she became aware that a shadow had flitted across the glory-flooded room: it must have been Harney passing the window against the sunset. . . . She half raised herself, and then dropped back on her folded arms. The combs had slipped from her hair, and it trailed in a rough dark rope across her breast. She lay quite still, a sleepy smile on her lips, her indolent lids half shut. There was a fumbling at the padlock and she called out: "Have you slipped the chain?" The door opened, and Mr. Royall walked into the room.

She started up, sitting back against the cushions, and they looked at each other without speaking. Then Mr. Royall closed the door-latch and advanced a few steps.

Charity jumped to her feet. "What have you come for?" she stammered.

The last glare of the sunset was on her guardian's face, which looked ash-coloured in the yellow radiance.

"Because I knew you were here," he answered simply.

She had become conscious of the hair hanging loose across her breast, and it seemed as though she could not speak to him till she had set herself in order. She groped for her combs, and tried to fasten up the coil. Mr. Royall silently watched her.

"Charity," he said, "he'll be here in a minute. Let me talk to you first."

"You've got no right to talk to me. I can do what I please."

"Yes. What is it you mean to do?"

"I needn't answer that, or anything else."

He had glanced away, and stood looking curiously about the illuminated room. Purple asters and red maple-leaves filled the jar on the table; on a shelf against the wall stood a lamp, the kettle, a little pile of cups and saucers. The canvas chairs were grouped about the table.

"So this is where you meet," he said.

His tone was quiet and controlled, and the fact disconcerted her. She had been ready to give him violence for violence, but this calm acceptance of things as they were left her without a weapon.

"See here, Charity—you're always telling me I've got no rights over you. There might be two ways of looking at that—but I ain't going to argue it. All I know is I raised you as good as I could, and meant fairly by you always—except once, for a bad half-hour. There's no justice in weighing that half-hour against the rest, and you know it. If you hadn't, you wouldn't have gone on living under my roof. Seems to me the fact of your doing that gives me some sort of a right; the right to try and keep you out of trouble. I'm not asking you to consider any other."

She listened in silence, and then gave a slight laugh. "Better wait till I'm in trouble," she said.

He paused a moment, as if weighing her words. "Is that all your answer?"

"Yes, that's all."

"Well—I'll wait."

He turned away slowly, but as he did so the thing she had been waiting for happened; the door opened again and Harney entered.

He stopped short with a face of astonishment, and then, quickly controlling himself, went up to Mr. Royall with a frank look.

"Have you come to see me, sir?" he said coolly, throwing his cap on the table with an air of proprietorship.

Mr. Royall again looked slowly about the room; then his eyes turned to the young man.

"Is this your house?" he inquired.

Harney laughed: "Well—as much as it's anybody's. I come here to sketch occasionally."

"And to receive Miss Royall's visits?"

"When she does me the honour——"

"Is this the home you propose to bring her to when you get married?"

There was an immense and oppressive silence. Charity, quivering with anger, started forward, and then stood silent, too humbled for speech. Harney's eyes had dropped under the old man's gaze; but he raised them presently, and looking steadily at Mr. Royall, said: "Miss Royall is not a child. Isn't it rather absurd to talk of her as if she were? I believe she considers herself free to come and go as she pleases, without any questions from anyone." He paused and added: "I'm ready to answer any she wishes to ask me."

Mr. Royall turned to her. "Ask him when he's going to marry you, then——" There was another silence, and he laughed in his turn—a broken laugh, with a scraping sound in it. "You darsn't!" he shouted out with sudden passion. He went close up to Charity, his right arm lifted, not in menace but in tragic exhortation.

"You darsn't, and you know it—and you know why!" He
swung back again upon the young man. "And you know
why you ain't asked her to marry you, and why you don't
mean to. It's because you hadn't need to; nor any other man
either. I'm the only one that was fool enough not to know
that; and I guess nobody'll repeat my mistake—not in Eagle
County, anyhow. They all know what she is, and what she
came from. They all know her mother was a woman of the
town from Nettleton, that followed one of those Mountain
fellows up to his place and lived there with him like a heathen. I saw her there sixteen years ago, when I went to
bring this child down. I went to save her from the kind of
life her mother was leading—but I'd better have left her in
the kennel she came from. . . ." He paused and stared
darkly at the two young people, and out beyond them, at
the menacing Mountain with its rim of fire; then he sat
down beside the table on which they had so often spread
their rustic supper, and covered his face with his hands. Harney leaned in the window, a frown on his face: he was twirling between his fingers a small package that dangled from a
loop of string. . . . Charity heard Mr. Royall draw a hard
breath or two, and his shoulders shook a little. Presently he
stood up and walked across the room. He did not look
again at the young people: they saw him feel his way to the
door and fumble for the latch; and then he went out into
the darkness.

After he had gone there was a long silence. Charity waited
for Harney to speak; but he seemed at first not to find anything to say. At length he broke out irrelevantly: "I wonder
how he found out?"

She made no answer and he tossed down the package he
had been holding, and went up to her.

"I'm so sorry, dear . . . that this should have happened. . . ."

She threw her head back proudly. "I ain't ever been sorry—
not a minute!"

"No."

She waited to be caught into his arms, but he turned away
from her irresolutely. The last glow was gone from behind
the Mountain. Everything in the room had turned grey and

indistinct, and an autumnal dampness crept up from the hollow below the orchard, laying its cold touch on their flushed faces. Harney walked the length of the room, and then turned back and sat down at the table.

"Come," he said imperiously.

She sat down beside him, and he untied the string about the package and spread out a pile of sandwiches.

"I stole them from the love-feast at Hamblin," he said with a laugh, pushing them over to her. She laughed too, and took one, and began to eat.

"Didn't you make the tea?"

"No," she said. "I forgot——"

"Oh, well—it's too late to boil the water now." He said nothing more, and sitting opposite to each other they went on silently eating the sandwiches. Darkness had descended in the little room, and Harney's face was a dim blur to Charity. Suddenly he leaned across the table and laid his hand on hers.

"I shall have to go off for a while—a month or two, perhaps—to arrange some things; and then I'll come back . . . and we'll get married."

His voice seemed like a stranger's: nothing was left in it of the vibrations she knew. Her hand lay inertly under his, and she left it there, and raised her head, trying to answer him. But the words died in her throat. They sat motionless, in their attitude of confident endearment, as if some strange death had surprised them. At length Harney sprang to his feet with a slight shiver. "God! it's damp—we couldn't have come here much longer." He went to the shelf, took down a tin candlestick and lit the candle; then he propped an unhinged shutter against the empty window-frame and put the candle on the table. It threw up a queer shadow on his frowning forehead, and made the smile on his lips a grimace.

"But it's been good, though, hasn't it, Charity? . . . What's the matter—why do you stand there staring at me? Haven't the days here been good?" He went up to her and caught her to his breast. "And there'll be others—lots of others . . . jollier . . . even jollier . . . won't there, darling?"

He turned her head back, feeling for the curve of her throat below the ear, and kissing her there, and on the hair and eyes and lips. She clung to him desperately, and as he drew her to his knees on the couch she felt as if they were being sucked down together into some bottomless abyss.

XV

HAT NIGHT, as usual, they said good-bye at the wood's edge.

Harney was to leave the next morning early. He asked Charity to say nothing of their plans till his return, and, strangely even to herself, she was glad of the postponement. A leaden weight of shame hung on her, benumbing every other sensation, and she bade him good-bye with hardly a sign of emotion. His reiterated promises to return seemed almost wounding. She had no doubt that he intended to come back; her doubts were far deeper and less definable.

Since the fanciful vision of the future that had flitted through her imagination at their first meeting she had hardly ever thought of his marrying her. She had not had to put the thought from her mind; it had not been there. If ever she looked ahead she felt instinctively that the gulf between them was too deep, and that the bridge their passion had flung across it was as insubstantial as a rainbow. But she seldom looked ahead; each day was so rich that it absorbed her. . . . Now her first feeling was that everything would be different, and that she herself would be a different being to Harney. Instead of remaining separate and absolute, she would be compared with other people, and unknown things would be expected of her. She was too proud to be afraid, but the freedom of her spirit drooped. . . .

Harney had not fixed any date for his return; he had said he would have to look about first, and settle things. He had promised to write as soon as there was anything definite to say, and had left her his address, and asked her to write also. But the address frightened her. It was in New York, at a club with a long name in Fifth Avenue: it seemed to raise an insurmountable barrier between them. Once or twice, in the first days, she got out a sheet of paper, and sat looking at it, and trying to think what to say; but she had the feeling that her letter would never reach its destination. She had never written to anyone farther away than Hepburn.

Harney's first letter came after he had been gone about ten days. It was tender but grave, and bore no resemblance to the

gay little notes he had sent her by the freckled boy from
Creston River. He spoke positively of his intention of coming
back, but named no date, and reminded Charity of their
agreement that their plans should not be divulged till he had
had time to "settle things." When that would be he could not
yet foresee; but she could count on his returning as soon as
the way was clear.

She read the letter with a strange sense of its coming from
immeasurable distances and having lost most of its meaning
on the way; and in reply she sent him a coloured post-card of
Creston Falls, on which she wrote: "With love from Charity."
She felt the pitiful inadequacy of this, and understood, with a
sense of despair, that in her inability to express herself she
must give him an impression of coldness and reluctance; but
she could not help it. She could not forget that he had never
spoken to her of marriage till Mr. Royall had forced the word
from his lips; though she had not had the strength to shake
off the spell that bound her to him she had lost all spontaneity of feeling, and seemed to herself to be passively awaiting a
fate she could not avert.

She had not seen Mr. Royall on her return to the red
house. The morning after her parting from Harney, when she
came down from her room, Verena told her that her guardian
had gone off to Worcester and Portland. It was the time of
year when he usually reported to the insurance agencies he
represented, and there was nothing unusual in his departure
except its suddenness. She thought little about him, except to
be glad he was not there. . . .

She kept to herself for the first days, while North Dormer
was recovering from its brief plunge into publicity, and the
subsiding agitation left her unnoticed. But the faithful Ally
could not be long avoided. For the first few days after the
close of the Old Home Week festivities Charity escaped her by
roaming the hills all day when she was not at her post in the
library; but after that a period of rain set in, and one pouring
afternoon Ally, sure that she would find her friend indoors,
came around to the red house with her sewing.

The two girls sat upstairs in Charity's room. Charity, her
idle hands in her lap, was sunk in a kind of leaden dream,
through which she was only half-conscious of Ally, who sat

opposite her in a low rush-bottomed chair, her work pinned to her knee, and her thin lips pursed up as she bent above it.

"It was my idea running a ribbon through the gauging," she said proudly, drawing back to contemplate the blouse she was trimming. "It's for Miss Balch: she was awfully pleased." She paused and then added, with a queer tremor in her piping voice: "I darsn't have told her I got the idea from one I saw on Julia."

Charity raised her eyes listlessly. "Do you still see Julia sometimes?"

Ally reddened, as if the allusion had escaped her unintentionally. "Oh, it was a long time ago I seen her with those gaugings. . . ."

Silence fell again, and Ally presently continued: "Miss Balch left me a whole lot of things to do over this time."

"Why—has she gone?" Charity inquired with an inner start of apprehension.

"Didn't you know? She went off the morning after they had the celebration at Hamblin. I seen her drive by early with Mr. Harney."

There was another silence, measured by the steady tick of the rain against the window, and, at intervals, by the snipping sound of Ally's scissors.

Ally gave a meditative laugh. "Do you know what she told me before she went away? She told me she was going to send for me to come over to Springfield and make some things for her wedding."

Charity again lifted her heavy lids and stared at Ally's pale pointed face, which moved to and fro above her moving fingers.

"Is she going to get married?"

Ally let the blouse sink to her knee, and sat gazing at it. Her lips seemed suddenly dry, and she moistened them a little with her tongue.

"Why, I presume so . . . from what she said. . . . Didn't you know?"

"Why should I know?"

Ally did not answer. She bent above the blouse, and began picking out a basting thread with the point of the scissors.

"Why should I know?" Charity repeated harshly.

"I didn't know but what . . . folks here say she's engaged to Mr. Harney."

Charity stood up with a laugh, and stretched her arms lazily above her head.

"If all the people got married that folks say are going to you'd have your time full making wedding-dresses," she said ironically.

"Why—don't you believe it?" Ally ventured.

"It wouldn't make it true if I did—nor prevent it if I didn't."

"That's so. . . . I only know I seen her crying the night of the party because her dress didn't set right. That was why she wouldn't dance any. . . ."

Charity stood absently gazing down at the lacy garment on Ally's knee. Abruptly she stooped and snatched it up.

"Well, I guess she won't dance in this either," she said with sudden violence; and grasping the blouse in her strong young hands she tore it in two and flung the tattered bits to the floor.

"Oh, Charity——" Ally cried, springing up. For a long interval the two girls faced each other across the ruined garment. Ally burst into tears.

"Oh, what'll I say to her? What'll I do? It was real lace!" she wailed between her piping sobs.

Charity glared at her unrelentingly. "You'd oughtn't to have brought it here," she said, breathing quickly. "I hate other people's clothes—it's just as if they was there themselves." The two stared at each other again over this avowal, till Charity brought out, in a gasp of anguish: "Oh, go—go—go—or I'll hate you too. . . ."

When Ally left her, she fell sobbing across her bed.

The long storm was followed by a north-west gale, and when it was over the hills took on their first umber tints, the sky grew more densely blue, and the big white clouds lay against the hills like snow-banks. The first crisp maple-leaves began to spin across Miss Hatchard's lawn, and the Virginia creeper on the Memorial splashed the white porch with scarlet. It was a golden triumphant September. Day by day the flame of the Virginia creeper spread to the hillsides in wider waves of carmine and crimson, the larches glowed like the thin yellow halo about a fire, the maples blazed and smouldered, and the black hemlocks turned to indigo against the incandescence of the forest.

The nights were cold, with a dry glitter of stars so high up that they seemed smaller and more vivid. Sometimes, as Charity lay sleepless on her bed through the long hours, she felt as though she were bound to those wheeling fires and swinging with them around the great black vault. At night she planned many things . . . it was then she wrote to Harney. But the letters were never put on paper, for she did not know how to express what she wanted to tell him. So she waited. Since her talk with Ally she had felt sure that Harney was engaged to Annabel Balch, and that the process of "settling things" would involve the breaking of this tie. Her first rage of jealousy over, she felt no fear on this score. She was still sure that Harney would come back, and she was equally sure that, for the moment at least, it was she whom he loved and not Miss Balch. Yet the girl, no less, remained a rival, since she represented all the things that Charity felt herself most incapable of understanding or achieving. Annabel Balch was, if not the girl Harney ought to marry, at least the kind of girl it would be natural for him to marry. Charity had never been able to picture herself as his wife; had never been able to arrest the vision and follow it out in its daily consequences; but she could perfectly imagine Annabel Balch in that relation to him.

The more she thought of these things the more the sense of fatality weighed on her: she felt the uselessness of struggling against the circumstances. She had never known how to adapt herself; she could only break and tear and destroy. The scene with Ally had left her stricken with shame at her own childish savagery. What would Harney have thought if he had witnessed it? But when she turned the incident over in her puzzled mind she could not imagine what a civilized person would have done in her place. She felt herself too unequally pitted against unknown forces. . . .

At length this feeling moved her to sudden action. She took a sheet of letter paper from Mr. Royall's office, and sitting by the kitchen lamp, one night after Verena had gone to bed, began her first letter to Harney. It was very short:

I want you should marry Annabel Balch if you promised to. I think maybe you were afraid I'd feel too bad about it. I feel I'd rather you acted right.

Your loving
CHARITY.

She posted the letter early the next morning, and for a few days her heart felt strangely light. Then she began to wonder why she received no answer.

One day as she sat alone in the library pondering these things the walls of books began to spin around her, and the rosewood desk to rock under her elbows. The dizziness was followed by a wave of nausea like that she had felt on the day of the exercises in the Town Hall. But the Town Hall had been crowded and stiflingly hot, and the library was empty, and so chilly that she had kept on her jacket. Five minutes before she had felt perfectly well; and now it seemed as if she were going to die. The bit of lace at which she still languidly worked dropped from her fingers, and the steel crochet hook clattered to the floor. She pressed her temples hard between her damp hands, steadying herself against the desk while the wave of sickness swept over her. Little by little it subsided, and after a few minutes she stood up, shaken and terrified, groped for her hat, and stumbled out into the air. But the whole sunlit autumn world reeled and roared around her as she dragged herself along the interminable length of the road home.

As she approached the red house she saw a buggy standing at the door, and her heart gave a leap. But it was only Mr. Royall who got out, his travelling-bag in hand. He saw her coming, and waited in the porch. She was conscious that he was looking at her intently, as if there was something strange in her appearance, and she threw back her head with a desperate effort at ease. Their eyes met, and she said: "You back?" as if nothing had happened, and he answered: "Yes, I'm back," and walked in ahead of her, pushing open the door of his office. She climbed to her room, every step of the stairs holding her fast as if her feet were lined with glue.

Two days later, she descended from the train at Nettleton, and walked out of the station into the dusty square. The brief interval of cold weather was over, and the day was as soft, and almost as hot, as when she and Harney had emerged on the same scene on the Fourth of July. In the square the same broken-down hacks and carry-alls stood drawn up in a despondent line, and the lank horses with fly-nets over their withers swayed their heads drearily to and fro. She recognized the staring signs over the eating-houses and billiard saloons, and the long lines of wires on lofty poles tapering down the main street to the park at its other end. Taking the way the wires pointed, she went on hastily, with bent head, till she reached a wide transverse street with a brick building at the corner. She crossed this street and glanced furtively up at the front of the brick building; then she returned, and entered a door opening on a flight of steep brass-rimmed stairs. On the second landing she rang a bell, and a mulatto girl with a bushy head and a frilled apron let her into a hall where a stuffed fox on his hind legs proffered a brass card-tray to visitors. At the back of the hall was a glazed door marked: "Office." After waiting a few minutes in a handsomely furnished room, with plush sofas surmounted by large gold-framed photographs of showy young women, Charity was shown into the office. . . .

When she came out of the glazed door Dr. Merkle followed, and led her into another room, smaller, and still more crowded with plush and gold frames. Dr. Merkle was a plump woman with small bright eyes, an immense mass of black hair coming down low on her forehead, and unnaturally white and even teeth. She wore a rich black dress, with gold chains and charms hanging from her bosom. Her hands were large and smooth, and quick in all their movements; and she smelt of musk and carbolic acid.

She smiled on Charity with all her faultless teeth. "Sit down, my dear. Wouldn't you like a little drop of something to pick you up? . . . No. . . . Well, just lay back a minute then. . . . There's nothing to be done just yet; but in about a month, if you'll step round again . . . I could take you right into my own house for two or three days, and there wouldn't be a mite of trouble. Mercy me! The next time you'll know better'n to fret like this. . . ."

Charity gazed at her with widening eyes. This woman with the false hair, the false teeth, the false murderous smile— what was she offering her but immunity from some unthinkable crime? Charity, till then, had been conscious only of a vague self-disgust and a frightening physical distress; now, of a sudden, there came to her the grave surprise of motherhood. She had come to this dreadful place because she knew of no other way of making sure that she was not mistaken about her state; and the woman had taken her for a miserable creature like Julia. . . . The thought was so horrible that she sprang up, white and shaking, one of her great rushes of anger sweeping over her.

Dr. Merkle, still smiling, also rose. "Why do you run off in such a hurry? You can stretch out right here on my sofa. . . ." She paused, and her smile grew more motherly. "Afterwards—if there's been any talk at home, and you want to get away for a while . . . I have a lady friend in Boston who's looking for a companion . . . you're the very one to suit her, my dear. . . ."

Charity had reached the door. "I don't want to stay. I don't want to come back here," she stammered, her hand on the knob; but with a swift movement Dr. Merkle edged her from the threshold.

"Oh, very well. Five dollars, please."

Charity looked helplessly at the doctor's tight lips and rigid face. Her last savings had gone in repaying Ally for the cost of Miss Balch's ruined blouse, and she had had to borrow four dollars from her friend to pay for her railway ticket and cover the doctor's fee. It had never occurred to her that medical advice could cost more than two dollars.

"I didn't know . . . I haven't got that much . . ." she faltered, bursting into tears.

Dr. Merkle gave a short laugh which did not show her teeth, and inquired with concision if Charity supposed she ran the establishment for her own amusement? She leaned her firm shoulders against the door as she spoke, like a grim gaoler making terms with her captive.

"You say you'll come round and settle later? I've heard that pretty often too. Give me your address, and if you can't pay me I'll send the bill to your folks. . . . What? I can't understand what you say. . . . That don't suit you either? My, you're pretty particular for a girl that ain't got enough to settle her own bills. . . ." She paused, and fixed her eyes on the brooch with a blue stone that Charity had pinned to her blouse.

"Ain't you ashamed to talk that way to a lady that's got to earn her living, when you go about with jewellery like that on you? . . . It ain't in my line, and I do it only as a favour . . . but if you're a mind to leave that brooch as a pledge, I don't say no. . . . Yes, of course, you can get it back when you bring me my money. . . ."

On the way home, she felt an immense and unexpected quietude. It had been horrible to have to leave Harney's gift in the woman's hands, but even at that price the news she brought away had not been too dearly bought. She sat with half-closed eyes as the train rushed through the familiar landscape; and now the memories of her former journey, instead of flying before her like dead leaves, seemed to be ripening in her blood like sleeping grain. She would never again know what it was to feel herself alone. Everything seemed to have grown suddenly clear and simple. She no longer had any difficulty in picturing herself as Harney's wife now that she was the mother of his child; and compared to her sovereign right Annabel Balch's claim seemed no more than a girl's sentimental fancy.

That evening, at the gate of the red house, she found Ally waiting in the dusk. "I was down at the post-office just as they were closing up, and Will Targatt said there was a letter for you, so I brought it."

Ally held out the letter, looking at Charity with piercing sympathy. Since the scene of the torn blouse there had been a new and fearful admiration in the eyes she bent on her friend.

Charity snatched the letter with a laugh. "Oh, thank you—good-night," she called out over her shoulder as she ran up the path. If she had lingered a moment she knew she would have had Ally at her heels.

She hurried upstairs and felt her way into her dark room. Her hands trembled as she groped for the matches and lit her candle, and the flap of the envelope was so closely stuck that she had to find her scissors and slit it open. At length she read:

DEAR CHARITY:

I have your letter, and it touches me more than I can say. Won't you trust me, in return, to do my best? There are things it is hard to explain, much less to justify; but your generosity makes everything easier. All I can do now is to thank you from my soul for understanding. Your telling me that you wanted me to do right has helped me beyond expression. If ever there is a hope of realizing what we dreamed of you will see me back on the instant; and I haven't yet lost that hope.

She read the letter with a rush; then she went over and over it, each time more slowly and painstakingly. It was so beautifully expressed that she found it almost as difficult to understand as the gentleman's explanation of the Bible pictures at Nettleton; but gradually she became aware that the gist of its meaning lay in the last few words. "If ever there is a hope of realizing what we dreamed of . . ."

But then he wasn't even sure of that? She understood now that every word and every reticence was an avowal of Annabel Balch's prior claim. It was true that he was engaged to her, and that he had not yet found a way of breaking his engagement.

As she read the letter over Charity understood what it must have cost him to write it. He was not trying to evade an importunate claim; he was honestly and contritely struggling between opposing duties. She did not even reproach him in her thoughts for having concealed from her that he was not free: she could not see anything more reprehensible in his conduct than in her own. From the first she had needed him more than he had wanted her, and the power that had swept them together had been as far beyond resistance as a great gale loosening the leaves of the forest. . . . Only, there stood between them, fixed and upright in the general upheaval, the indestructible figure of Annabel Balch. . . .

Face to face with his admission of the fact, she sat staring at the letter. A cold tremor ran over her, and the hard sobs struggled up into her throat and shook her from head to foot.

For a while she was caught and tossed on great waves of anguish that left her hardly conscious of anything but the blind struggle against their assaults. Then, little by little, she began to relive, with a dreadful poignancy, each separate stage of her poor romance. Foolish things she had said came back to her, gay answers Harney had made, his first kiss in the darkness between the fireworks, their choosing the blue brooch together, the way he had teased her about the letters she had dropped in her flight from the evangelist. All these memories, and a thousand others, hummed through her brain till his nearness grew so vivid that she felt his fingers in her hair, and his warm breath on her cheek as he bent her head back like a flower. These things were hers; they had passed into her blood, and become a part of her, they were building the child in her womb; it was impossible to tear asunder strands of life so interwoven.

The conviction gradually strengthened her, and she began to form in her mind the first words of the letter she meant to write to Harney. She wanted to write it at once, and with feverish hands she began to rummage in her drawer for a sheet of letter paper. But there was none left; she must go downstairs to get it. She had a superstitious feeling that the letter must be written on the instant, that setting down her secret in words would bring her reassurance and safety; and taking up her candle she went down to Mr. Royall's office.

At that hour she was not likely to find him there: he had probably had his supper and walked over to Carrick Fry's. She pushed open the door of the unlit room, and the light of her lifted candle fell on his figure, seated in the darkness in his high-backed chair. His arms lay along the arms of the chair, and his head was bent a little; but he lifted it quickly as Charity entered. She started back as their eyes met, remembering that her own were red with weeping, and that her face was livid with the fatigue and emotion of her journey. But it was too late to escape, and she stood and looked at him in silence.

He had risen from his chair, and came toward her with outstretched hands. The gesture was so unexpected that she let him take her hands in his, and they stood thus, without speaking, till Mr. Royall said gravely: "Charity—was you looking for me?"

She freed herself abruptly and fell back. "Me? No——" She set down the candle on his desk. "I wanted some letter-paper, that's all."

His face contracted, and the bushy brows jutted forward over his eyes. Without answering he opened the drawer of the desk, took out a sheet of paper and an envelope, and pushed them toward her. "Do you want a stamp too?" he asked.

She nodded, and he gave her the stamp. As he did so she felt that he was looking at her intently, and she knew that the candle light flickering up on her white face must be distorting her swollen features and exaggerating the dark rings about her eyes. She snatched up the paper, her reassurance dissolving under his pitiless gaze, in which she seemed to read the grim perception of her state, and the ironic recollection of the day when, in that very room, he had offered to compel Harney to marry her. His look seemed to say that he knew she had taken the paper to write to her lover, who had left her as he had warned her she would be left. She remembered the scorn with which she had turned from him that day, and knew, if he guessed the truth, what a list of old scores it must settle. She turned and fled upstairs; but when she got back to her room all the words that had been waiting had vanished. . . .

If she could have gone to Harney it would have been different; she would only have had to show herself to let his memories speak for her. But she had no money left, and there was no one from whom she could have borrowed enough for such a journey. There was nothing to do but to write, and await his reply. For a long time she sat bent above the blank page; but she found nothing to say that really expressed what she was feeling. . . .

Harney had written that she had made it easier for him, and she was glad it was so; she did not want to make things hard. She knew she had it in her power to do that; she held his fate in her hands. All she had to do was to tell him the truth; but that was the very fact that held her back. . . . Her five minutes face to face with Mr. Royall had stripped her of her last illusion, and brought her back to North Dormer's point of view. Distinctly and pitilessly there rose before her the fate of the girl who was married "to make things right."

She had seen too many village love-stories end in that way. Poor Rose Coles's miserable marriage was of the number; and what good had come of it for her or for Halston Skeff? They had hated each other from the day the minister married them; and whenever old Mrs. Skeff had a fancy to humiliate her daughter-in-law she had only to say: "Who'd ever think the baby's only two? And for a seven months' child—ain't it a wonder what a size he is?" North Dormer had treasures of indulgence for brands in the burning, but only derision for those who succeeded in getting snatched from it; and Charity had always understood Julia Hawes's refusal to be snatched. . . .

Only—was there no alternative but Julia's? Her soul recoiled from the vision of the white-faced woman among the plush sofas and gilt frames. In the established order of things as she knew them she saw no place for her individual adventure. . . .

She sat in her chair without undressing till faint grey streaks began to divide the black slats of the shutters. Then she stood up and pushed them open, letting in the light. The coming of a new day brought a sharper consciousness of ineluctable reality, and with it a sense of the need of action. She looked at herself in the glass, and saw her face, white in the autumn dawn, with pinched cheeks and dark-ringed eyes, and all the marks of her state that she herself would never have noticed, but that Dr. Merkle's diagnosis had made plain to her. She could not hope that those signs would escape the watchful village; even before her figure lost its shape she knew her face would betray her.

Leaning from her window she looked out on the dark and empty scene; the ashen houses with shuttered windows, the grey road climbing the slope to the hemlock belt above the cemetery, and the heavy mass of the Mountain black against a rainy sky. To the east a space of light was broadening above the forest; but over that also the clouds hung. Slowly her gaze travelled across the fields to the rugged curve of the hills. She had looked out so often on that lifeless circle, and wondered if anything could ever happen to anyone who was enclosed in it. . . .

Almost without conscious thought her decision had been

reached; as her eyes had followed the circle of the hills her mind had also travelled the old round. She supposed it was something in her blood that made the Mountain the only answer to her questioning, the inevitable escape from all that hemmed her in and beset her. At any rate it began to loom in her now as it loomed against the rainy dawn; and the longer she looked at it the more clearly she understood that now at last she was really going there.

XVI

Tʜᴇ ʀᴀɪɴ held off, and an hour later, when she started, wild gleams of sunlight were blowing across the fields.

After Harney's departure she had returned her bicycle to its owner at Creston, and she was not sure of being able to walk all the way to the Mountain. The deserted house was on the road; but the idea of spending the night there was unendurable, and she meant to try to push on to Hamblin, where she could sleep under a wood-shed if her strength should fail her. Her preparations had been made with quiet forethought. Before starting she had forced herself to swallow a glass of milk and eat a piece of bread; and she had put in her canvas satchel a little packet of the chocolate that Harney always carried in his bicycle bag. She wanted above all to keep up her strength, and reach her destination without attracting notice. . . .

Mile by mile she retraced the road over which she had so often flown to her lover. When she reached the turn where the wood-road branched off from the Creston highway she remembered the Gospel tent—long since folded up and transplanted—and her start of involuntary terror when the fat evangelist had said: "Your Saviour knows everything. Come and confess your guilt." There was no sense of guilt in her now, but only a desperate desire to defend her secret from irreverent eyes, and begin life again among people to whom the harsh code of the village was unknown. The impulse did not shape itself in thought: she only knew she must save her baby, and hide herself with it somewhere where no one would ever come to trouble them.

She walked on and on, growing more heavy-footed as the day advanced. It seemed a cruel chance that compelled her to retrace every step of the way to the deserted house; and when she came in sight of the orchard, and the silver-gray roof slanting crookedly through the laden branches, her strength failed her and she sat down by the roadside. She sat there a long time, trying to gather the courage to start again, and walk past the broken gate and the untrimmed rose-bushes strung with scarlet hips. A few drops of rain were falling, and she thought of the warm evenings when she and Harney had sat embraced in the shadowy room, and the noise of summer showers on the roof had rustled through their kisses. At length she understood that if she stayed any longer the rain might compel her to take shelter in the house overnight, and she got up and walked on, averting her eyes as she came abreast of the white gate and the tangled garden.

The hours wore on, and she walked more and more slowly, pausing now and then to rest, and to eat a little bread and an apple picked up from the roadside. Her body seemed to grow heavier with every yard of the way, and she wondered how she would be able to carry her child later, if already he laid such a burden on her. . . . A fresh wind had sprung up, scattering the rain and blowing down keenly from the mountain. Presently the clouds lowered again, and a few white darts struck her in the face: it was the first snow falling over Hamblin. The roofs of the lonely village were only half a mile ahead, and she was resolved to push beyond it, and try to reach the Mountain that night. She had no clear plan of action, except that, once in the settlement, she meant to look for Liff Hyatt, and get him to take her to her mother. She herself had been born as her own baby was going to be born; and whatever her mother's subsequent life had been, she could hardly help remembering the past, and receiving a daughter who was facing the trouble she had known.

Suddenly the deadly faintness came over her once more and she sat down on the bank and leaned her head against a tree-trunk. The long road and the cloudy landscape vanished from her eyes, and for a time she seemed to be circling about in some terrible wheeling darkness. Then that too faded.

She opened her eyes, and saw a buggy drawn up beside her, and a man who had jumped down from it and was gazing at her with a puzzled face. Slowly consciousness came back, and she saw that the man was Liff Hyatt.

She was dimly aware that he was asking her something, and she looked at him in silence, trying to find strength to speak. At length her voice stirred in her throat, and she said in a whisper: "I'm going up the Mountain."

"Up the Mountain?" he repeated, drawing aside a little; and as he moved she saw behind him, in the buggy, a heavily coated figure with a familiar pink face and gold spectacles on the bridge of a Grecian nose.

"Charity! What on earth are you doing here?" Mr. Miles exclaimed, throwing the reins on the horse's back and scrambling down from the buggy.

She lifted her heavy eyes to his. "I'm going to see my mother."

The two men glanced at each other, and for a moment neither of them spoke.

Then Mr. Miles said: "You look ill, my dear, and it's a long way. Do you think it's wise?"

Charity stood up. "I've got to go to her."

A vague mirthless grin contracted Liff Hyatt's face, and Mr. Miles again spoke uncertainly. "You know, then—you'd been told?"

She stared at him. "I don't know what you mean. I want to go to her."

Mr. Miles was examining her thoughtfully. She fancied she saw a change in his expression, and the blood rushed to her forehead. "I just want to go to her," she repeated.

He laid his hand on her arm. "My child, your mother is dying. Liff Hyatt came down to fetch me. . . . Get in and come with us."

He helped her up to the seat at his side, Liff Hyatt clambered in at the back, and they drove off toward Hamblin. At first Charity had hardly grasped what Mr. Miles was saying; the physical relief of finding herself seated in the buggy, and securely on her road to the Mountain, effaced the impression of his words. But as her head cleared she began to understand. She knew the Mountain had but the most infrequent intercourse with the valleys; she had often enough heard it said that no one ever went up there except the minister, when someone was dying. And now it was her mother who was dying . . . and she would find herself as much alone on the Mountain as anywhere else in the world. The sense of unescapable isolation was all she could feel for the moment; then she began to wonder at the strangeness of its being Mr. Miles who had undertaken to perform this grim errand. He did not seem in the least like the kind of man who would care to go up the Mountain. But here he was at her side, guiding the horse with a firm hand, and bending on her the kindly gleam of his spectacles, as if there were nothing unusual in their being together in such circumstances.

For a while she found it impossible to speak, and he seemed to understand this, and made no attempt to question her. But presently she felt her tears rise and flow down over her drawn cheeks; and he must have seen them too, for he laid his hand on hers, and said in a low voice: "Won't you tell me what is troubling you?"

She shook her head, and he did not insist: but after a while he said, in the same low tone, so that they should not be overheard: "Charity, what do you know of your childhood, before you came down to North Dormer?"

She controlled herself, and answered: "Nothing, only what I heard Mr. Royall say one day. He said he brought me down because my father went to prison."

"And you've never been up there since?"

"Never."

Mr. Miles was silent again, then he said: "I'm glad you're coming with me now. Perhaps we may find your mother alive, and she may know that you have come."

They had reached Hamblin, where the snow-flurry had left white patches in the rough grass on the roadside, and in the angles of the roofs facing north. It was a poor bleak village under the granite flank of the Mountain, and as soon as they left it they began to climb. The road was steep and full of ruts, and the horse settled down to a walk while they mounted and mounted, the world dropping away below them in great mottled stretches of forest and field, and stormy dark blue distances.

Charity had often had visions of this ascent of the Mountain but she had not known it would reveal so wide a country, and the sight of those strange lands reaching away on every side gave her a new sense of Harney's remoteness. She knew he must be miles and miles beyond the last range of hills that seemed to be the outmost verge of things, and she wondered how she had ever dreamed of going to New York to find him. . . .

As the road mounted the country grew bleaker, and they drove across fields of faded mountain grass bleached by long months beneath the snow. In the hollows a few white birches trembled, or a mountain ash lit its scarlet clusters; but only a scant growth of pines darkened the granite ledges. The wind was blowing fiercely across the open slopes; the horse faced it with bent head and straining flanks, and now and then the buggy swayed so that Charity had to clutch its side.

Mr. Miles had not spoken again; he seemed to understand that she wanted to be left alone. After a while the track they were following forked, and he pulled up the horse, as if uncertain of the way. Liff Hyatt craned his head around from the back, and shouted against the wind: "Left——" and they turned into a stunted pine-wood and began to drive down the other side of the Mountain.

A mile or two farther on they came out on a clearing where two or three low houses lay in stony fields, crouching among the rocks as if to brace themselves against the wind. They were hardly more than sheds, built of logs and rough boards, with tin stove-pipes sticking out of their roofs. The sun was setting, and dusk had already fallen on the lower world, but a yellow glare still lay on the lonely hillside and the crouching houses. The next moment it faded and left the landscape in dark autumn twilight.

"Over there," Liff called out, stretching his long arm over Mr. Miles's shoulder. The clergyman turned to the left, across a bit of bare ground overgrown with docks and nettles, and stopped before the most ruinous of the sheds. A stove-pipe reached its crooked arm out of one window, and the broken panes of the other were stuffed with rags and paper. In contrast to such a dwelling the brown house in the swamp might have stood for the home of plenty.

As the buggy drew up two or three mongrel dogs jumped out of the twilight with a great barking, and a young man slouched to the door and stood there staring. In the twilight Charity saw that his face had the same sodden look as Bash Hyatt's, the day she had seen him sleeping by the stove. He made no effort to silence the dogs, but leaned in the door, as if roused from a drunken lethargy, while Mr. Miles got out of the buggy.

"Is it here?" the clergyman asked Liff in a low voice; and Liff nodded.

Mr. Miles turned to Charity. "Just hold the horse a minute, my dear: I'll go in first," he said, putting the reins in her hands. She took them passively, and sat staring straight ahead of her at the darkening scene while Mr. Miles and Liff Hyatt went up to the house. They stood a few minutes talking with the man in the door, and then Mr. Miles came back. As he came close, Charity saw that his smooth pink face wore a frightened solemn look.

"Your mother is dead, Charity; you'd better come with me," he said.

She got down and followed him while Liff led the horse away. As she approached the door she said to herself: "This is where I was born . . . this is where I belong. . . ." She had said it to herself often enough as she looked across the sunlit valleys at the Mountain; but it had meant nothing then, and now it had become a reality. Mr. Miles took her gently by the arm, and they entered what appeared to be the only room in the house. It was so dark that she could just discern a group of a dozen people sitting or sprawling about a table made of boards laid across two barrels. They looked up listlessly as Mr. Miles and Charity came in, and a woman's thick voice said: "Here's the preacher." But no one moved.

Mr. Miles paused and looked about him; then he turned to the young man who had met them at the door.

"Is the body here?" he asked.

The young man, instead of answering, turned his head toward the group. "Where's the candle? I tole yer to bring a candle," he said with sudden harshness to a girl who was lolling against the table. She did not answer, but another man got up and took from some corner a candle stuck into a bottle.

"How'll I light it? The stove's out," the girl grumbled.

Mr. Miles fumbled under his heavy wrappings and drew out a match-box. He held a match to the candle, and in a moment or two a faint circle of light fell on the pale aguish heads that started out of the shadow like the heads of nocturnal animals.

"Mary's over there," someone said; and Mr. Miles, taking the bottle in his hand, passed behind the table. Charity followed him, and they stood before a mattress on the floor in a corner of the room. A woman lay on it, but she did not look like a dead woman; she seemed to have fallen across her squalid bed in a drunken sleep, and to have been left lying where she fell, in her ragged disordered clothes. One arm was flung above her head, one leg drawn up under a torn skirt that left the other bare to the knee: a swollen glistening leg with a ragged stocking rolled down about the ankle. The woman lay on her back, her eyes staring up unblinkingly at the candle that trembled in Mr. Miles's hand.

"She jus' dropped off," a woman said, over the shoulder of the others; and the young man added: "I jus' come in and found her."

An elderly man with lank hair and a feeble grin pushed between them. "It was like this: I says to her on'y the night before: if you don't take and quit, I says to her . . ."

Someone pulled him back and sent him reeling against a bench along the wall, where he dropped down muttering his unheeded narrative.

There was a silence; then the young woman who had been lolling against the table suddenly parted the group, and stood in front of Charity. She was healthier and robuster looking than the others, and her weather-beaten face had a certain sullen beauty.

"Who's the girl? Who brought her here?" she said, fixing her eyes mistrustfully on the young man who had rebuked her for not having a candle ready.

Mr. Miles spoke. "I brought her; she is Mary Hyatt's daughter."

"What? Her too?" the girl sneered; and the young man turned on her with an oath. "Shut your mouth, damn you, or get out of here," he said; then he relapsed into his former apathy, and dropped down on the bench, leaning his head against the wall.

Mr. Miles had set the candle on the floor and taken off his heavy coat. He turned to Charity. "Come and help me," he said.

He knelt down by the mattress, and pressed the lids over the dead woman's eyes. Charity, trembling and sick, knelt beside him, and tried to compose her mother's body. She drew the stocking over the dreadful glistening leg, and pulled the skirt down to the battered upturned boots. As she did so, she looked at her mother's face, thin yet swollen, with lips parted in a frozen gasp above the broken teeth. There was no sign in it of anything human: she lay there like a dead dog in a ditch. Charity's hands grew cold as they touched her.

Mr. Miles drew the woman's arms across her breast and laid his coat over her. Then he covered her face with his handkerchief, and placed the bottle with the candle in it at her head. Having done this he stood up.

"Is there no coffin?" he asked, turning to the group behind him.

There was a moment of bewildered silence; then the fierce girl spoke up. "You'd oughter brought it with you. Where'd we get one here, I'd like ter know?"

Mr. Miles, looking at the others, repeated: "Is it possible you have no coffin ready?"

"That's what I say: them that has it sleeps better," an old woman murmured. "But then she never had no bed. . . ."

"And the stove warn't hers," said the lank-haired man, on the defensive.

Mr. Miles turned away from them and moved a few steps apart. He had drawn a book from his pocket, and after a pause he opened it and began to read, holding the book at arm's length and low down, so that the pages caught the feeble light. Charity had remained on her knees by the mattress: now that her mother's face was covered it was easier to stay near her, and avoid the sight of the living faces which too horribly showed by what stages hers had lapsed into death.

"I am the Resurrection and the Life," Mr. Miles began; "he that believeth in me, though he were dead, yet shall he live. . . . Though after my skin worms destroy my body, yet in my flesh shall I see God. . . ."

In my flesh shall I see God! Charity thought of the gaping mouth and stony eyes under the handkerchief, and of the glistening leg over which she had drawn the stocking. . . .

"We brought nothing into this world and we shall take nothing out of it——"

There was a sudden muttering and a scuffle at the back of the group. "I brought the stove," said the elderly man with lank hair, pushing his way between the others. "I wen' down to Creston'n bought it . . . n' I got a right to take it outer here . . . n' I'll lick any feller says I ain't. . . ."

"Sit down, damn you!" shouted the tall youth who had been drowsing on the bench against the wall.

"For man walketh in a vain shadow, and disquieteth himself in vain; he heapeth up riches and cannot tell who shall gather them . . ."

"Well, it *are* his," a woman in the background interjected in a frightened whine.

The tall youth staggered to his feet. "If you don't hold your mouths I'll turn you all out o' here, the whole lot of you," he cried with many oaths. "G'wan, minister . . . don't let 'em faze you. . . ."

"Now is Christ risen from the dead and become the first-fruits of them that slept. . . . Behold, I show you a mystery. We shall not all sleep, but we shall all be changed, in a moment, in the twinkling of an eye, at the last trump. . . . For this corruptible must put on incorruption and this mortal must put on immortality. So when this corruption shall have put on incorruption, and when this mortal shall have put on immortality, then shall be brought to pass the saying that is written, Death is swallowed up in Victory. . . ."

One by one the mighty words fell on Charity's bowed head, soothing the horror, subduing the tumult, mastering her as they mastered the drink-dazed creatures at her back. Mr. Miles read to the last word, and then closed the book.

"Is the grave ready?" he asked.

Liff Hyatt, who had come in while he was reading, nodded a "Yes," and pushed forward to the side of the mattress. The young man on the bench, who seemed to assert some sort of right of kinship with the dead woman, got to his feet again, and the proprietor of the stove joined him. Between them they raised up the mattress; but their movements were unsteady, and the coat slipped to the floor, revealing the poor body in its helpless misery. Charity, picking up the coat, covered her mother once more. Liff had brought a lantern, and the old woman who had already spoken took it up, and opened the door to let the little procession pass out. The wind had dropped, and the night was very dark and bitterly cold. The old woman walked ahead, the lantern shaking in her hand and spreading out before her a pale patch of dead grass and coarse-leaved weeds enclosed in an immensity of blackness.

Mr. Miles took Charity by the arm, and side by side they walked behind the mattress. At length the old woman with the lantern stopped, and Charity saw the light fall on the stooping shoulders of the bearers and on a ridge of upheaved earth over which they were bending. Mr. Miles released her arm and approached the hollow on the other side of the ridge; and while the men stooped down, lowering the mattress into the grave, he began to speak again.

"Man that is born of woman hath but a short time to live and is full of misery. . . . He cometh up and is cut down . . . he fleeth as it were a shadow. . . . Yet, O Lord God most holy, O Lord most mighty, O holy and merciful Saviour, deliver us not into the bitter pains of eternal death . . ."

"Easy there . . . is she down?" piped the claimant to the stove; and the young man called over his shoulder: "Lift the light there, can't you?"

There was a pause, during which the light floated uncertainly over the open grave. Someone bent over and pulled out Mr. Miles's coat——("No, no—leave the handkerchief," he interposed)—and then Liff Hyatt, coming forward with a spade, began to shovel in the earth.

"Forasmuch as it hath pleased Almighty God of His great mercy to take unto Himself the soul of our dear sister here departed, we therefore commit her body to the ground; earth to earth, ashes to ashes, dust to dust . . ." Liff's gaunt shoulders rose and bent in the lantern light as he dashed the clods of earth into the grave. "God—it's froze a'ready," he muttered, spitting into his palm and passing his ragged shirt-sleeve across his perspiring face.

"Through our Lord Jesus Christ, who shall change our vile body that it may be like unto His glorious body, according to the mighty working, whereby He is able to subdue all things unto Himself . . ." The last spadeful of earth fell on the vile body of Mary Hyatt, and Liff rested on his spade, his shoulder blades still heaving with the effort.

"Lord, have mercy upon us, Christ have mercy upon us, Lord have mercy upon us. . . ."

Mr. Miles took the lantern from the old woman's hand and swept its light across the circle of bleared faces. "Now kneel down, all of you," he commanded, in a voice of authority that Charity had never heard. She knelt down at the edge of the grave, and the others, stiffly and hesitatingly, got to their knees beside her. Mr. Miles knelt, too. "And now pray with me—you know this prayer," he said, and he began: "Our Father which art in Heaven . . ." One or two of the women falteringly took the words up, and when he ended, the lank-haired man flung himself on the neck of the tall youth. "It was this way," he said. "I tole her the night before, I says to her . . ." The reminiscence ended in a sob.

Mr. Miles had been getting into his coat again. He came up to Charity, who had remained passively kneeling by the rough mound of earth.

"My child, you must come. It's very late."

She lifted her eyes to his face: he seemed to speak out of another world.

"I ain't coming: I'm going to stay here."

"Here? Where? What do you mean?"

"These are my folks. I'm going to stay with them."

Mr. Miles lowered his voice. "But it's not possible—you don't know what you are doing. You can't stay among these people: you must come with me."

She shook her head and rose from her knees. The group about the grave had scattered in the darkness, but the old woman with the lantern stood waiting. Her mournful withered face was not unkind, and Charity went up to her.

"Have you got a place where I can lie down for the night?" she asked. Liff came up, leading the buggy out of the night. He looked from one to the other with his feeble smile. "She's my mother. She'll take you home," he said; and he added, raising his voice to speak to the old woman: "It's the girl from lawyer Royall's—Mary's girl . . . you remember. . . ."

The woman nodded and raised her sad old eyes to Charity's. When Mr. Miles and Liff clambered into the buggy she went ahead with the lantern to show them the track they were to follow; then she turned back, and in silence she and Charity walked away together through the night.

XVII

C HARITY LAY on the floor on a mattress, as her dead mother's body had lain. The room in which she lay was cold and dark and low-ceilinged, and even poorer and barer than the scene of Mary Hyatt's earthly pilgrimage. On the other side of the fireless stove Liff Hyatt's mother slept on a blanket, with two children—her grandchildren, she said— rolled up against her like sleeping puppies. They had their thin clothes spread over them, having given the only other blanket to their guest.

Through the small square of glass in the opposite wall Charity saw a deep funnel of sky, so black, so remote, so palpitating with frosty stars that her very soul seemed to be sucked up into it. Up there somewhere, she supposed, the God whom Mr. Miles had invoked was waiting for Mary Hyatt to appear. What a long flight it was! And what would she have to say when she reached Him?

Charity's bewildered brain laboured with the attempt to picture her mother's past, and to relate it in any way to the designs of a just but merciful God; but it was impossible to imagine any link between them. She herself felt as remote from the poor creature she had seen lowered into her hastily dug grave as if the height of the heavens had divided them. She had seen poverty and misfortune in her life; but in a community where poor thrifty Mrs. Hawes and the industrious Ally represented the nearest approach to destitution there was nothing to suggest the savage misery of the Mountain farmers.

As she lay there, half-stunned by her tragic initiation, Charity vainly tried to think herself into the life about her. But she could not even make out what relationship these people bore to each other, or to her dead mother; they seemed to be herded together in a sort of passive promiscuity in which their common misery was the strongest link. She tried to picture to herself what her life would have been if she had grown up on the Mountain, running wild in rags, sleeping on the floor curled up against her mother, like the pale-faced children huddled against old Mrs. Hyatt, and turning into a fierce bewildered creature like the girl who had apostrophized her in such strange words. She was frightened by the secret affinity she had felt with this girl, and by the light it threw on her own beginnings. Then she remembered what Mr. Royall had said in telling her story to Lucius Harney: "Yes, there was a mother; but she was glad to have the child go. She'd have given her to anybody. . . ."

Well! after all, was her mother so much to blame? Charity, since that day, had always thought of her as destitute of all human feeling; now she seemed merely pitiful. What mother would not want to save her child from such a life? Charity thought of the future of her own child, and tears welled into her aching eyes, and ran down over her face. If she had been less exhausted, less burdened with his weight, she would have sprung up then and there and fled away. . . .

The grim hours of the night dragged themselves slowly by, and at last the sky paled and dawn threw a cold blue beam into the room. She lay in her corner staring at the dirty floor, the clothes-line hung with decaying rags, the old woman huddled against the cold stove, and the light gradually spreading across the wintry world, and bringing with it a new day in which she would have to live, to choose, to act, to make herself a place among these people—or to go back to the life she had left. A mortal lassitude weighed on her. There were moments when she felt that all she asked was to go on lying there unnoticed; then her mind revolted at the thought of becoming one of the miserable herd from which she sprang, and it seemed as though, to save her child from such a fate, she would find strength to travel any distance, and bear any burden life might put on her.

Vague thoughts of Nettleton flitted through her mind. She said to herself that she would find some quiet place where she could bear her child, and give it to decent people to keep; and then she would go out like Julia Hawes and earn its living and hers. She knew that girls of that kind sometimes made enough to have their children nicely cared for; and every other consideration disappeared in the vision of her baby, cleaned and combed and rosy, and hidden away

somewhere where she could run in and kiss it, and bring it
pretty things to wear. Anything, anything was better than to
add another life to the nest of misery on the Mountain. . . .

The old woman and the children were still sleeping when
Charity rose from her mattress. Her body was stiff with cold
and fatigue, and she moved slowly lest her heavy steps should
rouse them. She was faint with hunger, and had nothing left
in her satchel; but on the table she saw the half of a stale loaf.
No doubt it was to serve as the breakfast of old Mrs. Hyatt
and the children; but Charity did not care; she had her own
baby to think of. She broke off a piece of the bread and ate it
greedily; then her glance fell on the thin faces of the sleeping
children, and filled with compunction she rummaged in her
satchel for something with which to pay for what she had
taken. She found one of the pretty chemises that Ally had
made for her, with a blue ribbon run through its edging. It
was one of the dainty things on which she had squandered
her savings, and as she looked at it the blood rushed to her
forehead. She laid the chemise on the table, and stealing
across the floor lifted the latch and went out. . . .

The morning was icy cold and a pale sun was just rising
above the eastern shoulder of the Mountain. The houses scattered on the hillside lay cold and smokeless under the sun-
flecked clouds, and not a human being was in sight. Charity
paused on the threshold and tried to discover the road by
which she had come the night before. Across the field surrounding Mrs. Hyatt's shanty she saw the tumble-down
house in which she supposed the funeral service had taken
place. The trail ran across the ground between the two houses
and disappeared in the pine-wood on the flank of the Mountain; and a little way to the right, under a wind-beaten thorn,
a mound of fresh earth made a dark spot on the fawn-
coloured stubble. Charity walked across the field to the
mound. As she approached it she heard a bird's note in the still
air, and looking up she saw a brown song-sparrow perched in
an upper branch of the thorn above the grave. She stood a
minute listening to his small solitary song; then she rejoined
the trail and began to mount the hill to the pine-wood.

Thus far she had been impelled by the blind instinct of
flight; but each step seemed to bring her nearer to the realities

of which her feverish vigil had given only a shadowy image. Now that she walked again in a daylight world, on the way back to familiar things, her imagination moved more soberly. On one point she was still decided: she could not remain at North Dormer, and the sooner she got away from it the better. But everything beyond was darkness.

As she continued to climb the air grew keener, and when she passed from the shelter of the pines to the open grassy roof of the Mountain the cold wind of the night before sprang out on her. She bent her shoulders and struggled on against it for a while; but presently her breath failed, and she sat down under a ledge of rock overhung by shivering birches. From where she sat she saw the trail wandering across the bleached grass in the direction of Hamblin, and the granite wall of the Mountain falling away to infinite distances. On that side of the ridge the valleys still lay in wintry shadow; but in the plain beyond the sun was touching village roofs and steeples, and gilding the haze of smoke over far-off invisible towns.

Charity felt herself a mere speck in the lonely circle of the sky. The events of the last two days seemed to have divided her forever from her short dream of bliss. Even Harney's image had been blurred by that crushing experience: she thought of him as so remote from her that he seemed hardly more than a memory. In her fagged and floating mind only one sensation had the weight of reality; it was the bodily burden of her child. But for it she would have felt as rootless as the whiffs of thistledown the wind blew past her. Her child was like a load that held her down, and yet like a hand that pulled her to her feet. She said to herself that she must get up and struggle on. . . .

Her eyes turned back to the trail across the top of the Mountain, and in the distance she saw a buggy against the sky. She knew its antique outline, and the gaunt build of the old horse pressing forward with lowered head; and after a moment she recognized the heavy bulk of the man who held the reins. The buggy was following the trail and making straight for the pine-wood through which she had climbed; and she knew at once that the driver was in search of her. Her first impulse was to crouch down under the ledge till he had

passed; but the instinct of concealment was overruled by the
relief of feeling that someone was near her in the awful emptiness. She stood up and walked toward the buggy.

Mr. Royall saw her, and touched the horse with the whip.
A minute or two later he was abreast of Charity; their eyes
met, and without speaking he leaned over and helped her up
into the buggy. She tried to speak, to stammer out some explanation, but no words came to her; and as he drew the
cover over her knees he simply said: "The minister told me
he'd left you up here, so I come up for you."

He turned the horse's head, and they began to jog back
toward Hamblin. Charity sat speechless, staring straight
ahead of her, and Mr. Royall occasionally uttered a word of
encouragement to the horse: "Get along there, Dan. . . . I
gave him a rest at Hamblin; but I brought him along pretty
quick, and it's a stiff pull up here against the wind."

As he spoke it occurred to her for the first time that to
reach the top of the Mountain so early he must have left
North Dormer at the coldest hour of the night, and have travelled steadily but for the halt at Hamblin; and she felt a softness at her heart which no act of his had ever produced since
he had brought her the Crimson Rambler because she had
given up boarding-school to stay with him.

After an interval he began again: "It was a day just like this,
only spitting snow, when I come up here for you the first
time." Then, as if fearing that she might take his remark as a
reminder of past benefits, he added quickly: "I dunno's you
think it was such a good job, either."

"Yes, I do," she murmured, looking straight ahead of her.

"Well," he said, "I tried——"

He did not finish the sentence, and she could think of nothing more to say.

"Ho, there, Dan, step out," he muttered, jerking the bridle.
"We ain't home yet. — You cold?" he asked abruptly.

She shook her head, but he drew the cover higher up, and
stooped to tuck it in about the ankles. She continued to look
straight ahead. Tears of weariness and weakness were dim-
ming her eyes and beginning to run over, but she dared not
wipe them away lest he should observe the gesture.

They drove in silence, following the long loops of the

descent upon Hamblin, and Mr. Royall did not speak again till they reached the outskirts of the village. Then he let the reins droop on the dashboard and drew out his watch.

"Charity," he said, "you look fair done up, and North Dormer's a goodish way off. I've figured out that we'd do better to stop here long enough for you to get a mouthful of breakfast and then drive down to Creston and take the train."

She roused herself from her apathetic musing. "The train—what train?"

Mr. Royall, without answering, let the horse jog on till they reached the door of the first house in the village. "This is old Mrs. Hobart's place," he said. "She'll give us something hot to drink."

Charity, half unconsciously, found herself getting out of the buggy and following him in at the open door. They entered a decent kitchen with a fire crackling in the stove. An old woman with a kindly face was setting out cups and saucers on the table. She looked up and nodded as they came in, and Mr. Royall advanced to the stove, clapping his numb hands together.

"Well, Mrs. Hobart, you got any breakfast for this young lady? You can see she's cold and hungry."

Mrs. Hobart smiled on Charity and took a tin coffee-pot from the fire. "My, you do look pretty mean," she said compassionately.

Charity reddened, and sat down at the table. A feeling of complete passiveness had once more come over her, and she was conscious only of the pleasant animal sensations of warmth and rest.

Mrs. Hobart put bread and milk on the table, and then went out of the house: Charity saw her leading the horse away to the barn across the yard. She did not come back, and Mr. Royall and Charity sat alone at the table with the smoking coffee between them. He poured out a cup for her, and put a piece of bread in the saucer, and she began to eat.

As the warmth of the coffee flowed through her veins her thoughts cleared and she began to feel like a living being again; but the return to life was so painful that the food choked in her throat and she sat staring down at the table in silent anguish.

After a while Mr. Royall pushed back his chair. "Now, then," he said, "if you're a mind to go along——" She did not move, and he continued: "We can pick up the noon train for Nettleton if you say so."

The words sent the blood rushing to her face, and she raised her startled eyes to his. He was standing on the other side of the table looking at her kindly and gravely; and suddenly she understood what he was going to say. She continued to sit motionless, a leaden weight upon her lips.

"You and me have spoke some hard things to each other in our time, Charity; and there's no good that I can see in any more talking now. But I'll never feel any way but one about you; and if you say so we'll drive down in time to catch that train, and go straight to the minister's house; and when you come back home you'll come as Mrs. Royall."

His voice had the grave persuasive accent that had moved his hearers at the Home Week festival; she had a sense of depths of mournful tolerance under that easy tone. Her whole body began to tremble with the dread of her own weakness.

"Oh, I can't——" she burst out desperately.

"Can't what?"

She herself did not know: she was not sure if she was rejecting what he offered, or already struggling against the temptation of taking what she no longer had a right to. She stood up, shaking and bewildered, and began to speak:

"I know I ain't been fair to you always; but I want to be now. . . . I want you to know . . . I want . . ." Her voice failed her and she stopped.

Mr. Royall leaned against the wall. He was paler than usual, but his face was composed and kindly and her agitation did not appear to perturb him.

"What's all this about wanting?" he said as she paused. "Do you know what you really want? I'll tell you. You want to be took home and took care of. And I guess that's all there is to say."

"No . . . it's not all. . . ."

"Ain't it?" He looked at his watch. "Well, I'll tell you another thing. All *I* want is to know if you'll marry me. If there was anything else, I'd tell you so; but there ain't. Come to my age, a man knows the things that matter and the things that don't; that's about the only good turn life does us."

His tone was so strong and resolute that it was like a supporting arm about her. She felt her resistance melting, her strength slipping away from her as he spoke.

"Don't cry, Charity," he exclaimed in a shaken voice. She looked up, startled at his emotion, and their eyes met.

"See here," he said gently, "old Dan's come a long distance, and we've got to let him take it easy the rest of the way. . . ."

He picked up the cloak that had slipped to her chair and laid it about her shoulders. She followed him out of the house, and they walked across the yard to the shed, where the horse was tied. Mr. Royall unblanketed him and led him out into the road. Charity got into the buggy and he drew the cover about her and shook out the reins with a cluck. When they reached the end of the village he turned the horse's head toward Creston.

XVIII

THEY BEGAN to jog down the winding road to the valley at old Dan's languid pace. Charity felt herself sinking into deeper depths of weariness, and as they descended through the bare woods there were moments when she lost the exact sense of things, and seemed to be sitting beside her lover with the leafy arch of summer bending over them. But this illusion was faint and transitory. For the most part she had only a confused sensation of slipping down a smooth irresistible current; and she abandoned herself to the feeling as a refuge from the torment of thought.

Mr. Royall seldom spoke, but his silent presence gave her, for the first time, a sense of peace and security. She knew that where he was there would be warmth, rest, silence; and for the moment they were all she wanted. She shut her eyes, and even these things grew dim to her. . . .

In the train, during the short run from Creston to Nettleton, the warmth aroused her, and the consciousness of being under strange eyes gave her a momentary energy. She sat upright, facing Mr. Royall, and stared out of the window at the denuded country. Forty-eight hours earlier, when she had last traversed it, many of the trees still held their leaves; but the high wind of the last two nights had stripped them, and the lines of the landscape were as finely pencilled as in December. A few days of autumn cold had wiped out all trace of the rich fields and languid groves through which she had passed on the Fourth of July; and with the fading of the landscape those fervid hours had faded too. She could no longer believe that she was the being who had lived them; she was someone to whom something irreparable and overwhelming had happened, but the traces of the steps leading up to it had almost vanished.

When the train reached Nettleton and she walked out into the square at Mr. Royall's side the sense of unreality grew more overpowering. The physical strain of the night and day had left no room in her mind for new sensations and she followed Mr. Royall as passively as a tired child. As in a confused dream she presently found herself sitting with him in a pleasant room, at a table with a red and white table-cloth on which hot food and tea were placed. He filled her cup and plate and whenever she lifted her eyes from them she found his resting on her with the same steady tranquil gaze that had reassured and strengthened her when they had faced each other in old Mrs. Hobart's kitchen. As everything else in her consciousness grew more and more confused and immaterial, became more and more like the universal shimmer that dissolves the world to failing eyes, Mr. Royall's presence began to detach itself with rocky firmness from this elusive background. She had always thought of him—when she thought of him at all—as of someone hateful and obstructive, but whom she could outwit and dominate when she chose to make the effort. Only once, on the day of the Old Home Week celebration, while the stray fragments of his address drifted across her troubled mind, had she caught a glimpse of another being, a being so different from the dull-witted enemy with whom she had supposed herself to be living that even through the burning mist of her own dreams he had stood out with startling distinctness. For a moment, then, what he said—and something in his way of saying it—had made her see why he had always struck her as such a lonely man. But the mist of her dreams had hidden him again, and she had forgotten that fugitive impression.

It came back to her now, as they sat at the table, and gave her, through her own immeasurable desolation, a sudden sense of their nearness to each other. But all these feelings were only brief streaks of light in the grey blur of her physical weakness. Through it she was aware that Mr. Royall presently left her sitting by the table in the warm room, and came back after an interval with a carriage from the station—a closed "hack" with sunburnt blue silk blinds—in which they drove together to a house covered with creepers and standing next to a church with a carpet of turf before it. They got out at this house, and the carriage waited while they walked up the path and entered a wainscoted hall and then a room full of books. In this room a clergyman whom Charity had never seen received them pleasantly, and asked them to be seated for a few minutes while witnesses were being summoned.

Charity sat down obediently, and Mr. Royall, his hands

behind his back, paced slowly up and down the room. As he turned and faced Charity, she noticed that his lips were twitching a little; but the look in his eyes was grave and calm. Once he paused before her and said timidly: "Your hair's got kinder loose with the wind," and she lifted her hands and tried to smooth back the locks that had escaped from her braid. There was a looking-glass in a carved frame on the wall, but she was ashamed to look at herself in it, and she sat with her hands folded on her knee till the clergyman returned. Then they went out again, along a sort of arcaded passage, and into a low vaulted room with a cross on an altar, and rows of benches. The clergyman, who had left them at the door, presently reappeared before the altar in a surplice, and a lady who was probably his wife, and a man in a blue shirt who had been raking dead leaves on the lawn, came in and sat on one of the benches.

The clergyman opened a book and signed to Charity and Mr. Royall to approach. Mr. Royall advanced a few steps, and Charity followed him as she had followed him to the buggy when they went out of Mrs. Hobart's kitchen; she had the feeling that if she ceased to keep close to him, and do what he told her to do, the world would slip away from beneath her feet.

The clergyman began to read, and on her dazed mind there rose the memory of Mr. Miles, standing the night before in the desolate house of the Mountain, and reading out of the same book words that had the same dread sound of finality:

"I require and charge you both, as ye will answer at the dreadful day of judgment when the secrets of all hearts shall be disclosed, that if either of you know any impediment whereby ye may not be lawfully joined together . . ."

Charity raised her eyes and met Mr. Royall's. They were still looking at her kindly and steadily. "I will!" she heard him say a moment later, after another interval of words that she had failed to catch. She was so busy trying to understand the gestures the clergyman was signalling to her to make that she no longer heard what was being said. After another interval the lady on the bench stood up, and taking her hand put it in Mr. Royall's. It lay enclosed in his strong palm and she felt a

ring that was too big for her being slipped onto her thin finger. She understood then that she was married. . . .

Late that afternoon Charity sat alone in a bedroom of the
fashionable hotel where she and Harney had vainly sought a
table on the Fourth of July. She had never before been in so
handsomely furnished a room. The mirror above the dressing-
table reflected the high head-board and fluted pillow-slips of
the double bed, and a bedspread so spotlessly white that she
had hesitated to lay her hat and jacket on it. The humming
radiator diffused an atmosphere of drowsy warmth, and
through a half-open door she saw the glitter of the nickel taps
above twin marble basins.

For a while the long turmoil of the night and day had
slipped away from her and she sat with closed eyes, surrender-
ing herself to the spell of warmth and silence. But presently
this merciful apathy was succeeded by the sudden acuteness of
vision with which sick people sometimes wake out of a heavy
sleep. As she opened her eyes they rested on the picture that
hung above the bed. It was a large engraving with a dazzling
white margin enclosed in a wide frame of bird's-eye maple
with an inner scroll of gold. The engraving represented a
young man in a boat on a lake overhung with trees. He was
leaning over to gather water-lilies for the girl in a light dress
who lay among the cushions in the stern. The scene was full
of a drowsy midsummer radiance, and Charity averted her
eyes from it and, rising from her chair, began to wander restlessly about the room.

It was on the fifth floor, and its broad window of plate
glass looked over the roofs of the town. Beyond them
stretched a wooded landscape in which the last fires of sunset
were picking out a steely gleam. Charity gazed at the gleam
with startled eyes. Even through the gathering twilight she
recognized the contour of the soft hills encircling it, and the
way the meadows sloped to its edge. It was Nettleton Lake
that she was looking at.

She stood a long time in the window staring out at the
fading water. The sight of it had roused her for the first time
to a realization of what she had done. Even the feeling of
the ring on her hand had not brought her this sharp sense of
the irretrievable. For an instant the old impulse of flight

swept through her; but it was only the lift of a broken wing. She heard the door open behind her, and Mr. Royall came in.

He had gone to the barber's to be shaved, and his shaggy grey hair had been trimmed and smoothed. He moved strongly and quickly, squaring his shoulders and carrying his head high, as if he did not want to pass unnoticed.

"What are you doing in the dark?" he called out in a cheerful voice. Charity made no answer. He went up to the window to draw down the blind, and putting his finger on the wall flooded the room with a blaze of light from the central chandelier. In this unfamiliar illumination husband and wife faced each other awkwardly for a moment; then Mr. Royall said: "We'll step down and have some supper, if you say so."

The thought of food filled her with repugnance; but not daring to confess it she smoothed her hair and followed him to the lift.

An hour later, coming out of the glare of the dining-room, she waited in the marble-panelled hall while Mr. Royall, before the brass lattice of one of the corner counters, selected a cigar and bought an evening paper. Men were lounging in rocking chairs under the blazing chandeliers, travellers coming and going, bells ringing, porters shuffling by with luggage. Over Mr. Royall's shoulder, as he leaned against the counter, a girl with her hair puffed high smirked and nodded at a dapper drummer who was getting his key at the desk across the hall.

Charity stood among these cross-currents of life as motionless and inert as if she had been one of the tables screwed to the marble floor. All her soul was gathered up into one sick sense of coming doom, and she watched Mr. Royall in fascinated terror while he pinched the cigars in successive boxes and unfolded his evening paper with a steady hand.

Presently he turned and joined her. "You go right along up to bed—I'm going to sit down here and have my smoke," he said. He spoke as easily and naturally as if they had been an old couple, long used to each other's ways, and her contracted heart gave a flutter of relief. She followed him to the lift, and he put her in and enjoined the buttoned and braided boy to show her to her room.

She groped her way in through the darkness, forgetting where the electric button was, and not knowing how to manipulate it. But a white autumn moon had risen, and the illuminated sky put a pale light in the room. By it she undressed, and after folding up the ruffled pillow-slips crept timidly under the spotless counterpane. She had never felt such smooth sheets or such light warm blankets; but the softness of the bed did not soothe her. She lay there trembling with a fear that ran through her veins like ice. "What have I done? Oh, what have I done?" she whispered, shuddering to her pillow; and pressing her face against it to shut out the pale landscape beyond the window she lay in the darkness straining her ears, and shaking at every footstep that approached. . . .

Suddenly she sat up and pressed her hands against her frightened heart. A faint sound had told her that someone was in the room; but she must have slept in the interval, for she had heard no one enter. The moon was setting beyond the opposite roofs, and in the darkness, outlined against the grey square of the window, she saw a figure seated in the rocking-chair. The figure did not move: it was sunk deep in the chair, with bowed head and folded arms, and she saw that it was Mr. Royall who sat there. He had not undressed, but had taken the blanket from the foot of the bed and laid it across his knees. Trembling and holding her breath she watched him, fearing that he had been roused by her movement; but he did not stir, and she concluded that he wished her to think he was asleep.

As she continued to watch him ineffable relief stole slowly over her, relaxing her strained nerves and exhausted body. He knew, then . . . he knew . . . it was because he knew that he had married her, and that he sat there in the darkness to show her she was safe with him. A stir of something deeper than she had ever felt in thinking of him flitted through her tired brain, and cautiously, noiselessly, she let her head sink on the pillow. . . .

When she woke the room was full of morning light, and her first glance showed her that she was alone in it. She got up and dressed, and as she was fastening her dress the door opened, and Mr. Royall came in. He looked old and tired in the bright daylight, but his face wore the same expression of grave friendliness that had reassured her on the Mountain. It was as if all the dark spirits had gone out of him.

They went downstairs to the dining-room for breakfast, and after breakfast he told her he had some insurance business to attend to. "I guess while I'm doing it you'd better step out and buy yourself whatever you need." He smiled, and added with an embarrassed laugh: "You know I always wanted you to beat all the other girls." He drew something from his pocket, and pushed it across the table to her; and she saw that he had given her two twenty-dollar bills. "If it ain't enough there's more where that come from—I want you to beat 'em all hollow," he repeated.

She flushed and tried to stammer out her thanks, but he had pushed back his chair and was leading the way out of the dining-room. In the hall he paused a minute to say that if it suited her they would take the three o'clock train back to North Dormer; then he took his hat and coat from the rack and went out.

A few minutes later Charity went out too. She had watched to see in what direction he was going, and she took the opposite way and walked quickly down the main street to the brick building on the corner of Lake Avenue. There she paused to look cautiously up and down the thorough-fare, and then climbed the brass-bound stairs to Dr. Merkle's door. The same bushy-headed mulatto girl admitted her, and after the same interval of waiting in the red plush parlor she was once more summoned to Dr. Merkle's office. The doctor received her without surprise, and led her into the inner plush sanctuary.

"I thought you'd be back, but you've come a mite too soon: I told you to be patient and not fret," she observed, after a pause of penetrating scrutiny.

Charity drew the money from her breast. "I've come to get my blue brooch," she said, flushing.

"Your brooch?" Dr. Merkle appeared not to remember. "My, yes—I get so many things of that kind. Well, my dear, you'll have to wait while I get it out of the safe. I don't leave valuables like that laying round like the noospaper."

She disappeared for a moment, and returned with a bit of twisted-up tissue paper from which she unwrapped the brooch.

Charity, as she looked at it, felt a stir of warmth at her heart. She held out an eager hand.

"Have you got the change?" she asked a little breathlessly, laying one of the twenty-dollar bills on the table.

"Change? What'd I want to have change for? I only see two twenties there," Dr. Merkle answered brightly.

Charity paused, disconcerted. "I thought . . . you said it was five dollars a visit. . . ."

"For *you*, as a favour—I did. But how about the responsibility—*and* the insurance? I don't s'pose you ever thought of that? This pin's worth a hundred dollars easy. If it had got lost or stole, where'd I been when you come to claim it?"

Charity remained silent, puzzled and half-convinced by the argument, and Dr. Merkle promptly followed up her advantage. "I didn't ask you for your brooch, my dear. I'd a good deal ruther folks paid me my regular charge than have 'em put me to all this trouble."

She paused, and Charity, seized with a desperate longing to escape, rose to her feet and held out one of the bills.

"Will you take that?" she asked.

"No, I won't take that, my dear; but I'll take it with its mate, and hand you over a signed receipt if you don't trust me."

"Oh, but I can't—it's all I've got," Charity exclaimed.

Dr. Merkle looked up at her pleasantly from the plush sofa. "It seems you got married yesterday, up to the 'Piscopal church; I heard all about the wedding from the minister's chore-man. It would be a pity, wouldn't it, to let Mr. Royall know you had an account running here? I just put it to you as your own mother might."

Anger flamed up in Charity, and for an instant she thought of abandoning the brooch and letting Dr. Merkle do her worst. But how could she leave her only treasure with that evil woman? She wanted it for her baby: she meant it, in some mysterious way, to be a link between Harney's child and its unknown father. Trembling and hating herself while she did it, she laid Mr. Royall's money on the table, and catching up the brooch fled out of the room and the house. . . .

In the street she stood still, dazed by this last adventure. But the brooch lay in her bosom like a talisman, and she felt a secret lightness of heart. It gave her strength, after a moment, to walk on slowly in the direction of the post office, and go in through the swinging doors. At one of the windows she bought a sheet of letter-paper, an envelope and a stamp; then she sat down at a table and dipped the rusty post office pen in ink. She had come there possessed with a fear which had haunted her ever since she had felt Mr. Royall's ring on her finger: the fear that Harney might, after all, free himself and come back to her. It was a possibility which had never occurred to her during the dreadful hours after she had received his letter; only when the decisive step she had taken made longing turn to apprehension did such a contingency seem conceivable. She addressed the envelope, and on the sheet of paper she wrote:

I'm married to Mr. Royall. I'll always remember you.
CHARITY.

The last words were not in the least what she had meant to write; they had flowed from her pen irresistibly. She had not had the strength to complete her sacrifice; but, after all, what did it matter? Now that there was no chance of ever seeing Harney again, why should she not tell him the truth?

When she had put the letter in the box she went out into the busy sunlit street and began to walk to the hotel. Behind the plate-glass windows of the department stores she noticed the tempting display of dresses and dress-materials that had fired her imagination on the day when she and Harney had looked in at them together. They reminded her of Mr. Royall's injunction to go out and buy all she needed. She looked down at her shabby dress, and wondered what she should say when he saw her coming back empty-handed. As she drew near the hotel she saw him waiting on the doorstep, and her heart began to beat with apprehension.

He nodded and waved his hand at her approach, and they walked through the hall and went upstairs to collect their possessions, so that Mr. Royall might give up the key of the room when they went down again for their midday dinner. In the bedroom, while she was thrusting back into the satchel the few things she had brought away with her, she suddenly felt that his eyes were on her and that he was going to speak. She stood still, her half-folded night-gown in her hand, while the blood rushed up to her drawn cheeks.

"Well, did you rig yourself out handsomely? I haven't seen any bundles round," he said jocosely.

"Oh, I'd rather let Ally Hawes make the few things I want," she answered.

"That so?" He looked at her thoughtfully for a moment and his eye-brows projected in a scowl. Then his face grew friendly again. "Well, I wanted you to go back looking stylisher than any of them; but I guess you're right. You're a good girl, Charity."

Their eyes met, and something rose in his that she had never seen there: a look that made her feel ashamed and yet secure.

"I guess you're good, too," she said, shyly and quickly. He smiled without answering, and they went out of the room together and dropped down to the hall in the glittering lift.

Late that evening, in the cold autumn moonlight, they drove up to the door of the red house.

OLD NEW YORK

FALSE DAWN
(*The 'Forties*)

THE OLD MAID
(*The 'Fifties*)

THE SPARK
(*The 'Sixties*)

NEW YEAR'S DAY
(*The 'Seventies*)

FALSE DAWN

(*The 'Forties*)

I

H AY, VERBENA and mignonette scented the languid July
day. Large strawberries, crimsoning through sprigs of
mint, floated in a bowl of pale yellow cup on the verandah
table: an old Georgian bowl, with complex reflections on
polygonal flanks, engraved with the Raycie arms between lions'
heads. Now and again the gentlemen, warned by a menacing
hum, slapped their cheeks, their brows or their bald crowns;
but they did so as furtively as possible, for Mr. Halston Raycie, on whose verandah they sat, would not admit that there
were mosquitoes at High Point.

The strawberries came from Mr. Raycie's kitchen garden;
the Georgian bowl came from his great-grandfather (father of
the Signer); the verandah was that of his country-house,
which stood on a height above the Sound, at a convenient
driving distance from his town house in Canal Street.

"Another glass, Commodore," said Mr. Raycie, shaking out
a cambric handkerchief the size of a table-cloth, and applying
a corner of it to his steaming brow.

Mr. Jameson Ledgely smiled and took another glass. He
was known as "the Commodore" among his intimates because of having been in the Navy in his youth, and having
taken part, as a midshipman under Admiral Porter, in the war
of 1812. This jolly sunburnt bachelor, whose face resembled
that of one of the bronze idols he might have brought back
with him, had kept his naval air, though long retired from the
service; and his white duck trousers, his gold-braided cap and
shining teeth, still made him look as if he might be in command of a frigate. Instead of that, he had just sailed over a
party of friends from his own place on the Long Island shore;
and his trim white sloop was now lying in the bay below the
point.

The Halston Raycie house overlooked a lawn sloping to
the Sound. The lawn was Mr. Raycie's pride: it was mown
with a scythe once a fortnight, and rolled in the spring by an
old white horse specially shod for the purpose. Below the

verandah the turf was broken by three round beds of rose-geranium, heliotrope and Bengal roses, which Mrs. Raycie tended in gauntlet gloves, under a small hinged sunshade that folded back on its carved ivory handle. The house, remodelled and enlarged by Mr. Raycie on his marriage, had played a part in the Revolutionary war as the settler's cottage where Benedict Arnold had had his headquarters. A contemporary print of it hung in Mr. Raycie's study; but no one could have detected the humble outline of the old house in the majestic stone-coloured dwelling built of tongued-and-grooved boards, with an angle tower, tall narrow windows, and a verandah on chamfered posts, that figured so confidently as a "Tuscan Villa" in Downing's "Landscape Gardening in America." There was the same difference between the rude lithograph of the earlier house and the fine steel engraving of its successor (with a "specimen" weeping beech on the lawn) as between the buildings themselves. Mr. Raycie had reason to think well of his architect.

He thought well of most things related to himself by ties of blood or interest. No one had ever been quite sure that he made Mrs. Raycie happy, but he was known to have the highest opinion of her. So it was with his daughters, Sarah Anne and Mary Adeline, fresher replicas of the lymphatic Mrs. Raycie; no one would have sworn that they were quite at ease with their genial parent, yet every one knew how loud he was in their praises. But the most remarkable object within the range of Mr. Raycie's self-approval was his son Lewis. And yet, as Jameson Ledgely, who was given to speaking his mind, had once observed, you wouldn't have supposed young Lewis was exactly the kind of craft Halston would have turned out if he'd had the designing of his son and heir.

Mr. Raycie was a monumental man. His extent in height, width and thickness was so nearly the same that whichever way he was turned one had an almost equally broad view of him; and every inch of that mighty circumference was so exquisitely cared for that to a farmer's eye he might have suggested a great agricultural estate of which not an acre is untilled. Even his baldness, which was in proportion to the rest, looked as if it received a special daily polish; and on a hot day his whole person was like some wonderful example of the costliest irrigation. There was so much of him, and he had so many planes, that it was fascinating to watch each runnel of moisture follow its own particular watershed. Even on his large fresh-looking hands the drops divided, trickling in different ways from the ridges of the fingers; and as for his forehead and temples, and the raised cushion of cheek beneath each of his lower lids, every one of these slopes had its own particular stream, its hollow pools and sudden cataracts; and the sight was never unpleasant, because his whole vast bubbling surface was of such a clean and hearty pink, and the exuding moisture so perceptibly flavoured with expensive eau de Cologne and the best French soap.

Mrs. Raycie, though built on a less heroic scale, had a pale amplitude which, when she put on her best watered silk (the kind that stood alone), and framed her countenance in the innumerable blonde lace ruffles and clustered purple grapes of her newest Paris cap, almost balanced her husband's bulk. Yet from this full-rigged pair, as the Commodore would have put it, had issued the lean little runt of a Lewis, a shrimp of a baby, a shaver of a boy, and now a youth as scant as an ordinary man's midday shadow.

All these things, Lewis himself mused, dangling his legs from the verandah rail, were undoubtedly passing through the minds of the four gentlemen grouped about his father's bowl of cup.

Mr. Robert Huzzard, the banker, a tall broad man, who looked big in any company but Mr. Raycie's, leaned back, lifted his glass, and bowed to Lewis.

"Here's to the Grand Tour!"

"Don't perch on that rail like a sparrow, my boy," Mr. Raycie said reprovingly; and Lewis dropped to his feet, and returned Mr. Huzzard's bow.

"I wasn't thinking," he stammered. It was his too frequent excuse.

Mr. Ambrose Huzzard, the banker's younger brother, Mr. Ledgely and Mr. Donaldson Kent, all raised their glasses and cheerily echoed: "The Grand Tour!"

Lewis bowed again, and put his lips to the glass he had forgotten. In reality, he had eyes only for Mr. Donaldson Kent, his father's cousin, a silent man with a lean hawklike profile, who looked like a retired Revolutionary hero, and lived in daily fear of the most trifling risk or responsibility.

To this prudent and circumspect citizen had come, some years earlier, the unexpected and altogether inexcusable demand that he should look after the daughter of his only brother, Julius Kent. Julius had died in Italy—well, that was his own business, if he chose to live there. But to let his wife die before him, and to leave a minor daughter, and a will entrusting her to the guardianship of his esteemed elder brother, Donaldson Kent Esquire, of Kent's Point, Long Island, and Great Jones Street, New York—well, as Mr. Kent himself said, and as his wife said for him, there had never been anything, anything whatever, in Mr. Kent's attitude or behaviour, to justify the ungrateful Julius (whose debts he had more than once paid) in laying on him this final burden.

The girl came. She was fourteen, she was considered plain, she was small and black and skinny. Her name was Beatrice, which was bad enough, and made worse by the fact that it had been shortened by ignorant foreigners to Treeshy. But she was eager, serviceable and good-tempered, and as Mr. and Mrs. Kent's friends pointed out, her plainness made everything easy. There were two Kent boys growing up, Bill and Donald; and if this penniless cousin had been compounded of cream and roses—well, she would have taken more watching, and might have rewarded the kindness of her uncle and aunt by some act of wicked ingratitude. But this risk being obviated by her appearance, they could be goodnatured to her without afterthought, and to be goodnatured was natural to them. So, as the years passed, she gradually became the guardian of her guardians; since it was equally natural to Mr. and Mrs. Kent to throw themselves in helpless reliance on every one whom they did not nervously fear or mistrust.

"Yes, he's off on Monday," Mr. Raycie said, nodding sharply at Lewis, who had set down his glass after one sip. "Empty it, you shirk!" the nod commanded; and Lewis, throwing back his head, gulped down the draught, though it almost stuck in his lean throat. He had already had to take two glasses, and even this scant conviviality was too much for him, and likely to result in a mood of excited volubility, followed by a morose evening and a head the next morning.

And he wanted to keep his mind clear that day, and to think steadily and lucidly of Treeshy Kent.

Of course he couldn't marry her—yet. He was twenty-one that very day, and still entirely dependent on his father. And he wasn't altogether sorry to be going first on this Grand Tour. It was what he had always dreamed of, pined for, from the moment when his infant eyes had first been drawn to the prints of European cities in the long upper passage that smelt of matting. And all that Treeshy had told him about Italy had confirmed and intensified the longing. Oh, to have been going there with her—with her as his guide, his Beatrice! (For she had given him a little Dante of her father's, with a steel-engraved frontispiece of Beatrice; and his sister Mary Adeline, who had been taught Italian by one of the romantic Milanese exiles, had helped her brother out with the grammar.)

The thought of going to Italy with Treeshy was only a dream; but later, as man and wife, they would return there, and by that time, perhaps, it was Lewis who would be her guide, and reveal to her the historic marvels of her birthplace, of which after all she knew so little, except in minor domestic ways that were quaint but unimportant.

The prospect swelled her suitor's bosom, and reconciled him to the idea of their separation. After all, he secretly felt himself to be still a boy, and it was as a man that he would return: he meant to tell her that when they met the next day. When he came back his character would be formed, his knowledge of life (which he already thought considerable) would be complete; and then no one could keep them apart. He smiled in advance to think how little his father's shouting and booming would impress a man on his return from the Grand Tour. . .

The gentlemen were telling anecdotes about their own early experiences in Europe. None of them—not even Mr. Raycie—had travelled as extensively as it was intended that Lewis should; but the two Huzzards had been twice to England on banking matters, and Commodore Ledgely, a bold man, to France and Belgium as well—not to speak of his early experiences in the Far East. All three had kept a vivid and amused recollection, slightly tinged with disapprobation, of what they had seen— "Oh, those French wenches," the Commodore chuckled through his white teeth—but poor Mr. Kent, who had gone abroad on his honeymoon, had been caught in Paris by the revolution of 1830, had had the fever in Florence, and had nearly been arrested as a spy in Vienna; and the only satisfactory episode in this disastrous, and never repeated, adventure, had been the fact of his having been mistaken for the Duke of Wellington (as he was trying to slip out of a Viennese hotel in his courier's blue surtout) by a crowd who had been— "Well, very gratifying in their enthusiasm," Mr. Kent admitted.

"How my poor brother Julius could have lived in Europe! Well, look at the consequences—" he used to say, as if poor Treeshy's plainness gave an awful point to his moral.

"There's one thing in Paris, my boy, that you must be warned against: those gambling-hells in the Pally Royle," Mr. Kent insisted. "I never set foot in the places myself; but a glance at the outside was enough."

"I knew a feller that was fleeced of a fortune there," Mr. Henry Huzzard confirmed; while the Commodore, at his tenth glass, chuckled with moist eyes: "The trollops, oh, the trollops—"

"As for Vienna—" said Mr. Kent.

"Even in London," said Mr. Ambrose Huzzard, "a young man must be on his look-out against gamblers. Every form of swindling is practised, and the touts are always on the look-out for greenhorns; a term," he added apologetically, "which they apply to any traveller new to the country."

"In Paris," said Mr. Kent, "I was once within an ace of being challenged to fight a duel." He fetched a sigh of horror and relief, and glanced reassuredly down the Sound in the direction of his own peaceful roof-tree.

"Oh, a duel," laughed the Commodore. "A man can fight duels here. I fought a dozen when I was a young feller in New Erleens." The Commodore's mother had been a southern lady, and after his father's death had spent some years with her parents in Louisiana, so that her son's varied experiences had begun early. "'Bout women," he smiled confidentially, holding out his empty glass to Mr. Raycie.

"The ladies—!" exclaimed Mr. Kent in a voice of warning.

The gentlemen rose to their feet, the Commodore quite as promptly and steadily as the others. The drawing-room window opened, and from it emerged Mrs. Raycie, in a ruffled sarsenet dress and Point de Paris cap, followed by her two daughters in starched organdy with pink spencers. Mr. Raycie looked with proud approval at his womenkind.

"Gentlemen," said Mrs. Raycie, in a perfectly even voice, "supper is on the table, and if you will do Mr. Raycie and myself the favour—"

"The favour, ma'am," said Mr. Ambrose Huzzard, "is on your side, in so amiably inviting us."

Mrs. Raycie curtsied, the gentlemen bowed, and Mr. Raycie said: "Your arm to Mrs. Raycie, Huzzard. This little farewell party is a family affair, and the other gentlemen must content themselves with my two daughters. Sarah Anne, Mary Adeline—"

The Commodore and Mr. John Huzzard advanced ceremoniously toward the two girls, and Mr. Kent, being a cousin, closed the procession between Mr. Raycie and Lewis.

Oh, that supper-table! The vision of it used sometimes to rise before Lewis Raycie's eyes in outlandish foreign places; for though not a large or fastidious eater when he was at home, he was afterward, in lands of chestnut-flour and garlic and queer bearded sea-things, to suffer many pangs of hunger at the thought of that opulent board. In the centre stood the Raycie *épergne* of pierced silver, holding aloft a bunch of June roses surrounded by dangling baskets of sugared almonds and striped peppermints; and grouped about this decorative "motif" were Lowestoft platters heavy with piles of raspberries, strawberries and the first Delaware peaches. An outer flanking of heaped-up cookies, crullers, strawberry short-cake, piping hot corn-bread and deep golden butter in moist blocks still bedewed from the muslin swathings of the dairy, led the eye to the Virginia ham in front of Mr. Raycie, and the twin dishes of scrambled eggs on toast and broiled blue-fish over which his wife presided. Lewis could never afterward fit into this intricate pattern the "side-dishes" of devilled turkey-legs and creamed chicken hash, the sliced cucumbers and tomatoes, the heavy silver jugs of butter-coloured cream, the floating-island, "slips" and lemon jellies that were somehow interwoven with the solider elements of the design; but they were all there, either together or successively, and so were the towering piles of waffles reeling on their foundations, and the slender silver jugs of maple syrup perpetually escorting them about the table as black Dinah replenished the supply.

They ate—oh, how they all ate!—though the ladies were supposed only to nibble; but the good things on Lewis's plate remained untouched until, ever and again, an admonishing glance from Mr. Raycie, or an entreating one from Mary Adeline, made him insert a languid fork into the heap.

And all the while Mr. Raycie continued to hold forth.

"A young man, in my opinion, before setting up for himself, must see the world; form his taste; fortify his judgment. He must study the most famous monuments, examine the organization of foreign societies, and the habits and customs of those older civilizations whose yoke it has been our glory to cast off. Though he may see in them much to deplore and to reprove—" ("Some of the gals, though," Commodore Ledgely was heard to interject)—"much that will make him give thanks for the privilege of having been born and brought up under our own Free Institutions, yet I believe he will also"—Mr. Raycie conceded it with magnanimity—"be able to learn much."

"The Sundays, though," Mr. Kent hazarded warningly; and Mrs. Raycie breathed across to her son: "Ah, that's what *I* say!"

Mr. Raycie did not like interruption; and he met it by growing visibly larger. His huge bulk hung a moment, like an avalanche, above the silence which followed Mr. Kent's interjection and Mrs. Raycie's murmur; then he crashed down on both.

"The Sundays—the Sundays? Well, what of the Sundays? What is there to frighten a good Episcopalian in what we call the Continental Sunday? I presume that we're all Churchmen here, eh? No puling Methodists or atheistical Unitarians at my table tonight, that I'm aware of? Nor will I offend the ladies of my household by assuming that they have secretly lent an ear to the Baptist ranter in the chapel at the foot of our lane. No? I thought not! Well, then, I say, what's all this flutter about the Papists? Far be it from me to approve of their heathenish doctrines—but, damn it, they go to church, don't they? And they have a real service, as we do, don't they? And real clergy, and not a lot of nondescripts dressed like laymen, and damned badly at that, who chat familiarly with the Almighty in their own vulgar lingo? No, sir"—he swung about on the shrinking Mr. Kent—"it's not the Church I'm afraid of in foreign countries, it's the sewers, sir!"

Mrs. Raycie had grown very pale: Lewis knew that she too was deeply perturbed about the sewers. "And the night-air," she scarce-audibly sighed.

But Mr. Raycie had taken up his main theme again. "In my opinion, if a young man travels at all, he must travel as extensively as his—er—means permit; must see as much of the world as he can. Those are my son's sailing orders, Commodore; and here's to his carrying them out to the best of his powers!"

Black Dinah, removing the Virginia ham, or rather such of its bony structure as alone remained on the dish, had managed to make room for a bowl of punch from which Mr. Raycie poured deep ladlefuls of perfumed fire into the glasses ranged before him on a silver tray. The gentlemen rose, the ladies smiled and wept, and Lewis's health and the success of the Grand Tour were toasted with an eloquence which caused Mrs. Raycie, with a hasty nod to her daughters, and a covering rustle of starched flounces, to shepherd them softly from the room.

"After all," Lewis heard her murmur to them on the threshold, "your father's using such language shows that he's in the best of humour with dear Lewis."

II

I N SPITE OF his enforced potations, Lewis Raycie was up the next morning before sunrise.

Unlatching his shutters without noise, he looked forth over the wet lawn merged in a blur of shrubberies, and the waters of the Sound dimly seen beneath a sky full of stars. His head ached but his heart glowed; what was before him was thrilling enough to clear a heavier brain than his.

He dressed quickly and completely (save for his shoes), and then, stripping the flowered quilt from his high mahogany bed, rolled it in a tight bundle under his arm. Thus enigmatically equipped he was feeling his way, shoes in hand, through the darkness of the upper story to the slippery oak stairs, when he was startled by a candle-gleam in the pitch-blackness of the hall below. He held his breath, and leaning over the stair-rail saw with amazement his sister Mary Adeline come forth, cloaked and bonneted, but also in stocking-feet, from the passage leading to the pantry. She too carried a double burden: her shoes and the candle in one hand, in the other a large covered basket that weighed down her bare arm.

Brother and sister stopped and stared at each other in the blue dusk: the upward slant of the candle-light distorted Mary Adeline's mild features, twisting them into a frightened grin as Lewis stole down to join her.

"Oh—" she whispered. "What in the world are you doing here? I was just getting together a few things for that poor young Mrs. Poe down the lane, who's so ill—before mother goes to the store-room. You won't tell, will you?"

Lewis signalled his complicity, and cautiously slid open the bolt of the front door. They durst not say more till they were out of ear-shot. On the doorstep they sat down to put on their shoes; then they hastened on without a word through the ghostly shrubberies till they reached the gate into the lane.

"But you, Lewis?" the sister suddenly questioned, with an astonished stare at the rolled-up quilt under her brother's arm.

"Oh, I—. Look here, Addy—" he broke off and began to grope in his pocket—"I haven't much about me . . . the old gentleman keeps me as close as ever . . . but here's a dollar, if you think that poor Mrs. Poe could use it. . . I'd be too happy . . . consider it a privilege. . ."

"Oh, Lewis, Lewis, how noble, how generous of you! Of course I can buy a few extra things with it . . . they never see meat unless I can bring them a bit, you know . . . and I fear she's dying of a decline . . . and she and her mother are so fiery-proud. . ." She wept with gratitude, and Lewis drew a breath of relief. He had diverted her attention from the bed-quilt.

"Ah, there's the breeze," he murmured, sniffing the suddenly chilled air.

"Yes; I must be off; I must be back before the sun is up," said Mary Adeline anxiously, "and it would never do if mother knew—"

"She doesn't know of your visits to Mrs. Poe?"

A look of childish guile sharpened Mary Adeline's undeveloped face. "She *does*, of course; but yet she doesn't . . . we've arranged it so. You see, Mr. Poe's an Atheist; and so father—"

"I see," Lewis nodded. "Well, we part here; I'm off for a swim," he said glibly. But abruptly he turned back and caught his sister's arm. "Sister, tell Mrs. Poe, please, that I heard her husband give a reading from his poems in New York two nights ago—"

("Oh, Lewis—*you*? But father says he's a blasphemer!")

"—And that he's a great poet—a Great Poet. Tell her that from me, will you, please, Mary Adeline?"

"Oh, brother, I couldn't . . . we never speak of him," the startled girl faltered, hurrying away.

In the cove where the Commodore's sloop had ridden a few hours earlier a biggish rowing-boat took the waking ripples. Young Raycie paddled out to her, fastened his skiff to the moorings, and hastily clambered into the boat.

From various recesses of his pockets he produced rope, string, a carpet-layer's needle, and other unexpected and incongruous tackle; then, lashing one of the oars across the top of the other, and jamming the latter upright between the

forward thwart and the bow, he rigged the flowered bed-
quilt on this mast, knotted a rope to the free end of the quilt,
and sat down in the stern, one hand on the rudder, the other
on his improvised sheet.

Venus, brooding silverly above a line of pale green sky,
made a pool of glory in the sea as the dawn-breeze plumped
the lover's sail. . .

On the shelving pebbles of another cove, two or three miles
down the Sound, Lewis Raycie lowered his queer sail and
beached his boat. A clump of willows on the shingle-edge
mysteriously stirred and parted, and Treeshy Kent was in his
arms.

The sun was just pushing above a belt of low clouds in the
east, spattering them with liquid gold, and Venus blanched as
the light spread upward. But under the willows it was still
dusk, a watery green dusk in which the secret murmurs of the
night were caught.

"Treeshy—Treeshy!" the young man cried, kneeling beside
her—and then, a moment later: "My angel, are you sure that
no one guesses—?"

The girl gave a faint laugh which screwed up her funny
nose. She leaned her head on his shoulder, her round forehead and rough braids pressed against his cheek, her hands in
his, breathing quickly and joyfully.

"I thought I should never get here," Lewis grumbled,
"with that ridiculous bed-quilt—and it'll be broad day soon!
To think that I was of age yesterday, and must come to you in
a boat rigged like a child's toy on a duck-pond! If you knew
how it humiliates me—"

"What does it matter, dear, since you're of age now, and
your own master?"

"But am I, though? He says so—but it's only on his own
terms; only while I do what he wants! You'll see. . . I've a
credit of ten thousand dollars . . . ten . . . thou . . . sand
. . . d'you hear? . . . placed to my name in a London bank;
and not a penny here to bless myself with meanwhile. . .
Why, Treeshy darling, why, what's the matter?"

She flung her arms about his neck, and through their innocent kisses he could taste her tears. "What *is* it, Treeshy?" he implored her.

"I . . . oh, I'd forgotten it was to be our last day together till you spoke of London—cruel, cruel!" she reproached him; and through the green twilight of the willows her eyes blazed on him like two stormy stars. No other eyes he knew could express such elemental rage as Treeshy's.

"You little spitfire, you!" he laughed back somewhat chokingly. "Yes, it's our last day—but not for long; at our age two years are not so very long, after all, are they? And when I come back to you I'll come as my own master, independent, free—come to claim you in face of everything and everybody! Think of that, darling, and be brave for my sake . . . brave and patient . . . as I mean to be!" he declared heroically.

"Oh, but you—you'll see other girls; heaps and heaps of them; in those wicked old countries where they're so lovely. My uncle Kent says the European countries are all wicked, even my own poor Italy . . ."

"But *you*, Treeshy; you'll be seeing cousins Bill and Donald meanwhile—seeing them all day long and every day. And you know you've a weakness for that great hulk of a Bill. Ah, if only I stood six-foot-one in my stockings I'd go with an easier heart, you fickle child!" he tried to banter her.

"Fickle? Fickle? *Me*—oh, Lewis!"

He felt the premonitory sweep of sobs, and his untried courage failed him. It was delicious, in theory, to hold weeping beauty to one's breast, but terribly alarming, he found, in practice. There came a responsive twitching in his throat.

"No, no; firm as adamant, true as steel; that's what we both mean to be, isn't it, *cara*?"

"*Caro*, yes," she sighed, appeased.

"And you'll write to me regularly, Treeshy—long long letters? I may count on that, mayn't I, wherever I am? And they must all be numbered, every one of them, so that I shall know at once if I've missed one; remember!"

"And, Lewis, you'll wear them here?" (She touched his breast.) "Oh, not *all*," she added, laughing, "for they'd make such a big bundle that you'd soon have a hump in front like Pulcinella—but always at least the last one, just the last one. Promise!"

"Always, I promise—as long as they're kind," he said, still struggling to take a spirited line.

"Oh, Lewis, they will be, as long as yours are—and long long afterward. . ."

Venus failed and vanished in the sun's uprising.

III

THE CRUCIAL MOMENT, Lewis had always known, would be not that of his farewell to Treeshy, but of his final interview with his father.

On that everything hung: his immediate future as well as his more distant prospects. As he stole home in the early sunlight, over the dew-drenched grass, he glanced up apprehensively at Mr. Raycie's windows, and thanked his stars that they were still tightly shuttered.

There was no doubt, as Mrs. Raycie said, that her husband's "using language" before ladies showed him to be in high good humour, relaxed and slippered, as it were—a state his family so seldom saw him in that Lewis had sometimes impertinently wondered to what awful descent from the clouds he and his two sisters owed their timorous being.

It was all very well to tell himself, as he often did, that the bulk of the money was his mother's, and that he could turn her round his little finger. What difference did that make? Mr. Raycie, the day after his marriage, had quietly taken over the management of his wife's property, and deducted, from the very moderate allowance he accorded her, all her little personal expenses, even to the postage-stamps she used, and the dollar she put in the plate every Sunday. He called the allowance her "pin-money," since, as he often reminded her, he paid all the household bills himself, so that Mrs. Raycie's quarterly pittance could be entirely devoted, if she chose, to frills and feathers.

"And will be, if you respect my wishes, my dear," he always added. "I like to see a handsome figure well set-off, and not to have our friends imagine, when they come to dine, that Mrs. Raycie is sick above-stairs, and I've replaced her by a poor relation in *allapacca*." In compliance with which Mrs. Raycie, at once flattered and terrified, spent her last penny in adorning herself and her daughters, and had to stint their bedroom fires, and the servants' meals, in order to find a penny for any private necessity.

Mr. Raycie had long since convinced his wife that this method of dealing with her, if not lavish, was suitable, and in

fact "handsome"; when she spoke of the subject to her relations it was with tears of gratitude for her husband's kindness in assuming the management of her property. As he
managed it exceedingly well, her hard-headed brothers (glad
to have the responsibility off their hands, and convinced
that, if left to herself, she would have muddled her money
away in ill-advised charities) were disposed to share her approval of Mr. Raycie; though her old mother sometimes said
helplessly: "When I think that Lucy Ann can't as much as
have a drop of gruel brought up to her without his weighing the oatmeal. . ." But even that was only whispered, lest
Mr. Raycie's mysterious faculty of hearing what was said behind his back should bring sudden reprisals on the venerable
lady to whom he always alluded, with a tremor in his genial
voice, as "my dear mother-in-law—unless indeed she will
allow me to call her, more briefly but more truly, my dear
mother."

To Lewis, hitherto, Mr. Raycie had meted the same measure as to the females of the household. He had dressed him
well, educated him expensively, lauded him to the skies—and
counted every penny of his allowance. Yet there was a difference; and Lewis was as well aware of it as any one.

The dream, the ambition, the passion of Mr. Raycie's life,
was (as his son knew) to found a Family; and he had only
Lewis to found it with. He believed in primogeniture, in heirlooms, in entailed estates, in all the ritual of the English
"landed" tradition. No one was louder than he in praise of the
democratic institutions under which he lived; but he never
thought of them as affecting that more private but more important institution, the Family; and to the Family all his care
and all his thoughts were given. The result, as Lewis dimly
guessed, was, that upon his own shrinking and inadequate
head was centred all the passion contained in the vast expanse
of Mr. Raycie's breast. Lewis was his very own, and Lewis
represented what was most dear to him; and for both these
reasons Mr. Raycie set an inordinate value on the boy (a quite
different thing, Lewis thought, from loving him).

Mr. Raycie was particularly proud of his son's taste for letters. Himself not a wholly unread man, he admired intensely
what he called the "cultivated gentleman"—and that was

what Lewis was evidently going to be. Could he have combined with this tendency a manlier frame, and an interest in the few forms of sport then popular among gentlemen, Mr. Raycie's satisfaction would have been complete; but whose is, in this disappointing world? Meanwhile he flattered himself that, Lewis being still young and malleable, and his health certainly mending, two years of travel and adventure might send him back a very different figure, physically as well as mentally. Mr. Raycie had himself travelled in his youth, and was persuaded that the experience was formative; he secretly hoped for the return of a bronzed and broadened Lewis, seasoned by independence and adventure, and having discreetly sown his wild oats in foreign pastures, where they would not contaminate the home crop.

All this Lewis guessed; and he guessed as well that these two wander-years were intended by Mr. Raycie to lead up to a marriage and an establishment after Mr. Raycie's own heart, but in which Lewis's was not to have even a consulting voice.

"He's going to give me all the advantages—for his own purpose," the young man summed it up as he went down to join the family at the breakfast table.

Mr. Raycie was never more resplendent than at that moment of the day and season. His spotless white duck trousers, strapped under kid boots, his thin kerseymere coat, and drab *piqué* waistcoat crossed below a snowy stock, made him look as fresh as the morning and as appetizing as the peaches and cream banked before him.

Opposite sat Mrs. Raycie, immaculate also, but paler than usual, as became a mother about to part from her only son; and between the two was Sarah Anne, unusually pink, and apparently occupied in trying to screen her sister's empty seat. Lewis greeted them, and seated himself at his mother's right.

Mr. Raycie drew out his *guillochée* repeating watch, and detaching it from its heavy gold chain laid it on the table beside him.

"Mary Adeline is late again. It is a somewhat unusual thing for a sister to be late at the last meal she is to take—for two years—with her only brother."

"Oh, Mr. Raycie!" Mrs. Raycie faltered.

"I say, the idea is peculiar. Perhaps," said Mr. Raycie sarcastically, "I am going to be blessed with a *peculiar* daughter."

"I'm afraid Mary Adeline is beginning a sick headache, sir. She tried to get up, but really could not," said Sarah Anne in a rush.

Mr. Raycie's only reply was to arch ironic eyebrows, and Lewis hastily intervened: "I'm sorry, sir; but it may be my fault—"

Mrs. Raycie paled, Sarah Anne purpled, and Mr. Raycie echoed with punctilious incredulity: "Your—fault?"

"In being the occasion, sir, of last night's too-sumptuous festivity—"

"Ha—ha—ha!" Mr. Raycie laughed, his thunders instantly dispelled.

He pushed back his chair and nodded to his son with a smile; and the two, leaving the ladies to wash up the teacups (as was still the habit in genteel families) betook themselves to Mr. Raycie's study.

What Mr. Raycie studied in this apartment—except the accounts, and ways of making himself unpleasant to his family—Lewis had never been able to discover. It was a small bare formidable room; and the young man, who never crossed the threshold but with a sinking of his heart, felt it sink lower than ever. *"Now!"* he thought.

Mr. Raycie took the only easy-chair, and began.

"My dear fellow, our time is short, but long enough for what I have to say. In a few hours you will be setting out on your great journey: an important event in the life of any young man. Your talents and character—combined with your means of improving the opportunity—make me hope that in your case it will be decisive. I expect you to come home from this trip a man—"

So far, it was all to order, so to speak; Lewis could have recited it beforehand. He bent his head in acquiescence.

"A man," Mr. Raycie repeated, "prepared to play a part, a considerable part, in the social life of the community. I expect you to be a figure in New York; and I shall give you the means to be so." He cleared his throat. "But means are not enough—though you must never forget that they are essential. Education, polish, experience of the world; these are what so many of our men of standing lack. What do they know of Art or Letters? We have had little time here to produce either as yet—you spoke?" Mr. Raycie broke off with a crushing courtesy.

"I—oh, no," his son stammered.

"Ah; I thought you might be about to allude to certain blasphemous penny-a-liners whose poetic ravings are said to have given them a kind of pothouse notoriety."

Lewis reddened at the allusion but was silent, and his father went on:

"Where is our Byron—our Scott—our Shakespeare? And in painting it is the same. Where are our Old Masters? We are not without contemporary talent; but for works of genius we must still look to the past; we must, in most cases, content ourselves with copies. . . Ah, here, I know, my dear boy, I touch a responsive chord! Your love of the arts has not passed unperceived; and I mean, I desire, to do all I can to encourage it. Your future position in the world—your duties and obligations as a gentleman and a man of fortune—will not permit you to become, yourself, an eminent painter or a famous sculptor; but I shall raise no objection to your dabbling in these arts as an amateur—at least while you are travelling abroad. It will form your taste, strengthen your judgment, and give you, I hope, the discernment necessary to select for me a few masterpieces which shall *not* be copies. Copies," Mr. Raycie pursued with a deepening emphasis, "are for the less discriminating, or for those less blessed with this world's goods. Yes, my dear Lewis, I wish to create a gallery: a gallery of Heirlooms. Your mother participates in this ambition—she desires to see on our walls a few original specimens of the Italian genius. Raphael, I fear, we can hardly aspire to; but a Domenichino, an Albano, a Carlo Dolci, a Guercino, a Carlo Maratta—one or two of Salvator Rosa's noble landscapes . . . you see my idea? There shall be a Raycie Gallery; and it shall be your mission to get together its nucleus." Mr. Raycie paused, and mopped his flowing forehead. "I believe I could have given my son no task more to his liking."

"Oh, no, sir, none indeed!" Lewis cried, flushing and paling. He had in fact never suspected this part of his father's plan, and his heart swelled with the honour of so unforeseen a

mission. Nothing, in truth, could have made him prouder or
happier. For a moment he forgot love, forgot Treeshy, forgot
everything but the rapture of moving among the masterpieces
of which he had so long dreamed, moving not as a mere hungry spectator but as one whose privilege it should at least be
to single out and carry away some of the lesser treasures. He
could hardly take in what had happened, and the shock of the
announcement left him, as usual, inarticulate.

He heard his father booming on, developing the plan, explaining with his usual pompous precision that one of the
partners of the London bank in which Lewis's funds were
deposited was himself a noted collector, and had agreed to
provide the young traveller with letters of introduction to
other connoisseurs, both in France and Italy, so that Lewis's
acquisitions might be made under the most enlightened
guidance.

"It is," Mr. Raycie concluded, "in order to put you on a
footing of equality with the best collectors that I have placed
such a large sum at your disposal. I reckon that for ten thousand dollars you can travel for two years in the very best style;
and I mean to place another five thousand to your credit"
—he paused, and let the syllables drop slowly into his son's
brain: "five thousand dollars for the purchase of works of art,
which eventually—remember—will be yours; and will be
handed on, I trust, to your sons' sons as long as the name of
Raycie survives"—a length of time, Mr. Raycie's tone seemed
to imply, hardly to be measured in periods less extensive than
those of the Egyptian dynasties.

Lewis heard him with a whirling brain. *Five thousand dollars!* The sum seemed so enormous, even in dollars, and so
incalculably larger when translated into any continental currency, that he wondered why his father, in advance, had given
up all hope of a Raphael. . . "If I travel economically," he
said to himself, "and deny myself unnecessary luxuries, I may
yet be able to surprise him by bringing one back. And my
mother—how magnanimous, how splendid! Now I see why
she has consented to all the little economies that sometimes
seemed so paltry and so humiliating. . ."

The young man's eyes filled with tears, but he was still silent, though he longed as never before to express his gratitude

and admiration to his father. He had entered the study ex-pecting a parting sermon on the subject of thrift, coupled with the prospective announcement of a "suitable establish-ment" (he could even guess the particular Huzzard girl his father had in view); and instead he had been told to spend his princely allowance in a princely manner, and to return home with a gallery of masterpieces. "At least," he murmured to himself, "it shall contain a Correggio."

"Well, sir?" Mr. Raycie boomed.

"Oh, sir—" his son cried, and flung himself on the vast slope of the parental waistcoat.

Amid all these accumulated joys there murmured deep down in him the thought that nothing had been said or done to interfere with his secret plans about Treeshy. It seemed almost as if his father had tacitly accepted the idea of their unmentioned engagement; and Lewis felt half guilty at not confessing to it then and there. But the gods are formidable even when they unbend; never more so, perhaps, than at such moments. . .

PART II

IV

Lewis Raycie stood on a projecting rock and surveyed the sublime spectacle of Mont Blanc.

It was a brilliant August day, and the air, at that height, was already so sharp that he had had to put on his fur-lined pelisse. Behind him, at a respectful distance, was the travelling servant who, at a signal, had brought it up to him; below, in the bend of the mountain road, stood the light and elegant carriage which had carried him thus far on his travels.

Scarcely more than a year had passed since he had waved a farewell to New York from the deck of the packet-ship headed down the bay; yet, to the young man confidently facing Mont Blanc, nothing seemed left in him of that fluid and insubstantial being, the former Lewis Raycie, save a lurking and abeyant fear of Mr. Raycie senior. Even that, however, was so attenuated by distance and time, so far sunk below the horizon, and anchored on the far side of the globe, that it stirred in its sleep only when a handsomely folded and wafered letter in his parent's writing was handed out across the desk of some continental counting-house. Mr. Raycie senior did not write often, and when he did it was in a bland and stilted strain. He felt at a disadvantage on paper, and his natural sarcasm was swamped in the rolling periods which it cost him hours of labour to bring forth; so that the dreaded quality lurked for his son only in the curve of certain letters, and in a positively awful way of writing out, at full length, the word *Esquire*.

It was not that Lewis had broken with all the memories of his past of a year ago. Many still lingered in him, or rather had been transferred to the new man he had become—as for instance his tenderness for Treeshy Kent, which, somewhat to his surprise, had obstinately resisted all the assaults of English keepsake beauties and almond-eyed houris of the East. It startled him, at times, to find Treeshy's short dusky face, with its round forehead, the widely spaced eyes and the high cheek-bones, starting out at him suddenly in the street of some legendary town, or in a landscape of languid beauty, just as he had now and again been arrested in an exotic garden by the very scent of the verbena under the verandah at home. His travels had confirmed rather than weakened the family view of Treeshy's plainness; she could not be made to fit into any of the patterns of female beauty so far submitted to him; yet there she was, ensconced in his new heart and mind as deeply as in the old, though her kisses seemed less vivid, and the peculiar rough notes of her voice hardly reached him. Sometimes, half irritably, he said to himself that with an effort he could disperse her once for all; yet she lived on in him, unseen yet ineffaceable, like the image on a daguerreotype plate, no less there because so often invisible.

To the new Lewis, however, the whole business was less important than he had once thought it. His suddenly acquired maturity made Treeshy seem a petted child rather than the guide, the Beatrice, he had once considered her; and he promised himself, with an elderly smile, that as soon as he got to Italy he would write her the long letter for which he was now considerably in her debt.

His travels had first carried him to England. There he spent some weeks in collecting letters and recommendations for his tour, in purchasing his travelling-carriage and its numerous appurtenances, and in driving in it from cathedral town to storied castle, omitting nothing, from Abbotsford to Kenilworth, which deserved the attention of a cultivated mind. From England he crossed to Calais, moving slowly southward to the Mediterranean; and there, taking ship for the Piræus, he plunged into pure romance, and the tourist became a Giaour.

It was the East which had made him into a new Lewis Raycie; the East, so squalid and splendid, so pestilent and so poetic, so full of knavery and romance and fleas and nightingales, and so different, alike in its glories and its dirt, from what his studious youth had dreamed. After Smyrna and the bazaars, after Damascus and Palmyra, the Acropolis, Mytilene and Sunium, what could be left in his mind of Canal Street and the lawn above the Sound? Even the mosquitoes, which seemed at first the only connecting link, were different, because he fought with them in scenes so different; and a young gentleman who had journeyed across the desert in Arabian dress, slept under goats'-hair tents, been attacked by robbers in the Peloponnesus and despoiled by his own escort at Baalbek, and by customs' officials everywhere, could not but look with a smile on the terrors that walk New York and the Hudson river. Encased in security and monotony, that other Lewis Raycie, when his little figure bobbed up to the surface, seemed like a new-born babe preserved in alcohol. Even Mr. Raycie senior's thunders were now no more than the far-off murmur of summer lightning on a perfect evening. Had Mr. Raycie ever really frightened Lewis? Why, now he was not even frightened by Mont Blanc!

He was still gazing with a sense of easy equality at its awful pinnacles when another travelling-carriage paused near his own, and a young man, eagerly jumping from it, and also followed by a servant with a cloak, began to mount the slope. Lewis at once recognized the carriage, and the light springing figure of the young man, his blue coat and swelling stock, and the scar slightly distorting his handsome and eloquent mouth. It was the Englishman who had arrived at the Montanvert inn the night before with a valet, a guide, and such a cargo of books, maps and sketching-materials as threatened to overshadow even Lewis's outfit.

Lewis, at first, had not been greatly drawn to the newcomer, who, seated aloof in the dining-room, seemed not to see his fellow-traveller. The truth was that Lewis was dying for a little conversation. His astonishing experiences were so tightly packed in him (with no outlet save the meagre trickle of his nightly diary) that he felt they would soon melt into the vague blur of other people's travels unless he could give them fresh reality by talking them over. And the stranger with the deep-blue eyes that matched his coat, the scarred cheek and eloquent lip, seemed to Lewis a worthy listener. The Englishman appeared to think otherwise. He preserved an air of moody abstraction, which Lewis's vanity imagined him to have put on as the gods becloud themselves for their secret errands; and the curtness of his goodnight was (Lewis flattered himself) surpassed only by the young New Yorker's.

But today all was different. The stranger advanced affably, raised his hat from his tossed statue-like hair, and enquired with a smile: "Are you by any chance interested in the forms of cirrous clouds?"

His voice was as sweet as his smile, and the two were rein-forced by a glance so winning that it made the odd question seem not only pertinent but natural. Lewis, though surprised, was not disconcerted. He merely coloured with the unwonted sense of his ignorance, and replied ingenuously: "I believe, sir, I am interested in everything."

"A noble answer!" cried the other, and held out his hand.

"But I must add," Lewis continued with courageous hon-esty, "that I have never as yet had occasion to occupy myself particularly with the forms of cirrous clouds."

His companion looked at him merrily. "That," said he, "is no reason why you shouldn't begin to do so now!" To which Lewis as merrily agreed. "For in order to be interested in things," the other continued more gravely, "it is only neces-sary to see them; and I believe I am not wrong in saying that you are one of the privileged beings to whom the seeing eye has been given."

Lewis blushed his agreement, and his interlocutor contin-ued: "You are one of those who have been on the road to Damascus."

"On the road? I've been to the place itself!" the wanderer exclaimed, bursting with the particulars of his travels; and then blushed more deeply at the perception that the other's use of the name had of course been figurative.

The young Englishman's face lit up. "You've been to Da-mascus—literally been there yourself? But that may be almost as interesting, in its quite different way, as the formation of clouds or lichens. For the present," he continued with a ges-ture toward the mountain, "I must devote myself to the extremely inadequate rendering of some of these delicate *aiguilles*; a bit of drudgery not likely to interest you in the face of so sublime a scene. But perhaps this evening—if, as I think, we are staying in the same inn—you will give me a few minutes of your society, and tell me something of your trav-els. My father," he added with his engaging smile, "has had packed with my paint-brushes a few bottles of a wholly trustworthy Madeira; and if you will favour me with your company at dinner. . ."

He signed to his servant to undo the sketching materials, spread his cloak on the rock, and was already lost in his task as Lewis descended to the carriage.

The Madeira proved as trustworthy as his host had promised. Perhaps it was its exceptional quality which threw such a golden lustre over the dinner; unless it were rather the conversation of the blue-eyed Englishman which made Lewis Raycie, always a small drinker, feel that in his company every drop was nectar.

When Lewis joined his host it had been with the secret hope of at last being able to talk; but when the evening was over (and they kept it up to the small hours) he perceived that he had chiefly listened. Yet there had been no sense of suppression, of thwarted volubility; he had been given all the openings he wanted. Only, whenever he produced a little fact it was instantly overflowed by the other's imagination till it burned like a dull pebble tossed into a rushing stream. For whatever Lewis said was seen by his companion from a new angle, and suggested a new train of thought; each commonplace item of experience became a many-faceted crystal flashing with unexpected fires. The young Englishman's mind moved in a world of associations and references far more richly peopled than Lewis's; but his eager communicativeness, his directness of speech and manner, instantly opened its gates to the simpler youth. It was certainly not the Madeira which sped the hours and flooded them with magic; but the magic gave the Madeira—excellent, and reputed of its kind, as Lewis afterward learned—a taste no other vintage was to have for him.

"Oh, but we must meet again in Italy—there are many things there that I could perhaps help you to see," the young Englishman declared as they swore eternal friendship on the stairs of the sleeping inn.

V

I<small>T WAS</small> in a tiny Venetian church, no more than a chapel, that Lewis Raycie's eyes had been unsealed—in a dull-looking little church not even mentioned in the guide-books. But for his chance encounter with the young Englishman in the shadow of Mont Blanc, Lewis would never have heard of the place; but then what else that was worth knowing would he ever have heard of, he wondered?

He had stood a long time looking at the frescoes, put off at first—he could admit it now—by a certain stiffness in the attitudes of the people, by the childish elaboration of their dress (so different from the noble draperies which Sir Joshua's Discourses on Art had taught him to admire in the great painters), and by the innocent inexpressive look in their young faces—for even the gray-beards seemed young. And then suddenly his gaze had lit on one of these faces in particular: that of a girl with round cheeks, high cheek-bones and widely set eyes under an intricate head-dress of pearl-woven braids. Why, it was Treeshy—Treeshy Kent to the life! And so far from being thought "plain," the young lady was no other than the peerless princess about whom the tale revolved. And what a fairy-land she lived in—full of lithe youths and round-faced pouting maidens, rosy old men and burnished blackamoors, pretty birds and cats and nibbling rabbits—and all involved and enclosed in golden balustrades, in colonnades of pink and blue, laurel-garlands festooned from ivory balconies, and domes and minarets against summer seas! Lewis's imagination lost itself in the scene; he forgot to regret the noble draperies, the exalted sentiments, the fuliginous backgrounds, of the artists he had come to Italy to admire—forgot Sassoferrato, Guido Reni, Carlo Dolce, Lo Spagnoletto, the Carracci, and even the Transfiguration of Raphael, though he knew it to be the greatest picture in the world.

After that he had seen almost everything else that Italian art had to offer; had been to Florence, Naples, Rome; to Bologna to study the Eclectic School, to Parma to examine the Correggios and the Giulio Romanos. But that first vision had

laid a magic seed between his lips; the seed that makes you
hear what the birds say and the grasses whisper. Even if his
English friend had not continued at his side, pointing out,
explaining, inspiring, Lewis Raycie flattered himself that the
round face of the little Saint Ursula would have led him safely
and confidently past all her rivals. She had become his touchstone, his star: how insipid seemed to him all the sheep-faced
Virgins draped in red and blue paint after he had looked into
her wondering girlish eyes and traced the elaborate pattern of
her brocades! He could remember now, quite distinctly, the
day when he had given up even Beatrice Cenci . . . and as for
that fat naked Magdalen of Carlo Dolce's, lolling over the
book she was not reading, and ogling the spectator in the
good old way . . . faugh! Saint Ursula did not need to rescue
him from *her*. . .

His eyes had been opened to a new world of art. And this
world it was his mission to reveal to others—he, the insignificant and ignorant Lewis Raycie, as "but for the grace of
God," and that chance encounter on Mont Blanc, he might
have gone on being to the end! He shuddered to think of the
army of Neapolitan beggar-boys, bituminous monks, whirling
prophets, languishing Madonnas and pink-rumped *amorini*
who might have been travelling home with him in the hold of
the fast new steam-packet.

His excitement had something of the apostle's ecstasy. He
was not only, in a few hours, to embrace Treeshy, and be
reunited to his honoured parents; he was also to go forth and
preach the new gospel to them that sat in the darkness of
Salvator Rosa and Lo Spagnoletto. . .

The first thing that struck Lewis was the smallness of the
house on the Sound, and the largeness of Mr. Raycie.

He had expected to receive the opposite impression. In his
recollection the varnished Tuscan villa had retained something
of its impressiveness, even when compared to its supposed
originals. Perhaps the very contrast between their draughty
distances and naked floors, and the expensive carpets and
bright fires of High Point, magnified his memory of the
latter—there were moments when the thought of its groaning board certainly added to the effect. But the image of Mr.

Raycie had meanwhile dwindled. Everything about him, as his son looked back, seemed narrow, juvenile, almost childish. His bluster about Edgar Poe, for instance—true poet still to Lewis, though he had since heard richer notes; his fussy tyranny of his womenkind; his unconscious but total ignorance of most of the things, books, people, ideas, that now filled his son's mind; above all, the arrogance and incompetence of his artistic judgments. Beyond a narrow range of reading—mostly, Lewis suspected, culled in drowsy after-dinner snatches from Knight's "Half-hours with the Best Authors"—Mr. Raycie made no pretence to book-learning; left *that*, as he handsomely said, "to the professors." But on matters of art he was dogmatic and explicit, prepared to justify his opinions by the citing of eminent authorities and of market-prices, and quite clear, as his farewell talk with his son had shown, as to which Old Masters should be privileged to figure in the Raycie collection.

The young man felt no impatience of these judgments. America was a long way from Europe, and it was many years since Mr. Raycie had travelled. He could hardly be blamed for not knowing that the things he admired were no longer admirable, still less for not knowing why. The pictures before which Lewis had knelt in spirit had been virtually undiscovered, even by art-students and critics, in his father's youth. How was an American gentleman, filled with his own self-importance, and paying his courier the highest salary to show him the accredited "Masterpieces"—how was he to guess that whenever he stood rapt before a Sassoferrato or a Carlo Dolce one of those unknown treasures lurked near by under dust and cobwebs?

No; Lewis felt only tolerance and understanding. Such a view was not one to magnify the paternal image; but when the young man entered the study where Mr. Raycie sat immobilized by gout, the swathed leg stretched along his sofa seemed only another reason for indulgence . . .

Perhaps, Lewis thought afterward, it was his father's prone position, the way his great bulk billowed over the sofa, and the lame leg reached out like a mountain-ridge, that made him suddenly seem to fill the room; or else the sound of his voice booming irritably across the threshold, and scattering

Mrs. Raycie and the girls with a fierce: "And now, ladies, if the hugging and kissing are over, I should be glad of a moment with my son." But it was odd that, after mother and daughters had withdrawn with all their hoops and flounces, the study seemed to grow even smaller, and Lewis himself to feel more like a David without the pebble.

"Well, my boy," his father cried, crimson and puffing, "here you are at home again, with many adventures to relate, no doubt; and a few masterpieces to show me, as I gather from the drafts on my exchequer."

"Oh, as to the masterpieces, sir, certainly," Lewis simpered, wondering why his voice sounded so fluty, and his smile was produced with such a conscious muscular effort.

"Good—good," Mr. Raycie approved, waving a violet hand which seemed to be ripening for a bandage. "Reedy carried out my orders, I presume? Saw to it that the paintings were deposited with the bulk of your luggage in Canal Street?"

"Oh, yes, sir; Mr. Reedy was on the dock with precise instructions. You know he always carries out your orders," Lewis ventured with a faint irony.

Mr. Raycie stared. "Mr. Reedy," he said, "does what I tell him, if that's what you mean; otherwise he would hardly have been in my employ for over thirty years."

Lewis was silent, and his father examined him critically. "You appear to have filled out; your health is satisfactory? Well . . . well . . . Mr. Robert Huzzard and his daughters are dining here this evening, by the way, and will no doubt be expecting to see the latest French novelties in stocks and waistcoats. Malvina has become a very elegant figure, your sisters tell me." Mr. Raycie chuckled, and Lewis thought: "I *knew* it was the oldest Huzzard girl!" while a slight chill ran down his spine.

"As to the pictures," Mr. Raycie pursued with growing animation, "I am laid low, as you see, by this cursèd affliction, and till the doctors get me up again, here must I lie and try to imagine how your treasures will look in the new gallery. And meanwhile, my dear boy, I need hardly say that no one is to be admitted to see them till they have been inspected by me and suitably hung. Reedy shall begin unpacking at once; and when we move to town next month Mrs. Raycie, God willing, shall give the handsomest evening party New York has yet seen, to show my son's collection, and perhaps . . . eh, well? . . . to celebrate another interesting event in his history."

Lewis met this with a faint but respectful gurgle, and before his blurred eyes rose the wistful face of Treeshy Kent.

"Ah, well, I shall see her tomorrow," he thought, taking heart again as soon as he was out of his father's presence.

VI

MR. RAYCIE stood silent for a long time after making the round of the room in the Canal Street house where the unpacked pictures had been set out.

He had driven to town alone with Lewis, sternly rebuffing his daughters' timid hints, and Mrs. Raycie's mute but visible yearning to accompany him. Though the gout was over he was still weak and irritable, and Mrs. Raycie, fluttered at the thought of "crossing him," had swept the girls away at his first frown.

Lewis's hopes rose as he followed his parent's limping progress. The pictures, though standing on chairs and tables, and set clumsily askew to catch the light, bloomed out of the half-dusk of the empty house with a new and persuasive beauty. Ah, how right he had been—how inevitable that his father should own it!

Mr. Raycie halted in the middle of the room. He was still silent, and his face, so quick to frown and glare, wore the calm, almost expressionless look known to Lewis as the mask of inward perplexity. "Oh, of course it will take a little time," the son thought, tingling with the eagerness of youth.

At last, Mr. Raycie woke the echoes by clearing his throat; but the voice which issued from it was as inexpressive as his face. "It is singular," he said, "how little the best copies of the Old Masters resemble the originals. For these *are* Originals?" he questioned, suddenly swinging about on Lewis.

"Oh, absolutely, sir! Besides—" The young man was about to add: "No one would ever have taken the trouble to copy them"—but hastily checked himself.

"Besides——?"

"I meant, I had the most competent advice obtainable."

"So I assume; since it was the express condition on which I authorized your purchases."

Lewis felt himself shrinking and his father expanding; but he sent a glance along the wall, and beauty shed her reviving beam on him.

Mr. Raycie's brows projected ominously; but his face

remained smooth and dubious. Once more he cast a slow glance about him.

"Let us," he said pleasantly, "begin with the Raphael." And it was evident that he did not know which way to turn.

"Oh, sir, a Raphael nowadays—I warned you it would be far beyond my budget."

Mr. Raycie's face fell slightly. "I had hoped nevertheless . . . for an inferior specimen. . ." Then, with an effort: "The Sassoferrato, then."

Lewis felt more at his ease; he even ventured a respectful smile. "Sassoferrato is *all* inferior, isn't he? The fact is, he no longer stands . . . quite as he used to. . ."

Mr. Raycie stood motionless: his eyes were vacuously fixed on the nearest picture.

"Sassoferrato . . . no longer . . . ?"

"Well, sir, *no*; not for a collection of this quality."

Lewis saw that he had at last struck the right note. Something large and uncomfortable appeared to struggle in Mr. Raycie's throat; then he gave a cough which might almost have been said to cast out Sassoferrato.

There was another pause before he pointed with his stick to a small picture representing a snub-nosed young woman with a high forehead and jewelled coif, against a background of delicately interwoven columbines. "Is *that*," he questioned, "your Carlo Dolce? The style is much the same, I see; but it seems to me lacking in his peculiar sentiment."

"Oh, but it's not a Carlo Dolce: it's a Piero della Francesca, sir!" burst in triumph from the trembling Lewis.

His father sternly faced him. "It's a *copy*, you mean? I thought so!"

"No, no; not a copy; it's by a great painter . . . a much greater . . ."

Mr. Raycie had reddened sharply at his mistake. To conceal his natural annoyance he assumed a still more silken manner. "In that case," he said, "I think I should like to see the inferior painters first. Where *is* the Carlo Dolce?"

"There *is* no Carlo Dolce," said Lewis, white to the lips.

The young man's next distinct recollection was of standing, he knew not how long afterward, before the armchair in

which his father had sunk down, almost as white and shaken
as himself.

"This," stammered Mr. Raycie, "this is going to bring back
my gout. . ." But when Lewis entreated: "Oh, sir, do let us
drive back quietly to the country, and give me a chance later
to explain . . . to put my case" . . . the old gentleman had
struck through the pleading with a furious wave of his stick.

"Explain later? Put your case later? It's just what I insist
upon your doing here and now!" And Mr. Raycie added
hoarsely, and as if in actual physical anguish: "I understand
that young John Huzzard returned from Rome last week with
a Raphael."

After that, Lewis heard himself—as if with the icy detachment of a spectator—marshalling his arguments, pleading the
cause he hoped his pictures would have pleaded for him,
dethroning the old Powers and Principalities, and setting up
these new names in their place. It was first of all the names
that stuck in Mr. Raycie's throat: after spending a life-time in
committing to memory the correct pronunciation of words
like Lo Spagnoletto and Giulio Romano, it was bad enough,
his wrathful eyes seemed to say, to have to begin a new set of
verbal gymnastics before you could be sure of saying to a
friend with careless accuracy: "And *this* is my Giotto da
Bondone."

But that was only the first shock, soon forgotten in the rush
of greater tribulation. For one might conceivably learn how
to pronounce Giotto da Bondone, and even enjoy doing so,
provided the friend in question recognized the name and
bowed to its authority. But to have your effort received by a
blank stare, and the playful request: "You'll have to say that
over again, please"—to know that, in going the round of the
gallery (the Raycie Gallery!) the same stare and the same
request were likely to be repeated before each picture; the
bitterness of this was so great that Mr. Raycie, without exaggeration, might have likened his case to that of Agag.

"God! God! God! Carpatcher, you say this other fellow's
called? Kept him back till the last because it's the gem of the
collection, did you? Carpatcher—well, he'd have done better
to stick to his trade. Something to do with those new European steam-cars, I suppose, eh?" Mr. Raycie was so incensed

that his irony was less subtle than usual. "And Angelico you say did that kind of Noah's Ark soldier in pink armour on gold-leaf? Well, *there* I've caught you tripping, my boy. Not Angelico, Angelica; Angelica Kauffman was a lady. And the damned swindler who foisted that barbarous daub on you as a picture of hers deserves to be drawn and quartered—and shall be, sir, by God, if the law can reach him! He shall disgorge every penny he's rooked you out of, or my name's not Halston Raycie! A bargain . . . you say the thing was a *bargain*? Why, the price of a clean postage stamp would be too dear for it! God—my son; do you realize you had a *trust* to carry out?"

"Yes, sir, yes; and it's just because—"

"You might have written; you might at least have placed your views before me . . ."

How could Lewis say: "If I had, I knew you'd have refused to let me buy the pictures?" He could only stammer: "I *did* allude to the revolution in taste . . . new names coming up . . . you may remember . . ."

"Revolution! New names! Who says so? I had a letter last week from the London dealers to whom I especially recommended you, telling me that an undoubted Guido Reni was coming into the market this summer."

"Oh, the dealers—*they* don't know!"

"The dealers . . . don't? . . . Who does . . . except yourself?" Mr. Raycie pronounced in a white sneer.

Lewis, as white, still held his ground. "I wrote you, sir, about my friends; in Italy, and afterward in England."

"Well, God damn it, I never heard of one of *their* names before, either; no more'n of these painters of yours here. I supplied you with the names of all the advisers you needed, and all the painters, too; I all but made the collection for you myself, before you started. . . I was explicit enough, in all conscience, wasn't I?"

Lewis smiled faintly. "That's what I hoped the pictures would be . . ."

"What? Be what? What'd you mean?"

"Be explicit. . . Speak for themselves . . . make you see that their painters are already superseding some of the better-known . . ."

Mr. Raycie gave an awful laugh. "They are, are they? In whose estimation? Your friends', I suppose. What's the name, again, of that fellow you met in Italy, who picked 'em out for you?"

"Ruskin—John Ruskin," said Lewis.

Mr. Raycie's laugh, prolonged, gathered up into itself a fresh shower of expletives. "Ruskin—Ruskin—just plain John Ruskin, eh? And who *is* this great John Ruskin, who sets God A'mighty right in his judgments? Who'd you say John Ruskin's father was, now?"

"A respected wine-merchant in London, sir."

Mr. Raycie ceased to laugh: he looked at his son with an expression of unutterable disgust.

"Retail?"

"I . . . believe so . . ."

"Faugh!" said Mr. Raycie.

"It wasn't only Ruskin, father. . . . I told you of those other friends in London, whom I met on the way home. They inspected the pictures, and all of them agreed that . . . that the collection would some day be very valuable."

"*Some day*—did they give you a date . . . the month and the year? Ah, those other friends; yes. You said there was a Mr. Brown and a Mr. Hunt and a Mr. Rossiter, was it? Well, I never heard of any of those names, either—except perhaps in a trades' directory."

"It's not Rossiter, father: Dante Rossetti."

"Excuse me: Rossetti. And what does Mr. Dante Rossetti's father do? Sell macaroni, I presume?"

Lewis was silent, and Mr. Raycie went on, speaking now with a deadly steadiness: "The friends I sent you to were judges of art, sir; men who know what a picture's worth; not one of 'em but could pick out a genuine Raphael. Couldn't you find 'em when you got to England? Or hadn't they the time to spare for you? You'd better not," Mr. Raycie added, "tell me *that*, for I know how they'd have received your father's son."

"Oh, most kindly . . . they did indeed, sir . . ."

"Ay; but that didn't suit you. You didn't *want* to be advised. You wanted to show off before a lot of ignoramuses like yourself. You wanted—how'd I know what you wanted?

It's as if I'd never given you an instruction or laid a charge on you! And the money—God! Where'd it go to? Buying *this*? Nonsense—." Mr. Raycie raised himself heavily on his stick and fixed his angry eyes on his son. "Own up, Lewis; tell me they got it out of you at cards. Professional gamblers the lot, I make no doubt; your Ruskin and your Morris and your Rossiter. Make a business to pick up young American greenhorns on their travels, I daresay. . . No? Not that, you say? Then—women? . . . God A'mighty, Lewis," gasped Mr. Raycie, tottering toward his son with outstretched stick, "I'm no blue-nosed Puritan, sir, and I'd a damn sight rather you told me you'd spent it on a woman, every penny of it, than let yourself be fleeced like a simpleton, buying these things that look more like cuts out o' Foxe's Book of Martyrs than Originals of the Old Masters for a Gentleman's Gallery. . . Youth's youth. . . Gad, sir, I've been young myself . . . a fellow's got to go through his apprenticeship. . . Own up now: women?"

"Oh, not women——"

"Not even!" Mr. Raycie groaned. "All in pictures, then? Well, say no more to me now. . . I'll get home, I'll get home. . ." He cast a last apoplectic glance about the room. "The Raycie Gallery! That pack of bones and mummers' finery! . . . Why, let alone the rest, there's not a full-bodied female among 'em. . . Do you know what those Madonnas of yours are like, my son? Why, there ain't one of 'em that don't remind me of a bad likeness of poor Treeshy Kent. . . I should say you'd hired half the sign-painters of Europe to do her portrait for you—if I could imagine your wanting it. . . No, sir! I don't need your arm," Mr. Raycie snarled, heaving his great bulk painfully across the hall. He withered Lewis with a last look from the doorstep. "And to buy *that* you overdrew your account?—No, I'll drive home alone."

VII

M^{R.} R<small>AYCIE</small> did not die till nearly a year later; but New York agreed it was the affair of the pictures that had killed him.

The day after his first and only sight of them he sent for his lawyer, and it became known that he had made a new will. Then he took to his bed with a return of the gout, and grew so rapidly worse that it was thought "only proper" to postpone the party Mrs. Raycie was to have given that autumn to inaugurate the gallery. This enabled the family to pass over in silence the question of the works of art themselves; but outside of the Raycie house, where they were never mentioned, they formed, that winter, a frequent and fruitful topic of discussion.

Only two persons besides Mr. Raycie were known to have seen them. One was Mr. Donaldson Kent, who owed the privilege to the fact of having once been to Italy; the other, Mr. Reedy, the agent, who had unpacked the pictures. Mr. Reedy, beset by Raycie cousins and old family friends, had replied with genuine humility: "Why, the truth is, I never was taught to see any difference between one picture and another, except as regards the size of them; and these struck me as smallish . . . on the small side, I would say. . ."

Mr. Kent was known to have unbosomed himself to Mr. Raycie with considerable frankness—he went so far, it was rumoured, as to declare that he had never seen any pictures in Italy like those brought back by Lewis, and begged to doubt if they really came from there. But in public he maintained that noncommittal attitude which passed for prudence, but proceeded only from timidity; no one ever got anything from him but the guarded statement: "The subjects are wholly inoffensive."

It was believed that Mr. Raycie dared not consult the Huzzards. Young John Huzzard had just brought home a Raphael; it would have been hard not to avoid comparisons which would have been too galling. Neither to them, nor to any one else, did Mr. Raycie ever again allude to the Raycie Gallery. But when his will was opened it was found that he had bequeathed the pictures to his son. The rest of his property was left absolutely to his two daughters. The bulk of the estate was Mrs. Raycie's; but it was known that Mrs. Raycie had had her instructions, and among them, perhaps, was the order to fade away in her turn after six months of widowhood. When she had been laid beside her husband in Trinity church-yard her will (made in the same week as Mr. Raycie's, and obviously at his dictation) was found to allow five thousand dollars a year to Lewis during his life-time; the residue of the fortune, which Mr. Raycie's thrift and good management had made into one of the largest in New York, was divided between the daughters. Of these, the one promptly married a Kent and the other a Huzzard; and the latter, Sarah Ann (who had never been Lewis's favourite), was wont to say in later years: "Oh, no, I never grudged my poor brother those funny old pictures. You see, we have a Raphael."

The house stood on the corner of Third Avenue and Tenth Street. It had lately come to Lewis Raycie as his share in the property of a distant cousin, who had made an "old New York will" under which all his kin benefited in proportion to their consanguinity. The neighbourhood was unfashionable, and the house in bad repair; but Mr. and Mrs. Lewis Raycie, who, since their marriage, had been living in retirement at Tarrytown, immediately moved into it.

Their arrival excited small attention. Within a year of his father's death, Lewis had married Treeshy Kent. The alliance had not been encouraged by Mr. and Mrs. Kent, who went so far as to say that their niece might have done better; but as that one of their sons who was still unmarried had always shown a lively sympathy for Treeshy, they yielded to the prudent thought that, after all, it was better than having her entangle Bill.

The Lewis Raycies had been four years married, and during that time had dropped out of the memory of New York as completely as if their exile had covered half a century. Neither of them had ever cut a great figure there. Treeshy had been nothing but the Kents' Cinderella, and Lewis's ephemeral importance, as heir to the Raycie millions, had been effaced by the painful episode which resulted in his being deprived of them.

So secluded was their way of living, and so much had it come to be a habit, that when Lewis announced that he had inherited Uncle Ebenezer's house his wife hardly looked up from the baby-blanket she was embroidering.

"Uncle Ebenezer's house in New York?"

He drew a deep breath. "Now I shall be able to show the pictures."

"Oh, Lewis—" She dropped the blanket. "Are we going to live there?"

"Certainly. But the house is so large that I shall turn the two corner rooms on the ground floor into a gallery. They are very suitably lighted. It was there that Cousin Ebenezer was laid out."

"Oh, Lewis——"

If anything could have made Lewis Raycie believe in his own strength of will it was his wife's attitude. Merely to hear that unquestioning murmur of submission was to feel something of his father's tyrannous strength arise in him; but with the wish to use it more humanely.

"You'll like that, Treeshy? It's been dull for you here, I know."

She flushed up. "Dull? With *you*, darling? Besides, I like the country. But I shall like Tenth Street too. Only—you said there were repairs?"

He nodded sternly. "I shall borrow money to make them. If necessary—" he lowered his voice—"I shall mortgage the pictures."

He saw her eyes fill. "Oh, but it won't be! There are so many ways still in which I can economize."

He laid his hand on hers and turned his profile toward her, because he knew it was so much stronger than his full face. He did not feel sure that she quite grasped his intention about the pictures; was not even certain that he wished her to. He went in to New York every week now, occupying himself mysteriously and importantly with plans, specifications and other business transactions with long names; while Treeshy, through the hot summer months, sat in Tarrytown and waited for the baby.

A little girl was born at the end of the summer and christened Louisa; and when she was a few weeks old the Lewis Raycies left the country for New York.

"Now!" thought Lewis, as they bumped over the cobble-stones of Tenth Street in the direction of Cousin Ebenezer's house.

The carriage stopped, he handed out his wife, the nurse followed with the baby, and they all stood and looked up at the house-front.

"Oh, Lewis—" Treeshy gasped; and even little Louisa set up a sympathetic wail.

Over the door—over Cousin Ebenezer's respectable, conservative and intensely private front-door—hung a large sign-board bearing, in gold letters on a black ground, the inscription:

GALLERY OF CHRISTIAN ART

OPEN ON WEEK-DAYS FROM 2 TO 4

ADMISSION 25 CENTS. CHILDREN 10 CENTS

Lewis saw his wife turn pale, and pressed her arm in his. "Believe me, it's the only way to make the pictures known. And they *must* be made known," he said with a thrill of his old ardour.

"Yes, dear, of course. But . . . to every one? Publicly?"

"If we showed them only to our friends, of what use would it be? Their opinion is already formed."

She sighed her acknowledgment. "But the . . . the entrance fee . . ."

"If we can afford it later, the gallery will be free. But meanwhile——"

"Oh, Lewis, I quite understand!" And clinging to him, the still-protesting baby in her wake, she passed with a dauntless step under the awful sign-board.

"At last I shall see the pictures properly lighted!" she exclaimed, and turned in the hall to fling her arms about her husband.

"It's all they need . . . to be appreciated," he answered, aglow with her encouragement.

Since his withdrawal from the world it had been a part of Lewis's system never to read the daily papers. His wife eagerly conformed to his example, and they lived in a little air-tight circle of aloofness, as if the cottage at Tarrytown had been situated in another and happier planet.

Lewis, nevertheless, the day after the opening of the Gallery of Christian Art, deemed it his duty to derogate from this attitude, and sallied forth secretly to buy the principal journals. When he re-entered his house he went straight up to the nursery where he knew that, at that hour, Treeshy would be giving the little girl her bath. But it was later than he supposed. The rite was over, the baby lay asleep in its modest cot, and the mother sat crouched by the fire, her face hidden in her hands. Lewis instantly guessed that she too had seen the papers.

"Treeshy—you mustn't . . . consider this of any consequence. . . ," he stammered.

She lifted a tear-stained face. "Oh, my darling! I thought you never read the papers."

"Not usually. But I thought it my duty——"

"Yes; I see. But, as you say, what earthly consequence——?"

"None whatever; we must just be patient and persist."

She hesitated, and then, her arms about him, her head on his breast: "Only, dearest, I've been counting up again, ever so carefully; and even if we give up fires everywhere but in the nursery, I'm afraid the wages of the door-keeper and the guardian . . . especially if the gallery's open to the public every day . . ."

"I've thought of that already, too; and I myself shall hereafter act as doorkeeper and guardian."

He kept his eyes on hers as he spoke. "This is the test," he thought. Her face paled under its brown glow, and the eyes dilated in her effort to check her tears. Then she said gaily: "That will be . . . very interesting, won't it, Lewis? Hearing what the people say. . . Because, as they begin to know the pictures better, and to understand them, they can't fail to say very interesting things . . . can they?" She turned and caught up the sleeping Louisa. "Can they . . . oh, you darling—darling?"

Lewis turned away too. Not another woman in New York would have been capable of that. He could hear all the town echoing with this new scandal of his showing the pictures himself—and she, so much more sensitive to ridicule, so much less carried away by apostolic ardour, how much louder must that mocking echo ring in her ears! But his pang was only momentary. The one thought that possessed him for any length of time was that of vindicating himself by making the pictures known; he could no longer fix his attention on lesser matters. The derision of illiterate journalists was not a thing to wince at; once let the pictures be seen by educated and intelligent people, and they would speak for themselves— especially if he were at hand to interpret them.

VIII

OR A WEEK or two a great many people came to the gallery; but, even with Lewis as interpreter, the pictures failed to make themselves heard. During the first days, indeed, owing to the unprecedented idea of holding a paying exhibition in a private house, and to the mockery of the newspapers, the Gallery of Christian Art was thronged with noisy curiosity-seekers; once the astonished metropolitan police had to be invited in to calm their comments and control their movements. But the name of "Christian Art" soon chilled this class of sight-seer, and before long they were replaced by a dumb and respectable throng, who roamed vacantly through the rooms and out again, grumbling that it wasn't worth the money. Then these too diminished; and once the tide had turned, the ebb was rapid. Every day from two to four Lewis still sat shivering among his treasures, or patiently measured the length of the deserted gallery: as long as there was a chance of any one coming he would not admit that he was beaten. For the next visitor might always be the one who understood.

One snowy February day he had thus paced the rooms in unbroken solitude for above an hour when carriage-wheels stopped at the door. He hastened to open it, and in a great noise of silks his sister Sarah Anne Huzzard entered.

Lewis felt for a moment as he used to under his father's glance. Marriage and millions had given the moon-faced Sarah something of the Raycie awfulness; but her brother looked into her empty eyes, and his own kept their level.

"Well, Lewis," said Mrs. Huzzard with a simpering sternness, and caught her breath.

"Well, Sarah Anne—I'm happy that you've come to take a look at my pictures."

"I've come to see you and your wife." She gave another nervous gasp, shook out her flounces, and added in a rush: "And to ask you how much longer this . . . this spectacle is to continue. . . ."

"The exhibition?" Lewis smiled. She signed a flushed assent.

"Well, there has been a considerable falling-off lately in the number of visitors——"

"Thank heaven!" she interjected.

"But as long as I feel that any one wishes to come . . . I shall be here . . . to open the door, as you see."

She sent a shuddering glance about her. "Lewis—I wonder if you realize . . . ?"

"Oh, fully."

"Then *why* do you go on? Isn't it enough—aren't you satisfied?"

"With the effect they have produced?"

"With the effect *you* have produced—on your family and on the whole of New York. With the slur on poor Papa's memory."

"Papa left me the pictures, Sarah Anne."

"Yes. But not to make yourself a mountebank about them."

Lewis considered this impartially. "Are you sure? Perhaps, on the contrary, he did it for that very reason."

"Oh, don't heap more insults on our father's memory! Things are bad enough without that. How your wife can allow it I can't see. Do you ever consider the humiliation to *her*?"

Lewis gave another dry smile. "She's used to being humiliated. The Kents accustomed her to that."

Sarah Anne reddened. "I don't know why I should stay to be spoken to in this way. But I came with my husband's approval."

"Do you need that to come and see your brother?"

"I need it to—to make the offer I am about to make; and which he authorizes."

Lewis looked at her in surprise, and she purpled up to the lace ruffles inside her satin bonnet.

"Have you come to make an offer for my collection?" he asked her, humorously.

"You seem to take pleasure in insinuating preposterous things. But anything is better than this public slight on our name." Again she ran a shuddering glance over the pictures. "John and I," she announced, "are prepared to double the allowance mother left you on condition that this . . . this ends . . . for good. That that horrible sign is taken down tonight."

Lewis seemed mildly to weigh the proposal. "Thank you very much, Sarah Anne," he said at length. "I'm touched . . . touched and . . . and surprised . . . that you and John should have made this offer. But perhaps, before I decline it, you will accept *mine*: simply to show you my pictures. When once you've looked at them I think you'll understand——"

Mrs. Huzzard drew back hastily, her air of majesty collapsing. "Look at the pictures? Oh, thank you . . . but I can see them very well from here. And besides, I don't pretend to be a judge . . ."

"Then come up and see Treeshy and the baby," said Lewis quietly.

She stared at him, embarrassed. "Oh, thank you," she stammered again; and as she prepared to follow him: "Then it's *no*, really no, Lewis? Do consider, my dear! You say yourself that hardly any one comes. What harm can there be in closing the place?"

"What—when tomorrow the man may come who understands?"

Mrs. Huzzard tossed her plumes despairingly and followed him in silence.

"What—Mary Adeline?" she exclaimed, pausing abruptly on the threshold of the nursery. Treeshy, as usual, sat holding her baby by the fire; and from a low seat opposite her rose a lady as richly furred and feathered as Mrs. Huzzard, but with far less assurance to carry off her furbelows. Mrs. Kent ran to Lewis and laid her plump cheek against his, while Treeshy greeted Sarah Anne.

"I had no idea you were here, Mary Adeline," Mrs. Huzzard murmured. It was clear that she had not imparted her philanthropic project to her sister, and was disturbed at the idea that Lewis might be about to do so. "I just dropped in for a minute," she continued, "to see that darling little pet of an angel child—" and she enveloped the astonished baby in her ample rustlings and flutterings.

"I'm very glad to see you here, Sarah Anne," Mary Adeline answered with simplicity.

"Ah, it's not for want of wishing that I haven't come before! Treeshy knows that, I hope. But the cares of a household like mine . . ."

"Yes; and it's been so difficult to get about in the bad weather," Treeshy suggested sympathetically.

Mrs. Huzzard lifted the Raycie eyebrows. "Has it really? With two pairs of horses one hardly notices the weather. . . Oh, the pretty, pretty, *pretty* baby! . . . Mary Adeline," Sarah Anne continued, turning severely to her sister, "I shall be happy to offer you a seat in my carriage if you're thinking of leaving."

But Mary Adeline was a married woman too. She raised her mild head and her glance crossed her sister's quietly. "My own carriage is at the door, thank you kindly, Sarah Anne," she said; and the baffled Sarah Anne withdrew on Lewis's arm. But a moment later the old habit of subordination reasserted itself. Mary Adeline's gentle countenance grew as timorous as a child's, and she gathered up her cloak in haste.

"Perhaps I was too quick. . . I'm sure she meant it kindly," she exclaimed, overtaking Lewis as he turned to come up the stairs; and with a smile he stood watching his two sisters drive off together in the Huzzard coach.

He returned to the nursery, where Treeshy was still crooning over her daughter.

"Well, my dear," he said, "what do you suppose Sarah Anne came for?" And, in reply to her wondering gaze: "To buy me off from showing the pictures!"

His wife's indignation took just the form he could have wished. She simply went on with her rich cooing laugh and hugged the baby tighter. But Lewis felt the perverse desire to lay a still greater strain upon her loyalty.

"Offered to double my allowance, she and John, if only I'll take down the sign!"

"No one shall touch the sign!" Treeshy flamed.

"Not till I do," said her husband grimly.

She turned about and scanned him with anxious eyes. "Lewis . . . *you?*"

"Oh, my dear . . . they're right. . . It can't go on forever . . ." He went up to her, and put his arm about her and the child. "You've been braver than an army of heroes; but it won't do. The expenses have been a good deal heavier than

I was led to expect. And I . . . I can't raise a mortgage on the pictures. Nobody will touch them."

She met this quickly. "No; I know. That was what Mary Adeline came about."

The blood rushed angrily to Lewis's temples. "Mary Adeline—how the devil did *she* hear of it?"

"Through Mr. Reedy, I suppose. But you must not be angry. She was kindness itself: she doesn't want you to close the gallery, Lewis . . . that is, not as long as you really continue to believe in it. . . She and Donald Kent will lend us enough to go on with for a year longer. That is what she came to say."

For the first time since the struggle had begun, Lewis Raycie's throat was choked with tears. His faithful Mary Adeline! He had a sudden vision of her, stealing out of the house at High Point before daylight to carry a basket of scraps to the poor Mrs. Edgar Poe who was dying of a decline down the lane. . . He laughed aloud in his joy.

"Dear old Mary Adeline! How magnificent of her! Enough to give me a whole year more . . ." He pressed his wet cheek against his wife's in a long silence. "Well, dear," he said at length, "it's for you to say—do we accept?"

He held her off, questioningly, at arm's length, and her wan little smile met his own and mingled with it.

"Of course we accept!"

IX

O F THE RAYCIE FAMILY, which prevailed so powerfully in
the New York of the 'forties, only one of the name survived in my boyhood, half a century later. Like so many of
the descendants of the proud little Colonial society, the Raycies had totally vanished, forgotten by everyone but a few old
ladies, one or two genealogists and the sexton of Trinity
Church, who kept the record of their graves.

The Raycie blood was of course still to be traced in various
allied families: Kents, Huzzards, Cosbys and many others,
proud to claim cousinship with a "Signer," but already indifferent or incurious as to the fate of his progeny. These old
New Yorkers, who lived so well and spent their money so
liberally, vanished like a pinch of dust when they disappeared
from their pews and their dinner-tables.

If I happen to have been familiar with the name since my
youth, it is chiefly because its one survivor was a distant
cousin of my mother's, whom she sometimes took me to see
on days when she thought I was likely to be good because I
had been promised a treat for the morrow.

Old Miss Alethea Raycie lived in a house I had always
heard spoken of as "Cousin Ebenezer's." It had evidently, in
its day, been an admired specimen of domestic architecture;
but was now regarded as the hideous though venerable relic
of a bygone age. Miss Raycie, being crippled by rheumatism,
sat above stairs in a large cold room, meagrely furnished with
beadwork tables, rosewood étagères and portraits of pale sad-
looking people in odd clothes. She herself was large and sat-
urnine, with a battlemented black lace cap, and so deaf that
she seemed a survival of forgotten days, a Rosetta Stone to
which the clue was lost. Even to my mother, nursed in that
vanished tradition, and knowing instinctively to whom Miss
Raycie alluded when she spoke of Mary Adeline, Sarah Anne
or Uncle Doctor, intercourse with her was difficult and languishing, and my juvenile interruptions were oftener encouraged than reproved.

In the course of one of these visits my eye, listlessly roaming, singled out among the pallid portraits a three-crayon

drawing of a little girl with a large forehead and dark eyes, dressed in a plaid frock and embroidered pantalettes, and sitting on a grass-bank. I pulled my mother's sleeve to ask who she was, and my mother answered: "Ah, that was poor little Louisa Raycie, who died of a decline. How old was little Louisa when she died, Cousin Alethea?"

To batter this simple question into Cousin Alethea's brain was the affair of ten laborious minutes; and when the job was done, and Miss Raycie, with an air of mysterious displeasure, had dropped a deep "Eleven," my mother was too exhausted to continue. So she turned to me to add, with one of the private smiles we kept for each other: "It was the poor child who would have inherited the Raycie Gallery." But to a little boy of my age this item of information lacked interest, nor did I understand my mother's surreptitious amusement.

This far-off scene suddenly came back to me last year, when, on one of my infrequent visits to New York, I went to dine with my old friend, the banker, John Selwyn, and came to an astonished stand before the mantelpiece in his new library.

"Hal*lo*!" I said, looking up at the picture above the chimney.

My host squared his shoulders, thrust his hands into his pockets, and affected the air of modesty which people think it proper to assume when their possessions are admired. "The Macrino d'Alba? Y—yes . . . it was the only thing I managed to capture out of the Raycie collection."

"The only thing? Well——"

"Ah, but you should have seen the Mantegna; *and* the Giotto; *and* the Piero della Francesca—hang it, one of the most beautiful Piero della Francescas in the world. . . A girl in profile, with her hair in a pearl net, against a background of columbines; *that* went back to Europe—the National Gallery, I believe. And the Carpaccio, the most exquisite little St. George . . . that went to California . . . *Lord!*" He sat down with the sigh of a hungry man turned away from a groaning board. "Well, it nearly broke me buying *this*!" he murmured, as if at least that fact were some consolation.

I was turning over my early memories in quest of a clue to what he spoke of as the Raycie collection, in a tone which implied that he was alluding to objects familiar to all art-lovers.

Suddenly: "They weren't poor little Louisa's pictures, by any chance?" I asked, remembering my mother's cryptic smile.

Selwyn looked at me perplexedly. "Who the deuce is poor little Louisa?" And, without waiting for my answer, he went on: "They were that fool Netta Cosby's until a year ago—and she never even knew it."

We looked at each other interrogatively, my friend perplexed at my ignorance, and I now absorbed in trying to run down the genealogy of Netta Cosby. I did so finally. "Netta Cosby—you don't mean Netta Kent, the one who married Jim Cosby?"

"That's it. They were cousins of the Raycies', and she inherited the pictures."

I continued to ponder. "I wanted awfully to marry her, the year I left Harvard," I said presently, more to myself than to my hearer.

"Well, if you had you'd have annexed a prize fool; *and* one of the most beautiful collections of Italian Primitives in the world."

"In the world?"

"Well—you wait till you see them; if you haven't already. And I seem to make out that you haven't—that you can't have. How long have you been in Japan? Four years? I thought so. Well, it was only last winter that Netta found out."

"Found out what?"

"What there was in old Alethea Raycie's attic. You must remember the old Miss Raycie who lived in that hideous house in Tenth Street when we were children. She was a cousin of your mother's, wasn't she? Well, the old fool lived there for nearly half a century, with five millions' worth of pictures shut up in the attic over her head. It seems they'd been there ever since the death of a poor young Raycie who collected them in Italy years and years ago. I don't know much about the story; I never was strong on genealogy, and the Raycies have always been rather dim to me. They were everybody's cousins, of course; but as far as one can make out

that seems to have been their principal if not their only function. Oh—and I suppose the Raycie Building was called after
them; only *they* didn't build it!

"But there was this one young fellow—I wish I could find
out more about him. All that Netta seems to know (or to
care, for that matter) is that when he was very young—barely
out of college—he was sent to Italy by his father to buy Old
Masters—in the 'forties, it must have been—and came back
with this extraordinary, this unbelievable collection . . . a boy
of that age! . . . and was disinherited by the old gentleman
for bringing home such rubbish. The young fellow and his
wife died ever so many years ago, both of them. It seems he
was so laughed at for buying such pictures that they went
away and lived like hermits in the depths of the country.
There were some funny spectral portraits of them that old
Alethea had up in her bedroom. Netta showed me one of
them the last time I went to see her: a pathetic drawing of the
only child, an anæmic little girl with a big forehead. Jove, but
that must have been your little Louisa!"

I nodded. "In a plaid frock and embroidered pantalettes?"

"Yes, something of the sort. Well, when Louisa and her
parents died, I suppose the pictures went to old Miss Raycie.
At any rate, at some time or other—and it must have been
longer ago than you or I can remember—the old lady inherited them with the Tenth Street house; and when *she* died,
three or four years ago, her relations found she'd never even
been upstairs to look at them."

"Well——?"

"Well, she died intestate, and Netta Kent—Netta Cosby—
turned out to be the next of kin. There wasn't much to be got
out of the estate (or so they thought) and, as the Cosbys are
always hard up, the house in Tenth Street had to be sold, and
the pictures were very nearly sent off to the auction room
with all the rest of the stuff. But nobody supposed they
would bring anything, and the auctioneer said that if you
tried to sell pictures with carpets and bedding and kitchen
furniture it always depreciated the whole thing; and so, as the
Cosbys had some bare walls to cover, they sent for the lot—
there were about thirty—and decided to have them cleaned
and hang them up. 'After all,' Netta said, 'as well as I can

make out through the cobwebs, some of them look like rather
jolly copies of early Italian things.' But as she was short of
cash she decided to clean them at home instead of sending
them to an expert; and one day, while she was operating on
this very one before you, with her sleeves rolled up, the man
called who always *does* call on such occasions; the man who
knows. In the given case, it was a quiet fellow connected with
the Louvre, who'd brought her a letter from Paris, and whom
she'd invited to one of her stupid dinners. He was announced, and she thought it would be a joke to let him see
what she was doing; she has pretty arms, you may remember.
So he was asked into the dining-room, where he found her
with a pail of hot water and soap-suds, and *this* laid out on
the table; and the first thing he did was to grab her pretty arm
so tight that it was black and blue, while he shouted out:
'God in heaven! Not *hot* water!' "

My friend leaned back with a sigh of mingled resentment
and satisfaction, and we sat silently looking up at the lovely
"Adoration" above the mantelpiece.

"That's how I got it a little cheaper—most of the old var-
nish was gone for good. But luckily for her it was the first
picture she had attacked; and as for the others—you must see
them, that's all I can say. . . Wait; I've got the catalogue
somewhere about . . ."

He began to rummage for it, and I asked, remembering
how nearly I had married Netta Kent: "Do you mean to say
she didn't keep a single one of them?"

"Oh, yes—in the shape of pearls and Rolls-Royces. And
you've seen their new house in Fifth Avenue?" He ended with
a grin of irony: "The best of the joke is that Jim was just
thinking of divorcing her when the pictures were discovered."

"Poor little Louisa!" I sighed.

THE   END

THE OLD MAID

(The 'Fifties)

I

IN THE OLD New York of the 'fifties a few families ruled, in simplicity and affluence. Of these were the Ralstons.

The sturdy English and the rubicund and heavier Dutch had mingled to produce a prosperous, prudent and yet lavish society. To "do things handsomely" had always been a fundamental principle in this cautious world, built up on the fortunes of bankers, India merchants, ship-builders and ship-chandlers. Those well-fed slow-moving people, who seemed irritable and dyspeptic to European eyes only because the caprices of the climate had stripped them of superfluous flesh, and strung their nerves a little tighter, lived in a genteel monotony of which the surface was never stirred by the dumb dramas now and then enacted underground. Sensitive souls in those days were like muted key-boards, on which Fate played without a sound.

In this compact society, built of solidly welded blocks, one of the largest areas was filled by the Ralstons and their ramifications. The Ralstons were of middle-class English stock. They had not come to the colonies to die for a creed but to live for a bank-account. The result had been beyond their hopes, and their religion was tinged by their success. An edulcorated Church of England which, under the conciliatory name of the "Episcopal Church of the United States of America," left out the coarser allusions in the Marriage Service, slid over the comminatory passages in the Athanasian Creed, and thought it more respectful to say "Our Father *who*" than "*which*" in the Lord's Prayer, was exactly suited to the spirit of compromise whereon the Ralstons had built themselves up. There was in all the tribe the same instinctive recoil from new religions as from unaccounted-for people. Institutional to the core, they represented the conservative element that holds new societies together as seaplants bind the seashore.

Compared with the Ralstons, even such traditionalists as the Lovells, the Halseys or the Vandergraves appeared careless, indifferent to money, almost reckless in their impulses

and indecisions. Old John Frederick Ralston, the stout
founder of the race, had perceived the difference, and emphasized it to his son, Frederick John, in whom he had scented a
faint leaning toward the untried and unprofitable.

"You let the Lannings and the Dagonets and the Spenders
take risks and fly kites. It's the county-family blood in 'em:
we've nothing to do with that. Look how they're petering
out already—the men, I mean. Let your boys marry their
girls, if you like (they're wholesome and handsome); though
I'd sooner see my grandsons take a Lovell or a Vandergrave,
or any of our own kind. But don't let your sons go mooning
around after their young fellows, horse-racing, and running
down south to those d——d Springs, and gambling at New
Orleans, and all the rest of it. That's how you'll build up
the family, and keep the weather out. The way we've always
done it."

Frederick John listened, obeyed, married a Halsey, and
passively followed in his father's steps. He belonged to the
cautious generation of New York gentlemen who revered
Hamilton and served Jefferson, who longed to lay out New
York like Washington, and who laid it out instead like a gridiron, lest they should be thought "undemocratic" by people
they secretly looked down upon. Shop-keepers to the marrow, they put in their windows the wares there was most demand for, keeping their private opinions for the back-shop,
where through lack of use, they gradually lost substance and
colour.

The fourth generation of Ralstons had nothing left in the
way of convictions save an acute sense of honour in private
and business matters; on the life of the community and the
state they took their daily views from the newspapers, and the
newspapers they already despised. The Ralstons had done
little to shape the destiny of their country, except to finance the
Cause when it had become safe to do so. They were related to
many of the great men who had built the Republic; but no
Ralston had so far committed himself as to be great. As old
John Frederick said, it was safer to be satisfied with three per
cent: they regarded heroism as a form of gambling. Yet by
merely being so numerous and so similar they had come to
have a weight in the community. People said: "The Ralstons"

when they wished to invoke a precedent. This attribution of authority had gradually convinced the third generation of its collective importance, and the fourth, to which Delia Ralston's husband belonged, had the ease and simplicity of a ruling class.

Within the limits of their universal caution, the Ralstons fulfilled their obligations as rich and respected citizens. They figured on the boards of all the old-established charities, gave handsomely to thriving institutions, had the best cooks in New York, and when they travelled abroad ordered statuary of the American sculptors in Rome whose reputation was already established. The first Ralston who had brought home a statue had been regarded as a wild fellow; but when it became known that the sculptor had executed several orders for the British aristocracy it was felt in the family that this too was a three per cent investment.

Two marriages with the Dutch Vandergraves had consolidated these qualities of thrift and handsome living, and the carefully built-up Ralston character was now so congenital that Delia Ralston sometimes asked herself whether, were she to turn her own little boy loose in a wilderness, he would not create a small New York there, and be on all its boards of directors.

Delia Lovell had married James Ralston at twenty. The marriage, which had taken place in the month of September, 1840, had been solemnized, as was then the custom, in the drawing-room of the bride's country home, at what is now the corner of Avenue A and Ninety-first Street, overlooking the Sound. Thence her husband had driven her (in Grand-mamma Lovell's canary-coloured coach with a fringed hammer-cloth) through spreading suburbs and untidy elm-shaded streets to one of the new houses in Gramercy Park, which the pioneers of the younger set were just beginning to affect; and there, at five-and-twenty, she was established, the mother of two children, the possessor of a generous allowance of pin-money, and, by common consent, one of the handsomest and most popular "young matrons" (as they were called) of her day.

She was thinking placidly and gratefully of these things as she sat one afternoon in her handsome bedroom in Gramercy

Park. She was too near to the primitive Ralstons to have as clear a view of them as, for instance, the son in question might one day command: she lived under them as unthinkingly as one lives under the laws of one's country. Yet that tremor of the muted key-board, that secret questioning which sometimes beat in her like wings, would now and then so divide her from them that for a fleeting moment she could survey them in their relation to other things. The moment was always fleeting; she dropped back from it quickly, breathless and a little pale, to her children, her house-keeping, her new dresses and her kindly Jim.

She thought of him today with a smile of tenderness, remembering how he had told her to spare no expense on her new bonnet. Though she was twenty-five, and twice a mother, her image was still surprisingly fresh. The plumpness then thought seemly in a young wife stretched the grey silk across her bosom, and caused her heavy gold watch-chain—after it left the anchorage of the brooch of St. Peter's in mosaic that fastened her low-cut Cluny collar—to dangle perilously in the void above a tiny waist buckled into a velvet waist-band. But the shoulders above sloped youthfully under her Cashmere scarf, and every movement was as quick as a girl's.

Mrs. Jim Ralston approvingly examined the rosy-cheeked oval set in the blonde ruffles of the bonnet on which, in compliance with her husband's instructions, she had spared no expense. It was a cabriolet of white velvet tied with wide satin ribbons and plumed with a crystal-spangled marabout—a wedding bonnet ordered for the marriage of her cousin, Charlotte Lovell, which was to take place that week at St. Mark's-in-the-Bouwerie. Charlotte was making a match exactly like Delia's own: marrying a Ralston, of the Waverly Place branch, than which nothing could be safer, sounder or more—well, usual. Delia did not know why the word had occurred to her, for it could hardly be postulated, even of the young women of her own narrow clan, that they "usually" married Ralstons; but the soundness, safeness, suitability of the arrangement, did make it typical of the kind of alliance which a nice girl in the nicest set would serenely and blushingly forecast for herself.

Yes—and afterward?

Well—what? And what did this new question mean? Afterward: why, of course, there was the startled puzzled surrender to the incomprehensible exigencies of the young man to whom one had at most yielded a rosy cheek in return for an engagement ring; there was the large double-bed; the terror of seeing him shaving calmly the next morning, in his shirt-sleeves, through the dressing-room door; the evasions, insinuations, resigned smiles and Bible texts of one's Mamma; the reminder of the phrase "to obey" in the glittering blur of the Marriage Service; a week or a month of flushed distress, confusion, embarrassed pleasure; then the growth of habit, the insidious lulling of the matter-of-course, the dreamless double slumbers in the big white bed, the early morning discussions and consultations through that dressing-room door which had once seemed to open into a fiery pit scorching the brow of innocence.

And then, the babies; the babies who were supposed to "make up for everything," and didn't—though they were such darlings, and one had no definite notion as to what it was that one had missed, and that they were to make up for.

Yes: Charlotte's fate would be just like hers. Joe Ralston was so like his second cousin Jim (Delia's James), that Delia could see no reason why life in the squat brick house in Waverly Place should not exactly resemble life in the tall brownstone house in Gramercy Park. Only Charlotte's bed-room would certainly not be as pretty as hers.

She glanced complacently at the French wall-paper that reproduced a watered silk, with a "valanced" border, and tassels between the loops. The mahogany bedstead, covered with a white embroidered counterpane, was symmetrically reflected in the mirror of a wardrobe which matched it. Coloured lithographs of the "Four Seasons" by Léopold Robert surmounted groups of family daguerreotypes in deeply-recessed gilt frames. The ormolu clock represented a shepherdess sitting on a fallen trunk, a basket of flowers at her feet. A shepherd, stealing up, surprised her with a kiss, while her little dog barked at him from a clump of roses. One knew the profession of the lovers by their crooks and the shape of their hats. This frivolous time-piece had been a wedding-gift from

Delia's aunt, Mrs. Manson Mingott, a dashing widow who lived in Paris and was received at the Tuileries. It had been entrusted by Mrs. Mingott to young Clement Spender, who had come back from Italy for a short holiday just after Delia's marriage; the marriage which might never have been, if Clem Spender could have supported a wife, or if he had consented to give up painting and Rome for New York and the law. The young man (who looked, already, so odd and foreign and sarcastic) had laughingly assured the bride that her aunt's gift was "the newest thing in the Palais Royal"; and the family, who admired Mrs. Manson Mingott's taste though they disapproved of her "foreignness," had criticized Delia's putting the clock in her bedroom instead of displaying it on the drawing-room mantel. But she liked, when she woke in the morning, to see the bold shepherd stealing his kiss.

Charlotte would certainly not have such a pretty clock in her bedroom; but then she had not been used to pretty things. Her father, who had died at thirty of lung-fever, was one of the "poor Lovells." His widow, burdened with a young family, and living all the year round "up the River," could not do much for her eldest girl; and Charlotte had entered society in her mother's turned garments, and shod with satin sandals handed down from a defunct aunt who had "opened a ball" with General Washington. The old-fashioned Ralston furniture, which Delia already saw herself banishing, would seem sumptuous to Chatty; very likely she would think Delia's gay French time-piece somewhat frivolous, or even not "quite nice." Poor Charlotte had become so serious, so prudish almost, since she had given up balls and taken to visiting the poor! Delia remembered, with ever-recurring wonder, the abrupt change in her: the precise moment at which it had been privately agreed in the family that, after all, Charlotte Lovell was going to be an old maid.

They had not thought so when she came out. Though her mother could not afford to give her more than one new tarlatan dress, and though nearly everything in her appearance was regrettable, from the too bright red of her hair to the too pale brown of her eyes—not to mention the rounds of brick-rose on her cheek-bones, which almost (preposterous thought!) made her look as if she painted—yet these defects were redeemed by a slim waist, a light foot and a gay laugh; and when her hair was well oiled and brushed for an evening party, so that it looked almost brown, and lay smoothly along her delicate cheeks under a wreath of red and white camellias, several eligible young men (Joe Ralston among them) were known to have called her pretty.

Then came her illness. She caught cold on a moonlight sleighing-party, the brick-rose circles deepened, and she began to cough. There was a report that she was "going like her father," and she was hurried off to a remote village in Georgia, where she lived alone for a year with an old family governess. When she came back everyone felt at once that there was a change in her. She was pale, and thinner than ever, but with an exquisitely transparent cheek, darker eyes and redder hair; and the oddness of her appearance was increased by plain dresses of Quakerish cut. She had left off trinkets and watch-chains, always wore the same grey cloak and small close bonnet, and displayed a sudden zeal for visiting the indigent. The family explained that during her year in the south she had been shocked by the hopeless degradation of the "poor whites" and their children, and that this revelation of misery had made it impossible for her to return to the light-hearted life of her young friends. Everyone agreed, with significant glances, that this unnatural state of mind would "pass off in time"; and meanwhile old Mrs. Lovell, Chatty's grandmother, who understood her perhaps better than the others, gave her a little money for her paupers, and lent her a room in the Lovell stables (at the back of the old lady's Mercer Street house) where she gathered about her, in what would afterward have been called a "day-nursery," some of the destitute children of the neighbourhood. There was even, among them, the baby girl whose origin had excited such intense curiosity two or three years earlier, when a veiled lady in a handsome cloak had brought it to the hovel of Cyrus Washington, the negro handy-man whose wife Jessamine took in Dr. Lanskell's washing. Dr. Lanskell, the chief medical practitioner of the day, was presumably versed in the secret history of every household from the Battery to Union Square; but, though beset by inquisitive patients, he had invariably declared himself unable to identify Jessamine's "veiled lady," or to hazard a guess as to the origin of the hundred dollar bill pinned to the baby's bib.

The hundred dollars were never renewed, the lady never reappeared, but the baby lived healthily and happily with Jessamine's piccaninnies, and as soon as it could toddle was brought to Chatty Lovell's day-nursery, where it appeared (like its fellow paupers) in little garments cut down from her old dresses, and socks knitted by her untiring hands. Delia, absorbed in her own babies, had nevertheless dropped in once or twice at the nursery, and had come away wishing that Chatty's maternal instinct might find its normal outlet in marriage. The married cousin confusedly felt that her own affection for her handsome children was a mild and measured sentiment compared with Chatty's fierce passion for the waifs in Grandmamma Lovell's stable.

And then, to the general surprise, Charlotte Lovell engaged herself to Joe Ralston. It was known that Joe had "admired her" the year she came out. She was a graceful dancer, and Joe, who was tall and nimble, had footed it with her through many a reel and *schottische*. By the end of the winter all the match-makers were predicting that something would come of it; but when Delia sounded her cousin, the girl's evasive answer and burning brow seemed to imply that her suitor had changed his mind, and no further questions could be asked. Now it was clear that there had, in fact, been an old romance between them, probably followed by that exciting incident, a "misunderstanding"; but at last all was well, and the bells of St. Mark's were preparing to ring in happier days for Charlotte. "Ah, when she has her first baby," the Ralston mothers chorused . . .

"Chatty!" Delia exclaimed, pushing back her chair as she saw her cousin's image reflected in the glass over her shoulder.

Charlotte Lovell had paused in the doorway. "They told me you were here—so I ran up."

"Of course, darling. How handsome you do look in your poplin! I always said you needed rich materials. I'm so thankful to see you out of grey cashmere." Delia, lifting her hands, removed the white bonnet from her dark polished head, and shook it gently to make the crystals glitter.

"I hope you like it? It's for your wedding," she laughed.

Charlotte Lovell stood motionless. In her mother's old dove-coloured poplin, freshly banded with narrow rows of crimson velvet ribbon, an ermine tippet crossed on her bosom, and a new beaver bonnet with a falling feather, she had already something of the assurance and majesty of a married woman.

"And you know your hair certainly *is* darker, darling," Delia added, still hopefully surveying her.

"Darker? It's grey," Charlotte suddenly broke out in her deep voice. She pushed back one of the pommaded bands that framed her face, and showed a white lock on her temple. "You needn't save up your bonnet; I'm not going to be married," she added, with a smile that showed her small white teeth in a fleeting glare.

Delia had just enough presence of mind to lay down the bonnet, marabout-up, before she flung herself on her cousin.

"Not going to be married? Charlotte, are you perfectly crazy?"

"Why is it crazy to do what I think right?"

"But people said you were going to marry him the year you came out. And no one understood what happened then. And now—how can it possibly be right? You simply *can't!*" Delia incoherently cried.

"Oh—people!" said Charlotte Lovell wearily.

Her married cousin looked at her with a start. Something thrilled in her voice that Delia had never heard in it, or in any other human voice, before. Its echo seemed to set their familiar world rocking, and the Axminster carpet actually heaved under Delia's shrinking slippers.

Charlotte Lovell stood staring ahead of her with strained lids. In the pale brown of her eyes Delia noticed the green specks that floated there when she was angry or excited.

"Charlotte—where on earth have you come from?" she questioned, drawing the girl down to the sofa.

"Come from?"

"Yes. You look as if you had seen a ghost—an army of ghosts."

The same snarling smile drew up Charlotte's lip. "I've seen Joe," she said.

"Well?—Oh, Chatty," Delia exclaimed, abruptly illuminated, "you don't mean to say that you're going to let any little thing in Joe's past—? Not that I've ever heard the least hint; never. But even if there were. . ." She drew a deep breath, and bravely proceeded to extremities. "Even if you've heard that he's been . . . that he's had a child—of course he would have provided for it before . . ."

The girl shook her head. "I know: you needn't go on. 'Men will be men'; but it's not that."

"Tell me what it is."

Charlotte Lovell looked about the sunny prosperous room as if it were the image of her world, and that world were a prison she must break out of. She lowered her head. "I want—to get away," she panted.

"Get away? From Joe?"

"From his ideas—the Ralston ideas."

Delia bridled—after all, she was a Ralston! "The Ralston ideas? I haven't found them—so unbearably unpleasant to live with," she smiled a little tartly.

"No. But it was different with you: they didn't ask you to give up things."

"What things?" What in the world (Delia wondered) had poor Charlotte that any one could want her to give up? She had always been in the position of taking rather than of having to surrender. "Can't you explain to me, dear?" Delia urged.

"My poor children—he says I'm to give them up," cried the girl in a stricken whisper.

"Give them up? Give up helping them?"

"Seeing them—looking after them. Give them up altogether. He got his mother to explain to me. After—after we have children . . . he's afraid . . . afraid our children might catch things. . . . He'll give me money, of course, to pay some one . . . a hired person, to look after them. He thought that handsome," Charlotte broke out with a sob. She flung off her bonnet and smothered her prostrate weeping in the cushions.

Delia sat perplexed. Of all unforeseen complications this was surely the least imaginable. And with all the acquired Ralston that was in her she could not help seeing the force of

Joe's objection, could almost find herself agreeing with him. No one in New York had forgotten the death of the poor Henry van der Luydens' only child, who had caught small-pox at the circus to which an unprincipled nurse had surrep-titiously taken him. After such a warning as that, parents felt justified in every precaution against contagion. And poor people were so ignorant and careless, and their children, of course, so perpetually exposed to everything catching. No, Joe Ralston was certainly right, and Charlotte almost insanely un-reasonable. But it would be useless to tell her so now. Instinc-tively, Delia temporized.

"After all," she whispered to the prone ear, "if it's only after you have children—you may not have any—for some time."

"Oh, yes, I shall!" came back in anguish from the cushions.

Delia smiled with matronly superiority. "Really, Chatty, I don't quite see how you can know. You don't understand."

Charlotte Lovell lifted herself up. Her collar of Brussels lace had come undone and hung in a wisp on her crumpled bod-ice, and through the disorder of her hair the white lock glim-mered haggardly. In her pale brown eyes the little green specks floated like leaves in a trout-pool.

"Poor girl," Delia thought, "how old and ugly she looks! More than ever like an old maid; and she doesn't seem to realize in the least that she'll never have another chance."

"You must try to be sensible, Chatty dear. After all, one's own babies have the first claim."

"That's just it." The girl seized her fiercely by the wrists. "How can I give up my own baby?"

"Your—your—?" Delia's world again began to waver under her. "Which of the poor little waifs, dearest, do you call your own baby?" she questioned patiently.

Charlotte looked her straight in the eyes. "I call my own baby my own baby."

"Your own—? Take care—you're hurting my wrists, Chatty!" Delia freed herself, forcing a smile. "Your own—?"

"My own little girl. The one that Jessamine and Cyrus—"

"Oh—" Delia Ralston gasped.

The two cousins sat silent, facing each other; but Delia looked away. It came over her with a shudder of repugnance that such things, even if they had to be said, should not have been spoken in her bedroom, so near the spotless nursery across the passage. Mechanically she smoothed the organ-like folds of her silk skirt, which her cousin's embrace had tumbled. Then she looked again at Charlotte's eyes, and her own melted.

"Oh, poor Chatty—my poor Chatty!" She held out her arms to her cousin.

II

T HE SHEPHERD continued to steal his kiss from the shepherdess, and the clock in the fallen trunk continued to tick out the minutes.

Delia, petrified, sat unconscious of their passing, her cousin clasped to her. She was dumb with the horror and amazement of learning that her own blood ran in the veins of the anonymous foundling, the "hundred dollar baby" about whom New York had so long furtively jested and conjectured. It was her first contact with the nether side of the smooth social surface, and she sickened at the thought that such things were, and that she, Delia Ralston, should be hearing of them in her own house, and from the lips of the victim! For Chatty of course was a victim—but whose? She had spoken no name, and Delia could put no question: the horror of it sealed her lips. Her mind had instantly raced back over Chatty's past; but she saw no masculine figure in it but Joe Ralston's. And to connect Joe with the episode was obviously unthinkable. Some one in the south, then—? But no: Charlotte had been ill when she left—and in a flash Delia understood the real nature of that illness, and of the girl's disappearance. But from such speculations too her mind recoiled, and instinctively she fastened on something she could still grasp: Joe Ralston's attitude about Chatty's paupers. Of course Joe could not let his wife risk bringing contagion into their home—that was safe ground to dwell on. Her own Jim would have felt in the same way; and she would certainly have agreed with him.

Her eyes travelled back to the clock. She always thought of Clem Spender when she looked at the clock, and suddenly she wondered—if things had been different—what *he* would have said if she had made such an appeal to him as Charlotte had made to Joe. The thing was hard to imagine; yet in a flash of mental readjustment Delia saw herself as Clem's wife, she saw her children as his, she pictured herself asking him to let her go on caring for the poor waifs in the Mercer Street stable, and she distinctly heard his laugh and his light answer: "Why on earth did you ask, you little goose? Do you take me for such a Pharisee as that?"

Yes, that was Clem Spender all over—tolerant, reckless, indifferent to consequences, always doing the kind thing at the moment, and too often leaving others to pay the score. "There's something cheap about Clem," Jim had once said in his heavy way. Delia Ralston roused herself and pressed her cousin closer. "Chatty, tell me," she whispered.

"There's nothing more."

"I mean, about yourself . . . this thing . . . this. . ." Clem Spender's voice was still in her ears. "You loved some one," she breathed.

"Yes. That's over—. Now it's only the child. . . And I could love Joe—in another way." Chatty Lovell straightened herself, wan and frowning.

"I need the money—I must have it for my baby. Or else they'll send it to an Institution." She paused. "But that's not all. I want to marry—to be a wife, like all of you. I should have loved Joe's children—our children. Life doesn't stop . . ."

"No; I suppose not. But you speak as if . . . as if . . . the person who took advantage of you . . ."

"No one took advantage of me. I was lonely and unhappy. I met some one who was lonely and unhappy. People don't all have your luck. We were both too poor to marry each other . . . and mother would never have consented. And so one day . . . one day before he said goodbye . . ."

"He said goodbye?"

"Yes. He was going to leave the country."

"He left the country—knowing?"

"How was he to know? He doesn't live here. He'd just come back—come back to see his family—for a few weeks . . ." She broke off, her thin lips pressed together upon her secret.

There was a silence. Blindly Delia stared at the bold shepherd.

"Come back from where?" she asked at length in a low tone.

"Oh, what does it matter? You wouldn't understand," Charlotte broke off, in the very words her married cousin had compassionately addressed to her virginity.

A slow blush rose to Delia's cheek: she felt oddly humiliated by the rebuke conveyed in that contemptuous retort. She seemed to herself shy, ineffectual, as incapable as an ignorant girl of dealing with the abominations that Charlotte was thrusting on her. But suddenly some fierce feminine intuition struggled and woke in her. She forced her eyes upon her cousin's.

"You won't tell me who it was?"

"What's the use? I haven't told anybody."

"Then why have you come to me?"

Charlotte's stony face broke up in weeping. "It's for my baby . . . my baby . . ."

Delia did not heed her. "How can I help you if I don't know?" she insisted in a harsh dry voice: her heart-beats were so violent that they seemed to send up throttling hands to her throat.

Charlotte made no answer.

"Come back from where?" Delia doggedly repeated; and at that, with a long wail, the girl flung her hands up, screening her eyes. "He always thought you'd wait for him," she sobbed out, "and then, when he found you hadn't . . . and that you were marrying Jim. . . He heard it just as he was sailing. . . He didn't know it till Mrs. Mingott asked him to bring the clock back for your wedding . . ."

"Stop—stop," Delia cried, springing to her feet. She had provoked the avowal, and now that it had come she felt that it had been gratuitously and indecently thrust upon her. Was this New York, *her* New York, her safe friendly hypocritical New York, was this James Ralston's house, and this his wife listening to such revelations of dishonour?

Charlotte Lovell stood up in her turn. "I knew it—I knew it! You think worse of my baby now, instead of better. . . Oh, why did you make me tell you? I knew you'd never understand. I'd always cared for him, ever since I came out; that was why I wouldn't marry any one else. But I knew there was no hope for me . . . he never looked at anybody but you. And then, when he came back four years ago, and there was no *you* for him any more, he began to notice me, to be kind, to talk to me about his life and his painting. . ." She drew a deep breath, and her voice cleared. "That's over —all over. It's as if I couldn't either hate him or love him.

There's only the child now—my child. He doesn't even know of it—why should he? It's none of his business; it's nobody's business but mine. But surely you must see that I can't give up my baby."

Delia Ralston stood speechless, looking away from her cousin in a growing horror. She had lost all sense of reality, all feeling of safety and self-reliance. Her impulse was to close her ears to the other's appeal as a child buries its head from midnight terrors. At last she drew herself up, and spoke with dry lips.

"But what do you mean to do? Why have you come to me? Why have you told me all this?"

"Because he loved you!" Charlotte Lovell stammered out; and the two women stood and faced each other.

Slowly the tears rose to Delia's eyes and rolled down her cheeks, moistening her parched lips. Through the tears she saw her cousin's haggard countenance waver and droop like a drowning face under water. Things half-guessed, obscurely felt, surged up from unsuspected depths in her. It was almost as if, for a moment, this other woman were telling her of her own secret past, putting into crude words all the trembling silences of her own heart.

The worst of it was, as Charlotte said, that they must act now; there was not a day to lose. Chatty was right—it was impossible that she should marry Joe if to do so meant giving up the child. But, in any case, how could she marry him without telling him the truth? And was it conceivable that, after hearing it, he should not repudiate her? All these questions spun agonizingly through Delia's brain, and through them glimmered the persistent vision of the child—Clem Spender's child—growing up on charity in a negro hovel, or herded in one of the plague-houses they called Asylums. No: the child came first—she felt it in every fibre of her body. But what should she do, of whom take counsel, how advise the wretched creature who had come to her in Clement's name? Delia glanced about her desperately, and then turned back to her cousin.

"You must give me time. I must think. You ought not to marry him—and yet all the arrangements are made; and the wedding-presents. . . There would be a scandal . . . it would kill Granny Lovell . . ."

Charlotte answered in a low voice: "There *is* no time. I must decide now."

Delia pressed her hands against her breast. "I tell you I must think. I wish you would go home.—Or, no: stay here: your mother mustn't see your eyes. Jim's not coming home till late; you can wait in this room till I come back." She had opened the wardrobe and was reaching up for a plain bonnet and heavy veil.

"Stay here? But where are you going?"

"I don't know. I want to walk—to get the air. I think I want to be alone." Feverishly, Delia unfolded her Paisley shawl, tied on bonnet and veil, thrust her mittened hands into her muff. Charlotte, without moving, stared at her dumbly from the sofa.

"You'll wait," Delia insisted, on the threshold.

"Yes: I'll wait."

Delia shut the door and hurried down the stairs.

III

S HE HAD SPOKEN the truth in saying that she did not know where she was going. She simply wanted to get away from Charlotte's unbearable face, and from the immediate atmosphere of her tragedy. Outside, in the open, perhaps it would be easier to think.

As she skirted the park-rails she saw her rosy children playing, under their nurse's eye, with the pampered progeny of other square-dwellers. The little girl had on her new plaid velvet bonnet and white tippet, and the boy his Highland cap and broad-cloth spencer. How happy and jolly they looked! The nurse spied her, but she shook her head, waved at the group and hurried on.

She walked and walked through the familiar streets decked with bright winter sunshine. It was early afternoon, an hour when the gentlemen had just returned to their offices, and there were few pedestrians in Irving Place and Union Square. Delia crossed the Square to Broadway.

The Lovell house in Mercer Street was a sturdy old-fashioned brick dwelling. A large stable adjoined it, opening on an alley such as Delia, on her honey-moon trip to England, had heard called a "mews." She turned into the alley, entered the stable court, and pushed open a door. In a shabby white-washed room a dozen children, gathered about a stove, were playing with broken toys. The Irishwoman who had charge of them was cutting out small garments on a broken-legged deal table. She raised a friendly face, recognizing Delia as the lady who had once or twice been to see the children with Miss Charlotte.

Delia paused, embarrassed.

"I—I came to ask if you need any new toys," she stammered.

"That we do, ma'am. And many another thing too, though Miss Charlotte tells me I'm not to beg of the ladies that comes to see our poor darlin's."

"Oh, you may beg of me, Bridget," Mrs. Ralston answered, smiling. "Let me see your babies—it's so long since I've been here."

The children had stopped playing and, huddled against their nurse, gazed up open-mouthed at the rich rustling lady. One little girl with pale brown eyes and scarlet cheeks was dressed in a plaid alpaca frock trimmed with imitation coral buttons that Delia remembered. Those buttons had been on Charlotte's "best dress" the year she came out. Delia stopped and took up the child. Its curly hair was brown, the exact colour of the eyes—thank heaven! But the eyes had the same little green spangles floating in their transparency. Delia sat down, and the little girl, standing on her knee, gravely fingered her watch-chain.

"Oh, ma'am—maybe her shoes'll soil your skirt. The floor here ain't none too clean."

Delia shook her head, and pressed the child against her. She had forgotten the other gazing babies and their wardress. The little creature on her knee was made of different stuff—it had not needed the plaid alpaca and coral buttons to single her out. Her brown curls grew in points on her high forehead, exactly as Clement Spender's did. Delia laid a burning cheek against the forehead.

"Baby want my lovely yellow chain?"

Baby did.

Delia unfastened the gold chain and hung it about the child's neck. The other babies clapped and crowed, but the little girl, gravely dimpling, continued to finger the links in silence.

"Oh, ma'am, you can't leave that fine chain on little Teeny. When she has to go back to those blacks . . ."

"What is her name?"

"Teena they call her, I believe. It don't seem a Christian name, har'ly."

Delia was silent.

"What I say is, her cheeks is too red. And she coughs too easy. Always one cold and another. Here, Teeny, leave the lady go."

Delia stood up, loosening the tender arms.

"She doesn't want to leave go of you, ma'am. Miss Chatty ain't been in today, and the little thing's kinder lonesome without her. She don't play like the other children, somehow. . . Teeny, you look at that lovely chain you've got . . . there, there now . . ."

"Goodbye, Clementina," Delia whispered below her breath. She kissed the pale brown eyes, the curly crown, and dropped her veil on rushing tears. In the stable-yard she dried them on her large embroidered handkerchief, and stood hesitating. Then with a decided step she turned toward home.

The house was as she had left it, except that the children had come in; she heard them romping in the nursery as she went down the passage to her bedroom. Charlotte Lovell was seated on the sofa, upright and rigid, as Delia had left her.

"Chatty—Chatty, I've thought it out. Listen. Whatever happens, the baby shan't stay with those people. I mean to keep her."

Charlotte stood up, tall and white. The eyes in her thin face had grown so dark that they seemed like spectral hollows in a skull. She opened her lips to speak, and then, snatching at her handkerchief, pressed it to her mouth, and sank down again. A red trickle dripped through the handkerchief onto her poplin skirt.

"Charlotte—Charlotte," Delia screamed, on her knees beside her cousin. Charlotte's head slid back against the cushions and the trickle ceased. She closed her eyes, and Delia, seizing a vinaigrette from the dressing-table, held it to her pinched nostrils. The room was filled with an acrid aromatic scent.

Charlotte's lids lifted. "Don't be frightened. I still spit blood sometimes—not often. My lung is nearly healed. But it's the terror—"

"No, no: there's to be no more terror. I tell you I've thought it all out. Jim is going to let me take the baby."

The girl raised herself haggardly. "Jim? Have you told him? Is that where you've been?"

"No, darling. I've only been to see the baby."

"Oh," Charlotte moaned, leaning back again. Delia took her own handkerchief, and wiped away the tears that were raining down her cousin's cheeks.

"You mustn't cry, Chatty; you must be brave. Your little girl and his—how could you think? But you must give me time: I must manage it in my own way. . . Only trust me . . ."

Charlotte's lips stirred faintly.

"The tears . . . don't dry them, Delia. . . . I like to feel them . . ."

The two cousins continued to lean against each other without speaking. The ormolu clock ticked out the measure of their mute communion in minutes, quarters, a half-hour, then an hour: the day declined and darkened, the shadows lengthened across the garlands of the Axminster and the broad white bed. There was a knock.

"The children's waiting to say their grace before supper, ma'am."

"Yes, Eliza. Let them say it to you. I'll come later." As the nurse's steps receded Charlotte Lovell disengaged herself from Delia's embrace.

"Now I can go," she said.

"You're not too weak, dear? I can send for a coach to take you home."

"No, no; it would frighten mother. And I shall like walking now, in the darkness. Sometimes the world used to seem all one awful glare to me. There were days when I thought the sun would never set. And then there was the moon at night." She laid her hands on her cousin's shoulders. "Now it's different. By and bye I shan't hate the light."

The two women kissed each other, and Delia whispered: "Tomorrow."

IV

THE RALSTONS gave up old customs reluctantly, but once they had adopted a new one they found it impossible to understand why everyone else did not immediately do likewise.

When Delia, who came of the laxer Lovells, and was naturally inclined to novelty, had first proposed to her husband to dine at six o'clock instead of two, his malleable young face had become as relentless as that of the old original Ralston in his grim Colonial portrait. But after a two days' resistance he had come round to his wife's view, and now smiled contemptuously at the obstinacy of those who clung to a heavy midday meal and high tea.

"There's nothing I hate like narrow-mindedness. Let people eat when they like, for all I care: it's their narrow-mindedness that I can't stand."

Delia was thinking of this as she sat in the drawing-room (her mother would have called it the parlour) waiting for her husband's return. She had just had time to smooth her glossy braids, and slip on the black-and-white striped moire with cherry pipings which was his favourite dress. The drawing-room, with its Nottingham lace curtains looped back under florid gilt cornices, its marble centre-table on a carved rosewood foot, and its old-fashioned mahogany armchairs covered with one of the new French silk damasks in a tart shade of apple-green, was one for any young wife to be proud of. The rosewood what-nots on each side of the folding doors that led into the dining-room were adorned with tropical shells, feld-spar vases, an alabaster model of the Leaning Tower of Pisa, a pair of obelisks made of scraps of porphyry and serpentine picked up by the young couple in the Roman Forum, a bust of Clytie in chalk-white biscuit de Sèvres, and four old-fashioned figures of the Seasons in Chelsea ware, that had to be left among the newer ornaments because they had belonged to great-grandmamma Ralston. On the walls hung large dark steel-engravings of Cole's "Voyage of Life," and between the windows stood the life-size statue of "A Captive Maiden" executed for Jim Ralston's father by the celebrated Harriet Hosmer, immortalized in Hawthorne's novel of the Marble Faun. On the table lay handsomely tooled copies of Turner's Rivers of France, Drake's Culprit Fay, Crabbe's Tales, and the Book of Beauty containing portraits of the British peeresses who had participated in the Earl of Eglinton's tournament.

As Delia sat there, before the hard-coal fire in its arched opening of black marble, her citron-wood work-table at her side, and one of the new French lamps shedding a pleasant light on the centre-table from under a crystal-fringed shade, she asked herself how she could have passed, in such a short time, so completely out of her usual circle of impressions and convictions—so much farther than ever before beyond the Ralston horizon. Here it was, closing in on her again, as if the very plaster ornaments of the ceiling, the forms of the furniture, the cut of her dress, had been built out of Ralston prejudices, and turned to adamant by the touch of Ralston hands.

She must have been mad, she thought, to have committed herself so far to Charlotte; yet, turn about as she would in the ever-tightening circle of the problem, she could still find no other issue. Somehow, it lay with her to save Clem Spender's baby.

She heard the sound of the latch-key (her heart had never beat so high at it), and the putting down of a tall hat on the hall console—or of two tall hats, was it? The drawing-room door opened, and two high-stocked and ample-coated young men came in: two Jim Ralstons, so to speak. Delia had never before noticed how much her husband and his cousin Joe were alike; it made her feel how justified she was in always thinking of the Ralstons collectively.

She would not have been young and tender, and a happy wife, if she had not thought Joe but an indifferent copy of her Jim; yet, allowing for defects in the reproduction, there remained a striking likeness between the two tall athletic figures, the short sanguine faces with straight noses, straight whiskers, straight brows, candid blue eyes and sweet selfish smiles. Only, at the present moment, Joe looked like Jim with a tooth-ache.

"Look here, my dear: here's a young man who's asked to take pot-luck with us," Jim smiled, with the confidence of a

well-nourished husband who knows that he can always bring
a friend home.

"How nice of you, Joe!—Do you suppose he can put up
with oyster soup and a stuffed goose?" Delia beamed upon
her husband.

"I knew it! I told you so, my dear chap! He said you
wouldn't like it—that you'd be fussed about the dinner. Wait
till you're married, Joseph Ralston—." Jim brought down a
genial paw on his cousin's bottle-green shoulder, and Joe
grimaced as if the tooth had stabbed him.

"It's excessively kind of you, cousin Delia, to take me in
this evening. The fact is—"

"Dinner first, my boy, if you don't mind! A bottle of
Burgundy will brush away the blue devils. Your arm to your
cousin, please; I'll just go and see that the wine is brought
up."

Oyster soup, broiled bass, stuffed goose, apple fritters and
green peppers, followed by one of Grandmamma Ralston's
famous caramel custards: through all her mental anguish,
Delia was faintly aware of a secret pride in her achievement.
Certainly it would serve to confirm the rumour that Jim
Ralston could always bring a friend home to dine without
notice. The Ralston and Lovell wines rounded off the effect,
and even Joe's drawn face had mellowed by the time the Lovell
Madeira started westward. Delia marked the change when
the two young men rejoined her in the drawing-room.

"And now, my dear fellow, you'd better tell her the whole
story," Jim counselled, pushing an armchair toward his
cousin.

The young woman, bent above her wool-work, listened
with lowered lids and flushed cheeks. As a married woman—
as a mother—Joe hoped she would think him justified in
speaking to her frankly: he had her husband's authority to
do so.

"Oh, go ahead, go ahead," chafed the exuberant after-
dinner Jim from the hearth-rug.

Delia listened, considered, let the bridegroom flounder on
through his embarrassed exposition. Her needle hung like a
sword of Damocles above the canvas; she saw at once that Joe

depended on her trying to win Charlotte over to his way of thinking. But he was very much in love: at a word from Delia, she understood that he would yield, and Charlotte gain her point, save the child, and marry him . . .

How easy it was, after all! A friendly welcome, a good dinner, a ripe wine, and the memory of Charlotte's eyes—so much the more expressive for all that they had looked upon. A secret envy stabbed the wife who had lacked this last enlightenment.

How easy it was—and yet it must not be! Whatever happened, she could not let Charlotte Lovell marry Joe Ralston. All the traditions of honour and probity in which she had been brought up forbade her to connive at such a plan. She could conceive—had already conceived—of high-handed measures, swift and adroit defiances of precedent, subtle revolts against the heartlessness of the social routine. But a lie she could never connive at. The idea of Charlotte's marrying Joe Ralston—her own Jim's cousin—without revealing her past to him, seemed to Delia as dishonourable as it would have seemed to any Ralston. And to tell him the truth would at once put an end to the marriage; of that even Chatty was aware. Social tolerance was not dealt in the same measure to men and to women, and neither Delia nor Charlotte had ever wondered why: like all the young women of their class they simply bowed to the ineluctable.

No; there was no escape from the dilemma. As clearly as it was Delia's duty to save Clem Spender's child, so clearly, also, she seemed destined to sacrifice his mistress. As the thought pressed on her she remembered Charlotte's wistful cry: "I want to be married, like all of you," and her heart tightened. But yet it must not be.

"I make every allowance" (Joe was droning on) "for my sweet girl's ignorance and inexperience—for her lovely purity. How could a man wish his future wife to be—to be otherwise? You're with me, Jim? And Delia? I've told her, you understand, that she shall always have a special sum set apart for her poor children—in addition to her pin-money; on that she may absolutely count. God! I'm willing to draw up a deed, a settlement, before a lawyer, if she says so. I admire, I appreciate her generosity. But I ask you, Delia, as a mother—mind you, now, I want your frank opinion. If you think I can stretch a point—can let her go on giving her personal care to these children until . . . until . . ." A flush of pride suffused the potential father's brow . . . "till nearer duties claim her, why, I'm more than ready . . . if you'll tell her so. I undertake," Joe proclaimed, suddenly tingling with the memory of his last glass, "to make it right with my mother, whose prejudices, of course. while I respect them, I can never allow to—to come between me and my own convictions." He sprang to his feet, and beamed on his dauntless double in the chimney-mirror. "My convictions," he flung back at it.

"Hear, hear!" cried Jim emotionally.

Delia's needle gave the canvas a sharp prick, and she pushed her work aside.

"I think I understand you both, Joe. Certainly, in Charlotte's place, I could never give up those children."

"There you are, my dear fellow!" Jim triumphed, as proud of this vicarious courage as of the perfection of the dinner.

"Never," said Delia. "Especially, I mean, the foundlings—there are two, I think. Those children always die if they are sent to asylums. That is what is haunting Chatty."

"Poor innocents! How I love her for loving them! That there should be such scoundrels upon this earth unpunished—. Delia, will you tell her that I'll do whatever—"

"Gently, old man, gently," Jim admonished him, with a flash of Ralston caution.

"Well, that is to say, whatever—in reason—"

Delia lifted an arresting hand. "I'll tell her, Joe: she will be grateful. But it's of no use—"

"No use? What more—?"

"Nothing more: except this. Charlotte has had a return of her old illness. She coughed blood here today. You must not marry her."

There: it was done. She stood up, trembling in every bone, and feeling herself pale to the lips. Had she done right? Had she done wrong? And would she ever know?

Poor Joe turned on her a face as wan as hers: he clutched the back of his armchair, his head drooping forward like an old man's. His lips moved, but made no sound.

"My God!" Jim stammered. "But you know you've got to buck up, old boy."

"I'm—I'm so sorry for you, Joe. She'll tell you herself to-morrow," Delia faltered, while her husband continued to proffer heavy consolations.

"Take it like a man, old chap. Think of yourself—your future. Can't be, you know. Delia's right; she always *is*. Better get it over—better face the music now than later."

"Now than later," Joe echoed with a tortured grin; and it occurred to Delia that never before in the course of his easy good-natured life had he had—any more than her Jim—to give up anything his heart was set on. Even the vocabulary of renunciation, and its conventional gestures, were unfamiliar to him.

"But I don't understand. I can't give her up," he declared, blinking away a boyish tear.

"Think of the children, my dear fellow; it's your duty," Jim insisted, checking a glance of pride at Delia's wholesome comeliness.

In the long conversation that followed between the cousins—argument, counter-argument, sage counsel and hopeless protest—Delia took but an occasional part. She knew well enough what the end would be. The bridegroom who had feared that his bride might bring home contagion from her visits to the poor would not knowingly implant disease in his race. Nor was that all. Too many sad instances of mothers prematurely fading, and leaving their husbands alone with a young flock to rear, must be pressing upon Joe's memory. Ralstons, Lovells, Lannings, Archers, van der Luydens—which one of them had not some grave to care for in a distant cemetery: graves of young relatives "in a decline," sent abroad to be cured by balmy Italy? The Protestant grave-yards of Rome and Pisa were full of New York names; the vision of that familiar pilgrimage with a dying wife was one to turn the most ardent Ralston cold. And all the while, as she listened with bent head, Delia kept repeating to herself: "This is easy; but how am I going to tell Charlotte?"

When poor Joe, late that evening, wrung her hand with a stammered farewell, she called him back abruptly from the threshold.

"You must let me see her first, please; you must wait till she sends for you—" and she winced a little at the alacrity of his acceptance. But no amount of rhetorical bolstering-up could make it easy for a young man to face what lay ahead of Joe; and her final glance at him was one of compassion . . .

The front door closed upon Joe, and she was roused by her husband's touch on her shoulder.

"I never admired you more, darling. My wise Delia!"

Her head bent back, she took his kiss, and then drew apart. The sparkle in his eyes she understood to be as much an invitation to her bloom as a tribute to her sagacity.

She held him at arms' length. "What should you have done, Jim, if I'd had to tell you about myself what I've just told Joe about Chatty?"

A slight frown showed that he thought the question negligible, and hardly in her usual taste. "Come," his strong arm entreated her.

She continued to stand away from him, with grave eyes. "Poor Chatty! Nothing left now—"

His own eyes grew grave, in instant sympathy. At such moments he was still the sentimental boy whom she could manage.

"Ah, poor Chatty, indeed!" He groped for the readiest panacea. "Lucky, now, after all, that she has those paupers, isn't it? I suppose a woman *must* have children to love—somebody else's if not her own." It was evident that the thought of the remedy had already relieved his pain.

"Yes," Delia agreed, "I see no other comfort for her. I'm sure Joe will feel that too. Between us, darling—" and now she let him have her hands—"between us, you and I must see to it that she keeps her babies."

"Her babies?" He smiled at the possessive pronoun. "Of course, poor girl! Unless indeed she's sent to Italy?"

"Oh, she won't be that—where's the money to come from? And, besides, she'd never leave Aunt Lovell. But I thought, dear, if I might tell her tomorrow—you see, I'm not exactly looking forward to my talk with her—if I might tell her that you would let me look after the baby she's most worried about, the poor little foundling girl who has no name and no home—if I might put aside a fixed sum from my pin-money . . ."

Their hands flowed together, she lifted her flushing face to his. Manly tears were in his eyes; ah, how he triumphed in her health, her wisdom, her generosity!

"Not a penny from your pin-money—never!"

She feigned discouragement and wonder. "Think, dear—if I'd had to give you up!"

"Not a penny from your pin-money, I say—but as much more as you need, to help poor Chatty's pauper. There—will that content you?"

"Dearest! When I think of our own, upstairs!" They held each other, awed by that evocation.

V

CHARLOTTE LOVELL, at the sound of her cousin's step, lifted a fevered face from the pillow.

The bedroom, dim and close, smelt of eau de Cologne and fresh linen. Delia, blinking in from the bright winter sun, had to feel her way through a twilight obstructed by dark mahogany.

"I want to see your face, Chatty: unless your head aches too much?"

Charlotte signed "No," and Delia drew back the heavy window-curtains and let in a ray of light. In it she saw the girl's head, livid against the bed-linen, the brick-rose circles again visible under darkly shadowed lids. Just so, she remembered, poor cousin So-and-so had looked the week before she sailed for Italy!

"Delia!" Charlotte breathed.

Delia drew near the bed, and stood looking down at her cousin with new eyes. Yes: it had been easy enough, the night before, to dispose of Chatty's future as if it were her own. But now?

"Darling—"

"Oh, begin, please," the girl interrupted, "or I shall know that what's coming is too dreadful!"

"Chatty, dearest, if I promised you too much—"

"Jim won't let you take my child? I knew it! Shall I always go on dreaming things that can never be?"

Delia, her tears running down, knelt by the bed and gave her fresh hand into the other's burning clutch.

"Don't think that, dear: think only of what you'd like best . . ."

"Like best?" The girl sat up sharply against her pillows, alive to the hot fingertips.

"You can't marry Joe, dear—can you—and keep little Tina?" Delia continued.

"Not keep her with me, no: but somewhere where I could slip off to see her—oh, I had hoped such follies!"

"Give up follies, Charlotte. Keep her where? See your own

child in secret? Always in dread of disgrace? Of wrong to your other children? Have you ever thought of that?"

"Oh, my poor head won't think! You're trying to tell me that I must give her up?"

"No, dear; but that you must not marry Joe."

Charlotte sank back on the pillow, her eyes half-closed. "I tell you I must make my child a home. Delia, you're too blest to understand!"

"Think yourself blest too, Chatty. You shan't give up your baby. She shall live with you: you shall take care of her—for me."

"For you?"

"I promised you I'd take her, didn't I? But not that you should marry Joe. Only that I would make a home for your baby. Well, that's done; you two shall be always together."

Charlotte clung to her and sobbed. "But Joe—I can't tell him, I can't!" She put back Delia suddenly. "You haven't told him of my—of my baby? I couldn't bear to hurt him as much as that."

"I told him that you coughed blood yesterday. He'll see you presently: he's dreadfully unhappy. He has been given to understand that, in view of your bad health, the engagement is broken by your wish—and he accepts your decision; but if he weakens, or if you weaken, I can do nothing for you or for little Tina. For heaven's sake remember that!"

Delia released her hold, and Charlotte leaned back silent, with closed eyes and narrowed lips. Almost like a corpse she lay there. On a chair near the bed hung the poplin with red velvet ribbons which had been made over in honour of her betrothal. A pair of new slippers of bronze kid peeped from beneath it. Poor Chatty! She had hardly had time to be pretty . . .

Delia sat by the bed motionless, her eyes on her cousin's closed face. They followed the course of a tear that forced a way between Charlotte's tight lids, hung on the lashes, glittered slowly down the cheeks. As the tear reached the narrowed lips they spoke.

"Shall I live with her somewhere, do you mean? Just she and I together?"

"Just you and she."

"In a little house?"

"In a little house . . ."

"You're sure, Delia?"

"Sure, my dearest."

Charlotte once more raised herself on her elbow and sent a hand groping under the pillow. She drew out a narrow ribbon on which hung a diamond ring.

"I had taken it off already," she said simply, and handed it to Delia.

PART II

VI

Y OU COULD always have told, every one agreed afterward, that Charlotte Lovell was meant to be an old maid. Even before her illness it had been manifest: there was something prim about her in spite of her fiery hair. Lucky enough for her, poor girl, considering her wretched health in her youth: Mrs. James Ralston's contemporaries, for instance, remembered Charlotte as a mere ghost, coughing her lungs out— that, of course, had been the reason for her breaking her engagement with Joe Ralston.

True, she had recovered very rapidly, in spite of the peculiar treatment she was given. The Lovells, as every one knew, couldn't afford to send her to Italy; the previous experiment in Georgia had been unsuccessful; and so she was packed off to a farm-house on the Hudson—a little place on the James Ralstons' property—where she lived for five or six years with an Irish servant-woman and a foundling baby. The story of the foundling was another queer episode in Charlotte's history. From the time of her first illness, when she was only twenty-two or three, she had developed an almost morbid tenderness for children, especially for the children of the poor. It was said—Dr. Lanskell was understood to have said—that the baffled instinct of motherhood was peculiarly intense in cases where lung-disease prevented marriage. And so, when it was decided that Chatty must break her engagement to Joe Ralston and go to live in the country, the doctor had told her family that the only hope of saving her lay in not separating her entirely from her pauper children, but in letting her choose one of them, the youngest and most pitiable, and devote herself to its care. So the James Ralstons had lent her their little farm-house, and Mrs. Jim, with her extraordinary gift of taking things in at a glance, had at once arranged everything, and even pledged herself to look after the baby if Charlotte died.

Charlotte did not die. She lived to grow robust and middle-aged, energetic and even tyrannical. And as the trans-

formation in her character took place she became more and
more like the typical old maid: precise, methodical, absorbed
in trifles, and attaching an exaggerated importance to the
smallest social and domestic observances. Such was her reputation as a vigilant house-wife that, when poor Jim Ralston
was killed by a fall from his horse, and left Delia, still young,
with a boy and girl to bring up, it seemed perfectly natural
that the heart-broken widow should take her cousin to live
with her and share her task. But Delia Ralston never did
things quite like other people. When she took Charlotte she
took Charlotte's foundling too: a dark-haired child with pale
brown eyes, and the odd incisive manner of children who
have lived too much with their elders. The little girl was
called Tina Lovell: it was vaguely supposed that Charlotte
had adopted her. She grew up on terms of affectionate equality with her young Ralston cousins, and almost as much so—
it might be said—with the two women who mothered her.
But, impelled by an instinct of imitation which no one took
the trouble to correct, she always called Delia Ralston
"Mamma," and Charlotte Lovell "Aunt Chatty." She was a
brilliant and engaging creature, and people marvelled at poor
Chatty's luck in having chosen so interesting a specimen
among her foundlings (for she was by this time supposed to
have had a whole asylum-full to choose from).

The agreeable elderly bachelor, Sillerton Jackson, returning
from a prolonged sojourn in Paris (where he was understood
to have been made much of by the highest personages) was
immensely struck by Tina's charms when he saw her at her
coming-out ball, and asked Delia's permission to come some
evening and dine alone with her and her young people. He
complimented the widow on the rosy beauty of her own
young Delia; but the mother's keen eye perceived that all
the while he was watching Tina, and after dinner he confided to the older ladies that there was something "very
French" in the girl's way of doing her hair, and that in the
capital of all the Elegances she would have been pronounced
extremely stylish.

"Oh—" Delia deprecated, beamingly, while Charlotte Lovell sat bent over her work with pinched lips; but Tina, who

had been laughing with her cousins at the other end of the room, was around upon her elders in a flash.

"I heard what Mr. Sillerton said! Yes, I did, Mamma: he says I do my hair stylishly. Didn't I always tell you so? I *know* it's more becoming to let it curl as it wants to than to plaster it down with bandoline like Aunty's—"

"Tina, Tina—you always think people are admiring you!" Miss Lovell protested.

"Why shouldn't I, when they do?" the girl laughingly challenged; and, turning her mocking eyes on Sillerton Jackson: "Do tell Aunt Charlotte not to be so dreadfully old-maidish!"

Delia saw the blood rise to Charlotte Lovell's face. It no longer painted two brick-rose circles on her thin cheek-bones, but diffused a harsh flush over her whole countenance, from the collar fastened with an old-fashioned garnet brooch to the pepper-and-salt hair (with no trace of red left in it) flattened down over her hollow temples.

That evening, when they went up to bed, Delia called Tina into her room.

"You ought not to speak to your Aunt Charlotte as you did this evening, dear. It's disrespectful—you must see that it hurts her."

The girl overflowed with compunction. "Oh, I'm so sorry! Because I said she was an old maid? But she *is*, isn't she, Mamma? In her inmost soul, I mean. I don't believe she's ever been young—ever thought of fun or admiration or falling in love—do you? That's why she never understands me, and you always do, you darling dear Mamma." With one of her light movements, Tina was in the widow's arms.

"Child, child," Delia softly scolded, kissing the dark curls planted in five points on the girl's forehead.

There was a soft foot-fall in the passage, and Charlotte Lovell stood in the door. Delia, without moving, sent her a glance of welcome over Tina's shoulder.

"Come in, Charlotte. I'm scolding Tina for behaving like a spoilt baby before Sillerton Jackson. What will he think of her?"

"Just what she deserves, probably," Charlotte returned with a cold smile. Tina went toward her, and her thin lips touched the girl's proffered forehead just where Delia's warm kiss had rested. "Goodnight, child," she said in her dry tone of dismissal.

The door closed on the two women, and Delia signed to Charlotte to take the armchair opposite to her own.

"Not so near the fire," Miss Lovell answered. She chose a straight-backed seat, and sat down with folded hands. Delia's eyes rested absently on the thin ringless fingers: she wondered why Charlotte never wore her mother's jewels.

"I overheard what you were saying to Tina, Delia. You were scolding her because she called me an old maid."

It was Delia's turn to colour. "I scolded her for being disrespectful, dear; if you heard what I said you can't think that I was too severe."

"Not too severe: no. I've never thought you too severe with Tina; on the contrary."

"You think I spoil her?"

"Sometimes."

Delia felt an unreasoning resentment. "What was it I said that you object to?"

Charlotte returned her glance steadily. "I would rather she thought me an old maid than—"

"Oh—" Delia murmured. With one of her quick leaps of intuition she had entered into the other's soul, and once more measured its shuddering loneliness.

"What else," Charlotte inexorably pursued, "*can* she possibly be allowed to think me—ever?"

"I see . . . I see . . ." the widow faltered.

"A ridiculous narrow-minded old maid—nothing else," Charlotte Lovell insisted, getting to her feet, "or I shall never feel safe with her."

"Goodnight, my dear," Delia said compassionately. There were moments when she almost hated Charlotte for being Tina's mother, and others, such as this, when her heart was wrung by the tragic spectacle of that unavowed bond.

Charlotte seemed to have divined her thought.

"Oh, but don't pity me! She's mine," she murmured, going.

VII

DELIA RALSTON sometimes felt that the real events of her life did not begin until both her children had contracted—so safely and suitably—their irreproachable New York alliances. The boy had married first, choosing a Vandergrave in whose father's bank at Albany he was to have an immediate junior partnership; and young Delia (as her mother had foreseen she would) had selected John Junius, the safest and soundest of the many young Halseys, and followed him to his parents' house the year after her brother's marriage.

After young Delia had left the house in Gramercy Park it was inevitable that Tina should take the centre front of its narrow stage. Tina had reached the marriageable age, she was admired and sought after; but what hope was there of her finding a husband? The two watchful women did not propound this question to each other; but Delia Ralston, brooding over it day by day, and taking it up with her when she mounted at night to her bedroom, knew that Charlotte Lovell, at the same hour, carried the same problem with her to the floor above.

The two cousins, during their eight years of life together, had seldom openly disagreed. Indeed, it might almost have been said that there was nothing open in their relation. Delia would have had it otherwise: after they had once looked so deeply into each other's souls it seemed unnatural that a veil should fall between them. But she understood that Tina's ignorance of her origin must at all costs be preserved, and that Charlotte Lovell, abrupt, passionate and inarticulate, knew of no other security than to wall herself up in perpetual silence.

So far had she carried this self-imposed reticence that Mrs. Ralston was surprised at her suddenly asking, soon after young Delia's marriage, to be allowed to move down into the small bedroom next to Tina's that had been left vacant by the bride's departure.

"But you'll be so much less comfortable there, Chatty. Have you thought of that? Or is it on account of the stairs?"

"No; it's not the stairs," Charlotte answered with her usual

bluntness. How could she avail herself of the pretext Delia
offered her, when Delia knew that she still ran up and down
the three flights like a girl? "It's because I should be next to
Tina," she said, in a low voice that jarred like an untuned
string.

"Oh—very well. As you please." Mrs. Ralston could not
tell why she felt suddenly irritated by the request, unless it
were that she had already amused herself with the idea of
fitting up the vacant room as a sitting-room for Tina. She had
meant to do it in pink and pale green, like an opening flower.

"Of course, if there is any reason—" Charlotte suggested,
as if reading her thought.

"None whatever; except that—well, I'd meant to surprise
Tina by doing the room up as a sort of little boudoir where
she could have her books and things, and see her girl friends."

"You're too kind, Delia; but Tina mustn't have boudoirs,"
Miss Lovell answered ironically, the green specks showing in
her eyes.

"Very well: as you please," Delia repeated, in the same irritated tone. "I'll have your things brought down tomorrow."

Charlotte paused in the doorway. "You're sure there's no
other reason?"

"Other reason? Why should there be?" The two women
looked at each other almost with hostility, and Charlotte
turned to go.

The talk once over, Delia was annoyed with herself for
having yielded to Charlotte's wish. Why must it always be she
who gave in, she who, after all, was the mistress of the house,
and to whom both Charlotte and Tina might almost be said
to owe their very existence, or at least all that made it worth
having? Yet whenever any question arose about the girl it
was invariably Charlotte who gained her point, Delia who
yielded: it seemed as if Charlotte, in her mute obstinate way,
were determined to take every advantage of the dependence
that made it impossible for a woman of Delia's nature to oppose her.

In truth, Delia had looked forward more than she knew to
the quiet talks with Tina to which the little boudoir would
have lent itself. While her own daughter inhabited the room,
Mrs. Ralston had been in the habit of spending an hour there

every evening, chatting with the two girls while they undressed, and listening to their comments on the incidents of
the day. She always knew beforehand exactly what her own
girl would say; but Tina's views and opinions were a perpetual delicious shock to her. Not that they were strange or unfamiliar; there were moments when they seemed to well
straight up from the dumb depths of Delia's own past. Only
they expressed feelings she had never uttered, ideas she had
hardly avowed to herself: Tina sometimes said things which
Delia Ralston, in far-off self-communions, had imagined herself saying to Clement Spender.

And now there would be an end to these evening talks:
if Charlotte had asked to be lodged next to her daughter,
might it not conceivably be because she wished them to end?
It had never before occurred to Delia that her influence over
Tina might be resented; now the discovery flashed a light far
down into the abyss which had always divided the two
women. But a moment later Delia reproached herself for attributing feelings of jealousy to her cousin. Was it not rather
to herself that she should have ascribed them? Charlotte, as
Tina's mother, had every right to wish to be near her, near
her in all senses of the word; what claim had Delia to oppose
to that natural privilege? The next morning she gave the order
that Charlotte's things should be taken down to the room
next to Tina's.

That evening, when bedtime came, Charlotte and Tina
went upstairs together; but Delia lingered in the drawing-
room, on the pretext of having letters to write. In truth, she
dreaded to pass the threshold where, evening after evening,
the fresh laughter of the two girls used to waylay her while
Charlotte Lovell already slept her old-maid sleep on the floor
above. A pang went through Delia at the thought that henceforth she would be cut off from this means of keeping her
hold on Tina.

An hour later, when she mounted the stairs in her turn, she
was guiltily conscious of moving as noiselessly as she could
along the heavy carpet of the corridor, and of pausing longer
than was necessary over the putting out of the gas-jet on the
landing. As she lingered she strained her ears for the sound of

voices from the adjoining doors behind which Charlotte and
Tina slept; she would have been secretly hurt at hearing talk
and laughter from within. But none came, nor was there any
light beneath the doors. Evidently Charlotte, in her hard methodical way, had said goodnight to her daughter, and gone
straight to bed as usual. Perhaps she had never approved of
Tina's vigils, of the long undressing punctuated with mirth
and confidences; she might have asked for the room next to
her daughter's simply because she did not want the girl to
miss her "beauty sleep."

Whenever Delia tried to explore the secret of her cousin's
actions she returned from the adventure humiliated and
abashed by the base motives she found herself attributing to
Charlotte. How was it that she, Delia Ralston, whose happiness had been open and avowed to the world, so often found
herself envying poor Charlotte the secret of her scanted motherhood? She hated herself for this movement of envy whenever she detected it, and tried to atone for it by a softened
manner and a more anxious regard for Charlotte's feelings;
but the attempt was not always successful, and Delia sometimes wondered if Charlotte did not resent any show of sympathy as an indirect glance at her misfortune. The worst of
suffering such as hers was that it left one sore to the gentlest
touch . . .

Delia, slowly undressing before the same lace-draped toilet-
glass which had reflected her bridal image, was turning over
these thoughts when she heard a light knock. She opened the
door, and there stood Tina, in a dressing-gown, her dark curls
falling over her shoulders.

With a happy heart-beat Delia held out her arms.

"I had to say goodnight, Mamma," the girl whispered.

"Of course, dear." Delia pressed a long kiss on her lifted
forehead. "Run off now, or you might disturb your aunt. You
know she sleeps badly, and you must be as quiet as a mouse
now she's next to you."

"Yes, I know," Tina acquiesced, with a grave glance that
was almost of complicity.

She asked no further question, she did not linger: lifting
Delia's hand she held it a moment against her cheek, and then
stole out as noiselessly as she had come.

VIII

"BUT YOU must see," Charlotte Lovell insisted, laying aside the *Evening Post*, "that Tina has changed. You do see that?"

The two women were sitting alone by the drawing-room fire in Gramercy Park. Tina had gone to dine with her cousin, young Mrs. John Junius Halsey, and was to be taken afterward to a ball at the Vandergraves', from which the John Juniuses had promised to see her home. Mrs. Ralston and Charlotte, their early dinner finished, had the long evening to themselves. Their custom, on such occasions, was for Charlotte to read the news aloud to her cousin, while the latter embroidered; but tonight, all through Charlotte's conscientious progress from column to column, without a slip or an omission, Delia had felt her, for some special reason, alert to take advantage of her daughter's absence.

To gain time before answering, Mrs. Ralston bent over a stitch in her delicate white embroidery.

"Tina changed? Since when?" she questioned.

The answer flashed out instantly. "Since Lanning Halsey has been coming here so much."

"Lanning? I used to think he came for Delia," Mrs. Ralston mused, speaking at random to gain still more time.

"It's natural you should suppose that every one came for Delia," Charlotte rejoined dryly; "but as Lanning continues to seek every chance of being with Tina—"

Mrs. Ralston raised her head and stole a swift glance at her cousin. She had in truth noticed that Tina had changed, as a flower changes at the mysterious moment when the unopened petals flush from within. The girl had grown handsomer, shyer, more silent, at times more irrelevantly gay. But Delia had not associated these variations of mood with the presence of Lanning Halsey, one of the numerous youths who had haunted the house before young Delia's marriage. There had, indeed, been a moment when Mrs. Ralston's eyes had been fixed, with a certain apprehension, on the handsome Lanning. Among all the sturdy and stolid Halsey cousins he was the only one to whom a prudent mother might have hesitated to

413

entrust her daughter; it would have been hard to say why, except that he was handsomer and more conversable than the rest, chronically unpunctual, and totally unperturbed by the fact. Clem Spender had been like that; and what if young Delia—?

But young Delia's mother was speedily reassured. The girl, herself arch and appetizing, took no interest in the corresponding graces except when backed by more solid qualities. A Ralston to the core, she demanded the Ralston virtues, and chose the Halsey most worthy of a Ralston bride.

Mrs. Ralston felt that Charlotte was waiting for her to speak. "It will be hard to get used to the idea of Tina's marrying," she said gently. "I don't know what we two old women shall do, all alone in this empty house—for it will be an empty house then. But I suppose we ought to face the idea."

"I *do* face it," said Charlotte Lovell gravely.

"And you dislike Lanning? I mean, as a husband for Tina?"

Miss Lovell folded the evening paper, and stretched out a thin hand for her knitting. She glanced across the citron-wood work-table at her cousin. "Tina must not be too difficult—" she began.

"Oh—" Delia protested, reddening.

"Let us call things by their names," the other evenly pursued. "That's my way, when I speak at all. Usually, as you know, I say nothing."

The widow made a sign of assent, and Charlotte went on: "It's better so. But I've always known a time would come when we should have to talk this thing out."

"Talk this thing out? You and I? What thing?"

"Tina's future."

There was a silence. Delia Ralston, who always responded instantly to the least appeal to her sincerity, breathed a deep sigh of relief. At last the ice in Charlotte's breast was breaking up!

"My dear," Delia murmured, "you know how much Tina's happiness concerns me. If you disapprove of Lanning Halsey as a husband, have you any other candidate in mind?"

Miss Lovell smiled one of her faint hard smiles. "I am not

aware that there is a queue at the door. Nor do I disapprove
of Lanning Halsey as a husband. Personally, I find him very
agreeable; I understand his attraction for Tina."

"Ah—Tina *is* attracted?"

"Yes."

Mrs. Ralston pushed aside her work and thoughtfully considered her cousin's sharply-lined face. Never had Charlotte
Lovell more completely presented the typical image of the old
maid than as she sat there, upright on her straight-backed
chair, with narrowed elbows and clicking needles, and imper-
turbably discussed her daughter's marriage.

"I don't understand, Chatty. Whatever Lanning's faults
are—and I don't believe they're grave—I share your liking
for him. After all—" Mrs. Ralston paused—"what is it that
people find so reprehensible in him? Chiefly, as far as I can
hear, that he can't decide on the choice of a profession. The
New York view about that is rather narrow, as we know.
Young men may have other tastes . . . artistic . . . literary
. . . they may even have difficulty in deciding . . ."

Both women coloured slightly, and Delia guessed that
the same reminiscence which shook her own bosom also
throbbed under Charlotte's strait bodice.

Charlotte spoke. "Yes: I understand that. But hesitancy
about a profession may cause hesitancy about . . . other decisions . . ."

"What do you mean? Surely not that Lanning—?"

"Lanning has not asked Tina to marry him."

"And you think he's hesitating?"

Charlotte paused. The steady click of her needles punctuated the silence as once, years before, it had been punctuated
by the tick of the Parisian clock on Delia's mantel. As Delia's
memory fled back to that scene she felt its mysterious tension
in the air.

Charlotte spoke. "Lanning is not hesitating any longer: he
has decided *not* to marry Tina. But he has also decided—not
to give up seeing her."

Delia flushed abruptly; she was irritated and bewildered by
Charlotte's oracular phrases, doled out between parsimonious
lips.

"You don't mean that he has offered himself and then

drawn back? I can't think him capable of such an insult to
Tina."

"He has not insulted Tina. He has simply told her that he
can't afford to marry. Until he chooses a profession his father
will allow him only a few hundred dollars a year; and that
may be suppressed if—if he marries against his parents'
wishes."

It was Delia's turn to be silent. The past was too over-
whelmingly resuscitated in Charlotte's words. Clement
Spender stood before her, irresolute, impecunious, persuasive.
Ah, if only she had let herself be persuaded!

"I'm very sorry that this should have happened to Tina. But
as Lanning appears to have behaved honourably, and withdrawn without raising false expectations, we must hope . . .
we must hope. . ." Delia paused, not knowing what they
must hope.

Charlotte Lovell laid down her knitting. "You know as well
as I do, Delia, that every young man who is inclined to fall in
love with Tina will find as good reasons for not marrying
her."

"Then you think Lanning's excuses are a pretext?"

"Naturally. The first of many that will be found by his successors—for of course he will have successors. Tina—
attracts."

"Ah," Delia murmured.

Here they were at last face to face with the problem which,
through all the years of silence and evasiveness, had lain as
close to the surface as a corpse too hastily buried! Delia drew
another deep breath, which again was almost one of relief.
She had always known that it would be difficult, almost impossible, to find a husband for Tina; and much as she desired
Tina's happiness, some inmost selfishness whispered how
much less lonely and purposeless the close of her own life
would be should the girl be forced to share it. But how say
this to Tina's mother?

"I hope you exaggerate, Charlotte. There may be disinterested characters. . . But, in any case, surely Tina need not be
unhappy here, with us who love her so dearly."

"Tina an old maid? Never!" Charlotte Lovell rose abruptly,
her closed hand crashing down on the slender work-table.

"My child shall have her life . . . her own life . . . whatever it costs me . . ."

Delia's ready sympathy welled up. "I understand your feeling. I should want also . . . hard as it will be to let her go. But surely there is no hurry—no reason for looking so far ahead. The child is not twenty. Wait."

Charlotte stood before her, motionless, perpendicular. At such moments she made Delia think of lava struggling through granite: there seemed no issue for the fires within.

"Wait? But if *she* doesn't wait?"

"But if he has withdrawn—what do you mean?"

"He has given up marrying her—but not seeing her."

Delia sprang up in her turn, flushed and trembling.

"Charlotte! Do you know what you're insinuating?"

"Yes: I know."

"But it's too outrageous. No decent girl—"

The words died on Delia's lips. Charlotte Lovell held her eyes inexorably. "Girls are not always what you call decent," she declared.

Mrs. Ralston turned slowly back to her seat. Her tambour frame had fallen to the floor; she stooped heavily to pick it up. Charlotte's gaunt figure hung over her, relentless as doom.

"I can't imagine, Charlotte, what is gained by saying such things—even by hinting them. Surely you trust your own child."

Charlotte laughed. "My mother trusted me," she said.

"How dare you—how dare you?" Delia began; but her eyes fell, and she felt a tremor of weakness in her throat.

"Oh, I dare anything for Tina, even to judging her as she is," Tina's mother murmured.

"As she is? She's perfect!"

"Let us say then that she must pay for my imperfections. All I want is that she shouldn't pay too heavily."

Mrs. Ralston sat silent. It seemed to her that Charlotte spoke with the voice of all the dark destinies coiled under the safe surface of life; and that to such a voice there was no answer but an awed acquiescence.

"Poor Tina!" she breathed.

"Oh, I don't intend that she shall suffer! It's not for that

that I've waited . . . waited. Only I've made mistakes: mistakes that I understand now, and must remedy. You've been too good to us—and we must go."

"Go?" Delia gasped.

"Yes. Don't think me ungrateful. You saved my child once—do you suppose I can forget? But now it's my turn— it's I who must save her. And it's only by taking her away from everything here—from everything she's known till now—that I can do it. She's lived too long among unrealities: and she's like me. They won't content her."

"Unrealities?" Delia echoed vaguely.

"Unrealities for her. Young men who make love to her and can't marry her. Happy households where she's welcomed till she's suspected of designs on a brother or a husband—or else exposed to their insults. How could we ever have imagined, either of us, that the child could escape disaster? I thought only of her present happiness—of all the advantages, for both of us, of being with you. But this affair with young Halsey has opened my eyes. I must take Tina away. We must go and live somewhere where we're not known, where we shall be among plain people, leading plain lives. Somewhere where she can find a husband, and make herself a home."

Charlotte paused. She had spoken in a rapid monotonous tone, as if by rote; but now her voice broke and she repeated painfully: "I'm not ungrateful."

"Oh, don't let's speak of gratitude! What place has it between you and me?"

Delia had risen and begun to move uneasily about the room. She longed to plead with Charlotte, to implore her not to be in haste, to picture to her the cruelty of severing Tina from all her habits and associations, of carrying her inexplicably away to lead "a plain life among plain people." What chance was there, indeed, that a creature so radiant would tamely submit to such a fate, or find an acceptable husband in such conditions? The change might only precipitate a tragedy. Delia's experience was too limited for her to picture exactly what might happen to a girl like Tina, suddenly cut off from all that sweetened life for her; but vague visions of revolt and flight—of a "fall" deeper and more irretrievable than Charlotte's—flashed through her agonized imagination.

"It's too cruel—it's too cruel," she cried, speaking to herself rather than to Charlotte.

Charlotte, instead of answering, glanced abruptly at the clock.

"Do you know what time it is? Past midnight. I mustn't keep you sitting up for my foolish girl."

Delia's heart contracted. She saw that Charlotte wished to cut the conversation short, and to do so by reminding her that only Tina's mother had a right to decide what Tina's future should be. At that moment, though Delia had just protested that there could be no question of gratitude between them, Charlotte Lovell seemed to her a monster of ingratitude, and it was on the tip of her tongue to cry out: "Have all the years then given me no share in Tina?" But at the same instant she had put herself once more in Charlotte's place, and was feeling the mother's fierce terrors for her child. It was natural enough that Charlotte should resent the faintest attempt to usurp in private the authority she could never assert in public. With a pang of compassion Delia realized that she herself was literally the one being on earth before whom Charlotte could act the mother. "Poor thing—ah, let her!" she murmured inwardly.

"But why should you sit up for Tina? She has the key, and Delia is to bring her home."

Charlotte Lovell did not immediately answer. She rolled up her knitting, looked severely at one of the candelabra on the mantelpiece, and crossed over to straighten it. Then she picked up her work-bag.

"Yes, as you say—why should any one sit up for her?" She moved about the room, putting out the lamps, covering the fire, assuring herself that the windows were bolted, while Delia passively watched her. Then the two cousins lit their bedroom candles and walked upstairs through the darkened house. Charlotte seemed determined to make no further allusion to the subject of their talk. On the landing she paused, bending her head toward Delia's nightly kiss.

"I hope they've kept up your fire," she said, with her capable housekeeping air; and on Delia's hasty reassurance the two murmured a simultaneous "Goodnight," and Charlotte turned down the passage to her room.

IX

ELIA'S FIRE had been kept up, and her dressing-gown was warming on an arm-chair near the hearth. But she neither undressed nor yet seated herself. Her conversation with Charlotte had filled her with a deep unrest.

For a few moments she stood in the middle of the floor, looking slowly about her. Nothing had ever been changed in the room which, even as a bride, she had planned to modernize. All her dreams of renovation had faded long ago. Some deep central indifference had gradually made her regard herself as a third person, living the life meant for another woman, a woman totally unrelated to the vivid Delia Lovell who had entered that house so full of plans and visions. The fault, she knew, was not her husband's. With a little managing and a little wheedling she would have gained every point as easily as she had gained the capital one of taking the foundling baby under her wing. The difficulty was that, after that victory, nothing else seemed worth trying for. The first sight of little Tina had somehow decentralized Delia Ralston's whole life, making her indifferent to everything else, except indeed the welfare of her own husband and children. Ahead of her she saw only a future full of duties, and these she had gaily and faithfully accomplished. But her own life was over: she felt as detached as a cloistered nun.

The change in her was too deep not to be visible. The Ralstons openly gloried in dear Delia's conformity. Each acquiescence passed for a concession, and the family doctrine was fortified by such fresh proofs of its durability. Now, as Delia glanced about her at the Léopold Robert lithographs, the family daguerreotypes, the rosewood and mahogany, she understood that she was looking at the walls of her own grave.

The change had come on the day when Charlotte Lovell, cowering on that very lounge, had made her terrible avowal. Then for the first time Delia, with a kind of fearful exaltation, had heard the blind forces of life groping and crying underfoot. But on that day also she had known herself excluded from them, doomed to dwell among shadows. Life had passed her by, and left her with the Ralstons.

Very well, then! She would make the best of herself, and of the Ralstons. The vow was immediate and unflinching; and for nearly twenty years she had gone on observing it. Once only had she been not a Ralston but herself; once only had it seemed worth while. And now perhaps the same challenge had sounded again; again, for a moment, it might be worth while to live. Not for the sake of Clement Spender—poor Clement, married years ago to a plain determined cousin, who had hunted him down in Rome, and enclosing him in an unrelenting domesticity, had obliged all New York on the grand tour to buy his pictures with a resigned grimace. No, not for Clement Spender, hardly for Charlotte or even for Tina; but for her own sake, hers, Delia Ralston's, for the sake of her one missed vision, her forfeited reality, she would once more break down the Ralston barriers and reach out into the world.

A faint sound through the silent house disturbed her meditation. Listening, she heard Charlotte Lovell's door open and her stiff petticoats rustle toward the landing. A light glanced under the door and vanished; Charlotte had passed Delia's threshold on her way downstairs.

Without moving, Delia continued to listen. Perhaps the careful Charlotte had gone down to make sure that the front door was not bolted, or that she had really covered up the fire. If that were her object, her step would presently be heard returning. But no step sounded; and it became gradually evident that Charlotte had gone down to wait for her daughter. Why?

Delia's bedroom was at the front of the house. She stole across the heavy carpet, drew aside the curtains and cautiously folded back the inner shutters. Below her lay the empty square, white with moonlight, its tree-trunks patterned on a fresh sprinkling of snow. The houses opposite slept in darkness; not a footfall broke the white surface, not a wheel-track marred the brilliant street. Overhead a heaven full of stars swam in the moonlight.

Of the households around Gramercy Park Delia knew that only two others had gone to the ball: the Petrus Vandergraves and their cousins the young Parmly Ralstons. The Lucius Lannings had just entered on their three years of mourning for Mrs. Lucius's mother (it was hard on their daughter Kate, just eighteen, who would be unable to "come out" till she was twenty-one); young Mrs. Marcy Mingott was "expecting her third," and consequently secluded from the public eye for nearly a year; and the other denizens of the square belonged to the undifferentiated and uninvited.

Delia pressed her forehead against the pane. Before long carriages would turn the corner, the sleeping square ring with hoof-beats, fresh laughter and young farewells mount from the door-steps. But why was Charlotte waiting for her daughter downstairs in the darkness?

The Parisian clock struck one. Delia came back into the room, raked the fire, picked up a shawl, and, wrapped in it, returned to her vigil. Ah, how old she must have grown, that she should feel the cold at such a moment! It reminded her of what the future held for her: neuralgia, rheumatism, stiffness, accumulating infirmities. And never had she kept a moonlight watch with a lover's arms to warm her . . .

The square still lay silent. Yet the ball must surely be ending: the gayest dances did not last long after one in the morning, and the drive from University Place to Gramercy Park was a short one. Delia leaned in the embrasure and listened.

Hoof-beats, muffled by the snow, sounded in Irving Place, and the Petrus Vandergraves' family coach drew up before the opposite house. The Vandergrave girls and their brother sprang out and mounted the steps; then the coach stopped again a few doors farther on, and the Parmly Ralstons, brought home by their cousins, descended at their own door. The next carriage that rounded the corner must therefore be the John Juniuses', bringing Tina.

The gilt clock struck half-past one. Delia wondered, knowing that young Delia, out of regard for John Junius's business hours, never stayed late at evening parties. Doubtless Tina had delayed her; Mrs. Ralston felt a little annoyed with Tina's thoughtlessness in keeping her cousin up. But the feeling was swept away by an immediate wave of sympathy. "We must go away somewhere, and lead plain lives among plain people." If Charlotte carried out her threat—and Delia knew she would hardly have spoken unless her resolve had been taken—it might be that at that very moment poor Tina was dancing her last *valse*.

Another quarter of an hour passed; then, just as the cold was finding a way through Delia's shawl, she saw two people turn into the deserted square from Irving Place. One was a young man in opera hat and ample cloak. To his arm clung a figure so closely wrapped and muffled that, until the corner light fell on it, Delia hesitated. After that, she wondered that she had not at once recognized Tina's dancing step, and her manner of tilting her head a little sideways to look up at the person she was talking to.

Tina—Tina and Lanning Halsey, walking home alone in the small hours from the Vandergrave ball! Delia's first thought was of an accident: the carriage might have broken down, or else her daughter been taken ill and obliged to return home. But no; in the latter case she would have sent the carriage on with Tina. And if there had been an accident of any sort the young people would have been hastening to apprise Mrs. Ralston; instead of which, through the bitter brilliant night, they sauntered like lovers in a midsummer glade, and Tina's thin slippers might have been falling on daisies instead of snow.

Delia began to tremble like a girl. In a flash she had the answer to a question which had long been the subject of her secret conjectures. How did lovers like Charlotte and Clement Spender contrive to meet? What Latmian solitude hid their clandestine joys? In the exposed compact little society to which they all belonged, how was it possible—literally—for such encounters to take place? Delia would never have dared to put the question to Charlotte; there were moments when she almost preferred not to know, not even to hazard a guess. But now, at a glance, she understood. How often Charlotte Lovell, staying alone in town with her infirm grandmother, must have walked home from evening parties with Clement Spender, how often have let herself and him into the darkened house in Mercer Street, where there was no one to spy upon their coming but a deaf old lady and her aged servants, all securely sleeping overhead! Delia, at the thought, saw the grim drawing-room which had been their moonlit forest, the drawing-room into which old Mrs. Lovell no longer descended, with its swathed chandelier and hard Empire sofas, and the eyeless marble caryatids of the mantel; she pictured the shaft of moonlight falling across the swans and garlands of the faded carpet, and in that icy light two young figures in each other's arms.

Yes: it must have been some such memory that had roused Charlotte's suspicions, excited her fears, sent her down in the darkness to confront the culprits. Delia shivered at the irony of the confrontation. If Tina had but known! But to Tina, of course, Charlotte was still what she had long since resolved to be: the image of prudish spinsterhood. And Delia could imagine how quietly and decently the scene below stairs would presently be enacted: no astonishment, no reproaches, no insinuations, but a smiling and resolute ignoring of excuses.

"What, Tina? You walked home with Lanning? You imprudent child—in this wet snow! Ah, I see: Delia was worried about the baby, and ran off early, promising to send back the carriage—and it never came? Well, my dear, I congratulate you on finding Lanning to see you home. . . Yes—I sat up because I couldn't for the life of me remember whether you'd taken the latch-key—was there ever such a flighty old aunt? But don't tell your Mamma, dear, or she'd scold me for being so forgetful, and for staying downstairs in the cold. . . You're quite sure you have the key? Ah, Lanning has it? Thank you, Lanning; so kind! Goodnight—or one really ought to say, good morning."

As Delia reached this point in her mute representation of Charlotte's monologue the front door slammed below, and young Lanning Halsey walked slowly away across the square. Delia saw him pause on the opposite pavement, look up at the house-front, and then turn lingeringly away. His dismissal had taken exactly as long as Delia had calculated it would. A moment later she saw a passing light under her door, heard the starched rustle of Charlotte's petticoats, and knew that mother and daughter had reached their rooms.

Slowly, with stiff motions, she began to undress, blew out her candles, and knelt by her bedside, her face hidden.

X

L YING AWAKE till morning, Delia lived over every detail of the fateful day when she had assumed the charge of Charlotte's child. At the time she had been hardly more than a child herself, and there had been no one for her to turn to, no one to fortify her resolution, or to advise her how to put it into effect. Since then, the accumulated experiences of twenty years ought to have prepared her for emergencies, and taught her to advise others instead of seeking their guidance. But these years of experience weighed on her like chains binding her down to her narrow plot of life; independent action struck her as more dangerous, less conceivable, than when she had first ventured on it. There seemed to be so many more people to "consider" now ("consider" was the Ralston word): her children, their children, the families into which they had married. What would the Halseys say, and what the Ralstons? Had she then become a Ralston through and through?

A few hours later she sat in old Dr. Lanskell's library, her eyes on his sooty Smyrna rug. For some years now Dr. Lanskell had no longer practised: at most, he continued to go to a few old patients, and to give consultations in "difficult" cases. But he remained a power in his former kingdom, a sort of lay Pope or medical Elder to whom the patients he had once healed of physical ills often returned for moral medicine. People were agreed that Dr. Lanskell's judgment was sound; but what secretly drew them to him was the fact that, in the most totem-ridden of communities, he was known not to be afraid of anything.

Now, as Delia sat and watched his massive silver-headed figure moving ponderously about the room, between rows of medical books in calf bindings and the Dying Gladiators and Young Augustuses of grateful patients, she already felt the reassurance given by his mere bodily presence.

"You see, when I first took Tina I didn't perhaps consider sufficiently—"

The Doctor halted behind his desk and brought his fist

down on it with a genial thump. "Thank goodness you
didn't! There are considerers enough in this town without
you, Delia Lovell."

She looked up quickly. "Why do you call me Delia Lovell?"

"Well, because today I rather suspect you *are*," he rejoined
astutely; and she met this with a wistful laugh.

"Perhaps, if I hadn't been, once before—I mean, if I'd always been a prudent deliberate Ralston it would have been
kinder to Tina in the end."

Dr. Lanskell sank his gouty bulk into the armchair behind
his desk, and beamed at her through ironic spectacles. "I hate
in-the-end kindnesses: they're about as nourishing as the
third day of cold mutton."

She pondered. "Of course I realize that if I adopt Tina—"

"Yes?"

"Well, people will say. . ." A deep blush rose to her throat,
covered her cheeks and brow, and ran like fire under her
decently-parted hair.

He nodded: "Yes."

"Or else—" the blush darkened—"that she's Jim's—"

Again Dr. Lanskell nodded. "That's what they're more
likely to think; and what's the harm if they do? I know Jim:
he asked you no questions when you took the child—but he
knew whose she was."

She raised astonished eyes. "He knew—?"

"Yes: he came to me. And—well—in the baby's interest I
violated professional secrecy. That's how Tina got a home.
You're not going to denounce me, are you?"

"Oh, Dr. Lanskell—" Her eyes filled with painful tears.
"Jim knew? And didn't tell me?"

"No. People didn't tell each other things much in those
days, did they? But he admired you enormously for what you
did. And if you assume—as I suppose you do—that he's now
in a world of completer enlightenment, why not take it for
granted that he'll admire you still more for what you're going
to do? Presumably," the Doctor concluded sardonically,
"people realize in heaven that it's a devilish sight harder, on
earth, to do a brave thing at forty-five than at twenty-five."

"Ah, that's what I was thinking this morning," she confessed.

"Well, you're going to prove the contrary this afternoon." He looked at his watch, stood up and laid a fatherly hand on her shoulder. "Let people think what they choose; and send young Delia to me if she gives you any trouble. Your boy won't, you know, nor John Junius either; it must have been a woman who invented that third-and-fourth generation idea . . ."

An elderly maid-servant looked in, and Delia rose; but on the threshold she halted.

"I have an idea it's Charlotte I may have to send to you."

"Charlotte?"

"She'll hate what I'm going to do, you know."

Dr. Lanskell lifted his silver eye-brows. "Yes: poor Charlotte! I suppose she's jealous? That's where the truth of the third-and-fourth generation business comes in, after all. Somebody always has to foot the bill."

"Ah—if only Tina doesn't!"

"Well—that's just what Charlotte will come to recognize in time. So your course is clear."

He guided her out through the dining-room, where some poor people and one or two old patients were already waiting.

Delia's course, in truth, seemed clear enough till, that afternoon, she summoned Charlotte alone to her bedroom. Tina was lying down with a headache: it was in those days the accepted state of young ladies in sentimental dilemmas, and greatly simplified the communion of their elders.

Delia and Charlotte had exchanged only conventional phrases over their mid-day meal; but Delia still had the sense that her cousin's decision was final. The events of the previous evening had no doubt confirmed Charlotte's view that the time had come for such a decision.

Miss Lovell, closing the bedroom door with her dry deliberateness, advanced toward the chintz lounge between the windows.

"You wanted to see me, Delia?"

"Yes.—Oh, don't sit there," Mrs. Ralston exclaimed uncontrollably.

Charlotte stared: was it possible that she did not remember

the sobs of anguish she had once smothered in those very cushions?

"Not—?"

"No; come nearer to me. Sometimes I think I'm a little deaf," Delia nervously explained, pushing a chair up to her own.

"Ah." Charlotte seated herself. "I hadn't remarked it. But if you are, it may have saved you from hearing at what hour of the morning Tina came back from the Vandergraves' last night. She would never forgive herself—inconsiderate as she is—if she thought she'd waked you."

"She didn't wake me," Delia answered. Inwardly she thought: "Charlotte's mind is made up; I shan't be able to move her."

"I suppose Tina enjoyed herself very much at the ball?" she continued.

"Well, she's paying for it with a headache. Such excitements are not meant for her, I've already told you—"

"Yes," Mrs. Ralston interrupted. "It's to continue our talk of last night that I've asked you to come up."

"To continue it?" The brick-red circles appeared on Charlotte's dried cheeks. "Is it worth while? I think I ought to tell you at once that my mind's made up. I suppose you'll admit that I know what's best for Tina."

"Yes; of course. But won't you at least allow me a share in your decision?"

"A share?"

Delia leaned forward, laying a warm hand on her cousin's interlocked fingers. "Charlotte, once in this room, years ago, you asked me to help you—you believed I could. Won't you believe it again?"

Charlotte's lips grew rigid. "I believe the time has come for me to help myself."

"At the cost of Tina's happiness?"

"No; but to spare her greater unhappiness."

"But, Charlotte, Tina's happiness is all I want."

"Oh, I know. You've done all you could do for my child."

"No; not all." Delia rose, and stood before her cousin with a kind of solemnity. "But now I'm going to." It was as if she had pronounced a vow.

Charlotte Lovell looked up at her with a glitter of apprehension in her hunted eyes.

"If you mean that you're going to use your influence with the Halseys—I'm very grateful to you; I shall always be grateful. But I don't want a compulsory marriage for my child."

Delia flushed at the other's incomprehension. It seemed to her that her tremendous purpose must be written on her face. "I'm going to adopt Tina—give her my name," she announced.

Charlotte Lovell stared at her stonily. "Adopt her—adopt her?"

"Don't you see, dear, the difference it will make? There's my mother's money—the Lovell money; it's not much, to be sure; but Jim always wanted it to go back to the Lovells. And my Delia and her brother are so handsomely provided for. There's no reason why my little fortune shouldn't go to Tina. And why she shouldn't be known as Tina Ralston." Delia paused. "I believe—I think I know—that Jim would have approved of that too."

"*Approved?*"

"Yes. Can't you see that when he let me take the child he must have foreseen and accepted whatever—whatever might eventually come of it?"

Charlotte stood up also. "Thank you, Delia. But nothing more must come of it, except our leaving you; our leaving you now. I'm sure that's what Jim would have approved."

Mrs. Ralston drew back a step or two. Charlotte's cold resolution benumbed her courage, and she could find no immediate reply.

"Ah, then it's easier for you to sacrifice Tina's happiness than your pride?" she exclaimed.

"My pride? I've no right to any pride, except in my child. And that I'll never sacrifice."

"No one asks you to. You're not reasonable. You're cruel. All I want is to be allowed to help Tina, and you speak as if I were interfering with your rights."

"My rights?" Charlotte echoed the words with a desolate laugh. "What are they? I have no rights, either before the law or in the heart of my own child."

"How can you say such things? You know how Tina loves you."

"Yes; compassionately—as I used to love my old-maid aunts. There were two of them—you remember? Like withered babies! We children used to be warned never to say anything that might shock Aunt Josie or Aunt Nonie; exactly as I heard you telling Tina the other night—"

"Oh—" Delia murmured.

Charlotte Lovell continued to stand before her, haggard, rigid, unrelenting. "No, it's gone on long enough. I mean to tell her everything; and to take her away."

"To tell her about her birth?"

"I was never ashamed of it," Charlotte panted.

"You do sacrifice her, then—sacrifice her to your desire for mastery?"

The two women faced each other, both with weapons spent. Delia, through the tremor of her own indignation, saw her antagonist slowly waver, step backward, sink down with a broken murmur on the lounge. Charlotte hid her face in the cushions, clenching them with violent hands. The same fierce maternal passion that had once flung her down upon those same cushions was now bowing her still lower, in the throes of a bitterer renunciation. Delia seemed to hear the old cry: "But how can I give up my baby?" Her own momentary resentment melted, and she bent over the mother's labouring shoulders.

"Chatty—it won't be like giving her up this time. Can't we just go on loving her together?"

Charlotte did not answer. For a long time she lay silent, immovable, her face hidden: she seemed to fear to turn it to the face bent down to her. But presently Delia was aware of a gradual relaxing of the stretched muscles, and saw that one of her cousin's arms was faintly stirring and groping. She lowered her hand to the seeking fingers, and it was caught and pressed to Charlotte's lips.

XI

Tina Lovell—now Miss Clementina Ralston—was to be married in July to Lanning Halsey. The engagement had been announced only in the previous April; and the female elders of the tribe had begun by crying out against the indelicacy of so brief a betrothal. It was unanimously agreed in the New York of those times that "young people should be given the chance to get to know each other"; though the greater number of the couples constituting New York society had played together as children, and been born of parents as long and as familiarly acquainted, yet some mysterious law of decorum required that the newly affianced should always be regarded as being also newly known to each other. In the southern states things were differently conducted: headlong engagements, even runaway marriages, were not uncommon in their annals; but such rashness was less consonant with the sluggish blood of New York, where the pace of life was still set with a Dutch deliberateness.

In a case as unusual as Tina Ralston's, however, it was no great surprise to any one that tradition should have been disregarded. In the first place, everybody knew that she was no more Tina Ralston than you or I; unless, indeed, one were to credit the rumours about poor Jim's unsuspected "past," and his widow's magnanimity. But the opinion of the majority was against this. People were reluctant to charge a dead man with an offense from which he could not clear himself; and the Ralstons unanimously declared that, thoroughly as they disapproved of Mrs. James Ralston's action, they were convinced that she would not have adopted Tina if her doing so could have been construed as "casting a slur" on her late husband.

No: the girl was perhaps a Lovell—though even that idea was not generally held—but she was certainly not a Ralston. Her brown eyes and flighty ways too obviously excluded her from the clan for any formal excommunication to be needful. In fact, most people believed that—as Dr. Lanskell had always affirmed—her origin was really undiscoverable, that she represented one of the unsolved mysteries which occasionally

perplex and irritate well-regulated societies, and that her adoption by Delia Ralston was simply one more proof of the
Lovell clannishness, since the child had been taken in by Mrs.
Ralston only because her cousin Charlotte was so attached to
it. To say that Mrs. Ralston's son and daughter were pleased
with the idea of Tina's adoption would be an exaggeration;
but they abstained from comment, minimizing the effect of
their mother's whim by a dignified silence. It was the old
New York way for families thus to screen the eccentricities of
an individual member, and where there was "money enough
to go round" the heirs would have been thought vulgarly
grasping to protest at the alienation of a small sum from the
general inheritance.

Nevertheless, Delia Ralston, from the moment of Tina's
adoption, was perfectly aware of a different attitude on the
part of both her children. They dealt with her patiently, almost parentally, as with a minor in whom one juvenile lapse
has been condoned, but who must be subjected, in consequence, to a stricter vigilance; and society treated her in the
same indulgent but guarded manner.

She had (it was Sillerton Jackson who first phrased it) an
undoubted way of "carrying things off"; since that dauntless
woman, Mrs. Manson Mingott, had broken her husband's
will, nothing so like her attitude had been seen in New York.
But Mrs. Ralston's method was different, and less easy to
analyze. What Mrs. Manson Mingott had accomplished by
dint of epigram, invective, insistency and runnings to and
fro, the other achieved without raising her voice or seeming
to take a step from the beaten path. When she had persuaded Jim Ralston to take in the foundling baby, it had
been done in the turn of a hand, one didn't know when or
how; and the next day he and she were as untroubled and
beaming as usual. And now, this adoption—! Well, she had
pursued the same method; as Sillerton Jackson said, she behaved as if her adopting Tina had always been an understood thing, as if she wondered that people should wonder.
And in face of her wonder theirs seemed foolish, and they
gradually desisted.

In reality, behind Delia's assurance there was a tumult of
doubts and uncertainties. But she had once learned that one

can do almost anything (perhaps even murder) if one does not attempt to explain it; and the lesson had never been forgotten. She had never explained the taking over of the foundling baby; nor was she now going to explain its adoption. She was just going about her business as if nothing had happened that needed to be accounted for; and a long inheritance of moral modesty helped her to keep her questionings to herself.

These questionings were in fact less concerned with public opinion than with Charlotte Lovell's private thoughts. Charlotte, after her first moment of tragic resistance, had shown herself pathetically, almost painfully, grateful. That she had reason to be, Tina's attitude abundantly revealed. Tina, during the first days after her return from the Vandergrave ball, had shown a closed and darkened face that terribly reminded Delia of the ghastliness of Charlotte Lovell's sudden reflection, years before, in Delia's own bedroom mirror. The first chapter of the mother's history was already written in the daughter's eyes; and the Spender blood in Tina might well precipitate the sequence. During those few days of silent observation Delia discovered, with terror and compassion, the justification of Charlotte's fears. The girl had nearly been lost to them both: at all costs such a risk must not be renewed.

The Halseys, on the whole, had behaved admirably. Lanning wished to marry dear Delia Ralston's protégée—who was shortly, it was understood, to take her adopted mother's name, and inherit her fortune. To what better could a Halsey aspire than one more alliance with a Ralston? The families had always intermarried. The Halsey parents gave their blessing with a precipitation which showed that they too had their anxieties, and that the relief of seeing Lanning "settled" would more than compensate for the conceivable drawbacks of the marriage; though, once it was decided on, they would not admit even to themselves that such drawbacks existed. Old New York always thought away whatever interfered with the perfect propriety of its arrangements.

Charlotte Lovell of course perceived and recognized all this. She accepted the situation—in her private hours with Delia—as one more in the long list of mercies bestowed on an underserving sinner. And one phrase of hers perhaps gave the clue to her acceptance: "Now at least she'll never suspect the truth." It had come to be the poor creature's ruling purpose that her child should never guess the tie between them . . .

But Delia's chief support was the sight of Tina. The older woman, whose whole life had been shaped and coloured by the faint reflection of a rejected happiness, hung dazzled in the light of bliss accepted. Sometimes, as she watched Tina's changing face, she felt as though her own blood were beating in it, as though she could read every thought and emotion feeding those tumultuous currents. Tina's love was a stormy affair, with continual ups and downs of rapture and depression, arrogance and self-abasement; Delia saw displayed before her, with an artless frankness, all the visions, cravings and imaginings of her own stifled youth.

What the girl really thought of her adoption it was not easy to discover. She had been given, at fourteen, the current version of her origin, and had accepted it as carelessly as a happy child accepts some remote and inconceivable fact which does not alter the familiar order of things. And she accepted her adoption in the same spirit. She knew that the name of Ralston had been given to her to facilitate her marriage with Lanning Halsey; and Delia had the impression that all irrelevant questionings were submerged in an overwhelming gratitude. "I've always thought of you as my Mamma; and now, you dearest, you really are," Tina had whispered, her cheek against Delia's; and Delia had laughed back: "Well, if the lawyers can make me so!" But there the matter dropped, swept away on the current of Tina's bliss. They were all, in those days, Delia, Charlotte, even the gallant Lanning, rather like straws whirling about on a sunlit torrent.

The golden flood bore them onward, nearer and nearer to the enchanted date; and Delia, deep in bridal preparations, wondered at the comparative indifference with which she had ordered and inspected her own daughter's twelve-dozen-of-everything. There had been nothing to quicken the pulse in young Delia's placid bridal; but as Tina's wedding day approached imagination burgeoned like the year. The wedding was to be celebrated at Lovell Place, the old house on the Sound where Delia Lovell had herself been married, and where, since her mother's death, she spent her summers. Although the neighbourhood was already overspread with a net-work of mean streets, the old house, with its thin colonnaded verandah, still looked across an uncurtailed lawn and leafy shrubberies to the narrows of Hell Gate; and the drawing-rooms kept their frail slender settees, their Sheraton consoles and cabinets. It had been thought useless to discard them for more fashionable furniture, since the growth of the city made it certain that the place must eventually be sold.

Tina, like Mrs. Ralston, was to have a "house-wedding," though Episcopalian society was beginning to disapprove of such ceremonies, which were regarded as the despised *pis-aller* of Baptists, Methodists, Unitarians and the other altarless sects. In Tina's case, however, both Delia and Charlotte felt that the greater privacy of a marriage in the house made up for its more secular character; and the Halseys favoured their decision. The ladies accordingly settled themselves at Lovell Place before the end of June, and every morning young Lanning Halsey's cat-boat was seen beating across the bay, and furling its sail at the anchorage below the lawn.

There had never been a fairer June in any one's memory. The damask roses and mignonette below the verandah had never sent such a breath of summer through the tall French windows; the gnarled orange-trees brought out from the old arcaded orange-house had never been so thickly blossomed; the very haycocks on the lawn gave out whiffs of Araby.

The evening before the wedding Delia Ralston sat on the verandah watching the moon rise across the Sound. She was tired with the multitude of last preparations, and sad at the thought of Tina's going. On the following evening the house would be empty: till death came, she and Charlotte would sit alone together beside the evening lamp. Such repinings were foolish—they were, she reminded herself, "not like her." But too many memories stirred and murmured in her: her heart was haunted. As she closed the door on the silent drawing-room—already transformed into a chapel, with its lace-hung altar, the tall alabaster vases awaiting their white roses and June lilies, the strip of red carpet dividing the rows of chairs from door to chancel—she felt that it had perhaps been a mistake to come back to Lovell Place for the wedding. She saw herself again, in her high-waisted "India mull" embroidered with daisies, her flat satin sandals, her Brussels veil— saw again her reflection in the sallow pier-glass as she had left that same room on Jim Ralston's triumphant arm, and the one terrified glance she had exchanged with her own image before she took her stand under the bell of white roses in the hall, and smiled upon the congratulating company. Ah, what a different image the pier-glass would reflect tomorrow!

Charlotte Lovell's brisk step sounded indoors, and she came out and joined Mrs. Ralston.

"I've been to the kitchen to tell Melissa Grimes that she'd better count on at least two hundred plates of ice-cream."

"Two hundred? Yes—I suppose she had, with all the Philadelphia connection coming." Delia pondered. "How about the doylies?" she enquired.

"With your aunt Cecilia Vandergrave's we shall manage beautifully."

"Yes.—Thank you, Charlotte, for taking all this trouble."

"Oh—" Charlotte protested, with her flitting sneer; and Delia perceived the irony of thanking a mother for occupying herself with the details of her own daughter's wedding.

"Do sit down, Chatty," she murmured, feeling herself redden at her blunder.

Charlotte, with a sigh of fatigue, sat down on the nearest chair.

"We shall have a beautiful day tomorrow," she said, pensively surveying the placid heaven.

"Yes. Where is Tina?"

"She was very tired. I've sent her upstairs to lie down."

This seemed so eminently suitable that Delia made no immediate answer. After an interval she said: "We shall miss her."

Charlotte's reply was an inarticulate murmur.

The two cousins remained silent, Charlotte as usual bolt upright, her thin hands clutched on the arms of her old-fashioned rush-bottomed seat, Delia somewhat heavily sunk into the depths of a high-backed armchair. The two had exchanged their last remarks on the preparations for the morrow; nothing more remained to be said as to the number of guests, the brewing of the punch, the arrangements for the robing of the clergy, and the disposal of the presents in the best spare-room.

Only one subject had not yet been touched upon, and Delia, as she watched her cousin's profile grimly cut upon the melting twilight, waited for Charlotte to speak. But Charlotte remained silent.

"I have been thinking," Delia at length began, a slight tremor in her voice, "that I ought presently—"

She fancied she saw Charlotte's hands tighten on the knobs of the chair-arms.

"You ought presently—?"

"Well, before Tina goes to bed, perhaps go up for a few minutes—"

Charlotte remained silent, visibly resolved on making no effort to assist her.

"Tomorrow," Delia continued, "we shall be in such a rush from the earliest moment that I don't see how, in the midst of all the interruptions and excitement, I can possibly—"

"Possibly?" Charlotte monotonously echoed.

Delia felt her blush deepening through the dusk. "Well, I suppose you agree with me, don't you, that a word ought to be said to the child as to the new duties and responsibilities that—well—what is usual, in fact, at such a time?" she falteringly ended.

"Yes, I have thought of that," Charlotte answered. She said no more, but Delia divined in her tone the stirring of that obscure opposition which, at the crucial moments of Tina's life, seemed automatically to declare itself. She could not understand why Charlotte should, at such times, grow so enigmatic and inaccessible, and in the present case she saw no reason why this change of mood should interfere with what she deemed to be her own duty. Tina must long for her guiding hand into the new life as much as she herself yearned for the exchange of half-confidences which would be her real farewell to her adopted daughter. Her heart beating a little more quickly than usual, she rose and walked through the open window into the shadowy drawing-room. The moon, between the columns of the verandah, sent a broad band of light across the rows of chairs, irradiated the lace-decked altar with its empty candlesticks and vases, and outlined with silver Delia's heavy reflection in the pier-glass.

She crossed the room toward the hall.

"Delia!" Charlotte's voice sounded behind her. Delia turned, and the two women scrutinized each other in the revealing light. Charlotte's face looked as it had looked on the dreadful day when Delia had suddenly seen it in the looking-glass above her shoulder.

"You were going up now to speak to Tina?" Charlotte asked.

"I—yes. It's nearly nine. I thought . . ."

"Yes; I understand." Miss Lovell made a visible effort at self-control. "Please understand me too, Delia, if I ask you—not to."

Delia looked at her cousin with a vague sense of apprehension. What new mystery did this strange request conceal? But no—such a doubt as flitted across her mind was inadmissible. She was too sure of her Tina!

"I confess I don't understand, Charlotte. You surely feel that, on the night before her wedding, a girl ought to have a mother's counsel, a mother's . . ."

"Yes; I feel that." Charlotte Lovell took a hurried breath. "But the question is: *which of us is her mother?*"

Delia drew back involuntarily. "Which of us—?" she stammered.

"Yes. Oh, don't imagine it's the first time I've asked myself the question! There—I mean to be calm; quite calm. I don't intend to go back to the past. I've accepted—accepted everything—gratefully. Only tonight—just tonight . . ."

Delia felt the rush of pity which always prevailed over every other sensation in her rare interchanges of truth with Charlotte Lovell. Her throat filled with tears, and she remained silent.

"Just tonight," Charlotte concluded, "*I'm* her mother."

"Charlotte! You're not going to tell her so—not now?" broke involuntarily from Delia.

Charlotte gave a faint laugh. "If I did, should you hate it as much as all that?"

"Hate it? What a word, between us!"

"Between us? But it's the word that's been between us

since the beginning—the very beginning! Since the day when you discovered that Clement Spender hadn't quite broken his heart because he wasn't good enough for you; since you found your revenge and your triumph in keeping me at your mercy, and in taking his child from me!" Charlotte's words flamed up as if from the depth of the infernal fires; then the blaze dropped, her head sank forward, and she stood before Delia dumb and stricken.

Delia's first movement was one of an indignant recoil. Where she had felt only tenderness, compassion, the impulse to help and befriend, these darknesses had been smouldering in the other's breast! It was as if a poisonous smoke had swept over some pure summer landscape. . .

Usually such feelings were quickly followed by a reaction of sympathy. But now she felt none. An utter weariness possessed her.

"Yes," she said slowly, "I sometimes believe you really have hated me from the very first; hated me for everything I've tried to do for you."

Charlotte raised her head sharply. "To do for me? But everything you've done has been done for Clement Spender!"

Delia stared at her with a kind of terror. "You are horrible, Charlotte. Upon my honour, I haven't thought of Clement Spender for years."

"Ah, but you have—you have! You've always thought of him in thinking of Tina—of him and nobody else! A woman never stops thinking of the man she loves. She thinks of him years afterward, in all sorts of unconscious ways, in thinking of all sorts of things—books, pictures, sunsets, a flower or a ribbon—or a clock on the mantelpiece," Charlotte broke off with her sneering laugh. "That was what I gambled on, you see—that's why I came to you that day. I knew I was giving Tina another mother."

Again the poisonous smoke seemed to envelop Delia: that she and Charlotte, two spent old women, should be standing before Tina's bridal altar and talking to each other of hatred, seemed unimaginably hideous and degrading.

"You wicked woman—you *are* wicked!" she exclaimed.

Then the evil mist cleared away, and through it she saw the baffled pitiful figure of the mother who was not a mother, and who, for every benefit accepted, felt herself robbed of a privilege. She moved nearer to Charlotte and laid a hand on her arm.

"Not here! Don't let us talk like this here."

The other drew away from her. "Wherever you please, then. I'm not particular!"

"But tonight, Charlotte—the night before Tina's wedding? Isn't every place in this house full of her? How could we go on saying cruel things to each other anywhere?" Charlotte was silent, and Delia continued in a steadier voice: "Nothing you say can really hurt me—for long; and I don't want to hurt you—I never did."

"You tell me that—and you've left nothing undone to divide me from my daughter! Do you suppose it's been easy, all these years, to hear her call you 'mother'? Oh, I know, I know—it was agreed that she must never guess . . . but if you hadn't perpetually come between us she'd have had no one but me, she'd have felt about me as a child feels about its mother, she'd have *had* to love me better than any one else. With all your forbearances and your generosities you've ended by robbing me of my child. And I've put up with it all for her sake—because I knew I had to. But tonight—tonight she belongs to me. Tonight I can't bear that she should call you 'mother'."

Delia Ralston made no immediate reply. It seemed to her that for the first time she had sounded the deepest depths of maternal passion, and she stood awed at the echoes it gave back.

"How you must love her—to say such things to me," she murmured; then, with a final effort: "Yes, you're right. I won't go up to her. It's you who must go."

Charlotte started toward her impulsively; but with a hand lifted as if in defense, Delia moved across the room and out again to the verandah. As she sank down in her chair she heard the drawing-room door open and close, and the sound of Charlotte's feet on the stairs.

Delia sat alone in the night. The last drop of her magnanimity had been spent, and she tried to avert her shuddering mind from Charlotte. What was happening at this moment upstairs? With what dark revelations were Tina's bridal dreams to be defaced? Well, that was not matter for conjecture either. She, Delia Ralston, had played her part, done her utmost: there remained nothing now but to try to lift her spirit above the embittering sense of failure.

There was a strange element of truth in some of the things that Charlotte had said. With what divination her maternal passion had endowed her! Her jealousy seemed to have a million feelers. Yes; it was true that the sweetness and peace of Tina's bridal eve had been filled, for Delia, with visions of her own unrealized past. Softly, imperceptibly, it had reconciled her to the memory of what she had missed. All these last days she had been living the girl's life, she had been Tina, and Tina had been her own girlish self, the far-off Delia Lovell. Now for the first time, without shame, without self-reproach, without a pang or a scruple, Delia could yield to that vision of requited love from which her imagination had always turned away. She had made her choice in youth, and she had accepted it in maturity; and here in this bridal joy, so mysteriously her own, was the compensation for all she had missed and yet never renounced.

Delia understood now that Charlotte had guessed all this, and that the knowledge had filled her with a fierce resentment. Charlotte had said long ago that Clement Spender had never really belonged to her; now she had perceived that it was the same with Clement Spender's child. As the truth stole upon Delia her heart melted with the old compassion for Charlotte. She saw that it was a terrible, a sacrilegious thing to interfere with another's destiny, to lay the tenderest touch upon any human being's right to love and suffer after his own fashion. Delia had twice intervened in Charlotte Lovell's life: it was natural that Charlotte should be her enemy. If only she did not revenge herself by wounding Tina!

The adopted mother's thoughts reverted painfully to the little white room upstairs. She had meant her half-hour with Tina to leave the girl with thoughts as fragrant as the flowers she was to find beside her when she woke. And now—.

Delia started up from her musing. There was a step on the stair—Charlotte coming down through the silent house. Delia rose with a vague impulse of escape: she felt that she could not face her cousin's eyes. She turned the corner of the

verandah, hoping to find the shutters of the dining-room un-
latched, and to slip away unnoticed to her room; but in a
moment Charlotte was beside her.

"Delia!"

"Ah, it's you? I was going up to bed." For the life of her
Delia could not keep an edge of hardness from her voice.

"Yes: it's late. You must be very tired." Charlotte paused;
her own voice was strained and painful.

"I *am* tired," Delia acknowledged.

In the moonlit hush the other went up to her, laying a
timid touch on her arm.

"Not till you've seen Tina."

Delia stiffened. "Tina? But it's late! Isn't she sleeping? I
thought you'd stay with her until—"

"I don't know if she's sleeping." Charlotte paused. "I
haven't been in—but there's a light under her door."

"You haven't been in?"

"No: I just stood in the passage, and tried—"

"Tried—?"

"To think of something . . . something to say to her without . . . without her guessing. . ." A sob stopped her, but
she pressed on with a final effort. "It's no use. You were
right: there's nothing I can say. You're her real mother. Go to
her. It's not your fault—or mine."

"Oh—" Delia cried.

Charlotte clung to her in inarticulate abasement. "You said
I was wicked—I'm not wicked. After all, she was mine when
she was little!"

Delia put an arm about her shoulder.

"Hush, dear! We'll go to her together."

The other yielded automatically to her touch, and side by
side the two women mounted the stairs, Charlotte timing her
impetuous step to Delia's stiffened movements. They walked
down the passage to Tina's door; but there Charlotte Lovell
paused and shook her head.

"No—you," she whispered, and turned away.

Tina lay in bed, her arms folded under her head, her happy
eyes reflecting the silver space of sky which filled the window.
She smiled at Delia through her dream.

"I knew you'd come."

Delia sat down beside her, and their clasped hands lay upon the coverlet. They did not say much, after all; or else their communion had no need of words. Delia never knew how long she sat by the child's side: she abandoned herself to the spell of the moonlit hour.

But suddenly she thought of Charlotte, alone behind the shut door of her own room, watching, struggling, listening. Delia must not, for her own pleasure, prolong that tragic vigil. She bent down to kiss Tina goodnight; then she paused on the threshold and turned back.

"Darling! Just one thing more."

"Yes?" Tina murmured through her dream.

"I want you to promise me—"

"Everything, everything, you darling mother!"

"Well, then, that when you go away tomorrow—at the very last moment, you understand—"

"Yes?"

"After you've said goodbye to me, and to everybody else— just as Lanning helps you into the carriage—"

"Yes?"

"That you'll give your last kiss to Aunt Charlotte. Don't forget—the very last."

THE END

THE SPARK
(The 'Sixties)

I

Y OU IDIOT!" said his wife, and threw down her cards.
I turned my head away quickly, to avoid seeing Hayley
Delane's face; though why I wished to avoid it I could not
have told you, much less why I should have imagined (if I
did) that a man of his age and importance would notice what
was happening to the wholly negligible features of a youth
like myself.

I turned away so that he should not see how it hurt me to
hear him called an idiot, even in joke—well, at least half in
joke; yet I often thought him an idiot myself, and bad as my
own poker was, I knew enough of the game to judge that
his—when he wasn't attending—fully justified such an outburst from his wife. Why her sally disturbed me I couldn't
have said; nor why, when it was greeted by a shrill guffaw
from her "latest," young Bolton Byrne, I itched to cuff the
little bounder; nor why, when Hayley Delane, on whom
banter always dawned slowly but certainly, at length gave
forth his low rich gurgle of appreciation—why then, most
of all, I wanted to blot the whole scene from my memory.
Why?

There they sat, as I had so often seen them, in Jack Alstrop's luxurious bookless library (I'm sure the rich rows behind the glass doors were hollow), while beyond the windows
the pale twilight thickened to blue over Long Island lawns
and woods and a moonlit streak of sea. No one ever looked
out at *that*, except to conjecture what sort of weather there
would be the next day for polo, or hunting, or racing, or
whatever use the season required the face of nature to be put
to; no one was aware of the twilight, the moon or the blue
shadows—and Hayley Delane least of all. Day after day,
night after night, he sat anchored at somebody's poker-table,
and fumbled absently with his cards. . .

Yes; that was the man. He didn't even (as it was once said
of a great authority on heraldry) know his own silly business;
which was to hang about in his wife's train, play poker with
her friends, and giggle at her nonsense and theirs. No wonder
Mrs. Delane was sometimes exasperated. As she said, *she*

hadn't asked him to marry her! Rather not: all their contemporaries could remember what a thunderbolt it had been on his side. The first time he had seen her—at the theatre, I think: "Who's that? Over there—with the heaps of hair?"—"Oh, Leila Gracy? Why, she's not *really* pretty. . ." "Well, I'm going to marry her—" "Marry her? But her father's that old scoundrel Bill Gracy . . . the one. . ." "I'm going to marry her. . ." "The one who's had to resign from all his clubs. . ." "I'm going to marry her. . ." And he did; and it was she, if you please, who kept him dangling, and who would and who wouldn't, until some whipper-snapper of a youth, who was meanwhile making up his mind about *her*, had finally decided in the negative.

Such had been Hayley Delane's marriage; and such, I imagined, his way of conducting most of the transactions of his futile clumsy life. . . Big bursts of impulse—storms he couldn't control—then long periods of drowsing calm, during which, something made me feel, old regrets and remorses woke and stirred under the indolent surface of his nature. And yet, wasn't I simply romanticizing a commonplace case? I turned back from the window to look at the group. The bringing of candles to the card-tables had scattered pools of illumination throughout the shadowy room; in their radiance Delane's harsh head stood out like a cliff from a flowery plain. Perhaps it was only his bigness, his heaviness and swarthiness—perhaps his greater age, for he must have been at least fifteen years older than his wife and most of her friends; at any rate, I could never look at him without feeling that he belonged elsewhere, not so much in another society as in another age. For there was no doubt that the society he lived in suited him well enough. He shared cheerfully in all the amusements of his little set—rode, played polo, hunted and drove his four-in-hand with the best of them (you will see, by the last allusion, that we were still in the archaic 'nineties). Nor could I guess what other occupations he would have preferred, had he been given his choice. In spite of my admiration for him I could not bring myself to think it was Leila Gracy who had subdued him to what she worked in. What would he have chosen to do if he had not met her that night at the play? Why,

I rather thought, to meet and marry somebody else just like her. No; the difference in him was not in his tastes—it was in something ever so much deeper. Yet what is deeper in a man than his tastes?

In another age, then, he would probably have been doing the equivalent of what he was doing now: idling, taking much violent exercise, eating more than was good for him, laughing at the same kind of nonsense, and worshipping, with the same kind of dull routine-worship, the same kind of woman, whether dressed in a crinoline, a farthingale, a peplum or the skins of beasts—it didn't much matter under what sumptuary dispensation one placed her. Only in that other age there might have been outlets for other faculties, now dormant, perhaps even atrophied, but which must—yes, really must—have had something to do with the building of that big friendly forehead, the monumental nose, and the rich dimple which now and then furrowed his cheek with light. Did the dimple even mean no more than Leila Gracy?

Well, perhaps it was *I* who was the idiot, if she'd only known it; an idiot to believe in her husband, be obsessed by him, oppressed by him, when, for thirty years now, he'd been only the Hayley Delane whom everybody took for granted, and was glad to see, and immediately forgot. Turning from my contemplation of that great structural head, I looked at his wife. Her head was still like something in the making, something just flowering, a girl's head ringed with haze. Even the kindly candles betrayed the lines in her face, the paint on her lips, the peroxide on her hair; but they could not lessen her fluidity of outline, or the girlishness that lurked in her eyes, floating up from their depths like a startled Naïad. There was an irreducible innocence about her, as there so often is about women who have spent their time in amassing sentimental experiences. As I looked at the husband and wife, thus confronted above the cards, I marvelled more and more that it was she who ruled and he who bent the neck. You will see by this how young I still was.

So young, indeed, that Hayley Delane had dawned on me in my school-days as an accomplished fact, a finished monument: like Trinity Church, the Reservoir or the Knickerbocker Club. A New Yorker of my generation could no more imagine him altered or away than any of those venerable institutions. And so I had continued to take him for granted till, my Harvard days over, I had come back after an interval of world-wandering to settle down in New York, and he had broken on me afresh as something still not wholly accounted for, and more interesting than I had suspected.

I don't say the matter kept me awake. I had my own business (in a down-town office), and the pleasures of my age; I was hard at work discovering New York. But now and then the Hayley Delane riddle would thrust itself between me and my other interests, as it had done tonight just because his wife had sneered at him, and he had laughed and thought her funny. And at such times I found myself moved and excited out of all proportion to anything I knew about him, or had observed in him, to justify such emotions.

The game was over, the dressing-bell had rung. It rang again presently, with a discreet insistence: Alstrop, easy in all else, preferred that his guests should not be more than half an hour late for dinner.

"I say—*Leila!*" he finally remonstrated.

The golden coils drooped above her chips. "Yes—yes. Just a minute. Hayley, you'll have to pay for me.— There, I'm going!" She laughed and pushed back her chair.

Delane, laughing also, got up lazily. Byrne flew to open the door for Mrs. Delane; the other women trooped out with her. Delane, having settled her debts, picked up her gold-mesh bag and cigarette-case, and followed.

I turned toward a window opening on the lawn. There was just time to stretch my legs while curling-tongs and powder were being plied above stairs. Alstrop joined me, and we stood staring up at a soft dishevelled sky in which the first stars came and went.

"Curse it—looks rotten for our match tomorrow!"

"Yes—but what a good smell the coming rain does give to things!"

He laughed. "You're an optimist—like old Hayley."

We strolled across the lawn toward the woodland.

"Why like old Hayley?"

"Oh, he's a regular philosopher. I've never seen him put out, have you?"

"No. That must be what makes him look so sad," I exclaimed.

"Sad? Hayley? Why, I was just saying—"

"Yes, I know. But the only people who are never put out are the people who don't care; and not caring is about the saddest occupation there is. I'd like to see him in a rage just once."

My host gave a faint whistle, and remarked: "By Jove, I believe the wind's hauling round to the north. If it does—" He moistened his finger and held it up.

I knew there was no use in theorizing with Alstrop; but I tried another tack. "What on earth has ·Delane done with himself all these years?" I asked. Alstrop was forty, or thereabouts, and by a good many years better able than I to cast a backward glance over the problem.

But the effort seemed beyond him. "Why—what years?"

"Well—ever since he left college."

"Lord! How do I know? I wasn't there. Hayley must be well past fifty."

It sounded formidable to my youth; almost like a geological era. And that suited him, in a way—I could imagine him drifting, or silting, or something measurable by aeons, at the rate of about a millimetre a century.

"How long has he been married?" I asked.

"I don't know that either; nearly twenty years, I should say. The kids are growing up. The boys are both at Groton. Leila doesn't look it, I must say—not in some lights."

"Well, then, what's he been doing since he married?"

"Why, what should he have done? He's always had money enough to do what he likes. He's got his partnership in the bank, of course. They say that rascally old father-in-law, whom he refuses to see, gets a good deal of money out of him. You know he's awfully soft-hearted. But he can swing it all, I fancy. Then he sits on lots of boards—Blind Asylum, Children's Aid, S.P.C.A., and all the rest. And there isn't a better sport going."

"But that's not what I mean," I persisted.

Alstrop looked at me through the darkness. "You don't mean women? I never heard—but then one wouldn't, very likely. He's a shut-up fellow."

We turned back to dress for dinner. Yes, that was the word I wanted; he was a shut-up fellow. Even the rudimentary Alstrop felt it. But shut-up consciously, deliberately—or only instinctively, congenitally? There the mystery lay.

II

THE BIG POLO MATCH came off the next day. It was the first of the season, and, taking respectful note of the fact, the barometer, after a night of showers, jumped back to Fair.

All Fifth Avenue had poured down to see New York versus Hempstead. The beautifully rolled lawns and freshly painted club stand were sprinkled with spring dresses and abloom with sunshades, and coaches and other vehicles without number enclosed the farther side of the field.

Hayley Delane still played polo, though he had grown so heavy that the cost of providing himself with mounts must have been considerable. He was, of course, no longer regarded as in the first rank; indeed, in these later days, when the game has become an exact science, I hardly know to what use such a weighty body as his could be put. But in that far-off dawn of the sport his sureness and swiftness of stroke caused him to be still regarded as a useful back, besides being esteemed for the part he had taken in introducing and establishing the game.

I remember little of the beginning of the game, which resembled many others I had seen. I never played myself, and I had no money on: for me the principal interest of the scene lay in the May weather, the ripple of spring dresses over the turf, the sense of youth, fun, gaiety, of young manhood and womanhood weaving their eternal pattern under the conniving sky. Now and then they were interrupted for a moment by a quick "Oh" which turned all those tangled glances the same way, as two glittering streaks of men and horses dashed across the green, locked, swayed, rayed outward into starry figures, and rolled back. But it was for a moment only—then eyes wandered again, chatter began, and youth and sex had it their own way till the next charge shook them from their trance.

I was of the number of these divided watchers. Polo as a spectacle did not amuse me for long, and I saw about as little of it as the pretty girls perched beside their swains on coach-tops and club stand. But by chance my vague wanderings

brought me to the white palings enclosing the field, and
there, in a cluster of spectators, I caught sight of Leila Delane.

As I approached I was surprised to notice a familiar figure
shouldering away from her. One still saw old Bill Gracy often
enough in the outer purlieus of the big race-courses; but I
wondered how he had got into the enclosure of a fashionable
Polo Club. There he was, though, unmistakably; who could
forget that swelling chest under the shabby-smart racing-coat,
the gray top-hat always pushed back from his thin auburn
curls, and the mixture of furtiveness and swagger which made
his liquid glance so pitiful? Among the figures that rose here
and there like warning ruins from the dead-level of old New
York's respectability, none was more typical than Bill Gracy's;
my gaze followed him curiously as he shuffled away from his
daughter. "Trying to get more money out of her," I concluded; and remembered what Alstrop had said of Delane's
generosity.

"Well, if I were Delane," I thought, "I'd pay a good deal to
keep that old ruffian out of sight."

Mrs. Delane, turning to watch her father's retreat, saw me
and nodded. At the same moment Delane, on a tall deep-
chested poney, ambled across the field, stick on shoulder. As
he rode thus, heavily yet mightily, in his red-and-black shirt
and white breeches, his head standing out like a bronze
against the turf, I whimsically recalled the figure of Guidoriccio da Foligno, the famous mercenary, riding at a slow
powerful pace across the fortressed fresco of the Town Hall of
Siena. Why a New York banker of excessive weight and more
than middle age, jogging on a poney across a Long Island
polo field, should have reminded me of a martial figure on an
armoured war-horse, I find it hard to explain. As far as I knew
there were no turreted fortresses in Delane's background; and
his too juvenile polo cap and gaudy shirt were a poor substitute for Guidoriccio's coat of mail. But it was the kind of trick
the man was always playing; reminding me, in his lazy torpid
way, of times and scenes and people greater than he could
know. That was why he kept on interesting me.

It was this interest which caused me to pause by Mrs.
Delane, whom I generally avoided. After a vague smile she
had already turned her gaze on the field.

"You're admiring your husband?" I suggested, as Delane's trot carried him across our line of vision.

She glanced at me dubiously. "You think he's too fat to play, I suppose?" she retorted, a little snappishly.

"I think he's the finest figure in sight. He looks like a great general, a great soldier of fortune—in an old fresco, I mean."

She stared, perhaps suspecting irony, as she always did beneath the unintelligible.

"Ah, *he* can pay anything he likes for his mounts!" she murmured; and added, with a wandering laugh: "Do you mean it as a compliment? Shall I tell him what you say?"

"I wish you would."

But her eyes were off again, this time to the opposite end of the field. Of course—Bolton Byrne was playing on the other side! The fool of a woman was always like that—absorbed in her latest adventure. Yet there had been so many, and she must by this time have been so radiantly sure there would be more! But at every one the girl was born anew in her: she blushed, palpitated, "sat out" dances, plotted for tête-à-têtes, pressed flowers (I'll wager) in her copy of "Omar Khayyám," and was all white muslin and wild roses while it lasted. And the Byrne fever was then at its height.

It did not seem polite to leave her immediately, and I continued to watch the field at her side. "It's their last chance to score," she flung at me, leaving me to apply the ambiguous pronoun; and after that we remained silent.

The game had been a close one; the two sides were five each, and the crowd about the rails hung breathless on the last minutes. The struggle was short and swift, and dramatic enough to hold even the philanderers on the coach-tops. Once I stole a glance at Mrs. Delane, and saw the colour rush to her cheek. Byrne was hurling himself across the field, crouched on the neck of his somewhat weedy mount, his stick swung like a lance—a pretty enough sight, for he was young and supple, and light in the saddle.

"They're going to win!" she gasped with a happy cry.

But just then Byrne's poney, unequal to the pace, stumbled, faltered, and came down. His rider dropped from the saddle, hauled the animal to his feet, and stood for a minute half-dazed before he scrambled up again. That minute made the

difference. It gave the other side their chance. The knot of
men and horses tightened, wavered, grew loose, broke up in
arrowing flights; and suddenly a ball—Delane's—sped
through the enemy's goal, victorious. A roar of delight went
up; "Good for old Hayley!" voices shouted. Mrs. Delane gave
a little sour laugh. "That—that beastly poney; I warned him
it was no good—and the ground still so slippery," she broke
out.

"The poney? Why, he's a ripper. It's not every mount that
will carry Delane's weight," I said. She stared at me unseeingly and turned away with twitching lips. I saw her speeding
off toward the enclosure.

I followed hastily, wanting to see Delane in the moment of
his triumph. I knew he took all these little sporting successes
with an absurd seriousness, as if, mysteriously, they were the
shadow of more substantial achievements, dreamed of, or accomplished, in some previous life. And perhaps the elderly
man's vanity in holding his own with the youngsters was also
an element of his satisfaction; how could one tell, in a mind
of such monumental simplicity?

When I reached the saddling enclosure I did not at once
discover him; an unpleasant sight met my eyes instead. Bolton Byrne, livid and withered—his face like an old woman's,
I thought—rode across the empty field, angrily lashing his
poney's flanks. He slipped to the ground, and as he did so,
struck the shivering animal a last blow clean across the head.
An unpleasant sight—

But retribution fell. It came like a black-and-red thunderbolt descending on the wretch out of the heaven. Delane had
him by the collar, had struck him with his whip across the
shoulders, and then flung him off like a thing too mean for
human handling. It was over in the taking of a breath—then,
while the crowd hummed and closed in, leaving Byrne to
slink away as if he had become invisible, I saw my big Delane,
grown calm and apathetic, turn to the poney and lay a soothing hand on its neck.

I was pushing forward, moved by the impulse to press that
hand, when his wife went up to him. Though I was not far
off I could not hear what she said; people did not speak loud
in those days, or "make scenes," and the two or three words

which issued from Mrs. Delane's lips must have been inaudible to everyone but her husband. On his dark face they raised a sudden redness; he made a motion of his free arm (the other hand still on the poney's neck), as if to wave aside an importunate child; then he felt in his pocket, drew out a cigarette, and lit it. Mrs. Delane, white as a ghost, was hurrying back to Alstrop's coach.

I was turning away too when I saw her husband hailed again. This time it was Bill Gracy, shoving and yet effacing himself, as his manner was, who came up, a facile tear on his lashes, his smile half tremulous, half defiant, a yellow-gloved hand held out.

"God bless you for it, Hayley—God bless you, my dear boy!"

Delane's hand reluctantly left the poney's neck. It wavered for an instant, just touched the other's palm, and was instantly engulfed in it. Then Delane, without speaking, turned toward the shed where his mounts were being rubbed down, while his father-in-law swaggered from the scene.

I had promised, on the way home, to stop for tea at a friend's house half-way between the Polo Club and Alstrop's. Another friend, who was also going there, offered me a lift, and carried me on to Alstrop's afterward.

During our drive, and about the tea-table, the talk of course dwelt mainly on the awkward incident of Bolton Byrne's thrashing. The women were horrified or admiring, as their humour moved them; but the men all agreed that it was natural enough. In such a case any pretext was permissible, they said; though it was stupid of Hayley to air his grievance on a public occasion. But then he *was* stupid— that was the consensus of opinion. If there was a blundering way of doing a thing that needed to be done, trust him to hit on it! For the rest, everyone spoke of him affectionately, and agreed that Leila was a fool . . . and nobody particularly liked Byrne, an "outsider" who had pushed himself into society by means of cheek and showy horsemanship. But Leila, it was agreed, had always had a weakness for "outsiders," perhaps because their admiration flattered her extreme desire to be thought "in."

"Wonder how many of the party you'll find left—this affair must have caused a good deal of a shake-up," my friend said, as I got down at Alstrop's door; and the same thought was in my own mind. Byrne would be gone, of course; and no doubt, in another direction, Delane and Leila. I wished I had a chance to shake that blundering hand of Hayley's. . .

Hall and drawing-room were empty; the dressing-bell must have sounded its discreet appeal more than once, and I was relieved to find it had been heeded. I didn't want to stumble on any of my fellow-guests till I had seen our host. As I was dashing upstairs I heard him call me from the library, and turned back.

"No hurry—dinner put off till nine," he said cheerfully; and added, on a note of inexpressible relief: "We've had a tough job of it—*ouf!*"

The room looked as if they had: the card tables stood untouched, and the deep armchairs, gathered into confidential groups, seemed still deliberating on the knotty problem. I noticed that a good deal of whiskey and soda had gone toward its solution.

"What happened? Has Byrne left?"

"Byrne? No—thank goodness!" Alstrop looked at me almost reproachfully. "Why should he? That was just what we wanted to avoid."

"I don't understand. You don't mean that *he's* stayed and the Delanes have gone?"

"Lord forbid! Why should they, either? Hayley's apologized!"

My jaw fell, and I returned my host's stare.

"Apologized? To that hound? For what?"

Alstrop gave an impatient shrug. "Oh, for God's sake don't reopen the cursèd question," it seemed to say. Aloud he echoed: "For what? Why, after all, a man's got a right to thrash his own poney, hasn't he? It was beastly unsportsmanlike, of course—but it's nobody's business if Byrne chooses to be that kind of a cad. That's what Hayley saw—when he cooled down."

"Then I'm sorry he cooled down."

Alstrop looked distinctly annoyed. "I don't follow you. We had a hard enough job. You said you wanted to see him in a rage just once; but you don't want him to go on making an ass of himself, do you?"

"I don't call it making an ass of himself to thrash Byrne."

"And to advertise his conjugal difficulties all over Long Island, with twenty newspaper reporters at his heels?"

I stood silent, baffled but incredulous. "I don't believe he ever gave that a thought. I wonder who put it to him first in that way?"

Alstrop twisted his unlit cigarette about in his fingers. "We all did—as delicately as we could. But it was Leila who finally convinced him. I must say Leila was very game."

I still pondered: the scene in the paddock rose again before me, the quivering agonized animal, and the way Delane's big hand had been laid reassuringly on its neck.

"Nonsense! I don't believe a word of it!" I declared.

"A word of what I've been telling you?"

"Well, of the official version of the case."

To my surprise, Alstrop met my glance with an eye neither puzzled nor resentful. A shadow seemed to be lifted from his honest face.

"What *do* you believe?" he asked.

"Why, that Delane thrashed that cur for ill-treating the poney, and not in the least for being too attentive to Mrs. Delane. I was there, I tell you— I saw him."

Alstrop's brow cleared completely. "There's something to be said for that theory," he agreed, smiling over the match he was holding to his cigarette.

"Well, then—what was there to apologize for?"

"Why, for *that*—butting in between Byrne and his horse. Don't you see, you young idiot? If Hayley hadn't apologized, the mud was bound to stick to his wife. Everybody would have said the row was on her account. It's as plain as the knob on the door—there wasn't anything else for him to do. He saw it well enough after she'd said a dozen words to him—"

"I wonder what those words were," I muttered.

"Don't know. He and she came downstairs together. He looked a hundred years old, poor old chap. 'It's the cruelty, it's the cruelty,' he kept saying; 'I hate cruelty.' I rather think he knows we're all on his side. Anyhow, it's all patched up and well patched up; and I've ordered my last 'eighty-four Georges Goulet brought up for dinner. Meant to keep it for my own wedding-breakfast; but since this afternoon I've rather lost interest in that festivity," Alstrop concluded with a celibate grin.

"Well," I repeated, as though it were a relief to say, "I could swear he did it for the poney."

"Oh, so could I," my host acquiesced as we went upstairs together.

On my threshold, he took me by the arm and followed me in. I saw there was still something on his mind.

"Look here, old chap—you say you were in there when it happened?"

"Yes. Close by—"

"Well," he interrupted, "for the Lord's sake don't allude to the subject tonight, will you?"

"Of course not."

"Thanks a lot. Truth is, it was a narrow squeak, and I couldn't help admiring the way Leila played up. She was in a fury with Hayley; but she got herself in hand in no time, and behaved very decently. She told me privately he was often like that—flaring out all of a sudden like a madman. You wouldn't imagine it, would you, with that quiet way of his? She says she thinks it's his old wound."

"What old wound?"

"Didn't you know he was wounded—where was it? Bull Run, I believe. In the head—"

No, I hadn't known; hadn't even heard, or remembered, that Delane had been in the Civil War. I stood and stared in my astonishment.

"Hayley Delane? In the war?"

"Why, of course. All through it."

"But Bull Run—Bull Run was at the very beginning." I broke off to go through a rapid mental calculation. "Look here, Jack, it can't be; he's not over fifty-five. You told me so yourself. If he was in it from the beginning he must have gone into it as a schoolboy."

"Well, that's just what he did: ran away from school to volunteer. His family didn't know what had become of him till he was wounded. I remember hearing my people talk about it. Great old sport, Hayley. I'd have given a lot not to have this thing happen; not at my place anyhow; but it *has*, and there's no help for it. Look here, you swear you won't make a sign, will you? I've got all the others into line, and if you'll back us up we'll have a regular Happy Family Evening. Jump into your clothes—it's nearly nine."

III

THIS IS NOT a story-teller's story; it is not even the kind of episode capable of being shaped into one. Had it been, I should have reached my climax, or at any rate its first stage, in the incident at the Polo Club, and what I have left to tell would be the effect of that incident on the lives of the three persons concerned.

It is not a story, or anything in the semblance of a story, but merely an attempt to depict for you—and in so doing, perhaps make clearer to myself—the aspect and character of a man whom I loved, perplexedly but faithfully, for many years. I make no apology, therefore, for the fact that Bolton Byrne, whose evil shadow ought to fall across all my remaining pages, never again appears in them; and that the last I saw of him (for my purpose) was when, after our exaggeratedly cheerful and even noisy dinner that evening at Jack Alstrop's, I observed him shaking hands with Hayley Delane, and declaring, with pinched lips and a tone of falsetto cordiality: "Bear malice? Well, rather not—why, what rot! All's fair in—in polo, ain't it? I should say so! Yes—off first thing tomorrow. S'pose of course you're staying on with Jack over Sunday? I wish I hadn't promised the Gildermeres—." And therewith he vanishes, having served his purpose as a passing lantern-flash across the twilight of Hayley Delane's character.

All the while, I continued to feel that it was not Bolton Byrne who mattered. While clubs and drawing-rooms twittered with the episode, and friends grew portentous in trying to look unconscious, and said "I don't know what you mean," with eyes beseeching you to speak if you knew more than they did, I had already discarded the whole affair, as I was sure Delane had. "It *was* the poney, and nothing but the poney," I chuckled to myself, as pleased as if I had owed Mrs. Delane a grudge, and were exulting in her abasement; and still there ran through my mind the phrase which Alstrop said Delane had kept repeating: "It was the cruelty—it was the cruelty. I hate cruelty."

How it fitted in, now, with the other fact my host had let drop—the fact that Delane had fought all through the civil war! It seemed incredible that it should have come to me as a surprise; that I should have forgotten, or perhaps never even known, this phase of his history. Yet in young men like myself, just out of college in the 'nineties, such ignorance was more excusable than now seems possible.

That was the dark time of our national indifference, before the country's awakening; no doubt the war seemed much farther from us, much less a part of us, than it does to the young men of today. Such was the case, at any rate, in old New York, and more particularly, perhaps, in the little clan of well-to-do and indolent old New Yorkers among whom I had grown up. Some of these, indeed, had fought bravely through the four years: New York had borne her part, a memorable part, in the long struggle. But I remember with what perplexity I first wakened to the fact—it was in my school-days—that if certain of my father's kinsmen and contemporaries had been in the war, others—how many!—had stood aside. I recall especially the shock with which, at school, I had heard a boy explain his father's lameness: "He's never got over that shot in the leg he got at Chancellorsville."

I stared; for my friend's father was just my own father's age. At the moment (it was at a school foot-ball match) the two men were standing side by side, in full sight of us—*his* father stooping, halt and old, mine, even to filial eyes, straight and youthful. Only an hour before I had been bragging to my friend about the wonderful shot my father was (he had taken me down to his North Carolina shooting at Christmas); but now I stood abashed.

The next time I went home for the holidays I said to my mother, one day when we were alone: "Mother, why didn't father fight in the war?" My heart was beating so hard that I thought she must have seen my excitement and been shocked. But she raised an untroubled face from her embroidery.

"Your father, dear? Why, because he was a married man." She had a reminiscent smile. "Molly was born already—she was six months old when Fort Sumter fell. I remember I was nursing her when Papa came in with the news. We couldn't believe it." She paused to match a silk placidly. "Married men weren't called upon to fight," she explained.

"But they *did*, though, Mother! Payson Gray's father

fought. He was so badly wounded at Chancellorsville that he's had to walk with a stick ever since."

"Well, my dear, I don't suppose you would want your Papa to be like that, would you?" She paused again, and finding I made no answer, probably thought it pained me to be thus convicted of heartlessness, for she added, as if softening the rebuke: "Two of your father's cousins *did* fight: his cousins Harold and James. They were young men, with no family obligations. And poor Jamie was killed, you remember."

I listened in silence, and never again spoke to my mother of the war. Nor indeed to anyone—even myself. I buried the whole business out of sight, out of hearing, as I thought. After all, the war had all happened long ago; it had been over ten years when I was born. And nobody ever talked about it nowadays. Still, one did, of course, as one grew up, meet older men of whom it was said: "Yes, so-and-so was in the war." Many of them even continued to be known by the military titles with which they had left the service: Colonel Ruscott, Major Detrancy, old General Scole. People smiled a little, but admitted that, if it pleased them to keep their army rank, it was a right they had earned. Hayley Delane, it appeared, thought differently. He had never allowed himself to be called "Major" or "Colonel" (I think he had left the service a Colonel). And besides he was years younger than these veterans. To find that he had fought at their side was like discovering that the grandmother one could remember playing with had been lifted up by her nurse to see General Washington. I always thought of Hayley Delane as belonging to my own generation rather than to my father's; though I knew him to be so much older than myself, and occasionally called him "sir," I felt on an equality with him, the equality produced by sharing the same amusements and talking of them in the same slang. And indeed he must have been ten or fifteen years younger than the few men I knew who had been in the war, none of whom, I was sure, had had to run away from school to volunteer; so that my forgetfulness (or perhaps even ignorance) of his past was not inexcusable.

Broad and Delane had been, for two or three generations, one of the safe and conservative private banks of New York. My friend Hayley had been made a partner early in his career;

the post was almost hereditary in his family. It happened that, not long after the scene at Alstrop's, I was offered a position in the house. The offer came, not through Delane, but through Mr. Frederick Broad, the senior member, who was an old friend of my father's. The chance was too advantageous to be rejected, and I transferred to a desk at Broad and Delane's my middling capacities and my earnest desire to do my best. It was owing to this accidental change that there gradually grew up between Hayley Delane and myself a sentiment almost filial on my part, elder-brotherly on his—for paternal one could hardly call him, even with his children.

My job need not have thrown me in his way, for his business duties sat lightly on him, and his hours at the bank were neither long nor regular. But he appeared to take a liking to me, and soon began to call on me for the many small services which, in the world of affairs, a young man can render his elders. His great perplexity was the writing of business letters. He knew what he wanted to say; his sense of the proper use of words was clear and prompt; I never knew anyone more impatient of the hazy verbiage with which American primary culture was already corrupting our speech. He would put his finger at once on these laborious inaccuracies, growling: "For God's sake, translate it into English—" but when he had to write, or worse still dictate, a letter his friendly forehead and big hands grew damp, and he would mutter, half to himself and half to me: "How the devil shall I say: 'Your letter of the blankth came yesterday, and after thinking over what you propose I don't like the looks of it'?"—"Why, say just that," I would answer; but he would shake his head and object: "My dear fellow, you're as bad as I am. You don't know how *to write good English*." In his mind there was a gulf fixed between speaking and writing the language. I could never get his imagination to bridge this gulf, or to see that the phrases which fell from his lips were "better English" than the written version, produced after much toil and pen-biting, which consisted in translating the same statement into some such language as: "I am in receipt of your communication of the 30th ultimo, and regret to be compelled to inform you in reply that, after mature consideration of the proposals therein contained, I find myself unable to pronounce a favourable judgment upon the same"—usually sending a furious dash through "the same" as "counterjumper's lingo," and then groaning over his inability to find a more Johnsonian substitute.

"The trouble with me," he used to say, "is that both my parents were martinets on grammar, and never let any of us children use a vulgar expression without correcting us." (By "vulgar" he meant either familiar or inexact.) "We were brought up on the best books—Scott and Washington Irving, old what's-his-name who wrote the *Spectator*, and Gibbon and so forth; and though I'm not a literary man, and never set up to be, I can't forget my early training, and when I see the children reading a newspaper-fellow like Kipling I want to tear the rubbish out of their hands. Cheap journalism—that's what most modern books are. And you'll excuse my saying, dear boy, that even you are too young to know how English ought to be *written*."

It was quite true—though I had at first found it difficult to believe—that Delane must once have been a reader. He surprised me, one night, as we were walking home from a dinner where we had met, by apostrophizing the moon, as she rose, astonished, behind the steeple of the "Heavenly Rest," with "She walks in beauty like the night"; and he was fond of describing a victorious charge in a polo match by saying: "Tell you what, we came down on 'em like the Assyrian." Nor had Byron been his only fare. There had evidently been a time when he had known the whole of "Gray's Elegy" by heart, and I once heard him murmuring to himself, as we stood together one autumn evening on the terrace of his country-house:

> *Now fades the glimmering landscape on the sight,*
> *And all the air a solemn stillness holds . . .*

Little sympathy as I felt for Mrs. Delane, I could not believe it was his marriage which had checked Delane's interest in books. To judge from his very limited stock of allusions and quotations, his reading seemed to have ceased a good deal earlier than his first meeting with Leila Gracy. Exploring him like a geologist, I found, for several layers under the Leila stratum, no trace of any interest in letters; and I concluded that, like other men I knew, his mind had been receptive up to a certain age, and had then snapped shut on what it possessed, like a replete crustacean never reached by another high tide. People, I had by this time found, all stopped living at one time or another, however many years longer they continued to be alive; and I suspected that Delane had stopped at about nineteen. That date would roughly coincide with the end of the civil war, and with his return to the common-place existence from which he had never since deviated. Those four years had apparently filled to the brim every crevice of his being. For I could not hold that he had gone through them unawares, as some famous figures, puppets of fate, have been tossed from heights to depths of human experience without once knowing what was happening to them—forfeiting a crown by the insistence on some prescribed ceremonial, or by carrying on their flight a certain monumental dressing-case.

No, Hayley Delane had felt the war, had been made different by it; how different I saw only when I compared him to the other "veterans" who, from being regarded by me as the dullest of my father's dinner-guests, were now become figures of absorbing interest. Time was when, at my mother's announcement that General Scole or Major Detrancy was coming to dine, I had invariably found a pretext for absenting myself; now, when I knew they were expected, my chief object was to persuade her to invite Delane.

"But he's so much younger—he cares only for the sporting set. He won't be flattered at being asked with old gentlemen." And my mother, with a slight smile, would add: "If Hayley has a weakness, it's the wish to be thought younger than he is—on his wife's account, I suppose."

Once, however, she did invite him, and he accepted; and we got over having to ask Mrs. Delane (who undoubtedly *would* have been bored) by leaving out Mrs. Scole and Mrs. Ruscott, and making it a "man's dinner" of the old-fashioned sort, with canvas-backs, a bowl of punch, and my mother the only lady present—the kind of evening my father still liked best.

I remember, at that dinner, how attentively I studied the contrasts, and tried to detect the points of resemblance, between General Scole, old Detrancy and Delane. Allusions to

the war—anecdotes of Bull Run and Andersonville, of
Lincoln, Seward and MacClellan, were often on Major Detrancy's lips, especially after the punch had gone round.
"When a fellow's been through the war," he used to say as a
preface to almost everything, from expressing his opinion of
last Sunday's sermon to praising the roasting of a canvas-
back. Not so General Scole. No one knew exactly why he had
been raised to the rank he bore, but he tacitly proclaimed his
right to it by never alluding to the subject. He was a tall and
silent old gentleman with a handsome shock of white hair,
half-shut blue eyes glinting between veined lids, and an impressively upright carriage. His manners were perfect—so
perfect that they stood him in lieu of language, and people
would say afterward how agreeable he had been when he had
only bowed and smiled, and got up and sat down again, with
an absolute mastery of those difficult arts. He was said to be a
judge of horses and Madeira, but he never rode, and was reported to give very indifferent wines to the rare guests he
received in his grim old house in Irving Place.

He and Major Detrancy had one trait in common—the
extreme caution of the old New Yorker. They viewed with
instinctive distrust anything likely to derange their habits,
diminish their comfort, or lay on them any unwonted responsibilities, civic or social; and slow as their other mental
processes were, they showed a supernatural quickness in divining when a seemingly harmless conversation might draw
them into "signing a paper," backing up even the mildest attempt at municipal reform, or pledging them to support, on
however small a scale, any new and unfamiliar cause.

According to their creed, gentlemen subscribed as handsomely as their means allowed to the Charity Organization
Society, the Patriarchs Balls, the Children's Aid, and their
own parochial charities. Everything beyond savoured of
"politics," revivalist meetings, or the attempts of vulgar persons to buy their way into the circle of the elect; even the
Society for the Prevention of Cruelty to Animals, being of
more recent creation, seemed open to doubt, and they
thought it rash of certain members of the clergy to lend it
their names. "But then," as Major Detrancy said, "in this
noisy age some people will do anything to attract notice."

And they breathed a joint sigh over the vanished "Old New York" of their youth, the exclusive and impenetrable New York to which Rubini and Jenny Lind had sung and Mr. Thackeray lectured, the New York which had declined to receive Charles Dickens, and which, out of revenge, he had so scandalously ridiculed.

Yet Major Detrancy and General Scole had fought all through the war, had participated in horrors and agonies untold, endured all manner of hardships and privations, suffered the extremes of heat and cold, hunger, sickness and wounds; and it had all faded like an indigestion comfortably slept off, leaving them perfectly commonplace and happy.

The same was true, with a difference, of Colonel Ruscott, who, though not by birth of the same group, had long since been received into it, partly because he was a companion in arms, partly because of having married a Hayley connection. I can see Colonel Ruscott still: a dapper handsome little fellow, rather too much of both, with a lustrous wave to his hair (or was it a wig?), and a dash too much of Cologne on too-fine cambric. He had been in the New York militia in his youth, had "gone out" with the great Seventh; and the Seventh, ever since, had been the source and centre of his being, as still, to some octogenarians, their University dinner is.

Colonel Ruscott specialized in chivalry. For him the war was "the blue and the grey," the rescue of lovely Southern girls, anecdotes about Old Glory, and the carrying of vital despatches through the enemy lines. Enchantments seemed to have abounded in his path during the four years which had been so drab and desolate to many; and the punch (to the amusement of us youngsters, who were not above drawing him) always evoked from his memory countless situations in which by prompt, respectful yet insinuating action, he had stamped his image indelibly on some proud Southern heart, while at the same time discovering where Jackson's guerillas lay, or at what point the river was fordable.

And there sat Hayley Delane, so much younger than the others, yet seeming at such times so much their elder that I thought to myself: "But if *he* stopped growing up at nineteen, they're still in long-clothes!" But it was only morally that he had gone on growing. Intellectually they were all on a par.

When the last new play at Wallack's was discussed, or my mother tentatively alluded to the last new novel by the author of *Robert Elsmere* (it was her theory that, as long as the hostess was present at a man's dinner, she should keep the talk at the highest level), Delane's remarks were no more penetrating than his neighbours'—and he was almost sure not to have read the novel.

It was when any social question was raised: any of the problems concerning club administration, charity, or the relation between "gentlemen" and the community, that he suddenly stood out from them, not so much opposed as aloof.

He would sit listening, stroking my sister's long skye-terrier (who, defying all rules, had jumped up to his knees at dessert), with a grave half-absent look on his heavy face; and just as my mother (I knew) was thinking how bored he was, that big smile of his would reach out and light up his dimple, and he would say, with enough diffidence to mark his respect for his elders, yet a complete independence of their views: "After all, what does it matter who makes the first move? The thing is to get the business done."

That was always the gist of it. To everyone else, my father included, what mattered in everything, from Diocesan Meetings to Patriarchs Balls, was just what Delane seemed so heedless of: the standing of the people who made up the committee or headed the movement. To Delane, only the movement itself counted; if the thing was worth doing, he pronounced in his slow lazy way, get it done somehow, even if its backers *were* Methodists or Congregationalists, or people who dined in the middle of the day.

"If they were convicts from Sing Sing I shouldn't care," he affirmed, his hand lazily flattering the dog's neck as I had seen it caress Byrne's terrified poney.

"Or lunatics out of Bloomingdale—as these 'reformers' usually are," my father added, softening the remark with his indulgent smile.

"Oh, well," Delane murmured, his attention flagging, "I daresay we're well enough off as we are."

"Especially," added Major Detrancy with a playful sniff, "with the punch in the offing, as I perceive it to be."

The punch struck the note for my mother's withdrawal.

She rose with her shy circular smile, while the gentlemen, all on their feet, protested gallantly at her desertion.

"Abandoning us to go back to Mr. Elsmere—we shall be jealous of the gentleman!" Colonel Ruscott declared, chivalrously reaching the door first; and as he opened it my father said, again with his indulgent smile: "Ah, my wife—she's a great reader."

Then the punch was brought.

IV

"YOU'LL ADMIT," Mrs. Delane challenged me, "that Hayley's perfect."

Don't imagine you have yet done with Mrs. Delane, any more than Delane had, or I. Hitherto I have shown you only one side, or rather one phase, of her; that during which, for obvious reasons, Hayley became an obstacle or a burden. In the intervals between her great passions, when somebody had to occupy the vacant throne in her bosom, her husband was always re-instated there; and during these interlunar periods he and the children were her staple subjects of conversation. If you had met her then for the first time you would have taken her for the perfect wife and mother, and wondered if Hayley ever got a day off; and you would not have been far wrong in conjecturing that he seldom did.

Only these intervals were rather widely spaced, and usually of short duration; and at other times, his wife being elsewhere engaged, it was Delane who elder-brothered his big boys and their little sister. Sometimes, on these occasions—when Mrs. Delane was abroad or at Newport—Delane used to carry me off for a week to the quiet old house in the New Jersey hills, full of Hayley and Delane portraits, of heavy mahogany furniture and the mingled smell of lavender bags and leather—leather boots, leather gloves, leather luggage, all the aromas that emanate from the cupboards and passages of a house inhabited by hard riders.

When his wife was at home he never seemed to notice the family portraits or the old furniture. Leila carried off her own regrettable origin by professing a democratic scorn of ancestors in general. "I know enough bores in the flesh without bothering to remember all the dead ones," she said one day, when I had asked her the name of a stern-visaged old forbear in breast-plate and buff jerkin who hung on the library wall: and Delane, so practised in sentimental duplicities, winked jovially at the children, as who should say: "There's the proper American spirit for you, my dears! That's the way we all ought to feel."

Perhaps, however, he detected a tinge of irritation in my

own look, for that evening, as we sat over the fire after Leila had yawned herself off to bed, he glanced up at the armoured image, and said: "That's old Durward Hayley—the friend of Sir Harry Vane the Younger and all that lot. I have some curious letters somewhere. . . But Leila's right, you know," he added loyally.

"In not being interested?"

"In regarding all that old past as dead. It *is* dead. We've got no use for it over here. That's what that queer fellow in Washington always used to say to me. . ."

"What queer fellow in Washington?"

"Oh, a sort of big backwoodsman who was awfully good to me when I was in hospital . . . after Bull Run. . ."

I sat up abruptly. It was the first time that Delane had mentioned his life during the war. I thought my hand was on the clue; but it wasn't.

"You were in hospital in Washington?"

"Yes; for a longish time. They didn't know much about disinfecting wounds in those days. . . But Leila," he resumed, with his smiling obstinacy, "Leila's dead right, you know. It's a better world now. Think of what has been done to relieve suffering since then!" When he pronounced the word "suffering" the vertical furrows in his forehead deepened as though he felt the actual pang of his old wound. "Oh, I believe in progress every bit as much as *she* does—I believe we're working out toward something better. If we weren't. . ." He shrugged his mighty shoulders, reached lazily for the adjoining tray, and mixed my glass of whiskey-and-soda.

"But the war—you were wounded at Bull Run?"

"Yes." He looked at his watch. "But I'm off to bed now. I promised the children to take them for an early canter tomorrow, before lessons, and I have to have my seven or eight hours of sleep to feel fit. I'm getting on, you see. Put out the lights when you come up."

No; he wouldn't talk about the war.

It was not long afterward that Mrs. Delane appealed to me to testify to Hayley's perfection. She had come back from her last absence—a six weeks' flutter at Newport—

rather painfully subdued and pinched-looking. For the first time I saw in the corners of her mouth that middle-aged droop which has nothing to do with the loss of teeth. "How common-looking she'll be in a few years!" I thought uncharitably.

"Perfect—perfect," she insisted; and then, plaintively: "And yet—"

I echoed coldly: "And yet?"

"With the children, for instance. He's everything to them. He's cut me out with my own children." She was half joking, half whimpering.

Presently she stole an eye-lashed look at me, and added: "And at times he's so *hard*."

"Delane?"

"Oh, I know you won't believe it. But in business matters—have you never noticed? You wouldn't admit it, I suppose. But there are times when one simply can't move him." We were in the library, and she glanced up at the breast-plated forbear. "He's as hard to the touch as *that*." She pointed to the steel convexity.

"Not the Delane I know," I murmured, embarrassed by these confidences.

"Ah, you think you know him?" she half-sneered; then, with a dutiful accent: "I've always said he was a perfect father—and he's made the children think so. And yet—"

He came in, and dropping a pale smile on him she drifted away, calling to her children.

I thought to myself: "She's getting on, and something has told her so at Newport. Poor thing!"

Delane looked as preoccupied as she did; but he said nothing till after she had left us that evening. Then he suddenly turned to me.

"Look here. You're a good friend of ours. Will you help me to think out a rather bothersome question?"

"Me, sir?" I said, surprised by the "ours," and overcome by so solemn an appeal from my elder.

He made a wan grimace. "Oh, don't call me 'sir'; not during this talk." He paused, and then added: "You're remembering the difference in our ages. Well, that's just why I'm asking you. I want the opinion of somebody who hasn't had time to freeze into his rut—as most of my contemporaries have. The fact is, I'm trying to make my wife see that we've got to let her father come and live with us."

My open-mouthed amazement must have been marked enough to pierce his gloom, for he gave a slight laugh. "Well, yes—"

I sat dumbfounded. All New York knew what Delane thought of his suave father-in-law. He had married Leila in spite of her antecedents; but Bill Gracy, at the outset, had been given to understand that he would not be received under the Delane roof. Mollified by the regular payment of a handsome allowance, the old gentleman, with tears in his eyes, was wont to tell his familiars that personally he didn't blame his son-in-law. "Our tastes differ: that's all. Hayley's not a bad chap at heart; give you my word he isn't." And the familiars, touched by such magnanimity, would pledge Hayley in the champagne provided by his last remittance.

Delane, as I still remained silent, began to explain. "You see, somebody's got to look after him—who else is there?"

"But—" I stammered.

"You'll say he's always needed looking after? Well, I've done my best; short of having him here. For a long time that seemed impossible; I quite agreed with Leila—" (So it was Leila who had banished her father!) "But now," Delane continued, "it's different. The poor old chap's getting on: he's been breaking up very fast this last year. And some blood-sucker of a woman has got hold of him, and threatened to rake up old race-course rows, and I don't know what. If we don't take him in he's bound to go under. It's his last chance—he feels it is. He's scared; he wants to come."

I was still silent, and Delane went on: "You think, I suppose, what's the use? Why not let him stew in his own juice? With a decent allowance, of course. Well, I can't say . . . I can't tell you . . . only I feel it mustn't be. . ."

"And Mrs. Delane?"

"Oh, I see her point. The children are growing up; they've hardly known their grandfather. And having him in the house isn't going to be like having a nice old lady in a cap knitting by the fire. He takes up room, Gracy does; it's not going to be pleasant. She thinks we ought to consider the children first. But I don't agree. The world's too ugly a place; why should anyone grow up thinking it's a flower-garden? Let 'em take their chance. . . . And then"—he hesitated, as if embarrassed—"well, you know her; she's fond of society. Why shouldn't she be? She's made for it. And of course it'll cut us off, prevent our inviting people. She won't like that, though she doesn't admit that it has anything to do with her objecting."

So, after all, he judged the wife he still worshipped! I was beginning to see why he had that great structural head, those large quiet movements. There *was* something—

"What alternative does Mrs. Delane propose?"

He coloured. "Oh, more money. I sometimes fancy," he brought out, hardly above a whisper, "that she thinks I've suggested having him here because I don't want to give more money. She won't understand, you see, that more money would just precipitate things."

I coloured too, ashamed of my own thought. Had she not, perhaps, understood; was it not her perspicacity which made her hold out? If her father was doomed to go under, why prolong the process? I could not be sure, now, that Delane did not suspect this also, and allow for it. There was apparently no limit to what he allowed for.

"*You'll* never be frozen into a rut," I ventured, smiling.

"Perhaps not frozen; but sunk down deep. I'm that already. Give me a hand up, do!" He answered my smile.

I was still in the season of cocksureness, and at a distance could no doubt have dealt glibly with the problem. But at such short range, and under those melancholy eyes, I had a chastening sense of inexperience.

"You don't care to tell me what you think?" He spoke almost reproachfully.

"Oh, it's not that . . . I'm trying to. But it's so—so awfully evangelical," I brought out—for some of us were already beginning to read the Russians.

"Is it? Funny, that, too. For I have an idea I got it, with other things, from an old heathen; that chap I told you about, who used to come and talk to me by the hour in Washington."

My interest revived. "That chap in Washington—was he a heathen?"

"Well, he didn't go to church." Delane did, regularly taking the children, while Leila slept off the previous night's poker, and joining in the hymns in a robust barytone, always half a tone flat.

He seemed to guess that I found his reply inadequate, and added helplessly: "You know I'm no scholar: I don't know what you'd call him." He lowered his voice to add: "I don't think he believed in our Lord. Yet he taught me Christian charity."

"He must have been an unusual sort of man, to have made such an impression on you. What was his name?"

"There's the pity! I must have heard it, but I was all foggy with fever most of the time, and can't remember. Nor what became of him either. One day he didn't turn up— that's all I recall. And soon afterward I was off again, and didn't think of him for years. Then, one day, I had to settle something with myself, and, by George, there he was, telling me the right and wrong of it! Queer—he comes like that, at long intervals; turning-points, I suppose." He frowned, his heavy head sunk forward, his eyes distant, pursuing the vision.

"Well—hasn't he come this time?"

"Rather! That's my trouble—I can't see things in any way but his. And I want another eye to help me."

My heart was beating rather excitedly. I felt small, trivial and inadequate, like an intruder on some grave exchange of confidences.

I tried to postpone my reply, and at the same time to satisfy another curiosity. "Have you ever told Mrs. Delane about— about him?"

Delane roused himself and turned to look at me. He lifted his shaggy eyebrows slightly, protruded his lower lip, and sank once more into abstraction.

"Well, sir," I said, answering the look, "*I* believe in him."

The blood rose in his dark cheek. He turned to me again, and for a second the dimple twinkled through his gloom. "That's your answer?"

I nodded breathlessly.

He got up, walked the length of the room, and came back, pausing in front of me. "He just vanished. I never even knew his name. . ."

V

DELANE was right; having Bill Gracy under one's roof was not like harbouring a nice old lady. I looked on at the sequence of our talk and marvelled.

New York—the Delanes' New York—sided unhesitatingly with Leila. Society's attitude toward drink and dishonesty was still inflexible: a man who had had to resign from his clubs went down into a pit presumably bottomless. The two or three people who thought Delane's action "rather fine" made haste to add: "But he ought to have taken a house for the old man in some quiet place in the country." Bill Gracy cabined in a quiet place in the country! Within a week he would have set the neighbourhood on fire. He was simply not to be managed by proxy; Delane had understood that, and faced it.

Nothing in the whole unprecedented situation was more odd, more unexpected and interesting, than Mr. Gracy's own perception of it. He too had become aware that his case was without alternative.

"They *had* to have me here, by gad; I see that myself. Old firebrand like me . . . couldn't be trusted! Hayley saw it from the first—fine fellow, my son-in-law. He made no bones about telling me so. Said: 'I can't trust you, father' . . . said it right out to me. By gad, if he'd talked to me like that a few years sooner I don't answer for the consequences! But I ain't my own man any longer. . . I've got to put up with being treated like a baby. . . I forgave him on the spot, sir—on the spot." His fine eye filled, and he stretched a soft old hand, netted with veins and freckles, across the table to me.

In the virtual seclusion imposed by his presence I was one of the few friends the Delanes still saw. I knew Leila was grateful to me for coming; but I did not need that incentive. It was enough that I could give even a negative support to Delane. The first months were horrible; but he was evidently saying to himself: "Things will settle down gradually," and just squaring his great shoulders to the storm.

Things didn't settle down; as embodied in Bill Gracy they

continued in a state of effervescence. Filial care, good food and early hours restored the culprit to comparative health; he became exuberant, arrogant and sly. Happily his first imprudence caused a relapse alarming even to himself. He saw that his powers of resistance were gone, and, tremulously tender over his own plight, he relapsed into a plaintive burden. But he was never a passive one. Some part or other he had to play, usually to somebody's detriment.

One day a strikingly dressed lady forced her way in to see him, and the house echoed with her recriminations. Leila objected to the children's assisting at such scenes, and when Christmas brought the boys home she sent them to Canada with a tutor, and herself went with the little girl to Florida. Delane, Gracy and I sat down alone to our Christmas turkey, and I wondered what Delane's queer friend of the Washington hospital would have thought of that festivity. Mr. Gracy was in a melting mood, and reviewed his past with an edifying prolixity. "After all, women and children have always loved me," he summed up, a tear on his lashes. "But I've been a curse to you and Leila, and I know it, Hayley. That's my only merit, I suppose—that I *do* know it! Well, here's to turning over a new leaf . . ." and so forth.

One day, a few months later, Mr. Broad, the head of the firm, sent for me. I was surprised, and somewhat agitated, at the summons, for I was not often called into his august presence.

"Mr. Delane has a high regard for your ability," he began affably.

I bowed, thrilled at what I supposed to be a hint of promotion; but Mr. Broad went on: "I know you are at his house a great deal. In spite of the difference in age he always speaks of you as an old friend." Hopes of promotion faded, yet left me unregretful. Somehow, this was even better. I bowed again.

Mr. Broad was becoming embarrassed. "You see Mr. William Gracy rather frequently at his son-in-law's?"

"He's living there," I answered bluntly.

Mr. Broad heaved a sigh. "Yes. It's a fine thing of Mr. Delane . . . but does he quite realize the consequences? His own family side with his wife. You'll wonder at my speaking with such frankness . . . but I've been asked . . . it has been suggested . . ."

"If he weren't there he'd be in the gutter."

Mr. Broad sighed more deeply. "Ah, it's a problem. . . You may ask why I don't speak directly to Mr. Delane . . . but it's so delicate, and he's so uncommunicative. Still, there are Institutions. . . You don't feel there's anything to be done?"

I was silent, and he shook hands, murmured: "This is confidential," and made a motion of dismissal. I withdrew to my desk, feeling that the situation must indeed be grave if Mr. Broad could so emphasize it by consulting me.

New York, to ease its mind of the matter, had finally decided that Hayley Delane was "queer." There were the two of them, madmen both, hobnobbing together under his roof; no wonder poor Leila found the place untenable! That view, bruited about, as such things are, with a mysterious underground rapidity, prepared me for what was to follow.

One day during the Easter holidays I went to dine with the Delanes, and finding my host alone with old Gracy I concluded that Leila had again gone off with the children. She had: she had been gone a week, and had just sent a letter to her husband saying that she was sailing from Montreal with the little girl. The boys would be sent back to Groton with a trusted servant. She would add nothing more, as she did not wish to reflect unkindly on what his own family agreed with her in thinking an act of ill-advised generosity. He knew that she was worn out by the strain he had imposed on her, and would understand her wishing to get away for a while. . .

She had left him.

Such events were not, in those days, the matters of course they have since become; and I doubt if, on a man like Delane, the blow would ever have fallen lightly. Certainly that evening was the grimmest I ever passed in his company. I had the same impression as on the day of Bolton Byrne's chastisement: the sense that Delane did not care a fig for public opinion. His knowing that it sided with his wife did not, I believe, affect him in the least; nor did her own view of his conduct —and for that I was unprepared. What really ailed him, I discovered, was his loneliness. He missed her, he wanted her back—her trivial irritating presence was the thing in the world he could least dispense with. But when he told me what she had done he simply added: "I see no help for it; we've both of us got a right to our own opinion."

Again I looked at him with astonishment. Another voice seemed to be speaking through his lips, and I had it on mine to say: "Was that what your old friend in Washington would have told you?" But at the door of the dining-room, where we had lingered, Mr. Gracy's flushed countenance and unreverend auburn locks appeared between us.

"Look here, Hayley; what about our little game? If I'm to be packed off to bed at ten like a naughty boy you might at least give me my hand of poker first." He winked faintly at me as we passed into the library, and added, in a hoarse aside: "If he thinks he's going to boss me like Leila he's mistaken. Flesh and blood's one thing; now she's gone I'll be damned if I take any bullying."

That threat was the last flare of Mr. Gracy's indomitable spirit. The act of defiance which confirmed it brought on a severe attack of pleurisy. Delane nursed the old man with dogged patience, and he emerged from the illness diminished, wizened, the last trace of auburn gone from his scant curls, and nothing left of his old self but a harmless dribble of talk.

Delane taught him to play patience, and he used to sit for hours by the library fire, puzzling over the cards, or talking to the children's parrot, which he fed and tended with a touching regularity. He also devoted a good deal of time to collecting stamps for his youngest grandson, and his increasing gentleness and playful humour so endeared him to the servants that a trusted housemaid had to be dismissed for smuggling cocktails into his room. On fine days Delane, coming home earlier from the bank, would take him for a short stroll; and one day, happening to walk up Fifth Avenue behind them, I noticed that the younger man's broad shoulders were beginning to stoop like the other's, and that there was less lightness in his gait than in Bill Gracy's jaunty shamble. They looked like two old men doing their daily mile on the sunny side of the street. Bill Gracy was no longer a danger to the community, and Leila might have come home. But I understood from Delane that she was still abroad with her daughter.

Society soon grows used to any state of things which is imposed upon it without explanation. I had noticed that Delane never explained; his chief strength lay in that negative quality. He was probably hardly aware that people were beginning to say: "Poor old Gracy—after all, he's making a decent end. It was the proper thing for Hayley to do—but his wife ought to come back and share the burden with him." In important matters he was so careless of public opinion that he was not likely to notice its veering. He wanted Leila to come home; he missed her and the little girl more and more; but for him there was no "ought" about the matter.

And one day she came. Absence had rejuvenated her, she had some dazzling new clothes, she had made the acquaintance of a charming Italian nobleman who was coming to New York on the next steamer . . . she was ready to forgive her husband, to be tolerant, resigned and even fond. Delane, with his amazing simplicity, took all this for granted; the effect of her return was to make him feel he had somehow been in the wrong, and he was ready to bask in her forgiveness. Luckily for her own popularity she arrived in time to soothe her parent's declining moments. Mr. Gracy was now a mere mild old pensioner and Leila used to drive out with him regularly, and refuse dull invitations "because she had to be with Papa." After all, people said, she had a heart. Her husband thought so too, and triumphed in the conviction. At that time life under the Delane roof, though melancholy, was idyllic; it was a pity old Gracy could not have been kept alive longer, so miraculously did his presence unite the household it had once divided. But he was beyond being aware of this, and from a cheerful senility sank into coma and death. The funeral was attended by the whole of New York, and Leila's crape veil was of exactly the right length—a matter of great importance in those days.

Life has a way of overgrowing its achievements as well as its ruins. In less time than seemed possible in so slow-moving a society, the Delanes' family crisis had been smothered and forgotten. Nothing seemed changed in the mutual attitude of husband and wife, or in that of their little group toward the couple. If anything, Leila had gained in popular esteem by her assiduity at her father's bedside; though as a truthful chronicler I am bound to add that she partly forfeited this advantage by plunging into a flirtation with the Italian noble- man before her crape trimmings had been replaced by *passe- menterie*. On such fundamental observances old New York still took its stand.

As for Hayley Delane, he emerged older, heavier, more stooping, but otherwise unchanged, from the ordeal. I am not sure that anyone except myself was aware that there had been an ordeal. But my conviction remained. His wife's return had changed him back into a card-playing, ball-going, race- frequenting elderly gentleman; but I had seen the waters part, and a granite rock thrust up from them. Twice the upheaval had taken place; and each time in obedience to motives unin- telligible to the people he lived among. Almost any man can take a stand on a principle his fellow-citizens are already occu- pying; but Hayley Delane held out for things his friends could not comprehend, and did it for reasons he could not explain. The central puzzle subsisted.

Does it subsist for me to this day? Sometimes, walking up town from the bank where in my turn I have become an institution, I glance through the rails of Trinity churchyard and wonder. He has lain there ten years or more now; his wife has married the President of a rising Western Univer- sity, and grown intellectual and censorious; his children are scattered and established. Does the old Delane vault hold his secret, or did I surprise it one day; did he and I surprise it together?

It was one Sunday afternoon, I remember, not long after Bill Gracy's edifying end. I had not gone out of town that week-end, and after a long walk in the frosty blue twilight of Central Park I let myself into my little flat. To my surprise I saw Hayley Delane's big overcoat and tall hat in the hall. He used to drop in on me now and then, but mostly on the way home from a dinner where we happened to have met; and I was rather startled at his appearance at that hour and on a

Sunday. But he lifted an untroubled face from the morning paper.

"You didn't expect a call on a Sunday? Fact is, I'm out of a job. I wanted to go down to the country, as usual, but there's some grand concert or other that Leila was booked for this afternoon; and a dinner tonight at Alstrop's. So I dropped in to pass the time of day. What *is* there to do on a Sunday afternoon, anyhow?"

There he was, the same old usual Hayley, as much put to it as the merest fribble of his set to employ an hour unfilled by poker! I was glad he viewed me as a possible alternative, and laughingly told him so. He laughed too—we were on terms of brotherly equality—and told me to go ahead and read two or three notes which had arrived in my absence. "Gad—how they shower down on a fellow at your age!" he chuckled.

I broke the seals and was glancing through the letters when I heard an exclamation at my back.

"By Jove—there he is!" Hayley Delane shouted. I turned to see what he meant.

He had taken up a book—an unusual gesture, but it lay at his elbow, and I suppose he had squeezed the newspapers dry. He held the volume out to me without speaking, his forefinger resting on the open page; his swarthy face was in a glow, his hand shook a little. The page to which his finger pointed bore the steel engraving of a man's portrait.

"It's him to the life—I'd know those old clothes of his again anywhere," Delane exulted, jumping up from his seat.

I took the book and stared first at the portrait and then at my friend.

"Your pal in Washington?"

He nodded excitedly. "That chap I've often told you about—yes!" I shall never forget the way his smile flew out and reached the dimple. There seemed a net-work of them spangling his happy face. His eyes had grown absent, as if gazing down invisible vistas. At length they travelled back to me.

"How on earth did the old boy get his portrait in a book? Has somebody been writing something about him?" His sluggish curiosity awakened, he stretched his hand for the volume. But I held it back.

"Lots of people have written about him; but this book is his own."

"You mean he wrote it?" He smiled incredulously. "Why, the poor chap hadn't any education!"

"Perhaps he had more than you think. Let me keep the book a moment longer, and read you something from it."

He signed an assent, though I could see the apprehension of the printed page already clouding his interest.

"What sort of things did he write?"

"Things for *you*. Now listen."

He settled back into his armchair, composing a painfully attentive countenance, and I sat down and began:

A sight in camp in the day-break grey and dim.
As from my tent I emerge so early, sleepless,
As slow I walk in the cool fresh air, the path near by the hospital
*   tent,*
Three forms I see on stretchers lying, brought out there, untended
*   lying,*
Over each the blanket spread, ample brownish woollen blanket,
Grey and heavy blanket, folding, covering all.

Curious, I halt, and silent stand:
Then with light fingers I from the face of the nearest, the first,
*   just lift the blanket:*
Who are you, elderly man so gaunt and grim, with well-grey'd
*   hair, and flesh all sunken about the eyes?*
Who are you, my dear comrade?

Then to the second I step—And who are you, my child and
*   darling?*
Who are you, sweet boy, with cheeks yet blooming?

Then to the third—a face nor child, nor old, very calm, as of
*   beautiful yellow-white ivory;*
Young man, I think I know you—I think this face of yours is the
*   face of the Christ himself;*
Dead and divine, and brother of all, and here again he lies.

I laid the open book on my knee, and stole a glance at Delane. His face was a blank, still composed in the heavy folds of enforced attention. No spark had been struck from him. Evidently the distance was too great between the far-off point at which he and English poetry had parted company, and this new strange form it had put on. I must find something which would bring the matter closely enough home to surmount the unfamiliar medium.

> *Vigil strange I kept on the field one night,*
> *When you, my son and my comrade, dropt at my side. . .*

The starlit murmur of the verse flowed on, muffled, insistent; my throat filled with it, my eyes grew dim. I said to myself, as my voice sank on the last line: "He's reliving it all now, seeing it again—knowing for the first time that someone else saw it as he did."

Delane stirred uneasily in his seat, and shifted his crossed legs one over the other. One hand absently stroked the fold of his carefully ironed trousers. His face was still a blank. The distance had not yet been bridged between "Gray's Elegy" and this unintelligible harmony. But I was not discouraged. I ought not to have expected any of it to reach him—not just at first—except by way of the closest personal appeal. I turned from the "Lovely and Soothing Death," at which I had re-opened the book, and looked for another page. My listener leaned back resignedly.

> *Bearing the bandages, water and sponge,*
> *Straight and swift to my wounded I go. . .*

I read on to the end. Then I shut the book and looked up again. Delane sat silent, his great hands clasping the arms of his chair, his head slightly sunk on his breast. His lids were dropped, as I imagined reverentially. My own heart was beating with a religious emotion; I had never felt the oft-read lines as I felt them then.

A little timidly, he spoke at length. "Did *he* write that?"

"Yes; just about the time you were seeing him, probably."

Delane still brooded; his expression grew more and more timid. "What do you . . . er . . . call it . . . exactly?" he ventured.

I was puzzled for a moment; then: "Why, poetry . . . rather a free form, of course. . . You see, he was an originator of new verse-forms. . ."

"New verse-forms?" Delane echoed forlornly. He stood up in his heavy way, but did not offer to take the book from me again. I saw in his face the symptoms of approaching departure.

"Well, I'm glad to have seen his picture after all these years," he said; and on the threshold he paused to ask: "What was his name, by the way?"

When I told him he repeated it with a smile of slow relish. "Yes; that's it. Old Walt—that was what all the fellows used to call him. He was a great chap: I'll never forget him.—I rather wish, though," he added, in his mildest tone of reproach, "you hadn't told me that he wrote all that rubbish."

THE END

NEW YEAR'S DAY
(*The 'Seventies*)

I

"SHE WAS *bad* . . . always. They used to meet at the Fifth Avenue Hotel," said my mother, as if the scene of the offence added to the guilt of the couple whose past she was revealing. Her spectacles slanted on her knitting, she dropped the words in a hiss that might have singed the snowy baby-blanket which engaged her indefatigable fingers. (It was typical of my mother to be always employed in benevolent actions while she uttered uncharitable words.)

"They used to meet at the Fifth Avenue Hotel"; how the precision of the phrase characterized my old New York! A generation later, people would have said, in reporting an affair such as Lizzie Hazeldean's with Henry Prest: "They met in hotels"—and today who but a few superannuated spinsters, still feeding on the venom secreted in their youth, would take any interest in the tracing of such topographies?

Life has become too telegraphic for curiosity to linger on any given point in a sentimental relation; as old Sillerton Jackson, in response to my mother, grumbled through his perfect "china set": "Fifth Avenue Hotel? They might meet in the middle of Fifth Avenue nowadays, for all that anybody cares."

But what a flood of light my mother's tart phrase had suddenly focussed on an unremarked incident of my boyhood!

The Fifth Avenue Hotel . . . Mrs. Hazeldean and Henry Prest . . . the conjunction of these names had arrested her darting talk on a single point of my memory, as a search-light, suddenly checked in its gyrations, is held motionless while one notes each of the unnaturally sharp and lustrous images it picks out.

At the time I was a boy of twelve, at home from school for the holidays. My mother's mother, Grandmamma Parrett, still lived in the house in West Twenty-third Street which Grandpapa had built in his pioneering youth, in days when people shuddered at the perils of living north of Union Square— days that Grandmamma and my parents looked back to with a joking incredulity as the years passed and the new houses advanced steadily Park-ward, outstripping the Thirtieth Streets,

taking the Reservoir at a bound, and leaving us in what, in
my school-days, was already a dullish back-water between Aristocracy to the south and Money to the north.

Even then fashion moved quickly in New York, and my
infantile memory barely reached back to the time when
Grandmamma, in lace lappets and creaking "*moiré*," used to
receive on New Year's day, supported by her handsome married daughters. As for old Sillerton Jackson, who, once a social custom had dropped into disuse, always affected never to
have observed it, he stoutly maintained that the New Year's
day ceremonial had never been taken seriously except among
families of Dutch descent, and that that was why Mrs. Henry
van der Luyden had clung to it, in a reluctant half-apologetic
way, long after her friends had closed their doors on the first
of January, and the date had been chosen for those out-of-
town parties which are so often used as a pretext for absence
when the unfashionable are celebrating their rites.

Grandmamma, of course, no longer received. But it would
have seemed to her an exceedingly odd thing to go out of
town in winter, especially now that the New York houses
were luxuriously warmed by the new hot-air furnaces, and
searchingly illuminated by gas chandeliers. No, thank you—
no country winters for the chilblained generation of prunella
sandals and low-necked sarcenet, the generation brought up
in unwarmed and unlit houses, and shipped off to die in Italy
when they proved unequal to the struggle of living in New
York! Therefore Grandmamma, like most of her contemporaries, remained in town on the first of January, and marked
the day by a family reunion, a kind of supplementary Christmas—though to us juniors the absence of presents and plum-
pudding made it but a pale and moonlike reflection of the
Feast.

Still, the day was welcome as a lawful pretext for over-
eating, dawdling, and looking out of the window: a Dutch
habit still extensively practised in the best New York circles.
On the day in question, however, we had not yet placed ourselves behind the plate-glass whence it would presently be so
amusing to observe the funny gentlemen who trotted about,
their evening ties hardly concealed behind their overcoat collars, darting in and out of chocolate-coloured house-fronts on

their sacramental round of calls. We were still engaged in placidly digesting around the ravaged luncheon table when a servant dashed in to say that the Fifth Avenue Hotel was on fire.

Oh, then the fun began—and what fun it was! For Grandmamma's house was just opposite the noble edifice of white marble which I associated with such deep-piled carpets, and such a rich sultry smell of anthracite and coffee, whenever I was bidden to "step across" for a messenger-boy, or to buy the evening paper for my elders.

The hotel, for all its sober state, was no longer fashionable. No one, in my memory, had ever known any one who went there; it was frequented by "politicians" and "Westerners," two classes of citizens whom my mother's intonation always seemed to deprive of their vote by ranking them with illiterates and criminals.

But for that very reason there was all the more fun to be expected from the calamity in question; for had we not, with infinite amusement, watched the arrival, that morning, of monumental "floral pieces" and towering frosted cakes for the New Year's day reception across the way? The event was a communal one. All the ladies who were the hotel's "guests" were to receive together in the densely lace-curtained and heavily chandeliered public parlours, and gentlemen with long hair, imperials and white gloves had been hastening since two o'clock to the scene of revelry. And now, thanks to the opportune conflagration, we were going to have the excitement not only of seeing the Fire Brigade in action (supreme joy of the New York youngster), but of witnessing the flight of the ladies and their visitors, staggering out through the smoke in gala array. The idea that the fire might be dangerous did not mar these pleasing expectations. The house was solidly built; New York's invincible Brigade was already at the door, in a glare of polished brass, coruscating helmets and horses shining like table-silver; and my tall cousin Hubert Wesson, dashing across at the first alarm, had promptly returned to say that all risk was over, though the two lower floors were so full of smoke and water that the lodgers, in some confusion, were being transported to other hotels. How then could a small boy see in the event anything but an unlimited lark?

Our elders, once reassured, were of the same mind. As they

stood behind us in the windows, looking over our heads, we heard chuckles of amusement mingled with ironic comment.

"Oh, my dear, look—here they all come! The New Year ladies! Low neck and short sleeves in broad daylight, every one of them! Oh, and the fat one with the paper roses in her hair . . . they *are* paper, my dear . . . off the frosted cake, probably! Oh! Oh! Oh! *Oh!*"

Aunt Sabina Wesson was obliged to stuff her lace handkerchief between her lips, while her firm poplin-cased figure rocked with delight.

"Well, my dear," Grandmamma gently reminded her, "in my youth we wore low-necked dresses all day long and all the year round."

No one listened. My cousin Kate, who always imitated Aunt Sabina, was pinching my arm in an agony of mirth. "Look at them scuttling! The parlours must be full of smoke. Oh, but this one is still funnier; the one with the tall feather in her hair! Granny, did you wear feathers in your hair in the daytime? Oh, don't ask me to believe it! And the one with the diamond necklace! And all the gentlemen in white ties! Did Grandpapa wear a white tie at two o'clock in the afternoon?" Nothing was sacred to Kate, and she feigned not to notice Grandmamma's mild frown of reproval.

"Well, they do in Paris, to this day, at weddings—wear evening clothes and white ties," said Sillerton Jackson with authority. "When Minnie Transome of Charleston was married at the Madeleine to the Duc de . . ."

But no one listened even to Sillerton Jackson. One of the party had abruptly exclaimed: "Oh, there's a lady running out of the hotel who's not in evening dress!"

The exclamation caused all our eyes to turn toward the person indicated, who had just reached the threshold; and someone added, in an odd voice: "Why, her figure looks like Lizzie Hazeldean's—"

A dead silence followed. The lady who was not in evening dress paused. Standing on the door-step with lifted veil, she faced our window. Her dress was dark and plain—almost conspicuously plain—and in less time than it takes to tell she had put her hand to her closely-patterned veil and pulled it down over her face. But my young eyes were keen and far-

sighted; and in that hardly perceptible interval I had seen a
vision. Was she beautiful—or was she only someone apart? I
felt the shock of a small pale oval, dark eyebrows curved with
one sure stroke, lips made for warmth, and now drawn up in
a grimace of terror; and it seemed as if the mysterious something, rich, secret and insistent, that broods and murmurs behind a boy's conscious thoughts, had suddenly peered out at
me. . . As the dart reached me her veil dropped.

"But it *is* Lizzie Hazeldean!" Aunt Sabina gasped. She had
stopped laughing, and her crumpled handkerchief fell to the
carpet.

"Lizzie—*Lizzie?*" The name was echoed over my head with
varying intonations of reprobation, dismay and half-veiled
malice.

Lizzie Hazeldean? Running out of the Fifth Avenue Hotel
on New Year's day with all those dressed-up women? But
what on earth could she have been doing there? No; nonsense! It was impossible. . .

"There's Henry Prest with her," continued Aunt Sabina in
a precipitate whisper.

"With her?" someone gasped; and *"Oh—"* my mother
cried with a shudder.

The men of the family said nothing, but I saw Hubert Wesson's face crimson with surprise. Henry Prest! Hubert was
forever boring us youngsters with his Henry Prest! That was
the kind of chap Hubert meant to be at thirty: in his eyes
Henry Prest embodied all the manly graces. Married? No,
thank you! That kind of man wasn't made for the domestic
yoke. Too fond of ladies' society, Hubert hinted with his
undergraduate smirk; and handsome, rich, independent—an
all-round sportsman, good horseman, good shot, crack
yachtsman (had his pilot's certificate, and always sailed his
own sloop, whose cabin was full of racing trophies); gave the
most delightful little dinners, never more than six, with cigars
that beat old Beaufort's; was awfully decent to the younger
men, chaps of Hubert's age included—and combined, in
short, all the qualities, mental and physical, which make up,
in such eyes as Hubert's, that oracular and irresistible figure,
the man of the world. "Just the fellow," Hubert always solemnly concluded, "that I should go straight to if ever I got

into any kind of row that I didn't want the family to know about"; and our blood ran pleasantly cold at the idea of our old Hubert's ever being in such an unthinkable predicament.

I felt sorry to have missed a glimpse of this legendary figure; but my gaze had been enthralled by the lady, and now the couple had vanished in the crowd.

The group in our window continued to keep an embarrassed silence. They looked almost frightened; but what struck me even more deeply was that not one of them looked surprised. Even to my boyish sense it was clear that what they had just seen was only the confirmation of something they had long been prepared for. At length one of my uncles emitted a whistle, was checked by a severe glance from his wife, and muttered: "I'll be damned"; another uncle began an unheeded narrative of a fire at which he had been present in his youth, and my mother said to me severely: "You ought to be at home preparing your lessons—a big boy like you!"—a remark so obviously unfair that it served only to give the measure of her agitation.

"I don't believe it," said Grandmamma, in a low voice of warning, protest and appeal. I saw Hubert steal a grateful look at her.

But nobody else listened: every eye still strained through the window. Livery-stable "hacks," of the old blue-curtained variety, were driving up to carry off the fair fugitives; for the day was bitterly cold, and lit by one of those harsh New York suns of which every ray seems an icicle. Into these ancient vehicles the ladies, now regaining their composure, were being piled with their removable possessions, while their kid-gloved callers ("So like the White Rabbit!" Kate exulted) appeared and reappeared in the doorway, gallantly staggering after them under bags, reticules, bird-cages, pet dogs and heaped-up finery. But to all this—as even I, a little boy, was aware—nobody in Grandmamma's window paid the slightest attention. The thoughts of one and all, with a mute and guarded eagerness, were still following the movements of those two who were so obviously unrelated to the rest. The whole business—discovery, comment, silent visual pursuit— could hardly, all told, have filled a minute, perhaps not as much; before the sixty seconds were over, Mrs. Hazeldean and Henry Prest had been lost in the crowd, and, while the hotel continued to empty itself into the street, had gone their joint or separate ways. But in my grandmother's window the silence continued unbroken.

"Well, it's over: here are the firemen coming out again," someone said at length.

We youngsters were all alert at that; yet I felt that the grown-ups lent but a half-hearted attention to the splendid sight which was New York's only pageant: the piling of scarlet ladders on scarlet carts, the leaping up on the engine of the helmeted flame-fighters, and the disciplined plunge forward of each pair of broad-chested black steeds, as one after another the chariots of fire rattled off.

Silently, almost morosely, we withdrew to the drawing-room hearth; where, after an interval of languid monosyllables, my mother, rising first, slipped her knitting into its bag, and turning on me with renewed severity, said: "This racing after fire-engines is what makes you too sleepy to prepare your lessons"—a comment so wide of the mark that once again I perceived, without understanding, the extent of the havoc wrought in her mind by the sight of Mrs. Hazeldean and Henry Prest coming out of the Fifth Avenue Hotel together.

It was not until many years later that chance enabled me to relate this fugitive impression to what had preceded and what came after it.

II

M RS. HAZELDEAN paused at the corner of Fifth Avenue and Madison Square. The crowd attracted by the fire still enveloped her; it was safe to halt and take breath.

Her companion, she knew, had gone in the opposite direction. Their movements, on such occasions, were as well-ordered and as promptly executed as those of the New York Fire Brigade; and after their precipitate descent to the hall, the discovery that the police had barred their usual exit, and the quick: "You're all right?" to which her imperceptible nod had responded, she was sure he had turned down Twenty-third Street toward Sixth Avenue.

"The Parretts' windows were full of people," was her first thought.

She dwelt on it a moment, and then reflected: "Yes, but in all that crowd and excitement nobody would have been thinking of *me*!"

Instinctively she put her hand to her veil, as though recalling that her features had been exposed when she ran out, and unable to remember whether she had covered them in time or not.

"What a fool I am! It can't have been off my face for more than a second—" but immediately afterward another disquieting possibility assailed her. "I'm almost sure I saw Sillerton Jackson's head in one of the windows, just behind Sabina Wesson's. No one else has that particularly silvery gray hair." She shivered, for everyone in New York knew that Sillerton Jackson saw everything, and could piece together seemingly unrelated fragments of fact with the art of a skilled china-mender.

Meanwhile, after sending through her veil the circular glance which she always shot about her at that particular corner, she had begun to walk up Broadway. She walked well—fast, but not too fast; easily, assuredly, with the air of a woman who knows that she has a good figure, and expects rather than fears to be identified by it. But under this external appearance of ease she was covered with cold beads of sweat.

Broadway, as usual at that hour, and on a holiday, was

nearly deserted; the promenading public still slowly poured up and down Fifth Avenue.

"Luckily there was such a crowd when we came out of the hotel that no one could possibly have noticed me," she murmured over again, reassured by the sense of having the long thoroughfare to herself. Composure and presence of mind were so necessary to a woman in her situation that they had become almost a second nature to her, and in a few minutes her thick uneven heart-beats began to subside and to grow steadier. As if to test their regularity, she paused before a florist's window, and looked appreciatively at the jars of roses and forced lilac, the compact bunches of lilies-of-the-valley and violets, the first pots of close-budded azaleas. Finally she opened the shop-door, and after examining the Jacqueminots and Marshal Niels, selected with care two perfect specimens of a new silvery-pink rose, waited for the florist to wrap them in cotton-wool, and slipped their long stems into her muff for more complete protection.

"It's so simple, after all," she said to herself as she walked on. "I'll tell him that as I was coming up Fifth Avenue from Cousin Cecilia's I heard the fire-engines turning into Twenty-third Street, and ran after them. Just what *he* would have done . . . once . . ." she ended on a sigh.

At Thirty-first Street she turned the corner with a quicker step. The house she was approaching was low and narrow; but the Christmas holly glistening between frilled curtains, the well-scrubbed steps, the shining bell and door-knob, gave it a welcoming look. From garret to basement it beamed like the abode of a happy couple.

As Lizzie Hazeldean reached the door a curious change came over her. She was conscious of it at once—she had so often said to herself, when her little house rose before her: "It makes me feel younger as soon as I turn the corner." And it was true even today. In spite of her agitation she was aware that the lines between her eyebrows were smoothing themselves out, and that a kind of inner lightness was replacing the heavy tumult of her breast. The lightness revealed itself in her movements, which grew as quick as a girl's as she ran up the steps. She rang twice—it was her signal—and turned an unclouded smile on her elderly parlourmaid.

"Is Mr. Hazeldean in the library, Susan? I hope you've kept up the fire for him."

"Oh, yes, ma'am. But Mr. Hazeldean's not in," said Susan, returning the smile respectfully.

"*Not in?* With his cold—and in this weather?"

"That's what I told him, ma'am. But he just laughed—"

"Just laughed? What do you mean, Susan?" Lizzie Hazeldean felt herself turning pale. She rested her hand quickly on the hall table.

"Well, ma'am, the minute he heard the fire-engine, off he rushed like a boy. It seems the Fifth Avenue Hotel's on fire: there's where he's gone."

The blood left Mrs. Hazeldean's lips; she felt it shuddering back to her heart. But a second later she spoke in a tone of natural and good-humoured impatience.

"What madness! How long ago—can you remember?" Instantly, she felt the possible imprudence of the question, and added: "The doctor said he ought not to be out more than a quarter of an hour, and only at the sunniest time of the day."

"I know that, ma'am, and so I reminded him. But he's been gone nearly an hour, I should say."

A sense of deep fatigue overwhelmed Mrs. Hazeldean. She felt as if she had walked for miles against an icy gale: her breath came laboriously.

"How could you let him go?" she wailed; then, as the parlourmaid again smiled respectfully, she added: "Oh, I know—sometimes one can't stop him. He gets so restless, being shut up with these long colds."

"That's what I *do* feel, ma'am."

Mistress and maid exchanged a glance of sympathy, and Susan felt herself emboldened to suggest: "Perhaps the outing will do him good," with the tendency of her class to encourage favoured invalids in disobedience.

Mrs. Hazeldean's look grew severe. "Susan! I've often warned you against talking to him in that way—"

Susan reddened, and assumed a pained expression. "How can you think it, ma'am?—me that never say anything to anybody, as all in the house will bear witness."

Her mistress made an impatient movement. "Oh, well, I daresay he won't be long. The fire's over."

"Ah—you knew of it too, then, ma'am?"

"Of the fire? Why, of course. I *saw* it, even—" Mrs. Hazeldean smiled. "I was walking home from Washington Square—from Miss Cecilia Winter's—and at the corner of Twenty-third Street there was a huge crowd, and clouds of smoke. . . It's very odd that I shouldn't have run across Mr. Hazeldean." She looked limpidly at the parlourmaid. "But, then, of course, in all that crowd and confusion . . ."

Half-way up the stairs she turned to call back: "Make up a good fire in the library, please, and bring the tea up. It's too cold in the drawing-room."

The library was on the upper landing. She went in, drew the two roses from her muff, tenderly unswathed them, and put them in a slim glass on her husband's writing-table. In the doorway she paused to smile at this touch of summer in the firelit wintry room; but a moment later her frown of anxiety reappeared. She stood listening intently for the sound of a latch-key; then, hearing nothing, passed on to her bedroom.

It was a rosy room, hung with one of the new English chintzes, which also covered the deep sofa, and the bed with its rose-lined pillow-covers. The carpet was cherry red, the toilet-table ruffled and looped like a ball-dress. Ah, how she and Susan had ripped and sewn and hammered, and pieced together old scraps of lace and ribbon and muslin, in the making of that airy monument! For weeks after she had done over the room her husband never came into it without saying: "I can't think how you managed to squeeze all this loveliness out of that last cheque of your stepmother's."

On the dressing-table Lizzie Hazeldean noticed a long florist's box, one end of which had been cut open to give space to the still longer stems of a bunch of roses. She snipped the string, and extracted from the box an envelope which she flung into the fire without so much as a glance at its contents. Then she pushed the flowers aside, and after rearranging her dark hair before the mirror, carefully dressed herself in a loose garment of velvet and lace which lay awaiting her on the sofa, beside her high-heeled slippers and stockings of open-work silk.

She had been one of the first women in New York to have tea every afternoon at five, and to put off her walking-dress for a tea-gown.

III

S HE RETURNED to the library, where the fire was beginning to send a bright blaze through the twilight. It flashed on the bindings of Hazeldean's many books, and she smiled absently at the welcome it held out. A latch-key rattled, and she heard her husband's step, and the sound of his cough below in the hall.

"What madness—what madness!" she murmured.

Slowly—how slowly for a young man!—he mounted the stairs, and still coughing came into the library. She ran to him and took him in her arms.

"Charlie! How could you? In this weather? It's nearly dark!"

His long thin face lit up with a deprecating smile. "I suppose Susan's betrayed me, eh? Don't be cross. You've missed such a show! The Fifth Avenue Hotel's been on fire."

"Yes; I know." She paused, just perceptibly. "I *didn't* miss it, though—I rushed across Madison Square for a look at it myself."

"You did? You were there too? What fun!" The idea appeared to fill him with boyish amusement.

"Naturally I was! On my way home from Cousin Cecilia's . . ."

"Ah, of course. I'd forgotten you were going there. But how odd, then, that we didn't meet!"

"If we *had* I should have dragged you home long ago. I've been in at least half an hour, and the fire was already over when I got there. What a baby you are to have stayed out so long, staring at smoke and a fire-engine!"

He smiled, still holding her, and passing his gaunt hand softly and wistfully over her head. "Oh, don't worry. I've been indoors, safely sheltered, and drinking old Mrs. Parrett's punch. The old lady saw me from her window, and sent one of the Wesson boys across the street to fetch me in. They had just finished a family luncheon. And Sillerton Jackson, who was there, drove me home. So you see,—"

He released her, and moved toward the fire, and she stood

motionless, staring blindly ahead, while the thoughts spun through her mind like a mill-race.

"Sillerton Jackson—" she echoed, without in the least knowing what she said.

"Yes; he has the gout again—luckily for me!—and his sister's brougham came to the Parretts' to fetch him."

She collected herself. "You're coughing more than you did yesterday," she accused him.

"Oh, well—the air's sharpish. But I shall be all right presently. . . Oh, those roses!" He paused in admiration before his writing-table.

Her face glowed with a reflected pleasure, though all the while the names he had pronounced—"The Parretts, the Wessons, Sillerton Jackson"—were clanging through her brain like a death-knell.

"They *are* lovely, aren't they?" she beamed.

"Much too lovely for me. You must take them down to the drawing-room."

"No; we're going to have tea up here."

"That's jolly—it means there'll be no visitors, I hope?"

She nodded, smiling.

"Good! But the roses—no, they mustn't be wasted on this desert air. You'll wear them in your dress this evening?"

She started perceptibly, and moved slowly back toward the hearth.

"This evening? . . . Oh, I'm not going to Mrs. Struthers's," she said, remembering.

"Yes, you are. Dearest—I want you to!"

"But what shall you do alone all the evening? With that cough, you won't go to sleep till late."

"Well, if I don't, I've a lot of new books to keep me busy."

"Oh, your books—!" She made a little gesture, half teasing, half impatient, in the direction of the freshly cut volumes stacked up beside his student lamp. It was an old joke between them that she had never been able to believe anyone could really "care for reading." Long as she and her husband had lived together, this passion of his remained for her as much of a mystery as on the day when she had first surprised him, mute and absorbed, over what the people she had always lived with would have called "a deep book." It was her first encounter with a born reader; or at least, the few she had known had been, like her stepmother, the retired opera-singer, feverish devourers of circulating library fiction: she had never before lived in a house with books in it. Gradually she had learned to take a pride in Hazeldean's reading, as if it had been some rare accomplishment; she had perceived that it reflected credit on him, and was even conscious of its adding to the charm of his talk, a charm she had always felt without being able to define it. But still, in her heart of hearts she regarded books as a mere expedient, and felt sure that they were only an aid to patience, like jackstraws or a game of patience, with the disadvantage of requiring a greater mental effort.

"Shan't you be too tired to read tonight?" she questioned wistfully.

"Too tired? Why, you goose, reading is the greatest rest in the world!—I want you to go to Mrs. Struthers's, dear; I want to see you again in that black velvet dress," he added with his coaxing smile.

The parlourmaid brought in the tray, and Mrs. Hazeldean busied herself with the tea-caddy. Her husband had stretched himself out in the deep armchair which was his habitual seat. He crossed his arms behind his neck, leaning his head back wearily against them, so that, as she glanced at him across the hearth, she saw the salient muscles in his long neck, and the premature wrinkles about his ears and chin. The lower part of his face was singularly ravaged; only the eyes, those quiet ironic grey eyes, and the white forehead above them, re-minded her of what he had been seven years before. Only seven years!

She felt a rush of tears: no, there were times when fate was too cruel, the future too horrible to contemplate, and the past—the past, oh, how much worse! And there he sat, coughing, coughing—and thinking God knows what, behind those quiet half-closed lids. At such times he grew so mysteri-ously remote that she felt lonelier than when he was not in the room.

"Charlie!"

He roused himself. "Yes?"

"Here's your tea."

He took it from her in silence, and she began, nervously, to
wonder why he was not talking. Was it because he was afraid
it might make him cough again, afraid she would be worried,
and scold him? Or was it because he was thinking—thinking
of things he had heard at old Mrs. Parrett's, or on the drive
home with Sillerton Jackson . . . hints they might have
dropped . . . insinuations . . . she didn't know what . . . or
of something he had *seen*, perhaps, from old Mrs. Parrett's
window? She looked across at his white forehead, so smooth
and impenetrable in the lamplight, and thought: "Oh, God,
it's like a locked door. I shall dash my brains out against it
some day!"

For, after all, it was not impossible that he had actually seen
her, seen her from Mrs. Parrett's window, or even from the
crowd around the door of the hotel. For all she knew, he
might have been near enough, in that crowd, to put out his
hand and touch her. And he might have held back, benumbed, aghast, not believing his own eyes. . . She couldn't
tell. She had never yet made up her mind how he would look,
how he would behave, what he would say, if ever he *did* see
or hear anything. . .

No! That was the worst of it. They had lived together for
nearly nine years—and how closely!—and nothing that she
knew of him, or had observed in him, enabled her to forecast
exactly what, in that particular case, his state of mind and his
attitude would be. In his profession, she knew, he was celebrated for his shrewdness and insight; in personal matters he
often seemed, to her alert mind, oddly absent-minded and
indifferent. Yet that might be merely his instinctive way of
saving his strength for things he considered more important.
There were times when she was sure he was quite deliberate
and self-controlled enough to feel in one way and behave in
another: perhaps even to have thought out a course in advance—just as, at the first bad symptoms of illness, he had
calmly made his will, and planned everything about her future, the house and the servants. . . No, she couldn't tell;
there always hung over her the thin glittering menace of a
danger she could neither define nor localize—like that aveng-
ing lightning which groped for the lovers in the horrible
poem he had once read aloud to her (what a choice!) on a

lazy afternoon of their wedding journey, as they lay stretched under Italian stone-pines.

The maid came in to draw the curtains and light the lamps. The fire glowed, the scent of the roses drifted on the warm air, and the clock ticked out the minutes, and softly struck a half hour, while Mrs. Hazeldean continued to ask herself, as she so often had before: "Now, what would be the *natural* thing for me to say?"

And suddenly the words escaped from her, she didn't know how: "I wonder you didn't see me coming out of the hotel— for I actually squeezed my way in."

Her husband made no answer. Her heart jumped convulsively; then she lifted her eyes and saw that he was asleep. How placid his face looked—years younger than when he was awake! The immensity of her relief rushed over her in a warm glow, the counterpart of the icy sweat which had sent her chattering homeward from the fire. After all, if he could fall asleep, fall into such a peaceful sleep as that—tired, no doubt, by his imprudent walk, and the exposure to the cold— it meant, beyond all doubt, beyond all conceivable dread, that he knew nothing, had seen nothing, suspected nothing: that she was safe, safe, safe!

The violence of the reaction made her long to spring to her feet and move about the room. She saw a crooked picture that she wanted to straighten, she would have liked to give the roses another tilt in their glass. But there he sat, quietly sleeping, and the long habit of vigilance made her respect his rest, watching over it as patiently as if it had been a sick child's.

She drew a contented breath. Now she could afford to think of his outing only as it might affect his health; and she knew that this sudden drowsiness, even if it were a sign of extreme fatigue, was also the natural restorative for that fatigue. She continued to sit behind the tea-tray, her hands folded, her eyes on his face, while the peace of the scene entered into her, and held her under brooding wings.

IV

A<small>T</small> M<small>RS</small>. S<small>TRUTHERS'S</small>, at eleven o'clock that evening, the long over-lit drawing-rooms were already thronged with people.

Lizzie Hazeldean paused on the threshold and looked about her. The habit of pausing to get her bearings, of sending a circular glance around any assemblage of people, any drawing-room, concert-hall or theatre that she entered, had become so instinctive that she would have been surprised had anyone pointed out to her the unobservant expression and careless movements of the young women of her acquaintance, who also looked about them, it is true, but with the vague unseeing stare of youth, and of beauty conscious only of itself.

Lizzie Hazeldean had long since come to regard most women of her age as children in the art of life. Some savage instinct of self-defence, fostered by experience, had always made her more alert and perceiving than the charming creatures who passed from the nursery to marriage as if lifted from one rose-lined cradle into another. "Rocked to sleep—that's what they've always been," she used to think sometimes, listening to their innocuous talk during the long after-dinners in hot drawing-rooms, while their husbands, in the smoking-rooms below, exchanged ideas which, if no more striking, were at least based on more direct experiences.

But then, as all the old ladies said, Lizzie Hazeldean had always preferred the society of men.

The man she now sought was not visible, and she gave a little sigh of ease. "If only he has had the sense to stay away!" she thought.

She would have preferred to stay away herself; but it had been her husband's whim that she should come. "You know you always enjoy yourself at Mrs. Struthers's—everybody does. The old girl somehow manages to have the most amusing house in New York. Who is it who's going to sing to-night? . . . If you don't go, I shall know it's because I've coughed two or three times oftener than usual, and you're worrying about me. My dear girl, it will take more than the

Fifth Avenue Hotel fire to kill *me*. . . My heart's feeling unusually steady. . . Put on your black velvet, will you?—with
these two roses. . ."

So she had gone. And here she was, in her black velvet,
under the glitter of Mrs. Struthers's chandeliers, amid all the
youth and good looks and gaiety of New York; for, as Hazeldean said, Mrs. Struthers's house was more amusing than
anybody else's, and whenever she opened her doors the world
flocked through them.

As Mrs. Hazeldean reached the inner drawing-room the
last notes of a rich tenor were falling on the attentive silence.
She saw Campanini's low-necked throat subside into silence
above the piano, and the clapping of many tightly-fitting
gloves was succeeded by a general movement, and the usual
irrepressible outburst of talk.

In the breaking-up of groups she caught a glimpse of Sillerton Jackson's silvery crown. Their eyes met across bare shoulders, he bowed profoundly, and she fancied that a dry smile
lifted his moustache. "He doesn't usually bow to me as low as
that," she thought apprehensively.

But as she advanced into the room her self-possession returned. Among all these stupid pretty women she had such a
sense of power, of knowing almost everything better than
they did, from the way of doing her hair to the art of keeping
a secret! She felt a thrill of pride in the slope of her white
shoulders above the black velvet, in the one curl escaping
from her thick chignon, and the slant of the gold arrow
tipped with diamonds which she had thrust in to retain
it. And she had done it all without a maid, with no one cleverer than Susan to help her! Ah, as a woman she knew her
business. . .

Mrs. Struthers, plumed and ponderous, with diamond stars
studding her black wig like a pin-cushion, had worked her
resolute way back to the outer room. More people were coming in; and with her customary rough skill she was receiving,
distributing, introducing them. Suddenly her smile deepened;
she was evidently greeting an old friend. The group about her
scattered, and Mrs. Hazeldean saw that, in her cordial absent-
minded way, and while her wandering hostess-eye swept the

rooms, she was saying a confidential word to a tall man whose
hand she detained. They smiled at each other; then Mrs.
Struthers's glance turned toward the inner room, and her
smile seemed to say: "You'll find her there."

The tall man nodded. He looked about him composedly,
and began to move toward the centre of the throng, speaking
to everyone, appearing to have no object beyond that of
greeting the next person in his path, yet quietly, steadily pursuing that path, which led straight to the inner room.

Mrs. Hazeldean had found a seat near the piano. A good-
looking youth, seated beside her, was telling her at considerable length what he was going to wear at the Beauforts'
fancy-ball. She listened, approved, suggested; but her glance
never left the advancing figure of the tall man.

Handsome? Yes, she said to herself; she had to admit that
he was handsome. A trifle too broad and florid, perhaps;
though his air and his attitude so plainly denied it that, on
second thoughts, one agreed that a man of his height had,
after all, to carry some ballast. Yes; his assurance made him, as
a rule, appear to people exactly as he chose to appear; that is,
as a man over forty, but carrying his years carelessly, an active
muscular man, whose blue eyes were still clear, whose fair
hair waved ever so little less thickly than it used to on a low
sunburnt forehead, over eyebrows almost silvery in their
blondness, and blue eyes the bluer for their thatch. Stupid-
looking? By no means. His smile denied that. Just self-
sufficient enough to escape fatuity, yet so cool that one felt
the fundamental coldness, he steered his way through life as
easily and resolutely as he was now working his way through
Mrs. Struthers's drawing-rooms.

Half-way, he was detained by a tap of Mrs. Wesson's red
fan. Mrs. Wesson—surely, Mrs. Hazeldean reflected, Charles
had spoken of Mrs. Sabina Wesson's being with her mother,
old Mrs. Parrett, while they watched the fire? Sabina Wesson
was a redoubtable woman, one of the few of her generation
and her clan who had broken with tradition, and gone to
Mrs. Struthers's almost as soon as the Shoe-Polish Queen had
bought her house in Fifth Avenue, and issued her first challenge to society. Lizzie Hazeldean shut her eyes for an instant; then, rising from her seat, she joined the group about

the singer. From there she wandered on to another knot of acquaintances.

"Look here: the fellow's going to sing again. Let's get into that corner over there."

She felt ever so slight a touch on her arm, and met Henry Prest's composed glance.

A red-lit and palm-shaded recess divided the drawing-rooms from the dining-room, which ran across the width of the house at the back. Mrs. Hazeldean hesitated; then she caught Mrs. Wesson's watchful glance, lifted her head with a smile and followed her companion.

They sat down on a small sofa under the palms, and a couple, who had been in search of the same retreat, paused on the threshold, and with an interchange of glances passed on. Mrs. Hazeldean smiled more vividly.

"Where are my roses? Didn't you get them?" Prest asked. He had a way of looking her over from beneath lowered lids, while he affected to be examining a glove-button or contemplating the tip of his shining boot.

"Yes, I got them," she answered.

"You're not wearing them. I didn't order those."

"No."

"Whose are they, then?"

She unfolded her mother-of-pearl fan, and bent above its complicated traceries.

"Mine," she pronounced.

"Yours? Well, obviously. But I suppose someone sent them to you?"

"*I* did." She hesitated a second. "I sent them to myself."

He raised his eyebrows a little. "Well, they don't suit you—that washy pink! May I ask why you didn't wear mine?"

"I've already told you. . . I've often asked you never to send flowers . . . on the day. . ."

"Nonsense. That's the very day. . . What's the matter? Are you still nervous?"

She was silent for a moment; then she lowered her voice to say: "You ought not to have come here tonight."

"My dear girl, how unlike you! You *are* nervous."

"Didn't you see all those people in the Parretts' window?"

"What, opposite? Lord, no; I just took to my heels! It was

the deuce, the back way being barred. But what of it? In all that crowd, do you suppose for a moment—"

"My husband was in the window with them," she said, still lower.

His confident face fell for a moment, and then almost at once regained its look of easy arrogance.

"Well—?"

"Oh, nothing—as yet. Only I ask you . . . to go away now."

"Just as you asked me not to come! Yet *you* came, because you had the sense to see that if you didn't . . . and I came for the same reason. Look here, my dear, for God's sake don't lose your head!"

The challenge seemed to rouse her. She lifted her chin, glanced about the thronged room which they commanded from their corner, and nodded and smiled invitingly at several acquaintances, with the hope that some one of them might come up to her. But though they all returned her greetings with a somewhat elaborate cordiality, not one advanced toward her secluded seat.

She turned her head slightly toward her companion. "I ask you again to go," she repeated.

"Well, I will then, after the fellow's sung. But I'm bound to say you're a good deal pleasanter—"

The first bars of *"Salve, Dimora"* silenced him, and they sat side by side in the meditative rigidity of fashionable persons listening to expensive music. She had thrown herself into a corner of the sofa, and Henry Prest, about whom everything was discreet but his eyes, sat apart from her, one leg crossed over the other, one hand holding his folded opera-hat on his knee, while the other hand rested beside him on the sofa. But an end of her tulle scarf lay in the space between them; and without looking in his direction, without turning her glance from the singer, she was conscious that Prest's hand had reached and drawn the scarf toward him. She shivered a little, made an involuntary motion as though to gather it about her—and then desisted. As the song ended, he bent toward her slightly, said: "Darling" so low that it seemed no more than a breath on her cheek, and then, rising, bowed, and strolled into the other room.

She sighed faintly, and, settling herself once more in her corner, lifted her brilliant eyes to Sillerton Jackson, who was approaching. "It *was* good of you to bring Charlie home from the Parretts' this afternoon." She held out her hand, making way for him at her side.

"Good of me?" he laughed. "Why, I was glad of the chance of getting him safely home; it was rather naughty of *him* to be where he was, I suspect." She fancied a slight pause, as if he waited to see the effect of this, and her lashes beat her cheeks. But already he was going on: "Do you encourage him, with that cough, to run about town after fire-engines?"

She gave back the laugh.

"I don't discourage him—ever—if I can help it. But it *was* foolish of him to go out today," she agreed; and all the while she kept on asking herself, as she had that afternoon, in her talk with her husband: "Now, what would be the *natural* thing for me to say?"

Should she speak of having been at the fire herself—or should she not? The question dinned in her brain so loudly that she could hardly hear what her companion was saying; yet she had, at the same time, a queer feeling of his never having been so close to her, or rather so closely intent on her, as now. In her strange state of nervous lucidity, her eyes seemed to absorb with a new precision every facial detail of whoever approached her; and old Sillerton Jackson's narrow mask, his withered pink cheeks, the veins in the hollow of his temples, under the carefully-tended silvery hair, and the tiny blood-specks in the white of his eyes as he turned their cautious blue gaze on her, appeared as if presented under some powerful lens. With his eye-glasses dangling over one white-gloved hand, the other supporting his opera-hat on his knee, he suggested, behind that assumed carelessness of pose, the patient fixity of a naturalist holding his breath near the crack from which some tiny animal might suddenly issue—if one watched long enough, or gave it, completely enough, the impression of not looking for it, or dreaming it was anywhere near. The sense of that tireless attention made Mrs. Hazeldean's temples ache as if she sat under a glare of light even brighter than that of the Struthers' chandeliers—a glare in which each quiver of a half-formed thought might be as

visible behind her forehead as the faint lines wrinkling its surface into an uncontrollable frown of anxiety. Yes, Prest was
right; she was losing her head—losing it for the first time in
the dangerous year during which she had had such continual
need to keep it steady.

"What is it? What has happened to me?" she wondered.

There had been alarms before—how could it be otherwise?
But they had only stimulated her, made her more alert and
prompt; whereas tonight she felt herself quivering away into
she knew not what abyss of weakness. What was different,
then? Oh, she knew well enough! It was Charles . . . that
haggard look in his eyes, and the lines of his throat as he had
leaned back sleeping. She had never before admitted to herself
how ill she thought him; and now, to have to admit it, and
at the same time not to have the complete certainty that the
look in his eyes was caused by illness only, made the strain
unbearable.

She glanced about her with a sudden sense of despair. Of
all the people in those brilliant animated groups—of all the
women who called her Lizzie, and the men who were familiars at her house—she knew that not one, at that moment,
guessed, or could have understood, what she was feeling. . .
Her eyes fell on Henry Prest, who had come to the surface a
little way off, bending over the chair of the handsome Mrs.
Lyman. "And *you* least of all!" she thought. "Yet God knows,"
she added with a shiver, "they all have their theories about
me!"

"My dear Mrs. Hazeldean, you look a little pale. Are you
cold? Shall I get you some champagne?" Sillerton Jackson was
officiously suggesting.

"If you think the other women look blooming! My dear
man, it's this hideous vulgar overhead lighting. . ." She rose
impatiently. It had occurred to her that the thing to do—the
"natural" thing—would be to stroll up to Jinny Lyman, over
whom Prest was still attentively bending. *Then* people would
see if she was nervous, or ill—or afraid!

But half-way she stopped and thought: "Suppose the Parretts and Wessons *did* see me? Then my joining Jinny while
he's talking to her will look—how will it look?" She began to
regret not having had it out on the spot with Sillerton Jack-

son, who could be trusted to hold his tongue on occasion, especially if a pretty woman threw herself on his mercy. She glanced over her shoulder as if to call him back; but he had turned away, been absorbed into another group, and she found herself, instead, abruptly face to face with Sabina Wesson. Well, perhaps that was better still. After all, it all depended on how much Mrs. Wesson had seen, and what line she meant to take, supposing she *had* seen anything. She was not likely to be as inscrutable as old Sillerton. Lizzie wished now that she had not forgotten to go to Mrs. Wesson's last party.

"Dear Mrs. Wesson, it was so kind of you—"

But Mrs. Wesson was not there. By the exercise of that mysterious protective power which enables a woman desirous of not being waylaid to make herself invisible, or to transport herself, by means imperceptible, to another part of the earth's surface, Mrs. Wesson, who, two seconds earlier, appeared in all her hard handsomeness to be bearing straight down on Mrs. Hazeldean, with a scant yard of clear *parquet* between them—Mrs. Wesson, as her animated back and her active red fan now called on all the company to notice, had never been there at all, had never seen Mrs. Hazeldean ("*Was* she at Mrs. Struthers's last Sunday? How odd! I must have left before she got there—"), but was busily engaged, on the farther side of the piano, in examining a picture to which her attention appeared to have been called by the persons nearest her.

"Ah, how *life-like*! That's what I always feel when I see a Meissonier," she was heard to exclaim, with her well-known instinct for the fitting epithet.

Lizzie Hazeldean stood motionless. Her eyes dazzled as if she had received a blow on the forehead. "So *that's* what it feels like!" she thought. She lifted her head very high, looked about her again, tried to signal to Henry Prest, but saw him still engaged with the lovely Mrs. Lyman, and at the same moment caught the glance of young Hubert Wesson, Sabina's eldest, who was standing in disengaged expectancy near the supper-room door.

Hubert Wesson, as his eyes met Mrs. Hazeldean's, crimsoned to the forehead, hung back a moment, and then came forward, bowing low—again that too low bow! "So *he* saw me too," she thought. She put her hand on his arm with a laugh. "Dear me, how ceremonious you are! Really, I'm not as old as that bow of yours implies. My dear boy, I hope you want to take me in to supper at once. I was out in the cold all the afternoon, gazing at the Fifth Avenue Hotel fire, and I'm simply dying of hunger and fatigue."

There, the die was cast—she had said it loud enough for all the people nearest her to hear! And she was sure now that it was the right, the "natural" thing to do.

Her spirits rose, and she sailed into the supper-room like a goddess, steering Hubert to an unoccupied table in a flowery corner.

"No—I think we're very well by ourselves, don't you? Do you want that fat old bore of a Lucy Vanderlow to join us? If you *do*, of course . . . I can see she's dying to . . . but then, I warn you, I shall ask a young man! Let me see—shall I ask Henry Prest? You see he's hovering! No, it *is* jollier with just you and me, isn't it?" She leaned forward a little, resting her chin on her clasped hands, her elbows on the table, in an attitude which the older women thought shockingly free, but the younger ones were beginning to imitate.

"And now, some champagne, please—and *hot* terrapin! . . . But I suppose you were at the fire yourself, weren't you?" she leaned still a little nearer to say.

The blush again swept over young Wesson's face, rose to his forehead, and turned the lobes of his large ears to balls of fire ("It looks," she thought, "as if he had on huge coral earrings."). But she forced him to look at her, laughed straight into his eyes, and went on: "Did you ever see a funnier sight than all those dressed-up absurdities rushing out into the cold? It looked like the end of an Inauguration Ball! I was so fascinated that I actually pushed my way into the hall. The firemen were furious, but they couldn't stop me—nobody can stop me at a fire! You should have seen the ladies scuttling downstairs—the fat ones! Oh, but I beg your pardon; I'd forgotten that you admire . . . avoirdupois. No? But . . . Mrs. Van . . . so stupid of me! Why, you're actually blushing! I assure you, you're as red as your mother's fan—and visible from as great a distance! Yes, please; a little more champagne. . ."

And then the inevitable began. She forgot the fire, forgot her anxieties, forgot Mrs. Wesson's affront, forgot everything but the amusement, the passing childish amusement, of twirling around her little finger this shy clumsy boy, as she had twirled so many others, old and young, not caring afterward if she ever saw them again, but so absorbed in the sport, and in her sense of knowing how to do it better than the other women—more quietly, more insidiously, without ogling, bridling or grimacing—that sometimes she used to ask herself with a shiver: "What was the gift given to me for?" Yes; it always amused her at first: the gradual dawn of attraction in eyes that had regarded her with indifference, the blood rising to the face, the way she could turn and twist the talk as though she had her victim on a leash, spinning him after her down winding paths of sentimentality, irony, caprice . . . and leaving him, with beating heart and dazzled eyes, to visions of an all-promising morrow. . . "My only accomplishment!" she murmured to herself as she rose from the table followed by young Wesson's fascinated gaze, while already, on her own lips, she felt the taste of cinders.

"But at any rate," she thought, "he'll hold his tongue about having seen me at the fire."

V

SHE LET herself in with her latch-key, glanced at the notes and letters on the hall-table (the old habit of allowing nothing to escape her), and stole up through the darkness to her room.

A fire still glowed in the chimney, and its light fell on two vases of crimson roses. The room was full of their scent.

Mrs. Hazeldean frowned, and then shrugged her shoulders. It had been a mistake, after all, to let it appear that she was indifferent to the flowers; she must remember to thank Susan for rescuing them. She began to undress, hastily yet clumsily, as if her deft fingers were all thumbs; but first, detaching the two faded pink roses from her bosom, she put them with a reverent touch into a glass on the toilet-table. Then, slipping on her dressing-gown, she stole to her husband's door. It was shut, and she leaned her ear to the keyhole. After a moment she caught his breathing, heavy, as it always was when he had a cold, but regular, untroubled. . . With a sigh of relief she tiptoed back. Her uncovered bed, with its fresh pillows and satin coverlet, sent her a rosy invitation; but she cowered down by the fire, hugging her knees and staring into the coals.

"So *that's* what it feels like!" she repeated.

It was the first time in her life that she had ever been deliberately "cut"; and the cut was a deadly injury in old New York. For Sabina Wesson to have used it, consciously, deliberately—for there was no doubt that she had purposely advanced toward her victim—she must have done so with intent to kill. And to risk that, she must have been sure of her facts, sure of corroborating witnesses, sure of being backed up by all her clan.

Lizzie Hazeldean had her clan too—but it was a small and weak one, and she hung on its outer fringe by a thread of little-regarded cousinship. As for the Hazeldean tribe, which was larger and stronger (though nothing like the great organized Wesson-Parrett *gens*, with half New York and all Albany at its back)—well, the Hazeldeans were not much to be counted on, and would even, perhaps, in a furtive negative

518

way, be not too sorry ("if it were not for poor Charlie") that poor Charlie's wife should at last be made to pay for her good looks, her popularity, above all for being, in spite of her origin, treated by poor Charlie as if she were one of them!

Her origin was, of course, respectable enough. Everybody knew all about the Winters—she had been Lizzie Winter. But the Winters were very small people, and her father, the Reverend Arcadius Winter, the sentimental over-popular Rector of a fashionable New York church, after a few seasons of too great success as preacher and director of female consciences, had suddenly had to resign and go to Bermuda for his health—or was it France?—to some obscure watering-place, it was rumoured. At any rate, Lizzie, who went with him (with a crushed bed-ridden mother), was ultimately, after the mother's death, fished out of a girls' school in Brussels—they seemed to have been in so many countries at once!—and brought back to New York by a former parishioner of poor Arcadius's, who had always "believed in him," in spite of the Bishop, and who took pity on his lonely daughter.

The parishioner, Mrs. Mant, was "one of the Hazeldeans." She was a rich widow, given to generous gestures which she was often at a loss how to complete; and when she had brought Lizzie Winter home, and sufficiently celebrated her own courage in doing so, she did not quite know what step to take next. She had fancied it would be pleasant to have a clever handsome girl about the house; but her housekeeper was not of the same mind. The spare-room sheets had not been out of lavender for twenty years—and Miss Winter always left the blinds up in her room, and the carpet and curtains, unused to such exposure, suffered accordingly. Then young men began to call—they called in numbers. Mrs. Mant had not supposed that the daughter of a clergyman—and a clergyman "under a cloud"—would expect visitors. She had imagined herself taking Lizzie Winter to Church Fairs, and having the stitches of her knitting picked up by the young girl, whose "eyes were better" than her benefactress's. But Lizzie did not know how to knit—she possessed no useful accomplishments—and she was visibly bored by Church Fairs, where her presence was of little use, since she had no money to spend. Mrs. Mant began to see her mistake; and the

discovery made her dislike her protégée, whom she secretly
regarded as having intentionally misled her.

In Mrs. Mant's life, the transition from one enthusiasm to
another was always marked by an interval of disillusionment,
during which, Providence having failed to fulfill her requirements, its existence was openly called into question. But in
this flux of moods there was one fixed point: Mrs. Mant was
a woman whose life revolved about a bunch of keys. What
treasures they gave access to, what disasters would have ensued had they been forever lost, was not quite clear; but
whenever they were missed the household was in an uproar,
and as Mrs. Mant would trust them to no one but herself,
these occasions were frequent. One of them arose at the very
moment when Mrs. Mant was recovering from her enthusiasm for Miss Winter. A minute before, the keys had been
there, in a pocket of her work-table; she had actually
touched them in hunting for her buttonhole-scissors. She
had been called away to speak to the plumber about the
bath-room leak, and when she left the room there was no
one in it but Miss Winter. When she returned, the keys were
gone. The house had been turned inside out; everyone had
been, if not accused, at least suspected; and in a rash moment Mrs. Mant had spoken of the police. The housemaid
had thereupon given warning, and her own maid threatened
to follow; when suddenly the Bishop's hints recurred to
Mrs. Mant. The Bishop had always implied that there had
been something irregular in Dr. Winter's accounts, besides
the other unfortunate business. . .

Very mildly, she had asked Miss Winter if she might not
have seen the keys, and "picked them up without thinking."
Miss Winter permitted herself to smile in denying the suggestion; the smile irritated Mrs. Mant; and in a moment the
flood-gates were opened. She saw nothing to smile at in her
question—unless it was of a kind that Miss Winter was already used to, prepared for . . . with that sort of background
. . . her unfortunate father. . .

"Stop!" Lizzie Winter cried. She remembered now, as if it
had happened yesterday, the abyss suddenly opening at her
feet. It was her first direct contact with human cruelty. Suffering, weakness, frailties other than Mrs. Mant's restricted

fancy could have pictured, the girl had known, or at least suspected; but she had found as much kindness as folly in her path, and no one had ever before attempted to visit upon her the dimly-guessed shortcomings of her poor old father. She shook with horror as much as with indignation, and her "Stop!" blazed out so violently that Mrs. Mant, turning white, feebly groped for the bell.

And it was then, at that very moment, that Charles Hazeldean came in—Charles Hazeldean, the favourite nephew, the pride of the tribe. Lizzie had seen him only once or twice, for he had been absent since her return to New York. She had thought him distinguished-looking, but rather serious and sarcastic; and he had apparently taken little notice of her—which perhaps accounted for her opinion.

"Oh, Charles, dearest Charles—that you should be here to hear such things said to me!" his aunt gasped, her hand on her outraged heart.

"What things? Said by whom? I see no one here to say them but Miss Winter," Charles had laughed, taking the girl's icy hand.

"Don't shake hands with her! She has insulted me! She has ordered me to keep silence—in my own house. 'Stop!' she said, when I was trying, in the kindness of my heart, to get her to admit privately . . . Well, if she prefers to have the police. . ."

"I do! I ask you to send for them!" Lizzie cried.

How vividly she remembered all that followed: the finding of the keys, Mrs. Mant's reluctant apologies, her own cold acceptance of them, and the sense on both sides of the impossibility of continuing their life together! She had been wounded to the soul, and her own plight first revealed to her in all its destitution. Before that, despite the ups and downs of a wandering life, her youth, her good looks, the sense of a certain bright power over people and events, had hurried her along on a spring tide of confidence; she had never thought of herself as the dependent, the beneficiary, of the persons who were kind to her. Now she saw herself, at twenty, a penniless girl, with a feeble discredited father carrying his snowy head, his unctuous voice, his edifying manner from one cheap watering-place to another, through an endless succession of sentimental and pecuniary entanglements. To him she could be of no more help than he to her; and save for him she was alone. The Winter cousins, as much humiliated by his disgrace as they had been puffed-up by his triumphs, let it be understood, when the breach with Mrs. Mant became known, that they were not in a position to interfere; and among Dr. Winter's former parishioners none was left to champion him. Almost at the same time, Lizzie heard that he was about to marry a Portuguese opera-singer and be received into the Church of Rome; and this crowning scandal too promptly justified his family.

The situation was a grave one, and called for energetic measures. Lizzie understood it—and a week later she was engaged to Charles Hazeldean.

She always said afterward that but for the keys he would never have thought of marrying her; while he laughingly affirmed that, on the contrary, but for the keys she would never have looked at *him*.

But what did it all matter, in the complete and blessed understanding which was to follow on their hasty union? If all the advantages on both sides had been weighed and found equal by judicious advisers, harmony more complete could hardly have been predicted. As a matter of fact, the advisers, had they been judicious, would probably have found only elements of discord in the characters concerned. Charles Hazeldean was by nature an observer and a student, brooding and curious of mind: Lizzie Winter (as she looked back at herself)—what was she, what would she ever be, but a quick, ephemeral creature, in whom a perpetual and adaptable activity simulated mind, as her grace, her swiftness, her expressiveness simulated beauty? So others would have judged her; so, now, she judged herself. And she knew that in fundamental things she was still the same. And yet she had satisfied him: satisfied him, to all appearances, as completely in the quiet later years as in the first flushed hours. As completely, or perhaps even more so. In the early months, dazzled gratitude made her the humbler, fonder worshipper; but as her powers expanded in the warm air of comprehension, as she felt herself grow handsomer, cleverer, more competent and more companionable than he had hoped, or she had dreamed herself capable of becoming, the balance was imperceptibly reversed, and the triumph in his eyes when they rested on her.

The Hazeldeans were conquered; they had to admit it. Such a brilliant recruit to the clan was not to be disowned. Mrs. Mant was left to nurse her grievance in solitude, till she too fell into line, carelessly but handsomely forgiven.

Ah, those first years of triumph! They frightened Lizzie now as she looked back. One day, the friendless defenceless daughter of a discredited man; the next, almost, the wife of Charlie Hazeldean, the popular successful young lawyer, with a good practice already assured, and the best of professional and private prospects. His own parents were dead, and had died poor; but two or three childless relatives were understood to be letting their capital accumulate for his benefit, and meanwhile in Lizzie's thrifty hands his earnings were largely sufficient.

Ah, those first years! There had been barely six; but even now there were moments when their sweetness drenched her to the soul. . . Barely six; and then the sharp re-awakening of an inherited weakness of the heart that Hazeldean and his doctors had imagined to be completely cured. Once before, for the same cause, he had been sent off, suddenly, for a year of travel in mild climates and distant scenes; and his first return had coincided with the close of Lizzie's sojourn at Mrs. Mant's. The young man felt sure enough of the future to marry and take up his professional duties again, and for the following six years he had led, without interruption, the busy life of a successful lawyer; then had come a second breakdown, more unexpectedly, and with more alarming symptoms. The "Hazeldean heart" was a proverbial boast in the family; the Hazeldeans privately considered it more distinguished than the Sillerton gout, and far more refined than the Wesson liver; and it had permitted most of them to survive, in valetudinarian ease, to a ripe old age, when they died of some quite other disorder. But Charles Hazeldean had defied it, and it took its revenge, and took it savagely.

One by one, hopes and plans faded. The Hazeldeans went south for a winter; he lay on a deck-chair in a Florida garden, and read and dreamed, and was happy with Lizzie beside him. So the months passed; and by the following autumn he was better, returned to New York, and took up his profession. Intermittently but obstinately, he had continued the struggle for two more years; but before they were over husband and wife understood that the good days were done.

He could be at his office only at lengthening intervals; he sank gradually into invalidism without submitting to it. His income dwindled; and, indifferent for himself, he fretted ceaselessly at the thought of depriving Lizzie of the least of her luxuries.

At heart she was indifferent to them too; but she could not convince him of it. He had been brought up in the old New York tradition, which decreed that a man, at whatever cost, must provide his wife with what she had always "been accustomed to"; and he had gloried too much in her prettiness, her elegance, her easy way of wearing her expensive dresses, and his friends' enjoyment of the good dinners she knew how to order, not to accustom her to everything which could enhance such graces. Mrs. Mant's secret satisfaction rankled in him. She sent him Baltimore terrapin, and her famous clam broth, and a dozen of the old Hazeldean port, and said "I told you so" to her confidants when Lizzie was mentioned; and Charles Hazeldean knew it, and swore at it.

"I won't be pauperized by her!" he declared; but Lizzie smiled away his anger, and persuaded him to taste the terrapin and sip the port.

She was smiling faintly at the memory of the last passage between him and Mrs. Mant when the turning of the bedroom door-handle startled her. She jumped up, and he stood there. The blood rushed to her forehead; his expression frightened her; for an instant she stared at him as if he had been an enemy. Then she saw that the look in his face was only the remote lost look of excessive physical pain.

She was at his side at once, supporting him, guiding him to the nearest armchair. He sank into it, and she flung a shawl over him, and knelt at his side while his inscrutable eyes continued to repel her.

"Charles . . . Charles," she pleaded.

For a while he could not speak; and she said to herself that she would perhaps never know whether he had sought her because he was ill, or whether illness had seized him as he entered her room to question, accuse, or reveal what he had seen or heard that afternoon.

Suddenly he lifted his hand and pressed back her forehead, so that her face lay bare under his eyes.

"Love, love—you've been happy?"

"Happy?" The word choked her. She clung to him, burying her anguish against his knees. His hand stirred weakly in her hair, and gathering her whole strength into the gesture, she raised her head again, looked into his eyes, and breathed back: "And you?"

He gave her one full look; all their life together was in it, from the first day to the last. His hand brushed her once more, like a blessing, and then dropped. The moment of their communion was over; the next she was preparing remedies, ringing for the servants, ordering the doctor to be called. Her husband was once more the harmless helpless captive that sickness makes of the most dreaded and the most loved.

VI

IT WAS in Mrs. Mant's drawing-room that, some half-year later, Mrs. Charles Hazeldean, after a moment's hesitation, said to the servant that, yes, he might show in Mr. Prest.

Mrs. Mant was away. She had been leaving for Washington to visit a new protégée when Mrs. Hazeldean arrived from Europe, and after a rapid consultation with the clan had decided that it would not be "decent" to let poor Charles's widow go to an hotel. Lizzie had therefore the strange sensation of returning, after nearly nine years, to the house from which her husband had triumphantly rescued her; of returning there, to be sure, in comparative independence, and without danger of falling into her former bondage, yet with every nerve shrinking from all that the scene revived.

Mrs. Mant, the next day, had left for Washington; but before starting she had tossed a note across the breakfast-table to her visitor.

"Very proper—he was one of Charlie's oldest friends, I believe?" she said, with her mild frosty smile. Mrs. Hazeldean glanced at the note, turned it over as if to examine the signature, and restored it to her hostess.

"Yes. But I don't think I care to see anyone just yet."

There was a pause, during which the butler brought in fresh griddle-cakes, replenished the hot milk, and withdrew. As the door closed on him, Mrs. Mant said, with a dangerous cordiality: "No one would misunderstand your receiving an old friend of your husband's . . . like Mr. Prest."

Lizzie Hazeldean cast a sharp glance at the large empty mysterious face across the table. They *wanted* her to receive Henry Prest, then? Ah, well . . . perhaps she understood. . .

"Shall I answer this for you, my dear? Or will you?" Mrs. Mant pursued.

"Oh, as you like. But don't fix a day, please. Later—"

Mrs. Mant's face again became vacuous. She murmured: "You must not shut yourself up too much. It will not do to be morbid. I'm sorry to have to leave you here alone—"

Lizzie's eyes filled: Mrs. Mant's sympathy seemed more cruel than her cruelty. Every word that she used had a veiled taunt for its counterpart.

"Oh, you mustn't think of giving up your visit—"

"My dear, how can I? It's a *duty*. I'll send a line to Henry Prest, then. . . If you would sip a little port at luncheon and dinner we should have you looking less like a ghost. . ."

Mrs. Mant departed; and two days later—the interval was "decent"—Mr. Henry Prest was announced. Mrs. Hazeldean had not seen him since the previous New Year's day. Their last words had been exchanged in Mrs. Struthers's crimson boudoir, and since then half a year had elapsed. Charles Hazeldean had lingered for a fortnight; but though there had been ups and downs, and intervals of hope when none could have criticised his wife for seeing her friends, her door had been barred against everyone. She had not excluded Henry Prest more rigorously than the others; he had simply been one of the many who received, day by day, the same answer: "Mrs. Hazeldean sees no one but the family."

Almost immediately after her husband's death she had sailed for Europe on a long-deferred visit to her father, who was now settled at Nice; but from this expedition she had presumably brought back little comfort, for when she arrived in New York her relations were struck by her air of ill-health and depression. It spoke in her favour, however; they were agreed that she was behaving with propriety.

She looked at Henry Prest as if he were a stranger: so difficult was it, at the first moment, to fit his robust and splendid person into the region of twilight shades which, for the last months, she had inhabited. She was beginning to find that everyone had an air of remoteness; she seemed to see people and life through the confusing blur of the long crape veil in which it was a widow's duty to shroud her affliction. But she gave him her hand without perceptible reluctance.

He lifted it toward his lips, in an obvious attempt to combine gallantry with condolence, and then, half-way up, seemed to feel that the occasion required him to release it.

"Well—you'll admit that I've been patient!" he exclaimed.

"Patient? Yes. What else was there to be?" she rejoined with a faint smile, as he seated himself beside her, a little too near.

"Oh, well . . . of course! I understood all that, I hope you'll believe. But mightn't you at least have answered my letters—one or two of them?"

She shook her head. "I couldn't write."

"Not to anyone? Or not to me?" he queried, with ironic emphasis.

"I wrote only the letters I had to—no others."

"Ah, I see." He laughed slightly. "And you didn't consider that letters to *me* were among them?"

She was silent, and he stood up and took a turn across the room. His face was redder than usual, and now and then a twitch passed over it. She saw that he felt the barrier of her crape, and that it left him baffled and resentful. A struggle was still perceptibly going on in him between his traditional standard of behaviour at such a meeting, and primitive impulses renewed by the memory of their last hours together. When he turned back and paused before her his ruddy flush had paled, and he stood there, frowning, uncertain, and visibly resenting the fact that she made him so.

"You sit there like a stone!" he said.

"I feel like a stone."

"Oh, come—!"

She knew well enough what he was thinking: that the only way to bridge over such a bad beginning was to get the woman into your arms—and talk afterward. It was the classic move. He had done it dozens of times, no doubt, and was evidently asking himself why the deuce he couldn't do it now. . . But something in her look must have benumbed him. He sat down again beside her.

"What you must have been through, dearest!" He waited and coughed. "I can understand your being—all broken up. But I know nothing; remember, I know nothing as to what actually happened. . ."

"Nothing happened."

"As to—what we feared? No hint—?"

She shook her head.

He cleared his throat before the next question. "And you

don't think that in your absence he may have spoken—to anyone?"

"Never!"

"Then, my dear, we seem to have had the most unbelievable good luck; and I can't see—"

He had edged slowly nearer, and now laid a large ringed hand on her sleeve. How well she knew those rings—the two dull gold snakes with malevolent jewelled eyes! She sat as motionless as if their coils were about her, till slowly his tentative grasp relaxed.

"Lizzie, you know"—his tone was discouraged—"this is morbid. . ."

"Morbid?"

"When you're safe out of the worst scrape . . . and free, my darling, *free!* Don't you realize it? I suppose the strain's been too much for you; but I want you to feel that now—"

She stood up suddenly, and put half the length of the room between them.

"Stop! Stop! Stop!" she almost screamed, as she had screamed long ago at Mrs. Mant.

He stood up also, darkly red under his rich sunburn, and forced a smile.

"Really," he protested, "all things considered—and after a separation of six months!" She was silent. "My dear," he continued mildly, "will you tell me what you expect me to think?"

"Oh, don't take that tone," she murmured.

"What tone?"

"As if—as if—you still imagined we could go back—"

She saw his face fall. Had he ever before, she wondered, stumbled upon an obstacle in that smooth walk of his? It flashed over her that this was the danger besetting men who had a "way with women"—the day came when they might follow it too blindly.

The reflection evidently occurred to him almost as soon as it did to her. He summoned another propitiatory smile, and drawing near, took her hand gently. "But I don't want to go back. . . I want to go forward, dearest. . . Now that at last you're free."

She seized on the word as if she had been waiting for her cue. "Free! Oh, that's it—*free!* Can't you see, can't you understand, that I mean to stay free?"

Again a shadow of distrust crossed his face, and the smile he had begun for her reassurance seemed to remain on his lips for his own.

"But of course! Can you imagine that I want to put you in chains? I want you to be as free as you please—free to love me as much as you choose!" He was visibly pleased with the last phrase.

She drew away her hand, but not unkindly. "I'm sorry—I *am* sorry, Henry. But you don't understand."

"What don't I understand?"

"That what you ask is quite impossible—ever. I can't go on . . . in the old way. . ."

She saw his face working nervously. "In the old way? You mean—?" Before she could explain he hurried on with an increasing majesty of manner: "Don't answer! I see—I understand. When you spoke of freedom just now I was misled for a moment—I frankly own I was—into thinking that, after your wretched marriage, you might prefer discreeter ties . . . an apparent independence which would leave us both. . . I say *apparent*, for on my side there has never been the least wish to conceal. . . But if I was mistaken, if on the contrary what you wish is . . . . is to take advantage of your freedom to regularize our . . . our attachment. . ."

She said nothing, not because she had any desire to have him complete the phrase, but because she found nothing to say. To all that concerned their common past she was aware of offering a numbed soul. But her silence evidently perplexed him, and in his perplexity he began to lose his footing, and to flounder in a sea of words.

"Lizzie! Do you hear me? If I was mistaken, I say—and I hope I'm not above owning that at times I *may* be mistaken; if I was—why, by God, my dear, no woman ever heard me speak the words before; but here I am to have and to hold, as the Book says! Why, hadn't you realized it? Lizzie, look up—! *I'm asking you to marry me.*"

Still, for a moment, she made no reply, but stood gazing about her as if she had the sudden sense of unseen presences between them. At length she gave a faint laugh. It visibly ruffled her visitor.

"I'm not conscious," he began again, "of having said anything particularly laughable—" He stopped and scrutinized her narrowly, as though checked by the thought that there might be something not quite normal. . . Then, apparently reassured, he half-murmured his only French phrase: "*La joie fait peur* . . . eh?"

She did not seem to hear. "I wasn't laughing at you," she said, "but only at the coincidences of life. It was in this room that my husband asked me to marry him."

"Ah?" Her suitor appeared politely doubtful of the good taste, or the opportunity, of producing this reminiscence. But he made another call on his magnanimity. "Really? But, I say, my dear, I couldn't be expected to know it, could I? If I'd guessed that such a painful association—"

"Painful?" She turned upon him. "A painful association? Do you think that was what I meant?" Her voice sank. "This room is sacred to me."

She had her eyes on his face, which, perhaps because of its architectural completeness, seemed to lack the mobility necessary to follow such a leap of thought. It was so ostensibly a solid building, and not a nomad's tent. He struggled with a ruffled pride, rose again to playful magnanimity, and murmured: "Compassionate angel!"

"Oh, compassionate? To whom? Do you imagine—did I ever say anything to make you doubt the truth of what I'm telling you?"

His brows fretted: his temper was up. "*Say* anything? No," he insinuated ironically; then, in a hasty plunge after his lost forbearance, added with exquisite mildness: "Your tact was perfect . . . always. I've invariably done you that justice. No one could have been more thoroughly the . . . the lady. I never failed to admire your good-breeding in avoiding any reference to your . . . your other life."

She faced him steadily. "Well, that other life *was* my life—my only life! Now you know."

There was a silence. Henry Prest drew out a monogrammed handkerchief and passed it over his dry lips. As he did so, a whiff of his eau de Cologne reached her, and she winced a little. It was evident that he was seeking what to say next; wondering, rather helplessly, how to get back his lost command of the situation. He finally induced his features to break again into a persuasive smile.

"Not your *only* life, dearest," he reproached her.

She met it instantly. "Yes; so you thought—because I chose you should."

"You chose—?" The smile became incredulous.

"Oh, deliberately. But I suppose I've no excuse that you would not dislike to hear. . . Why shouldn't we break off now?"

"Break off . . . this conversation?" His tone was aggrieved. "Of course I've no wish to force myself—"

She interrupted him with a raised hand. "Break off for good, Henry."

"For good?" He stared, and gave a quick swallow, as though the dose were choking him. "For good? Are you really—? You and I? Is this serious, Lizzie?"

"Perfectly. But if you prefer to hear . . . what can only be painful. . ."

He straightened himself, threw back his shoulders, and said in an uncertain voice: "I hope you don't take me for a coward."

She made no direct reply, but continued: "Well, then, you thought I loved you, I suppose—"

He smiled again, revived his moustache with a slight twist, and gave a hardly perceptible shrug. "You . . . ah . . . managed to produce the illusion. . ."

"Oh, well, yes: a woman *can*—so easily! That's what men often forget. You thought I was a lovelorn mistress; and I was only an expensive prostitute."

"Elizabeth!" he gasped, pale now to the ruddy eyelids. She saw that the word had wounded more than his pride, and that, before realizing the insult to his love, he was shuddering at the offence to his taste. Mistress! Prostitute! Such words were banned. No one reproved coarseness of language in women more than Henry Prest; one of Mrs. Hazeldean's greatest charms (as he had just told her) had been her way of remaining, "through it all," so ineffably "the lady." He looked at her as if a fresh doubt of her sanity had assailed him.

"Shall I go on?" she smiled.

He bent his head stiffly. "I am still at a loss to imagine for what purpose you made a fool of me."

"Well, then, it was as I say. I wanted money—money for my husband."

He moistened his lips. "For your husband?"

"Yes; when he began to be so ill; when he needed comforts, luxury, the opportunity to get away. He saved me, when I was a girl, from untold humiliation and wretchedness. No one else lifted a finger to help me—not one of my own family. I hadn't a penny or a friend. Mrs. Mant had grown sick of me, and was trying to find an excuse to throw me over. Oh, you don't know what a girl has to put up with—a girl alone in the world—who depends for her clothes, and her food, and the roof over her head, on the whims of a vain capricious old woman! It was because *he* knew, because he understood, that he married me. . . He took me out of misery into blessedness. He put me up above them all . . . he put me beside himself. I didn't care for anything but that; I didn't care for the money or the freedom; I cared only for him. I would have followed him into the desert—I would have gone barefoot to be with him. I would have starved, begged, done anything for him—*anything*." She broke off, her voice lost in a sob. She was no longer aware of Prest's presence—all her consciousness was absorbed in the vision she had evoked. "It was *he* who cared—who wanted me to be rich and independent and admired! He wanted to heap everything on me—during the first years I could hardly persuade him to keep enough money for himself. . . And then he was taken ill; and as he got worse, and gradually dropped out of affairs, his income grew smaller, and then stopped altogether; and all the while there were new expenses piling up—nurses, doctors, travel; and he grew frightened; frightened not for himself but for me. . . And what was I to do? I had to pay for things somehow. For the first year I managed to put off paying—then I borrowed small sums here and there. But that couldn't last. And all the while I had to keep on looking pretty and prosperous, or else he began to worry, and think we were ruined, and wonder what would become of me if he didn't get well. By the time you came I was desperate—I would have done anything, anything! He thought the money came from my Portuguese stepmother. She really was rich, as it happens. Unluckily my poor father tried to invest her money, and lost it all; but when they were first married she sent a thousand dollars—and all the rest, all you gave me, I built on that."

She paused pantingly, as if her tale were at an end. Gradually her consciousness of present things returned, and she saw Henry Prest, as if far off, a small indistinct figure looming through the mist of her blurred eyes. She thought to herself: "He doesn't believe me," and the thought exasperated her.

"You wonder, I suppose," she began again, "that a woman should dare confess such things about herself—"

He cleared his throat. "About herself? No; perhaps not. But about her husband."

The blood rushed to her forehead. "About her husband? But you don't dare to imagine—?"

"You leave me," he rejoined icily, "no other inference that I can see." She stood dumbfounded, and he added: "At any rate, it certainly explains your extraordinary coolness—pluck, I used to think it. I perceive that I needn't have taken such precautions."

She considered this. "You think, then, that he knew? You think, perhaps, that I knew he did?" She pondered again painfully, and then her face lit up. "He never knew—never! That's enough for me—and for you it doesn't matter. Think what you please. He was happy to the end—that's all I care for."

"There can be no doubt about your frankness," he said with pinched lips.

"There's no longer any reason for not being frank."

He picked up his hat, and studiously considered its lining; then he took the gloves he had laid in it, and drew them thoughtfully through his hands. She thought: "Thank God, he's going!"

But he set the hat and gloves down on a table, and moved a little nearer to her. His face looked as ravaged as a reveller's at daybreak.

"You—leave positively nothing to the imagination!" he murmured.

"I told you it was useless—" she began; but he interrupted her: "Nothing, that is—if I believed you." He moistened his lips again, and tapped them with his handkerchief. Again she had a whiff of the eau de Cologne. "But I don't!" he proclaimed. "Too many memories . . . too many . . . proofs, my dearest. . ." He stopped, smiling somewhat convulsively. She saw that he imagined the smile would soothe her.

She remained silent, and he began once more, as if appealing to her against her own verdict: "I know better, Lizzie. In spite of everything, *I know you're not that kind of woman.*"

"I took your money—"

"As a favour. I knew the difficulties of your position. . . I understood completely. I beg of you never again to allude to—all that." It dawned on her that anything would be more endurable to him than to think he had been a dupe—and one of two dupes! The part was not one that he could conceive of having played. His pride was up in arms to defend her, not so much for her sake as for his own. The discovery gave her a baffling sense of helplessness; against that impenetrable self-sufficiency all her affirmations might spend themselves in vain.

"No man who has had the privilege of being loved by you could ever for a moment. . ."

She raised her head and looked at him. "You have never had that privilege," she interrupted.

His jaw fell. She saw his eyes pass from uneasy supplication to a cold anger. He gave a little inarticulate grunt before his voice came back to him.

"You spare no pains in degrading yourself in my eyes."

"I am not degrading myself. I am telling you the truth. I needed money. I knew no way of earning it. You were willing to give it . . . for what you call the privilege. . ."

"Lizzie," he interrupted solemnly, "don't go on! I believe I enter into all your feelings—I believe I always have. In so sensitive, so hypersensitive a nature, there are moments when every other feeling is swept away by scruples. . . For those scruples I only honour you the more. But I won't hear another word now. If I allowed you to go on in your present state of . . . nervous exaltation . . . you might be the first to deplore. . . I wish to forget everything you have said . . . I wish to look forward, not back. . ." He squared his shoulders, took a deep breath, and fixed her with a glance of recovered confidence. "How little you know me if you believe that I could fail you *now!*"

She returned his look with a weary steadiness. "You are kind—you mean to be generous, I'm sure. But don't you see that I *can't* marry you?"

"I only see that, in the natural rush of your remorse—"

"Remorse? Remorse?" She broke in with a laugh. "Do you imagine I feel any remorse? I'd do it all over again tomorrow—for the same object! I got what I wanted—I gave him that last year, that last good year. It was the relief from anxiety that kept him alive, that kept him happy. Oh, he *was* happy—I know that!" She turned to Prest with a strange smile. "I do thank you for that—I'm not ungrateful."

"You . . . you . . . *ungrateful?* This . . . is really . . . indecent. . ." He took up his hat again, and stood in the middle of the room as if waiting to be waked from a bad dream.

"You are—rejecting an opportunity—" he began.

She made a faint motion of assent.

"You do realize it? I'm still prepared to—to help you, if you should. . ." She made no answer, and he continued: "How do you expect to live—since you have chosen to drag in such considerations?"

"I don't care how I live. I never wanted the money for myself."

He raised a deprecating hand. "Oh, don't—*again!* The woman I had meant to. . ." Suddenly, to her surprise, she saw a glitter of moisture on his lower lids. He applied his handkerchief to them, and the waft of scent checked her momentary impulse of compunction. That Cologne water! It called up picture after picture with a hideous precision. "Well, it was worth it," she murmured doggedly.

Henry Prest restored his handkerchief to his pocket. He waited, glanced about the room, turned back to her.

"If your decision is final—"

"Oh, final!"

He bowed. "There is one thing more—which I should have mentioned if you had ever given me the opportunity of seeing you after—after last New Year's day. Something I preferred not to commit to writing—"

"Yes?" she questioned indifferently.

"Your husband, you are positively convinced, had no idea . . . that day . . . ?"

"None."

"Well, others, it appears, had." He paused. "Mrs. Wesson saw us."

"So I supposed. I remember now that she went out of her way to cut me that evening at Mrs. Struthers's."

"Exactly. And she was not the only person who saw us. If people had not been disarmed by your husband's falling ill that very day you would have found yourself—ostracized."

She made no comment, and he pursued, with a last effort: "In your grief, your solitude, you haven't yet realized what your future will be—how difficult. It is what I wished to guard you against—it was my purpose in asking you to marry me." He drew himself up and smiled as if he were look-ing at his own reflection in a mirror, and thought favourably of it. "A man who has had the misfortune to compromise a woman is bound in honour—Even if my own inclination were not what it is, I should consider. . ."

She turned to him with a softened smile. Yes, he had really brought himself to think that he was proposing to marry her to save her reputation. At this glimpse of the old hackneyed axioms on which he actually believed that his conduct was based, she felt anew her remoteness from the life he would have drawn her back to.

"My poor Henry, don't you see how far I've got beyond the Mrs. Wessons? If all New York wants to ostracize me, let it! I've had my day . . . no woman has more than one. Why shouldn't I have to pay for it? I'm ready."

"Good heavens!" he murmured.

She was aware that he had put forth his last effort. The wound she had inflicted had gone to the most vital spot; she had prevented his being magnanimous, and the injury was unforgivable. He was glad, yes, actually glad now, to have her know that New York meant to cut her; but, strive as she might, she could not bring herself to care either for the fact, or for his secret pleasure in it. Her own secret pleasures were beyond New York's reach and his.

"I'm sorry," she reiterated gently. He bowed, without trying to take her hand, and left the room.

As the door closed she looked after him with a dazed stare. "He's right, I suppose; I don't realize yet—" She heard the shutting of the outer door, and dropped to the sofa, pressing her hands against her aching eyes. At that moment, for the first time, she asked herself what the next day, and the next, would be like. . .

"If only I cared more about reading," she moaned, remembering how vainly she had tried to acquire her husband's tastes, and how gently and humorously he had smiled at her efforts. "Well—there are always cards; and when I get older, knitting and patience, I suppose. And if everybody cuts me I shan't need any evening dresses. That will be an economy, at any rate," she concluded with a little shiver.

. . . . . .

S HE WAS *bad* . . . always. They used to meet at the Fifth Avenue Hotel."

I must go back now to this phrase of my mother's—the phrase from which, at the opening of my narrative, I broke away for a time in order to project more vividly on the scene that anxious moving vision of Lizzie Hazeldean: a vision in which memories of my one boyish glimpse of her were pieced together with hints collected afterward.

When my mother uttered her condemnatory judgment I was a young man of twenty-one, newly graduated from Harvard, and at home again under the family roof in New York. It was long since I had heard Mrs. Hazeldean spoken of. I had been away, at school and at Harvard, for the greater part of the interval, and in the holidays she was probably not considered a fitting subject of conversation, especially now that my sisters came to the table.

At any rate, I had forgotten everything I might ever have picked up about her when, on the evening after my return, my cousin Hubert Wesson—now towering above me as a pillar of the Knickerbocker Club, and a final authority on the ways of the world—suggested our joining her at the opera.

"Mrs. Hazeldean? But I don't know her. What will she think?"

"That it's all right. Come along. She's the jolliest woman I know. We'll go back afterward and have supper with her— jolliest house I know." Hubert twirled a self-conscious moustache.

We were dining at the Knickerbocker, to which I had just been elected, and the bottle of Pommery we were finishing disposed me to think that nothing could be more fitting for two men of the world than to end their evening in the box of the jolliest woman Hubert knew. I groped for my own moustache, gave a twirl in the void, and followed him, after meticulously sliding my overcoat sleeve around my silk hat as I had seen him do.

But once in Mrs. Hazeldean's box I was only an overgrown

boy again, bathed in such blushes as used, at the same age, to
visit Hubert, forgetting that I had a moustache to twirl, and
knocking my hat from the peg on which I had just hung it, in
my zeal to pick up a programme she had not dropped.

For she was really too lovely—too formidably lovely. I was
used by now to mere unadjectived loveliness, the kind that
youth and spirits hang like a rosy veil over commonplace features, an average outline and a pointless merriment. But this
was something calculated, accomplished, finished—and just a
little worn. It frightened me with my first glimpse of the in-
finity of beauty and the multiplicity of her pit-falls. What!
There were women who need not fear crow's-feet, were more
beautiful for being pale, could let a silver hair or two show
among the dark, and their eyes brood inwardly while they
smiled and chatted? But then no young man was safe for a
moment! But then the world I had hitherto known had been
only a warm pink nursery, while this new one was a place of
darkness, perils and enchantments. . .

It was the next day that one of my sisters asked me where I
had been the evening before, and that I puffed out my chest
to answer: "With Mrs. Hazeldean—at the opera." My
mother looked up, but did not speak till the governess had
swept the girls off; then she said with pinched lips: "Hubert
Wesson took you to Mrs. Hazeldean's box?"

"Yes."

"Well, a young man may go where he pleases. I hear Hubert is still infatuated; it serves Sabina right for not letting
him marry the youngest Lyman girl. But don't mention Mrs.
Hazeldean again before your sisters. . . They say her husband
never knew—I suppose if he *had* she would never have got
old Miss Cecilia Winter's money." And it was then that my
mother pronounced the name of Henry Prest, and added that
phrase about the Fifth Avenue Hotel which suddenly woke
my boyish memories. . .

In a flash I saw again, under its quickly-lowered veil, the
face with the exposed eyes and the frozen smile, and felt
through my grown-up waistcoat the stab to my boy's heart
and the loosened murmur of my soul; felt all this, and at the
same moment tried to relate that former face, so fresh and

clear despite its anguish, to the smiling guarded countenance of Hubert's "jolliest woman I know."

I was familiar with Hubert's indiscriminate use of his one adjective, and had not expected to find Mrs. Hazeldean "jolly" in the literal sense: in the case of the lady he happened to be in love with the epithet simply meant that she justified his choice. Nevertheless, as I compared Mrs. Hazeldean's earlier face to this one, I had my first sense of what may befall in the long years between youth and maturity, and of how short a distance I had travelled on that mysterious journey. If only she would take me by the hand!

I was not wholly unprepared for my mother's comment. There was no other lady in Mrs. Hazeldean's box when we entered; none joined her during the evening, and our hostess offered no apology for her isolation. In the New York of my youth every one knew what to think of a woman who was seen "alone at the opera"; if Mrs. Hazeldean was not openly classed with Fanny Ring, our one conspicuous "professional," it was because, out of respect for her social origin, New York preferred to avoid such juxtapositions. Young as I was, I knew this social law, and had guessed, before the evening was over, that Mrs. Hazeldean was not a lady on whom other ladies called, though she was not, on the other hand, a lady whom it was forbidden to mention to other ladies. So I did mention her, with bravado.

No ladies showed themselves at the opera with Mrs. Hazeldean; but one or two dropped in to the jolly supper announced by Hubert, an entertainment whose jollity consisted in a good deal of harmless banter over broiled canvas-backs and celery, with the best of champagne. These same ladies I sometimes met at her house afterward. They were mostly younger than their hostess, and still, though precariously, within the social pale: pretty trivial creatures, bored with a monotonous prosperity, and yearning for such unlawful joys as cigarettes, plain speaking, and a drive home in the small hours with the young man of the moment. But such daring spirits were few in old New York, their appearances infrequent and somewhat furtive. Mrs. Hazeldean's society consisted mainly of men, men of all ages, from her bald or grey-headed contemporaries to youths of Hubert's accomplished years and raw novices of mine.

A great dignity and decency prevailed in her little circle. It was not the oppressive respectability which weighs on the reformed *déclassée*, but the air of ease imparted by a woman of distinction who has wearied of society and closed her doors to all save her intimates. One always felt, at Lizzie Hazeldean's, that the next moment one's grandmother and aunts might be announced; and yet so pleasantly certain that they wouldn't be.

What is there in the atmosphere of such houses that makes them so enchanting to a fastidious and imaginative youth? Why is it that "those women" (as the others call them) alone know how to put the awkward at ease, check the familiar, smile a little at the over-knowing, and yet encourage naturalness in all? The difference of atmosphere is felt on the very threshold. The flowers grow differently in their vases, the lamps and easy-chairs have found a cleverer way of coming together, the books on the table are the very ones that one is longing to get hold of. The most perilous coquetry may not be in a woman's way of arranging her dress but in her way of arranging her drawing-room; and in this art Mrs. Hazeldean excelled.

I have spoken of books; even then they were usually the first objects to attract me in a room, whatever else of beauty it contained; and I remember, on the evening of that first "jolly supper," coming to an astonished pause before the crowded shelves that took up one wall of the drawing-room. What! The goddess read, then? She could accompany one on those flights too? Lead one, no doubt? My heart beat high. . .

But I soon learned that Lizzie Hazeldean did not read. She turned but languidly even the pages of the last Ouida novel; and I remember seeing Mallock's *New Republic* uncut on her table for weeks. It took me no long time to make the discovery: at my very next visit she caught my glance of surprise in the direction of the rich shelves, smiled, coloured a little, and met it with the confession: "No, I can't read them. I've tried—I *have* tried—but print makes me sleepy. Even novels do. . ." "They" were the accumulated treasures of English poetry, and a rich and varied selection of history, criticism, letters, in English, French and Italian—she spoke these languages, I knew—books evidently assembled by a sensitive and widely-ranging reader. We were alone at the time, and Mrs. Hazeldean went on in a lower tone: "I kept just the few he liked best—my husband, you know." It was the first time that Charles Hazeldean's name had been spoken between us, and my surprise was so great that my candid cheek must have reflected the blush on hers. I had fancied that women in her situation avoided alluding to their husbands. But she continued to look at me, wistfully, humbly almost, as if there were something more that she wanted to say, and was inwardly entreating me to understand.

"He was a great reader: a student. And he tried so hard to make me read too—he wanted to share everything with me. And I *did* like poetry—some poetry—when he read it aloud to me. After his death I thought: 'There'll be his books. I can go back to them—I shall find him there.' And I tried—oh, so hard—but it's no use. They've lost their meaning . . . as most things have." She stood up, lit a cigarette, pushed back a log on the hearth. I felt that she was waiting for me to speak. If life had but taught me how to answer her, what was there of her story I might not have learned? But I was too inexperienced; I could not shake off my bewilderment. What! This woman whom I had been pitying for matrimonial miseries which seemed to justify her seeking solace elsewhere—this woman could speak of her husband in such a tone! I had instantly perceived that the tone was not feigned; and a confused sense of the complexity—or the chaos—of human relations held me as tongue-tied as a schoolboy to whom a problem beyond his grasp is suddenly propounded.

Before the thought took shape she had read it, and with the smile which drew such sad lines about her mouth, had continued gaily: "What are you up to this evening, by the way? What do you say to going to the 'Black Crook' with your cousin Hubert and one or two others? I have a box."

It was inevitable that, not long after this candid confession, I should have persuaded myself that a taste for reading was boring in a woman, and that one of Mrs. Hazeldean's chief charms lay in her freedom from literary pretensions. The truth was, of course, that it lay in her sincerity; in her humble yet fearless estimate of her own qualities and short-comings. I had never met its like in a woman of any age, and coming to me in such early days, and clothed in such looks and intonations, it saved me, in after years, from all peril of meaner beauties.

But before I had come to understand that, or to guess what falling in love with Lizzie Hazeldean was to do for me, I had quite unwittingly and fatuously done the falling. The affair turned out, in the perspective of the years, to be but an incident of our long friendship; and if I touch on it here it is only to illustrate another of my poor friend's gifts. If she could not read books she could read hearts; and she bent a playful yet compassionate gaze on mine while it still floundered in unawareness.

I remember it all as if it were yesterday. We were sitting alone in her drawing-room, in the winter twilight, over the fire. We had reached—in her company it was not difficult—the degree of fellowship when friendly talk lapses naturally into a friendlier silence, and she had taken up the evening paper while I glowered dumbly at the embers. One little foot, just emerging below her dress, swung, I remember, between me and the fire, and seemed to hold her all in the spring of its instep. . .

"Oh," she exclaimed, "poor Henry Prest—". She dropped the paper. "His wife is dead—poor fellow," she said simply.

The blood rushed to my forehead: my heart was in my throat. She had named him—named him at last, the recreant lover, the man who had "dishonoured" her! My hands were clenched: if he had entered the room they would have been at his throat. . .

And then, after a quick interval, I had again the humiliating disheartening sense of not understanding: of being too young, too inexperienced, to know. This woman, who spoke of her deceived husband with tenderness, spoke compassionately of her faithless lover! And she did the one as naturally as the other, not as if this impartial charity were an attitude she had determined to assume, but as if it were part of the lesson life had taught her.

"I didn't know he was married," I growled between my teeth.

She meditated absently. "Married? Oh, yes; when was it? The year after . . ." her voice dropped again . . . "after my husband died. He married a quiet cousin, who had always been in love with him, I believe. They had two boys.—You knew him?" she abruptly questioned.

I nodded grimly.

"People always thought he would never marry—he used to say so himself," she went on, still absently.

I burst out: "The—hound!"

"*Oh!*" she exclaimed. I started up, our eyes met, and hers filled with tears of reproach and understanding. We sat looking at each other in silence. Two of the tears overflowed, hung on her lashes, melted down her cheeks. I continued to stare at her shamefacedly; then I got to my feet, drew out my handkerchief, and tremblingly, reverently, as if I had touched a sacred image, I wiped them away.

My love-making went no farther. In another moment she had contrived to put a safe distance between us. She did not want to turn a boy's head; long since (she told me afterward) such amusements had ceased to excite her. But she did want my sympathy, wanted it overwhelmingly: amid the various feelings she was aware of arousing, she let me see that sympathy, in the sense of a moved understanding, had always been lacking. "But then," she added ingenuously, "I've never really been sure, because I've never told anyone my story. Only I take it for granted that, if I haven't, it's *their* fault rather than mine. . ." She smiled half-deprecatingly, and my bosom swelled, acknowledging the distinction. "And now I want to tell *you*—" she began.

I have said that my love for Mrs. Hazeldean was a brief episode in our long relation. At my age, it was inevitable that it should be so. The "fresher face" soon came, and in its light I saw my old friend as a middle-aged woman, turning grey, with a mechanical smile and haunted eyes. But it was in the first glow of my feeling that she had told me her story; and when the glow subsided, and in the afternoon light of a long intimacy I judged and tested her statements, I found that each detail fitted into the earlier picture.

My opportunities were many; for once she had told the tale she always wanted to be retelling it. A perpetual longing to relive the past, a perpetual need to explain and justify her-self—the satisfaction of these two cravings, once she had permitted herself to indulge them, became the luxury of her empty life. She had kept it empty—emotionally, sentimen-tally empty—from the day of her husband's death, as the guardian of an abandoned temple might go on forever sweep-ing and tending what had once been the god's abode. But this duty performed, she had no other. She had done one great— or abominable—thing; rank it as you please, it had been done heroically. But there was nothing in her to keep her at that height. Her tastes, her interests, her conceivable occupa-tions, were all on the level of a middling domesticity; she did not know how to create for herself any inner life in keeping with that one unprecedented impulse.

Soon after her husband's death, one of her cousins, the Miss Cecilia Winter of Washington Square to whom my mother had referred, had died also, and left Mrs. Hazeldean a handsome legacy. And a year or two later Charles Hazeldean's small estate had undergone the favourable change that befell New York realty in the 'eighties. The property he had be-queathed to his wife had doubled, then tripled, in value; and she found herself, after a few years of widowhood, in posses-sion of an income large enough to supply her with all the luxuries which her husband had struggled so hard to provide. It was the peculiar irony of her lot to be secured from temp-tation when all danger of temptation was over; for she would never, I am certain, have held out the tip of her finger to any man to obtain such luxuries for her own enjoyment. But if she did not value her money for itself, she owed to it—and the service was perhaps greater than she was aware—the power of mitigating her solitude, and filling it with the trivial distractions without which she was less and less able to live.

She had been put into the world, apparently, to amuse men and enchant them; yet, her husband dead, her sacrifice accom-plished, she would have preferred, I am sure, to shut herself up in a lonely monumental attitude, with thoughts and pur-suits on a scale with her one great hour. But what was she to do? She had known of no way of earning money except by her graces; and now she knew no way of filling her days ex-cept with cards and chatter and theatre-going. Not one of the men who approached her passed beyond the friendly barrier she had opposed to me. Of that I was sure. She had not shut out Henry Prest in order to replace him—her face grew white at the suggestion. But what else was there to do, she asked me; what? The days had to be spent somehow; and she was incurably, disconsolately sociable.

So she lived, in a cold celibacy that passed for I don't know what licence; so she lived, withdrawn from us all, yet needing us so desperately, inwardly faithful to her one high impulse, yet so incapable of attuning her daily behaviour to it! And so, at the very moment when she ceased to deserve the blame of society, she found herself cut off from it, and reduced to the status of the "fast" widow noted for her jolly suppers.

I bent bewildered over the depths of her plight. What else, at any stage of her career, could she have done, I often wondered? Among the young women now growing up about me I find none with enough imagination to picture the helpless incapacity of the pretty girl of the 'seventies, the girl without money or vocation, seemingly put into the world only to please, and unlearned in any way of maintaining herself there by her own efforts. Marriage alone could save such a girl from starvation, unless she happened to run across an old lady who wanted her dogs exercised and her *Churchman* read aloud to her. Even the day of painting wild-roses on fans, of colouring photographs to "look like" miniatures, of manufacturing lamp-shades and trimming hats for more fortunate friends— even this precarious beginning of feminine independence had not dawned. It was inconceivable to my mother's generation that a portionless girl should not be provided for by her relations until she found a husband; and that, having found him, she should have to help him to earn a living, was more inconceivable still. The self-sufficing little society of that vanished New York attached no great importance to wealth, but regarded poverty as so distasteful that it simply took no account of it.

These things pleaded in favour of poor Lizzie Hazeldean, though to superficial observers her daily life seemed to belie the plea. She had known no way of smoothing her husband's last years but by being false to him; but once he was dead, she expiated her betrayal by a rigidity of conduct for which she asked no reward but her own inner satisfaction. As she grew older, and her friends scattered, married, or were kept away from one cause or another, she filled her depleted circle with a less fastidious hand. One met in her drawing-room dull men, common men, men who too obviously came there because they were not invited elsewhere, and hoped to use her as a social stepping-stone. She was aware of the difference—her eyes said so whenever I found one of these newcomers installed in my arm-chair—but never, by word or sign, did she admit it. She said to me once: "You find it duller here than it used to be. It's my fault, perhaps; I think I knew better how to draw out my old friends." And another day: "Remember, the people you meet here now come out of kindness. I'm an old woman, and I consider nothing else." That was all.

She went more assiduously than ever to the theatre and the opera; she performed for her friends a hundred trivial services; in her eagerness to be always busy she invented superfluous attentions, oppressed people by offering assistance they did not need, verged at times—for all her tact—on the officiousness of the desperately lonely. At her little suppers she surprised us with exquisite flowers and novel delicacies. The champagne and cigars grew better and better as the quality of the guests declined; and sometimes, as the last of her dull company dispersed, I used to see her, among the scattered ash-trays and liqueur decanters, turn a stealthy glance at her reflection in the mirror, with haggard eyes which seemed to ask: "Will even *these* come back tomorrow?"

I should be loth to leave the picture at this point; my last vision of her is more satisfying. I had been away, travelling for a year at the other end of the world; the day I came back I ran across Hubert Wesson at my club. Hubert had grown pompous and heavy. He drew me into a corner, and said, turning red, and glancing cautiously over his shoulder: "Have you seen our old friend Mrs. Hazeldean? She's very ill, I hear."

I was about to take up the "I hear"; then I remembered that in my absence Hubert had married, and that his caution was probably a tribute to his new state. I hurried at once to Mrs. Hazeldean's; and on her door-step, to my surprise, I ran against a Catholic priest, who looked gravely at me, bowed and passed out.

I was unprepared for such an encounter, for my old friend had never spoken to me of religious matters. The spectacle of her father's career had presumably shaken whatever incipient faith was in her; though in her little-girlhood, as she often told me, she had been as deeply impressed by Dr. Winter's eloquence as any grown-up member of his flock. But now, as soon as I laid eyes on her, I understood. She was very ill, she was visibly dying; and in her extremity, fate, not always kind, had sent her the solace which she needed. Had some obscure inheritance of religious feeling awaked in her? Had she remembered that her poor father, after his long life of mental and moral vagabondage, had finally found rest in the ancient fold? I never knew the explanation—she probably never knew it herself.

But she knew that she had found what she wanted. At last she could talk of Charles, she could confess her sin, she could be absolved of it. Since cards and suppers and chatter were over, what more blessed barrier could she find against solitude? All her life, henceforth, was a long preparation for that daily hour of expansion and consolation. And then this merciful visitor, who understood her so well, could also tell her things about Charles: knew where he was, how he felt, what exquisite daily attentions could still be paid to him, and how, with all unworthiness washed away, she might at last hope to reach him. Heaven could never seem strange, so interpreted; each time that I saw her, during the weeks of her slow fading, she was more and more like a traveller with her face turned homeward, yet smilingly resigned to await her summons. The house no longer seemed lonely, nor the hours tedious; there had even been found for her, among the books she had so often tried to read, those books which had long looked at her with such hostile faces, two or three (they were always on her bed) containing messages from the world where Charles was waiting.

Thus provided and led, one day she went to him.

THE END

THE MOTHER'S RECOMPENSE

Desolation is a delicate thing.
SHELLEY.

My excuses are due to the decorous shade of Grace Aguilar, loved of our grandmothers, for deliberately appropriating, and applying to uses so different, the title of one of the most admired of her tales.

E. W.

I.

KATE CLEPHANE was wakened, as usual, by the slant of Riviera sun across her bed.

It was the thing she liked best about her shabby cramped room in the third-rate Hôtel de Minorque et de l'Univers: that the morning sun came in at her window, and yet that it didn't come too early.

No more sunrises for Kate Clephane. They were associated with too many lost joys—coming home from balls where one had danced one's self to tatters, or from suppers where one had lingered, counting one's winnings (it was wonderful, in the old days, how often she had won, or friends had won for her, staking a *louis* just for fun, and cramming her hands with thousand franc bills); associated, too, with the scramble up hill through the whitening gray of the garden, flicked by scented shrubs, caught on perfidious prickles, up to the shuttered villa askew on its heat-soaked rock—and then, at the door, in the laurustinus-shade that smelt of honey, that unexpected kiss (well honestly, yes, unexpected, since it had long been settled that one was to remain "just friends"); and the pulling away from an insistent arm, and the one more pressure on hers of lips young enough to be fresh after a night of drinking and play and more drinking. And she had never let Chris come in with her at that hour, no, not once, though at the time there was only Julie the cook in the house, and goodness knew. . . Oh, but she had always had her pride—people ought to remember *that* when they said such things about her. . .

That was what the sunrise reminded Kate Clephane of—as she supposed it did most women of forty-two or so (or was it really forty-four last week?) For nearly twenty years now she had lived chiefly with women of her own kind, and she no longer very sincerely believed there were any others, that is to say among women properly so called. Her female world was made up of three categories: frumps, hypocrites and the "good sort"—like herself. After all, the last was the one she preferred to be in.

Not that she could not picture another life—if only one had met the right man at the right hour. She remembered her one week—that tiny little week of seven days, just six years ago—when she and Chris had gone together to a lost place in Normandy where there wasn't a railway within ten miles, and you had to drive in the farmer's cart to the farm-house smothered in apple-blossoms; and Chris and she had gone off every morning for the whole day, while he sketched by willowy river-banks, and under the flank of mossy village churches; and every day for seven days she had watched the farm-yard life waking at dawn under their windows, while she dashed herself with cold water and did her hair and touched up her face before he was awake, because the early light is so pitiless after thirty. She remembered it all, and how sure she had been then that she was meant to live on a farm and keep chickens; just as sure as he was that he was meant to be a painter, and would already have made a name if his parents hadn't called him back to Baltimore and shoved him into a broker's office after Harvard—to have him off their minds, as he said.

Yes, she could still picture that kind of life: every fibre in her kept its glow. But she didn't believe in it; she knew now that "things didn't happen like that" for long, that reality and durability were attributes of the humdrum, the prosaic and the dreary. And it was to escape from reality and durability that one plunged into cards, gossip, flirtation, and all the artificial excitements which society so lavishly provides for people who want to forget.

She and Chris had never repeated that week. He had never suggested doing so, and had let her hints fall unheeded, or turned them off with a laugh, whenever she tried, with shy tentative allusions, to coax him back to the idea; for she had found out early that one could never ask him anything point-blank—it just put his back up, as he said himself. One had to manœuvre and wait; but when didn't a woman have to manœuvre and wait? Ever since she had left her husband, eighteen years ago, what else had she ever done? Sometimes, nowadays, waking alone and unrefreshed in her dreary hotel room, she shivered at the memory of all the scheming, planning, ignoring, enduring, accepting, which had led her in the end to—this.

Ah, well—

"Aline!"

After all, there was the sun in her window, there was the triangular glimpse of blue wind-bitten sea between the roofs, and a new day beginning, and hot chocolate coming, and a new hat to try on at the milliner's, and—

"Aline!"

She had come to this cheap hotel just in order to keep her maid. One couldn't afford everything, especially since the war, and she preferred veal for dinner every night to having to do her own mending and dress her hair: the unmanageable abundant hair which had so uncannily survived her youth, and sometimes, in her happier moods, made her feel that perhaps, after all, in the eyes of her friends, other of its attributes survived also. And besides, it looked better for a lone woman who, after having been thirty-nine for a number of years, had suddenly become forty-four, to have a respectable-looking servant in the background; to be able, for instance, when one arrived in new places, to say to supercilious hotel-clerks: "My maid is following with the luggage."

"Aline!"

Aline, ugly, neat and enigmatic, appeared with the breakfast-tray. A delicious scent preceded her.

Mrs. Clephane raised herself on a pink elbow, shook her hair over her shoulders, and exclaimed: "Violets?"

Aline permitted herself her dry smile. "From a gentleman."

Colour flooded her mistress's face. Hadn't she known that something good was going to happen to her that morning—hadn't she felt it in every touch of the sunshine, as its golden finger-tips pressed her lids open and wound their way through her hair? She supposed she was superstitious. She laughed expectantly.

"A gentleman?"

"The little lame boy with the newspapers that Madame was kind to," the maid continued, arranging the tray with her spare Taylorized gestures.

"Oh, poor child!" Mrs. Clephane's voice had a quaver which she tried to deflect to the lame boy, though she knew how impossible it was to deceive Aline. Of course Aline knew everything—well, yes, that was the other side of the medal. She often said to her mistress: "Madame is too much alone—Madame ought to make some new friends—" and what did that mean, except that Aline knew she had lost the old ones?

But it was characteristic of Kate that, after a moment, the quaver in her voice did instinctively tilt in the direction of the lame boy who sold newspapers; and when the tears reached her eyes it was over his wistful image, and not her own, that they flowed. She had a way of getting desperately fond of people she had been kind to, and exaggeratedly touched by the least sign of their appreciation. It was her weakness—or her strength: she wondered which?

"Poor, poor little chap. But his mother'll beat him if she finds out. Aline, you must hunt him up this very day and pay back what the flowers must have cost him." She lifted the violets and pressed them to her face. As she did so she caught sight of a telegram beneath them.

A telegram—for her? It didn't often happen nowadays. But after all there was no reason why it shouldn't happen once again—at least once. There was no reason why, this very day, this day on which the sunshine had waked her with such a promise, there shouldn't be a message at last, the message for which she had waited for two years, three years; yes, exactly three years and one month—just a word from him to say: *"Take me back."*

She snatched up the telegram, and then turned her head toward the wall, seeking, while she read, to hide her face from Aline. The maid, on whom such hints were never lost, immediately transferred her attention to the dressing-table, skilfully deploying the glittering troops on that last battlefield where the daily struggle still renewed itself.

Aline's eyes averted, her mistress tore open the blue fold and read: "Mrs. Clephane dead—"

A shiver ran over her. *Mrs. Clephane dead?* Not if Mrs. Clephane knew it! Never more alive than today, with the sun crisping her hair, the violet scent enveloping her, and that jolly north-west gale rioting out there on the Mediterranean. What was the meaning of this grim joke?

The first shock over, she read on more calmly and understood. It was the other Mrs. Clephane who was dead: the one who used to be her mother-in-law. Her first thought was: "Well, serve her right"—since, if it was so desirable to be alive on such a morning it must be correspondingly undesirable to be dead, and she could draw the agreeable conclusion that the other Mrs. Clephane had at last been come up with—oh, but thoroughly.

She lingered awhile on this pleasing fancy, and then began to reach out to wider inferences. "But if—but if—but little Anne—"

At the murmur of the name her eyes filled again. For years now she had barricaded her heart against her daughter's presence; and here it was, suddenly in possession again, crowding out everything else, yes, effacing even Chris as though he were the thinnest of ghosts, and the cable in her hand a cockcrow. "But perhaps now they'll let me see her," the mother thought.

She didn't even know who "they" were, now that their formidable chieftain, her mother-in-law, was dead. Lawyers, judges, trustees, guardians, she supposed—all the natural enemies of woman. She wrinkled her brows, trying to remember who, at the death of the child's father, had been appointed the child's other guardian—old Mrs. Clephane's overpowering assumption of the office having so completely effaced her associate that it took a few minutes to fish him up out of the far-off past.

"Why, poor old Fred Landers, of course!" She smiled retrospectively. "I don't believe he'd prevent my seeing the child if he were left to himself. Besides, isn't she nearly grown up? Why, I do believe she must be."

The telegram fell from her hands, both of which she now impressed into a complicated finger-reckoning of how old little Anne must be, if Chris were thirty-three, as he certainly was—no, thirty-one, he couldn't be more than thirty-one, because *she*, Kate, was only forty-two . . . yes, forty-two . . . and she'd always acknowledged to herself that there were nine years between them; no, eleven years, if she were really forty-two; yes, but was she? Or, goodness, was she actually forty-five? Well, then, if she was forty-five—just supposing it for a minute—and had married John Clephane at twenty-one, as she knew she had, and little Anne had been born the second summer afterward, then little Anne must be nearly twenty . . . why, quite twenty, wasn't it? But then, how old would *that* make Chris? Oh, well, he *must* be older than he looked . . . she'd always thought he was. That boyish way of his, she had sometimes fancied, was put on to make her imagine there was a greater difference of age between them than there really was—a device he was perfectly capable of making use of for ulterior purposes. And of course she'd never been that dreadful kind of woman they called a "baby-snatcher". . . But if Chris were thirty-one, and she forty-five, then how old *was* Anne?

With impatient fingers she began all over again.

The maid's voice, seeming to come from a long way off, respectfully reminded her that the chocolate would be getting cold. Mrs. Clephane roused herself, looked about the room, and exclaimed: "My looking-glass, please." She wanted to settle that question of ages.

As Aline approached with the glass there was a knock at the door. The maid went to it, and came back with her small inward smile.

"Another telegram."

Another? This time Mrs. Clephane sat bolt upright. What could it be, now, but a word from him, a message at last? Oh, but she was ashamed of herself for thinking of such a thing at such a moment. Solitude had demoralized her, she supposed. And then her child was so far away, so invisible, so unknown—and Chris of a sudden had become so near and real again, though it was three whole years and one month since he had left her. And at her age— She opened the second message, trembling. Since Armistice Day her heart had not beat so hard.

"New York. Dearest mother," it ran, "I want you to come home at once. I want you to come and live with me. Your daughter Anne."

"You asked for the looking-glass, Madame," Aline patiently reminded her.

Mrs. Clephane took the proffered glass, stared into it with eyes at first unseeing, and then gradually made out the reflection of her radiant irrepressible hair, a new smile on her lips, the first streak of gray on her temples, and the first tears—oh, she couldn't remember for how long—running down over her transfigured face.

"Aline—" The maid was watching her with narrowed eyes. "The Rachel powder, please—"

Suddenly she dropped the glass and the powder-puff, buried her face in her hands, and sobbed.

II.

S HE WENT OUT an hour later, her thoughts waltzing and eddying like the sunlit dust which the wind kept whirling round the corners in spasmodic gusts. Everything in her mind was hot and cold, and beating and blowing about, like the weather on that dancing draughty day; the very pavement of the familiar streets, and the angles of the buildings, seemed to be spinning with the rest, as if the heaviest substances had suddenly grown imponderable.

"It must," she thought, "be a little like the way the gravestones will behave on the Day of Judgment."

To make sure of where she was she had to turn down one of the white streets leading to the sea, and fix her eyes on that wedge of blue between the houses, as if it were the only ballast to her brain, the only substantial thing left. "I'm glad it's one of the days when the sea is firm," she thought. The glittering expanse, flattened by the gale and solidified by the light, rose up to meet her as she walked toward it, the pavement lifting her and flying under her like wings till it dropped her down in the glare of the Promenade, where the top-knots of the struggling palms swam on the wind like chained and long-finned sea-things against that sapphire wall climbing half-way up the sky.

She sat down on a bench, clinging sideways as if lashed to a boat's deck, and continued to steady her eyes on the Mediterranean. To collect her thoughts she tried to imagine that nothing had happened, that neither of the two cables had come, and that she was preparing to lead her usual life, as mapped out in the miniature engagement-book in her handbag. She had her "set" now in the big Riviera town where she had taken refuge in 1916, after the final break with Chris, and where, after two years of war-work and a "Reconnaissance Française" medal, she could carry her head fairly high, and even condescend a little to certain newcomers.

She drew forth the engagement-book, smiling at her childish game of "pretending." At eleven, a hat to try on; eleven-thirty, a dress; from then to two o'clock, nothing; at two, a slow solemn drive with poor old Mrs. Minity (in the last-surviving private victoria in the town); tea and bridge at Countess Lanska's from four to six; a look in at the Rectory of the American church, where there was a Ladies' Guild meeting about the Devastated Regions' Fancy Fair; lastly a little dinner at the Casino, with the Horace Betterlys and a few other pals. Yes—a rather-better-than-the-average day. And now— Why, now she could kick over the whole apple-cart if she chose; chuck it all (except the new dress and hat!): the tedious drive with the prosy patronizing old woman; the bridge, which was costing her more than it ought, with that third-rate cosmopolitan set of Laura Lanska's; the long dis-cussion at the Rectory as to whether it would "do" to ask Mrs. Schlachtberger to take a stall at the Fair in spite of her unfortunate name; and the little dinner with the Horace Bet-terlys and their dull noisy friends, who wanted to "see life" and didn't know that you can't see it unless you've first had the brains to imagine it. . . Yes, she could drop it all now, and never never see one of them again . . .

"My daughter . . . my daughter Anne. . . Oh, you don't know my little girl? She *has* changed, hasn't she? Growing up is a way the children have. . . Yes, it is ageing for a poor mother to trot about such a young giantess . . . Oh, I'm going gray already, you know—here, on the temples. *Fred Landers?* It is you, really? Dear old Fred! No, of course I've never forgotten you . . . Known me anywhere? You would? Oh, nonsense! Look at my gray hair. But *men* don't change— lucky men! Why, I remember even that Egyptian seal-ring of yours. . . My daughter . . . my daughter Anne . . . let me introduce you to this big girl of mine . . . my little Anne. . ."

It was curious: for the first time she realized that, in think-ing back over the years since she had been parted from Anne, she seldom, nowadays, went farther than the episode with Chris. Yet it was long before—it was eighteen years ago— that she had "lost" Anne: "lost" was the euphemism she had invented (as people called the Furies The Amiable Ones), be-cause a mother couldn't confess, even to her most secret self, that she had willingly deserted her child. Yet that was what she had done; and now her thoughts, shrinking and shiver-ing, were being forced back upon the fact. She had left Anne when Anne was a baby of three; left her with a dreadful pang, a rending of the inmost fibres, and yet a sense of unutterable relief, because to do so was to escape from the oppression of her married life, the thick atmosphere of self-approval and un-perceivingness which emanated from John Clephane like coal-gas from a leaking furnace. So she had put it at the time—so, in her closest soul-scrutiny, she had to put it still. "I couldn't breathe—" that was all she had to say in her own defence. She had said it first—more's the pity—to Hylton Davies; with the result that two months later she was on his yacht, headed for the West Indies . . . And even then she couldn't breathe any better; not after the first week or two. The as-phyxiation was of a different kind, that was all.

It was a year later that she wrote to her husband. There was no answer: she wrote again. "At any rate, let me see Anne. . . I can't live without Anne. . . I'll go and live with her any-where you decide. . ." Again no answer. . . She wrote to her mother-in-law, and Mrs. Clephane's lawyer sent the letter back unopened. She wrote, in her madness, to the child's nurse, and got a reply from the same legal firm, requesting her to cease to annoy her husband's family. She ceased.

Of all this she recalled now only the parting from Anne, and the subsequent vain efforts to recover her. Of the agent of her release, of Hylton Davies, she remembered, in the deep sense of remembering, nothing. He had become to her, with his flourish and his yachting-clothes, and the big shining yacht, and the cocoa-palms and general setting of cool drinks and tropical luxury, as unreal as somebody in a novel, the highly coloured hero (or villain) on the "jacket". From her inmost life he had vanished into a sort of remote pictorial perspective, where a woman of her name figured with him, in muslin dresses and white sunshades, herself as unreal as a lady on a "jacket". . . Dim also had grown the years that fol-lowed: lonely humdrum years at St.-Jean-de-Luz, at Bordi-ghera, at Dinard. She would settle in a cheap place where there were a circulating library, a mild climate, a few quiet bridge-playing couples whom one got to know through the doctor or the clergyman; then would grow tired and drift away again. Once she went back to America, at the time of her mother's death. . . It was in midsummer, and Anne (now ten years old) was in Canada with her father and grand-mother. Kate Clephane, not herself a New Yorker, and with only two or three elderly and disapproving relatives left in the small southern city of her origin, stood alone before the elaborately organized defences of a vast New York clan, and knew herself helpless. But in her madness she dreamed of a dash to Canada, an abduction—schemes requiring money, friends, support, all the power and ruse she was so lacking in. She gave that up in favour of a midnight visit (inspired by *Anna Karénine*) to the child's nursery; but on the way to Quebec she heard that the family had left in a private car for the Rocky Mountains. She turned about and took the first steamer to France.

All this, too, had become dim to her since she had known Chris. For the first time, when she met him, her soul's lungs seemed full of air. Life still dated for her from that day—in spite of the way he had hurt her, of his having inflicted on her the bitterest pain she had ever suffered, he had yet given her more than he could take away. At thirty-nine her real self had been born; without him she would never have had a self. . . And yet, at what a cost she had bought it! All the secluded penitential years that had gone before wiped out at a stroke—stained, defiled by follies she could not bear to think of, among people from whom her soul recoiled. Poor Chris! It was not that he was what is called "vicious"—but he was never happy without what he regarded as excitement; he was always telling her that an artist had to have excitement. She could not reconcile his idea of what this stimulus consisted in with his other tastes and ideas—with that flashing play of intelligence which had caught her up into an air she had never breathed before. To be capable of that thought-play, of those flights, and yet to need gambling, casinos, rowdy crowds, and all the pursuits devised to kill time for the uninventive and lethargic! He said he saw things in that kind of life that she couldn't see—but since he also saw this unseeable (and she knew he did) in nature, in poetry and painting, in their shared sunsets and moonrises, in their first long dreaming days, far from jazz-bands and baccarat tables, why wasn't that enough, and how could the other rubbishy things excite the same kind of emotions in him? It had been the torment of her torments, the inmost pang of her misery, that she had never understood; and that when she thought of him now it was through that blur of noise and glare and popping corks and screaming bands that she had to grope back to the first fleeting Chris who had loved her and waked her.

At eleven o'clock she found herself, she didn't know how, at the milliner's. Other women, envious or undecided, were already flattening their noses against the panes. "That bird of Paradise . . . what they cost nowadays!" But she went in, cool and confident, and asked gaily to try on her new hat. She must have been smiling, for the sales-woman received her with a smile.

"What a complexion, ma'am! One sees you're not afraid of the wind."

But when the hat was produced, though it was the copy of one she had already tried on, it struck Mrs. Clephane as absurdly youthful, even ridiculous. Had she really been dressing all this time like a girl in her teens?

"You forget that I've a grown-up daughter, Madame Berthe."

"Allons, Madame plaisante!"

She drew herself up with dignity. "A daughter of twenty-one; I'm joining her in New York next week. What would she think of me if I arrived in a hat more youthful than hers? Show me something darker, please: yes, the one with the autumn leaves. See, I'm growing gray on the temples—don't try to make me look like a flapper. What's the price of that blue fox over there? I like a gray fur with gray hair."

In the end she stalked out, offended by the milliner's refusal to take her gray hair seriously, and reflecting, with a retrospective shiver, that her way of dressing and her demeanour must have thoroughly fixed in all these people's minds the idea that she was one of the silly vain fools who imagine they look like their own daughters.

At the dress-maker's, the scene repeated itself. The dashing little frock prepared for her—an orange silk handkerchief peeping from the breast-pocket on which an anchor was embroidered—made her actually blush; and reflecting that money wouldn't "matter" now (the thought of the money had really not come to her before) she persuaded the dressmaker to take the inappropriate garment back, and ordered, instead, something sober but elaborate, and ever so much more expensive. It seemed a part of the general unreal rapture that even the money-worry should have vanished.

Where should she lunch? She inclined to a quiet restaurant in a back street; then the old habit of following the throng, the need of rubbing shoulders with a crowd of unknown people, swept her automatically toward the Casino, and sat her down, in a blare of brass instruments and hard sunshine, at the only table left. After all, as she had often heard Chris say, one could feel more alone in a crowd. . . But gradually it came over her that to feel alone was not in the least what she wanted. She had never, for years at any rate, been able to bear it for long; the crowd, formerly a solace and an escape, had become a habit, and being face to face with her own thoughts was like facing a stranger. Oppressed and embarrassed, she tried to "make conversation" with herself; but the soundless words died unuttered, and she sought distraction in staring about her at the unknown faces.

Their number became oppressive: it made her feel small and insignificant to think that, of all this vulgar feasting throng, not one knew the amazing thing which had befallen her, knew that she was awaited by an only daughter in a big house in New York, a house she would re-enter in a few days—yes, actually in a few days—with the ease of a long-absent mistress, a mistress returning from an immense journey, but to whom it seems perfectly natural and familiar to be once again smiling on old friends from the head of her table.

The longing to be with people to whom she could tell her news made her decide, after all, to live out her day as she had originally planned it. Before leaving the hotel she had announced her departure to the astonished Aline (it was agreeable, for once, to astonish Aline) and despatched her to the post office with a cable for New York and a telegram for a Paris steamship company. In the cable she had said simply: "Coming darling." They were the words with which she used to answer little Anne's calls from the nursery: that impatient reiterated "Mummy—Mummy—I want my *Mummy!*" which had kept on echoing in her ears through so many sleepless nights. The phrase had flashed into her head the moment she sat down to write the cable, and she had kept murmuring to herself ever since: "Mummy—Mummy—I want my *Mummy!*" She would have liked to quote the words to Mrs. Minity, whose door she was now approaching; but how could she explain to the old lady, who was deaf and self-absorbed, and thought it a privilege for any one to go driving with her, why little Anne's cry had echoed so long in the void? No; she could not speak of that to any one: she must stick to her old "take-it-for-granted" attitude, the attitude which had carried her successfully over so many slippery places.

Mrs. Minity was very much pre-occupied about her foot-warmer. She spent the first quarter of an hour in telling Mrs. Clephane that the Rector's wife, whom she had taken out the day before, had possessed herself of the object without so much as a "may I," and kept her big feet on it till Mrs. Minity had had to stop the carriage and ask the coachman in a loud voice how it was that *The Foot-warmer* had not been put in as usual. Whereupon, if you please, Mrs. Merriman had simply said: "Oh, I have it, thanks, dear Mrs. Minity—such a comfort, on these windy days!" "Though why a woman who keeps no carriage, and has to tramp the streets at all hours, should have cold feet I can't imagine—nor, in fact, wholly believe her when she says so," said Mrs. Minity, in the tone of one to whom a defective circulation is the recognized prerogative of carriage-owners. "I notice, my dear, that *you* never complain of being cold," she added approvingly, relegating Kate, as an enforced pedestrian, to Mrs. Merriman's class, but acknowledging in her a superior sense of propriety. "I'm always glad," she added, "to take you out on windy days, for battling with the *mistral* on foot must be so very exhausting, and in the carriage, of course, it is so easy to reach a sheltered place."

Mrs. Minity was still persuaded that to sit in her hired victoria, behind its somnolent old pair, was one of the most rapid modes of progression devised by modern science. She talked as if her carriage were an aeroplane, and was as particular in avoiding narrow streets, and waiting at the corner when she called for friends who lived in them, as if she had to choose a safe alighting-ground.

Mrs. Minity had come to the Riviera thirty years before, after an attack of bronchitis, and finding the climate milder and the life easier than in Brooklyn, had not gone back. Mrs. Clephane never knew what roots she had broken in the upheaval, for everything immediately surrounding her assumed such colossal proportions that remoter facts, even concerning herself, soon faded to the vanishing-point. Only now and then, when a niece from Bridgeport sent her a bottle of brandy-peaches, or a nephew from Brooklyn wrote to say that her income had been reduced by the foreclosure of a mortgage, did the family emerge from its transatlantic mists, and Mrs. Minity become, for a moment, gratified or irate at the intrusion. But such emotions, at their acutest, were but faint shadows of those aroused by the absence of her foot-warmer, or the Salvation Army's having called twice in the same month for her subscription, or one of the horses having a stiff shoulder, and being replaced, for a long hazardous week, by another, known to the same stable for twenty years, and whom the *patron* himself undertook to drive, so that Mrs. Minity should not miss her airing. She *had* thought of staying in till her *own* horse recovered; but the doctor had absolutely forbidden it, so she had taken her courage in both hands, and gone out with the substitute, who was not even of the same colour as the horse she was used to. "But I took valerian every night," she added, "and doubled my digitalis."

Kate Clephane, as she listened (for the hundredth time), remembered that she had once thought Mrs. Minity a rather impressive old lady, somewhat arrogant and very prosy, but with a distinct "atmosphere," and a charming half-obsolete vocabulary, suggesting "Signers" and Colonial generals, which was a refreshing change from the over-refinement of Mrs. Merriman and the Betterlys' monotonous slang. Now, compared to certain long-vanished figures of the Clephane background—compared even to the hated figure of old Mrs. Clephane—Mrs. Minity shrank to the semblance of a vulgar fussy old woman.

"Old Mrs. Clephane never bragged, whatever she did,"

Kate thought: "how ridiculous all that fuss about driving behind a strange horse would have seemed to her. After all, good breeding, even in the odious, implies a certain courage. . ." Her mother-in-law, as she mused, assumed the commanding yet not unamiable shape of a Roman matron of heroic mould, a kind of "It-hurts-not-O-my-Pætus," falling first upon the sword.

The bridge-players in Countess Lanska's pastille-scented and smoke-blurred drawing-room seemed to have undergone the same change as Mrs. Minity. The very room, as Kate entered, on fire from the wind, seemed stuffier, untidier and, yes—vulgarer—than she had remembered. The empty glasses with drowned lemon-peel, the perpetually unemptied ash-trays, the sketches by the Countess's latest protégé—splashy flower markets, rococo churches, white balustrades, umbrella-pines and cobalt seas—the musical instruments tossed about on threadbare cashmere shawls covering still more threadbare sofas, even the heart-rending gaze of the outspread white bear with the torn-off ear which, ever since Kate had known him, had clung to his flattened head by the same greasy thread: all this disorder was now, for the first time, reflected in the faces about the card-tables. Not one of them, men or women, if asked where they had come from, where they were going, or why they had done such and such things, or refrained from doing such other, would have answered truthfully; not, as Kate knew, from any particular, or at any rate permanent, need of concealment, but because they lived in a chronic state of mental inaccuracy, excitement and inertia, which made it vaguely exhilarating to lie and definitely fatiguing to be truthful.

She had not meant to stay long, for her first glance at their new faces told her that to them also she would not be able to speak of what had happened. But, to subdue her own agitation and divert their heavy eyes, the easiest thing was to take her usual hand at bridge; and once she had dropped into her place, the familiar murmur of "No trumps . . . yes . . . diamonds. . . Who dealt? . . . No bid . . . No . . . yes . . . no . . .", held her to her seat, soothed by the mesmeric touch of habit.

*   *   *

At the Rectory Mrs. Merriman exclaimed: "Oh, *there* she is!" in a tone implying that she had had to stand between Mrs. Clephane and the assembled committee.

Kate remembered that she was secretary, and expected to read the minutes.

"Have I kept you all waiting? So sorry," she beamed, in a voice that sang hallelujahs. Mrs. Merriman pushed the book toward her with a protecting smile; and Mrs. Parley Plush of the Villa Mimosa (she always told you it had been quite her own idea, calling it that) visibly wondered that Mrs. Merriman should be so tolerant.

They were all there: the American Consul's wife, mild, plump and irreproachable; the lovely Mrs. Prentiss of San Francisco, who "took things" and had been involved in a drug scandal; the Comtesse de Sainte Maxime, who had been a Loach of Philadelphia, and had figured briefly on the operatic stage; the Consul's sister, who dressed like a flapper, and had been engaged during the war to a series of American officers, all of whom seemed to have given her celluloid bangles; and a pale Mrs. Marsh, who used to be seen about with a tall tired man called "the Colonel", whose family-name was not Marsh, but for whom she wore mourning when he died, explaining—somewhat belatedly—that he was a cousin. Lastly, there was Mrs. Fred Langly of Albany, whose husband was "wanted" at home for misappropriation of funds, and who, emerging from the long seclusion consequent on this unfortunate episode, had now blossomed into a "prominent war-worker", while Mr. Langly devoted himself to the composition of patriotic poems, which he read (flanked by the civil and military authorities) at all the allied Inaugurations and Commemorations; so that by the close of the war he had become its recognized bard, and his "Lafayette, can we forget?" was quoted with tears by the very widows and orphans he had defrauded. Facing Mrs. Merriman sat the Rector, in clerical pepper-and-salt clothes and a secular pepper-and-salt moustache, talking cheerful slang in a pulpit voice.

Mrs. Clephane looked about her with new eyes. Save for their hostess, the Consul's wife and Mrs. Langly, "things" had been said of all the women; even concerning Mrs. Parley

Plush, the older inhabitants (though they all went to her teas at the Villa Mimosa) smiled and hinted. And they all knew each other's stories, or at least the current versions, and affected to disapprove of each other and yet be tolerant; thus following the example of Mrs. Merriman, who simply wouldn't *listen* to any of those horrors, and of Mr. Merriman, whose principle it was to "believe the best" till the worst stared him in the face, and then to say: "I understand it all happened a long while ago."

To all of them the Rectory was a social nucleus. One after another they had found their way there, subscribed to parochial charities, sent Mrs. Merriman fruit and flowers, and suppressed their yawns at Mothers' Meetings and Sewing Circles. It was part of the long long toll they had to pay to the outraged goddess of Respectability. And at the Rectory they had made each other's acquaintance, and thus gradually widened their circle, and saved more hours from solitude, their most dreaded enemy. Kate Clephane knew it all by heart: for eighteen years she had trodden that round. The Rector knew too; if ever a still youngish and still prettyish woman, in quiet but perfect clothes with a scent of violets, asked to see him after service, he knew she was one more recruit. In all the fashionable Riviera colonies these ladies were among the staunchest supporters of their respective churches. Even the oldest, stoutest, grimmest of his flock had had her day; Mr. Merriman remembered what his predecessor had hinted of old Mrs. Orbitt's past, and how he had smiled at the idea, seeing Mrs. Orbitt, that first Sunday, planted in her front pew like a very Deborah.

Some of the prettiest—or who had been, at least—exchanged parishes, as it were; like that sweet Lady de Tracey, who joined the American fold, while Miss Julia Jettridge, from New York, attended the Anglican services. They both said it was because they preferred "the nearest church"; but the Rector knew better than that.

Then the war came; the war which, in those bland southern places and to those uprooted drifting women, was chiefly a healing and amalgamating influence. It was awful, of course, to admit even to one's self that it could be that; but, in the light of her own deliverance, Kate Clephane knew that she and all the others had so viewed it. They had shuddered and wept, toiled hard, and made their sacrifices; of clothes and bridge, of butter and sweets and carriage-hire—but all the while they were creeping slowly back into the once impregnable stronghold of Social Position, getting to know people who used to cut them, being invited to the Préfecture and the Consulate, and lots of houses of which they used to say with feigned indifference: "Go to *those* dreary people? Not for the world!" because they knew they had no chance of getting there.

Yes: the war had brought them peace, strange and horrible as it was to think it. Kate's eyes filled as she looked about the table at those haggard powdered masks which had once glittered with youth and insolence and pleasure. All they wanted now was what she herself wanted only a few short hours ago: to be bowed to when they caught certain people's eyes; to be invited to one more dull house; to be put on the Rector's Executive Committees, and pour tea at the Consuless's "afternoons".

"May I?" a man's voice fluted; and a noble silver-thatched head with a beak-like nose and soft double chin was thrust into the doorway.

"Oh, Mr. Paly!" cried Mrs. Merriman; and murmured to the nearest ladies: "For the music— I thought he'd better come today."

Every one greeted Mr. Paly with enthusiasm. It *was* poky, being only women and the Rector. And Mr. Paly had the dearest little flat in one of the old houses of the "Vieux Port", such a tiny flat that one wondered how any one so large, manly and yet full of quick womanish movements, managed to fit in between the bric-a-brac. Mr. Paly clasped his hostess's hand in a soft palm. "I've brought my young friend Lion Carstairs; you won't mind? He's going to help me with the programme."

But one glance at Mr. Carstairs made it clear that he did not mean to help any one with anything. He held out two lax fingers to Mrs. Merriman, sank into an armchair, and let his Antinous-lids droop over his sullen deep gray eyes. "He's awfully good on Sicilian music . . . noted down folk-songs at Taormina. . ." Mr. Paly whispered, his leonine head with its

bushy eye-brows and silver crown bending confidentially to
his neighbour.

"Order!" rapped the Rector; and the meeting began.

At the Casino that night Kate Clephane, on the whole,
was more bored than at the Rectory. After all, at the Merrimans' there was a rather anxious atmosphere of kindliness,
of a desire to help, and a retrospective piety about the war
which had served them such a good turn, and of which they
were still trying, in their tiny measure, to alleviate the ravages.

Whereas the Betterlys—

"What? Another begging-list? No, my dear Kate; you
don't! Stony-broke; that's what I am, and so's Harry—ain't
you, Harry?" Marcia Betterly would scream, clanking her jewelled bangles, twisting one heavy hand through her pearls,
and clutching with the other the platinum-and-diamond
wrist-bag on which she always jokingly pretended that Kate
Clephane had her eye. "Look out, Sid, she's a regular train-
robber; hold you up at your own door. I believe she's squared
the police: if she hadn't she'd 'a been run in long ago. . . Oh,
the *war*? *What war*? Is there another war on? What, that old
one? Why, I thought *that* one was over long ago. . . You
can't get anybody *I* know to talk about it even!"

"Guess we've got our work cut out paying for it," added
Horace Betterly, stretching a begemmed and bloated hand toward the wine-list.

"Well, I should *say*!" his wife agreed with him.

"Sid, what form of liquid refreshment?" And "Sid", a puffy
Chicago business man, grew pink in his effort to look knowing and not name the wrong champagne . . .

It was odd: during her drive with Mrs. Minity, at Madame
Lanska's, and again at the Rectory, Kate Clephane had meant
to proclaim her great news—and she had not yet breathed a
word of it. The fact was, it was too great; too precious to
waste on Mrs. Minity's inattention, too sacred to reveal to
Madame Lanska's bridge players, and too glorious to over-
whelm those poor women at the Rectory with. And now, in
the glare and clatter of the Casino, with the Sids and Harrys
exchanging winks, and the Mrs. Sids and Harrys craning fat

necks to see the last new cocotte, or the young Prince about whom there were such awful stories—here, of all places, to unbare her secret, name her daughter: how could she ever have thought it possible?

Only toward the end of the long deafening dinner, when Marcia and Mrs. Sid began to make plans for a week at Monte Carlo, and she found herself being impressed into the party (as she had, so often and so willingly, before) did Mrs. Clephane suddenly find herself assuming the defensive.

"You can't? Or you *won't*? Now, you Kate-cat you," Marcia threatened her with a scented cigarette, "own up now—what's doing? What you onto this time? Ain't she naughty? *We* ain't grand enough for her, girls!" And then, suddenly, at a sign from Horace, and lowering her voice, but not quite enough to make the communication private: "See here, Kate darling—of course, you know, *as our guest*: why, of course, naturally." While, on the other side, Mrs. Sid drawled: "What I want to know is: where else *can* anybody go at this season?"

Mrs. Clephane surveyed her calmly. "To New York—at least I can."

They all screamed it at her at once: "N'York?" and again she dropped the two syllables slowly from disdainful lips.

"Well, I never! Whaffor, though?" questioned Horace from the depths of a fresh bumper.

Mrs. Clephane swept the table with a cool eye. "Business—family business," she said.

"*Criky!*" burst from Horace. And: "Say, Sid, a drop of *fine*, just to help us over the shock? Well, here's to the success of the lady's Family Business!" he concluded with a just perceptible wink, emptying his champagne goblet and replacing it by the big bubble-shaped liqueur glass into which a thoughtful waiter had already measured out the proper quantity of the most expensive *fine*.

III.

As KATE CLEPHANE stood on deck, straining her eyes at the Babylonian New York which seemed to sway and totter toward her menacingly, she felt a light hand on her arm.

"Anne!"

She barely suppressed the questioning lift of her voice; for the length of a heart-beat she had not been absolutely certain. Then . . . yes, there was her whole youth, her whole married past, in that small pale oval—her own hair, but duskier, stronger; something of her smile too, she fancied; and John Clephane's straight rather heavy nose, beneath old Mrs. Clephane's awful brows.

"But the eyes—you chose your own eyes, my darling!" She had the girl at arms'-length, her own head thrown back a little: Anne was slightly the taller, and her pale face hung over her mother's like a young moon seen through mist.

"So wise of you! Such an improvement on anything we had in stock. . ." How absurd! When she thought of the things she had meant to say! What would her child think her? Incurably frivolous, of course. Well, if she stopped to consider *that* she was lost. . . She flung both arms about Anne and laid a long kiss on her fresh cheek.

"My Anne . . . little Anne. . ."

She thirsted to have the girl to herself, where she could touch her hair, stroke her face, draw the gloves from her hands, kiss her over and over again, and little by little, from that tall black-swathed figure, disengage the round child's body she had so long continued to feel against her own, like a warmth and an ache, as the amputated feel the life in a lost limb.

"Come, mother: this way. And here's Mr. Landers," the girl said. Her voice was not unkind; it was not cold; it was only muffled in fold on fold of shyness, embarrassment and constraint. After all, Kate thought, it was just as well that the crowd, the confusion and Fred Landers were there to help them over those first moments.

"Fred Landers! Dear old Fred! Is it you, really? Known me

anywhere? Oh, nonsense! Look at my gray hair. But *you*—"
She had said the words over so often in enacting this imagined scene that they were on her lips in a rush; but some
contradictory impulse checked them there, and let her just
murmur "Fred" as her hand dropped into that of the heavy
grizzled man with a red-and-yellow complexion and screwed-
up blue eyes whom Time had substituted for the thin loose-
jointed friend of her youth.

Landers beamed on her, silent also; a common instinct
seemed to have told all three that for the moment there was
nothing to say—that they must just let propinquity do its
mysterious work without trying to hasten the process.

In the motor Mrs. Clephane's agony began. "What do
they think of *me*?" she wondered. She felt so sure, so safe, so
enfolded, with them; or she would have, if only she could
have guessed what impression she was making. She put it in
the plural, because, though at that moment all she cared for
was what Anne thought, she had guessed instantly that, for
a time at least, Anne's view would be influenced by her
guardian's.

The very tone in which he had said, facing them from his
seat between the piled-up bags: "You'll find this young
woman a handful—I'm not sorry to resign my trust—"
showed the terms the two were on. And so did Anne's rejoin-
der: "I'm not a handful now to any one but myself— I'm in
my own hands, Uncle Fred."

He laughed, and the girl smiled. Kate wished her daughter
and she had been facing each other, so that she could have
seen the whole stretch of the smile, instead of only the tip
dimpling away into a half-turned cheek. So much depended,
for the mother, on that smile—on the smile, and the motion
of those grave brows. The whole point was, how far did the
one offset the other?

"Yes," Mr. Landers assented, "you're a free agent now—
been one for just three weeks, haven't you? So far you've
made fairly good use of your liberty."

Guardian and ward exchanged another smile, in which
Kate felt herself generously included; then Landers's eye
turned to hers. "You're not a bit changed, you know."

"Oh, come! Nonsense." Again she checked that silly "look

at my gray hair." "I hope one never is, to old friends—after the first shock, at any rate."

"There wasn't any first shock. I spotted you at once, from the pier."

Anne intervened in her calm voice. "I recognized mother too—from such a funny old photograph, in a dress with puffed sleeves."

Mrs. Clephane tried to smile. "I don't know, darling, if I recognized you. . . You were just there . . . in me . . . where you've always been . . ." She felt her voice breaking, and was glad to have Mr. Landers burst in with: "And what do you say to our new Fifth Avenue?"

She stood surveying its upper reaches, that afternoon, from the window of the sitting-room Anne had assigned to her. Yes; Fred Landers was right, it was a new, an absolutely new, Fifth Avenue; but there was nothing new about Anne's house. Incongruously enough—in that fluid city, where the stoutest buildings seemed like atoms forever shaken into new patterns by the rumble of Undergrounds and Elevateds—the house was the very one which had once been Kate's, the home to which, four-and-twenty years earlier, she had been brought as a bride.

Her house, since she had been its mistress; but never hers in the sense of her having helped to make it. John Clephane lived by proverbs. One was that fools built houses for wise men to live in; so he had bought a fool's house, furniture and all, and moved into it on his marriage. But if it had been built by a fool, Kate sometimes used to wonder, how was it that her husband found it to be planned and furnished so exactly as he would have chosen? He never tired of boasting of the fact, seemingly unconscious of the unflattering inference to be drawn; perhaps, if pressed, he would have said there was no contradiction, since the house had cost the fool a great deal to build, and him, the wise man, very little to buy. It had been, he was never tired of repeating, a bargain, the biggest kind of a bargain; and that, somehow, seemed a reason (again Kate didn't see why) for leaving everything in it unchanged, even to the heraldic stained glass on the stairs and the Jacobean mantel in a drawing-room that ran to Aubusson. . . And

here it all was again, untouched, unworn—the only difference being that she, Kate, was installed in the visitor's suite
on the third floor (swung up to it in a little jewel-box of a
lift), instead of occupying the rooms below which had once
been "Papa's and Mamma's". The change struck her at once—
and the fact that Anne, taking her up, had first pressed the
wrong button, the one for the floor below, and then reddened in correcting her mistake. The girl evidently guessed
that her mother would prefer not to go back to those other
rooms; her having done so gave Kate a quick thrill.

"You don't mind being so high up, mother?"

"I like it ever so much better, dear."

"I'm so glad!" Anne was making an evident effort at expan-
siveness. "That's jolly of you—like this we shall be on the
same floor."

"Ah, you've kept the rooms you had—?" Kate didn't know
how to put it.

"Yes: the old nursery. First it was turned into a schoolroom, then into my den. One gets attached to places. I never
should have felt at home anywhere else. Come and see."

Ah, here, at last, in the grim middle-aged house, were
youth and renovation! The nursery, having changed its use,
had perforce had to change its appearance. Japanese walls of
reddish gold; a few modern pictures; books; a budding wis-
taria in a vase of Corean pottery; big tables, capacious arm-
chairs, an ungirlish absence of photographs and personal
trifles. Not particularly original; but a sober handsome room,
and comfortable, though so far from "cosy." Kate wondered:
"Is it her own idea, or is this what the new girl likes?" She
recalled the pink and white trifles congesting her maiden
bower, and felt as if a rather serious-minded son were showing her his study. An Airedale terrier, stretched before the
fire, reinforced the impression. She didn't believe many of the
new girls had rooms like this.

"It's all your own idea, isn't it?" she asked, almost shyly.

"I don't know—yes. Uncle Fred helped me, of course. He
knows a lot about Oriental pottery. I called him 'Uncle' after
father died," Anne explained, "because there's nothing else to
call a guardian, is there?"

On the wall Kate noticed a rough but vivid oil-sketch of a

branch of magnolias. She went up to it, attracted by its purity of colour. "I like that," she said.

Anne's eyes deepened. "Do you? I did it."

"You, dear? I didn't know you painted." Kate felt herself suddenly blushing; the abyss of all she didn't know about her daughter had once more opened before her, and she just managed to murmur: "I mean, not like *this*. It's very broad—very sure. You must have worked. . ."

The girl laughed, caught in the contagion of her mother's embarrassment. "Yes, I've worked hard—I care for it a great deal."

Kate sighed and turned from the picture. The few words they had exchanged—the technical phrases she had used—had called up a time when the vocabulary of the studio was forever in her ears, and she wanted, at that moment, to escape from it as quickly as she could.

Against the opposite wall was a deep sofa, books and a reading-lamp beside it. Kate paused. "That's just where your crib used to stand!" She turned to the fireplace with an unsteady laugh. "I can see you by the hearth, in your little chair, with the fire shining through your bush of hair, and your toys on the shelf in front of you. You thought the sparks were red birds in a cage, and you used to try to coax them through the fender with bits of sugar."

"Oh, did I? You darling, to remember!" The girl put an arm about Kate. It seemed to the mother, as the young warmth flowed through her, that everything else had vanished, and that together they were watching the little girl with the bush of hair coaxing the sparks through the fender.

Anne had left her, and Mrs. Clephane, alone in her window, looked down on the new Fifth Avenue. As it surged past, a huge lava-flow of interlaced traffic, her tired bewildered eyes seemed to see the buildings move with the vehicles, as a stationary train appears to move to travellers on another line. She fancied that presently even the little Washington Square Arch would trot by, heading the tide of skyscrapers from the lower reaches of the city. . . Oppressed and confused, she rejected the restless vision and called up in its place the old Fifth Avenue, the Fifth Avenue still intact at her marriage, a thoroughfare of monotonously ugly brown houses divided by a thin trickle of horse-drawn carriages; and she saw her mother-in-law, in just such a richly-curtained window, looking down, with dry mental comments, on old Mrs. Chivers's C-spring barouche and Mrs. Beaufort's new chestnut steppers, and knowing how long ago the barouche had been imported from Paris, and how much had been paid for the steppers—for Mrs. Clephane senior belonged to the generation which still surveyed its world from an upper window, like the Dutch ancestresses to whom the doings of the street were reported by a little mirror.

The contrast was too great; Kate Clephane felt herself too much a part of that earlier day. The overwhelming changes had all happened, in a whirl, during the years of her absence; and meanwhile she had been living in quiet backwaters, or in the steady European capitals where renewals make so little mark on the unyielding surface of the past. She turned back into the room, seeking refuge in its familiar big-patterned chintz, the tufted lounge, the woolly architecture of the carpet. It was thoughtful of Anne to have left her. . . They were both beginning to be oppressed again by a sense of obstruction: the packed memories of their so different pasts had jammed the passages between them. Anne had visibly felt that, and with a light kiss slipped out. "She's perfect," her mother thought, a little frightened. . .

She said to herself: "I'm dead tired—" put on a dressing-gown, dismissed the hovering Aline, and lay down by the fire. Then, in the silence, when the door had shut, she understood how excited she was, and how impossible it would be to rest.

Her eyes wandered about the unchanged scene, and into the equally familiar bedroom beyond—the "best spare-room" of old days. There hung the same red-eyed Beatrice Cenci above the double bed. John Clephane's parents had travelled in the days when people still brought home copies of the Old Masters; and a mixture of thrift and filial piety had caused John Clephane to preserve their collection in the obscurer corners of his house. Kate smiled at the presiding genius selected to guard the slumbers of married visitors (as Ribera monks and Caravaggio gamblers darkened the digestive processes in the dining-room); she smiled, as she so often had—but now without bitterness—at the naïve incongruities of that innocent and inquisitorial past. Then her eye lit on the one novelty in the room: the telephone at her elbow. Oh, to talk to some one—to talk to Fred Landers, instantly! "There are too many things I don't know . . . I'm too utterly in the dark," she murmured. She rushed through the directory, found his number, and assailed his parlour-maid with questions. But Mr. Landers was not at home; the parlour-maid's inflexion signified: "At this hour?" and a glance at the clock showed Kate that the endless day had barely reached mid-afternoon. Of course he would not be at home. But the parlour-maid added: "He's always at his office till five."

His office! Fred Landers had an office—had one still! Kate remembered that two-and-twenty years ago, after lunching with them, he used always to glance at his watch and say: "Time to get back to the office." And he was well-off—always had been. He needn't—needn't! What on earth did he do there, she wondered? What results, pecuniary or other, had he to show for his quarter-century of "regular hours"? She remembered that his profession had been legal— most of one's men friends, in those remote days, were lawyers. But she didn't fancy he had ever appeared in court; people consulted him about investments, he looked after estates. For the last years, very likely, his chief business had been to look after Anne's; no doubt he was one of John Clephane's executors, and also old Mrs. Clephane's. One pictured him as deeply versed in will-making and will-interpreting: he had always, in his dry mumbling way, rather enjoyed a quibble over words. Kate thought, by the way, that he mumbled less, spoke more "straight from the shoulder," than he used to. Perhaps it was experience, authority, the fact of being consulted and looked up to, that had changed the gaunt shambling Fred Landers of old days into the four-square sort of man who had met her on the pier and disentangled her luggage with so little fuss. Oh, yes, she was sure the new Fred Landers could help her—advice was just what she wanted, and what, she suspected, he liked to give.

She called up his office, and in less than a minute there was his calm voice asking what he could do.

"Come at once—oh, Fred, you must!"

She heard: "Is there anything wrong?" and sent him a re-assuring laugh.

"Nothing—except *me*. I don't yet know how to fit in. There are so many things I ought to be told. Remember, I'm so unprepared—"

She fancied she felt a tremor of disapproval along the wire. Ought she not to have gone even as far as that on the telephone?

"Anne's out," she added hastily. "I was tired, and she told me to rest. But I can't. How can I? Can't you come?"

He returned, without the least acceleration of the syllables: "I never leave the office until—"

"Five. I know. But just today—"

There was a pause. "Yes; I'll come, of course. But you know there's nothing in the world to bother about," he added patiently. ("He's saying to himself," she thought, " 'that's the sort of fuss that used to drive poor Clephane out of his wits'.")

But when he came he did not strike her as having probably said anything of the sort. There was no trace of "the office", or of any other preoccupation, in the friendly voice in which he asked her if she wouldn't please stay lying down, and let him do the talking.

"Yes, I want you to. I want you to tell me everything. And first of all—" She paused to gather up her courage. "What does Anne know?" she flung at him.

Her visitor had seated himself in the armchair facing her. The late afternoon light fell on his thick ruddy face, in which the small eyes, between white lids, looked startlingly blue. At her question the blood rose from his cheeks to his forehead, and invaded the thin pepper-and-salt hair carefully brushed over his solidly moulded head.

"Don't—don't try to find out, I beg of you; I haven't," he stammered.

She felt his blush reflected on her own pale cheek, and the tears rose to her eyes. How was he to help her if he took that tone? He did not give her time to answer, but went on, in a voice laboriously cheerful: "Look forward, not back: that's the thing to do. Living with young people, isn't it the natural attitude? And Anne is not the kind to dig and brood: thank goodness, she's health itself, body and soul. She asks no questions; never has. Why should I have put it into her head that there were any to ask? Her grandmother didn't. It was her policy . . . as it's been mine. If we didn't always agree, the old lady and I, we did on *that*." He stood up and leaned against the mantel, his gaze embracing the pyramidal bronze clock on which a heavily-draped Muse with an Etruscan necklace rested her lyre. "Anne was simply given to understand that you and her father didn't agree; that's all. A girl," he went on in an embarrassed tone, "can't grow up nowadays without seeing a good many cases of the kind about her; Lord forgive me, they're getting to be the rule rather than the exception. Lots of things that you, at her age, might have puzzled over and thought mysterious, she probably takes for granted. At any rate she behaves as if she did.

"Things didn't always go smoothly between her and her grandmother. The child has talents, you know; developed 'em early. She paints cleverly, and the old lady had her taught; but when she wanted a studio of her own there was a row—I was sent for. Mrs. Clephane had never heard of anybody in the family having a studio; that settled it. Well, Anne's going to have one now. And so it was with everything. In the end Anne invariably gets what she wants. She knew of course that you and her grandmother were not the best of friends—my idea is that she tried to see you not long after her father died, and was told by the old lady that she must wait till she was of age. They neither of them told me so—but, well, it was in the air. And Anne waited. But now she's doubly free—and you see the first use she's made of her freedom." He had recovered his ease, and sat down again, his hands on his knees, his trouser-hem rather too high above wrinkled socks and solemn square-toed boots. "I may say," he added smiling, "that she cabled to you without consulting me—without consulting anybody. I heard about it only when she showed me your answer. That ought to tell you," he concluded gaily, "as much as anything can, about Anne. Only take her for granted, as she will you, and you've got your happiest days ahead of you—see if you haven't."

As he blinked at her with kindly brotherly eyes she saw in their ingenuous depths the terror of the man who has tried to buy off fate by one optimistic evasion after another, till it has become second nature to hand out his watch and pocket-book whenever reality waylays him.

She exchanged one glance with that lurking fear; then she said: "Yes; you're right, I suppose. But there's not only Anne. What do other people know? I ought to be told."

His face clouded again, though not with irritation. He seemed to understand that the appeal was reasonable, and to want to help her, yet to feel with every word she was making it more difficult.

"What they know? Why . . . why . . . what they *had* to . . . merely that. . ." ("What you yourself forced on them," his tone seemed to imply.)

"That I went away. . ."

He nodded.

"With another man. . ."

Reluctantly he brought the words out after her: "With another man."

"With Hylton Davies. . ."

"Hylton Davies. . ."

"And travelled with him—for nearly two years."

He frowned, but immediately fetched a sigh of relief. "Oh, well—abroad. And he's dead." He glanced at her cautiously, and then added: "He's not a man that many people remember."

But she insisted: "After that. . . —"

Mr. Landers lifted his hand in a gesture of reassurance; the cloud was lifted from his brow. "After that, we all know what your life was. You'll forgive my putting it bluntly: but your living in that quiet way—all these years—gradually produced a change of opinion . . . told immensely in your favour. Even among the Clephane relations . . . especially those who had glimpses of you abroad . . . or heard of you when they were there. Some of the family distinctly disapproved of—of John's attitude; his persistent refusal . . . yes, the Tresseltons even, and the Drovers— I know they all did what they could—especially Enid Drover—"

Her blood rushed up and the pulses drummed in her temples. "If I cry," she thought "it will upset him—" but the tears rose in a warm gush about her heart.

"Enid Drover? I never knew—"

"Oh, yes; so that for a long time I hoped . . . we all hoped. . ."

She began to tremble. Even her husband's sister Enid Drover! She had remembered the Hendrik Drovers, both husband and wife, as among the narrowest, the most inexorable of the Clephane tribe. But then, it suddenly flashed across her, if it hadn't been for the episode with Chris perhaps she might have come back years before. What mocking twists fate gave to one's poor little life-pattern!

"Well—?" she questioned, breathless.

He met her gaze now without a shadow of constraint. "Oh, well, you know what John was—always the slave of anything he'd once said. Once he'd found a phrase for a thing, the phrase ruled him. He never could be got beyond that first vision of you . . . you and Davies. . ."

"Never—?"

"No. All the years after made no difference to him. He wouldn't listen. 'Burnt child dreads the fire' was all he would say. And after he died his mother kept it up. She seemed to regard it as a duty to his memory. . . She might have had your life spread out before her eyes, day by day, hour by hour . . . it wouldn't have changed her." He reddened again. "Some of your friends kept on trying . . . but nothing made any difference."

Kate Clephane lay silent, staring at the fire. Tentatively, fearfully, she was building up out of her visitor's tones, his words, his reticences, the incredible fact that, for him and all her husband's family—that huge imperious clan—her life, after she had left them, had been divided into two sharply differentiated parts: the brief lapse with Hylton Davies, the long expiation alone. Of that third episode, which for her was the central fact of her experience, apparently not a hint had reached them. She was the woman who had once "stooped to folly", and then, regaining her natural uprightness, had retained it inflexibly through all the succeeding years. As the truth penetrated her mind she was more frightened than relieved. Was she not returning on false pretences to these kindly forgiving relations? Was it not possible, indeed almost certain, that a man like Frederick

Landers, had he known about Chris, would have used all his influence to dissuade Anne from sending for her, instead of exerting it in the opposite sense, as he avowedly had? And, that being so, was she not taking them all unawares, actually abusing their good faith, in passing herself off as the penitential figure whom the passage of blameless years had gradually changed from the offending into the offended? Yet was it, after all, possible that the affair with Chris, and the life she had led with him, could so completely have escaped their notice? Rumour has a million eyes, and though she had preserved appearances in certain, almost superstitious, ways, she had braved them recklessly in others, especially toward the end, when the fear of losing Chris had swept away all her precautions. Then suddenly the explanation dawned on her. She had met Chris for the first time less than a year before the outbreak of the war, and the last of their months together, the most reckless and fervid, had been overshadowed, blotted out of everybody's sight, in that universal eclipse.

She had never before thought of it in that way: for her the war had begun only when Chris left her. During its first months she and he had been in Spain and Italy, shut off by the safe Alps or the neutral indifference; and the devouring need to keep Chris amused, and herself amusing, had made her fall into the easy life of the Italian watering-places, and the careless animation of Rome, without any real sense of being in an altered world. Around them they found only the like-minded; the cheerful, who refused to be "worried", or the argumentative and paradoxical, like Chris himself, who thought it their duty as "artists" or "thinkers" to ignore the barbarian commotion. It was only in 1915, when Chris's own attitude was mysteriously altered, and she found him muttering that after all a fellow couldn't stand aside when all his friends and the chaps of his own age were getting killed— only then did the artificial defences fall, and the reality stream in on her. Was his change of mind genuine? He often said that his opinions hadn't altered, but that there were times when opinions didn't count . . . when a fellow just had to *act*. It was her own secret thought (had been, perhaps, for longer than she knew); but with Chris—could one ever tell?

Whatever he was doing, he was sure, after a given time, to want to be doing something else, and to find plausible reasons for it: even the war might be serving merely as a pretext for his unrest. Unless . . . unless he used it as an excuse for leaving her? Unless being with *her* was what it offered an escape from? If only she could have judged him more clearly, known him better! But between herself and any clear understanding of him there had hung, from the first, the obscuring mist of her passion, muffling his face, touch, speech (so that now, at times, she could not even rebuild his features or recall his voice), obscuring every fold and cranny of his character, every trick of phrase, every doubling and dodging of his restless mind and capricious fancy. Sometimes, in looking back, she thought there was only one sign she had ever read clearly in him, and that was the first sign of his growing tired of her. Disguise that as she would, avert her eyes from it, argue it away, there the menace always was again, faint but persistent, like the tiny intermittent pang which first announces a mortal malady.

And of all this none of the people watching her from across the sea had had a suspicion. The war had swallowed her up, her and all her little concerns, as it had engulfed so many million others. It seemed written that, till the end, she should have to be thankful for the war.

Her eyes travelled back to Fred Landers, whose sturdy bulk, planted opposite her, seemed to have grown so far off and immaterial. Did he really guess nothing of that rainbow world she had sent her memory back to? And what would he think or say if she lifted the veil and let him into it?

"He'll hate me for it—but I must," she murmured. She raised herself on her elbow: "Fred—"

The door opened softly to admit Anne, with the Airedale at her heels. They brought in a glow of winter air and the strange cold perfume of the dusk.

"Uncle Fred? How jolly of you to have come! I was afraid I'd left mother alone too long," the girl said, bending to her mother's cheek. At the caress the blood flowed back into Kate's heart. She looked up and her eyes drank in her daughter's image.

Anne hung above her for a moment, tall, black-cloaked,

remote in the faint light; then she dropped on her knees beside the couch.

"But you're *tired* . . . you're utterly done up and worn out!" she exclaimed, slipping an arm protectingly behind her mother. There was a note of reproach and indignation in her voice. "You must never be tired or worried about things any more; I won't have it; we won't any of us have it. Remember, I'm here to look after you now—and so is Uncle Fred," she added gaily.

"That's what I tell her—nothing on earth to worry about *now*," Mr. Landers corroborated, getting up from his chair and making for the door with muffled steps.

"Nothing, nothing—ever again! You'll promise me that, mother, won't you?"

Kate Clephane let her hand droop against the strong young shoulder. She felt herself sinking down into a very Bethesda-pool of forgetfulness and peace. From its depths she raised herself just far enough to say: "I promise."

IV.

A NNE, withdrawing from her mother's embrace, had decreed, in a decisive tone: "And now I'm going to ring for Aline to tuck you up in bed. And presently your dinner will be brought; consommé and chicken and champagne. Is that what you'll like?"

"Exactly what I shall like. But why not share it with you downstairs?"

But the girl had been firm, in a sweet yet almost obstinate way. "No, dearest—you're really tired out. You don't know it yet; but you will presently. I want you just to lie here, and enjoy the fire and the paper; and go to sleep as soon as you can."

Where did her fresh flexible voice get its note of finality? It was—yes, without doubt—an echo of old Mrs. Clephane's way of saying: "We'll consider that *settled*, I think."

Kate shivered a little; but it was only a passing chill. The use the girl made of her authority was so different—as if the old Mrs. Clephane in her spoke from a milder sphere—and it was so sweet to be compelled, to have things decided for one, to be told what one wanted and what was best for one. For years Kate Clephane had had to order herself about: to tell herself to rest and not to worry, to eat when she wasn't hungry, to sleep when she felt staring wide-awake. She would have preferred, on the whole, that evening, to slip into a tea-gown and go down to a quiet dinner, alone with her daughter and perhaps Fred Landers; she shrank from the hurricane that would start up in her head as soon as she was alone; yet she liked better still to be "mothered" in that fond blundering way the young have of mothering their elders. And besides, Anne perhaps felt—not unwisely—that again, for the moment, she and her mother had nothing more to say to each other; that to close on that soft note was better, just then, than farther effort.

At any rate, Anne evidently did not expect to have her decision questioned. It was that hint of finality in her solicitude that made Kate, as she sank into the lavender-scented pillows, feel—perhaps evoked by the familiar scent of cared-for linen—the closing-in on her of all the old bounds.

The next morning banished the sensation. She felt only, now, the novelty, the strangeness. Anne, entering in the wake of a perfect breakfast tray, announced that Uncle Hendrik and Aunt Enid Drover were coming to dine, with their eldest son, Alan, with Lilla Gates (Lilla Gates, Kate recalled, was their married daughter) and Uncle Fred Landers. "No one else, dear, on account of this—" the girl touched her mourning dress—"but you'll like to begin quietly, I know—after the fatigue of the crossing, I mean," she added hastily, lest her words should seem to imply that her mother might have other reasons for shrinking from people. "No one else," she continued, "but Joe and Nollie. Joe Tresselton, you know, married Nollie Shriner—yes, one of the Fourteenth Street Shriners, the one who was first married to Frank Haverford. She was divorced two years ago, and married Joe immediately afterward." The words dropped from her as indifferently as if she had said: "She came out two years ago, and married Joe at the end of her first season."

"Nollie Tresselton's everything to me," Anne began after a pause. "You'll see—she's transformed Joe. Everybody in the family adores her. She's waked them all up. Even Aunt Enid, you know—. And when Lilla came to grief—"

"Lilla? Lilla Gates?"

"Yes. Didn't you know? It was really dreadful for Aunt Enid—especially with her ideas. Lilla behaved really badly; even Nollie thinks she did. But Nollie arranged it as well as she could. . . Oh, but I'm boring you with all this family gossip." The girl paused, suddenly embarrassed; then, glancing out of the window: "It's a lovely morning, and not too cold. What do you say to my running you up to Bronx Park and back before lunch, just to give you a glimpse of what Nollie calls our *New* York? Or would you rather take another day to rest?"

The rush through the vivid air; the spectacle of the new sumptuous city; of the long reaches above the Hudson with their showy architecture and towering "Institutions"; of the

smooth Boulevards flowing out to cared-for prosperous suburbs; the vista of Fifth Avenue, as they returned, stretching
southward, interminably, between monumental façades and
resplendent shop-fronts—all this and the tone of Anne's talk,
her unconscious allusions, revelations of herself and her surroundings, acted like champagne on Kate Clephane's brain,
making the world reel about her in a headlong dance that
challenged her to join it. The way they all took their mourning, for instance! She, Anne, being her grandmother's heiress
(she explained) would of course not wear colours till Easter,
or go to the Opera (except to matinées) for at least another
month. Didn't her mother think she was right? "Nollie thinks
it awfully archaic of me to mix up music and mourning; what
have they got to do with each other, as she says? But I know
Aunt Enid wouldn't like it . . . and she's been so kind to me.
Don't you agree that I'd better not?"

"But of course, dear; and I think your aunt's right."

Inwardly, Kate was recalling the inexorable laws which had
governed family affliction in the New York to which she had
come as a bride: three crape-walled years for a parent, two for
sister or brother, at least twelve solid months of black for
grandparent or aunt, and half a year (to the full) for cousins,
even if you counted them by dozens, as the Clephanes did. As
for the weeds of widowhood, they were supposed to be measured only by the extent of the survivor's affliction, and *that*
was expected to last as long, and proclaim itself as unmistakably in crape and seclusion, as the most intolerant censor in
the family decreed—unless you were prepared to flout the
whole clan, and could bear to be severely reminded that your
veil was a quarter of a yard shorter than cousin Julia's, though
her bereavement antedated yours by six months. Much as
Kate Clephane had suffered under the old dispensation, she
felt a slight recoil from the indifference that had succeeded it.
She herself, just before sailing, had replaced the coloured
finery hastily bought on the Riviera by a few dresses of un-
noticeable black, which, without suggesting the hypocrisy of
her wearing mourning for old Mrs. Clephane, yet kept her
appearance in harmony with her daughter's; and Anne's
question made her glad that she had done so.

The new tolerance, she soon began to see, applied to everything; or, if it didn't, she had not yet discovered the new prohibitions, and during all that first glittering day seemed to move through a millennium where the lamb of pleasure lay down with the lion of propriety. . . After all, this New York into which she was being reinducted had never, in any of its stages, been hers; and the fact, which had facilitated her flight from it, leaving fewer broken ties and uprooted habits, would now, she saw, in an equal measure simplify her return. Her absence, during all those years, had counted, for the Clephanes, only in terms of her husband's humiliation; there had been no family of her own to lament her fall, take up her defence, quarrel with the clan over the rights and wrongs of the case, force people to take sides, and leave a ramification of vague rancours to which her return would give new life. The old aunts and indifferent cousins at Meridia—her remote inland town—had bowed their heads before the scandal, thanking fortune that the people they visited would probably never hear of it. And now she came back free of everything and every one, and rather like a politician resuming office than a prodigal returning to his own.

The sense of it was so rejuvenating that she was almost sure she was looking her best (and with less help than usual from Aline) when she went down to dinner to meet the clan. Enid Drover's appearance gave a momentary check to her illusion: Enid, after eighteen years, seemed alarmingly the same— pursed-up lips, pure vocabulary and all. She had even kept, to an astonishing degree, the physical air of her always middle-aged youth, the smooth complexion, symmetrically-waved hair and empty eyes that made her plump small-nosed face like a statue's. Yet the mere fact of her daughter Lilla profoundly altered her—the fact that she could sit beaming maternally across the table at that impudent stripped version of herself, with dyed hair, dyed lashes, drugged eyes and unintelligible dialect. And her husband, Hendrik Drover—the typical old New Yorker—that he too should accept this outlawed daughter, laugh at her slang, and greet her belated entrance with the remark: "Top-notch get-up tonight, Lil!"

"Oh, Lilla's going on," laughed Mrs. Joe Tresselton, slipping her thin brown arm through her cousin's heavy white one.

Lilla laughed indolently. "Ain't *you*?"

"No—I mean to stay and bore Aunt Kate till the small hours, if she'll let me."

Aunt Kate! How sweet it sounded, in that endearing young voice! No wonder Anne had spoken as she did of Nollie. Whatever Mrs. Joe Tresselton's past had been, it had left on her no traces like those which had smirched and deadened Lilla. Kate smiled back at Nollie and loved her. She was prepared to love Joe Tresselton too, if only for having brought this live thing into the family. Personally, Joe didn't at first offer many points of contact: he was so hopelessly like his cousin Alan Drover, and like all the young American officers Kate had seen on leave on the Riviera, and all the young men who showed off collars or fountain-pens or golf-clubs in the backs of American magazines. But then Kate had been away so long that, as yet, the few people she had seen were always on the point of being merged into a collective American Face. She wondered if Anne would marry an American Face, and hoped, before that, to learn to differentiate them; meanwhile, she would begin by practising on Joe, who, seating himself beside her with the collective smile, seemed about to remark: "See that Arrow?"

Instead he said: "Anne's great, isn't she, Aunt Kate?" and thereby acquired an immediate individuality for Anne's mother.

Dinner was announced, and at the dining-room door Kate wavered, startled by the discovery that it was still exactly the same room—black and gold, with imitation tapestries and a staring white bust niched in a red marble over-mantel—and feeling once more uncertain as to what was expected of her. But already Anne was guiding her to her old seat at the head of the table, and waiting for her to assign their places to the others. The girl did it without a word; just a glance and the least touch. If this were indeed a mannerless age, how miraculously Anne's manners had been preserved!

And now the dinner was progressing, John Clephane's champagne bubbling in their glasses (it seemed oddest of all to be drinking her husband's Veuve Clicquot), Lilla steadily smoking, both elbows on the table, and Nollie Tresselton leading an exchange of chaff between the younger cousins, with the object, as Kate Clephane guessed, of giving her, the newcomer, time to take breath and get her bearings. It was wonderful, sitting there, to recall the old "family dinners", when Enid's small censorious smile (Enid, then in her twenties!) seemed as inaccessible to pity as the forbidding line of old Mrs. Clephane's lips; when even Joe Tresselton's mother (that lazy fat Alethea Tresselton) had taken her cue from the others, and echoed their severities with a mouth made for kissing and forgiving; and John Clephane, at the foot of the table, proud of his house, proud of his wine, proud of his cook, still half-proud of his wife, was visibly saying to himself, as he looked about on his healthy handsome relatives: "After all, blood is thicker than water."

The contrast was the more curious because nothing, after all, could really alter people like the Drovers. Enid was still gently censorious, though with her range of criticism so deflected by the huge exception to be made for her daughter that her fault-finding had an odd remoteness: and Hendrik Drover, Kate guessed, would be as easily shocked as of old by allusions to the "kind of thing they did in Europe", though what they did at home was so vividly present to him in Lilla's person, and in the fact of Joe Tresselton's having married a Fourteenth Street Shriner, and a divorced one at that.

It was all too bewildering for a poor exile to come to terms with—Mrs. Clephane could only smile and listen, and be thankful that her own case was so evidently included in the new range of their indulgence.

But the young people—what did they think? That would be the interesting thing to know. They had all, she gathered, far more interests and ideas than had scantily furnished her own youth, but all so broken up, scattered, and perpetually interrupted by the strenuous labour of their endless forms of sport, that they reminded her of a band of young entomologists, equipped with the newest thing in nets, but in far too great a hurry ever to catch anything. Yet perhaps it seemed so only to the slower motions of middle-age.

Kate's glance wandered from Lilla Gates, the most obvious and least interesting of the group, to Nollie Shriner (one of the "awful" Fourteenth Street Shriners); Nollie Shriner first, then Nollie Haverford, wife of a strait-laced Albany Haverford, and now Nollie Tresselton, though she still looked, with her brown squirrel-face and slim little body, like a girl in the schoolroom. Yes, even Nollie seemed to be in a great hurry; one felt her perpetually ordering and sorting and marshalling things in her mind, and the fact, Kate presently perceived, now and then gave an odd worn look of fixity to her uncannily youthful face. Kate wondered when there was ever time to enjoy anything, with that perpetual alarm-clock in one's breast.

Her glance travelled on to her own daughter. Anne seemed eager too, but not at such a pace, or about such a multiplicity of unrelated things. Perhaps, though, it was only the fact of being taller, statelier—old-fashioned words still fitted Anne—which gave her that air of boyish aloofness. But no; it was the mystery of her eyes—those eyes which, as Kate had told her, she had chosen for herself from some forgotten ancestral treasury into which none of the others had dipped. Between olive and brown, but flecked with golden lights, a little too deep-set, the lower lid flowing up smooth and flat from the cheek, and the black lashes as evenly set as the microscopic plumes in a Peruvian feather-ornament; and above them, too prominent, even threatening, yet melting at times to curves of maiden wonder, the obstinate brows of old Mrs. Clephane. What did those eyes portend?

Kate Clephane glanced away, frightened at the riddle, and absorbed herself in the preoccupying fact that the only way to tell the Drovers from the Tresseltons was to remember that the Drovers' noses were even smaller than the Tresseltons' (but *would* that help, if one met one of either tribe alone?). She was roused by hearing Enid Drover question plaintively, as the ladies regained the drawing-room: "But after all, why *shouldn't* Anne go too?"

The women formed an interrogative group around Mrs. Clephane, who found herself suddenly being scrutinized as if for a verdict. She cast a puzzled glance at Anne, and her daughter slipped an arm through hers but addressed Mrs. Drover.

"Go to Madge Glenver's cabaret-party with Lilla? But there's no real reason at all why I shouldn't—except that my preference, like Nollie's, happens to be for staying at home this evening."

Mrs. Drover heaved a faint sigh of relief, but her daughter, shrugging impatient shoulders out of her too-willing shoulder-straps, grumbled: "Then why doesn't Aunt Kate come too? You'll talk her to death if you all stay here all the evening."

Nollie Tresselton smiled. "So much for what Lilla thinks of the charm of our conversation!"

Lilla shrugged again. "Not *your* conversation particularly. I hate talking. I only like noises that don't mean anything."

"Does that rule out talking—*quite?*"

"Well, I hate cleverness, then; you and Anne are always being clever. You'll tire Aunt Kate a lot more than Madge's party would." She stood there, large and fair, the features of her small inexpressive face so like her mother's, the lines of her relaxed inviting body so different from Mrs. Drover's righteous curves. Her painted eyes rested curiously on Mrs. Clephane. "You don't suppose she spent her time in Europe sitting at home like this, do you?" she asked the company with simplicity.

There was a stricken pause. Kate filled it by saying with a laugh: "You'll think I might as well have, when I tell you I've never in my life been to a cabaret-party."

Lilla's stare deepened; she seemed hardly able to take the statement in. "What *did* you do with your evenings, then?" she questioned, after an apparently hopeless search for alternatives.

Mrs. Drover had grown pink and pursed-up; even Nollie Tresselton's quick smile seemed congealed. But Kate felt herself carrying it off on wings. "Very often I just sat at home alone, and thought of you all here, and of our first evening together—this very evening."

She saw Anne colour a little, and felt the quick pressure of her arm. That they should have found each other again, she and Anne!

The butler threw open the drawing-room door with solemnity. "A gentleman has called in his motor for Mrs. Gates; he sends word that he's in a hurry, madam, please."

"Oh," said Lilla, leaping upon her fan and vanity bag. She

was out of the room before the butler had rounded off his sentence.

Mrs. Drover, her complacency restored, sank down on a plump Clephane sofa that corresponded in richness and ponderosity with her own person. "Lilla's such a baby!" she sighed; then, with a freer breath, addressed herself to sympathetic enquiries as to Mrs. Clephane's voyage. It was evident that, as far as the family were concerned, Anne's mother had been born again, seven days earlier, on the gang-plank of the liner that had brought her home. On these terms they were all delighted to have her back; and Mrs. Drover declared herself particularly thankful that the voyage had been so smooth.

V.

SMOOTHNESS, Kate Clephane could see, was going to mark the first stage of her re-embarkation on the waters of life. The truth came to her, after that first evening, with the surprised discovery that the family had refrained from touching on her past not so much from prudery, or discretion even, as because such retrogressions were jolting uncomfortable affairs, and the line of least resistance flowed forward, not back. She had been right in guessing that her questions as to what people thought of her past were embarrassing to Landers, but wrong in the interpretation of his embarrassment. Like every one else about her, he was caught up in the irresistible flow of existence, which somehow reminded her less of a mighty river tending seaward than of a moving stairway revolving on itself. "Only they all think it's a river . . ." she mused.

But such thoughts barely lit on her tired mind and were gone. In the first days, after she had grasped (without seeking its explanation) the fact that she need no longer be on her guard, that henceforth there would be nothing to conjure away, or explain, or disguise, her chief feeling was one of illimitable relief. The rapture with which she let herself sink into the sensation showed her for the first time how tired she was, and for how long she had been tired. It was almost as if this sense of relaxation were totally new to her, so far back did her memory have to travel to recover a time when she had not waked to apprehension, and fallen asleep rehearsing fresh precautions for the morrow. In the first years of her marriage there had been the continual vain effort to adapt herself to her husband's point of view, to her mother-in-law's standards, to all the unintelligible ritual with which they barricaded themselves against the alarming business of living. After that had come the bitterness of her first disenchantment, and the insatiable longing to be back on the nursery floor with Anne; then, through all the ensuing years, the many austere and lonely years, and the few consumed with her last passion, the ever-recurring need of one form of vigilance or another, the effort to keep hold of something that might at any moment slip from her, whether it were her painfully-regained "respectability" or the lover for whom she had forgone it. Yes; as she looked back, she saw herself always with taut muscles and the grimace of ease; always pretending that she felt herself free, and secretly knowing that the prison of her marriage had been liberty compared with what she had exchanged it for.

That was as far as her thoughts travelled in the first days. She abandoned herself with the others to the flood of material ease, the torrent of facilities on which they were all embarked. She had been scornful of luxury when it had symbolized the lack of everything else; now that it was an adjunct of her recovered peace she began to enjoy it with the rest, and to feel that the daily perfection of her breakfast-tray, the punctual renewal of the flowers in her sitting-room, the inexhaustible hot water in her bath, the swift gliding of Anne's motor, and the attentions of her household of servants, were essential elements of this new life.

At last she was at rest. Even the nature of her sleep was changed. Waking one morning—not with a jerk, but slowly, voluntarily, as it were—out of a soundless, dreamless night, a miraculous draught of sleep, she understood that for years even her rest had been unrestful. She recalled the uncertainty and apprehension always woven through her dreams, the sudden nocturnal wakings to a blinding, inextinguishable sense of her fate, her future, her past; and the shallow turbid half-consciousness of her morning sleep, which would leave her, when she finally woke from it, emptied of all power of action, all hope and joy. Then every sound that broke the night-hush had been irritating, had pierced her rest like an insect's nagging hum; now the noises that accompanied her falling asleep and awakening seemed to issue harmoniously out of the silence, and the late and early roar of Fifth Avenue to rock her like the great reiterations of the sea.

"This is peace . . . this *must* be peace," she repeated to herself, like a botanist arrested by an unknown flower, and at once guessing it to be the rare exquisite thing he has spent half his life in seeking.

Of course she would not have felt any of these things if Anne had not been the Anne she was. It was from Anne's presence, her smile, her voice, the mystery of her eyes even, that the healing flowed. If Kate Clephane had an apprehension left, it was her awe—almost—of that completeness of Anne's. Was it possible, humanly possible, that one could cast away one's best treasure, and come back after nearly twenty years to find it there, not only as rare as one had remembered it, but ripened, enriched, as only beautiful things are enriched and ripened by time? It was as if one had set out some delicate plant under one's window, so that it might be an object of constant vigilance, and then gone away, leaving it unwatched, unpruned, unwatered—how could one hope to find more than a dead stick in the dust when one returned? But Anne was real; she was not a mirage or a mockery; as the days passed, and her mother's life and hers became adjusted to each other, Kate felt as if they were two parts of some delicate instrument which fitted together as perfectly as if they had never been disjoined—as if Anne were that other half of her life, the half she had dreamed of and never lived. To see Anne living it would be almost the same as if it were her own; would be better, almost; since she would be there, with her experience, and tenderness, to hold out a guiding hand, to help shape the perfection she had sought and missed.

These thoughts came back to her with particular force on the evening of Anne's reappearance at the Opera. During the weeks since old Mrs. Clephane's death the Clephane box had stood severely empty; even when the Opera House was hired for some charity entertainment, Anne sent a cheque but refused to give the box. It was awfully "archaic", as Nollie Tresselton said; but somehow it suited Anne, was as much in her "style" as the close braids folded about her temples. "After all, it's not so easy to be statuesque, and I like Anne's memorial manner," Nollie concluded.

Tonight the period of formal mourning for old Mrs. Clephane was over, and Anne was to go to the Opera with her mother. She had asked the Joe Tresseltons and her guardian to join them first at a little dinner, and Kate Clephane had gone up to dress rather earlier than usual. It was her first public appearance, also, and—as on each occasion of her new life when she came on some unexpected survival of her youth, a face, a voice, a point of view, a room in which the furniture had not been changed—she was astonished, and curiously agitated, at setting out from the very same house for the very same Opera box. The only difference would be in the mode of progression; she remembered the Parisian landau and sixteen-hand chestnuts with glittering plated harness that had waited at the door in her early married days. Then she had a vision of her own toilet, of the elaborate business it used to be: Aline's predecessor, with cunning fingers, dividing and coiling the generous ripples of her hair, and building nests of curls about the temples and in the nape; then the dash up in her dressing-gown to Anne's nursery for a last kiss, and the hurrying back to get into her splendid brocade, to fasten the diamond coronet, the ruby "sunburst", the triple pearls. John Clephane was fond of jewels, and particularly proud of his wife's, first because he had chosen them, and secondly because he had given them to her. She sometimes thought he really admired her only when she had them all on, and she often reflected ironically on Esther's wifely guile in donning her regal finery before she ventured to importune Ahasuerus. It certainly increased Kate Clephane's importance in her husband's eyes to know that, when she entered her box, no pearls could hold their own against hers except Mrs. Beaufort's and old Mrs. Goldmere's.

It was years since Kate Clephane had thought of those jewels. She smiled at the memory, and at the contrast between the unobtrusive dress Aline had just prepared for her, and all those earlier splendours. The jewels, she supposed, were Anne's now; since modern young girls dressed as richly as their elders, Anne had no doubt had them reset for her own use. Mrs. Clephane closed her eyes with a smile of pleasure, picturing Anne (as she had not yet seen her) with bare arms and shoulders, and the orient of the pearls merging in that of her young skin. It was lucky that Anne was tall enough to look her best in jewels. Thence the mother's fancy wandered to the effect Anne must produce on other imaginations; on those, particularly, of young men. Was she already, as they used to say, "interested"? Among the young men Mrs. Clephane had seen, either calling at the house, or in the course of informal dinners at the Tresseltons', the Drovers', and other cousins or "in-laws", she had remarked none who seemed to fix her daughter's attention. But there had been, as yet, few opportunities: the mitigated mourning for old Mrs. Clephane did at least seclude them from general society, and when a girl as aloof as Anne was attracted, the law of contrasts might draw her to some one unfamiliar and undulled by propinquity.

"Or an older man, perhaps?" Kate considered. She thought of Anne's half-daughterly, half-feminine ways with her former guardian, and then shrugged away the possibility that her old stolid Fred could exercise a sentimental charm. Yet the young men of Anne's generation, those her mother had hitherto met, seemed curiously undifferentiated and immature, as if they had been kept too long in some pure and enlightened school, eternally preparing for a life into which their parents and professors could never decide to let them plunge. . . It struck Mrs. Clephane that Chris, when she first met him, must have been about the age of these beautiful inarticulate athletes . . . and Heaven knew how many lives he had already run through! As he said himself, he felt every morning when he woke as if he had come into a new fortune, and had somehow got to "blow it all in" before night.

Kate Clephane sat up and brushed her hand over her eyes. It was the first time Chris had been present to her, in that insistent immediate way, since her return to New York. She had thought of him, of course—how could she cast even a glance over her own past without seeing him there, woven into its very texture? But he seemed to have receded to the plane of that past: from his torturing actual presence her new life had delivered her. . . She pressed both hands against her eyes, as if to crush and disperse the image stealthily forming; then she rose and went into her bedroom, where, a moment before, she had heard Aline laying out her dress.

The maid had finished and gone; the bedroom was empty. The change of scene, the mere passage from one room to another, the sight of the evening dress and opera-cloak on the bed, and of Beatrice Cenci looking down on them through her perpetual sniffle, sufficed to recall Kate to the present. She turned to the dressing-table, and noticed a box which had been placed before her mirror. It was of ebony and citron-wood, embossed with agates and cornelians, and heavily clasped with chiselled silver; and from the summit of the lid a silver Cupid bent his shaft at her.

Kate broke into a faint laugh. How well she remembered that box! She did not have to lift the lid to see its padded trays and tufted sky-blue satin lining! It was old Mrs. Clephane's jewel-box, and on Kate's marriage the dowager had solemnly handed it over to her daughter-in-law with all that it contained.

"I wonder where Anne found it?" Kate conjectured, amused by the sight of one more odd survival in that museum of the past which John Clephane's house had become. A little key hung on one of the handles, and she put it in the lock, and saw all her jewels lying before her. On a slip of paper Anne had written: "Darling, these belong to you. Please wear some of them tonight. . ."

As she entered the opera-box Kate Clephane felt as if the great central chandelier were raying all its shafts upon her, as if she were somehow caught up into and bound on the wheel of its devouring blaze. But only for a moment—after that it seemed perfectly natural to be sitting there with her daughter and Nollie Tresselton, backed by the usual cluster of white waistcoats. After all, in this new existence it was Anne who mattered, not Anne's mother; instantly, after the first plunge, Mrs. Clephane felt herself merged in the blessed anonymity of motherhood. She had never before understood how exposed and defenceless her poor unsupported personality had been through all the lonely years. Her eyes rested on Anne with a new tenderness; the glance crossed Nollie Tresselton's, and the two triumphed in their shared admiration. "Oh, there's no one like Anne," their four eyes told each other.

Anne looked round and intercepted the exchange. Her eyes smiled too, and turned with a childish pleasure to the pearls hanging down over her mother's black dress.

"Isn't she beautiful, Nollie?"

Young Mrs. Tresselton laughed. "You two were made for each other," she said.

Mrs. Clephane closed her lids for an instant; she wanted to drop a curtain between herself and the stir and brightness, and to keep in her eyes the look of Anne's as they fell on the pearls. The episode of the jewels had moved the mother strangely. It had brought Anne closer than a hundred confidences or endearments. As Kate sat there in the dark, she saw, detached against the blackness of her closed lids, a child stumbling with unsteady steps across a windy beach, a funny flushed child with sand in her hair and in the creases of her fat legs, who clutched to her breast something she was bringing to her mother. "It's for mummy," she said solemnly, opening her pink palms on a dead star-fish. Kate saw again the child's rapturous look, and felt the throb of catching her up, star-fish and all, and devouring with kisses the rosy body and tousled head.

In themselves the jewels were nothing. If Anne had handed her a bit of coal—or another dead star-fish—with that look and that intention, the gift would have seemed as priceless. Probably it would have been impossible to convey to Anne how indifferent her mother had grown to the Clephane jewels. In her other life—that confused intermediate life which now seemed so much more remote than the day when the little girl had given her the star-fish—jewels, she supposed, might have pleased her, as pretty clothes had, or flowers, or anything that flattered the eye. Yet she could never remember having regretted John Clephane's jewels; and now they would have filled her with disgust, with abhorrence almost, had they not, in the interval, become Anne's. . . It was the girl who gave them their beauty, made them exquisite to the mother's sight and touch, as though they had been a part of her daughter's loveliness, the expression of something she could not speak.

Mrs. Clephane suddenly exclaimed to herself: "I am rewarded!" It was a queer, almost blasphemous, fancy—but it came to her so. She was rewarded for having given up her daughter; if she had not, could she ever have known such a moment as this? She had been too careless and impetuous in her own youth to be worthy to form and guide this rare creature; and while she seemed to be rushing blindly to her destruction, Providence had saved the best part of her in saving Anne. All these scrupulous self-controlled people—Enid and Hendrik Drover, Fred Landers, even the arch enemy, old Mrs. Clephane—had taken up the task she had flung aside, and carried it out as she could never have done. And she had somehow run the mad course allotted to her, and come out of it sane and sound, to find them all waiting there to give her back her daughter. It was incredible, but there it was. She bowed her head in self-abasement.

The box door was opening and shutting softly, on the stage voices and instruments soared and fell. She did not know how long she sat there in a kind of brooding rapture. But presently she was roused by hearing a different voice at her elbow. She half opened her eyes, and saw a newcomer sitting by Anne. It was one of the young men who came to the house; his fresh blunt face was as inexpressive as a foot-ball; he might have been made by a manufacturer of sporting-goods.

"—in the box over there; but he's gone now; bolted. Said he was too shy to come over and speak to you. Give you my word, he's got it bad; we couldn't get him off the subject."

"*Shy?*" Anne murmured ironically.

"That's what he said. Said he's never had the microbe before. Anyhow, he's bolted off home. Says he don't know when he'll come back to New York."

Kate Clephane, watching her daughter through narrowed lids, perceived a subtle change in her face. Anne did not blush—that close-textured skin of hers seldom revealed the motions of her blood. Her delicate profile remained shut, immovable; she merely lowered her lids as if to keep in a vision. It was Kate's own gesture, and the mother recognized it with a start. She had been right, then; there *was* some one—some one whom Anne had to close her eyes to see! But who was he? Why had he been too shy to come to the box? Where did he come from, and whither had he fled?

Kate glanced at Nollie Tresselton, wondering if she had overheard; but Nollie, in the far corner of the box, leaned forward, deep in the music. Joe Tresselton had vanished, Landers slumbered in the rear. With a little tremor of satisfaction, Kate saw that she had her daughter's secret to herself: if there was no one to enlighten her about it at least there was no one to share it with her, and she was glad. For the first time she felt a little nearer to Anne than all the others.

"It's odd," she thought, "I always knew it would be some one from a distance." But there are no real distances nowadays, and she reflected with an inward smile that the fugitive would doubtless soon reappear, and her curiosity be satisfied.

That evening, when Anne followed her into her bedroom, Mrs. Clephane opened the wardrobe in which she had placed the jewel-box. "Here, my dear; you shall choose one thing for me to wear. But I want you to take back all the rest."

The girl's face clouded. "You won't keep them, then? But they're all yours!"

"Even if they were, I shouldn't want them any longer. But they're not, they're only a trust—" she paused, half smiling—"a trust till your wedding."

She had tried to say the word lightly, but it echoed on through the silence like a peal of silver bells.

"Oh, my wedding! But I shall never marry," said Anne, laughing joyously, and catching her mother in her arms. It was the first time she had made so impulsive a movement; Kate Clephane, trembling a little, held her close.

It brought the girl nearer, made her less aloof, to hear that familiar old denial. "Some day before long," the mother thought, "she'll tell me who he is."

VI.

Kate Clephane lay awake all night thinking of the man who had been too shy to come into the box.

Her sense of security, of permanence, was gone. She understood now that it had been based on the idea that her life would henceforth go on just as it had for the two months since her return; that she and Anne would always remain side by side. The idea was absurd, of course; if she followed it up, her mind recoiled from it. To keep Anne for the rest of her life unchanged, and undesirous of change — the aspiration was inconceivable. She wanted for her daughter the common human round, no more, but certainly no less. Only she did not want her to marry yet — not till they two had grown to know each other better, till Kate had had time to establish herself in her new life.

So she put it to herself; but she knew that what she felt was just an abject fear of change, more change — of being uprooted again, cast once more upon her own resources.

No! She could not picture herself living alone in a little house in New York, dependent on Drovers and Tresseltons, and on the good Fred Landers, for her moral sustenance. To be with Anne, to play the part of Anne's mother — the one part, she now saw, that fate had meant her for — that was what she wanted with all her starved and world-worn soul. To be the background, the atmosphere, of her daughter's life; to depend on Anne, to feel that Anne depended on her; it was the one perfect companionship she had ever known, the only close tie unmarred by dissimulation and distrust. The mere restfulness of it had made her contracted soul expand as if it were sinking into a deep warm bath.

Now the sense of restfulness was gone. From the moment when she had seen Anne's lids drop on that secret vision, the mother had known that her days of quietude were over. Anne's choice might be perfect; she, Kate Clephane, might live out the rest of her days in peace between Anne and Anne's husband. But the mere possibility of a husband made everything incalculable again.

The morning brought better counsel. There was Anne

herself, in her riding-habit, aglow from an early canter, and bringing in her mother's breakfast, without a trace of mystery in her clear eyes. There was the day's pleasant routine, easy and insidious, the planning and adjusting of engagements, notes to be answered, invitations to be sent out; the habitual took Mrs. Clephane into its soothing hold. "After all," she reflected, "young men don't run away nowadays from falling in love." Probably the whole thing had been some cryptic chaff of the youth with the football face; Nollie, indirectly, might enlighten her.

Indirectly; for it was clear to Kate that whatever she learned about her daughter must be learned through observing her, and not through questioning others. The mother could not picture herself as having any rights over the girl, as being, under that roof, anything more than a privileged guest. Anne's very insistence on treating her as the mistress of the house only emphasized her sense of not being so by right: it was the verbal courtesy of the Spaniard who puts all his possessions at the disposal of a casual visitor.

Not that there was anything in Anne's manner to suggest this; but that to Kate it seemed inherent in the situation. It was absurd to assume that her mere return to John Clephane's house could invest her, in any one else's eyes, and much less in her own, with the authority she had lost in leaving it; she would never have dreamed of behaving as if she thought so. Her task, she knew, was gradually, patiently, to win back, of all she had forfeited, the one thing she really valued: her daughter's love and confidence. The love, in a measure, was hers already; could the confidence fail to follow?

Meanwhile, at any rate, she could be no more than the fondest of lookers-on, the discreetest of listeners; and for the moment she neither saw nor heard anything to explain that secret tremor of Anne's eyelids.

At the Joe Tresseltons', a few nights later, she had hoped for a glimpse, a hint. Nollie had invited mother and daughter (with affectionate insistence on the mother's presence) to a little evening party at which some one who was not Russian was to sing—for Nollie was original in everything. The Joe Tresseltons had managed to lend a freshly picturesque air to a dull old Tresselton house near Washington Square, of which the stable had become a studio, and other apartments suffered like transformations, without too much loss of character. It was typical of Nollie that she could give an appearance of stability to her modern furnishings, just as her modern manner kept its repose.

The party was easy and amusing, but even Lilla Gates (whom Nollie always included) took her tone from the mistress of the house, and, dressed with a kind of savage soberness, sat there in her heavy lustreless beauty, bored but triumphant. It was evident that, though at Nollie's she was not in her element, she would not for the world have been left out.

Kate Clephane, while the music immobilized the groups scattered about the great shadowy room, found herself scanning them with a fresh intensity of attention. She no longer thought of herself as an object of curiosity to any of these careless self-engrossed young people; she had learned that a woman of her age, however conspicuous her past, and whatever her present claims to notice, is fated to pass unremarked in a society where youth so undisputedly rules. The discovery had come with a slight shock; then she blessed the anonymity which made observation so much easier.

Only—what was there to observe? Again the sameness of the American Face encompassed her with its innocent uniformity. How many of them it seemed to take to make up a single individuality! Most of them were like the miles and miles between two railway stations. She saw again, with gathering wonder, that one may be young and handsome and healthy and eager, and yet unable, out of such rich elements, to evolve a personality.

Her thoughts wandered back to the shabby faces peopling her former life. She knew every seam of their shabbiness, but now for the first time she seemed to see that they had been worn down by emotions and passions, however selfish, however sordid, and not merely by ice-water and dyspepsia.

"Since the Americans have ceased to have dyspepsia," she reflected, "they have lost the only thing that gave them any expression."

Landers came up as the thought flashed through her mind, and apparently caught its reflection in her smile.

"You look at me as if you'd never seen me before; is it because my tie's crooked?" he asked, sitting down beside her.

"No; your tie is absolutely straight. So is everything else about you. That's the reason I was looking at you in that way. I can't get used to it!"

He reddened a little, as if unaccustomed to such insistent scrutiny. "Used to what?"

"The universal straightness. You're all so young and—and so regular! I feel as if I were in a gallery of marble master-pieces."

"As that can hardly apply to our features, I suppose it's intended to describe our morals," he said with a faint gri-mace.

"I don't know— I wish I did! What I'm trying to do, of course," she added abruptly and unguardedly, "is to guess how I should feel about all these young men—if I were Anne."

She was vexed with herself that the words should have slipped out, and yet not altogether sorry. After all, one could always trust Landers to hold his tongue—and almost always to understand. His smile showed that he understood now.

"Of course you're trying; we all are. But, as far as I know, Sister Anne hasn't yet seen any one from her tower."

A breath of relief expanded the mother's heart.

"Ah, well, you'd be sure to know—especially as, when she does, it ought to be some one visible a long way off!"

"It ought to be, yes. The more so as she seems to be in no hurry." He looked away. "But don't build too much on that," he added. "I learned long ago, in such matters, to expect only the unexpected."

Kate Clephane glanced at him quickly; his ingenuous coun-tenance wore an unaccustomed shadow. She remembered that, in old days, John Clephane had always jokingly de-clared—in a tone proclaiming the matter to be one mention-able only as a joke—that Fred Landers was in love with her; and she said to herself that the lesson her old friend referred to was perhaps the one she had unwittingly given him when she went away with another man.

It was on the tip of her tongue to exclaim: "Oh, but I didn't know anything then— I wasn't anybody! My real life,

my only life, began years later—" but she checked herself
with a start. Why, in the very act of thinking of her daughter,
had she suddenly strayed away into thinking of Chris? It
was the first time it had happened to her to confront the
two images, and she felt as if she had committed a sort of
profanation.

She took refuge in another thought that Landers's last
words had suggested—the thought that if she herself had
matured late, why so might Anne. The idea was faintly reassuring.

"No; I won't build on any theory," she said, answering
him. "But one can't help hoping she'll wait till some one turns
up good enough for what she's going to be."

"Oh, these mothers!" he laughed, his face smoothing out
into its usual guileless lines.

The music was over. The groups flowed past them toward
the little tables in another picturesque room, and Lilla Gates
swept by in a cluster of guffawing youths. She seemed to have
attracted all the kindred spirits in the room, and her sluggish
stare was shot with provocation. Ah, there was another mystery! No one explained Lilla—every one seemed to take her
for granted. Not that it really mattered; Kate had seen
enough of Anne to feel sure she would never be in danger of
falling under Lilla's influence. The perils in wait for her would
wear a subtler form. But, as a matter of curiosity, and a possible light on the new America, Kate would have liked to
know why her husband's niece—surprising offshoot of the
prudent Clephanes and stolid Drovers—had been singled
out, in this new easy-going society, to be at once reproved
and countenanced. Lilla in herself was too uninteresting to
stimulate curiosity; but as a symptom she might prove enlightening. Only, here again, Kate had the sense that she, of
all the world, was least in a position to ask questions. What if
people should turn around and ask them about *her*? Since she
had been living under her old roof, and at her daughter's
side, the mere suggestion made her tremble. It was curious—
and she herself was aware of it—how quickly, unconsciously
almost, she had slipped at last into the very attitude the Clephanes had so long tried to force upon her: the attitude of
caution and conservatism.

Her glance, in following Lilla, caught Fred Landers's, and he smiled again, but with a slight constraint. Instantly she thought: "He'd like to tell me her whole story, but he doesn't dare, because very likely it began like my own. And it will always go on being like that: whatever I'm afraid to ask they'll be equally afraid to tell." Well, that was what people called "starting with a clean slate", she supposed; would no one ever again scribble anything unguardedly on hers? She felt indescribably alone.

On the way home the mere feeling of Anne's arm against hers drew her out of her solitariness. After all, she had only to wait. The new life was but a few weeks old; and already Anne's nearness seemed to fill it. If only she could keep Anne near enough!

"Did you like it, mother? How do we all strike you, I wonder?" the girl asked suddenly.

"As kinder than anything I ever dreamed."

She thought she felt Anne's surprised glance in the darkness. "Oh, *that*! But why not? It's you who must try to be kind to us. I feel as if we must be so hard to tell apart. In Europe there are more contrasts, I suppose. I saw Uncle Fred helping you to sort us out this evening."

"You mean you caught me staring? I dare say I do. I want so much not to miss anything . . . anything that's a part of your life. . ." Her voice shook with the avowal.

She was answered by a closer pressure. "You wonderful mother! I don't believe you ever will." She was conscious in Anne, mysteriously, of a tension answering her own. "Isn't it splendid to be two to talk things over?" the girl said joyously.

"*What things?*" Kate Clephane thought; but dared not speak. Her hand on Anne's, she sat silent, feeling her child's heart tremble nearer.

VII.

EVERY ONE noticed how beautifully it worked; the way, as Fred Landers said, she and Anne had hit it off from their first look at each other on the deck of the steamer.

Enid Drover was almost emotional about it, one evening when she and Kate sat alone in the Clephane drawing-room. It was after one of Anne's "young" dinners, and the other guests, with Anne herself, had been whirled off to some form of midnight entertainment.

"It's wonderful, my dear, how you've done it. Poor mother didn't always find Anne easy, you know. But she's taken a tremendous fancy to you."

Kate felt herself redden with pride. "I suppose it's the novelty, partly," Mrs. Drover continued, with her heavy-stepping simplicity. "Perhaps that's an advantage, in a way." But she pulled up, apparently feeling that, in some obscure manner, she might be offending where she sought to please. "Anne admires your looks so much, you know; and your slightness." A sigh came from her adipose depths. "I do believe it gives one more hold over one's girls to have kept one's figure. One can at least go on wearing the kind of clothes they like."

Kate felt an inward glow of satisfaction. The irony of the situation hardly touched her: the fact that the youth and elasticity she had clung to so desperately should prove one of the chief assets of her new venture. It was beginning to seem natural that everything should lead up to Anne.

"This business of setting up a studio, now; Anne's so pleased that you approve. She had a struggle with her grandmother about it; but poor mother wouldn't give in. She was too horrified. She thought paint so messy—and then how could she have got up all those stairs?"

"Ah, well"—it was so easy to be generous!—"that sort of thing did seem horrifying to Mrs. Clephane's generation. After all, it was not so long before her day that Dr. Johnson said portrait-painting was indelicate in a female."

Mrs. Drover gave her sister-in-law a puzzled look. Her mind seldom retained more than one word in any sentence, and her answer was based on the reaction that particular word provoked. *"Female —"* she murmured— "is that word being used again? I never thought it very nice to apply it to women, did you? I suppose I'm old-fashioned. Nothing shocks the young people nowadays—not even the Bible."

Nothing could have given Kate Clephane greater confidence in her own success than this little talk with Enid Drover. She had been feeling her way so patiently, so stealthily almost, among the outworks and defences of her daughter's character; and here she was actually instated in the citadel.

Anne's "studio-warming" strengthened the conviction. Mrs. Clephane had not been allowed to see the studio; Anne and Nollie and Joe Tresselton, for a breathless week, had locked themselves in with nails and hammers and pots of paint, sealing their ears against all questioning. Then one afternoon the doors were opened, and Kate, coming out of the winter twilight, found herself in a great half-lit room with a single wide window overlooking the reaches of the Sound all jewelled and netted with lights, the fairy span of the Brooklyn Bridge, and the dark roof-forest of the intervening city. It all seemed strangely significant and mysterious in that disguising dusk—full of shadows, distances, invitations. Kate leaned in the window, surprised at this brush of the wings of poetry.

In the room, Anne had had the good taste to let the sense of space prolong itself. It looked more like a great library waiting for its books than a modern studio; as though the girl had measured the distance between that mighty nocturne and her own timid attempts, and wanted the implements of her art to pass unnoticed.

They were sitting—Mrs. Clephane, the Joe Tresseltons and one or two others—about the tea-cups set out at one end of a long oak table, when the door opened and Lilla Gates appeared, tawny and staring, in white furs and big pendulous earrings. She brought with her a mingled smell of cigarettes and Houbigant, and as she stood there, circling the room with her sulky contemptuous gaze, Kate felt a movement of annoyance.

"Why must one forever go on being sorry for Lilla?" she

wondered, wincing a little as Anne's lips touched her cousin's mauve cheek.

"It was nice of you to come, Lilla."

"Well—I chucked something bang-up for you," said Lilla coolly. It was evidently her pride to be perpetually invited, perpetually swamped in a multiplicity of boring engagements. She looked about her again, and then dropped into an armchair. "Mercy—you *have* cleared the decks!" she remarked. "Ain't there going to be any more furniture than this?"

"Oh, the furniture's all outside—and the pictures too," Anne said, pointing to the great window.

"What—Brooklyn Bridge? Lord!—Oh, but I see: you've kept the place clear for dancing. Good girl, Anne! Can I bring in some of my little boys sometimes? Is that a pianola?" she added, with a pounce toward the grand piano in a shadowy corner. "I like this kindergarten," she pronounced.

Nollie Tresselton laughed. "If you come, Anne won't let you dance. You'll all have to sit for her—for hours and hours."

"Well, we'll sit between the dances then. Ain't I going to have a latch-key, Anne?"

She stood leaning against the piano, sipping the cock-tail some one had handed her, her head thrown back, and the light from a shaded lamp striking up at her columnar throat and the green glitter of her earrings, which suggested to Kate Clephane the poisonous antennæ of some giant insect. Anne stood close to her, slender, erect, her small head clasped in close braids, her hands hanging at her sides, dead-white against the straight dark folds of her dress. There was something distinctly unpleasant to Kate Clephane in the proximity of the two, and she rose and moved toward the piano.

As she sat down before it, letting her hands drift into the opening bars of a half-remembered melody, she saw Lilla, in her vague lounging way, draw nearer to Anne, who held out a hand for the empty cock-tail glass. The gesture brought them so close that Lilla, slightly drooping her head, could let fall, hardly above her breath, but audibly to Kate: "He's back again. He bothered the life out of me to bring him here today."

Again Kate saw that quick drop of her daughter's lids; this

time it was accompanied by a just-perceptible tremor of the hand that received the glass.

"Nonsense, Lilla!"

"Well, what on earth am I to do about it? I can't get the police to run him in, can I?"

Anne laughed—the faintest half-pleased laugh of impatience and dismissal. "You may have to," she said.

Nollie Tresselton, in the interval, had glided up and slipped an arm through Lilla's.

"Come along, my dear. There's to be no dancing here today." Her little brown face had the worn sharp look it often took on when she was mothering Lilla. But Lilla's feet were firmly planted. "I don't budge till I get another cock-tail."

One of the young men hastened to supply her, and Anne turned to her other guests. A few minutes later the Tresseltons and Lilla went away, and one by one the remaining visitors followed, leaving mother and daughter alone in the recovered serenity of the empty room.

But there was no serenity in Kate. That half-whispered exchange between Lilla Gates and Anne had stirred all her old apprehensions and awakened new ones. The idea that her daughter was one of Lilla's confidants was inexpressibly disturbing. Yet the more she considered, the less she knew how to convey her anxiety to her daughter.

"If I only knew how intimate they really are—what she really thinks of Lilla!"

For the first time she understood on what unknown foundations her fellowship with Anne was built. Were they solid? Would they hold? Was Anne's feeling for her more than a sudden girlish enthusiasm for an agreeable older woman, the kind of sympathy based on things one can enumerate, and may change one's mind about, rather than the blind warmth of habit?

She stood musing while Anne moved about the studio, putting away the music, straightening a picture here and there.

"And this is where you're going to work—"

Anne nodded joyously.

"Lilla apparently expects you to turn it into a dance-hall for her benefit."

"Poor Lilla! She can't see a new room without wanting to fox-trot in it. Life, for her, wherever she is, consists in going somewhere else in order to do exactly the same thing."

Kate was relieved: there was no mistaking the half-disdainful pity of the tone.

"Well—don't give her that latch-key!" she laughed, gathering up her furs.

Anne echoed the laugh. "There are to be only two latch-keys—yours and mine," she said; and mother and daughter went gaily down the steep stairs.

The days, after that, moved on with the undefinable reassurance of habit. Kate Clephane was beginning to feel herself part of an old-established routine. She had tried to organize her life in such a way that it should fit into Anne's without awkward overlapping. Anne, nowadays, after her early canter, went daily to the studio and painted till lunch; sometimes, as the days lengthened, she went back for another two hours' work in the afternoon. When the going was too bad for her morning ride she usually walked to the studio, and Kate sometimes walked with her, or went through the Park to meet her on her return. When she painted in the afternoon, Kate would occasionally drop in for tea, and they would return home together on foot in the dusk. But Mrs. Clephane was scrupulously careful not to intrude on her daughter's working-hours; she held back, not with any tiresome display of discretion, but with the air of caring for her own independence too much not to respect Anne's.

Sometimes, now that she had settled down into this new way of life, she was secretly aware of feeling a little lonely; there were hours when the sense of being only a visitor in the house where her life ought to have been lived gave her the same drifting uprooted feeling which had been the curse of her other existence. It was not Anne's fault; nor that, in this new life, every moment was not interesting and even purposeful, since each might give her the chance of serving Anne, pleasing Anne, in some way or another getting closer to Anne. But this very feeling took a morbid intensity from the fact of having no common memories, no shared associations, to feed on. Kate was frightened, sometimes, by its likeness to that other isolated and devouring emotion which her love for Chris had been. Everything might have been different, she thought, if she had had more to do, or more friends of her own to occupy her. But Anne's establishment, which had been her grandmother's, still travelled smoothly enough on its own momentum, and though the girl insisted that her mother was now the head of the house, the headship involved little more than ordering dinner, and talking over linen and carpets and curtains with old Mrs. Clephane's house-keeper.

Then, as to friends—was it because she was too much engrossed in her daughter to make any? Or because her life had been too incommunicably different from that of her bustling middle-aged contemporaries, absorbed by local and domestic questions she had no part in? Or had she been too suddenly changed from a self-centred woman, insatiable for personal excitements, into that new being, a mother, her centre of gravity in a life not hers?

She did not know; she felt only that she no longer had time for anything but motherhood, and must be content to bridge over, as best she could, the unoccupied intervals. And, after all, the intervals were not many. Her daughter never appeared without instantly filling up every crevice of the present, and overflowing into the past and the future, so that, even in the mother's rare lapses into despondency, life without Anne, like life before Anne, had become unthinkable.

She was revolving this for the thousandth time as she turned into the Park one afternoon to meet Anne on the latter's way homeward. The days were already much longer; the difference in the light, and that premature languor of the air which comes, in America, before the sleeping earth seems to expect it, made Mrs. Clephane feel that the year had turned, that a new season was opening in her new life. She walked on with the vague sense of confidence in the future which the first touch of spring gives. The worst of the way was past—how easily, how smoothly to the feet! Where misunderstanding and failure had been so probable, she was increasingly sure of having understood and succeeded. And already she and Anne were making delightful plans for the spring. . .

Ahead of her, in a transverse alley, she was disagreeably surprised by the sight of Lilla Gates. There was no mistaking that tall lounging figure, though it was moving slowly away from her. Lilla at that hour in the Park? It seemed curious and improbable. Yet Lilla it was; and Mrs. Clephane's conclusion was drawn immediately. "Who is she waiting for?"

Whoever it was had not come; the perspective beyond Lilla was empty. After a moment she hastened her step, and vanished behind a clump of evergreens at the crossing of the paths. Kate did not linger to watch for her reappearance. The incident was too trifling to fix the attention; after all, what had one ever expected of Lilla but that she might be found loitering in unlikely places, in quest of objectionable people? There was nothing new in that—nor did Kate even regret not having a glimpse of the objectionable person. In her growing reassurance about Anne, Lilla's affairs had lost whatever slight interest they once offered.

She walked on—but her mood was altered. The sight of Lilla lingering in that deserted path had called up old associations. She remembered meetings of the same kind—but was it her own young figure she saw fading down those far-off perspectives? Well—if it were, let it go! She owned no kinship with that unhappy ghost. Serene, middle-aged, respected and respectable, she walked on again out of that vanishing past into the warm tangible present. And at any moment now she might meet Anne.

She had turned down a wide walk leading to one of the Fifth Avenue entrances of the Park. One could see a long way ahead; there were people coming and going. Two women passed, with some noisy children racing before them, a milliner's boy, whistling, his boxes slung over his shoulder, a paralytic pushing himself along in a wheeled chair; then, coming toward her from the direction of Fifth Avenue, a man who half-stopped, recognized her, and raised his hat.

BOOK II

VIII.

"CHRIS!" she said.

She felt herself trembling all over; then, abruptly, mysteriously, and in the very act of uttering his name, she ceased to tremble, and it came flooding in on her with a shock of wonder that the worst was already over—that at last she was going to be free.

"Well, well," she heard him saying, in that round full voice which always became fuller and more melodious when it had any inner uncertainty to mask; and "If only," she thought, "it doesn't all come back when he laughs!"

He laughed. "I'm so glad . . . *glad*," he reiterated, as if explaining; and with the laugh in her ears she still felt herself as lucidly, as incredibly remote from him.

"Glad?" she echoed, a little less sure of her speech than of her thoughts, and remembering how sometimes the smile in his eyes used to break up her words into little meaningless splinters that she could never put together again till he was gone.

"Of your good luck, I mean. . . I've heard, of course." And now she had him, for the first time, actually reddening and stammering as she herself used to do, and catching at the splinters of his own words! Ah, the trick was done—she could even see, as they continued to face each other in the searching spring light, that he had reddened, thickened, hardened—as if the old Chris had been walled into this new one, and were not even looking at her out of the windows of his prison.

"My good luck?" she echoed again, while the truth still danced in her ears: the truth that she was free, free, free—away from him at last, far enough off to see him and judge him!

It must have been his bad taste—the bad taste that could lead him into such an opening as that—which, from the very first, she had felt in him, and tried not to feel, even when she was worshipping him most blindly.

But, after all, if she felt so free, why be so cruel? Ah, because the terror was still there—it had only shifted its ground. What frightened her now was not the thought of their past but of their future. And she must not let him see that it frightened her. What had his last words been? Ah, yes—. She answered: "Of course I'm very happy to be at home again."

He lowered his voice to murmur: "And I'm happy *for* you."

Yes; she remembered now; it was always in emotional moments that his tact failed him, his subtlety vanished, and he seemed to be reciting speeches learned by heart out of some sentimental novel—the very kind he was so clever at ridiculing.

They continued to stand facing each other, their inspiration spent, as if waiting for the accident that had swept them together to whirl them apart again.

Suddenly she risked (since it was better to know): "So you're living now in New York?"

He shook his head with an air of melancholy. "No such luck. I'm back in Baltimore again. Come full circle. For a time, after the war, I was on a newspaper there; interviewing film-stars and base-ball fans and female prohibitionists. Then I tried to run a Country Club—awful job! All book-keeping, and rows between members. Now Horace Maclew has taken pity on me; I'm what I suppose you'd call his private secretary. No eight-hour day: he keeps me pretty close. It's only once in a blue moon I can get away."

She felt her tightened heart dilating. Baltimore wasn't very far away; but it was far enough as long as he had anything to keep him there. She knew about Horace Maclew, an elderly wealthy bibliophile and philanthropist, with countless municipal and social interests in his own town, and a big country-place just outside it. No; Mr. Maclew's private secretary was not likely to have many holidays. But how long would Chris resign himself to such drudgery? She wanted to be kind and say: "And your painting? Your writing?" but she didn't dare. Besides, he had probably left both phases far behind him, and there was no need, really, for her to concern herself with his new hobbies, whatever they might be. Of course she knew

that he and she would have to stand there staring at one another till she made a gesture of dismissal; but on what note
was she to make it? The natural thing (since she felt so safe
and easy with him) would have been to say: "The next time
you're in town you must be sure to look me up—". But, with
him, how could one be certain of not having such a suggestion taken literally? Now that he had seen she was not afraid
of him he would probably not be afraid of *her*; if he wanted a
good dinner, or an evening at the Opera, he'd be as likely as
not to call her up and ask for it.

And suddenly, as they hung there, she caught, over his
shoulder, a glimpse of another figure just turning into the
Park from the same direction; Anne, with her quick step, her
intent inward air, as she always moved and looked when she
had just left her easel. In another moment Anne would be
upon them.

Mrs. Clephane held out her hand: for a fraction of a second
it lay in his. "Well, goodbye; I'm glad to know you've got a
job that must be so interesting."

"Oh—interesting!" He dismissed it with a gesture. "But
I'm glad to see you," he added; "just to *see* you," with a clever
shifting of the emphasis. He paused a moment, and then
risked a smile. "You don't look a day older, you know."

She threw her head back with an answering smile. "Why
should I, when I feel years younger?"

Thank heaven, an approaching group of people must have
obstructed her daughter's view! Mrs. Clephane hurried on,
wanting to put as much distance as she could between herself
and Chris's retreating figure before she came up with her
daughter. When she did, she plunged straight into the girl's
eyes, and saw that they were still turned on her inward vision.
"Dearest," she cried gaily, "I can see by your look that you've
been doing a good day's work."

Anne's soul rose slowly to the surface, shining out between
deep lashes. "How do you know, I wonder? I suppose you
must have been a great deal with somebody who painted. For
a long time afterward one carries the thing about with one
wherever one goes." She slipped her arm in Kate's, and
turned unresistingly as the latter guided her back toward Fifth
Avenue.

"It's dusty in the Park, and I feel as if I wanted a quick walk home. I like Fifth Avenue when the lights are just coming out," Mrs. Clephane explained.

All night long she lay awake in the great bed of the Clephane spare-room, and stared at Chris. While they still faced each other—and after her first confused impression of his having thickened and reddened—she had seen him only through the blur of her fears and tremors. Even after they had parted, and she was walking home with Anne, the shock of the encounter still tingling in her, he remained far off, almost imponderable, less close and importunate than her memories of him. It was as if his actual presence had exorcised his ghost. But now—

He had not vanished; he had only been waiting. Waiting till she was alone in her room in the sleeping house, in the un-heeding city. How alone, she had never more acutely felt. Who on earth was there to intervene between them, when there was not a soul to whom she could even breathe that she had met him? She lay in the darkness with terrified staring eyes, and there he stood, his smile deriding her—a strange composite figure, made equally of the old Chris and the new. . .

It was of no use to shut her eyes; he was between lid and ball. It was of no use to murmur disjointed phrases to herself, conjure him away with the language of her new life, with allusions and incantations unknown to him; he just stood there and waited. Well, then—she would face it out now, would deal with him! But how? What was he to her, and what did he want of her?

Yes: it all came to the question of what he wanted; it always had. When had there ever been a question of what *she* wanted? He took what he chose from life, gathered and let drop and went on: it was the artist's way, he told her. But what could he possibly want of her now, and why did she imagine that he wanted anything, when by his own showing he was so busy and so provided for?

She pulled herself together, suddenly ashamed of her own thoughts. In pity for herself she would have liked to draw the old tattered glamour over him; but there must always have

been rents and cracks in it, and now it couldn't by any tugging be made to cover him. No; she didn't love him any
longer; she was sure of that. Like a traveller who has just
skirted an abyss, she could lean over without dizziness and
measure the depth into which she had not fallen. But if that
were so, why was she so afraid of him? If it were a mere
question of her own social safety, a mean dread of having her
past suspected, why, she was more ashamed of that than of
having loved him. She would almost rather have endured the
misery of still loving him than of seeing what he and she
looked like, now that the tide had ebbed from them. She had
been a coward; she had been stiff and frightened and conventional, when, from the vantage-ground of her new security,
she could so easily have been friendly and generous; she felt
like rushing out into the streets to find him, to speak to him
as she ought to have spoken, to tell him that she was not in
the least afraid of him.

And yet she *was*! She supposed it was the old incalculable
element in him, that profound fundamental difference in their
natures which used to make their closest nearness seem more
like a spell than a reality. She understood now that if she had
always been afraid of him it was just because she could never
tell what she was afraid of. . .

If only there had been some one to whom she could confess herself, some one who would laugh away her terrors!
Fred Landers? But she would frighten him more than he reassured her. And the others—the kindly approving family?
What would they do but avert their eyes and beg her to be
reasonable and remember her daughter? Well—and her
daughter, then? And Anne? Was there any one on earth but
Anne who would understand her?

The oppression of the night and the silence, and the rumour of her own fears, were becoming intolerable. She could
not endure them any longer. She jumped up, flung on her
dressing-gown, and stole out of her room. The corridor was
empty and obscure; only a faint light from the lower hall cast
its reflection upward on the ceiling of the stairs. From below
came the pompous tick of the hall clock, as loud as a knocking
in the silence.

She stole to her daughter's door, and kneeling down laid

her ear against the crack. Presently, through the hush, she caught the soft rhythmic breath of youthful sleep, and pictured Anne, slim and motionless, her dark hair in orderly braids along the pillow. The vision startled the mother back to sanity. She got up stiffly and stood looking about her with dazed eyes.

Suddenly the light on the stairs, the nocturnal ticking, swept another vision through her throbbing brain. In just such a silence, before the first cold sounds of the winter daylight, she had crept down those very stairs, unchained the front door, slipped back one after another of John Clephane's patent bolts, and let herself out of his house for the last time. Ah, what business had she in it now, her hand on her daughter's door? She dragged herself back to her own room, switched on the light, and sat hunched up in the great bed, mechanically turning over the pages of a fashion-paper she had picked up on her sitting-room table. Skirts were certainly going to be narrower that spring. . .

IX

ILLA—but of course he comes for Lilla!" she exclaimed.

She raised herself on her elbow, saw the bed-lamp still burning, and the fashion-paper on the floor beside the bed. The night was not over; there was no grayness yet between the curtains. She must have dropped into a short uneasy sleep, from which Lilla's loitering expectant figure, floating away from her down an alley of the Park, had detached itself with such emphasis that the shock awoke her.

Lilla and Chris . . . but of course they had gone to the Park to meet each other! Why should he have happened to turn in at that particular gate, at that particular hour, unless to find some one who, a few yards off, careless and unconcerned, was so obviously lingering there to be found?

The discovery gave Kate Clephane a sensation of actual physical nausea. She sat up in bed, pushed her hair back from her damp forehead, and repeated the two names slowly, as if trying from those conjoined syllables to disentangle the clue to the mystery. For mystery there was; she was sure of it now! People like Lilla Gates and Chris did not wander aimlessly through Central Park at the secret hour when the winter dusk begins to blur its paths. Every moment of such purposeless lives was portioned out, packed with futilities. Kate had seen enough of that in her enforced association with the idlers of a dozen watering-places, her dreary participation in their idling.

And how the clue, now she held it, explained everything! Explained, first of all, why Chris, the ready, the resourceful, had been so tongue-tied and halting when they met. Why had she not been struck by that before? She saw now that, if she was afraid of him, he was a thousand times more afraid of her! And how could she have imagined that, to a man like Chris, the mere fact of running across a discarded mistress would be disconcerting, or even wholly unpleasant? Who better than he should know how to deal with such emergencies? His past must be strewn with precedents. As her memory travelled back over their life together she recalled their having met, one day at Hadrian's Villa, a little woman, a Mrs. Guy

So-and-so—she had even forgotten the name! She and Chris
had been wandering, close-linked—for the tourist season was
over, and besides, they cared so little who saw them—
through the rich garlanded ruins, all perfume and enchantment; and there, in their path, had stood a solitary figure, the
figure of a young woman, pretty, well-dressed, with a hungry
melancholy face. A little way behind her, a heavy elderly gentleman in blue goggles and an overcoat was having archæological explanations shouted into his deaf ear and curved
hand by a guide with a rasping German accent—and Chris,
exclaiming: "By Jove, there are the So-and-sos!" had advanced
with outstretched hand, introduced the two women, and
poured out upon the melancholy newcomer a flood of laughing allusive talk, half chaff, half sentiment, and all as easily, as
unconcernedly as if her great eyes had not, all the while, been
pleading, pleading with him to remember.

And then, afterward, when Kate had said to him: "But
wasn't that the woman you told me about once, who was so
desperately unhappy, and wanted to run away with you?" he
had merely answered: "Oh, not particularly with *me*, as far as
I remember—" and she had hugged his arm closer, and
thought how funny he was, and luxuriously pitied the other
woman.

Yes; that was the real Chris; always on the spot, easy-going
and gay. The stammering evasive apparition in the Park had
no resemblance to that Chris; Kate knew instinctively that it
was not the fact of meeting her that had so disturbed him,
but the fact that, for some reason, the meeting might interfere
with his plans. But what plans? Why, his plans with Lilla—
which would necessarily bring him in contact with the clan,
since they so resolutely backed Lilla up, and thus expose him
to—to what? To Kate's betraying him? For a moment she
half-laughed at the idea.

For what could she do to injure him, after all? And, whatever his plans were, how could he ever imagine her interfering
with them, when to do so would be to betray her own secret?
She lay there in the dreary dawn and tried to work her way
through the labyrinth. And then, all at once, it came to her:
what if he wanted to marry Lilla? And what more probable
than that he did? It was evident that living with his people

and administering Mr. Maclew's philanthropies was not a life that he would have called "fit for a dog". He liked money, she knew, for all his careless way; he wanted to have it, but he hated to earn it. And if he married Lilla there would be plenty of money. The Drovers would see to that—Kate could imagine nothing more likely to unloose their purse-strings than the possibility of "settling" Lilla, and getting rid of the perpetual menace that her roving fancies hung over her mother's neatly-waved head. Chris, of course, was far too clever not to have seen that, and worked out the consequences in his own mind. If Lilla had been plain and dowdy he wouldn't even have considered it—Kate did him that justice. If he liked money he liked it in a large lordly way, and only as one among several things which it was convenient but not essential to have. He would never do a base thing for money; but, after all, there was nothing base in marrying Lilla if he liked her looks and was amused by her talk, as he probably was. There was one side of Chris, the side Kate Clephane had least explored, and was least capable of understanding, which might very well find its complement in Lilla. . .

Kate's aching eyes continued to strain into the future. If that were really his plan, of course he would be afraid of her! For he knew her too, knew her ever so much better than she did him, and would be sure to guess that, much as she would want to cover up their past, she would not hesitate a moment between revealing it and doing what she called her duty. Her duty—how he used to laugh at the phrase! He told her she had run away from her real duties only for the pleasure of inventing new ones, and that to her they were none the less duties because she imagined them to be defiances. It was one of the paradoxes that most amused him: the picture of her flying from her conscience and always meeting it again in her path, barely disguised by the audacities she had dressed it up in.

Yes; evidently he had asked himself, on the instant, what she would do about Lilla; and the mere fact made her feel, with a fierce desperation, that she must do something. Not that she cared a straw about Lilla, or felt the least "call" to save her—but to have Chris in the family, in the group, to have to smile at him across the Clephane dinner-table, the

Drover dinner-table, all the family dinner-tables, to have to keep up, for all the rest of her life, the double pretence of never having liked him too much, and of now liking him enough to gratify the pride and allay the suspicions of the family—no, she could not imagine herself doing it! She was right to be afraid of him; he was right to be afraid of her.

The return to daylight made her nocturnal logic seem absurd; but several days passed before her agitation subsided. It was only when she found life continuing undisturbed about her, Anne painting for long rapturous hours, Lilla following her same bored round of pleasure, the others placidly engaged in their usual pursuits, and no one mentioning Chris's name, or apparently aware of his existence, that the shadow of her midnight imaginings was lifted.

Once or twice, as the sense of security returned, she thought of letting Chris's name fall, ever so casually, in Fred Landers's hearing. She never got as far as that; but one day she contrived, in speaking of some famous collection of books just coming into the market, to mention Horace Maclew.

Landers's eye kindled. "Ah, what books! His Italian antiphonals are probably the best in the world."

"You know him, then? How—is it long since you last saw his library?" she stammered.

He considered. "Oh, years; not since before the war."

Her heart rose on the mounting hope. "Oh, not since then? . . . I suppose he must have a very good librarian?"

"Used to have; the poor chap was killed in the war, I believe. That reminds me that I heard the other day he was looking for some one."

"Looking for a librarian?" She heard her voice shake. "Not for a private secretary?"

She thought he looked surprised. "I don't think so; but I really don't remember. I know he always has a lot of scribes about him; naturally, with so many irons in the fire. Did you happen to hear of any one who was looking for that sort of job? It might be a kindness to let Maclew know."

She drew her brows together, affecting to consider. "Where did I hear of some one? I can't remember either. One is always hearing nowadays of people looking for something to do."

"Yes; but of few who can do anything. And Maclew's the last man to put up with incompetence. You must come and see him with me. He's not an easy customer, but he and I are old members of the Grolier Club and he lets me bring a friend to see his library occasionally. I've always promised to take Anne, some day when she's going on to Washington."

Kate's heart gave a sharp downward plunge. That "Take Anne" reverberated in her like a knell. What a fool she had been to bring the subject up! If she had not mentioned Horace Maclew's name Landers might never have thought of his library again; at least not of the promise to take Anne there. Well, it was a lesson to hold her tongue, to let things follow their course without fearing or interfering. Happily Anne, more and more absorbed in her painting, seemed to have no idea of a visit to Washington; she had never mentioned such a plan, beyond once casually saying: "Oh, the Washington magnolias . . . some spring I must go there and paint them."

Some spring . . . well, that was pleasantly indefinite. For Chris was not likely to remain long with Horace Maclew. Where had Chris ever remained long? Kate Clephane did not know, now, whether to tremble at that impermanence or be glad of it. She did not know what to think about anything, now that the thought of Chris had suddenly re-introduced itself into the smooth-running wheels of her existence.

Then, as the days passed, her reassurance returned again, and it was with a stupefied start that one afternoon, crossing the Park on her way to the studio, she once more caught sight of Lilla Gates. This time the person for whom she had presumably been waiting was with her, and the two stood in close communion. The man's back was turned, but his figure, his attitude, were so familiar to Kate that she stopped short, trembling lest she should see his face.

She did not see it. He and Mrs. Gates were in the act of leave-taking. Their hands met, they lingered for a last word, and then separated, each hastening away in a direction other than Kate's. She continued to stand motionless after they had vanished, uncertain yet certain. It was Chris— but of course it was Chris! He came often to New York, then, in spite of what he had said about the difficulty of getting away. If he had said that, it was probably just because he wanted to keep his comings and goings from Mrs. Clephane's knowledge. And that again would tally with what she suspected as to his motives. She turned sick, and stood with compressed lips and lowered head, as if to close her senses against what was coming. At length she roused herself and walked on.

Lilla. . . Lilla. . . Chris and Lilla!

She kept on her way northward, following the less frequented by-ways of the Park. It was early yet, and she wanted to walk off her agitation before joining Anne at the studio.

Lilla. . . Lilla. . . Chris and Lilla!

Something must be done about it, something must be said — it was impossible that this affair, whatever it was, should go on unchecked. But had she, Kate Clephane, any power to prevent it? Probably not — her intervention might serve only to precipitate events. Well, at least she must know what was coming — must find out what the others knew. . . Her excitement increased instead of subsiding: as she walked on she felt the tears running down her face. Life had seemed, at last, so simple, so merciful, so soothing; and here were all the old mysteries and duplicities pressing on her again. She stopped, out of breath, and finding herself at the extreme northern end of the Park, with the first street-lights beginning to gem the bare trees. The need to be with Anne suddenly seized her. Perhaps, by dropping a careless word or two, she might learn something from her daughter — learn at least if the baleful Lilla were using the girl as a confidant, as that brief scene in the studio had once suggested. On that point, at any rate, it was the mother's right, her duty even, to be informed. She had made no appointment to meet Anne that afternoon; and she hastened her pace, fearing to find that her daughter had already left the studio. . .

A light through the transom reassured her. She put her key in the lock, threw off her cloak in the little entrance-hall, and pushed open the door beyond. The studio was unlit except by the city's constellated lamps, hung like a golden vintage from an invisible trellising of towers and poles, and by the rosy gleam of the hearth. Anne's easel had been pushed aside, and Anne and another person were sitting near each other in low chairs, duskily outlined against the fire. As Mrs. Clephane crossed the threshold a man's voice was saying gaily: "What I want is a rhyme for *astrolabe*. I must have it! And apparently there is none; at least none except *babe*. And so there won't be any poem. That's always my luck. I find something . . . or somebody . . . who's just what I want, and then. . ."

Kate Clephane stood still, enveloped by the voice. It was the first time she had heard those laughing confiding in-flexions addressed to any ear but hers. Southern sunshine scorched her; the air seemed full of flowers. She hung there for a moment, netted in tightening memories; then she loosed her hold on the door-handle and advanced a few steps into the room. Her heels clicked on the bare floor, and the two by the fire rose and turned to her. She fancied her daughter's glance conveyed a faint surprise—was it even a faint annoy-ance at her intrusion?

"Mother, this is Major Fenno. I think you know him," the girl said.

Chris came forward, simple, natural, unembarrassed. There was no trace of constraint in his glance or tone; he looked at Mrs. Clephane almost fraternally.

"Dear Mrs. Clephane—a rhyme for *astrolabe*!" he en-treated, with that half-humorous way he had of flinging the lasso of his own thought over anybody who happened to stray within range; and then, with one of his usual quick tran-sitions: "I got a chance to run over to New York unexpect-edly, and I heard you were in town, and went to see you. At your house they told me you might be here, so I came, and Miss Clephane was kind enough to let me wait."

"I was afraid you weren't coming," the girl added, looking gravely at her mother.

In spite of the blood drumming in her head, and the way his airy fib about having heard she was in town had drawn her again into the old net of their complicities, Kate was steadied by his composure. She looked from him to Anne; and Anne's face was also composed.

"I had the luck," Chris added, "to meet Miss Clephane after I was invalided home. She took pity on me when I was in hospital on Long Island, and I've wanted to thank her ever since. But my boss keeps me on a pretty short chain, and I can't often get away."

"It's wonderful," said the girl, with her quiet smile, "how you've got over your lameness."

"Oh, well—" he had one of his easy gestures— "lameness isn't the hardest thing in the world to get over. Especially not with the care I had."

Silence fell. Kate struggled to break it, feeling that she was expected to speak, to say something, anything; but there was an obstruction in her throat, as if her voice were a ghost vainly struggling to raise its own grave-stone.

Their visitor made the automatic motion of consulting his wrist-watch. "Jove! I hadn't an idea it was so late. I've got barely time to dash for my train!" He stood looking in his easy way from mother to daughter; then he turned once more to Kate.

"Aren't you coming over to see the great Maclew library one of these days? I was just telling Miss Clephane—"

"Uncle Fred has always promised to take me," the girl threw in.

"Well, that settles it; doesn't it, Mrs. Clephane?" This time he wavered a second before the "Mrs.", and then carried it off triumphantly. "As soon as you can make a date, will you wire me? Good!" He was holding out his hand. Kate put hers in it; she did not mind. It was as if she had laid a stone in his palm.

"It's a go, then?" he repeated gaily, as he shook hands with Anne; and the door closed on him.

"Major Fenno"—. Kate repeated the name slowly as she turned back toward the fire. She had never heard of his military rank. "Was he wounded?" she asked her daughter suddenly.

"At Belleau Wood—didn't you know? I thought you might have—he was mentioned in despatches. He has the Legion of Honour and the D.S.M." Anne's voice had an unwonted vibration. "But he never talks of all that; all he cares about is his writing," she added.

She was gathering up her brushes, rubbing her palette with a rag, going through all the habitual last gestures with her usual somewhat pedantic precision. She found something wrong with one of the brushes, and bent over the lamp with it, her black brows jutting. At that moment she reminded her mother of old Mrs. Clephane; somehow, there was an odd solace in the likeness.

"If he comes for anybody it's for Lilla," the mother thought, as her eyes rested on her daughter's stern young profile; and again she felt the necessity of clearing up the mystery. On the whole, it might be easier to question Anne, now that the name had been pronounced between them.

Major Fenno—and he had been wounded. . . And all he cared about was his writing.

X.

AFTER ALL, she was not going to be able to question Anne about Lilla. As she faced the situation the next day—as she faced the new Chris in her path—Kate Clephane saw the impossibility of using him as a key to her daughter's confidence. There was one thing much closer to her now than any conceivable act of Chris's could ever be; and that was her own relation to Anne. She simply could not talk to Anne about Chris—not yet. It was not that she regarded that episode in her life as a thing to be in itself ashamed of. She was not going, even now, to deny or disown it; she wanted only to deny and disown Chris. Quite conceivably, she might have said to her daughter: "Yes, I loved once—and the man I loved was not your father." But to say it about Chris! To see the slow look of wonder in those inscrutable depths of Anne's eyes: a look that said, not "I blame you", or even "I disapprove you", but, so much more scathingly, just: "You, mother—and *Chris*?"

Yes; that was it. It was necessary for her pride and dignity, for her moral safety almost, that what people like Enid Drover would have called her "past" should remain unidentified, unembodied—or at least not embodied in Chris Fenno. Yet to know—to know!

There were, of course, other sources of enlightenment; if there were anything in her theory of a love-affair between Lilla and Chris, the family were probably not unaware of it. Kate had the sense that they never had their eyes off Lilla for long. But it was all very well to plan to talk to them— the question remained, how to begin? Before trying to find out about Lilla she would first have to find out about them. What did she know of any one of them? Nothing more, she now understood, than their glazed and impenetrable surfaces.

She was still a guest among them; she was a guest even in her daughter's house. It was the character she had herself chosen; in her dread of seeming to assert rights she had forfeited, to thrust herself into a place she had deserted, she had perhaps erred in the other sense, held back too much, been too readily content with the easy part of the week-end visitor.

Well—it had all grown out of the other choice she had made when, years ago, she had said: "Thy gods shall *not* be my gods." And now she but dimly guessed who their gods were. At the moment when her very life depended on her knowing their passwords, holding the clue to their labyrinth, she stood outside the mysterious circle and vainly groped for a way in.

Nollie Tresselton, of course, could have put the clue in her hand; but to speak to Nollie was too nearly like speaking to Anne. Not that Nollie would betray a confidence; but to be divined and judged by her would be almost as searing an experience as being divined and judged by Anne. And so Kate Clephane continued to sit there between them, hugging her new self in her anxious arms, turning its smooth face toward them, and furtively regulating its non-committal gestures and the sounds that issued from its lips.

Only the long nights of dreamless sleep were gone; and her heart stood still each time she slipped the key into the studio door.

"Mother, Uncle Fred wants to take us to Baltimore next week to see the Maclew library; you and Lilla and me."

Anne threw it over her shoulder as she stood before her easel, frowning and narrowing her lips at the difficulty of a branch of red pyrus japonica in a brass pot, haloed with the light of the sunlit window.

Kate, behind her, was leaning back indolently in a deep wicker armchair. She started, and echoed in a blank voice: "Next week?"

"Well, you see, I've promised to spend a few days in Washington with Madge Glenver, who has taken a house at Rock Creek for the spring. This is just the moment for the magnolias; and I thought we might stop at Baltimore on the way, and Uncle Fred could bring you and Lilla back from there."

It sounded perfectly simple and sensible; Anne spoke of it in her usual matter-of-course tone. Her mother tried for the same intonation in answering, with a faint touch of surprise: "Lilla too?"

Anne turned around completely and smiled. "Oh, Lilla particularly! You mustn't speak of it yet, please—not even to Aunt Enid—but there's a chance . . . a chance of Lilla's marrying."

Kate's heart gave a great bound of relief or resentment—which? Why, relief, she instantly assured herself. She had been right then—that was the key to the mystery! And why not? After all, what did it matter to her? Had she, Kate, ever imagined that Chris's love-affairs would cease when she passed from his life? Wasn't it most probably in pursuit of a new one that he had left her? To think so had been, at any rate, in spite of the torturing images evoked, more bearable than believing he had gone because he was tired of her. For years, as she now saw, she had been sustained by her belief in that "other woman"; only, that she should take shape in Lilla was unbelievably humiliating.

Anne continued to smile softly down on her mother. In her smile there was something veiled and tender, as faint as sunlight refracted from water—a radiance striking up from those mysterious depths that Kate had never yet reached. "We should all be so glad if it happened," the girl continued; and Kate said to herself: "What she's really thinking of when she smiles in that way is her own marriage. . ." She remembered the cryptic allusion of the football-faced youth at the Opera, and the way those vigilant lids of Anne's had shut down on her vision.

"Of course—poor Lilla!" Mrs. Clephane absently assented. Inwardly she was saying to herself that it would be impossible for her to go to Baltimore on that particular errand. Chris and Lilla—Chris and Lilla! The coupled names began again to jangle maddeningly through her brain. She stood up and moved away to the window. No, she couldn't!

"Next week, dear? It doesn't matter—but I think you'll have to go without me." She spoke from the window, without turning her head toward her daughter, who had gone back to the easel.

"Oh—." There was distinct disappointment in Anne's voice.

"The fact is I've made two or three dinner engagements; I don't think I can very well break them, do you? People have been so awfully kind—all my old friends," Kate stammered, while the "couldn't, couldn't" kept booming on in her ears. "Besides," she added, "why not take Nollie instead? A young party will be more amusing for Mr. Maclew."

Anne laughed. "Oh, I don't believe he'll notice Nollie and me," she said with a gay significance; but added at once: "Of course you must do exactly as you please. That's the foundation of our agreement, isn't it?"

"Our agreement?"

"To be the two most perfect pals that ever were."

Mrs. Clephane sprang up impulsively and moved toward her daughter. "We *are* that, aren't we, Anne?"

Anne's lids dropped; she nodded, screwed her mouth up, and opened her other eyes—her painter's eyes—on the branch of pyrus with its coral-like studding of red cups. "From the very first," she agreed.

The young party went, Fred Landers beaming in attendance. The family thought it a pity that Mrs. Clephane should miss such a chance, for Horace Maclew was chary of exhibiting his books. But there was something absent-minded and perfunctory in the tone of these regrets; Kate could see that the family interest was passionately centred in Lilla. And she felt, more and more, that in the circumstances she herself was better out of the way. For, at the last moment, the party had been invited to stay at Horace Maclew's; and to have assisted, in an almost official capacity, at the betrothal of Chris and Lilla, with all the solemnity and champagne likely to ensue in such a setting, was more than her newly healed nerves could have endured. It was easier to sit at home and wait, and try to prepare herself for this new and unbelievable situation. Chris and Lilla—!

It was on the third day that Aline, bringing in the breakfast-tray with a bunch of violets (Anne's daily attention since she had been gone), produced also a telegram; as on that far-off morning, four months ago, when the girl's first message had come to her mother with the same flowers.

Kate held the envelope for a moment before opening it, as she had done on that other occasion—but not because she wanted to prolong her illusion. This time there was no illusion in the thin envelope between her fingers; she could feel through it the hard knife-edge of reality. If she delayed she did so from cowardice. Chris and Lilla—

She tore open the envelope and read: "Engaged to Horace Maclew madly happy Lilla."

The telegram fluttered to the floor, and Kate Clephane leaned back on her pillows, feeling a little light-headed.

"Is Madame not well?" Aline sharply questioned.

"Oh, yes; perfectly well. Perfectly well!" Kate repeated joyously. But she continued to lean back, staring vacantly ahead of her, till Aline admonished her, as she had done when the other message came, that the chocolate would be getting cold.

A respite—a respite. Oh, yes, it was at least a respite!

XI.

THERE WAS something so established and reassuring in the mere look of Enid Drover's drawing-room that Kate Clephane, waiting there that afternoon for her sister-in-law to come in, felt a distinct renewal of confidence.

The house was old Mrs. Clephane's wedding gift to her daughter, and everything in it had obviously been selected by some one whose first thought concerning any work of art was to ask if it would chip or fade. Nothing in the solid and costly drawing-room had chipped or faded; it had retained something of Enid's invulnerable youthfulness, and, like herself, had looked as primly old-fashioned in its first bloom as in its well-kept maturity.

It was odd that so stable a setting should have produced that hurricane of a Lilla; and Kate smiled at the thought of the satisfaction with which the very armchairs, in their cushioned permanence, would welcome her back to domesticity.

But Mrs. Drover, when she appeared, took it on a higher plane. Had Lilla ever been unstable, or in any way failed to excel? If so, her mother, and her mother's background, showed no signs of remembering. The armchairs stood there stolidly, as if asking what you meant by such ideas. Enid was a little troubled—she confessed—by the fact that Horace Maclew was a widower, and so much older than her child. "I'm not sure if such a difference of age is not always a risk. . . But then Mr. Maclew is a man of such strong character, and has behaved so generously. . . There will be such opportunities for doing good. . ."

Opportunities for doing good! It was on the tip of Kate's tongue to say: "Ah, that must have been Lilla's reason for accepting him!"; but Mrs. Drover was serenely continuing: "He has given her all the pearls already. She's bringing them back tomorrow to be restrung." And Kate understood that, for the present, the opportunities for doing good lay rather with the bridegroom than the bride.

"Of course," Mrs. Drover went on, "it will be a great sacrifice for her father and me to let her go; though luckily Baltimore is not far off. And it will be a serious kind of life; a life full of responsibilities. Hendrik is afraid that, just at first, Lilla may miss the excitements of New York; but I think I know my child better. When Lilla is *really happy* no one cares less than she does for excitement."

The phrase gave Kate's nerves a sudden twist. It was just what Chris used to say when she urged him to settle down to his painting—at least on the days when he didn't say that excitement was necessary to the artist. . . She looked at her sister-in-law's impenetrable pinkness, and thought: "It might be Mrs. Minity speaking."

Fred Landers had telephoned that he had got back and was coming to dine; she fancied he had it on his mind not to let her feel her solitude while Anne was away; and she said to herself that from him at least she would get a glimpse of the truth.

Fred Landers, as became a friend of the family, was also beaming; but he called Lilla's engagement a "solution" and not a "sacrifice"; and this made it easier for Kate at last to put her question: "How did it happen?"

He leaned back, pulling placidly at his after-dinner cigar, his old-fashioned square-toed pumps comfortably stretched to the fire; and for an instant Kate thought: "It might be pleasant to have him in that armchair every evening." It was the first time such a possibility had occurred to her.

"How did she pull it off, you mean?" He screwed up his friendly blue eyes in a confidential grin. "Well, I'm naturally not initiated; but I suppose in one of the good old ways. Lilla probably knows most of the tricks—and I rather think Nollie Tresselton's been aiding and abetting her. It's been going on for the last six months, I know, and a shooting-box in South Carolina is mixed up with it. Of course they all have a theory that Lilla need only be happy to be good."

"And what do you think about it?"

He shrugged. "Why, I think it's an experiment for which Maclew is to furnish the *corpus vile*. But he's a thick-skinned subject, and it may not hurt him much, and may help Lilla. We can only look on and hope."

Kate sat pondering her next question. At length she said: "Was Mr. Maclew's private secretary there?"

"That fellow Fenno? Yes; he was on duty." She fancied he frowned a little.

"Why do you call him 'that fellow'?"

He turned toward her, and she saw that his friendly brows were beetling. "Is it necessary to speak of him more respectfully? The fact is, I don't fancy him—never did."

"You knew him before, then?" She felt the blood creeping to her forehead, and reached out for a painted hand-screen that she might seem to hold between her eyes and the fire.

Landers reflected. "Oh, yes. I've run across him now and then. I rather fancy he's been mixed up in this too; stirring the brew with the others. That's my impression."

"Yes.— I wonder why," said Kate suddenly.

Landers smiled a little, though his brows continued to jut. "To please Anne, perhaps."

"Anne—*Anne*?"

The name, after she had uttered it, continued to ring on between them, and she leaned back, pressing the screen against her closed lids. "Why?" she managed to question.

"Well—a good many people have wanted to please Anne, first and last. I simply conjectured that Fenno might be among them."

"Oh, no; I'm sure you're quite wrong. I wonder—." She hesitated, and then went on with a rush: "The fact is, I wonder you haven't noticed that he and Lilla—"

Landers sat up and flung his cigar-end into the embers. "Fenno and Lilla? By Jove—you might be right. I hadn't thought of it—"

"Well, I have; I've met them together; when they didn't expect to be met—." She hurried it out with a kind of violence. Her heart was beating to suffocation; she had to utter her suspicion, to give it life and substance.

"The idea sheds floods of light—no doubt of that. Poor Maclew! I'm beginning to be sorry for him. But I think the lot of them are capable of taking pretty good care of themselves. On the whole," Landers added with a sudden sigh of relief, "I'm jolly glad it's Lilla—if it's anybody."

"I *know* it's Lilla." Kate spoke with a passionate emphasis. She had to prove to some one that Chris was Lilla's lover in order to believe it herself, and she had to believe it herself in order to dispel the dreadful supposition raised by Landers's words. She found herself, now, able to smile away his suggestion quite easily, to understand that he had meant it only as a random joke. People in America were always making jokes of that kind, juvenile jokes about flirtations and engagements; they were the staple topic of the comic papers. But the shock of finding herself for a second over that abyss sent her stumbling back half-dazed to the safe footing of reality. If she were going to let her imagination run away at any chance word, what peace would there ever be for her?

The next day Nollie Tresselton reappeared, smiling and fresh, like a sick-nurse whose patient has "turned the corner". With Lilla off her hands her keen boyish face had lost its expression of premature vigilance, and she looked positively rejuvenated. She was more outspoken than Landers.

"At last we can talk about it—thank goodness!" And she began. Horace Maclew and Lilla had met the previous autumn, duck-shooting in South Carolina. Lilla was a wonderful shot when she wasn't . . . well, when she was in training . . . and Maclew, like most heavy solemn men of his type, who theoretically admire helpless feminine women, had been bowled over by the sight of this bold huntress, who damned up and down the birds she missed, smoked and drank with the men, and in the evening lay back silent, with lids half-dropped over smouldering sullen eyes, and didn't bore one with sporting chatter or sentimental airs. It had been a revelation, the traditional thunderbolt; only, once back in Baltimore, Maclew had been caught in the usual network of habits and associations; or perhaps other influences had intervened. No doubt, with a man like that, there would be a "settled attachment" in the background. Then Lilla, for a while, was more outrageous than ever, and when he came to New York to see her, dragged him to one of her rowdiest parties, and went away from it in the small hours with another man, leaving Maclew and his super-Rolls to find their way home uncompanioned. After that the suitor had vanished, and it had taken the combined efforts of all the family, and the family's friends, to draw him back. ("And no one helped us more than Major Fenno," Nollie added with a grateful sigh.)

The name, dropping suddenly into their talk, made Lilla and her wooer and all the other figures in the tale shrivel up like toy balloons. Kate Clephane felt her blood rising again; would she never be able to hear Chris mentioned without this rush of the pulses?

"He was so clever and tactful about it," Nollie was going on. "And he really *believes* in Lilla, just as I do. Otherwise, of course, he couldn't have done what he did—when Horace Maclew has been such a friend to him. He believes she'll keep straight, and that they'll be awfully happy. I fancy he knows a good deal about women, don't you?"

"About women like Lilla, perhaps." The words had flashed out before Kate even knew the thought had formed itself. It must have welled up from some depth of bitterness she had long thought dry.

Nollie's eyes looked grieved. "Oh—you don't like him?"

"I haven't seen him for years," Kate answered lifelessly.

"He admires you so much; he says he used to look up to you so when he was a boy. But I daresay he wasn't half as interesting then; he says himself he was a sort of intellectual rolling stone, never sure of what he wanted to be or to do, and always hurting and offending people in his perpetual efforts to find himself. That's how he puts it."

Look up to her when he was a boy! Yes; that's how he *would* put it. And the rest too; how often she had heard that old analogy of the rolling stone and its victims!

"I think the war transformed him; made a man of him. He says so himself. And now he believes he's really found his vocation; he doesn't think of anything but his writing, and some of his poetry seems to me very beautiful. I'm only sorry," Nollie continued thoughtfully, "that he feels obliged to give up his present job. It seems a pity, when he has so little money, and has been looking so long for a post of the sort—"

"Ah . . . he's giving it up?"

"Well, yes; he says he must have more mental elbow-room; for his writing, I mean. He can't be tied down to hours and places."

"Ah, no; he never could—" Again the words had nearly slipped out. The effort to suppress them left Kate dumb for a moment, though she felt that Nollie was waiting for her to speak.

"Then of course he must go," she assented. Inwardly she was thinking: "After all, if I'm right—and this seems to prove I'm right—about him and Lilla, it's only decent of him to give up his job." And her eyes suddenly filled with tears at the thought of his making a sacrifice, behaving at a crucial moment as her old ideal of him would have had him behave. After all, he was perhaps right in saying that the war had made a man of him.

"Yes; but it's a pity. And not only for him, I mean. I think he had a good influence on Lilla," Nollie went on.

Ah, now, really they were too simple—even Nollie was! Kate could hardly keep from shouting it out at her: "But can't you see, you simpleton, that they're lovers, the two of them, and have cooked up this match for their own convenience, and that your stupid Maclew is their dupe, as all the rest of you are?"

But something in her—was it pride or prudence?— recoiled from such an outburst, and from the need of justifying it. In God's name, what did it matter to her—what did it matter? The risk was removed, the dreadful risk; she was safe again—as safe as she would ever be—unless some suicidal madness drove her to self-betrayal.

With dry lips and an aching smile she said: "You must help me to choose my wedding-present for Lilla."

XII.

ANNE'S SOJOURN in Washington prolonged itself for a fortnight. Her letters to her mother, though punctual, were
inexpressive; but that was not her fault, Kate knew. She had
inherited from her father a certain heaviness of pen, an inability to convey on paper shades of meaning or of feeling,
and having said: "Isn't it splendid about Lilla?" had evidently exhausted the subject, or rather her power of developing it.

At length she returned, bringing with her some studies of
magnolias that were freer and more vigorous than any of her
previous work. She greeted her mother with her usual tenderness, and to Kate her coming was like a lifting of clouds and
opening of windows; the mother had never supposed that
anything in her life could ever again strike such deep roots as
this passion for her daughter. *Perfect love casteth out fear!*
"Does it? *How does any one know?*" she had often incredulously
asked herself. But now, for the first time, love and security
dwelt together in her in a kind of millennial quiet.

She grudged having to dine out on the evening of Anne's
return; but Mrs. Porter Lanfrey was celebrating Lilla's betrothal by a big dinner, with music afterward, and Anne, arriving by a late train, had barely time to dress before the
motor was announced. There was no way of avoiding the festivity; its social significance was immeasurable. Mrs. Lanfrey
was one of the hostesses who had dropped Lilla from their
lists after the divorce, and Mrs. Lanfrey's yea or nay was almost the last survival of the old social code in New York.
Those she invited, at any rate, said that hers was the only
house where there was a "tradition" left; and though Lilla, at
this, used to growl: "Yes, the tradition of how to bore
people," her reinstatement visibly elated her as much as it did
her family. To Enid Drover—resplendent in all her jewels—
the event had already reversed the parts in her daughter's
matrimonial drama, and relegated all the obloquy to the outraged Gates. "Of course this evening shows what Jessie Lanfrey really thinks of Phil Gates," Enid whispered to Mrs.
Clephane as the sisters-in-law took off their cloaks in the

marble hall; and Kate inwardly emended, with a faint smile:
"Or what she really thinks of Horace Maclew."

Mrs. Clephane had entered the vast Lanfrey drawing-room
with a shrinking not produced by the presence of most of
her own former censors and judges—now transformed into
staunch champions or carelessly benevolent acquaintances—
but by the dread of seeing, behind Mr. Maclew's momentous bulk, a slighter figure and more vivid face. But the
moment of suspense was not long; Chris was not there; nor
was his name announced after her arrival. The guests were
all assembled; the dining-room doors were thrown open,
and Mrs. Lanfrey, taking Mr. Maclew's arm, majestically
closed the procession from walnut-and-gold to gold-and-
marble—for the Lanfrey house was "tradition" made visible,
and even the *menu* was exactly what a previous transmitter
of the faith had thought a *menu* ought to be when Mrs.
Lanfrey gave her first dinner.

For a moment Kate Clephane felt herself in the faint bewildered world between waking and sleeping. There they all
were, the faces that had walled in her youth; she was not sure,
at first, if they belonged to the same persons, or had been
handed on, as part of the tradition, to a new generation. It
even occurred to her that, by the mere act of entering Mrs.
Lanfrey's drawing-room, the latter's guests acquired a facial
conformity that belonged to the Lanfrey plan as much as the
fat prima-donna islanded in a sea of Aubusson who warbled
an air from *La Tosca* exactly as a previous fat prima-donna had
warbled it on the same spot years before. It seemed as if even
Lilla, seated on a gilt sofa beside her betrothed, had smoothed
her rebellious countenance to an official smirk. Only Anne
and Nollie Tresselton resisted the enveloping conformity;
Kate wondered if she herself were not stealthily beginning to
resemble Enid Drover. "This is what I ran away from," she
thought; and found more reasons than ever for her flight.
"And after all, I have Anne back," she murmured blissfully
. . . for that still justified the rest. Ah, how fate, in creating
Anne, had baffled its own designs against Anne's mother!

On the way home the girl was unusually silent. She leaned
back against the cushions and let her lids drop. Was it because

she was tired after her long day, or only because she was holding in her vision? Kate could not tell. In the passing flashes of the arc-lights the head at her side, bound about with dark braids, looked as firm and young as a Greek marble; Anne was still at the age when neither weariness nor anxiety mars the surface.

Kate Clephane always respected her daughter's silences, and never felt herself excluded from them; but she was glad when, as they neared their door, Anne's hand stole out to her. How many old breaches the touch healed! It was almost as if the girl had guessed how often Kate had driven up to that door inertly huddled in her corner, with her husband's profile like a wall between her and the world beyond the windows.

"Dear! You seem to have been gone for months," the mother said as they reached her sitting-room.

"Yes. So much has happened." Anne spoke from far off, as if she were groping through a dream.

"But there'll be time for all that tomorrow. You're dead tired now—you're falling with sleep."

The girl opened her eyes wide, in the way she had when she came out of one of her fits of abstraction. "I'm not tired; I'm not sleepy." She seemed to waver. "Can't I come in and sit with you a little while?"

"Of course, dear." Kate slipped an arm through hers, and they entered the shadowy welcoming room, lit by one veiled lamp and the faint red of the hearth. "After all, this is the best hour of the twenty-four for a talk," the mother said, throwing herself back luxuriously on her lounge. It was delicious, after her fortnight of solitude, to think of talking things over with Anne. "And now tell me about everything," she said.

"Yes; I want to." Anne stood leaning against the chimney-piece, her head on her lifted arm. "There's so much to say, isn't there? Always, I mean—now that you and I are to-gether. You don't know the difference it makes, coming home to you, instead—" She broke off, and crossing the hearth knelt down by her mother. Their hands met, and the girl leant her forehead against Kate's shoulder.

"I've been lonely too!" The confession sprang to Kate's lips. Oh, if at last she might say it! But she dared not. The bond between her and her daughter was still too fragile; and how would such an avowal sound on her lips? It was better to let Anne guess—

Anne did guess. "You *have* been happy here, haven't you?"

"Happy? Little Anne!"

"And what a beautiful mother you are! Nollie was saying tonight that you're younger looking every day. And nobody wears their clothes as you do. I knew from that old photograph that you were lovely; but I couldn't guess that you hadn't grown any older since it was taken."

Kate lay still, letting the warmth of the words and the embrace flow through her. What praise had ever seemed as sweet? All the past faded in the sunset radiance of the present. "Little Anne," she sighed again. The three syllables summed it all up.

Anne was silent for a moment; then she continued, her cheek still pressed against her mother: "I want you to stay here always, you know; I want the house to belong to you."

"The house—?" Kate sat up with a start. The girl's shoulder slipped from hers and they remained looking at each other, the space between them abruptly widened. "This house—belong to me? Why, what in the world—"

It was the first time such a question had arisen. On her arrival in America, when Landers, at Anne's request, had tentatively broached the matter of financial arrangements, Kate had cut him short with the declaration that she would gladly accept her daughter's hospitality, but preferred not to receive any money beyond the small allowance she had always had from the Clephane estate. After some argument Landers had understood the uselessness of insisting, and had doubtless made Anne understand it; for the girl had never spoken of the subject to her mother.

Kate put out an encircling arm. "What in the world should I do with this house, dear? Besides—need we look so far ahead?"

For a moment Anne remained somewhat passively in her mother's embrace; then she freed herself and went back to lean against the mantel. "That's just it, dear; I think we must," she said. "With such years and years before you—and all that lovely hair!" Her eyes still lingered smilingly on her mother.

Kate sat upright again, and brushed back the lovely hair from her bewildered temples. What did Anne mean? What was it she was trying to say? The mother began to tremble with an undefined apprehension; then the truth flashed over her.

"Dearest—you mean you may be married?"

The girl nodded, with the quick drop of the lids that called up such memories to her mother. "I couldn't write it; I'm so bad at writing. I want you to be happy with me, darling. I'm going to marry Major Fenno."

XIII.

BALTIMORE—the conductor called it out as the train
ground its way into the station.

Kate Clephane, on her feet in the long swaying Pullman,
looked about her at the faces of all the people in the other
seats—the people *who didn't know*. The whole world was divided, now, between people such as those, and the only two
who did know: herself and one other. All lesser differences
seemed to have been swallowed up in that. . .

She pushed her way between the seats, in the wake of
the other travellers who were getting out—she wondered
why!—at Baltimore. No one noticed her; she had no luggage; in a moment or two she was out of the station. She
stood there, staring in a dazed way at the meaningless traffic
of the streets. Where were all these people going, what could
they possibly want, or hope for, or strive for, in a world such
as she now knew it to be?

There was a spring mildness in the air, and presently, walking on through the hurrying crowd, she found herself in a
quiet park-like square, with budding trees, and bulbs pushing
up in the mounded flower-beds. She sat down on a bench.

Strength had been given her to get through that first hour
with Anne . . . she didn't know how, but somehow, all at
once, the shabby years of dissimulation, of manœuvring, of
concealing, had leapt to her defence like a mercenary army
roused in a righteous cause. She had to deceive Anne, to lull
Anne's suspicions, though she were to die in the attempt.
And she had not died—

That was the worst of it.

She had never been more quiveringly, comprehensively
alive than as she sat there, in that alien place, staring out alone
into an alien future. She felt strong and light enough to jump
up and walk for miles and miles—if only she had known
where to go! They said grief was ageing—well, this agony
seemed to have plunged her into a very Fountain of Youth.

No one could possibly know where she was. She had told
her daughter that one of the aunts at Meridia was very ill;
dying, she believed she had said. To reach Meridia one passed

through Baltimore—it had all been simple enough. Luckily she had once or twice talked of the aunts to Anne; had said vaguely: "There was never much intimacy, but some day I ought to go and see them"—so that now it seemed quite natural, and Anne, like all her generation, was too used to sudden comings and goings, and violent changes of plan, to do more than ring up the motor to take her mother to the first train, and recommend carrying a warm wrap.

The hush, the solitude, the sense of being alone and un-known in a strange place to which no one knew she had gone, gradually steadied Kate Clephane's mind, and fragments torn from the last hours began to drift through it, one by one. Curiously enough, it was Anne's awkward little speech about giving her the house that came first—perhaps because it might so easily be the key to the rest.

Kate Clephane had never thought of money since she had been under her daughter's roof, save on the one occasion when she had refused to have her allowance increased. Her disregard of the matter came not so much from conventional scruples as from a natural gay improvidence. If one were poor, and lived from hand to mouth, one had to think about money—worse luck! But once relieved from the need of doing so, she had dismissed the whole matter from her thoughts. Safely sheltered, becomingly arrayed, she cared no more than a child for the abstract power of possession. And the possession of money, in particular, had always been so associated in her mind with moral and mental dependence that after her break with Hylton Davies poverty had seemed one of the chief attributes of freedom.

It was Anne's suggestion of giving her the house which had flung a sudden revealing glare on the situation. Anne was rich, then—very rich! Such a house—one of the few surviving from the time when Fifth Avenue had been New York's fashionable quarter—must have grown greatly in value with the invasion of business. What could it be worth? Mrs. Clephane couldn't conjecture . . . could only feel that, to offer it in that way (and with it, of course, the means of living in it), Anne, who had none of her mother's improvidence, must be securely and immensely wealthy. And if she were—

The mother stood up and stared about her. What she was

now on the verge of thinking was worse, almost, than all the dreadful things she had thought before. If it were the money he wanted, she might conceivably buy him off—that was what she was thinking! And a nausea crept over her as she thought it; for he had never seemed to care any more for money than she did. His gay scorn of it, not only expressed but acted upon, had been one of his chief charms to her, after all her years in the Clephane atmosphere of thrifty wealth, and the showy opulence of the months with Hylton Davies. Chris Fenno, quite simply and naturally, had laughed with her at the cares of the anxious rich, and rejoiced that those, at least, would never weigh on either of them. But that was long ago; long at least in a life as full of chances and changes as his. Compared with the reckless boy she had known he struck her now as having something of the weight and prudence of middle-age. Might not his respect for money have increased with the increasing need of it? At any rate, she had to think of him, to believe it of him, if she could, for the possibility held out her one hope in a welter of darkness.

Her mind flagged. She averted her sickened eyes from the thought, and began to turn once more on the racking wheel of reiteration. "*I must see him. . . I must see him. . . I must see him.*" . . That was as far as she had got. She looked at her watch, and went up to a policeman to ask the way.

He was not to be found at Horace Maclew's, and to her surprise she learned that he did not live there. Careless as he had always been of money in itself, he was by no means averse to what it provided. No one was more appreciative of the amenities of living when they came his way without his having to take thought; and she had pictured him quartered in a pleasant corner of Horace Maclew's house, and participating in all the luxuries of his larder and cellar. But no; a super-butler, summoned at her request, informed her that Major Fenno had telephoned not to expect him that day, and that, as for his home address, the fact was he had never given it.

A new emotion shot through her, half sharper anguish, half relief. If he were not lodged under the Maclew roof, if his private address were not to be obtained there, might it not be because he was involved in some new tie, perhaps actually living with some unavowable woman? What a solution— Kate Clephane leapt on it—to be able to return to Anne with that announcement! It seemed to clear the way in a flash— but as a hurricane does, by ploughing its path through the ruins it makes. She supposed she would never, as long as she lived, be able to think evil of Chris without its hurting her.

She turned away from the wrought-iron and plate-glass portals that were so exactly what she had known the Maclew portals would be. Perhaps she would find his address at a post-office. She asked the way to the nearest one, and vainly sought for his name in the telephone book. Well, it was not likely that he would proclaim his whereabouts if what she suspected were true. But as her eye travelled down the page she caught his father's name, and an address she remembered. Chris Fenno, though so habitually at odds with his parents, was fond of them in his easy way—especially fond of his mother. Kate had often posted letters for him to that address. She might hear of him there—if necessary she would ask for Mrs. Fenno.

A trolley carried her to a Quakerish quarter of low plain-faced brick houses: streets and streets of them there seemed to be, all alike. Here and there a tree budded before one; but the house at which she rang had an unbroken view of its dispir-ited duplicates. Kate Clephane was not surprised at the shab-biness of the neighbourhood. She knew that the Fennos, never well-off according to Clephane standards, had of late years been greatly straitened, partly, no doubt, through their son's own exigencies, and his cheerful inability to curtail them. Her heart contracted as she stood looking down at Mrs. Fenno's dingy door-mat—the kind on which only tired feet seem to have wiped themselves—and remembered her radiant idle months with Mrs. Fenno's son.

She had to ring twice. Then the door was opened by an elderly negress with gray hair, who stood wiping her hands on a greasy apron, and repeating slowly: "Mr. Chris?"

"Yes. I suppose you can tell me where he lives?"

The woman stared. "Mr. Chris? Where'd he live? Why, right here."

Kate returned the stare. Through the half-open door came

the smell of chronic cooking; a mournful waterproof hung against the wall. "Major Fenno—here?"

Major Fenno; yes; the woman repeated it. Mr. Chris they always called him, she added with a toothless smile. Of course he lived there; she kinder thought he was upstairs now. His mother, she added gratuitously, had gone out—stepped round to the market, she presumed. She'd go and look for Mr. Chris. Would the lady please walk in?

Kate was shown into a small dull sitting-room. All she remembered of it afterward was that there were funny tufted armchairs, blinds half down, a rosewood "what-not," and other relics of vanished ease. Above the fireless chimney stood a too handsome photograph of Chris in uniform.

After all, it was natural enough to find that he was living there. He had always hated any dependence on other people's plans and moods; she remembered how irritably he had spoken of his servitude as Mr. Maclew's secretary, light as the yoke must be. And it was like him, since he was settled in Baltimore, to have returned to his parents. There was something in him—on the side she had always groped for, and occasionally known in happy glimpses—that would make him dislike to live in luxury in the same town in which his father and mother were struggling on the scant income his own follies had reduced them too. He would probably never relate cause and effect, or be much troubled if he did; he would merely say to himself: "It would be beastly wallowing in things here, when it's such hard sledding for the old people"—in the same tone in which he used to say to Kate, on their lazy Riviera Sundays: "If I were at home now I'd be getting ready to take the old lady to church. I always go with her." And no doubt he did. He loved his parents tenderly whenever they were near enough to be loved.

There was a step in the passage. She turned with a start and he came in. At sight of her he closed the door quickly. He was very pale. "Kate!" he said, stopping on the threshold. She had been standing in the window, and she remained there, the width of the room between them. She was silenced by the curious deep shock of remembrance that his actual presence always gave her, and began to tremble lest it should weaken her resolve. "Didn't you expect me?" she finally said.

He looked at her as if he hardly saw her. "Yes; I suppose I did," he answered at length in a slow dragging voice. "I was going to write; to ask when I could see you." As he stood there he seemed like some one snatched out of a trance. To her surprise she felt him singularly in her power. Their parts were reversed for the first time, and she said to herself: "I must act quickly, before he can collect himself." Aloud she asked: "What have you got to say?"

"To say——" he began; and then, suddenly, with a quick change of voice, and moving toward her with outstretched hands: "For God's sake don't take that tone. It's bad enough. . ."

She knew every modulation; he had pleaded with her so often before! His trying it now only hardened her mind and cleared her faculties; and with that flash of vision came the sense that she was actually seeing him for the first time. There he stood, stripped of her dreams, while she registered in a clear objective way all the strength and weakness, the flaws and graces of his person, marked the premature thinning of his smooth brown hair, the incipient crows'-feet about the lids, their too tender droop over eyes not tender enough, and that slight slackness of the mouth that had once seemed a half-persuasive pout, and was now only a sign of secret uncertainties and indulgences. She saw it all, and under the rich glaze of a greater prosperity, a harder maturity, a prompter self-assurance and resourcefulness, she reached to the central failure.

That was what she became aware of—and aware too that the awful fact of actually seeing another human being might happen to one for the first time only after years of intimacy. She averted her eyes as from a sight not meant for her.

"It's bad enough," she heard him repeat.

She turned back to him and her answer caught up his unfinished phrase. "Ah—you do realize how bad it is? That's the reason why you've given up your job? Because you see that you must go? Are you going now—going at once?"

"Going—going?" He echoed the word in his flat sleepwalking voice. "How on earth can I go?"

The question completely hardened whatever his appear-

ance, the startled beaten look of him, had begun to soften in
her. She stood gazing at him and laughed.

"How can you go? Are you mad? Why, what else on earth
can you do?"

As he stood before her she began to be aware that he had
somehow achieved the attitude of dignity for which she was
still struggling. He looked like an unhappy man, a cowed
man; but not a guilty one.

"If you'd waited I should myself have asked you to let me
explain—" he began.

"Explain? What is there to explain?"

"For one thing, why I can't go away—go for good, as you
suggest."

"Suggest? I don't suggest! I order it."

"Well—I must disobey your order."

They stood facing each other while she tried to gather up
the shattered fragments of her authority. She had said to herself that what lay before her was horrible beyond human
imagining; but never once had she imagined that, if she had
the strength to speak, he would have the strength to defy her.
She opened her lips, but no sound came.

"You seem ready to think the worst of me; I suppose that's
natural," he continued. "The best's bad enough. But at any
rate, before ordering me to go, perhaps you ought to know
that I *did* go—once."

She echoed the word blankly. "Once?"

He smiled a little. "You didn't suppose—or did you?—
that I'd drifted into this without a fight; a long fight? At the
hospital, where I first met her, I hadn't any idea who she was.
I'm not a New Yorker; I knew nothing of your set of people
in New York. You never spoke to me of her—I never even
knew you had a daughter."

It was true. In that other life she had led she had never
spoken to any one of Anne. She had never been able to. From
the time when she had returned to Europe, frustrated in her
final attempt to get the child back, or even to have one last
glimpse of her, to the day when her daughter's cable had
summoned her home, that daughter's name had never been
uttered by her except in the depths of her heart.

A darkness was about her feet; her head swam. She looked

around her vaguely, and put out her hand for something to lean on. Chris Fenno moved a chair forward, and she sat down on it without knowing what she was doing.

He continued to stand in front of her. "You do believe me?" he repeated.

"Oh, yes—I believe you." She was beginning to feel, now, the relief of finding him less base than he had at first appeared. She lifted her eyes to his. "But afterward—"

"Well; afterward—" He stopped, as if hoping she would help him to fill in the pause. But she made no sign, and he went on. "As I say, we met first in the hospital where she nursed me. It began there. Afterward she asked me to come and see her at her grandmother's. It was only then that I found out—"

"Well, and then—?"

"Then I went away; went as soon as I found out."

"Of course—"

"Yes; of course; only—"

"Only—you came back. You knew; and yet you came back."

She saw his lips hardening again to doggedness. He had dropped into a chair facing hers, and sat there with lowered head, his hands clenched on his knees.

"Naturally you're bound to think the worst of me—"

She interrupted him. "I'm still waiting to know what to think of you. Don't let it be the worst!"

He made a hopeless gesture. "What is the worst?"

"The worst is that, having gone, you should ever have come back. Why did you?"

He stood up, and this time their eyes met. "You have the right to question me about my own feelings; but not about any one else's."

"Feelings? *Your* feelings?" She laughed again. "And my own daughter's—ah, but I didn't mean to name her even!" she exclaimed.

"Well, I'm glad you've named her. You've answered your own question." He paused, and then added in a low voice: "You know what she is when she cares. . ."

"Ah, don't *you* name her—I forbid you! You say you loved her, not knowing. I believe you. . . I pity you. . . I want to pity you. . . But nothing can change the facts, can change the past. There's nothing for you now but to go."

He stood before her, his eyes on the ground. At last he raised them again, but only for the length of a quick glance. "You think then . . . a past like that . . . irrevocable?"

She sprang to her feet, strong now in her unmitigated scorn. "Irrevocable? Irrevocable? And you ask me this . . . with *her* in your mind? Ah—but you're abominable!"

"Am I? I don't know . . . my head reels with it. She's terribly young; she feels things terribly. She won't give up—she wouldn't before."

"Don't—don't! Leave her out of this. I'm not here to discuss her with you; I'm here to tell you to go, and to go at once."

He made no answer, but turned and walked across the room and back. Then he sank into his chair, and renewed his study of the carpet. Finally he looked up again, with one of the tentative glances she knew so well: those glances that seemed to meet one's answer half-way in their desire to say what one would expect of him. "Is there any use in your taking this tone?"

Again that appeal—it was too preposterous! But suddenly, her eyes on the huddled misery of his attitude, the weakness of his fallen features, she understood that the cry was real; that he was in agony, and had turned to her for help. She crossed the room and laid her hand on his shoulder.

"No; you're right; it's of no use. If you'll listen I'll try to be calm. I want to spare you—why shouldn't I want to?"

She felt her hand doubtfully taken and laid for a moment against his cheek. The cheek was wet. "I'll listen."

"Well, then; I won't reproach you; I won't argue with you. Why should I," she exclaimed with a flash of inspiration, "when all the power is mine? If I came in anger, in abhorrence . . . well, I feel only pity now. Don't reject it—don't reject my pity. This awful thing has fallen on both of us together; as much on me as on you. Let me help you—let us try to help each other."

He pressed the hand closer to his face and then dropped it. "Ah, you're merciful. . . I think I understand the abhorrence better. I've been a cad and a blackguard, and everything else

you like. I've been living with the thought of it day and night.
Only, now—"

"Well, now," she panted, "let me help you; let me—Chris,"
she cried, "let me make it possible for you to go. I know there
may be all sorts of difficulties—material as well as others—
and those at least—"

He looked up at her sharply, as if slow to grasp her words.
Then his face hardened and grew red. "You're bribing me? I
see. I didn't at first. Well—you've the right to, I suppose;
there's hardly any indignity you haven't the right to lay on
me. Only—it's not so simple. I've already told you—"

"Don't name her again! Don't make me remember. . .
Chris, I want to help you as if this were . . . were any other
difficulty. . . Can't we look at it together in that way?"

But she felt the speciousness of her words. How could one
face the Gorgon-image of this difficulty as if it were like any
other? His silence seemed to echo her thought. Slowly he rose
again from his chair, plunged his hands deeply into his pockets, with a gesture she remembered when he was troubled,
and went and leaned in the jamb of the window. What was he
thinking, she wondered, as he glanced vacantly up and down
the long featureless street? Smiling inwardly, perhaps, at the
crudeness of her methods, the emptiness of her threats. For,
after all—putting the case at its basest—if the money were
really what had tempted him, how, with that fortune at his
feet, could any offer of hers divert his purpose?

A clock she had not noticed began to tick insistently. It
seemed to be measuring out the last seconds before some
nightmare crash that she felt herself powerless to arrest. Powerless, at least—

She saw his expression change, and he turned and moved
back quickly into the room. "There's my mother coming
down the street. She's been to market—my mother does her
own marketing." He spoke with a faint smile of irony. "But
you needn't be afraid of meeting her. She won't come in here;
she never does at this hour. She'll go straight to the kitchen."

Kate had begun to tremble again. "Afraid? Why should I
be afraid of your mother? Or she of me? It's you who are
afraid now!" she exclaimed.

His face seemed to age as she watched it. "Well, yes, I am," he acknowledged. "I've been a good deal of a nuisance to her first and last; and she's old and ill. Let's leave her out too, if we can."

As he spoke, they heard, through the thin wall, the fumbling of a latch-key in the outer lock. Kate moved to the door; her decision was taken.

"You want to leave her out? Then promise me—give me your word that you'll go. You know you can count on me if you need help. Only you must promise now; if not, I shall call your mother in— I shall tell her everything." Her hand was on the doorknob when he caught it back.

"Don't!"

The street door opened and closed again, a dragging step passed through the narrow hall, and a door was opened into the region from which the negress with the greasy apron had emerged in a waft of cooking.

"Phemia!" they heard Mrs. Fenno call in a tired elderly voice.

"I promise," her son said, loosening his hold on Kate's wrist.

The two continued to stand opposite each other with lowered heads. At length Mrs. Clephane moved away.

"I'm going now. You understand that you must leave at once . . . tomorrow?" She paused. "I'll do all I can for you as long as you keep your word; if you break it I won't spare you. I've got the means to beat you in the end; only don't make me use them—don't make me!"

He stood a few feet away from her, his eyes on the ground. Decidedly, she had beaten him, and he understood it. If there were any degrees left in such misery she supposed that the worst of it was over.

XIV.

As Kate Clephane drove up late that night to the house in Fifth Avenue she seemed to be reliving all her former anguished returns there, real or imaginary, from the days when she had said to herself: "Shall I never escape?" to those others when, from far off, she had dreamed of the hated threshold, and yearned for it, and thought: "Shall I never get back?"

She had said she might be late in returning, and had begged that no one should stay up for her. Her wish, as usual, had been respected, and she let herself into the hushed house, put out the lights, and stole up past the door where Anne lay sleeping her last young sleep.

Ah, that thought of Anne's awakening! The thought of seeing Anne's face once again in all its radiant unawareness, and then assisting helpless at the darkening of its light! How would the blow fall? Suddenly and directly, or gradually, circuitously? Would the girl learn her fate on the instant, or be obliged to piece it together, bit by bit, through all the slow agonies of conjecture? What pretext would Chris give for the break? He was skilled enough in evasions and subterfuges—but what if he had decided to practise them on Anne's mother, and not on Anne? What if the word he had given were already forfeited? What assurance had any promise of his ever conveyed?

Kate Clephane sat in her midnight room alone with these questions. She had forgotten to go to bed, she had forgotten to undress. She sat there, in her travelling dress and hat, as she had stepped from the train: it was as if this house which people called her own were itself no more than the waiting-room of a railway station where she was listening for the coming of another train that was to carry her—whither?

Ah, but she had forgotten—forgotten that she had him in her power! She had said to him: "I've got the means to beat you in the end," and he had bowed his head to the warning and given his word. Why, the mere threat that she would tell his mother had thrown him on her mercy—what would it be if she were to threaten to tell Anne? She knew him

. . . under all his emancipated airs, his professed contempt for traditions and conformities, lurked an uneasy fear of being thought less than his own romantic image of himself. . . No; even if his designs on Anne were wholly interested, it would kill him to have her know. There was no danger there.

The bitterness of death was passed; yes—but the bitterness of what came after? What of the time to come, when mother and daughter were left facing each other like two ghosts in a gray world of disenchantment? Well, the girl was young— time would help—they would travel. . . Ah, no; her tortured nerves cried out that there could not be, in any woman's life, another such hour as the one she had just lived through!

Toward dawn she roused herself, undressed, and crawled into bed; and there she lay in the darkness, sharpening her aching wits for the continuation of the struggle.

"A telegram—" Aline always said it with the same slightly ironic intonation, as if it were still matter of wonder and amusement to her that any one should be in such haste to communicate with her mistress. Mrs. Clephane, in sables and pearls, with a great house at her orders, was evidently a more considerable person than the stray tenant of the little third-floor room at the Hotel de Minorque, and no one was more competent to measure the distance between them than Aline. But still—a telegram!

Kate opened the envelope with bloodless fingers. "I am going." That was all—there was not even a signature. He had kept his word; and he wanted her to know it.

She felt the loosening of the cords about her heart; a deep breath of relief welled up in her. He had kept his word.

There was a tap on the door, and Anne, radiant, confident, came in.

"You've had a telegram? Not about Aunt Janey—"

Aunt Janey? For a second Kate could not remember, could not associate the question with anything related to the last hours. Then she collected herself, just in time to restrain a self-betraying clutch at the telegram. With a superhuman effort at composure she kept her hands from moving, and left the message lying, face up, on the coverlet between herself and Anne. Yet what if Anne were to read the *Baltimore* above the unsigned words?

"No; it's not about Aunt Janey." She made a farther effort at recollection. "The fact is, the aunts had a panic . . . an absurd panic. . . Aunt Janey's failed a good deal, of course; it's the beginning of the end. But there's no danger of anything sudden—not the least. . . I'm glad I went, though; it comforted them to see me. . . And it was really rather wrong of me not to have been before."

Ah, now, at last she remembered, and how thankfully, that she had, after all, been to Meridia; had, automatically, after leaving Chris, continued her journey, surprised and flattered the aunts by her unannounced appearance, and spent an hour with them before taking the train back to New York. She had had the wit, at the time, to see how useful such an alibi might be, and then, in the disorder of her dreadful vigil, had forgotten about it till Anne's question recalled her to herself. The complete gap in her memory frightened her, and made her feel more than ever unfitted to deal with what might still be coming—what must be coming.

Anne still shed about her the reflected radiance of her bliss. "I'm so glad it's all right—so glad you went. And of course, dear, you didn't tell them anything, did you?"

"Tell them anything—?"

"About me." The lids dropped, the lashes clasped her vision. How could her mother have forgotten?—that flutter of the lids seemed to say.

"Darling! But of course not." Kate Clephane brought the words out with dry lips. Her hand stole out to Anne's, then drew back, affecting to pick up the telegram. She could not put her hand in her daughter's just yet.

The girl sat down beside her on the bed. "I want it to be our secret, remember—just yours and mine—till he comes next week. He can't get away before."

Ah, thank God for that! The mother remembered now that Anne had told her this during their first talk—the talk of which, at the time, no details had remained in her shattered mind. Now, as she listened, those details came back, bit by bit, phantasmagorically mingled.

No one was to be told of the engagement; no, not even

Nollie Tresselton; not till Chris came to New York. And that was not to be for another week. He could not get away sooner, and Anne had decreed that he must see her mother before their betrothal was made public. "I suppose I'm absurdly out-of-date—but I want it to be like that," the girl had said; and Kate Clephane understood that it was out of regard for her, with the desire to "situate" her again, and once for all, as the head of the house, that her daughter had insisted on this almost obsolete formality, had stipulated that her suitor should ask Mrs. Clephane's consent in the solemn old-fashioned way.

The girl bent nearer, her radiance veiled in tenderness. "If you knew, mother, how I want you to like him—" ah, the familiar cruel words!—"You did, didn't you, in old times, when you used to know him so well? Though he says he was just a silly conceited boy then, and wonders that anybody could endure his floods of nonsense. . ."

Ah, God, how long would it go on? Kate Clephane again reached out her hand, and this time clasped her daughter's with a silent nod of assent. Speech was impossible. She moistened her parched lips, but no sound came from them; and suddenly she felt everything slipping away from her in a great gulf of oblivion.

"Mother! You're ill—you're over-tired. . ." She was just aware, through the twilight of her faintness, that Anne's arm was under her, that Anne was ringing the bell and moistening her forehead.

BOOK III

XV.

FANTASTIC SHAPES of heavy leaf-shadows on blinding whiteness. Torrents of blue and lilac and crimson foaming over the branches of unknown trees. Azure distances, snow-peaks, silver reefs, and an unbroken glare of dead-white sunshine merging into a moonlight hardly whiter. Was there never any night, real, black, obliterating, in all these dazzling latitudes in which two desperate women had sought refuge?

They had "travelled." It had been very interesting; and Anne was better. Certainly she was much better. They were on their way home now, moving at a leisurely pace—what was there to return for?—from one scene of gorgeous unreality to another. And all the while Anne had never spoken—never really spoken! She had simply, a day or two after Mrs. Clephane's furtive trip to Baltimore, told her mother that her engagement was broken: "by mutual agreement" were the stiff old-fashioned words she used. As no one else, even among their nearest, had been let into the secret of that fleeting bond, there was no one to whom explanations were due; and the girl, her curt confidence to her mother once made, had withdrawn instantly into the rigid reserve she had maintained ever since. Just so, in former days, Kate Clephane had seen old Mrs. Clephane meet calamity. After her favourite daughter's death the old woman had never spoken her name. And thus with Anne; her soul seemed to freeze about its secret. Even the physical resemblance to old Mrs. Clephane reappeared, and with it a certain asperity of speech, a sharp intolerance of trifles, breaking every now and again upon long intervals of smiling apathy.

During their travels the girl was more than ever attentive to her mother; but her solicitude seemed the result of a lesson in manners inculcated long ago (with the rest of her creed) by old Mrs. Clephane. It was impossible for a creature so young and eager to pass unseeingly through the scenes of their journey; but it was clear that each momentary enthusiasm only deepened the inner pang. And from all participation in that hidden conflict between youth and suffering the mother continued to feel herself shut out.

Nevertheless, she began to imagine that time was working its usual miracle. Anne's face was certainly less drawn— Anne's manner perhaps a shade less guarded. Lately she had begun to sketch again . . . she had suggested one day their crossing from Rio to Marseilles, continuing their wanderings in the Mediterranean . . . had spoken of Egypt and Crete for the winter. . .

Mrs. Clephane acquiesced, bought guide-books, read up furtively, and tried to temper zeal with patience. It would not do to seem too eager; she held her breath, waiting on her daughter's moods, and praying for the appearance of the "some one else" whose coming mothers invoke in such contingencies. That very afternoon, sitting on the hotel balcony above a sea of flowers, she had suffered herself to wonder if Anne, who was off on a long riding excursion with a party of young people, might not return with a different look, the clear happy look of the last year's Anne. The young English planter to whose *hacienda* they had gone had certainly interested her more than any one they had hitherto met.

The mother, late that evening, was still alone on the balcony when, from behind her, Anne's shadow fell across the moonlight. The girl dropped into a seat. No, she wasn't tired—wasn't hungry—they had supped, on the way back, at a glorious place high up over Rio. Yes, the day had been wonderful; the beauty incredible; and the moonlit descent through the forest. . . Anne lapsed into silence, her profile turned from her mother. Perhaps—who could tell? Her silence seemed heavy with promise. Suddenly she put out a hand to Kate.

"Mother, I want to make over all my money to you. It would have been yours if things had been different. It *is* yours, really; and I don't want it—I hate it!" Her hand was trembling.

Mrs. Clephane trembled too. "But, Anne—how absurd! What can it matter? What difference can it make?"

"All the difference." The girl lowered her voice. "It's because I was too rich that he wouldn't marry me." It broke from her in a sob. "I can't bear it—I can't bear it!" She stretched her hand to the silver splendours beneath them. "All this beauty and glory in the world—and nothing in me but cold and darkness!"

Kate Clephane sat speechless. She remembered just such flashes of wild revolt in her own youth, when sea and earth and sky seemed joined in a vast conspiracy of beauty, and within her too all was darkness. For months she had been praying for this hour of recovered communion with her daughter; yet now that it had come, now that the barriers were down, she felt powerless to face what was beyond. If it had been any other man! Paralysed by the fact that it was just that one, she continued to sit silent, her hand on Anne's sunken head.

"Why should you think it's the money?" she whispered at last, to gain time.

"I know it—I know it! He told Nollie once that nothing would induce him to marry a girl with a fortune. He thought it an impossible position for a poor man."

"Did he tell *you* so?"

"Not in so many words. But it was easy to guess. When he wrote to . . . to give me back my freedom, he said he'd been mad to think we might marry . . . that it was impossible . . . there would always be an obstacle between us. . ." The girl lifted her head, her agonized eyes on her mother's. "What obstacle could there be but my money?"

Kate Clephane had turned as cold as marble. At the word "obstacle" she stood up, almost pushing the girl from her. In that searching moonlight, what might not Anne read in her eyes?

"Come indoors, dear," she said.

Anne followed her mechanically. In the high-ceilinged shadowy room Mrs. Clephane sat down in a wooden rocking-chair and the girl stood before her, tall and ghostly in her white linen riding-habit, the dark hair damp on her forehead.

"Come and sit by me, Anne."

"No. I want you to answer me first—to promise."

"But, my dear, what you suggest is madness. How can I promise such a thing? And why should it make any difference? Why should any man be humiliated by the fact of marrying a girl with money?"

"Ah, but Chris is different! You don't know him."

The mother locked her hands about the chair-arms. She sat looking down at the bare brick floor of the room, and at Anne's two feet, slim and imperious, planted just before her in an attitude of challenge, of resistance. She did not dare to raise her eyes higher. *"I don't know him!"* she repeated to herself.

"Mother, answer me—you've got to answer me!" The girl's low-pitched voice had grown shrill; her swaying tall white presence seemed to disengage some fiery fluid. Kate Clephane suddenly recalled the baby Anne's lightning-flashes of rage, and understood what reserves of violence still underlay her daughter's calm exterior.

"How can I answer? I know what you're suffering—but I can't pretend to think that what you propose would make any difference."

"You don't think it was the money?"

Kate Clephane drew a deep breath, and clasped the chair-arms tighter. "No."

"What *was* it, then?" Anne had once more sunk on her knees beside her mother. "I can't bear not to know. I can't bear it an hour longer," she gasped out.

"It's hard, dear. . . I know how hard. . ." Kate put her arms about the shuddering body.

"What shall I do, mother? I've written, and he doesn't answer. I've written three times. And yet I know—"

"You know?"

"He *did* love me, mother."

"Yes, dear."

"And there wasn't any one else; I know that too."

"Yes."

"No one else that he cared about . . . or who had any claim . . . I asked him that before I promised to marry him."

"Then, dear, there's nothing more to say—or to do. You can only conclude that he gave you back your freedom because he wanted his."

"But it was all so quick! How can anybody love one day, and not the next?"

Kate winced. "It does happen so—sometimes."

"I don't believe it—not of him and me! And there *was* the money; I know that. Mother, let me try; let me tell him that you've agreed to take it all back; that I shall have only the allowance you choose to make me."

Mrs. Clephane again sat silent, with lowered head. She had not foreseen this torture.

"Don't you think, dear, as you've written three times and had no answer, that you'd better wait? Better try to forget?"

The girl shook herself free and stood up with a tragic laugh. "You don't know me either, mother!"

That word was crueller than the other; the mother shrank from it as if she had received a blow.

"I do know that, in such cases, there's never any remedy but one. If your courage fails you, there's your pride."

"My pride? What's pride, if one cares? I'd do anything to get him back. I only want you to do what I ask!"

Kate Clephane rose to her feet also. Her own pride seemed suddenly to start up from its long lethargy, and she looked almost defiantly at her defiant daughter.

"I can't do what you ask."

"You won't?"

"I can't."

"You want me to go on suffering, then? You want to kill me?" The girl was close to her, in a white glare of passion. "Ah, it's true—why should you care what happens to me? After all, we're only strangers to each other."

Kate Clephane's first thought was: "I mustn't let her see how it hurts—" not because of the fear of increasing her daughter's suffering, but to prevent her finding out how she could inflict more pain. Anne, at that moment, looked as if the discovery would have been exquisite to her.

The mother dared not speak; she feared her whole agony would break from her with her first word. The two stood facing each other for a moment; then Mrs. Clephane put her hand out blindly. But the girl turned from it with a fierce "Don't!" that seemed to thrust her mother still farther from her, and swept out of the room without a look.

XVI.

Anne had decreed that they should return home; and they returned.

The day after the scene at Rio the girl had faltered out an apology, and the mother had received it with a silent kiss. After that neither had alluded to the subject of their midnight talk. Anne was as solicitous as ever for her mother's comfort and enjoyment, but the daughter had vanished in the travelling companion. Sometimes, during those last weary weeks of travel, Kate Clephane wondered if any closer relation would ever be possible between them. But it was not often that she dared to look ahead. She felt like a traveller crawling along a narrow ledge above a precipice; a glance forward or down might plunge her into the depths.

As they drew near New York she recalled her other return there, less than a year before, and the reckless confidence with which she had entered on her new life. She recalled her first meeting with her daughter, her sense of an instant understanding on the part of each, and the way her own past had fallen from her at the girl's embrace.

Now Anne seemed remoter than ever, and it was the mother's past which had divided them. She shuddered at the fatuity with which she had listened to Enid Drover and Fred Landers when they assured her that she had won her daughter's heart. "She's taken a tremendous fancy to you—" Was it possible that that absurd phrase had ever satisfied her? But daughters, she said to herself, don't take a fancy to their mothers! Mothers and daughters are part of each other's consciousness, in different degrees and in a different way, but still with the mutual sense of something which has always been there. A real mother is just a habit of thought to her children.

Well—this mother must put up with what she had, and make the most of it. Yes; for Anne's sake she must try to make the most of it, to grope her own way and the girl's through this ghastly labyrinth without imperilling whatever affection Anne still felt for her. So a conscientious chaperon might have reasoned—and what more had Kate Clephane the right to call herself?

They reached New York early in October. None of the family were in town; even Fred Landers, uninformed of the exact date of their return, was off shooting with Horace Maclew in South Carolina. Anne had wanted their arrival to pass unperceived; she told her mother that they would remain in town for a day or two, and then decide where to spend the rest of the autumn. On the steamer they languidly discussed alternatives; but, from the girl's inability to decide, the mother guessed that she was waiting for something—probably a letter. "She's written to him after all; she expects to find the answer when we arrive."

They reached the house and went upstairs to their respective apartments. Everything in Anne's establishment was as discreetly ordered as in a club; each lady found her correspondence in her sitting-room, and Kate Clephane, while she glanced indifferently over her own letters, sat with an anguished heart wondering what message awaited Anne.

They met at dinner, and she fancied the girl looked paler and more distant than usual. After dinner the two went to Kate's sitting-room. Aline had already laid out some of the presents they had brought home: a Mexican turquoise ornament for Lilla, an exotic head-band of kingfishers' feathers for Nollie, an old Spanish chronicle for Fred Landers. Mother and daughter turned them over with affected interest; then talk languished, and Anne rose and said goodnight.

On the threshold she paused. "Mother, I was odious to you that night at Rio."

Kate started up with an impulsive gesture. "Oh, my darling, what does that matter? It was all forgotten long ago."

"I haven't forgotten it. I'm more and more ashamed of what I said. But I was dreadfully unhappy. . ."

"I know, dear, I know."

The girl still stood by the door, clutching the knob in an unconscious hand. "I wanted to tell you that now I'm cured—quite cured." Her smile was heart-breaking. "I didn't follow your advice; I wrote to him. I told him—I pretended—that you were going to accept my plan of giving you back the money, and that I should have only a moderate allowance, so that he needn't feel any inequality . . . any sense of obligation. . ."

Kate listened with lowered head. "Perhaps you were right to write to him."

"Yes, I was right," Anne answered with a faint touch of self-derision. "For now I know. It was not the money; he has told me so. I've had a letter."

"Ah—"

"I'm dismissed," said the girl with an abrupt laugh.

"What do you mean, dear, when you say I was right?"

"I mean that there was another woman." Anne came close to her, with the same white vehement face as she had shown during their nocturnal talk at Rio.

Kate's heart stood still. "Another woman?"

"Yes. And you made me feel that you'd always suspected it."

"No, dear . . . really. . ."

"You *didn't*?" She saw the terrible flame of hope rekindling in Anne's eyes.

"Not—not about any one in particular. But of course, with a man . . . a man like that. . ." (Should she go on, or should she stop?)

Anne was upon her with a cry. *"Mother, what kind of a man?"*

Fool that she was, not to have foreseen the consequences of such a slip! She sat before her daughter like a criminal under cross-examination, feeling that whatever word she chose would fatally lead her deeper into the slough of avowal.

Anne repeated her question with insistence. "You knew him before I did," she added.

"Yes; but it's so long ago."

"But what makes you suspect him now?"

"Suspect? I suspect nothing!"

The girl stood looking at her fixedly under dark menacing brows. "I do, then! I wouldn't allow myself to before; but all the while I knew there was another woman." Between the sentences she drew short panting breaths, as though with every word speech grew more difficult. "Mother," she broke out, "the day I went to Baltimore to see him the maid who opened the door didn't want to let me in because there'd been a woman there two days before who'd made a scene. A scene—that's what she said! Isn't it horrible?" She burst into tears.

Kate Clephane sat stupefied. She could not yet grasp the significance of the words her daughter was pouring out, and repeated dully: "You went to Baltimore?" How secret Anne must be, she thought, not only to have concealed her visit at the time, but even to have refrained from any allusion to it during their stormy talk at Rio! How secret, since, even in moments of seeming self-abandonment, she could refrain from revealing whatever she chose to keep to herself! More acutely than ever, the mother had the sense of being at arm's length from her child.

"Yes, I went to Baltimore," said Anne, speaking now in a controlled incisive voice. "I didn't tell you at the time because you were not well. It was just after you came back from Meridia, and had that nervous break-down—you remember? I didn't want to bother you about my own affairs. But as soon as I got his letter saying the engagement was off I jumped into the first train, and went straight to Baltimore to see him."

"And you did?" It slipped from Kate irresistibly.

"No. He was away; he'd left. But I didn't believe it at the time; I thought the maid-servant had had orders not to let me in. . ." She paused. "Mother, it was too horrible; she took me for the woman who had made the scene. She said I looked just like her."

Kate gasped: "The negress said so?"

Her question seemed to drop into the silence like a shout; it was as if she had let fall a platter of brass on a marble floor.

"The negress?" Anne echoed.

Kate Clephane sank down into the depths of her chair as if she had been withered by a touch. She pressed her elbows against her sides to try to hide the trembling of her body.

"How did you know it was a negress, mother?"

Kate sat helpless, battling with confused possibilities of fear; and in that moment Anne leapt on the truth.

"It was *you*, mother—*you* were the other woman? You went to see him the day you said you'd been to Meridia?" The girl stood before her now like a blanched Fury.

"I *did* go to Meridia!" Kate Clephane declared.

"You went to Baltimore too, then. You went to his house; you saw him. You were the woman who made the scene."

Anne's voice had mounted to a cry; but suddenly she seemed to regain a sense of her surroundings. At the very moment when Kate Clephane felt the flash of the blade over her head it was arrested within a hair's-breadth of her neck. Anne's voice sank to a whisper.

"Mother—you did that? It was really you—it was your doing? You've always hated him, then? Hated him enough for that?"

Ah, that blessed word—*hated!* When the other had trembled in the very air! The mother, bowed there, her shrunken body drawn in on itself, felt a faint expanding of the heart.

"No, dear; no; not hate," she stammered.

"But it *was* you?" She suddenly understood that, all the while, Anne had not really believed it. But the moment for pretense was past.

"I did go to see him; yes."

"To persuade him to break our engagement?"

"Anne—"

"Answer me, please."

"To ask him—to try to make him see. . ."

The girl interrupted her with a laugh. "You made him break our engagement—you did it. And all this time—all these dreadful months—you let me think it was because he was tired of me!" She sprang to her mother and caught her by the wrists. Her hot fingers seemed to burn into Kate's shivering flesh.

"Look at me, please, mother; no, straight in the eyes. I want to try to find out which of us you hated most; which of us you most wanted to see suffer."

The mother disengaged herself and stood up. "As for suffering—if you look at me, you'll see I've had my share."

The girl seemed not to hear. "But why—why—why?" she wailed.

A reaction of self-defence came over Kate Clephane. Anne's white-heat of ire seemed to turn her cold, and her self-possession returned.

"What is it you want me to tell you? I did go to see Major Fenno—yes. I wanted to speak to him privately; to ask him to reconsider his decision. I didn't believe he could make you happy. He came round to my way of thinking.

That's all. Any mother would have done as much. I had the right—"

"The right?" Anne shrilled. "What right? You gave up all your rights over me when you left my father for another man!"

Mrs. Clephane rose with uncertain steps, and moved toward the door of her bedroom. On the threshold she paused and turned toward her daughter. Strength had come back to her with the thought that after all the only thing that mattered was to prevent this marriage. And that she might still do.

"The right of a friend, then, Anne. Won't you even allow me that? You've treated me as a friend since you asked me to come back. You've trusted me, or seemed to. Trust me now. I did what I did because I knew you ought not to marry Major Fenno. I've known him for a great many years. I knew he couldn't make you happy—make any woman happy. Some men are not meant to marry; he's one of them. I know enough of his history to know that. And you see he recognized that I was right—"

Anne was still staring at her with the same fixed implacable brows. Then her face broke up into the furrows of young anguish, and she became again a helpless grief-tossed girl, battling blindly with her first sorrow. She flung up her arms, buried her head in them, and sank down by the sofa. Kate watched her for a moment, hesitating; then she stole up and laid an arm about the bowed neck. But Anne shook her off and sprang up.

"No—no—no!" she cried. They stood facing each other, as on that other cruel night.

"You don't know me; you don't understand me. What right have you to interfere with my happiness? Won't you please say nothing more now? It was my own fault to imagine that we could ever live together like mother and daughter. A relation like that can't be improvised in a day." She flung a tragic look at her mother. "If you've suffered, I suppose it was my fault for asking you to make the experiment. Excuse me if I've said anything to hurt you. But you must leave me to manage my life in my own way." She turned toward the door.

"Goodnight—my child," Kate whispered.

XVII.

TWO DAYS LATER Fred Landers returned.

Mrs. Clephane had sent a note begging him to call her up as soon as he arrived. When his call came she asked if she might dine with him that night, and he replied that she ought to have come without asking. Anne, he supposed, would honour him too?

No, she answered; Anne, the day before, had gone down to the Drovers' on Long Island. She would probably be away for a few days. And would Fred please ask no one else to dine? He assured her that such an idea would never have occurred to him.

He received her in the comfortable shabby drawing-room which he had never changed since his mother and an old-maid sister had vanished from it years before. He indulged his own tastes in the library upstairs, leaving this chintzy room, with its many armchairs, the Steinway piano and the family Chippendale, much as Kate had known it when old Mrs. Landers had given her a bridal dinner. The memory of that dinner, and of Mrs. Landers, large, silvery, demonstrative, flashed through Mrs. Clephane's mind. She saw herself in an elaborately looped gown, proudly followed by her husband, and enclosed in her hostess's rustling embrace, while her present host, crimson with emotion and admiration, hung shyly behind his mother; and the memory gave her a pang of self-pity.

In the middle of the room she paused and looked about her. "It feels like home," she said, without knowing what she was saying.

A flush almost as agitated as the one she remembered mounted to Landers's forehead. She saw his confusion and pleasure, and was remotely touched by them.

"You see, I'm homeless," she explained with a faint smile.

"Homeless?"

"Oh, I can't remember when I was ever anything else. I've been a wanderer for so many years."

"But not any more," he smiled.

The double mahogany doors were thrown open. Landers,

with his stiff little bow, offered her an arm, and they passed into a dusky flock-papered dining-room which seemed to borrow most of its lighting from the sturdy silver and monumental cut-glass of the dinner-table. A bunch of violets, compact and massive, lay by her plate. Everything about Fred Landers was old-fashioned, solid and authentic. She sank into her chair with a sense of its being a place of momentary refuge. She did not mean to speak till after dinner—then she would tell him everything, she thought. "How delicious they are!" she murmured, smelling the violets.

In the library, after dinner, Landers settled her in his deepest armchair, moved the lamp away, pressed a glass of old Chartreuse on her, and said: "And now, what's wrong?"

The suddenness and the perspicacity of the question took her by surprise. She had imagined he would leave the preliminaries to her, or at any rate beat about the subject in a clumsy effort to get at it. But she perceived that, awkward and almost timorous as he remained in smaller ways, the mere habit of life had given him a certain self-assurance at important moments. It was she who now felt a tremor of reluctance. How could she tell him—what could she tell him?

"Well, you know, I really *am* homeless," she began. "Or at least, in remaining where I am I'm forfeiting my last shred of self-respect. Anne has told me that her experiment has been a mistake."

"What experiment?"

"Having me back."

"Is that what she calls it—an experiment?"

Mrs. Clephane nodded.

Fred Landers stood leaning against the mantelpiece, an unlit cigar in his hand. His face expressed perplexity and perturbation. "I don't understand. What has happened? She seemed to adore you."

"Yes; as a visitor; a chaperon; a travelling companion."

"Well—that's not so bad to begin with."

"No; but it has nothing on earth to do with the real relation between a mother and daughter."

"Oh, *that*—"

It was her turn to flush. "You agree with Anne, then, that I've forfeited all right to claim it?"

He seemed embarrassed. "What do you mean by claiming it?"

She hesitated a moment; then she began. It was not the story she had meant to tell; she had hardly opened her lips before she understood that it would be as impossible to tell that to Fred Landers as to Anne. For an instant, as he welcomed her to the familiar house, so full of friendly memories, she had had the illusion of nearness to him, the sense of a brotherly reassuring presence. But as she began to speak of Chris every one else in her new life except her daughter became remote and indistinct to her. She supposed it could not be otherwise. She had chosen to cast her lot elsewhere, and now, coming back after so many years, she found the sense of intimacy and confidence irreparably destroyed. What did she really know of the present Fred Landers, or he of her? All she found herself able to say was that when she had heard that Anne meant to marry Chris Fenno she had thought it her duty to try to prevent the marriage; and that the girl had guessed her interference and could not forgive her. She elaborated on this, lingering over the relatively insignificant details of her successive talks with her daughter in the attempt to delay the moment when Landers should begin to question her.

She saw that he was deeply disturbed, but perhaps not altogether sorry. He had never liked Chris, she knew, and the news of the engagement was clearly a shock to him. He said he had seen and heard nothing of Fenno since Anne and her mother had left. Landers, who could not recall that either Horace Maclew or Lilla had ever mentioned him, had concluded that the young man was no longer a member of their household, and probably not even in Baltimore. If he were, Lilla would have been sure to keep her hold on him; he was too useful a diner and dancer to be lost sight of— and much more in Lilla's line, one would have fancied, than in Anne's.

Kate Clephane winced at the unconscious criticism. "He gave me his word that he would go," she said with a faint sigh of relief.

Fred Landers continued to lean meditatively against the chimney-piece.

"You said nothing at all to Anne herself at the time?" he asked, after another interval.

"No. Perhaps I was wrong; but I was afraid to. I felt I didn't know her well enough—yet."

Instantly she saw how he would interpret her avowal, and her colour rose again. She must have felt, then, that she knew Major Fenno better; the inference was inevitable.

"You found it easier to speak to Fenno?"

She hesitated. "I cared so much less for what he felt."

"Of course," he sighed. "And you knew damaging things about him? Evidently, since he broke the engagement when you told him to."

Again she faltered. "I knew something of his past life—enough to be sure he wasn't the kind of husband for Anne. I made him understand it. That's all."

"Ah. Well, I'm not surprised. I suspected he was trying for her, and I own I hated the idea. But now I suppose there's no help for it—"

"No help?" She looked up in dismay.

"Well—is there? To be so savage with you she must be pretty well determined to have him back. How the devil are you going to stop it?"

"I can't. But *you*—oh, Fred, you must!"— Her eyes clung imploringly to his troubled face.

"But I don't know anything definite! If there *is* anything—anything one can really take hold of—you'll have to tell me. I'll do all I can; but if I interfere without good reason, I know it will only make Anne more determined. Have you forgotten what the Clephanes are like?"

She had lowered her head again, and sat desolately staring at the floor. With the little wood-fire playing on the hearth, and this honest kindly man looking down at her, how safe and homelike the room seemed! Yet her real self was not in it at all, but blown about on a lonely wind of anguish, outside in the night. And so it would always be, she supposed.

"Won't you tell me exactly what there is against him?" she heard Landers repeat.

The answer choked in her throat. Finally she brought out: "Oh, I don't know . . . women . . . the usual thing. . . He's light. . ."

"But is it all just hearsay? Or have you proof—proof of any one particular rotten thing?"

"Isn't his giving up and going away sufficient proof?"

"Not if he comes back now when she sends for him."

The words shot through her like a stab. "Oh, but she mustn't—she can't!"

"You're fairly sure he will come if she does?"

Kate Clephane put up her hands and pressed them against her ears. She could not bear to hear another question. What had been the use of coming to Fred Landers? He had no help to give her, and his insight had only served to crystallize her hazy terrors. She rose slowly from her armchair and held out her hand with a struggling smile.

"You're right. I suppose there's nothing more to do."

"But you're not going?"

"Yes; I'm tired. And I want to be by myself—to think. I must decide about my own future."

"Your own future? Oh, nonsense! Let all this blow over. Wait till Anne comes back. The chief thing, of course, is that you should stay with her, whatever happens."

She put her hand in his. "Goodbye, Fred. And thank you."

"I'll do all I can, you know," he said, as he followed her down the stairs. "But you mustn't desert Anne."

The taxi he had called carried her back to her desolate house.

XVIII.

HER PLACE was beside Anne—that was all she had got out of Fred Landers. And in that respect she was by no means convinced that her instinct was not surer than his, that she was not right in agreeing with her daughter that their experiment had been a failure.

Yet, even if it had, she could not leave Anne now; not till she had made sure there was no further danger from Chris. Ah—if she were once certain of that, it would perhaps be easiest and simplest to go! But not till then.

She did not know when Anne was coming back; no word had come from her. Mrs. Clephane had an idea that the house-keeper knew; but she could not ask the house-keeper. So for another twenty-four hours she remained on, with a curious sense of ghostly unconcern, while she watched Aline unpack her trunks and "settle" her into her rooms for the winter.

It was on the third day that Nollie Tresselton telephoned. She was in town, and asked if she might see Mrs. Clephane at once. The very sound of her voice brought reassurance; and Kate Clephane sat counting the minutes till she appeared.

She had come up from the Drovers', as Kate had guessed; and she brought an embarrassed message of apology from Anne. "She couldn't write—she's too upset. But she's so sorry for what she said . . . for the way she said it. You must try to forgive her. . ."

"Oh, forgive her—that's nothing!" the mother cried, her eyes searching the other's face. But Nollie's vivid features were obscured by the embarrassment of the message she had brought. She looked as if she were tangled in Anne's confusion.

"That's nothing," Kate Clephane repeated. "I hurt her horribly too—I had to. I couldn't expect her to understand."

Mrs. Tresselton looked relieved. "Ah, you do see that? I knew you would! I told her so—" She hesitated, and then went on, with a slight tremor in her voice: "Your taking it in that way will make it all so much easier—"

But she stopped again, and Kate, with a sinking heart, stood up. "Nollie; she wants me to go?"

"No, no! How could you imagine it? She wants you to look upon this house as yours; she has always wanted it."

"But she's not coming back to it?"

The younger woman laid a pleading hand on Mrs. Clephane's arm. "Aunt Kate—you must be patient. She feels she can't; not now, at any rate."

"Not now? Then it's *she* who hasn't forgiven?"

"She would, you know—oh, so gladly!—she'd never think again of what's happened. Only she fears—"

"Fears?"

"Well—that your feeling about Chris is still the same. . ."

Mrs. Clephane caught at the hand that lay on her arm. "Nollie! She knows where he is? She's seen him?"

"No; but she means to. He's been very ill—he's had a bad time since the engagement was broken. And that makes her feel still more strongly—" The younger woman broke off and looked at Mrs. Clephane compassionately, as if trying to make her understand the hopelessness of the struggle. "Aunt Kate, really . . . what's the use?"

"The use? Where is he, Nollie? Here—now—in New York?"

Mrs. Tresselton was silent; the pity in her gaze had turned to a guarded coolness. Of course Nollie couldn't understand—never would! Of course they were all on Anne's side. Kate Clephane stood looking helplessly about her. The memory of old scenes under that same roof—threats, discussions, dissimulations and inward revolts—arose within her, and she felt on her shoulders the whole oppression of the past.

"Don't think," Nollie continued, her expression softening, "that Anne hasn't tried to understand . . . to make allowances. The boy you knew must have been so different from the Major Fenno we all like and respect—yes, respect. He's 'made good', you see. It's not only his war record, but everything since. He's worked so hard—done so well at his various jobs—and Anne's sure that if he had the chance he would make himself a name in the literary world. All that naturally makes it more difficult for her to understand your objection—or your way of asserting it."

Mrs. Clephane lifted imploring eyes to her face. "I don't expect Anne to understand; not yet. But you must try to, Nollie; you must help me."

"I want to, Aunt Kate." The young woman stood before her, affectionately perplexed. "If there's anything . . . anything really wrong . . . you ought to tell me."

"I *do* tell you," Kate panted.

"Well—what is it?"

Silence fell—always the same silence. Kate glanced desperately about the imprisoning room. Every panel and moulding of its walls, every uncompromising angle or portly curve of its decorous furniture, seemed equally leagued against her, forbidding her, defying her, to speak.

"Ask Fred Landers," she said, at bay.

"But I have; I saw him on my way here. And he says he doesn't know—that you wouldn't explain."

"Why should I have to explain? I've said Major Fenno ought not to marry Anne. I've known him longer than any of you. Isn't it likely that I know him better?"

The words came from her precipitate and shrill; she felt she was losing all control of her face and voice, and lifted her handkerchief to her lips to hide their twitching.

"Aunt Kate—!" Nollie Tresselton gasped it out on a new note of terror; then she too fell silent, slowly turning her eyes away.

In that instant Kate Clephane saw that she had guessed, or if not, was at least on the point of guessing; and fresh alarm possessed the mother. She tried to steady herself, to raise new defences against this new danger. "Some men are not meant to marry: they're sure to make their wives unhappy. Isn't that reason enough? It's a question of character. In those ways, I don't believe character ever changes. That's all."

"That's all." The word was said. She had been challenged again, and had again shrunk away from the challenge.

Nollie Tresselton drew a deep breath of relief. "After knowing him so well as a boy, you naturally don't want to say anything more; but you think they're unsuited to each other."

"Yes—that's it. You do see?"

The younger woman considered; then she took Mrs.

Clephane by the hand. "I do see. And I'll try to help—to persuade Anne to put off deciding. Perhaps after she's seen him it will be easier. . ."

Nollie was again silent, and Mrs. Clephane understood that, whatever happened, the secret of Chris's exact whereabouts was to be kept from her. She thought: "Anne's afraid to have me meet him again," and there was a sort of fierce satisfaction in the thought.

Nollie was gathering up her wrap and hand-bag. She had to get back to Long Island, she said; Kate understood that she meant to return to the Drovers'. As she reached the door a last impulse of avowal seized the older woman. What if, by giving Nollie a hint of the truth, she could make sure of her support and thus secure Anne's safety? But what argument against the marriage would be more efficacious on Nollie's lips than on her own? One only—the one that no one must ever use. The terror lest Nollie, possessed of that truth, and sickened by it, should after all reveal it in a final effort to prevent the marriage, prevailed over Mrs. Clephane's other fears. Once Nollie knew, Anne would surely get to know; the horror of that possibility sealed the mother's lips.

Nollie, from the threshold, still looked at her wistfully, expectantly, as if half-awaiting the confession; but Mrs. Clephane held out her hand without a word.

"I must find out where he is." It was Kate's first thought after the door had closed on her visitor. If he were in New York—and he evidently was—she, Kate Clephane, must run him down, must get speech with him, before he had been able to see her daughter.

But how was she to set about it? Fred Landers did not even know if he were still with Horace Maclew or not—for the mere fact of Maclew's not alluding to him while they were together meant nothing, less than nothing. And even if he had left the Maclews, the chances were that Lilla knew where he was, and had already transmitted Anne's summons.

Mrs. Clephane consulted the telephone-book, but of course in vain. Then, after some hesitation, she rang up Horace Maclew's house in Baltimore. No one was there, but she finally elicited from the servant who answered the telephone that

Mrs. Maclew was away on a motor trip. Perhaps Mr. Maclew could be reached at his country-place. . . Kate tried the country-place, but Mr. Maclew had gone to Chicago.

The sense of loneliness and helplessness closed in on her more impenetrably than ever. Night came, and Aline reminded her that she had asked to have her dinner brought up on a tray. Solitary meals in John Clephane's dining-room were impossible to her.

"I don't want any dinner."

Aline's look seemed to say that she knew why, and her mistress hastily emended: "Or just some bouillon and toast. Whatever's ready—"

She sat down to it without changing her dress. Every gesture, every act, denoting intimacy with that house, or the air of permanence in her relation to it, would also have been impossible. Again she had the feeling of sitting in a railway station, waiting for a train to come in. But now she knew for what she was waiting.

At the close of her brief meal Aline entered briskly with fruit and coffee. Her harsh face illuminated with curiosity, she handed her mistress a card. "The gentleman is downstairs. He hopes Madame will excuse the hour." Her tone seemed to imply: "Madame, in this case, will excuse *everything!*" and Kate cast a startled glance at the name.

He had come to her, then—had come of his own accord! She felt dizzy with relief and fear. Fear uppermost—yes; was she not always afraid of him?

XIX.

CHRIS FENNO stood in the drawing-room. The servant who received him had turned on a blast of lamps and wall-lights, and in the hard overhead glare he looked drawn and worn, like a man recovering from severe illness. His clothes, too, Kate fancied, were shabbier; everything in his appearance showed a decline, a defeat.

She had not much believed in his illness when Nollie spoke of it; the old habit of incredulity was too strong in her. But now his appearance moved her. She felt herself responsible, almost guilty. But for her folly, she thought, he might have been standing before her with a high head, on easy terms with the world.

"You've been ill!" she exclaimed.

His gesture brushed that aside. "I'm well now, thanks." He looked her in the face and added: "May we have a few minutes' talk?"

She faltered: "If you think it necessary." Inwardly she had already begun to tremble. When his blue eyes turned to that harsh slate-gray, and the two perpendicular lines deepened between his brows, she had always trembled.

"You've made it necessary," he retorted, his voice as harsh as his eyes.

"I?"

"You've broken our compact. It's not my doing. I stuck to my side of it." He flung out the short sentences like blows.

Her heart was beating so wildly that she could not follow what he said. "What do you mean?" she stammered.

"That you agreed to help me if I gave up Anne. God knows what your idea of helping me was. To me it meant only one thing: your keeping quiet, keeping out of the whole business, and trusting me to carry out my side of the bargain—as I did. I broke our engagement, chucked my job, went away. And you? Instead of keeping out of it, of saying nothing, you've talked against me, insinuated God knows what, and then refused to explain your insinuations. You've put me in such a position that I've got to take back my word to you, or appear to your daughter and your family as a man who has run away because he knew he couldn't face the charge hanging over him."

It was only in the white heat of anger that he spoke with such violence, and at such length; he seemed spent, and desperately at bay, and the thought gave Kate Clephane courage.

"Well—*can* you face it?" she asked.

His expression changed, as she had so often seen it change. From menace it passed to petulance and then became almost pleading in its perplexity. She said to herself: "It's the first time I've ever been brave with him, and he doesn't know how to take it." But even then she felt the precariousness of the advantage. His ready wit had so often served him instead of resolution. It served him now.

"You do mean to make the charge, then?" he retorted.

She stood silent, feeling herself defeated, and at the same time humiliated that their angry thoughts should have dragged them down to such a level.

"Don't sneer—" she faltered.

"Sneer? At what? I'm in dead earnest—can't you see it? You've ruined me—or very nearly. I'm not speaking now of my feelings; that would make *you* sneer, probably. At any rate, this is no time for discussing them. I'm merely putting my case as a poor devil who has to earn his living, a man who has his good name to defend. On both counts you've done me all the harm you could."

"I had to stop this marriage."

"Very well. I agreed to that. I did what I'd promised. Couldn't you let it alone?"

"No. Because Anne wouldn't. She wanted to ask you to come back. She saw I couldn't bear it—she suspected me of knowing something. She insisted."

"And you sacrificed my good name rather—"

"Oh, I'd sacrifice anything. You'd better understand that."

"I do understand it. That's why I'm here. To tell you I consider that what you've done has freed me from my promise."

She stretched out her hands as if to catch him back. "Chris—no, stay! You can't! You can't! You know you can't!"

He stood leaning against the chimney-piece, his arms crossed, his head a little bent and thrust forward, in the atti-

tude of sullen obstinacy that she knew so well. And all at once
in her own cry she heard the echo of other cries, other en-
treaties. She saw herself in another scene, stretching her arms
to him in the same desperate entreaty, with the same sense of
her inability to move him, even to reach him. Her tears overflowed and ran down.

"You don't mean you'll tell her?" she whispered.

He kept his dogged attitude. "I've got to clear myself—
somehow."

"Oh, don't tell her, don't tell her! Chris, don't tell her!"

As the cry died on her lips she understood that, in uttering
it, she had at last cast herself completely on his mercy. For it
was not impossible that, if other means failed, he would risk
justifying himself to Anne by revealing the truth. There were
times when he was reckless enough to risk anything. And if
Kate were right in her conjecture—if he had the audacity he
affected—then his hold over her was complete, and he knew
it. If any one else told Anne, the girl's horror would turn her
from him at once. But what if he himself told her? All this
flashed on Kate Clephane in the same glare of enlightenment.

There was a long silence. She had sunk into a chair and
hidden her face in her hands. Presently, through the enveloping cloud of her misery, she felt his nearness, and a touch on
her shoulder.

"Kate—won't you try to understand; to listen quietly?"

She lifted her eyes and met his fugitively. They had lost
their harshness, and were almost frightened. "I was angry
when I came here—a man would be," he continued. "But
what's to be gained by our talking to each other in this way?
You were awfully kind to me in old times; I haven't forgotten.
But is that a reason for being so hard on me now? I didn't
bring this situation on myself—you're my witness that I
didn't. But here it is; it's a fact; we've got to face it."

She lowered her eyes and voice to whisper painfully: "To
face Anne's love for you?"

"Yes."

"Her determination—?"

"Her absolute determination."

His words made her tremble again; there had always been
moments when his reasonableness alarmed her more than his

anger, because she knew that, to be so gentle, he must be certain of eventually gaining his point. But she gathered resolution to say: "And if I take back my threats, as you call them? If I take back all I've said—'clear' you entirely? That's what you want, I understand? If I promise that," she panted, "will you promise too—promise me to find a way out?"

His hand fell from her shoulder, and he drew back a step. "A way out—now? But there isn't any."

Mrs. Clephane stood up. She remembered wondering long ago—one day when he had been very tender—how cruel Chris could be. The conjecture, then, had seemed whimsical, almost morbid; now she understood that she had guessed in him from the outset this genius for reaching, at the first thrust, to the central point of his antagonist's misery.

"You've seen my daughter, then?"

"I've seen her—yes. This morning. It was she who sent me here."

"If she's made up her mind, why did she send you?"

"To tell you how she's suffering. She thinks, you know—" He wavered again for a second or two, and then brought out: "She's very unhappy about the stand you take. She thinks you ought to say something to . . . to clear up. . ."

"What difference will it make, if she means to marry you?"

"Why—the immense difference of her feeling for *you*. She's dreadfully hurt . . . she's very miserable. . . ."

"But absolutely determined?"

Again he made an embarrassed gesture of acquiescence.

Kate Clephane stood looking about the rich glaring room. She felt like a dizzy moth battering itself to death against that implacable blaze. She closed her lids for an instant.

"I shall tell her, then; I shall tell her the truth," she said suddenly.

He stood in the doorway, his hard gaze upon her. "Well, tell her—do tell her; if you want never to see her again," he said.

XX.

H E MUST have been very sure of her not acting on his final challenge, or he would not have dared to make it. That was the continuous refrain of Kate Clephane's thoughts as the train carried her down to Long Island the next morning.

"He's convinced I shall never tell her; but what if I do?" The thought sustained her through the long sleepless night, and gave her the strength and clearness of mind to decide that she must at once see Anne, however little her daughter might desire the meeting. After all, she still had that weapon in her depleted armoury: she could reveal the truth.

At the station she found one of the Drover motors, and remembered with a start that it was a Saturday, and that she would probably come upon a large house-party at her sister-in-law's. But to her relief she learned that the motor had only brought a departing visitor to the up-train. She asked to be driven back in it, and in a few moments was rolling between the wrought-iron gates and down the long drive to the house. The front door stood open, and she went into the hall. The long oak tables were so laden with golf-sticks, tennis racquets and homespun garments that she saw she had been right in guessing she would encounter a houseful. But it was too late to turn back; and besides, what did the other people matter? They might, if they were numerous enough, make it easier for her to isolate herself with Anne.

The hall seemed empty; but as she advanced she saw a woman's figure lazily outstretched in a deep armchair before the fire. Lilla Maclew rose from the chair to greet her.

"Hallo—Aunt Kate?" Mrs. Clephane caught the embarrassment in her niece's rich careless voice, and guessed that the family had already been made aware of the situation existing between Anne and Anne's mother, and probably, therefore, of the girl's engagement. But Lilla Maclew was even more easy, self-confident and indifferent than Lilla Gates had been. The bolder dash of peroxyde on her hair, and the glint of jewels on her dusky skin, made her look like a tall bronze statue with traces of gilding on it.

"Hallo," she repeated, rather blankly; "have you come to lunch?"

"I've come to see Anne," Anne's mother answered.

Lilla's constraint visibly increased, and with it her sullen reluctance to make any unnecessary effort. One hadn't married money, her tone proclaimed, to be loaded up like this with family bothers.

"Anne's out. She's gone off with Nollie to a tennis match or something. I'm just down; we played bridge till nearly daylight, and I haven't seen anybody this morning. I suppose mother must be somewhere about."

She glanced irritably around her, as if her look ought to have been potent enough to summon her mother to the spot; and apparently it was, for a door opened, and Mrs. Drover appeared.

"Kate! I didn't know you were here! How did you come?" Her hostess's mild countenance betrayed the same embarrassment as Lilla's, and under it Mrs. Clephane detected the same aggrieved surprise. Having at last settled her own daughter's difficulties, Mrs. Drover's eyes seemed to ask, why should she so soon be called upon to deal with another family disturbance? Even juries, after a protracted trial, are excused from service for seven years; yet here she was being drawn into the thick of a new quarrel when the old one was barely composed.

"Anne's out," she added, offering a cool pink cheek to her sister-in-law.

"May I wait, then? I came to see her," Kate said timidly.

"Of course, my dear! You must stay to lunch." Mrs. Drover's naturally ceremonious manner became stiff with apprehension. "You look tired, you know; this continuous travelling must be very exhausting. And the food! . . . Yes; Anne ought to be back for lunch. She and Nollie went off to the Glenvers' to see the tennis finals; didn't they, Lilla? Of course I can't *promise* they'll be back . . . but you must stay. . ." She rang and gave orders that another seat should be put at table. "We're rather a large party; you won't mind? The men are off at a polo practice at Hempstead. Dawson, how many shall we be for lunch?" she asked the butler. Under her breath she added: "Yes; champagne." If we ever need it, she concluded in a parenthetic glance, it will be to-day!

The hall was already filling up with a jocund bustle of Drovers and Tresseltons. Young, middle-aged and elderly, they poured out of successive motors, all ruddy, prosperous, clamouring for food. Hardly distinguishable from the family were the week-end friends returning with them from one sportive spectacle or another. As Kate Clephane stood among them, going through the mechanical gestures of greeting and small-talk, she felt so tenuous and spectral that she almost wondered how she could be visible to their hearty senses. They were all glad to see her, all a little sur-prised at her being there, and all soon forgetful of their own surprise in discussing the more important questions of polo, tennis and lunch. Once more she had the impression of be-ing hurried with them down a huge sliding stairway that perpetually revolved upon itself, and once more she recalled her difficulty in telling one of them from another, and in deciding whether it was the Tresseltons or the Drovers who had the smallest noses.

"But Anne—where's Anne?" Hendrik Drover enquired, steering the tide of arrivals toward the shining stretch of a long luncheon-table. He put Mrs. Clephane at his left, and added, as he settled her in her seat: "Anne and Nollie went off early to the Glenver finals. But Joe was there too—weren't you, Joe?"

He did not wait for Joe Tresselton's answer, but addressed himself hurriedly to the lady on his right. Kate had the feel-ing that they all thought she had committed an error of taste in appearing among them at that particular moment, but that it was no business of theirs, after all, and they must act in concert in affecting that nothing could be more natural. The Drovers and Tresseltons were great at acting in concert, and at pretending that whatever happened was natural, usual, and not of a character to interfere with one's lunch. When a member of the tribe was ill, the best doctors and most expensive nurses were summoned, but the illness was spoken of as a trifling indisposition; when misfortune be-fell any one of them, it was not spoken of at all. Taking Lilla for granted had brought this art to the highest point of perfection, and her capture of Horace Maclew had fully confirmed its usefulness.

All this flashed through Kate Clephane while she refused the champagne ordered on her behalf, and pretended to eat Newburgh lobster and corn *soufflé*; but under the surface-rattle of her thoughts a watchful spirit brooded haggardly on the strangeness and unreality of the scene. She had come, in agony of soul, to seek her daughter, to have speech with her at all costs; and the daughter was away watching a tennis match, and no one seemed surprised or concerned. Life, even Anne's life, was going on in its usual easy way. The girl had found her betrothed again, and been reunited to him; what would it matter to her, or to her approving family, if the intruder who for a few months had gone through the pretence of being one of them, and whose delusion they had good-naturedly abetted, should vanish again from the group? As she looked at them all, so obtuse and so powerful, so sure of themselves and each other, her own claim to belong to them became incredible even to herself. She had made her choice long ago, and she had not chosen them; and now their friendly indifference made the fact clear.

Well—perhaps it also made her own course clearer. She was as much divided from them already as death could divide her. Why not die, then—die altogether? She would tell Anne the truth, and then go away and never see her again; and that would be death. . .

"Ah, here they are!" Hendrik Drover called out genially. Lunch was over; the guests, scattered about in the hall and billiard-room, were lighting their cigarettes over coffee and liqueurs. Mrs. Clephane, who had drifted out with the rest, and mechanically taken her cup of coffee as the tray passed her, lifted her head and saw Anne and Nollie Tresselton. Anne entered first. She paused to take off her motor coat, glanced indifferently about her, and said to Mrs. Drover: "You didn't wait for us, Aunt Enid? We were so late that we stopped to lunch at Madge's—." Then she saw her mother and her pale cheek whitened.

Mrs. Clephane's eyes filled, and she stood motionless. Everything about her was so blurred and wavering that she dared not stir, or even attempt to set down her cup.

"Mother!" the girl exclaimed. With a quick movement she made her way through the cluster of welcoming people, and went up with outstretched arms to Mrs. Clephane.

For a moment the two held each other; then Mrs. Drover, beaming up to them, said benevolently: "Your mother must be awfully tired, Anne. Do carry her off to your own quarters for a quiet talk—" and dazed, trembling, half-fearing she was in a dream from which the waking would be worse than death, Mrs. Clephane found herself mounting the stairs with her daughter.

On the first landing she regained her senses, said to herself: "She thinks I've come to take back what I said," and tried to stiffen her soul against this new form of anguish. Anne moved silently at her side. After the first cry and the first kiss she had drawn back into herself, perhaps obscurely conscious of some inward resistance in her mother. But when the bedroom door had closed on them she drew Mrs. Clephane down into an armchair, dropped on her knees beside it, and whispered: "Mother—how could you and I ever give each other up?"

The words sounded like an echo of the dear unuttered things the mother had heard said to herself long ago, in her endless dialogues with an invisible Anne. No tears rose to her eyes, but their flood seemed to fill her thirsty breast. She drew Anne's head against it. "Anne . . . little Anne. . ." Her fingers crept through the warm crinklings of hair, wound about the turn of the temples, and slipped down the cheeks. She shut her eyes, softly saying over her daughter's name.

Anne was the first to speak. "I've been so unhappy. I wanted you so to come."

"Darling, you were sure I would?"

"How could I tell? You seemed so angry."

"With you? Never, child!"

There was a slight pause; then, raising herself, the girl slipped her arms about her mother's neck.

"Nor with him, any longer?"

The chill of reality smote through Mrs. Clephane's happy trance. She felt herself turning again into the desolate stranger who had stood below watching for Anne's return.

"Mother—you see, I want you both," she heard the girl entreating; and *"Now!"* the inward voice admonished her.

Now indeed was the time to speak; to make an end. It was clear that no compromise would be of any use. Anne had obviously imagined that her mother had come to forgive and be forgiven, and that Chris was to be included in the general amnesty. On no other terms would any amnesty be accepted. Through the girl's endearments Kate felt, as never before, the steely muscles of her resolution.

Anne pressed her closer. "Can't we agree, mother, that I must take my chance—and that, if the risks are as great as you think, you'll be there to help me? After all, we've all got to buy our own experience, haven't we? And perhaps the point of view about . . . about early mistakes . . . is more indulgent now than in your time. But I don't want to discuss that," the girl hurried on. "Can't we agree not to discuss any-thing—not even Chris—and just be the perfect friends we were before? You'd say yes if you knew the difference it has made, this last year, to have you back!" She lifted her face close to Mrs. Clephane's to add, with a half-whimsical smile: "Mothers oughtn't ever to leave their daughters."

Kate Clephane sat motionless in that persuasive hold. It did not seem to her, at the moment, as if she and her child were two, but as if her whole self had passed into the young body pressed pleadingly against her.

"How can I leave her—how can I ever leave her?" was her only thought.

"You see," the cajoling voice went on, "when I asked you to come back and live with me, though I *did* want you to, most awfully, I wasn't as sure . . . well, as sure as Uncle Fred was . . . that the experiment would be a success—a perfect success. My life had been rather lonely, but it had been very independent too, in spite of Granny, and I didn't know how well I should behave to my new mother, or whether she'd like me, or whether we'd be happy together. And then you came, and the very first day I forgot all my doubts—didn't *you*?"

Kate Clephane assented: "The very first day."

"And every day afterward, as I saw how right Uncle Fred had been, and how perfectly he'd remembered what you were, and what you would have been to me if we hadn't been separated when I was a baby, I was more and more grateful to you for coming, and more and more anxious to make you forget that we hadn't always been together."

"You did make me forget it—"

"And then, suddenly, the great gulf opened again, and there I was on one side of it, and you on the other, just as it was in all those dreary years when I was without you; and it seemed as if it was you who had chosen again that we should be divided, and in my unhappiness I said dreadful things. . . I know I did. . ."

Kate felt as if it were her own sobs that were shaking her daughter's body. She held her fast, saying over and over, as a mother would to a child that has fallen and hurt itself: "There, there . . . don't cry." She no longer knew what she herself was feeling. All her consciousness had passed into Anne. This young anguish, which is the hardest of all to bear, must be allayed: she was ready to utter any words that should lift that broken head from her breast.

"My Anne—how could I ever leave you?" she whispered. And as she spoke she felt herself instantly caught in the tight net of her renunciation. If she did not tell Anne now she would never tell her—and it was exactly on this that Chris had counted. He had known that she would never speak.

XXI.

IT HAD been decided that Mrs. Clephane must, of course, stay over the Sunday; on Monday morning she would return to town with Anne. Meanwhile Aline was summoned with week-end raiment; and Kate Clephane, after watching the house-party drive off to a distant polo match, remained alone in the great house with her sister-in-law.

Mrs. Drover's countenance, though worn from the strain of incessant hospitality, had lost its look of perturbation. It was clear that the affectionate meeting between mother and daughter had been a relief to the whole family, and Mrs. Drover's ingenuous eye declared that since now, thank heaven, that matter was settled, there need be no farther pretence of mystery. She invited her sister-in-law to join her in her own sitting-room over a quiet cup of tea, and as she poured it out observed with a smile that she supposed the wedding would take place before Christmas.

"The wedding? Anne's wedding?"

"Why, my dear, isn't everything settled? We all supposed that was what you'd come down for. She told us of her engagement as soon as she arrived." Wrinkles of apprehension reluctantly reformed themselves on Mrs. Drover's brow. "At least you might have let me have my tea without this new worry!" her look seemed to protest. "Hendrik has the highest opinion of Major Fenno, you know," she continued, in a tone that amicably sought to dismiss the subject.

Kate Clephane put down her untasted cup. What could she answer? What was the use of answering at all?

Misled by her silence, Mrs. Drover pursued with a clearing brow: "Of course nowadays, with the cut of everything changing every six months, there's no use in ordering a huge trousseau. Besides, Anne tells me they mean to go to Europe almost immediately; and whatever people say, it *is* more satisfactory to get the latest models on the spot. . ."

"Oh, Enid—Anne mustn't marry him!" Kate Clephane cried, starting to her feet.

Mrs. Drover set down her own cup. Lines of disapproval hardened about her small concise mouth; but she had evidently resolved to restrain herself to the last limit of sisterly forbearance.

"Now, my dear, do sit down again and drink your tea quietly. What good will all this worrying do? You look feverish—and as thin as a rail. Are you sure you haven't picked up one of those dreadful tropical microbes? . . . Of course, I understand your being unhappy at parting so soon again with Anne. . . She feels it too; I know she does. It's a pity you couldn't have been together a little longer, just you two; but then—. And, after all, since Anne wants you to keep the Fifth Avenue house for yourself, why shouldn't the young people buy that property just round the corner? Then the lower floors of the two houses could be thrown into one for entertaining. I'm not clever about plans, but Lilla'll tell you exactly how it could be done. She's got hold of such a clever young architect to modernize their Baltimore house. Of course, though Horace didn't realize it, it was *all* library; no room for dancing. And I daresay Anne—not that Anne ever cared much for dancing. . . But I hear Major Fenno likes going out, and a young wife can't make a greater mistake than to have a dull house if her husband is fond of gaiety. Lilla, now, has quite converted Horace—"

Kate Clephane had reseated herself and was automatically turning the spoon about in her cup. "It won't happen; it can't be; he'll never dare." The thought, flashing in on her aching brain, suddenly quieted her, helped her to compose her features, and even to interject the occasional vague murmur which was all her sister-in-law needed to feed her flow of talk. The mention of the Maclews and their clever architect had served to deflect the current of Mrs. Drover's thoughts, and presently she was describing how wonderfully Lilla managed Horace, and how she and the architect had got him to think he could not live without the very alterations he had begun by resolutely opposing, on the ground that they were both extravagant and unnecessary.

"Just an innocent little conspiracy, you know. . . They completely got the better of him, and now he's delighted, and tells everybody it was his own idea," Mrs. Drover chuckled; and then, her voice softening, and a plump hand reassuringly outstretched to Mrs. Clephane: "You'll see, my dear, after you get over the first loneliness, what a lovely thing it is to have one's child happily married."

"It won't happen; it can't be; he'll never dare!" the other mother continued to murmur to herself.

Horace Maclew, among numerous other guests, arrived for dinner. He sat nearly opposite Mrs. Clephane, and in the strange whirl and dazzle that surrounded her she instinctively anchored her gaze on his broad frame and ponderous countenance. What had his marriage done to him, she wondered, and what weight had it given him in the counsels of his new family? She had known of him but vaguely before, as the conscientious millionaire who collects works of art and relieves suffering; she imagined him as having been brought up by equally conscientious parents, themselves wealthy and scrupulous, and sincerely anxious to transmit their scruples, with their millions, to their only son. But other influences and tendencies had also been in play; one could fancy him rather heavily adjusting them to his inherited principles, with the "After all" designed to cover venial lapses. His marriage with Lilla must have been the outcome, the climax, of these private concessions, and have prepared him to view most of the problems of life from an easier angle. Undoubtedly, among the men present, though no quicker-witted than the others, he would have been the one most likely to understand Kate Clephane's case, could she have put it to him. But to do so—one had only to intercept their glances across the table to be sure of it—would have been to take Lilla also into her confidence; and it suddenly became clear to Mrs. Clephane that no recoil of horror, and no Pharisaical disapproval, would be as intolerable to her as Lilla's careless stare and Lilla's lazy: "Why, what on earth's all the fuss about? Don't that sort of thing happen all the time?"

It did, no doubt; Mrs. Clephane had already tried to adjust her own mind to that. She had known such cases; everybody had; she had seen them smoothed over and lived down; but that she and Anne should ever figure as one of them was beyond human imagining. She would have felt herself befouled to the depths by Lilla's tolerance.

Her unquiet eyes wandered from Horace Maclew to her

daughter. Anne shone with recovered joy. Her anxiety had left only the happy traces of a summer shower on a drooping garden. Every now and then she smiled across the table at her mother, and Kate felt herself irresistibly smiling back. There was something so rich, dense and impregnable in the fact of possessing Anne's heart that the mother could not remember to be alarmed when their eyes met.

Suddenly she noticed that Anne was absorbed in conversation with one of her neighbours. This was the Reverend Dr. Arklow, Rector of St. Stephen's, the New York church of the Clephane and Drover clan. Old Mrs. Clephane had been a pillar of St. Stephen's, and had bequeathed a handsome sum to the parish. Dr. Arklow, formerly the curate, had come back a few years previously as Rector of the church, and was now regarded as one of the foremost lights of the diocese, with a strong possibility of being named its Coadjutor, or possibly Bishop of the American Episcopal Churches in Europe.

The Drovers and all their tribe took their religion with moderation: they subscribed handsomely to parochial charities, the older members of the family still went to church on Sunday mornings, and once in the winter each of the family invited the Rector to a big dinner. But their relations with him, though amicable, were purely formal, and Kate concluded that his presence at one of the Drover week-ends was to be attributed to the prestige he had acquired as a certain Coadjutor or possible Bishop. The Drover social scheme was like a game of chess in which Bishops counted considerably more than Rectors.

The Rector of St. Stephen's struck Mrs. Clephane, who had met him only once before, as a man accustomed to good company, and eager to prove it. He had a face as extensive as Mr. Maclew's but running to length instead of width. His thin gray hair was carefully brushed back from a narrow benevolent forehead, and though he loved a good cigar, and wore a pepper-and-salt suit on his travels, he knew his value as a decorative element, and was fastidiously clerical on social occasions. His manly chest seemed outspread to receive the pectoral cross, and all his gestures were round and full, like the sleeves for which they were preparing.

As he leaned back, listening to Anne with lowered lids, and

finger-tips thoughtfully laid against each other, his occasional faint smile and murmur of assent suggested to Mrs. Clephane that the girl was discussing with him the arrangements for the wedding; and the mother, laying down her fork, closed her eyes for an instant while the big resonant room reeled about her. Then she said to herself that, after all, this was only what was to be expected, and that if she hadn't the courage to face such a possibility, and many others like it, she would assuredly never have the courage to carry out the plan which, all through the afternoon and evening, had been slowly forming in her mind. That plan was simply, for the present, to hold fast to Anne, and let things follow their course. She would return to New York the next day with Anne, she would passively assist at her daughter's preparations—for an active share in them seemed beyond her powers—and she would be there when Chris came, and when they announced the engagement. Whatever happened, she would be there. She would let Chris see at once that he would have to reckon with that. And how would he be able to reckon with it? How could he stand it, day after day? They would perhaps never exchange another word in private—she prayed they might not—but he would understand by her mere presence what she meant, what she was determined on. He would understand that in the end he would have to give up Anne because she herself would never do so. The struggle between them would become a definite, practical, circumscribed thing; and, knowing Chris as she did, she felt almost sure she could hold out longer than he.

This new resolve gave her a sort of light-headed self-confidence: when she left the dinner-table she felt so easy and careless that she was surprised to see that the glass of champagne beside her plate was untouched. She felt as if all its sparkles were whirling through her.

On the return of the gentlemen to the drawing-room Dr. Arklow moved to her side, and she welcomed him with a smile. He opened with some mild generalities, and she said to herself that he was too anxiously observant of the social rules to speak of her daughter's marriage before she herself alluded to it. For a few minutes she strove to find a word which should provide him with an opening; but to say to any one:

"My daughter is going to be married" was beyond her, and they lingered on among slumbrous platitudes.

Suddenly Anne drifted up, sat down an on arm of her mother's chair, and took her mother's hand. Kate's eyes filled, and through their mist she fancied she saw Dr. Arklow looking at her attentively. For the first time it occurred to her that, behind the scrupulous social puppet, there might be a simple-hearted man, familiar with the humble realities of pain and perplexity, and experienced in dealing with them. The thought gave her a sense of relief, and she said to herself: "I will try to speak to him alone. I will go to see him when we get to New York." But meanwhile she merely continued to smile up at her daughter, and Dr. Arklow to say: "Our young lady has been telling me about the big tennis finals. There's no doubt all these sports are going to be a great factor in building up a healthier, happier world."

None of the three made any allusion to Anne's engagement.

XXII.

"MISS ANNE CLEPHANE weds War Hero. Announces engagement to Major Christopher Fenno, D.S.M., Chevalier of Legion of Honour."

The headline glared at Kate Clephane from the first page of the paper she had absently picked up from the table of her sitting-room. She and Anne, that morning, had journeyed back from Long Island in Hendrik Drover's motor, separated by his genial bulk, and shielded by it from the peril of private talk. On the day before—that aching endless Sunday—Anne, when with her mother, had steadily avoided the point at issue. She seemed too happy in their reunion to risk disturbing its first hours; perhaps, Kate thought, she was counting on the spell of that reunion to break down her mother's opposition. But as they neared New York every mile brought them closer to the reality they were trying not to see; and here it was at last, deriding the mother from those hideous headlines. She heard Anne's step behind her, and their glance crossed above the paragraph. A flush rose to the girl's cheek, while her eyes hesitatingly questioned her mother.

The decisive moment in their struggle was at hand. Kate felt that everything depended on her holding fast to the line she had resolved to follow, and her voice sounded thin and small in the effort to steady it.

"Is Major Fenno in New York?"

"No. He went back to Baltimore on Saturday." Anne wavered. "He's waiting to hear from me . . . before he comes."

A hope leapt up in the mother's breast, then sank its ineffectual wings. She glanced back slowly at the newspaper.

"This announcement was made with your permission?"

The unwonted colour still burned in the girl's cheek. She made a motion of assent, and added, after another pause: "Uncle Hendrik and Aunt Enid thought it only fair."

"Fair to Major Fenno?"

"Yes."

The silence prolonged itself. At length the mother brought out: "But if you've announced your engagement he has a right to be with you."

Anne looked at her almost timidly. "I wanted first . . . we both wanted . . . to feel that when he came you would . . . would be ready to receive him."

Kate Clephane turned away from her daughter's eyes. The look in them was too intolerably sweet to her. Anne was imploring her approval—Anne could not bear to be happy without it. Yes; but she wanted her other happiness also; she wanted that more than anything else; she would not hesitate to sacrifice her mother to it if there were no other way.

All this rushed over Kate in a final flash of illumination. "I want you both!" Anne had said; but she wanted Chris Fenno infinitely the more.

"Dear—." At her mother's first syllable Anne was at her side again, beseechingly. Kate Clephane lifted her hands to the girl's shoulders. "You've made your choice, dearest. When Major Fenno comes of course I will receive him." Her lips felt dry and stiff as she uttered her prevarication. But all her old arts of casuistry had come back; what was the use of having practised them so long if they were not to serve her now? She let herself yield to Anne's embrace.

That afternoon, as Mrs. Clephane sat alone upstairs, Fred Landers telephoned to ask if she would receive him. Anne was out, and her mother sent word that when Mr. Landers came he was to be shown up to her sitting-room. He entered it, presently, with outstretched hands and a smile of satisfaction.

"Well, it's all settled, then? Thank God! You've done just the right thing; I knew you would."

Her hand fell lifelessly into his; she could not answer.

He drew up an armchair to the little autumnal fire, and continued to contemplate her approvingly.

"I know how hard it must have been. But there was only one thing to be considered: Anne needs you!"

"She needs Major Fenno more."

"Oh, well—that's the law of life, isn't it?" His tone seemed to say: "At any rate, it's the one you obeyed in your own youth." And again she found no answer.

She was conscious that the gaze he still fixed on her had

passed from benevolence to wistfulness. "Do you still mind it so awfully?"

His question made her tears rise; but she was determined not to return upon the past. She had proved the uselessness of the attempt.

"Anne has announced her engagement. What more is there to say? You tell me she needs me; well, here I am with her."

"And you don't know how she appreciates it. She rang me up as soon as you got back this morning. She's overcome by your generosity in going down to the Drovers' after what had taken place between you—after her putting herself so completely in the wrong." He paused again, as if weighing his next words. "You know I'm not any keener than you are about this marriage; but, my dear, I believe it had to be."

"Had to be?"

His capacious forehead crimsoned with the effort to explain. "Well, Anne's a young woman of considerable violence of feeling . . . of . . . of. . . In short, there's no knowing what she might have ended by doing if we'd all backed you up in opposing her. And I confess I didn't feel sure enough of the young man to count on his not taking advantage of her . . . her impetuosity, as it were, if he thought there was no other chance. . . You understand?"

She understood. What he was trying to say was that, on the whole, given the girl's self-will, and taking into account her . . . well, her peculiar heredity . . . taking into account, in fact, Kate Clephane herself . . . the family had probably adopted the safest course in accepting the situation.

"Not that I mean to imply—of course not! Only the young people nowadays settle most questions for themselves, don't they? And in this case. . . Well, all's well that ends well. We all know that some of the most successful marriages have had . . . er . . . rather risky preliminaries."

Kate Clephane sat listening in a state of acquiescent lassitude. She felt as if she had been given a drug which had left her intelligence clear but paralyzed her will. What was the use of arguing, discussing, opposing? Later, of course, if everything else failed, Fred Landers was after all the person she would have to turn to, to whom her avowal would have to be made; but for the moment he was of no more use to her than any of the others. The game she had resolved to play must be played between herself and Chris Fenno; everything else was the vainest expenditure of breath.

"You *do* agree, don't you?" she heard Landers rather nervously insisting; and: "Oh, I daresay you're right," she assented.

"And the great thing, you know, is that Anne shouldn't lose you, or you lose Anne, because of this. All the rest will arrange itself somehow. Life generally does arrange things. And if it shouldn't—"

He stood up rather awkwardly, and she was aware of his advancing toward her. His face had grown long and solemn, and his broad bulk seemed to have narrowed to the proportions of the lank youth suffused with blushes who had taken shelter behind his mother when old Mrs. Landers had offered a bridal banquet to the John Clephanes.

"If it doesn't work out for you as we hope . . . there's my house . . . that's been waiting for you for ever so long . . . though I shouldn't ever have ventured to suggest it. . ."

"Oh—" she faltered out, the clutch of pain relaxing a little about her heart.

"Well, well," her visitor stammered, rubbing his hands together deprecatingly, "I only suggest it as a sort of last expedient . . . a forlorn hope. . ." His nervous laugh tried to give the words a humorous turn, but his eyes were still grave. Kate rose and put her hand in his.

"You're awfully good to me," was all she found to say. Inwardly she was thinking, with a fresh thrill of anguish: "And now I shall never be able to tell him—never!"

He had caught the note of dismissal in her voice, and was trying to gather up the scattered fragments of his self-possession. "Of course, at our age . . . *my* age, I mean . . . all that kind of thing is rather. . . But there: I didn't want you to feel there was no one you could turn to. That's all. You won't bear me a grudge, though? Now then; that's all right. And you'll see: this other business will shake down in time. Bound to, you know. I daresay the young man has merits that you and I don't see. And you'll let me go on dropping in as usual? After all, I'm Anne's guardian!" he ended with his clumsy laugh.

"I shall want you more than ever, Fred," Mrs. Clephane said simply.

The next evening, as she looked down the long dinner-table from her seat at its head, she was fantastically reminded of the first family dinner over which she had presided after her marriage.

The background was the same; the faces were the same, or so like that they seemed merely rejuvenated issues of the same coinage. Hendrik Drover sat in his brother-in-law's place; but even that change was not marked enough to disturb the illusion. Hendrik Drover's heavy good-natured face belonged to the same type as John Clephane's; one saw that the two had gone to the same schools and the same University, frequented the same clubs, fished the same salmon rivers; Hendrik Drover might have been the ghost of John Clephane revisiting the scene of his earthly trials in a mood softened by celestial influences. And as for herself—Kate Clephane—if she had conformed to the plan of life prepared for her, instead of turning from it and denying it, might she not reasonably have hoped to reappear on the scene in the form of Enid Drover?

These grotesque fancies had begun to weave their spirals through her brain only after a first impact had emptied it of everything else, swept it suddenly clear of all meaning and all reason. That moment had come when Chris Fenno had entered in the wake of the other guests; when she had heard his name announced like that of any other member of the family; had seen him advance across the interminable length of the room, all the lights in it converging upon him as she felt that all the eyes in it converged on her; when she had seen Anne at his side, felt her presence between them, heard the girl's voice, imperious, beseeching: "Mother—here's Chris," and felt her hand drop into that other hand with the awful plunge that the heart makes when a sudden shock flings it from its seat.

She had lived through all that; she and he had faced each other; had exchanged greetings, she supposed; had even, perhaps, said something to each other about Anne, and about their future relation. She did not know what; she judged only, from the undisturbed faces about them, that there had been nothing alarming, nothing to scandalize or grieve; that it had all, to the tribal eye, passed off decently and what they called "suitably". Her past training had served her—his boundless assurance had served him. It was what the French called "a moment to pass"; they had passed it. And in that mad world beyond the abyss, where she now found herself, here they all were with the old faces, saying the same old things with the same old complacency, eating their way through the same Clephane courses, expressing the same approval of the Clephane cellar ("It was Hendrik, you know, who advised John to lay down that ninety-five Clicquot," she caught Enid Drover breathing across the bubbles to her son-in-law). It was all, in short, as natural and unnatural, as horrible, intolerable and unescapable, as if she had become young again, with all her desolate and unavoidable life stretching away ahead of her to—this.

And, in the mad phantasmagoria, there was Chris himself, symbolizing what she had flown to in her wild escape; representing, in some horrible duality, at once her sin and its harvest, her flight and her return. At the thought, her brain began to spin again, and she saw her own youth embodied before her in Anne, with Anne's uncompromising scorns and scruples, Anne's confident forward-looking gaze.

"Ah, well," she heard Hendrik Drover say as they rose from the table, "these occasions will come round from time to time in the best-regulated families, and I suppose we all feel—" while, at the other side of the table, Enid Drover, pink and melting from a last libation, sighed to Horace Maclew: "I only wish dear mother and John could have been here with us!" and Lilla, overhearing her, bracketed the observation in an ironic laugh.

It had all gone off wonderfully; thanks to Anne's tact the meeting between her mother and her betrothed had been thickly swaddled in layer on layer of non-conducting, non-explosive "family". A sense of mutual congratulation was in the air as the groups formed themselves again in the drawing-room. The girl herself moved from one to another, pale, vigilant, radiant; Chris Fenno, in a distant corner, was settled with coffee-cup and cigarette at Lilla Maclew's side; Mrs. Clephane found herself barricaded behind Hendrik Drover and one of the older Tresseltons. They were the very two men, she remembered, between whom she had spent her evening after that first family dinner in which this one was so hallucinatingly merged.

Not until the party was breaking up, and farewells filled the hall, did she suddenly find herself—she knew not how—isolated in the inner drawing-room with Chris Fenno. He stood there before her, and she seemed to hear his voice for the first time.

"I want to thank you. . ." He appeared to feel it was a bad beginning, and tried again. "Shan't I have the chance, some day soon, of finding you—for a word or two, quietly?" he asked.

She faced him, erect and unflinching; she dragged her eyes up to his.

"A chance? But as soon as you like—as many chances as you like! You'll always find me—I shall always be here. I'm never going to leave Anne," she announced.

It had been almost worth the agony she had bought it with to see the look in his eyes when he heard that.

XXIII.

EXTREME EXHAUSTION—the sense of having reached the last limit of endurable emotion—plunged Kate Clephane, that night, into a dreamless sleep. It was months and months since she had reached those nethermost levels below sound or image or any mental movement; and she rose from them revived, renewed—and then suddenly understood that they had been only a grief-drugged mockery.

The return to reality was as painful as that of a traveller who has fallen asleep in the snow. One by one she had to readjust all her frozen faculties to the unchanged and intolerable situation; and she felt weaker, less able to contend with it. The thought that that very day she might have to face Chris Fenno paralyzed her. He had asked to see her alone—and she lay there, in the desolate dawn, rehearsing to herself all the cruel things he would find to say; for his ways of being cruel were innumerable. The day before she had felt almost light-heartedly confident of being able to outface, to outlast him; of her power of making the situation even more intolerable to him than he could make it to her. Now, in the merciless morning light, she had a new view of their respective situations. Who had suffered most the previous evening, he or she? Whose wakening that morning was most oppressed by fears? He had proposed to have a talk with her; he had had the courage to do that; and she felt that by having that courage he had already gained another point in their silent struggle.

Slowly the days dragged by; their hours were filled, for mother and daughter, by the crowding obligations and preoccupations natural to such times. Mrs. Clephane was helping her daughter with the wedding preparations; a spectacle to charm and edify the rest of the family.

Chris Fenno, two or three days after the announcement of the engagement, had returned to Baltimore, where he had accepted a temporary job on a newspaper, and where he had that, and other matters, to wind up before his marriage. During his stay in New York, Mrs. Clephane had had but two or three brief glimpses of him, and always in the presence of others. It was natural that he should wish to devote the greater part of his time to his betrothed. He and Anne went off in the early afternoon, and when they returned were, on each evening, engaged to dine with some member of the family. It was easy for Mrs. Clephane to excuse herself from these entertainments. The fact of her having presided at the dinner at which the engagement was announced had sealed it with her approval; and at the little dinners organized by Nollie Tresselton and the other cousins her presence was hardly expected, and readily dispensed with.

All this fitted in with the new times. The old days of introspections and explanations were over; the era of taking things for granted was the only one that Anne's generation knew, and in that respect Anne was of her day.

After the betrothal dinner she had said a tender goodnight to her mother, and the next evening, as she rushed up to dress after her long outing with Chris, had stopped at Kate's door to wave a loving hand and call out: "He says you've been so perfect to him—" That was all. Kate Clephane's own memories told her that to some natures happiness comes like a huge landslide burying all the past and spreading a fresh surface to life's sowings: and it was from herself, she reflected, that Anne had inherited her capacity for such all-obliterating bliss.

The days passed, and Chris Fenno at length came back. He was staying with the Joe Tresseltons, and there was a constant coming and going of the young people between the two houses. Opportunities were not lacking to see Mrs. Clephane in private, and for the first days after his return she waited in numb terror for the inevitable, the incalculable moment. But it did not come; and gradually she understood that it never would. His little speech had been a mere formula; he had nothing to say to her; no desire was farther from him than the wish to speak with her alone. What she had dreaded past expression, but supposed to be inevitable, he had probably never even seriously considered. Explanations? What was the use of explanations? He had gained his point; the thing now was to live at peace with everybody.

She saw that all her calculations had been mistaken. She had fancied that her tactics would render his situation intolerable; that if only she could bear to spend a few weeks in his presence she would demonstrate to him the impossibility of his spending the rest of his life in hers. But his reasoning reached a good deal farther, and embraced certain essential elements in human nature that hers had left out. He had said to himself—she was sure of it now—: "The next few weeks will be pretty bad, but after that I'll have the upper hand." He had only to hold out till the wedding; after that she would be a mere mother-in-law, and mothers-in-law are not a serious problem in modern life. How could she ever have imagined that he would not see through her game and out-manœuvre her, when he had done it so often before, and when his whole future depended on his doing it just once more? She felt herself beaten at every point.

Unless—unless she told the truth to Anne. Every day was making that impossible thing more impossible; yet every day was bringing them nearer to the day when not to do so—if all other measures failed—would be most impossible of all. She seemed to have reached that moment when, one morning, Anne came into her room and caught her by the hand.

"Dearest—you've got to come with me this very minute."

Kate, yielding to the girl's hand, was drawn along the corridor to her bedroom. There, on the bed, in a dazzle of whiteness, lay the wedding-dress.

"Will you help me to try it on?" Anne asked.

Kate Clephane rang the Rectory bell and found herself in the Rectory sitting-room. As she sat there, among photogravures of Botticelli Virgins and etchings of English cathedrals, she could not immediately remember why she had come, and looked with a kind of detached curiosity at the volumes of memoirs and sermons on the table at her elbow, at the perpendicular Gothic chairs against the wall, and the Morris armchairs which had superseded them. She had not been in a rectory sitting-room since the committee meeting at the Merrimans', on the day when she had received Anne's cable.

Her lapse of memory lasted only for a few seconds, but during that time she relived with intensity the sensations of that other day, she felt her happy heart dancing against the message folded under her dress, she saw the southern sun gilding the dull faces about the table, and smelt the violets and mimosa in Mrs. Merriman's vases. She woke again to the present just as an austere parlour-maid was requesting her to step this way.

Dr. Arklow's study was full of books, of signed photographs of Church dignitaries, of more English cathedrals, of worn leather armchairs and scattered pipes and tobacco-pouches. The Rector himself, on the hearth, loomed before her at once bland and formidable. He had guessed, of course, that she had come to talk about the date and hour of the wedding, and all the formulas incidental to such visits fell from his large benevolent lips. The visit really passed off more easily than she had expected, and she was on her feet again and feeling him behind her like a gentle trade-wind accustomed to waft a succession of visitors to the door, when she stopped abruptly and faced him.

"Dr. Arklow—"

He waited benevolently.

"There's something else—a case I've always wanted to put to you. . ."

"Dear Mrs. Clephane—do put it now." He was waving her back into her armchair; but she stood before him, unconscious of the gesture.

"It's about a friend of mine—"

"Yes: a friend? Do sit down."

She sat down, still unaware of her movements or his.

"A most unhappy woman. . . I told her I would ask . . . ask what could be done. . . She had an idea that you could tell her. . ."

He bowed expectantly.

Her parched lips brought out: "Of course it's confidential," and his gesture replied that communications, in that room, were always held to be so. "Whatever I can do—" he added.

"Yes. My friend thought—her position is really desperate." She stopped, her voice failing her; then the words came forth in panting jerks. "She was most unhappily married . . . things went against her—everything did. She tried . . . tried her best. . . Then she met him . . . it was too difficult. . . He was her lover; only for a short time. After that her life was perfectly . . . was all it should be. She never saw him—oh, for years. Now her daughter wants to marry him. . ."

"Marry him? *The same man?*" The Rector's voice swelled above her like a wave; his presence towered, blurred and gigantic. She felt the tears in her throat; but again she was seized by the besetting desire that her secret should not be guessed, and a desperate effort at self-control drove the tears back and cleared her voice.

Dr. Arklow still loomed and brooded. "And the man—"

A slow flush of agony rose to her forehead; but she remembered that she was seated with her back to the light, and took courage. "He—he is determined." She paused, and then went on: "It's too horrible. But at first he didn't know . . . when he first met the girl. Neither of them knew. And when he found out—"

"Yes?"

"Then—it was too late, he said. The girl doesn't know even now; she doesn't dream; and she's grown to care—care desperately."

"That's his defence?"

Her voice failed her again, and she signed her assent.

There was another long pause. She sat motionless, looking down at her own interlocked hands. She felt that Dr. Arklow was uneasily pacing the hearth-rug; at last she was aware that he was once more standing before her.

"The lady you speak of—your friend—is she here?"

She started. *"Here?"*

"In New York, I mean?"

"No; no; she's not here," Kate cried precipitately. "That's the reason why I offered to come—"

"I see." She thought she caught a faint note of relief in his voice. "She wished you to consult me?"

"Yes."

"And she's done everything—everything, of course, to stop this abomination?"

"Oh, everything . . . everything."

"Except to tell her daughter?"

She made another sign of assent.

Dr. Arklow cleared his throat, and declared with emphasis: "It is her duty to tell her daughter."

"Yes," Kate Clephane faltered. She got to her feet and looked about her blindly for the door.

"She must tell her daughter," the Rector repeated with rising vehemence. "Such a shocking situation must be avoided; avoided at all costs."

"Yes," she repeated. She was on the threshold now; automatically she held out her hand.

"Unless," the Rector continued uncertainly, his eyes upon her, "she is absolutely convinced that less harm will come to all concerned if she has the courage to keep silence—always." There was a pause. "As far as I can see into the blackness of it," he went on, gaining firmness, "the whole problem turns on that. I may be mistaken; perhaps I am. But when a man has looked for thirty or forty years into pretty nearly every phase of human suffering and error, as men of my cloth have to do, he comes to see that there must be adjustments . . . adjustments in the balance of evil. Compromises, politicians would call them. Well, I'm not afraid of the word." He stood leaning against the jamb of the door; her hand was on the doorknob, and she listened with lowered head.

"The thing in the world I'm most afraid of is sterile pain," he said after a moment. "I should never want any one to be the cause of that."

She lifted her eyes with an effort, and saw in his face the same look of understanding she had caught there for a moment while she talked with him at the Drovers' after dinner.

"Sterile pain—" she murmured. She had crossed the threshold now; she felt that he was holding out his hand. His face once more wore the expression of worldly benevolence that was as much the badge of his profession as his dress. After all, she perceived, he was glad that she had said nothing more definite, glad that their talk was safely over. Yet she had caught that other look.

"If your friend were here; if there were anything I could do for her, or say to her—anything to help—"

"Oh, she's not here; she won't be here," Kate repeated.

"In that case—" Again she caught the relief in his voice.

"But I will tell her—tell her what you've said." She was aware that they were shaking hands, and that he was averting his apprehensive eyes from hers. "For God's sake," the eyes seemed to entreat her, "let's get through with this before you betray yourself—if there's anything further to betray."

At the front door he bowed her out, repeating cordially: "And about a date for Anne's wedding; as soon as you and she are absolutely decided, remember I'm completely at your service."

The door closed, and she found herself in the street.

XXIV.

S HE TURNED AWAY from the Rectory and walked aimlessly up Madison Avenue. It was a warm summer-coloured October day. At Fifty-ninth Street she turned into the Park and wandered on over the yellowing leaf-drifts of the ramble. In just such a state of blind bewilderment she had followed those paths on the day when she had first caught sight of Chris Fenno and Lilla Gates in the twilight ahead of her. That was less than a year ago, and she looked back with amazement at the effect which that chance encounter had had on her. She seemed hardly to be suffering more now than she had suffered then. It had seemed unbearable, impossible, at the moment, that Chris Fenno should enter, even so episodically, so remotely, into her new life; and here he was, ensconced in its very centre, in complete possession of it.

She tried to think the situation out; but, as always, her trembling thoughts recoiled, just as she had seen Dr. Arklow's recoil.

Every one to whom she had tried to communicate her secret without betraying it had had the same instantaneous revulsion. "Not that—don't tell me that!" their averted eyes, their shrinking voices seemed to say. It was too horrible for any ears.

How then was she to obey Dr. Arklow's bidding and impart the secret to Anne? He had said it as positively as if he were handing down a commandment from Sinai: "The daughter must be told."

How easy to lay down abstract rules for other people's guidance: "The daughter" was just an imaginary person—a convenient conversational pawn. But Kate Clephane's daughter—her own Anne! She closed her eyes and tried to face the look in Anne's as the truth dawned on her.

"You—*you*, mother? The mother I've come to adore—the mother I can't live without, even with all my other happiness? *You?*"

Yes—perhaps that would be the worst of it, the way Anne would look at her and say "*You?*" For, once the girl knew the truth, her healthy youth might so revolt from Chris's base-

ness, Chris's duplicity, that the shock of the discovery would
be its own cure. But when the blow had fallen, when Anne's
life had crashed about her, and the ruins been cleared away—
what then of her mother? Why, her mother would be buried
under those ruins; her life would be over; but a hideous indestructible image of her would remain, overshadowing, darkening the daughter's future.

"This man you are going to marry has—"

No; Kate Clephane could go no farther than that. Such
confessions were not to be made; were not for a daughter's
ears. She began the phrase to herself again and again, but
could not end it. . .

And, after all, she suddenly thought, Dr. Arklow himself,
having given the injunction, had at once qualified, had virtually withdrawn it. In declaring that such an abomination must
at all costs be prevented he had spoken with the firmness of a
priest; but almost at once the man had intervened, and had
suggested to the hypothetical mother the alternative of not
speaking at all, if only she could be sure of never betraying
herself in the future, of sacrificing everything to the supreme
object of avoiding what he called sterile pain. Those tentative,
half-apologetic words now effaced the others in Kate's mind.
Though spoken without the accent of authority—and almost
under his breath—she knew they represented what he really
felt. But where should she find the courage to conform to
them?

She had left the Park, aimlessly, unseeingly, and was walking eastward through a half-built street in the upper Nineties.
The thought of returning home—re-entering that house
where the white dress still lay on the bed—was unbearable.
She walked on and on. . . Suddenly she came upon an ugly
sandstone church-front with a cross above the doorway. The
leathern swing-doors were flapping back and forth, women
passing in and out. Kate Clephane pushed open one of the
doors and looked in. The day was fading, and in the dusky
interior lights fluttered like butterflies about the paper flowers
of the altar. There was no service, but praying figures were
scattered here and there. Against the brown-washed walls of
the aisles she observed a row of confessionals of varnished
wood, like cigar-boxes set on end; before one or two, women

were expectantly kneeling. Mrs. Clephane wondered what they had to tell.

Leaning against one of the piers of the nave she evoked all those imaginary confessions, and thought how trivial, how childish they would seem, compared to what she carried in her breast. . . What a help it must be to turn to somebody who could tell one firmly, positively what to do—to be able to lay down one's moral torture like a heavy load at the end of the day! Dr. Arklow had none of the authority which the habit of the confessional must give. He could only vaguely sympathize and deplore, and try to shuffle the horror out of sight as soon as he caught an unwilling glimpse of it. But these men whose office it was to bind and to unbind—who spoke as the mere impersonal mouth-pieces of a mighty Arbitrator, letting neither moral repugnance nor false delicacy interfere with the sacred task of alleviation and purification— how different must they be! Her eyes filled at the thought of laying her burden in such hands.

And why not? Why not entrust her anonymous secret to one of those anonymous ears? In talking to Dr. Arklow she had felt that both he and she were paralyzed by the personal relation, and all the embarrassments and complications arising from it. When she spoke of her friend in distress, and he replied with the same evasive formula, both were conscious of the evasion, and hampered by it. And so it had been from the first—there was not an ear into which she dared pour her agony. What if, now, at once, she were to join those unknown penitents? It was possible, she knew—she had but a step to take. . .

She did not take it. Her unrest drove her forth again into the darkening street, drove her homeward with uncertain steps, in the mood of forlorn expectancy of those who, having failed to exert their will, wait helplessly on the unforeseen. After all, how could one tell? Chris must, in his own degree, be suffering as she was suffering. Why not stick to her old plan of waiting, holding on, enduring everything, in the hope of wearing him out? She reached the door of her house, set her teeth, and went in. Overhead, she remembered with a shudder, the white dress waited, with all that it implied. . .

The drawing-room was empty, and she went up to her own

room. There, as usual, the fire shone invitingly, fresh flowers opened in the lamplight. All was warmth, peace, intimacy. As she sat down by the fireside she seemed to see Fred Landers's heavy figure in the opposite armchair, his sturdy square-toed boots turned to the hearth. She remembered how, one day, as he sat there, she had said to herself that it might be pleasant to see him there always. Now, in the extremity of her loneliness, the thought returned. Since then he had confessed his own hope to her—shyly, obliquely, apologetically; but under his stammering words she had recognized the echo of a long desire. She knew he had always loved her; had not Anne betrayed that it was her guardian who had persuaded her to recall her unknown mother? Kate Clephane owed him everything, then—all her happiness and all her sorrow! He knew everything of her life—or nearly everything. To whom else could she turn with the peculiar sense of security which that certitude gave? She felt sorry that she had received his tentative advance so coldly, so inarticulately. After all, he might yet be her refuge—her escape. She closed her eyes, and tried to imagine what life would be—years and years of it—at Fred Landers's side. To feel the nearness of that rugged patient kindness; would it not lighten her misery, make the thoughts and images that were torturing her less palpable, less acute, less real?

She sat there for a long time, brooding. Now and then a step passing her door, or a burst of voices on the landing, told her that Anne was probably receiving some of her friends in her own rooms at the other end of the passage. The wedding presents were already arriving; Anne, with a childish pleasure that was unlike her usual aloofness from material things, had set them out on a long table in her sitting-room. The mother pictured the eager group inspecting and admiring, the talk of future plans, the discussion of all the details of the wedding. The date for it would soon be fixed; ostensibly, her own visit to Dr. Arklow had been made for the purpose. But at the last moment her courage had failed her, and she had said vaguely, in leaving, that she would let him know.

As she sat there, she saw her daughter's pale illuminated face as though it were before her. Anne's happiness shone through her, making her opaque and guarded features lumi-

nous and transparent; and the mother could measure, from
her own experience, the amount of heat and force that fed
that incandescence. She herself had always had a terrible way
of being happy—and that way was Anne's.

She simply could not bear to picture to herself the change,
in Anne's face, from ecstasy to anguish. She had seen that
change once, and the sight had burned itself into her eye-
balls. To destroy Anne's happiness seemed an act of murderous cruelty. What did it matter—as the chances of life
went—of what elements such happiness was made? Had she,
Kate Clephane, ever shrunk from her own bliss because of the
hidden risks it contained? She had played high, staked everything—and lost. Could she blame her daughter for choosing
to take the same risks? No; there was, in all great happiness,
or the illusion momentarily passing for it, a quality so beatific,
so supernatural, that no pain with which it might have to be
paid could, at the time, seem too dear; could hardly, perhaps,
ever seem so, to headlong hearts like hers and Anne's.

Her own heart had begun to tremble and dilate with her
new resolve; the resolve to accept the idea of Anne's marriage,
to cease her inward struggle against it, and try to be in reality
what she was already pretending to be: the acquiescent, approving mother. . . After all, why not? Legally, technically,
there was nothing wrong, nothing socially punishable, in the
case. And what was there on the higher, the more private
grounds where she pretended to take her stand and deliver
her judgment? Chris Fenno was a young man—she was old
enough to be, if not his mother, at least his mother-in-law.
What had she ever hoped or expected to be to him but a
passing incident, a pleasant memory? From the first, she had
pitched their relation in that key; had insisted on the difference in their ages, on her own sense of the necessary tran-
siency of the tie, on the fact that she would not have it
otherwise. Anything rather than to be the old woman clutching at an impossible prolongation of bliss—anything rather
than be remembered as a burden instead of being regretted as
a delight! How often had she told him that she wanted to
remain with him like the memory of a flowering branch
brushed by at night? "You won't quite know if it was lilac
or laburnum, or both—you'll only know it was something

vanishing and sweet." Vanishing and sweet—that was what she had meant to be! And she had kept to her resolution till the blow fell—

Well, and was he so much to blame for its falling? She herself had been the witness of his resistance, of his loyal efforts to escape. The vehemence of Anne's passion had thwarted him, had baffled them both; if he loved her as passionately as she loved him, was he not justified in accepting the happiness forced upon him? And how refuse it without destroying the girl's life?

"If any one is to be destroyed, oh God, don't let it be Anne!" the mother cried. She seemed at last to have reached a clearer height, a more breathable air. Renunciation—renunciation. If she could attain to that, what real obstacle was there to her daughter's happiness?

"I would sell my soul for her—why not my memories?" she reflected.

The sound of steps and voices outside had ceased. From the landing had come a "Goodbye, dearest!" in Nollie Tresselton's voice; no doubt she had been the last visitor to leave, and Anne was now alone; perhaps alone with her betrothed. Well; to that thought also Kate Clephane must accustom herself; by and bye they would be always alone, those two, in the sense of being nearer to each other than either of them was to any one else. The mother could bear that too. Not to lose Anne— at all costs to keep her hold on the girl's confidence and tenderness: that was all that really mattered. She would go to Anne now. She herself would ask the girl to fix the date for the wedding.

She got up and walked along the deep-piled carpet of the corridor. The door of Anne's sitting-room was ajar, but no sound came from within. Every one was gone, then; even Chris Fenno. With a breath of relief the mother pushed the door open. The room was empty. One of the tall vases was full of branching chrysanthemums and autumn berries. In a corner stood a tea-table with scattered cups and plates. The Airedale drowsed by the hearth. As she stood there, Kate Clephane saw the little Anne who used to sit by that same fire trying to coax the red birds through the fender. The vision melted the last spot of resistance in her heart. The door of

Anne's bedroom was also ajar, but no sound came from there either. Perhaps the girl had gone out with her last visitors, escaping for a starlit rush up the Riverside Drive before dinner. These sudden sallies at queer hours were a way the young people had.

The mother listened a moment longer, then laid her hand on the bedroom door. Before her, directly in the line of her vision, was Anne's narrow bed. On it the wedding-dress still lay, in a dazzle of whiteness; and between Mrs. Clephane and the bed, looking also at the dress, stood Anne and Chris Fenno. They had not heard her cross the sitting-room or push open the bedroom door; they did not hear her now. All their faculties were absorbed in each other. The young man's arms were around the girl, her cheek was against his. One of his hands reached about her shoulder and, making a cup for her chin, pressed her face closer. They were looking at the dress; but the curves of their lips, hardly detached, were like those of a fruit that has burst apart of its own ripeness.

Kate Clephane stood behind them like a ghost. It made her feel like a ghost to be so invisible and inaudible. Then a furious flame of life rushed through her; in every cell of her body she felt that same embrace, felt the very texture of her lover's cheek against her own, burned with the heat of his palm as it clasped Anne's chin to press her closer.

"Oh, not that—not that—not that!" Mrs. Clephane imagined she had shrieked it out at them, and pressed her hands to her mouth to stifle the cry; then she became aware that it was only a dumb whisper within her. For a time which seemed without end she continued to stand there, invisible, inaudible, and they remained in each other's embrace, motionless, speechless. Then she turned and went. They did not hear her.

A dark fermentation boiled up into her brain; every thought and feeling was clogged with thick entangling memories. . . Jealous? Was she jealous of her daughter? Was she physically jealous? Was that the real secret of her repugnance, her instinctive revulsion? Was that why she had felt from the first as if some incestuous horror hung between them?

She did not know—it was impossible to analyze her anguish. She knew only that she must fly from it, fly as far as she could from the setting of these last indelible impressions. How had she ever imagined that she could keep her place at Anne's side—that she could either outstay Chris, or continue to live under the same roof with them? Both projects seemed to her, now, equally nebulous and impossible. She must put the world between them—the whole width of the world was not enough. The very grave, she thought, would be hardly black enough to blot out that scene.

She found herself, she hardly knew how, at the foot of the stairs, in the front hall. Her precipitate descent recalled the early winter morning when, as hastily, almost as unconsciously, she had descended those same stairs, flying from her husband's house. Nothing was changed in the hall: her eyes, once again morbidly receptive of details, noted on the door the same patent locks with which her fingers had then struggled. Now, as then, a man's hat and stick lay on the hall table; on that other day they had been John Clephane's, now they were Chris Fenno's. That was the only difference.

She stood there, looking about her, wondering why she did not push back the bolts and rush out into the night, hatless and cloakless as she was. What else was there to do but to go straight to the river, or to some tram line with its mortal headlights bearing straight down on one? One didn't have to have a hat and cloak to go out in search of annihilation. . .

As she stood there the door-bell rang, and she heard the step of a servant coming to open the door. She shrank back into the drawing-room, and in another moment Enid Drover had rustled in, her pink cheeks varnished with the cold, her furs full of the autumn freshness. Her little eyes were sharp with excitement.

"My dear Kate! I've rushed in with such good news: I shall be late for dinner, Hendrik will be furious. But never mind; I had to tell you. The house next door really *is* for sale! Isn't it too perfect? The agent thinks it could be got for a fairly reasonable price. But Hendrik says it may be snapped up at any minute, and Anne ought to decide at once. Then you could stay on comfortably here, and you and she and Chris would always be together, just as she wants you to be. . . No; don't send for her; I can't wait. And besides, I want you to have the pleasure of telling her." On the doorstep Mrs. Drover turned to call back: "Remember, Hendrik says she must decide." Her limousine engulfed her.

XXV.

MRS. CLEPHANE excused herself from coming down to dinner; Aline was to say that she was very tired, and begged that no one should disturb her. The next morning, she knew, Chris was returning to Baltimore. Perhaps in his absence she would be able to breathe more freely, see more clearly.

Anne, as usual, respected her mother's wishes; she neither came up nor sent to enquire. But the next morning, in the old way, fresh and shining, she appeared with Mrs. Clephane's breakfast tray. She wanted to be reassured as to her mother's health, and Kate, under her solicitous eye, poured out a cup of tea and forced down a bit of toast.

"You look tired, mother. It's only that?"

"Only that, dear."

"You didn't tell me that Aunt Enid had been in last night about the house next door—" Anne spoke the least little reproachfully.

"I'm sorry. I had such a headache that when she left I went straight to my room. Did she telephone you?"

"Uncle Hendrik did. Isn't it the greatest luck? It will be such fun arranging it all." The girl paused and looked at her mother. "And this will make you decide, darling, won't it?"

"Decide?"

"To stay on here. To keep this house for yourself. It will be almost like our all being together."

"Yes—almost."

"You will stay, won't you?"

"Stay here? I can't—I can't!" The words escaped before Mrs. Clephane could repress them. Her heart began to rush about in her like a caged animal.

Anne's brows darkened and drew together. "But I don't understand. You told Chris you would—"

"Did I? Perhaps I did. But I must sometimes be allowed to change my mind," Mrs. Clephane murmured, forcing a thin smile.

"To change your mind about being with us? You don't want to, then, after all?"

Mrs. Clephane pushed the tray away and propped herself on her elbow. "No, I don't want to."

"How you say it, mother! As if I were a stranger. I don't understand. . ." The girl's lip was beginning to tremble. "I thought. . . Chris and I both thought. . ."

"I'm sorry. But I must really decide as I think best. When you are married you won't need me."

"And shan't you need me, mother? Not a little?" Anne hesitated, and then ventured, timidly: "You're so alone—so awfully alone."

"I've always been that. It can't be otherwise. You've chosen . . . you've chosen to be married. . ."

Anne stood up and looked down on her with searching imperious eyes. "Is it my being married—or my being married to Chris?"

"Ah—don't let us talk of that again!"

The girl continued to scrutinize her strangely. "Once for all—you won't tell me?"

Mrs. Clephane did not speak.

"Then I shall ask him—I shall ask him in your presence," Anne exclaimed in a shaking voice.

At the sound of that break in her voice the dread of seeing her suffer once more superseded every other feeling in the mother's breast. She leaned against the pillows, speechless for a moment; then she held out her hand, seeking Anne's.

"There's nothing to ask, dear; nothing to tell."

"You don't hate him, mother? You really don't?"

Slowly Kate Clephane articulated: "I don't—hate him."

"But why won't you see him with me, then? Why won't you talk it all out with us once for all? Mother, what *is* it? I must know."

Mrs. Clephane, under her daughter's relentless eyes, felt the blood rising from her throat to her pale lips and drawn cheeks, and to the forehead in which her pulses must be visibly beating. She lay there, bathed in a self-accusing crimson, and it seemed to her that those clear young eyes were like steel blades plunging into the deepest folds of her conscience.

"You don't hate him? But then you're in love with him—you're in love with him, and I've known it all along!" The girl shrilled it out suddenly, and hid her face in her hands.

Kate Clephane lay without speaking. In the first shock of the outcry all her defences had crashed together about her head, and it had been almost a relief to feel them going, to feel that pretences and disguises were at an end. Then Anne's hands dropped to her side, and the mother, meeting her gaze, lost the sense of her own plight in the sight of that other woe. All at once she felt herself strong and resolute; all the old forces of dissimulation were pouring back through her veins. The accusing red faded from her face, and she lay there and quietly met the question in Anne's eyes.

"*Anne!*" she simply said, with a little shrug.

"Oh, mother—mother! I think I must be going mad!" Anne was on her knees at the bedside, her face buried in the coverlet. It was easier to speak to her while her eyes were hidden, and Kate laid a hand on her hair.

"Not mad, dear; but decidedly over-strung." She heard the note of magnanimity in her own voice.

"But can you forgive me—ever?"

"Nonsense, dear; can I do anything else?"

"But then—if you *do* forgive me, really—why must you go away? Why won't you promise to stay with us?"

Kate Clephane lay against her pillows and meditated. Her hand was still in Anne's hair; she held the girl's head gently against the coverlet, still not wishing her own face to be too closely scrutinized. At length she spoke.

"I didn't mean to tell you just yet; and you must tell no one." She paused, and rallied her failing courage. "I can't promise to stay with you, dear, because I may be going to get married too." The first words were the most difficult to say; after that she heard her voice going on steadily. "Fred Landers has asked me to marry him; and I think I shall accept. . . No; don't hug me too hard, child; my head still aches— There; now you understand, don't you? And you won't scold me any more? But remember, it's a secret from every one. It's not to be spoken of till after you're married. . . Now go."

After Anne had left her, subdued but jubilant, she lay there and remembered, with a twinge of humiliation, that the night before she had hurried downstairs in a mad rush to death. Anything—anything to escape from the coil of horror closing

in on her! . . . And it had sufficed to her to meet Enid
Drover in the hall, with that silly chatter about the house next
door, to check the impulse, drive her back into the life she
was flying from. . . She reflected with self-derision that all
her suicidal impulses seemed to end in the same way; by landing her in the arms of some man she didn't care for. Then she
remembered Anne's illuminated face, and lay listening to the
renewed life of the house, the bustle of happy preparations
going on all about her.

"Poor Fred! Well—if it's what he wants—" she thought.
What she herself wanted, all she now wanted, was never again
to see that dreadful question in Anne's eyes. And she had
found no other way of evading it.

XXVI.

N ow that a day for the wedding was fixed, the preparations went on more rapidly. Soon there was only a fortnight left; then only ten days; then a week.

Chris Fenno's parents were to have come to New York to
make the acquaintance of their son's betrothed; but though a
date had several times been appointed for their visit, Mrs.
Fenno, whose health was not good, had never been well
enough to come, and finally it was arranged that Anne should
go to Baltimore to see them. She was to stay with the Maclews, who immediately seized the opportunity to organize a
series of festivities in celebration of the event.

Lilla invited Mrs. Clephane to come with her daughter; but
Kate declined, on the plea that she herself was not well. People were beginning to notice how tired and thin she looked.
Her glass showed streaks of gray in her redundant hair, and
about her lips and eyes the little lines she had so long kept at
bay. Everybody in the family agreed that it would be a good
thing for her to have a few days' rest before the wedding.

With regard to her own future she had sworn Anne to unconditional secrecy. She explained that she did not intend to
give Fred Landers a definite answer till after the wedding, and
Anne, who had all the Clephane reticence, understood her
wish to keep the matter quiet, and even in her guardian's
presence was careful not to betray that she knew of his hopes.
She only made him feel that he was more than ever welcome,
and touched him by showing an added cordiality at a moment
when most girls are deaf and blind to all human concerns but
their own.

"It's so like Anne to find time to remember an old derelict
just when she might be excused for forgetting that any of us
exist." He said it with a gentle complacency as he sat in Mrs.
Clephane's sitting-room one evening during Anne's absence.
"She's like you—very like you," he added, looking at Kate
Clephane with shy beseeching eyes.

She smiled back at him, wondering if she would ever have
the courage to tell him that she meant to marry him. He was
thinking of that too, she knew. Why not tell him now, at

once? She had only to lean forward and lay her hand on his. No words would be necessary. And surely she would feel less alone. . . But she remained silent; it was easier to think of speaking than to speak.

It was he who questioned: "And afterward—have you decided what you're going to do?"

She continued to smile. "There'll be time to decide afterward."

"Anne tells me you've definitely refused to remain in this house."

"This house hasn't many pleasant associations for me."

He coloured as if she had caught him in a failure of tact. "I understand that. But with the young people here . . . or next door . . . she hoped you'd feel less lonely."

Again she perceived that he was trying to remind her of a possible alternative, and again she let the allusion drop, answering merely: "I'm used to being lonely. It's not as bad as people think."

"You've known worse, you mean?" He seldom risked anything as direct as that. "And it would be worse for you, being with Anne after she's married? You still hate the idea as much as ever?"

She rose impatiently and went to lean against the mantelpiece. "Fred, what's the use? I shall never hate it less. But that's all over—I've accepted it."

"Yes, and made Anne so happy."

"Oh, love is what is making Anne happy!" She hardly knew how she brought the word from her lips.

"Well—loving Fenno hasn't made her cease to love you."

"Anne is perfect. But suppose we talk of something else. At my age I find this bridal atmosphere a little suffocating. I shall go abroad again, probably—I don't know."

She turned and looked at herself in the glass above the mantel, seeing the gray streaks and the accusing crows'-feet. And as she stood there, she remembered how once, when she was standing in the same way before a mirror, Chris had come up behind her, and they had laughed at seeing their reflections kiss. How young she had been then—how young! Now, as she looked at herself, she saw behind her the reflection of Fred Landers's comfortable bulk, sunk in an armchair in after-dinner repose, his shirt-front bulging a little, the lamp-light varnishing the top of his head through the thinning hair. A middle-aged couple—perfectly suited to each other in age and appearance. She turned back and sat down beside him.

"Shall we try a Patience?" she said.

He accepted with a wistful alacrity which seemed to say it was the most he hoped for, and they drew up a table and sat down opposite each other, calmly disposing the little cards in elaborate patterns.

They had been playing for about half an hour when she rumpled up the cards abruptly, and sweeping them together into a passionate heap cried out: "I want it to be a gay wedding—the gayest wedding that ever was! I'm determined it shall be a gay wedding."

She dropped her face into her hands, and sat there propping her elbows on the card-table, and laughing out between her intercrossed fingers: "A really gay wedding, you know. . ."

XXVII.

ONLY THREE DAYS more now; for just three days more
she and Anne would live under one roof.

And then?

The interrogation was not Anne's. The news of Mrs. Clephane's intended marriage had completely restored the girl's
serenity. Chris Fenno, detained in Baltimore by his mother's
sudden and somewhat alarming illness, had not yet reappeared; it seemed likely now that he would arrive in New
York only the day before the wedding. Anne was to have her
mother to herself to the last; and with every art of tenderness
and dependence she tried to show her appreciation of these
final days, sweet with the sweetness of dear things ending, yet
without pain because they were not to precede a real separation. Her only anxiety—the alarm about Mrs. Fenno—had
been allayed by a reassuring telegram, and she moved within
that rainbow bubble that once or twice in life contrives to
pass itself off as the real horizon.

The sight of her, Kate Clephane reasoned, ought to have
been justification enough. Anything was worth doing or sacrificing to keep the bubble unbroken. And the last three days
would pass—the Day itself would pass. The world, after it
was over, would go on in the same old way. What was all the
flurry about?

Mrs. Drover did not find it easy to maintain so detached an
attitude. She, for one, could not conceive how her sister-in-
law could remain so calm at such a moment.

"Of course Nollie's wonderfully capable; she and Lilla have
taken almost all the worry on their shoulders, haven't they? I
never could have struggled alone with that immense list of
invitations. But still I don't think you ought to assume that
everything's settled. After all, there are only three days left!
And no one seems to have even begun to think who's going
to take you up the aisle. . ."

"Up the aisle?" Mrs. Clephane echoed blankly.

"Well, yes, my dear. There *is* an aisle at St. Stephen's,"
Enid Drover chirped with one of her rare attempts at irony.

"And of course Hendrik must take up the bride, and you must be there, ready to receive her and give her away. . ."

"Give her away?"

"Hadn't you thought of that either?" Mrs. Drover's little laugh had a tinge of condescension. Though all the family had conspired to make Mrs. Clephane forget that she had lived for nearly twenty years outside the social pale, the fact remained; she *had*. And it was on just such occasions as this that she betrayed it, somewhat embarrassingly to her sister-in-law. Not even to know that, when a bride's father was dead, it was her mother who gave her away!

"You didn't expect Hendrik to do it?" Mrs. Drover rippled on, half compassionate, half contemptuous. It was hard to understand how some people contrived to remain in ignorance of the most elementary rules of behaviour!

"Hendrik—well, why shouldn't he?" Kate Clephane said.

Anne was passing through the room, a pile of belated presents in her arms.

"Do you hear, my dear? Your uncle Hendrik will be very much flattered." Mrs. Drover's little eyes grew sharp with the vision of Hendrik's broad back and glossy collar playing the leading part in the ceremony. "The bride was given away by her uncle, Mr. Hendrik Drover, of—" It really would read very well.

"Flattered about what?" Anne paused to question.

"Your mother seems to think it's your uncle who ought to give you away."

"Not you, mother?" Kate Clephane caught the instant drop in the girl's voice. Underneath her radiant security, what suspicion, what dread, still lingered?

"I'm so stupid, dear; I hadn't realized it was the custom."

"Don't you want it to be?"

"I want what you want." Their thin-edged smiles seemed to cross like blades.

"I want it to be you, mother."

"Then of course, dear—"

Mrs. Drover heaved a faintly disappointed sigh. Hendrik would certainly have looked the part better. "Well, *that's* settled," she said, in the tone of one who strikes one more item off an invisible list. "And now the question is, who's to take your mother up the aisle?"

Anne and her mother were still exchanging smiles. "Why, Uncle Fred of course, isn't he?" Anne cried.

"That's the point. If your mother's cousin comes from Meridia—"

Mrs. Clephane brushed aside the possible cousin from Meridia. "Fred shall take me up," she declared; and Anne's smile lost its nervous edge.

"Now, is there anything else left to settle?" the girl gaily challenged her aunt; and Mrs. Drover groaned back: "Anything else? But it seems as if we'd only just begun. If it weren't for Nollie and Lilla I shouldn't feel sure of *anybody's* being at the church when the time comes. . ."

The time had almost come: the sun had risen on the day before the wedding. It rose, mounted up in a serene heaven, bent its golden arch over an untroubled indifferent world, and stooped westward in splendid unawareness. The day, so full of outward bustle, of bell-ringing, telephone calls, rushings back and forth of friends, satellites and servants, had drooped to its close in the unnatural emptiness of such conclusions. Everything was done; every question was settled; every last order given; and Anne, with a kiss for her mother, had gone off with Nollie and Joe Tresselton for one of the crepuscular motor-dashes that clear the cobwebs from modern brains.

Anne had resolutely refused to have either bridesmaids or the conventional family dinner of the bridal eve. She wanted to strip the occasion of all its meaningless formalities, and Chris Fenno was of the same mind. He was to spend the evening alone with his parents at their hotel, and Anne had invited no one but Fred Landers to dine. She had warned her mother that she might be a little late in getting home, and had asked her, in view of Mr. Landers's excessive punctuality, to be downstairs in time to receive and pacify him.

Mrs. Clephane had seen through the simple manœuvre, and had not resented it. After all, it would be the best opportunity to tell Fred Landers what she had decided to tell him. As she sat by the drawing-room fire listening for the door-bell she felt a curious sense of aloofness, almost of pacification. It might be only the quiet of exhaustion; she half-suspected it was, but she was too exhausted to feel sure. Yet one thing was clear to her; she had suffered less savagely since she had known that Dr. Arklow had guessed what she was suffering. The problem had been almost too difficult for him; but it was enough that he had perceived its difficulty, had seen that it was too deeply rooted in living fibres to be torn out without mortal hurt.

"Sterile pain. . . I should never want any one to be the cause of sterile pain. . ." That phrase of his helped her even now; her mind clung fast to it as she sat waiting for Landers's ring.

It came punctually, even sooner than the hour, as Anne had foreseen; and in another moment he was advancing across the room in his slow bulky way, with excuses for his early arrival.

"But I did it on purpose. I was sure Anne would be late—"

"Anne! She isn't even in—"

"I knew it! They're all a pack of vagabonds. And I hoped you'd be punctual," he continued, letting himself down into an armchair as if he were lowering a bale of goods over the side of a ship. "After all, you and I belong to the punctual generation."

She winced a little at being so definitely relegated to the rank where she belonged. Yes: he and she were nearly of an age. She remembered, in her newly-married precocity, thinking of him as a shy shambling boy, years younger than herself. Now he had the deliberate movements of the elderly, and though he shot, fished, played golf, and kept up the activities common to his age, his mind, in maturing, had grown heavier, and seemed to have communicated its prudent motions to his body. She shut her eyes for a second from the vision. Her own body still seemed so supple, free and imponderable. If it had not been for her looking-glass she would never have known she was more than twenty.

She glanced up at the clock; a quarter to eight. Very likely Anne would not be back for another half hour. How would the evening ever drag itself to an end?

They exchanged a few words about the wedding, but the

topic was intolerable to Mrs. Clephane. She had managed to face the situation as a whole: to consider its details was still beyond her. Yet if she left that subject, just beyond it lay the question her companion was waiting to ask; and that alternative was intolerable too. She got up from her seat, moved aimlessly across the room, straightened a flower in a vase, put out a superfluous wall-light.

"That's enough illumination—at our age," she said, coming back to her seat.

"Oh—*you!*" He threw all his unspoken worship into the word. "With that hair of yours. . ."

"My hair—my hair!" Her hands went up to the rich mass as if she would have liked to tear it from her head. At that moment she hated it, as she did everything else that mocked her with the barren illusion of youth.

Fred Landers had coloured to the edge of his own thin hair; no doubt he was afraid of her resenting even this expression of admiration. His embarrassment irritated yet touched her, and raising her eyes she looked into his.

"I never knew till the other day that it's to you I owe the fact of being here," she said.

He was evidently unprepared for this, and did not know whether to be distressed or gratified. His faint blush turned to crimson.

"To me?"

"Oh, well—I'm not sorry it should be," she rejoined, her voice softening.

"But it's all nonsense. Anne was determined to get you back."

"Yes; because you told her she must. She owned up frankly. She said she wasn't sure, at first, how the plan would work; but you were. You backed me for all you were worth."

"Oh, if you mean that; of course I backed you. You see, she didn't know you; and I did."

She continued to look at him thoughtfully, almost tenderly. "Very few people have taken the trouble to care what became of me. And you hadn't seen me for nearly twenty years."

"No; but I remembered; and I knew you'd had a rotten bad start."

"Lots of women have that, and nobody bothers. But you did; you remembered and you brought me here."

She turned again, restlessly, and went and stood by the chimney-piece, resting her chin on her hand.

Landers smiled up at her, half deprecatingly. "If I did, don't be too hard on me."

"Why should I be? I've had over a year. As happiness goes, that's a lifetime."

"Don't speak as if yours were over."

"Oh, it's been good enough to be worth while!"

He sat silent for a while, meditatively considering his honest boot-tips. At length he spoke again, in a tone of sudden authority, such as came into his voice when business matters were being discussed. "You mustn't come back alone to this empty house."

She looked slowly about her. "No; I never want to see this house again."

"Where shall you go, then?"

"After tomorrow? There's a steamer sailing for the Mediterranean the next day. I think I shall just go down and get on board."

"Alone?"

She shed a sudden smile on him. "Will you come with me?"

At the question he sprang up out of his armchair with the headlong haste of a young man. The movement upset a little table at his elbow; but he let the table lie.

"By God, yes!" he shouted, reaching out to her with both hands.

She shrank back a little, not from reluctance but from a sense of paralyzing inadequacy. "It's I who am old now," she thought with a shiver.

"What—you really would come with me? The day after tomorrow?" she said.

"I'd come with you today, if there was enough of it left to get us anywhere." He stood looking at her, waiting for her to speak; then, as she remained silent, he slowly drew back a step or two. "Kate—this isn't one of your jokes?"

As she returned his look she was aware that her sight of him was becoming faintly blurred. "Perhaps it was, when I began. It isn't now." She put her hands in his.

XXVIII.

I N THE STILLNESS of the sleeping house she sat up with a start, plucked out of a tormented sleep.

"But it can't be—it can't be—it can't be!"

She jumped out of bed, turned on the light, and stared about her. What secret warning had waked her with that cry on her lips? She could not recall having dreamed: she had only tossed and fought with some impalpable oppression. And now, as she stood there, in that hideously familiar room, the silence went on echoing with her cry. All the excuses, accommodations, mitigations, mufflings, disguisings, had dropped away from the bare fact that her lover was going to marry her daughter, and that nothing she could do would prevent it.

A few hours ago she had still counted on the blessed interval of time, the lulling possibilities of delay. She had kissed Anne goodnight very quietly, she remembered. Then it was eleven o'clock of the night before; now it was the morning of the day. A pitch-black winter morning: there would be no daylight for another three hours. No daylight—but the Day was here!

She glanced at the clock. Half-past four. The longing seized her to go and look at Anne for the last time; but the next moment she felt that hardly a sight in the world would be less bearable.

She turned back into her room, wrapped herself in her dressing-gown, and went and sat in the window.

What did Fifth Avenue look like nowadays at half-past four o'clock of a winter morning? Much as it had when she had kept the same vigil nearly twenty years earlier, on the morning of her flight with Hylton Davies. That night too she had not slept, and for the same reason: the thought of Anne. On that other day she had deserted her daughter for the first time—and now it seemed as though she were deserting her again. One betrayal of trust had led inexorably to the other.

Fifth Avenue was much more brilliantly lit than on that other far-off morning. Long streamers of radiance floated on the glittering asphalt like tropical sea-weeds on a leaden sea.

But overhead the canopy of darkness was as dense, except for the tall lights hanging it here and there with a planetary glory.

The street itself was empty. In old times one would have heard the desolate nocturnal sound of a lame hoof-beat as a market-gardener's cart went by: they always brought out in the small hours the horses that were too bad to be seen by day. But all that was changed. The last lame horse had probably long since gone to the knacker's yard, and no link of sound was left between the Niagara-roar of the day and the hush before dawn.

On that other morning a hansom-cab had been waiting around the corner for young Mrs. Clephane. It had all been very well arranged—Hylton Davies had a gift for arranging. His yacht was a marvel of luxury: food, service, appointments. He was the kind of man who would lean across the table to say confidentially: "I particularly recommend that sauce." He had the soul of a club steward. It was curious to be thinking of him now. . .

She remembered that, as she jumped into the hansom on that fateful morning, she had thought to herself: "Now I shall never again hear my mother-in-law say: 'I do think, my dear, you make a mistake not to humour John's prejudices a little more'." She had fixed her mind with intensity on the things she most detested in the life she was leaving; it struck her now that she had thought hardly at all of the life she was going to. Above all, that day, she had crammed into her head every possible thought that might crowd out the image of little Anne: John Clephane's bad temper, his pettiness about money, his obstinacy, his obtuseness, the detested sound of his latch-key when he came home, flown with self-importance, from his club. "Thank God," she remembered thinking, "there can't possibly be a latch-key on a yacht!"

Now she suddenly reminded herself that before long she would have to get used to the click of another key. Dear Fred Landers! That click would symbolize all the securities and placidities: all the thick layers of affection enfolding her from loneliness, from regret, from remorse. It comforted her already to know that, after tomorrow, there would always be some one between herself and her thoughts. In that mild warmth she would bask like one of those late bunches of grapes that have just time, before they drop, to turn from sourness to insipidity.

Now again she was at the old game of packing into her mind every thought that might crowd out the thought of Anne; but her mind was like a vast echoing vault, and the thoughts she had to put into it would not have filled the palm of her hand.

Where would she and Landers live? A few months of travel, no doubt; and then—New York. Could she picture him any-where else? Would it be materially possible for him to give up his profession—renounce "the office"? Her mind refused to see him in any other setting. And yet—and yet. . . But no; it was useless to linger on that. Nothing, nothing that she could invent would crowd out the thought of Anne.

She sat in the window, and watched the sky turn from black to gray, and then to the blank absence of colour before daylight. . .

In the motor, on the way to St. Stephen's, the silence had become oppressive, and Kate suddenly laid her hand on her daughter's.

"My darling, I wish you all the happiness there ever was in the world—happiness beyond all imagining."

"Oh, mother, take care! Not too much! You frighten me. . ." Through the white mist of tulle Kate caught the girl's constrained smile. She had been too vehement, then? She had over-emphasized? Doubtless she would never get ex-actly the right note. She heard herself murmuring vaguely: "But there can't be too much, can there?" and Anne's answer: "Oh, I don't know . . ." and mercifully that brought them to the verge of the crimson carpet and the awning.

In the vestibule of the church they were received into a flutter of family. No bridesmaids; but Fred Landers and Hen-drik Drover, stationed there as participants in the bridal pro-cession, amid a cluster of Drovers and Tresseltons who had lingered for a glimpse of the bride before making their way to the front pews. A pervading lustre of pearls and tall hats; a cloud of expensive furs, a gradual vague impression of some-thing having possibly gone wrong, and no one wishing to be the first to suggest it. Finally Joe Tresselton approached to say in Mrs. Clephane's ear: "He's not here yet—"

Anne had caught the whisper. Her mother saw her lips whiten as they framed a laugh. "Chris late? How like him! Or is it that we're too indecently punctual—?"

Oh, the tidal rush in the mother's breast! The *Not here! Not here! Not here!* shouted down at her from every shaft and curve of the vaulting, rained down on her from the accomplice heavens! And she had called the sky indifferent! But of course he was not here—he would not be here. She had always known that she would wear him out in the end. Her case was so much stronger than his. In a flash all her torturing doubts fell away from her.

All about her, wrist-watches were being furtively consulted. Anne stood between the groups, a pillar of snow.

"Anne always *is* indecently punctual," Nollie Tresselton laughed; Uncle Hendrik mumbled something ponderous about traffic obstruction. Once or twice the sexton's black gown fluttered enquiringly out of an aisle door and back; the bridal group began to be aware of the pressure, behind them, of late arrivals checked in the doorway till the procession should have passed into the church.

Kate Clephane caught Fred Landers's eyes anxiously fixed on her; she suspected her own of shooting out rays of triumph, and bent down hurriedly to straighten a fold of Anne's train. *Not here! Not here! Not here!* the sky shouted down at her. And none of them—except perhaps Anne—knew why. . . Anne—yes; Anne's suffering would be terrible. But she was young—she was young; and some day she would know what she had been saved from. . .

The central doors were suddenly flung open; the Mendelssohn march rolled out. Mrs. Clephane started up from her stooping posture to signal to Fred Landers that the doors must be shut . . . the music stopped . . . since the bridegroom was not coming.

But the folds of Anne's train were already slipping through her mother's fingers, Anne was in motion on Uncle Hendrik's stalwart arm. The rest of the family had drifted up to their front pews: Fred Landers, a little flushed, stood before Mrs. Clephane, his arm bent to receive her hand. The bride, softly smiling, drew aside to let her mother pass into the church before her. At the far end of the nave, on the chancel-steps, two figures had appeared against a background of lawn sleeves and lilies.

Blindly Kate Clephane moved forward, keeping step with Landers's slow stride. At the chancel-steps he left her, taking his seat with Mrs. Drover. The mother stood alone and waited for her daughter.

XXIX.

THE DROVERS had wanted Mrs. Clephane to return to Long Island with them that afternoon; Nollie Tresselton had added her prayer; Anne herself had urged her mother to accept.

"How can I drive away thinking of you here all alone?" the girl had said; and Kate had managed to smile back: "You won't be thinking of me at all!" and had added that she wanted to rest, and have time to gather up her things before sailing.

It had been settled, in the last days before the wedding, that she was to go abroad for the winter: to Italy, perhaps, or the south of France. The young couple, after a brief dash to Florida, were off for India, by Marseilles and Suez; it seemed only reasonable that Mrs. Clephane should not care to remain in New York. And Anne knew—though no one else did— that when her mother went abroad she would not go alone. Nothing was to be said . . . not a word to any one; though by this time—an hour after bride and groom had driven away to the Palm Beach express—Chris Fenno was no doubt in the secret.

Anne had left without anxiety; she understood her mother's wish to keep her plans to herself, and respected it. And in a few days now the family would be reassembling at St. Stephen's for another, even quieter wedding.

Aline came downstairs to the long drawing-room, where Mrs. Clephane was sitting alone in a litter of fallen rose-petals, grains of rice and ends of wedding-cake ribbon. Beyond, in the dining-room, the servants were moving away the small tables, and carrying off the silver in green-lined baskets.

The housekeeper had come in to give the butler the address of the hospital to which Mrs. Fenno wished the flowers to be sent, and a footman was already removing the baskets and bouquets from the drawing-room.

"Madame will be much more comfortable upstairs than in all this untidiness; and Mr. Landers has telephoned to ask if he may see Madame in about half an hour."

Aline, of course, knew everything; news reached her by every pore, as it circulates through an Eastern bazaar. Erect in the handsome dress that Mrs. Clephane had given her for the wedding, she smiled drily but approvingly upon her mistress. It was understood that Mr. Landers was *un bon parti*; and the servants' hall knew him to be generous. So did Aline, whose gown was fastened by the diamond arrow he had offered her that morning.

"There's a nice fire in Madame's sitting-room," she added persuasively.

Kate Clephane sat motionless, without looking up. She heard what the maid was saying, and could have repeated her exact words; but they conveyed no meaning.

"Madame must come up," Aline again insisted.

The humiliation of being treated like a sick person at length roused Mrs. Clephane, and she got to her feet and followed the maid. On the way upstairs she said to her: "Presently I will tell you what I shall need on the steamer." Then she turned into the sitting-room, and Aline softly closed the door on her.

The fire was burning briskly; Anne's last bunch of violets stood on the low table near the lounge. Outside the windows the winter light was waning. Kate Clephane, sitting down on the lounge, remembered that the room had worn that same look of soothing intimacy on the day when Anne had first led her into it, little more than a year ago; and she remembered that then, also, Fred Landers had joined her there, hurriedly summoned to reassure her loneliness. It was curious, in what neatly recurring patterns events often worked themselves out.

The door opened and he came in. He still wore his wedding clothes, and the dark morning coat and the pearl in his tie suited him, gave him a certain air of self-confidence and importance. He looked like a man who would smooth one's way, manage all the tiresome details of life admirably, without fuss or bluster. The small point of consciousness left alive in Kate Clephane registered the fact, and was dimly comforted by it. Steamer chairs, for instance, and the right table in a ventilated corner of the dining-saloon—one wouldn't have to bother about anything. . .

"I wish we could have got off tomorrow," he said, sitting down beside her, and looking at her with a smile. "I would have, you know, if you'd thought it feasible. Why shouldn't we have been married in Liverpool?"

"Or on board! Don't they provide a registry office on these modern boats?" she jested with pale lips.

"But next week—next week I shall carry you off," he continued with authority.

"Yes; next week." She tried to add a word of sympathy, of affection; the word he was waiting for. But she could only turn her wan smile on him.

"My dear, you're dead-beat; don't you want me to go?"

She shook her head.

"No? You'd rather I stayed—you really would?" His face lit up. "You needn't pretend with me, Kate, you know."

"Needn't I? Are you sure? All my life I seem never to have done anything but pretend," she suddenly exclaimed.

"Well, you needn't now; I'm sure." He sealed it with his quiet smile, leaning toward her a little, but without moving his chair nearer. There was something infinitely reassuring in the way he took things for granted, without undue emphasis or enthusiasm.

"Lie down now; let me pull that shawl up. A cigarette— may I? I suppose there'll be tea presently? We needn't talk about plans till tomorrow."

She tried to smile back. "But what else is there to talk about?" Her eyes rested on his face, and she read in it his effort to remain the unobtrusive and undemanding friend. The sight gave her a little twinge of compunction. "I mean, there's nothing to say about me. Let's talk about you," she suggested.

The blood mounted to his temples, congesting his cheekbones and the elderly fold above his stiff collar. He made a movement as if to rise, and then settled back resolutely into his chair. "About me? There's nothing to say about me either—except in relation to you. And there there's too much! Don't get me going. Better take me for granted."

"I do; that's my comfort." She was beginning to smile on him less painfully. "All your goodness to me—"

But now he stood up, his pink deepening to purple.

"Oh, not that, please! It rather hurts; even at my age. And I assure you I can be trusted to remind myself of it at proper intervals."

She raised herself on her elbow, looking up at him in surprise.

"I've hurt you? I didn't mean to."

"Well—goodness, you know! A man doesn't care to be eternally reminded of his goodness; not even if it's supposed to be all he has to offer—in exchange for everything."

"Oh—*everything!*" She gave a little shrug. "If ever a woman came to a man empty-handed. . ."

With a slight break in his voice he said: "You come with yourself."

The answer, and his tone, woke in her a painful sense of his intense participation in their talk and her own remoteness from it. The phrase "come with yourself" shed a lightning-flash of irony on their reciprocal attitude. What self had she left to come with? She knew he was waiting for an answer; she felt the cruelty of letting his exclamation drop as if un-heard; but what more had she to say to him—unless she should say everything?

The thought shot through her for the first time. Had she really meant to marry him without his knowing? Perhaps she had; she was not sure; she felt she would never again be very sure of her own intentions. But now, through all the confusion and exhaustion of her mind, one fact had become abruptly clear: that she would have to tell him. Whether she married him or not seemed a small matter in comparison. First she must look into those honest eyes with eyes as honest.

"Myself?" she said, echoing his last word. "What do you know of that self, I wonder?"

He continued to stand before her in the same absorbed and brooding attitude. "All I need to know is how unhappy you've been."

She leaned on her arm, still looking up at him. "Yes; I've been unhappy; horribly unhappy. Beyond anything you can imagine. Beyond anything you've ever guessed."

This did not seem to surprise him. He continued to return her gaze with the same tranquil eyes. "But I rather think I *have* guessed," he said.

Something in his voice seemed to tell her that after all she had not been alone in her struggle; it was as if he had turned a key in the most secret ward of her heart. Oh, if he had really guessed—if she were to be suddenly lifted beyond that miserable moment of avowal into a quiet heaven of understanding and compassion!

"You have guessed—you've understood?"

Yes; his face was still unperturbed, his eyes were indulgent. The tears rushed to her own; she wanted to sit down and cry her heart out. Instead, she got to her feet and went to him with outstretched hands. She must thank him; she would find the words now; she would be able to tell him what that perfect trust was to her, or at least what it would be when the present was far enough away for anything on earth to help her.

"Oh, Fred—you knew all the while? You saw I tried to the utmost, you saw I couldn't do anything to stop it?"

He had her hands in his, and was holding them against his breast. "Stop it—the marriage? Is that what's troubling you?" He was speaking now as if to a frightened disconsolate child. "Of course you couldn't stop it. I know how you must have loathed it; all you must have suffered. But Anne's happiness had to come first."

He did understand, then; did pity her! She let herself lie in his hold. The relief of avowal was too exquisite, now that all peril of explanation was over and she could just yield herself up to his pity. But though he held her she no longer saw him; all her attention was centred on her own torturing problem. She thought of him only as of some one kinder and more understanding than any one else, and her heart overflowed.

"But wasn't it just cowardice on my part? Wasn't it wicked of me not to dare to tell her?"

"Of course it wasn't wicked. What good would it have done? It's hard that she made the choice she did; but a girl with a will like Anne's has to take her chance. I always felt you'd end by seeing it. And you will, when you're less tired and overwrought. Only trust me to look after you," he said.

Her tears rose and began to run down. She would have liked to go on listening without having to attend to what he said. But again she felt that he was waiting for her to speak, and she tried to smile back at him. "I do trust you . . . you do help me. You can't tell the agony of the secret. . ." She hardly knew what she was saying.

"It needn't be a secret now. Doesn't that help?"

"Your knowing, and not loathing me? Oh, *that*—." She gave a faint laugh. "You're the only one of them all who's not afraid of me."

"Afraid of you?"

"Of what I might let out—if they hadn't always stopped me. That's my torture now; that I let them stop me. It always will be. I shall go over it and over it; I shall never be sure I oughtn't to have told them."

"Told *what*?"

"Why—what you know."

She looked up at him, surprised, and saw that a faint veil had fallen over the light in his eyes. His face had grown pale and she felt that he was holding her hands without knowing that he held them.

"I know you've been most unhappy . . . most cruelly treated. . ." He straightened his shoulders and looked at her. "That there've been things in the past that you regret . . . must regret. . ." He paused, as if waiting for her to speak; then, with a visible effort, went on: "In all those lonely years—when you were so friendless—I've naturally supposed you were not always . . . alone. . ."

She freed herself gently and moved away from him.

"Is that all?"

She was conscious in him of a slowly dawning surprise. "All—what else is there?"

"What else? The shame . . . the misery . . . the truth. . ."

For a moment he seemed hardly to take in the words she was flinging at him. He looked like a man who has not yet felt the pain of the wound he has received.

"I certainly don't know—of any shame," he answered slowly.

"Then you don't know anything. You don't know any more than the others." She had almost laughed out as she said it.

He seemed to be struggling with an inconceivable idea: an idea for which there were no terms in his vocabulary. His lips moved once or twice before he became articulate. "You mean: some sort of complicity—some sort of secret—between you and—and Anne's husband?"

She made a faint gesture of assent.

"Something—" he still wavered over it—"something you ought to have told Anne before . . . before she. . ." Abruptly he broke off, took a few steps away from her, and came back. "Not you—not you and that man?" She was silent.

The silence continued. He stood without moving, turned away from her. She had dropped down on the foot of the lounge, and sat gazing at the pattern of the carpet. He put his hands over his eyes. Presently, hearing him move, she looked up. He had uncovered his eyes and was staring about the room as if he had never seen it before, and could not remember what had brought him there. His face had shrunk and yellowed; he seemed years older.

As she looked at him, she marvelled at her folly in imagining even for a moment that he had read any farther into her secret than the others. She remembered his first visit after her return; remembered how she had plied him with uncomfortable questions, and detected in his kindly eyes the terror of the man who, all his life, has tried to buy off fate by optimistic evasions. Fate had caught up with him now—Kate Clephane would have given the world if it had not been through her agency. Sterile pain—it appeared that she was to inflict it after all, and on the one being who really loved her, who would really have helped her had he known how!

He moved nearer, and stood in front of her, forcing a thin smile. "You'll think me as obtuse as the rest of them," he said.

She could not find anything to answer. Her tears had stopped, and she sat dry-eyed, counting the circles in the carpet. When she had reached the fifteenth she heard him speaking again in the same stiff concise tone. "I—I was unprepared, I confess."

"Yes. I ought to have known—" She stood up, and continued in a low colourless voice, as if the words were being dictated to her: "I meant to tell you; I really did; at least I suppose I did. But I've lived so long with the idea of the thing that I wasn't surprised when you said you knew—knew everything. I thought you meant that you'd guessed. There were times when I thought everybody must have guessed—"

"Oh, God forbid!" he ejaculated.

She smiled faintly. "I don't know that it much matters. Except that I want to keep it from Anne—that I must keep it from her now. I daresay it was wicked of me not to stop the marriage at any cost; but when I tried to, and saw her agony, I couldn't. The only way would have been to tell her outright; and I couldn't do that—I couldn't! Coming back to her was like dying and going to heaven. It *was* heaven to me here till he came. Then I tried . . . I tried. . . But how can I ever make you understand? For nearly twenty years no one had thought much of me—I hadn't thought much of myself. I'd never really forgiven myself for leaving Anne. And then, when she sent for me, and I came, and we were so happy together, and she seemed so fond of me, I thought . . . I thought perhaps after all it hadn't made any difference. But as soon as the struggle began I saw I hadn't any power—any hold over her. She told me so herself: she said I was a stranger to her. She said I'd given up any claim on her, any right to influence her, when I went away and left her years ago. And so she wouldn't listen to me. That was my punishment: that I couldn't stop her."

"Oh, Anne—Anne can look out for herself. What do I care for Anne?" he exclaimed harshly. "But you—you—you— and that man!" He dropped down into his armchair and hid his eyes again.

She waited a minute or two; then she ventured: "Don't mind so much."

He made no answer. At length he lifted his head, but without looking directly at her.

"It was—long ago?"

"Yes. Six years—eight years. I don't know. . ." She heard herself pushing the date back farther and farther, but she could not help it.

"At a time when you were desperately lonely and unhappy?"

"Oh—not much more than usual." She added, after a moment: "I don't claim any extenuating circumstances."

"The cad—the blackguard! I—"

She interrupted him. "Not that either—quite. When he first met Anne he didn't know; didn't know she was even related to me. When he found out he went away; he went away twice. She made him come back. She reproached me for separating them. Nothing could have stopped her except my telling her. And I couldn't tell her when I saw how she cared."

"No—" There was a slight break in the harshness of his voice.

Again she was silent, not through the wish to avoid speaking, but from sheer inability to find anything more to say.

Suddenly he lifted his miserable eyes, and looked at her for a second. "You've been through hell," he said.

"Yes. I'm there still." She stopped, and then, drawn by the pity in his tone, once more felt herself slipping down the inevitable slope of confession. "It's not only *that* hell—there's another. I want to tell you everything now. It was not only for fear of Anne's suffering that I couldn't speak; it was because I couldn't bear the thought of what she would think of me if I did. It was so sweet being her mother—I couldn't bear to give it up. And the triumph of your all thinking she'd done right to bring me back—I couldn't give that up either, because I knew how much it counted in her feeling for me. Somehow, it turned me once more into the person I was meant to be—or thought I was meant to be. That's all. I'm glad I've told you. . . Only you mustn't let it hurt you; not for long. . ."

After she had ended he continued to sit without moving; she had the impression that he had not heard what she had said. His attention, his receptive capacity, were still engrossed by the stark fact of her confession: her image and Chris Fenno's were slowly burning themselves into his shrinking vision. To assist at the process was like peeping into a torture-chamber, and for the moment she lost the sense of her own misery in the helpless contemplation of his. Sterile pain, if ever there was—

At last she crossed over to where he sat, and laid a touch on his shoulder.

"Fred—you mustn't let this hurt you. It has done me good

to tell you . . . it has helped. Your being so sorry has helped. And now it's all over . . . it's ended. . ."

He did not change his attitude or even look up again. She still doubted if he heard her. After a minute or two she withdrew her hand and moved away. The strain had been too great; she had imposed on him more than he could bear. She saw that clearly now: she said to herself that their talk was over, that they were already leagues apart. Her sentimental experience had shown her how often two people still in the act of exchanging tender or violent words are in reality at the opposite ends of the earth, and she reflected, ironically, how much success in human affairs depends on the power to detect such displacements. She herself had no such successes to her credit; hers was at best the doubtful gift of discerning, perhaps more quickly than most people, why she failed. But to all such shades of suffering her friend was impervious: he was taking his ordeal in bulk.

She sat down and waited. Curiously enough, she was less unhappy than for a long time past. His pain and his pity were perhaps what she had most needed from him: the centre of her wretchedness seemed the point at which they were meant to meet. If only she could have put it in words simple enough to reach him—but to thank him for what he was suffering would have seemed like mockery; and she could only wait and say to herself that perhaps before long he would go.

After a while he lifted his head and slowly got to his feet. For a moment he seemed to waver; then he crossed the space between them, and stood before her. She rose too, and held out her hand; but he did not appear to notice the gesture, though his eyes were now intensely fixed on her.

"The time will come," he said, "when all this will seem very far off from both of us. That's all I want to think of now."

She looked up, not understanding. Then she began to tremble in all her body; her very lips trembled, and the lids of her dazzled eyes. He was still looking at her, and she saw the dawn of the old kindness in his. He seemed to have come out on the other side of a great darkness. But all she found to say was the denial of what she was feeling. "Oh, no—no—no—"; and she put him from her.

"No?"

"It's enough; enough; what you've just said is enough." She stammered it out incoherently. "Don't you see that I can't bear any more?"

He stood rooted there in his mild obstinate kindness. "There's got to be a great deal more, though."

"Not now—not now!" She caught his hand, and just laid it to her cheek. Then she drew back, with a sense of resolution, of finality, that must have shown itself in her face and air. "Now you're to go; you're to leave me. I'm dreadfully tired." She said it almost like a child who asks to be taken up and carried. It seemed to her that for the first time in her life she had been picked up out of the dust and weariness, and set down in a quiet place where no harm could come.

He was still looking at her, uncertainly, pleadingly. "To-morrow, then? Tomorrow morning?"

She hesitated. "Tomorrow afternoon."

"And now you'll rest?"

"Now I'll rest."

With that—their hands just clasping—she guided him gently to the door, and stood waiting till she heard his step go down the stair. Then she turned back into the room and opened the door of her bedroom.

The maid was there, preparing a becoming tea-gown. She had no doubt conjectured that Mr. Landers would be coming back for dinner.

"Aline! Tomorrow's steamer—it's not too late to call up the office?"

The maid stood staring, incredulous, the shimmering dress on her arm.

"The steamer—not tomorrow's steamer?"

"The steamer on which I had taken passages," Mrs. Clephane explained, hurriedly reaching for the telephone book.

Aline's look seemed to say that this was beyond all reasonable explanation.

"But those passages—Madame ordered me to give them up. Madame said we were not to sail till next week."

"Never mind. At this season there's no crowd. You must call up at once and get them back."

"Madame is not really thinking of sailing tomorrow? The boat leaves at six in the morning."

Mrs. Clephane almost laughed in her face. "I'm not thinking of doing it; I'm going to do it. Ah, here's the number—" She unhooked the receiver.

XXX.

KATE CLEPHANE was wakened by the slant of Riviera sun across her bed.

The hotel was different; it was several rungs higher on the ladder than the Minorque et l'Univers, as its name—the Petit Palais—plainly indicated. The bedroom, too, was bigger, more modern, more freshly painted; and the corner window of the tiny adjoining *salon* actually clipped a wedge of sea in its narrow frame.

So much was changed for the better in Mrs. Clephane's condition; in other respects, she had the feeling of having simply turned back a chapter, and begun again at the top of the same dull page.

Her maid, Aline, was obviously of the same opinion; in spite of the more commodious room, and the sitting-room with its costly inset of sea, Mrs. Clephane had not recovered her lost prestige in Aline's estimation. "What was the good of all the fuss if it was to end in *this*?" Aline's look seemed to say, every morning when she brought in the breakfast-tray. Even the fact that letters now lay on it more frequently, and that telegrams were no longer considered epoch-making, did not compensate for the general collapse of Aline's plans and ambitions. When one had had a good roof over one's head, and a good motor at one's door, what was the sense of bolting away from them at a moment's notice and coming back to second-rate hotels and rattling taxis, with all the loss of consequence implied? Aline remained icily silent when her mistress, after a few weeks at the Petit Palais, mentioned that she had written to enquire about prices at Dinard for the summer.

Kate Clephane, on the whole, took the change more philosophically. To begin with, it had been her own choice to fly as she had; and that in itself was a help—at times; and then— well, yes,—already, after the first weeks, she had begun to be aware that she was slipping back without too much discomfort into the old groove.

The first month after her arrival wouldn't yet bear thinking about; but it was well behind her now, and habit was working its usual miracle. She had been touched by the welcome her old friends and acquaintances had given her, and exquisitely relieved—after the first plunge—to find herself again among people who asked no questions about her absence, betrayed no curiosity about it, and probably felt none. They were all very much occupied with each other's doings when they were together, but the group was so continually breaking up and reshaping itself, with the addition of new elements, and the departing scattered in so many different directions, and toward destinations so unguessable, that once out of sight they seemed to have no more substance or permanence than figures twitching by on a film.

This sense of unsubstantiality had eased Kate Clephane's taut nerves, and helped her to sink back almost unaware into her old way of life. Enough was known of her own existence in the interval—a shadowy glimpse of New York opulence, an Opera box, a massive and important family, a beautiful daughter married to a War Hero—to add considerably to her standing in the group; but her Riviera friends were all pleasantly incurious as to details. In most of their lives there were episodes to be bridged over by verbal acrobatics, and they were all accustomed to taking each other's fibs at their face-value. Of Mrs. Clephane they did not even ask any: she came back handsomer, better dressed—yes, my dear, actually *sables!*—and she offered them cock-tails and Mah-Jongg in her own sitting-room (with a view of the sea thrown in). They were glad of so useful a recruit, and the distance between her social state and theirs was not wide enough to awaken acrimony or envy.

"Aline!"

The maid's door was just across the passage now; she appeared almost at once, bearing a breakfast-tray on which were several letters.

"Violets!" she announced with a smile; Aline's severity had of late been tempered by an occasional smile. But Mrs. Clephane did not turn her head; her colour did not change. These violets were not from the little lame boy whose bouquet had flushed her with mysterious hopes on the day when her daughter's cable had called her home; the boy she had set up for life (it had been her first thought after landing) because of that happy coincidence. Today's violets embodied neither hope nor mystery. She knew from whom they came, and what stage in what game they represented; and lifting them from the tray after a brief sniff, she poured out her chocolate with a steady hand. Aline, perceptibly rebuffed, but not defeated, put the flowers into a glass on her mistress's dressing-table. "There," the gesture said, "she can't help seeing them."

Mrs. Clephane leaned back against her pink-lined pillows, and sipped her chocolate with deliberation. She had not yet opened the letters, or done more than briefly muster their superscriptions. None from her daughter: Anne, at the moment, was half-way across the Red Sea, on her way to India, and there would be no news of her for several weeks to come. None of the letters was interesting enough to be worth a glance. Mrs. Clephane went over them once or twice, as if looking for one that was missing; then she pushed them aside and took up the local newspaper.

She had got back into her old habit of lingering on every little daily act, making the most of it, spreading it out over as many minutes as possible, in the effort to cram her hours so full that there should be no time for introspection or remembrance; and she read the paper carefully, from the grandiloquent leading article on the wonders of the approaching Carnival to the column in which the doings of the local and foreign society were glowingly recorded.

"The flower of the American colony and the most distinguished French and foreign notabilities of the Riviera will meet this afternoon at the brilliant reception which Mrs. Parley Plush has organized at her magnificent Villa Mimosa in honour of the Bishop of the American Episcopal churches in Europe."

Ah—to be sure; it was today! Kate Clephane laid down the newspaper with a smile. She was recalling Mrs. Minity's wrath when it had been announced that the reception for the new Bishop was to be given by Mrs. Parley Plush—Mrs. Plush, of all people! Mrs. Minity was not an active member of the Reverend Mr. Merriman's parochial committees; her bodily inertia, and the haunting fear of what might happen if her coachman tried to turn the horses in the narrow street in which the Rectory stood, debarred her from such participation; but she was nevertheless a pillar of the church, by reason of a small but regular donation to its fund and a large and equally regular commentary on its affairs. Mr. Merriman gave her opinions almost the importance she thought they deserved; and a dozen times in the season Mrs. Merriman was expected to bear the brunt of her criticisms, and persuade her not to give up her pew and stop her subscription. "That woman," Mrs. Minity would cry, "whom I have taken regularly for a drive once a fortnight all winter, and supplied with brandy-peaches when I had to go without myself!"

Mrs. Minity, on the occasion of the last drive, had not failed to tell Mrs. Merriman what she thought of the idea—put forward, of course, by Mrs. Plush herself—of that lady's being chosen to entertain the new Bishop on his first tour of his diocese. The scandal was bad enough: did Mrs. Merriman want Mrs. Minity to tell her what the woman had been, what her reputation was? No; Mrs. Merriman would rather not. She probably knew well enough herself, if she had chosen to admit it . . . but for Mrs. Minity the real bitterness of the situation lay in the fact that she herself could not eclipse Mrs. Plush by giving the reception because she lived in a small flat instead of a large—a vulgarly large—villa.

"No; don't try to explain it away, my dear"; (this to Kate Clephane, the day after Mrs. Merriman had been taken on the latest of her penitential drives); "don't try to put me off with that Rectory humbug. Everybody at home knows that Mrs. Parley Plush came from Anaconda, Georgia, and everybody in Anaconda knows *what* she came from. And now, because she has a big showy villa (at least, so they tell me—for naturally I've never set foot in it, and never shall); now that she's been white-washed by those poor simple-minded Merrimans, who have lived in this place for twenty years as if it were a Quaker colony, the woman dares to put herself forward as the proper person—Mrs. Parley Plush *proper*!—to welcome our new Bishop in the name of the American Colony! Well," said Mrs. Minity in the voice of Cassandra, "if the Bishop knew a quarter of what I do about her—and what I daresay it is my duty, as a member of this diocese, to tell him. . . But there: what am I to do, my dear, with a doctor who *absolutely forbids* all agitating discussions, and warns me that if anybody should say anything disagreeable to me I might be snuffed out on the spot?"

Kate Clephane had smiled; these little rivalries were beginning to amuse her again. And the amusement of seeing Mrs. Minity appear (as of course she would) at Mrs. Plush's that afternoon made it seem almost worth while to go there. Mrs. Clephane reached out for her engagement-book, scrutinized the day's page, and found—with another smile, this one at herself—that she had already noted down: "Plush". Yes; it was true; she knew it herself: she still had to go on cramming things into her days, things good, bad or indifferent, it hardly mattered which as long as they were crammed tight enough to leave no chinks for backward glances. Her old training in the art of taking things easily—all the narcotic tricks of evasion and ignoring—had come gradually to her help in the struggle to remake her life. Of course she would go to Mrs. Plush's . . . just as surely as Mrs. Minity would.

The day was glorious; exactly the kind of day, all the ladies said, on which one would want the dear Bishop to have his first sight of his new diocese. The whole strength of the Anglo-American colony was assembled on Mrs. Plush's flowery terraces, among the beds of cineraria and cyclamen, and the giant blue china frogs which, as Mrs. Plush said, made the garden look "more natural". Mrs. Plush herself sailed majestically from group to group, keeping one eye on the loggia through which the Bishop and Mr. Merriman were to arrive.

"Ah, dear Lord Charles—this is kind! You'll find *all* your friends here. Yes, Mrs. Clephane is over there at the other end of the terrace," Mrs. Plush beamed, waving a tall disenchanted-looking man in the direction of a palm-tree emerging from a cushion of pansies.

Mrs. Clephane, from under the palm, had seen the manœuvre, and smiled at that also. She knew she was Lord Charles's pretext for coming to the reception, but she knew, also, that he was glad to have a pretext, because if he hadn't come he wouldn't have known any more than she did what to do with the afternoon. There was nothing, she sometimes felt, that she didn't know about Lord Charles, though they had met only three months ago. He was so exactly what medical men call "a typical case," and she had had such unlimited time and opportunity for the study of his particular type. The only difference was that he was a gentleman—a gentleman still; while the others, most of them, never had been, or else had long since abdicated that with the rest.

As he moved over the sunlit gravel in her direction she asked herself for the hundredth time what she meant to do about it. Marry him? God forbid! Even if she had been sure—and in her heart of hearts she wasn't—that he intended to give her the chance. Fall in love with him? That too she shrugged away. Let him make love to her? Well a little . . . perhaps . . . when one was too lonely . . . and because he was the only man at all "possible" in their set. . . But what she most wanted of him was simply to fill certain empty hours; to know that when she came home at five he would be waiting there, half the days of the week, by her tea-table; that when she dined out, people would be sure to invite him and put him next to her; that when there was no bridge or Mah-Jongg going he would always be ready for a tour of the antiquity shops, and so sharp at picking up bargains for the little flat she had in view.

That was all she wanted of him; perhaps all he wanted of her. But the possibility of his wanting more (at which the violets seemed to hint) produced an uncertainty not wholly disagreeable, especially when he and she met in company, and she guessed the other women's envy. "One has to have something to help one out—" It was the old argument of the drug-takers: well, call Lord Charles her drug! Why not, when she was so visibly his?

She settled herself in a garden-chair and watched his approach. It was a skilful bit of manœuvring: she knew he intended to "eliminate the bores" and join her only when there was no danger of their being disturbed. She could imagine how, in old days, he would have stalked contemptuously through such a company, without a glance to right or left. But not now. He had reached a phase in his decline when it became prudent to pause and admire the view at Mrs. Plush's side, exchange affabilities with the Consul's wife, nod familiarly to Mr. Paly, and even suffer himself to be boisterously hailed by Mrs. Horace Betterly, who came clinking down the loggia steps to shout out a reminder that they counted on him for dinner that evening. It was the fate of those who had to stuff their days full, and could no longer be particular about the quality of the stuffing. Kate could almost see the time when Lord Charles, very lean and wizened, would be collecting china frogs for Mrs. Plush.

He was half-way across the terrace when a sudden expanding and agitating of Mrs. Plush's plumes seemed to forerun the approach of the Bishop. An impressive black figure appeared under the central arch of the loggia. Mrs. Plush surged forward, every fold of her draperies swelling: but the new arrival was not the Bishop—it was only Mrs. Minity who, clothed in black cashmere and majesty, paused and looked about her.

Mrs. Plush, checked in her forward plunge, stood an instant rigid, almost tilted backward; her right hand sketched the gesture of two barely extended fingers; then her just resentment of Mrs. Minity's strictures was swept away in the triumph of having her there at last, and Mrs. Plush swept on full sail, welcoming her unexpected guest as obsequiously as if Mrs. Minity had been the Bishop.

Kate Clephane looked on with lazy amusement. She could enjoy the humours of her little world now that her mind was more at leisure. She hoped the scene between Mrs. Plush and Mrs. Minity would prolong itself, and was getting up to move within ear-shot when the Bishop, supported by Mr. and Mrs. Merriman, at length appeared.

Mrs. Clephane stopped short half-way across the terrace. She had never dreamed of this—never once thought it possible. Yet now she remembered that Dr. Arklow had been spoken of at the Drovers' as one of the candidates for this new diocese; and there he stood, on the steps just above her, benignant and impressive as when she had last seen him, at St. Stephen's, placing Anne's hand in Chris Fenno's. . .

Mrs. Clephane's first impulse was to turn and lose herself in the crowd. The sight of that figure brought with it too many banished scenes and obliterated memories. Back they all rushed on her, fiercely importunate; she felt their cruel fingers at her throat. For a moment she stood irresolute, detached in the middle of the terrace; then, just as she was turning, she heard Mrs. Plush's trumpet-call: "Mrs. Clephane? Yes, of course; there she is! Dear Mrs. Clephane, the Bishop has spied you out already!"

He seemed to reach her in a stride, so completely did his approach span distances and wipe out time. She saw herself sitting again in a deep leather armchair, under the photogravure of Salisbury Cathedral, while he paced the worn rug before the hearth, and his preacher's voice broke on the words: "Sterile pain. . ."

"Shall we walk a little way? The garden seems very beautiful," the Bishop suggested.

They stood by a white balustrade under mimosa boughs, and exchanged futilities about the blueness of the sea and the heat of the sun. "A New York February . . . brr . . ." "Yes, don't you envy us? Day after day of this. . . Oh, of course a puff of *mistral* now and then . . . but then that's healthy . . . and the flowers!"

He laid his large hand deliberately on hers. "My dear—when are you coming home to New York?" She felt her face just brushed by the understanding look she had caught twice before in his eyes.

"To New York? Never."

He waited as if to weigh the answer, and then turned his eyes on the Mediterranean.

"Never is a long word. There is some one there who would be very happy if you did."

She answered precipitately: "It would never have been what he imagines. . ."

"Isn't he the best judge of that? He thinks you ought to have given him the chance."

She dropped her voice to say: "I wonder he can ask me to think of ever living in New York again."

"He doesn't ask it of you; I'm charged to say so. He understands fully. . . He would be prepared to begin his life again anywhere. . . It lies with you. . ."

There was a silence. At length she mastered her voice enough to say: "Yes; I know. I'm very grateful. It's a comfort to me. . ."

"No more?"

She waited again, and then, lifting her eyes, caught once more the understanding look in his.

"I don't know how to tell you—how to explain. It seems to me . . . my refusing . . ." she lowered her voice still more . . . "the one thing that keeps me from being too hopeless, too unhappy."

She saw the first tinge of perplexity in his gaze. "The fact of refusing?"

"The fact of refusing."

Ah, it was useless; he would never understand! How could she have imagined that he would?

"But is this really your last word; the very last?" he questioned mildly.

"Oh, it has to be—it has to be. It's what I live by," she almost sobbed.

No; he would never understand. His face had once more become blank and benedictory. He pressed her hand, said: "My dear child, I must see you again—we must talk of this!" and passed on, urbane and unperceiving.

Her eyes filled; for a moment her loneliness came down on her like a pall. It was always so whenever she tried to explain, not only to others but even to herself. Yet deep down in her, deeper far than her poor understanding could reach, there was something that said "No" whenever that particular temptation stirred in her. Something that told her that, as Fred Landers's pity had been the most precious thing he had to give her, so her refusal to accept it, her precipitate flight from it, was the most precious thing she could give him in return. He had overcome his strongest feelings, his most deep-rooted repugnance; he had held out his hand to her, in the extremity of her need, across the whole width of his traditions and his convictions; and she had blessed him for it, and stood fast on her own side. And this afternoon, when she returned home and found his weekly letter—as she was sure she would, since it had not come with that morning's post—she would bless him again, bless him both for writing the letter, and for giving her the strength to hold out against its pleadings.

Perhaps no one else would ever understand; assuredly he would never understand himself. But there it was. Nothing on earth would ever again help her—help to blot out the old horrors and the new loneliness—as much as the fact of being able to take her stand on that resolve, of being able to say to herself, whenever she began to drift toward new uncertainties and fresh concessions, that once at least she had stood fast, shutting away in a little space of peace and light the best thing that had ever happened to her.

THE   END

A BACKWARD GLANCE

A backward glance o'er travell'd roads.
Walt Whitman

Je veux remonter le penchant de mes belles
années . . .
Châteaubriand: *Mémoires d'Outre Tombe*

Kein Genuss ist vorübergehend.
Goethe: *Wilhelm Meister*

THE AUTHOR

TO THE FRIENDS
WHO EVERY YEAR ON ALL SOULS' NIGHT
COME AND SIT WITH ME
BY THE FIRE

A First Word

Years ago I said to myself: "There's no such thing as old age; there is only sorrow."

I have learned with the passing of time that this, though true, is not the whole truth. The other producer of old age is habit: the deathly process of doing the same thing in the same way at the same hour day after day, first from carelessness, then from inclination, at last from cowardice or inertia. Luckily the inconsequent life is not the only alternative; for caprice is as ruinous as routine. Habit is necessary; it is the habit of having habits, of turning a trail into a rut, that must be incessantly fought against if one is to remain alive.

In spite of illness, in spite even of the arch-enemy sorrow, one *can* remain alive long past the usual date of disintegration if one is unafraid of change, insatiable in intellectual curiosity, interested in big things, and happy in small ways. In the course of sorting and setting down of my memories I have learned that these advantages are usually independent of one's merits, and that I probably owe my happy old age to the ancestor who accidentally endowed me with these qualities.

Another advantage (equally accidental) is that I do not remember long to be angry. I seldom forget a bruise to the soul—who does? But life puts a quick balm on it, and it is recorded in a book I seldom open. Not long ago I read a number of reviews of a recently published autobiography. All the reviewers united in praising it on the score that here at last was an autobiographer who was not afraid to tell the truth! And what gave the book this air of truthfulness? Simply the fact that the memorialist "spared no one", set down in detail every defect and absurdity in others, and every resentment in the writer. That was the kind of autobiography worth reading!

Judged by that standard mine, I fear, will find few readers. I have not escaped contact with the uncongenial; but the antipathy they aroused was usually reciprocal, and this simplified and restricted our intercourse. Nor do I remember that these unappreciative persons ever marked their lack of interest in me by anything more harmful than indifference. I recall no sensational grievances. Everywhere on my path I have met with kindness and furtherance; and from the few dearest to me an exquisite understanding. It will be seen, then, that in telling my story I have had to make the best of unsensational material; and if what I have to tell interests my readers, that merit at least will be my own.

Madame Swetchine, that eminent Christian, was once asked how she managed to feel Christianly toward her enemies. She looked surprised. *"Un ennemi? Mais de tous les accidents c'est le plus rare!"*

So I have found it.

E. W.

Contents

Illustrations

I

The Background

Gute Gesellschaft hab ich gesehen; man nennt sie die gute
Wenn sie zum kleinsten Gedicht nicht die Gelegenheit giebt.
                              GOETHE: *Venezianische Epigrammen*

I

IT WAS ON a bright day of midwinter, in New York. The
little girl who eventually became me, but as yet was neither me nor anybody else in particular, but merely a soft
anonymous morsel of humanity—this little girl, who bore my
name, was going for a walk with her father. The episode is
literally the first thing I can remember about her, and therefore I date the birth of her identity from that day.

She had been put into her warmest coat, and into a new
and very pretty bonnet, which she had surveyed in the glass
with considerable satisfaction. The bonnet (I can see it
today) was of white satin, patterned with a pink and green
plaid in raised velvet. It was all drawn into close gathers,
with a *bavolet* in the neck to keep out the cold, and thick
ruffles of silky *blonde* lace under the brim in front. As the air
was very cold a gossamer veil of the finest white Shetland
wool was drawn about the bonnet and hung down over the
wearer's round red cheeks like the white paper filigree over a
Valentine; and her hands were encased in white woollen
mittens.

One of them lay in the large safe hollow of her father's bare
hand; her tall handsome father, who was so warm-blooded
that in the coldest weather he always went out without
gloves, and whose head, with its ruddy complexion and intensely blue eyes, was so far aloft that when she walked beside
him she was too near to see his face. It was always an event in
the little girl's life to take a walk with her father, and more
particularly so today, because she had on her new winter bonnet, which was so beautiful (and so becoming) that for the
first time she woke to the importance of dress, and of herself
as a subject for adornment—so that I may date from that

hour the birth of the conscious and feminine *me* in the little girl's vague soul.

The little girl and her father walked up Fifth Avenue: the old Fifth Avenue with its double line of low brown-stone houses, of a desperate uniformity of style, broken only—and surprisingly—by two equally unexpected features: the fenced-in plot of ground where the old Miss Kennedys' cows were pastured, and the truncated Egyptian pyramid which so strangely served as a reservoir for New York's water supply. The Fifth Avenue of that day was a placid and uneventful thoroughfare, along which genteel landaus, broughams and victorias, and more countrified vehicles of the "carry-all" and "surrey" type, moved up and down at decent intervals and a decorous pace. On Sundays after church the fashionable of various denominations paraded there on foot, in gathered satin bonnets and tall hats; but at other times it presented long stretches of empty pavement, so that the little girl, advancing at her father's side was able to see at a considerable distance the approach of another pair of legs, not as long but considerably stockier than her father's. The little girl was so very little that she never got much higher than the knees in her survey of grown-up people, and would not have known, if her father had not told her, that the approaching legs belonged to his cousin Henry. The news was very interesting, because in attendance on Cousin Henry was a small person, no bigger than herself, who must obviously be Cousin Henry's little boy Daniel, and therefore somehow belong to the little girl. So when the tall legs and the stocky ones halted for a talk, which took place somewhere high up in the air, and the small Daniel and Edith found themselves face to face close to the pavement, the little girl peered with interest at the little boy through the white woollen mist over her face. The little boy, who was very round and rosy, looked back with equal interest; and suddenly he put out a chubby hand, lifted the little girl's veil, and boldly planted a kiss on her cheek. It was the first time—and the little girl found it very pleasant.

This is my earliest definite memory of anything happening to me; and it will be seen that I was wakened to conscious life by the two tremendous forces of love and vanity.

It may have been just after this memorable day—at any rate it was nearly at the same time—that a snowy-headed old gentleman with a red face and a spun-sugar moustache and imperial gave me a white Spitz puppy which looked as if its coat had been woven out of the donor's luxuriant locks. The old gentleman, in whose veins ran the purest blood of Dutch Colonial New York, was called Mr. Lydig Suydam, and I should like his name to survive till this page has crumbled, for with his gift a new life began for me. The owning of my first dog made me into a conscious sentient person, fiercely possessive, anxiously watchful, and woke in me that long ache of pity for animals, and for all inarticulate beings, which nothing has ever stilled. How I loved that first "Foxy" of mine, how I cherished and yearned over and understood him! And how quickly he relegated all dolls and other inanimate toys to the region of my everlasting indifference!

I never cared much in my little-childhood for fairy tales, or any appeals to my fancy through the fabulous or legendary. My imagination lay there, coiled and sleeping, a mute hibernating creature, and at the least touch of common things—flowers, animals, words, especially the sound of words, apart from their meaning—it already stirred in its sleep, and then sank back into its own rich dream, which needed so little feeding from the outside that it instinctively rejected whatever another imagination had already adorned and completed. There was, however, one fairy tale at which I always thrilled—the story of the boy who could talk with the birds and hear what the grasses said. Very early, earlier than my conscious memory can reach, I must have felt myself to be of kin to that happy child. I cannot remember when the grasses first spoke to me, though I think it was when, a few years later, one of my uncles took me, with some little cousins, to spend a long spring day in some marshy woods near Mamaroneck, where the earth was starred with pink trailing arbutus, where pouch-like white and rosy flowers grew in a swamp, and leafless branches against the sky were netted with buds of mother-of-pearl; but on the day when Foxy was given to me I learned what the animals say to each other, and to us. . . .

2

The readers (and I should doubtless have been among them) who twenty years ago would have smiled at the idea that time could transform a group of *bourgeois* colonials and their republican descendants into a sort of social aristocracy, are now better able to measure the formative value of nearly three hundred years of social observance: the concerted living up to long-established standards of honour and conduct, of education and manners. The value of duration is slowly asserting itself against the welter of change, and sociologists without a drop of American blood in them have been the first to recognize what the traditions of three centuries have contributed to the moral wealth of our country. Even negatively, these traditions have acquired, with the passing of time, an unsuspected value. When I was young it used to seem to me that the group in which I grew up was like an empty vessel into which no new wine would ever again be poured. Now I see that one of its uses lay in preserving a few drops of an old vintage too rare to be savoured by a youthful palate; and I should like to atone for my unappreciativeness by trying to revive that faint fragrance.

If any one had suggested to me, before 1914, to write my reminiscences, I should have answered that my life had been too uneventful to be worth recording. Indeed, I had never even thought of recording it for my own amusement, and the fact that until 1918 I never kept even the briefest of diaries has greatly hampered this tardy reconstruction. Not until the successive upheavals which culminated in the catastrophe of 1914 had "cut all likeness from the name" of my old New York, did I begin to see its pathetic picturesqueness. The first change came in the 'eighties, with the earliest detachment of big money-makers from the West, soon to be followed by the lords of Pittsburgh. But their infiltration did not greatly affect old manners and customs, since the dearest ambition of the newcomers was to assimilate existing traditions. Social life, with us as in the rest of the world, went on with hardly perceptible changes till the war abruptly tore down the old frame-work, and what had seemed unalterable rules of conduct became of a sudden observances as quaintly arbitrary as the domestic rites of the Pharaohs. Between the point of view of my Huguenot great-great-grandfather, who came from the French Palatinate to participate in the founding of New Rochelle, and my own father, who died in 1882, there were fewer differences than between my father and the post-war generation of Americans. That I was born into a world in which telephones, motors, electric light, central heating (except by hot-air furnaces), X-rays, cinemas, radium, aeroplanes and wireless telegraphy were not only unknown but still mostly unforeseen, may seem the most striking difference between then and now; but the really vital change is that, in my youth, the Americans of the original States, who in moments of crisis still shaped the national point of view, were the heirs of an old tradition of European culture which the country has now totally rejected. This rejection (which Mr. Walter Lippmann regards as the chief cause of the country's present moral impoverishment) has opened a gulf between those days and these. The compact world of my youth has receded into a past from which it can only be dug up in bits by the assiduous relic-hunter; and its smallest fragments begin to be worth collecting and putting together before the last of those who knew the live structure are swept away with it.

3

My little-girl life, safe, guarded, monotonous, was cradled in the only world about which, according to Goethe, it is impossible to write poetry. The small society into which I was born was "good" in the most prosaic sense of the term, and its only interest, for the generality of readers, lies in the fact of its sudden and total extinction, and for the imaginative few in the recognition of the moral treasures that went with it. Let me try to call it back. . . .

Once, when I was about fifteen, my parents took me to Annapolis for the graduating ceremonies of the Naval Academy. In my infancy I had travelled extensively on the farther side of the globe, and it was thought high time that I should begin to see something of my own half.

I recall with delight the charming old Academic buildings grouped about turf and trees, and the smartness of the cadets (among whom were some of my young friends) in their dress uniforms; and thrilling memories of speeches, marchings, military music and strawberry ice, flutter pleasingly about the scene. On the way back we stopped in Baltimore and Washington; but neither city offered much to youthful eyes formed by the spectacle of Rome and Paris. Washington, in the days before Charles McKim had seen its possibilities, and resolved to develop them on Major L'Enfant's lines, was in truth a doleful desert; and it was a weary and bored little girl who trailed after her parents through the echoing emptiness of the Capitol, and at last into the famous Rotunda with its paintings of Revolutionary victories. Trumbull was little thought of as a painter in those days (Munkacsky would doubtless have been preferred to him), and when one great panel after another was pointed out to me, and I was led up first to the "Surrender of Burgoyne" and then to the "Surrender of Cornwallis", and told: "There's your great-grandfather," the tall thin young man in the sober uniform of a general of artillery, leaning against a cannon in the foreground of one picture, in the other galloping across the battlefield, impressed me much less than the beautiful youths to whom I had just said good-bye at Annapolis. If anything, I was vaguely sorry to have any one belonging to me represented in those stiff old-fashioned pictures, so visibly inferior to the battle-scenes of Horace Vernet and Detaille. I remember feeling no curiosity about my great-grandfather, and my parents said nothing to rouse my interest in him. The New Yorker of that day was singularly, inexplicably indifferent to his descent, and my father and mother were no exception to the rule.

It was many years later that I began to suspect that Trumbull was very nearly a great painter, and my great-grandfather Stevens very nearly a great man; but by that time all who had known him, and could have spoken of him familiarly, had long been dead, and he was no more than a museum-piece to me. It is a pity, for he must have been worth knowing, even at second hand.

On both sides our colonial ancestry goes back for nearly three hundred years, and on both sides the colonists in question seem to have been identified since early days with New York, though my earliest Stevens forbears went first to Massachusetts. Some of the first Stevens's grandsons, however, probably not being of the stripe of religious fanatic or political reformer to breathe easily in that passionate province, transferred their activities to the easier-going New York, where people seem from the outset to have been more interested in making money and acquiring property than in Predestination and witch-burning. I have always wondered if those old New Yorkers did not owe their greater suavity and tolerance to the fact that the Church of England (so little changed under its later name of Episcopal Church of America) provided from the first their prevalent form of worship. May not the matchless beauty of an ancient rite have protected our ancestors from what Huxley called the "fissiparous tendency of the Protestant sects", sparing them sanguinary wrangles over uncomprehended points of doctrine, and all those extravagances of self-constituted prophets and evangelists which rent and harrowed New England? Milder manners, a greater love of ease, and a franker interest in money-making and good food, certainly distinguished the colonial New Yorkers from the conscience-searching children of the "Mayflower". Apart from some of the old Dutch colonial families, who continued to follow the "Dutch Reformed" rite, the New York of my youth was distinctively Episcopalian; and to this happy chance I owe my early saturation with the noble cadences of the Book of Common Prayer, and my reverence for an ordered ritual in which the officiant's personality is strictly subordinated to the rite he performs.

Colonial New York was mostly composed of merchants and bankers; my own ancestors were mainly merchant ship-owners, and my great-grandmother Stevens's wedding-dress, a gauzy Directoire web of embroidered "India mull", was made for her in India and brought to New York on one of her father's merchant-men. My mother, who had a hearty contempt for the tardy discovery of aristocratic genealogies, always said that old New York was composed of Dutch and British middle-class families, and that only four or five could show a pedigree leading back to the aristocracy of their ancestral country. These, if I remember rightly, were the Duers, the Livingstons, the Rutherfurds, the de Grasses and the Van Rensselaers (descendants, these latter, of the original Dutch

"Patroon"). I name here only families settled in colonial New York; others, from the southern states, but well known in New York—such as the Fairfaxes, Carys, Calverts and Whartons—should be added if the list included the other colonies.

My own ancestry, as far as I know, was purely middle-class; though my family belonged to the same group as this little aristocratic nucleus I do not think there was any blood-relationship with it. The Schermerhorns, Joneses, Pendletons, on my father's side, the Stevenses, Ledyards, Rhinelanders on my mother's, the Gallatins on both, seem all to have belonged to the same prosperous class of merchants, bankers and lawyers. It was a society from which all dealers in retail business were excluded as a matter of course. The man who "kept a shop" was more rigorously shut out of polite society in the original Thirteen States than in post-revolutionary France—witness the surprise (and amusement) of the Paris solicitor, Moreau de St Méry, who, fleeing from the Terror, earned his living by keeping a bookshop in Philadelphia, and for this reason, though his shop was the meeting-place of the most blue-blooded of his fellow *émigrés*, and Talleyrand and the Marquis de la Tour du Pin were among his intimates, yet could not be invited to the ball given for Washington's inauguration. So little did the Revolution revolutionize a society at once middle-class and provincial that no retail dealer, no matter how palatial his shop-front or how tempting his millions, was received in New York society until long after I was grown up.

My great-grandfather, the Major-General Ebenezer Stevens of the Rotunda, seems to have been the only marked figure among my forbears. He was born in Boston in 1751 and, having a pronounced tendency to mechanical pursuits, was naturally drafted into the artillery at the Revolution. He served in Lieutenant Adino Paddock's artillery company, and took part in the "Boston tea-party", where, as he told one of his sons, "none of the party was painted as Indians, nor, that I know of, disguised; though," (he adds a trifle casuistically) "some of them stopped at a paint-shop on the way and daubed their faces with paint." Thereafter he is heard of as a house-builder and contractor in Rhode Island; but at the news of the battle of Lexington he abandoned his business and began the raising

MY GREAT-GRANDMOTHER STEVENS AND HER SON
(MINIATURE, PAINTER UNKNOWN)

and organizing of artillery companies. He was a first lieutenant in the Rhode Island artillery, then in that of Massachusetts, and in 1776 was transferred as captain to the regiment
besieging Quebec. At Ticonderoga, Stillwater and Saratoga
he commanded a division of artillery, and it was he who directed the operations leading to General Burgoyne's surrender. For these feats he was specially commended by Generals
Knox, Gates and Schuyler, and in 1778 he was in command of
the entire artillery service of the northern department. Under
Lafayette he took part in the expedition which ended in the
defeat of Lord Cornwallis; his skilful manoeuvres are said to
have broken the English blockade at Annapolis, and when the
English evacuated New York he was among the first to enter
the city.

The war over, he declined further military advancement and
returned to civil life. His services, however, were still frequently required, and in 1812 he was put in command of the
New York Brigade of artillery. One of the forts built at this
time for the defence of New York harbour was called Fort
Stevens, in his honour, and after the laying of the foundation
stone he "gave the party a dinner at his country seat, 'Mount
Buonaparte'", which he had named after the hero who restored order in France.

My great-grandfather next became an East-India merchant,
and carried on a large and successful trade with foreign
ports. The United States War Department still entrusted him
with important private missions; he was a confidential agent
of both the French and English governments, and at the
same time took a leading part in the municipal business of
New York, and served on numerous commissions dealing
with public affairs. He divided his year between his New
York house in Warren Street, and Mount Buonaparte, the
country place on Long Island created by the fortune he had
made as a merchant; but when his hero dropped the *u* from
his name and became Emperor, my scandalized great-
grandfather, irrevocably committed to the Republican idea,
indignantly re-named his place "The Mount". It stood, as its
name suggests, on a terraced height in what is now the
dreary waste of Astoria, and my mother could remember the
stately colonnaded orangery, and the big orange-trees in tubs

that were set out every summer on the upper terrace. But in her day the classical mantelpieces imported from Italy, with designs in white marble relieved against red or green, had already been torn out and replaced by black marble arches and ugly grates, and she recalled seeing the old mantelpieces stacked away in the stables. In his Bonapartist days General Stevens must have imported a good deal of Empire furniture from Paris, and one relic, a pair of fine gilt andirons crowned with Napoleonic eagles, has descended to his distant great-grand-daughter; but much was doubtless discarded when the mantelpieces went, and the stuffy day of Regency upholstery set in.

If I have dwelt too long on the career of this model citizen it is because of a secret partiality for him—for his stern high-nosed good looks, his gallantry in war, his love of luxury, his tireless commercial activities. I like above all the abounding energy, the swift adaptability and the *joie de vivre* which hurried him from one adventure to another, with war, commerce and domesticity (he had two wives and fourteen children) all carried on to the same heroic tune. But perhaps I feel nearest to him when I look at my eagle andirons, and think of the exquisite polychrome mantels that he found the time to bring all the way from Italy, to keep company with the orange-trees on his terrace.

In his delightful book on Walter Scott Mr. John Buchan, excusing Scott's inability to create a lifelike woman of his own class, says that, after all, to the men of his generation, gentlewomen were "a toast" and little else. Nothing could be truer. Child-bearing was their task, fine needlework their recreation, being respected their privilege. Only in aristocratic society, and in the most sophisticated capitals of Europe, had they added to this repertory a good many private distractions. In the upper middle class "the ladies, God bless 'em", sums it up. And so it happens that I know less than nothing of the particular virtues, gifts and modest accomplishments of the young women with pearls in their looped hair or cambric ruffs round their slim necks, who prepared the way for my generation. A few shreds of anecdote, no more than the faded flowers between the leaves of a great-grandmother's Bible, are all that remain to me.

Painting by Samuel Lovett Waldo

MY GREAT-GRANDFATHER,
GENERAL STEVENS

Painting by Samuel Lovett Waldo

MY GREAT-GRANDMOTHER,
MRS. STEVENS
(LUCRETIA AUSTIN)

Of my lovely great-grandmother Rhinelander (Mary Robart) I know only that she was of French descent, as her spirited profile declares, and properly jealous of her rights; for if she chanced to drive to New York in her yellow coach with its fringed hammer-cloth at the same hour when her daughter-in-law, from lower down the East River, was following the same road, the latter's carriage had to take the old lady's dust all the way, even though her horses were faster and her errand might be more urgent. I may add that once, several years after my marriage, a new coachman, who did not know my mother's carriage by sight, accidentally drove me past it on the fashionable Ocean Drive at Newport, and that I had to hasten the next morning to apologize to my mother, whose only comment was, when I explained that the coachman could not have known the offence he was committing: "You might have told him".

One of my great-grandmothers, Lucretia Ledyard (the second wife of General Stevens), lost her "handsome sable cloak" one day when she was driving out General Washington in her sleigh, while on another occasion, when she was walking on the Battery in 1812, the gentleman who was with her, glancing seaward, suddenly exclaimed: "My God, madam, there are the British!"

Meagre relics of the past; and when it comes to the next generation, that of my own grandparents, I am little better informed. My maternal grandfather Rhinelander, son of the proud dame of the yellow coach, married Mary Stevens, daughter of the General and his dusky handsome Ledyard wife. The young pair had four children, and then my grandfather died, when he was little more than thirty. He too was handsome, with frank blue eyes and a wide intelligent brow. My mother said he "loved reading", and that particular drop of his blood must have descended to my veins, for I know of no other bookworm in the family. His young widow and her children continued to live at the country place at Hell Gate, lived there, in fact, from motives of economy, in winter as well as summer while the children were young; for my grandmother, whose property was left to the management of her husband's eldest brother, remained poor though her brother-in-law grew rich. The children, however, were carefully educated by English governesses and tutors; and to one of the latter is owing the charming study of the view across Hell Gate to Long Island, taken from my grandmother's lawn, which is here reproduced.

The little girls were taught needle-work, music, drawing and "the languages" (their Italian teacher was Professor Foresti, a distinguished fugitive from the Austrian political prisons). In winter their "best dresses" were low-necked and short-sleeved frocks, of pea-green merino, with gray beaver hats trimmed with tartan ribbons, white cotton stockings and heelless prunella slippers. When they walked in the snow hand-knitted woollen stockings were drawn over this frail footgear, and woollen shawls wrapped about their poor bare shoulders. They suffered, like all young ladies of their day, from chilblains and excruciating sick-headaches, yet all lived to a vigorous old age. When the eldest (my mother) "came out", she wore a home-made gown of white tarlatan, looped up with red and white camellias from the greenhouse, and her mother's old white satin slippers; and her feet being of a different shape from grandmamma's, she suffered martyrdom, and never ceased to resent the indignity inflicted on her, and the impediment to her dancing, the more so as her younger sisters, who were prettier and probably more indulged, were given new slippers when their turn came. The girls appear to have had their horses (in that almost roadless day Americans still went everywhere in the saddle), and my mother, whose memory for the details of dress was inexhaustible, told me that she wore a beaver hat with a drooping ostrich plume, and a green veil to protect her complexion, and that from motives of modesty riding-habits were cut to trail on the ground, so that it was almost impossible to mount unassisted.

A little lower down the Sound (on the actual site of East Eighty-first Street) stood my grandfather Jones's pretty country house with classic pilasters and balustraded roof. A print in my possession shows a low-studded log-cabin adjoining it under the elms, described as the aboriginal Jones habitation; but it was more probably the slaves' quarter. In this pleasant house lived a young man of twenty, handsome, simple and kind, who was madly in love with Lucretia, the eldest of the "poor Rhinelander" girls. George Frederic's parents thought

MY GREAT-GRANDMOTHER,
MRS. RHINELANDER
(MARY ROBART)

MY GRANDFATHER,
FREDERIC WILLIAM RHINELANDER

him too young to marry; perhaps they had other ambitions for him; they bade him break off his attentions to Miss Rhinelander of Hell Gate. But George Frederic was the owner of a rowing-boat. His stern papa, perhaps on account of the proximity of the beloved, refused to give him a sailing-craft, though every youth of the day had his "cat-boat", and the smiling expanse of the Sound was flecked with the coming and going of white wings. But George was not to be thwarted. He contrived to turn an oar into a mast; he stole down before dawn, his bed-quilt under his arm, rigged it to the oar in guise of a sail, and flying over the waters of the Sound hurried to his lady's feet across the lawn depicted in the tutor's painting. His devotion at last overcame the paternal opposition, and George and "Lou" were married when they were respectively twenty-one and nineteen. My grandfather was rich, and must have made his sons a generous allowance; for the young couple, after an adventurous honeymoon in Cuba (of which my father kept a conscientious record, full of drives in *volantes* and visits to fashionable plantations) set up a house of their own in Gramercy Park, then just within the built-on limits of New York, and Mrs. George Frederic took her place among the most elegant young married women of her day. At last the home-made tarlatans and the inherited satin shoes were avenged, and there began a long career of hospitality at home and travels abroad. My father, as a boy, had been to Europe with his father on one of the last of the great sailing passenger-ships; and he often told me of the delights of that crossing, on a yacht-like vessel with few passengers and spacious airy cabins, as compared with subsequent voyages on the cramped foul-smelling steamers that superseded the sailing ships. A year or so after the birth of my eldest brother my parents went abroad on a long tour. The new railways were beginning to transform continental travel, and after driving by *diligence* from Calais to Amiens my family journeyed thence by rail to Paris. Later they took train from Paris to Brussels, a day or two after the inauguration of this line; and my father notes in his diary: "We were told to be at the station at one o'clock, *and by four we were actually off.*" By various means of conveyance the young couple with their infant son pursued their way through France, Belgium,

Germany and Italy. They met other young New Yorkers of fashion, also on their travels, and would have had a merry time of it had not little Freddy's youthful ailments so frequently altered their plans—sometimes to a degree so disturbing that the patient young father (of twenty-three) confides to his diary how "awful a thing it is to travel in Europe with an infant of twenty months".

In spite of Freddy they saw many cities and countries, and on February 24, 1848, toward the hour of noon, incidentally witnessed, from the balcony of their hotel in the rue de Rivoli, the flight of Louis Philippe and Queen Marie Amélie across the Tuileries gardens. Though my mother often described this scene to me, I suspect that the study of the Paris fashions made a more vivid impression on her than the fall of monarchies. The humiliation of the pea-green merino and the maternal slippers led to a good many extravagances; among them there is the white satin bonnet trimmed with white marabout and crystal drops in which the bride made her wedding visits, and a "capeline" of *gorge de pigeon* taffetas with a wreath of flowers in shiny brown kid, which was one of the triumphs of her Paris shopping. She had a beautiful carriage, and her sloping shoulders and slim waist were becomingly set off by the wonderful gowns brought home from that first visit to the capital of fashion. All this happened years before I was born; but the tradition of elegance was never abandoned, and when we finally returned to live in New York (in 1872) I shared the excitement caused by the annual arrival of the "trunk from Paris", and the enchantment of seeing one resplendent dress after another shaken out of its tissue-paper. Once, when I was a small child, my mother's younger sister, my beautiful and serious-minded Aunt Mary Newbold, asked me, with edifying interest: "What would you like to be when you grow up?" and on my replying in all good faith, and with a dutiful air: "The best-dressed woman in New York," she uttered the horrified cry: "Oh, don't say that, darling!" to which I could only rejoin in wonder: "But, Auntie, you know Mamma *is*."

When my grandfather died my father came into an independent fortune; but even before that my father and uncles seem to have had allowances permitting them to lead a life of

VIEW FROM MY GRANDMOTHER RHINELANDER'S COUNTRY-PLACE AT
HELL GATE (ABOUT 1835)

leisure and amiable hospitality. The customs of the day were simple, and in my father's set the chief diversions were sea-fishing, boat-racing and wild-fowl shooting. There were no clubs as yet in New York, and my mother, whose view of life was incurably prosaic, always said that this accounted for the early marriages, as the young men of that day "had nowhere else to go". The young married couples, Langdons, Hones, Newbolds, Edgars, Joneses, Gallatins, etc., entertained each other a good deal, and my mother's sloping shoulders were often displayed above the elegant fringed and ruffled "berthas" of her Parisian dinner gowns. The amusing diary of Mr. Philip Hone gives a good idea of the simple but incessant exchange of hospitality between the young people who ruled New York society before the Civil War.

My readers, by this time, may be wondering what were the particular merits, private or civic, of these amiable persons. Their lives, as one looks back, certainly seem lacking in relief; but I believe their value lay in upholding two standards of importance in any community, that of education and good manners, and of scrupulous probity in business and private affairs. New York has always been a commercial community, and in my infancy the merits and defects of its citizens were those of a mercantile middle class. The first duty of such a class was to maintain a strict standard of uprightness in affairs; and the gentlemen of my father's day did maintain it, whether in the law, in banking, shipping or wholesale commercial enterprises. I well remember the horror excited by any irregularity in affairs, and the relentless social ostracism inflicted on the families of those who lapsed from professional or business integrity. In one case, where two or three men of high social standing were involved in a discreditable bank failure, their families were made to suffer to a degree that would seem merciless to our modern judgment. But perhaps the New Yorkers of that day were unconsciously trying to atone for their culpable neglect of state and national politics, from which they had long disdainfully held aloof, by upholding the sternest principles of business probity, and inflicting the severest social penalties on whoever lapsed from them. At any rate I should say that the qualities justifying the existence of our old society were social amenity and financial incorruptibility; and we have travelled far enough from both to begin to estimate their value.

The weakness of the social structure of my parents' day was a blind dread of innovation, an instinctive shrinking from responsibility. In 1824 (or thereabouts) a group of New York gentlemen who were appointed to examine various plans for the proposed laying-out of the city, and whose private sympathies were notoriously anti-Jeffersonian and undemocratic, decided against reproducing the beautiful system of squares, circles and radiating avenues which Major L'Enfant, the brilliant French engineer, had designed for Washington, because it was thought "undemocratic" for citizens of the new republic to own building-plots which were not all of exactly the same shape, size—and *value!* This naïf document, shown to me by Robert Minturn, a descendant of a member of the original committee, and doubtless often since published, typified the prudent attitude of a society of prosperous business men who have no desire to row against the current.

A little world so well-ordered and well-to-do does not often produce either eagles or fanatics, and both seem to have been conspicuously absent from the circle in which my forbears moved. In old-established and powerful societies originality of character is smiled at, and even encouraged to assert itself; but conformity is the bane of middle-class communities, and as far as I can recall, only two of my relations stepped out of the strait path of the usual. One was a mild and inoffensive old bachelor cousin, very small and frail, and reputed of immense wealth and morbid miserliness, who built himself a fine house in his youth, and lived in it for fifty or sixty years, in a state of negativeness and insignificance which made him proverbial even in our conforming class—and then, in his last years (so we children were told) *sat on a marble shelf, and thought he was a bust of Napoleon.*

Cousin Edmund's final illusion was not without pathos, but as a source of inspiration to my childish fancy he was a poor thing compared with George Alfred. George Alfred was another cousin, but one whom I had never seen, and could never hope to see, because years before he had—vanished. Vanished, that is, out of society, out of respectability, out of the safe daylight world of "nice people" and reputable doings.

MY GRANDFATHER, EDWARD RENSHAW JONES

Before naming George Alfred my mother altered her expression and lowered her voice. Thank heaven *she* was not responsible for him—he belonged to my father's side of the family! But they too had long since washed their hands of George Alfred—had ceased even to be aware of his existence. If my mother pronounced his name it was solely, I believe, out of malice, out of the child's naughty desire to evoke some nursery hobgoblin by muttering a dark incantation like *Eena Meena Mina Mo*, and then darting away with affrighted backward looks to see if there is anything there.

My mother always darted away from George Alfred's name after pronouncing it, and it was not until I was grown up, and had acquired greater courage and persistency, that one day I drove her to the wall by suddenly asking: "But, Mamma, *what did he do*?" "Some woman"—my mother muttered; and no one accustomed to the innocuous word as now used can imagine the shades of disapproval, scorn and yet excited curiosity, that "some" could then connote on the lips of virtue.

George Alfred—and some woman! Who was she? From what heights had she fallen with him, to what depths dragged him down? For in those simple days it was always a case of "the woman tempted me". To her respectable sisters her culpability was as certain in advance as Predestination to the Calvinist. But I was not fated to know more—thank heaven I was not! For our shadowy Paolo and Francesca, circling together on the "accursèd air", somewhere outside the safe boundaries of our old New York, gave me, I verily believe, my earliest glimpse of the poetry that Goethe missed in the respectable world of the Hirschgraben, and that my ancestors assuredly failed to find, or to create, between the Battery and Union Square. The vision of poor featureless unknown Alfred and his siren, lurking in some cranny of my imagination, hinted at regions perilous, dark and yet lit with mysterious fires, just outside the world of copy-book axioms, and the old obediences that were in my blood; and the hint was useful—for a novelist.

II

Knee-High

PEOPLING the background of these earliest scenes there were the tall splendid father who was always so kind, and whose strong arms lifted one so high, and held one so safely; and my mother, who wore such beautiful flounced dresses, and had painted and carved fans in sandalwood boxes, and ermine scarves, and perfumed yellowish laces pinned up in blue paper, and kept in a marquetry chiffonier, and all the other dim impersonal attributes of a Mother, without, as yet, anything much more definite; and two big brothers who were mostly away (the eldest already at college); but in the foreground with Foxy there was one rich all-permeating presence: Doyley. How I pity all children who have not had a Doyley—a nurse who has always been there, who is as established as the sky and as warm as the sun, who understands everything, feels everything, can arrange everything, and combines all the powers of the Divinity with the compassion of a mortal heart like one's own! Doyley's presence was the warm cocoon in which my infancy lived safe and sheltered; the atmosphere without which I could not have breathed. It is thanks to Doyley that not one bitter memory, one uncomprehended injustice, darkened the days when the soul's flesh is so tender, and the remembrance of wrongs so acute.

I was born in New York, in my parents' house in West Twenty-third Street, and we lived there in winter, and (I suppose) at Newport in summer, during the first three years of my life. But no memories of those years survive, save those I have mentioned, and one other, a good deal dimmer, of going to stay one summer with my Aunt Elizabeth, my father's unmarried sister, who had a house at Rhinebeck-on-the-Hudson. This aunt, whom I remember as a ramrod-backed old lady compounded of steel and granite, had been threatened in her youth with the "consumption" which had already carried off a brother and sister. Few families in that day escaped the scourge of tuberculosis, and the Protestant cemeteries of Pisa and Rome are full of the graves of wretched exiles sent to end their days by the supposedly mild shores of Arno or Tiber. My poor Aunt Margaret, my poor Uncle Joshua, both snatched in their early flower, already slept beside the Pyramid of Caius Cestius, where my grandmother was later to join them; and when Elizabeth in her turn began to pine, her parents, no doubt discouraged by the Italian experiment, decided to try curing her at home. They therefore shut her up one October in her bedroom in the New York house in Mercer Street, lit the fire, sealed up the windows, and did not let her out again till the following June, when she emerged in perfect health, to live till seventy.

My aunt's house, called Rhinecliff, afterward became a vivid picture in the gallery of my little girlhood; but among those earliest impressions only one is connected with it; that of a night when, as I was ready to affirm, there was a Wolf under my bed. This business of the Wolf was the first of other similar terrifying experiences, and since most imaginative children know these hauntings by tribal animals, I mention it only because from the moment of that adventure it became necessary, whenever I "read" the story of Red Riding Hood (that is, looked at the pictures), to carry my little nursery stool from one room to another, in pursuit of Doyley or my mother, so that I should never again be exposed to meeting the family Totem when I sat down alone to my book.

The effect of terror produced by the house of Rhinecliff was no doubt partly due to what seemed to me its intolerable ugliness. My visual sensibility must always have been too keen for middling pleasures; my photographic memory of rooms and houses—even those seen but briefly, or at long intervals—was from my earliest years a source of inarticulate misery, for I was always vaguely frightened by ugliness. I can still remember hating everything at Rhinecliff, which, as I saw, on rediscovering it some years later, was an expensive but dour specimen of Hudson River Gothic; and from the first I was obscurely conscious of a queer resemblance between the granitic exterior of Aunt Elizabeth and her grimly comfortable home, between her battlemented caps and the turrets of Rhinecliff. But all this is merged in a blur, for by the time I

was four years old I was playing in the Roman Forum instead
of on the lawns of Rhinecliff.

2

The transition woke no surprise, for almost everything that
constituted my world was still about me: my handsome
father, my beautifully dressed mother, and the warmth and
sunshine that were Doyley. The chief difference was that the
things about me were now not ugly but incredibly beautiful.
That old Rome of the mid-nineteenth century was still the
city of romantic ruins in which Clive Newcome's "J. J." had
depicted the Trasteverina dancing before a *locanda* to the music of a *pifferaro*. I remember, through the trailing clouds of
infancy, the steps of the Piazza di Spagna thronged with
Thackerayan artists' models, and heaped with early violets,
daffodils and tulips; I remember long sunlit wanderings on
the springy turf of great Roman villas; heavy coaches of Car-
dinals flashing in scarlet and gold through the twilight of
narrow streets; the flowery bombardment of the Carnival
procession watched with shrieks of infant ecstasy from a balcony of the Corso. But the liveliest hours were those spent
with my nurse on the Monte Pincio, where I played with
Marion Crawford's little half-sister, Daisy Terry, and her
brother Arthur. Other children, long since dim and nameless,
flit by as supernumeraries of the band; but only Daisy and her
brother have remained alive to me. There we played, dodging
in and out among old stone benches, racing, rolling hoops,
whirling through skipping ropes, or pausing out of breath to
watch the toy procession of stately barouches and glossy
saddle-horses which, on every fine afternoon of winter, carried the flower of Roman beauty and nobility round and
round and round the restricted meanderings of the hill-top.

Those hours were the jolliest; yet deeper impressions were
gathered in walks with my mother on the daisy-strewn lawns
of the Villa Doria-Pamphili, among the statues and stone-
pines of the Villa Borghese, or hunting on the slopes of the
Palatine for the mysterious bits of blue and green and rosy
stone which cropped up through the turf as violets and anem-
ones did in other places, and turned out to be precious frag-

ments of porphyry, lapis lazuli, verde antico, and all the mineral flora of the Palace of the Cæsars. In those days every traveller of artistic sensibility gathered baskets-full of these marble blossoms, and had them transformed into the paper-weights, inkstands and circular "sofa-tables" without which no gentleman's home was complete. All the glory seemed to forsake my treasures when they were forced into these lapidary combinations; but the hunt was thrilling, and it occurred to no one that these exquisite relics of ruined *opus alexandrinum*, and of Imperial vases and statues, should have been treated with more reverence. The buffaloes of Piranesi had vanished from the Forum and the Palatine, but the ruins of Imperial Rome were still a free stamping ground for the human herd.

There were other days when we drove out on the Campagna, and wandered over the short grass between the tombs of the Appian way; still others among the fountains of Frascati; and some, particularly vivid, when, in the million-tapered blaze of St Peter's, the Pope floated ethereally above a long train of ecclesiastics seen through an incense haze so golden that it seemed to pour from the blinding luminary behind the High Altar.

What clung closest in after years, when I thought of the lost Rome of my infancy? It is hard to say; perhaps simply the warm scent of the box hedges on the Pincian, and the texture of weather-worn sun-gilt stone. Those, at least, are the two impressions which, for many years after, the mightiest of names instantly conjured up for me.

3

My Roman impressions are followed by others, improbably picturesque, of a journey to Spain. It must have taken place just before or after the Roman year; I remember that the Spanish tour was still considered an arduous adventure, and to attempt it with a young child the merest folly. But my father had been reading Prescott and Washington Irving; the Alhambra was more of a novelty than the Colosseum; and as the offspring of born travellers I was expected, even in infancy, to know how to travel. I suppose I acquitted myself

better than the unhappy Freddy; for from that wild early pilgrimage I brought back an incurable passion for the road.
What a journey it must have been! Presumably there was already a railway from the frontier to Madrid; but I recall only
the incessant jingle of *diligence* bells, the cracking of whips,
the yells of gaunt muleteers hurling stones at their gaunter
mules to urge them up interminable and almost unscaleable
hills. It is all a jumble of excited impressions: breaking down
on wind-swept sierras; arriving late and hungry at squalid
posadas; flea-hunting, chocolate-drinking (I believe there was
nothing but chocolate and olives to feed me on), being pursued wherever we went by touts, guides, deformed beggars,
and all sorts of jabbering and confusing people; and, through
the chaos and fatigue, a fantastic vision of the columns of
Cordova, the tower of the Giralda, the pools and fountains of
the Alhambra, the orange groves of Seville, the awful icy penumbra of the Escorial, and everywhere shadowy aisles undu-
lating with incense and processions. . . Perhaps, after all, it is
not a bad thing to begin one's travels at four.

4

In the course of time we exchanged the Piazza di Spagna
for the Champs Elysées. It probably happened the very next
winter; but life in Paris must have seemed colourless after the
sunny violet-scented Italian days, for I remember far less of it
than of Rome.

Two episodes, however, stand out vividly. One was the
coming to dine every Sunday evening of a kindly gentleman
with curly gray hair and a long moustache, an old friend and
Rhode Island neighbour of the family. This was Mr. Henry
Bedlow, whose chief title to fame seems to have been that he
lived in an old house "up the island" called Malbone, which
he had inherited from his grandfather or great-uncle, the celebrated miniature painter of that name. When Mr. Bedlow
dined with us I was always led in with the dessert, my red hair
rolled into sausages, and the sleeves of my best frock looped
up with pink coral, and was allowed to perch on his knee
while he "told me mythology". What blessings I have since
called down on the teller! Fairy stories, even Mother Goose,

even Andersen's tales and the Contes de Perrault, still left me inattentive and indifferent, but the domestic dramas of the Olympians roused all my creative energy. Perhaps I scented an indefinable condescension (and often a great lack of discernment) in the stories which big people have invented about little ones; and besides, the doings of children were always intrinsically less interesting to me than those of grownups, and I felt more at home with the gods and goddesses of Olympus, who behaved so much like the ladies and gentlemen who came to dine, whom I saw riding and driving in the Bois de Boulogne, and about whom I was forever weaving stories of my own.

The other Parisian event concerns this story-telling. The imagining of tales (about grown-up people, "real people", I called them—children always seemed to me incompletely realized) had gone on in me since my first conscious moments; I cannot remember the time when I did not want to "make up" stories. But it was in Paris that I found the necessary formula. Oddly enough, I had no desire to write my stories down (even had I known how to write, and I couldn't yet form a letter); but from the first I had to have a book in my hand to "make up" with, and from the first it had to be a certain sort of book. The page had to be closely printed, with rather heavy black type, and not much margin. Certain densely printed novels in the early Tauchnitz editions, Harrison Ainsworth's for instance, would have been my richest sources of inspiration had I not hit one day on something even better: Washington Irving's "Alhambra". These shaggy volumes, printed in close black characters on rough-edged yellowish pages, and bound in coarse dark-blue paper covers (probably a production of the old Galignani Press in Paris) must have been a relic of our Spanish adventure. Washington Irving was an old friend of my family's, and his collected works, in comely type and handsome binding, adorned our library shelves at home. But these would not have been of much use to me as a source of inspiration. The rude companion of our travels was the book I needed; I had only to open it for the Pierian fount to flow. There was richness and mystery in the thick black type, a hint of bursting overflowing material in the serried lines and scant margin. To this day I am bored by the sight of widely spaced type, and a little islet of text in a sailless sea of white paper.

Well—the "Alhambra" once in hand, making up was ecstasy. At any moment the impulse might seize me; and then, if the book was in reach, I had only to walk the floor, turning the pages as I walked, to be swept off full sail on the sea of dreams. The fact that I could not read added to the completeness of the illusion, for from those mysterious blank pages I could evoke whatever my fancy chose. Parents and nurses, peeping at me through the cracks of doors (I always had to be alone to "make up"), noticed that I often held the book upside down, but that I never failed to turn the pages, and that I turned them at about the right pace for a person reading aloud as passionately and precipitately as was my habit.

There was something almost ritualistic in the performance. The call came regularly and imperiously; and though, when it caught me at inconvenient moments, I would struggle against it conscientiously—for I was beginning to be a very conscientious little girl—the struggle was always a losing one. I had to obey the furious Muse; and there are deplorable tales of my abandoning the "nice" playmates who had been invited to "spend the day", and rushing to my mother with the desperate cry: "Mamma, you must go and entertain that little girl for me. *I've got to make up.*"

My parents, distressed by my solitude (my two brothers being by this time grown up and away) were always trying to establish relations for me with "nice" children, and I was willing enough to play in the Champs Elysées with such specimens as were produced or (more reluctantly) to meet them at little parties or dancing classes; but I did not want them to intrude on my privacy, and there was not one I would not have renounced forever rather than have my "making up" interfered with. What I really preferred was to be alone with Washington Irving and my dream.

The peculiar purpose for which books served me probably made me indifferent to what was in them. At any rate, I can remember feeling no curiosity about it. But my father, by dint of patience, managed to drum the alphabet into me; and one day I was found sitting under a table, absorbed in a volume which I did not appear to be using for improvisation. My immobility attracted attention, and when asked what I was doing, I replied: "Reading". This was received with incredulity; but on being called upon to read a few lines aloud I appear to have responded to the challenge, and it was then discovered that the work over which I was poring was a play by Ludovic Halévy, called "Fanny Lear", which was having a *succès de scandale* in Paris owing to the fact that the heroine was what ladies of my mother's day called "one of those women". Thereafter the books I used for "making up" were carefully inspected before being entrusted to me; and an arduous business it must have been, for no book ever came my way without being instantly pounced on, and now that I could read I divided my time between my own improvisations and the printed inventions of others.

It was in Paris that I took my first dancing-lessons. I was no Isadora, and these beginnings would not be worth a word but for the light they throw on the manners and customs of my infancy. I used to go, with a group of little friends, children English and American, to the private *cours* of an ex-ballerina of the Grand Opera, Mademoiselle Michelet, a large stern woman with a heavy black moustache, in whom it would have been hard for the most imaginative to detect even a trace of her early calling. To us she was the severest of instructresses. The waltz and mazurka had long since been introduced into the ball-room, without even a lingering remembrance of Byron's reprobation; but they were not thought difficult enough to train the young, and we were persistently exercised in the *menuet*, the shawl dance (with a lace scarf) and the *cachucha*—of course with castanets. Mademoiselle Michelet's quarters were very small; and I can still see myself, an isolated figure in the centre of her shining *parquet*, helplessly waving my scarf or uncertainly clacking my castanets, while my fellow pupils hedged me about as rather bored spectators, and Mademoiselle Michelet's wizened little old mother, in a cap turreted with loops of purple ribbon, tinkled out the tunes at a piano squeezed into a corner of the room.

During one of our Paris winters (I think there were two or three) my dear old grandmother, my mother's mother, paid us a long visit. I call her "old", though it is probably that at the time she was under sixty; but I had never seen her except in lace cap and lappets, a bunch of gold charms dangling from her massive watch-chain, among the folds of a rich black silk dress, and a black japanned ear-trumpet at her ear — the abstract type of an ancestress as the function was then understood.

I always recall her seated in an arm-chair, her undimmed eyes bent over some exquisitely fine needle-work. I hope she sometimes went for a walk or a drive, and enjoyed a few glimpses of grown-up society; but for me she exists only as a motionless and gently smiling figure, whose one gesture was to lay aside her stitching for her ear-trumpet at my approach. When she was with us I was constantly in her room; and my way of returning her affection was to read aloud to her. I had just discovered a volume of Tennyson among my father's books, and for hours I used to shout the "Idyls of the King", and "The Lord of Burleigh" through the trumpet of my long-suffering ancestress. Not being more than six or seven years old I understood hardly anything of what I was reading, or rather I understood it in my own way, which was most often not the poet's; as in the line from "The Lord of Burleigh", "and he made a loving consort", where I read *concert* for consort, and concluded (being already addicted to rash generalizations) that a gentleman's first act after marriage was to give his spouse a concert, in gratitude for which "a faithful wife was she". But I enjoyed all the sonorities as much as if I had known what they meant, and perhaps even more, since my own interpretations so often enriched the text; and probably such shrill scraps as travelled through the windings of my grandmother's trumpet troubled her no more than they did me. To one whose preferred poetic reading was "The Christian Year", the "Idyls of the King" must have been almost as full of mystery and obscurity as Browning was to the next generation, and the rhythmic raptures tingling through me probably woke no echo in the dear old head bent to mine.

I suspect that no one else in the house could bear to be read aloud to by me, for I do not remember attempting it on any one but my grandmother; and indeed poetry did not play much part in our lives. My father knew Macaulay's "Lays" by heart, and

> Ho, Philip, send for charity thy Mexican pistoles,

and

> Where ride Massilia's triremes
> Heavy with fair-haired slaves,

had already thrummed their march-tunes into my infant ears. The new Tennysonian rhythms also moved my father greatly; and I imagine there was a time when his rather rudimentary love of verse might have been developed had he had any one with whom to share it. But my mother's matter-of-factness must have shrivelled up any such buds of fancy; and in later years I remember his reading only Macaulay, Prescott, Washington Irving, and every book of travel he could find. Arctic explorations especially absorbed him, and I have wondered since what stifled cravings had once germinated in him, and what manner of man he was really meant to be. That he was a lonely one, haunted by something always unexpressed and unattained, I am sure.

5

I remember nothing else of my Paris life except one vision over which after-events shed a tragic glare. It was the sight, one autumn afternoon, of a beautiful lady driving down the Champs Elysées in a beautiful open carriage, a little boy in uniform beside her on a pony, and a glittering escort of officers. The carriage, of the kind called a *daumont*, was preceded by outriders, and swayed gracefully on its big C-springs to the rhythm of four high-stepping and highly-groomed horses, a postilion on one of the leaders, and two tremendous footmen perched high at the back. But all I had eyes for was the lady herself, leaning back as ladies of those days leaned in their indolently-hung carriages, flounces of *feuille-morte* taffetas billowing out about her, and on her rich auburn hair a tiny black lace bonnet with a tea-rose above one ear. I still see her serene elegance of attitude and expression, her conscious air of being, with her little boy, and the shining horses, and the flashing officers and outriders, the centre of the sumptuous spectacle. The next year she and her procession had vanished in a crimson hurricane; and the whole setting of swaying carriages and outstretched ladies, of young men caracoling on thorough-breds past stately houses glimpsed through clustering horse-chestnut foliage, has long since been rolled up in the lumber-room of discarded pageants.

We must have remained in Paris till the outbreak of the Franco-Prussian War, at which fateful moment we chanced to be at Bad Wildbad, in the Black Forest, a primitive watering-place just coming into fashion, where my mother had been sent for a cure. With a young German nursery governess who had been added to our party I took happy rambles in the pine-forests, and learned from her to make wild-flower garlands, to knit and to tat, and to practise (for the only time in my life) other Gretchenish arts. She also taught me (out of the New Testament) how to read German; and in our Bible reading I came across a phrase which has always delighted me because of the quaint contrast between its impulsive German *Gemüthlichkeit* and the majestic phraseology of our Authorized Version. When, on the Mount of Transfiguration, the disciples cry out: "Lord, it is good for us to be here; if Thou wilt, let us make here three tabernacles", the German version causes them to say: *"So lasset uns Hütten bauen!"* The cry, which suggested to me something fresh and leafy and adventurous, like a Mayne Reid story or "The Swiss Family Robinson", is a picturesque instance of the way in which racial character colours alien formulas.

But one morning, climbing a woodland path with my governess and some other children, I was seized by an agony of pain—and after that for many long weeks life was a confused and feverish misery. I was desperately ill with typhoid fever, and I mention the fact only because of one incredible circumstance. All the doctors of Wildbad (they were doubtless few) had already been mobilized, save one super-annuated practitioner; and he had never before seen a case of typhoid! His son, also a doctor, was with the army; and all that his father could do was to despatch bulletins to him, asking how I was to be treated. The replies, one may suppose, were long in arriving; and in the interval death came near. But at the same time a celebrated Russian physician arrived at Wildbad for a day, at the call of a princely patient. My parents persuaded him to see me, and he prescribed the new treatment: plunging the patient in baths of ice-cold water. At the suggestion my mother's courage failed her; but she wrapped me in wet sheets, and I was saved.

6

My childish world, though so well filled, lacked completeness, for my dog Foxy had not come to Europe with us. His absence left such a void that my parents finally gave me a Florentine *lupetto*, as white as Foxy, but much smaller. By that time (I think in 1870) we had exchanged Paris for Florence, and he was known as Florence Foxy. He was the joyous companion of a comparatively dull winter; for the return to Italy did not bring back the joys of Rome. Florence was much colder and less sunny; there were no children to replace the jolly Pincianites, and the Cascine Gardens are associated only with sedate walks with my elders, monotonous enough if I had not had Foxy to race with, and violets to gather.

The other high lights of those gray months were the increased enchantment of "making up", and the fainter glow of the hours spent with a charming young lady who taught me Italian. My lessons amused me, and the new language came to me as naturally as breathing, as French and German had already. Why do so few parents know what a fortune they could bestow on their children by teaching them the modern languages in babyhood, when a playmate is the only professor needed, and the speech acquired is never afterward lost, however deep below the surface it may be embedded?

But discovering Italian, though it was to be the source of such joys, was nothing to the ecstasy of "making up". Learning to read, instead of distracting me from this passion, had only fed it; and during that Florentine winter it became a frenzy. Our vast and cheerless suite in the high-ceilinged *piano nobile* of an hotel overlooking the Arno was scantily furnished with threadbare carpets and heavy consoles and sofas; but the long vista of rooms, each communicating with the next through tall folding doors, was a matchless track for my sport. When the grown-ups were out, and Doyley safe with her sewing, I had the field to myself; and I still feel the rap-

ture (greater than any I have ever known in writing) of pouring forth undisturbed the tireless torrent of my stories. The
"Faster, faster, O Circe, Goddess" of "The Strayed Reveller"
always reminds me of those youthful gallops around the race-
course of my imagination. The speed at which I travelled was
so great that my mother tried in vain to take down my "stories", and posterity will never know what it has lost! All I
remember is that my tales were about what I still thought of
as "real people" (that is, grown-up people, resembling in appearance and habits my family and their friends, and caught
in the same daily coil of "things that might have happened").
My imagination was still closed to the appeal of the purely
fabulous and fairy-like, and though I was already an ardent
reader of poetry I felt no desire to write it. But all that was
soon to be changed; for the next year we were to go home to
New York, and I was to enter into the kingdom of my father's
library.

III

Little Girl

I

THE DEPRECIATION of American currency at the close of the Civil War had so much reduced my father's income that, in common with many of his friends and relations, he had gone to Europe to economize, letting his town and country houses for six years to some of the profiteers of the day; but I did not learn till much later to how prosaic a cause I owed my early years in Europe. Happy misfortune, which gave me, for the rest of my life, that background of beauty and old-established order! I did not know how deeply I had felt the nobility and harmony of the great European cities till our steamer was docked at New York.

I remember once asking an old New Yorker why he never went abroad, and his answering: "Because I can't bear to cross Murray Street." It was indeed an unsavoury experience, and the shameless squalor of the purlieus of the New York docks in the 'seventies dismayed my childish eyes, stored with the glories of Rome and the architectural majesty of Paris. But it was summer; we were soon at Newport, under the friendly gables of Pencraig; and to a little girl long pent up in hotels and flats there was inexhaustible delight in the freedom of a staircase to run up and down, of lawns and trees, a meadow full of clover and daisies, a pony to ride, terriers to romp with, a sheltered cove to bathe in, flower-beds spicy with "carnation, lily, rose", and a kitchen-garden crimson with strawberries and sweet as honey with Seckel pears.

The roomy and pleasant house of Pencraig was surrounded by a verandah wreathed in clematis and honeysuckle, and below it a lawn sloped to a deep daisied meadow, beyond which were a private bathing-beach and boat-landing. From the landing we used to fish for "scuppers" and "porgies", succulent little fish that were grilled or fried for high tea; and off the rocky point lay my father's and brothers' "cat-boats", the graceful wide-sailed craft that flecked the bay like sea-gulls.

Adjoining our property was Edgerston, the country home
of Lewis Rutherfurd, the distinguished astronomer, notable
in his day for his remarkable photographs of the moon. He
and his wife were lifelong friends of my parents', and in
their household, besides two grown-up daughters of singular
beauty, there were two little boys, the youngest of my own
age. There were also two young governesses, French and
German; and as I was alone, and the German governess who
had been imported for me was unsympathetic and unsatis-
fied, she was soon sent home, and the Rutherfurd governesses (the daughters of the house being "out," and off their
hands) took me on for French, German, and whatever else,
in those ancient days, composed a little girl's curriculum.
This drew the two households still closer, for though I did
not study with the little boys I seem to remember that I
went to Edgerston for my lessons. There was certainly a
continual coming and going through the private gate between the properties; but I recall a good deal more of our
games than of my lessons.

Most vivid is my memory of the picturesque archery club
meetings of which the grown daughters of the house, Margaret (afterward Mrs. Henry White) and her sister Louisa
were among the most brilliant performers. When the club
met we children were allowed to be present, and to circulate
among the grown-ups (usually all three of us astride of one
patient donkey); and a pretty sight the meeting was, with
parents and elders seated in a semicircle on the turf behind
the lovely archeresses in floating silks or muslins, with their
wide leghorn hats, and heavy veils flung back only at the
moment of aiming. These veils are associated with all the
summer festivities of my childhood. In that simple society
there was an almost pagan worship of physical beauty, and
the first question asked about any youthful newcomer on the
social scene was invariably: "Is she pretty?" or: "Is he handsome?"—for good looks were as much prized in young men
as in maidens. For the latter no grace was rated as high as "a
complexion". It is hard to picture nowadays the shell-like
transparence, the luminous red-and-white, of those young
cheeks untouched by paint or powder, in which the blood
came and went like the lights of an aurora. Beauty was un-

thinkable without "a complexion", and to defend that treasure against sun and wind, and the arch-enemy sea air, veils
as thick as curtains (some actually of woollen barège) were
habitually worn. It must have been very uncomfortable for
the wearers, who could hardly see or breathe; but even to
my childish eyes the effect was dazzling when the curtain
was drawn, and young beauty shone forth. My dear friend
Howard Sturgis used to laugh at the "heavily veiled" heroines who lingered on so late in Victorian fiction, and were
supposed to preserve their incognito until they threw back
their veils; but if he had known fashionable Newport in my
infancy he would have seen that the novelists' formula was
based on what was once a reality.

    Those archery meetings greatly heightened my infantile de-
sire to "tell a story", and the young gods and goddesses I
used to watch strolling across the Edgerston lawn were the
prototypes of my first novels. The spectacle was a charming
one to an imaginative child already caught in the toils of romance; no wonder I remember it better than my studies. Not
that I was not eager to learn; but my long and weary illness
had made my parents unduly anxious about my health, and
they forbade my being taught anything that required a mental
effort. Committing to memory, and preparing lessons in advance, were ruled out; it was thought that I read too much
(as if a born reader could!), and that my mind must be spared
all "strain". This was doubtless partly due to the solicitude of
parents for a late-born child, partly to a natural reaction
against the severities of their own early training. The sentimental theory that children must not be made to study anything that does not interest them was already in the air, and
reinforced by the fear of "fatiguing" my brain, it made my
parents turn my work into play. Being deprived of the irreplaceable grounding of Greek and Latin, I never learned to
concentrate except on subjects naturally interesting to me, and
developed a restless curiosity which prevented my fixing my
thoughts for long even on these. Of benefits I see only one.
To most of my contemporaries the enforced committing to
memory of famous poems must have forever robbed some of
the loveliest of their bloom; but this being forbidden me,
great poetry—English, French, German and Italian—came

to me fresh as the morning, with the dew on it, and has never lost that early glow.

The drawbacks were far greater than this advantage. But for the wisdom of Fräulein Bahlmann, my beloved German teacher, who saw which way my fancy turned, and fed it with all the wealth of German literature, from the Minnesingers to Heine—but for this, and the leave to range in my father's library, my mind would have starved at the age when the mental muscles are most in need of feeding.

I used to say that I had been taught only two things in my childhood: the modern languages and good manners. Now that I have lived to see both these branches of culture dispensed with, I perceive that there are worse systems of education. But in justice to my parents I ought to have named a third element in my training; a reverence for the English language as spoken according to the best usage. Usage, in my childhood, was as authoritative an element in speaking English as tradition was in social conduct. And it was because our little society still lived in the reflected light of a long-established culture that my parents, who were far from intellectual, who read little and studied not at all, nevertheless spoke their mother tongue with scrupulous perfection, and insisted that their children should do the same.

This reverence for the best tradition of spoken English—an easy idiomatic English, neither pedantic nor "literary"—was no doubt partly due to the fact that, in the old New York families of my parents' day, the children's teachers were often English. My mother and her sisters and brother had English tutors and governesses, and my own brothers were educated at home by an extremely cultivated English tutor. In my mother's family, more than one member of the generation preceding hers had been educated at Oxford or Cambridge, and one of my own brothers went to Cambridge.

Even so, however, I have never quite understood how two people so little preoccupied with letters as my father and mother had such sensitive ears for pure English. The example they set me was never forgotten; I still wince under my mother's ironic smile when I said that some visitor had stayed "quite a while", and her dry: "Where did you pick *that* up?" The wholesome derision of my grown-up brothers saved me from pomposity as my mother's smile guarded me against slovenliness; I still tingle with the sting of their ridicule when, excusing myself for having forgotten something I had been told to do, I said, with an assumption of grown-up dignity (*aetat* ten or eleven): "I didn't know that it was *imperative*."

Such elementary problems as (judging from the letters I receive from unknown readers) disturb present-day users of English in America—perplexity as to the distinction between "should" and "would", and the display of such half-educated pedantry as saying "gotten" and "you would better"—never embarrassed our speech. We spoke naturally, instinctively good English, but my parents always wanted it to be better, that is, easier, more flexible and idiomatic. This excessive respect for the language never led to priggishness, or precluded the enjoyment of racy innovations. Long words were always smiled away as pedantic, and any really expressive slang was welcomed with amusement—but used as slang, as it were between quotation marks, and not carelessly admitted into our speech. Luckily we all had a lively sense of humour, and now that my brothers were at home again the house rang with laughter. We all knew by heart "Alice in Wonderland", "The Hunting of the Snark", and whole pages of Lear's "Nonsense Book", and our sensitiveness to the quality of the English we spoke doubled our enjoyment of the incredible verbal gymnastics of those immortal works. Dear to us also, though in a lesser degree, were "Innocents Abroad", Bret Harte's parodies of novels, and, in their much later day, George Ade's "Arty", and the first volumes of that great philosopher, Mr. Dooley. I cannot remember a time when we did not, every one of us, revel in the humorous and expressive side of American slang; what my parents abhorred was not the picturesque use of new terms, if they were vivid and expressive, but the habitual slovenliness of those who picked up the slang of the year without having any idea that they were not speaking in the purest tradition. But above all abhorrent to ears piously attuned to all the inflexions and shades of meaning of our rich speech were such mean substitutes as "back of" for behind, "dirt" for earth (i.e., a "dirt road"), "any place" for anywhere, or slovenly phrases like "a great ways", soon, alas, to be followed by the still more inexcusable "a *barracks*", "a *woods*", and even "a

strata", "a phenomena", which, as I grew up, a new class of
the uneducated rich were rapidly introducing.

This feeling for good English was more than reverence, and
nearer: it was love. My parents' ears were wounded by an
unsuitable word as those of the musical are hurt by a false
note. My mother, herself so little of a reader, was exaggeratedly scrupulous about the books I read; not so much the
"grown-up" books as those written for children. I was never
allowed to read the popular American children's books of my
day because, as my mother said, the children spoke bad English *without the author's knowing it*. You could do what you
liked with the language if you did it consciously, and for a
given purpose—but if you went shuffling along, trailing it
after you like a rag in the dust, tramping over it, as Henry
James said, like the emigrant tramping over his kitchen oil-
cloth—that was unpardonable, there deterioration and corruption lurked. I remember it was only with reluctance, and
because "all the other children read them", that my mother
consented to my reading "Little Women" and "Little Men";
and my ears, trained to the fresh racy English of "Alice in
Wonderland," "The Water Babies" and "The Princess and the
Goblin", were exasperated by the laxities of the great Louisa.

Perhaps our love of good English may be partly explained
by the background of books which was an essential part of
the old New York household. In my grand-parents' day every
gentleman had what was called "a gentleman's library". In my
father's day, these libraries still existed, though they were often only a background; but in our case Macaulay, Prescott,
Motley, Sainte-Beuve, Augustin Thierry, Victor Hugo, the
Brontës, Mrs. Gaskell, Ruskin, Coleridge, had been added to
the French and English classics in their stately calf bindings.
Were these latter ever read? Not often, I imagine; but they
were there; they represented a standard; and perhaps some
mysterious emanation disengaged itself from them, obscurely
fighting for the protection of the languages they had illustrated.

A standard; the word perhaps gives me my clue. When I
said, in my resentful youth, that I had been taught only languages and manners, I did not know how closely, in my parents' minds, the two were related. Bringing-up in those days

was based on what was called "good breeding". One was polite, considerate of others, careful of the accepted formulas,
because such were the principles of the well-bred. And probably the regard of my parents for the niceties of speech was a
part of their breeding. They treated their language with the
same rather ceremonious courtesy as their friends. It would
have been "bad manners" to speak "bad" English, and "bad
manners" were the supreme offence.

This fastidiousness of speech came chiefly from my mother's side, and my father probably acquired it under her influence. His own people, though they spoke good English, had
disagreeable voices. I have noticed that wherever, in old New
York families, there was a strong admixture of Dutch blood,
the voices were flat, the diction was careless. My mother's
stock was English, without Dutch blood, and this may account for the greater sensitiveness of all her people to the
finer shades of English speech. In an article on Conrad which
appeared in the *Times Literary Supplement* after his death, the
author said (I quote from memory): "Conrad had worshipped
the English language all his life like a lover, but he had never
romped with her in the nursery"; and this it was my happy
fate to do.

To the modern child my little-girl life at Pencraig would
seem sadly tame and uneventful, for its chief distractions were
the simple ones of swimming and riding. My mother, like
most married women of her day, had long since given up
exercise, my father's only active pursuits were boating and
shooting, and there was no one to ride with me but the
coachman—nor was our end of the island a happy place for
equestrianism. I enjoyed scampering on my pony over the
hard dull roads; but it was better fun to swim in our own
cove, in the jolly company of brothers, cousins and young
neighbours. There were always two or three "cat-boats"
moored off our point, but I never shared the passion of my
father and brothers for sailing. To be a passenger was too
sedentary, and I felt no desire to sail the boat myself, being
too wrapt in dreams to burden my mind with so exact a science. Best of all I liked our weekly walks with Mr. Rutherfurd
over what we called the Rocks—the rough moorland country, at that time without roads or houses, extending from the

placid blue expanse of Narragansett bay to the gray rollers of the Atlantic. Every Sunday he used to collect the children of the few friends living near us, and take them, with his own, for a tramp across this rugged country to the sea.

Yet what I recall of those rambles is not so much the comradeship of the other children, or the wise and friendly talk of our guide, as my secret sensitiveness to the landscape—something in me quite incommunicable to others, that was tremblingly and inarticulately awake to every detail of wind-warped fern and wide-eyed briar rose, yet more profoundly alive to a unifying magic beneath the diversities of the visible scene—a power with which I was in deep and solitary communion whenever I was alone with nature. It was the same tremor that had stirred in me in the spring woods of Mamaroneck, when I heard the whisper of the arbutus and the starry choir of the dogwood; and it has never since been still.

2

The old New York to which I came back as a little girl meant to me chiefly my father's library. Now for the first time I had my fill of books. Out of doors, in the mean monotonous streets, without architecture, without great churches or palaces, or any visible memorials of an historic past, what could New York offer to a child whose eyes had been filled with shapes of immortal beauty and immemorial significance? One of the most depressing impressions of my childhood is my recollection of the intolerable ugliness of New York, of its untended streets and the narrow houses so lacking in external dignity, so crammed with smug and suffocating upholstery. How could I understand that people who had seen Rome and Seville, Paris and London, could come back to live contentedly between Washington Square and the Central Park? What I could not guess was that this little low-studded rectangular New York, cursed with its universal chocolate-coloured coating of the most hideous stone ever quarried, this cramped horizontal gridiron of a town without towers, porticoes, fountains or perspectives, hide-bound in its deadly uniformity of mean ugliness, would fifty years later be as much a vanished city as Atlantis or the lowest layer of Schliemann's Troy,

THE AUTHOR AT EIGHT

THE AUTHOR AT SIXTEEN

or that the social organization which that prosaic setting had slowly secreted would have been swept to oblivion with the rest. Nothing but the Atlantis-fate of old New York, the New York which had slowly but continuously developed from the early seventeenth century to my own childhood, makes that childhood worth recalling now.

Looking back at that little world, and remembering the "hoard of petty maxims" with which its elders preached down every sort of initiative, I have often wondered at such lassitude in the descendants of the men who first cleared a place for themselves in a new world, and then fought for the right to be masters there. What had become of the spirit of the pioneers and the revolutionaries? Perhaps the very violence of their effort had caused it to exhaust itself in the next generation, or the too great prosperity succeeding on almost unexampled hardships had produced, if not inertia, at least indifference in all matters except business or family affairs.

Even the acquiring of wealth had ceased to interest the little society into which I was born. In the case of some of its members, such as the Astors and Goelets, great fortunes, originating in a fabulous increase of New York real estate values, had been fostered by judicious investments and prudent administration; but of feverish money-making, in Wall Street or in railway, shipping or industrial enterprises, I heard nothing in my youth. Some of my father's friends may have been bankers, others have followed one of the liberal professions, usually the law; in fact almost all the young men I knew read law for a while after leaving college, though comparatively few practised it in after years. But for the most part my father's contemporaries, and those of my brothers also, were men of leisure—a term now almost as obsolete as the state it describes. It will probably seem unbelievable to present-day readers that only one of my own near relations, and not one of my husband's, was "in business". The group to which we belonged was composed of families to whom a middling prosperity had come, usually by the rapid rise in value of inherited real estate, and none of whom, apparently, aspired to be more than moderately well-off. I never in my early life came in contact with the gold-fever in any form, and when I hear that nowadays business life in New York is so strenuous that men and women never meet socially before the dinner hour, I remember the delightful week-day luncheons of my early married years, where the men were as numerous as the women, and where one of the first rules of conversation was the one early instilled in me by my mother: "Never talk about money, and think about it as little as possible."

The child of the well-to-do, hedged in by nurses and governesses, seldom knows much of its parents' activities. I have only the vaguest recollection of the way in which my father and mother spent their days. I know that my father was a director on the principal charitable boards of New York—the Blind Asylum and the Bloomingdale Insane Asylum among others; and that during Lent a ladies' "sewing class" met at our house to work with my mother for the poor. I also recall frequent drives with my mother, when the usual afternoon round of card-leaving was followed by a walk in the Central Park, and a hunt for violets and hepaticas in the secluded dells of the Ramble. In the evenings my parents went occasionally to the theatre, but never, as far as I remember, to a concert, or any kind of musical performance, until the Opera, then only sporadic, became an established entertainment, to which one went (as in eighteenth century Italy) chiefly if not solely for the pleasure of conversing with one's friends. Their most frequent distraction was dining out or dinner giving. Sometimes the dinners were stately and ceremonious (with engraved invitations issued three weeks in advance, soups, "thick" and "clear", and a Roman punch half way through the *menu*), but more often they were intimate and sociable, though always the occasion of much excellent food and old wine being admirably served, and discussed with suitable gravity.

My father had inherited from his family a serious tradition of good cooking, with a cellar of vintage clarets, and of Madeira which had rounded the Cape. The "Jones" Madeira (my father's) and the "Newbold" (my uncle's) enjoyed a particular celebrity even in that day of noted cellars. The following generation, interested only in champagne and claret, foolishly dispersed these precious stores. My brothers sold my father's cellar soon after his death; and after my marriage, dining in a *nouveau riche* house of which the master was unfamiliar with old New York cousinships, I had pressed on me, as a treat not likely to have come the way of one of my modest condition, a glass of "the famous Newbold Madeira".

My mother, if left to herself, would probably not have been much interested in the pleasures of the table. My father's Dutch blood accounted for his gastronomic enthusiasm; his mother, who was a Schermerhorn, was reputed to have the best cook in New York. But to know about good cooking was a part of every young wife's equipment, and my mother's favourite cookery books (Francatelli's and Mrs. Leslie's) are thickly interleaved with sheets of yellowing note paper, on which, in a script of ethereal elegance, she records the making of "Mrs. Joshua Jones's scalloped oysters with cream", "Aunt Fanny Gallatin's fried chicken", "William Edgar's punch", and the special recipes of our two famous negro cooks, Mary Johnson and Susan Minneman. These great artists stand out, brilliantly turbaned and ear-ringed, from a Snyders-like background of game, fish and vegetables transformed into a succession of succulent repasts by their indefatigable blue-nailed hands: Mary Johnson, a gaunt towering woman of a rich bronzy black, with huge golden hoops in her ears, and crisp African crinkles under vividly patterned kerchiefs; Susan Minneman, a small smiling mulatto, more quietly attired, but as great a cook as her predecessor.

Ah, what artists they were! How simple yet sure were their methods—the mere perfection of broiling, roasting and basting—and what an unexampled wealth of material, vegetable and animal, their genius had to draw upon! Who will ever again taste anything in the whole range of gastronomy to equal their corned beef, their boiled turkeys with stewed celery and oyster sauce, their fried chickens, broiled red-heads, corn fritters, stewed tomatoes, rice griddle cakes, strawberry short-cake and vanilla ices? I am now enumerating only our daily fare, that from which even my tender years did not exclude me; but when my parents "gave a dinner", and terrapin and canvas-back ducks, or (in their season) broiled Spanish mackerel, soft-shelled crabs with a mayonnaise of celery, and peach-fed Virginia hams cooked in champagne (I am no doubt confusing all the seasons in this allegoric evocation of their riches), lima-beans in cream, corn soufflés and salads of oyster-crabs, poured in varied succulence from Mary Johnson's lifted cornucopia—ah, then, the *gourmet* of that long-lost day, when cream was cream and butter butter and coffee coffee, and meat fresh every day, and game hung just for the proper number of hours, might lean back in his chair and murmur "Fate cannot harm me" over his cup of Moka and his glass of authentic Chartreuse.

I have lingered over these details because they formed a part—a most important and honourable part—of that ancient curriculum of house-keeping which, at least in Anglo-Saxon countries, was so soon to be swept aside by the "monstrous regiment" of the emancipated: young women taught by their elders to despise the kitchen and the linen room, and to substitute the acquiring of University degrees for the more complex art of civilized living. The movement began when I was young, and now that I am old, and have watched it and noted its results, I mourn more than ever the extinction of the household arts. Cold storage, deplorable as it is, has done far less harm to the home than the Higher Education.

And what of the guests who gathered at my father's table to enjoy the achievements of the Dark Ladies? I remember a mild blur of rosy and white-whiskered gentlemen, of ladies with bare sloping shoulders rising flower-like from voluminous skirts, peeped at from the stair-top while wraps were removed in the hall below. A great sense of leisure emanated from their kindly faces and voices. No motors waited to rush them on to ball or opera; balls were few and widely spaced, the opera just beginning; and "Opera night" would not have been chosen for one of my mother's big dinners. There being no haste, and a prodigious amount of good food to be disposed of, the guests sat long at table; and when my mother bowed slightly to the lady facing her on my father's right, and flounces and trains floated up the red velvet stair-carpet to the white-and-gold drawing-room with tufted purple satin arm-chairs, and voluminous purple satin curtains festooned with buttercup yellow fringe, the gentlemen settled down again to claret and Madeira, sent duly westward, and followed by coffee and Havana cigars.

My parents' guests ate well, and drank good wine with

discernment; but a more fastidious taste had shortened the enormous repasts and deep bumpers of colonial days, and in twenty minutes the whiskered gentlemen had joined the flounced ladies on the purple settees for another half hour of amiable chat, accompanied by the cup of tea which always rounded off the evening. How mild and leisurely it all seems in the glare of our new century! Small parochial concerns no doubt formed the staple of the talk. Art and music and literature were rather timorously avoided (unless Trollope's last novel were touched upon, or a discreet allusion made to Mr. William Astor's audacious acquisition of a Bouguereau Venus), and the topics chiefly dwelt on were personal: the thoughtful discussion of food, wine, horses ("high steppers" were beginning to be much sought after), the laying out and planting of country-seats, the selection of "specimen" copper beeches and fern-leaved maples for lawns just beginning to be shorn smooth by the new hand-mowers, and those plans of European travel which filled so large a space in the thought of old New Yorkers. From my earliest infancy I had always seen about me people who were either just arriving from "abroad" or just embarking on a European tour. The old New Yorker was in continual contact with the land of his fathers, and it was not until I went to Boston on my marriage that I found myself in a community of wealthy and sedentary people seemingly too lacking in intellectual curiosity to have any desire to see the world.

I have always been perplexed by the incuriosity of New England with regard to the rest of the world, for New Yorkers of my day were never so happy as when they were hurrying on board the ocean liner which was to carry them to new lands. Those whose society my parents frequented did not, perhaps, profit much by the artistic and intellectual advantages of European travel, and to social opportunities they were half-resentfully indifferent. It was thought vulgar and snobbish to try to make the acquaintance, in London, Paris or Rome, of people of the class corresponding to their own. The Americans who forced their way into good society in Europe were said to be those who were shut out from it at home; and the self-respecting American on his travels frequented only the little "colonies" of his compatriots already settled in the European capitals, and only their most irreproachable members! What these artless travellers chiefly enjoyed were scenery, ruins and historic sites; places about which some sentimental legend hung, and to which Scott, Byron, Hans Andersen, Bulwer, Washington Irving or Hawthorne gently led the timid sight-seer. Public ceremonials also, ecclesiastical or royal, were much appreciated, though of the latter only distant glimpses could be caught, since it would have been snobbish to ask, through one's Legation, for reserved seats or invitations. And as for the American women who had themselves presented at the English Court—well, one had only to see with whom they associated at home!

However, ruins, snow-mountains, lakes and water-falls— especially water-falls—were endlessly enjoyable; and in the great cities there were the shops! In them, as Henry James acutely noted in "The Pension Beaurepas", the American woman found inexhaustible consolation for the loneliness and inconveniences of life in foreign lands. But, lest I seem to lay undue stress on the limitations of my compatriots, it must be remembered that, even in more sophisticated societies, cultivated sight-seeing was hardly known in those days. One need only glance through the "Travels" of the early nineteenth century to see how little, before Ruskin, the average well-educated tourist of any country was prepared to observe and enjoy. The intellectual few, at the end of the eighteenth century, had been taught by Arthur Young to travel with an eye to agriculture and geology; and Goethe, in Sicily, struck Syracuse and Girgenti from his itinerary, and took the monotonous and exhausting route across the middle of the island, in order to see with his own eyes why it had been called the granary of Rome. Meanwhile the simpler majority collected scraps of marble from the Forum, pressed maidenhair fern from the temple of Vesta at Tivoli, or daisies from the grave of Shelley, and bought edelweiss gummed on card-board from the guides of Chamonix, and copies of Guido's "Aurora" and Caravaggio's "Gamesters" from the Roman picture-dealers.

At that very time a handsome blue-eyed young man with a scarred mouth was driving across the continent in his parents' travelling carriage, and looking with wondering eyes at the

Giottos of the Arena Chapel and the Cimabues of Assisi; at that time a young architect, poor and unknown, was toiling through the by-ways of Castile, Galicia and Andalusia in jolting *diligences*, or over stony mule-tracks, and recording in a series of exquisite drawings the unknown wonders of Spanish architecture; and Browning was dreaming of "The Ring and the Book"—and Shelley had long since written "The Cenci". But to the average well-to-do traveller Hawthorne's "Marble Faun", Bulwer's "Last Days of Pompeii" and Washington Irving's "Alhambra" were still the last word on Spain and Italy.

3

I have wandered far from my father's library. Though it had the leading share in my growth I have let myself be drawn from it by one scene after another of my parents' life in New York or on their travels. But the library calls me back, and I pause on its threshold, averting my eyes from the monstrous oak mantel supported on the heads of vizored knights, and looking past them at the rows of handsome bindings and familiar names. The library probably did not contain more than seven or eight hundred volumes. My father was a younger son, and my mother had a brother to whom most of the books on her side of the family went. (I remember on my uncle's shelves an unexpurgated Hogarth, splendidly bound in eighteenth century crushed Levant, with which my little cousins and I quite innocently and unharmedly beguiled ourselves.) The library to which I had access contained therefore few inherited books; I remember chiefly, in the warm shabby calf of the period, complete editions of Swift, Sterne, Defoe, the "Spectator", Shakespeare, Milton, the Percy Reliques—and Hannah More! Most of the other books must have been acquired by my father. Though few they were well-chosen, and the fact that their number was so limited probably helped to fix their contents in my memory. At any rate, long before the passing of years and a succession of deaths brought them back to me, I could at any moment visualize the books contained in those low oak bookcases. My mother, perplexed by the discovery that she had produced an omnivorous reader, and not knowing how to direct my reading, had perhaps expected the governess to do it for her. Being an indolent woman, she finally turned the difficulty by reviving a rule of her own schoolroom days, and decreeing that I should never read a novel without asking her permission. I was a painfully conscientious child and, conforming literally to this decree, I submitted to her every work of fiction which attracted my fancy. In order to save further trouble she almost always refused to let me read it—a fact hardly to be wondered at, since her own mother had forbidden her to read any of Scott's novels, except "Waverley", till after she was married! At all events, of the many prohibitions imposed on me—most of which, as I look back, I see little reason to regret—there is none for which I am more grateful than this, though it extended its rigours even to one of the works of Charlotte M. Yonge! By denying me the opportunity of wasting my time over ephemeral rubbish my mother threw me back on the great classics, and thereby helped to give my mind a temper which my too-easy studies could not have produced. I was forbidden to read Whyte Melville, Rhoda Broughton, "The Duchess", and all the lesser novelists of the day; but before me stretched the wide expanse of the classics, English, French and German, and into that sea of wonders I plunged at will. Nowadays a reader might see only the *lacunae* of the little library in which my mind was formed; but, small as it was, it included most of the essentials. The principal historians were Plutarch, Macaulay, Prescott, Parkman, Froude, Carlyle, Lamartine, Thiers; the diaries and letters included Evelyn, Pepys, White of Selborne, Cowper, Mme de Sévigné, Fanny Burney, Moore, the Journals of the Misses Berry; the "poetical works" (in addition to several anthologies, such as Knight's "Half Hours with the Best Authors" and Lamb's precious selections from the Elizabethan dramatists) were those of Homer (in Pope's and Lord Derby's versions), Longfellow's Dante, Milton, Herbert, Pope, Cowper, Gray, Thomson, Byron, Moore, Scott, Burns, Wordsworth, Campbell, Coleridge, Shelley (I wonder how or why?), Longfellow, Mrs. Hemans and Mrs. Browning—though not as yet the writer described in one of the anthologies of the period as "the husband of Elizabeth Barrett, and himself no mean poet". He was to come later, as a present from my sister-in-law, and to be one of the great Awakeners of my childhood.

Among the French poets were Corneille, Racine, Lafontaine and Victor Hugo, though, oddly enough, of Lamartine the poet there was not a page, nor yet of Chénier, Vigny or Musset. Among French prose classics there were, of course, Sainte-Beuve's "Lundis", bracing fare for a young mind, Sévigné the divinely loitering, Augustin Thierry and Philarète Chasles. Art history and criticism were represented by Lacroix's big volumes, so richly and exquisitely illustrated, on art, architecture and costume in the Middle Ages, by Schliemann's "Ilias" and "Troja", by Gwilt's Encyclopaedia of Architecture, by Kugler, Mrs. Jameson, P. G. Hamerton, and the Ruskin of "Modern Painters" and the "Seven Lamps", together with a volume of "Selections" (appropriately bound in purple cloth) of all his purplest patches; to which my father, for my benefit, added "Stones of Venice" and "Walks in Florence" when we returned to Europe and the too-short days of our joint sightseeing began.

In philosophy, I recall little but Victor Cousin and Coleridge ("The Friend" and "Aids to Reflection"); among essayists, besides Addison, there were Lamb and Macaulay; in the way of travel, I remember chiefly Arctic explorations. As for fiction, after the eighteenth century classics, Miss Burney and Scott of course led the list; but, mysteriously enough, Richardson was lacking, save for an abridged version of "Clarissa Harlowe" (and a masterly performance that abridgement was, as I remember it). No doubt Richardson, with Smollett and Fielding, fell to my uncle's share, and were too much out-of-date to be thought worth replacing. Thus, except for Scott, there was a great gap until one came to Washington Irving, that charming hybrid on whom my parents' thoughts could dwell at ease, because, in spite of the disturbing fact that he "wrote", he was a gentleman, and a friend of the family. For my parents and their group, though they held literature in great esteem, stood in nervous dread of those who produced it. Washington Irving, Fitz-Greene Halleck and William Dana were the only representatives of the disquieting art who were deemed uncontaminated by it; though Longfellow, they admitted, if a popular poet, was nevertheless a gentleman. As for Herman Melville, a cousin of the Van Rensselaers, and qualified by birth to figure in the best society, he was doubtless excluded from it by his deplorable Bohemianism, for I never heard his name mentioned, or saw one of his books. Banished probably for the same reasons were Poe, that drunken and demoralized Baltimorean, and the brilliant wastrel Fitz James O'Brien, who was still further debased by "writing for the newspapers". But worse still perhaps in my parents' eyes was the case of such unhappy persons as Joseph Drake, author of "The Culprit Fay", balanced between "fame and infamy" as not quite of the best society, and writing not quite the best poetry. I cannot hope to render the tone in which my mother pronounced the names of such unfortunates, or, on the other hand, that of Mrs. Beecher Stowe, who was so "common" yet so successful. On the whole, my mother doubtless thought, it would be simpler if people one might be exposed to meeting would refrain from meddling with literature.

Considering the stacks of novels which she, my aunts and my grandmother annually devoured, their attitude seems singularly ungrateful; but it was probably prompted by the sort of diffidence which, thank heaven, no psycho-analyst had yet arisen to call a "complex". In the eyes of our provincial society authorship was still regarded as something between a black art and a form of manual labour. My father and mother and their friends were only one generation away from Sir Walter Scott, who thought it necessary to drape his literary identity in countless clumsy subterfuges, and almost contemporary with the Brontës, who shrank in agony from being suspected of successful novel-writing. But I am sure the chief element in their reluctance to encounter the literary was an awe-struck dread of the intellectual effort that might be required of them. They were genuinely modest and shy in the presence of any one who wrote or painted. To sing was still a drawing-room accomplishment, and I had two warbling cousins who had studied with the great opera singers; but authors and painters lived in a world unknown and incalculable. In addition to its mental atmosphere, its political and moral ideas might be contaminating, and there was a Kilmeny-touch about those who adventured into it and came back.

Meanwhile, though living authors were so remote, the dead were my most living companions. I was a healthy little girl who loved riding, swimming and romping; yet no children of my own age, and none even among the nearest of my grown-ups, were as close to me as the great voices that spoke to me from books. Whenever I try to recall my childhood it is in my father's library that it comes to life. I am squatting again on the thick Turkey rug, pulling open one after another the glass doors of the low bookcases, and dragging out book after book in a secret ecstasy of communion. I say "secret", for I cannot remember ever speaking to any one of these enraptured sessions. The child knows instinctively when it will be understood, and from the first I kept my adventures with books to myself. But perhaps it was not only the "misunderstood" element, so common in meditative infancy, that kept me from talking of my discoveries. There was in me a secret retreat where I wished no one to intrude, or at least no one whom I had yet encountered. Words and cadences haunted it like song-birds in a magic wood, and I wanted to be able to steal away and listen when they called. When I was about fifteen or sixteen I tried to write an essay on English verse rhythms. I never got beyond the opening paragraph, but that came straight out of my secret wood. It ran: "No one who cannot feel the enchantment of 'Yet once more, O ye laurels, and once more', without knowing even the next line, or having any idea whatever of the context of the poem, has begun to understand the beauty of English poetry." For the moment that was enough of ecstasy; but I wanted to be always free to steal away to it.

It was obvious that a little girl with such cravings, and to whom the Old Testament, the Apocalypse and the Elizabethan dramatists were open, could not long pine for Whyte Melville or even Rhoda Broughton. Ah, the long music-drunken hours on that library floor, with Isaiah and the Song of Solomon and the Book of Esther, and "Modern Painters", and Augustin Thierry's Merovingians, and Knight's "Half Hours", and that rich mine of music, Dana's "Household Book of Poetry"! Presently kind friends began to endow me with a little library of my own, and I was reading "Faust" and "Wilhelm Meister", "Philip Van Arteveld", "Men and

Women" and "Dramatis Personæ" in the intervals between "The Broken Heart" and "The Duchess of Malfy", "Phèdre" and "Andromaque". And there was one supreme day when, my mother having despairingly asked our old literary adviser, Mr. North at Scribner's, "what she could give the child for her birthday", I woke to find beside my bed Buxton Forman's great editions of Keats and Shelley! Then the gates of the realms of gold swung wide, and from that day to this I don't believe I was ever again, in my inmost self, wholly lonely or unhappy.

By the time I was seventeen, though I had not read every book in my father's library, I had looked into them all. Those I devoured first were the poets and the few literary critics, foremost of course Sainte-Beuve. Ruskin fed me with visions of the Italy for which I had never ceased to pine, and Freeman's delightful "Subject and Neighbour Lands of Venice", Mrs. Jameson's amiable volumes, and Kugler's "Handbook of Italian Painting", gave a firmer outline to these visions. But the books which made the strongest impression on me—doubtless because they reached a part of my mind that no one had thought of arousing—were two shabby volumes unearthed among my brother's college text-books: an abridgement of Sir William Hamilton's "History of Philosophy" and a totally forgotten work called "Coppée's Elements of Logic". This first introduction to the technique of thinking developed the bony structure about which my vague gelatinous musings could cling and take shape; and Darwin and Pascal, Hamilton and Coppée ranked foremost among my Awakeners.

In a day when youthful innocence was rated so high my mother may be thought to have chosen a singular way of preserving mine when she deprived me of the Victorian novel but made me free of the Old Testament and the Elizabethans. Her plan was certainly not premeditated; but had it been, she could not have shown more insight. Those great pages, those high themes, purged my imagination; and I cannot recall ever trying to puzzle out allusions which in tamer garb might have roused my curiosity. Once, at the house of a little girl friend, rummaging with her through a neglected collection of books which her parents had acquired with the property, and never

since looked at, we came upon a small volume which seemed
to burst into fiery bloom in our hands.

Forth, ballad, and take roses in both arms,
  Even till the top rose touch thee in the throat
Where the least thornprick harms;
  And girdled in thy golden singing-coat,
Come thou before my lady and say this:
  Borgia, thy gold hair's colour burns in me,
Thy mouth makes beat my blood in feverish rhymes;
  Therefore so many as these roses be,
    Kiss me so many times.

But this, like all the rest, merely enriched the complex music of my strange inner world. I do not mean to defend the
sheltered education against the system which expounds phys-
iological mysteries in the nursery; I am not sure which is best.
But I am sure that great literature does not excite premature
curiosities in normally constituted children; and I can give a
comic proof of the fact, for though "The White Devil",
"Faust" and "Poems and Ballads" were among my early story-
books, all I knew about adultery (against which we were
warned every week in church) was that those who "committed" it were penalized by having to pay higher fares in travelling: a conclusion arrived at by my once seeing on a ferry-
boat the sign: "Adults 50 cents; children 25 cents"!

This ferment of reading revived my story-telling fever; but
now I wanted to write and not to improvise. My first attempt
(at the age of eleven) was a novel, which began: " 'Oh, how
do you do, Mrs. Brown?' said Mrs. Tompkins. 'If only I had
known you were going to call I should have tidied up the
drawing-room'." Timorously I submitted this to my mother,
and never shall I forget the sudden drop of my creative frenzy
when she returned it with the icy comment: "Drawing-rooms
are always tidy."

This was so crushing to a would-be novelist of manners
that it shook me rudely out of my dream of writing fiction,
and I took to poetry instead. It was not thought necessary to
feed my literary ambitions with foolscap, and for lack of paper
I was driven to begging for the wrappings of the parcels
delivered at the house. After a while these were regarded as

belonging to me, and I always kept a stack in my room. It never occurred to me to fold and cut the big brown sheets, and I used to spread them on the floor and travel over them on my hands and knees, building up long parallel columns of blank verse headed: "Scene: A Venetian palace", or "Dramatis Personæ" (which I never knew how to pronounce).

My dear governess, seeing my perplexity over the structure of English verse, gave me a work called "Quackenbos's Rhetoric", which warned one not to speak of the oyster as a "succulent bivalve", and pointed out that even Shakespeare nodded when he made Hamlet "take arms against a sea of troubles". Mr. Quackenbos disposed of the delicate problems of English metric by squeezing them firmly into the classic categories, so that Milton was supposed to have written in "iambic pentameters", and all superfluous syllables were got rid of (as in the eighteenth century) by elisions and apostrophes. Always respectful of the rules of the game, I tried to cabin my Muse within these bounds, and once when, in a moment of unheard-of audacity, I sent a poem to a newspaper (I think "The World"), I wrote to the editor apologizing for the fact that my metre was "irregular", but adding firmly that, though I was only a little girl, I wished this irregularity to be respected, as it was "intentional". The editor published the poem, and wrote back politely that he had no objection to irregular metres himself; and thereafter I breathed more freely. My poetic experiments, however, were destined to meet with the same discouragement as my fiction. Having vainly attempted a tragedy in five acts I turned my mind to short lyrics, which I poured out with a lamentable facility. My brother showed some of these to one of his friends, an amiable and cultivated Bostonian named Allen Thorndike Rice, who afterward became the owner and editor of the "North American Review". Allen Rice very kindly sent the poems to the aged Longfellow, to whom his mother's family were related; and on the bard's recommendation some of my babblings appeared in the "Atlantic Monthly". Happily this experiment was not repeated; and any undue pride I might have felt in it was speedily dashed by my young patron's remarking to me one day: "You know, writing lyrics won't lead you anywhere. What you want to do is to write an epic. All the great poets have written epics. Homer . . . Milton . . . Byron. Why don't you try your hand at something like 'Don Juan'?" This was a hard saying to a dreamy girl of fifteen, and I shrank back into my secret retreat, convinced that I was unfitted to be either a poet or a novelist. I did, indeed, attempt another novel, and carried this one to its close; but it was destined for the private enjoyment of a girl friend, and was never exposed to the garish light of print. It exists to this day, beautifully written out in a thick copy-book, with a title page inscribed "Fast and Loose", and an epigraph from Owen Meredith's "Lucile":

> Let Woman beware
> How she plays fast and loose with human despair,
> And the storm in Man's heart.

Title and epigraph were terrifyingly exemplified in the tale, but it closed on a note of mournful resignation, with the words: "And every year when April comes the violets bloom again on Georgie's grave."

After this I withdrew to secret communion with the Muse. I continued to cover vast expanses of wrapping paper with prose and verse, but the dream of a literary career, momentarily shadowed forth by one miraculous adventure, soon faded into unreality. How could I ever have supposed I could be an author? I had never even seen one in the flesh!

IV

Unreluctant Feet

IN ONE of the most famous poems of my first literary protector the Maiden is supposed to arrive with reluctant feet "where the brook and river meet". I cannot say that my own feet were thus hampered. I was contented enough with swimming and riding, with my dogs, and my reading and dreaming, but I longed to travel and see new places, and, short of that, was by no means averse to seeing new people, and especially to being regarded as "grown up".

I had not long to wait, for when I was seventeen my parents decided that I spent too much time in reading, and that I was to come out a year before the accepted age. The New York mothers of that day usually gave a series of "coming-out" entertainments for *débutante* daughters, leading off with a huge tea and an expensive ball. My mother thought this absurd. She said her daughter could meet all the people she need know without being advertised by a general entertainment; and as my family kept open house, and as the younger of my two brothers was very popular in society, it was easy enough to launch me in this informal way. I was therefore put into a low-necked bodice of pale green brocade, above a white muslin skirt ruffled with rows and rows of Valenciennes, my hair was piled up on top of my head, some friend of the family sent me a large bouquet of lilies-of-the-valley, and thus adorned I was taken by my parents to a ball at Mrs. Morton's, in Fifth Avenue. Houses with ball-rooms were still few in New York: almost the only ones were those of the Astors, the Mortons, the Belmonts and my cousins the Schermerhorns. As a rule, hostesses who wished to give a dance hired the ball-room at Delmonico's restaurant; but my mother would never have consented to my making my first appearance in a public room, so to Mrs. Morton's we went. To me the evening was a long cold agony of shyness. All my brother's friends asked me to dance, but I was too much frightened to accept, and cowered beside my mother in speechless misery, unable even to exchange a word with the friendly young men whom I regarded as elder brothers when they lunched and dined at our house.

This shyness, though it long troubled me in general company, soon vanished when I was with my friends. New York society was not at that time divided into water-tight compartments by differences of age. The pleasantest houses were those of a group of young married women who all through the season gave a succession of small dinners, informal Sunday lunches and after-theatre suppers. They were all friendly and welcoming to any young girl "who could talk", and the great ambition of the *débutante* was to be invited to their houses and treated on an equal footing by them, and by the "older men" whose attentions were thought so much more flattering than those of callow youths just out of college. This luck befell me, thanks chiefly to my brother Harry's popularity, and invitations poured in after my first sad evening. Like all agreeable societies, ours was small, and the people composing it met almost every day, and always sought each other out in any larger company. Some of the hostesses had drawing-rooms big enough for informal dances, and to be invited to these was the privilege of a half-dozen of the younger girls. A season of opera at the old Academy of Music was now an established event of the winter, and on Mondays and Fridays we met each other there; Wednesday being, for some obscure tribal reason, the night on which boxes were sent to dull relations and visitors from out of town, while the inner circle disported itself elsewhere. Our society was, in short, a little "set" with its private catch-words, observances and amusements, and its indifference to anything outside of its charmed circle; and no really entertaining social group has ever been anything else. The ages of the people composing it ranged from eighteen to fifty; but all were young in spirit, mostly good-looking, and full of gaiety and humour. The talk was never intellectual and seldom brilliant, but it was always easy and sometimes witty, and a charming informality had replaced the ceremonious dulness of my parents' day. I doubt if New York society was ever simpler, gayer, or more pleasantly sophisticated, than it was then.

I enjoyed myself thoroughly that winter, and still more so the following summer, when Pencraig was full of merry young people, and the new game of lawn tennis, played on our lawn by young gentlemen in tail coats and young ladies in tight whale-boned dresses, began to supersede the hitherto fashionable archery. Every room in our house was always full in summer, and I remember jolly bathing parties from the floating boat-landing at the foot of the lawn, mackerel-fishing, races in rival "cat-boats", and an occasional excursion up the bay, or out to sea when the weather was calm enough, on one of the pretty white steam-yachts which were beginning to be the favourite toys of the rich.

On one of these yachting-parties I made an acquaintance which some unlucky chance kept me from renewing. A thin young man with intelligent eyes was brought up and introduced as Cecil Spring-Rice, then, I think, a secretary at the British Legation in Washington. Spring-Rice was already—or became soon afterward—the friend of several of my most intimate friends, and the affectionate nickname of "Springy" was as familiar to me as that of one of my own intimates. But, to my loss, we were never to meet again; and I record our single encounter only because his delightful talk so illuminated an otherwise dull afternoon that I have never forgotten the meeting. It also left me in possession of two nearly perfect stories—Spring-Rice was a great story-teller—one of which I never heard from any one else, while the other is usually repeated in a far less effective form. Here they are.

A young physician who was also a student of chemistry, and a dabbler in strange experiments, employed a little orphan boy as assistant. One day he ordered the boy to watch over, and stir without stopping, a certain chemical mixture which was to serve for a very delicate experiment. At the appointed time the chemist came back, and found the mixture successfully blent—but beside it lay the little boy, dead of the poisonous fumes.

The young man, who was very fond of his assistant, was horrified at his death, and in despair at having involuntarily caused it. He could not understand why the fumes should have proved fatal, and wishing to find out, in the interest of science, he performed an autopsy, and discovered that the boy's heart had been transformed into a mysterious jewel, the like of which he had never seen before. The young man had a mistress whom he adored, and full of grief, yet excited by this strange discovery, he brought her the tragic jewel, which was very beautiful, and told her how it had been produced. The lady examined it, and agreed that it was beautiful. "But," she added carelessly, "you must have noticed that I wear no ornaments but earrings. If you want me to wear this jewel, you must get me another one just like it."

The other story is that of a young man who went to spend a week-end at a big country-house where he had never been before. His train was late, and when he came down the party had already gone in to dinner. He was shown into the dining-room, and his hostess asked him to take the only remaining vacant seat. On one side of him sat a very dull and disagreeable man, on the other one of the most captivating young women he had ever met. Naturally it was to her that he devoted all his attention, and so fascinated was he that he did not even stop to wonder who she was—he simply felt that he and she must always have been friends.

They wandered delightedly from one subject to another, and toward the end of dinner the conversation touched on the supernatural. "Do you believe in ghosts?" the young lady asked. "No," said he with a laugh; "do you?" "I am one," she replied—and suddenly the seat she had occupied was empty. After dinner his hostess apologized for putting him next to an empty chair. "We expected my dear friend, Mrs. ——; but just as you arrived we had a telegram announcing her sudden death—and there was not even time to take away her seat."

The regular afternoon diversion at Newport was a drive. Every day all the elderly ladies, leaning back in victoria or barouche, or the new-fangled *vis-à-vis*, a four-seated carriage with a rumble for the footman, drove down the whole length of Bellevue Avenue, where the most fashionable villas then stood, and around the newly laid-out "Ocean Drive", which skirted for several miles the wild rocky region between Narragansett bay and the Atlantic. For this drive it was customary to dress as elegantly as for a race-meeting at Auteuil or Ascot. A brocaded or satin-striped dress, powerfully whale-boned, a small flower-trimmed bonnet tied with a large tulle bow under the chin, a dotted tulle veil and a fringed silk or velvet sunshade, sometimes with a jointed handle of elaborately carved ivory, composed what was thought a suitable toilet for this daily circuit between wilderness and waves.

If these occupations seem to us insufficient to fill a day, it must be remembered that the onerous and endless business of "calling" took up every spare hour. I can hardly picture a lady of my mother's generation without her card-case in her hand. Calling was then a formidable affair, since many ladies had weekly "days" from which there was no possible escape, and others cultivated an exasperating habit of being at home on the very afternoon when, according to every reasonable calculation, one might have expected them to be at Polo, or at Mrs. Belmont's archery party, or abroad on their own sempiternal card-leaving. By the time I grew up the younger married women had emancipated themselves, and simply drove from house to house depositing their cards, duly turned down in the upper left-hand corner, to the indignation of stay-at-home hostesses, many of whom made their servants keep a list of the callers who "did not ask", so that these might be struck off the next season's invitation list—a punishment borne by the young and gay with perfect equanimity, as it was only the dull hostesses who inflicted it.

In my mother's day, however, there were no palliatives to calling. The footman had to ask if Mrs. So-and-so was at home, and if she was, there ensued a half hour's visit in a cool shaded drawing-room, or on a wide verandah overlooking the sea. As this had to be repeated after every lunch, dinner or ball, and even the young men were not exempt (though they usually got a mother or sister to leave their cards for them), it may be imagined how much those daughters of Danaus, the dowagers leaning back in their victorias, needed the refreshment of a "turn" around the Ocean Drive in the intervals of their unending labour.

Still more striking than the dowagers' parade was the sight of the young ladies, married or single, who, when they were guests at a Newport villa, expected to be taken for an afternoon drive by the master of the house or one of his sons. The vehicles of the fashionable young men were either dog-carts (drawn by a pair driven tandem) or a high four-wheeled conveyance called a T-cart, which, if I am not mistaken, was drawn by one big stepper; while the older men drove handsome phaetons, with a showy pair, and an impressive groom with folded arms in the rumble.

Carriages, horses, harnesses and grooms were all of the latest and most irreproachable cut, and Bellevue Avenue was a pretty scene when the double line of glittering vehicles and showy horse-flesh paraded between green lawns and scarlet geranium-borders. The dress of the young ladies perched on the precarious height of a dog-cart or phaeton was no less elegant than that of the dowagers; and I remember, one hot summer afternoon, seeing one of the damsels who were staying at Pencraig appear for the drive arrayed in a heavy white silk dress with a broad black satin stripe, and a huge hat wreathed with crimson roses and draped with a green veil against the sun. It is only fair to add that my brother, who helped her to the giddy summit of the T-cart, and climbed to her side while a tiny groom in snowy breeches clung to the bridle of the impatient chestnut—my brother, like all the young gentlemen of his day, was arrayed in a frock-coat, a tall hat and pearl-gray trousers. What wonder that an eager-eyed little girl, watching these stately comings and goings from the verandah of Pencraig, still thought that old Mr. Bedlow's Olympian gods and goddesses must have looked like her brother Harry and his lovely companion when they started off for a turn along some supernal Ocean Drive?

2

Such delights faded before what the next autumn brought. During the long eight years since our return from Europe, how often had I not said to my father: "Papa, when are we going back?" and how sadly had I not listened to his answer: "My dear, whenever we can afford it." Now, unhappily, his health made it necessary that he should not spend another winter in New York; but the doctors seemed to think that in a warmer climate he might live for years, and, dearly as I loved him, the impending joys of travel were much more vivid to me than any fears for his health.

To my last day I shall never forget how the prospect thrilled me. What were society and dancing and tennis compared to the rapture of seeing again all that, for eight years, my eyes had pined for? A happier pilgrim has never set foot in the November fogs of London; for what I had dimly loved as a child I was now to look on again with grown-up eyes (as I then thought them!).

My governess came with us, and I can still retravel with her every step of our first journey through the National Gallery. It was on that day, the first after our arrival in London, that I discovered my life-long friend, Franciabigio's "Knight of Malta", with his poignant motto, *Tar ublia chi bien eima*; that day that I fitted the "Santa Conversazione" of Bellini with the lines which Milton must have meant for it:

> There entertain him all the saints above,
> In solemn troops and sweet societies—

that day that I was first caught in the airy web of Pinturic-chio's weaving Penelope, and swept upward in the serenely circling heavens of Botticini's Assumption. But it was not only among pictures that I felt the stir of old associations. The streets, the houses, the people of the countries I had lived in as a child, met me with the faces of old friends, and every voice was music. I longed, of course, to travel, above all to go to Italy; but on my father's account we had to start almost immediately for the Riviera. My parents had meant to spend the winter at Nice, but I could not bear the thought of being pent up in a city when all the country-side was full of roses and jasmine. I was allowed to go with my governess to Cannes, then a small colony of villas in leafy gardens, and there we found a quiet hotel with terraces of flowers, where I persuaded my parents to establish themselves. My mother was cheered by discovering in near-by villas two old friends from Boston, the Countess de Sartiges and the Countess de Bañue-los. In both families there were girls a year or two older than myself; and though my mother would not go out herself she was persuaded to put me under the care of the Countess de Bañuelos, who took me everywhere with her own daughters. The small and intimate society we frequented was made up of French and English families, mostly connected by old friend-ship, and some by blood. Our amusements were simple and

MY FATHER, GEORGE FREDERIC JONES
(PAINTED BY JOHN W. EHNINGER)

informal, as social pleasures were in those days, and picnics on the shore, or among the red rocks and pine forests of the Esterel, lawn tennis parties and small dinners, united the same young people day after day, under the guardianship of a pleasant group of their elders. The wooded background of Cannes still descended almost to the shore, and my amusements were diversified by long country walks with my governess, and delightful rides through the cork and pine-woods with Tonita de Bañuelos. I was received with extreme friendliness into this little circle, which, allowing for the difference in race and traditions, was so like the one I had left in New York: made up of kindly and rather frivolous people, to whom my secret dreams would have been as unintelligible as to my friends at home. I was very happy among them, however, and twenty-five years later, when my husband and I went to Paris to spend a winter, those who remained of the old group welcomed me as affectionately as though weeks and not years had intervened since our young days in Cannes.

The following summer we spent at Homburg, then a fashionable but quiet little watering-place with gardens full of roses, where my mother had been sent for the cure. My father's health, to my young eyes at least, seemed neither to improve nor to grow worse; I became accustomed to his patient inactivity, and probably thought of him as old rather than ill. That autumn we went to Venice and Florence, and it must have been then that he gave me "Stones of Venice" and "Walks in Florence", and gently lent himself to my whim of following step by step Ruskin's arbitrary itineraries. But probably even this mild sight-seeing was beyond his strength, for I do not recall many walks with him; and by the time we returned to Cannes he had grown distinctly worse, and failed slowly during the winter. He died there in the early spring, suddenly stricken by paralysis; and I am still haunted by the look in his dear blue eyes, which had followed me so tenderly for nineteen years, and now tried to convey the goodbye messages he could not speak. Twice in my life I have been at the death-bed of some one I dearly loved, who has vainly tried to say a last word to me; and I doubt if life holds a subtler anguish.

*   *   *

My mother and I went home to Pencraig. In those days the rules of family mourning were severe, and I went out very little; but in the autumn my mother hired a house in Washington Square, and subsequently bought one in West Twenty-Fifth Street, which she altered and added to. My old friends welcomed me on our return, and there followed two gay but uneventful New York winters. I had never ceased to be a great reader, but had almost forgotten my literary dreams. I could not believe that a girl like myself could ever write anything worth reading, and my friends would certainly have agreed with me. No one in our set had any intellectual interests, though most of the men were better read than the average young American of today. Many of the group, however, were quicker and more amusing than I was, and though I was popular, and enjoyed myself in their company, I never dreamed that I was in any way their superior. Indeed, being much less pretty than many of the girls, and less quick at the up-take than the young men, I might have suffered from an inferiority complex had such ailments been known. But my powers of enjoyment have always been many-sided, and the mere fact of being alive and young and active was so exhilarating that I could seldom spare the time to listen to my inner voices. Yet when they made themselves heard again they had become irresistible.

V

Friendships and Travels

I

AT THE END of my second winter in New York I was married; and thenceforth my thirst for travel was to be gratified. My husband, whose family came from Virginia, but whose father had married in Boston and settled there, was an intimate friend of my brother's, and had long been an annual visitor at Pencraig. He was thirteen years older than myself, but the difference in age was lessened by his natural youthfulness, his good humour and gaiety, and the fact that he shared my love of animals and out-door life, and was soon to catch my travel-fever. It was not that, either then or later, I was restless, or eager for change for its own sake. My first care was to create a home of my own; and a few months after our marriage my husband and I moved into a little cottage in the grounds of Pencraig, and re-arranged it in accordance with our tastes. I was never very happy at Newport. The climate did not agree with me, and I did not care for watering-place mundanities, and always longed for the real country; but the place and the life suited my husband, and in any case we could not have afforded to buy a property of our own. So we settled down at Pencraig Cottage, and for a few years always lived there from June till February; and I was too busy with my little house and garden ever to find the time long. But every year we went abroad in February for four months of travel; and it was then that I really felt alive. Vernon Lee, John Addington Symonds and "John Inglesant" had been added to my library of Italian travel, and "Euphorion" and "The Italian Renaissance" had given me joys I should be ungrateful not to record. Another book, of a totally different kind, figured among my more recent Awakeners; and that was James Fergusson's "History of Architecture", at that time one of the most stimulating books that could fall into a young student's hands. A generation nourished on learned monographs, monumental histories, and works of reference covering every period of art from Babylonian prehistory to the present day, would find it hard to believe how few books of the sort, especially on architecture and sculpture, were available in my youth. Fergusson's "History of Architecture" was an amazing innovation in its day. It shed on my misty haunting sense of the beauty of old buildings the light of historical and technical precision, and cleared and extended my horizon as Hamilton's "History of Philosophy", and my little old handbook of logic, had done in another way.

Hitherto my best beloved companions had been books, and to leave one out of this record seems like omitting the name of a human friend. But to enumerate even a fraction would turn my tale into a library catalogue, for I never stopped reading, and having new adventures in the realms of gold; and meanwhile the fate which had so long denied me any other intellectual companionship suddenly relented, and gave me a friend.

Books are alive enough to an imagination which knows how to animate them; but living companions are more living still, as I was to discover when I passed for the first time from the somewhat cramping companionship of the kindly set I had grown up in, and the cool solitude of my studies, into the warm glow of a cultivated intelligence. The man to whom I owe this was Egerton Winthrop, an old friend of my family's. He was a direct descendant of Governor Stuyvesant of New York, and of John Winthrop, first Colonial Governor of Massachusetts; but he belonged to the branch of the latter family long established in New York. Having married early, and been soon left a widower, he had lived for many years in Paris; but his children were growing up, the time had come for his sons to enter Harvard, and the year of my marriage he returned to New York, where he had built himself a charming house. Besides being an ardent bibliophile he was a discriminating collector of works of art, especially of the eighteenth century, and his house was the first in New York in which an educated taste had replaced stuffy upholstery and rubbishy "ornaments" with objects of real beauty in a simply designed setting. He delighted to receive his friends, and was one of the most popular hosts in New York. But the more I ponder over our long friendship the more I despair of portraying him; for never, I believe, have an intelligence so distinguished and a character so admirable been combined with interests for the most part so trivial. In spite of his worldly tastes he was subject, with all but his intimates, to fits of shyness which made him appear either stiff or affected; and I always said that when he came to see me nothing was safe in my small drawing-room, for if he found other visitors there he invariably stumbled across a foot-stool, or made straight for any fragile object in his path. Yet this man, so self-conscious and ill at ease with insignificant people, was the most stimulating of talkers in a congenial group. But though he was nervous and preoccupied in the company of the commonplace, and at his best only with people who shared his deeper interests, yet he attached far more importance to his merely mundane relations, and took far more trouble about the finish and perfection of his dinners than about the choice of his guests. The truth is, he was an intensely social being, and to such the New York of the day offered few intellectual resources. As in most provincial societies, the scholars, artists and men of letters shut themselves obstinately away from the people they despised as "fashionable", and the latter did not know how to make the necessary advances to those who lived outside of their little conventions. It is only in sophisticated societies that the intellectual recognize the uses of the frivolous, and that the frivolous know how to make their houses attractive to their betters.

Though, like Egerton Winthrop, I had always lived among the worldly, I had never been much impressed by them, and he was always pleading with me to fill the part he thought I ought to play in New York, where my husband and I now had the smallest of small houses; but I suspect that he was secretly envious of an indifference to the world of fashion which he was never able to acquire. Though he was nearly twice my age, in this one respect I was his senior, and I think he knew it. But the man who was my friend was so different from the diner-out and ball-giver that I was aware of the latter's existence only when he took me to task for my disregard of society. When we were alone I saw only the lover of books and pictures, the accomplished linguist and eager reader, whose ever-youthful curiosities first taught my mind to ana-

lyze and my eyes to see. It was too late for me to acquire the
mental discipline I had missed in the schoolroom, but my
new friend directed and systematized my reading, and filled
some of the worst gaps in my education. Through him I first
came to know the great French novelists and the French historians and literary critics of the day; but his chief gift was to
introduce me to the wonder-world of nineteenth century science. He it was who gave me Wallace's "Darwin and Darwin-
ism", and "The Origin of Species", and made known to me
Huxley, Herbert Spencer, Romanes, Haeckel, Westermarck,
and the various popular exponents of the great evolutionary
movement. But it is idle to prolong the list, and hopeless to
convey to a younger generation the first overwhelming sense
of cosmic vastnesses which such "magic casements" let into
our little geocentric universe.

My friendship with Egerton Winthrop was perhaps the
happiest I was to know, since it was the least troubled by the
perturbations which mar most intimacies. From our first
meeting to the last—a period of over thirty years—he was
the most perfect of friends. As the years passed, and the difference in our ages made itself felt, the coming of younger
friends into my life caused us to be less often together; but,
though I knew he suffered from the change, it never lessened
his friendly devotion, and to the day of his death we wrote
often and fully to each other.

I have dwelt on our long comradeship not only because I
want to record my gratitude to so dear a friend, but because,
alike in his faults and his qualities, Egerton Winthrop was
typical of the American gentleman of his day. The type has
vanished with the conditions that produced it; but in my
young days New York could show a group of men, such as
my old friend Bayard Cutting, Robert Minturn, John Cadwalader, George Rives, Stephen Olin and their like, who,
without having Egerton Winthrop's range of interests, combined a cultivated taste with marked social gifts. Their weakness was that, save in a few cases, they made so little use of
their abilities. A few were distinguished lawyers or bankers,
with busy professional careers, but too many, like Egerton
Winthrop, lived in dilettantish leisure. The best class of New
Yorkers had shaken off the strange apathy following on the

Civil War, and begun to develop a municipal conscience, and all the men I have mentioned were active in administering the new museums, libraries and charities of New York; but the idea that gentlemen could stoop to meddle with politics had hardly begun to make its way, and none of my friends rendered the public services that a more enlightened social system would have exacted of them. In every society there is the room, and the need, for a cultivated leisure class; but from the first the spirit of our institutions has caused us to waste this class instead of using it.

In our little group Egerton Winthrop's was by far the most sensitive intelligence, and it transformed my life to find my vague enthusiasms canalized, my roving curiosities supplied with the food they needed, and a glow of participation reflected back over all my years of solitary reading. But he helped me also in other ways; for though so easily entangled in worldly trifles, he was full of wisdom in serious matters. Sternly exacting toward himself, he was humorously indulgent toward others. Throughout our friendship I found him, in difficult moments, the surest of counsellors; and even now that I am old, and he has been so many years dead, it still happens to me, when faced by a difficulty, to ask myself: "What would Egerton have done?"

2

My husband, though a Bostonian by birth, was by blood a Virginian, and while he was greatly attached to his Boston friends, he did not care for the place, and had no desire to live there. Like most Bostonians he had travelled very little; but he soon caught my love of the road, though he too cared for travelling only as an occasional change from our quiet months at home.

After several seasons of happy wandering in Italy we both felt the longing to go farther, and one day I happened to say to our old friend James Van Alen: "I would give everything I own to make a cruise in the Mediterranean!"

I was not prepared for his prompt reply: "You needn't do that if you'll let me charter a yacht, and come with me."

At first we took the suggestion as a joke; but when we

found that it was made in earnest it began to fascinate our imagination. However, though we were fond of James Van Alen, and grateful for his invitation, we were not disposed to make so long a voyage as his guests, or that of any other friend. In so momentous an adventure we preferred to have our say about the itinerary, the choice of places to be seen (since, alas, it was necessary to choose), and the general arrangements for the trip. We asked Van Alen to calculate exactly how much a four months' cruise would cost, learned that to pay half of the expenses would consume our whole income for the year—and promptly decided to do so!

Loud was the outcry in our respective families. My brothers, who were my trustees under my father's will, asked, not unnaturally, what we proposed to live on for the rest of the year—and there was no answer! But the most indignant protests came from my husband's family. In Boston married couples, after a brief honeymoon abroad, were expected to divide the rest of their lives between Boston in winter and its suburbs, or the neighbouring sea-shore, in summer; and it was told of an old Mr. Russell that on driving away from the church on his wedding day he remarked to his bride, perhaps rather wistfully: "And now, my dear, there is nothing before us but Mount Auburn" (the family cemetery). For the Bostonians have never been backward in satirizing their own peculiarities.

But, of all mad schemes, our families protested, why a cruise in the Mediterranean? Who had ever before heard of such an idea? Though there were many American yacht owners with swift and beautiful craft, they cruised mainly in home waters, or if they crossed the Atlantic, did so not for sight-seeing but to try their luck in international racing. Such a voyage as we planned was almost unheard of, and in any case only a fad for the wealthy. I was more impressed than my husband by these arguments. I had been taught to treat my brothers, who were so much older than myself, with filial deference, and it seemed a sacrilege to go against their judgment and my mother's. We could not raise a loan, since my property was in trust, and my husband had only a small allowance from his father. In those days it was thought dishonourable to take financial risks one might be unable to meet; and how were we to live for the rest of the year, since neither of us could have earned a penny? But my husband said: "Do you really want to go?" and when I nodded, he rejoined: "All right. Come along, then." And we went.

Those four months in the Ægean were the greatest step forward in my making. I shall not enlarge here on the wonders of the cruise, or expatiate on the inexhaustible memories it left with me; but I must add, in justification of our families' astonishment at our adventure, that we met hardly any pleasure craft (and, except in the big ports, no passenger steamers), and that at Astypalæa, one of the islands we visited, the parish priest, the mayor and all the inhabitants came out on the Venetian ramparts in solemn procession to receive us, explaining that it was a great day for the island, as no steamer had ever before touched there, and many of the islanders had never seen one in the distance!

I must also say a word of our travelling companion, who not only took on himself all the trouble of chartering and provisioning our delightful little yacht, the "Vanadis", but, although he did not altogether share my archæological ardours, bore with them with unvarying good-nature, allowing me the necessary time, between Girgenti and Sunium, to see all but the most inaccessible Greek temples, and to explore nearly every one of the then little visited Ægean islands.

James Van Alen had travelled all over the Peloponnesus in his youth, and to my imagination he was a living link with the old trackless dangerous Greece of Byron's day, for he had been invited to join the ill-fated party of Englishmen who were seized by brigands near Athens early in the 'seventies, and of whom only one (Lord Muncaster) escaped alive. Van Alen had accepted the invitation, but at the last moment an attack of malaria had prevented his going. Those perilous days were over; but at the time of our cruise their memory was still preserved in the current edition of Murray's Guide, and when one day, being driven by a gale into the gulf of Maïna (formerly one of the most dangerous regions in Greece) we consulted that invaluable work to see if the village frowning on the cliff above were worth visiting, we were rewarded by the following information: "The Maïnotes are a brave, generous and hospitable race, but much given to acts of treachery, piracy, wreckage, robbery and murder." The day was hot, the path was steep—and we decided to stay on the yacht.

My husband and I were so lost in enjoyment that neither of us gave a thought to the unsolved financial problem awaiting us at the end of the cruise. Only twice in my life have I been able to put all practical cares out of my mind for months, and each time it has been on a voyage in the Ægean. We reached Athens only toward the end of the cruise, and among the letters which awaited us was one telling me that a little dog we had left in America was dead, and another announcing the demise of a cousin of my father's, an old gentleman I had never seen, and hardly knew by name. This excellent man had lived all his life in one room in the old New York Hotel, and gone without a fire in winter to save money; and this enabled him to divide among his many cousins a fortune enormously increased by his privations— proving (as my sister-in-law remarked) that what we had always regarded as miserliness was only a wise economy! My share was more than enough to pay for our taste of heaven; but my husband complained that in my grief for the dog I forgot to be grateful to my cousin. It was in fact some time before I grasped my good luck, and when my gratitude woke it took, as often happens, the form of doing exactly what my benefactor would most have reproved. He had been a miser, and he nearly turned me into a spendthrift! At any rate he taught me that never again, when I had the chance to do something difficult and wonderful, must I hesitate to trust to my star—the only condition being that the risk should not be run for anything not really worth it.

Acting on this conviction we threw our families into fresh alarms by deciding, a year or two later, to charter a sailing vessel, head for the West Indies, pick up the trades for the Canaries, and thence, by way of the Azores, make for Portugal and Spain. The schooner was chosen, the charter drawn up— and what a glorious adventure it would have been! But, alas, it was not to come off, for there was cholera at the Canaries or the Azores, and we were warned that quarantine difficulties would waylay us everywhere. Our families drew a breath of relief—but we never ceased to regret our lost adventure.

Our Mediterranean cruise took place in 1888; but, owing to my not having kept a diary, I find it impossible to disentangle the chronology of our travels in Italy. We used to go there every spring, and each year we explored some new and relatively unfamiliar region, choosing in preference places which offered examples of seventeenth and eighteenth century architecture. A trifling incident had given this turn to my studies. Not long after our marriage, my husband asked his old friend Julian Story, who had a studio in Paris, to paint my portrait. I was sitting to him one day—restless, and desperately bored, for I saw the picture was going to be a failure—when my eye lit on an arm-chair, the most artlessly simple and graceful arm-chair I had ever seen. I knew a little about French eighteenth century furniture, and saw at once that this chair was different: less skilful in execution, yet freer and more individual in movement. I asked where it came from, and Story answered: "Oh, eighteenth century Venetian. It's a pity no one knows or cares anything about eighteenth century Italian furniture or architecture. In fact everybody behaves—the historians as well as the art critics—as if Italy had ceased to exist at the end of the Renaissance."

The words struck my imagination, for though I had read Vernon Lee's enchanting "Eighteenth Century in Italy," and soon afterward was to discover Gurlitt's excellent "Barockstil in Italien", I knew it was true in the main that, to the traveller of average reading, the eighteenth century seemed at that time to belong as exclusively to France as the Cinque Cento to Italy. The new turn thus given to my curiosity made us devote our subsequent holidays to the study of eighteenth century painting and architecture in Italy. In these pleasant explorations Egerton Winthrop was our constant companion, and among comrades of the road I have known few as responsive to beauty, as patient over disappointments and discomforts. Among many good wanderings I remember especially our drive one spring from Florence to Urbino and the Adriatic, by way of San Marino, San Leo, Loreto, Ancona, Pesaro and Rimini. Nowadays it is a quick motor-jaunt over smooth roads leading to comfortable inns, but forty years ago it was a toilsome expedition, in a heavy carriage drawn by tired horses, a journey full of the enchantments of discovery but also of fatigue and discomfort, since the well-organized travel of coaching days was over, and the inns off the direct railway routes had been almost abandoned.

I was not always patient under such discomfort. Once, in a now defunct hotel at Parma, where the conditions below stairs were so unappetizing that we persuaded the waiter to serve our dinner in Egerton's bedroom, I may have grumbled a little more than usual, for I remember his saying with gentle irony: "My dear, no doubt your standards of cleanliness are higher than this hotel-keeper's; but I daresay the Princess of Wales [Queen Alexandra] would not consider your toilet appointments good enough for her; and the angels may think even Her Royal Highness insufficiently clean." Another day, when my irresistible tendency to improve and organize led me, in some forlorn French hotel, to remark on the slovenly incompetence of the waiter, my old friend observed: "If the poor man were as intelligent as he would have to be to please you, he wouldn't be a waiter in this inn, but President of the French Republic."

Sometimes the Paul Bourgets were our companions on these wanderings. Bourget, soon after his marriage (about 1893, I think) had been commissioned by Gordon Bennett to write for the New York "Herald" the series of articles on the United States subsequently collected in the volume called "Outremer". The preparation for this book sent him and his young wife to America, and a friend in Paris gave them a letter for me. Bourget had been specially instructed to do his "fashionable watering place" article at Newport, and as soon as he and his wife arrived they came to lunch, and that very day our long friendship began, a friendship as close with the brilliant and stimulating husband as with his quiet and exquisite companion. I shall never forget Minnie Bourget as I first saw her, with her little aquiline nose, her grave remote gray eyes and sensitive mouth, in the delicate oval of a small face crowned by heavy braids of brown hair. I used to call her the "Tanagra Madonna", so curiously did that little head combine the gravity of a mediaeval Virgin with the miniature elegance of a Greek figurine. Everything about her was shy, elusive and somehow personal to herself. I have never known any one like her, and can hardly imagine any one more unlike myself; yet from our very first meeting a deep-down under-standing established itself between us.

When my husband and I first joined the Bourgets for an Italian tour, Bourget had already published his "Sensations d'Italie", and was still much interested in the art of mediaeval and Renaissance Italy; but perhaps his wife was more sensi-tive to the minor magic of scenes and places, the little un-noted exquisitenesses that waylaid one at every turn of the paths we followed. Minnie Bourget was a being so rare, so full of delicate and secret vibrations, yet so convinced that she had been put on earth only to be her husband's attentive shadow, that I never knew by what happy accident I pene-trated what might be called her voluntary invisibility, and found myself made free of her real self. But so it was; and from our first acquaintance to the day when her last tragic illness shut her finally into the seclusion she had always sought, I never knocked at that gate in vain. We disagreed on many subjects, and she could never tolerate any discussion of a point which her convictions made sacred; but we agreed so deeply on essentials that the disagreements did not matter. I am not sure what it was that united us—perhaps poetry, perhaps pictures, and old storied scenes, and yet something deeper and more exquisite, of which the visible beauty we loved was merely a fugitive token. But I find no words deli-cate and imponderable enough to describe the Psyche-like tremor of those folded but never quiet wings of hers; and now that she is dead, and the wings are shut, there is a part of me which is dead also.

One enchanting journey, which I afterward sketched in a book called "Italian Backgrounds", carried us to the hills of northern Italy. I had always maintained that in the choice of an itinerary one should be guided by the sound of names, and that in doing so I had never been disappointed. Just then I was under the spell of the phrase "the Bergamasque Alps" (perhaps because of a recent encounter with Verlaine), and I persuaded the Bourgets to make an excursion through this mysterious region. It led us, of course, away from the rail-ways, so we hired (for the last time, probably) an old-time travelling carriage, and my husband went ahead as *éclaireur* on his bicycle, engaging rooms and ordering dinner for the rest of the party. The excursion was full of delight, and it was only after it was over, and I returned to the study of my maps, that I found we had only skirted the magic region of "Masques et Bergamasques", instead of travelling through it. But its magic had overflowed on us, and though we agreed to make the real trip another year, we never dared, lest it should turn out to be less perfect.

All this was soon to result in the writing of my first novel, "The Valley of Decision", and a few years later in my "Italian Villas and Their Gardens", and "Italian Backgrounds". But before reaching this stage of my literary life I must turn back and take it up at its odd and unexpected beginning.

3

Thanks to my late cousin's testamentary discernment my husband and I had been able to buy a home of our own at Newport. It was an ugly wooden house with half an acre of rock and illimitable miles of Atlantic Ocean; for, as its name, "Land's End", denoted, it stood on the edge of Rhode Island's easternmost cliffs, and our windows looked straight across to the west coast of Ireland. I disliked the relaxing and depressing climate, and the vapid watering-place amusements in which the days were wasted; but I loved Land's End, with its windows framing the endlessly changing moods of the misty Atlantic, and the night-long sound of the surges against the cliffs.

The outside of the house was incurably ugly, but we helped it to a certain dignity by laying out a circular court with high hedges and trellis-work niches (the whole promptly done away with by our successors!); and within doors there were interesting possibilities. My husband and I talked them over with a clever young Boston architect, Ogden Codman, and we asked him to alter and decorate the house—a somewhat new departure, since the architects of that day looked down on house-decoration as a branch of dress-making, and left the field to the upholsterers, who crammed every room with curtains, lambrequins, jardinières of artificial plants, wobbly velvet-covered tables littered with silver gewgaws, and festoons of lace on mantelpieces and dressing-tables.

Codman shared my dislike of these sumptuary excesses, and thought as I did that interior decoration should be simple and architectural; and finding that we had the same views we drifted, I hardly know how, toward the notion of putting them into a book.

We went into every detail of our argument: the idea, novel at the time though now self-evident, that the interior of a house is as much a part of its organic structure as the outside, and that its treatment ought, in the same measure, to be based on right proportion, balance of door and window spacing, and simple unconfused lines. We developed this argument logically, and I think forcibly, and then sat down to write the book—only to discover that neither of us knew how to write! This was excusable in an architect, whose business it was to build in bricks, not words, but deeply discouraging to a young woman who had in her desk a large collection of blank verse dramas and manuscript fiction. Happily I had the saving sense to know that I didn't know—that I literally could not write out in simple and precise English the ideas which seemed so clear in my mind.

The year before my marriage I had made friends with a young man named Walter Berry, the son of an old friend of my family's (and indeed a distant cousin). We had seen a great deal of each other for a few weeks, and the encounter had given me a fleeting hint of what the communion of kindred intelligences might be. But chance separated us, and we were not to meet again, but for intermittent glimpses, till he happened to come and stay with us at Land's End the very summer that Codman and I were struggling with our book. Walter Berry was born with an exceptionally sensitive literary instinct, but also with a critical sense so far outweighing his creative gift that he had early renounced the idea of writing. But though he was already a hard-working young lawyer, with a promising future at the bar, the service of letters was still his joy in his moments of leisure. I remember shyly asking him to look at my lumpy pages; and I remember his first shout of laughter (for he never flattered or pretended), and then his saying good-naturedly: "Come, let's see what can be done", and settling down beside me to try to model the lump into a book.

In a few weeks the modelling was done, and in those weeks, as I afterward discovered, I had been taught whatever I know about the writing of clear concise English. The book was re-read by my friend, and found fit for publication; and we proceeded to seek a publisher.

Neither Codman nor I knew any of these formidable people, but my sister-in-law had her entry at Macmillan's, and she offered to submit the manuscript to them. It was promptly rejected, with the brief comment that the architect to whom they had shown it (simply to oblige my sister-in-law) had received it with cries of derision. Nobody was likely to buy an amateur work on house-decoration by two totally unknown writers, and they advised her not to continue her friendly efforts. This was a blow. To whom should we turn?

The previous year a small literary adventure of my own had introduced me to "Scribner's Magazine". I had suddenly taken to writing poetry again, and one day I decided to send three of my poems to three of the leading magazines of the day: "Scribner's", "Harper's" and the "Century". I can remember only one of these poems, the longest, called "The Last Giustiniani", which I chanced to send to "Scribner's". I did not know how authors communicated with editors, but I copied out the verses in my fairest hand, and enclosed each in an envelope with my visiting card! A week or two elapsed, and then I received the three answers, telling me that all three poems had been accepted. We had a little house in Madison Avenue that winter (it was our first trial of New York), and as long as I live I shall never forget my sensations when I opened the first of the three letters, and learned that I was to appear in print. I can still see the narrow hall, the letter-box out of which I fished the letters, and the flight of stairs up and down which I ran, senselessly and incessantly, in the attempt to give my excitement some muscular outlet!

The letter accepting "The Last Giustiniani" was written by Edward Burlingame, editor of "Scribner's Magazine", who became one of my most helpful guides in the world of letters. He not only accepted my verses, but (oh, rapture!) wanted to know what else I had written; and this encouraged me to go to see him, and laid the foundation of a friendship which lasted till his death. It was naturally to him that I turned after

Macmillan's rejection of "The Decoration of Houses"; but I did so with little hope, since I knew he was not connected with the publishing department of the firm, and in any case there was little chance of the Scribners' being interested in a book of so technical a character, and one already rejected by the Macmillans. However, I took the manuscript to Mr. Burlingame, he passed it on to the publishing department, where it fell into the hands of another dear friend-to-be, William Brownell—and after some hesitation it was accepted, chiefly, I suspect because Mr. Burlingame and Mr. Brownell liked my poetry.

The Scribners brought out a very small and tentative edition, produced with great typographical care, probably thinking that the book was more likely to succeed as a gift book among my personal friends than as a practical manual. But the first edition was sold out at once; Batsford immediately asked for the book for England; and from that day to this it has gone on from edition to edition, and still, after nearly forty years, brings in an annual tribute to its astonished authors!

Our success was not unmerited. Codman had been at great pains to cite suitable instances in support of his principles, and revolutionary as these were, we found that people of taste were only too eager to follow any guidance that would not only free them from the suffocating upholsterer, but tell them how to replace him. It became the fashion to use our volume as a touchstone of taste, and I was often taxed by my friends with not applying to the arrangement of my own rooms the rigorous rules laid down in "The Decoration of Houses". The popularity of the work may be judged by the fact that, a good many years later, after I had published "The House of Mirth" and several other novels, an enthusiastic lady one day sailed up to me to say: "I'm so glad to meet you at last, because Ogden Codman is such an old friend of mine that I've read every one of the wonderful novels he and you have written together!"

VI

Life and Letters

I

THE DOING of "The Decoration of Houses" amused me very much, but can hardly be regarded as a part of my literary career. That began with the publishing, in "Scribner's Magazine", of two or three short stories. The first was called "Mrs. Manstey's View", the second "The Fulness of Life". Both attracted attention, and gave me the pleasant flutter incidental to first seeing one's self in print; but they brought me no nearer to other workers in the same field. I continued to live my old life, for my husband was as fond of society as ever, and I knew of no other existence, except in our annual escapes to Italy. I had as yet no real personality of my own, and was not to acquire one till my first volume of short stories was published—and that was not until 1899. This volume, called "The Greater Inclination", contained none of my earliest tales, all of which I had rejected as not worth reprinting. I had gone on working hard at the *nouvelle* form, and the stories making up my first volume were chosen after protracted consultations with Walter Berry, the friend who had shown me how to put "The Decoration of Houses" into shape. From that day until his death, twenty-seven years later, through all his busy professional life, he followed each of my literary steps with the same patient interest, and I doubt if a beginner in the art ever had a sterner yet more stimulating guide.

And now the incredible had happened! Out of the Pelion and Ossa of slowly accumulating manuscripts, plays, novels and dramas, had blossomed a little volume of stories—stories which editors had wanted for their magazines, and a publisher now actually wanted for a volume! I had been astonished enough to see the stories in print, but the idea that they might in the course of time be collected in a book never occurred to me till Mr. Brownell transmitted the Scribner proposal.

I had written short stories that were thought worthy of

868

preservation! Was it the same insignificant *I* that I had always known? Any one walking along the streets might go into any bookshop, and say: "Please give me Edith Wharton's book", and the clerk, without bursting into incredulous laughter, would produce it, and be paid for it, and the purchaser would walk home with it and read it, and talk of it, and pass it on to other people to read! The whole business seemed too unreal to be anything but a practical joke played on me by some occult humourist; and my friends could not have been more astonished and incredulous than I was. I opened the first notices of the book with trembling hands and a suffocated heart. What I had done was actually thought important enough to be not only printed but reviewed! With a sense of mingled guilt and self-satisfaction I glanced at one article after another. They were unbelievably kind, but for the most part their praise only humbled me; and often I found it bewildering. But at length I came on a notice which suddenly stiffened my limp spine. "When Mrs. Wharton," the condescending critic wrote, "has learned the rudiments of her art, she will know that a short story should always begin with dialogue."

"Always"? I rubbed my eyes. Here was a professional critic who seemed to think that works of art should be produced by rule of thumb, that there could be a fixed formula for the design of every short story ever written or to be written! Even I already knew that this was ridiculous. I had never consciously formulated the principles of my craft, but during my years of experimenting I had pondered on them deeply, and this egregious commentary did me the immense service of giving my ponderings an axiomatic form. Every short story, I now saw, like every other work of art, contains within itself the germ of its own particular form and dimensions, and *ab ovo* is the artist's only rule. In an instant I was free forever from the bogey of the omniscient reviewer, and though I was always interested in what was said of my books, and sometimes (though rarely) helped by the comments of the professional critics, never did they influence me against my judgment, or deflect me by a hair's-breadth from what I knew to be "the real right" way.

In this I was much helped by Walter Berry. No critic was ever severer, but none had more respect for the artist's liberty. He taught me never to be satisfied with my own work, but never to let my inward conviction as to the rightness of anything I had done be affected by outside opinion. I remember, after writing the first chapters of "The Valley of Decision", which I had begun in a burst of lyric rapture and didn't know how to go on with, confessing to him my difficulty and my discouragement. He looked through what I had written, handed it back, and said simply: "Don't worry about how you're to go on. Just write down everything you feel like telling." The advice freed me once for all from the incubus of an artificially pre-designed plan, and sent me rushing ahead with my tale, letting each incident create the next, and keeping in sight only the novelist's essential sign-post; the inner significance of the "case" selected. Yet when the novel was done, I remember how meticulously he studied it from the point of view of language, marking down faulty syntax and false metaphors, smiling away over-emphasis and unnecessary repetitions, helping me patiently through the beginner's verbal perplexities, yet never laying hands on what he considered sacred: the *soul* of the novel, which is (or should be) the writer's own soul.

I suppose there is one friend in the life of each of us who seems not a separate person, however dear and beloved, but an expansion, an interpretation, of one's self, the very meaning of one's soul. Such a friend I found in Walter Berry, and though the chances of life then separated us, and later his successful professional career, first in Washington, afterward as one of the Judges of the International Tribunal in Cairo, for long years put frequent intervals between our meetings, yet whenever we did meet the same deep understanding drew us together. That understanding lasted as long as my friend lived; and no words can say, because such things are unsayable, how the influence of his thought, his character, his deepest personality, were interwoven with mine.

He alone not only encouraged me to write, as others had already done, but had the patience and the intelligence to teach me how. Others praised, some flattered—he alone took the trouble to analyze and criticize. The instinct to write had always been there; it was he who drew it forth, shaped it and set it free. From my first volume of short stories to "Twilight

Sleep", the novel I published just before his death, nothing in
my work escaped him, no detail was too trifling to be examined and discussed, gently ridiculed or quietly praised. He
never overlooked a defect, and there were times when his silence had the weight of a page of censure; yet I never remember to have been disheartened by it, for he had so deep a
respect for the artist's liberty that he never sought to restrict
my imagination or to check its flight. His invariable rule,
though he prized above all things concision and austerity, was
to encourage me to write as my own instinct impelled me;
and it was only after the story or the book was done that we
set out together on the "adjective hunts" from which we often
brought back such heavy bags.

Once I had found my footing and had my material in hand,
his criticisms became increasingly searching. With each book
he exacted a higher standard in economy of expression, in
purity of language, in the avoidance of the hackneyed and the
precious. Sometimes I was not able to show him a novel
before publication, and in that case he confined himself to
friendly generalities, often helping me to avoid, in my next
book, the faults he gently hinted at. When he could follow
my work in manuscript he left no detail unnoticed; but
though I sometimes caught a faint smile over a situation
which he did not see from my angle, or a point of view he did
not share, his only care was to help me do better whatever I
had set out to do.

But perhaps our long, our ever-recurring talks about the
masters of fiction, helped me even more than his advice. I had
never known any one so instantly and unerringly moved by all
that was finest in literature. His praise of great work was like
a trumpet-call. I never heard it without discovering new beauties in the work he praised; he was one of those commenta-
tors who unseal one's eyes. I remember his once saying to me,
when I was very young: "It is easy to see superficial resem-
blances between things. It takes a first-rate mind to perceive
the differences underneath." Nothing has ever sharpened my
own critical sense as much as that.

The comrade that he was to me in my work, he was also in
the enjoyment of all things beautiful, stirring and exalting. He
was tireless in his appreciation of beauty—beauty of architec-

ture, of painting, of landscape. Whatever I saw with him, in
the many lands we wandered through, I saw with a keenness
doubled by his, and studied afterward with an ardour with
which his always kept pace. To the end, through prolonged
ill-health and the bitter consciousness of failing powers, his
soul still struggled out to beauty; and I remember that, summoned to him at the first attack of his fatal illness, I found
him lying speechless, motionless and barely able to look up,
but yet able to whisper, as he recognized me: "Bamberg—in
the hall". After a moment's bewilderment I guessed that he
must be speaking of a new book—there was not a day when
they did not pour in to his admirably chosen and ever-
growing library; and going out into the hall I found a newly
published quarto on the sculptures of Bamberg cathedral,
which he had received only the day before. I brought it to
him, and as I sat beside him with the open volume he whispered one by one the names of the most beautiful statues, and
signed to me to hold the book up so that he could see them.

During his arduous professional life we had met only at
long intervals; but when ill-health obliged him to resign from
the International Tribunal of Cairo he came to live in Paris,
and after that we were more often together. During all his
working years, frequently interrupted by months of serious
illness, he had managed to find time to read my manuscripts
and send me long letters of criticism and encouragement; but
from the time when he came to Paris, where I was then living,
he was able to follow my work more closely, and his reading
of each chapter as it was written, and the listening to his comments as he read, gave fresh life to my writing.

Another joy was the discovering of the newest and most
worth while books, and the talking them over together. He
was a good linguist, and one of the most insatiable readers I
have ever known; in science, history, biography, travels, archæological explorations, and the newest books on art and
letters, little of real value escaped him. But best of all (when
he could be induced to do it) was his reading of poetry; a
reading wholly different from Henry James's, a thing apart,
and unforgettable, more reticent, less emphatic, yet equally
sensitive and moving.

I cannot picture what the life of the spirit would have been

to me without him. He found me when my mind and soul
were hungry and thirsty, and he fed them till our last hour
together. It is such comradeships, made of seeing and dreaming, and thinking and laughing together, that make one feel
that for those who have shared them there can be no parting.

But I must return to "The Greater Inclination", and to my
discovery of that soul of mine which the publication of my
first volume called to life. At last I had groped my way
through to my vocation, and thereafter I never questioned
that story-telling was my job, though I doubted whether I
should be able to cross the chasm which separated the *nouvelle*
from the novel. Meanwhile I felt like some homeless waif
who, after trying for years to take out naturalization papers,
and being rejected by every country, has finally acquired a
nationality. The Land of Letters was henceforth to be my
country, and I gloried in my new citizenship.

I remember once saying that I was a failure in Boston
(where we used to go to stay with my husband's family) because they thought I was too fashionable to be intelligent,
and a failure in New York because they were afraid I was too
intelligent to be fashionable. An amusing instance of this
point of view happened not long after my first book had
come out—at a moment, that is, when I probably seemed to
my New York friends at once more formidable and less
"smart" than before I had appeared in print. I met a girl
friend, herself the epitome of all "smartness", who told me
that one of New York's most fashionable hostesses had, rather
apologetically, invited her to dine "with a few people who
write". "It will be rather Bohemian, I'm afraid," the inviter
added, "but they say one ought to see something of those
people. I hope you won't mind coming to help me out?" My
young friend, who knew something of Paris and London society, was delighted at an innovation which promised to take
us out of the New York rut, and so was I, for it chanced that I
had been invited for the same evening. "Oh, what fun! Who
do you suppose they'll be?" I exulted, racking my brains to
guess how our hostess, who was my cousin, could have made
the acquaintance of the very people I was still vainly longing
to know. The evening came, we assembled in the ornate
drawing-room (one of those from which "The Decoration of

Houses" had not cleared a single gewgaw!) and I discovered
that the Bohemians were my old friend Eliot Gregory, most
popular of New York diners-out (but who had the audacity to
write an occasional article in a review or daily paper), George
Smalley, the New York correspondent of the London
"Times"—and myself! To emphasize our common peculiarity
we were seated together, slightly below the salt, while up and
down the rest of the long table the tiara-ed heads and bulging
white waistcoats of the most accredited millionaires glittered
between gold plate and orchids. Such was Fifth Avenue's first
glimpse of Bohemia, as personified by myself and two old
friends!

I have often wondered, in looking back at the slow stammering beginnings of my literary life, whether or not it is a
good thing for the creative artist to grow up in an atmosphere
where the arts are simply nonexistent. Violent opposition
might be a stimulus—but was it helpful or the reverse to have
every aspiration ignored, or looked at askance? I have thought
over this many times, as I have over most problems of creative
art, in the fascinating but probably idle attempt to discover
how it is all done, and exactly what happens at that "fine point
of the soul" where the creative act, like the mystic's union
with the Unknowable, really seems to take place. And as I
have grown older my point of view has necessarily changed,
since I have seen more and more would-be creators, whether
in painting, music or letters, whose way has been made
smooth from the cradle, geniuses whose families were prostrate before them before they had written a line or composed
a measure, and who, in middle age, still sat in ineffectual ecstasy before the blank page or the empty canvas; while, on
the other hand, more and more of the baffled, the derided or
the ignored have fought their way to achievement. The conclusion is that I am no believer in pampered vocations, and
that Schopenhauer's *Was Einer ist* seems to me the gist of the
matter. But as regards a case like my own, where a development no doubt naturally slow was certainly retarded by the
indifference of every one about me, it is hard to say whether
or no I was really hindered. I am inclined to think the drawbacks were outweighed by the advantages; chief among these
being the fact that I escaped all premature flattery, all local

celebrity, that I had to fight my way to expression through a
thick fog of indifference, if not of tacit disapproval, and that
when at last I met one or two kindred minds their criticisms
were to me as sharp and searching as if they had been profes-
sionals in the exercise of their calling. Fortunately the fact that
they were personal friends did not affect their judgment, and
my craft was held in such small account in the only world I
knew that I was always able to take the severest criticism
without undue sensitiveness, and not unusually to profit by it.
The criticism I have in mind is that given in the course of
private talk, and not imparted by the reviews. I have no quarrel with the professional critics, who have often praised me
beyond my merits; but the man who has to review fifty books
a week, often on a great variety of subjects, can hardly deal as
satisfactorily with any one of them as the friend talking over a
book with a friend, and I have always found this kind of comment the most helpful.

2

The publishing of "The Greater Inclination" broke the
chains which had held me so long in a kind of torpor. For
nearly twelve years I had tried to adjust myself to the life I
had led since my marriage; but now I was overmastered by
the longing to meet people who shared my interests. I had
found two delightful friends, who had helped to educate me
and to widen my interests; but one was a busy lawyer who
did not live in New York, and who, as his practice grew, had
less and less leisure; while the other, a man many years older
than myself, and of very worldly tastes, could not understand
my longing to break away from the world of fashion and be
with my own spiritual kin. What I wanted above all was to
get to know other writers, to be welcomed among people
who lived for the things I had always secretly lived for. I
knew only one novelist, Paul Bourget, one of the most stimulating and cultivated intelligences I have ever met, and perhaps the most brilliant talker I have known; but we saw each
other for only two or three weeks in the year, and he too was
always rebuking me for my apathy in continuing a life of wea-
risome frivolity, and telling me that at the formative stage of

my career I ought to be with people who were thinking and creating. Egerton Winthrop was too generous not to come round also to this view, and in the end it was he who urged my husband to go to London with me for a few weeks every year, so that I might at least meet a few men of letters, and have a taste of an old society in which the various elements had been fused for generations.

These arguments prevailed, and we went to London the year that "The Greater Inclination" appeared. Shortly after our arrival a friend gave me the address of James Bain, the well-known bookseller, and one day I dropped in at his shop to ask what interesting new books there were. In reply Mr. Bain handed me my own little volume, with the remark: "This is what everybody in London is talking about just now." As Mr. Bain had no idea who I was, his astonishment on learning my identity was as great as mine when he tried to sell me my own first-born as the book of the day! I should have enjoyed intensely following up this first glimpse of success; but my husband was bored in London, where he would have been amused only among the sporting set, while I wanted to know the writers. It is always depressing to live with the dissatisfied, and my powers of enjoyment are so varied that when I was young I did not find it hard to adapt myself to the preferences of any one I was fond of. The people about me were so indifferent to everything I really cared for that complying with the tastes of others had become a habit, and it was only some years later, when I had written several books, that I finally rebelled, and pleaded for the right to something better. Meanwhile we soon left London to take up again the Italian wanderings which we both enjoyed, and out of which, in 1904, "The Valley of Decision" was to grow.

Before this happened, another change had come. We sold our Newport house, and built one near Lenox, in the hills of western Massachusetts, and at last I escaped from watering-place trivialities to the real country. If I could have made the change sooner I daresay I should never have given a thought to the literary delights of Paris or London; for life in the country is the only state which has always completely satisfied me, and I had never been allowed to gratify it, even for a few weeks at a time. Now I was to know the joys of six or seven

PENCRAIG, NEWPORT, RHODE ISLAND

THE MOUNT, LENOX, MASSACHUSETTS

months a year among fields and woods of my own, and the childish ecstasy of that first spring outing at Mamaroneck swept away all restlessness in the deep joy of communion with the earth. On a slope overlooking the dark waters and densely wooded shores of Laurel Lake we built a spacious and dignified house, to which we gave the name of my great-grandfather's place, the Mount. There was a big kitchen-garden with a grape pergola, a little farm, and a flower-garden outspread below the wide terrace overlooking the lake. There for over ten years I lived and gardened and wrote content-edly, and should doubtless have ended my days there had not a grave change in my husband's health made the burden of the property too heavy. But meanwhile the Mount was to give me country cares and joys, long happy rides and drives through the wooded lanes of that loveliest region, the com-panionship of a few dear friends, and the freedom from trivial obligations which was necessary if I was to go on with my writing. The Mount was my first real home, and though it is nearly twenty years since I last saw it (for I was too happy there ever to want to revisit it as a stranger) its blessed influ-ence still lives in me.

The country quiet stimulated my creative zeal; and since the publication of "The Greater Inclination" I was naturally in the first fever of authorship. A year later, in 1900, I brought out my earliest attempt at a novel—a long tale, rather—and, the year after, a second collection of short stories, under the title of "Crucial Instances". The long tale, which was called "The Touchstone"—a quiet title carefully chosen for one of the quietest of my stories—had little success in America. John Lane bought the English rights, and thinking the title too colourless he renamed the book (naturally taking care not to consult me!) "A Gift from the Grave". This seductive but mis-leading label must have been exactly to the taste of the senti-mental novel-reader of the day, for to my mingled wrath and amusement the book sold rapidly in England, and I have often chuckled to think how defrauded the purchasers must have felt themselves after reading the first few pages.

My short stories had attracted the attention denied to "The Touchstone", and I think it was in reference to a tale in "Crucial Instances" that I received what is surely one of the tersest and most vigorous letters ever penned by an amateur critic. "Dear Madam," my unknown correspondent wrote, "have you never known a respectable woman? If you have, in the name of decency write about her!" It seems a long way from that comminatory cry to the point of view of the critic who, referring the other day to the republication (in an anthology of ghost stories) of one of my tales, "The Lady's Maid's Bell", scathingly said it was hard to believe that a ghost created by so refined a writer as Mrs. Wharton would do anything so gross as to ring a bell! My career began in the days when Thomas Hardy, in order to bring out "Jude the Obscure" in a leading New York periodical, was compelled to turn the children of Jude and Sue into adopted orphans; when the most popular young people's magazine in America excluded all stories containing any reference to "religion, love, politics, alcohol or fairies" (this is textual); the days when a well-known New York editor, offering me a large sum for the serial rights of a projected novel, stipulated only that no reference to "an unlawful attachment" should figure in it; when Theodore Roosevelt gently rebuked me for not having caused the reigning Duke of Pianura (in "The Valley of Decision") to make an honest woman of the humble bookseller's daughter who loved him; and when the translator of Dante, my beloved friend, Professor Charles Eliot Norton, hearing (after the appearance of "The House of Mirth") that I was preparing another "society" novel, wrote in alarm imploring me to remember that "no great work of the imagination has ever been based on illicit passion"!

The poor novelists who were my contemporaries (in English-speaking countries) had to fight hard for the right to turn the wooden dolls about which they were expected to make believe into struggling suffering human beings; but we have been avenged, and more than avenged, not only by life but by the novelists, and I hope the latter will see before long that it is as hard to get dramatic interest out of a mob of irresponsible criminals as out of the Puritan marionettes who formed our stock-in-trade. Authentic human nature lies somewhere between the two, and is always there for a new great novelist to rediscover.

The amusing thing about this turn of the wheel is that we

who fought the good fight are now jeered at as the prigs and prudes who barred the way to complete expression—as perhaps we should have tried to do, had we known it was to cause creative art to be abandoned for pathology! But I must return to the reigning Duke of Pianura, who about this time was more real to me than most of the people I talked and walked with in my daily life.

I have often been asked whether the writing of "The Valley of Decision" was not preceded by months of hard study. I had never studied hard in my life, and it was far too late to learn how when I began to write "The Valley of Decision"; but whenever I make this reply it is received with polite incredulity. The truth is that I have always found it hard to explain that gradual absorption into my pores of a myriad details— details of landscape, architecture, old furniture and eighteenth century portraits, the gossip of contemporary diarists and travellers, all vivified by repeated spring wanderings guided by Goethe and the Chevalier de Brosses, by Goldoni and Gozzi, Arthur Young, Dr. Burney and Ippolito Nievo, out of which the tale grew. I did not travel and look and read with the writing of the book in mind; but my years of intimacy with the Italian eighteenth century gradually and imperceptibly fashioned the tale and compelled me to write it; and whatever its faults—and they are many—it is saturated with the atmosphere I had so long lived in.

Professor Norton, who had by this time become one of my great friends, followed the development of the tale with interest, and helped it on by one of the most graceful *gestes* ever made by a distinguished scholar to a beginner. I happened to tell him that, though I had been picking up second-hand books on eighteenth century Italy whenever I could find them (hardly any of the classics of the period being then reprinted), there were a few that I had been unable to buy, and one or two that even the public libraries could not supply. Among these were the original (French) version of Goldoni's memoirs, and the memoirs of Lorenzo da Ponte, published in Boston (of all places!) about 1824. A few weeks later there came to the Mount a box containing these unattainable treasures, and many other books, almost as rare, from the great library of travels at Shady Hill. For a whole summer these extremely valuable books, some quite irreplaceable, were left at the disposal of a young scribbler who was just starting on her first novel—and to Charles Norton it seemed perfectly natural, and almost an obligation, to hold out such help to a beginner.

The year after the publication of "The Valley of Decision" the "Century Magazine" asked me, to my great delight, to write the text for a series of water-colours of Italian villas by Mr. Maxfield Parrish. The suggestion had originated in the unexpected popularity of "The Decoration of Houses", and also of "The Valley of Decision", which was now rewarding me for the long months of toil and perplexity I had undergone in writing it. I was only beginning to be known as a novelist, but on Italian seventeenth and eighteenth century architecture, about which so little had been written, I was thought to be fairly competent.

Armed with this commission I set out with my husband for Rome in the winter of 1903, and began my work in all seriousness.

3

Before telling the story of "Italian Villas" I must speak of the friend whose kindness made its writing possible. Several years earlier, on starting on our annual pilgrimage to Italy, I had taken with me a letter from Paul Bourget to Vernon Lee (Miss Violet Paget), the author of "Studies of the Eighteenth Century in Italy", "Belcaro" and "Euphorion", three of my best-loved companions of the road. Bourget warned me that, though Miss Paget was an old friend of his, he could not promise that his introduction would be of any use, as her time was so much taken up by her invalid half-brother, Eugene Lee-Hamilton, who lived with her, that she saw very few people, and those only among her intimates. It was therefore with little hope of success that I drove out from Florence to Il Palmerino, the long low villa on the hillside of San Domenico where Miss Paget has so long made her home. I left Bourget's letter, took a yearning look at the primrose-yellow house-front and the homely box-scented garden, and drove away with no expectation of ever seeing them again. But the next day Miss Paget wrote that, though her brother's illness prevented her receiving visitors, yet if I chanced to be the Edith Wharton who had written a certain sonnet (I forget its name) which had attracted his attention in "Scribner's Magazine," she begged me to come as soon as possible, as he wished to make my acquaintance. Luckily I *was* the author of the sonnet, and I hastened back to Il Palmerino, where I was affectionately welcomed by its mistress, and led to the darkened room where her brother lay on the mattress that seemed so likely to be a grave.

Eugene Lee-Hamilton, who was then a middle-aged man, had been one of Lord Lyons's secretaries of Embassy in Paris during the Franco-Prussian war. The long period of overstrain and over-work, followed by the privations and horrors of the siege of Paris, had brought about a bad nervous breakdown, of a kind which the doctors of that day had not learned to deal with. Lee-Hamilton, his career cut short, lapsed into what seemed hopeless invalidism, and for years had lain motionless on the mattress on which I first saw him. By that time he had grown so weak that he could see only an occasional visitor, and for a very few moments. He was one of the most amusing talkers and *raconteurs* I have ever known, and a great lover of letters, and especially of poetry; but when I first met him he could neither read nor write, and was in such a state of weakness that his sister could only read a few lines to him at a time. These brief readings were usually chosen among the poets, and his literary curiosity had remained so alert that, in addition to the classics, he kept up with the new poets, even with those who had figured only in the reviews. It was in the course of these explorations that he happened on the sonnet which did me the great good turn of bringing me into contact with two of the most brilliant minds I have ever met.

His long years of suffering and helplessness had made Eugene Lee-Hamilton himself into a poet, and I have never understood why the poignant verse written during his illness, and published in a volume called "Sonnets of the Wingless Hours", is not more widely known. I was proud to have any verse of mine praised by a poet of such quality, and I look back gratefully to the moments spent at his bedside, talking of the things of the spirit.

To lighten the gloom of the picture I must add that a few

years later he rose miraculously from his mattress, learned again to walk, to write, and finally to ride a bicycle, and not long afterward came to America, where he paid us a visit to Land's End, rejoicing in his recovered vigour, and keeping us and our guests in shouts of laughter by his high spirits and inimitable stories. I have often wished that the after-death resurrection, if it comes to us, might resemble the recovery of lost youth which made Lee-Hamilton's return to life so exhilarating to all about him.

Thanks to him, my acquaintance with his sister had grown into a friendship which has never flagged, though we are so seldom together. Hitherto all my intellectual friendships had been with men, and Vernon Lee was the first highly cultivated and brilliant woman I had ever known. I stood a little in awe of her, as I always did in the presence of intellectual superiority, and liked best to sit silent and listen to a conversation which I still think almost the best of its day. I have been fortunate in knowing intimately some great talkers among men, but I have met only three women who had the real gift. They were Vernon Lee, Matilde Serao, the Neapolitan journalist and novelist, and the French poetess, the Comtesse de Noailles. It is hard to establish any comparison between beings so unlike in race, traditions and culture—but one might suggest the difference by saying that Matilde Serao's talk was like the noonday glow of her own Mediterranean, while Vernon Lee's has the opalescent play of a northerly sky, and Madame de Noailles' resembled the most expensive fireworks.

No one welcomed "The Valley of Decision" more warmly than Vernon Lee, and it was a great encouragement to be praised by a writer whom I so much admired, and who was so unquestioned an authority on the country and the period I had dealt with. A year or two later the editor of the *Nuova Antologia*, then the leading Italian literary review, proposed to me to bring out an Italian translation of my novel, and Vernon Lee at once offered to write the introduction. For a reason I was never able to fathom (probably owing to a change in the administration of the review), the translation never appeared; but Vernon Lee's admirable preface is in my possession, and I still hope it may serve to introduce Italian readers to my book.

These years were perhaps the happiest I was to know as regards literary hopes and achievements. My long experimenting had resulted in two or three books which brought me more encouragement than I had ever dreamed of obtaining, and were the means of my making some of the happiest friendships of my life. The reception of my books gave me the self-confidence I had so long lacked, and in the company of people who shared my tastes, and treated me as their equal, I ceased to suffer from the agonizing shyness which used to rob such encounters of all pleasure. It was in this mood that I arrived in Italy in 1903, and turned to Vernon Lee for help in preparing my new book.

Always generous to younger writers, she was doubly so to me because of my friendship with her brother, and of her interest in the task I had undertaken. At that time little had been written on Italian villa and garden architecture, and only the most famous country-seats, mostly royal or princely, had been photographed and studied. As, in "The Decoration of Houses", Ogden Codman and I had purposely excluded palaces and royal *châteaux* from our list, and directed the attention of our readers to the study of small and simple houses, so I wished that my new book should make known the simpler and less familiar type of villa. At Frascati, for instance, I passed hurriedly over the familiar splendours of Falconieri and Mondragone in order to give more space to the lovely Muti gardens, which at that time were almost unknown; and wherever I went I followed the same plan. At first I found it difficult to get helpful information from Italians, even from those living on the spot; a "garden" to them still meant a humpy lawn with oval beds of cannas encircling a banana-plant, and I wasted a good deal of time before learning that I must ask for "*giardini tagliati*", and not be discouraged by the usual reply: "Oh, you mean the old-fashioned garden with clipped shrubs? Well, we believe there *is* one at the Villa So-and-so—but what can you find in that to interest you?"

Vernon Lee's long familiarity with the Italian country-side, and the wide circle of her Italian friendships, made it easy for her to guide me to the right places, and put me in relation with people who could enable me to visit them. She herself took me to nearly all the villas I wished to visit near Florence, and it was thanks to her recommendation that wherever I went, from the Lakes to the Roman Campagna, I found open doors and a helpful hospitality.

Among the friendships then made I should like to record with particular gratitude that of the Countess Papafava of Padua, from whom I first heard of the fantastic Castle of Cattajo, and through whose kindness the intricately lovely gardens of Val San Zibio were opened to me; of Don Guido Cagnola of Varese, an authority on Italian villa architecture, and himself the owner of La Gazzada, the beautiful villa near Varese of which there is a painting by Canaletto in the Brera; of the Countess Rasponi, who lived in the noble villa of Font'allerta, above Florence, and supplemented Vernon Lee in guiding me among the Florentine and Sienese villas; of the great Enrico Boito, whose powerful protection opened the doors of some little-known villas of the Brianza and the Naviglio; and lastly of Countess Rasponi's sister, my old friend the Countess Maria Pasolini of Rome and Ravenna, great lover of seventeenth and eighteenth century architecture, and an indefatigable guide in such a search as I was making. I have named them all here, because, although with the exception of the Countess Rasponi and Boito they are still alive, and I now and then have the pleasure of seeing them, I feel that I have never properly expressed my appreciation of their helpfulness. Their intelligent collaboration gave "Italian Villas" its chief value, and I like to recall the joy I had in making the book by naming the friends who helped me.

The day of the motor was not yet, and in addition to the difficulty of discovering the type of villa I was in search of there remained the problem of how to get to it when found. I never enjoyed any work more than the preparing of that book, but neither do I remember any task so associated with physical fatigue. Most of the places I wished to visit were far from the principal railway lines, and could be reached only by a combination of slow trains and broken-down horse conveyances, and we seemed to be always either rushing through the villas in order not to miss our train, or else, the villas exhaustively inspected, kicking our heels for hours in some musty railway-station. I remember that once, after a particularly fatiguing day, we were waiting at the Pavia station to catch a crowded express back to Milan. We had taken the tea-basket, but there was no time for tea till we reached the station. There, feeling on the verge of inanition, I started to brew it, in spite of my husband's protests; but just as I filled our cups the express roared into the station, and we had to leap on board and force our way into a crowded compartment carrying the basket, the plates and the brimming cups! How we accomplished this I cannot imagine; but we did, to the astonishment and indignation of our fellow travellers.

I have said there were no motors in 1903; but as a toy of the rich they were beginning to appear, and my old friend George Meyer, then American Ambassador in Rome, was the owner of a magnificent specimen. Knowing that I wished to visit the Villa Caprarola, now familiar to every sight-seer, but then visible only to the privileged, he suggested taking me there in his car. I had never been in a motor before, and could hardly believe that we were to do the run to Caprarola and back (fifty miles each way) in an afternoon, and still have time to inspect the villa and gardens; but we did—we did with a vengeance! The car was probably the most luxurious, and certainly one of the fastest, then procurable; but that meant only a sort of high-perched phaeton without hood or screen, or any protection from the wind. My husband was put behind with the chauffeur, while I had the high seat like a coachman's box beside the Ambassador. In a thin spring dress, a sailor hat balanced on my chignon, and a two-inch tulle veil over my nose, I climbed proudly to my perch, and off we tore across the Campagna, over humps and bumps, through ditches and across gutters, wind-swept, dust-enveloped, I clinging to my sailor-hat, and George Meyer (luckily) to the wheel. We did the run in an hour, and I was able to see the villa and gardens fairly well before we tore back to Rome, in time for a big dinner to which he and we happened to be going. It was great fun doing the Witch of Atlas, and blissful not to have to worry about tired horses or inconvenient trains; but when I reached the dinner my voice was entirely gone, and I spent the next days in bed, fighting an acute laryngitis. In spite of this I swore then and there that as soon as I could make money enough I would buy a motor; and so I did—and having a delicate throat, scoured the country in the hottest weather swaddled in a stifling hood with a mica window, till some benefactor of the race invented the wind-screen and made motoring an unmixed joy.

Meanwhile my first article had appeared in the "Century", illustrated by a number of photographs, and by one of Maxfield Parrish's brilliant idealisations of the Italian scene. Thanks to the latter, the article attracted much attention, but a note of warning soon came to me in the form of a distracted letter from the editor of the "Century", Richard Watson Gilder, an old friend and a country neighbour in the Berkshires. It appeared that in the editorial offices of the "Century" Mr. Parrish's fairy-tale pictures were justly admired, but it was agreed that the accompanying text was too dry and technical. Would I not, Mr. Gilder pleaded, introduce into the next number a few anecdotes, and a touch of human interest?

I am afraid my answer was curt. I had prepared for my task conscientiously; I knew that, at least in English, there was no serious work on Italian villa and garden architecture, and I meant, as far as I was able, to fill the want. I wrote back that if the "Century" wanted a series of sentimental and anecdotic commentaries on Mr. Parrish's illustrations, I was surprised that one of the authors of "The Decoration of Houses" should have been commissioned to write them. But I added that if, on reflection, my articles were thought unsuitable to the illustrations (as they certainly were!) I was quite willing to annul my contract. This was not accepted, and the articles continued to appear, my only punishment being that the Century Company refused (when the volume came out) to publish the plans of certain little-known but important gardens, such as those of the Villas Muti at Frascati and Gori at Siena, which I had taken great pains to procure, because, according to the publishers, the public "did not care for plans". I mention this because, when "Italian Villas" became, as it soon did, a working manual for architectural students and landscape gardeners, I was often reproached for not having provided the book with plans. In a sense, of course, the editors of the "Century" were right. My articles were quite out of keeping with the Parrish pictures, which should have been used to illustrate some fanciful tale of Lamotte-Fouqué, or Andersen's "Improvisatore"; but I knew that, even had I had an

architectural draughtsman as illustrator, the editorial scruples
would not have been allayed, for what really roused them was
not the lack of harmony between text and pictures but the
fear their readers would be bored by the serious technical
treatment of a subject associated with moonlight and nightingales. Therefore, having been given the opportunity to do a
book that needed doing, I resolutely took it; and I hope the
success of "Italian Villas", which still has a steady sale, has
made the publishers forgive me.

Again and again in my literary life I have encountered the
same kind of editorial timidity. I think it was Edwin Godkin,
then the masterly editor of the New York "Evening Post",
who said that the choice of articles published in American
magazines was entirely determined by the fear of scandalizing
a non-existent clergyman in the Mississippi Valley; and I
made up my mind from the first that I would never sacrifice
my literary conscience to this ghostly censor. Not being
obliged to live solely by my pen I thought I owed it to less
lucky colleagues to fight for the independence they might not
always be in a position to assert. A higher standard of taste in
letters can be achieved only if authors will refuse to write
down to the particular Mississippi Valley level of the day (for
there is always a censorship of the same sort, though it is now
at the other end of the moral register), and the greatest service
a writer can render to letters is to follow his conscience.

In the intervals of my work on "Italian Villas" I had
published a number of short articles which I collected and
brought out in 1905 in a volume called "Italian Backgrounds".
I do not intend to burden these pages with an account of
every book I have written and I speak of "Italian Backgrounds" only because it is a convenient peg on which to
hang an interesting discussion. In the 'seventies and 'eighties
there had appeared a series of agreeable volumes of travel and
art-criticism of the cultured dilettante type, which had found
thousands of eager readers. From Pater's "Renaissance", and
Symonds' "Sketches in Italy and Greece", to the deliciously
desultory volumes of Vernon Lee, and Bourget's delicate
"Sensations d'Italie", though ranging through varying degrees
of erudition, they all represented a high but unspecialized
standard of culture; all were in a sense the work of amateurs,

and based on the assumption that it is mainly to the cultured amateur that the creative artist must look for appreciation, and that such appreciation ought to be, and often is, worth recording.

But while the cultivated reader continued to enjoy these books, and to ask for more, the voice of the trained scholar was sounding a note of resistance. Literary "appreciations" of works of art were being smiled away by experts trained in Bertillon-Morelli methods, and my deep contempt for picturesque books about architecture naturally made me side with those who wished to banish sentiment from the study of painting and sculpture. Then, with the publication of Berenson's first volumes on Italian painting, lovers of Italy learned that aesthetic sensibility may be combined with the sternest scientific accuracy, and I began to feel almost guilty for having read Pater and even Symonds with such zest, and ashamed of having added my own facile vibrations to the chorus. The application of scholarly standards to the judgment of works of art certainly helped to clear away the sentimental undergrowth which had sprung up in the wake of the gifted amateur; but nowadays, as was almost certain to happen, the very critics who did the necessary clearing have come to recognize that, their task once done, there remains the imponderable something, the very soul of the work contemplated, and that this something may be felt and registered by certain cultivated sensibilities, whether or not they have been disciplined by technical training. There remains a field of observation wherein the mere lover of beauty can open the eyes and sharpen the hearing of the receptive traveller, as Pater, Symonds and Vernon Lee had done to readers of my generation. The combination of gifts required is seldom found, and the volumes which guided my early wanderings were succeeded by minor dithyrambs to which I never again felt tempted to add my own pipe of ecstasy; but there is certainly room for the gifted amateur in the field of artistic impressions—if only he is sufficiently gifted.

VII

New York and the Mount

I

W E HAD NOW organized our summers at the Mount, and
had acquired a small house—we used to say it was
actually the smallest—in New York. I had grown very weary
of our annual wanderings, and now that I had definite work
to do I felt the need of a winter home where I could continue
my writing, instead of having to pack up every autumn, as we
had been doing for over fifteen years. Personally I should have
preferred to live all the year round at the Mount, but my
husband's fondness for society, and his dislike of the New
England winter cold, made this impossible; and a few years
later, when he found even the climate of New York too trying, we decided to spend all our winters abroad. But meanwhile I had the amusement of adorning our sixteen-foot-wide
house in New York with the modest spoils of our Italian travels, and my summers being quiet I did not so much mind the
social demands of the winter. Besides, life in New York, with
its theatres and opera, and its new interests of all kinds, was
very different from the flat frivolity of Newport; and I was
happy in my work, and in the new sense of confidence in my
powers.

My literary success puzzled and embarrassed my old friends
far more than it impressed them, and in my own family it
created a kind of constraint which increased with the years.
None of my relations ever spoke to me of my books, either to
praise or blame—they simply ignored them; and among the
immense tribe of my New York cousins, though it included
many with whom I was on terms of affectionate intimacy, the
subject was avoided as though it were a kind of family disgrace, which might be condoned but could not be forgotten.
Only one eccentric widowed cousin, living a life of lonely invalidism, turned to my novels for occasional distraction, and
had the courage to tell me so.

At first I had felt this indifference acutely; but now I no

longer cared, for my recognition as a writer had transformed my life. I had made my own friends, and my books were beginning to serve as an introduction to my fellow-writers. But it was amusing to think that, whereas in London even my modest achievements would have opened many doors, in my native New York they were felt only as a drawback and an embarrassment. The literary life of New York had changed very little since my youth. The literary men foregathered at the Century Club, and continued to turn a contemptuous shoulder on society. Our most distinguished man of letters, William Brownell, led the life of a recluse, and though he became a dear friend it was chiefly by letter that we communicated, and only on rare occasions that I could persuade him to come to our house. I have always regretted that our friendly meetings were so rare, and so seldom occurred in a more sympathetic setting than his cramped and crowded office at Scribner's. When he died in 1928 I tried to put into an article contributed to "Scribner's Magazine" something of my deep admiration for the scholar and critic; but I found it difficult to convey the exquisite quality of the man. There was always an aloofness, an elusiveness in Brownell's manner and personality, something shy and crepuscular, as though his real self dwelt in a closely-guarded recess of contemplation from which it emerged more easily and freely in writing than in speech; and indeed his letters to me, which were long and frequent, always brought him nearer than our actual encounters. As these letters concern only, or chiefly, my own works, their interest for the general reader would obviously be less than for their recipient; but to me they were a precious link with one of the rarest intelligences I have ever known.

In writing of Brownell after his death it was inevitable that I should associate with his name that of Edward Burlingame, for many years Brownell's colleague in the house of Scribner, where he edited the magazine. I said of the two: "I do not think I have ever forgotten one word of the counsels they gave me", and the assertion is as true today as it would have been in my youth. In Edward Burlingame also I found a devoted personal friend, as well as a literary adviser. During his editorship he raised "Scribner's Magazine" to the highest level compatible with the tastes of the American magazine public—then apparently a higher one than now. Burlingame, who used to come and dine now and then with his wife, was far more sociably inclined than his colleague. He was a man of real cultivation, a good linguist, and genuinely interested in modern literature. It was thanks to him that Scribner had published Stevenson's best prose, and Burlingame's ambition was to keep his magazine on a level with the standard then established. He was a good-looking man whose quiet dignity of manner masked an acute sense of humour and a patient cordiality which many a young author must have had reason to bless as I did. I remember once saying to him (à propos of some young woman in straitened circumstances, whose manuscript he had reluctantly had to refuse): "How hard it must be to say 'no' in such cases!" But he answered quietly: "Not as hard as you think, because if one isn't cruel at first one has to be so much crueller afterward." Another of his wise answers was occasioned by my coming to him one day (in the new flush of my success) bearing with me, as it were, an armful of unwritten short stories. He listened patiently to my plans, and then said: "If I were you I wouldn't be in such a hurry. You mustn't risk becoming *a magazine bore*." Lastly I owe to him the neatest formulation I know of one of the first principles of every art: "You can ask your reader to believe whatever you can induce him to believe." These axioms have remained with me as applicable not only to literature but to life: and Burlingame abounded in such wisdom.

W. D. Howells was (partly, I believe, owing to his wife's chronic ill-health) another irreducible recluse, and though I was in a way accredited to him by my friendship with his two old friends, Charles Norton and Henry James, I seldom met him. I always regretted this, for I had a great admiration for "A Modern Instance" and "Silas Lapham", and should have liked to talk with their author about the art in which he stood so nearly among the first; and he himself, whenever we met, was full of a quiet friendliness. But I suppose my timidity and his social aloofness kept us apart; for though I felt that he was amicably disposed he remained inaccessible. Once, however, he did me a great kindness. I invited him to come with us to the first night (in New York) of Clyde Fitch's dramatization of "The House of Mirth". The play had already been tried out on the road, and in spite of Fay Davis's exquisite representation of Lily Bart I knew that (owing to my refusal to let the heroine survive) it was foredoomed to failure. Howells doubtless knew it also, and not improbably accepted my invitation for that very reason; a fact worth recording as an instance of his friendliness to young authors, and also on account of the lapidary phrase in which, as we left the theatre, he summed up the reason of the play's failure. "Yes—what the American public always wants is a tragedy with a happy ending".

Still another friend from the world of letters (and a life-long intimate of all my husband's family), was Judge Robert Grant of Boston, who, in his rare moments of escape from the duties of the Probate Court, used to come to New York on flying visits. I have always had a great admiration for his early novel, "Unleavened Bread", which, with W. D. Howells's "A Modern Instance", was the forerunner of "Main Street", of "Babbitt", of that unjustly forgotten masterpiece "Susan Lenox", of the best of Frank Norris, and of Dreiser's "American Tragedy". Howells was the first to feel the tragic potentialities of life in the drab American small town; but the incurable moral timidity which again and again checked him on the verge of a masterpiece drew him back even from the logical conclusion of "A Modern Instance", and left Robert Grant the first in the field which he was eventually to share with Lewis and Dreiser.

But though there was little change in the attitude of the literary group, the merely fashionable were beginning to enlarge their interests. With the coming of the new millionaires the building of big houses had begun, in New York and in the country, bringing with it (though not always to those for whom the building was done) a keen interest in architecture, furniture and works of art in general. The Metropolitan Museum was waking up from its long lethargy, and the leading picture dealers from London and Paris were seizing the opportunity of educating a new clientèle, opening branch houses in New York and getting up loan exhibitions. With the coming of Edward Robinson (formerly of the Boston Museum) as Director of the Metropolitan, and the growth of the Hewitt sisters' activities in organizing their Museum of Decorative Art at the Cooper Union, the doctrines first preached by "The Decoration of Houses" were beginning to find general expression; and in many houses there was already a new interest in letters as well as art. Men like my friends Bayard Cutting and John Cadwalader, in addition to preparing the way for the great new Public Library, and taking an active part in its creation, were forming valuable libraries of their own; others were collecting prints and pictures, and several of the younger architects were acquiring the important professional libraries which have been one of the chief elements in forming American taste in architecture, and making it the foremost influence in modern building. A few men of exceptional intelligence, such as Egerton Winthrop, Bayard Cutting, John Cadwalader, Walter Maynard, Charles McKim, Stanford White and Ogden Codman, had at last stirred the stagnant air of old New York, and in their particular circle it was full of the dust of new ideas.

This circle had happily always been mine, and I enjoyed its renovated air all the more now that I had found my own line in life; but though I liked New York well enough it was only at the Mount that I was really happy. There, every summer, I gathered about me my own group of intimates, of whom the number was slowly growing. Chief among the newcomers was a youth who, though many years my junior, at once became the closest of comrades. Walter Berry, who lived and exercised his profession, in Washington, first put me in touch with his young friend, George Cabot Lodge (always "Bay" to his intimates). We met in Washington, where I had gone on a short visit; and from that first encounter till the day of his death Bay and I were fast friends. Bay Lodge (the eldest son of Henry Cabot Lodge, the Senator from Massachusetts) was one of the most brilliant and versatile youths I have ever known. In what direction he would eventually have developed I have never been sure; his sudden death at the age of thirty-six cut short such conjectures. He believed himself to be meant for poetry and letters; and he wrote, and published, several volumes of poetry marked by a grave rhetorical beauty. Though I admired certain lines and passages, I felt, as did most of his friends, that they showed only one side, perhaps not the most personal, of his rich and eager intelligence, and that if poetry was to be his ultimate form he must pass beyond the imitative stage into fuller self-expression. But he had a naturally scholarly mind, and might have turned in the end to history and archæology; unless indeed he was simply intended to be the most sensitive of contemplators, as he was the most varied and dazzling of talkers. In our hurried world too little value is attached to the part of the connoisseur and dilettante, and it never occurred to Bay's family that he was not meant for an active task in letters. His fate, in fact, was the reverse of mine, for he grew up in a hot-house of intensive culture, and was one of the most complete examples I have ever known of the young genius before whom an adoring family unites in smoothing the way. This kept him out of the struggle of life, and consequently out of its experiences, and to the end his intellectual precocity was combined with a boyishness of spirit at once delightful and pathetic. He had always lived in Washington, where, at the time when he was growing up, his father, Henry Adams, John Hay, and the eccentric Sturgis Bigelow of Boston, whose erudition so far exceeded his mental capacity, formed a close group of intimates. Until Theodore Roosevelt came to Washington theirs were almost the only houses where one breathed a cosmopolitan air, and where such men as Sir Cecil Spring-Rice, J. J. Jusserand and Lord Bryce felt themselves immediately at home. But Washington, even then, save for the politician and the government official, was a place to retire to, not to be young in; and Bay often complained of the lack of friends of his own age. Even more than from the narrowness of his opportunities he suffered from the slightly rarefied atmosphere of mutual admiration, and disdain of the rest of the world, that prevailed in his immediate surroundings. John Hay was by nature the most open-minded of the group, and his diplomatic years in London had enlarged his outlook; but the dominating spirits were Henry Adams and Cabot Lodge, and though they were extremely kind to me, and my pleasantest hours in Washington were spent at their houses, I always felt that the influences prevailing there kept Bay in a state of brilliant immaturity. He was at his best when he came to stay with us at the Mount, where small parties of congenial friends succeeded each other through the summer, and he was brought in contact with minds as active as his own, but more unprejudiced.

Another friend of this time was young Bayard Cutting, the son of my old friend. He was then recently married, and already menaced by the illness which cut him off a few years later. Bayard was as different as possible from his contemporary, Bay Lodge, as quiet and retiring as Bay was brilliant and exuberant; and his main interests, had he lived, would probably have been political rather than literary, though he was a great reader, and a passionate lover of letters. He was extremely intelligent and eagerly responsive to all intellectual appeals, but his rarest quality was a sort of quiet radiance which sent its beam through the dark fog of weakness and pain enveloping the years that ought to have been his happiest.

During those years, so quickly consumed by suffering, I never once heard him complain. He never ceased to struggle against his malady, trying every country and every climate in the effort to throw it off, but at the same time he took life on the normal terms of a healthy man—doing his best to get well, yet behaving, talking, and apparently thinking, as if he *were* well. In his wanderings in the pursuit of health he and his wife once spent a summer at Lenox, and during those months I learned of how fine and delicate a substance he was made. We have always needed such men sorely in American public life, and Bayard Cutting's death was a loss far beyond the immediate circle of his friends.

2

About this time we set up a motor, or perhaps I should say a series of them, for in those days it was difficult to find one which did not rapidly develop some organic defect; and selling, buying and exchanging went on continuously, though without appreciably better results. One summer, when we were all engaged on the first volumes of Mme Karénine's absorbing life of George Sand, we had a large showy car which always started off brilliantly and then broke down at the first hill, and this we christened "Alfred de Musset", while the small but indefatigable motor which subsequently replaced "Alfred" was naturally named "George". But those were the days when motor-guides still contained carefully drawn gradient-maps like fever-charts, and even "George" sometimes balked at the state of the country roads about Lenox; I remember in particular one summer night when Henry James, Walter Berry, my husband and I sat by the roadside till near dawn while our chauffeur tried to persuade "George" to carry us back to the Mount. The other day, in going over some old letters written to Bay Lodge by Walter Berry, I came on one dated from the Mount. "Great fun here," the writer exulted; "we motor every day, and yesterday *we did sixty-five miles*" (in triumphant italics). In those epic days roads and motors were an equally unknown quantity, and one set out on a ten-mile run with more apprehension than would now attend a journey across Africa. But the range of country-lovers like myself had hitherto been so limited, and our imagination so tantalized by the mystery beyond the next blue hills, that there was inexhaustible delight in penetrating to the remoter parts of Massachusetts and New Hampshire, discovering derelict villages with Georgian churches and balustraded house-fronts, exploring slumbrous mountain valleys, and coming back, weary but laden with a new harvest of beauty, after sticking fast in ruts, having to push the car up hill, to rout out the village blacksmith for repairs, and suffer the jeers of horse-drawn travellers trotting gaily past us. My two New England tales, "Ethan Frome" and "Summer", were the result of explorations among villages still bedrowsed in a decaying rural existence, and sad slow-speaking people living in conditions hardly changed since their forbears held those villages against the Indians.

A frequent excursion was to Ashfield, where Charles Eliot Norton spent the summer with his daughters in his little mountain farmhouse, and where there was always a friendly welcome, and the joy of long hours of invigorating talk. What I have said of the underrated value of the connoisseur and disseminator of ideas is even more applicable to a man like Charles Eliot Norton, whose long life proved what can only be regretfully surmised in regard to a career as short as Bay Lodge's. Charles Norton of course led an active life of letters in conjunction with his teaching as Professor of Fine Arts at Harvard; but his animating influence on my generation in

America was exerted through what he himself was, and what he made his pupils see and feel with him. Among those of my intimate friends who came under Norton's influence at Harvard there was none who did not regard the encounter as a turning point in his own growth. Norton was supremely gifted as an awakener, and no thoughtful mind can recall without a thrill the notes of the first voice which has called it out of its morning dream.

In his prime Charles Norton, to be really known, had to be seen in the Shady Hill library, at Cambridge, where the ripest years of his intellectual life were lived. Against that noble background of books his frail presence, the low voice, the ascetic features so full of scholarly distinction, acquired their full meaning, and his talk was at its richest and happiest. But the rusticity of the Ashfield cottage, with its rocky slopes of orchard and woodland looking out to the blue distances of his beloved New England, formed an even fitter setting to his serene old age. It was there that I was oftenest in his company, for my most intimate friends were his friends also. One such pilgrimage is delightfully recorded in a letter written from the Mount by Henry James, and others were made with Walter Berry, Gaillard Lapsley, and divers devotees and disciples; memories radiant with the beauty of the long mountain drive from Lenox to Ashfield, with sunsets watched from the summit of "High Pasture" (where Norton always dreamed of building a house that should command the wide landscape), and the slow descent through the orchards at dusk, the lights twinkling under the eaves, a happy group gathered for high tea, and an evening of quiet talk about the fire. Charles Norton was not a great talker; he had none of the sweep and impetus of the born conversationalist; but he was one of the best guides to good conversation that I have ever known. Every word he spoke, every question he asked, was like a signal pointing to the next height, and his silences were of the kind which serve to carry on the talk.

He was too old, when I began to know him intimately, to care to travel. He often promised to come to the Mount, but I cannot remember that he ever did, though his daughter Sally was so beloved and frequent a visitor. I never failed, however, when I was in Boston, to make the pilgrimage to

Shady Hill, or to go to Ashfield in summer; and in the intervals between our meetings we wrote to each other, or kept in touch through my correspondence with Sally. He never ceased to interest himself in my work, or to encourage me to go forward, although the more I developed the more, in literary matters, our points of view diverged. He was obviously disturbed by my increasing "realism", my exclusive interest, as a novelist, in the life about me, which seemed to him so devoid of the stuff of romance; he would have been happier if I had never come any nearer to the nineteenth century than I did in "The Valley of Decision". But no friendly pressure, even from the critics I most esteemed, could turn me from the way I seemed meant to follow; and with a magnanimity unusual in a man of his age Charles Norton accepted this, and kept me in his heart.

In the intervals between our meetings we wrote to each other, and, though our actual hours together were not many, I had to the end the warm enveloping sense of his friendship, and the last letter he ever wrote (or dictated, for he was past writing) was addressed to me.

One of Charles Norton's great friends, Edward Robinson, came often to the Mount with his wife. Since he had given up the directorship of the Boston Museum, and been placed at the head of the Metropolitan, I had naturally more frequent opportunities of seeing him; and he was welcome not only on his own account but as a link with other Boston friends, the Nortons, Robert Grant, Barrett Wendell, and many others. Edward Robinson, tall, spare and pale, with his blond hair cut short "en brosse", bore the physical imprint of his German University formation, and might almost have sat for the portrait of a Teutonic *Gelehrter* but for the quiet twinkle perceptible behind his eyeglasses. He had, indeed, an extremely delicate sense of humour, combined with the boyish love of pure nonsense only to be found in Anglo-Saxons. He was one of the people for whom I used to hoard up my best stories, but his own were generally better, for his professional experiences gave him many humorous sidelights on human nature, and no one could rival the dry pedantic manner in which he poked fun at pedantry. I remember particularly one story, not especially relevant to this, but which has remained with me because of its strangeness, and Robinson's dramatic way of telling it. The young Heir Apparent of a Far Eastern Empire, who was making an official tour of the United States, was taken with his suite to the Metropolitan, and shown about by Robinson and the Museum staff. For two mortal hours Robinson marched the little procession from one work of art to another, pausing before each to give the necessary explanations to the aide-de-camp (the only one of the visitors who spoke English), who transmitted them to his Imperial master. During the whole of the tour the latter's face remained as immovable as that of the Emperor Constantius entering Rome, in Gibbon's famous description. The Prince never asked a question, or glanced to right or left, and this slow and awful progress through the endless galleries was beginning to tell on Robinson's nerves when they halted before a fine piece of fifteenth century sculpture, a Pietà, or a Deposition, with a peculiarly moving figure of the dead Christ. Here His Imperial Highness opened his lips to ask, through his aide-de-camp, what the group represented, and Robinson hastened to explain: "It is the figure of our dead God, after His enemies have crucified Him". The Prince listened, stared, and then burst into loud and prolonged laughter. Peal after peal echoed uncannily through the startled galleries; then his features resumed their imperial rigidity and the melancholy procession moved on through new vistas of silence.

Edward Robinson's presence in New York helped to centralize the growing interest in art and architecture, and he was one of the most sympathetic among the group of friends who used to gather in my small New York drawing-room, or join in our adventurous motor trips at the Mount. If I have dwelt chiefly on the homely familiar traits of his character, the fun, the irony, the gentle malice, leaving it to others to praise his scholarship and recount his public services, it is because in trying to tell the story of my life I have found that it is these little personal characteristics (and above all others, the ironic sense of the pity and mystery of things) which have always created the closest ties between myself and my friends.

Robert Minturn, of New York, whom I had known slightly all through my girlhood, was now frequently at the Mount, or at our house in New York. He and I belonged by birth to the same "old New York", and I hardly know what had kept us so long from becoming friends, unless perhaps the somewhat austere Minturn *milieu* (with its Boston-Abolitionist affiliations) regarded mine as incorrigibly frivolous. At any rate, as soon as I went to live in New York and began to see more of this grave young man, whose pensive dusky head was so like that of a Titian portrait, we found that we were meant to be friends—and often have I grieved that we had not discovered sooner, for Bob Minturn's was one of the affections I am proudest of having inspired. Once, as a child, I was severely rebuked for saying of a dull kindly servant, whom my father was defending because he was "so good": "Of course he's good—he's too stupid to be bad". The rebuke was no doubt very salutary; yet experience has shown me that there was a grain of truth in my comment, for the intellectually eager and enquiring are seldom serenely and unquestioningly good. But Robert Minturn belonged to the happy few who have found a way of harmonizing the dissecting intellect with the accepting soul, and whose daily life reveals the inner harmony "through chinks that grief has made".

Bob Minturn's grief was his health; it was already menaced when our friendship began, and during his last years he was an invalid, accepting infirmity and facing death with complete serenity. One by one he had given up the activities and enjoyments of a young man's life; but he never allowed these renunciations to dull his appreciation of what remained—the love of art and letters, the love of nature, and above all, exquisitely vigilant and tender, the love of his friends. If he had kept his health he would no doubt have taken an active part in political and municipal life, for he had a lively sense of civic obligation and a natural interest in public affairs; but his activities, deprived of this outlet, had canalized themselves in an exquisite culture. He was an accomplished linguist, widely read in certain lines, a sensitive lover of words, indefatigable in the quest of their uses and meanings, handling them as a gardener does his flowers, or a collector precious jewels or porcelain, and deploring above all their barbarous misuse by our countrymen. Linguistic problems had such a fascination for him that even the letters to me which he dictated in the last months of his life, when he was too ill to write, are full of eagerly propounded etymological questions. To the last his interest in all the worth-while things kept his poor worn body aglow, and if ever a craft went down with colours flying it was that which bore the shining soul of Bob Minturn.

3

Another visitor of a very different type, but highly endowed with the sense of humour common to most of our group, was the popular playwright, Clyde Fitch. Though I had not escaped the novelist's usual temptation to write for the stage I had never taken my dramatic impulses very seriously, and after the appearance of my second novel, "The House of Mirth", I thought no more of the theatre—indeed, as nothing in the way of drama between the extremes of Racine's "Phèdre" and "The Private Secretary" has ever given me much pleasure, I went to the play as seldom as possible.

Once "The House of Mirth" had started on its prosperous career I was of course besieged with applications for leave to dramatize it; but I refused them all, convinced that (apart from the intrinsic weakness of most plays drawn from books) there was nothing in this particular book out of which to make a play. Great was my surprise, therefore, when I heard that Clyde Fitch, then at the height of his career, was eager to undertake the task, though he had never before consented to adapt any one else's material. I did not know Clyde Fitch, and had seen, I think, only one of his plays; but I had read a number of them, and though they were all disappointing, yet I thought him more gifted than was generally supposed. His sense of the theatre was keen, but that interested me less than his sense of the irony of life, his happy choice of the incidents by means of which he threw light on the human predicament. I still think the first act of one of his plays (I forget its title), in which the scene is laid in the rotunda of the Apollo Belvedere, at the Vatican, one of the most humorous exhibitions of human vacuity that I know of; and if he had written for a more sensitive and critical public, and been less tempted by easy success, he might have gone far in both mirth and pathos. As it was, he was the playwright of the hour in America, and being naturally flattered by his proposal I accepted it.

He stipulated that I should write every word of the dialogue, and as I was too much of a novice not to need continual guidance in interpreting his scenario, this led to many
meetings, and to his coming several times to stay. His visits
laid the foundation of a real friendship, and my husband and
I both became very much attached to the plump showily
dressed little man, with his olive complexion, and his beautiful Oriental eyes full of wit and understanding.

The work was longer and more difficult than he had probably foreseen. We were both fastidious, and both frank in our
criticisms of each other; and one day I burst out, rather despairingly: "I can't see how you could ever have thought there
was a play in this book!"

"But I never did!" he exclaimed, his beautiful eyes wide
with astonishment.

"You *didn't*? But they told me you wanted so much to
do it."

He gave a sigh of understanding. "Oh, I see! That's exactly
what they told me about *you*. They said you wanted me to
dramatize your novel, and had refused the rights to everybody
else in the hope that I could be induced to do it."

We sat and stared at each other, seeing that we had been
tricked into collaboration by an unscrupulous intermediary.
Then we both burst out laughing. "I was so flattered—" I
gasped.

"So was I!" he echoed; and we laughed again.

The play was written, the actors were bespoken, and it was
too late to withdraw; but I don't think either of us had a
moment's illusion as to the ultimate result. Clyde Fitch was
leaving the Mount that afternoon; under my laughter he
probably detected my annoyance at having been thus misrep-
resented to him, and the next day he sent me one of the kindest letters that one human being ever wrote to another. He
told me how sorry he was to have taken up so much of my
time on false pretenses (as though I had not taken up as much
of his!), and begged me to believe that, whatever befell the
play (and in theatrical matters, he reminded me, one could
never foretell), he would always be grateful for the accident
which had brought us together, since our collaboration had
given him so much pleasure, and taught him so much, that

the possible failure of the play mattered nothing in comparison. From an experienced playwright to an amateur no words could have been more generous; and he confirmed them by working over the staging and rehearsing as hard as if nothing had happened to disillusionize us.

In spite of his loyal efforts, and of Fay Davis's valiant and beautiful acting, the play failed; but I felt, as he did, that in the attempt I had gained a friend, and that nothing else greatly mattered.

Clyde Fitch was one of the most amusing story-tellers I ever met, and his rich treasures of observation and unfailing enjoyment of the human situation made him a delightful talker. I remember, in particular, one tale which delighted us. He had built himself a country house in Connecticut, probably, like his town house, rather over-ornate and too full of rococo Italian furniture. After a while he decided to sell it furnished, and a newly-rich Western couple having asked to visit it, his secretary was delegated to receive them. They liked the house; but the husband had never heard of the *sette cento* (or perhaps of Italy) and was puzzled and put off by the furniture, and his remarks were so disparaging that his wife was obviously distressed. In one bedroom there was a delicately carved and gilded four-poster, hung with old brocade, its tester decorated with amorous allegories. This was the show room of the house, but the husband said he'd never seen a bed like that, and what the devil could anybody do with it? The scandalized secretary replied that Mr. Fitch had brought it back from Venice, and considered it his best piece; and the wife, to disguise her husband's ignorance, hastily remarked: "Why, I think it's a perfectly lovely bed! Can't you just see one of those old monks in it?"

My theatrical contacts having been so few, I had better record them all here, though the next antedates by many years the production of "The House of Mirth". It must have been shortly after my marriage that my husband and I encountered in Paris an old friend of his family's, Arthur Dexter, a finished specimen of the contemplator-and-appreciator type. He had always been interested in the theatre, and was intimate with several of the great actors of the Théâtre Français—in particular with Got, Coquelin the elder and Delaunay. Delaunay had, I think, already retired, but I had an exquisite recollection of his last performances in the Musset comedies (in which I think he succeeded Bressant), and in the last plays of his modern repertory. My father, who was very fond of the theatre, often took me to the Français when I was a girl of eighteen (the year before his death), and I then saw, in the last faint light of their setting, the great stars of the old group: Madeleine Brohan, Delaunay, Got, with their juniors, Reichemberg, Baretta, Worms and Coquelin.

When, therefore, Arthur Dexter asked me if I would like to go to one of Delaunay's dramatic classes at the Conservatoire, I could hardly believe my luck. It was not easy to obtain permission to assist at any of these classes, and to be admitted to Delaunay's was particularly difficult; but being much attached to Dexter he had consented to make an exception in my favour. I don't believe he often did so; that day, at any rate, no one was present in the dreary *salle* but the young students, men and girls, and the mothers (seemingly authentic) of the latter—for in those days even budding actresses were chaperoned when they went to their classes! They all looked so surprised at our intrusion that shyness overcame me; but I forgot this as soon as one of the pupils mounted to the stage, and Delaunay sat down facing it. It was all so long ago that I recall but few details; but at the moment I had the sense of assisting at something masterly. Delaunay was very small, very withered, very old and rheumatic, and the golden voice was cracked; but the old fire still burned in him. One episode interested me particularly. A young man had prepared a scene (from Corneille's "Menteur", I think) in which his dropping his handkerchief formed an important episode. For some time the would-be comedian failed to drop the handkerchief to Delaunay's satisfaction: the gesture was not charged with all the significance the master thought it should contain. Delaunay explained his point carefully, gave his reasons, took the stage himself to enact the dropping of the handkerchief, and finally clenched his exposition by saying: "We know that this was the way in which it has always been dropped since the play was first acted"—giving the names of the actors by whom the tradition had been handed down unbroken since the seventeenth century.

Still more interesting was the great love scene from "Phè-dre", in which the unhappy Queen declares (shades of the Mississippi Valley clergyman!) her unholy passion for her stepson. The young girl who played Phaedra was beautiful, and had a good voice; but the famous apostrophe which should have poured from her like lava—"*Oui, Prince, je brûle, je languis pour Thésée*", and all the rest of it—failed to become incandescent on the actress's inexperienced lips. Patiently, repeatedly, Delaunay tried to ignite her with the sacred flame, but it was like striking a succession of damp matches; she remained blankly lovely and uncomprehending. At last he took the stage again, pushed her quietly aside, and saying in a sad but unreproachful voice: "*Que voulez-vous, Mademoiselle? Vous êtes trop jeune pour comprendre l'inceste*", proceeded to transform himself into the guilty Queen avowing her desperate desire to its loved and hated object. I saw Sarah Bernhardt afterward in "Phèdre"—and she could not woo and cajole, and taunt and curse and rave, like the old Delaunay.

My other experiences of the stage were few and fleeting. I was once asked—though how it came about I no longer remember—to make a play out of "Manon Lescaut" for that delightful actress, Marie Tempest. It must have happened very long ago, for I have forgotten who the intermediary was, or how Miss Tempest happened to think of me. There is no doubt that I did the play, however, for the manuscript still exists; and I remember, as the chief result, a very pleasant little supper after the theatre, at Miss Tempest's house near Regent's Park, for the purpose of talking the matter over. Soon afterward her manager notified me that she had decided to renounce "costume plays" for modern comedy, a resolve I could not but applaud; and that was the end of that.

Oddly different was the end of my last theatrical venture, which, like the others, was thrust on me and not solicited. A good many years after "Manon"—at the time when we were living in New York—Mrs. Patrick Campbell asked me to translate for her Sudermann's new play, "Es lebe das Leben", of which she had acquired the rights. I admired Mrs. Campbell's acting greatly, but after reading the play I felt obliged to tell her that I did not see how a tragedy based on the German "point of honour" in duelling, a convention which had so long since vanished from our customs, could be intelligible or interesting to English or American audiences. However she insisted, and the translation was made and delivered. I told her that the German title ("Long Live Life", in its most bitterly ironic sense) was virtually untranslatable; but some one persuaded her that it meant "The Joy of Living"! I protested vehemently, not wishing the dramatic critics to accuse me of such a flagrant error; but I was overruled, the play was brought out under that comic title, and in spite of Mrs. Campbell's brilliant acting, it promptly failed—not without the critics having seized the occasion to remark that, if the accuracy of the rest of Mrs. Wharton's translation was on a par with that of the title, etc., etc. . . .

But the odd conclusion was that, the Scribners having, to my surprise, proposed to publish my translation, that work, with its absurd title (which they said it was then too late to change), and its unintelligible discussions on the technical why-and-why-not of duelling, has gone on selling steadily in America ever since (a matter of over twenty-five years); indeed it figured as usual, on a modest scale, in my last royalty returns a few months ago. I have often, but always vainly, asked for a credible explanation of this phenomenon, which I am sure is as unintelligible to my publishers as to me— though they are too polite to tell me so.

In spite of the ill-success of this experiment I enjoyed my brief association with Mrs. Campbell; and in fact my experience of the stage has left me none but kindly memories of the theatre-folk with whom I had to do, though in each case the doing rendered them so little service.

VIII

Henry James

WHAT IS one's personality, detached from that of the friends with whom fate happens to have linked one? I cannot think of myself apart from the influence of the two or three greatest friendships of my life, and any account of my own growth must be that of their stimulating and enlightening influence. From a childhood and youth of complete intellectual isolation—so complete that it accustomed me never to be lonely except in company—I passed, in my early thirties, into an atmosphere of the rarest understanding, the richest and most varied mental comradeship. Some of my friends were men exceptionally distinguished in their own walk of life, without being public figures; others were already celebrated when I first knew them, and of these I shall find it difficult to give an adequate account because of my unhappy lack of verbal memory. Once I had emerged from my long inner solitude my opportunities, though limited in extent (for I have always been fundamentally un-"social"), were of a quality so rare that it ought to illuminate all my pages. I have lived in intimate friendship with two or three great intelligences; but I am not a Boswell myself, and have never had a Boswell of my own, both of which facts I deplore, since in the former case I might have set down the dazzling talk I spent such enchanted hours in absorbing, and in the latter have handed it on to my recording satellite. As it is, having a tendency to pass, when in high company, into a state of exhilaration that precludes anything as precise as taking notes, I enjoy the commerce with great minds as a painter enchanted by the glories of an Alpine meadow rather than as a botanist cataloguing its specimens.

Once, happening to sit next to M. Bergson at a dinner, I confided to him my distress and perplexity over the odd holes in my memory. How was it, I asked, that I could remember, with exasperating accuracy, the most useless and insignificant things, such as the address of every one I knew, and the author of the libretto of every opera I had ever heard since the age of eighteen—while, when it came to poetry, my chiefest passion and my greatest joy, my verbal memory failed me completely, and I heard only the inner cadence, and could hardly ever fill it out with the right words?

I had the impression, before I ended, that my problem did not greatly interest my eminent neighbour; and his reply was distinctly disappointing. *"Mais c'est précisément parce que vous êtes éblouie"* ("It's just because you are dazzled"), he answered quietly, turning to examine the dish which was being handed to him, and making no effort to pursue the subject. It was only afterward that I saw he had really said all there was to say: that the gift of precision in ecstasy (the best definition I can find for the highest poetry) is probably almost as rare in the appreciator as in the creator, and that my years of intellectual solitude had made me so super-sensitive to the joys of great talk that precise recording was impossible to me. Good talk seems, instead, to pass into my mind with a gradual nutritive force sometimes felt only long afterward; it permeates me as a power, an influence, it encloses my universe in a dome of many-coloured glass from which I can detach but few fragments while it builds itself up about me. The reader may here object that I have taken more than a page to say that I have a bad memory; but to say only that would not quite cover the case, since the talk I hear is not forgotten, but stored in some depth from which it still returns in its essential implications, though so seldom in its verbal shape.

Since I have already spoken of Henry James's visits to the Mount, it is perhaps best to put his name first on the list of the friends who composed my closest group during the years I spent there, and those that followed. In fact, however, my first meeting with Henry James happened many years earlier, probably in the late 'eighties; though it is at the Mount that he first comes into the foreground of the picture.

For a long time there seemed small hope of his ever figuring there, for when we first met I was still struck dumb in the presence of greatness, and I had never doubted that Henry James was great, though how great I could not guess till I came to know the man as well as I did his books. The

THE AUTHOR, ABOUT 1884

encounter took place at the house of Edward Boit, the brilliant water-colour painter whose talent Sargent so much admired. Boit and his wife, both Bostonians, and old friends of my husband's, had lived for many years in Paris, and it was there that one day they asked us to dine with Henry James. I could hardly believe that such a privilege could befall me, and I could think of only one way of deserving it—to put on my newest Doucet dress, and try to look my prettiest! I was probably not more than twenty-five, those were the principles in which I had been brought up, and it would never have occurred to me that I had anything but my youth, and my pretty frock, to commend me to the man whose shoe-strings I thought myself unworthy to unloose. I can see the dress still—and it *was* pretty; a tea-rose pink, embroidered with iridescent beads. But, alas, it neither gave me the courage to speak, nor attracted the attention of the great man. The evening was a failure, and I went home humbled and discouraged.

A year or two later, in Venice (probably in 1889 or 1890), the same opportunity came my way. Another friend of my husband's, Ralph Curtis of Boston, had the happy thought of inviting us to meet Henry James, who was, I think, staying either with Curtis at the Palazzo Barbaro, or with Robert Browning's old friend, Mrs. Arthur Bronson. Again fortune held out her hand—and again mine slipped out of it. Once more I thought: How can I make myself pretty enough for him to notice me? Well—this time I had a new hat; *a beautiful new hat!* I was almost sure it was becoming, and I felt that if he would only tell me so I might at last pluck up courage to blurt out my admiration for "Daisy Miller" and "The Portrait of a Lady". But he noticed neither the hat nor its wearer— and the second of our meetings fell as flat as the first. When I spoke to him of them years afterward he owned that he could not even remember having seen me on either occasion! And as for the date of the meeting which finally drew us together, without hesitations or preliminaries, we could neither of us ever recall when or where that happened. All we knew was that suddenly it was as if we had always been friends, and were to go on being (as he wrote to me in February 1910) "more and more never apart".

The explanation, of course, was that in the interval I had found myself, and was no longer afraid to talk to Henry James of the things we both cared about; while he, always so helpful and hospitable to younger writers, at once used his magic faculty of drawing out his interlocutor's inmost self. Perhaps it was our common sense of fun that first brought about our understanding. The real marriage of true minds is for any two people to possess a sense of humour or irony pitched in exactly the same key, so that their joint glances at any subject cross like interarching search-lights. I have had good friends between whom and myself that bond was lacking, but they were never really intimate friends; and in that sense Henry James was perhaps the most intimate friend I ever had, though in many ways we were so different.

The Henry James of the early meetings was the bearded Penseroso of Sargent's delicate drawing, soberly fastidious in dress and manner, cut on the approved pattern of the *homme du monde* of the 'eighties; whereas by the time we got to know each other well the compact upright figure had expanded to a rolling and voluminous outline, and the elegance of dress given way to the dictates of comfort, while a clean shave had revealed in all its sculptural beauty the noble Roman mask and the big dramatic mouth. The change typified something deep beneath the surface. In the interval two things had happened: Henry James had taken the measure of the fashionable society which in youth had subjugated his imagination, as it had Balzac's, and was later to subjugate Proust's, and had fled from it to live in the country, carrying with him all the loot his adventure could yield; and in his new solitude he had come to grips with his genius. Exquisite as the early novels are—and in point of perfection probably none can touch "The Portrait of a Lady"—yet measured by what was to come Henry James, when he wrote them, had but skimmed the surface of life and of his art. Even the man who wrote, in "The Portrait of a Lady", the chapter in which Isabel broods over her fate at night by the fire, was far from the man in whom was already ripening that greater night-piece, the picture of Maggie looking in from the terrace at Fawns at the four bridge-players, and renouncing her vengeance as "nothing nearer to experience than a wild eastern caravan, looming into view with crude colours in the sun, fierce pipes in the air, high spears against the sky . . . but turning off short before it reached her and plunging into other defiles".

But though he had found his genius and broken away from the social routine, he never emancipated himself in small matters from the conformities. Though he now affected to humour the lumbering frame whose physical ease must be considered first, he remained spasmodically fastidious about his dress, and about other trifling social observances, and once when he was motoring with us in France in 1907, and suddenly made up his mind (at Poitiers, of all places!) that he must then and there buy a new hat, almost insuperable difficulties attended its selection. It was not until he had announced his despair of ever making the hatter understand "that what he wanted was a hat like everybody else's", and I had rather impatiently suggested his asking for a head-covering *"pour l'homme moyen sensuel"*, that the joke broke through his indecisions, and to a rich accompaniment of chuckles the hat was bought.

Still more particular about his figure than his dress, he resented any suggestion that his silhouette had lost firmness and acquired volume; and once, when my friend Jacques-Emile Blanche was doing the fine seated profile portrait which is the only one that renders him *as he really was*, he privately implored me to suggest to Blanche "not to lay such stress on the resemblance to Daniel Lambert".

The truth is that he belonged irrevocably to the old America out of which I also came, and of which—almost—it might paradoxically be said that to follow up its last traces one had to come to Europe; as I discovered when my French and English friends told me, on reading "The Age of Innocence", that they had no idea New York life in the 'seventies had been so like that of the English cathedral town, or the French *"ville de province"*, of the same date. As for the nonsense talked by critics of a later generation, who never knew James, much less the world he grew up in, about his having thwarted his genius by living in Europe, and having understood his mistake too late, as a witness of his long sojourns in America in 1904, 1905 and 1910, and of the reactions they produced (expressed in all the letters written at the time), I can affirm that he was never really happy or at home there. He came several times for long visits to the Mount, and during his first visit to America, in 1904–5, he also stayed with us for some time in New York; and responsive as he always was, interested, curious, and heroically hospitable to new ideas, new aspects, new people, the nostalgia of which he speaks so poignantly in one of his letters to Sir Edmund Gosse (written from the Mount) was never for a moment stilled. Henry James was essentially a novelist of manners, and the manners he was qualified by nature and situation to observe were those of the little vanishing group of people among whom he had grown up, or their more picturesque prototypes in older societies. For better or worse he had to seek that food where he could find it, for it was the only food his imagination could fully assimilate. He was acutely conscious of this limitation, and often bewailed to me his total inability to use the "material", financial and industrial, of modern American life. Wall Street, and everything connected with the big business world, remained an impenetrable mystery to him, and knowing this he felt he could never have dealt fully in fiction with the "American scene", and always frankly acknowledged it. The attempt to portray the retired financier in Mr. Verver, and to relate either him or his native "American City" to any sort of concrete reality, is perhaps proof enough of the difficulties James would have found in trying to depict the American money-maker in action.

On his first visit, however, he was still in fairly good health, and in excellent spirits, exhilarated (at first) by the novelty of the adventure, the success of his revolt against his own sedentary habit (he called me "the pendulum-woman" because I crossed the Atlantic every year!), and, above all, captivated by the new experience of motoring. It was the summer when we were experimenting with "Alfred de Musset" and "George"; in spite of many frustrations there were beautiful tours successfully carried out "in the Whartons' commodious new motor, which has fairly converted me to the sense of all the thing may do for one and one may get from it"; and this mode of locomotion seemed to him, as it had to me, an immense enlargement of life.

2

It is particularly regrettable in the case of Henry James that no one among his intimates had a recording mind, or rather that those who had did not apply it to noting down his conversation, for I have never known a case in which an author's talk and his books so enlarged and supplemented each other. Talent is often like an ornamental excrescence; but the quality loosely called genius usually irradiates the whole character. "If he but so much as cut his nails," was Goethe's homely phrase of Schiller, "one saw at once that he was a greater man than any of them." This irradiation, so abundantly basked in by the friends of Henry James, was hidden from those who knew him slightly by a peculiarity due to merely physical causes. His slow way of speech, sometimes mistaken for affectation— or, more quaintly, for an artless form of Anglomania!—was really the partial victory over a stammer which in his boyhood had been thought incurable. The elaborate politeness and the involved phraseology that made off-hand intercourse with him so difficult to casual acquaintances probably sprang from the same defect. To have too much time in which to weigh each word before uttering it could not but lead, in the case of the alertest and most sensitive of minds, to self-consciousness and self-criticism; and this fact explains the hesitating manner that often passed for a mannerism. Once, in New York, when I had arranged a meeting between him and the great Mr. Dooley, whose comments on the world's ways he greatly enjoyed, I perceived, as I watched them after dinner, that Peter Dunne was floundering helplessly in the heavy seas of James's parentheses; and the next time we met, after speaking of his delight in having at last seen James, he added mournfully: "What a pity it takes him so long to say anything! Everything he said was so splendid—but I felt like telling him all the time: 'Just 'pit it right up into Popper's hand'."

To James's intimates, however, these elaborate hesitancies, far from being an obstacle, were like a cobweb bridge flung from his mind to theirs, an invisible passage over which one knew that silver-footed ironies, veiled jokes, tiptoe malices, were stealing to explode a huge laugh at one's feet. This moment of suspense, in which there was time to watch the forces of malice and merriment assembling over the mobile land-scape of his face, was perhaps the rarest of all in the unique experience of a talk with Henry James.

His letters, delightful as they are, give but hints and frag-ments of his talk; the talk that, to his closest friends, when his health and the surrounding conditions were favourable, poured out in a series of images so vivid and appreciations so penetrating, the whole so sunned over by irony, sympathy and wide-flashing fun, that those who heard him at his best will probably agree in saying of him what he once said to me of M. Paul Bourget: "He was the first, easily, of all the talkers I ever encountered."

Of the qualities most impossible to preserve in his letters, because so impossible to explain with whatever fulness of foot-notes, was the quality of fun—often of sheer abstract "fooling"—that was the delicious surprise of his talk. His let-ter to Walter Berry "on the gift of a dressing-bag" is almost the only instance of this genial play that is intelligible to the general reader. From many of the letters to his most intimate group it was necessary to excise long passages of chaff, and recurring references to old heaped-up pyramidal jokes, huge cairns of hoarded nonsense. Henry James's memory for a joke was prodigious; when he got hold of a good one, he not only preserved it piously, but raised upon it an intricate superstruc-ture of kindred nonsense, into which every addition offered by a friend was skilfully incorporated. Into his nonsense-world, as four-dimensional as that of the Looking Glass, or the Land where the Jumblies live, the reader could hardly have groped his way without a preparatory course in each correspondent's private history and casual experience. The merest hint was usually enough to fire the train; and, as in the writing of his tales a tiny mustard-seed of allusion spread into a many-branched "subject", so his best nonsense flowered out of unremembered trifles.

I recall a bubbling over of this nonsense on one of our happy motor-trips among the hills of Western Massachusetts. We had motored so much together in Europe that allusions to Roman ruins and Gothic cathedrals furnished a great part of the jests with which his mind played over what he has called "the thin empty lonely American beauty"; and one day, when his eye caught the fine peak rising alone in the vale between Deerfield and Springfield, with a wooden barrack of a "summer hotel" on its highest ledge, I told him that the hill was Mount Tom, and the building "the famous Carthusian monastery". "Yes, where the monks make Moxie," he flashed back, referring to a temperance drink that was blighting the landscape that summer from a thousand hoardings.

Sometimes his chaff was not untinged with malice. I remember a painful moment, during one of his visits, when my husband imprudently blurted out an allusion to "Edith's new story—you've seen it in the last 'Scribner'?" My heart sank; I knew it always embarrassed James to be called on, in the author's presence, for an "appreciation". He was himself so engrossed in questions of technique and construction—and so increasingly detached from the short-story form as a medium—that very few "fictions" (as he called them) but his own were of interest to him, except indeed Mr. Wells's, for which he once avowed to me an incurable liking, "because everything he writes is so alive and kicking". At any rate I always tried to keep my own work out of his way, and once accused him of ferreting out and reading it just to annoy me—to which charge his sole response was a guilty chuckle. In the present instance, as usual, he instantly replied: "Oh, yes, my dear Edward, I've read the little work—of course I've read it." A gentle pause, which I knew boded no good; then he softly continued: "Admirable, admirable; a masterly little achievement." He turned to me, full of a terrifying benevolence. "Of course so accomplished a mistress of the art would not, without deliberate intention, have given the tale so curiously conventional a treatment. Though indeed, in the given case, no treatment *but* the conventional was possible; which might conceivably, my dear lady, on further consideration, have led you to reject your subject as—er—in itself a totally unsuitable one."

I will not deny that he may have added a silent twinkle to the shout of laughter with which—on that dear wide sunny terrace of the Mount—his fellow-guests greeted my "dressing-down". Yet it would be a mistake to imagine that he had deliberately started out to destroy my wretched tale. He had begun, I am sure, with the sincere intention of praising it; but no sooner had he opened his lips than he was over-mastered by the need to speak the truth, and the whole truth, about anything connected with the art which was sacred to him. Simplicity of heart was combined in him with a brain that Mr. Percy Lubbock has justly called robust, and his tender regard for his friends' feelings was equalled only by the faithfulness with which, on literary questions, he gave them his view of their case when they asked for it—and sometimes when they did not. On all subjects but that of letters his sincerity was tempered by an almost exaggerated tenderness; but when *le métier* was in question no gentler emotion prevailed.

Another day—somewhat later in our friendship, since this time the work under his scalpel was "The Custom of the Country"—after prolonged and really generous praise of my book, he suddenly and irrepressibly burst forth: "But of course you know—as how should you, with your infernal keenness of perception, *not* know?—that in doing your tale you had under your hand a magnificent subject, which ought to have been your main theme, and that you used it as a mere incident and then passed it by?"

He meant by this that for him the chief interest of the book, and its most original theme, was that of a crude young woman such as Undine Spragg entering, all unprepared and unperceiving, into the mysterious labyrinth of family life in the old French aristocracy. I saw his point, and recognized that the contact between the Undine Spraggs and the French families they marry into was, as the French themselves would say, an "actuality" of immense interest to the novelist of manners, and one which as yet had been little dealt with; but I argued that in "The Custom of the Country" I was chronicling the career of a particular young woman, and that to whatever hemisphere her fortunes carried her, my task was to record her ravages and pass on to her next phase. This, however, was no argument to James; he had long since lost all interest in the chronicle-novel, and cared only for the elaborate working out on all sides of a central situation, so that he could merely answer, by implication if not openly: "Then, my dear child, you chose the wrong kind of subject."

Once when he was staying with us in Paris I had a still more amusing experience of this irresistible tendency to speak the truth. He had chanced to nose out the fact that, responding to an S.O.S. from the *Revue des Deux Mondes*, for a given number of which a promised translation of one of my tales had not been ready, I had offered to replace it by writing a story myself—in French! I knew what James would feel about such an experiment, and there was nothing I did not do to conceal the horrid secret from him; but he had found it out before arriving, and when in my presence some idiot challenged him with: "Well, Mr. James, don't you think it's remarkable that Mrs. Wharton should have written a story in French for the *Revue*?" the twinkle which began in the corner of his eyes and trickled slowly down to his twitching lips showed that his answer was ready. "Remarkable—most remarkable! An altogether astonishing feat." He swung around on me slowly. "I do congratulate you, my dear, on the way in which you've picked up every old worn-out literary phrase that's been lying about the streets of Paris for the last twenty years, and managed to pack them all into those few pages." To this withering comment, in talking over the story afterward with one of my friends, he added more seriously, and with singular good sense: "A very creditable episode in her career. *But she must never do it again.*"

He knew I enjoyed our literary rough-and-tumbles, and no doubt for that reason scrupled the less to hit straight from the shoulder; but with others, though he tried to be more merciful, what he really thought was no less manifest. My own experience has taught me that nothing is more difficult than to talk indifferently or insincerely on the subject of one's craft. The writer, without much effort, can reel off polite humbug about pictures, the painter about books; but to fib about the art one practises is incredibly painful, and James's overscrupulous conscience, and passionate reverence for letters, while always inclining him to mercy, made deception doubly impossible.

I think it was James who first made me understand that genius is not an indivisible element, but one variously apportioned, so that the popular system of dividing humanity into geniuses and non-geniuses is a singularly inadequate way of estimating human complexity. In connection with this, I once brought him a phrase culled in a literary review.

"Mr. ⸺ has *almost a streak* of genius". James, always an eager collector of verbal oddities, fell on the phrase with rapture, and earnest requests to every one to define the exact extent of "almost a streak" caused him amusement for months afterward. I mention this because so few people seem to have known in Henry James the ever-bubbling fountain of fun which was the delight of his intimates.

One of our joys, when the talk touched on any great example of prose or verse, was to get the book from the shelf, and ask one of the company to read the passage aloud. There were some admirable readers in the group, in whose gift I had long delighted; but I had never heard Henry James read aloud—or known that he enjoyed doing so—till one night some one alluded to Emily Brontë's poems, and I said I had never read "Remembrance". Immediately he took the volume from my hand, and, his eyes filling, and some far-away emotion deepening his rich and flexible voice, he began:

> Cold in the earth, and the deep snow piled above thee,
> Far, far removed, cold in the dreary grave,
> Have I forgot, my only Love, to love thee,
> Severed at last by Time's all-severing wave?

I had never before heard poetry read as he read it; and I never have since. He chanted it, and he was not afraid to chant it, as many good readers are, who, though they instinctively feel that the genius of the English poetical idiom requires it to be spoken *as poetry*, are yet afraid of yielding to their instinct because the present-day fashion is to chatter high verse as though it were colloquial prose. James, on the contrary, far from shirking the rhythmic emphasis, gave it full expression. His stammer ceased as by magic as soon as he began to read, and his ear, so sensitive to the convolutions of an intricate prose style, never allowed him to falter over the most complex prosody, but swept him forward on great rollers of sound till the full weight of his voice fell on the last cadence.

James's reading was a thing apart, an emanation of his inmost self, unaffected by fashion or elocutionary artifice. He read from his soul, and no one who never heard him read poetry knows what that soul was. Another day some one spoke of Whitman, and it was a joy to me to discover that James thought him, as I did, the greatest of American poets. "Leaves of Grass" was put into his hands, and all that evening we sat rapt while he wandered from "The Song of Myself" to "When lilacs last in the door-yard bloomed" (when he read "Lovely and soothing Death" his voice filled the hushed room like an organ adagio), and thence let himself be lured on to the mysterious music of "Out of the Cradle", reading, or rather crooning it in a mood of subdued ecstasy till the five-fold invocation to Death tolled out like the knocks in the opening bars of the Fifth Symphony.

James's admiration of Whitman, his immediate response to that mighty appeal, was a new proof of the way in which, above a certain level, the most divergent intelligences walk together like gods. We talked long that night of "Leaves of Grass", tossing back and forth to each other treasure after treasure; but finally James, in one of his sudden humorous drops from the heights, flung up his hands and cried out with the old stammer and twinkle: "Oh, yes, a great genius; undoubtedly a very great genius! Only one cannot help deploring his too-extensive acquaintance with the foreign languages."

3

I believe James enjoyed those days at the Mount as much as he did (or could) anything connected with the American scene; and the proof of it is the length of his visits and their frequency. But on one occasion his stay with us coincided with a protracted heat-wave; a wave of such unusual intensity that even the nights, usually cool and airy at the Mount, were as stifling as the days. My own dislike of heat filled me with sympathy for James, whose sufferings were acute and uncontrollable. Like many men of genius he had a singular inability for dealing with the most ordinary daily incidents, such as giving an order to a servant, deciding what to wear, taking a railway ticket, or getting from one place to another; and I have often smiled to think how far nearer the truth than he could possibly have known was the author of that cataclysmic sketch in the famous "If—" series: "If Henry James had written Bradshaw."

During a heat-wave this curious inadaptability to conditions or situations became positively tragic. His bodily surface, already broad, seemed to expand to meet it, and his imagination to become a part of his body, so that the one dripped words of distress as the other did moisture. Always uneasy about his health, he became visibly anxious in hot weather, and this anxiety added so much to his sufferings that his state was pitiful. Electric fans, iced drinks and cold baths seemed to give no relief; and finally we discovered that the only panacea was incessant motoring. Luckily by that time we had a car which would really go, and go we did, daily, incessantly, over miles and miles of lustrous landscape lying motionless under the still glaze of heat. While we were moving he was refreshed and happy, his spirits rose, the twinkle returned to lips and eyes; and we never halted except for tea on a high hillside, or for a "cooling drink" at a village apothecary's—on one of which occasions he instructed one of us to bring him "something less innocent than Apollinaris", and was enchanted when this was interpreted as meaning an "orange phosphate", a most sophisticated beverage for that day.

On another afternoon we had encamped for tea on a mossy ledge in the shade of great trees, and as he seemed less uneasy than usual somebody pulled out an anthology, and I asked one of the party to read aloud Swinburne's "Triumph of Time", which I knew to be a favourite of James's; but after a stanza or two I saw the twinkle of beatitude fade, and an agonized hand was lifted up. "Perhaps, in view of the abnormal state of the weather, our young friend would have done better to choose a poem of less inordinate length—" and immediately we were all bundled back into the car and started off again on the incessant quest for air.

James was to leave for England in about a fortnight; but his sufferings distressed me so much that, the day after this expedition, feeling sure that there was nothing to detain him in America if he chose to go, I asked a friend who was staying in the house to propose my telephoning for a passage on a Boston steamer which was sailing within two days. My ambassador executed the commission, and hurried back with the report that the mere hint of such a plan had thrown James into a state of helpless perturbation. To change his sailing date at two days' notice—to get from the Mount to Boston (four hours by train) in *two days*—how could I lightly suggest anything so impracticable? And what about his heavy luggage, which was at his brother William's in New Hampshire? And his wash, which had been sent to the laundry only the afternoon before? Between the electric fan clutched in his hand, and the pile of sucked oranges at his elbow, he cowered there, a mountain of misery, repeating in a sort of low despairing chant: "Good God, what a woman—what a woman! Her imagination boggles at nothing! She does not even scruple to project me in a naked flight across the Atlantic . . ." The heat collapse had been as nothing to the depths into which my rash proposal plunged him, and it took several hours to quiet him down and persuade him that, if he preferred enduring the weather to flying from it, we were only too glad to keep him at the Mount.

A similar perturbation could be produced (I later learned, to my cost) by asking him to explain any phrase in his books that did not seem quite clear, or any situation of which the motive was not adequately developed; and still more disastrous was the effect of letting him know that any of his writings had been parodied. I had always regarded the fact of being parodied as one of the surest evidences of fame, and once, when he was staying with us in New York, I brought him with glee a deliciously droll article on his novels by poor Frank Colby, the author of "Imaginary Obligations". The effect was disastrous. I shall never forget the misery, the mortification even, which tried to conceal itself behind an air of offended dignity. His ever-bubbling sense of fun failed him completely on such occasions; as it did also (I was afterward to find) when one questioned him, in a way that even remotely implied criticism, on any point in the novels. It was in England, I think—when he and I, and a party of intimate friends, were staying together at Howard Sturgis's—that I brought him, in all innocence, a passage from one of his books which, after repeated readings, I still found unintelligible. He took the book from me, read over the passage to himself, and handed it back with a lame attempt at a joke; but I saw—we all saw—that even this slight, and quite involuntary, criticism, had wounded his morbidly delicate sensibility.

Once again—and again unintentionally—I was guilty of a similar blunder. I was naturally much interested in James's technical theories and experiments, though I thought, and still think, that he tended to sacrifice to them that spontaneity which is the life of fiction. Everything, in the latest novels, had to be fitted into a predestined design, and design, in his strict geometrical sense, is to me one of the least important things in fiction. Therefore, though I greatly admired some of the principles he had formulated, such as that of always letting the tale, as it unfolded, be seen through the mind most capable of reaching to its periphery, I thought it was paying too dear even for such a principle to subordinate to it the irregular and irrelevant movements of life. And one result of the application of his theories puzzled and troubled me. His latest novels, for all their profound moral beauty, seemed to me more and more lacking in atmosphere, more and more severed from that thick nourishing human air in which we all live and move. The characters in "The Wings of the Dove" and "The Golden Bowl" seem isolated in a Crookes tube for our inspection: his stage was cleared like that of the Théâtre Français in the good old days when no chair or table was introduced that was not *relevant to the action* (a good rule for the stage, but an unnecessary embarrassment to fiction). Preoccupied by this, I one day said to him: "What was your idea in suspending the four principal characters in 'The Golden Bowl' in the void? What sort of life did they lead when they were not watching each other, and fencing with each other? Why have you stripped them of all the *human fringes* we necessarily trail after us through life?"

He looked at me in surprise, and I saw at once that the surprise was painful, and wished I had not spoken. I had assumed that his system was a deliberate one, carefully thought out, and had been genuinely anxious to hear his reasons. But after a pause of reflection he answered in a disturbed voice: "My dear—I didn't know I had!" and I saw that my question, instead of starting one of our absorbing literary discussions,

HENRY JAMES
(SNAP-SHOT TAKEN IN SCOTLAND BY A GAMEKEEPER
ON JOHN CADWALADER'S MOOR)

had only turned his startled attention on a peculiarity of which he had been completely unconscious.

This sensitiveness to criticism or comment of any sort had nothing to do with vanity; it was caused by the great artist's deep consciousness of his powers, combined with a bitter, a life-long disappointment at his lack of popular recognition. I am not sure that Henry James had not secretly dreamed of being a "best seller" in the days when that odd form of literary fame was at its height; at any rate he certainly suffered all his life—and more and more as time went on—from the lack of recognition among the very readers who had most warmly welcomed his early novels. He could not understand why the success achieved by "Daisy Miller" and "The Portrait of a Lady" should be denied to the great novels of his maturity: and the sense of protracted failure made him miserably alive to the least hint of criticism, even from those who most completely understood, and sympathized with, his later experiments in technique and style.

4

Those long days at the Mount, in the deep summer glow or the crisp glitter of autumn, the walks in the woods, motor-flights over hill and dale, evening talks on the moonlit terrace and readings around the library fire, come back with a mocking radiance as I write—and with them the figures of our other most beloved guests, Walter Berry, Bay Lodge, and three dear friends from England, Gaillard Lapsley, Robert Norton and John Hugh Smith.

Still others, friendly and delightful also, came and went; but these, with Henry James, if not by the actual frequency of their visits, yet from some secret quality of participation, had formed from the first the nucleus of what I have called the inner group. In this group an almost immediate sympathy had established itself between the various members, so that our common stock of allusions, cross-references, pleasantries was always increasing, and new waves of interest in the same book or picture, or any sort of dramatic event in life or letters, would simultaneously flood through our minds.

I think I may safely say that Henry James was never so

good as with this little party at the Mount, or when some of its members were reunited, as often happened in after years, under Howard Sturgis's welcoming roof at Windsor. The mere fact that we had in common so many topics, and such innumerable allusions, made James's talk on such occasions easier and wider-ranging than I ever heard it elsewhere; and the free and rapid give-and-take of ideas animated his mind, which so easily drooped in dull company.

In one respect Henry James stood alone among the great talkers I have known, for while he was inexhaustible in repartee, and never had the least tendency to monopolize the talk, yet it was really in monologue that he was most himself. I remember in particular one summer evening, when we sat late on the terrace at the Mount, with the lake shining palely through dark trees, and one of us suddenly said to him (in response to some chance allusion to his Albany relations): "And now tell us about the Emmets—tell us all about them."

The Emmet and Temple families composed, as we knew, the main element of his vast and labyrinthine cousinship— "the Emmetry", as he called it—and for a moment he stood there brooding in the darkness, murmuring over to himself: "Ah, my dear, the Emmets—ah, the Emmets!" Then he began, forgetting us, forgetting the place, forgetting everything but the vision of his lost youth that the question had evoked, the long train of ghosts flung with his enchanter's wand across the wide stage of the summer night. Ghostlike indeed at first, wavering and indistinct, they glimmered at us through a series of disconnected ejaculations, epithets, allusions, parenthetical rectifications and restatements, till not only our brains but the clear night itself seemed filled with a palpable fog; and then, suddenly, by some miracle of shifted lights and accumulated strokes, there they stood before us as they lived, drawn with a million filament-like lines, yet sharp as an Ingres, dense as a Rembrandt; or, to call upon his own art for an analogy, minute and massive as the people of Balzac.

I often saw the trick repeated; saw figures obscure or famous summoned to the white square of his magic-lantern, flickering and wavering there, and slowly solidifying under the turn of his lens; but never perhaps anything so ample, so sustained, as that summoning to life of dead-and-gone Emmets and Temples, old lovelinesses, old follies, old failures, all long laid away and forgotten under old crumbling gravestones. I wonder if it may not have been that very night, the place and his re-awakened associations aiding, that they first came to him and constrained him to make them live for us again in the pages of "A Small Boy" and "A Son and Brother"?

5

In New York James was a different being. He hated the place, as his letters abundantly testify; its aimless ugliness, its noisy irrelevance, wore on his nerves; but he was amused by the social scene, and eager to leave nothing of it unobserved. During his visits, therefore, we invited many people to the house, and he dined out frequently, and went to the play— for he was still intensely interested in the theatre. But this mundane James, his attention scattered, his long and complex periods breaking against a dull wall of incomprehension, and dispersing themselves in nervous politenesses, was a totally different being from our leisurely companion at the Mount. I always enjoyed having him under my roof, wherever that good fortune befell me; but my hurried preoccupied New York guest seemed a mere fragment of the great "Henry" of our country hours.

New York in those days, though more cosmopolitan than in my youth, was still a small place, with so limited a range of intellectual interests and allusions that dinner-table talk was a good deal like the "local items" column in a country newspaper; and I remember depressing evenings when the hosts, contributing orchids and gold plate, remained totally unconscious of the royal gifts their guest had brought them in exchange.

James knew that his treasures were largely unmarketable in Fifth Avenue, but it perplexed and saddened him that they should, as a rule, be equally so in the world of letters, which he was naturally even more eager to explore. I remember one occasion when a dinner was especially arranged to make known to him a brilliant essayist whose books he greatly enjoyed. Unhappily the essayist's opaque countenance revealed nothing of the keenness within, and he on his part, though appreciative of James's genius, was obviously put off by his laborious hesitations. Their comments on the meeting were, on the essayist's side, a joke about James's stammer, and on James's the melancholy exclamation: "What a mug!"

I suspect that he was much happier, and more at his ease, in Boston than in New York. At Cambridge, in the houses of his brother, William James, and of Charles Eliot Norton, and their kindred circles, he had the best of Boston; and in Boston itself, where the sense of the past has always been so much stronger than in New York, he found all sorts of old affinities and relations, and early Beacon Hill traditions, to act as life-belts in the vast ocean of strangeness. He had always clung to his cousinage, and to any one who represented old friendly associations, whether in Albany, New York or Boston, and I remember his once saying: "You see, my dear, they're so much easier to talk to, because I can always ask them questions about uncles and aunts, and other cousins." He had brought this question-asking system to a high state of perfection, and practised it not only on relations and old friends, but on transatlantic pilgrims to Lamb House, whom he would literally silence by a friendly volley of interrogations as to what train they had taken to come down, and whether they had seen all the cathedral towns yet, and what plays they had done; so that they went away aglow with the great man's cordiality, "and, you see, my dear, they hadn't time to talk to me about my books"—the calamity at all costs to be averted.

IX

The Secret Garden

This wielding of the unreal trowel.
Walter Scott's Diary (December 26, 1825)

I

I HAVE hesitated for some time before beginning this chapter, since any attempt to analyze work of one's own doing seems to imply that one regards it as likely to be of lasting interest, and I wish at once to repudiate such an assumption. Every artist works, like the Gobelins weavers, on the wrong side of the tapestry, and if now and then he comes around to the right side, and catches what seems a happy glow of colour, or a firm sweep of design, he must instantly retreat again, if encouraged yet still uncertain; and once the work is done, and he hopes to contemplate it dispassionately, the result of his toil too often presses on his tired eyes with the nightmare weight of a cinema "close-up".

Nevertheless, no picture of myself would be more than a profile if it failed to give some account of the teeming visions which, ever since my small-childhood, and even at the busiest and most agitated periods of my outward life, have incessantly peopled my inner world. I shall therefore try to describe, as simply as I can, what seems to have gone to the making of my books; and there is the more reason for doing so because so few writers seem to have watched themselves while they wrote, or if they did, to have set down their observations. Not a few painters have painted themselves at their easels, but I can think of nothing corresponding to these self-confessions in the world of letters, or at any rate of fiction, except the prefaces of Henry James. These, however, are mainly analyses of the way in which he focussed a given subject, and of the technical procedure employed, his angle of vision once determined. Even that deeply moving fragment, the appeal to his Genius, the knowledge of which we owe to Percy Lubbock, is an invocation to the goddess and not an objective notation of her descent into his soul. What I mean to try for is the observation of that strange moment when the vaguely adumbrated characters whose adventures one is preparing to record are suddenly *there*, themselves, in the flesh, in possession of one, and in command of one's voice and hand. It is there that the central mystery lies, and perhaps it is as impossible to fix in words as that other mystery of what happens in the brain at the precise moment when one falls over the edge of consciousness into sleep.

My impression is that, among English and American novelists, few are greatly interested in these deeper processes of their art; their conscious investigations of method seldom seem to go deeper than syntax, and it is immeasurably deeper that the vital interest begins. Therefore I shall try to depict the growth and unfolding of the plants in my secret garden, from the seed to the shrub-top—for I have no intention of magnifying my vegetation into trees!

When I began to talk with novelists about the art of fiction I was amazed at the frequently repeated phrase: "I've been hunting about for months for a good subject". Hunting about for a subject! Good heavens! I remember once, when an old friend of the pen made this rather wistful complaint, carelessly rejoining: "Subjects? But they swarm about me like mosquitoes! I'm sick of them; they stifle me. I wish I could get rid of them!" And only years afterward, when I had learned more from both life and letters, did I understand how presumptuous such an answer must have sounded. The truth is that I have never attached much importance to subject, partly because every incident, every situation, presents itself to me in the light of story-telling material, and partly from the conviction that the possibilities of a given subject are—whatever a given imagination can make of them. But by the time I had written three or four novels I had learned to keep silence on this point.

The analysis of the story-telling process may be divided into two parts: that which concerns the technique of fiction (in the widest sense), and that which tries to look into what, for want of a simpler term, one must call by the old bardic name of inspiration. On the subject of technique I have found only two novelists explicitly and deeply interested: Henry James and Paul Bourget. I have talked long and frequently with both, and profitably also, I hope, though on certain points we always disagreed. I have also, to the best of my ability, analyzed this process, as I understood it, in my book, "The Writing of Fiction"; and therefore I shall deal here not with any general theory of technique but simply with the question of how some of my own novels happened to me, how each little volcanic island shot up from the unknown depths, or each coral-atoll slowly built itself. But first I will try to capture the elusive moment of the arrival of the characters.

In the birth of fiction, it is sometimes the situation, the "case", which first presents itself, and sometimes the characters who appear, asking to be fitted into a situation. It is hard to say what conditions are likely to give the priority to one or the other, and I doubt if fiction can be usefully divided into novels of situation and of character, since a novel, if worth anything at all, is always both, in inextricable combination. In my own case a situation sometimes occurs to me first, and sometimes a single figure suddenly walks into my mind. If the situation takes the lead, I leave it lying about, as it were, in a quiet place, and wait till the characters creep stealthily up and wriggle themselves into it. All I seem to have done is to say, at the outset: "This thing happened—but to whom?" Then I wait, holding my breath, and one by one the people appear and take possession of the case. When it happens in the other way, I may be strolling about casually in my mind, and suddenly a character will start up, coming seemingly from nowhere. Again, but more breathlessly, I watch; and presently the character draws nearer, and seems to become aware of me, and to feel the shy but desperate need to unfold his or her tale. I cannot say in which way a subject is most likely to present itself—though perhaps in short stories the situation, in novels one of the characters, generally appears first.

But this is not the most interesting point of the adventure. Compared with what follows it is not interesting at all, though it has, in my case, one odd feature I have not heard of elsewhere—that is, that my characters always appear with their names. Sometimes these names seem to me affected, sometimes almost ridiculous; but I am obliged to own that they are never fundamentally unsuitable. And the proof that they are not, that they really belong to the people, is the difficulty I have in trying to substitute other names. For many years the attempt always ended fatally; any character I unchristened instantly died on my hands, as if it were some kind of sensitive crustacean, and the name it brought with it were its shell. Only gradually, and in very few cases, have I gained enough mastery over my creatures to be able to effect the change; and even now, when I do, I have to resort to hypodermics and oxygen, and not always successfully.

These names are hardly ever what I call "real names", that is, the current patronymics one would find in an address-book or a telephone directory; and it is their excessive oddness which often makes me try to change them. When in a book by some one else I meet people called by current names I always say to myself: "Ah, those names were tied on afterward"; and I often find that the characters thus labelled are less living than the others. Yet there seems to be no general rule, for in the case of certain famous novelists whose characters have out-of-the-way names, many are tied on too. Balzac had to hunt the streets of Paris for names on shop-signs; and Thackeray and Trollope bent their genius to the invention of the most laboured and dreary pleasantries in the pointless attempt to characterize their people in advance. Yet Captain Deuceace and the Rev. Mr. Quiverful are alive enough, and I can only suppose that this odd fact of the prenamed characters is a peculiarity of my own mental make-up. But I often wonder how the novelist whose people arrive without names manages to establish relations with them!

A still more spectral element in my creative life is the sudden appearance of names without characters. Several times, in this way, a name to which I can attach no known association of ideas has forced itself upon me in a furtive shadowy way, not succeeding in making its bearer visible, yet hanging about obstinately for years in the background of my thoughts. The Princess Estradina was such a name. I knew nothing of its origin, and still less of the invisible character to whom it presumably belonged. Who was she, what were her nationality, her history, her claims on my attention? She must have been there, lurking and haunting me, for years before she walked into "The Custom of the Country", in high-coloured flesh and blood, cool, dominant and thoroughly at home. Another such character haunts me today. Her name is still odder: Laura Testvalley. How I should like to change that name! But it has been attached for some time now to a strongly outlined material form, the form of a character figuring largely in an adventure I know all about, and have long wanted to relate. Several times I have tried to give Miss Testvalley another name, since the one she bears, should it appear ever in print, will be even more troublesome to my readers than to me. But she is strong-willed, and even obstinate, and turns sulky and unmanageable whenever I hint at the advantages of a change; and I foresee that she will eventually force her way into my tale burdened with her impossible patronymic.

But this is a mere parenthesis; what I want to try to capture is an impression of the elusive moment when these people who haunt my brain actually begin to speak within me with their own voices. The situating of my tale, and its descriptive and narrative portions, I am conscious of conducting, though often unaware of how the story first came to me, pleading to be told; but as soon as the dialogue begins, I become merely a recording instrument, and my hand never hesitates because my mind has not to choose, but only to set down what these stupid or intelligent, lethargic or passionate, people say to each other in a language, and with arguments, that appear to be all their own. It is because of this that I attach such importance to dialogue, and yet regard it as an effect to be sparingly used. By dialogue I do not mean the pages of "Yes" and "No", of platitudes and repetitions, of which most actual talk is composed, and which any writer with a photographic mind and a good memory can set down by the yard (and does, in most modern fiction). The vital dialogue is that exchanged by characters whom their creator has really vitalized, and his instinct will be to record only the significant passages of their talk, in high relief against the narrative, and not uselessly embedded in it.

These moments of high tension, when the creature lives and its creator listens to it, have nothing in common with the "walking away with the subject", the "settling it in their own way", with which some novelists so oddly charge their characters. It is always a necessity to me that the note of inevitableness should be sounded at the very opening of my tale, and that my characters should go forward to their ineluctable doom like the "murdered man" in "The Pot of Basil". From the first I know exactly what is going to happen to every one of them; their fate is settled beyond rescue, and I have but to watch and record. When I read that great novelists like Dickens and Trollope "killed off" a character, or changed the conclusion of a tale, in response to the request or the criticism of a reader, I am dumbfounded. What then was their own relation to their subject? But to show how mysterious and incalculable the whole business is, one has only to remember that Trollope "went home and killed" Mrs. Proudie because he had overheard some fool at his club complaining that she had lived long enough; and yet that the death scene thus arbitrarily brought about is one of the greatest pages he ever wrote, and places him momentarily on a level with Balzac and Tolstoy!

But these people of mine, whose ultimate destiny I know so well, walk to it by ways unrevealed to me beforehand. Not only their speech, but what I might call their subsidiary action, seems to be their very own, and I am sometimes startled at the dramatic effect of a word or gesture which would never have occurred to me if I had been pondering over an abstract "situation", as yet uninhabited by its "characters".

I do not think I can get any nearer than this to the sources of my story-telling; I can only say that the process, though it takes place in some secret region on the sheer edge of consciousness, is always illuminated by the full light of my critical attention. What happens there is as real and as tangible as my encounters with my friends and neighbours, often more so, though on an entirely different plane. It produces in me a great emotional excitement, quite unrelated to the joy or sorrow caused by real happenings, but as intense, and with as great an appearance of reality; and my two lives, divided between these equally real yet totally unrelated worlds, have gone on thus, side by side, equally absorbing, but wholly isolated from each other, ever since in my infancy I "read stories" aloud to myself out of Washington Irving's "Alhambra", which I generally held upside down.

2

After "The Valley of Decision", and my book on Italian villas, the idea of attempting a novel of contemporary life in New York began to fascinate me. Still, I hesitated. "The Valley of Decision" was not, in my sense of the term, a novel at all, but only a romantic chronicle, unrolling its episodes like the frescoed legends on the palace-walls which formed its background; my idea of a novel was something very different, something far more compact and centripetal, and I doubted whether I should ever have enough constructive power to achieve anything beyond isolated character studies, or the stringing together of picturesque episodes. But my mind was full of my new subject, and whatever else I was about, I went on, in Tyndall's brooding phrase, trying to "look into it till it became luminous".

Fate had planted me in New York, and my instinct as a story-teller counselled me to use the material nearest to hand, and most familiarly my own. Novelists of my generation must have noticed, in recent years, as one of the unforeseen results of "crowd-mentality" and standardizing, that the modern critic requires every novelist to treat the same kind of subject, and relegates to insignificance the author who declines to conform. At present the demand is that only the man with the dinner pail shall be deemed worthy of attention, and fiction is classed according to its degree of conformity to this rule.

There could be no greater critical ineptitude than to judge a novel according to *what it ought to have been about*. The bigger the imagination, the more powerful the intellectual equipment, the more different subjects will come within the novelist's reach; and Balzac spread his net over nearly every class and situation in the French social system. As a matter of fact, there are but two essential rules: one, that the novelist should deal only with what is within his reach, literally or figuratively (in most cases the two are synonymous), and the other that the value of a subject depends almost wholly on what the author sees in it, and how deeply he is able to see *into* it. Almost—but not quite; for there are certain subjects too shallow to yield anything to the most searching gaze. I had always felt this, and now my problem was how to make use of a subject—fashionable New York—which, of all others, seemed most completely to fall within the condemned category. There it was before me, in all its flatness and futility, asking to be dealt with as the theme most available to my hand, since I had been steeped in it from infancy, and should not have to get it up out of note-books and encyclopaedias—and yet!

The problem was how to extract from such a subject the typical human significance which is the story-teller's reason for telling one story rather than another. In what aspect could a society of irresponsible pleasure-seekers be said to have, on the "old woe of the world", any deeper bearing than the people composing such a society could guess? The answer was that a frivolous society can acquire dramatic significance only through what its frivolity destroys. Its tragic implication lies in its power of debasing people and ideals. The answer, in short, was my heroine, Lily Bart.

Once I had understood that, the tale rushed on toward its climax. I already had definite ideas as to how any given subject should be viewed, and from what angle approached; my trouble was that the story kept drawing into its web so many subordinate themes that to show their organic connection with the main issue, yet keep them from crowding to the front, was a heavy task for a beginner. The novel was already promised to "Scribner's Magazine", but no date had been fixed for its delivery, and between my critical dissatisfaction with the work, and the distractions of a busy and hospitable life, full of friends and travel, reading and gardening, I had let the months drift by without really tackling my subject. And then, one day, Mr. Burlingame came to my rescue by asking me to come to his. A novel which was to have preceded mine in the magazine could not be ready in time, and I was asked to replace it. The first chapters of my tale would have to appear almost at once, and it must be completed within four or five months! I have always been a slow worker, and was then a very inexperienced one, and I was to be put to the severest test to which a novelist can be subjected: my novel was to be exposed to public comment before I had worked it out to its climax. What that climax was to be I had known before I began. My last page is always latent in my first; but the intervening windings of the way become clear only as I write, and now I was asked to gallop over them before I had even traced them out! I had expected to devote another year or eighteen months to the task, instead of which I was asked to be ready within six months; and nothing short of "the hand of God" must be suffered to interrupt my labours, since my first chapters would already be in print!

I hesitated for a day, and then accepted, and buckled down to my job; and of all the friendly turns that Mr. Burlingame ever did me, his exacting this effort was undoubtedly the most helpful. Not only did it give me what I most lacked—self-confidence—but it bent me to the discipline of the daily task, that inscrutable "inspiration of the writing table" which Baudelaire, most untrammelled and nerve-racked of geniuses, proclaimed as insistently as Trollope. When the first chapters appeared I had written hardly fifty thousand words; but I kept at it, and finished and delivered my novel on time.

It was good to be turned from a drifting amateur into a professional; but that was nothing compared to the effect on my imagination of systematic daily effort. I was really like Saul the son of Kish, who went out to find an ass, and came back with a kingdom: the kingdom of mastery over my tools. When the book was done I remember saying to myself: "I don't yet know how to write a novel; *but I know how to find out how to.*"

I went on steadily trying to 'find out how to'; but I wrote two or three novels without feeling that I had made much progress. It was not until I wrote "Ethan Frome" that I suddenly felt the artisan's full control of his implements. When "Ethan Frome" first appeared I was severely criticized by the reviewers for what was considered the clumsy structure of the tale. I had pondered long on this structure, had felt its peculiar difficulties, and possible awkwardness, but could think of no alternative which would serve as well in the given case; and though I am far from thinking "Ethan Frome" my best novel, and am bored and even exasperated when I am told that it is, I am still sure that its structure is not its weak point.

From that day until now I have always felt that I had my material fairly well in hand, though so often, alas, I am conscious that the strange beings who have commissioned me

to tell their story are not satisfied with the portraits I have
drawn of them. I think it was Sargent who said that, when a
portrait was submitted to the sitter's family, the comment of
the latter was always: "There's something wrong about the
mouth". It is the same with my sitters; though they are free to
talk and even to behave, in their own way, the image of them
reflected in my pages is often, I fear, wavering, or at least
blurred. "There is something wrong about the mouth"—and
the great masters of portraiture, Balzac, Tolstoy, Thackeray,
Trollope, have neglected to tell us by what means they not
only "caught the likeness", but carried it on, in all its flesh-
and-blood actuality and changefulness, to the very last page.

<h2 style="text-align:center">3</h2>

All novelists who describe (whether from without or
within) what is called "society life", are pursued by the exasperating accusation of putting flesh-and-blood people into
their books. Any one gifted with the least creative faculty
knows the absurdity of such a charge. "Real people" transported into a work of the imagination would instantly cease
to be real; only those born of the creator's brain can give the
least illusion of reality. But it is hopeless to persuade the unimaginative—who make up the bulk of novel-readers—that
to introduce actual people into a novel would be exactly like
gumming their snapshots into the vibrating human throng of
a Guardi picture. If one did, they would be the only dead and
unreal objects in a scene quivering with life. The low order, in
fiction, of the genuine *roman à clef* (which is never written by
a born novelist) naturally makes any serious writer of fiction
indignant at being suspected of such methods. Nothing can
be more trying to the creative writer than to have a clumsy
finger point at one of the beings born in that mysterious
other-world of invention, with the playful accusation: "Of
course we all recognize your aunt Eliza!", or to be told (and
this has more than once happened to me): "We all thought
your heroine must be meant for Mrs. X., *because their hair is
exactly the same colour.*"

Of what, then, are the mysterious creatures compounded
who come to life (sometimes) under the novelist's pen? Well,

it would be insincere to deny that there are bits of Aunt Eliza in this one, of Mrs. X. in that—though in the case of Mrs. X. it is hardly likely that the psychological novelist would use the colour of her hair as a mark of identity, and more than probable that the bits of Mrs. X. which have actually served him are embedded in some character where the reader alive only to outward signs would never think of seeking them. The process is in fact inexplicable enough to the author, and doubly so to his readers. No "character" can be made out of nothing, still less can it be successfully pieced together out of heterogeneous scraps of the "real", like dismembered statues of which the fragments have been hopelessly mixed up by the restorer. The process is more like that by which sham Tanagra statuettes used formerly, I have been told, to be manufactured for the unsuspecting. The experts having discovered that ancient terra-cotta acquires, through long burial, a peculiar flavour, were in the habit of assuring themselves of the genuineness of the piece by *tasting it*; and the forgers, discovering this, ground fragments of old Tanagras into powder, ran the powder into one of the old moulds, and fearlessly presented the result as an antique. Experience, observation, the looks and ways and words of "real people", all melted and fused in the white heat of the creative fires—such is the mingled stuff which the novelist pours into the firm mould of his narrative. And yet even this does not wholly solve the problem; it is only a step or two nearer the truth than the exasperating attributions of the simple-minded . . .

These attributions are exasperating, no doubt; but they are less so because of the accidental annoyance that may result in a given case than because they bring home to the creator, each time with a fresh shock, the lack of imaginative response to his effort. It is discouraging to know that the books into the making of which so much of one's soul has entered will be snatched at by readers curious only to discover which of the heroes and heroines of the "society column" are to be found in it. But I made up my mind long ago that it is foolish and illogical to resent so puerile a form of criticism. If one has sought the publicity of print, and sold one's wares in the open market, one has sold to the purchasers the right to think what they choose about one's books; and the novelist's best safeguard is to put out of his mind the quality of the praise or blame bestowed on him by reviewers and readers, and to write only for that dispassionate and ironic critic who dwells within the breast.

X

London, "Qu'acre" and "Lamb"

I

I MUST GO BACK a long way to recover the threads leading to my earliest acquaintance with London society. My husband and I took our first dip into it just after the appearance of "The Greater Inclination"; but a dip so brief that I brought back from it hardly more than a list of names. It was then, probably, that I first met Lady Jeune, afterward Lady St Helier, whose friendly interest put me in relation with her large and ever-varying throng of guests. The tastes and interests of Lady St Helier, one of the best-known London hostesses of her day, could hardly have been more remote from my own. She was a born "entertainer" according to the traditional London idea, which regarded (and perhaps still regards) the act of fighting one's way through a struggling crowd of celebrities as the finest expression of social intercourse. I have always hated "general society", and Lady St Helier could conceive of no society that was not general. She took a frank and indefatigable interest in celebrities, and was determined to have them all at her house, whereas I was shy, or indifferent, and without any desire to meet any of them, at any rate on such wholesale occasions, except one or two of my own craft. Yet Lady Jeune and I at once became fast friends, and my affection and admiration for her grew with the growth of our friendship. For many years I stayed with her whenever I went to London, gladly undergoing the inevitable series of big lunches and dinners for the sake of the real pleasure I had in being with her. Others have done justice to her tireless and intelligent activities on the London County Council, and in every good cause, political, municipal or philanthropic, which appealed to her wide sympathies. What I wish to record is that this woman, who figured to hundreds merely as the most indefatigable and imperturbable of hostesses, a sort of automatic entertaining machine, had a vigorous personality of her own, and the most generous and

independent character. Psychologically, the professional hostess and celebrity-seeker will always remain an enigma to me;
but I have known intimately three who were famous in their
day, and though nothing could be more divergent than their
tastes and mine, yet I was drawn to all three by the same large
and generous character, the same capacity for strong individual friendships.

Lady St Helier was perfectly aware of her own foible for
hospitality on a large scale, and I remember her being amused
and touched by an incident which happened just before one
of my visits to her. One of her two married daughters shared
her interest in the literary and artistic figures of the day, and
as this daughter lived in the country she depended on her
mother for her glimpses of the passing show. One day she
wrote begging Lady St Helier to invite to dinner, at a date
when she, the daughter, was to be in London, a young writer
whose first book had caused a passing flutter. Lady St Helier,
delighted at the pretext, wrote to the young man, who was a
total stranger to her, telling him of her daughter's admiration, and her own, for his book, and begging him to dine
with her the following week. The novelist replied that he
could not accept her invitation; he hated dining out, and
moreover owned no evening clothes; but he added that he
was desperately hard up, and as Lady St Helier had liked his
book he hoped she would not mind lending him five pounds.
His would-be hostess was disappointed at his refusing her invitation, but delighted with his frankness; and I am certain
she sent him the five pounds—and not as a loan.

She would, I am sure, have been equally amused if she had
ever heard (as I daresay she did) the story of the cannibal
chief who, on the point of consigning a captive explorer to
the pot, snatched him back to safety with the exclamation:
"But I think I've met you at Lady St Helier's!"

Among the friends I made at that friendly table I remember
chiefly Sir George Trevelyan, the historian, Lord Haldane and
Lord Goschen—the two latter, I imagine, interested by the
accident of my familiarity with German literature. I saw at
Lady St Helier's a long line of men famous in letters and
public affairs, but our meetings were seldom renewed, for my
visits to London were so crowded and hurried, owing to my

husband's unwillingness to remain in England for more than a few days at a time, that the encounters were at best but passing glimpses. Thomas Hardy, however, I met several times, and though he was as remote and uncommunicative as our most unsocial American men of letters, his silence seemed due to an unconquerable shyness rather than to the great man's disdain for humbler neighbours. I sometimes sat next to him at luncheon at Lady St Helier's, and I found it comparatively easy to carry on a mild chat on literary matters. I remember once asking him if it were really true that the editor of the American magazine which had the privilege of publishing "Jude the Obscure" had insisted on his transforming the illegitimate children of Jude and Sue into adopted orphans. He smiled, and said yes, it was a fact; but he added philosophically that he was not much surprised, as the editor of the Scottish magazine which had published his first short story had objected to his making his hero and heroine go for a walk on a Sunday, and obliged him to transfer the stroll to a weekday! He seemed to take little interest in the literary movements of the day, or in fact in any critical discussion of his craft, and I felt that he was completely enclosed in his own creative dream, through which I imagine few voices or influences ever reached him.

One of the things that most struck me when I began to go into general society in England was this indifference of the kind and friendly people whom I met to any but their individual occupations or hobbies. At that time—over thirty years ago—an interest in general ideas, and indeed in any topic whatever outside of the political and social preoccupations of the England of the day, was almost non-existent, except in a small group with which I was not thrown until later. There were, of course, brilliant exceptions, and many of the most cultivated and widely ranging intelligences I have known have been among the Englishmen of that generation. But in general, in the big politico-worldly society in which men of all sorts, sportsmen, soldiers, lawyers, scholars and statesmen, were mingled with the merely frivolous, I found the greater number rather narrowly confined to their own particular topics, and general conversation as rigorously excluded as general ideas.

I remember, at one big dinner in this portion of the London world, hearing some one name Lord Basil Blackwood as we entered the dining-room, and turning eagerly to my neighbour (a famous polo-player, I think) with the question: "Oh, *can* you tell me if that is the wonderful Basil Blackwood who did the pictures for 'The Bad Child's Book of Beasts'?" My neighbour gave me a glance of undisguised dismay, and hastily replied: "Oh, please don't ask me that sort of question! I'm not in the least literary." His hostess, in sending him in with me, had probably whispered to the unhappy man: "*She writes*", and he was determined to make his position clear from the outset.

On another evening I had as neighbour, at another big dinner in the same set, a friendly young army officer, evidently much engrossed in his profession, who at once disarmed me by confessing that he didn't know how to talk anything but "shop". As I foresaw at least ten courses (I think the dinner was at Lord Rothschild's) I was somewhat disconcerted; but the encounter must have taken place not long after the Boer War, and having just read Conan Doyle's vivid narrative of that campaign I plunged at once into the subject, and thus kept more or less afloat for the first half hour. But what in the world were we to talk of next—? My neighbour knew I was an American, and I thought his manifest interest in military history might have led him to hear of the American Revolution. I therefore asked him if he had read Sir George Trevelyan's lately published history of that event. He had never heard of the book or of the author, and to rouse his interest I said I had been told that Lord Wolseley regarded Sir George's account of the battle of Bunker Hill as the finest description of a military engagement written in our day.

"Ah," said my neighbour, with awakening interest—"the author's a soldier himself, then, I suppose?"

"No, he's not; which makes it all the more remarkable," I replied (though at the moment I was not sure that it did!).

My reply plunged the young officer into perplexity; then his face lit up. "Ah—I see; he was out there as military correspondent, was he?"

2

Now and then, of course, there were rich compensations for such evenings. I always said that London dinners reminded me of Clärchen's song; they could be so *"freudvoll"* or so *"leidvoll"*—though *"gedankenvoll"* they seldom were. But in the course of my London visits I gradually made friends with various intelligent people of the world whose interests were much nearer my own. Most of them figured among the "Souls", who prided themselves on a title which had been ironically conferred, or among a kindred set of fashionable cosmopolitans, always ready to welcome new ideas, though they could seldom spare the time to understand them. The latter group, though not affiliated to the "Souls", yet for the most part had the same interests and amusements, and I passed some pleasant hours with both.

One night at a dinner in this *milieu*—I think at Lady Ripon's—I found myself next to a man of about thirty-five or forty, whose name I had not caught. We fell into conversation, and within five minutes I was being whirled away on such a quick current of talk as I had not dipped into for many a day. My neighbour moved with dazzling agility from topic to topic, tossing them to and fro like glittering glass balls, always making me share in the game, yet directing it with a practised hand. We soon discovered a common love of letters, and I think it was our main theme that evening. At all events, what I chiefly remember is our having matched, so to speak, the most famous kisses in literature, and my producing as my crowning effect, and to my neighbour's great admiration, the kiss on the stairs in "The Spoils of Poynton" (which I have always thought one of the most moving love-scenes in fiction), while he quoted in exchange the last desperate embrace of Troilus:

> Injurious Time now with a robber's haste
> Crams his rich thievery up, he knows not how;
> As many farewells as be stars in heaven . . .
> He fumbles up into a loose adieu,
> And scants us with a single famished kiss
> Distasted with the salt of broken tears.

Only at the end of the evening did I learn that I had sat next to Harry Cust, one of the most eager and radio-active intelligences in London, unhappily too favoured by fortune to have been forced to canalize his gifts, but a captivating talker and delightful companion in the small circle of his intimates. We struck up a prompt friendship, and thereafter I seldom missed seeing him when I was in London, and keep the memory of delightful lunches and dinners at his picturesque house, looking out over a quiet rose-garden, a stone's throw from the roar of Knightsbridge.

Among these fashionable cosmopolitans (of whom Lady Ripon was one of the most accomplished) I found again an old friend and contemporary, the beautiful Lady Essex, who had been Adèle Grant of New York. She lived at that time at Bourdon House, Mayfair, the charming little brick manor of a famous heiress who, in the seventeenth century, brought her immense estates to the Dukes of Westminster; one of the last, I suppose, of the old country houses to survive till our day in that intensely urban quarter. There, in the friendly setting of old pictures and old furniture of which her friends keep so happy a memory, I met a number of well-known people, among whom I remember especially Claude Phillips, the witty and agreeable director of the Wallace collection, Sir Edmund Gosse, who always showed me great kindness, Mr. H. G. Wells, most stirring and responsive of talkers, the silent William Archer, dramatic critic and translator of Ibsen, and Max Beerbohm the matchless. It was not my good luck to meet the latter often, though he was still living in London, and far from being the recluse he has since (like myself) become. But when we did sit next to each other at lunch or dinner, it was like suddenly growing wings! I don't, alas, after all these years, remember many of our topics of conversation, or of his lapidary comments; but one of the latter still delights me. We were discussing the works of a well-known novelist whose talk was full of irony and humour, but whose fiction was heavy, and overburdened with unnecessary detail. I remarked that a woman friend of his, who was aware of this defect, had once said to me: "I believe X.'s insistence on detail is caused by his having to look at everything too closely, owing to his being so short-sighted."

Max looked at me gravely. "Ah, really? She thinks it's because he's so short-sighted? I should have said it was because he was so long-winded!"

The Essexes at that time were in the habit of entertaining big week-end parties at Cassiobury, Lord Essex's place near St Albans, and one Sunday at the end of a brilliant London season, when my husband and I motored down there to lunch, we found, scattered on the lawn under the great cedars, the very flower and pinnacle of the London world: Mr. Balfour, Lady Desborough, Lady Poynder (now Lady Islington), Lady Wemyss (then Lady Elcho), and John Sargent, Henry James, and many others of that shining galaxy—but one and all so exhausted by the social labours of the last weeks, so talked out with each other and with all the world, that beyond benevolent smiles they had little to give; and I remarked that evening to my husband that meeting them in such circumstances was like seeing their garments hung up in a row, with nobody inside.

To Adèle Essex, always a devoted friend and responsive companion, and to Lady Ripon, whose sense of fun and quick enthusiasms always delighted me, I owed on the whole the pleasantest hours of my London visits; though I should be ungrateful not to add to their names those of Sir George Trevelyan, who kept up till his death a friendly interest in my books, of Mrs. Wilfrid Meynell, Mrs. Humphry Ward and my shrewd and independent old friend, Mrs. Alfred Austin. Mrs. Meynell, whose poems I admired far more than her delicate but too self-conscious essays, became interested in me, I think, through her liking for "The Valley of Decision", and always showed me great kindness when I was in London. On one occasion, knowing my admiration for the poetry of Francis Thompson, she carried her kindness so far as to invite me to lunch with that elusive being (having previously extracted from him a promise that he would really come). But, alas, though Mr. Meynell, for greater security, called at Thompson's lodgings to fetch him, the poor poet was in an opium dream from which he was not to be roused; and I never met him.

The first time I lunched at Mrs. Meynell's I was struck by the solemnity with which this tall thin sweet-voiced woman, with melancholy eyes and rather catafalque-like garb, was treated by her husband and children. Mr. Meynell, small and brisk, bustled in ahead of her, as though preceding a sovereign; and all through the luncheon Mrs. Meynell's utterances, murmured with soft deliberation, were received in an attentive silence punctuated by: "My wife was saying the other day," "My wife always thinks"—as though each syllable from those lips were final.

I, who had been accustomed at home to dissemble my literary pursuits (as though, to borrow Dr. Johnson's phrase about portrait painting, they were "indelicate in a female"), was astonished at the prestige surrounding Mrs. Meynell in her own family; and at the Humphry Wards' I found the same affectionate deference toward the household celebrity.

I was often a guest of the Wards, in London or at their peaceful country-house near Tring. There were many ties of old friendship, English and American, between us, and Mrs. Ward was unfailingly kind in her estimation of my work, and always eager to make me known to interesting people. Indeed, whenever I have been in England I have found there kindness, hospitality, and a disposition to put me at once on a footing of old friendship. I should be sorry to leave out the names of any to whom I am thus indebted, and at least must add those of Sir Ian and Lady Hamilton, still my friends and my kind hosts on my frequent visits to England, of those dear friends of my childhood, now both dead, Henry and Margaret White (he was then first secretary of our Embassy in London), of Lord and Lady Charles Beresford, Sir Edmund Gosse, Lord and Lady Burghclere, and my husband's hospitable cousin, Mrs. Adair. Of country life I saw next to nothing, for we were never in England in the autumn and winter, and at the season when we *were* there my husband's dates were so unalterable that we once missed a week-end at Mentmore with Lord Rosebery because it was considered impossible that we should postpone our sailing for a few days. I have always regretted this, as well as my having been unable to accept two or three invitations to Lord Rosebery's house in London; for as a girl of seventeen I had met him when he came to America after his marriage, and I had a vivid memory of the light and air he let into the stuffy atmosphere of a Newport season. Unhappily I never saw him again.

Much as I enjoyed these London glimpses they are now no more than a golden blur. So many years have gone by, and that old world of my youth has been so convulsed and shattered, that as I look back, and try to recapture the details of particular scenes and talks, they dissolve into the distance. But in any case I was not made to extract more than a passing amusement from such fugitive dips into a foreign society. My idea of society was (and still is) the daily companionship of the same five or six friends, and its pleasure is based on continuity, whereas the hospitable people who opened their doors to me in London, though of course they all had their own intimate circles, were as much exhilarated by the yearly stream of new faces as a successful shot by the size of his bag. Most of my intimate friendships in England were made later, and in circumstances more favourable (to me, at any rate) than the rush and confusion of a London season. Some of the dearest of them I owe to Howard Sturgis, and to him, and to Queen's Acre, his house at Windsor, I turn for the setting of my next scene.

3

A long low drawing-room; white-panelled walls hung with water-colours of varying merit; curtains and furniture of faded slippery chintz; French windows opening on a crazy wooden verandah, through which, on one side, one caught a glimpse of a weedy lawn and a shrubbery edged with an unsuccessful herbaceous border, on the other, of a not too successful rose garden, with a dancing faun poised above an incongruously "arty" blue-tiled pool. Within, profound chintz arm-chairs drawn up about a hearth on which a fire always smouldered; a big table piled with popular novels and picture-magazines; and near the table a lounge on which lay outstretched, his legs covered by a thick shawl, his hands occupied with knitting-needles or embroidery silks, a sturdily-built handsome man with brilliantly white wavy hair, a girlishly clear complexion, a black moustache, and tender mocking eyes under the bold arch of his black brows.

Such was Howard Sturgis, perfect host, matchless friend, drollest, kindest and strangest of men, as he appeared to the startled eyes of newcomers on their first introduction to Queen's Acre.

It was not there, but at a dinner at Newport, that I first met him, a few years after my marriage. I did not even know who he was; but if ever there was a case of friendship at first sight it was struck up between us then and there. Like me he was a great lover of good talk, and shared my inability to enjoy it except in a small and intimate circle. Continuity in friendship he valued also as much as I did, and from that day until his death, many years later, he and I shared the same small group of intimates.

Howard Sturgis was the youngest son of Mr. Russell Sturgis, of the old Boston family of that name, who for many years had been at the head of an important American banking-house in London. Mr. Sturgis, as became an international banker, was rich, popular and hospitable, kept up a large household, and entertained a great deal in London and at Givens Grove, his country place near Leatherhead. Howard, I think, was born in England, and had probably never been to America till he came out on a visit to his Boston relations, the year I met him at Newport. His mother, Mr. Sturgis's third wife, was also a Bostonian, and his cousinage was as large as mine in New York, and far more assiduously cultivated. Howard's closest associations, however, were English, for he had been sent to Eton and thence to Cambridge. At Eton he had been a pupil of Mr. Ainger's, a privilege never forgotten by an Etonian fortunate enough to have enjoyed it; and Mr. Ainger, whom I often met at Queen's Acre, had remained one of his most devoted friends. Another friend of his youth was the eccentric and tragic William Cory Johnson, an Eton master of a different stamp, and an exquisite poet in a minor strain; and it is to Howard that I owe my precious first edition of "Ionica", royally clothed in crimson morocco.

Mr. Russell Sturgis died when Howard was still a youth, and after his father's death, and the marriages of his brothers and his sister, he found himself alone at home with his mother. Mrs. Sturgis, whom I never knew, is said to have been a very beautiful woman. She was as luxurious in her tastes as her husband, but, I imagine, without his gift of easy hospitality. She continued to keep up handsome establishments at Givens and in London; but she and her son, who was her devoted slave, were frequently absent from England, and when at home kept more and more to themselves; and her death left him, a middle-aged man, as lost and helpless as a child.

When I first knew him this sad phase was past; the London house had been sold, Givens had gone to Howard's eldest half-brother, and Howard was happily settled in a roomy friendly house on the edge of Windsor Park, where he had gathered about him a company of devoted friends, some of whom were soon to become mine. He detested pomp and circumstance as much as his parents had valued it, and his life was already organized on the simple easy lines from which it never afterward departed. Some of his mother's old servants remained with him, and when he went to Windsor he took with him Hall, the majestic butler. Hall had been with the family for many years, and was devoted to Howard; but after a few months at Queen's Acre he announced his intention of leaving. Howard, much distressed, said he supposed Hall did not care to remain in so small an establishment; but Hall replied sadly: "Oh, no, sir, it's not that; it's only that I can't bear never to 'ear you ring a bell, and 'ave you always putting your 'ead out of the door and 'ollering 'all [Hall] down the passage."

Howard felt the justice of the rebuke, but also the impossibility of living up to the old butler's standards. Always impatient of conventional observances, he could never ring a bell when " 'ollering" brought the necessary response; so Hall departed, and was replaced by a small thin worried man, more in scale with the reduced household whose burdens (and they were not light) he was to bear till death relieved him, soon after the loss of his beloved master. This excellent man, whose name was Robinson, but who had been baptized by Henry James "the little saint and angel", was dear to all visitors to Queen's Acre, as were the admirable cook, Mrs. Lees (shall I ever again eat the like of her braised tongue?), and the sturdy old Scottish housemaid, Christina.

There was also, I believe, an old family coachman in the stable behind the shrubbery; but he and his "old family" horses, and the still older and more decayed family brougham, had reached a decrepitude so advanced that they hardly ever emerged from the stable-yard, and guests at Queen's Acre depended chiefly on station flies, or, in motoring days, on their own cars. Howard, though his means permitted every comfort, would never introduce electric light into the house, much less the telephone and central heating; and his reluctance to repair, to repaint or in any way renovate his dear old house, must have been part of the deep-seated "complex" which made him unwilling to take any decision on whatever subject; for he was the most generous of men, and as careless of money as he was indifferent to all material comforts except good food.

I have sometimes thought that Howard's old servants represented not inaptly the odd duality of his nature: Robinson his long-suffering sweetness and unselfishness, and the devoted but dour Christina the streak of asperity which sometimes came to the surface. Once when I was staying at Queen's Acre I was at work on a novel, and writing in bed in the early morning, as my reprehensible habit is, with my inkstand balanced on a writing board. An inadvertent movement caused me to upset the ink, and instantly it poured over my sumptuously monogrammed sheet—doubtless a survival from Mrs. Sturgis's stores of fine linen. Inkstands and teacups are never as full as when one upsets them, and seeing that the disaster was beyond the help of blotting-paper, I hastily rang for Christina. At the sight she threw up her hands in horror, and was seizing the sheet to fly with it to the tub, when I said: "Just a moment, Christina. I want you first to take the sheet to Mr. Sturgis, with this note from me."

Christina's jaw fell, and her look said: "Is there no limit to the craziness of these Americans?"

"Did ye say I was to tek a note, mem, to Mr. Sturgis?"

"*With* the sheet."

"Not the sheet, mem? There's no reason for Mr. Sturgis to be told about the accident, mem—" in the conciliatory tone of one who remembers that it is safer to humour lunatics than to oppose them.

"Yes, please, Christina; note *and* sheet."

Reluctantly Christina departed on this insane mission. In the note I had written: "Dearest Howard, the book has been going slowly of late; but the stimulating air of Queen's Acre has had its usual effect, and as you will see this morning's chapter has come with a rush."

A jubilant message of congratulation was brought back, with a clean sheet, by Christina. When the sheet was in place she lingered, perplexity on her face; then, determined to protect her master's interests, though suspecting that he would be horrified at her means of doing so, she broke out in her fiercest Scots: "I dinna suppose ye mean to replace it, mem? But if ye *did*, they coom from Marshall's."

The sheet was promptly duplicated by Marshall and Snelgrove, and when it arrived Christina's heart was softened, and thereafter we were the best of friends.

At Queen's Acre some of the happiest hours of my life were passed, some of my dearest friendships formed or consolidated, and my own old friends welcomed because they were mine. For Howard Sturgis was not only one of the most amusing and lovable of companions, but untiring in hospitality to the friends of his friends. Indolent and unambitious though he was, his social gifts were irresistible, and his drawing-room—where he spent most of his hours, not from ill-health but through inertia—was always full of visitors. There one found all that was most intelligent and agreeable in the world of Eton, as well as a chosen few from London, and mingled with them a continual and somewhat incongruous stream of cousins from Boston and New York—for Howard cherished with sentimental fervour the ties of consanguinity. There were also other cousins, long established in England and old habitués of Queen's Acre; chief among them the three daughters of Motley, the historian, Lily Lady Harcourt, Mrs. Sheridan, the kindly hostess of Frampton Court, and Mrs. Mildmay; besides a succession of amiable nieces and nephews, children of Howard's brothers and sister. But among the transients the chief current was fed by Bostonians and New Yorkers of the old school, whom Howard welcomed with effusion, undismayed by the difficulty of harmonizing them at short notice with the small intimate group who were *de fondation* about his fireside.

This inner group I see now, gathered around him as the lamps are brought in at the end of a foggy autumn afternoon. In one of the arm-chairs by the fire is sunk the long-limbed frame of the young Percy Lubbock, still carrying in his mind the delightful books he has since given us, and perhaps as yet hardly aware that he was ever to put them on paper; in another sits Gaillard Lapsley, down for the week-end from his tutorial duties at Cambridge, while John Hugh-Smith faces Percy across the fireside, and Robert Norton and I share the corners of the wide chintz sofa behind the tea-table; and dominating the hearth, and all of us, Henry James stands, or heavily pads about the room, listening, muttering, groaning disapproval, or chuckling assent to the paradoxes of the other tea-drinkers. And then, when tea is over, and the tray has disappeared, he stops his prowling to lean against the mantel-piece and plunge into reminiscences of the Paris or London of his youth, or into some slowly elaborated literary disquisition, perhaps on the art of fiction or the theatre, on Balzac, on Tolstoy, or, better still, on one of his own contemporaries. I remember, especially, one afternoon when the question: "And Meredith—?" suddenly freed a "full-length" of that master which, I imagine, still hangs in the mental picture-galleries of all who heard him.

It began, mildly enough, with a discussion of Meredith's importance as a novelist, in which I think Howard was his principal champion. James, deep-sunk in an arm-chair and in silence, sat listening, and weighing our views, till he suddenly pounced on my avowal that, much as I admired some of the novels, I had never been able to find out what any of them, except "The Egoist" and "Harry Richmond", were about. I tried to temper this by adding that in many passages, and especially the descriptive ones, the author's style rose to a height of poetic imagery which—but here James broke in with the cry that I had put my finger on the central weakness of Meredith's art, its unconscious insincerity. Words—words—poetic imagery, metaphors, epigrams, descriptive passages! How much did any of them weigh in the baggage of the authentic novelist? (By this time he was on his feet, swaying agitatedly to and fro before the fire.) Meredith, he continued, was a sentimental rhetorician, whose natural indolence or congenital insufficiency, or both, made him, in life as in his art, shirk every climax, dodge around it, and veil its absence in a fog of eloquence. Of course, he pursued, neither I nor any other reader could make out what Meredith's tales were about; and not only what they were about, but even in what country and what century they were situated, all these prosaic details being hopelessly befogged by the famous poetic imagery. He himself, James said, when he read Meredith, was always at a loss to know where he was, or what causes had led to which events, or even to discover by what form of conveyance the elusive characters he was struggling to identify moved from one point of the globe to another (except, Howard interpolated, that the heroines always did so on horseback); till at last the practical exigencies of the subject forced the author to provide some specific means of transport, and suddenly, through the fog of his verbiage, the reader caught the far-off tinkle of a bell that (here there was a dramatic pause of suspense)—that turned out to be that of a mere vulgar hansom-cab: "Into which," James concluded with his wicked twinkle, "I always manage to leap before the hero, and drive straight out of the story."

Such *boutades* implied no lack of appreciation of Meredith the poet, still less of regard for the man. James liked and admired Meredith, and esteemed him greatly for the courage and dignity with which he endured the trial of his long illness; but, when the sacred question of the craft was touched upon, all personal sympathies seemed irrelevant, and our friend pronounced his judgments without regard to them.

4

In Howard Sturgis's case, even more than in that of James, the lack of a Boswell is to be deplored, for in his talk there was the same odd blending of the whimsical and the shrewd, of scepticism and emotion, as in his character, and the chosen friends who frequented Qu'acre (as its intimates called it) were always at their best in his company. But he has now been dead for over twelve years, and since voices more qualified to speak are still silent, I cannot part from his dear shade without trying to call it back for a moment.

Everything in Howard Sturgis's life was contradictory, perplexing, and in a sense incomplete. He had begun by writing two charming, if slightly over-sentimental tales, "Tim" and "All That Was Possible", both of which had been greatly admired by a small circle of appreciative readers, while the latter had won him a wider public. Thereafter he was silent for a number of years, and then, about 1906, he published a long novel called "Belchamber", which to my mind stands very nearly in the first rank. But "Belchamber" had no success with the public, and less than his other books with most of his friends. Henry James (never to be trusted about the value of any "fiction" which was not built according to his own rigid plan) pointed out with some truth that Howard had failed to utilize what should have been his central effect, and privately pronounced the book old-fashioned and feebly Thackerayan; while the reviewers dismissed it as too "painful" and "unnecessarily disagreeable", meaning thereby that it "faced the facts" at a time when English fiction had not begun to practise that now too common exercise. The book was in truth a striking study of fashionable London in the 'nineties, lifted above the level of anecdote by a touch of tragedy, and rising in certain scenes to the quiet power of great fiction. But it was born out of its due time, and sank almost at once into an obscurity from which I am persuaded it will some day emerge, with that entirely different but equally neglected masterpiece, Graham Phillips's "Susan Lenox".

Howard, after the failure of "Belchamber", apparently lost all interest in writing. He was unduly distressed by Henry James's criticism, and it was in vain that I pointed out how foolish it was to be discouraged by the opinion of a novelist who could no longer judge impartially any novel not built according to his own theories. Howard, by the way, was to see those theories suddenly demolished when, a good many years later, I sent James a copy of *Du Côté de chez Swann* on its first appearance, and all his principles and prejudices went down like straws in the free wind of Proust's genius; but that was long afterward, and meanwhile, Howard's native indolence and genuine humility aiding, he accepted James's verdict and relapsed into knitting and embroidery.

For the joy of his friends this was hardly to be regretted, since it left him free to give them his whole time. Intellectually he combined a kind of sentimental socialism with a hard lucidity of judgment, emotionally he was at once tender and malicious, indulgent and penetrating, and one felt that he saw through one to the marrow at the very moment when, in all sincerity, he was smothering one under exaggerated praise. There was nothing perfidious or calculated in these sudden changes; his affection for his friends co-existed with a pitiless discernment of their weaknesses, but his heart always poured balm on what his tongue could not refrain from lashing.

Howard's days, once he had abandoned literature, were methodically divided into brief moments of exercise and long hours of immobility. Every morning at the same hour he took a short toddle in Windsor Park with the sad little dog Misery and her rickety out-of-wedlock son, who was the cause of her being so named; Howard's Puritan blood having compelled him to put this brand on his frail pet. He walked very slowly and potteringly, and I have known few more chilly forms of exercise, on a cold damp day, than a "constitutional" with him and James, the latter stopping short every few yards to elaborate a point or propound a problem, while, just as one had got James moving again, Howard was sure to dive into the bushes in pursuit of Misery or her illegitimate offspring.

The walk ended, and an excellent luncheon enjoyed, Howard returned to his lounge and his embroidery, seldom leaving the drawing-room again till it was time to dress for dinner, and gently deriding the vain activities of those who did. I remember, in particular, one occasion when he had invited down for the day my friend Jacques-Emile Blanche and his wife, who were staying in London. It was a lovely summer day, and my impression is that the charms of the Thames valley were unknown to our French guests. At any rate, it was suggested that I should take them, after luncheon, to see the beautiful old alms-houses at Bray, and when this brief excursion was over, and I had driven them back to the railway station, I returned to King's Road to find Howard in his usual place on the lounge. The afternoon was still young, and as I entered the room I cried out: "Come along, Howard! Put on your bonnet and shawl, and let's walk down to Eton!"

Cries of dismay and incredulity from Howard. "Walk down to Eton with you? *Now*—at this hour of the day? But you went for a walk this morning; and you've been motoring all over the place all the afternoon with the Blanches; and now you're actually suggesting that I should walk all the way to Eton with you before dinner?"

So horrified was he at my mad proposal that it rankled in him for the rest of the evening, and every now and then, as we sat in the drawing-room after dinner, he would appeal plaintively to his other guests: "Did you ever hear of such a thing? After motoring all over the place all the afternoon with the Blanches, she actually came back and said to me: 'Put on your bonnet and shawl, and let's walk down to Eton!'"

In my day Howard's social relations with Eton were limited, at least as far as his guests were concerned, to taking us to call now and then on Mrs. Cornish or Mr. Ainger. But on one occasion we were bidden there for a public ceremony, and one I would not willingly have missed: the inauguration by King Edward VII of the beautiful hall which had been recently built in commemoration of the Etonians who fell in the Boer War. I had never seen King Edward before, and my recollection of the simple and dignified ceremony is naturally centred in his stout but stately figure. I remember being at first slightly shocked by the thick guttural intonation so reminiscent of his Hanoverian descent, and then captivated by the simplicity of his manner and the genuine emotion which his words expressed. Between the King's disquietingly Teutonic presence, and his audience of so deeply English subjects, the mourning relatives of the dead, one felt at once the current of understanding, the sharing of private grief and national pride, which gives such symbolic value to inherited rule.

As far as I can remember I was taken only once to see Mrs. Cornish, and on this occasion, as so often happened, my incorrigible shyness turned the meeting into a damp-match affair. Mrs. Cornish, wife of the distinguished Vice-Provost of

Eton, was one of the most striking figures of that highly specialized world; wherever Eton was mentioned people always said: "You don't know Mrs. Cornish? Oh, but you *must* know her!"

Mrs. Cornish had once been thrown with the Bourgets, of whom she kept an admiring recollection, and when she heard that I was an intimate friend of theirs she instructed Howard to bring me to tea at the Vice-Provost's Lodge. The only day on which I was free was one on which she happened to have invited a party of Eton boys, and she excused herself for this; but I thought their rosy faces and shining collars well suited to the serene and studious beauty of The Cloisters, with its long low-studded drawing-room, and the flowers and turf of the garden seen through mullioned windows. Mrs. Cornish was eager to hear all I could tell her of the Bourgets, but in spite of my desire to enjoy (and be enjoyed), the silent pink audience communicated its shyness to me. At any rate, no other topic of interest occurred to me or to my hostess when we had used up the theme of our serviceable friends; and after a while Mrs. Cornish, visibly aware of my distress, and herself affected by it, caught at the Bourgets again, like a man overboard swimming back to the spar he has abandoned. One of the Eton boys, a dark good-looking lad, who had been introduced to us as Prince Ruspoli, suddenly fixed her attention, and she swept around on him with her great dominant air.

"And you, Carlo Ruspoli—have you ever read the novels of Paul Bourget?" she abruptly challenged him. All the boys turned pinker at the startling enquiry, and the young prince pinkest.

"I—n-no—I'm afraid I haven't," he stammered, disconcerted.

Mrs. Cornish's inquiring gaze darkened to disapproval. "What, you've not read them? Not any of them? Then you should, Carlo Ruspoli; you should read *all of them* immediately," she surprisingly commanded—for a counsel from Mrs. Cornish was always a command. An inarticulate murmur and a deeper blush were the only response; and thereafter the conversation so excitingly begun trailed off again into commonplaces—or I fear it must have, no doubt through my fault, for I remember of it nothing else of moment.

5

Not infrequently, on my annual visit to Qu'acre, I "took off" from Lamb House, where I also went annually for a visit to Henry James. The motor run between Rye and Windsor being an easy one, I was often accompanied by Henry James, who generally arranged to have his visit to Qu'acre coincide with mine. James, who was a frequent companion on our English motor-trips, was firmly convinced that, because he lived in England, and our chauffeur (an American) did not, it was necessary that the latter should be guided by him through the intricacies of the English country-side. Sign-posts were rare in England in those days, and for many years afterward, and a truly British reserve seemed to make the local authorities reluctant to communicate with the invading stranger. Indeed, considerable difficulty existed as to the formulating of advice and instructions, and I remember in one village the agitated warning: "Motorists! Beware of the children!"—while in general there was a marked absence of indications as to the whereabouts of the next village.

It chanced, however, that Charles Cook, our faithful and skilful driver, was a born path-finder, while James's sense of direction was non-existent, or rather actively but always erroneously alert; and the consequences of his intervention were always bewildering, and sometimes extremely fatiguing. The first time that my husband and I went to Lamb House by motor (coming from France) James, who had travelled to Folkestone by train to meet us, insisted on seating himself next to Cook, on the plea that the roads across Romney marsh formed such a tangle that only an old inhabitant could guide us to Rye. The suggestion resulted in our turning around and around in our tracks till long after dark, though Rye, conspicuous on its conical hill, was just ahead of us, and Cook could easily have landed us there in time for tea.

Another year we had been motoring in the west country, and on the way back were to spend a night at Malvern. As we approached (at the close of a dark rainy afternoon) I saw James growing restless, and was not surprised to hear him say: "My dear, I once spent a summer at Malvern, and know it very well; and as it is rather difficult to find the way to the hotel, it might be well if Edward were to changes places with me, and let me sit beside Cook." My husband of course acceded (though with doubt in his heart), and James having taken his place, we awaited the result. Malvern, if I am not mistaken, is encircled by a sort of upper boulevard, of the kind called in Italy a *strada di circonvallazione*, and for an hour we circled about above the outspread city, while James vainly tried to remember which particular street led down most directly to our hotel. At each corner (literally) he stopped the motor, and we heard a muttering, first confident and then anguished. "This—this, my dear Cook, yes . . . this certainly is the right corner. But no; stay! A moment longer, please— in this light it's so difficult . . . appearances are so misleading . . . It may be . . . yes! I think it *is* the next turn . . . 'a little farther lend thy guiding hand' . . . that is, drive on; but slowly, please, my dear Cook; *very* slowly!" And at the next corner the same agitated monologue would be repeated; till at length Cook, the mildest of men, interrupted gently: "I guess any turn'll get us down into the town, Mr. James, and after that I can ask—" and late, hungry and exhausted we arrived at length at our destination, James still convinced that the next turn would have been the right one, if only we had been more patient.

The most absurd of these episodes occurred on another rainy evening, when James and I chanced to arrive at Windsor long after dark. We must have been driven by a strange chauffeur—perhaps Cook was on a holiday; at any rate, having fallen into the lazy habit of trusting to him to know the way, I found myself at a loss to direct his substitute to the King's Road. While I was hesitating, and peering out into the darkness, James spied an ancient doddering man who had stopped in the rain to gaze at us. "Wait a moment, my dear—I'll ask him where we are"; and leaning out he signalled to the spectator.

"My good man, if you'll be good enough to come here, please; a little nearer—so," and as the old man came up: "My friend, to put it to you in two words, this lady and I have just arrived here from *Slough*; that is to say, to be more strictly accurate, we have recently *passed through* Slough on our way here, having actually motored to Windsor from Rye, which was our point of departure; and the darkness having over-taken us, we should be much obliged if you would tell us where we now are in relation, say, to the High Street, which, as you of course know, leads to the Castle, after leaving on the left hand the turn down to the railway station."

I was not surprised to have this extraordinary appeal met by silence, and a dazed expression on the old wrinkled face at the window; nor to have James go on: "In short" (his invariable prelude to a fresh series of explanatory ramifications), "in short, my good man, what I want to put to you in a word is this: supposing we have already (as I have reason to think we have) driven past the turn down to the railway station (which, in that case, by the way, would probably not have been on our left hand, but on our right), where are we now in relation to. . ."

"Oh, please," I interrupted, feeling myself utterly unable to sit through another parenthesis, "do ask him where the King's Road is."

"Ah—? The King's Road? Just so! Quite right! Can you, as a matter of fact, my good man, tell us where, in relation to our present position, the King's Road exactly *is*?"

"Ye're in it," said the aged face at the window.

6

It would be hard to imagine a greater contrast than between the hospitality of Queen's Acre and that of Lamb House. In the former a cheerful lavishness prevailed, and a cook enamoured of her art set a variety of inviting dishes before a table-full of guests, generally reinforced by transients from London or the country. At Lamb House an anxious frugality was combined with the wish that the usually solitary guest (there were never, at most, more than two at a time) should not suffer too greatly from the contrast between his or her supposed habits of luxury, and the privations imposed by the host's conviction that he was on the brink of ruin. If any one in a pecuniary difficulty appealed to James for help, he gave it without counting; but in his daily life he was haunted by the spectre of impoverishment, and the dreary pudding or pie of which a quarter or half had been consumed at dinner reappeared on the table the next day with its ravages unrepaired.

We used to laugh at Howard Sturgis because, when any new subject was touched on in our talks, he always interrupted us to cry out: "Now please remember that I've read nothing, and know nothing, and am not in the least quick or clever or cultivated"; and one day, when I prefaced a remark with "Of course, to people as intelligent as we all are," he broke in with a sort of passionate terror: "Oh, how can you say such things about us, Edith?"—as though my remark had been a challenge to the Furies.

The same scruples weighed on Henry James; but in his case the pride that apes humility concerned itself (oddly enough) with material things. He lived in terror of being thought rich, worldly or luxurious, and was forever contrasting his visitors' supposed opulence and self-indulgence with his own hermit-like asceticism, and apologizing for his poor food while he trembled lest it should be thought too good. I have often since wondered if he did not find our visits more of a burden than a pleasure, and if the hospitality he so conscientiously offered and we so carelessly enjoyed did not give him more sleepless nights than happy days.

I hope not; for some of my richest hours were spent under his roof. From the moment when I turned the corner of the grass-grown street mounting steeply between squat brick houses, and caught sight, at its upper end, of the wide Palladian window of the garden-room, a sense of joyous liberation bore me on. There *he* stood on the doorstep, the white-panelled hall with its old prints and crowded book-cases forming a background to his heavy loosely-clothed figure. Arms outstretched, lips and eyes twinkling, he came down to the car, uttering cries of mock amazement and mock humility at the undeserved honour of my visit. The arrival at Lamb House was an almost ritual performance, from those first ejaculations to the large hug and the two solemn kisses executed in the middle of the hall rug. Then, arm in arm, through the oak-panelled morning-room we wandered out onto the thin worn turf of the garden, with its ancient mulberry tree, its unkempt flower-borders, the gables of Watchbell Street peeping like village gossips over the creeper-clad walls, and the scent of roses spiced with a strong smell of the sea. Up and down the lawn we strolled with many pauses, exchanging news, answering each other's questions, delivering messages from the other members of the group, inspecting the strawberries and lettuces in the tiny kitchen-garden, and the chrysanthemums "coming along" in pots in the greenhouse; till at length the parlour-maid appeared with a tea-tray, and I was led up the rickety outside steps to the garden-room, that stately and unexpected appendage to the unadorned cube of the house.

In summer the garden-room, with its high ceiling, its triple window commanding the grass-grown declivity of West Street, and its other window looking along another ancient street to the Gothic mass of the parish church, was the centre of life at Lamb House. Here, in the morning, James dictated to his secretary, striding incessantly up and down the room, and in the afternoon and evening, when the weather was too cool for the garden, sat with outstretched legs in his deep arm-chair before the hearth, laughing and talking with his guests.

On the whole, he was very happy at Rye, and in spite of the house-keeping cares which he took so hard the change was all to the good for a man who could never resist invitations, yet was wearied and irritated by the incessant strain of social life in London. At Rye, in summer at least, he had as many guests as his nerves could endure, and his sociable relations with his neighbours—among whom were, at one time, his beloved friends, Sir George and Lady Prothero—must have prevented his feeling lonely. He was very proud of his old house, the best of its sober and stately sort in the town, and he who thought himself so detached from material things tasted the simple joys of proprietorship when, with a deprecating air, he showed his fine Georgian panelling and his ancient brick walls to admiring visitors.

Like Howard Sturgis he was waited upon by two or three faithful servants. Foremost among them was the valet and factotum, Burgess, always spoken of by his employer as "poor little Burgess". Burgess's broad squat figure and phlegmatic countenance are a familiar memory to all who frequented Lamb House, and James's friends gratefully recall his devotion to his master during the last unhappy years of nervous break-down and illness. He had been preceded by a man-servant whom I did not know, but of whom James spoke with regard as an excellent fellow. "The only trouble was that, when I gave him an order, he had to go through three successive mental processes before he could understand what I was say-ing. First he had to register the fact that he was being spoken to, then to assimilate the meaning of the order given to him, and lastly to think out what practical consequences might be expected to follow if he obeyed it."

Perhaps these mental gymnastics were excusable in the cir-cumstances; but Burgess apparently soon learned to dispense with them, and without any outward appearance of having understood what his master was saying, carried out his instructions with stolid exactitude. Stolidity was his most marked characteristic. He seldom gave any sign of compre-hension when spoken to, and I remember once saying to my Alsatian maid, who was always as quick as a flash at the up-take: "Do you know, I think Burgess must be very stupid. When I speak to him I'm never even sure that he's heard what I've said."

My maid looked at me gravely. "Oh, no, Madam: Burgess is remarkably intelligent. *He always understands what Mr. James says.*" And that argument was certainly conclusive.

At Lamb House my host and I usually kept to ourselves until luncheon. Our working hours were the same, and it was only now and then that we went out before one o'clock to take a look at the green peas in the kitchen-garden, or to stroll down the High Street to the Post Office. But as soon as lun-cheon was despatched (amid unnecessary apologies for its meagreness, and sarcastic allusions to my own supposed culi-nary extravagances) the real business of the day began. Henry James, an indifferent walker, and incurably sedentary in his habits, had a passion for motoring. He denied himself (I be-lieve quite needlessly) the pleasure and relaxation which a car of his own might have given him, but took advantage, to the last drop of petrol, of the travelling capacity of any visitor's car. When, a few years after his death, I stayed at Lamb House with the friend who was then its tenant, I got to know for the first time the rosy old town and its sea-blown neighbourhood. In Henry James's day I was never given the chance, for as soon as luncheon was over we were always whirled miles away, throwing out over the country-side what he called our "great loops" of exploration. Sometimes we went off for two or three days. I remember one beautiful pilgrimage to Winchester, Gloucester and beyond; another long day carried us to the ancient house of Brede, to lunch with the Morton Frewens, another to spend a day near Ashford with the Alfred Austins, in their pleasant old house full of books and flowers. Usually, however, to avoid an interruption to the morning's work, we lunched at Lamb House, and starting out immediately afterward pushed our explorations of down and weald and seashore to the last limit of the summer twilight.

James was as jubilant as a child. Everything pleased him— the easy locomotion (which often cradled him into a brief nap), the bosky softness of the landscape, the discovery of towns and villages hitherto beyond his range, the magic of ancient names, quaint or impressive, crabbed or melodious. These he would murmur over and over to himself in a low chant, finally creating characters to fit them, and sometimes whole families, with their domestic complications and matrimonial alliances, such as the Dymmes of Dymchurch, one of whom married a Sparkle, and was the mother of little Scintilla Dymme-Sparkle, subject of much mirth and many anecdotes. Except during his naps, nothing escaped him, and I suppose no one ever felt more imaginatively, or with deeper poetic emotion, the beauty of sea and sky, the serenities of the landscape, the sober charm of villages, manor-houses and humble churches, and all the implications of that much-storied corner of England.

One perfect afternoon we spent at Bodiam—my first visit there. It was still the old spell-bound ruin, unrestored, guarded by great trees, and by a network of lanes which baffled the invading charabancs. Tranquil white clouds hung above it in a windless sky, and the silence and solitude were complete as we sat looking across at the crumbling towers, and at their reflection in a moat starred with water-lilies, and danced over by great blue dragon-flies. For a long time no one spoke; then James turned to me and said solemnly:

"Summer afternoon—summer afternoon; to me those have always been the two most beautiful words in the English language." They were the essence of that hushed scene, those ancient walls; and I never hear them spoken without seeing the towers of Bodiam mirrored in their enchanted moat.

Another day was memorable in another way. We were motoring from Rye to Windsor, to stay, as usual, with Howard Sturgis, and suddenly James said: "The day is so beautiful that I should like to make a little *détour*, and show you Box Hill." I was delighted at the prospect of seeing a new bit of English scenery, and perhaps catching a glimpse of George Meredith's cottage on its leafy hillside. But James's next words chilled my ardour: "I want you to know Meredith," he added.

"Oh, no, no!" I protested. I knew enough, by this time, of my inability to profit by such encounters. I was always benumbed by them, and unable to find the right look or the right word, while inwardly I bubbled with fervour, and the longing to express it. I remember once being taken to see Miss Jekyll's famous garden at Great Warley. On that long-desired day I had a hundred questions to ask, a thousand things to learn. I went with a party of fashionable and indifferent people, all totally ignorant of gardens and gardening; I put one timid question to Miss Jekyll, who answered curtly, and turned her back on me to point out a hybrid iris to an eminent statesman who knew neither what a hybrid nor an iris was; and for the rest of the visit she gave me no chance of exchanging a word with her.

To see Meredith and talk with him was a more important affair. In spite of all reservations, my admiration for certain parts of his work was very great. I delighted in his poetry, and treasured two of his novels—"The Egoist" and "Harry Richmond"—and I should have enjoyed telling him just what it was that I most admired in them. But I foresaw the impossibility of doing so at a first meeting which would probably also be the last. I told James this, and added that the great man's deafness was in itself an insurmountable obstacle, since I cannot make myself heard even by the moderately deaf. James pleaded with me, but I was firm. For months he had been announcing his visit to Meredith, but had always been deterred by the difficulty of getting from Rye to Box Hill without going up to London; and I should really be doing him a great service by allowing him to call there on the way to Windsor. To this, of course, I was obliged to consent; but I stipulated that I should be allowed to wait in the car, and though he tried to convince me that "just to have taken a look at the great man" would be an interesting memory, he knew I hated that kind of human sight-seeing, and did not insist. So we deflected our course to take in Box Hill, and the car climbed the steep ascent to the garden-gate where James was to get out. As he did so he turned to me and said: "Come, my dear! I can't leave you sitting here alone. I should have you on my mind all the time; and supposing somebody were to come out of the house and find you?"

There was nothing for it but to comply; and somewhat sulkily I followed him up the narrow path, between clumps of sweetwilliam and Scotch pinks. It was a tiny garden patch, and a few steps brought us to the door of a low-studded cottage in a gap of the hanging woods. It was useless to notify Meredith in advance when one went to see him; he had long since been immobilized by illness, and was always there, and always, apparently, delighted to receive his old friends. The maid who announced us at once returned to say that we were to come in, and we were shown into a very small low-ceilinged room, so small and so low that it seemed crowded though there were only four people in it. The four were the great man himself, white of head and beard, and statuesquely throned in a Bath chair; his daughter, the handsome Mrs. Henry Sturgis (wife of Howard's eldest brother), another man who seemed to me larger than life, perhaps on account of the exiguity of the room, and who turned out to be Mr. Morley Roberts—and lastly a trained nurse, calmly eating her supper at a table only a foot or two from her patient's chair.

It was the nurse's presence—and the way she went on steadily eating and drinking—that I found most disconcerting. The house was very small indeed; but was it really so small that there was not a corner of it in which she could have been fed, instead of consuming her evening repast under our eyes and noses? I have always wondered, and never found the answer.

Meanwhile I was being led up and explained by James and

Mrs. Sturgis—a laborious business, and agonizing to me, as the room rang and rang again with my unintelligible name. But finally the syllables reached their destination; and then, as they say in detective novels, the unexpected happened. The invalid stretched out a beautiful strong hand—everything about him was strong and beautiful—and lifting up a book which lay open at his elbow, held it out with a smile. I read the title, and the blood rushed over me like fire. It was my own "Motor Flight through France", then lately published; and he had not known I was to be brought to see him, and he had actually been reading my book when I came in!

At once, in his rich organ tones, he began to say the kindest, most appreciative things; to ask questions, to want particulars—but, alas, my unresonant voice found no crack in the wall of his deafness. I longed to tell him that Henry James had been our companion on most of the travels described in my modest work; and James, joining in, tried to explain, to say kind things also; but it was all useless, and Meredith, accustomed to steering a way through these first difficult moments, had presently taken easy hold of the conversation, never again letting it go till we left.

The beauty, the richness, the flexibility of his voice held me captive, and it is that which I remember, not what he said; except that he was all amenity, all kindliness, as if the voice were poured in a healing tide over the misery of my shyness. But the object of the visit was, of course, to give him a chance of talking with James, and presently I drew back and chatted with Mrs. Sturgis and Morley Roberts, while the great bright tide of monologue swept on over my friend. After all, it had been worth coming for; but the really interesting thing about the visit was James's presence, and the chance of watching from my corner the nobly confronted profiles of the two old friends: Meredith's so classically distinguished, from the spring of the wavy hair to the line of the straight nose, and the modelling of cheek and throat, but all like a slightly idealized bas-relief "after" a greater original; and James's heavy Roman head, so realistically and vigorously his own, not a bas-relief but a bust, wrought in the round by harsher but more powerful hands. As they sat there, James benignly listening, Meredith eloquently discoursing, and their old deep regard for each other burning steadily through the surface eloquence and the surface attentiveness, I felt I was in great company, and was glad.

"Well, my dear," James said to me, as we went out into the dusk, "wasn't I right?" Yes, he had been right, and I had to own it.

7

Henry James, after buying Lamb House, had given up his flat in London; but in the autumn and winter he often went up to town for a short visit, staying at his club (the Athenaeum) and "doing" as many lunches and dinners as he could crowd in, besides anything new at the theatres—for his interest in matters theatrical had not waned. Now that he had given up London he returned to it on these occasions with the zest of a truant school-boy. Everything he did exhilarated him, every one he saw amused him, everything he ate agreed with him—and when it was over he would go back, feeling guilty but rejuvenated, to a long stretch of work, and a diet of herbs and cold pudding.

When I was in London he generally joined me there for a day or two, especially if any theatrical event were impending; and I remember going one evening with him to see Mr. Knoblock's Arabian Nights' fantasy, "Kismet", then an innovation in stage-setting and lighting. We were enchanted with this lovely evocation of the bazaars, to which all London was thronging; it was the first time we had either of us seen what was in some sort a dematerialized pantomime, freed of its too realistic trappings—a first bud in the coming springtide of the Russian ballet. Another evening we went to "Androcles and the Lion", and I think James laughed as much as I did at that enormous fooling, though doubtless with more self-restraint. In reality he was a much better theatre-goer than I, for the material limitations of the stage, and its violent foreshortenings, which always contract my vision, and cut rudely into my dream, seemed to stimulate his imagination, however much he found to criticize in a given play or its acting.

Sometimes, too, our little knot of friends would contrive to be in London at the same time, and I recall one happy evening when Howard Sturgis, Walter Berry, Percy Lubbock and Gaillard Lapsley were dining with me at my hotel. We had hoped that James would join us; but he was already booked for a fashionable dinner from which it was useless to try to detach him. Hardly had we sat down when, to our astonishment, in he walked, resplendent in white waistcoat and white tie, and rubbing his hands as though he nursed between his palms the smile striking up into his face. He had made a mistake in his date; had presented himself at the great house, and been told the dinner was not till the next evening; so here he was, and did we still want him, and was there room for him at the table—oh, he could squeeze into the least little corner, if we'd only let him! And let him we did; and how he enjoyed his dinner, and his glass of champagne (he who, at Rye, thought he could digest nothing heavier than a squeeze of orange juice!), and what a good evening of talk and laughter we had! As I write I yearn back to those lost hours, all the while aware that those who read of them must take their gaiety, their jokes and laughter, on faith, yet unable to detach my memory from them, and loath not to give others a glimpse of that jolliest of comrades, the laughing, chaffing, jubilant yet malicious James, who was so different from the grave personage known to less intimate eyes.

XI

Paris

A YEAR or two after the publication of "The House of Mirth" my husband and I decided to exchange our little house in New York for a flat in Paris. My husband suffered increasingly from the harsh winds and sudden changes of temperature of the New York winter, and latterly we had spent the cold months in rather aimless drifting on the French and the Italian Rivieras. Alassio, San Remo, Bordighera, Menton, Monte Carlo, Cannes; we knew them all to satiety, and in none could I hope to find the kind of human communion I cared for. In none, that is, but Hyères, where we had begun to go nearly every year since the Paul Bourgets had acquired there a little peach-coloured villa above the peach-orchards of Costebelle. But even the companionship of these friends could not fill the emptiness of life in a Riviera hotel. A house and garden of my own, anywhere on the coast between Marseilles and Fréjus, would have made me happy; since that could not be, my preference was for a flat in Paris, where I could see people who shared my tastes, and whence it was easy to go south for sunshine when the weather grew too damp for my husband. On this, therefore, we decided in 1907, thereafter spending our winters in Paris, and going back to the Mount every summer. For two years we occupied an apartment sublet to us by American friends, in a stately Louis XIV *hôtel* of the rue de Varenne; then we hired a flat in a modern house in the same street, and there I remained till 1920, so that my thirteen years of Paris life were spent entirely in the rue de Varenne; and all those years rise up to meet me whenever I turn the corner of the street. Rich years, crowded and happy years; for though I should have preferred London, I should have been hard to please had I not discovered many compensations in my life in Paris.

I found myself at once among friends, both old and new. The Bourgets always spent a part of the winter in the quiet and leafy rue Barbet de Jouy, a short walk from our door; and in other houses of the old Faubourg I found three or four of the French girl friends I had known in my youth at Cannes, and who had long since married, and settled in Paris. Their welcome, and that of the Bourgets, at once made me feel at home, and thanks to their kindness I soon enlarged my circle of acquaintances. My new friends came from worlds as widely different as the University, the literary and Academic *milieux*, and the old and aloof society of the Faubourg Saint-Germain, to which my early companions at Cannes all belonged. As a stranger and newcomer, not only outside of all groups and coteries, but hardly aware of their existence, I enjoyed a freedom not possible in those days to the native-born, who were still enclosed in the old social pigeon-holes, which they had begun to laugh at, but to which they still flew back.

If in those days any authentic member of the Faubourg Saint-Germain had been asked what really constituted Paris society, the answer would undoubtedly have been: "There is no Paris society any longer—there is just a welter of people from heaven knows where." In a once famous play by Alexandre Dumas *fils*, "L'Etrangère", written, I suppose, in the 'sixties, the Duke (a Duke of the proudest and most ancient nobility) forces his equally proud and perfectly irreproachable wife to invite his foreign mistress (Mrs. Clarkson) to an evening party. The Duchess is seen receiving her guests in the high-ceilinged *salon* of their old *hôtel*, with tall French windows opening to the floor. Mrs. Clarkson arrives, elegant, arrogant and nervous; the Duchess receives her simply and courteously; then she rings for the major-domo, and gives the order: *"Ouvrez les fenêtres! Que tout le monde entre maintenant!"*

In the Paris I knew, the Paris of twenty-five years ago, everybody would have told me that those windows had remained wide open ever since, that *tout le monde* had long since come in, that all the old social conventions were tottering or already demolished, and that the Faubourg had become as promiscuous as the Fair of Neuilly. The same thing was no doubt said a hundred years earlier, and two hundred years even, and probably something not unlike it was heard in the more exclusive *salons* of Babylon and Ur.

At any rate, as I look back at it across the chasm of the war, and all the ruins since heaped up, every convention of that compact and amiable little world seems still to have been standing, though few were rigid enough to hinder social enjoyment. I remember, however, one amusing instance of this rigidity. Soon after coming to Paris my husband and I, wishing to make some return for the welcome my old friends had given us, invited a dozen of them to dine. They were all intimate with each other, and members of the same group; but, being new to the job, and aware of the delicate problems which beset the question of precedence in French society, I begged one of the young women I had invited to advise me as to the seating of my guests. The next day she came to me in perplexity.

"My dear, I really don't know! It's so difficult that I think I'd better consult my uncle, the Duc de D." That venerable nobleman, who had represented his country as Ambassador to one or two of the great powers, was, I knew, the final authority in the Faubourg on ceremonial questions, and though surprised that he should be invoked in so unimportant a matter, I gratefully awaited his decision. The next day my friend brought it. "My uncle was very much perplexed. He *thinks* on the whole you had better place your guests in this way." (She handed me a plan of the table.) "But he said: 'My dear child, Mrs. Wharton ought *never* to have invited them together' "—not that they were not all good and even intimate friends, and in the habit of meeting daily, but because the shades of difference in their rank were so slight, and so difficult to adjust, that even the diplomatist Duke recoiled from the attempt.

It took me, naturally, some time to acquire even the rudiments of this "unwritten law"; to remember, for instance, that an Academician takes precedence of every one but a Duke or an Ambassador (though what happens if he is both a Duke and an Academician I can't remember, if I ever knew); that the next-but-two most honoured guest sits on the right of the lady who is on the host's right; that a foreigner of no rank whatever takes precedence of every rank but that of an Academician, a Cardinal or an Ambassador (or does he? Again I can't remember!); and that, under the most exquisite surface urbanity, resentment may rankle for years in the bosom of a guest whose claims have been disregarded. As almost all the rules are exactly the opposite of those prevailing in England, my path was no doubt strewn with blunders; but such indulgence as may have been needed was accorded because of my girlish intimacy with a small group belonging to the inner circle of the Faubourg, and because I had written a successful novel, a translation of which had recently appeared, with a flattering introduction by Bourget. Herein lay one of the many distinctions between the social worlds of New York and Paris. In Paris no one could live without literature, and the fact that I was a professional writer, instead of frightening my fashionable friends, interested them. If the French Academy had served no other purpose than the highly civilizing one of linking together society and letters, that service would justify its existence. But it is a delusion to think that a similar institution could render the same service in other societies. Culture in France is an eminently social quality, while in Anglo-Saxon countries it might also be called anti-social. In France, where politics so sharply divide the different classes and coteries, artistic and literary interests unite them; and wherever two or three educated French people are gathered together, a *salon* immediately comes into being.

2

In the numberless books I had read about social life in France—memoirs, history, essays, from Sainte-Beuve to Jules Lemaître and after—I had been told that the *salon* had vanished forever, first with the famous *douceur de vivre* of the Old Régime, then with the downfall of the Bourbons, then with the end of the House of Orleans, and finally on the disastrous day of Sedan. Each of these catastrophes doubtless took with it something of the exclusiveness, the intimacy and continuity of the traditional *salon*; but before I had lived a year in Paris I had discovered that most of the old catch-words were still in circulation, most of the old rules still observed, and that the ineradicable passion for good talk, and for seeing the same people every day, was as strong at the opening of the twentieth century as when the *Précieuses* met at the Hôtel de

Rambouillet. When I first went to live in Paris, old ladies with dowdy cashmere "mantles", and bonnets tied under their chins, were pointed out to me as still receiving every afternoon or evening, at the same hour, the same five or six men who had been the "foundation" of their group nearly half a century earlier. Though circles as small as these scarcely formed a *salon*, they were composed of the same elements, and capable of the same expansion. Occasionally even the most exclusive felt the need of a blood-transfusion, and more than once it happened to me to be invited, and as it were tested, by the prudent guardian of the hearth.

The typical *salon*, the *salon* in action, was of course a larger and more elastic organization. It presupposed a moderate admixture of new elements, judiciously combined with the permanent ones, those which were called *de fondation*. But these recognized *salons* were based on the same belief that intimacy and continuity were the first requisites of social enjoyment. To attain the perfection of this enjoyment the Parisian hostess would exercise incessant watchfulness over all the members of her own group, as well as over other groups which might supply her with the necessary new blood, and would put up with many whims and humours on the part of her chief performers; and I remember, when I once said to a French friend: "How can Madame A. endure the crotchets of Monsieur X.? Why doesn't she stop inviting him?" his astonished reply: *"Mais elle ne veut pas dégarnir son salon!"*

This continuity of social relations was what particularly appealed to me. In London, where another ideal prevailed, and perpetual novelty was sought for, the stream of new faces rushing past me often made me feel as if I were in a railway station rather than a drawing-room; whereas after I had got my bearings in Paris I found myself, as usual, settling down into a small circle of friends with whom, through all my years in the rue de Varenne, I kept up a delightful intimacy.

Paul Bourget was then at the height of his social popularity. He was one of the most interesting and versatile of talkers, and much in demand by ambitious hostesses; but he too preferred a small group to general society, and was always at his best among his intimates. Far more than I was aware of at the time, he smoothed my social path in Paris, bringing me into

contact with the people he thought most likely to interest
me, and putting me at once on a footing of intimacy in the
houses where he was most at home. Through all the changes
which have since befallen us both, his friendship has never
failed me; and in looking back at those mirage-like years I
like to think how much of their happiness I owed to him
and to his wife.

Early in our first winter he did me an exceptionally good
turn. A new Academician—I forget who—was to be received
under the famous "Cupola", and Bourget invited me to the
ceremony. I had never seen an Academic reception—still one
of the most unchanged and distinctive events of Parisian
life—and was naturally delighted, as invitations are few, and
much sought after if the candidate happens to be (as he was
in this case) a familiar and popular Parisian figure. For some
reason Minnie Bourget could not go with me, and as I had
never been to the Institut, and did not know how to find my
way in, or to manoeuvre for a seat, Bourget asked an old
friend of his, the Comtesse Robert de Fitz-James, to take me
under her wing. She invited me to luncheon, I think—or
came to lunch with us; at any rate, before we had struggled to
our places through the fashionable throng battling in the
circuitous corridors of the Institut, she and I had become
friends.

The widowed Comtesse de Fitz-James, known as "Rosa"
among her intimates, was a small thin woman, then perhaps
forty-five years old, with a slight limp which obliged her to
lean on a stick, hair prematurely white, sharp features, eager
dark eyes and a disarmingly guileless smile. Belonging by
birth to the wealthy Viennese banking family of the Gut-
manns, she had the easy cosmopolitanism of a rich Austrian
Jewess, and though she had married early, and since her marriage had always lived in Paris, she spoke English almost perfectly, and was always eager to welcome any foreigners likely
to fit into the carefully-adjusted design of her *salon*, which, at
that time, was the meeting-place of some of the most distinguished people in Paris. There were still, among the irreduc-
ibles of the Faubourg, a few who held out, declined to risk
themselves among such international promiscuities, and received the mention of the hostess's name with raised eye-

brows, and an affectation of hearing it for the first time. But they were few even then, and now that the world we then knew has come to an end, even they would probably agree that in the last ten or fifteen years before the war Madame de Fitz-James' *salon* had a prestige which no Parisian hostess, since 1918, has succeeded in recovering.

When I first knew it, the *salon* in question looked out on the mossy turf and trees of an eighteenth century *hôtel* standing between court and garden in the rue de Grenelle. A few years later it was transferred to a modern building in the Place des Invalides, to which Madame de Fitz-James had moved her fine collection of eighteenth century furniture and pictures at the suggestion of her old friends, the Comte and Comtesse d'Haussonville, who lived on the floor above. The rue de Grenelle apartment, which had much more character, faced north, and her Anglo-Saxon friends thought she had left in search of sunlight, and congratulated her on the change. But she looked surprised, and said: "Oh, no; I hate the sun; it's such a bore always having to keep the blinds down." To regard the sun as the housewife's enemy, fader of hangings and devourer of old stuffs, is common on the continent, and Madame de Fitz-James' cream-coloured silk blinds were lowered, even in winter, whenever the sun became intrusive. The three drawing-rooms, which opened into one another, were as commonplace as rooms can be in which every piece of furniture, every picture and every ornament is in itself a beautiful thing, yet the whole reveals no trace of the owner's personality. In the first drawing-room, a small room hung with red damask, Madame de Fitz-James, seated by the fire, her lame leg supported on a foot-rest, received her intimates. Beyond was the big drawing-room, with pictures by Ingres and David on the pale walls, and tapestry sofas and arm-chairs; it was there that the dinner guests assembled. Opening out of it was another small room, lined with ornate Louis XV bookcases in which rows of rare books in precious bindings stood in undisturbed order—for Madame de Fitz-James was a book-collector, not a reader. She made no secret of this—or indeed of any of her idiosyncrasies—for she was one of the most honest women I have ever known, and genuinely and unaffectedly modest. Her books were an ornament and an investment; she never pretended that they were anything else. If one of her guests was raised to Academic honours she bought his last work and tried to read it—usually with negative results; and her intimates were all familiar with the confidential question: "I've just read So-and-So's new book. *Tell me, my dear: is it good?*"

This model hostess was almost always at home; in fact she very nearly realized the definition of the perfect hostess once given me by an old frequenter of Parisian *salons*. "A woman should never go out—*never*—if she expects people to come to her," he declared; and on my protesting that this cloistered ideal must, on merely practical grounds, be hard for a Parisian hostess to live up to, he replied with surprise: "But why? If a woman once positively resolves never to go to a funeral or a wedding, why should she ever leave her house?"

Why indeed? And Madame de Fitz-James, though she fell short of this counsel of perfection, and missed few funerals and weddings, and occasionally went to an afternoon tea, seldom lunched or dined out. When she did, she preferred big banquets, where the food and the plate were more interesting than the conversation. This, I am sure, was not because she was unduly impressed by the display of wealth, but because it was less of an effort to talk to the fashionable and the over-fed, and the crowd gave her the shelter of anonymity which she seemed to crave outside of her own doors. Occasionally—but very seldom—she came to dine with us; and these small informal parties, though always composed of her own friends, seemed to embarrass and fatigue her. She appeared to feel that she ought to be directing the conversation, signing to the butler to refill the wine-glasses, trying to reshape the groups into which the guests had drifted after dinner; and the effort to repress this impulse was so tiring that she always fled early, with an apologetic murmur. As with most of the famous hostesses I have known, her hospitality seemed to be a blind overpowering instinct, hardly ever to be curbed, and then only with evident distress. When I saw her in other people's houses she always made me think of the story of the English naturalist who kept two tame beavers, and one day, having absented himself for an hour or two, found on his return that the dear creatures had built a dam across the drawing-room floor. That is exactly what Madame de Fitz-James blindly yearned to do in other people's drawing-rooms.

3

She and Bourget had a real regard for each other, and it was thanks to him that I soon became an habitual guest at her weekly lunches and dinners. These always took place on fixed days; a dinner of fourteen or sixteen, with a small reception afterward, on a certain evening of the week, a smaller dinner on another, and on Fridays an informal and extremely agreeable luncheon, at which her accomplished cook served two *menus* of equal exquisiteness, one for those who abstained from meat on Fridays, the other for heretics and nonconformers. More than once, in the excitement and delight of the good talk, I have eaten my way unknowingly through the fat and the lean *menus*, with no subsequent ill-effects beyond a slight reluctance to begin again at dinner; and I was not the only guest whom intellectual enjoyment led into this gastronomic oversight.

Certainly, in my limited experience, I have never known easier and more agreeable social relations than at Rosa de Fitz-James'. Lists of names are not of much help in evoking an atmosphere; but the pre-war society of the Faubourg Saint-Germain has been so utterly dispersed and wiped out that as a group the frequenters of Madame de Fitz-James' drawing-room have an almost historic interest. Among the Academicians — in such cases, I suppose, entitled to be named first — were, of course, Bourget himself, the Comte d'Haussonville (Madame de Staël's grandson and biographer), the two popular playwrights, Paul Hervieu and the Marquis de Flers, the former gaunt, caustic and somewhat melancholy, the latter rotund, witty and cordial to the brink of exuberance; the poet and novelist Henri de Régnier, and my dear friend the Marquis de Ségur, a charming talker in his discreet and finely-shaded way, and the author, among other historical studies, of a remarkable book on Julie de Lespinasse. The Institut was represented by two eminent members, the Comte Alexandre de Laborde, the learned bibliophile and authority on illuminated manuscripts, whom his old friend, Gustave Schlumberger, has characterized as "the most worldly of scholars, and the most scholarly of men of the world"; the other, also a friend of mine, the Baron Ernest Seillière, a tall quiet man with keen eyes under a vertical shock of white hair, who had studied in a German University, and whose interest in the *Sturm-und-Drang* of the German Romantics, and its effect on European culture, has resulted in a number of erudite and interesting volumes.

Diplomacy (combined with the Academy) shone at Madame de Fitz-James' in the person of the French Ambassador in Berlin, the wise and witty Jules Cambon, whom I had known since his far-off days in Washington, and who was a much sought-for guest whenever his leave brought him to Paris; by Maurice Paléologue, who, after filling important posts at the Foreign Office, was to be the last French Ambassador at St Petersburg before the war, and soon after its close to enter the Academy; by the German and Austrian Ambassadors, Prince Radolin and Count Czechen; by Don Enrique Larreta, the Argentine Ambassador, a real lover of letters, and author of that enchanting chronicle-novel, "The Glory of Don Ramiro" (of which Rémy de Gourmont's French version is a triumph of literary interpretation); and, among Secretaries of Embassy, by Mr. George Grahame, attached to the British Embassy in Paris, the cultivated and indefatigably brilliant Charles de Chambrun (now French Ambassador to the Quirinal), and the gay and ironic Olivier Taigny, whose ill-health unfortunately shortened his diplomatic career, but left him his incisive wit.

I have probably left out far more names than I have recorded; but I am impatient to escape from the seats of honour to that despised yet favoured quarter of the French dining-room, the *bout de table*. As I have already said, in France, where everything connected with food is treated with a proper seriousness, the seating of the guests has a corresponding importance—or had, at any rate, in pre-war days. In London, even in those remote times, though the old rules of precedence still prevailed at big dinners (and may yet, for all I know), they were relaxed on intimate occasions, and one of the first to go was that compelling host and hostess always to face each other from the head and foot of the table. In

France, all this is reversed. Host and hostess sit opposite one another in the middle of the table (a rule always maintained, in my time, at whatever cost to the harmonious grouping of the party), and the guests descend right and left in dwindling importance to the table-ends, where the untitled, unofficial, unclassified, but usually young, humorous and voluble, are assembled. These *bouts de table* are at once the shame and glory of the French dinner-table; the shame of those who think they deserve a better place, or are annoyed with themselves and the world because they have not yet earned it; the glory of hostesses ambitious to receive the quickest wits in Paris, and aware that most of the brilliant sallies, bold paradoxes and racy anecdotes emanate from that cluster of independents.

The Parisian table-end deserves a chapter to itself, so many are the famous sayings originating there, and so various is the attitude of the table-enders. At first, of course, it is good fun to be among them, and a sought-after table-ender has his own special prestige; but as the years pass, he grows more and more ready to make way for the rising generation, and work upward to the seats of the successful. Not long ago I met at dinner a new Academician, elected after many efforts and long years of waiting, and who had risen without intermediate stages from the table-end to his hostess's right hand. As the guests seated themselves, an old and unpromoted table-ender, passing behind the new Academician, laid a hand on his shoulder, and said: "Ah, my dear B., after so many years of table-end I shall feel terribly lonely without my old neighbour!" Every one burst out laughing except the Academician, who silently unfolded his napkin with an acid smile, and the mistress of the house, who was flurried by this free-and-easy treatment of a guest now raised to the highest rank. A good story is told of the Comte A. de R., a nobleman known as a fierce stickler for the seat to which his armorial bearings entitled him, and who on one occasion was placed, as he thought, too near the table-end. He watched for a lull in the talk, and then, turning to the lady next to him, asked in a piercing voice: "Do you suppose, *chère Madame*, the dishes will be handed as far down the table as this?" (It was this same Comte de R. who, on leaving another dinner, said to a guest of equally aristocratic descent, who lived in his neighbour-hood: "Are you walking home? Good! Let us walk together, then, *and talk of rank.*")

In those old days at Madame de Fitz-James' there were, I imagine, few malcontents at the table-ends, for the great rushes of talk and laughter that swept up from there sent a corresponding animation through all the occupants of the high seats. The habitual holders of the ends were the young André Tardieu, then the masterly political leader-writer of the *Temps*, his governmental honours still far ahead of him, the young André Chaumeix, in those days also of the *Temps*, Abel Bonnard, almost the only talker I have known in a French *salon* who was allowed to go on talking as long as he wanted on the same subject (the conventional time-allowance being not more than five minutes), Etienne Grosclaude, the well-known journalist and wit, and only a seat or two farther up (when the company was small) Alexandre de Gabriac, Charles de Chambrun, Taigny and the Marquis du Tillet, each alert to catch and send back the ball flung by their irrepressible juniors.

The whole *raison d'être* of the French *salon* is based on the national taste for general conversation. The two-and-two talks which cut up Anglo-Saxon dinners, and isolate guests at table and in the drawing-room, would be considered not only stupid but ill-bred in a society where social intercourse is a perpetual exchange, a market to which every one is expected to bring his best for barter. How often have I seen such transactions blighted by the presence of an English or American guest, perhaps full of interesting things to say, but unpractised in the accustomed sport, and blocking all circulation by imprisoning his or her restive but helpless neighbour in a relentless duologue!

At Madame de Fitz-James' the men always outnumbered the women, and this also helped to stimulate general talk. The few women present were mostly old friends, and *de fondation*; none very brilliant talkers, but all intelligent, observant and ready to listen. In a French *salon* the women are expected to listen, and enjoy doing so, since they love good talk, and are prepared by a long social experience to seize every allusion, and when necessary to cap it by another. This power of absorbed and intelligent attention is one of the Frenchwoman's greatest gifts, and makes a perfect background for the talk of the men. And how good that talk is—or was, at any rate—only those can say who have frequented such a *salon* as that of Madame de Fitz-James. Almost all the guests knew each other well, all could drop into the conversation at any stage, without groping or blundering, and each had something worth saying, from Bourget's serious talk, all threaded with golden streaks of irony and humour, to the incessant fire-works of Tardieu, the quiet epigrams of Henri de Régnier, the anecdotes of Taigny and Gabriac, the whimsical and half-melancholy gaiety of Abel Bonnard.

The creator of a French *salon* may be moved by divers ambitions; she may wish to make it predominantly political, or literary and artistic, or merely mundane—though the worldly *salon* hardly counts, and is, at any rate, not worth commemorating. Any hostess, however, who intends to specialize, particularly in politics, runs the risk of making her *salon* dull; and dullest of all is that exclusively devoted to manufacturing Academicians, an industry inexhaustibly fascinating to many Frenchwomen. Few can resist political or academic intrigues as an ingredient in their social mixture; but the great art is to combine the ingredients so that none predominates, and to flavour the composition with an occasional dash of novelty. The transients introduced as seasoning must not be too numerous, or rashly chosen; they must be interesting for one reason or another, and above all they must blend agreeably with the "foundation" mixture. In describing French society one has to borrow one's imagery from the French *cuisine*, so similar are the principles involved, and so equally minute is the care required, in preparing a *soufflé* or a *salon*.

Madame de Fitz-James chose her transients with exceptional skill. The few women she added now and then to her habitual group usually possessed some striking quality. The most stimulating and vivid was the Princesse Lucien Murat, and the two most charming were the daughter and the sister of famous poets; the subtle and exquisite Madame Henri de Régnier (one of the three daughters of Hérédia) and my dear friend Jeanne de Margerie, sister of Edmond Rostand, and an intimate of old days, for her husband, until recently French

Ambassador in Berlin, had been for many years secretary of Embassy in Washington. Jeanne de Margerie's gifts were of a quieter order, but she was exceptionally quick and responsive, with an unfailing sense of fun; and when she died, not long after the war, a soft but warm radiance vanished from the Parisian scene, and from the lives of her friends.

I do not remember ever seeing Madame de Noailles, the poetess, at Madame de Fitz-James'. Poets are usually shy of *salons*, and so are monologuists like Madame de Noailles, whose dazzling talk was always intolerant of the slightest interruption. Among the women I met there by far the most remarkable was Matilde Serao, the Neapolitan novelist and journalist. She was an old friend of Bourget's, by whom she was first introduced to Madame de Fitz-James, who at once recognized her, in spite of certain external oddities, as an invaluable addition to her parties. Matilde Serao, for a number of years before the war, made an annual visit to Paris, and had many friends there. She was a broad squat woman, with a red face on a short red neck between round cushiony shoulders. Her black hair, as elaborately dressed as a Neapolitan peasant's, looked like a wig, and must have been dyed or false. Her age was unguessable, though the fact that she was accompanied by a young daughter in short skirts led one to assume that she was under fifty. This strange half-Spanish figure, oddly akin to the *Meniñas* of Velasquez, and described by Bourget as "Dr. Johnson in a ball-dress", was always arrayed in low-necked dresses rather in the style of Mrs. Tom Thumb's—I remember in particular a spreading scarlet silk festooned with black lace, on which her short arms and chubby hands rested like a cherub's on a sunset cloud. With her strident dress and intonation she seemed an incongruous figure in that drawing-room, where everything was in half-shades and semi-tones—but when she began to speak we had found our master. In Latin countries the few women who shine as conversationalists often do so at the expense of the rapid give-and-take of good talk. Not so Matilde Serao. She never tried to vaticinate or to predominate; what interested her was exchanging ideas with intelligent people. Her training as a journalist, first on her husband Edoardo Scarfoglio's newspaper, *Il Mattino*, and later as editor of a sheet of her own, *Il Giorno*, had given her a rough-and-ready knowledge of life, and an experience of public affairs, totally lacking in the drawing-room Corinnes whom she outrivalled in wit and eloquence. She had a man's sense of fair play, listened attentively, never dwelt too long on one point, but placed her sallies at the right moment, and made way for the next competitor. But when she was encouraged to talk, and given the field—as, alone with Abel Bonnard, she often was—then her monologues rose to greater heights than the talk of any other woman I have known. The novelist's eager imagination (two or three of her novels are masterly) was nourished on wide reading, and on the varied experience of classes and types supplied by her journalistic career; and culture and experience were fused in the glow of her powerful intelligence.

Another of Madame de Fitz-James' distinguished transients was Count Keyserling, who came often to her house when he was in Paris, as did his charming sister. There were also not a few agreeable Austrians, Count Fritz Hoyos and his sisters among them; none perhaps particularly interested in ideas, but all with that gift of ease and receptivity which made the pre-war Austrian so accomplished a social being. I remember, by the way, asking Theodore Roosevelt, at the end of his triumphal passage across Europe, what type of person he had found most sympathetic on his travels, and my momentary surprise at his unexpected reply: "The Austrian gentlemen."

Henry James was another outlander who, when he came to stay with us, at once became *de fondation*, as did Walter Berry and my friend Bernard Berenson; and from Rumania came Princess Marthe Bibesco and her cousin Prince Antoine (afterward Rumanian Minister in Washington)—but the list is too long to be continued. Instead, I wish to evoke at its close the figure of the most beloved, the kindliest and one of the wittiest of Madame de Fitz-James' "foundation" guests—the Abbé Mugnier (afterward made a Canon of Notre Dame), without whom no reunion at Rosa's would have been complete. The Abbé's sensitive intelligence was a solvent for the conflicting ideas and opinions of the other visitors, since no matter how much they disagreed with each other, they were one in appreciating "Monsieur l'Abbé", and at the approach of his small figure, with eyes always smiling behind their spectacles, and a tuft of gray hair vibrating flame-wise above his forehead, every group opened to welcome him.

Even for those who know the Abbé Mugnier well, it is not easy to define the qualities which thus single him out. Profound kindness and keen intelligence are too seldom blent in the same person for a word to have been coined describing that rare combination. I can only say that as vicar of the ultra-fashionable church of Sainte Clotilde, and then as chaplain of a convent in a remote street beyond Montparnasse, he seemed equally in his proper setting; and his quick sense of fun and irony is so lined with tender human sympathy that the good priest is always visible behind the shrewd social observer.

The Abbé Mugnier had an hour of celebrity when he converted Huysmans; he has since made other noted converts, and his concern for souls, and his wise dealings with them, cause him to be much sought after as the consoler of the dying, though those who have met him only in the world would not at first associate him with such scenes—at least not until they catch the tone of his voice in speaking of grief and suffering. His tolerance and sociability have indeed occasionally led people to risk in his presence remarks slightly inappropriate to his cloth; and it is good to see the quiet way in which, without the least air of offence, he gives the talk a more suitable turn.

His wise and kindly sayings—so quietly spoken that they sometimes escape the inattentive—are celebrated in Paris; but they have doubtless been recorded by many, and I will cite only two or three, which were said in my hearing. The Abbé, in spite of his social leanings, has a Franciscan soul, and is one of the few Frenchmen I have known with a genuine love of trees and flowers and animals. Before his sight began to fail he used to come out every year in June to my little garden near Paris, to see the long walk when the Candidum lilies were in bloom; and he really *did* see them, which is more than some visitors do, who make the pilgrimage for the same purpose. His tenderness for flowers and birds is so un-French that he might have imbibed it in the Thuringian forests where he used to wander on his summer holidays in the path of Goethe (Goethe and Châteaubriand, both forest-lovers, are his two literary passions); and it seems appropriate, therefore, that two of his sayings to me should be about birds.

We were speaking one day of the difficult moral problems which priests call *cas de conscience*, and he said: "Ah, a very difficult one presented itself to me once, for which I knew of no precedent. I was administering the Sacrament to a dying parishioner, and at that moment the poor woman's pet canary escaped from its cage, and lighting suddenly on her shoulder, pecked at the Host."

"Oh, Monsieur l'Abbé—and what did you do?"

"I blessed the bird," he answered with his quiet smile.

Another day he was talking of the great frost in Paris, when the Seine was frozen over for days, and of the sufferings it had caused among the poor. "I shall never forget the feeling of that cold. On one of the worst nights—or rather at three in the morning, the coldest hour of the twenty-four—I was called out of bed by the sacristan of Sainte Clotilde, who came to fetch me to take the viaticum to a poor parishioner. The sick man lived a long way off, and oh, how cold we were on the way there, Lalouette and I—the old sacristan's name was Lalouette (the lark)," he added with a reminiscent laugh.

The play on the name was irresistible, and I exclaimed: "Oh, how tempted you must have been, when he came for you, to cry out: ' 'Tis not the lark, it is the nightingale'—" I broke off, fearing that my quotation might be thought inappropriate; but with his usual calm smile the Abbé answered: "Unfortunately, Madame, we were not in Verona."

Once, in another vein, he was describing the marriage of two social "climbers" who had invited all fashionable Paris to their nuptial Mass, and had asked the Abbé (much sought after on such occasions also) to perform the ceremony. At the last moment, when the guests were already assembled, he discovered (what had perhaps been purposely slurred over), that the couple were in some way technically disqualified for a church marriage. "So," said the Abbé drily, "I blessed them in the sacristy, between two sterilized palms; and of course I could not prevent their assisting afterward at Mass with the rest of the company."

Another day we were lunching together at a friend's

house, and the talk having turned on the survival in the French provinces of the old-fashioned village atheist and anti-clerical (in the style of Flaubert's immortal Monsieur Homais), our hostess told us that she had known an old village chemist near her father's place in the Roussillon who was a perfect type of this kind. His family were much distressed by his sentiments, and when he lay on his death-bed besought him to receive the parish priest; but he refused indignantly, and to his wife's question: "But what can you have against our poor *Curé*?", replied with a last gust of fury: "Your *curés*—your *curés*, indeed! Don't tell me! I know all about your *curés*—"

"But what do you know against them?"

"Why, I read in a history book long ago that ten thousand *curés* died fighting for the beautiful Helen under the walls of Troy."

A shout of mirth received this prodigious bit of history, and as our laughter subsided we heard the Abbé's chuckle, and saw the little flame-like tuft quiver excitedly on his crest.

"Well, Monsieur l'Abbé, what do you think of that?"

"Ah, would to heaven it were true!" the Abbé murmured sadly.

The war broke up that company of friendly people; death followed on war, and now the whole scene seems as remote as if it had belonged to a past century, and I linger with a kind of piety over the picture of that pleasant gray-panelled room, with its pictures and soft lights, and arm-chairs of faded tapestry. I see Bourget and James talking together before the fire, soon to be joined by the Abbé Mugnier, Bonnard and Walter Berry; Monsieur d'Haussonville, Hervieu and Larreta listening to Matilde Serao, and Chambrun, Berenson and Tardieu forming another group; and in and out among her guests Madame de Fitz-James weaving her quiet way, leaning on her stick, watching, prodding, interfering, re-shaping the groups, building and rebuilding her dam, yet somehow never in the way, because, in spite of her incomprehension of the talk, she always manages to bring the right people together and diffuses about her such an atmosphere of kindly hospitality that her very blunders add to the general ease and good humour.

4

I have dwelt so long on one pre-war *salon* that it might seem as if the greater part of my life in Paris had been spent in it; but I risked producing this impression because I wished to put first among my Parisian glimpses the vision of a little society in which the old *douceur de vivre* was combined with an intelligent interest in current ideas and events.

Naturally, in the course of my Parisian years, I saw other typical scenes, and came to know many people in other circles, and to form friendships quite outside of Madame de Fitz-James' agreeable drawing-room; but hers remains with me as peculiarly characteristic of a vanished order.

One of the first friends I made was Jacques-Emile Blanche, the distinguished painter and man of letters, in whose house one met not only most of the worth-while in Paris, but an interesting admixture of literary and artistic London. Blanche speaks and writes English fluently, and he and Madame Blanche often went to London, and had many English friends in the world of society and letters, as well as among painters; and before the war their picturesque half-timbered house at Auteuil welcomed all that was newest and most amusing in cosmopolitan society. In such houses as the Blanches', and that of another friend, Monsieur André Chevrillon (the nephew of Taine), pre-war Paris was first brought into familiar contact with English artists, savants and men of letters, and made aware of the riches of intellectual and artistic life in England. It is hard to realize now how few those contacts were before the war, and how completely, except for a handful of Parisians, France remained enclosed in her own culture.

Blanche, besides being an excellent linguist, and a writer of exceptional discernment on contemporary art, is also a cultivated musician; and in those happy days painters, composers, novelists, playwrights—Diaghilew, the creator of the Russian *ballet*, Henry Bernstein, whose plays were the sensation of the hour, George Moore, André Gide, my dear friend Mrs. Charles Hunter, the painters Walter Sickert and Ricketts, and countless other well-known people, mostly of the cosmopolitan type—met on Sundays in the delightful informality of his studio, or about a tea-table under the spreading trees of the garden. The lofty studio-living-room (his real painting room is tucked away in a corner upstairs) was in those days the most perfect setting for such meetings. Everything in it was harmonious in colour and tone, from the tall Coromandel screens, the old Chinese rugs on the floor, and the early Chinese bronzes and monochrome porcelains, to the crowning glory of the walls, hung with pictures by Renoir, Degas, Manet, Corot, Boudin, Alfred Stevens and Whistler—the "Bathing Women" of Renoir, the sombre and powerful "Young Woman with the Glove" of Manet (a portrait of one of Madame Blanche's aunts in her youth), and an early Gainsborough landscape of a peculiar hazy loveliness; and among them, or else in the upper gallery, some of the most notable of our host's own portraits; the perfect study of Thomas Hardy, the Degas, the Debussy, the Aubrey Beardsley, the George Moore and the young Marcel Proust—for Blanche, with singular insight, began long ago that unique series of portraits of his famous contemporaries which ought some day to be permanently grouped as a whole.

On other afternoons there met at the Blanches' a small company of music-lovers ("Les Amis de la Musique", I think they were called), and it was enchanting to listen to Bach and Beethoven, Franck, Debussy or Chausson, with those great pictures looking down from the walls, and the glimpse of lawn and shady trees deepening the impression of the music by enclosing it in a country solitude.

The Blanches, for years, have spent their summers in a charming little stone manor-house in the village of Offranville, near Dieppe. A garden bursting with flowers divides the house from the village street, and at the back the windows look out on a beautiful orchard where the calves from the neighbouring farm caper under the apple-blossoms. I used to go there often to stay, and the first time I went I met a young man of nineteen or twenty, who at that time vibrated with all the youth of the world. This was Jean Cocteau, then a passionately imaginative youth to whom every great line of poetry was a sunrise, every sunset the foundations of the Heavenly City. Excepting Bay Lodge I have known no other young man who so recalled Wordsworth's "Bliss was it in that dawn to be alive". Every subject touched on—and in his

company they were countless—was lit up by his young enthusiasm, and it is one of the regrets of later years to have
watched the fading of that light. Life in general, and Parisian
life in particular, is the cause of many such effacements—or
defacements; but in Cocteau's case the pity is particularly
great because his gifts were so many, and his fervours so genuine. For many years I saw a great deal of him; he came often
to the rue de Varenne, and to many of my friends' houses; but
I never enjoyed his talk as much as in the leafy quiet of Offranville. I wish now that I had set down a thousand of his
sayings; but all have vanished, save one strangely beautiful
story, which he told me he had read somewhere, but which I
have never been able to trace.

One day when the Sultan was in his palace at Damascus a
beautiful youth who was his favourite rushed into his presence, crying out in great agitation that he must fly at once to
Baghdad, and imploring leave to borrow his Majesty's swift-
est horse.

The Sultan asked why he was in such haste to go to Baghdad. "Because," the youth answered, "as I passed through the
garden of the Palace just now, Death was standing there, and
when he saw me he stretched out his arms as if to threaten
me, and I must lose no time in escaping from him."

The young man was given leave to take the Sultan's horse
and fly; and when he was gone the Sultan went down indignantly into the garden, and found Death still there. "How
dare you make threatening gestures at my favourite?" he
cried; but Death, astonished, answered: "I assure your Majesty I did not threaten him. I only threw up my arms in surprise at seeing him here, because I have a tryst with him
tonight in Baghdad."

Many of my other encounters at the Blanches' were full of
interest; and so were other adventures in the more specialized
world of letters, and of the University. Bourget one day
brought to see me (two years or more before we came to live
in Paris) a young friend of his, Charles Du Bos, who was
anxious to translate my recently published novel, "The House
of Mirth". Charles Du Bos, being Anglo-American on his
mother's side, was exceptionally proficient in English, and he
desired to follow a literary career without yet knowing pre-

cisely what turn it would take. Bourget, who was an old friend of his family, and naturally in sympathy with this ambition, suggested his getting his hand in by translating my book; and so it happened that "The House of Mirth" was given to French readers by the future literary critic, and biographer of Byron, who in the course of the work became one of my closest friends.

5

When we finally settled in the rue de Varenne "The House of Mirth," then appearing in the *Revue de Paris*, was attracting attention in its French dress, partly because few modern English and American novels had as yet been translated, but chiefly because it depicted a society utterly unknown to French readers. The success of the book was so great that translations of my short stories (I had as yet written but two novels) were in great demand in the principal French reviews, and to this I owe an interesting glimpse of the Parisian life of letters. Those were the days when the *Revue de Paris*, edited by that remarkable man, Louis Ganderax, rivalled (if it did not out-rival) the *Revue des Deux Mondes* in interest and importance, and I was lucky enough to be made welcome in the editorial groups of both reviews, and to be much invited out in those agreeable circles.

Oddly enough, it was an old American friend of my husband's who enlarged my range in this direction. Archibald Coolidge (future Librarian of Harvard) was giving the Hyde Lectures that winter at the Sorbonne, and as soon as he found we were in Paris he decided that I must be made known to his friends in the University. So indefatigable was this kindly being in bringing to the house the most agreeable among his colleagues, as well as other acquaintances, that my husband and I christened him "the retriever". It was thanks to him, I think, that I first met Monsieur André Chevrillon, the author of a number of delightful books on English literature, and two or three exceptionally sensitive records of travel in India and North Africa. All the Taine nephews and nieces inherited the great man's English culture, spoke the language fluently, and were thoroughly versed in English literature; and it was

Monsieur Chevrillon who first made not only Ruskin but Kipling known to French readers. It was in the cosmopolitan atmosphere of his house at Saint Cloud that I first met, among other interesting people, the Comte Robert d'Humières, whose translations of Kipling rank with Scott Moncrieff's of Proust. Robert d'Humières was one of the most versatile of that alert and cultivated group; an admirable linguist, quick, well-read and responsive to new ideas, he combined great social gifts with a real love of letters. He wrote a brilliant little volume on the English in India, and another, equally remarkable, on contemporary England. He and his charming wife went often to England, and on one of their visits I gave them a letter for James. He asked them down to Lamb House, and a letter to me (published in Percy Lubbock's edition of the Letters) records his delighted impression of the pair. Robert d'Humières and I became great friends. He came very often to the rue de Varenne, and in 1914 he began a translation of my recently published novel, "The Custom of the Country". I had had many offers to translate this book, but had always refused, as I thought it almost impossible to make a tale so intensely American intelligible to French readers. But Robert d'Humières was perfectly fitted for the task, and judging from the first chapters his translation would have been masterly. The war sent him at once to the front; but in 1916 a bad attack of rheumatism obliged him to return to Paris, and he sent me word to come and see him. I found him, though very ill and worn, hard at work again on "The Custom of the Country"; but as soon as he was discharged he asked to go back to the trenches, and almost immediately fell in leading an attack. His broken-hearted wife died soon afterward.

Another friend whom I got to know through the devoted "retriever" was Victor Bérard, the eminent director of the *Ecole des Hautes Etudes*, whose speculative and picturesque interpretation of the Odyssey (*Les Phéniciens et l'Odyssée*) had aroused great interest far beyond University circles. Victor Bérard was a big handsome man, with a brain bursting with intellectual enthusiasms and rash hypotheses. He had the indefatigable activity, the almost limitless powers of work, of the typical French scholar, and his wife told me that, winter and summer, he was always at his desk at five in the morning, and that his working and teaching day often did not end till midnight. In spite of this he and Madame Bérard dispensed a tireless hospitality, receiving in their big old-fashioned house, which overlooked the neighbouring gardens of the Observatoire, many of the most distinguished men of letters, historians and archæologists of the day—and eminent painters as well, for Bérard was the intimate friend of Lucien Simon, Cottet and René Ménard, who were also great friends of each other, and consequently often to be seen together at his house.

These gatherings at the Bérards', and also at the Ganderaxes', the René Doumics', and other houses in the old closely-shut Parisian world of science and letters, were naturally of great interest to a stranger like myself; but they lacked—as such societies have wherever I have known them—the ease and amenity to be found only where intelligent people of various callings, with a few cultivated idlers among them, predominate over the highly-trained specialist. The only completely agreeable society I have ever known is that wherein the elements are selected and blent by a woman of the world, instinctively alert for every shade of suitability, and whose light hand never suffers the mixture to stiffen or grow heavy. At that time in Paris the appearance of a "foreigner" in any society not slightly cosmopolitanized still caused a certain constraint, especially among its womenkind; and I gradually perceived that in University circles the presence of an American woman was almost paralyzing to the ladies of the party. As the men, immediately after the meal was over, always fled with coffee and cigarettes to the farthest corner of the room, leaving the women to themselves, I was subjected on such occasions to an hour's desolating conversation, which invariably began with the three questions: "Are you soon to give us the pleasure of reading another of your wonderful novels?", "Do you write in French, and then have your books translated into English?" and "Have you already seen all the new plays?"—after which the talk languished into silence, my burdensome presence preventing the natural interchange of remarks on children, servants and prices which would otherwise have gone on between the ladies.

In many different sets I continued to make friends, and I keep a special niche in my memory for some of these. Among the dearest was Gustave Schlumberger, the celebrated archæologist and historian of the Byzantine Empire, who looked like a descendant of one of the Gauls on the arch of Titus, and who was cherished by a large group of devoted friends for the inexhaustible interest of his talk as much as he was dreaded by others for his uncurbed violence of speech. To me he was invariably kind, partly no doubt because of my interest in the archæological wonders of his beloved country; and during the last years of his life I saw him frequently. Another dear friend, very different in character though they shared certain artistic interest, was Auguste Laugel, whose acquaintance I made through Etta Reubell, my old friend, and Henry James's. Monsieur Laugel, the devoted friend of the Orléans family, who was especially attached to the Duc d'Aumale, and to whose learning and taste the Duke was indebted for the creation of the famous library at Chantilly, was an old man when I first knew him, and lived a quiet meditative life among his books and his friends. But his early years had been full of distinguished and successful activities, as a graduate of *Polytechnique*, as civil engineer, and professor at the *Ecole des Mines*, as a linguist, a traveller, and a writer on scientific subjects. To these interests he added a keen love of art and letters, and that highly specialized knowledge of books and of their makers which made of him one of the most accomplished bibliophiles of his day.

During a long sojourn in America, at the time of our Civil War, he was in frequent and intimate contact with the leading Northern generals and statesmen, and the result of those experiences was summed up in a series of notable articles in the Parisian press. Subsequently he followed the fortunes of the Duc d'Aumale, twice accompanying him into exile, and returning to France only when the Prince was finally allowed to re-establish himself at Chantilly.

Of all these years of labour and adventure there remained, when I knew him, only the mellowing influences left by a life of fruitful activity. Monsieur Laugel had married an American lady who had been very beautiful. They were a devoted couple, and after her death he had privately printed a small volume of poems, not addressed to the young bride in her freshness, but to the old and dying wife, as she lay helpless and motionless, for months, like the statue on her own grave. He did me the honour of giving me this book, as well as other treasures from his private library, and in particular one of its most precious volumes. I happened one day to mention that another of my friends, also a learned bibliophile, knowing my admiration for Racine, had given me the rare first editions of "Athalie" and "Esther", but had never been able to add to them a copy of the far rarer, the almost unfindable, "Phèdre". The next day Monsieur Laugel sent me the missing treasure; and I never look at the slim exquisite volume without a grateful thought for my delightful old friend, the perfect model of the distinguished and cultivated French gentleman of his day.

XII

Widening Waters

THESE NEW FRIENDSHIPS, and many others, added much to my enjoyment of Paris; but the core of my life was under my own roof, among my books and my intimate friends. Above all it was in my work, which was growing and spreading, and absorbing more and more of my time and my imagination.

I had continued steadily at my story-telling, from which nothing could ever distract me for long, and during the busy happy Parisian years, and especially after the appearance of "The House of Mirth", a growing sense of mastery made the work more and more absorbing. In 1908 I published "The Hermit and the Wild Woman", a volume of short stories, in 1910 another, called "Tales of Men and Ghosts", and between the two the record of some of our early motor journeys in France.

But the book to the making of which I brought the greatest joy and the fullest ease was "Ethan Frome". For years I had wanted to draw life as it really was in the derelict mountain villages of New England, a life even in my time, and a thousandfold more a generation earlier, utterly unlike that seen through the rose-coloured spectacles of my predecessors, Mary Wilkins and Sarah Orne Jewett. In those days the snowbound villages of Western Massachusetts were still grim places, morally and physically: insanity, incest and slow mental and moral starvation were hidden away behind the paintless wooden house-fronts of the long village street, or in the isolated farm-houses on the neighbouring hills; and Emily Brontë would have found as savage tragedies in our remoter valleys as on her Yorkshire moors. In this connection, I may mention that every detail about the colony of drunken mountain outlaws described in "Summer" was given to me by the rector of the church at Lenox (near which we lived), and that the lonely peak I have called "the Mountain" was in reality

Bear Mountain, an isolated summit not more than twelve miles from our own home. The rector had been fetched there by one of the mountain outlaws to read the Burial Service over a woman of evil reputation; and when he arrived every one in the house of mourning was drunk, and the service was performed as I have related it. The rector's predecessor in the fashionable parish of Lenox had, I believe, once been called for on a similar errand, but had prudently refused to go; my friend, however, thought it his duty to do so, and drove off alone with the outlaw—coming back with his eyes full of horror and his heart of anguish and pity. Needless to say, when "Summer" appeared, this chapter was received with indignant denial by many reviewers and readers; and not the least vociferous were the New Englanders who had for years sought the reflection of local life in the rose-and-lavender pages of their favourite authoresses—and had forgotten to look into Hawthorne's.

"Ethan Frome" shocked my readers less than "Summer"; but it was frequently criticized as "painful", and at first had much less success than my previous books. I have a clearer recollection of its beginnings than of those of my other tales, through the singular accident that its first pages were written—in French! I had determined, when we came to live in Paris, to polish and enlarge my French vocabulary; for though I had spoken the language since the age of four I had never had much occasion to talk it, for any length of time, with cultivated people, having usually, since my marriage, wandered through France as a tourist. The result was that I had kept up the language chiefly through reading, and the favourite French authors of my early youth being Bossuet, Racine, Corneille and La Bruyère, most of my polite locutions dated from the seventeenth century, and Bourget used to laugh at me for speaking "the purest Louis Quatorze". To bring my idioms up to date I asked Charles Du Bos to find, among his friends, a young professor who would come and talk with me two or three times a week. An amiable young man was found; but, being too amiable ever to correct my spoken mistakes, he finally hit on the expedient of asking me to prepare an "exercise" before each visit. The easiest thing for me was to write a story; and thus the French version of "Ethan Frome" was begun, and carried on for a few weeks. Then the lessons were given up, and the copy-book containing my "exercise" vanished forever. But a few years later, during one of our summer sojourns at the Mount, a distant glimpse of Bear Mountain brought Ethan back to my memory, and the following winter in Paris I wrote the tale as it now stands, reading my morning's work aloud each evening to Walter Berry, who was as familiar as I was with the lives led in those half-deserted villages before the coming of motor and telephone. We talked the tale over page by page, so that its accuracy of "atmosphere" is doubly assured—and I mention this because not long since, in an article by an American literary critic, I saw "Ethan Frome" cited as an interesting example of a successful New England story written by some one who knew nothing of New England! "Ethan Frome" was written after I had spent ten years in the hill-region where the scene is laid, during which years I had come to know well the aspect, dialect, and mental and moral attitude of the hill-people. The fact that "Summer" deals with the same class and type as those portrayed in "Ethan Frome", and has the same setting, might have sufficed to disprove the legend—but once such a legend is started it echoes on as long as its subject survives.

2

Almost all my intimate friends from England and America used to come to stay with us in Paris; Walter Berry, whenever he could escape from his hard work as one of the Judges of the International Tribunal at Cairo; Henry James, Howard Sturgis, Percy Lubbock, Gaillard Lapsley, Robert Norton and John Hugh-Smith. I also continued to see a great deal of Egerton Winthrop, Robert Minturn, and many other old friends from America, who came annually to Paris; and usually, before going back to the Mount for the summer, or on my return from America in the autumn, I snatched a few weeks in England, dividing them between Lamb House, Queen's Acre, and Hill Hall, Mrs. Charles Hunter's place in Essex.

Mrs. Charles Hunter was so much a part of my annual English holiday, so much the centre of my picture of the English world, that when she died the other day, for me at least, almost the whole fabric went with her. Henry James, who was her devoted friend, had long wanted us to meet; but knowing of her only as a fashionable hostess and indefatigable entertainer, and not wishing to plunge again into the world of big house-parties and London "crushes", I had evaded all suggestions and invitations. And then suddenly—I forgot when or where—we met, and became friends.

Sargent's portrait (given by her to the Tate Gallery) renders Mary Hunter's fair abundant beauty in all its harvest brightness; and it was thus that I first knew her—still beautiful, wealthy, hospitable and boundlessly generous, with no clear idea about money except that, if one had it, it was to be spent for the pleasure of others. Later, when her fortune, which was entirely in coal, dwindled to nothing with the other great English mining-fortunes, she bore the loss with dauntless good humour, a spirit of "the Lord gave, and the Lord hath taken away", of which I know few finer examples; but her notion of money remained as hazy when every penny mattered as when wealth poured uncounted through her lavish hands. As one of her friends said: "Mary is a cornucopia"; and to the end of her life generosity, pity, eagerness to help and to make happy, kept spilling out of her in words and deeds when they could no longer be expressed in cheques.

A year or two before her death we were staying at the same house in the country, and having broken her motoring spectacles she asked me to take her to an optician's to buy another pair. She was already ruined, and living in such narrow circumstances that I thought it quite natural for her to consider the price. "How much do you suppose they'll cost, my dear? Not above two or three pounds?" she asked anxiously. I burst out laughing. "Bless you, no! Not above two or three shillings." I expected a sigh of relief; but she gave no sign of seeing any difference, and to the very end such shades of more-or-less remained too microscopic for her notice.

The golden waves of prosperity were rolling higher and higher about her when our acquaintance began. Her husband, who adored her, wished her to enjoy every luxury; but he had always refused to give her a town house, fearing, as he said, that life in London would lead to extravagance beyond even his resources. He bestowed on her, instead, Hill Hall, a William-and-Mary house of stately proportions, built about a great interior quadrangle, and dominating the blue distances of Essex; and for the London season she hired one of the ornate seventeenth century houses attached to the Burlington Hotel. This she furnished luxuriously, and lived in it exactly as if it were her own—save that the upkeep stopped when she was not in town.

At Hill no limits were set, but the house was not expensively furnished, though arranged with much taste, and containing a few good pictures. Life there was on a large scale, for there were many rooms, and in addition to the perpetual come-and-go of married daughters, grandchildren and other relations, there was a succession of friends for a good part of the year, and a big house-party for every week-end.

I used sometimes to wonder what Rosa de Fitz-James, with her careful sense of conformity, of selection, her French cult of the *ce-qui-se-fait*, would have thought of those happy-go-lucky week-ends, with friends tumbling in unexpectedly from everywhere, extra seats being hastily crowded into the long dining-room, fresh provisions hurried to the already groaning tea-table, spare-rooms prepared, messages telephoned, people passing in and out with a sort of smiling fatalism, no questions asked, no explanations expected, just a continuous surge of easy good-humoured life through the big house, the broad flagged terraces and the crowded tennis-courts. I was about to add "and the gardens" when I remembered that, oddly enough for an Englishwoman, Mary Hunter was congenitally incapable of interesting herself in horticulture, her only attempt in that line at Hill being a made-to-order rose-garden of which Percy Lubbock remarked that it looked "as if no one had ever said a kind word to it".

Mary Hunter's hospitality was more comprehensive than Madame de Fitz-James', not only because her nature was larger and more impetuous, but because all the meticulous French discriminations would have been meaningless to her, and to her world, where numbers had a secret magic, and even to the intelligent the sense of being in a crowd was more stimulating than that of being too carefully shielded from it. Mrs. Hunter's guests, however, were combined with unusual discrimination, for though she herself had—as far as I could see—no particular pleasure in good talk, she enjoyed it vicariously, as a good hostess, and, as a clever one, managed to get together the elements to create it. Even her most haphazard parties contained a nucleus of intimate friends with literary and artistic tastes, and this saved the week-ends of Hill from the dullness usual in such assemblages. Moreover, Mrs. Hunter's watchful solicitude made her combine her inner group with a view to the enjoyment of all its members, and when I went to Hill I usually found there some of my own friends, among whom Henry James, Percy Lubbock and Howard Sturgis were the most frequent.

In earlier days she had gathered about her many painters and musicians, and more than once, especially among the painters, her generous encouragement gave the first impetus to a successful career. Sargent's portrait of herself, and the famous one of her three daughters (now in the National Gallery), are known to every one; but she and her family were also repeatedly painted by Mancini, and by Mrs. Swinnerton; and she was the life-long friend of Sargent, Walter Sickert, Rodin (who made a fine bust of her), Professor Tonks, Mr. Steer, Claude Monet and Jacques-Emile Blanche. As is usual with hostesses of her kind, the thought of the illustrious unsociable would not let her sleep, and she was determined not only to admire and help her celebrities (and help them she did, in every possible way) but to enjoy their society on her own terms; that is, in the crowd and tumult of the Hill weekends. She had all the tenacity and inventiveness of the celebrity-collector, and there is a tale of her, already a legend when I heard it, but so characteristic that it may well be true. She was a great admirer of Mancini's art, and hearing that he was staying in London she immediately introduced herself by telephone, and besought him to come down to Hill for the following Sunday. But he was poor, solitary-minded, and unable to speak English; and to excuse himself he enumerated all these objections. Go to stay with Mrs. Hunter—but he couldn't possibly! Why, to begin with, he didn't even own a dress-coat.

"Is that all? Nonsense! My husband'll lend you one."

"Oh, but that's nothing. I don't speak English—not more

than two words. And I don't understand anything that is said to me."

"Well, that doesn't matter either. So-and-so and so-and-so, who are coming, both speak Italian perfectly."

"Ah, but you don't understand. I couldn't even buy my railway-ticket, or find my way from my hotel to the station."

"My dear Signor Mancini, don't worry about that. I have an Italian footman—a perfect genius of a footman. He'll be at your hotel with a cab tomorrow afternoon at four; he'll pack your things, take you to the train, bring you down, and wait on you while you're here."

There was a faint murmur of surrender from Mancini, and Mary Hunter instantly called up a London tailoring establishment and ordered a dress-suit (it is not recorded how she obtained the measures). She then telephoned to an employment agency for an Italian footman, and on being told that they had none on their list, and could not possibly engage to produce one at such short notice, replied calmly: "You *must* find me one at any price, and he must bring Signor Mancini down to Hill tomorrow afternoon." And he was found, and brought Mancini down—with the dress-clothes smuggled into the latter's suit-case.

When I first went to Hill those epic days were over. Most of the painter friends of my hostess's youth were already middle-aged and illustrious, and except in two or three cases the intimacy, though not the friendship, had probably declined; or else Mrs. Hunter may have divided her friends into separate groups, for I seldom met any painters or musicians at Hill, and the "nucleus" in my time was usually literary. James was, of course, its central figure, welcomed and delighted in by all the family, and enveloped by the most discerning affection. The rival luminary, who hated and envied James, and missed no chance to belittle and sneer at him, was George Moore. I shall never forget a luncheon at Hill when John Hugh-Smith with seeming artlessness drew Moore out on his great contemporaries, and James, Conrad, Hardy, and all others of any worth, were swept away on a torrent of venom. It was the tone of "The Dunciad" without its wit. But that was George Moore's way; and I recall another instance of it at the house of Jacques Blanche, one of his most devoted and long-suffering friends. My husband and I often went to the Blanches' literary and artistic luncheons, and one day George Moore was of the party. When we returned to the big studio after luncheon, and coffee and cigarettes were served, Moore ostentatiously drew out his cigar-case, lit a big cigar, and offered one to my husband. The latter, though he loved a good cigar, declined, and Moore said in a loud voice: "If you haven't brought any of your own you'd better take one of mine. They never give them here." "I know," replied my husband quietly; "that's why I never bring one."

Mary Hunter could not resist baiting her hospitable hook with a name like James's. She loved and admired him so much that she wanted his glory to shine over as many of her parties as possible, and forgetting that its light, if intense, was not far-spread, she sometimes mentioned him as an inducement to guests who had never even heard his name. I was at Hill on one such occasion, when, on the arrival of a fashionable beauty, her hostess welcomed her with: "And tomorrow, you know, you're going to see Henry James!"

The lady's perplexity was great, but so also was her frankness. Who in the world, she asked, was Henry James, and why should she particularly want to see him? Mrs. Hunter was dumbfounded: was it possible that dear Lady —— really didn't know? No; she really didn't. But she was good-naturedly ready to be enlightened, and having been told that Henry James was one of the greatest of living novelists, she suffered "The Wings of the Dove" and "The Golden Bowl" to be pressed into her submissive hands, and obediently agreed to read them both before the next afternoon!

When she came down the following day, just before luncheon, I was sitting in the hall. The four fat volumes were under her arm, and she thumped them down on the table, and turned her lovely smile on me. "Well—of all the *tosh*!" she said gaily.

Knowing that Henry James, though he suffered acutely from the criticisms of the literary, would enjoy this fresh breeze out of Philistia, I told him the tale as soon as he arrived. He welcomed it with a joyful chuckle; and when he and the lady met that evening they at once became the best of friends.

This anecdote leads me to two others which I may as well insert at this point into my English picture. Once when James and I were staying together in the country our host suggested taking us to call on a charming neighbour, formerly, I think, a celebrated music-hall artist. James, I believe, had met the lady at a theatrical supper some twenty years earlier, and he declared himself delighted to renew the acquaintance. The lady, who also remembered the far-off supper, welcomed him cordially; and in the course of the visit, drawing me aside, she expressed her pleasure at seeing dear Mr. James again after so many years, and added: "I've so often wondered what had happened to him since. Do tell me—*has he kept up his writing?*"

My other tale concerns Lamb House, but at a much later time, when, after James's death, it was tenanted for some years by Robert Norton, who had known James well, and treated the house and its contents with the same veneration as the guardian of "The Birthplace" treated that shrine in James's story. Robert Norton happened one day to run across a London great lady, an old acquaintance of his, who was staying near Rye. She told him she had been longing for years to visit Lamb House, of which she had heard so much, and begged him to let her come to see it. She came, and he took her all over, showing each room, each piece of furniture, each relic, and explaining: "Here James dictated to his secretary every morning; under this weeping ash he used to sit in hot weather; this silver-point was done of him by Sargent before he shaved his beard; this is a replica of his bust by ——" till finally the great lady, grateful but bewildered, interrupted him to ask: "I've heard so much of Lamb House, as a particularly charming specimen of a small Georgian house—but *would* you mind telling me who this Mr. Henry James is, who appears to have lived here?"

The keeper of the "Birthplace" remembered "The Death of the Lion", and answered her question with a smile.

3

Henry James's visits to the rue de Varenne were always a busy time for me. He had been much in Paris in his youth, had frequented the great generation of the Goncourt "garret", met Flaubert frequently, and been intimate with Turgeniev, and later with Alphonse Daudet, and of course with Bourget. His description of taking Daudet down to Box Hill to see Meredith, and of the two great writers, both stricken with the same fatal malady, advancing painfully toward each other across the platform of the little country station, was one of the most moving things I ever heard him relate. He also piloted Bourget about London and Oxford, on the latter's first visit to England, when he was preparing the English impressions afterward included in *Etudes et Portraits*; and all these contacts had made James's name familiar among French intellectuals long before they struggled to decipher his books.

James's unusual social gifts, and keen enjoyment of society (once he had escaped from its tyrannous routine), lent a school-boy's zest to his Paris visits. The first time he stayed with us there must have been in 1905, before the rue de Varenne days, when my brother Harry, who had a flat in Paris, lent it to us during a temporary absence. It was in that year, I think, that James, through my intervention, sat to Blanche for the admirable portrait which distressed the sitter because of the "Daniel Lambert" curve of the rather florid waist-coat; and during those sittings, and on other occasions at the Blanches', he made many new acquaintances, and renewed some old friendships.

James's simple cordiality would have made him welcome anywhere; but he was particularly popular among his French friends, not only on account of his quickness and adaptability, but because his youthful frequentations in the French world of letters, following on the school-years in Geneva, had so steeped him in continental culture that the cautious and inhospitable French intelligence felt at once at ease with him. This feeling was increased by his mastery of the language. French people have told me that they had never met an Anglo-Saxon who spoke French like James; not only correctly and fluently, but—well, just as they did themselves; avoiding alike platitudes and pomposity, and using the language as spontaneously as if it were his own.

It was no wonder therefore that James enjoyed his French

holidays. He was invited out continually, and the only difficulty was to capture him now and then for an evening in the rue de Varenne. The contrast to the severe winter routine of Rye, the change of scene, of food, of point of view—the very differences in the houses and streets, in the mental attitude and the moral conventions—of all these nothing escaped him, nothing failed to amuse him. In the intervals between dining out he liked a dash in the motor; and among other jolly expeditions, I remember a visit to Nohant, when he saw for the first time George Sand's house. I had been there before, and knew how to ingratiate myself with the tall impressive guardian of the shrine, a handsome *Berrichonne* who could remember, as a very little girl, helping "Madame" to dress Maurice's marionettes, which still dangled wistfully from their hooks in the little theatre below stairs.

James, who shared my delight in the enchanting *Histoire de ma Vie* and the *Lettres d'un Voyageur*, had known personally a number of the illustrious pilgrims—Flaubert, Maupassant, Alexandre Dumas fils and others—who used to come to Nohant in the serene old age of its tumultuous châtelaine. He was therefore fascinated by every detail of the scene, deeply moved by the inscriptions on the family grave-stones under the wall of the tiny ancient church—especially in the tragic Solange's: *La Mère de Jeanne*—and absorbed in the study of the family portraits, from the Elector of Saxony and the Mlles Verrier to Maurice and his children. He lingered delightedly over the puppet theatre with Maurice's grimacing dolls, and the gay costumes stitched by his mother; then we wandered out into the garden, and looking up at the plain old house, tried to guess behind which windows the various famous visitors had slept. James stood there a long time, gazing and brooding beneath the row of closed shutters. "And in which of those rooms, I wonder, did George herself sleep?" I heard him suddenly mutter. "Though in which, indeed—" with a twinkle—"in which indeed, my dear, did she *not*?"

A vision especially dear to me is associated with one of James's visits to the rue de Varenne. It is that of the exquisite picture of Paris by night in the tale—perhaps the most beautiful of his later short stories—called "The Velvet Glove". He and I had often talked over the subject of this story, which was suggested by the fact that a very beautiful young English-woman of great position, and unappeased literary ambitions, had once tried to beguile him into contributing an introduction to a novel she was writing—or else into reviewing the book; I forget which. She had sought from him, at any rate, a literary "boost" which all his admiration and liking for her could not, he thought, justify his giving; and they parted, though still friends, with evidences on her part of visible disappointment—and surprise. The incident certainly gave him a theme "to his hand"; but it lay unused for lack of a setting, for he wanted to make of it, not a mere ironic anecdote—that was too easy—but a little episode steeped in wistfulness and poetry. And then, one soft spring evening, after we had dined somewhere out of town—possibly at Versailles, or at a restaurant in the Bois—knowing his love for motoring at night, I proposed a circuit in the environs, which finally brought us home by way of Saint Cloud; and as we hung there, high above the moonlit lamplit city and the gleaming curves of the Seine, he suddenly "held" his setting, as the painters say, and, though I knew nothing of it till long afterward, "The Velvet Glove" took shape that night.

The theatre was of course one of James's great interests when he was in Paris; but he was so much invited out, and so much amused by his glimpses of a new and stimulating social scene, that he could seldom spare an evening. When he did, it was usually for the first night of some well-known dramatist, such as Paul Hervieu, or in later years Henry Bataille or Henry Bernstein. James's interest in the theatre was sustained by the conviction (which it took so many bitter disappointments to eradicate) that he would one day achieve popular success as a playwright. It is an illusion often nursed by novelists, especially those who, like James, are gradually dominated by the sense of "situation", the strictly scenic element, in their subjects. It is difficult to understand that there is little connection between the novelist's sense of a situation and that of the playwright, and James was persuaded to the end that his constructive instinct ought to have served in play-building as well as in story-telling. Perhaps it might have, if he had not been so oddly enslaved by what might be called the Dumas-fils convention (a tradition from which the French have now so wholly emancipated themselves). The typical Dumas-fils play was a miracle of neat joinery, culminating in a "moral" of which all his characters were merely the subservient tools. It seems odd that James, whose conception of the novel was so independent and original, regarded these stage conventions as inevitable. He admired Ibsen, but seems never to have felt any incongruity between the two conceptions of the theatre, much less to have contemplated the possibility of creating a formula of his own for his plays, as he had for his novels.

James's interest in the stage naturally included the world of the theatre, with its rivalries and scandals, its generosities and absurdities, and all its *grandeurs et misères*. He was always particularly amused by anecdotes about theatrical people, and I remember a report of one conversation with a retired actress which delighted his listeners. The lady in question, in far-off days, had had a brief career on the London stage in classical tragedy, but long before James's coming to England she had married a man who had given her a place in the most conservative circles of early Victorian London. Always irreproachable in conduct and reputation, she yet yearned now and then for an opportunity to speak of her theatrical years, and especially to dwell on the perils to which the virtuous actress is exposed. On one occasion she had been detailing these at some length to James, and after complacently enumerating the various forms of temptation she had successfully resisted, she added: "And would you believe it, Mr. James? *One fiend in human shape actually offered me cameos.*"

There were many amusing incidents connected with Henry James's visits to Paris. I was the object of much attention on the part of hostesses who wished to use him as a social "draw", and of literary ladies who aspired to translate his novels; and among the advances made by the latter I remember two over which, when they were reported to him, his chuckles were particularly prolonged. In one case a fervent translatress besought me to recommend her to the Master as particularly qualified to translate "The Golden Bowl" because she had just dealt successfully with a work called "The Filigree Box"; while another tried to ingratiate herself by assuring me that her deep appreciation of my own great work,

"The House of the Myrtles", was surpassed only by her un-bounded admiration for that supreme anatomical masterpiece, "The Golden Bowel".

Ah, how we used to come back from those parties bearing our sheaves of laughter—and how the laughter still rings in my ears as I call up the scenes that provoked it!

4

"Well, I *am* glad to welcome to the White House some one to whom I can quote 'The Hunting of the Snark' without being asked what I mean!"

Such was my first greeting from Theodore Roosevelt after his accession to the Presidency—a date so much earlier than that of my sojourn in Paris that I ought to have introduced it before, had it not seemed simpler to gather into one chapter the record of our too infrequent meetings. Though I had known Theodore Roosevelt since my first youth, and though his second wife is my distant cousin, I had met him only at long intervals—usually at my sister-in-law's, in New York—and we had never "hooked" (in the French sense of the *atômes crochus*) until after the publication of "The Valley of Decision". He had a great liking for the book, which he wanted, after his usual fashion, to rearrange in conformity with his theory of domestic morals and the strenuous life; but when I pointed out that these ideals did not happen to prevail in the decadent Italian principalities which Napoleon was so soon to wipe out or to remodel, he laughingly acknowledged the fact, and thereafter we became great friends. My intimacy with Bay Lodge, and with the Jusserands, with whom my friendship dated back to my childhood, created other links between the Roosevelts and myself, and the first time I went to Washington after they were installed in the White House I was promptly summoned to lunch, and welcomed on the threshold by the President's vehement cry: "At last I can quote 'The Hunting of the Snark'!

"Would you believe it," he added, "no one in the Administration has ever heard of Alice, much less of the Snark, and the other day, when I said to the Secretary of the Navy: 'Mr. Secretary, *What I say three times is true*', he did not recognize the allusion, and answered with an aggrieved air: 'Mr. President, it would never for a moment have occurred to me to impugn your veracity'!"

These whirlwind welcomes were very characteristic, for Theodore Roosevelt had in his mind so clear a vision of each interlocutor's range of subjects, and his own was so extensive and so varied, that when he met any one who interested him he could never bear to waste a moment in preliminaries.

I remember another instance of this impatient desire to get to his point, however remote from the topics of the moment. Many years ago, that charming old institution, Williams College, conferred an honorary degree on Roosevelt, and the college authorities invited me to the Commencement ceremonies. I motored from the Mount to Williamstown, and when I appeared at the reception, which took place after the conferring of the degrees, the President, who probably did not expect to meet me there, uttered an exclamation of surprise, and cried out: "But you're the very person I wanted to see! Of course you've read that wonderful new book of de la Gorce's, the 'History of the Second Empire'? What an amazing thing! Let's go off into a corner at once and have a good talk about it."

And go off into a corner we did, and talked about it at some length, to the visible interruption of the academic formalities; but that was the President's way, and as everybody loved him, everybody forgave him; and moreover they all knew that in another ten minutes he would be cornering somebody else on some other equally absorbing subject. What he could not and would not endure was talking about things which did not interest him when there were so many that *did*—so far too many for the brief time he had to spare for them. One feels, in looking back, something premonitory in this impatience, this thirst to slake an intellectual curiosity almost as fervent as his moral ardours.

With his faculty of instantly extracting the best that each person had to give, he seldom failed, when we met, to turn the talk to books. So much of his time was spent among the bookless that many people never suspected either the range of his literary culture or his learned interest in the natural sciences; and in Washington they were probably fully known only to the small group of people to whom he turned for intellectual stimulus—such as the Cabot Lodges, Henry Adams, Walter Berry, the Jusserands and Spring-Rice.

But there was another tie between us. Theodore Roosevelt was one of the most humorous *raconteurs* I ever knew, and a very good mimic; and when we were among a little band of fun-lovers—say with Bay Lodge, the President's sister, Mrs. Douglas Robinson, and a few other collectors of good nonsense—he kept us rocking with his cow-boy tales and his evocations of White House visitors. His liberty of speech, even in mixed company, was startling. Once, at a moment of acute tension between the President and the Senate, I was lunching at the White House with a big and haphazard party, among whom were several guests who had never before met the President, and at least one journalist; and suddenly I heard him break out to the assembled table: "Well, yes, I'm tired; I'm terribly tired. I don't know exactly what's the matter with me; but if only we could revive the good old Roman customs, I know a bath in Senator ——'s blood would set me right in no time."

He was noted for speaking recklessly before people incapable of appreciating either his humour or his irony, and to whom it must often have been a temptation to quote his personal comments; yet it was always said that during his two terms of office no public advantage was ever taken of these indiscretions, and in a country like ours there could be no greater proof of the degree to which he was loved and respected.

One of our last meetings was in the rue de Varenne, in the course of the astonishing world-tour of 1909–10, when, after completing his second term of office as the most famous man in America, he discovered that his celebrity also embraced the other side of the globe. On this tour, during which, in spite of his repeated protests that he was only a private citizen, he was received with sovereign honours by every European government, he came to Paris to give a lecture at the Sorbonne. Through his old friend Jusserand, then Ambassador in Washington, who had arranged to meet him in Paris, I was notified that he would like to come to the rue de Varenne. He sent me word to invite a few people to meet him—not governmental or *"universitaire"*, since he was sure to see them elsewhere, but my own group of friends; and every one I summoned answered to the call, for the desire to meet him was intense. I tried to choose, in the literary and academic line, principally those who spoke English; but unhappily they were few; and though Roosevelt knew French well, he spoke it badly, and with a rather bewildering pronunciation. The consequence was that, having found among my guests an Academician (I forget who) who was a specialist on some subject which particularly interested him, and could talk to him about it in English, he broke up the royal "circle" (of which he was of course expected to go the round), and by isolating himself too long with this particular interlocutor caused much disappointment to some of my other guests.

Such an omission was not easily understood or forgiven; but it was difficult to stem the current of the President's eloquence, and the President he still was, to all intents and purposes. I was made to feel afterward that Jusserand and I had failed in our duty in not organizing the party in such a way that each guest should have a few minutes' talk with the great man; for it was inconceivable to my amiable but highly disciplined guests that either the President or his hostess should unintentionally omit a single move of the traditional game they had been invited to play with him.

I was only once at Sagamore—and I think it was there that I saw Theodore Roosevelt for the last time. There could not have been a fitter setting for what turned out to be our goodbye; for it was only at Sagamore that the least known side of his character was revealed, and *ranchero* and statesman both made way for the private man, absorbed in books and nature, and in the quiet interests of a country life.

What a good day that was! My husband and I went down to lunch, and found no one but the family (a term which, as in my own house, always included two or three busy and extremely interested dogs). The house was like one big library, and the whole tranquil place breathed of the love of books and of the country, so that I felt immediately at home there. After luncheon Mr. Roosevelt, with a good deal of simple amusement, showed us the photographs taken of himself and the Emperor William during the famous German manœuvres.

He was perfectly aware of the studied impertinence of the Kaiser's famous inscription on one of the photographs—it read, I think: "President Roosevelt shows the Emperor of Germany how to command an attack", or something of the kind—but he treated it as an imperial appeal to his sense of humour, which indeed it probably was.

In looking back over my memories of Theodore Roosevelt I am surprised to find how very seldom I saw him, and yet how sure I am that he was my friend. He had the rare gift of bridging over in an instant those long intervals between meetings that so often benumb even the best of friends, and he was so alive at all points, and so gifted with the rare faculty of living intensely and entirely in every moment as it passed, that each of those encounters glows in me like a tiny morsel of radium.

5

During our first years in Paris the friend of my childhood, Henry White, was our Ambassador there. He had married our beautiful neighbour at Newport, Margaret Rutherfurd, whose two equally beautiful young brothers, Lewis and Winthrop, had been (with the exception of Madame Jusserand and Daisy Terry) my earliest playmates. The intimacy between the two families had never relaxed, and during the years when Henry White was first Secretary at our London Embassy he and his wife were the means of my meeting many interesting people whenever I went to England. The Whites, in their youth, and even in their middle age, were one of the handsomest couples I have ever seen, and on the Rutherfurd side the beauty of the whole family was proverbial. The story was told of an Englishman and an American who were strolling down Piccadilly together, and discussing the relative degree of good looks of their respective compatriots. "I grant you," the Englishman said, "that your women are lovely; perhaps not as regularly beautiful as ours, but often prettier and more graceful. But your men—yes, of course, I've seen very good-looking American men; but nothing—if you'll excuse my saying so—to compare with our young Englishmen of the Public School and University type, our splendid young athletes: there, like these two who are just coming toward us—" and the two in question were Margaret White's brothers, the young Rutherfurds.

Another story, also turning on young masculine beauty, was told to me by one of two other proverbially handsome brothers, Grafton and Howard Cushing of Boston. Once, when these two ambrosial youths were staying in London, the eldest, Grafton, was asked by Queen Victoria's niece, the Countess Feo Gleichen, who was a sculptor of talent, to sit to her for a bust. The sittings took place in Countess Gleichen's apartment in Saint James's Palace; and Howard, who lived in lodgings with his brother, told me how one morning very early he was awakened by a hammering at the door, and heard the excited voice of the lodging-house buttons crying out: "If you please, sir, her Majesty has sent word to say that she expects you at Buckingham Palace this morning at nine o'clock sharp, and you're to wear the same shirt that you wore yesterday."

In Paris our Embassy, as long as the Whites were there, was a second home to me, and Harry, who was never happier than in contriving happiness for others, was always arranging for me to meet interesting people. I remember, in particular, lunching at the Embassy one day with Orville Wright, the survivor of the two famous brothers, who had come to Paris, I think, for the inauguration of the statue at Le Mans commemorative of their first flight on French soil. Walter Berry, who was also at the lunch, had for many years been the counsel of the French Embassy in Washington. He was the intimate friend of Jusserand, and when, in 1905, or thereabouts, the French Government sent a military mission to America to investigate the queer new "flying machine" which two unknown craftsmen of Dayton, Ohio, had invented, Walter Berry was requested by the Ambassador to accompany the mission to Dayton as legal adviser. He stayed there for three weeks, saw the machine "levitate" a few inches above the earth, and came back awed by the possibility of the "strange futures beautiful and new" folded up within those clumsy wings, and much impressed by the two shy taciturn men who had called the monster into being. I remember his telling me that when he discussed with Wilbur Wright the future of aviation, the latter said: "I can conceive that aeroplanes might possibly be of some use in war, but never for any commercial purpose, or as a regular means of communication."

It must have been about the same time that I was invited by the Marquis de Polignac to see an exhibition of flying in the aerodrome he had constructed at Reims. I went there with Walter Berry, and in the presence of a large assemblage of scientific notabilities we saw several glorious "aces" (whose names, alas, I have forgotten) execute, at a height of a few yards above the ground, non-stop flights around the aerodrome, which, as I remember it, must have had about the dimensions of an ordinary polo-field. And that was only two or three years before the war!

6

Fate seemed to have conspired to fill those last years of peace with every charm and pleasure. "Eyes, look your last"—in and about Paris all things seemed to utter the same cry: the smiling suburbs unmarred by hideous advertisements, the unravaged cornfields of Millet and Monet, still spreading in sunny opulence to the city's edge, the Champs-Elysées in their last expiring elegance, and the great buildings, statues and fountains withdrawn at dusk into silence and secrecy, instead of being torn from their mystery by the vulgar intrusion of flood-lighting.

One of the loveliest flowers on the bough so soon to be broken was the dancing of Isadora Duncan. Hardly any one in Paris had heard of her when she first appeared there, but in me her name woke an old memory. Years before, a philanthropic Boston lady who spent her summers at Newport had invited her friends to a garden party at which Isadora Duncan was to dance. "Isadora Duncan?" People repeated the unknown name, wondering why it had been used to bait Miss Mason's invitation. Only two kinds of dancing were familiar to that generation: waltzing in the ball-room and pirouetting on the stage. I hated pirouetting, and did not go to Miss Mason's. Those who did smiled, and said they supposed their hostess had asked the young woman to dance out of charity—as I daresay she did. Nobody had ever seen anything like it; you couldn't call it dancing, they said. No other Newport hostess engaged Miss Duncan, and her name vanished from everybody's mind. And then, nearly twenty years later, I went one night to the Opera in Paris, to see a strange new dancer about whom the artists were beginning to talk . . .

I suppose that liking or not liking the conventional form of ballet-dancing is as little to be accounted for as one's feeling about olives or caviar. To me the word "dancing" had always suggested a joyful *abandon*, a plastic improvisation, the visual equivalent of

> Like to a moving vintage down they came,
> Crowned with green leaves, and faces all on flame . . .

in Keats's glorious bacchanal. The traditional ballet-dancing, the swollen feet in ugly shoes performing impossible *tours de force* of poising and bounding, reminded me, on the contrary, of "But, oh, what labour—Prince, what pain!", and except in Carpeaux's intoxicating group, and Titian's "Triumph of Bacchus", I had never seen dancing as I inwardly imagined it. And then, when the curtain was drawn back from the great stage of the Opera, and before a background of grayish-green hangings a single figure appeared—a tall, rather awkwardly made woman, dragging a scarf after her—then suddenly I beheld the dance I had always dreamed of, a flowing of movement into movement, an endless interweaving of motion and music, satisfying every sense as a flower does, or a phrase of Mozart's.

That first sight of Isadora's dancing was a white milestone to me. It shed a light on every kind of beauty, and showed me for the first time how each flows into the other as the music merged with her dancing. All through the immense rapt audience one felt the rush of her inspiration, as one feels the blowing open of the door in the "Walkyrie," when Sieglinde cries out: *"Wer ging?"* and Sigmund answers: *"Einer kam. Es war der Lenz!"*

Yes; it was the spring, the bursting into bloom of acres and acres of silver fruit-blossom where a week before there had been only dead boughs. And I believe it was that fertilizing magic which evoked our next and last vision of beauty before the war: the Russian Ballet. Every one who saw the Imperial ballet in St Petersburg, in its official setting, has assured me that when Diaghilew brought his dancers to Paris he infused new life into them, broke down old barriers of convention, and taught their exquisitely disciplined steps to flow into wild free measures. It is hard to believe that Isadora's inspiration had no part in the change.

It seemed as if those years contained some generative fire which called forth masterpieces; for close on Isadora, and on Diaghilew's dancers, came Proust's first volume. Proust—a name almost as unfamiliar as Isadora's, and destined, like hers, to fly through our imaginations on a shower of spring blossoms: the hawthorn hedge of *Du Côté de chez Swann*. At the moment it merely recalled to me some clever skits on contemporary writers which I had glanced at from time to time in the *Figaro*. I forget who first spoke to me about the book, but it may have been Blanche, who was one of Proust's earliest friends and admirers. I began to read languidly, felt myself, after two pages, in the hands of a master, and was presently trembling with the excitement which only genius can communicate.

I sent the book immediately to James, and his letter to me shows how deeply it impressed him. James, at that time, was already an old man and, as I have said, his literary judgments had long been hampered by his increasing preoccupation with the structure of the novel, and his unwillingness to concede that the vital centre (when there was any) could lie elsewhere. Even when I first knew him he read contemporary novels (except Wells's and a few of Conrad's) rarely, and with ill-concealed impatience; and as time passed, and intricate problems of form and structure engrossed him more deeply, it became almost impossible to persuade him that there might be merit in the work of writers apparently insensible to these sterner demands of the art. I remember, for instance, that when he published his "Notes on Novelists", one of our friends, who had been greatly struck by Lawrence's "Sons and Lovers", reproached James for having dealt so summarily with a new novelist who was beginning to attract the attention of intelligent readers. James's reply was evasive and unsatisfactory, and at last his interlocutor exclaimed: "Come, now! Have you ever read any of Lawrence's novels—really read them?" James's most mischievous smile crept down from his eyes to his lips. "I—I have trifled with the exordia," he murmured with a wicked twinkle.

No one but a novelist knows how hard it is for one of the craft to read other people's novels; but in the presence of a masterpiece all of James's prejudices and reluctances vanished. He seized upon *Du Côté de chez Swann* and devoured it in a passion of curiosity and admiration. Here, in the first volume of a long chronicle-novel—the very type of the unrolling tapestry which was so contrary to his own conception of form— he instantly recognized a new mastery, a new vision, and a structural design as yet unintelligible to him, but as surely there as hard bone under soft flesh in a living organism. I wonder if in any other art the joy of such recognition is as great as it is to the born novelist who loves his craft, and sees its subtle and Protean form so often stretched out of shape by insensitive hands. I look back with peculiar pleasure at having made Proust known to James, for the encounter gave him his last, and one of his strongest, artistic emotions.

Neither James nor I ever met Proust. In my case the meeting could have been easily arranged, for he was the friend of some of my most intimate friends. But what I heard about him, even from the people who were fondest of him, did not increase my desire to meet him. I did not then know how ill he already was—at that time even his intimates scarcely guessed it—and to be told that the only people who really interested him were Dukes and Duchesses, and that the only place where one could hope to find him was at the Ritz, after midnight, was enough to put me off. When I first read *Du Côté de chez Swann* I was on the point of pouring out my admiration in a letter; but supposing that many readers must have yielded to the same impulse, I remained silent. When I read Proust's correspondence, and discovered that "Swann" (on the whole the most perfect of the series) had fallen flat even among his intimates, and that a word of praise, though from a casual stranger, would have been priceless to him, I bitterly regretted my discretion. But by the time I had found out who he was, and through whom I could have made his acquaintance, his books were already the fashion in the very circles least capable of reading or understanding him—and on the whole I am glad I did not try to pursue him there. His greatness lay in his art, his incredible littleness in the quality of his social admirations. But in this, after all, he merely exemplified the tendency not infrequent in novelists of manners—Balzac and Thackeray among them—to be dazzled by contact with the very society they satirize. If it is true that *pour comprendre il faut aimer* this seeming inconsistency may, in some, be a deep necessity of the creative imagination.

7

We still went home every summer to the Mount, and all our old friends returned year after year to stay with us: chief among them, as usual, Egerton Winthrop, Walter Berry, Robert Minturn, the Jusserands from Washington, Robert Grant and his wife from Boston, Bay Lodge and his beautiful Bessy, and another old Boston friend, William Richardson. But much as I loved the place, the glowing summer weeks, and the woodland pageantry of our matchless New England autumn, it was all darkened by my husband's growing ill-health. Since the first years of our marriage his condition, in spite of intervals of apparent health, had become steadily graver. His sweetness of temper and boyish enjoyment of life struggled long against the creeping darkness of neurasthenia, but all the neurologists we consulted were of the opinion that there could be no real recovery; and time confirmed their verdict. Such borderland cases are notoriously difficult, and for a long time my husband's family would not see, or at any rate acknowledge, the gravity of his state, and any kind of consecutive treatment was therefore impossible. But at length they understood that he could no longer lead a life of normal activity, and in bringing them to recognize this I had the help of some of his oldest friends, whose affectionate sympathy never failed me in those difficult years.

The care of the Mount had been my husband's chief interest and occupation, and the place had now to be sold, for much as I loved it the burden would have been too heavy for me to carry alone. It was sad to leave that lovely country, and for the moment I did not feel like making another country home for myself; so I lingered on in the rue de Varenne during the last two or three years before the war, going away only for a few weeks now and then, to visit friends or to travel.

Among the friends made at this time I must put first the Berensons. I had known them slightly for some years, but our real friendship dated from my first visit to their villa near Florence, in 1910, or thereabouts; and since then a pilgrimage to I Tatti has been one of my annual joys. I had never before stayed in a house where I could lead exactly the same life as in my own; working in the morning, and browsing at all hours in a library which, though incalculably bigger and more important than mine, was based on the same requirements; a broad and firm foundation of books of reference constantly replenished and kept up to date; all the still *living* classics, in Greek, Latin and the principal modern languages, and an annual influx of the best in current letters. Henry James and Howard Sturgis had nothing nearer to a library than a few dozen shelves of heterogeneous volumes; and indeed, even in houses commonly held to be "booky" one finds, nine times out of ten, not a library but a book-dump. But such a library as that of I Tatti is the book-worm's heaven: the fulfilment of all he has dreamed that a great working library ought to be, continually weeded out and renewed, "not made of spent deeds but of doing", not a dusty mausoleum of dead authors but a glorious assemblage of eternally living ones.

This "great good place", which at first consisted in one noble room, lined with books to the high vaulted ceiling, and used not only as a library but as a living-room, was added to the original house by my dear friend Geoffrey Scott, and Cecil Pinsent, his partner; and they presently built out from it a wing containing two long conventual book-rooms with tall doors leading out to a terrace of clipped box.

When I first knew Geoffrey Scott he was still practising as an architect, and not long afterward he brought out that perfect book—or shall I say, that perfect introduction to a book?—"The Architecture of Humanism". My interest in the Italian architecture of the Renaissance, and the styles deriving from it, created one of the first links between us, and led to many delightful pilgrimages. Geoffrey Scott was at that time established in Florence with his partner, and whenever I

went to stay with the Berensons we used to go off on architectural excursions and garden hunts, to Siena, Montepul-
ciano, and all through Tuscany and Umbria. But one of our
most amusing journeys took us to the Emilia, when I introduced Geoffrey to the little fairy-tale town of Sabbioneta,
then so far from the beaten track that it had remained undisturbed in its decaying beauty. There are people who,
wherever they go, attract droll adventures, little lurking
picturesquenesses of incident. Geoffrey was one of them, and
all our excursions were spangled with laughter. At Sabbioneta, when we arrived, the village boys were having a bicycle
race about the green facing the little garden-palace of the
Dukes of Sabbioneta (a junior branch of the Mantuan
Gonzagas). The instant we appeared racers and spectators
abandoned the track for the more novel sport of hunting us
through the deserted grassy streets, yelling out comments on
our nationality, speech and appearance, crowding in upon us
in the crumbling palaces and hushed church, and rudely
breaking the spell of the sleepy place.

Finally I could stand it no longer, and having run down in
his den the local *carabiniere*, I besought him to come to our
protection. Such was my respect for those beautifully uni-
formed and highly varnished guardians of the peace that I
doubted not but one word from him would scatter our enemies; but he was alone, and could not leave his post. He assured me, however, that he would send his comrade to our
relief as soon as the latter returned.

So on we surged, the mob triumphant at our discomfiture,
and finally, in despair, ended up at the little garden-palace.
There, just as our persecutors were crowding in with us, the
promised *carabiniere* did appear. He wore spectacles, he carried a book in his hand—but still, he represented the law in a
land accustomed (as I thought) to respect it. "*Now* you'll see!"
I triumphed to Geoffrey.

The *carabiniere* saluted us and turned to face the pack. He
looked at them over his spectacles, he opened his mouth, and
spoke. "*Bisogna*," he said, "*adoperare un po' più di prudenza.*"
("You must really try to conduct yourselves with more
circumspection".) Whereupon he stretched one arm across the
threshold, pulled us in with the other, and hastily locked out

the yelping band. In the palace he followed us about, listened attentively to the explanations of the custodian, and studied his little volume—which was apparently a local guide-book!

During those last pre-war years I travelled more, and in more different directions than ever before. Breaking with the seductive habit of going always and only to Italy, I made, one spring, a motor-trip to Spain with Madame de Fitz-James and a dear friend of hers and mine, Jean du Breuil de Saint Germain. Before the war motoring in Spain was still something of an adventure; the roads were notoriously bad, motor-maps were few and unreliable, the village inns dubious. However, we set forth, and having carefully worked out our itinerary I was delighted to find that we were following, stage by stage, Théophile Gautier's route of sixty or seventy years earlier, and that so little was changed in the character of the towns and villages through which we passed that his charming "Voyage en Espagne" was still a perfect guide-book. We went by way of Pamplona, Burgos, Avila and Salamanca to Madrid; but there we were held up by the impossibility of going farther south on wheels. Even the few miles from Madrid to Toledo were impassable, and we were warned that we must make the trip by train!

Spain was enriched for me by a rush of juvenile memories which made me exclaim at each step: "But I've been here before! I've seen this already!" Whenever I go back there everything I see is suffused in this faint glow of old associations, as if my receptive faculties were afloat in a rich thick medium like the *fond de cuisson* without which no good French cook will practise his art. A child of four stores up by anticipation so much of what the mature self is later to enjoy that the adventures of a little girl may incalculably enrich the inner life of an old woman.

I was eager to return to Spain in more adventurous company, and go to more out-of-the-way places; and I made two more Spanish journeys before 1914. Each year the roads were improving, and it was becoming easier to get information about their condition; and being with a companion who was not afraid of the unknown, and wanted to see what I did, I managed to enlarge my map very considerably. These travels took in, on the east coast, the Seo d'Urgel, Ripoll, Gerona

and Barcelona; and we even motored to Montserrat, though
at that time the road thither from Barcelona was so hard to
find, and so nearly impracticable, that the ascent took the best
part of a day, and we had to spend the night at the monastery. Foreign visitors, other than pilgrims, were still infrequent, and the brother who received us explained that there
were two hostelries for pilgrims, and asked us to choose between the one with a communal kitchen, where we could
cook our own food, and the other, and more expensive one,
to which a restaurant was attached. Feeling rather vulgar and
purse-proud, we chose the latter, and having asked for four
rooms were shown into an icy vaulted chamber with a stone
floor, and four niches in the walls, each containing a bed. Our
Spanish was not adequate to dealing with this difficulty, but
supplementing it by pantomime we finally induced the
brother to give us two four-niched rooms instead of one! I
have never since cared to return to Montserrat, which may
now be reached from Barcelona in an hour, by a perfect road
lined with cafés and places of amusement, and leading to the
luxurious hotels on the summit.

Thence we went to Jaca and Huesca, returned to Burgos
and Avila, and managed, on the way back, to get from the
Alcalde of Santillana the keys of the prehistoric cave of Altamira, then still abandoned to the care of a local peasant, who
guided us through it with one smoky candle, which he held
up recklessly to show the brilliant and delicate paintings. I
think it was only after the war that the Duke of Alba succeeded in convincing King Alfonso of the necessity of giving
proper protection to this incomparable treasure, and lighting
it with electricity.

In the summer of 1912 or 1913 I went to Germany with Bernard Berenson. We motored to Berlin by the lovely route of
the Rhine and the Thuringian forest, and for the first time I
saw Weimar, so small and smiling in its leafy quiet, and
Wetzlar, with Lotte's quaint wedge-shaped house, unchanged
without and within since she lived there. In Berlin we spent
eight crowded days, during which I trotted about the great
Museums after my learned companion (who has always accused me of not properly appreciating the privilege), and was
rewarded by a holiday in Dresden, and a day's dash to the

picturesque heights of Saxon Switzerland. But the evenings in
Berlin also brought their reward, for we not only heard "The
Ring" admirably given at the Opera but saw a memorable
performance of Tolstoy's "Living Corpse", and an enchanting
one of the first part of Faust at the *Kleines Theater*, with
charming scenery by Reinhardt, a Gretchen of eighteen,
a Faust to match, and a Mephistopheles of twenty-
five—budding understudies of the stars who were away on
their summer holiday. But the crowning joy was *Der Rosenkavalier*, which neither Berenson nor I had yet heard, even in
snatches on the gramophone. The sensations of that evening
rank with my first sight of Isadora's dancing, my first Russian
ballet, my first reading of *Du Côte de chez Swann*. They were
vernal hours—*es war der Lenz!* But already the sickles were
sharpening for the harvest . . .

One afternoon at the Adlon, just before leaving Berlin, we
came upon a quietly dressed elderly lady who greeted Berenson as an old friend, and introduced to us the silent and
rather sad-looking young man who was with her. The lady
was the Princess of Thurn and Taxis, and the young man
Rainer Maria Rilke, the exquisite poet, whose work I already
knew and admired, though his greatest poems, the *Duineser
Elegien*, written at the Princess's castle of Duino, near Trieste,
were still in manuscript. She spoke to me, I remember, of
their remote and mysterious beauty, while Berenson was talking to Rilke; and I longed for a better chance of seeing him
than that hurried encounter over clattering tea-cups. The better chance never came. Rilke died soon after the war, and
once more I cursed the shyness which had prevented my telling him then and there how much I cared for his writings.

I had the luck, in those years, to make two other enchanting journeys. The first, in 1913, took us through the length
and breadth of Sicily, of which hitherto I had seen only Pa-
lermo and the towns of the east coast. Now we explored also
the great central ridge across which Goethe laboured on
horse-back, and from there went to Segesta, Trapani and Seli-
nonte, then still a desert beach strewn with prone columns
and mighty architectural fragments. The other tour, in the
early spring of 1914, was made with Percy Lubbock and Gaillard Lapsley. We started by motor from Algiers, and after a

day at the exquisite oasis of Bou-Saada, in southern Algeria, turned eastward across the mountains of Kabylia to Timgad, Constantine and Tunis, and from Tunis, by Sfax and Souss, to Kairouan the fabulous, and thence to El Djem, Gabès (whence we tried in vain to cross to Djerba, the Lotus-eaters' island), and southward to the mysterious town of Médénine, beyond which there were then no roads for motor-travel.

I have yielded to the temptation of setting down these names for the sake of their magic properties; but such a journey is now a commonplace of North African travel, and a dash across the desert from Tozeur to Gardaïa less of an adventure than our run from Gabès to Médénine. Though such recollections constitute the traveller's joy they may easily become the reader's weariness. In writing one's personal reminiscences it is not always easy to discriminate between one's self and one's audience, and the peril of prolixity lies in wait for the writer who begins his first paragraph with "I remember". As long as the scenes or incidents remembered are distant enough to revive a lost touch of local colour, or of vanished customs, to enlarge on them may be excusable; and if I could recall the details of my *diligence* journey through Spain at the age of four I might conceivably produce a tale as captivating as Théophile Gautier's or Washington Irving's. But to readers who may fly to Ur, or motor across the Atlas to Timbuctoo, in the course of an ordinary holiday excursion, it can be of little interest to learn how Timgad looked to me under a full moon, or what song the siren sang when I tried to pick up a passage from Gabès to the Lotus-eaters. All this is locked away in me in a safe place; but I must go there alone to count my treasures, for if I offered them to other eyes they might turn into a pinch of dust, like that beautiful Etruscan queen too rashly dragged from her painted tomb into the daylight.

XIII

The War

ONE BEAUTIFUL AFTERNOON toward the end of June 1914, I stopped at the gate of Jacques Blanche's house at Auteuil. It was a perfect summer day; brightly dressed groups were gathered at tea-tables beneath the over-hanging boughs, or walking up and down the flower-bordered turf. Broad bands of blue forget-me-nots edged the shrubberies, old-fashioned *corbeilles* of yellow and bronze wall-flowers dotted the lawn, the climbing roses were budding on the pillars of the porch. Outside in the quiet street stood a long line of motors, and on the lawn and about the tea-tables there was a happy stir of talk. An exceptionally gay season was drawing to its close, the air was full of new literary and artistic emotions, and that dust of ideas with which the atmosphere of Paris is always laden sparkled like motes in the sun.

I joined a party at one of the tables, and as we sat there a cloud-shadow swept over us, abruptly darkening bright flowers and bright dresses. "Haven't you heard? The Archduke Ferdinand assassinated . . . at Serajevo . . . where *is* Serajevo? His wife was with him. What was her name? Both shot dead."

A momentary shiver ran through the company. But to most of us the Archduke Ferdinand was no more than a name; only one or two elderly diplomatists shook their heads and murmured of Austrian reprisals. What if Germany should seize the opportunity—? There would be more particulars in next morning's papers. The talk wandered away to the interests of the hour . . . the last play, the newest exhibition, the Louvre's most recent acquisitions . . .

I was leaving in a day for a quick dash to Barcelona and the Balearic islands, before going to England, where I had taken a house in the country, carrying out at last my life-long dream of a summer in England. All my old friends had promised to come and stay; we were to motor to Scotland, to Wales, to all the places I had longed to see for so many years. How happy and safe the future seemed!

After some radiant days among the Pyrenees we descended into the burning summer of Catalonia. Even the transparent Spanish air had never seemed so saturated with pure light. I remember a day when we picnicked in the scant shade of a group of cork-trees above a vineyard where an iridescent heat-shimmer hung visibly over the fiery red earth. But at Barcelona we had a disappointment. For three weeks ahead not a berth was to be had on the little boat crossing every night from there to Majorca. The Balearics had not yet been discovered by foreign trippers, but Spanish holiday-makers took possession of the islands in summer. It was too sultry to linger in Barcelona, and the few hotels then existing at Palma were sure to be crammed with excursionists; so we wandered about in the Spanish Pyrenees, and then made for the Atlantic coast at Bilbao. The days were long and shining, the new roads lured us on. We gave little thought to the poor murdered Archduke, and international politics seemed as remote as the moon. My servants had already closed my apartment in Paris, and gone to the house I had taken in England, and I was to follow early in August. Slowly we began to loiter northward.

During the last days in Spain we felt the chill of the same cold cloud which had darkened the Blanches' garden-party. The belated French newspapers were beginning to be disquieting, and we decided to hasten our return. On July 30th we slept at Poitiers, and all night long I lay listening to the crowds singing the *Marseillaise* in the square in front of the hotel. "What nonsense! It can't be war," we said to each other the next morning; but we started early and rushed through to Paris, where the air was already thick with rumours. Everything seemed strange, ominous and unreal, like the yellow glare which precedes a storm. There were moments when I felt as if I had died, and waked up in an unknown world. And so I had. Two days later war was declared.

2

When I am told—as I am not infrequently—by people who were in the nursery, or not born, in that fatal year, that the world went gaily to war, or when I have served up to me the more recent legend that France and England actually wanted war, and forced it on the peace-loving and reluctant Central Empires, I recall those first days of August 1914, and am dumb with indignation.

France was paralyzed with horror. France had never wanted war, had never believed that it would be forced upon her, had proved her good faith by the absurd but sublime act of ordering her covering troops ten miles back from the frontier as soon as she heard of Austria's ultimatum to Servia! It may be useless to revive such controversies now; but not, I believe, to put the facts once more on record for a future generation who may study them with eyes cleared of prejudice. The criminal mistakes made by the Allies were made in 1919, not in 1914.

I have related, in a little book written during the first two years of the war, the impressions produced by those dark and bewildering days of August 1914, and I will not return to them here, except to describe my personal situation. This was rather absurdly conditioned by the fact that I had no money—a disability shared at the moment by many other foreigners in France. When I reached Paris I had about two hundred francs in my pocket, and was preparing to call at the bank for my usual remittance when I learned that the banks would make no payments. I borrowed a small sum from Walter Berry, who happened to have some cash in hand; but other penniless friends assailed him, and I could not ask for enough to send to my servants in England, who were expecting me to arrive with funds to pay the previous month's expenses. My old friend Frederick Whitridge was staying at his house in Hertfordshire, close to the place I had hired, and I wired him to give my servants enough to go on with. He replied: "Very sorry. Have no money." I cabled to my bank in New York to send me at least a small sum, and the bank cabled back: "Impossible."

At last, after a long delay—I forget how many days it took—I managed to get five hundred dollars from New York, by paying another five hundred for the transmission! To retransmit to England what remained would have been, if not impossible, at any rate so costly that little would have been left to settle my tradesmen's bills. I had never had a house in England before, and accustomed to the suspiciousness of French tradespeople I was wondering how much longer my poor servants, who were totally unknown in the neighbourhood, would be able to obtain credit, and I realized that the only thing to do was to get to England myself as quickly as possible—not an easy undertaking either.

As I had no money to pay any more hotel bills I moved back to my shrouded quarters in the rue de Varenne, and camped there until I could get a permit to go to England. At that time it was believed in the highest quarters that the war would be fought out on Belgian soil, that it would last at the longest not more than six weeks, and that one decisive battle might probably end it sooner. My friends all advised me, if I could get to England, to stay there "till the war was over"— that is, presumably, till some time in October; and the first news of the battle of the Marne made it seem for two or three delirious days as though this prediction might come true.

While I was waiting to get to England I was asked by the Comtesse d'Haussonville, President of one of the branches of the French Red Cross (*Secours aux Blessés Militaires*) to organize a work-room for such work-women of my *arrondissement* as were not yet receiving government assistance. Almost all the hotels, restaurants, shops and work-rooms had closed with the drafting of the men for the army, and there remained a large number of women and children without means of livelihood, for whom immediate provision had to be made. I was totally inexperienced in every form of relief work, and not least in the management of anything like a work-room for seamstresses and *lingères*; and I had no money to do it with! But by this time it was possible for those who had a deposit in a French bank (which at the moment I had not), to draw it out in small amounts, and I assailed all my American friends who were either living in Paris, or still stranded there. I collected about twelve thousand francs (the first of many raids on the pockets of my compatriots), some one lent us a big empty flat in the Faubourg Saint-Germain, and luckily I came across two clever sisters (nieces of Professor Landormy, the well-known musical critic), who gave the aid of their quick wits and youthful energy. All this did not teach me how to run a big work-room, where we soon had about ninety women; but there was an ardour in the air which made it seem easy to accomplish whatever one attempted. There were several skilled *lingères* among our workers, and we decided to try for orders for fashionable *lingerie*, instead of competing with the other *ouvroirs* by making hospital supplies; and by dint of badgering my friends I extracted from them a rush of orders later supplemented by more from America. Our *lingerie* soon became well-known, and as I had told my assistants never on any account to refuse an order, whatever might be asked for, we were soon doing a thriving trade in unexpected lines, including men's shirts (in the low-neck Byronic style) for young American artists from Montparnasse!

This work was barely started when I got my visa for England, and a permit from the French War Office to motor to Calais (trains being slow and uncertain). At Folkestone Henry James met me and took me back to Lamb House for the night; then I hurried on to Stocks, the place I had hired. It was a charming old house in beautiful gardens, belonging at that time to the Humphry Wards. I knew the place well, and had looked forward to seeing all my friends about me in those pleasant rooms. How little could I have imagined in what conditions I was to arrive there! The country was deserted, and I was alone in the big echoing rooms, looking out on gardens radiant with flowers which I had no heart to enjoy. To the honour of the British race let it be recorded that all through those agonizing days Mrs. Ward's upper housemaid (whom I had taken on with the house) kept every room filled with bowls of flowers arranged with the most exquisite art; also that the local tradesmen had given my butler and cook unlimited credit, and would probably have gone on trusting them to the end of the summer. In what other country could such faith in an unknown customer have been found?

The loneliness of those days at Stocks was indescribable. The wireless was not yet, and for news we had to await the arrival of the London papers, which came late and irregularly. Every day I walked to the village post office to fetch the papers. The hours were endless—for the first time in my life I could not read, and sat unoccupied in Mrs. Ward's pleasant library. Henry James came to stay for a day or two; so, I think, did Percy Lubbock and Gaillard Lapsley. But no one could bear to remain—it was too far from London and the news, and there was something oppressive, unnatural, in the serene loveliness of the old gardens, the cedars spreading wide branches over deserted lawns, the borders glowing with un-heeded flowers. Besides, our separate lonelinesses seemed to merge in one great sense of solitude, of being cut off forever from the old untroubled world we had always known, so that my friends and I felt that our being together was really not much help to any of us.

I had never intended to follow the advice to stay in En-gland "till the end of the war". I meant to pay my bills, hand back Stocks to its owners, and return immediately to Paris, where I could be of use, and should have the blessed drug of hard work. But suddenly the way back was barred. I went up to London, I saw Mr. Page at our Embassy, and Monsieur Paul Cambon at his, and both could only bid me be patient. For the moment, they told me, even if I succeeded in crossing to Calais I should not be allowed to go a yard farther. There began to be rumours of a big battle —*the* decisive battle—not far from Paris. As soon as that was over it might be possible to give me my permit.

My solitude at Stocks became more and more unbearable. Mrs. Ward, who was at her house in London, understood this, and as she, on the other hand, had assumed war duties in the country, she proposed that we should exchange houses, and I gratefully installed myself under her roof in Grosvenor Place. There at least I could see people who fancied them-selves well-informed, could pick up scraps of news, and could importune my Embassy and Monsieur Cambon. So the days dragged on, lit up for a moment by the glorious news of the Marne, but darkened again—only too soon—by the indeci-sive results of an action which was at first believed to have been a final victory. I have but a blurred memory of those weeks of suspense, and recall distinctly only the last days of my stay in England. From the moment when I was sum-moned by Mr. Page, and told that my return to Paris was authorized, the rushing back and forth to the two Embassies kept me blissfully busy. Ours was crammed with travellers waiting for similar permissions, and it was hard to fix the attention of the over-worked officials. At last one of them told me that I must have myself photographed for my permit (I imagine there were no regular passports as yet). He hurriedly gave me the address of the photographer usually employed by the Embassy, who, he said, being used to the job, would deliver my photograph the same day.

I hastened to the address given—a vague street somewhere in Millbank. The houses were all exactly alike, but on the one bearing the number given me I read the sign "Photographer", and confidently rang the bell. A small shy man with pale hair and eyes admitted me, and showed me into a parlour furnished with aspidistras and antimacassars. Thence, after a long delay, he summoned me with the request to follow him to the roof. I was slightly surprised; but in those days everything was unexpected, and I climbed obediently up a ladder to the top of an outbuilding behind the house. Here this strange photographer seated me on a kitchen chair, and ducking under his voluminous black draperies took aim. But apparently something did not work, and after repeated duckings, and rumpled reappearances, he said in a tone of apology: "I'm so sorry, madam; but the truth is, I've always specialized in photographing wild beasts, and this is the first time I've ever done a human being."

I had evidently come to the wrong address; but there was nothing for it but to receive his excuses with a shout of laughter, and implore him to go on all the same. He did, and the portrait bore painful witness to the truth of his statement; but though it looked like a wild-cat robbed of her young it was sufficiently like to get me safely through to Paris.

3

On leaving Paris I had entrusted all the money I had collected to a young lady recommended to me by the Red Cross for the post of treasurer. During the German advance before the Marne many people had followed the example of the government, and moved rapidly in the direction of Bordeaux. Our treasurer was among them—and in the haste of departure she carried off all our funds! Ready money being still difficult to obtain, or to transmit, long and complicated negotiations were necessary before the Red Cross could recover my capital; and thereafter I acted as my own treasurer. But meanwhile the German advance, which had sent so many rich residents out of Paris, had driven into it the lamentable horde of the Belgian and French refugees. The Red Cross was engrossed by its immense task in the field and in the military hospitals, the government relief services were disorganized and totally unprepared for the sudden influx of refugees, and immediate help had to be given. Charles Du Bos, with a group of French and Belgian friends, had improvised an emergency work called *L'Accueil Franco-Belge*, which had already rendered great service, but risked being swamped by the increasing throng of applicants, and the lack of funds. I was asked to form an American committee, and to raise money; I did both, and speedily found myself, inexperienced as I was, unable to carry this new burden as well as my big *ouvroir*. But friends came to my aid, giving money and time, and before many months the relief work was on a sound basis, though none of us (luckily) foresaw the huge proportions it was to assume, and the repeated appeals for financial aid that our over-worked committee would have to make.

It is unnecessary to chronicle our labours in detail. The *Accueil Franco-Belge* (afterward the *Accueil Franco-Américain*) was only one among many war-charities created to supplement the inadequate and over-tasked administrative effort; but a few points in its growth and organization are worth recording. When it became necessary to divide the work into separate departments—registration bureau, centre for distribution of clothing, medical dispensary, cheap restaurants, etc.,—we installed our central bureau in the large and handsome business offices in the Champs-Elysées which were put at our disposal by the Comtesse de Béhague. Here the refugees were registered, and given tickets for food, clothing and lodging; and among the hard-worked functionaries who performed this drudgery were not only Charles Du Bos himself, but Darius Milhaud, the well-known composer, Geoffrey Scott, André Gide and Percy Lubbock. These were among our punctual and faithful volunteers; but others—how many!—came and went, speedily overcome by the boredom of the task, or the inability to keep regular hours (and what hours!—our office was often open from 9 A.M. till after midnight).

My greatest difficulty was that of divining beforehand on which of our volunteers we should be able to count. Some would drift in vaguely, saying: "I'll try for a few days—but don't expect too much from me," and would turn out to be the future corner-stones of the building. Others, lucid, precise and self-confident, would point out our deficiencies, offer to remedy them, and fade away after a week. I recall one rich compatriot, long established in Paris, who offered to take over the management of our chaotic clothes-distribution, where, as she pointed out, everything needed sorting, listing and super-intending. I was enchanted! Here at last, I thought, is a prac-tical intelligence, some one who knows instinctively all that I am vainly trying to learn. I drew a deep breath of relief, and made an appointment to meet her the next morning at the *Vestiaire*. She came for about a week, increased the confusion she had offered to dispel—and then disappeared.

Such experiences were discouraging, and I was beginning to fear that my lack of discernment in choosing my helpers, and my innate distaste for anything like "social service", were a hopeless handicap to my usefulness. But by this time I was President of our committee, and the work had to be kept going.

One day Mrs. Royall Tyler came to see me. I had met her husband before the war at the house of my friend Raymond Koechlin, the distinguished archæologist and collector, but my acquaintance with her was very slight. Royall Tyler, al-ready an accomplished archivist, was at that time employed by the British Record Office in editing the State Papers bearing on the diplomatic relations between England and Spain in the sixteenth century. Soon after the outbreak of the war he and his wife came to Paris, and Mrs. Tyler called on me, and said simply: "My husband and I want to help you. How can you use us?" I was touched by the offer, but uncertain what to say. I knew them both too little to guess at their capacity, and above all at their staying powers. But I had begun to suspect that intelligence is a valuable asset even in assigning lodgings and food-tickets to refugees, and I liked the simple way in which the offer was made. I "took on" both husband and wife, and Royall Tyler rendered me immense help until our entry into the war enrolled him in the United States Intelligence service; while of his wife I can only say that she found the *Accueil* a tottering house of cards, and turned it into solid bricks and mortar. Never once did she fail me for an hour, never did we disagree, never did her energy flag or her discernment and promptness of action grow less through those weary years. The real "Magic City" was that which her inexhaustible resourcefulness raised out of our humble beginnings, and it was thanks to her that each fresh emergency was met by new and far-seeing measures of relief, so that in 1918, when the war ended, we had, in addition to five thousand refugees permanently cared for in Paris, and four big colonies for old people and children, four large and well-staffed sanatoria for tuberculous women and children. The most important of these, *La Tuyolle*, was handed over in 1920 to the Department of the Seine and is still running under the staff originally selected and trained by Mrs. Tyler; and it still has the reputation of being one of the best sanatoria in France.

More and more funds had to be raised for our ever-growing work, and when the ardour of our supporters began to flag Mrs. Tyler offered to go to America and beg for more. Beg she did, valiantly and successfully, returning with spoils beyond my hopes, and the lasting good-will of the friends to whom I had commended her. Another effort was presently required, and this time it fell to my lot to put together "The Book of the Homeless", a collection of original poems, articles and drawings, contributed by literary and artistic celebrities in Europe and America. I appealed right and left for contributions, and met with only one refusal—but I will not name the eminent and successful author who went by on the other side.

"The Book of the Homeless", and the subsequent auction sale in New York of the original manuscripts and sketches, brought us in another large sum; but I ached with the labour of translating (in a few weeks' time) all but one of the French and Italian contributions! I am at best a slow worker, and with all the other tasks I had shouldered I could have cried for weariness at the mere thought of taking up my pen; but the overwhelming needs of the hour doubled every one's strength, and the book was ready on time.

I cannot end this summary of our war-labours without speaking of the response from America which alone made it possible for me to go on with the work. From my cousin Lewis Ledyard and his friend Payne Whitney, whose generosity built for us the sanatorium of *La Tuyolle*, to the woman doctor who sold her tiny scrap of radium because she had no other means of helping, and the French and English servants in New York who again and again sent us their joint savings, we met on every side with inexhaustible encouragement and sympathy. "Edith Wharton" committees were formed in New York, Boston, Washington, Philadelphia and Providence, and friends and strangers worked with me at a distance as untiringly as those who were close at hand. I should like to tell them all now that I have never forgotten what they did.

4

A year or two ago my friend Madame Octave Homberg, President of the Mozart Society of Paris, brought out to dine with me one summer evening that most magical of flute-players, René Leroy, and Félix Raugel, the distinguished organizer and conductor of the Mozart Society's concerts.

René Leroy I knew already; Raugel was a stranger, except by reputation, and when he entered the room I had no sense of ever having seen him before. But he came straight up to me with beaming smile and hands outstretched. "Madame! What an age since we last met! Do you remember? It was in August 1915, when you rode up a mountain in the Vosges, astride on an army mule, and suddenly appeared in the camp of the Blue Devils [*Chasseurs Alpins*] on top of the Col de la Chapelotte!"

I stared at him in wonder; and as he spoke the peaceful room vanished, and the twilight shadows of my suburban garden, and I saw myself, an eager grotesque figure, bestriding a mule in the long tight skirts of 1915, and suddenly appearing, a prosaic Walkyrie laden with cigarettes, in the heart of the mountain fastness held by the famous *Chasseurs Alpins*,

already among the legendary troops of the French army. Seeing Félix Raugel again brought back to me with startling viv-
idness the scenes of my repeated journeys to the front; the
scarred torn land behind the trenches, the faces of the men
who held it, the terrible and interminable epic of France's
long defence. I remembered the emotion of my arrival at the
posts I was permitted to visit, the speechless astonishment of
officers and men at the sight of a wandering woman, their
friendly greetings, the questions, the laughter, the jolly picnic
lunches around boards resting on trestles, the reluctant good-
byes, the burden of messages to wives and mothers with
which I returned to the rear . . .

Early in 1915 the French Red Cross asked me to report on
the needs of some military hospitals near the front. Common
prudence should have made me refuse to beg for more
money; but in those days it never occurred to any one to
evade a request of that kind. Armed with the needful permits,
and my car laden to the roof with bundles of hospital supplies, I set out in February 1915 to inspect the fever-hospital at
Châlons-sur-Marne. What I saw there made me feel the ur-
gency of telling my rich and generous compatriots something
of the desperate needs of the hospitals in the war-zone, and I
proposed to Monsieur Jules Cambon to make other trips to
the front, and recount my experiences in a series of magazine
articles.

Foreign correspondents were still rigorously excluded from
the war-zone; but Monsieur Cambon, after talking the matter
over with General Joffre's chief-of-staff, General Pellé, succeeded in convincing him that, even if in my ignorance I
should stumble on some important military secret, there
would be little risk of its betrayal in articles which could not
possibly be ready for publication until several months later;
while the description of what I saw might bring home to
American readers some of the dreadful realities of war. I was
given leave to visit the rear of the whole fighting line, all the
way from Dunkerque to Belfort, and did so in the course of
six expeditions, some of which actually took me into the
front-line trenches; and, wishing to lose no time in publishing
my impressions, I managed to scribble the articles between
my other tasks, and they appeared in "Scribner's Magazine"

in 1915, and immediately afterwards in a volume called "Fighting France".

When the book was published it was not permissible to give too precise details about places or people, and I have sometimes thought of bringing out a new edition in which the gaps should be filled in with more personal touches: such as the moment when I was received at La Panne, in a little wind-rocked sand-girt villa, by the Queen of the Belgians, who had summoned me to talk of the Belgian child-refugees committed to our care; or the day when Monsieur Paul Boncour (afterward French Minister of Foreign Affairs), in a particularly impeccable uniform, escorted me to the first-line trenches in Alsace; or the other when Monsieur Henry de Jouvenel (lately French Ambassador to Italy), receiving at Sainte Menehoulde my request to go on to Verdun, at first positively refused, and then, returning from a consultation with the General of the division, said with a smile: "Are you the author of 'The House of Mirth'? If you are, the General says you shall have a pass: but for heaven's sake drive as fast as you can, for we don't want any civilians on the road today." (It was on February 28, 1915, the day the French retook the heights of Vauquois, on the road to Verdun; and, as I have related in my book, we actually witnessed the victorious assault from a cottage garden at Clermont-en-Argonne.)

In Lorraine I was guided by an old friend, Raymond Recouly, then on the staff of General Humbert, one of the heroes of the Marne; and it was thanks to Recouly's disobedience of his chief's orders that we had a risky and exciting hour at Pont-à-Mousson, then close under the German guns, and rigorously closed to civilians. Nor, if I am giving thanks, must I omit to record my gratitude to another friend, Jean-Louis Vaudoyer, the well-known poet and novelist, whom I had already visited somewhere in a shelter at the rear of the front lines, I think in Alsace. On our return to Châlons-sur-Marne, after a second trip to Verdun, it chanced that we found Vaudoyer on the staff of the General in command in that region. It was a bitter winter evening when we arrived at Châlons, where we were to spend the night before returning to Paris. To our dismay we found the place thronged with troops, and were not surprised to hear, on applying at the hotel of the Haute Mère Dieu, the only one open, that there was not a single room free. We insisted, and the landlady at last replied: "We are under military orders always to keep two rooms at the disposal of staff-officers. If they are not required tonight you may induce the General in command to let you have them."

At Headquarters, in the stately Préfecture of Châlons, we found the great hall and monumental staircase swarming with officers, messengers and orderlies, and in spite of our high recommendations we were told that the rooms were not available, and that probably we should not find one in all Châlons. The only alternative was to sleep in the motor on a night of bitter frost (as my good chauffeur eventually did), for no civilian car was allowed on the roads after dark, and we were prisoners till the next day. Never shall I forget the relief of running across Jean-Louis Vaudoyer at the very moment when we were disconsolately leaving the Préfecture, and hearing him hurriedly whisper: "I know what has happened, and I can lend you my little lodging for the night, for I'm on duty here at Headquarters. You ought not to be in the streets at this hour, but I'll give you the password. If you can manage to wake up the landlady she'll let you in; if you càn't—well," his shrug seemed to say, "there is really nothing else that I can do for you."

We did get to the door of his lodgings unchallenged, we did rouse the landlady without making too much noise; and oh, the sight of those peaceful rooms, the clean sheets, the warm stove! I don't think I ever slept as deeply and completely as that night in Vaudoyer's blessed bed.

The noting of my impressions at the front had the effect of rousing in me an intense longing to write, at a moment when my mind was burdened with practical responsibilities, and my soul wrung with the anguish of the war. Even had I had the leisure to take up my story-telling I should have had no heart for it; yet I was tormented with a fever of creation.

After two years of war we all became strangely inured to a state which at first made intellectual detachment impossible. It would be inexact to say that the sufferings and the suspense were less acutely felt; but the mysterious adaptability of the human animal gradually made it possible for war-workers at the rear, while they went on slaving at their job with redoubled energy, to create within themselves an escape from the surrounding horror. This was possible only to real workers, as it is possible for a nurse on a hard case to bear the sight of the patient's sufferings because she is doing all she can to relieve them. All the pessimism and the lamentations came from the idlers, while those who were labouring to the limit possessed their souls, and faced the future with confidence.

Gradually my intellectual unrest sobered down into activity. I began to write a short novel, "Summer", as remote as possible in setting and subject from the scenes about me; and the work made my other tasks seem lighter. The tale was written at a high pitch of creative joy, but amid a thousand interruptions, and while the rest of my being was steeped in the tragic realities of the war; yet I do not remember ever visualizing with more intensity the inner scene, or the creatures peopling it.

Many women with whom I was in contact during the war had obviously found their vocation in nursing the wounded, or in other philanthropic activities. The call on their co-operation had developed unexpected aptitudes which, in some cases, turned them forever from a life of discontented idling, and made them into happy people. Some developed a real genius for organization, and a passion for self-sacrifice that made all selfish pleasures appear insipid. I cannot honestly say that I was of the number. I was already in the clutches of an inexorable calling, and though individual cases of distress appeal to me strongly I am conscious of lukewarmness in regard to organized beneficence. Everything I did during the war in the way of charitable work was forced on me by the necessities of the hour, but always with the sense that others would have done it far better; and my first respite came when I felt free to return to my own work.

Such freedom was seldom to be achieved during those terrible years, and between 1914 and 1918 I had time only for "Fighting France", "Summer", a short tale called "The Marne", and a series of articles, "French Ways and Their Meaning", which I was asked to write after our entry into the war, with the idea of making France and things French more intelligible to the American soldier. These articles appeared in a volume in 1919.

In 1917 I had my only real holiday. General Lyautey, then Resident General in Morocco, had held since 1914, in one or another of the Moroccan cities, an annual industrial exhibition, destined to impress upon France's North African subjects the fact that the war she was carrying on in no way affected her normal activities. The idea was admirable, the result wholly successful. To these exhibitions, which were carried out with the greatest taste and intelligence, the Resident annually invited a certain number of guests from allied and neutral countries. I was among those who were asked to visit the exhibition at Rabat; and General Lyautey carried his kindness to the extent of sending me on a three weeks' motor tour of the colony. The brief enchantment of this journey through a country still completely untouched by foreign travel, and almost destitute of roads and hotels, was like a burst of sunlight between storm-clouds. I returned from it to the crushing gloom of the last dark winter, to the night which was not to lift again until the following September, and I had no time to set down the story of my wonderful journey until 1920, when it appeared in a volume called "In Morocco".

5

One evening at the end of July 1918 Royall Tyler and I were sitting in my drawing-room in the rue de Varenne. He had been staying with me for a few days; and I suppose that as usual we were talking of the war, though his responsible position in our Paris Intelligence Bureau made confidential communications impossible. At any rate, as we sat there our talk was suddenly interrupted by the sound of a distant cannonade. We broke off and stared at each other.

Four years of war had inured Parisians to every kind of noise connected with air-raids, from the boom of warning maroons to the smashing roar of the bombs. The rue de Varenne was close to the Chamber of Deputies, to the Ministries of War and of the Interior, and to other important government offices, and bombs had rained about us and upon us since 1914; and as we were on Big Bertha's deathly trajectory her evil roar was also a well-known sound.

But this new noise came neither from maroon, from aeroplane nor from the throat of the dark Walkyrie; it was the level throb of distant artillery, a sound with which my expeditions to the front had made me painfully familiar. And this was the first time that I had heard it in Paris! The firing along the front was often distinctly audible on the south coast of England, and sometimes, I believe, at certain points in Surrey; but though familiar to dwellers in the south-western suburbs of Paris, it had never before, to my knowledge, reached the city itself. My guest and I sprang up and rushed to a long window opening on a balcony. There we stood and listened to that far-off rumour, relentless, unbroken, portentous; and suddenly Tyler turned to me with an illuminated face. "It's the opening of Foch's big offensive!"

Some three months later, on a hushed November day, another unwonted sound called me to the same balcony. The quarter I lived in was so quiet in those days that, except for the crash of aerial battles few sounds disturbed it; but now I was startled to hear, at an unusual hour, the familiar bell of our nearest church, Sainte Clotilde. I went to the balcony, and all the household followed me. Through the deep expectant hush we heard, one after another, the bells of Paris calling to each other; first those of our own quarter, Saint Thomas d'Aquin, Saint Louis des Invalides, Saint François Xavier, Saint Sulpice, Saint Etienne du Mont, Saint Séverin; then others, more distant, joining in from all around the city's great periphery, from Notre Dame to the Sacré Cœur, from the Madeleine to Saint Augustin, from Saint Louis-en-l'Ile to Notre-Dame de Passy; at first, as it seemed, softly, questioningly, almost incredulously; then with a gathering rush of sound and speed, precipitately, exultantly, till all their voices met and mingled in a crash of triumph.

We had fared so long on the thin diet of hope deferred that for a moment or two our hearts wavered and doubted. Then, like the bells, they swelled to bursting, and we knew the war was over.

XIV

And After

O N THE 14TH of July 1919 I stood on the high balcony of a friend's house in the Champs Elysées, and saw the Allied Armies ride under the Arch of Triumph, and down the storied avenue to the misty distance of the Place de la Concorde and its obelisk of flame.

As I stood there, high over the surging crowds and the great procession, the midsummer sun blinding my eyes, and the significance of that incredible spectacle dazzling my heart, I remembered what Bergson had once said of my inability to memorize great poetry: "You're dazzled by it."

Yes, I thought; I shan't remember all this except as a golden blur of emotion. Even now I can't catch the details, I can't separate the massed flags, or distinguish the famous generals as they ride by, or the names of the regiments as they pass. I remember thankfully that a *grand mutilé* for whom I have secured a wheeled chair must have received it just in time to join his group in the Place de la Concorde. . . The rest is all a glory of shooting sun-rays reflected from shining arms and helmets, from the flanks of glossy chargers, the dark glitter of the 'seventy-fives, of machine-guns and tanks. But all those I had seen at the front, dusty, dirty, mud-encrusted, blood-stained, spent and struggling on; when I try to remember, the two visions merge into one, and my heart is broken with them.

2

The war was over, and we thought we were returning to the world we had so abruptly passed out of four years earlier. Perhaps it was as well that, at first, we were sustained by that illusion.

My chief feeling, I confess, was that I was tired—oh, so tired! I wanted first of all, and beyond all, to get away from

Paris, away from streets and houses altogether and for always, into the country, or at least the near-country of a Paris suburb. In motoring out to visit our group of refugee colonies to the north of Paris I had sometimes passed through a little village near Ecouen. In one of its streets stood a quiet house which I had never noticed, but which had not escaped the quick eye of my friend Mrs. Tyler. She stopped one day and asked the concierge if by chance it were for sale. The answer was a foregone conclusion: of course it was for sale. Every house in the northern suburbs of Paris was to be bought at that darkest moment of the spring of 1918. They had all been deserted by their owners since the last German advance, for they were in the direct line of the approach to Paris, and the little house in question was also on Bertha's trajectory. But Mrs. Tyler, the next day, told me she had found just the house for me, and we drove out to see it. The way there—now, alas, disfigured by the growth of Paris— was through pleasant market-gardens, and acres of pear and apple orchard. The orchards were just bursting into bloom, and we seemed to pass through a rosy snow-storm to reach what was soon to be my own door. I saw the house, and fell in love with it in spite of its dirt and squalour—and before the end of the war it was mine. At last I was to have a garden again—and a big old kitchen-garden as well, planted with ancient pear and apple trees, espaliered and in cordon, and an old pool full of fat old gold-fish; and silence and rest under big trees! It was Saint Martin's summer after the long storm.

The little house has never failed me since. As soon as I was settled in it peace and order came back into my life. At last I had leisure for the two pursuits which never palled, writing and gardening; and through all the years I have gone on gardening and writing. From the day when (to the scandal of the village!) I chopped down a giant araucaria on the lawn, until this moment, I have never ceased to worry and pet and dress up and smooth down my two or three acres; and when winter comes, and rain and mud possess the Seine Valley for six months, I fly south to another garden, as stony and soilless as my northern territory is moist and deep with loam. But to do justice to my two gardens, or at least to my enjoyment of

PAVILLON COLOMBE

"LA TOUR JEANNE" IN THE PARK AT
SAINTE-CLAIRE LE CHÂTEAU

them, would require not a chapter but a book; and pending that I must pass on to the other branch of my activity.

3

The brief rapture that came with the cessation of war—the blissful thought: "Now there will be no more killing!"—soon gave way to a growing sense of the waste and loss wrought by those irreparable years. Death and mourning darkened the houses of all my friends, and I mourned with them, and mingled my private grief with the general sorrow. I myself had lost a charming young cousin, Newbold Rhinelander, shot down in an aeroplane battle in September 1917, and three dear friends. Of these, Jean du Breuil de Saint Germain and Robert d'Humières both fell leading their men though in each case their age would have assured them a safe berth as staff officers, had they been willing to accept it. The third of my friends was a young American, Ronald Simmons, excluded from active service by a weak heart, and appointed head of the American Intelligence service at the important post of Marseilles. He did admirable work there till the Spanish grippe swept over France; then his heart gave way, and he died in three days.

But sorrows come "not single spies but in battalions", and while I was mourning the friends killed in the war, more intimate griefs befell me. In 1916 died Henry James, the perfect friend of so many years, and in 1920 my beloved Howard Sturgis. By the loss of these two friends, and that of Egerton Winthrop, who died suddenly at about the same time, my life was greatly impoverished. In recent years I had seen less of Egerton Winthrop; but a friendship such as ours is made of many elements, and there remained, I believe, on his side a great affection, and on mine a gratitude which went back to the first days of what I might call my conscious life. To the purblind creature he had found me he had been the first to hold out a wise and tender hand; and the loss of his wisdom and tenderness made a darkness in my life.

But with Henry James and Howard Sturgis the sorrow was present, was poignant. They were part of my daily thoughts and plans, and my roots were torn up with theirs. In Howard Sturgis's case a fatal illness had declared itself, and much suffering was inevitable; so that his best friends could only pray for the end to come quickly. Happily it did, and he faced it with lucid serenity. It added to my grief that it was impossible for me to go to him; not that a last meeting would have helped either of us much, but simply because I knew he would have liked the fact of my coming.

In Henry James's case, though he was so much older, it was harder for his friends to resign themselves, for it seemed as though a man of his powerful frame and unimpaired intellectual vitality ought to have lived longer. We all knew that for years he had suffered from the evil effects of a dangerous dietary system, called (after the name of its egregious inventor) "Fletcherizing". The system resulted in intestinal atrophy, and when a doctor at last persuaded him to return to a normal way of eating he could no longer digest, and his nervous system had been undermined by years of malnutrition. The Fletcher fad, moreover, had bred others, as usually happens; and James's incessant preoccupation with his health gradually led to periods of nervous depression. The death of his brother William shook him to the soul, not only because of their deep attachment to each other, but because Henry, following the phases of his brother's fatal malady, had become convinced that he had the same organic heart-disease as William. The intense disappointment caused by his successive theatrical failures may also have had a share in weakening his health. Mr. Leon Edel, in his suggestive essay on James's play-writing, has made out so good a case for him as a dramatist (if only circumstances had been more favourable) that I sometimes wonder if I was not wrong in thinking these theatrical experiments a mistake. James, at any rate, never thought them so. He believed himself gifted for the drama, and, apart from the creative joy that the writing of his plays gave him, he longed intensely, incurably, for the shouting and the garlands so persistently refused to his great novels, and which, had he succeeded in his theatrical venture, would have come to him in a grosser but more substantial form. I once said that Anglo-Saxons had no notion of what the French mean when they speak of *la gloire*; but in that respect James was a Latin,

and the last infirmity of noble minds was never quite renounced by his.

His dying was slow and harrowing. The final stroke had
been preceded by one or two premonitory ones, each causing
a diminution just marked enough for the still conscious intelligence to register it, and the sense of disintegration must
have been tragically intensified to a man like James, who had
so often and deeply pondered on it, so intently watched for
its first symptoms. He is said to have told his old friend Lady
Prothero, when she saw him after the first stroke, that in the
very act of falling (he was dressing at the time) he heard in the
room a voice which was distinctly, it seemed, not his own,
saying: "So here it is at last, the distinguished thing!" The
phrase is too beautifully characteristic not to be recorded. He
saw the distinguished thing coming, faced it, and received it
with words worthy of all his dealings with life.

But what really gave him his death-blow was the war. He
struggled through two years of it, then veiled his eyes from
the endless perspective of destruction. It was the gesture of
Agamemnon, covering his face with his cloak before the unbearable.

Before James died he bore witness, in his own moving way,
to the depth of his grief. He loved England, naturally, as his
home of many years, as the scene of his greatest work, and of
his dearest friendships; but he loved America also, and the
longing for a better understanding between his native and his
adopted countries possessed him more and more as the war
dragged on. His one consolation was the knowledge that Mr.
Page, for whom he had a great regard, was fighting valiantly
in the same cause; but after the "Lusitania", and the American
government's supine attitude at that time, James felt the need
to make manifest by some visible, symbolic act, his indignant
sympathy with England. The only way open to him, he
thought, was to renounce his American citizenship and be
naturalized in England; and he did this. At the time I considered it a mistake; it seemed to me rather puerile, and altogether unlike him. Not knowing what to say I refrained from
writing to him; and I regret it now, for I think the act comforted him, and it deeply touched his old friends in England.

I have never seen any one else who, without a private

personal stake in that awful struggle, suffered from it as he did. He had not my solace of hard work, though he did all he had strength for, and gave all the pecuniary help he could. But it was not enough. His devouring imagination was never at rest, and the agony was more than he could bear. As far as I know the only letters of mine which he kept were those in which I described my various journeys to the front, and when these were sent back to me after his death they were worn with much handing about. His sensitiveness about his own physical disabilities gave him an exaggerated idea of what his friends were able to do, and he never tired of talking of what he regarded as their superhuman activities. But still the black cloud hung over the world, and to him it was soon to be a pall. Perhaps it was better so. I should have liked to have him standing beside me the day the victorious armies rode by; but when I think of the years intervening between his death and that brief burst of radiance I have not the heart to wish that he had seen it. The waiting would have been too bitter.

4

My spirit was heavy with these losses, but I could not sit still and brood over them. I wanted to put them into words, and in doing so I saw the years of the war, as I had lived them in Paris, with a new intensity of vision, in all their fantastic heights and depths of self-devotion and ardour, of pessimism, triviality and selfishness. A study of the world at the rear during a long war seemed to me worth doing, and I pondered over it till it took shape in "A Son at the Front". But before I could settle down to this tale, before I could begin to deal objectively with the stored-up emotions of those years, I had to get away from the present altogether; and though I began planning and brooding over "A Son at the Front" in 1917 it was not finished until four years later. Meanwhile I found a momentary escape in going back to my childish memories of a long-vanished America, and wrote "The Age of Innocence". I showed it chapter by chapter to Walter Berry; and when he had finished reading it he said: "Yes; it's good. But of course you and I are the only people who will ever read it. We are the last people left who can remember New York and Newport as they were then, and nobody else will be interested."

I secretly agreed with him as to the chances of the book's success; but it "had its fate", and that was—to be one of my rare best-sellers! I still had the writing-fever on me and the next outbreak came in 1922, when I published "The Glimpses of the Moon", a still further flight from the last grim years, though its setting and situation were ultra-modern. After that I settled down to "A Son at the Front"; and although I had waited so long to begin it, the book was written in a white heat of emotion, and may perhaps live as a picture of that strange war-world of the rear, with its unnatural sharpness of outline and over-heightening of colour.

After "A Son at the Front" I intended to take a long holiday—perhaps to cease from writing altogether. It was growing more and more evident that the world I had grown up in and been formed by had been destroyed in 1914, and I felt myself incapable of transmuting the raw material of the after-war world into a work of art. Gardening, reading and travel seemed the only solace left; and during the first years after the war I did a good deal of all three.

Years earlier, the reading of Monsieur Joseph Bédier's famous book, "Les Chansons Epiques", had roused in me a longing to follow the mediaeval pilgrims across the Pyrenees to the glorious shrine of Compostela; and after the war this desire, and the resolve to satisfy it, were reawakened by the appearance of two new books, Kingsley Porter's "Romanesque Sculpture of the Pilgrimage Roads", and Miss Georgiana King's "The Way of St James".

We began our pilgrimage at Saint Jean-Pied-de-Port, in the western Pyrenees, and descended thence into Spain by Roncevaux and Jaca. We were resolved to miss no stage of the ancient way, and from Jaca we went to Eunate, Logroño, Estella, Puente de la Reina and Burgos, and thence, by way of Fromista, Carrión de los Condes and Sahagun, to Leon, and across the Cantabrian Mountains to Oviedo. The roads in the Asturias and Galicia were still mediaeval, and our progress was slow; but our determination to carry out the pilgrimage to its end (or, I should rather say, to its beginning) bore us on over interminable humps and bumps to La Coruña, and thence to the solitary and mysterious point of Finisterre (*Nuestra Señora de Finibus Terrae*), where, as readers of the Golden Legend know, the decapitated body of St James the Greater landed in the boat carved out of stone in which it had been reverently laid on the distant shore of Palestine. From Finisterre, with imaginations raised to a high pitch of expectancy, we followed the saint back, past his halting-place at Padròn, to the mighty church which enshrines him; and on arriving at Santiago de Compostela we found that our expectations had not been pitched high enough! Perhaps because this was the first journey of any length which I had made since the war, every mile of the way seemed fabulous and beautiful. But even the impression left by the Panteòn de los Reyes at Leon, and the incomparable Camara Santa of Oviedo, faded in the radiance which streams from the singing sculptures of the Portico de la Gloria. Yet when I returned to Compostela a few years later, over smooth roads, and without the excitement of plunging into the unknown, the strange grandeur of that isolated city of palaces and monasteries, and the glory of its great church, impressed me more deeply than ever, and I rank Compostela not far behind Rome in the mysterious power of drawing back the traveller who has once seen it.

5

For years and years—ever since our first cruise in the Ægean—I had dreamed the impossible dream of going on another. Youth had passed, and middle-age was going, in the vain cherishing of that dream, when suddenly, unexpectedly, a stroke of literary luck made it seem that I might repeat the adventure. In going on our first cruise we had been reckless to the point of folly; but we were young, we were two, we were ready to face any financial consequences. Now I was old, I was alone, and I had learned the necessity of living within one's means. But when a friend wrote me that he had seen at Southampton a delightful little yacht of the same tonnage and draft as our dear old "Vanadis", my prudence vanished like a puff of smoke, and I felt as reckless (and as young!) as when I had first set foot on the deck of the latter, nearly forty years earlier.

So the yacht "Osprey" was chartered, and we set out from the Old Port of Hyères, the same from which Saint Louis, King of France, sailed forth on his last crusade. The date was March 31 1926, the day serene and sunny, and we were a congenial party, with lots of books, a full set of Admiralty charts, a stock of good provisions and *vins du pays* in the hold, and happiness in our hearts. From that day until we disembarked at the same port, two months and one week later, I lived in a state of euphoria which I suppose would seem inconceivable to most people. But I am born happy every morning, and during that magical cruise nothing ever seemed to occur during the day to diminish my beatitude, so that it went on rolling up like the interest on a millionaire's capital. Now and then, it is true, a twinge passed through me at the thought of the reckoning; but I said to myself: "Never mind! As soon as I get home I'll write the story of the cruise, and call it 'The Sapphire Way', and it will be such enchanting reading that it will immediately become a best-seller, and pay all the expenses of the journey."

Would it have, I wonder? The book is not yet written, and probably never will be; for I returned to fiction as soon as I got home, as I always do when no more pressing task prevents. Yet what a charming book it would have been—like so many that have never been written!

At any rate, the intention of doing it sent my conscience to sleep, and I lived in unbroken bliss as we wandered from island to island, from shore to shore, always "under a roof of blue Ionian weather", retracing the stages of the former cruise, and seeing many new wonders which had then been difficult of access, such as Delphi, Mistra, Cyprus and Crete. Not the least interesting part of the adventure was the following out, stage by stage, of our old itinerary, and noting the changes produced either by the hand of man (as at Rhodes and the renovated islands of the Dodecanese), or by that other Hand, always written with a capital, which scatters earthquakes and volcanic eruptions throughout those lovely lands as freely as man distributes his administrative changes.

At Rhodes, which I had seen in the depths of Turkish

squalour and *laissez-faire*, we now found a city magically restored to its ancient beauty, without the overdoing so irresistible to most restorers; and in the islands of the Dodecanese,
taken over with Rhodes by Italy, the same touch has given
order and cleanliness even to such human rabbit-warrens as
the mediaeval citadel of Astypalaea.

A fortunate change in our travelling equipment was the
substitution of oil for coal as fuel; so that, instead of having
to lose hours in coaling, the "Osprey" glided from port to
port without delay or discomfort; and had her oil-tank been
slightly larger we should not even have had the small incon-
venience of replenishing it. Even the Hand of God fell on us
lightly and as it were playfully; for we had the luck to slip into
Santorin and Crete between two earthquakes of considerable
violence, one of which occurred only a few weeks before our
visit, and the other just afterward. So it was that in Santorin's
mysterious harbour we lay close to a new lava-island still visibly edged with subterranean fires, and at Candia, in Crete,
beheld in all their plastic perfection the glorious Minoan jars
garlanded with sea-weed and sea-monsters, the slim Prince
Charming of the lilies, and the frivolous young ladies leaning
from their box above the arena to watch the young acrobats
leap from bull to bull, where, a few weeks after our visit, the
Museum floor was strewn with their shattered fragments.

But I am writing my reminiscences, and not that memorable work, "The Sapphire Way", which, if ever it is done, will
require several hundred pages, and all the colours of Turner's
palette; so I will conclude by saying that this cruise proved to
me again what the first had so fully shown: that *Kein Genuss
ist vorübergehend*, and that no treasure-house of Atreus was
ever as rich as a well-stored memory.

6

These and other wanderings have been the high lights of
the last years; when I turn from them the sky darkens. The
disappearance of one dear friend after another must always be
the chief sadness of a life bound up in a few close personal
ties. Such losses seem doubly poignant in the brave new
world predicted by Aldous Huxley, and already here in its

main elements—a world in which so many sources of peace and joy are already dried up that the few remaining have a more piercing sweetness. Saddest of all is it, as the years pass, to see the premature ending of lives which seemed meant to widen into usefulness and beauty. Such a life I had hoped Geoffrey Scott's would be. Since our first meeting, more than twenty years earlier, I had always found him a delightful comrade. I had rejoiced, with his other friends, in the appearance of those two well-nigh perfect books, "The Architecture of Humanism" and "The Story of Zélide", so little appreciated at first beyond a small circle of readers, so tardily discovered by the general public; yet, accomplished as these books were, I felt in him something dispersed and tentative, as though the balance between his creative and critical faculties had not yet been struck. This discord ran through his whole character, and though no one could be gayer, more flashingly responsive to every appeal of life's ironies and beauties (and for him, as for all subtler intelligences, the two were always interwoven), yet under this laughing surface lay a desert of gloom and despondency—

> A country where the lights are low,
> And where the roads are hard to find,

as he once wrote of his own mind. Even his work, though he brought to it such a scrupulous art, ceased to interest him as soon as he had exteriorized the emotions producing it; and I used to tell him he was like an over-fed squirrel, who only cared to crack every nut, and then threw them away. But I was mistaken; he was not over-fed, but only groping for the right nourishment.

After the war he used to stay with me for long weeks, and we made various motor-flights together in Umbria and the North of Italy. In 1926, when he spent a month with me in the country near Paris, he was planning a book on Benjamin Constant—and what a book it would have been! I can imagine no subject better suited to him, and no one better fitted to interpret that unquiet and elusive character. I took him to the drowsy hill-village of Saint Michel-du-Tertre, where Benjamin Constant had once lived, and to the Abbaye d'Hérivaux, which he had bought after the Revolution; but all through

Geoffrey's eager inquiries, and his keen interest in the projected work, ran the same streak of agitation and uncertainty. He had been asked for a life of Boswell for the English Men of Letters series, and the suggestion delighted him. But he was reluctant to begin the book because he knew of the existence, in private hands, of a quantity of unexplored Boswellian material, as yet inaccessible to scholars, but which, through the friendly intervention of Sir Edmund Gosse, he hoped one day to examine. I remember his once saying sadly: "If I put off the Boswell in the hope of seeing those papers, some one else will write the book instead, and every one will say, as they always do, that I'm lazy and undecided; yet to set to work without being able to use this new material seems hardly worth while. What do you advise?"

I answered at once: "Never mind what people say. Don't do the book till you can consult all the material available. Never do anything against your better judgment simply to prove that you're not lazy." As far as his own welfare was concerned, it might have been better for him to tie himself down to any definite task, rather than drift longer on the old sea of alternatives; but since the question was one of literary probity it seemed impossible to hesitate.

I have never seen him more adrift, more undecided and disenchanted, than during those weeks; and it was a relief to hear, I think that same autumn, that the Boswell documents had been bought by an American collector who, at Geoffrey's request, had agreed to let him examine them. The rest of the story is known; the unforeseen importance of the discovery, the new owner's invitation to Geoffrey to return to America with him and edit the whole collection, and Geoffrey's immediate acceptance. To his friends there is a certain irony in the fact that the sensitive and imaginative art-critic and biographer, master of a perfect prose and of a delicate lyrical gift, should have become known to the general public only through an editorial task. The first Boswell volumes met with unqualified praise, and Geoffrey's letters showed the steadying effect of the welcome given to his labours. I had feared the strain, and the long exile from Europe, in conditions scarcely made for peace of mind; but I soon felt that he was gaining strength from the effort. His letters were not altogether happy, but they gave no hint of uncertainty; he was determined to carry the work through, and buoyed up by knowing that the need to be near the British Museum must soon bring him back to England.

One day in London, in July 1929, I suddenly came across Geoffrey. There was so little trace in his strong erect figure and smiling face of the worn unquiet being I had parted from three years earlier that at first I hardly recognized him. He had taken an unexpected holiday from his work, and as he was not to be in England more than a fortnight he had notified no one in advance. He told me he was to sail in two days for America, where he intended to settle down again to a year's work, with the hope, after that, of continuing his labours in England. We spent the afternoon together, wandering from one picture gallery to another in happy talk—the happiest I ever had with him. He had found his work, and himself. The old irony, the old mockery and subtlety were there, but tempered by a new and confident hope in the future. He felt his strength equal to his task, and was happy with that best happiness, the sense of mastery over one's work. We parted full of plans for the future, and the next morning he sailed for New York—and ten days later lay there dead.

But he had felt his hand on the wheel, had guided Fortune where he chose; and his friends, when they remember him, must think of that.

7

The world is a welter and has always been one; but though all the cranks and the theorists cannot master the old floundering monster, or force it for long into any of their neat plans of readjustment, here and there a saint or a genius suddenly sends a little ray through the fog, and helps humanity to stumble on, and perhaps up.

The welter is always there, and the present generation hears close underfoot the growling of the volcano on which ours danced so long; but in our individual lives, though the years are sad, the days have a way of being jubilant. Life is the saddest thing there is, next to death; yet there are always new countries to see, new books to read (and, I hope, to write), a thousand little daily wonders to marvel at and rejoice in, and those magical moments when the mere discovery that "the woodspurge has a cup of three" brings not despair but delight. The visible world is a daily miracle for those who have eyes and ears; and I still warm my hands thankfully at the old fire, though every year it is fed with the dry wood of more old memories.

Index

LIFE AND I

I

MY FIRST conscious recollection is of being kissed in Fifth Avenue by my cousin Dan Fearing.

It was a winter day, I was walking with my father, & I was a little less than four years old, when this momentous event took place. My cousin, a very round & rosy little boy, two or three years older, was also walking with his father; & I remember distinctly his running up to me, & kissing me, & the extremely pleasant sensation which his salute produced. With equal distinctness, I recall the satisfaction I felt in knowing that *I had on my best bonnet*, a very handsome bonnet made of a bright Tartan velvet with a white satin ground, with a full ruffling of blonde lace under the brim. Thus I may truly say that my first conscious sensations were produced by the two deepest-seated instincts of my nature—the desire to love & to look pretty.

I say "to look pretty" instead of "to be admired", because I really believe it has always been an aesthetic desire, rather than a form of vanity. I always saw the visible world as a series of pictures, more or less harmoniously composed, & the wish *to make the picture prettier* was, as nearly as I can define it, the form my feminine instinct of pleasing took.

I am able to date this first adventure with precision, because it happened before we went to Europe to live, & I was four years old when we left America. I believe we went because my father's income was reduced by "bad times" (& also, probably, by bad management of his property), & he wished to economize for a time, & to let his newly-built country-house at Newport, & our town house as well. I imagine that the expense of these two establishments weighed rather heavily on him, & that my mother, who was a very indolent woman—though she could be spasmodically active when anything amused her for the moment—preferred the drifting European life to the care of two houses & the obligations which my father's taste for society laid upon her when they were at home. . . . Of the first two or three years of our life abroad I remember chiefly vague pictures of travel—for my visual sensibility seems to me, as I look back, to have been as intense then as it is now—& the most excruciating moral tortures. The visual impressions were received in the course of our varied wanderings in Italy, Spain, France, Germany & England. It is difficult, of course, to disentangle these from the palimpsest of later impressions received in the same scenes; but I recall certain images—impressions of scenery, & more sharply-drawn visions of rooms—which must belong to the primitive period. I think my suffering from ugliness developed earlier than my sense of beauty, though it would seem that, one being the complement of the other, they must have coincided in my consciousness. At any rate, the ugliness stamped itself more deeply on my brain, & I remember *hating* certain rooms in a London house of my aunt's, & feeling for ugly people an abhorrence, a kind of cold cruel hate, that I have never been able to overcome.

One of the first results of this detestation of physical ugliness was an incident which will explain what I meant just now in saying that I suffered moral tortures in my childhood. When my parents settled down in Paris—I must have been six or seven at the time—I was sent to a small private dancing-class kept by a certain Mlle Michelet, who had been a danseuse at the Grand Opera. Mlle Michelet was a large good-humoured swarthy person, who, while destitute of beauty, inspired in me no physical repugnance; but she had a small shrivelled bearded mother whom I could not look at without disgust. This disgust I confidentially revealed to the little boy I was in love with at the time (I was always in love with some little boy, & he was generally in love with another little girl.) I described Mlle Michelet as looking like "une vieille chèvre", & the description was greeted with such approval that, if I had been a normal child, I should have been delighted with the success of my witticism. Instead of this, however, I was seized with immediate horror at my guilt; for I had said something *about* Mlle Michelet's mother which I would not have said *to her*, & which it was consequently "naughty" to say, or even to think.

Now the only possible interest connected with this anecdote lies in the curious fact that my compunction was entirely self-evolved. I had been brought up in an atmosphere of truthfulness, & of moral fierté, but I had never been subjected to any severe moral discipline, or even to the religious instruction which develops self-scrutiny in many children. I had an easy-going affectionate nurse, who had been with us since my brothers were babies, & a succession of gentle young nursery-governesses, who never preached or scolded, or evoked moral bogeys; & my parents were profoundly indifferent to the subtler problems of the conscience. They had what might be called the code of worldly probity, but the Christian sense of an abstract law of conduct, of any religious counsel of perfection, was completely absent from their talk, & probably from their consciousness. My mother's rule of behaviour was that we should be "polite"—my father's that we should be kind. Ill-breeding—any departure from the social rules of conduct—was the only form of wrong-doing I can remember hearing condemned. I had never, as far as I know, been told that it was "naughty" to lie (perhaps because I had never conceived it possible to do so); but I had often been told that it was naughty to snatch, to interrupt, not to "shake hands nicely", & to tear the lace ruffles out of my bonnets (what fun it was to hear them crack!)—I had, nevertheless, worked out of my inner mind a rigid rule of absolute, unmitigated truth-telling, the least imperceptible deviation from which would inevitably be punished by the dark Power I knew as "God". Not content with this, I had further evolved the principle that it was "naughty" to say, or to think, anything about any one that one could not, without offense, avow to the person in question; with the grim deduction that this very act of avowal would, in such cases, be the only adequate expiation of one's offense. I therefore nerved myself—with what anguish, I still recall!—to the act of publicly confessing to Mlle Michelet, before the assembled dancing-class, that I had called her mother an old goat; & I perfectly remember (such are the sophistries of the infant heart) a distinct sense of disappointment when, instead of recognizing & commending the heroism of my conduct, she gave me a furious scolding for my impertinence. My distress was increased by the conviction that my mother would have disapproved of the whole thing—& of the act more than the thought leading up to it; & I believe my first sense of moral bewilderment—of the seeming impossibility of reconciling an ideal of conduct with the unexpectedness of human experience—dates from this unhappy incident. At any rate, for years afterward I was never free from the oppressive sense that I had two absolutely inscrutable beings to please—God & my mother—who, while ostensibly upholding the same principles of behaviour, differed totally as to their application. And my mother was the most inscrutable of the two.

Nothing I have suffered since has equalled the darkness of horror that weighed on my childhood in respect to this vexed problem of truth-telling, & the impossibility of reconciling "Gods" standard of truthfulness with the conventional obligation to be "polite" & not hurt any one's feelings. Between these conflicting rules of conduct I suffered an untold anguish of perplexity, & suffered alone, as imaginative children generally do, without daring to tell any one of my trouble, because I vaguely felt that I *ought* to know what was right, & that it was probably "naughty" not to. It is difficult to imagine how the sternest Presbyterian training could have produced different or more depressing results. I was indeed "God-intoxicated", in the medical sense of the word.

Happily I had two means of escape from this chronic moral malady. One was provided by my love of pretty things—pretty clothes, pretty pictures, pretty sights—& the other by my learning to read. How I learned no one ever knew. My father taught me my alphabet, & was planning to lead me on to "cat" and "bat" when one day I was found seated in the drawing-room, reading a play called "Fanny Lear", by Halévy, I think. Of the intermediate stages neither I nor any one in my family had been conscious; & I can remember nothing of the process except the fact—as clear to me as if it had happened yesterday—of perusing Mr Halévy's pages with an apparent mastery of the meaning of the short words & the sound of the long ones. When I recall how carefully my reading was supervised from that hour to the day of my marriage, it seems odd that it should have begun with the story of a prostitute!

From that moment I was enthralled by *words*. It mattered very little whether I understood them or not: the sound was the essential thing. Wherever I went, they sang to me like the birds in an enchanted forest. And they had *looks* as well as sound: each one had its own gestures & physiognomy. What were dolls to a child who had such marvellous toys, & who knew that as fast as one wearied of the familiar ones, there were others, more wonderful still, to take their place?

When I read my first poetry I felt that "bliss was it in that dawn to be alive". Here were words transfigured, lifted from earth to heaven! I think my first experience of rhyme was the hearing of the "Lays of Ancient Rome" read aloud by my father. The movement of the metre was intoxicating: I can still feel the thump thump of my little heart as I listened to it!

But this first taste only sharpened my appetite, & I plunged into Tennyson, the only other accessible poet. Here indeed were "realms of gold." My enjoyment of the rhythmic beauty of "Locksley Hall" & "In Memoriam" was undisturbed by any intellectual effort, as I understood hardly a word of what I was reading. The simpler poems, which I could partially understand—The Queen of the May, & Clara Vere de Vere, for instance—interested me far less; though I confess to a weakness for "The Lord of Burleigh", based, I think, on its documentary interest as a picture of love & marriage. (Subjects which already interested me profoundly.) From this poem I drew the inference that a husband's first act after marriage was to give his wife a concert. ("And a gentle *consort* made he.") As I never asked the meaning of an unknown word, & never hesitated to supply my own definitions, I had a stock of remarkable "readings" of this kind; & I remember, for instance, that many years later, I still thought that persons who had "committed adultery" had to *pay higher rates in travelling* (probably as a punishment of their guilt), because I had seen somewhere, in a train or a ferry-boat, the notice: "*Adults* 50 cents, children 25 cents."

But this increase of knowledge was as nought compared to the sensuous rapture produced by the sound & sight of the words. I never for a moment ceased to be conscious of them. They were visible, almost tangible presences, with faces as distinct as those of the persons among whom I lived. And, like the Erlkönig's daughters, they sang to me so bewitchingly that they almost lured me from the wholesome noonday air of childhood into some strange supernatural region, where the normal pleasures of my age seemed as insipid as the fruits of

the earth to Persephone after she had eaten of the pomegran-
ate seed.

But I perceive that in setting down this record of my
youthful emotions I have not put them in their proper order,
for one of the most intense & enduring awoke in me before I
learned to read. It was the passion for story-telling; a taste so
common to solitary children that it would hardly be worth
mentioning if it had not taken so curious a form in my case.
The peculiarity in question was my associating the act of fiction with the printed page before I could decipher a word of
the latter. I did not want to *tell* the stories I was forever inventing, I wanted to *read them aloud*; & every day for hours I
paced the nursery floor, engaged in the absorbing occupation
of reading these inexhaustible tales from a book which, as
often as not, I held upside down, but of which I never failed
to turn the pages. This strange pursuit was called "making
up", & was carried on long after I learned to read, & always
book in hand. My mother often tried to note down the narratives I poured out, but I "read aloud" so fast that she was
never able to capture more than a few words. I was very particular about the book I used, & my invention flagged unless
I had what I called "the right print"—rather a small type,
with a full page. I remember that some of the Tauchnitz
Trollopes were peculiarly inspiring.

This devastating passion grew on me to such an extent that
my parents became alarmed, & called in the aid of toys &
play-mates to distract me. But the only toys I cared for were
animals, & the only play-mates little boys. Dolls & little girls I
frankly despised, though I tried to be "polite" when their
company was forced upon me. Never shall I forget the long-
drawn weariness of the hours passed with "nice" little girls,
brought in to "spend the day," & unable to converse with me
about Tennyson, Macaulay, or anything that "really mattered". I used to struggle as long as I could against my perilous obsession, & then, when the "pull" became too strong, I
would politely ask my unsuspecting companions to excuse me
while I "went to speak to mamma", & dashing into the
drawing-room would pant out, "Mamma, please go & amuse
those children. *I must make up.*" And in another instant I
would be shut up in her bedroom, & measuring its floor with

rapid strides, while I poured out to my tattered Tauchnitz the accumulated floods of my pent-up eloquence. Oh, the exquisite relief of those moments of escape from the effort of trying to "be like other children"! The rapture of finding myself again in my own rich world of dreams! I don't think I exaggerate or embellish in retrospect the ecstasy which transported my little body & soul when I shut myself in & caught up my precious Tauchnitz. It was really the Pythoness-fury that possessed me!

Of the substance of these endless improvisations I remember nothing, save that they were always about "real people", & *never* about fairies. Fairy-tales bored me, & as I have always had a sense of the "au delà", & of casements opening on the perilous foam of the seas of magic, I can account for the fact only by supposing that I had heard of fairies only through "children's books," a form of literature which I despised, as any intelligent child does after a taste of "real books." Certainly my youthful realism was due to no absence of the anthropomorphic fancy, for the gods of Greece peopled my earliest dreams. When I was not more than five or six, a friend of my father's, who came to dine every Sunday, used to take me on his knee after dinner (one wonders how I came to be up at that hour!), & "tell me mythology". I looked forward to this event during the whole week, for it came next to "making up" in the order of my emotional experiences. It stands out, moreover, as the only glimpse my childhood ever had of the imaginative faculty in others. My parents & my teachers *read* me stories, but were the mere mouth-pieces of what they read; no one else ever *told* me a story, or gave a personal interpretation to the narrative; & our Sunday evening guest was the only person who ever showed signs of knowing anything about the secret story-world in which I lived. No doubt my complete mental isolation intensified all my sensations, & perhaps it now leads me to regard as singular many experiences that may be common to all fanciful children. I can only say that none of the children I knew had the clue to my labyrinth.

I think my parents by this time were beginning to regard me with fear, like some pale predestined child who disappears at night to dance with "the little people". They need not have felt any such anxiety, for all the normal instincts of my sex were strong in me. When my mother died I found among her papers several "brouillons" of letters I had indited to aunts & godmothers. They are all concerned with the "pretty dresses" I wore at various children's parties, & one contains the fatuous phrase "I wish you could have seen me in my white muslin at Elise's birthday party". (Elise Jusserand.) And then the objective world could never lose its charm to me while it contained puppy-dogs & little boys. I loved all forms of young animals, but gave my preference to these two. (Canary-birds I classed with dolls & little girls, as negligible if one could get anything better.) Games in which dogs & little boys took part were the chief joy of what I may call my external life; & I still meet in the alleys of the Champs Elysées, & in the "boschi" of the Pincio & the Boboli gardens, the ghosts of the romping children—the Harrys & Willies & Georgies—with a view to whose subjugation I practised the arts of the ball & the skipping-rope, & shook out my red hair so that it caught the sun!

II

WHEN I WAS nine years old I fell ill of typhoid fever, & lay for weeks at the point of death. We were at Mildbad in the Black Forest, then a small unfashionable "Bad", where my mother was taking the cure. The leading physician of the place (the only one, perhaps) had never seen a case of typhoid, & was obliged to write daily for advice to his son, also a physician, who was with the German army (it was just before the close of the Franco-Prussian war.)

This method of "absent treatment" was not successful, & at last the D^r told my parents that I was dying. That very day they happened to hear that the physician of the Czar of Russia was passing through Mildbad. In their despair they appealed to him, & on his way to the train he stopped at our hotel for five minute, looked at me, changed the treatment— & saved my life.

This illness formed the dividing line between my little-childhood, & the next stage. It obliterated—as far as I can recall—the torturing moral scruples which had darkened my life hitherto, but left me the prey to an intense & unreasoning physical timidity. During my convalescence, my one prayer was to be allowed to read, & among the books given me was one of the detestable "children's books" which poison the youthful mind when they do not hopelessly weaken it. I must do my mother the justice to say that, though wholly indifferent to literature, she had a wholesome horror of what she called "silly books", & always kept them from me; but the volume in question was lent by two little playmates, a brother & sister, who were very "nicely" brought up, & of whom it was to be assumed that they would have only "nice" stories in their possession. To an unimaginative child the tale would no doubt have been harmless; but it was a "robber-story", & with my intense Celtic sense of the super-natural, tales of robbers & ghosts were perilous reading. This one brought on a serious relapse, & again my life was in danger; & when I came to myself, it was to enter a world haunted by formless horrors. I had been naturally a fearless child; now I lived in a state of chronic fear. Fear of *what*? I cannot say—& even at the time, I was never able to formulate my terror. It was like some dark undefinable menace, forever dogging my steps, lurking, & threatening; I was conscious of it wherever I went by day, & at night it made sleep impossible, unless a light & a nurse-maid were in the room. But, whatever it was, it was most formidable & pressing when I was returning from my daily walk (which I always took with a maid or governess, or with my father.) During the last few yards, & while I waited on the door-step for the door to be opened, I could feel it behind me, upon me; & if there was any delay in the opening of the door I was seized by a choking agony of terror. It did not matter who was with me, for no one could protect me; but, oh, the rapture of relief if my companion had a latch-key, & we could get in at once, before It caught me!

This species of hallucination lasted seven or eight years, & I was a "young lady" with long skirts & my hair up before my heart ceased to beat with fear if I had to stand for half a minute on a door-step! I am often inclined—like most people—to think my parents might have brought me up in a manner more suited to my tastes & disposition; but I owe them the deepest gratitude for their treatment of me during this difficult phase. They made as light of my fears as they could, without hurting my feelings; but they never scolded or ridiculed me for them, or tried to "harden" me by making me sleep in the dark, or doing any of things which are supposed to give courage to timid children. I believe it is owing to this kindness & forbearance that my terror gradually wore off, & that I became what I am now—a woman hardly conscious of physical fear. But how long the traces of my illness lasted may be judged from the fact that, till I was twenty-seven or eight, I could not sleep in the room with a book containing a ghost-story, & that I have frequently had to burn books of this kind, because it frightened me to know that they were down-stairs in the library!

Shortly after I recovered from the typhoid fever we went back to America to live. I was keenly interested in this change in our existence, but I shall never forget the bitter disappoint-ment produced by the first impressions of my native country. I was only ten years old, but I had been fed on beauty since my babyhood, & my first thought was: *How ugly it is!*" I have never since thought otherwise, or felt otherwise than as an exile in America; & that this is no retrospective delusion is proved by the fact that I used to dream at frequent intervals that we were going back to Europe, & to wake from this dream in a state of exhilaration which the reality turned to deep depression.

Yet there was much to interest me in our new life, & I was always passionately interested in things! From a wandering existence in continental hotels we went to a comfortable town-house, luxuriously mounted, & a charming country-place on Narrangansett Bay, in the outskirts of Newport, where I found everything to delight the heart of a happy, healthy child—cows, a kitchen-garden full of pears & quinces & straw-berries, a beautiful rose-garden, a stable full of horses (with a dear little poney of my own), a boat, a bath-house, a beautiful sheltered cove to swim in, & best of all, two glorious little boys to swim with! I wonder now that I did not forget all about Europe.

The little boys were our neighbours, the children of Mr Lewis Rutherfurd, the distinguished astronomer (father of Mrs Henry White) whose place "marched" with ours, & who was an intimate friend of my parents. The younger of the two boys, Winthrop Rutherfurd, was just my age, the elder, Lewis, three or four years older. They were two of the most beautiful young creatures it is possible to imagine, the younger espiègle, gay & audacious, the elder grave, tender-hearted & shy. Need I say that I fell in love with the former, & that the latter fell in love with me?

With these delightful companions all my days were spent; for the German governess whom we had brought from Europe having proved unsympathetic & dissatisfied, my parents sent her home, & arranged that I should study with the governess of the Rutherfurd children, who became afterward my own dear pedagogue—Anna Bahlmann. Under such conditions work was pleasant enough; but play was of course infinitely better! *How* we played! I had a poney, Lewis & Winthrop had a donkey, & *everybody* had dogs! Dogs of all ages, sizes & characters swarmed through my early years—& how I loved them! The first—a furry Spitz puppy—was given me before I was four years old, & from that moment I was never without one, except during a brief interval in Europe, when a delicious brown rabbit named "Bonaparte" ruled alone in my heart. I always had a deep, instinctive understanding of animals, a yearning to hold them in my arms, a fierce desire to protect them against pain & cruelty. This feeling seemed to have its source in a curious sense of being somehow, myself, an intermediate creature between human beings & animals, & nearer, on the whole, to the furry tribes than to homo sapiens. I felt that I *knew things about them*— their sensations, desires & sensibilities—that other bipeds could not guess; & this seemed to lay on me the obligation to defend them against their human oppressors. The feeling grew in intensity until it became a morbid preoccupation, and I passed out of the phase of physical fear that I have just described only to be possessed by a haunting consciousness of the sufferings of animals. This lasted for years, & was the last stage of imaginative misery that I passed through before reaching a completely normal & balanced state of mind. I helped to cure myself by working as hard as I could to better the condition of animals wherever I happened to be living, & above all to make the work for their protection take a practical rather than a sentimental form.

Meanwhile at Pencraig (our country place) I was developing a happy healthy young body, learning to row, to swim & to ride, & taking long walks over the rolling rocky wilderness that extended between our place & the Atlantic. Two other little boys (the step-sons of Colonel Jérôme Bonaparte), who were also our neighbours, were admitted to the band; but they were stolid ugly little animals, & played a minor part in our adventures.

Unluckily for me, none of my companions had any imagination, or any taste for books or pictures. I lived one side of life with them, gaily & thoroughly, with every drop of my blood, & every inch of my joyous little body; but of the other wonderful side they never had so much as a guess! I often wonder if any other child possessed of that "other side" was ever so alone in it as I. Certainly none in my experience. All the people I have known who have cared for "les choses de l'esprit" have found some degree of sympathy & companionship either in their families or among their youthful friends. But I never exchanged a word with a really intelligent human being until I was over twenty—& then, alas, I had only a short glimpse of what such communion might be! . . .

So I lived my two lives, the one of physical exercise & healthy natural "fun", & the other, parallel with it, but known to none but myself—a life of dreams & visions, set to the rhythm of the poets, & peopled with thronging images of beauty. I cannot say that either of these lives occupied more space than the other; & perhaps the most curious thing about my youth is the equilibrium preserved between my solitary intellectual sympathies, & the sociable instincts which made me desire to be with other children, & to shine in their company. This eagerness to excel is one of the marked traits of my youth. I wanted to lead, to influence, I wanted—it must be owned!—to *épater*! There is nothing unusual in this, on the part of a clever child; but usually such strongly marked characteristics persist, & in my case the desire to be admired & to dominate died out before I was thirty.

Our return to America had brought me one untold boon— the possibility of access to a library. In the country we had few books, but in town there must have been five or six hundred, which but for me would have slumbered undisturbed behind the glass doors of the book-cases. My mother read nothing but novels & books on horticulture; my father read sermons, & narratives of Arctic exploration. But at that time every gentleman, whether he was a reader or not, possessed what was known as "a gentleman's library"; that is, a fair collection of the "standard" works in French & English. As there were *no novels* on the library shelves (except Scott & Disraeli), I was at once given free access to them, my mother's rule being that I must never read a novel without asking permission, but that "poetry & history" (her rough classification of the rest of literature) could do no harm. I must add that, having been thus put on my honour, I never once failed to observe the compact, & never read a novel without asking leave until the day of my marriage.

Oh, the rapture of my first explorations in that dear dear library! I can see now where almost every volume stood, from the beautiful old Swift & Fielding & Sterne in eighteenth century bindings (from my grandfather's library) to the white vellum Macaulay, with gold tooling & red morocco labels! I can *feel* the rough shaggy surface of the Turkey rug on which I used to lie stretched by the hour, my chin in my hands, poring over one precious volume after the other, & forming fantastic conceptions of life from the heterogeneous wisdom thus absorbed. I could make out a fairly complete list of the volumes; but instead of this, I will try to name, in the order of their importance, those from which I drew my chief intellectual sustenance. First, unquestionably, came Chambers's Encyclopaedia of English Literature, that admirable storehouse of great prose & poetry, in which I learned the cadences of the Areopagitica & the Urn-Burial, & caught fragmentary glimpses of the Elizabethan drama. Oh, how I longed for *more* of Ford & Marlowe & Webster! But the idea that they were obtainable in any other form apparently never occurred to me; & so I read & re-read the great scenes of the Duchess of Malfy, & the Broken Heart & Faustus & Edward II, & tried to write others like them . . . Next came—Coleridge's "Friend". Let no one ask me why! I can only suppose it answered to some hidden need to order my thoughts, & get things into some kind of logical relation to each other: a need which developed in me almost as early as the desire to be kissed & thought pretty! It originated, perhaps, in the sense that weighed on my whole childhood—the sense of bewilderment, of the need of guidance, the longing to understand *what it was all about*. My little corner of the cosmos seemed like a dark trackless region "where ignorant armies clash by night", & I was oppressed by the sense that I was too small & ignorant & alone ever to find my way about in it . . . After Coleridge, came Sainte Beuve, Corneille, Racine, & a very good anthology of French prose & verse. Some of Macaulay's essays I enjoyed, & parts of Augustin Thierry's History. (The vivid Merovingian pictures.) I don't remember trying Gibbon, but I read bits of Carlyle without much enthusiasm (I hated his blustering, bullying tone)—& then I came upon Ruskin! His wonderful cloudy pages gave me back the image of the beautiful Europe I had lost, & woke in me the habit of precise visual observation. The ethical & aesthetical *fatras* were easily enough got rid of later, & as an interpreter of visual impressions he did me incomparable service.

There seem to have been few poets in the library, for I remember reading only Wordsworth (without enthusiasm then.) But soon after this I fell in love with our clergyman, & thereby opened wide the gates of literature. The Revd Dr Washburn, rector of Calvary Church, must have been a man of about fifty-five. He was a scholar & a linguist, & had a beautiful voice. I have always been very sensitive to qualities of intonation, & to beauty of diction, & it was ecstasy to me to sit in the dusky shadowy church, & hear him roll out: "What though I have fought with the beasts at Ephesus?" or "Canst thou loose the sweet influences of the Pleiades?" I was about thirteen when this consuming passion fell upon me, & it raged for three or four years to the exclusion of every other affection. I am not aware that it was ever known to its object; but it led to my making the acquaintance of his daughter, a queer, shy, invalid girl of twenty or so, in whom I suspect there were strong traces of degeneracy. This daughter became passionately, morbidly attached to me; & as she was extremely cultivated, & a great reader (though not really intelligent) she soon saw that I was starving for mental nourishment, & poured it out upon me in reckless profusion. There was no measure to my appetite, & as I knew French, German & Italian as well as English (having learnt them all in my babyhood in Europe), we ranged through four literatures—though chiefly absorbed in German & English. At the same time I was "studying" German literature with Miss Bahlmann, & learning to read Middle High German in order to enjoy the Niebelungen in the original. This led me to read the Edda, & then Miss Washburn suggested that I should learn Anglo-Saxon, in order to "enjoy" (ye gods!) the Saxon Chronicle & Layamon's Brut in the original. "Gesagtgethan"—I was soon fluent in Anglo-Saxon, but, apart from the pleasure derived from "The Battle of Brunanburh", which is glorious, I remember getting no especial satisfaction from this new acquirement, save the hope that Dr Washburn might fall in love with me when he knew that I had learned Anglo-Saxon!

This hope was not fulfilled—but my time was not wasted, since my studies led me naturally to philology, & Skeat, Kemble, Morris, Earle &c, admitted me to new delights. Here I was back in the realm of words, my own native country, as it were; & for the next year or two I was steeped in comparative philology—Marsh, Max Müller, & lutti quanti: all the obsolete "authorities" whose very names I have forgotten! These worthies introduced me to their protégé the Aryan, & in that elusive being & his migrations I long took a passionate interest. Meanwhile my love of poetry & letters was fed by all these studies, & I plunged with rapture into the great ocean of Goethe. At fifteen I had read every word of his plays & poems, Dichtung und Wahrheit, & Wilhelm Meister. (The other novels were *novels*, & therefore prohibited!)

Faust was one of the "epoch-making" encounters for me—another was Keats. A third was—a little volume called "Coppée's Elements of Logic", which I discovered among the books my brother Harry had brought back from Trinity Hall; & of the three, *at the time* it was Coppée who made the greatest difference to me! Here again—explain who will; I can only state the fact. I shall never forget the thrill with which my eye first lit on those arid pages, one day when, in my brother's absence, I was ferreting about in his book-shelves (carefully avoiding the *novels*.) I felt at last as if I had found the clue to life—as if nothing would ever be so dark & bewildering again! As I read, it seemed as if I had known it all before—my mind kept on saying "Of course, of course", as my fascinated eyes flew on from page to page. And when, much later, I read:

"How charming is divine Philosophy;
      Not harsh & crabbèd, as dull fools suppose,
      But musical as is Apollo's lute",
I thought of Coppée, & gave a full assent!

It was certainly providential that, on the same shelf with Coppée, & almost at the same moment, I found an abridged edition of Sir William Hamilton's History of Philosophy! Oh, thrice-blest discovery! Now I was going to know all about life! Now I should never be that helpless blundering thing, a mere "little girl", again! The two little black cloth volumes, with their yellow paper & small black type, were more precious to me than anything I possessed . . .

And all the while Life, real Life, was ringing in my ears, humming in my blood, flushing my cheeks & waving in my hair—sending me messages & signals from every beautiful face & musical voice, & running over me in vague tremors when I rode my poney, or swam through the short bright ripples of the bay, or raced & danced & tumbled with "the boys". And I didn't know—& if, by any chance, I came across the shadow of a reality, & asked my mother "What does it mean?" I was always told "You're too little to understand", or else "It's not nice to ask about such things" . . . Once, when I was seven or eight, an older cousin had told me that babies were not found in flowers but in people. This information had been given unsought, but as I had been told by Mamma that it was "not nice" to enquire into such matters, I had a vague sense of contamination, & went immediately to confess my involuntary offense. I received a severe scolding, & was left with a penetrating sense of "not-niceness" which effectually kept me from pursuing my investigations farther; & this was literally all I knew of the processes of generation till I had been married for several weeks—the explanation which I had meanwhile worked out for myself being that married people "had children" because God saw the clergyman marrying them through the roof of the church!

While I am speaking of this, I will add that, a few days before my marriage, I was seized with such a dread of the whole dark mystery, that I summoned up courage to appeal to my mother, & begged her, with a heart beating to suffocation, to tell me "what being married was like." Her handsome face at once took on the look of icy disapproval which I most dreaded. "I never heard such a ridiculous question!" she said impatiently; & I felt at once how vulgar she thought me.

But in the extremity of my need I persisted. "I'm afraid, Mamma—I want to know what will happen to me!"

The coldness of her expression deepened to disgust. She was silent for a dreadful moment; then she said with an effort: "You've seen enough pictures & statues in your life. Haven't you noticed that men are—made differently from women?"

"Yes," I faltered blankly.

"Well, then—?"

I was silent, from sheer inability to follow, & she brought

out sharply: "Then for heaven's sake don't ask me any more silly questions. You can't be as stupid as you pretend!"

The dreadful moment was over, & the only result was that I had been convicted of stupidity for not knowing what I had been expressly forbidden to ask about, or even to think of! . . . . I record this brief conversation, because the training of which it was the beautiful & logical conclusion did more than anything else to falsify & misdirect my whole life . . . And, since, in the end, it did neither, it only strengthens the conclusion that one is what one is, & that education may delay but cannot deflect one's growth. Only, what possibilities of tragedy may lie in the delay! . . . .

III

ALL THIS TIME my two ruling sentiments—the desire to learn & the desire to "look pretty"—received not the least encouragement. It never occurred to my parents to give me anything beyond the ordinary teaching—French, German, music & drawing—or to have these acquirements made interesting by first-rate teachers. If I had only had a tutor—some one with whom I could talk of what I read, & who would have roused my ambition to study! My good little governess was cultivated & conscientious, but she never struck a spark from me, she never threw a new light on any subject, or made me see the relation of things to each other. My childhood & youth were an intellectual desert.

This fact did not make me feel any superiority to my playmates or to the grown persons about me. On the contrary, it humiliated me to be so "different". I was not a "bright" child in talk, & I often felt at a disadvantage with livelier companions. Yet I had the sense that I had more will, more strength than they. Only I did not care to use it, or know to what use to put it. I did not want to dominate—I wanted to be adored! And yet I detested the admiration of those I did not care for, & unsought demonstrations of affection filled me with repugnance. I was frequently told—perhaps on this account—that I had less "heart" than my brothers. Perhaps I had. Yet if I had been praised a little now & then I might have softened & grown more expressive. But it was thought, at that time, "injudicious" to commend children for their good looks or their intelligence, & wholesome to ridicule them for their supposed defects & affectations. I was laughed at by my brothers for my red hair, & for the supposed abnormal size of my hands & feet; & as I was much the least good-looking of the family, the consciousness of my physical short-comings was heightened by the beauty of the persons about me. My parents—or at least my mother—laughed at me for using "long words", & for caring for dress (in which heaven knows she set me the example!); & under this perpetual cross-fire of criticism I became a painfully shy self-conscious child.

But meanwhile I had found a new refuge from these outward miseries—I had begun to write! My earliest efforts date from my tenth year, & are in the form of poems & stories. Writing paper was apparently hard to obtain, but I begged the right to all the wrapping paper that came into the house, & my earliest works were laboriously inscribed on large brown sheets which I was not clever enough to fold & cut up into "cahiers". I began by sentimental poems, & mawkish stories about little girls who "got lost", but soon passed on to blank verse tragedies—& sermons! I loved writing sermons, & I really think I should have been an ornament to the pulpit.

My mother took an odd inarticulate interest in these youthful productions, & kept a blank book in which she copied many of them. She also perpetrated the folly of having a "selection" privately printed when I was sixteen; & from a recent perusal of these two volumes I am reluctantly obliged to conclude that, with one exception, nothing in my oeuvre de jeunesse showed the slightest spark of originality or talent. The exception is a little poem called "Opportunity", which I wrote when I was about sixteen; & as it is very short I transcribe it here.

—Opportunity—

Who knows his opportunities? They come
Not trumpet-tongued from heaven, but small & dumb,
Not beckoning from the future's promised land,
But in the narrow present close at hand.
They walk beside us with unsounding feet,
And like those two that trod the Eastern street,
And with their Master bartered thought for thought,
Our eyes are holden, & we know them not.

———

Meanwhile my religious preoccupations were increasing, probably because of my absorbing passion for our venerable Rector; & I read, à tort et à travers, every "religious" work I could lay hands on, from the sermons of Frederick Robertson to those of a Revd Dr Cumming, who belonged to some dissenting sect in England, & devoted floods of fiery eloquence to expounding—literally—the number of the Beast & other cryptic allusions of the Apocalypse. As religion was never mentioned in the family (though we went to church regularly every Sunday) I had but the vaguest idea of differences of creed, & did not learn till long afterward that to members of the Episcopalian Church the lucubrations of Dr Cumming represented the rankest heresy. But passionately as I was interested in Christianity, I was always horrified by the sanguinary conception of the Atonement. I remember saying to myself again & again, in moments of deep perplexity: "But if the servants did anything to annoy Mamma, it would be no satisfaction to her to kill Harry or me." Capricious as my mother was, I could not picture her as carrying her illogicalness to that extreme; & it was appalling to think that God must be even more inconsequent. Nevertheless, it never occurred to me then to question the reality of this dreadful Being: I accepted his existence as one of the dark fatalities that seemed to weigh on the lives of mortals; & I think it was at about this time that I wrote in one of my note-books the lugubrious phrase: "If I ever have children I shall deprive them of *every pleasure*, in order to prepare them for the inevitable unhappiness of life"!

The picture I have drawn of myself in these last pages is that of a morbid, self-scrutinizing & unhappy child. I *was* that—& yet I was also, at the same time, a creature of shouts & laughter, of ceaseless physical activity, of little wholesome vanities & glowing girlish enthusiasms. And I was also—& this most of all—the rapt creature who heard the choiring of the spheres, & trembled with a sensuous ecstasy at the sight of beautiful objects, or the sound of noble verse. I was all this in one, & at once, because I was like Egmont's Clärchen, "now wildly exultant, now deeply downcast," & always tossed on the waves of a passionate inner life. I never felt anything *calmly*—& I never have to this day!

Meanwhile a great event had happened in my life—I had been *printed* (not privately, by an admiring parent, but publicly, by a real Editor!) This incident took place when I was about seventeen. I had read an account of a little boy who had been put in the "lock-up" for some childish offense, & had hanged himself in the night. This appealed to the morbid strain in my nature, & I wrote a poem on the subject, which I sent to the Editor of one of the New York papers—I think the World. I had been given, a year or two before, that stimulating work, Quackenbos's rhetoric, & had learned from it the difference between the forms of English (or rather Latin) verse. I knew now when I was writing in Iambic pentameters, & when a dactyl or a spondee fell from my pen. I was proud of this knowledge, & zealous to conform to the "rules of English versification"; and yet—and yet—I couldn't see that Shakespeare or Milton had! This was almost as dark a problem as the Atonement—life & art seemed equally beset with difficulties for a little girl! And whenever I took to poetry myself, I found the lawless "redundant syllables" slipping in—& I generally let them stay. But it was one thing to write for one's own pleasure, another to appear in print; & knowing that the Editor of the World would probably have a sharp eye for metrical irregularities I was much troubled by the loose construction of my poem on the little boy. Yet my deepest instinct told me that it was right as it was, & after much debate I finally enclosed with it a note to the Editor in which I carefully explained that I "knew the rules of English versification", but that I had put in the extra syllables *on purpose!* I received a kind note, in which my course was fully approved; & the poem was published in all its native redundancy! It must have been at about the same time that Allan Rice, a friend of my brother Harry's, & at that time Editor of the North American Review, took a friendly interest in my scribblings, & sent some of them to Longfellow, who wrote in reply that they "showed promise", or some equally non-committal phrase. On the strength of this my friend sent them to Mr Howells, who was then Editor of the Atlantic, & Mr Howells politely published them. I can't remember what the poems were about, or when they appeared.

At this point my literary activity was checked by a much more important event: I "came out." Conventionally speaking—& everything in our family life was ordered according to convention—this important experience should have been postponed till I was eighteen; but (as I learned afterward) my parents were alarmed at my growing shyness, at my passion for study, & my indifference to the companionship of young people of my own age, and it was therefore decided that, contrary to all precedent, I should be taken into the world at seventeen. The step decided on, there followed a feverish period of dress-making; & at last one evening, with my shoulders bare, & my head coiffée, for the first time, I followed my father & mother to a ball at the house of Mrs L. P. Morton (the mother of the Duchess de Valençay.) I had hardly crossed the threshold of the ball-room before three men asked me to dance; I refused the first two in an agony of shyness, but consented to dance the Cotillion with the third, because he was "much older", & I had always known him. That evening was a pink blur of emotion—but after it was over my mother had no fears for me! For the rest of the winter, I don't think I missed a ball; & wherever I went I had all the dancers I wanted. There was nothing wonderful in this, for I had grown up among my brother Harry's friends, handsome gay young men some ten or twelve years older than I, & all of them among the leading "valseurs" of fashionable New York. It amused them to be kind to their friend's young sister, & as plenty of youths of my own age were naturally soon added to the group, I tasted all the sweets of popularity. Oh, how I loved it all—my pretty frocks, the flowers, the music, the sense that everybody "liked" me, & wanted to talk to me & dance with me! But I was not asked only to balls—I was invited constantly to dinners, with "the older girls" & the young married women. In those days the young married women ruled New York society, & the girl who found favour in their eyes, & was taken into their intimate circle, had a lot far more agreeable & interesting than that of the average "débutante". This good luck befell me at once—partly, no doubt, owing to the fact that my handsome brother Harry was at that time one of the most popular men in society—& I thus passed immediately from the pink-&-white anonymity of the girl in her first season into the group of the specific & the chosen.

In spite of these privileges, no very brilliant adventures happened to me. As it had been in my little-girlhood, so it was now: I led, I dominated, I was conscious of "counting" wherever I went—but I inspired no romantic passions! It may be added that I felt none, & that the two or three young men who—in the natural course of things—honoured me with their devotion, inspired me with no feelings but that of a friendly liking. I did not fall in love till I was twenty-one.

It was as well for me that I was allowed this premature dip into the world, for the following summer my dear kind father fell ill, & it was decreed by the Doctors that he must spend the winter in a warm climate . . . So we were going back to Europe at last! During our seven years at home, through all my other interests & emotions, the longing to return had persisted; & now all the delights of society — & heaven knows I didn't underrate them! — were as nothing to the joy of knowing that my wish was to be fulfilled. Without a pang I gave up the prospect of a "gay" winter, & turned my back on the various pretendants who had occupied my leisure without stirring my heart. I was going to see pictures & beautiful things again, & odd contradictory creature that I was, I went without a backward glance! . . . . . I remember, as distinctly as if it were all happening to me now, the emotions with which I found myself standing in the Salon Carré, soon after our arrival in Paris. I had spent rapturous hours in the National Gallery, on our way through London, & had made there a memorable acquaintance — that of Franciabigio's Knight of Malta, whose motto, Tar Ublia chi bien eima, I had written down in my diary — but, vividly as I remember my first moments there, they come back to me with less intensity than that first rush of sensation before the Giorgione, the Titian & the Mona Lisa. I felt as if all the great waves of the sea of Beauty were breaking over me at once — & at the same time I remember being conscious of the notice of the persons about me, & wondering whether I should be "thought pretty in Paris"!

From that day I never had a pang of regret for "society" — I was drunk with seeing & learning! We went to Cannes in December, & settled ourselves there for the winter, & the mild climate & open-air life did my father so much good that we became hopeful of his complete recovery. At Cannes we met my mother's old friends, the Comtesse de Bañuelos (mother of the Comtesse de Suzannet & the Comtesse d'Alcedo), & her sister, the Comtesse de Sartiges (mother of Mrs Lee-Childe.) Through these friends I was taken into the little set of amiable & hospitable French & English families constituting Cannes "society" — the Duchesse de Luynes, the Duchesse de Vallembrosa, Lady Kinnoull, Lady Blanche

Baillie, Admiral Glyn & his son & daughter, (now Lord Wolverton & Lady Norreys) the Comte de St Priest, & others whom I have forgotten. The most agreeable house at Cannes was the Villa Luynes, & there I went constantly, & made friends with the group of young girls—cousins of the Duchess's—who were always to be found there; & more especially with Yvonne de Contades (now the Marquise de Montboissier), Marie de Contades, (Ctesse Arthur de Vogüé), & the P^{cesse} Jeanne de Polignac (Ctesse d'Oilliamson.) The Prince de Poix, & the present Duc de Luynes & his sister (the Duchesse de Noailles) were the youngest members of the band—& we all used to be together constantly, playing tennis, going on picnics, &c . . . I mention this because it is rather curious that, after losing sight of this little group for over twenty years, I came back to Paris & took up my friendship with them all—except the P^{ce} de Poix, who was dead.

It was all very pleasant, but it was not intellectually stimulating, & in regard to "les choses de l'esprit" I was no better off than I had been at home. In fact, all my keenest pleasure in Cannes came from my joy in the scenery & the flowers, & in the wonderful white poodle, "Mouton", whom my father had bought for me in Paris. Two of the young men who had wanted to marry me in New York the previous year appeared in the course of the winter; but though I found them agreeable companions on our trips to Monte Carlo, I felt no wish to unite myself with either of them.

In the spring my father was better, & we started on a trip to Italy. I had been saturated in Ruskin, & the result was that, at least, I saw many things which the average Baedeker-led tourist of that day certainly missed. When I remember the hours I spent at San Giorgio dei Schiavoni, when I recall my thrill of delight at the first sight of "Ilaria del Caretto" at Lucca, & the joy of puzzling out the stories of the frescoes at Santa Maria Novella & in the Spanish Chapel, I cannot disown my debt to Ruskin. To Florence & Venice his little volumes gave a meaning, a sense of organic relation, which no other books attainable by me at that time could possibly have conveyed. Even if I had known of Burckhardt's Cultur der Renaissance in Italien I doubt if its compact form & serried array of facts would not have discouraged me, & if Ruskin was not the best possible preparation for the enjoyment of the authors who afterward led me away from him. My father, who had a vague enjoyment in "sight-seeing", unaccompanied by any artistic or intellectual curiosity, or any sense of the relations of things to each other, was delighted to take me about, & with our Ruskin in hand we explored every corner of Florence & Venice. Milan I did not appreciate till later, & I don't think we saw many of the smaller towns; at any rate, later visits have effaced my first impressions of all save Pisa & Lucca.

In the summer we went to Germany, to Mildbad & Homburg, where my parents took the cure. Here I was rather bored, & tried to distract myself by the only "flirtation" which I have ever indulged in. Among our acquaintances at Homburg was the Livingston family, of New York. The daughter, a dull & rather solemn girl of about my age was engaged to a very good-looking & amusing young man (Geraldyn R.—) also of New York, who was known to be in pursuit of an heiress. The engagement was not announced, (I believe because the L. parents wanted a richer prétendant), & the young lady, who was desperately éprise, was therefore unable to assert any exclusive right to her fiancé's society. It was visible at a glance that she loved him, & the situation appealed to my sense of humour, as one which it might be amusing to complicate a little. I had never cared for "flirting," since I was totally indifferent to the admiration of men whom I did not like, & far too proud to pay any man the honour of feigning to like him more than I really did. But Geraldyn R. was a very amusing companion, & found me very much to his taste. I knew he would never give up his heiress, & that the whole episode would be a mere intermezzo in both our lives; but I liked his admiration, & he liked my sense of fun, & I believe it amused us both to keep his poor fiancée on the rack for a few weeks. It was an innocent enough adventure, but it is the only one on which I ever embarked with malice prepense—& I *did* make the other girl miserable!

Chronology

1862   Born January 24 at 14 West 23rd Street, New York City, and baptized Edith Newbold Jones; third and last child of George Frederic Jones and Lucretia Stevens Rhinelander (brothers are Frederic, b. 1846, and Henry, b. 1850). Parents belong to long-established, socially prominent New York families. Father's income based on Manhattan land-holdings.

1865   Receives gift of spitz puppy, beginning a lifelong passion for small dogs.

1866   Post–Civil War depression in real estate market causes family to move to Europe for prolonged residence. Sails to England in November with parents, nurse Hannah Doyle ("Doyley"), and brother Henry, who begins law studies at Trinity Hall College, Cambridge.

1867   Family spends year in Rome.

1868   Family travels through Spain and settles in Paris. Taught to read by father; recites Tennyson for visiting maternal grandmother. Begins "making up," inventing stories using parents and their friends as characters.

1870–71   Stays at Wildbad, a spa in Württemberg, while mother takes water cure. Studies New Testament in German, takes walks in Black Forest. Suffers severe attack of typhoid fever (later remembers convalescence as beginning of recurrent apprehension of "some dark undefinable menace forever dogging my steps, lurking and threatening"). Family settles in Florence at end of 1870.

1872–75   Family returns to the United States, dividing year between three-story brownstone on West 23rd Street, New York, and Pencraig, their summer home in Newport, Rhode Island. At Pencraig rides pony, swims in cove, watches archery contests, visits neighboring family of astronomer Lewis Rutherfurd. Studies French, medieval and romantic German poetry with Rutherfurd family governess, Anna Bahlmann (who later becomes her governess). Begins life-long friendship with sister-in-law Mary Cadwalader Jones, wife (later divorced) of brother Frederic. In father's eight-hundred-volume New York library finds histories (including Plutarch, Macaulay, Carlyle, Parkman), diaries and correspondence (Pepys, Cowper, Madame de Sévigné), criticism (Sainte-Beuve), art history and archaeology (Ruskin, Schliemann), poetry (Homer and Dante in translation, most English poets, some French), and a few novels (Scott, Irving). Mother forbids the reading of contemporary fiction. Later remembers reading as "a secret ecstasy of communion." Summer 1875, forms close friendship with Emelyn, daughter of Edward Abiel Washburn, rector of Calvary Church, New York.

1876–77   Begins *Fast and Loose*, 30,000-word novella about trials of ill-starred young lovers, autumn 1876. Keeps enterprise secret from everyone except Emelyn Washburn. Finished January 1877, manuscript includes mock hostile reviews ("every character is a failure, the plot a vacuum").

1878–79   *Verses*, volume of twenty-nine poems, printed in Newport, arranged and paid for by mother. Summer 1879, Newport neighbor Allen Thorndike Rice shows some of the poems to Henry Wadsworth Longfellow and then sends them to William Dean Howells. Howells publishes one in *Atlantic Monthly*. Makes social debut.

1880–81   Two poems appear in the New York *World*. Courted in New York, Newport, and Bar Harbor, Maine, by Henry Leyden Stevens, twenty-one-year-old son of prominent social figure, Mrs. Paran Stevens. November 1880, goes to southern France with mother and ailing father. Henry Stevens joins them September 1881.

1882   Father, age sixty-one, dies in Cannes in March. Inherits over $20,000 in trust fund. August, engagement to Henry Stevens announced in Newport, with marriage scheduled for autumn. Engagement is broken off, apparently at insistence of Mrs. Stevens. Travels with mother to Paris.

1883   Spends summer at Bar Harbor. Meets Walter Van Rensselaer Berry, twenty-four-year-old Harvard graduate studying for admission to the District of Columbia bar.

They become close, but Berry leaves without proposing marriage. In August, Edward Robbins ("Teddy") Wharton, friend of brother Henry, arrives in Bar Harbor and begins courtship. A thirty-three-year-old Harvard graduate interested mainly in camping, hunting, fishing, and riding, he lives with his family in Boston and receives a $2,000 annuity from them.

1884   Hires Catherine Gross, Alsatian immigrant, as personal attendant (she will be Wharton's companion and housekeeper for over four decades).

1885–88   Marries Edward Wharton April 29, 1885, at Trinity Chapel, New York City. Henry Stevens dies of tuberculosis, July 18, 1885. Whartons move into Pencraig Cottage, small house on mother's Newport estate, leaving every February for four months of European travel, mostly in Italy. Introduced by Egerton Winthrop, wealthy New York art collector and their occasional traveling companion, to contemporary French literature and works of Darwin, Huxley, Spencer, Haeckel, and other writers on evolution. Whartons spend a year's income (about $10,000) on four-month Aegean cruise, 1888. Learns in Athens that she has inherited $120,000 from reclusive New York cousin Joshua Jones.

1889   Rents small house on Madison Avenue, New York City. Four poems accepted for publication by *Scribner's Magazine*, *Harper's Monthly*, and *Century Illustrated Monthly Magazine*.

1890–92   Suffers intermittently from inexplicable nausea and fatigue. Short story, "Mrs. Manstey's View," accepted by *Scribner's* May 1890, published July 1891. Purchases narrow house on Fourth Avenue near 78th Street (eventually 884 Park Avenue) for $19,670 in November 1891. (A few years later acquires its adjoining twin at 882 Park for the household staff to live in.) Works on long short story, "Bunner Sisters." It is rejected by *Scribner's*, December 1892.

1893   Buys Land's End, Newport estate overlooking the Atlantic, for $80,000 in March. Works with Boston architect Ogden Codman on decoration of its interior. French novelist Paul Bourget and his wife are guests. Three stories, "That Good May Come," "The Fulness of Life," and "The Lamp of Psyche," accepted by *Scribner's*, whose editor, Edward Burlingame, proposes a short-story volume for Charles Scribner's Sons. Wharton agrees, suggesting inclusion of "Bunner Sisters." Sails for Europe in December.

1894–95   Burlingame rejects "Something Exquisite" (later revised and published as "Friends"). Writes to him from Florence, expressing gratitude for his criticism and doubt about her own abilities. Travels through Tuscany. Visits Violet Paget ("Vernon Lee"), English novelist and historian of eighteenth-century Italy. After research at monastery of San Vivaldo and in Florence museums, identifies group of terra-cotta sculptures, previously thought to date from the seventeenth century, as work of the late fifteenth–early sixteenth century school of the Robbias. Writes article for *Scribner's* on her findings and surrounding Tuscan landscape. Notifies Burlingame in July 1894 that short-story volume will need another six months to prepare. Suffering from intense exhaustion, nausea, and melancholia, breaks off correspondence with Burlingame for sixteen months. Mother moves to Paris (brothers Frederic and Henry both live in Europe); meetings and correspondence with her become infrequent. Writes "The Valley of Childish Things, and Other Emblems," collection of ten short fables, and sends it in December 1895 to Burlingame, who rejects it.

1896–97   Writes, with architect Ogden Codman, *The Decoration of Houses*, study of interior arrangements and furnishings in upper-class city homes. Shows incomplete manuscript to Burlingame, who gives it to William Brownell, senior editor at Scribner's. Summer 1897, resumes friendship with Walter Berry, who stays for a month at Land's End, assisting Wharton in the revision of *The Decoration of Houses* (Codman is incapacitated by sunstroke). Wharton persuades Brownell to increase the number of halftone plates and makes extensive recommendations concerning the book's design. Published by Scribner's December 1897; sales are unexpectedly good.

1898   Writes and revises seven stories between March and July, despite recurring illness. In letter to Burlingame, discusses her earliest stories: "I regard them as the excesses of youth. They were all written 'at the top of my voice,' & The Fulness of Life is one long shriek—I may not write any better, but at least I hope that I write in a lower key . . ." Suffers mental and physical breakdown in August. Goes to Philadelphia in October to take the "rest cure" invented by Dr. S. Weir Mitchell and is treated as an outpatient under Mitchell's supervision. Therapy involves massage, electrical stimulation of the muscles, abundant eating, and near total isolation.

1899   January, settles with Edward for four-month stay in house at 1329 K Street in Washington, found for them by Walter Berry, who becomes close literary adviser and supporter. *The Greater Inclination*, long-delayed collection of short stories, published by Scribner's in March to enthusiastic reviews; sales exceed 3,000 copies. Protests to Scribner's that book has been insufficiently advertised. Begins extensive correspondence with Sara Norton, daughter of Harvard professor Charles Eliot Norton. Summer, travels in Europe, joined by the Bourgets in Switzerland; tours northern Italy with them, through Bergamo and Val Camonica. Returns to Land's End in September. Seeking escape from Newport climate, visits Lenox, Massachusetts, in fall.

1900   Novella, *The Touchstone* (in England, *A Gift from the Grave*), appears in the March and April *Scribner's*; published by Scribner's in April, selling 5,000 copies by year's end. Travels in England, Paris, and northern Italy, again accompanied by the Bourgets. Spends summer and fall at inn in Lenox while Edward goes on yachting trip. Begins concerted work on novel *The Valley of Decision*. Sends Henry James copy of "The Line of Least Resistance"; he responds with praise and detailed criticism, encouraging further effort. Wharton removes story from volume being prepared.

1901   February to June, negotiates purchase for $40,600 of 113-acre Lenox property extending into the village of Lee. After breaking with Codman over his fee, hires architect Francis V. L. Hoppin to design house modeled on Christopher Wren's Belton House in Lincolnshire, England.

Oversees landscaping and gardening. *Crucial Instances*, second volume of stories, published by Scribner's in April. Mother dies in Paris, age seventy-six, on June 28. Her will leaves large sums outright to Frederic and Henry but creates a trust fund for Wharton's share of the remainder of the estate. Trust eventually amounts to $90,000; total annual income from parents' and Joshua Jones's trusts is about $22,000. Wharton visits London and Paris and persuades her brothers to make husband Edward co-trustee with brother Henry. Works on play *The Man of Genius* (never finished) and on dramatization of Prosper Mérimée's *Manon Lescaut* (never produced).

1902   *The Valley of Decision*, historical novel set in eighteenth-century Italy, published by Scribner's in February. Wharton criticizes its design while it is being prepared. Suffers collapse (nausea, depression, fatigue) after publication. Reviews are generally enthusiastic and sales are good. Begins *Disintegration*, novel set in contemporary New York society, but does not finish it. Writes travel articles, poetry, theatrical reviews, and literary criticism, including essays on Gabriele D'Annunzio and George Eliot. Translates Hermann Sudermann's play *Es Lebe das Leben* as *The Joy of Living* (it runs briefly on Broadway and sells in book form for a number of years). Henry James writes Wharton in August that *The Valley of Decision* is "accomplished, pondered, saturated" and "brilliant and interesting from a literary point of view," but urges her to abandon historical subject matter "in favour of the American subject. There it is round you. Don't pass it by—the immediate, the real, the only, the yours, the novelist's that it waits for. Take hold of it and keep hold and let it pull you where it will . . . *Do New York!* The 1st-hand account is precious." Meets Theodore Roosevelt in Newport at christening of his godchild, son of Wharton's friends Margaret and Winthrop Chanler, beginning a long friendship. Moves into Lenox house, named "The Mount" after Long Island home of Revolutionary War ancestor Ebenezer Stevens, in September. Edward suffers first of series of nervous collapses.

1903   January, sails for Italy with ailing husband. Travels slowly north from Rome through Tuscany, the Veneto, and

Lombardy, inspecting estates for series of articles commissioned by R. W. Gilder for *Century*. Enjoys her first automobile ride. Visits Violet Paget at Villa Pomerino outside of Florence. Meets art expert Bernhard Berenson, who strongly dislikes her. Goes to Salsomaggiore, west of Parma, for treatment of her asthma. Spends summer and fall at The Mount, with interval at Newport. Sells Land's End for $122,500, June 13. Begins *The House of Mirth*. Novella *Sanctuary* published by Scribner's in October. Sails for England, early December. First conversations with Henry James, who comes up from Rye to London in mid-December.

1904   Purchases her first automobile, a Panhard-Levassor. With Edward driving, travels south to Hyères for a stay with the Bourgets, then to Cannes and Monte Carlo and back across France. In England, visits Henry James in Rye and tours Sussex with him. Returns to Lenox in late spring. Enthusiastic about motor travel, hires Charles Cook as a permanent chauffeur (he retains this position until 1921, when he suffers a stroke). *The Descent of Man*, collection of stories, published by Scribner's in April. After reading reviews, writes Brownell that "the continued cry that I am an echo of Mr. James (whose books of the last ten years I can't read, much as I delight in the man) . . . makes me feel rather hopeless." Hires Anna Bahlmann as secretary and literary assistant. Agrees with Burlingame in August to begin serialization of *The House of Mirth* in January 1905 *Scribner's*; undertakes schedule of intense work (usually writing in the morning) to meet deadline. (Finishes in March 1905; serialized Jan.–Nov.) House guests at The Mount include Brooks Adams and his wife, George Cabot Lodge (son of Senator Henry Cabot Lodge), Walter Berry, and Gaillard Lapsley, American-born don of medieval history at Trinity College, Cambridge. Henry James arrives in October with his friend Howard Sturgis, whom Wharton calls "the kindest and strangest of men." *Italian Villas and Their Gardens*, based on magazine articles, published by The Century Company in November. Returns to New York just before Christmas.

1905   Henry James visits at 884 Park Avenue for a few days in January. Whartons dine at the White House with President Roosevelt in March. *Italian Backgrounds*, sketches written since 1894, published by Scribner's in March. After European trip in spring, including visit to Salsomaggiore for asthma treatment, returns to The Mount. House guests include printer Berkeley Updike, illustrator Moncure Robinson, publisher Walter Maynard, Robert Grant, novelist and judge of the probate court in Boston, and Henry James. Visits Sara and Charles Eliot Norton. *The House of Mirth* published by Scribner's, October 14, in first printing of 40,000; 140,000 copies in print by the end of the year, "the most rapid sale of any book ever published by Scribner," according to Brownell. Literary earnings for year exceed $20,000. Henry James writes Wharton that the novel is an "altogether superior thing" but "better written than composed." Reviews generally favorable. December, undertakes collaboration on stage version with playwright Clyde Fitch.

1906   Sails for France, March 10. Through Paul Bourget, enters intellectual and social circles of Paris, especially those of the Faubourg St. Germain. Among new acquaintances are poet Comtesse Anna de Noailles, historian Gustave Schlumberger, and his close friend, Comtesse Charlotte de Cossé-Brissac. Goes to England at the end of April. Whartons and Henry James make short motor tour of England. Visits Queen's Acre, Howard Sturgis's home in Windsor, for the first time (it soon becomes the center of her English social life). Meets Percy Lubbock, young writer and disciple of Henry James. Returns to France and takes motor tour with brother Henry, visiting cathedrals at Amiens and Beauvais, and Nohant, home of George Sand. Returns to Lenox in June. Works on novel *Justine Brent* (later retitled *The Fruit of the Tree*). Novella *Madame de Treymes* appears in the August *Scribner's* (published by Scribner's in February 1907). September, goes to Detroit with Edward and Walter Berry to see first performance of stage version of *The House of Mirth*. October opening in New York is a critical and commercial failure; Wharton calls the experience "instructive." Edward is away from Lenox, hunting and fishing, during much of the fall. Literary earnings for the year total almost $32,000.

1907   Returns to Paris in January and rents the apartment of the George Vanderbilts at 58 Rue de Varenne, in the heart of

the Faubourg St. Germain. *The Fruit of the Tree* serialized
in *Scribner's*, January–November. March, takes a "motor-
flight" through France with Edward and Henry James,
visiting Nohant and touring southern France. Invites
James to stay for another month, and takes a short automobile trip with James and Gaillard Lapsley. Engages in-
structor to teach her contemporary French; for a lesson
exercise, writes a precursor sketch of *Ethan Frome*. April,
sees much of William Morton Fullerton, forty-two-year-
old Paris correspondent for the London *Times*, former student of Charles Eliot Norton, and disciple of Henry
James. Spends summer at The Mount. Sales of *The Fruit of
the Tree*, published by Scribner's in October, reach 60,000.
Reviews are good. Fullerton arrives at The Mount in October for a visit of several days. Wharton begins a journal
addressed to him. Returns to Paris in December. *The
House of Mirth* appears as *Chez les Heureux du Monde* in
the *Revue de Paris*, translated by Charles du Bos, a young
follower of Bourget.

1908   January–February, Edward afflicted by "nervous depres-
            sion." Wharton leads active social life, seeing linguist Vi-
            comte Robert d'Humières, American ambassador Henry
            White, watercolorist Walter Gay and his wife, Matilda,
            James Van Alen, Fullerton, Comtesse Rosa de Fitz-James,
            Bourget, playwright Paul Hervieu, Charles du Bos, and
            others. February, spends time with Fullerton while Ed-
            ward is away, and begins an affair with him in March.
            Edward, suffering from depression and pervasive pain,
            leaves for spa at Hot Springs, Arkansas, March 21. Whar-
            ton writes Brownell that Edward's illness has prevented
            her from making much progress on new novel, *The Cus-
            tom of the Country*, and doubts that it will be ready for
            serial publication by January 1909. April, moves to brother
            Henry's townhouse on Place des Etats-Unis when he goes
            to America on business. Egerton Winthrop visits. When
            Henry James visits, arranges to have Jacques Emile
            Blanche paint portrait that she considers the best ever
            done of him. May, has first significant meetings with
            Henry Adams. Meditates in her journal on the propriety
            of her affair with Fullerton; writes series of love sonnets.
            May 22, gives Fullerton journal addressed to him; he re-
            turns it the following day as she leaves for America. On
            fifth day of crossing, writes story "The Choice"; resumes

work on *The Custom of the Country*. In Lenox, has difficulty breathing for six weeks. Scribner's publishes *The
Hermit and the Wild Woman*, fourth collection of stories,
in September, *A Motor-Flight Through France*, travel account, in October. Writes poetry, enjoys reading Nietz-
sche's *Jenseits von Gut und Böse (Beyond Good and Evil)*.
Leaves for Europe, October 30. Introduced by Henry
James to aging George Meredith at Box Hill, near London, goes with James Barrie to see performance of his play
What Every Woman Knows. At Stanway, Gloucestershire
home of Lady Mary Elcho, meets two young Englishmen
who become close friends: Robert Norton, a landscape
painter, and John Hugh Smith, a banker expert in Anglo-
Russian financial affairs. Sees much of Henry James, who
soon professes exhaustion from her visits, referring to her
as "the Angel of Devastation." Crosses to France with
Howard Sturgis for Christmas. Literary earnings for year
are about $15,000.

1909   January, Edward arrives in Paris, suffering from insomnia
and inexplicable pain in his face and limbs. Work on *The
Custom of the Country* again interrupted. Edward returns
to Lenox in mid-April. *Artemis to Actaeon*, book of poetry,
published by Scribner's in late April. Continues to write
poetry, including "Ogrin the Hermit," long narrative
based on a portion of the Tristan and Iseult legend. When
lease on 58 Rue de Varenne expires, moves to large suite
in Hotel Crillon, Place de la Concorde, April. Involves
Henry James and Frederick Macmillan, Fullerton's publisher, in complicated scheme to conceal gift of money to
Fullerton to meet blackmail demands of an ex-mistress.
June, goes to London with Fullerton; they spend the
night at the Charing Cross Hotel. After Fullerton leaves
for America, writes "Terminus," fifty-two-line love poem.
Stays in England until mid-July, visiting with Sturgis,
Lapsley, and James. When Fullerton returns, they spend
night in Rye at James's Lamb House. September, Henry
Adams arranges another meeting between Wharton and
Bernhard Berenson. Friendship develops. Edward arrives
in Paris with his sister Nancy in November; soon confesses
to Wharton that during the summer he sold some of her
holdings, bought property in Boston, and lived there with
his mistress. Edward returns to Boston. Later admits to
embezzling $50,000 from Wharton's trust funds; makes

restitution by drawing upon $67,000 recently inherited from his mother.

1910   Moves into apartment at 53 Rue de Varenne, January. Writes stories "The Eyes" and "The Triumph of Night." Sells New York houses. Goes to England in March to see Henry James, who is recovering from a nervous breakdown. Edward returns to Paris, agrees to enter Swiss sanatorium for treatment of his depression. Begins short novel *Ethan Frome*. Walter Berry moves to Paris, stays in Whartons' guest suite for several months. July 3, sees Nijinsky dance in *L'Oiseau de Feu*. Affair with Fullerton ends. Visits Henry and William James at Lamb House in August. Sails in September to New York with Edward. October, Edward departs on trip around the world; Wharton returns to Paris, ill and exhausted. *Tales of Men and Ghosts* published by Scribner's in October; sells about 4,000 copies.

1911   January, confesses to Hugh Smith that "my writing tires and preoccupies me more than it used to." Tries unsuccessfully with William Dean Howells and Edmund Gosse to secure the Nobel Prize for Henry James. May, at Salsomaggiore for hay fever; resumes concerted work on *The Custom of the Country*. Returns to Lenox at end of June. Has Henry James, Hugh Smith, and Lapsley as guests. Wharton and Edward agree to formal separation in late July, then reverse decision. Returns to Europe in September after entrusting Edward with power to sell The Mount. *Ethan Frome* serialized in *Scribner's* from August through October, published by Scribner's in September. Reviewers in America and England call it one of her finest achievements. Disappointed with Scribner's reports of sales (4,200 copies by mid-November), Wharton protests lack of advertising, poor distribution, and bad typesetting. Tours central Italy and visits Berenson for the first time at his home, Villa I Tatti, near Florence, in October. Puts *The Custom of the Country* aside in November to work on novel *The Reef*.

1912   Edward arrives in February at Rue de Varenne and stays until May. Relations remain distant and strained. Visits La Verna, monastery in Tuscany mountains, with Berry; their car must be lowered by ropes for them to return. Sale of The Mount for undisclosed sum completed in June. Offers to live with Edward in United States, but he refuses. Summer, sees much of Henry James during visits to England. Arranges with Charles Scribner for $8,000 of her royalties to be given to James under the guise of an advance for his novel-in-progress, *The Ivory Tower*. (James receives $3,600 in 1913; the novel is never completed.) *The Reef* published by D. Appleton and Company, which had given her $15,000 advance. Reviews are relatively poor; sales reach 7,000. Resumes work on *The Custom of the Country*.

1913　　　*The Custom of the Country* appears in *Scribner's*, January–November. Receives unexpected letter from brother Henry denouncing her for coldness toward Countess Tecla, his mistress and intended wife. Sues Edward for divorce on grounds of adultery; Paris tribunal grants decree, April 16. Helps to initiate effort to raise gift of $5,000 for Henry James's seventieth birthday; effort abandoned when James discovers and angrily rejects it. Drives across Sicily with Berry in April. Friendship develops with Geoffrey Scott, author of *The Architecture of Humanism*. Favorably impressed by premiere of Igor Stravinsky's ballet *Le Sacre du Printemps* in Paris, May 29. Considers buying house outside of London, but eventually decides against it. August, finishes *The Custom of the Country*. Travels with Berenson through Luxembourg and Germany, stopping at Cologne, Dresden, and Berlin. Begins novel *Literature*, never completed. *The Custom of the Country* published by Scribner's in October; sales reach nearly 60,000. December, attends wedding of niece, landscape gardener Beatrix Jones (daughter of brother Frederic and Mary Cadwalader) and Yale historian Max Farrand, in New York. Finds New York "queer, rootless" and "overwhelming."

1914　　　Returns to Paris in January. Sends Henry James copy of Marcel Proust's recently published *Du Côté de chez Swann*. March, sails from Marseilles to Algiers with Percy Lubbock and Anna Bahlmann. Drives through northern Algeria and Tunisia, "an unexpurgated page of the Arabian Nights!" Frightened in Timgad, Algeria, by intruder in her room, who flees when she screams. July, tours Spain with Berry for three weeks, viewing cave paintings at

Altamira. Returns to Paris July 31, three days before outbreak of war between France and Germany. August, establishes workroom near Rue de Varenne for seamstresses and other women thrown out of work by the economic disruption of general mobilization. Collects funds, selects supervisory staff, arranges for supply of work orders, free lunches, and coal allotments. Late August, goes to Stocks, English country house rented from novelist Mrs. Humphry Ward, a trip planned before the war. Sees Henry James at Rye. After learning of battle of the Marne, makes arrangements, with difficulty, to return to Paris; succeeds by end of September. November, establishes and directs American Hostels for Refugees. Selects Elisina Tyler, friend since 1912, as administrative deputy; raises $100,000 in first twelve months. (Hostels assist 9,330 refugees by end of 1915, providing free or low-cost food, clothing, coal, housing, medical and child care, and assistance in finding work.)

1915   February, visits the front in the Argonne and at Verdun. Tours hospitals, investigating need for blankets and clothing; watches French assault on village of Vauquois. Makes five more visits to front in next six months, including tour of forward trenches in the Vosges; describes them in articles for *Scribner's* (collected in *Fighting France, from Dunkerque to Belfort*, published by Scribner's in November). April, organizes Children of Flanders Rescue Committee with Tyler, establishing six homes between Paris and the Normandy coast. Committee sets up classes in lace-making for girls, industrial training for boys, French for Flemish speakers. Nearly 750 Flemish children, many of them tubercular, cared for in 1915. Increasingly concentrates on fund-raising and creation of sponsoring committees in France and the United States, delegating daily administration to Tyler. Arranges benefit concerts and an art exhibition. Edits *The Book of the Homeless* (published by Scribner's early in 1916), with introductions by Marshal Joffre and Theodore Roosevelt. Contributors of poetry, essays, art, fiction, and musical scores include Cocteau, Conrad, Howells, Anna de Noailles, Hardy, Yeats, Eleanora Duse, Sarah Bernhardt, Henry James, Max Beerbohm, Paul Claudel, Edmond Rostand, Monet, Leon Bakst, and Stravinsky. Wharton does most of the translations. Proceeds (approximately $8,000 from the book,

$7,000 from the sale of art and manuscripts) go to Hos-
tels and Rescue Committee. Friendship develops with
André Gide, who serves on a Hostels committee. October,
makes short visit to England. Learns in December that
Henry James is dying; writes Lapsley: "His friendship has
been the pride & honour of my life."

1916   Henry James dies February 28. Spring, helps establish
treatment program for tubercular French soldiers. Made
Chevalier of the Legion of Honor, April 8. Mourns deaths
of Egerton Winthrop (tells Berenson that Winthrop and
Henry James "made up the sum of the best I have known
in human nature") and secretary Anna Bahlmann. Informs
Charles Scribner that she is working on novel *The Glimpses
of the Moon* and a work "of the dimensions of *Ethan
Frome*. It deals with the same kind of life in a midsummer
landscape." Offers the latter for serial publication, but
Charles Scribner declines, having already scheduled her
1892 "Bunner Sisters" for fall; accepts offer from Appleton
for book and from *McClure's* for serial. Feels financial
pressure due to expense of refugee work, reduced literary
earnings, and effects of American income tax. *Xingu and
Other Stories* (all except one story written before the war)
published in October by Scribner's.

1917   *Summer*, companion piece to *Ethan Frome*, serialized in
McClure's for $7,000, February–August; published by
Appleton July 2. Grows fond of Ronald Simmons, young
American officer and painter. After tuberculosis treatment
centers are taken over by the Red Cross, establishes four
convalescent homes for tubercular civilians. September,
makes month-long tour of French Morocco with Walter
Berry. Witnesses self-lacerative ritual dances and visits
harem, noting its air of "somewhat melancholy respectability."

1918   Inspired by success of American troops, gives public lecture on American life. Summer, brother Frederic dies;
Wharton, long estranged from him, writes sadly of her
brother Henry's failure to contact her. Deeply grieved by
death from pneumonia of Ronald Simmons, August 12.
Finds Paris increasingly noisy. After long negotiation, purchases Jean-Marie, house in village of St. Brice-sous-Fôret,

outside of Paris (will restore its original name, Pavillon Colombe). Novel *The Marne* published by Appleton.

1919   Rising expenses, support of financially troubled Mary Cadwalader Jones, establishment of trust fund for three Belgian children, together with changing New York real estate market and effects of American income tax, create financial pressure. Accepts offer of $18,000 from *The Pictorial Review* for serial rights to her next novel. Unable to finish *The Glimpses of the Moon*, suggests *A Son at the Front*, but both magazine and book editors feel that the public is tired of war material. Proposes novel *Old New York* (later retitled *The Age of Innocence*), set in 1875. Magazine accepts, and Appleton advances $15,000 against royalties. Leases Ste. Claire du Vieux Château in Hyères, overlooking Mediterranean. Moves into Pavillon Colombe in August. *French Ways and Their Meaning*, collection of magazine articles, published by Appleton. "Beatrice Palmato" outline and fragment, explicit treatment of father-daughter incest, probably written at this time (the story is never finished).

1920   Howard Sturgis dies in January; end of Queen's Acre gatherings. *In Morocco*, travel account, published by Scribner's in October. *The Age of Innocence*, serialized in *The Pictorial Review* July–October, published by Appleton in October, sells 66,000 copies in six months (by 1922 it earns Wharton nearly $70,000). December, moves to Hyères for several months.

1921   Resumes work on *The Glimpses of the Moon*. Writes *The Old Maid*, novella about out-of-wedlock birth (rejected by *Ladies' Home Journal* for being "a bit too vigorous for us"). Begins long friendship with Philomène de Lévis-Mirepoix (later Philomène de la Forest-Divonne, who will write journalism and novels under the name Claude Sylve). *The Age of Innocence* awarded Pulitzer Prize in May. Later learns that the jury had originally voted for Sinclair Lewis's *Main Street*, but had been overruled by the trustees of Columbia University, who thought it too controversial. Writes to Lewis in August of her "disgust" at the action and invites him to St. Brice (he makes the first of several visits in October). *The Old Maid* bought by

Red Book for $2,250 (serialized Feb.–April 1922). Septem-
ber, finishes *The Glimpses of the Moon*. Goes to Hyères in
mid-December.

1922   At Hyères until late May; June to mid-December at St.
Brice. Summer, long-time friend and correspondent Sara
Norton dies. When estranged brother Henry dies in August Wharton writes Berenson that "he was the dearest of
brothers to all my youth . . ." *The Glimpses of the Moon*
serialized in *The Pictorial Review*; published by Appleton
in August, sells more than 100,000 copies in America and
Britain in six months, earning her $60,000 from various
rights and royalties.

1923   Film version of *The Glimpses of the Moon*, with dialogue
titles by F. Scott Fitzgerald, released in April. (Six other
films were made from Wharton's works between 1918 and
1934; she had no involvement in any of the productions.)
Invited by Yale University to receive honorary Doctor of
Letters degree. Although reluctant to attend, decides she
needs to see United States if she is to continue writing
about it. Accepts degree (the first to be awarded to a
woman by Yale) at commencement in New Haven, June
20. Returns to France after eleven-day visit, her first since
1913 and her last. Novel *A Son at the Front* published by
Scribner's in September, fulfilling promise made a decade
earlier to give Scribner's another novel after *The Custom
of the Country*. Works on novel *The Mother's Recompense*.

1924   *Old New York*, collection of four novellas, published by
Appleton in May in boxed sets of four volumes. Titles are
False Dawn (The 'Forties), *The Old Maid (The 'Fifties)*, *The
Spark (The 'Sixties)*, *New Year's Day (The 'Seventies)*. About
26,000 sets sold in six months, with another 3,000 volumes sold individually. Awarded Gold Medal for "distinguished service" by National Institute of Arts and Letters.

1925   *The Mother's Recompense* published by Appleton in April
after serialization in *The Pictorial Review* October
1924–March 1925. Sales are good. June, receives inscribed
copy of *The Great Gatsby* from F. Scott Fitzgerald. July,
Fitzgerald visits St. Brice; the encounter is strained and
awkward. *The Writing of Fiction*, collection of five essays,

including long appreciation of Proust, published by Scribner's in the late summer.

1926   Charters 360-ton steam yacht *Osprey* for ten-week cruise with guests through the Mediterranean and Aegean, March–June. *Here and Beyond*, collection of short stories, published by Appleton in summer. *Twelve Poems* published in London by The Medici Society. Elected to the National Institute of Arts and Letters. September, travels with Berry through northern Italy. Finishes novel *Twilight Sleep* in November. Buys Ste. Claire, Hyères home, for $40,000.

1927   January, Berry suffers mild stroke; convalesces at Hyères for two months, depressed and irritable. *The Pictorial Review* pays $40,000 for serial rights to novel *The Children* after *Delineator* offers $42,000; promises *Delineator* the novel *The Keys of Heaven*. *Twilight Sleep* published by Appleton in June; sells well. Walter Berry suffers second stroke in Paris, October 2. Wharton visits him on his deathbed; he dies October 12. Writes Lapsley: "No words can tell of my desolation. He had been to me in turn all that one being can be to another, in love, in friendship, in understanding."

1928   Edward Wharton dies in New York, February 7. *The Children* is serialized in *The Pictorial Review* April–July, published by Appleton in September; earns $95,000 from sales and film rights. Begins novel *Hudson River Bracketed* after abandoning *The Keys of Heaven*. Friendship develops with Desmond MacCarthy, British writer and editor. December, *The Age of Innocence*, dramatized by Margaret Ayer Barnes, opens on Broadway, runs until June 1929, then tours for four months, earning Wharton $23,500.

1929   Severe winter storms devastate Ste. Claire gardens; describes effect as "torture." February, learns that *Delineator* began serialization of *Hudson River Bracketed* in September 1928, six months ahead of schedule. Contracts severe pneumonia in March and nearly dies. Recovers by midsummer. Saddened by death of Geoffrey Scott in August. Finishes *Hudson River Bracketed* (published by Appleton in Nov.) and begins restoration of Ste. Claire gardens.

Awarded Gold Medal for "special distinction in literature" by American Academy of Arts and Letters.

1930   Elected to the American Academy of Arts and Letters. *Certain People*, collection of short stories, published by Appleton in summer. Autumn, meets art critic and historian Kenneth Clark while traveling in Tuscany; deep friendship develops. December, meets Aldous Huxley, who introduces her to anthropologist Bronislaw Malinowski.

1931   Visits England in July and sees H. G. Wells, Harold Nicolson, and Osbert, Sacheverell, and Dame Edith Sitwell. Attends several Roman Catholic services during visit to Rome in November.

1932   January, finishes novel *The Gods Arrive*, sequel to *Hudson River Bracketed*. Rejected for serial publication by *The Saturday Evening Post*, *Liberty*, and *Collier's* because it features an unmarried couple living together. Sold to *Delineator* for $50,000 despite Wharton's anger over handling of *Hudson River Bracketed*, appearing February–August. Published by Appleton later in year, it sells poorly. Begins autobiography, *A Backward Glance*. Effects of the Depression begin to be felt in greatly diminished literary earnings; magazine offers for short stories fall drastically. Visits Rome in May. Becomes godmother to Kenneth Clark's son Colin.

1933   Catherine Gross, Wharton's companion since 1884, falls into paranoid dementia in April, dies in October. Elise Duvlenck, her personal maid since 1914, dies May 29. *Human Nature*, collection of short stories, published by Appleton. By threat of legal action, forces *Ladies' Home Journal* to honor pre-Depression agreement to pay $25,000 for her autobiography; installments appear October 1933–April 1934. June, vacations in England with Gaillard Lapsely, visits Wales for the first time; August goes to Salzburg for a week and in October visits Holland. Begins novel *The Buccaneers* (never finished, but published by Appleton-Century in 1938 with Wharton's long outline of the remainder of the story and an afterword by Gaillard Lapsley).

1934   Tours England and Scotland. Guided through National
          Gallery in London by Kenneth Clark. *A Backward Glance*
          published by Appleton-Century. Breaks with Appleton
          editor Rutger Jewett, who had acted as her agent without
          commission for over a decade, blaming him for decreased
          literary earnings; engages James Pinker as new agent.

1935   *The Old Maid*, dramatized by Zoë Akins, opens in New
          York for successful run. April, suffers mild stroke, with
          temporary loss of sight in left eye. September, Mary Cad-
          walader Jones dies.

1936   *Ethan Frome*, dramatized by Owen and Donald Davis,
          tours United States after successful New York run. Income
          from both plays is about $130,000, ending financial worry.
          Visits England in the summer. *The World Over*, collection
          of short stories, published by Appleton-Century.

1937   Sends last completed short story, "All Souls," to her
          agent, February. Health declines; suffers stroke, June 1.
          Dies at St. Brice on the evening of August 11. Buried near
          Walter Berry in the Cimetière des Gonards, Versailles,
          August 14.

Note on the Texts

By the time Edith Wharton was writing the novellas, novels, and autobiography included in this volume, she had established a regular working routine. She wrote by hand while still in bed in the morning, often dropping the pages onto the floor as she finished them. The manuscript was then typed by her secretary, and Wharton would revise the typed pages and have them retyped. This process would continue until she felt that the manuscript was ready to be sent to her New York publishers, either Charles Scribner's Sons or D. Appleton and Company. Except for the work published in *Scribner's Magazine*, the editor she worked with for book publication also acted as her agent for serial publication, transmitting serial proofs as well as book proofs and pages to her and receiving her corrected copy in return. Wharton did not oversee the English editions of her works. Macmillan, her English publisher until Appleton opened up an English office in 1921, imported and bound sheets of the American editions or used them for setting new editions. Wharton continued revising and correcting a work after the serial version was published and never considered that version to be final. She would also sometimes make further, but fewer, corrections and revisions in her works after they were published in book form; these changes would usually appear in later printings.

Madame de Treymes was published in the August 1906 number of *Scribner's Magazine*. After Wharton made corrections in the book proofs, it was printed by Wharton's friend, D. B. Updike, at The Merrymount Press, Boston, and published by Charles Scribner's Sons on February 20, 1907. Wharton made no further revisions in the work, so the text of that first book edition is printed here.

Edith Wharton first began *Ethan Frome* in 1907 as a writing exercise in French when she was living in Paris and wanted to gain a more idiomatic grasp of the contemporary language. After a short time she discontinued the French exercise, but several years later she again took up the story, writing to a friend on June 20, 1910, that she was "hard at work on a short novel. . . ." The work was finished early in 1911, and in April she read the proofs for the serial version, which appeared in the August through October 1911 numbers of *Scribner's Magazine*. Wharton made further revisions and corrections in the proofs for the book, which was published by Charles Scribner's Sons on September 30, 1911. The first printing of 6,000 copies was followed by two printings in November, one of 1,700 copies and the other of 3,400 copies. Although the book was favorably reviewed, the sales of *Ethan Frome* were initially much lower than those of many of her previous works. Seven additional printings appeared through August 1921, ranging from 300 to 1,000 copies, but no corrections or revisions were made in these printings. It was not until arrangements were made by Scribner's to bring out a special edition of *Ethan Frome* that Wharton made the corrections and revisions that she often made soon after a book had first appeared in print. Her sixty or so changes included a few revisions in wording, the alteration of the American "gray" to her preferred English form, "grey," and some shifts in punctuation. Wharton also wrote a short introduction for the new edition (this introduction is included in the notes to the present volume). The edition, published in 1922, included a notice stating: "This edition, designed by Bruce Rogers, consists of two thousand copies printed from type, which has been distributed." Though Scribner's continued to print copies from the first-edition plates (in fact a new printing of 1,000 copies was ordered the next month) and brought out new editions after Wharton's death, none of these included the corrections and revisions Wharton made for the limited second edition. The text of the limited second edition, therefore, is printed here.

Edith Wharton wrote *Summer* in 1916 in the midst of her war work and offered it to *Scribner's Magazine* for serial publication. *Scribner's*, however, was unable to take it at that time because the magazine was already publishing her story "Bunner Sisters" in the fall and was waiting for her to complete another novel, *Literature* (a work she never completed). When Charles Scribner asked about book publication of the novel, Wharton explained in a letter to him on January 15, 1917, that she had taken up "a long standing offer of Messrs Appleton, which combined serial publication in one of several magazines with book publication by them, on terms so advantageous" that she would "not have felt justified in rejecting the opportunity." Joseph Sears, her editor at D. Appleton and Company, arranged for the novel to be serialized in *McClure's* in its February through August 1917 numbers (payment for serialization was $7,000). *McClure's* Americanized her spellings and altered some of her preferred punctuation, adding commas between adjectives and deleting some commas before conjunctions. The book edition, set from her original typescript, maintains her preferred English spellings and punctuation and includes further revisions she made and sent to Sears while the novel was being serialized. Soon after D. Appleton and Company published *Summer* on July 2, 1917, Wharton discovered errors in the printing and cabled Sears on August 20 that she was sending a list of corrections by mail. Sears replied that *Summer* had already been reprinted once, and was about to be reprinted again, but that he would hold off the next printing until her corrections arrived. On September 4, Wharton again wrote Sears to tell him that she had found "about a dozen more misprints" and that she was enclosing a list of corrections. Wharton's lists have not been found, but collation of the first and second printings with later corrected printings shows which corrections were made. In several instances a repetition of words had been dropped out of a sentence; for example, at 205.6–7, "always full of scruples, and of scruples about her scruples" had been printed in the first and second printings as "always full of scruples about her scruples." Other changes correct errors in wording, restore English spellings, place commas before conjunctions, and make other punctuation changes. All together, Wharton made approximately fifty alterations that were incorporated into the text by D. Appleton and Company. The text of *Summer* printed here is that of the corrected first edition.

Each of the four novellas that make up *Old New York* was first published serially. *False Dawn (The 'Forties)* appeared in the November 1923 number of *The Ladies' Home Journal*; *The Old Maid (The 'Fifties)* appeared in the February 1922 number of *Red Book Magazine*; *The Spark (The 'Sixties)* appeared in the May 1924 number of *The Ladies' Home Journal*; and *New Year's Day (The 'Seventies)* appeared in the July 1923 number of *Red Book Magazine*. Wharton dealt directly only with Rutger

Jewett, her Appleton editor, transmitting all manuscripts and corrected proofs through his office, and receiving from him the proofs for correction. Collations of the serial versions with the book editions show numerous differences, most of them caused by the strong house-styling imposed by the editors at *Red Book Magazine* and *The Ladies' Home Journal.* Wharton's sister-in-law and close friend, Mary Cadwalader Jones, helped with the proofreading. Wharton wanted the four novellas to appear under a single cover but was persuaded by Jewett to allow them to be published both as a boxed set and as separate volumes, with the understanding that later they would be brought out in one volume. (However, *Old New York* did not appear as a single volume until Scribner's brought out an edition in 1952, fifteen years after Wharton had died.) D. Appleton and Company published the boxed set of *Old New York* and the four separate novellas on May 16, 1924. No corrections or revisions were ever made in the plates. The texts of the first book editions are printed here.

In April 1923 Edith Wharton sent a summary and the first three chapters of *The Mother's Recompense* to Rutger B. Jewett, her Appleton editor, so that he could negotiate a contract for serial rights to the novel with *The Pictorial Review.* The magazine paid her $27,000 for the rights, and—because time was needed to prepare illustrations for the novel, which would appear from October 1924 through March 1925—requested that a large portion of it be sent nine months in advance. As usual the transmission of manuscripts and proofs was handled exclusively through the Appleton office. Wharton continued the process of revision during this time, but many of her revisions arrived too late to be made in the serial version. She had her own copy of the typescript into which she had incorporated further revisions, and it was from this copy that the book was set. She read galley and page proofs, assisted in the last weeks before publication by her sister-in-law and Jewett himself. *The Mother's Recompense* was published by D. Appleton and Company in April 1925. Soon after receiving her copy in May, Wharton noticed a number of misprints, though fewer than she had found in previous works, and sent in several lists of corrections. These corrections, however, were not made until the fourth printing. The first three printings, for example, repeat at 623.26 a line that had occurred two lines above, "she felt like rushing out into the streets to find him," instead of printing the correct words, "him that she was not in the least afraid of him." Other serious errors were also corrected: for example, at 637.13, "Anne's lips dropped" was corrected to "Anne's lids dropped," and at 718.23, "with the accent" was corrected to "without the accent." Seven of the thirteen corrections she made were in punctuation: for example, at 677.9 "everything she thought" was corrected to "everything, she thought." Two of the changes she made were revisions in wording: at 654.7, "presumed" had been "reckoned" in the first three printings; and at 693.5, "Newburgh lobster" had originally been "Maryland chicken." Wharton made no other corrections or revisions after the fourth printing, and that text of the *The Mother's Recompense* is printed here.

The history of the serialization of her autobiography, *A Backward Glance*, is more complicated than that of the other works in this volume. Jewett had arranged early in 1932 for its serialization in *The Ladies' Home Journal*, for which Wharton was to receive $25,000, but after she had sent in her manuscript in March 1933, she learned that the magazine's editors wanted to cut it by forty percent and reduce the money paid to her by $5,000. Wharton finally agreed to the cuts, and a compromise was made on her payment. The editors at *The Ladies' Home Journal* cut the manuscript at their own discretion and sent typescript and galleys of the sections they used to Wharton for her approval. The serial version appeared from October 1933 through April 1934. A version of Chapter IX, "The Secret Garden," was published in the April 1933 number of *The Atlantic Monthly* with the title "Confessions of a Novelist." At Jewett's request, Wharton prepared a separate typescript for the book setting by Appleton. She began reading proofs for the book in January 1934 and finished on March 18, when she sent the last page proofs to Jewett. *A Backward Glance* was published by D. Appleton and Company in late April 1934. She received her copy in May and soon after sent in lists of misprints she wanted corrected. The lists are missing from the Appleton correspondence, but collation shows that in the index of the second printing, *La Tuvolle* was corrected to *La Tuyolle*. Additional corrections were made in the third printing: the artist Francia was corrected to Franciabigio at 848.10; the spelling of Lamothe-Fouqué was changed to Lamotte-Fouqué at 888.40; "ignored who have" was corrected to "ignored have" at 874.32; "usually often" was revised to "not unusually" at 875.9; and "along against" was corrected to "long against" at 1025.22. A few other stylistic revisions were made in references to her old friends, Lady Poynder and Lady Elcho, at 951.10-11. Three more corrections were made in the fourth printing: "cadences" was changed to "cadence" at 910.5, a comma was inserted after "think" at 1011.21, and "Sigurd" was changed to "Sigmund" at 1022.33. No other corrections were made by Wharton after the fourth printing, and that text of *A Backward Glance* is printed here.

This volume presents the texts of the original printings chosen for inclusion here but does not attempt to reproduce features of their typographic design, such as the display capitalization of chapter openings. The texts are printed without change except for the correction of typographical errors. Spelling, punctuation, and capitalization are often expressive features, and they are not altered, even when inconsistent or irregular. The following is a list of typographical errors corrected, cited by page and line number: 19.7, *négres*; 20.38, Boykins; 48.34, whereever; 51.21, makes; 99.1, finger's ends; 99.18, forsaw; 107.22, detatched; 121.6, it . . . ; 137.18, husband; 268.1, here there; 286.14, Nothing; 332.37, thought; 334.9, Anne,; 352.1, they?"; 367.6, Sedwyn; 421.32, moonnight; 451.9, It it; 457.7, coach; 484.1, Delane's; 503.24, Cecilia's . . .' ; 543.34, "Black Crook"; 637.34, breakfast- tray; 742.34, shut . . . ; 746.7, be; 764.26, Lander's; 848.10, Franciabigio,; 1016.17, expect meet; 1016.19, you're; 1044.18, "The; 1058.16, Ovideo; 1081.21, placed; 1089.3, pretty—"; 1089.21, I I.

Notes

In the notes below, the reference numbers denote page and line of the present volume (the line count includes chapter headings). No note is made for material included in a standard desk-reference book. For more detailed notes, references to other studies, and further biographical background than is included in the Chronology, see: R.W.B. Lewis, *Edith Wharton: A Biography* (New York: Harper & Row, 1975); *The Letters of Edith Wharton* (New York: Charles Scribner's Sons, 1975), edited by R.W.B. Lewis and Nancy Lewis; and Cynthia Griffin Wolff, *A Feast of Words: The Triumph of Edith Wharton* (Oxford: Oxford University Press, 1977).

MADAME DE TREYMES

4.17   yellow-backed fiction] Inexpensive editions of popular novels bound in yellow covers.

12.39   *contra mundum*!] Against the world!

14.7   *retentissement*] Reverberation, stir.

17.29   Bon Marché] The first modern department store in France, established c. 1860.

19.1   *jeunes filles*] Girls.

19.7   *là . . . nègres*] Over there, in the manner of the blacks (with a negative connotation).

21.36   *ventes de charité*] Charity bazaars.

22.23   *La suite. . . numéro*] To be continued in our next issue.

23.7   *fine lame*] A fine swordsman.

23.32–33   *rien que cela!*] Merely that! No more than that!

27.29   *écarts*] Digressions, mistakes.

30.21   *empressée*] Assiduous, earnest.

49.32–33   *morte saison*] The dead, i.e., slack or off, social season.

50.21–22   *que voulez vous?*] What can you expect?

56.39–40   *de loin*] From a distance.

ETHAN FROME

The following Introduction was written for the 1922 edition printed here:

I had known something of New England village life long before I made my home in the same county as my imaginary Starkfield; though, during the years spent there, certain of its aspects became much more familiar to me.

Even before that final initiation, however, I had had an uneasy sense that the New England of fiction bore little—except a vague botanical and dialectical—resemblance to the harsh and beautiful land as I had seen it. Even the abundant enumeration of sweet-fern, asters and mountain-laurel, and the conscientious reproduction of the vernacular, left me with the feeling that the outcropping granite had in both cases been overlooked. I give the impression merely as a personal one; it accounts for Ethan Frome, and may, to some readers, in a measure justify it.

So much for the origin of the story; there is nothing else of interest to say of it, except as concerns its construction.

The problem before me, as I saw in the first flash, was this: I had to deal with a subject of which the dramatic climax, or rather the anti-climax, occurs a generation later than the first acts of the tragedy. This enforced lapse of time would seem to anyone persuaded—as I have always been—that every subject (in the novelist's sense of the term) implicitly *contains its own form and dimensions*, to mark "Ethan Frome" as the subject for a novel. But I never thought this for a moment, for I had felt, at the same time, that the theme of my tale was not one on which many variations could be played. It must be treated as starkly and summarily as life had always presented itself to my protagonists; any attempt to elaborate and complicate their sentiments would necessarily have falsified the whole. They were, in truth, these figures, my *granite outcroppings*; but half-emerged from the soil, and scarcely more articulate.

This incompatibility between subject and plan would perhaps have seemed to suggest that my "situation" was after all one to be rejected. Every novelist has been visited by the insinuating wraiths of false "good situations," siren-subjects luring his cockle-shell to the rocks; their voice is oftenest heard, and their mirage-sea beheld, as he traverses the waterless desert which awaits him half-way through whatever work is actually in hand. I knew well enough what song those sirens sang, and had often tied myself to my dull job till they were out of hearing—perhaps carrying a lost masterpiece in their rainbow veils. But I had no such fear of them in the case of Ethan Frome. It was the first subject I had ever approached with full confidence in its value, for my own purpose, and a relative faith in my power to render at least a part of what I saw in it.

Every novelist, again, who "intends upon" his art, has lit upon such subjects, and been fascinated by the difficulty of presenting them in the fullest relief, yet without an added ornament, or a trick of drapery or lighting. This was my task, if I were to tell the story of Ethan Frome; and my scheme of construction—which met with the immediate and unqualified disapproval of the few friends to whom I tentatively outlined it—I still think justified in the given case. It appears to me, indeed, that, while an air of artificiality is lent to a tale of complex and sophisticated people which the novelist causes to be guessed at and interpreted by any mere looker-on, there need be no such drawback if the looker-on is sophisticated, and the people he interprets are simple. If he is capable of seeing all around them, no violence is done to probability in allowing him to exercise this faculty; it is natural enough that he should act as the sympathizing intermediary between his rudimentary characters and the more complicated minds to whom he is trying to present them. But this is all self-evident, and needs explaining only to those who have never thought of fiction as an art of composition.

The real merit of my construction seems to me to lie in a minor detail. I had to find means to bring my tragedy, in a way at once natural and picture-making, to the knowledge of its narrator. I might have sat him down before a village gossip who would have poured out the whole affair to him in a breath, but in doing this I should have been false to two essential elements of my picture: first, the deep-rooted reticence and inarticulateness of the people I was trying to draw, and secondly the effect of "roundness" (in the plastic sense) produced by letting their case be seen through eyes as different as those of Harmon Gow and Mrs. Ned Hale. Each of my chroniclers contributes to the narrative *just so much as he or she is capable of understanding* of what, to them, is a complicated and mysterious case; and only the narrator of the tale has scope enough to see it all, to resolve it back into simplicity, and to put it in its rightful place among his larger categories.

I make no claim for originality in following a method of which "La Grande Bretêche" and "The Ring and the Book" had set me the magnificent example; my one merit is, perhaps, to have guessed that the proceeding there employed was also applicable to my small tale.

I have written this brief analysis—the first I have ever published of any of my books—because, as an author's introduction to his work, I can imagine nothing of any value to his readers except a statement as to why he decided to attempt the work in question, and why he selected one form rather than another for its embodiment.

These primary aims, the only ones that can be explicitly stated, must, by the artist, be almost instinctively felt and acted upon before there can pass into his creation that imponderable something more which causes life to circulate in it, and preserves it for a little from decay.

March 31st, 1922.   EDITH WHARTON.

66.29   Carcel lamp]   The Carcel, also known as the French or mechanical, lamp was named for its inventor, Bertrand Carcel (1750–1812). It is fueled by oil which is pumped up a tube to the wick by clockwork.

92.24–25   "Curfew . . . Chord"]   "Curfew Must Not Ring Tonight," a ballad by Rose Hartwick Thorpe (1850–1939), was first published in 1867. The popular sentimental verse "A Lost Chord" by Adelaide Anne Proctor (1825–64) was set to music by Sir Arthur Sullivan (1842–1900).

113.34   traveller's joy]   *Clematis Vitalba*, a wild plant, was given its popular name because its tendrils trailed over and appeared to decorate England's roadside hedges.

SUMMER

167.2–3   "Opening . . . Burr,"]   *The Opening of a Chestnut Burr* (1874) was the second novel written by the New York clergyman Edward Payson Roe (1838–88), who then resigned the ministry to become a professional writer.

256.21   "Home, Sweet Home."]   John Payne (1791–1852) wrote the words for the music by Sir Henry Bishop (1786–1855). The popular song was originally part of the opera *Clari, or The Maid of Milan* (1823).

OLD NEW YORK

FALSE DAWN (*The 'Forties*)

319.14   watered silk]   Silk with a wavy, shiny, damask-like finish.

322.3–4   Paris . . . 1830]   On July 26, 1830, the publication of three reactionary decrees by Charles X sparked an insurrection in Paris. After three days of street fighting around barricades, Charles abdicated and was replaced by the duc d'Orléans, Louis-Philippe.

322.16   gambling-hells . . . Royle]   The arcades housing shops, restaurants, gaming houses, and apartments on three sides of the public garden of the Palais Royal were frequented by gamblers and prostitutes during the Revolution and early 19th century.

329.39   Pulcinella]   A comic character in commedia dell'arte and later professional improvisational Italian theater productions (also the Punch of

"Punch and Judy" puppet theater). Pulcinella is often characterized by a humped back and fat stomach.

333.34   *guillochée* repeating watch]   Ornamentally patterned watch with a repeating spring that strikes the hour.

339.37–38   Mytilene and Sunium]   Mytilene is an alternate name for Lesbos, an island in the Aegean Sea off the northwest coast of Turkey, and the name of its chief town, a site of Roman remains. Sunium Promontorium, the ancient name for Cape Colonna in east central Greece, is the site of an ancient temple.

341.23–24   road to Damascus]   The conversion of Saul (later called Paul) began on the road to Damascus. See Acts 9:3.

343.12–13   Sir . . . Art]   *Discourses on Art* (1769–90) had been delivered to the Royal Academy of Art by its first president, the portrait painter Sir Joshua Reynolds (1723–92).

343.36–37   Bologna . . . School]   The Bolognese painters chiefly associated with the eclectic school, which advocated incorporating the most important characteristics of individual great masters, were Ludovico Carracci (1555–1619) and his cousins Annibale (1560–1609) and Agostino (1557–1602), founders of the Accademia degli Incamminati in Bologna, and Domenichino (1581–1641), who studied there.

344.11   Beatrice Cenci]   The painting believed to represent Beatrice Cenci (1577–99) was attributed to Guido Reni (1575–1642).

344.22   *amorini*]   Cupids.

345.10–11   Knight's . . . Authors"]   Selections from and about great works of literature, edited by the English publisher Charles Knight (1791–1873).

350.35   Agag]   Agag, king of the Amalekites, was spared by Saul from a decree of death, then cut to pieces by Samuel. See I Samuel 15:32–33.

350.36   Carpatcher]   Venetian painter Vittore Carpaccio (c. 1460–?1525), whose works show the influence of Bellini and Gentile.

365.11   "Signer"]   A "signer" of the Declaration of Independence.

THE OLD MAID (*The 'Fifties*)

376.19   Cluny]   Lace.

395.4–6   Book . . . tournament]   Peeresses who participated in the tournament were among prominent women of the day who appeared in *Heath's Book of Beauty*, edited by Marguerite Gardiner, the Countess of Blessington

(1789–1849). Portraits and poems, stories, and essays, by or about them, were included.

423.26   Latmian solitude] In Greek mythology, a goddess fell in love with the shepherd Endymion on Mount Latmos. Keats uses the myth in his poem *Endymion* (1818).

427.6–7   third-and-fourth generation] Exodus 20:5 and 34:7, Numbers 14:18, and Deuteronomy 5:9.

THE SPARK (*The 'Sixties*)

449.39–40   Trinity . . . Club] Trinity Church on Broadway at the head of Wall Street, the first Anglican, later Episcopal, church in New York City, was consecrated in 1689. The church was rebuilt in 1788–90 and in 1839–46. The Reservoir of the Croton Aqueduct between 40th and 42d streets, on the site where the New York Public Library now stands, was completed in 1842 and demolished 1899–1901. The Knickerbocker Club for men, founded in 1871 by John Jacob Astor and others, was originally at 32d Street and Fifth Avenue.

466.2   "counterjumper's lingo"] Store clerk's jargon.

466.10   what's-his-name . . . *Spectator*] Joseph Addison (1672–1719), with Richard Steele (1672–1729), was the major contributor to the London daily periodical *The Spectator*, which they published 1711–12. Addison briefly revived the periodical in 1714.

466.22   "Heavenly Rest,"] The Episcopal Church of the Heavenly Rest was then on Fifth Avenue between 45th and 46th streets.

466.23–26   "She . . . Byron] "She Walks in Beauty" (June 12, 1814), line 1, and "The Destruction of Sennacherib" (1815), line 1: "The Assyrian came down like the wolf on the fold, . . ."

470.2–3   author . . . *Elsmere*] Mary Augusta (Mrs. Humphry) Ward (1851–1920). *Robert Elsmere* (1888) was her most popular novel.

470.33   lunatics . . . Bloomingdale] Bloomingdale Insane Asylum, a branch of New York Hospital, was built 1818–20 on Manhattan's upper west side. In 1894 it was moved to White Plains, N.Y., and its former site became the new campus of Columbia University.

486.13–487.7   *A sight . . . side*] The first lines serve as titles for both poems. These and "The Dresser," noted below, were first published in *Drum-Taps* (1865) and finally in the "Drum-Taps" cluster in *Leaves of Grass*.

487.20   "Lovely . . . Death,"] "Come, lovely and soothing Death" is from "When Lilacs Last in the Dooryard Bloom'd," first published in *Sequel to Drum-Taps* (1865–66). The poem later appeared in the "Memories of President Lincoln" cluster in *Leaves of Grass*.

487.23–24   *Bearing . . . go*]   Lines from "The Dresser." Whitman changed the title to "The Wound-Dresser" in 1876.

NEW YEAR'S DAY (*The 'Seventies*)

494.27   Madeleine]   A large church in Paris (built 1764–1842).

531.7–8   *La joie fait peur*]   Happiness creates fear.

539.21   Knickerbocker Club]   See note to 449.39–40.

542.33   Mallock's *New Republic*]   *New Republic: or culture, faith and philosophy in an English country house* (1877), a satire on English society and ideas, by William Mallock (1849–1923).

543.34   'Black Crook']   *The Black Crook*, the dramatic musical/dance spectacular that opened at Niblo's Garden in New York on September 12, 1866, was an enormous popular success. Productions began to open almost immediately throughout the country, and it was revived many times.

THE MOTHER'S RECOMPENSE

551.3   *Desolation . . . thing.*]   *Prometheus Unbound* (1818–19), Act I, line 772.

555.40   Taylorized gestures]   Mechanized gestures, after the American efficiency engineer Frederick Taylor (1856–1915).

564.22   *"Allons, Madame plaisante!"*]   Go on, Madame is joking!

568.5–7   Roman . . . sword.]   According to an account in the *Letters* of Pliny the Younger (Book III:16, To Maecilius Nepos), Arria chose to die with her husband, Paetus Caecina, who was condemned to death in A.D. 42 for involvement in a revolt against Claudius I. She stabbed herself, then pulled the dagger from her breast and gave it to her husband with the words "Paete, non dolet."

570.28–29   planted . . . Deborah]   See Judges 4:4–5.

584.35   "stooped to folly"]   Oliver Goldsmith's (?1730–74) poem "When lovely woman stoops to folly" first appeared in his novel *The Vicar of Wakefield* (1766).

600.17–18   Esther's . . . Ahasuerus]   Cf. Esther 5:1.

629.6   Grolier Club]   The New York club for bibliophiles, founded in
1884.

635.4–5   "Thy . . . gods."]   Cf. Ruth 1:16: ". . . thy people shall be my
people, and thy God my God."

645.16   *Perfect . . . fear!*]   I John 4:18.

745.5   *un bon parti*]   A good match.

A BACKWARD GLANCE

767.2   A backward . . . roads.]   The essay "A Backward Glance o'er Travel'd Roads" (1888) appears as an epilogue to the "death-bed edition" (1891–92)
of *Leaves of Grass*.

767.4–6   Je . . . *Tombe*]   I want to reascend the slope of my beautiful
years.—*Memoirs from Beyond the Tomb* (1849–50.)

767.7   Kein . . . vorübergehend.]   No pleasure is transitory.

772.7–10   Madame . . . *rare!*]   *"An enemy? But of all the accidents that is
the most rare!"* Anne Sophie Swetchine (1782–1857) was a French-Russian
writer and convert to Catholicism.

772.11   found it.]   After a text break, the following paragraph of acknowledgment is appended:

Several chapters of this book have already appeared in the "Atlantic
Monthly" and "The Ladies' Home Journal." I have also to thank Sir John
Murray for kindly permitting me to incorporate in the book two or three
passages from an essay on Henry James, published in "The Quarterly Review" of July 1920 and the Editor of "The Colophon" for the use of a few
paragraphs on the writing of "Ethan Frome."

777.3–5   Gute . . . *Epigrammen*]   I've seen good society; one calls it
good / When it gives no occasion for even the slightest poem.—*Venetian
Epigrams* (1795), 75.

777.19   *bavolet*]   A piece of trim at the back of a bonnet.

778.8–9   truncated . . . supply.]   The Croton Reservoir. See note to
449.39–40.

782.13   Munkacsky]   Mihály Munkácsy (1844–1909), a Hungarian genre
painter whose later works were often of religious and historical subjects
painted in a dramatic style.

795.19   *volantes*]   Two-wheeled hooded carriages guided by postilions.

796.19   *gorge de pigeon*]   Throat of pigeon, i.e., iridescent or streaked with
color.

803.26–27   Paolo . . . air"]   *The Divine Comedy, The Inferno*, Canto V.

803.30   Hirschgraben]   The name given by Goethe's father to their home in Frankfurt am Main. See Goethe's autobiography *Poetry and Truth* (1811–32).

806.10–12   Clive . . . *pifferaro*]   In William Thackeray's novel *The New-comes* (1853–55). A *locanda* is an inn, and a *pifferaro*, a piper.

812.31   "The Christian Year"]   The English clergyman and poet John Keble (1792–1866) based his book of sacred poetry, *The Christian Year* (1827), on the Anglican Book of Common Prayer.

813.1–4   Ho, . . . slaves,]   "Ivry: A Song of the Huguenots," line 63, and "Horatius," lines 3–4, in *Lays of Ancient Rome* (1842), by Thomas Babington Macaulay (1800–59).

813.30   *feuille-morte*]   Of a dead-leaf, i.e., yellow-brown color.

814.22–25   "So . . . Robinson"]   "Let us build tabernacles!" (Matthew 17:4) *Hütten*, in biblical usage, means "tabernacles" or "tents," but in ordinary speech means huts, cabins, shelters. The Irish-born Mayne Reid (1818–83) was the author of many popular adventures and romances, including *The Castaways* (1870). *The Swiss Family Robinson* (pub. in Zurich 1812–13) was written by Johann David Wyss (1743–1818) and edited and completed by his son, Johann Rudolf Wyss (1781–1830).

816.3   "Faster . . . Reveller"]   Lines 1 and 2 of the poem (1849) by Matthew Arnold (1822–88).

821.26–27   "Innocents . . . novels]   *The Innocents Abroad* (1869), an autobiographical account of his trip around the Mediterranean by Mark Twain (1835–1910), and *Condensed Novels and Other Papers* (1867) by Harte (1836–1902).

822.21–22   "The Water . . . Goblin"]   *The Water Babies* (1863) by Charles Kingsley (1819–75) and *The Princess and the Goblin* (1872) by George MacDonald (1824–1905).

832.38   young man]   John Ruskin.

833.29–30   the "Spectator" . . . Reliques"]   *The Spectator* was a periodical published by Addison and Steele (see note to 466.10). *Reliques of Ancient English Poetry* (pub. 1765) was edited by Thomas Percy (1729–1811).

834.29–30   Journals . . . Berry]   The writer Mary (1763–1852) and her sister Agnes (1764–1852) held a salon in their home that was "a feature of London society," and were friends of Horace Walpole. The journals of Mary Berry were included in *Extracts of the Journals and Correspondance of Miss Berry* (three volumes, 1865) edited by Lady Theresa Lewis.

836.39   Kilmeny-touch]   In the poem *The Queen's Wake* (1813), "Thirteenth Bard's Song—Kilmeny" by James Hogg (1770–1835), bonnie Kilmeny is taken into a land of love and light from which she views evil and sin in the world. She returns transformed to warn her friends of what she has seen, singing "in ecstasy of sweet reason," but they cannot tell whether she is alive or a spirit. No longer at home in the world, Kilmeny again disappears into "the land of thought."

837.24–25   'Yet . . . more'] John Milton (1608–74), "Lycidas" (1637), line 1.

837.35–838.3   "Modern . . . Andromaque"] *Modern Painters,* five volumes (1843–60), by John Ruskin (1819–1900); *Récits des temps mérovingiens* (two volumes, 1840, translated *Narratives of the Merovingian Era* in 1845) by Thierry (1795–1856); *Faust* (1808–32) and *Wilhelm Meister* (1777–1829) by Goethe (1749–1832); *Philip van Artevelde* (1834) by Sir Henry Taylor (1800–86); *Men and Women* (1855) and *Dramatis Personæ* (1864) by Robert Browning (1812–89); *The Broken Heart* (1633) by John Ford (1586–c.1640); *The Tragedy of the Dutchesse of Malfy* (1612/13) by John Webster (c. 1578–c.1632); *Phèdre* (1677) and *Andromaque* (1667) by Jean Racine (1639–99).

839.1–11   small . . . times.] "Ballad of Life," lines 71–79, in *Poems and Ballads* (first series—1866) by Algernon Charles Swinburne (1837–1909). The second series was published in 1878, the third in 1889.

839.18   "The White Devil"] The tragedy (1612) by John Webster.

842.5–6   Maiden . . . meet"] Cf. "Maidenhood," lines 7–8, by Henry Wadsworth Longfellow (1807–82).

846.31   daughters of Danaus] In Greek myth, forty-nine of Danaüs's fifty daughters are condemned to spend eternity pouring water into a sieve.

848.10–11   Franciabigio's . . . *eima*] "Portrait of a Knight of Saint John'" (c. 1514), also known as the "Knight of Rhodes," is by the Florentine painter Francesco di Cristofano (1482/3–1525), called Franciabigio. The words TAR. UBLIA. CHI. BIEN. EIMA, inscribed on a parapet on which the knight's arm is resting, appear to be an Italian phonetic spelling of the French, or Provençal, and have been translated "Slowly forgets he who loves well."("Qui bien aime à tard oublie"—"Who loves well is slow to forget"—is an old French saying, probably from a song.) The portrait was once referred to as "Knight of Malta," a name acquired by the Knights of Saint John of Jerusalem after their move to the island from Rhodes in 1530.

848.14–15   There . . . societies—] John Milton (1608–74), *Lycidas* (1637), lines 178–79.

853.27–30   Vernon . . . Renaissance"] The novel *John Inglesant* (1880) by Joseph Henry Shorthouse (1834–1903) is set in 17th-century England and Italy. Lee's *Euphorion* (1884) was subtitled *Being Studies of the Antiquities and the Medieval in the Renaissance* (see page 882.23–25). *History of the*

Renaissance in Italy (seven volumes, 1875–86) is the major work of Symonds (1840–93).

868.28–29   Pelion and Ossa] The mountains which the Aloade, two giants, piled on Mount Olympus in an attempt to scale heaven and overthrow the gods.

874.21–22   "fine . . . soul"] In a letter to John Hamilton Reynolds (1796–1852), November 22, 1817, John Keats (1795–1821) wrote: "A man should have the fine point of his soul taken off to become fit for this world."

874.34   *Was Einer ist*] What one is.

880.11–12   "Jude . . . periodical] Hardy's novel was titled *Hearts Insurgent* when it appeared in *Harper's New Monthly Magazine* (1894–95).

894.16–18   "Main . . . Lenox"] *Main Street* (1920) and *Babbitt* (1922) by Sinclair Lewis (1885–1951) and *Susan Lenox: Her Fall and Rise* (pub. 1917) by David Phillips (1867–1911).

900.29   "en brosse"] In a brush cut.

900.31   *Gelehrter*] Scholar, learned pundit.

902.20   "through . . . made"] "Old Age," line 8, in *Divine Poems* (1685) by Edmund Waller (1606–87).

903.14   "The Private Secretary"] The enormously popular play, which ran in London from 1884–86 and was often revived, featured broad jokes and physical comedy. It was adapted by the actor-producer Charles Hawtrey (1858–1923) from the farce *Der Bibliothekar* (1878) by German playwright Gustav von Moser (1825–1903).

905.19   *sette cento*] The 18th century.

907.6–7   *"Oui, . . . Thésée"*] "Yes, Prince, I burn, I languish for Thésée."

907.13–14   *"Que . . . l'inceste"*] "What do you want, Mademoiselle? You are too young to understand incest."

907.21   "Manon Lescaut"] A novel (1731) by Abbé Prévost (1697–1763).

914.38–915.4   Maggie . . . defiles"] In *The Golden Bowl* (1904).

916.23   Mr. Verver] Maggie's father in *The Golden Bowl*.

918.28   Land . . . live] "The Jumblies" in *Nonsense Songs, Stories, Botany and Alphabets* (1871) by Edward Lear (1812–88).

924.2   Bradshaw."] *Bradshaw's Monthly Railway Guide* (1841–1961).

936.21–24   Thackeray . . . Quiverful] Captain Deuceace appears in

William Thackeray's satirical novel *The Luck of Barry Lyndon* (1844). Mr. Quiverful appears in Anthony Trollope's *Barchester Towers* (1857).

938.4   "The Pot of Basil"] John Keats's narrative poem *Isabella, or the Pot of Basil* (1820), based on a tale in Boccaccio's *Decameron.*

938.13   Trollope . . . Proudie] Mrs. Proudie, a main character in the "Barsetshire" series, dies in *The Last Chronicle of Barset* (1867).

948.2–6   Lord . . . Beasts'] The book of verse (1896) by Hilaire Belloc (1870–1953), and illustrated by Blackwood (1870–1917).

949.4–5   Clärchen's . . . *"gedankenvoll"*] So *"delightful"* or so *"sorrowful"* —though *"thoughtful"* . . . Clärchen is a character in Goethe's play *Egmont* (1788).

949.9   "Souls"] The name used beginning in the late 1880s by the press and in society for the circle of about forty friends that included Arthur J. Balfour, Henry Cust, Lady Desborough, George Curzon, Lord and Lady Elcho, and Henry and Margaret White. The group was sometimes joined by others such as Henry James, Oscar Wilde, and Wharton.

949.29   "The Spoils of Poynton"] By Henry James (1897).

949.33–38   Injurious . . . tears.] *Troilus and Cressida,* IV, iv, 42–44 and 46–48.

952.10–11   Dr. . . . female"] James Boswell (1740–95), *Life of Samuel Johnson* (1791), Tuesday, April 18, 1775.

977.30–31   *"Ouvrez . . . maintenant!"*] "Open the windows! Let everyone come in now!"

979.28   *douceur de vivre*] Pleasure or sweet things of life.

979.31   day of Sedan] On September 1, 1870, during the Franco-Prussian War, the French suffered a major defeat at Sedan. The following day Napoleon III surrendered with 83,000 of his men, and on September 4 he was deposed and the Third Republic was proclaimed in Paris.

979.38–980.1   *Précieuses* . . . Rambouillet.] The salon held at the townhouse (hôtel) of the Marquise de Rambouillet (1588–1665) became a model for those that followed. It included members of the nobility and writers such as Sévigné, La Fayette, Scudéry, Longueville, and Montpensier among the women (the *précieuses*), and Corneille, Malherbe, and Richelieu among the men (the *précieux*), and was considered the intellectual center of Paris. Members of the circle were concerned with good taste and refinement and precision in language.

980.26   *"Mais . . . salon!"*] But she does not want to deplete her salon!

992.25   ' 'Tis . . . nightingale'] Cf. *Romeo and Juliet,* III, v, 1: "It was the nightingale, and not the lark."

995.39–40   "Bliss . . . alive"] *The Prelude* (1850), Book XI, line 108.

996.14–31   One . . . Baghdad."] Jean Cocteau (1889–1963) used a version of the story in *Le Grand Écart* (1923).

1008.38   "The Dunciad"] Various authors are held up to ridicule and their literary vices revealed in the satirical poem in four books (1728–42), an attack on "Dulness," by Alexander Pope (1688–1744).

1015.38   *What . . . true*'] Cf. *The Hunting of the Snark* (1876), Fit. 1, "The Landing," by Lewis Carroll (1832–98).

1022.11–12   Like . . . flame] *Endymion* (1818), Book IV, lines 200–201.

1022.32–34   "Walkyrie," . . . *Lenz!*"] *Die Walküre* (*The Valkyrie*) (performed 1870) is the second opera in the tetralogy *Der Ring des Nibelungen* (first complete performance, 1876) composed by Richard Wagner (1813–83). The conversation is translated: "Who went?" "One came. It was the Spring!"

1025.7   *pour . . . aimer*] In order to understand, it is necessary to love.

1030.2–10   "The Ring . . . *Rosenkavalier*] See note to 1022.32–34. *The Ring* also included *Das Rheingold* (performed 1869), *Siegfried* and *Gotterdämmerung* (*Twilight of the Gods*) (both first performed 1876). *Der Rosenkavalier* (1911) was composed by Richard Strauss (1864–1949).

1035.21   (*Secours . . . Militaires*)] Help to Wounded Soldiers.

1047.34–35   warning maroons] Charges of gun powder, a warning to take cover during air raids.

1048.1–2   Big . . . sound.] On March 23, 1918, the Germans began shelling Paris at a range of over seventy miles, using a specially built 210 mm. gun. The bombardment continued intermittently until August 12, 1918, by which time 367 shells had been fired, killing 256 people. "Big Bertha" was the name popularly used by the Allies both for the long-range guns used in the Paris bombardment and for the shorter-range 420 mm. siege mortars used by the Germans earlier in the war. The Germans, however, called only the siege mortars "Berthas," after Bertha Krupp von Bohlen und Halbach (1886–1957), owner of the Krupp steel and munitions works.

1053.22   "not . . . battalions"] *Hamlet*, IV, v, 78–79.

1054.15   "Fletcherizing"] The practice of eating only when hungry and chewing food thoroughly, preferably until liquified, was introduced by the nutritionist Horace Fletcher (1849–1919).

1058.4   Golden Legend] A medieval handbook of church teaching and lore, including lives of the saints.

1060.29–30   *Kein . . . vorübergehend*] See note to 767.7.

1061.10   "The Story of Zélide"] *The Portrait of Zélide*. This correction of
the title was made in a later printing.

1064.3–4   "the woodspurge . . . three"] "The Woodspurge," last line,
by Dante Gabriel Rossetti (1828–82).

LIFE AND I

This autobiographical fragment, never completed and covering only Wharton's early years, is printed here for the first time; the manuscript usage (su-
perscripts, abbreviations, etc.) is retained. Wharton may have begun it before
she wrote to her Appleton editor Rutger B. Jewett on February 21, 1923,
about a magazine's proposal for a series of articles on her "recollections of
New York Society": "[It] reminds me of a plan which has been vaguely floating through my mind for some time: namely, the writing of my own early
memories, from 1865 to 1885 or 1890, in which I should like to interweave the
recollections of my childhood and the beginnings of my literary life . . . My
original idea was to jot down these remembrances, and put them away for
use after my death; but as they would be concerned only with the picture of
my family life as a child and young girl, and with my literary development, I
see no particular reason for keeping them back. The whole plan is still vague
in my mind . . ."

1075.8   "Lays . . . Rome"] The book of poems (1842) by Thomas Babington Macaulay (1800–59).

1075.37   Erlkönig's daughters] In Goethe's poem "Erl-könig" or "Elf-
King," which provided the theme for Franz Schubert's song "Erlkönig"
(1816).

1077.13   the "au delà"] The beyond.

1078.3   "brouillons"] Rough drafts.

1082.38   "les . . . l'esprit"] Things of the spirit.

1083.15   *épater*] To amaze.

1084.12   Areopagitica . . . Urn-Burial] *Areopagitica* (1644), a speech by
John Milton against licensing books, and *Hydriotaphia* or *Urn Burial* (1658),
an archaeological treatise by Sir Thomas Browne (1605–82).

1084.32–33   Augustin . . . pictures)] *Narratives of the Merovingian Era*.
See note to 837.35–838.3.

1084.38   *fatras*] Rubbish.

1085.10–11   "What . . . Pleiades?"] Cf. I Corinthians 15:32 and Job 38:31.

1085.28–33   Niebelungen . . . Brunanburh"] The 13th-century poem *Ni-*
belungenlied tells a story that also appears in both the Old Norse *Prose Edda*
or *Younger Edda* (c. 1222) by Snorri Sturluson and the *Poetic Edda* or *Elder*

Edda (compiled c. 1270), which contains poems written c. 800–c. 1200. The Old English *Battle of Brunanburh* (c. 937) appears in *The Anglo-Saxon Chronicle*. *Brut*, in early Middle English by the priest and poet Layamon (fl. 1200), tells stories that would appear in later literature, including those of Arthur, Lear, and Cymbeline.

1085.31–32   "Gesagt-gethan"]   No sooner said than done.

1086.3   lutti quanti]   So much mire.

1086.10   Dichtung und Wahrheit]   The autobiography, *Truth and Poetry*.

1086.27–29   "How . . . lute"]   *Comus* (1637), lines 476–78, by John Milton (1608–74).

1090.34   Revd Dr Cumming]   John Cumming (1807–81), the Scottish divine, was a popular preacher at the National Scottish Church at Crown Court, Covent Garden, London. He was perhaps the most widely read theological writer of his time.

1091.28   Egmont's Clärchen]   See note to 949.4–5.

1094.19–20   Franciabigio's . . . eima,]   See note to 848.10–11.

1096.21   éprise]   In love, smitten.

CATALOGING INFORMATION

Wharton, Edith, 1862–1937.
  Novellas and Other Writings.
  Edited by Cynthia Griffin Wolff.

  (The Library of America ; 47)
  Contents: Madame de Treymes—Ethan Frome—Summer—
  Old New York—The mother's recompense—A backward glance.
  I. Title: Madame de Treymes. II. Title: Ethan Frome. III. Title:
  Summer. IV. Title: Old New York. V. Title: The mother's
  recompense. VI. Title: A backward glance. VII. Series.
  PS3545.H16A6   1990b   813'.52—dc20   89–62930
  ISBN 0–940450–53–4 (alk. paper)

For a list of titles in The Library of America, write:
The Library of America
14 East 60th Street
New York, New York 10022

*This book is set in 10 point Linotron Galliard,
a face designed for photocomposition by Matthew Carter
and based on the sixteenth-century face Granjon. The paper
is acid-free Ecusta Nyalite and meets the requirements for permanence of the American National Standards Institute. The binding
material is Brillianta, a 100% woven rayon cloth made by
Van Heek-Scholco Textielfabrieken, Holland. The composition is by Haddon Craftsmen, Inc., and The
Clarinda Company. Printing and binding
by R. R. Donnelley & Sons Company.
Designed by Bruce Campbell.*

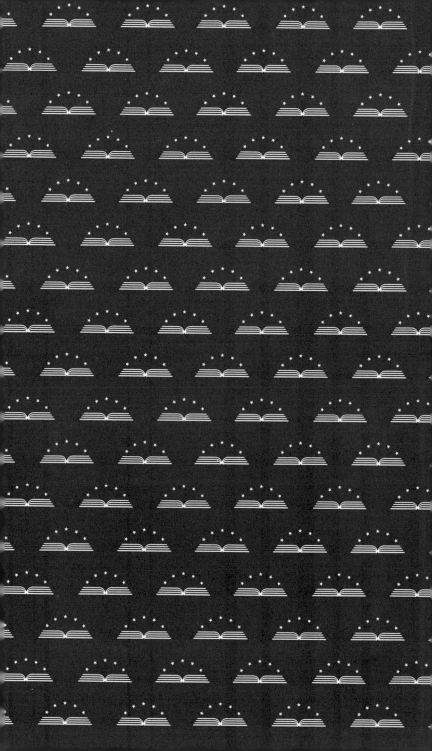